PENGUIN CLASSICS

THE BROTHERS KARAMAZOV

FYODOR MIKHAILOVICH DOSTOYEVSKY was born in Moscow in 1821, the second of a physician's seven children. His mother died in 1837 and his father was murdered a little over two years later. When he left his private boarding school in Moscow he studied from 1838 to 1843 at the Military Engineering College in St Petersburg, graduating with officer's rank. His first story to be published, 'Poor Folk' (1846), was a great success. In 1849 he was arrested and sentenced to death for participating in the 'Petrashevsky circle'; he was reprieved at the last moment but sentenced to penal servitude, and until 1854 he lived in a convict prison at Omsk, Siberia. In the decade following his return from exile he wrote *The Village of Stepanchikovo* (1859) and *The House of the Dead* (1860). Whereas the latter draws heavily on his experiences in prison, the former inhabits a completely different world, shot through with comedy and satire. In 1861 he began the review *Vremya* (*Time*) with his brother; in 1862 and 1863 he went abroad, where he strengthened his anti-European outlook, met Mlle Suslova, who was the model for many of his heroines, and gave way to his passion for gambling. In the following years he fell deeply in debt, but in 1867 he married Anna Grigoryevna Snitkina (his second wife), who helped to rescue him from his financial morass. They lived abroad for four years, then in 1873 he was invited to edit *Grazhdanin* (*The Citizen*), to which he contributed his *Diary of a Writer*. From 1876 the latter was issued separately and had a large circulation. In 1880 he delivered his famous address at the unveiling of Pushkin's memorial in Moscow; he died six months later in 1881. Most of his important works were written after 1864: *Notes from Underground* (1864), *Crime and Punishment* (1865–6), *The Gambler* (1866), *The Idiot* (1869), *The Devils* (1871) and *The Brothers Karamazov* (1880).

DAVID MCDUFF was born in 1945 and was educated at the University of Edinburgh. His publications comprise a large number of translations of foreign verse and prose, including poems by Joseph Brodsky and Tomas Venclova, as well as contemporary Scandinavian work; *Selected Poems* of Osip Mandelstam; *Complete Poems* of Edith Södergran; and *No I'm Not Afraid*, the selected poems of Irina Ratushinskaya. His first book of verse, *Words in Nature*, appeared in 1972. He has translated a number of nineteenth-century Russian prose works for the Penguin Classics series. These include Dostoyevsky's *The Brothers Karamazov*, *Crime and Punishment*, *The House of the Dead*, *Poor Folk and Other Stories* and *Uncle's Dream and Other Stories*, Tolstoy's *The Kreutzer Sonata and Other Stories* and *The Sebastopol Sketches*, and Nikolai Leskov's *Lady Macbeth of Mtsensk*. He has also translated Babel's *Collected Stories* and Bely's *Petersburg* for Penguin.

Fyodor Dostoyevsky

THE BROTHERS KARAMAZOV

*A Novel in Four Parts and
an Epilogue*

TRANSLATED WITH
AN INTRODUCTION AND NOTES
BY DAVID McDUFF

PENGUIN BOOKS

PENGUIN BOOKS

Published by the Penguin Group
Penguin Books Ltd, 27 Wrights Lane, London W8 5TZ, England
Penguin Putnam Inc., 375 Hudson Street, New York, New York 10014, USA
Penguin Books Australia Ltd, Ringwood, Victoria, Australia
Penguin Books Canada Ltd, 10 Alcorn Avenue, Toronto, Ontario, Canada M4V 3B2
Penguin Books India (P) Ltd, 11, Community Centre, Panchsheel Park, New Delhi – 110 017, India
Penguin Books (NZ) Ltd, Private Bag 102902, NSMC, Auckland, New Zealand
Penguin Books (South Africa) (Pty) Ltd, 5 Watkins Street, Denver Ext 4, Johannesburg 2094, South Africa

Penguin Books Ltd, Registered Offices: Harmondsworth, Middlesex, England

First published 1880
This translation first published 1993

11

This translation, Introduction and Notes copyright © David McDuff, 1993
All rights reserved

The moral right of the translator has been asserted

Typeset by Datix International Limited, Bungay, Suffolk
Set in Monophoto Fournier
Made and printed in Great Britain by Clays Ltd, St Ives plc

Contents

Epilogue

A Note on the Text

THE text used for the present translation is that contained in F. M. Dostoyevsky, *Polnoye sobranie sochineniy v tridtsati tomakh*, vols. 14–15, *Izdatel'stvo 'Nauka'*, Leningrad, 1976. The scholarly notes, essays and draft materials in that edition have been consulted, as have the important textual comments included in *A Karamazov Companion* (1981) by Victor Terras.

Introduction

The Brothers Karamazov was originally planned as a novel about children and childhood. On 16 March 1878 Dostoyevsky wrote in a letter to the writer and pedagogue V. V. Mikhailov:

> I have conceived and will soon begin a large novel in which, *inter alia*, a major role will be played by children – minors, aged from about seven to fifteen. There will be much portrayal of children. I am studying them, I have been studying them all my life, and love them very much, I have some of my own. But the observations of a man such as yourself will be precious to me (I understand this). Therefore, write to me *of children* what you yourself know.

On 16 May of the same year, Dostoyevsky's son, Alyosha, died of epilepsy at the age of two years and nine months. For a long time the writer was unable to work. 'In order to bring Fyodor Mikhailovich at least a little calm and to draw his mind away from melancholy thoughts,' A. G. Dostoyevskaya, the writer's widow, wrote in her memoirs, 'I prevailed upon Vladimir S. Solovyov, who was visiting us in those days of our grief, to persuade Fyodor Mikhailovich to travel with him to the Optina Hermitage, where Solovyov was preparing to go that summer. A visit to the Optina Hermitage had long been a dream of Fyodor Mikhailovich's.'

Dostoyevsky left Moscow with the philosopher and theologian Vladimir Solovyov on 18 June 1878. The journey to the Optina Hermitage took seven days, which were to prove of major significance to the way in which the project of the novel developed. In the course of the journey Dostoyevsky discussed with Solovyov his plans for the work he had begun, and Solovyov later asserted that 'the Church as a positive social ideal was to constitute the central idea of the new novel or new series of novels, of which only the first – *The Brothers Karamazov* – has been written'.

These twin themes, of childhood and the Church – were at the fore-front of Dostoyevsky's mind when, returning from the Optina Hermitage at the beginning of July – the actual stay at the hermitage had been, perhaps significantly, of only two days' duration – he began the opening chapters of the new novel. Yet as the work developed it came increasingly to embrace nearly all the concerns and preoccupations that had stayed with the writer throughout his long and often agonizingly tormented career, so that in its final form the novel represents a kind of sum-total of Dostoyevsky's creative, philosophical and ideological thinking. For example, one of the central themes of *The Brothers Karamazov* – that of the problem of freedom, dealt with at length in the chapter entitled 'The Grand Inquisitor' – is derived from a passage in the tale *The Landlady* (to be found in *Poor Folk and Other Stories*), published some forty years earlier, where the old man Murin says:

> You know, master, a weak man cannot control himself on his own.
> Give him everything, and he'll come of his own accord and give it back to you; give him half the world, just try it, and what do you think he'll do? He'll hide himself in your shoe immediately, that small will he make himself. Give a weak man freedom and he'll fetter it himself and give it back to you. A foolish heart has no use for freedom!

Similarly, the theme of 'the double', first elaborated by Dostoyevsky in 1846 in the famous 'St Petersburg Poem' of that name, is clearly reinvoked and referred to by the chapter in *The Brothers Karamazov* entitled 'The Devil'. And the all-pervasive theme of parricide has its origins in a passage in the first chapter of *The House of the Dead*:

> One man who had murdered his father stays particularly in my memory. He was of noble origin, had worked in government service and had been something of a prodigal son to his sixty-year-old father. His behaviour had been thoroughly dissipated, he had become embroiled in debt. His father had tried to exert a restraining influence on him, had tried to make him see reason; but the father had a house and a farm, it was suspected he had money, and – his son murdered him in order to get his hands on the inheritance . . . He had made no confession; had been stripped of his nobility and government service rank, and had been sentenced to twenty years' deportation and penal servitude . . . He was an unbalanced, flippant man, unreasoning in the extreme, though by no means stupid. I never observed any particular signs of cruelty in him. The prisoners despised him, not for his crime, of which no mention was ever made, but for his silliness, for his not knowing how to behave.

Thus, the original plan of a novel about children and childhood gradually became supplanted by a much larger and more complex project, a work in which the writer's entire life and career were put at stake and re-examined by himself in a kind of personal 'last judgement'.

The 'novel about children' survived into the final version of *The Brothers Karamazov* in several forms. Perhaps the least important of these is the story of the schoolboy Kolya Krasotkin and his friend Ilyusha, a tale which, taken on its own, is frequently reminiscent of the pages of a children's journal, though it has a tender humour and a deep insight into the interrelation between children and animals, and its conclusion raises it to a higher level. Far more significant is the story of the 'Russian boys', the 'brothers Karamazov' themselves – overgrown children, representative of their generation, who are in search of a spiritual goal and a true father, but who cannot find either. This story is made all the more painfully immediate by a fragmentary sociological sub-plot that focuses on the sufferings of children in nineteenth-century Russian society, sometimes in cruel and sickening detail. This is the soil, the social and spiritual climate, from which the 'Russian boys' must grow.

The sense of personal and generational suffering that is so much a feature of the novel's tone and timbre makes itself felt in a certain emotional distancing, as though the pain of the events described, both inner and outer, were too great to bear in an unmediated form. Dostoyevsky had used the device of an amateur literary 'chronicler' to such an end before, most particularly in *The House of the Dead*, where the voice of Goryanchikov, the narrator, has a curiously deadened, dispassionate quality. In *The Brothers Karamazov*, we are confronted with an 'author' who, from a lonely corner of a remote, provincial town (somewhat resembling Staraya Russa, the town of Dostoyevsky's childhood), in a crabbed and eccentric style that suggests the oddity of some column in an obscure local newspaper, succeeds in chronicling not only a parricide of Shakespearean dramatic force and vividness, but also the moral and spiritual collapse of an entire world. In order that the novel may be read in the sense in which it was intended, Dostoyevsky's narrator must first be taken account of. He is not Dostoyevsky himself, but a grotesque and even slightly Hoffmannesque *Phantasiegebilde* – a solitary, retired bachelor of partial, old-fashioned education and reactionary political and social views, his hobbies 'philology' and local history, set in his ways, with a resentment against women (one senses an unhappy love in his past) and a dislike of both social radicals and religious fanatics, in particular monks and the monkhood. It is the narrow, prejudiced but none the less curiously

perceptive eye of this contemporary observer, who is in his way a
somewhat jaded connoisseur and classifier of human nature, that is
brought to bear on the story of the 'Russian boys'; and the brain of the
same observer, ruminating on events that took place some thirteen years
earlier, composes from it both a 'life-chronicle' (the Russian word, *zhizne-
opisanie*, is an alternative, though rather more workaday, to the word
biografiya, 'biography') and a 'novel' (like the French *roman*, the Russian
word, *roman*, also has the meaning of 'romance', sometimes used in a
disparaging way). The matter is complicated further by the fact that in
having recourse to the device of a narrator, Dostoyevsky in this instance
wishes to imitate the ancient Russian *zhitiya*, or 'Lives' of the saints. The
irony of this – for none of the brothers can be considered to be particularly
saintly – casts a curious light over the entire narrative, filling it in many
places with ambivalence and an ironic, capricious humour that at times
verges on the sarcastic. Although Dostoyevsky's voice interweaves with
that of his narrator, the latter is very much in charge of things, to an
extent that some readers may find puzzling.

From the very outset of the novel's action the ambivalence and irony
make themselves evident. Neither the 'little family' (the narrator purposely
uses the deprecatory form *semeyka*) which has assembled for a gathering,
nor the 'Elder' whom they have come to visit appear in a very flattering
light. The Elder Zosima, apparently modelled by Dostoyevsky on Father
Amvrosy of the Optina Hermitage, and adored by Alyosha as a saint, is
described in slightly unpleasant terms as someone one might rather not
meet:

> Indeed, there was about the Elder's person something to which many
> people, and not only Miusov, might have taken a dislike. He was a
> short, hunched-up little man with very frail legs, only sixty-five years of
> age but whom illness made appear much older, at least by some ten
> years. The whole of his face, a very gaunt one, was peppered with little
> wrinkles, of which there were particularly many around his eyes. These
> eyes were small, of the clear variety, swift and brilliant, like two
> brilliant points of light. Grey wisps of hair remained only at his temples,
> he had a little, straggling, wedge-shaped beard, and his lips, which often
> bore an ironic smile, were as thin as two pieces of string. His nose could
> not have been described as long, but was rather sharp and watchful, like
> the beak of a bird.

The whole atmosphere of the monastery, with its rather sour and
secretive monks and *hieroschemonachs* (a Slavonic version of the Greek

schemahieromonachos, or priests who wear the robes of monks), its collection of fine wines and its smugly modest banquets, is hardly calculated to inspire the reader with respect, and makes Alyosha's devotion to it all the more absurd — the infatuation of a 'raw youth'. Alyosha's far from innocent involvement with Liza Khokhlakova is not what one might expect in a 'man of God', and establishes an affinity between him and the Elder, with his 'Mount Athos tricks' and 'dances'. Disconcerting details about the Elder's decidedly murky past are served up before us by Alyosha himself at the end of Part Two in the 'biographical information' contained in 'From the Life of the Departed in God the Hieroschemonach the Elder Zosima'. In the light of all this the 'scandalous' behaviour of the 'monster', Fyodor Pavlovich Karamazov, seems less shocking than it might otherwise do. There is a sense of a universal moral failure, where neither sinners nor saved have any valid context in which to perceive themselves as such, and where the whole social–religious edifice threatens to break down amidst sinister and mocking laughter.

Clearly, the death of his son and the two-day visit to the Optina Hermitage had influenced the course of Dostoyevsky's work on the 'novel about children' in such a way as to turn it far from the direction he had intended it to take. An important point to consider here is that the picture of the Optina Hermitage that emerges from the novel is not at all in consonance with the reality of the place, as documented by others at the time. Dostoyevsky's narrator distorts to the point of unrecognizability — the question must be: why? Some have seen the answer in a conflict between Dostoyevsky the artist and Dostoyevsky the publicist and aspirant religious adviser, who associated and corresponded with Konstantin Pobedonostsev and wished for acceptance by the Tsarist political establishment. Pobedonostsev's misgivings about the novel are well known and have been described in detail elsewhere. Pobedonostsev was not alone in finding Dostoyevsky's 'theodicy' and his portrayal of the monks problematical. Dostoyevsky himself, in a letter to Pobedonostsev of 24 August 1879, made no secret of his doubts:

> Your opinion of what you have read of *Karamazov* flattered me greatly (regarding the strength and energy of what has been written), but at the same time you raise a most necessary question: that there has as yet occurred to me no reply to all these atheistic theses, and they need one. Indeed so, and it is in that that now lie all my concern and all my unease. For this sixth book, 'The Russian Monk', which is to appear on 31 August, I have proposed as a reply to this whole *negative aspect*. And therefore I also tremble for it in the sense – will it be a *sufficient* reply?

All the more so as this reply is, after all, not direct, not point by point to the theses that were enunciated earlier (in 'the G. Inquisitor' and before), but is only indirect. Here there is presented something that is directly opposed to the world-outlook expressed above, but again it is presented not point by point, but, so to speak, in an artistic tableau. This it is that causes me unease, that is to say, will I be understood and will I attain even one small drop of my aim? And here in addition there are further obligations of artistry: it was required that I present a modest and majestic figure, whereas life is full of the comic and is majestic only in its inner sense, so that in the biography of my monk I was involuntarily compelled by artistic demands to touch upon even the most vulgar aspects so as not to infringe artistic realism. Then, too, there are several teachings of the monk against which people will simply cry out that they are absurd, for they are all too ecstatic; of course, they are absurd in an everyday sense, but in another, inward sense, I think they are true.

The prosaist, literary critic and Orthodox convert Konstantin Leontiev also found much to object to in this aspect of the novel. Whatever one's opinion of Leontiev's personal and political convictions, the fact remains that he was a man of intensely perceptive literary judgement, with, in addition, an almost unerring sense for the truth about life and human affairs, and an instinctive eye for falsehood. It may therefore be instructive to examine Leontiev's reaction to Dostoyevsky's 'Orthodoxy'.

In his article 'About Universal Love' (1880), Leontiev criticizes Dosto-yevsky's doctrine of universal brotherly love as it is put into the mouth of Father Zosima, considering it to be a distortion of true Christian love, a modified and altered form of socialist humanitarianism. Leontiev perceives the essence of Dostoyevsky's novel to be a revelation of the 'intolerable tragism of life', and considers the chapters concerning the monks and the monastery to be an unsuccessful attempt to present a 'positive' counterpart to it, a striving for cosmic 'harmony' that is really no more than an artist's desire to paint in shades of light and dark:

On the one hand, sorrows, injuries, the storm of the passions, crimes, jealousy, envy, acts of oppression, mistakes, and on the other – unex-pected consolations, kindness, forgiveness, the heart's repose, impulses and deeds of selflessness, simplicity and gaiety of heart! Here is *life*, here is the only possible *harmony* on this earth and under this heaven. *The harmonic law of compensation – and nothing more*. The poetic, living concordance of bright colours with dark ones – *and nothing more*. And in the highest degree integral semi-tragic, semi-serene opera, in which menacing and melancholy sounds alternate with tender and touching ones – and *nothing more!*

Leontiev believes that Dostoyevsky's attitude to the monks, who 'play a most important role' in the novel, is one of 'deep veneration', and sees in this an advance on the writer's path towards true Orthodoxy. Yet he is compelled to acknowledge that 'the monks do not quite, or, to be more precise, *do not at all* say the things that *very good* monks say both in Russia and on Mount Athos . . . To be sure, here there is rather little mention of worship, of monastic vows of obedience . . .' Later, after Dostoyevsky's death, Leontiev went even further. Attempting to dissuade his friend Vasily Rozanov from swallowing Dostoyevsky's 'Orthodoxy' whole, he wrote in a letter:

> . . . I zealously pray to God that you will soon *outgrow Dostoyevsky* and his 'harmonies', which will never be, and indeed are, unneeded. His monks are an invention. Even the teachings of Father Zosima are erroneous; and the whole style of his discourses is false . . . Though your article about the 'Grand Inquisitor' contains a great number of things that are beautiful and true, and in itself the 'Legend', too, is a beautiful fantasy, none the less the inflections of Dostoyevsky himself in his views on Catholicism and on Christianity in general are mistaken, false and obscure; and pray God that you will soon free yourself from his *unhealthy and overpowering* influence! Too complex, obscure and inapplicable to life. At Optina *The Brothers Karamazov* is *not considered to be a correct Orthodox work, and the Elder Zosima does not in any way either in his teaching or in his character resemble Father Amvrosy* . . .

In his memoirs, Leontiev wrote: '*The Brothers Karamazov* can be considered an Orthodox novel only by those who are little acquainted with true Orthodoxy, with the Christianity of the Holy Fathers and the Elders of Athos and Optina.' In Leontiev's view (he himself became an Orthodox monk and lived at Optina for the last six months of his life), the work of Zola (in *La Faute de l'abbé Mouret*) is 'far closer to the spirit of true personal monkhood than the superficial and sentimental inventions of Dostoyevsky in *The Brothers Karamazov*.'

In giving Dostoyevsky the benefit of the doubt, and considering the novelist to be guilty of mere 'humanitarian idealization' in his treatment of Optina and its monks, Leontiev tends to evade the question of whether Dostoyevsky may not, either consciously of semi-subconsciously, have been indulging in his familiar habit of irony at their expense. There is a level at which one may, in associating the character of the youngest

Karamazov with the world of the sick and dying Elder Zosima and his retinue of shadowy intellectual priests, religious fanatics and female admirer–supplicants, wonder whether Dostoyevsky is not asking: is this perhaps only the best Alyosha can hope for in a world that has 'gone on to another track'? Again, as earlier, one wonders why, if the monastery is supposed to represent a centre of health and wisdom in an otherwise corrupt world, so many of the features of the Alyosha–Zosima story bear such a morbid hue: Zosima owes his religious career to a common criminal and murderer, and after his death his body emits a 'putrid smell', calling to mind the novel's theme of 'stinking', and the lackey Smerdyakov. Alyosha is characterized by the narrator as 'a pretty strange fellow', and Dostoyevsky originally styled him on the 'idiot' Prince Myshkin from the novel of that name. Perhaps at least a part of the answer to the question of this ambivalence may be obtained from a glance at Dostoyevsky's notes and jottings for *The Brothers Karamazov*, in particular those relating to the sayings and character of the Elder Zosima. These indicate that in trying to portray a religious life and a body of spiritual belief that was adequate to the times in which he lived, Dostoyevsky – influenced, no doubt, by questions of censorship – originally went considerably further than he did in the final version of the novel. For example, in the section of the notebooks headed 'The Elder's Confession', one entry reads: 'Love human beings in their sins. *Love even their sins.*' And later: 'Love sins! Verily, life is paradise. Is given once in a myriad of ages.'

This 'love of sin' advocated by the Elder Zosima – and presumably also by Dostoyevsky – is what gives *The Brothers Karamazov* its strange and troubling quality of ambivalence, that passes through its entire plot, characterization and structure, making them impossible to define and determine with any degree of positive certainty. This becomes quite evident when we consider the story of the murder that forms the principal building-block of the novel's development.

According to the formal plot-scheme of the novel, the murder of Fyodor Pavlovich Karamazov is carried out by the lackey Smerdyakov at the instigation of Ivan. Mitya is found guilty of the murder only in consequence of 'a judicial error' committed by the jury at his trial. Some critics have insisted that Mitya's character is at bottom essentially innocent, that although he is a self-admitted 'scoundrel' he could never have murdered his father. This argument is lent support by the fact that Dostoyevsky appears to have modelled Mitya's character to some extent on that of the nobleman D. N. Ilyinsky, a supposed 'parricide' who was sent into penal servitude for someone else's crime, whom the author met in Siberia, and whom he describes in *The House of the Dead*. The 'publisher's note' that precedes Chapter 7 of Part II of that work seems to express a genuine and wholehearted indignation that an innocent man should have been punished unjustly:

> The other day the publisher of *Notes from the House of the Dead* received notification from Siberia that this criminal really had been in the right all along, and had suffered ten years of penal servitude for no reason. His innocence had been established officially, according to the processes of the law. The true perpetrators of the crime had apparently been found and had confessed, and the unfortunate man had been released from prison . . . There is no need to add any more. No need to expatiate on the tragic profundity of this case, on the young life ruined by such a dreadful accusation . . . We are of the opinion, too, that if a case such as this is possible, this very possibility adds a new and glaring facet to the overall picture of the House of the Dead . . .

Yet in the overall context of Dostoyevsky's life and work the theme of crime and punishment has a rather different perspective, one that is essentially subjective, moral and inward, and bears only a token relation to the external, social criteria of guilt and innocence. Thus, for example, in the novel *Crime and Punishment* what matters first and foremost is not Raskolnikov's guilt of the crime he has committed, but his own willingness to admit that he has committed a crime, and is inwardly guilty in terms that are absolute, not judicial – it is in that willingness, that admission, that the seeds of his future resurrection lie. Or, to return to *The House of the Dead* for a moment: its narrator, Goryanchikov, who murdered his wife, is only a cover for Dostoyevsky himself, who believed that his own political crime bore an inner significance that involved the whole of his fate, personality and soul. Like the axe-murderer Raskolnikov, Goryanchikov exists in a metaphysical region where the reality of suffering and the ability to accept it are the primary determining factors, the condition of a true humanity, and the only pointers to salvation. When we come to the case of Mitya in *The Brothers Karamazov*, Dostoyevsky already presupposes that the reader will not read the story, the *roman*, in literal terms, but rather in the Dantesque, Gogolian tradition of a tale concerning the 'contiguity with other worlds'. The character of Mitya is drawn with an intensity, passion and love that are almost unparalleled in the rest of Dostoyevsky's writing. This Promethean, ecstatic, drunken 'ardent heart' and fiery soul is a portrait of the universal man, unredeemed and possibly doomed for eternity.

Mitya's crime involves the 'murder of the fathers' in the sense in which it was defined by Dostoyevsky's contemporary, the nineteenth-century Russian thinker N. F. Fyodorov, who believed in a literal, real and personal resurrection that will take place on the earth, and will be brought about by the efforts of living sons to resurrect their dead fathers. In the world of late nineteenth-century Russia Fyodorov perceived one of the principal social sicknesses to be the hatred with which the educated youth viewed the concepts of 'father' and 'son', rejecting these with contempt in their frenzied aspiration towards social 'progress' and revolution. Fyodorov considered that the true revolution would be brought about by science and technology in a universal project involving the transformation of nature into the Kingdom of God by the resurrected brotherhood of man, the God–man. In *The Brothers Karamazov*, Dostoyevsky charts, in Mitya's story, the beginning of that process of resurrection out of a state of fall and shame. Mitya is not innocent, nor is he a mere 'scoundrel' – from the early pages of the novel it is made clear that his ultimate intent is the criminal one of killing his father, and the sadistic, bloody and murderous attack described in Chapter 9 of Book III leaves us in no doubt of this. Mitya's vow in Chapter 5 of Book VIII – 'I punish myself for the whole of my life, the whole of my life I punish!' indicates his overwhelming sense of guilt at being alive at all, at having received life from his father, and also his desire to punish his father for having given it to him. There is in all this, of course, an element of grand, Schillerean theatricality, the heroism of 'one against all'. In an outburst to the public procurator during the 'Third Torment' (Book IX, Chapter 5), Mitya states in existential terms his conviction that the murderer could not have been Smerdyakov, and it is based on the latter's deficiency in heroism and ardent emotion:

'But why do you so firmly and with such insistence assert that it is not he?'

'Because I am convinced. Because that is my impression. Because Smerdyakov is a man of the basest nature, and a coward. Or rather, not a coward but a combination of all the manifestations of cowardliness in the world taken together, walking on two legs. He was born of a hen. When he spoke to me, on each occasion he trembled lest I kill him, while I never even raised a finger against him. He fell at my feet and wept, he kissed these very boots, literally, begging me not to "frighten him" – what kind of a remark is that? And I even tried to give him money. He is a sickly hen with the falling sickness and a weak mind, a fellow whom an eight-year-old schoolboy could flatten to the ground. Is that a human being? . . .'

A few lines further on, confronted by the revelation that Smerdyakov had apparently been unconscious in a fit of epilepsy at the time of the murder, Mitya utters the revealing statement: 'Well, in that case it was the Devil who killed my father!'

And indeed, this is the conclusion that Dostoyevsky appears to be working towards in the novel. By the agency of the 'infernaless' Grushenka, whose cold, cruel, and animal nature takes hold of Mitya and drives him on to excess, the Devil enters Mitya's soul and brings about the death of his father. Yet Mitya is aware that in practical terms it is *not he* who has killed. To the eyes of the world, however, he is the murderer, and inwardly he feels himself to be such, and is perceived as such by Dostoyevsky. This may help to account for the vastly elaborate, persuasive and lengthy manner in which the assertion and 'proof' of Mitya's guilt are made by the public procurator at the novel's conclusion, spanning four chapters, for the comparatively perfunctory and unpersuasive speech of the defence counsel Fetyukovich (whose very name inspires a Gogolian shiver of revulsion, with its initial 'F' or 'Theta' suggesting an obscenity), and for the resolute and final way in which Dostoyevsky makes the jury of 'muzhiks' find Mitya guilty. In one sense, of course, the entire account of the trial is a satirical attack on provincial justice, in particular as it manifested itself under the influence of the newly introduced 'public courts' with their trial by jury. Neither prosecution nor defence emerge from the narrator's reminiscences with any degree of dignity: the proceedings are an elaborate sham, a cold-blooded attempt by the State to deny the spiritual, living content of a crime – the 'murder of the fathers' – and its consequences. Indeed, the world of the public procurator and the state investigator, with its *'soirées'* and 'legal experts', its games of cards and glasses of tea, is every bit as dubious from a moral point of view as the world of the monks and the monastery. It is not for nothing that Dostoyevsky names the 'little town' in which the action of his novel takes place Skotoprigonyevsk – which roughly translates as 'Brutesville'.

Amidst all the ambivalence and moral uncertainty, the sense of a world and a society in a state of break-up and disintegration, in which *The Brothers Karamazov* abounds, the injunction to 'love sins' is one of the few notes that rings out clearly and unequivocally. We are enjoined to love Alyosha, Mitya and Ivan in the extremity of their despair and their inability to transcend their own weakness and sinfulness, and to realize that behind their helplessness, their tormented humanity lie forces that are darker and greater. It is the Devil, not Mitya or Ivan, nor even the lackey Smerdyakov, who kills Fyodor Pavlovich, just as it is the Devil, not Ivan who dreams up the Byronic, God-denying fantasy of the Grand Inquisitor, the Devil, not Alyosha, who is the true 'novice' in the monasteries of Russia. We are to love these three brothers because in the sincerity of their passion, the warmth of their natures, the desperation of their souls they have confronted the great and sinister reality from which the rest of the world is hiding: the reality which the poet Lermontov called 'the spirit of banishment' and which Goethe made a protagonist of his most important drama.

The Devil is the central character in *The Brothers Karamazov*. For the most part concealed, he emerges from time to time throughout the novel in flashes and allusions, throwing light – or shadow – on the thoughts and actions of the brothers and those whom they encounter. Thus, for example, the title of an early chapter in Book II, 'The Old Buffoon', where 'buffoon' translates the Russian word *shut*, could also be conceived as meaning 'The Old Devil', for *shut* also carries that meaning in colloquial Russian – thus Fyodor Pavlovich emerges early on in a 'Satanic' light, appropriately enough, in the circumstances. The Devil appears again in the many invocations of his name that crop up in the text – 'the devil', and 'devil take it' (*chort, chort voz'mi*), are common enough Russian expletives, but Dostoyevsky uses them in his dialogue like a symphonic motif. Whereas in his earlier novels this diabolism has a somewhat arbitrary character, merely hinting at something that is never fully revealed or realized, in *The Brothers Karamazov* it is a studied and conscious theme and technique, leading inexorably to the actual appearance of the Devil himself.

It is to Ivan Karamazov, in formal plot terms the 'Murderer' (this is the name he bears in the early rough drafts of the novel), that the Devil at last makes his appearance. The fact that this is so adds yet another twist of irony to the narrative, for of the three brothers, the atheistic, sceptical and rationalist Ivan would seem the least likely to suffer from visions of a religious kind. One of the points Dostoyevsky is making here is that for all his efforts to 'improve' himself by means of Western education and 'Enlightenment' Ivan, too, is a Karamazov, with the Karamazovian weaknesses. 'You are like Fyodor Pavlovich, more than any of them, sir, more than any of his other children you have turned out like him, with the same soul as his honour had, sir,' Smerdyakov tells

Ivan at their third 'meeting', and the blood 'leaps to Ivan's face' in shocked recognition of the lackey's perceptiveness. The nature of Ivan's illness, though admittedly problematical, is none the less in linguistic terms a further pointer to his Karamazovian 'baseness'. The Russian term employed by Dostoyevsky, *belaya goryachka* (literally 'white fever'), is traditionally used to refer to the alcohol-related hallucinatory disorder known to medicine as *delirium tremens*, and this definition is given even in nineteenth-century Russian dictionaries and encyclopaedias, such as those of Dal' and Brockhaus-Efron. It is curious that a physician such as A. F. Blagonravov was able to write to Dostoyevsky following the novel's appearance in 1880, praising him for his skill in describing 'a form of mental illness, well-known to science under the name of hallucinations, so naturally and also so artistically', without ever mentioning the alcoholic root of the disorder. Yet it is surely doubtful that Dostoyevsky intended any other interpretation to be put on the 'illness' – the implications raised during Alyosha's talk with Ivan at the inn (Book V, Chapters 3, 4 and 5), with reference to 'dashing the cup to the floor', seem too obvious. So does the way in which Ivan's secret vice is mocked and shadowed in the paralytic drunkenness of the peasant in the snow near the house where Smerdyakov lives (Book XI, Chapter 8). Dostoyevsky himself intended to explain the illness in a special article for *Diary of a Writer*, but died before he was able to do so. Whatever the truth of the matter, the very formulation *belaya goryachka* suggests 'depravity' of some kind, and is an important element in establishing the author's ambivalence towards the character of Ivan, which might otherwise assume too lordly a profile. In 'loving sin', Dostoyevsky constantly deflates the protagonists of his drama, as though there were a danger that their mythic grandeur might obscure their weakness and humanity. Even the 'Legend of the Grand Inquisitor' is only the terrifyingly elaborate delirium of a man in despair.

The Devil himself, who is responsible for all this confusion and diminution, is subject to his own laws and limits. It is of the utmost importance to him that he be perceived as having concrete reality, equivalent to that of Christ, or the brothers. This is why Dostoyevsky lavishes such detailed attention on the Devil's outward appearance, portraying him as some kind of '*gospodin*, or rather, a certain kind of Russian "gentleman", no longer young in years, "*qui frisait la cinquantaine*", as the French say, with a not so very noticeable trace of grey in his hair that still was long and thick, and in his short and wedge-shaped beard', and paying studious heed to the Devil's mode of speech, with its Gallicisms and phrases of somewhat dated radical jargon. Critics have speculated that Dostoyevsky based his portrayal on the character of the radical publicist and writer Alexander Herzen. Much of the 'Devil' chapter is taken up with arguments about reality and non-reality:

'Not for one moment do I take you for a truth that is real,' Ivan exclaimed in what even amounted to fury. 'You are a falsehood, you are my illness, you are a ghost. Only I do not know how to destroy you, and perceive that for a certain time I must suffer you. You are a hallucination I am having. You are the embodiment of myself, but only of one side of me . . . of my thoughts and emotions, though only those that are most loathsome and stupid. In that regard you might even be of interest to me, if only I had time to throw away on you.'

'With your permission, with your permission, I shall demonstrate to you that you are wrong: back there by the lamp-post, when you turned on Alyosha and shouted at him: "You discovered it from *him*! How did you know that *he* comes to visit me?" I mean, that was me you were referring to, was it not? So you see, for just one teensy little moment you believed, believed that I really existed,' the gentleman laughed mildly.

'Yes, that was due to a weakness of nature . . . but it is out of the question that I believed in your existence. I am unsure whether I was asleep or on my feet last time. It is possible that I dreamed of you then, but I certainly did not see you when I was awake . . .'

Yet in the end, the Devil loses – for *le diable n'existe point*, and, subject to his own law of negation, in spite of all his yearning 'to take fleshly form in the person of a seven-pood merchant's wife and set up candles to God in church', he disappears into the snowstorm leaving nothing but a pair of burned-out candles and an empty tea-glass.

The Devil's function is to make man suffer, and perhaps unwittingly to drive him in the direction of free choice and love. That second part of the function is only a 'perhaps', however. What we see in *The Brothers Karamazov* – in itself only the first part of a much larger projected novel that was never written – is a complex depiction of suffering – the suffering of a world in which the good that lies concealed in the children cannot manifest itself because of the sins of the fathers, and where the fathers cannot be resurrected because of those sins. Ivan goes mad, but may recover; Mitya chooses twenty years of suffering; and Alyosha, the 'idiot', is left, for want of any other audience, proclaiming the gospel of universal brotherhood to a flock of Russian schoolchildren.

*

Early reactions to the novel in Russian were mixed, but numerous and animated. 'The novel is read everywhere, people send me letters, the youth reads it, it is read in high society, in literature it is abused or praised, and never yet, to judge by the impression it has made all round, have I experienced such success,' Dostoyevsky wrote on 8 December 1879. Yet all the time up to the work's publication, the author was in a state of anxiety about how it would be received: '. . . I am in a fever,' he wrote to Pobedonostsev on 16 August 1880.

> It is not that I do not believe what I myself have written, but I am always tormented by the question: how will it be received, will people be willing to comprehend the essence of the matter, and may bad, not good, result from my having *published* my intimate convictions? All the more so because I am always compelled to express certain ideas only in their basic form, a form that is highly in need of greater development and conclusivity.

While many of Dostoyevsky's contemporaries were enthusiastic about *The Brothers Karamazov* — a typical reaction was to see it as a gallery of Russian 'types' *à la* Gogol — some reviewers took exception to what they felt to be the writer's excessive 'psychologism' and preoccupation with human iniquity. In 1879, before the whole novel had yet appeared, one commentator remarked:

> . . . the author does not leave in the sinful Karamazovs one single small wrinkle untouched by his psychological analysis. What the author will develop in future and create on the soil he has prepared, we do not know, but from several circumstances it is possible to draw the conclusion that he is preparing for his readers a terrible drama, in which one of the principal roles will be played by Grushenka.

Others felt that the only positive characters in the novel were the monks, and that this was taking condemnation of human nature too far. Perhaps the most famous 'review' of *The Brothers Karamazov* is that by the writer and publicist N. K. Mikhailovsky, who coined the phrase 'a cruel talent' to characterize Dostoyevsky, making it the title of his critical article. 'Having selected a suitable victim,' Mikhailovsky wrote,

> Dostoyevsky removes God from him and does this as simply and mechanically . . . as though he were taking the lid off a soup tureen. He removes God and looks: how will the victim behave in this situation? It goes without saying that the examinee immediately begins to commit a series of more or less infamous crimes. But this is no matter: for crimes

there is redeeming suffering, followed by all-forgiving love. Not for everyone, however, and in this lies the nub of the matter. If the examinee, left without God, begins to writhe in convulsions of pricked conscience, Dostoyevsky acts with comparative mercy towards him: having dragged the victim through a whole series of infamies, he sends him into penal servitude or to a 'monk-counsellor' and there, self-abased and humble, spreads over him the wing of all-forgiving love ... If the victim is stubborn and to the end creates 'mutiny', as one characteristic chapter of *The Brothers Karamazov* is entitled, mutiny against God, the order of things and the obligatoriness of suffering ... Dostoyevsky makes him hang himself, shoot himself, drown himself, first having once again made him run the gauntlet of villainy and crimes ...

Turgenev's judgement of the novel is well known, and was even more extreme − he considered Dostoyevsky to have revealed himself in it as a Russian de Sade. We have already considered the more sympathetic but critical reactions of Konstantin Leontiev. But perhaps the most sensitive nineteenth-century interpretation of all came some ten years after the novel's publication from Leontiev's Dostoyevskian acquaintance, the enigmatic philosopher Vasily Rozanov. In his *The Legend of the Grand Inquisitor* (1890), Rozanov reconstructs the novel in terms of one of its chapters, the one in which Ivan relates his '*poema*' to Alyosha. Rozanov sees this as the heart of the work, from which it derives all its meaning and creative energy: 'the "Legend",' he writes, 'constitutes as it were the soul of the entire work, which merely groups itself around it, like variations around their theme, in it is concealed the writer's intimate thought, without which not only this novel, but also many other works of his would never have been written ...' The long essay, which contains a masterly analysis of the '*poema*', seeing in the despair of its message an ultimate and paradoxical push towards moral regeneration through a recognition that after all, man's nature as originally constituted must be regarded as benevolent and good, concludes with the words:

The Legend itself is his bitter lament, when, having lost his innocence and been abandoned by God, he suddenly realizes that now he is completely alone, with his weakness, with his sin, with the struggle of light and darkness within his soul. To overcome this darkness, to help this light − that is all that man can do on his earthly wandering, and what he must do, in order to calm his distressed conscience, so burdened, so sick, so incapable of enduring its sufferings any longer. The clear perception of whence this light proceeds and whence this darkness, may more than anything strengthen him with the hope that he is not doomed to remain eternally the arena of their struggle.

Rozanov sounds a note of distant optimism. Yet Dostoyevsky himself, for all the boisterous pathos of the finale with which he provided the novel, was less sanguine. In his notebook for 1880–81 we come across the following passage:

The Devil. (Psychological and *detailed* critical explanation of Ivan Fyodorovich and the appearance of the Devil.) Ivan Fyodorovich is deep, this is not the contemporary atheists, who demonstrate by their unbelief only the narrowness of their world-outlook and the dimness of their dim-witted abilities ... Nihilism appeared among us because we are *all nihilists*. We were merely frightened by the new, original form of its manifestation. (All to a man Fyodor Pavloviches.) ... Conscience without God is a horror, it may lose its way to the point of utter immorality ... The Inquisitor is only immoral because in his heart, in his conscience there has managed to accommodate itself the idea of the necessity of burning human beings ... The Inquisitor and the chapter about children. In view of these chapters you could take a scholarly, yet not so haughty approach to me where philosophy is concerned, though philosophy is not my speciality. Not even in Europe is there such a power of atheistic *expressions, nor has there been*. So it is not as a boy, then, that I believe in Christ and confess Him, but through the great *crucible of doubt* has my *hosannah* passed, as I have him say, in that same novel of mine, the Devil.

Dedicated to

Anna Grigoryevna Dostoyevskaya*

Verily, verily, I say unto you, Except a corn of wheat fall into the ground and die, it abideth alone: but if it die, it bringeth forth much fruit.

JOHN 12:24

FROM THE AUTHOR

As I begin the life-chronicle of my hero, Aleksey Fyodorovich Karamazov, I find myself in something of a quandary. To wit: though I call Aleksey Fyodorovich my hero, I am nevertheless aware that he is in no way a man of greatness, and thus do I anticipate inevitable questions of a kind such as: 'In what respect does your Aleksey Fyodorovich stand out from the common run of men, that you have selected him as your hero? What has he done that is so special? Who has ever heard of him, and for what reasons? Why must I, the reader, expend my time in the study of the facts and events of his life?'

The last question is the most fateful one, for to it I am able to reply only: 'Perhaps you will see when you read the novel.' Well, and what if the novel is read and nothing at all is seen, the notability of my Aleksey Fyodorovich unconceded? Thus do I put it, as I regretfully anticipate that it will be so. For me he is notable, but I decidedly doubt whether I shall be able to prove it to the reader. The problem is that while this man is, perhaps, an activist, his status as such is vague and unclear. Though in fact it would be strange in times like ours to demand clarity of men. One thing is, perhaps, fairly beyond doubt: this is a strange man, an oddity, even. But strangeness and oddness are sooner a cause of harm to their possessor than any guarantee of attention, particularly in a time when all are striving to unite the details of existence and to discover at least some kind of general meaning in the universal muddle. For in most cases an oddity is a detail and an isolated instance. Is it not so?

The point is, you see, that if you do not concur with this last thesis and reply: 'Not true', or 'not always true', then I shall perhaps take encouragement with regard to the significance of my hero Aleksey Fyodorovich. For not only is an oddity 'not always' a detail and an isolated instance – on the contrary, it may occasionally transpire that he it is who bears within him, perhaps, the very heartwood of the whole, while, for some reason, the other men of his epoch have all of them been wrenched loose from it for a time as by some tidal gale . . .

I should, as a matter of fact, have much preferred not to embark upon these thoroughly vague and uninteresting explanations at all, but quite simply and without ceremony to begin without a preface: if it meets with approval, the thing will be read anyway; but the trouble is that while I have one life-chronicle to write, it consists of two novels. The principal novel is the second — an account of my hero's doings in our own times, that is to say, at our present-day current moment. The first novel, on the other hand, took place thirteen years ago and is almost not even a novel at all, but merely a single moment in my hero's early youth. It is out of the question for me to dispense with this first novel, as much in the second would become incomprehensible. But in this fashion my original predicament is rendered the more complex: for if I — the biographer himself, that is to say — consider that even one novel might possibly be excessive for such a modest and ill-defined hero, then what do I think I am about in appearing with two, and how is such presumption on my part to be explained?

At a loss in the attempt to solve these problems, I have determined to pass them over without solution. The sagacious reader will of course have long ago divined that this is the point to which I have been coming from the very outset, and has merely been irritated with me for wasting fruitless words and precious time. To this at least I shall deliver a precise reply. I have wasted fruitless words and precious time in the first instance out of courtesy, and in the second out of stratagem: as if to say, 'Well, I did give you some warning.' As a matter of fact, I am even glad that my novel should of its own accord have broken itself into two narratives 'in spite of the essential unity of the whole': having acquainted himself with the first narrative, the reader may then himself decide whether it is worth his while to begin upon the second. Of course, no one is obliged in any respect whatsoever; anyone may cast the book aside after only two pages of the first narrative, never to reopen it. But then again, there are, after all, such scrupulous readers as will wish to read the book to its end in order not to err in their dispassionate judgement — as, for example, all the Russian critics. Before readers such as these my heart is, I must say, lighter: in spite of all their exactitude and scruple I give them the most legitimate pretext for casting the narrative aside at the novel's first episode. Well, so much for the preface. I entirely agree that it is superfluous, but as it has now been written, there let it stay.

And now to business.

PART ONE

BOOK I
THE STORY OF A CERTAIN LITTLE FAMILY

I

Fyodor Pavlovich Karamazov

ALEKSEY Fyodorovich Karamazov was the third son of a landowner in our district, Fyodor Pavlovich Karamazov, so noted in his time (and even now still recollected among us) for his tragic and fishy death, which occurred just thirteen years ago and which I shall report in its proper context. All I shall say now about this 'landowner' (as he was called among us, though for most of his life he hardly ever lived on his estate at all) is that he was a strange type, one that is, however, rather often encountered, namely the type of man who is not only empty and depraved but also muddle-headed — belonging, though, to the class of muddle-headed men who are perfectly well able to handle their little property affairs, and, it would seem, these alone. Fyodor Pavlovich, for example, began with practically nothing, was a landowner of the very least important category, went trotting around other people's dinner tables, aspired to the rank of sponge, but at the moment of his decease turned out to possess something to the tune of one hundred thousand roubles in ready money. And yet at the same time he had persisted all his life in being one of the most muddle-headed madcaps in the whole of our district. I repeat: here there was no question of stupidity; the bulk of these madcaps are really quite sharp and clever — but plain muddle-headedness, and, moreover, of a peculiar, national variety.

He was married twice, and he had three sons — Dmitry Fyodorovich, the eldest, by his first spouse, and the other two, Ivan and Aleksey by his second. Fyodor Pavlovich's first spouse came from a rather well-to-do and aristocratic tribe of gentlefolk, the Miusovs, who were also landowners in our district. Just how it came to transpire that a girl with a dowry, who was also attractive and was, moreover, one of those pert, clever girls so frequently encountered in our present generation, though not entirely absent from our last, could have given her hand in marriage to such an insignificant 'weakling', as everyone called him then, I shall not labour to explain. You see, I once knew a certain young unmarried woman, back in the last 'romantic' generation, who after several years of mysterious love for a certain gentleman, whom, incidentally, she could have taken to the altar at the time of her choosing with a modicum of fuss, ended by inventing insuperable obstacles, and on a stormy night throwing herself from a lofty bank, resembling a cliff, into a rather deep and fast-flowing river and perished in it really for no other reason than her own caprice, solely in order to emulate Shakespeare's Ophelia; and one might even say that had this cliff, so long ago selected and favoured by her, been not so picturesque, and had there been on its site merely a flat, prosaic bank, then her suicide might possibly never have taken place at all. This is an authentic case, and one may suppose that in our Russian life there has, over the past two or three generations, occurred no small number of such cases, or cases of a similar nature. As in those other instances, Adelaida Ivanovna Miusova's behaviour was, without doubt, an echo of trends and ideas acquired elsewhere and also the 'fretting of a captive mind'.* It may be that she wished to demonstrate her female independence, to protest against the conditions imposed on her by society, against the despotism of her blood and family, and for one single instant, let us suppose, her complaisant imagination persuaded her that Fyodor Pavlovich, his rank of sponge notwithstanding, was none the less one of the boldest and most rapier-tongued men of that era, transitional as it was to all that was finest, while he was really only a nasty buffoon, and nothing more. Another piquant aspect of the marriage was the fact that it took place following an elopement, and Adelaida Ivanovna had found this enticing. Where Fyodor Pavlovich was concerned, his social position at the time made him thoroughly prepared for strange adventures of this kind, for he entertained a passionate wish to secure his future career by any means that lay to hand; when it came to sucking up to a good family and acquiring a dowry, this was a very alluring prospect. With regard to mutual love, it appears to have been entirely absent – both on the part of the bride and of himself, for all Adelaida Ivanovna's attractiveness. So it may have been that this incident was the only one of its kind in the life of Fyodor Pavlovich, all his life the most voluptuous-tempered of men, ready in a trice to cling to any skirt at all, no sooner did it lead him on. Yet it appears that this woman alone failed to make any particular impression on him from the voluptuary point of view.

Adelaida Ivanovna realized in a flash, immediately after the elopement, that she merely despised her husband, and that was all. In this fashion the consequences of the marriage showed themselves with extreme rapidity. Even though the family rather quickly came to regard the event as a *fait accompli* and apportioned the fugitive girl her dowry, the couple began together a disorderly existence that involved eternal scenes and rows. It was related that in the process of these the young female spouse demonstrated an incomparably greater degree of good breeding and elevation than did Fyodor Pavlovich, who, as is now notorious, diddled her right there and then, in one fell swoop, out of all her wretched money, to the tune of twenty-five thousand, as soon as she received it, with the result that as far as she was concerned, from that day on those dear little thousands might as well have sunk in the river. As for the small estate and the rather elegant town house which were also included in her dowry, for a long time he strove his utmost to have these transferred to his own name by the formulation of some suitable deed and would most likely have attained his end by the mere, as it were, contempt and revulsion he inspired in his spouse every moment with his shameless beggings and blackmailings, by the mere psychological exhaustion she endured, praying only that he would let her alone. Luckily, however, Adelaida Ivanovna's family entered the fray and placed a check on the marauder. It has been positively established that frequent fights occurred between the couple, but legend will have it that it was not Fyodor Pavlovich who administered the blows but Adelaida Ivanovna, a lady hot-blooded, audacious, dark-haired, impatient and endowed with remarkable physical strength. At last she forsook the house and ran away from Fyodor Pavlovich with a certain schoolteacher—seminarian who was practically dying of poverty, leaving her three-year-old son Mitya in the arms of her husband. In no time at all Fyodor Pavlovich had set up an entire harem in the house and begun to embark upon the most dissolute of drunken excesses, in the entr'actes of which be traversed very nearly the entire province, tearfully complaining to each and every one about his Adelaida Ivanovna's desertion, imparting as he did so details that it would be positively shameful for any married man to give about his conjugal life. The main thing was that he seemed to find it enjoyable and even flattering to act out before everyone the preposterous rôle of injured spouse and even to depict with colourful additions the details of his injury. 'Anyone would think you'd got a promotion, Fyodor Pavlovich, so pleased you are in spite of all your misfortune,' the mockers would say to him. Many would even add that in their opinion he enjoyed appearing in the revamped guise of a buffoon and that he was purposely pretending, in order to intensify their mirth, not to be aware of the comical position in which he found himself. Who can tell, however − perhaps it really was a genuine naïveté on his part. Finally he succeeded in uncovering the traces of his fugitive spouse. The poor thing was found to be in St Petersburg, whither she had moved with her seminarian and where she had wholeheartedly launched herself upon a process of the most complete emancipation. Fyodor Pavlovich had at once bestirred himself and set about making ready for the journey to St Petersburg − for what reason? − it hardly needs adding that he himself did not know. In truth, he might actually have gone; but, having taken a decision of such moment, he at once considered himself peculiarly enfranchised, for the sake of keeping up his spirits and for the road, to launch himself upon another most unbridled drunken excess. And then it was that the family of his spouse received the news of her death in St Petersburg. She had died suddenly, in a garret somewhere, according to some versions of the story of typhus, according to others − of hunger. Fyodor Pavlovich learned of the death of his spouse while drunk; some say that he went racing off down the street and began to shout, lifting his arms to the heavens in joy: 'Lord, now lettest thou!',* and others that he sobbed violently like a small child to the point where it grieved one just to look at him, all the revulsion he inspired notwithstanding. It may very well be that both the one and the other took place, that is to say, that he exulted in his liberation and wept for his liberatress − both at the same time. In the majority of instances human beings, even the evil-doers among them, are far more naïve and straightforward than we suppose. And that includes ourselves.

2

He Gets the First Son Off His Hands

It may, of course, be imagined what kind of an educator and father such a man would make. From a fatherly viewpoint he did what he was bound to do, that is to say he utterly and completely abandoned the child he had begotten with Adelaida Ivanovna, not out of any ill-feeling towards him, or any resentments of an injured spouse, but simply because he altogether forgot about him. While he was making everyone's lives a misery with his tears and complaints and was turning his house into a den of depravity, the three-year-old Mitya was taken into care by Grigory, the faithful manservant of that house, and had the latter not tended to him there might very well have been no one to change the little boy's wretched shirt. To make matters worse it at first appeared that the relatives of the child on his mother's side had also somehow contrived to forget him. His grandfather, that is to say old Miusov Senior himself, Adelaida Ivanovna's father, was no longer alive at this time; his widowed spouse, Mitya's grandmother, had moved to Moscow and fallen gravely ill, and as for the sisters, they were by now married, with the result that Mitya had to stay for almost a whole year in the care of the manservant Grigory, living with him in an *izba** in the yard. As a matter of fact, even had his father remembered him (and after all, it is impossible that he was totally unaware of his existence), he would have personally sent him back to the *izba* again, as the boy would have been a hindrance to his debaucheries. But it so happened that from Paris there returned a cousin of Adelaida Ivanovna's, Pyotr Aleksandrovich Miusov, who later lived for many years abroad but was then still a very young man, a man, however, unique among the Miusovs, being enlightened, metropolitan, foreign-educated and, moreover, all his life a European, and towards the end of his days a 'forties-and-'fifties liberal to boot. In the passage of his career he had established links with many of the most liberal men of his era, both inside Russia and out, been personally acquainted with Proudhon and Bakunin* and had, though this was now towards the end of his peregrinations, a special fondness for recollecting and relating the three days of the Paris February Revolution of the year 'forty-eight, letting it drop that he himself had very nearly been a participant of the barricades. This was one of the most gratifying memories of his youth. He possessed an independent fortune consisting of about a thousand souls on the old ratio.* His magnificent estate was situated right at the gates of our town and lay adjacent to the grounds of our illustrious monastery, with which Pyotr Aleksandrovich, back in his very early days, as soon as he had acquired his inheritance, had instantly begun a never-ending lawsuit connected with some kind of rights over river fishing or forest wood-felling, for a certainty I do not know which; all I do know is that he positively considered it his civic and enlightened obligation to instigate legal proceedings against the 'clericals'. Upon hearing all the details about Adelaida Ivanovna, whom naturally he remembered and had once even favoured with his attention, and upon learning that Mitya had been abandoned, he became – his youthful indignation and his contempt for Fyodor Pavlovich notwithstanding – actively involved in the affair. It was at this point that he met Fyodor Pavlovich for the first time. He declared to him openly that he wished to take upon himself the boy's education and upbringing. For many years afterwards he used to relate, as a characteristic detail, that when he began to talk to Fyodor Pavlovich about Mitya, Fyodor

Pavlovich looked for a while as though he could not for the life of him think what child was being discussed, and was even somewhat surprised to learn that he had in some portion of his manor a small son. Though Pyotr Aleksandrovich's story might have contained an element of exaggeration, there was in it also something that undeniably resembled the truth. But indeed, all his life Fyodor Pavlovich had a fondness for pretending, for suddenly playing out before one some unexpected rôle, something which more often than not – and here lay the essence of it – was quite unnecessary and even plain detrimental to himself, as in the present instance. This feature is, as a matter of fact, common to very many people, even the highly intelligent, and not only to the Fyodor Pavloviches of this world. Pyotr Aleksandrovich carried out his task with zeal and was even appointed (together with Fyodor Pavlovich) guardian of the little boy, as in spite of everything his mother had left behind her a small estate, with a house and land. And indeed Mitya was transferred to the custody of this uncle once-removed; but the latter had no family of his own, and as, having just settled and secured the regular payment to himself of the financial receipts from his estates, he was in a hurry to get back to a long *séjour* in Paris without delay, he entrusted the child to the care of one of his aunts twice-removed, a certain upper-class Moscow lady. It so transpired that, having put down roots in Paris, he also forgot about the boy, particularly when there came along that very same February Revolution which so stuck his imagination and which he was unable to forget for the rest of his life. As for the upper-class Moscow lady, she died, and Mitya was transferred to the home of one of her married daughters. It appears that he subsequently changed nests yet a fourth time. On this I shall not now expand, the more so as there still remains much for me to tell about this first-born son of Fyodor Pavlovich; for the present I shall instead restrict myself to giving the most salient information about him, without which it is impossible for me even to begin the novel.

The first point is that this Dmitry Fyodorovich was the only one of Fyodor Pavlovich's three sons who grew up in the conviction that in spite of everything he possessed a certain fortune and that when he attained his maturity would be independent. His boyhood and youth took a disorderly course: after dropping out of the gymnasium he subsequently ended up in a military academy, then served in the Caucasus, rose in the ranks, fought a duel, was demoted, rose in the ranks again, led a most extravagant life and spent a relatively large amount of money. He did not begin to receive any from Fyodor Pavlovich until he was twenty-one, and so ran himself badly into debt. The first time he set eyes on Fyodor Pavlovich, his own father, was after his maturity, when he came especially to our parts in order to discuss with him the question of his property. He seems to have disliked his parent even then; he stayed with him only for a short time and left quickly, having done no more than obtain from him a certain sum and enter into some kind of deal with him concerning the subsequent receipt of income from the estate, neither the profit nor the value of which (a fact that deserves to be noted) he was able to ascertain from his father at that time. Fyodor Pavlovich perceived then, at first glance (this too needs to be borne in mind), that Mitya had an exaggerated and erroneous notion of the size of his fortune. Fyodor Pavlovich was very pleased about this, seeing in it particular advantages for himself. He deduced merely that the young man was thoughtless, turbulent, at the mercy of his passions, impatient, the kind of debauchee who needs only to be given temporary, short-term handouts in order, though for no more than a brief period, of course, to be kept happy. This it was that Fyodor Pavlovich proceeded to take advantage of, getting rid of his son with small handouts, remittances to tide him over, until in the end it so transpired that when, some four years later, Mitya, his patience at an end, appeared in our little town for the second time in order now finally to settle the matter with his parent, it turned out, to his very great bewilderment, that he owned precisely nothing, that it was even hard to get any precise figures, that he had already received from Fyodor Pavlovich in cash the entire value of his property and might even owe him money; that according to the terms of certain arrangements and deals into which he had entered on certain dates of his own accord he was not entitled to demand any more, etcetera, etcetera. The young man was horror-struck, suspected lying and deceit, became nearly beside himself and almost lost his reason. This was the event that led to the catastrophe, the description of which constitutes the subject of my first, introductory novel or rather its outer aspect. Before I proceed to that novel, however, I must first relate a thing or two concerning Fyodor Pavlovich's other two sons, Mitya's brothers, and explain where they, too, sprang from.

3

A Second Marriage and Second Children

HAVING got the four-year-old Mitya off his hands, Fyodor Pavlovich very soon after married a second time. This second marriage endured for some eight years. He took this second spouse of his, also a very young lady, Sofya Ivanovna by name, from another province, where he had gone in order to attend to some minor contracting business with a little Jew associate. Fyodor Pavlovich, though he spent extravagantly, drank and indulged in debauchery, never ceased to concern himself with the investment of his capital and always arranged his business affairs successfully though, it went without saying, almost invariably with more than a touch of shabbiness. Sofya Ivanovna was of that category known as 'orphan', without kith or kin since childhood; the daughter of some obscure deacon she had grown up in the rich household of her benefactress, governess and tormentress, an old lady of noble family, the widow of a General Vorokhov. The details I do not know — I have heard only that the foster-child, a meek, forgiving creature who would not say boo to a goose, was once taken down from a rope on which she had tried to hang herself from a nail in the storeroom — so hard had she found it to endure the wilfulness and perpetual scoldings of the old woman who by all accounts bore no malice but whom idleness had turned into a most insufferable petty tyrant. Fyodor Pavlovich offered his hand, his background was investigated, and he was chased from the doorstep; at that point, as in his first marriage, he proposed an elopement to the orphan girl. It is very, very possible that she too would on no account have agreed to marry him had she known a few more facts about him in proper time. But the marriage took place in another province; and in any case what could a sixteen-year-old girl possibly make of it all beyond realizing that she would be better off throwing herself in the river than staying with her benefactress? And so the poor thing exchanged benefactress for benefactor. On this occasion Fyodor Pavlovich received not a groat, as the general's widow became angry, refused to part with any money and, what was more, railed at them both; but he had not been counting on money, and made do with succumbing to the innocent young girl's remarkable beauty and, in particular, to her innocent air which had startled him, voluptuary that he was, and hitherto the dissolute fancier of only the grosser kind of female beauty. 'Those innocent little eyes slashed my soul like a razor,' he would say later on with a loathsome snigger that was all his own. As a matter of fact, in a profligate like him this could simply have been a lustful attraction. Having received no dowry money, Fyodor Pavlovich lost no time on empty ceremonies with his spouse and, exploiting the fact that she was, in a manner of speaking, 'guilty' in his regard and that he had practically 'taken her from the rope', and exploiting, what was more, her phenomenal humility and meekness, trod underfoot the most basic conjugal proprieties. Women of ill-repute flocked into the house, right there, in front of his wife, and orgies took place. In order to add a touch of detail, I shall relate that the manservant Grigory, a stupid, morose and stubborn answerer-back who had hated his previous mistress, Adelaida Ivanovna, on this occasion took the part of his new mistress, spoke out in her support and quarrelled with Fyodor Pavlovich on account of her in a fashion almost unallowable for a servant, and once even broke up the orgy and shooed the troops of viragos from the doorstep by force. The unhappy young woman, who had been intimidated from her childhood, subsequently fell prey to a kind of female nervous disorder that is most frequently encountered among the common folk, in country women, who because of it are named 'wailers'.* At times this disorder, with its terrible attacks of hysteria, even made the sick woman lose her reason. Nevertheless, she bore Karamazov two sons, Ivan and Aleksey, the former in the first year of their marriage, and the latter three years thereafter. The little boy Aleksey was not yet four when she died, yet strange as it may seem, I know that he later remembered his mother all his life – as in a dream, needless to say. Upon her death both boys suffered almost precisely the same fate as that endured by the first son, Mitya: they were completely forgotten and neglected by their father and also ended up with Grigory in his outbuilding. In the outbuilding they, too, were found by the old petty tyrant of a general's widow, their mother's benefactress and educatrix. She was still alive and during all that time, a whole eight years, had been unable to forget the offence that had been inflicted on her. Throughout all of those eight years she had had at her fingertips the most precise information concerning the life of her 'Sofya' and, hearing that she was ill and surrounded by such disgraceful goings-on, she said out loud to her retainers two or three times: 'She's got what she deserved, that's what God has sent her for her ingratitude.'

Exactly three months from the day of Sofya Ivanovna's death, the general's widow suddenly arrived in our town and presented herself directly and in person at Fyodor Pavlovich's quarters and, though she only remained in the town for half an hour in all, achieved much. It was the evening hour. Fyodor Pavlovich, on whom she had not set eyes for a whole eight years, came out to greet her – yes, drunk. They say that in an instant, without any explanations, as soon as she caught sight of him, she gave him two noble and resounding slaps on the face, tugged him three times by the forelock, up and down – and then, without adding a word, set off straight for the outbuilding and the two boys. Having

observed from one glance that they were unwashed and in dirty underwear, she immediately delivered another slap to Grigory, announced to
him that she was removing both children into her own custody, then led
them out in their underwear, swathed them in a rug, seated them in her
carriage and drove them away to her town. Grigory endured this blow
like a devoted vassal, offering not so much as a word of crude invective,
and as he was escorting the old mistress to her carriage, bowed from the
waist before her and imposingly declared: 'God will recompense you for
the orphans.' 'I don't care what you say, you're an idle dunderhead!' the
general's widow cried to him as she drove off. Pondering the whole
arrangement afterwards, Fyodor Pavlovich decided that it was a good
one, and in granting his subsequent formal consent to having his children
brought up in the home of the general's widow, he did not renege on a
single point. As for the slaps he had received, he himself drove around
the whole town telling people about them.

It came to pass that the general's widow, too, died soon after this —
not, however, before stipulating in her will that both urchins should
receive the sum of a thousand roubles, 'for their education, and that this
money shall be expended upon them without fail, but in such a way that
there be enough to last them until their maturity, for even a dole such as
this is excessive for such children, and if anyone shall feel so inclined,
then let him loosen his purse-strings as he thinks fit', and so on, and so
forth. I myself have not read the will, but I have heard that it really did
contain some strange passage of this kind, phrased in a rather curious
manner. But the old lady's principal inheritor turned out to be an honest
man, Yefim Petrovich Polyonov, the marshal of nobility in that province.
Having exchanged letters with Fyodor Pavlovich and having instantly
divined that nothing would be forthcoming from him to support the
upbringing of his own children (though Fyodor Pavlovich never openly
refused, but merely employed delaying tactics as he always did in such
cases, sometimes with a positive outpouring of sentimentalities), he took
a personal concern for the orphans, developing a particular fondness for
the younger of them, Aleksey, with the result that the latter actually
spent a long time growing up in his household. This fact I ask the reader
to observe right from the very start. And if there was one person to
whom the young men owed a lifelong debt for their upbringing and
education, it was namely to this Yefim Petrovich, a most decent and
humane man of a kind that is seldom encountered. He preserved the
thousand-rouble doles that had been left the urchins by the general's
widow untouched, so that by the advent of their maturity these sums had

grown by the addition of interest to twice their original size, brought
them up on his own money and, of course, spent far more than a
thousand roubles on each. I shall not for the moment embark upon the
detailed story of their childhood and youth, but will chart only the main
points. Indeed, concerning the elder boy, Ivan, I shall say only that he
grew up a rather gloomy lad, closed off in himself, far from being timid,
but having even at the age of ten perceived that they were growing up in
someone else's family and at the mercy of someone else's good graces and
that their father was someone whom it was shameful even to speak of, and
so on and so forth. This boy very quickly, almost in infancy (so it was
related, at least), began to manifest certain unusual and brilliant learning
abilities. The exact details I do not know, it somehow transpired that
he parted company with Yefim Petrovich's family when he was scarcely
thirteen years old, passing on to one of the Moscow gymnasia and
boarding in the home of an experienced and renowned pedagogue of the
time who had been a friend of Yefim Petrovich's since childhood. Ivan
himself would tell people later on that it was all the result, as it were, of
the 'passion for good deeds' nourished by Yefim Petrovich, who had
been enthralled by the idea that the boy's genius-like abilities required to
be fostered by an educator of genius. As a matter of fact, however,
neither Yefim Petrovich nor the educator of genius were still alive by the
time the young man, his gymnasium studies completed, began university.
Since Yefim Petrovich had ordered things badly and the receipt of the
money that had been bequeathed to the boys by the petty tyrant of a
general's widow, money that had now increased to twice its value, was
delayed because of various formalities and procrastinations quite inevitable
in our country, the young man had a pretty hard time of it during his
first two years at the university, as he was during all this period compelled
to feed and maintain himself as well as perform his studies. It should be
observed that during these years he made not the slightest attempt to
communicate with his father by letter – possibly out of pride, and
contempt for him, but possibly also as an outcome of a cold, common-
sense reasoning, which whispered in his ear that he could expect to
receive from his papa nothing even approaching a serious level of support.
For all this, the young man did not in any way lose his presence of mind
and managed to obtain work, initially giving lessons at twenty-five
copecks an hour, and then going around the editorial offices of the
newspapers and delivering short articles of a dozen lines about street
incidents under the *nom de plume* 'Eyewitness'. It is said that these articles
were always so interestingly and piquantly composed that they quickly

gained currency, and already in this alone the young man showed his practical and intellectual superiority over that numerous, forever wanting and unhappy portion of our scholastic youth of both sexes which in our capital cities usually haunts the thresholds of the various newspapers and journals, unable to think up anything better than the eternal repetition of the same old plea for French translation or copying. Having introduced himself to the editorial offices, Ivan Fyodorovich maintained his contacts with them throughout all the time that followed and during his last years at university began to publish thoroughly talented critiques of books on various specialized themes, with the result that he actually even became well-known in certain literary coteries. Only very lately, however, had he succeeded in drawing to himself quite suddenly the particular attention of a much larger circle of readers, so that a great many people noticed and remembered him at the same time. This was a rather curious event. At the time of his leaving the university and preparing to travel abroad on his two thousand, Ivan Fyodorovich suddenly published in one of the main newspapers a certain strange article which drew the attention even of non-specialists and was particularly remarkable for concerning a subject about which, on the face of it, he might have been thought to know nothing at all, as his degree had been in natural science. The article had been written about the question, universally discussed at the time, of the Ecclesiastical Court.* In a discussion of several already received opinions on this subject, he also stated his own personal view. The principal thing was the tone of the piece and its remarkably unexpected conclusion. Many of the proponents of the Church's cause really considered the author to be one of their own. And then suddenly, along with them, not only the proponents of the civic cause but also the atheists themselves began for their part to applaud. Eventually one or two astute men decided that the entire article was merely an insolent farce and a piece of mockery. I make particular mention of the said event for the reason that this article also penetrated to the famous monastery that lies just outside our town, where there was a general interest in the current question of the Ecclesiastical Court – penetrated there and caused total bafflement. The author's name being learned, interest was also aroused by the fact that he was a native of our town and a son of 'that Fyodor Pavlovich fellow'. And then suddenly at around this time the author himself turned up in our midst.

The reason for Ivan Fyodorovich's having come to us at that time was, I recall, even then a question I asked myself almost with a kind of uneasiness. This arrival which was so fateful and which was to serve as the origin of so many consequences for me long afterwards, the rest of my life, almost, remained to me a matter of obscurity. Speaking quite generally, it was strange that a young man, so proud, so learned and possessed of such apparent caution, should suddenly present himself on the doorstep of such a disgraceful household, to such a father, who had all his life ignored, neglected and forgotten him, and who even though he would not on any account have parted with money, not even if his sons had asked him for it, had nevertheless lived all his life in fear that his sons Ivan and Aleksey might one day come and do just that. And now here was the young man settling into the house of such a father, living with him from one month to the next, and both getting along with each other as well as could possibly be imagined. This latter circumstance was a source of especial surprise not only to myself, but to many other people as well. Pyotr Aleksandrovich Miusov, of whom I have already spoken above, a distant relative of Fyodor Pavlovich's on the side of his first wife, happened to be among us again at that time on his out-of-town estate, gracing us with a visit from Paris, where he had by now completely made himself at home. I remember that he was really more surprised than anyone to make the acquaintance of the young man who interested him in the extreme and with whom he sometimes, not without inner chagrin, exchanged caustic displays of general knowledge. 'He's proud,' he used to tell us concerning him. 'He'll always be able to get hold of a copeck or two, even now he has enough to go abroad – so what's he doing here? It's clear to everyone that he hasn't come to his father for money, because on no account will his father give him any. He doesn't like drinking and fornicating, yet the old man can't manage without him, they're on such good terms!' This was true; the young man had an almost visible influence on his old father, who sometimes almost seemed to act in obedience to him, though he was now and then extremely and even aggressively wilful; he even sometimes started to behave with more decorum . . .

Only subsequently was it explained that Ivan Fyodorovich had arrived partly at the request and on the business of his elder brother, Dmitry Fyodorovich, on whom he had set eyes for the first time in his life almost at this very same time, the occasion of his arrival from Moscow, but with whom, however, he had even before this entered into correspondence on a certain important matter which was of primary concern to Dmitry Fyodorovich. As to what the details of this matter were the reader will be fully apprised in good time. All the same I must say that even when I learned about this peculiar circumstance, Ivan Fyodorovich still appeared an enigma to me, and his arrival among us none the less inexplicable.

I shall also add that at the time in question Ivan Fyodorovich performed the rôle of mediator and conciliator between his father and his elder brother, Dmitry Fyodorovich, who had started a major quarrel with his father and had even begun a formal legal action against him.

I repeat that during the days in question this little family met together for the first time in its life, and that several of its members saw each other for the first time in theirs. Only the youngest son, Aleksey Fyodorovich, had lived among us for a year previous to this and had thus come to us first of the brothers. It is this Aleksey who presents me with the greatest difficulty in speaking of in my prefatory narrative, before I lead him out upon the boards of the novel proper. But about him, too, I must write a preface, if only to cast some light in advance upon a certain very strange circumstance, to wit: that right from the novel's first scene I am constrained to present my future hero to the reader garbed in the cassock of a novice. Yes, for about a year now he had been living in our monastery and, it appeared, was preparing to lock himself up in it for the rest of his days.

4

The Third Son Alyosha

AT that time he was only twenty years old (his brother Ivan was then in his twenty-fourth year, while their eldest brother, Dmitry, was in his twenty-eighth). Before anything else I declare that this youth, Alyosha, was in no sense a fanatic, nor even in my opinion at any rate a mystic at all. I shall state in advance my complete opinion: he was simply an early lover of mankind,* and if he had struck out along the monastery road it was only because it had at that time made a strong impression on him and presented itself to him as, so to speak, an ideal of deliverance for his soul, straining as it was out of the murk of worldly hatred unto the light of love. And this very road had only made such a strong impression on him because he had at that time encountered a being by his estimate unusual – Father Zosima, the renowned Elder of our monastery, to whom he had attached himself with all the first ardent love of his quenchless heart. Actually, I will not argue that even then he was a pretty strange fellow, and had been thus since the cradle. I have, incidentally, already said of him that, having lost his mother when he was in his fourth year, he remembered her all the rest of his life, her face, her caresses, 'every bit as though she stood before me in real life'. Images of this kind may be recalled (and this is no secret) from a yet earlier age, as far back as the age of two, but in such a manner that they emerge all one's life only as bright points in the dark, like a tiny corner torn from an enormous picture which has all faded and disappeared, apart from that one little corner. Exactly so it was with him: he remembered a certain evening, aestival, calm, an open window, the oblique rays of the setting sun* (those oblique rays were what he remembered most of all), in a corner of a room an icon, before it a lighted lamp, and in front of the icon on her knees, sobbing as in a fit of hysterics, with screechings and shriekings, his mother, gripping him with both hands, embracing him tightly to the point of pain and supplicating for him to the Mother of God, stretching him forth out of her embraces with both hands towards the icon as though into the protection of the Mother . . . and suddenly the nurse running in and tearing him from her arms in panic. There was a picture! Alyosha also remembered his mother's face at that instant: he would say that it was frenzied but magnificent, to judge by what he could remember. But he seldom liked to confide this memory to anyone. In childhood and youth he was not very expansive, nor even very talkative, but not because of suspicion, timidity or morose aversion to human company, quite the opposite indeed, but because of something other than this, a kind of inner concern, purely private and not affecting others, but so important to him that because of it he seemed to forget other people. But he liked human beings: he seemed to live all his life with a complete faith in them, and yet no one ever thought him a simpleton or a naïf. About him there was something that said and suggested (and was to do so for the rest of his life) that he did not want to be a judge of men, that he did not want to take upon himself the task of censure and would not apportion it on any account. He even seemed to tolerate anything, without the slightest condemnation, though often with bitter sadness. Moreover, in this respect he came to the point where no one could either frighten or astonish him, and this while he was still in the very earliest part of his youth. In presenting himself at the age of twenty on his father's doorstep and entering a positive den of filthy lewdness he, the chaste and pure one, only moved away without a word when to look was unendurable, but without the slightest air of contempt or censure in anyone's regard. On the other hand his father, a one-time retainer and for that reason a man sensitive and quick to detect injury, having initially greeted him with sullen suspicion (as though to say: 'he doesn't talk much and keeps a lot to himself'), soon found himself, after no more than a couple of weeks, embracing and kissing the lad unconscionably often, with drunken tears it is true, in maudlin sentimentality, but clearly having grown deeply and sincerely fond of him and in such a manner, of course, as a man such as he had never succeeded in liking anyone . . .

Indeed, everyone liked this youth wherever he showed his face, and this had been true ever since his most childish years. Finding himself in the home of his benefactor and educator, Yefim Petrovich Polyonov, he had won the attachment of every member of that household to such a degree that he had well and truly been considered there as one of its own children. Yet at such immature years had he entered that household that it was quite out of the question for anyone to suspect any calculating slyness or pushing in the child, any proficiency in the art of fawning, ingratiating behaviour, of making himself be liked. So it must have been that he contained within himself by his very nature, as it were, directly and without artifice, the gift of arousing an especial affection towards him. The same thing had also happened to him at school, and yet it would appear that he was precisely the sort of child that arouses the mistrust, the occasional mockery and possibly even the hatred of its companions. He used, for example, to lapse into reflection and seemingly to cut himself off. From an early age he liked to withdraw into a corner and read books, yet so well-liked was he by his companions that he really could have been described as a universal favourite during the entire period of his attendance at the school. He was seldom frolicsome, seldom even cheerful, but one look at him instantly told them all that this was not because of any moroseness on his part, but that, on the contrary, he was equable and serene. He never made any attempt to show off among his coevals. It may have been for this reason that he was never afraid of anyone, yet the boys at once understood that he by no means took pride in his fearlessness, but gazed at them as though he did not know he was bold and fearless. He never remembered an insult. It would transpire that an hour after the insult he would reply to its deliverer or personally engage him in conversation with such a serene and trustful air as to indicate that nothing was amiss between them at all. And it was not that in doing so he wore an air which said he had casually forgotten or purposely forgiven the insult, but that he simply did not view it as an insult at all, and it was this that really captivated the children and subdued them. He possessed, though, a certain feature which throughout all the forms of the gymnasium, from the lowest to the highest, aroused in his companions a constant desire to make fun of him – not out of spiteful mockery, however, but because they thought it hilarious. This feature of his was a savage, frenzied modesty and chastity. He could not

abide certain words and certain kinds of stories about women. These
'certain' words and stories are, unfortunately, impossible to eradicate in
schools. Boys who are pure of soul and heart, still children really, very
often like to talk in the classroom among themselves and even within
earshot about things, images and scenes of which not even soldiers will
invariably talk, quite apart from the fact that soldiers are an ignorant lot
and do not understand much of what in this sphere is already common
knowledge to the still so youthful offspring of our intelligentsia and
higher social orders. There is probably as yet no perversion of morals
here, and there is also no real cynicism of the ingrained, lascivious kind;
it is sooner external in nature and is not infrequently considered among
them as something positively delicate, subtle, mettlesome and worthy of
imitation. When they saw that 'that Alyosha Karamazov' quickly put his
fingers in his ears whenever they began to talk about 'you know what',
they would sometimes purposely stand around him in a crowd and,
forcibly removing his hands from his ears, shout foul things into them,
while he strained to break free, sank to the floor, lay down, covered
himself up, and all this without saying a single word to them, without
returning a word of abuse, and enduring the outrage in silence. Eventually,
however, they left him in peace and stopped teasing him for being a
'girl', and even viewed him with compassion in this regard. In his classes
he was, by the way, invariably one of the best students, but he never
came first.

    When Yefim Petrovich died, Alyosha continued to attend the provin-
cial gymnasium for another two years. Yefim Petrovich's inconsolable
spouse set off almost immediately after his death for a long stay in Italy
accompanied by her entire household, which consisted exclusively of
female persons, and Alyosha ended up in the home of two ladies he had
never seen in his life before, some kind of distant relatives of Yefim
Petrovich; though on what conditions, he himself did not know. It was
also a characteristic feature of him, one exceedingly so, in fact, that he
never worried about whose means he was living on. In this he was the
complete opposite of his elder brother, Ivan Fyodorovich, who had spent
his first two years at university in poverty, supporting himself by his
own efforts, and had since early childhood sensed bitterly that he was
living as a dependant on his benefactor. Yet it seems wrong to be too
hard on this strange feature of Aleksey's character, because everyone who
got to know him even slightly, as soon as this question arose at once
became certain that here was a youth who almost resembled a holy fool
and who, even if he were suddenly to be landed with an entire capital

fortune, would have no difficulty in giving it away at the first demand to some good cause, or perhaps simply to a clever old fox, if the latter should ask him for it. As a general matter, indeed, it was as if he had no idea at all of the value of money, if we leave aside the literal sense of that expression. When he was given pocket money, for which he himself never asked, either he kept it for weeks on end, uncertain of what to do with it, or was alarmingly spendthrift of it, and it vanished in a trice. Pyotr Aleksandrovich Miusov, a man of great sensitivity on the subject of money and bourgeois rectitude, once subsequently, having taken a good look at Aleksey, pronounced the following aphorism concerning him: 'Behold possibly the only man in the world who if one were suddenly to abandon him alone and without money on a square in an unfamiliar city of a million inhabitants, would on no account go under or die of hunger and cold, because he would instantly be fed, instantly be settled, and, if he were not, then would himself instantly see to it that he was, and this would cost him no effort and no degradation, and the person who settled him would find it no burden, but might, on the contrary, view it as a pleasure.'

He did not complete the course at his gymnasium; he still had a whole year to put in when he suddenly declared to his ladies that he was going to see his father on a certain business matter that had come into his head. The ladies cherished him greatly and were reluctant to let him go. The cost of the journey was very little, and the ladies would not hear of him pawning his watch – a gift he had received from the family of his benefactor before their departure abroad, but granted him generous provision of means, even of new clothing and linen. He, however, returned to them half of the money, declaring that he wished without fail to travel third class. On arriving in our little town and facing the demand of his parent to know why he had come to see him without having completed his course he was, so they say, more than usually reflective. It soon came to light that he was searching for his mother's grave. He himself more or less admitted at the time that that was the sole reason for his arrival. But this can hardly have been so. It is far more probable that he himself did not know what it was and could not for the life of him have explained just what had suddenly stirred within his soul, inexorably drawing him along some new, unknown but now unavoidable road. Fyodor Pavlovich was unable to point out to him the spot where he had buried his second spouse as he had never been to her grave again after the day of her funeral, and through fault of the years had completely forgotten where that day they had buried her . . .

Some incidental comments about Fyodor Pavlovich. For a long time previous to this he had lived in places other than our town. Some three or four years after the death of his second wife he had set off for the south of Russia and had ultimately ended up in Odessa, where he passed several years in succession. At first he had made the acquaintance, to employ his own words, 'of a lot of big Yids, little Yids, Yiddikins and Yidlets', and had ended by being 'the guest of the Jews as well'. One must suppose that it was at this period of his life that he developed in himself a particular talent for the scraping together and extortion of the lucre. He had finally returned to our little town again only some three years before Alyosha's arrival. His former acquaintances found he had aged terribly, though he was by no means yet an old man. Not that his behaviour was any more decent than it had been — it was if anything more insolent. There had appeared in the old buffoon, for example, a brazen compulsion to make buffoons of others. Far from having given up his disgraceful carryings-on with the female sex, if anything he continued it in a more loathsome manner. It was not long before he became the founder of a large number of new drinking-houses in the district. One could see that he was worth possibly something like a hundred thousand roubles or only slightly less. Many of the inhabitants of our town and district immediately borrowed from him — on the most reliable security, needless to say. Just lately, though, he seemed to have run to fat, had somehow begun to lose his equability, his self-accountability, had even fallen into a kind of light-mindedness, beginning one thing and ending with another, somehow spilling out of his mould and more and more often drinking himself under the table, until had it not been for that very same manservant Grigory, who had also by this time aged and sometimes looked after him almost like a *gouverneur*, Fyodor Pavlovich would not have got by without especial difficulty. Alyosha's arrival even seemed to have an effect on him from the moral point of view, as though inside this premature dotard there had awoken some element of that which had long ago expired within his soul: 'Do you realize,' he often began to say to Alyosha, taking a good look at him, 'that you look like her, the "wailer"?' This was the name he had given his deceased wife, Alyosha's mother. In the end it was the manservant Grigory who pointed out to Alyosha the 'wailer's' little grave. He had taken him to our municipal cemetery and there, in a remote little corner had shown him the cheap but tidy cast-iron slab on which there was even an inscription with her name, estate, age and year of death, with at the bottom something akin to the old four-line rhyming epitaphs that are commonly found on the graves of bourgeois townsfolk. Surprisingly, this slab turned out to be the work of Grigory. He himself had erected it over the grave of the poor 'wailer' at his own expense, after Fyodor Pavlovich, whom he had on numerous occasions exasperated by mentioning this little sepulchre, finally departed for Odessa, shrugging his shoulders not only at the grave, but at all his memories as well. Alyosha had displayed no particular emotion at his mother's little grave; he simply listened to Grigory's pompous and moralistic tale concerning the erection of the slab, stood for a while with his head lowered and left without having uttered a word. Ever since that time, for a whole year almost, he had not been back to the cemetery. But this minor episode had also produced its effect on Fyodor Pavlovich, and it was a very singular one. He suddenly picked up a thousand roubles and took it to our monastery, donating it in memory of his spouse's soul – but it was not his second spouse he meant, not Alyosha's mother, the 'wailer', but his first, Adelaida Ivanovna, the one who had given him beatings. On the evening of that day he got himself drunk and vilified the monks to Alyosha. He himself was far from being one of the religious; the man had in all likelihood never placed so much as a five-copeck candle in front of an icon. Strange bursts of sudden emotion and sudden ideas are common in such types.

I have already said that he had grown very fat and flabby. His physiognomy had by this time acquired something that bore sharp witness to the essential characteristics of the entire kind of life he had lived. Not only were there long, meaty pouches under his little eyes, which were forever brazen, suspicious and mocking; not only was there a host of deep wrinkles on his small but pudgy face: beneath his jutting chin there hung a large Adam's apple, fleshy and oblong, like a purse, which somehow gave him a loathsomely concupiscent air. Add to this a long, carnivorous mouth with puffy lips, behind which could be glimpsed small fragments of black teeth that had almost entirely rotted away. Each time he began to speak he emitted a spray of spittle. As a matter of fact, he himself liked to make jokes about his face, though he seemed content with it. He particularly liked to draw attention to his nose, which was not very large but was very elegant and had a strongly pronounced hook-form: 'A real Roman one,' he would say, 'which together with my Adam's apple reproduces the true physiognomy of an Ancient Roman patrician of the period of the decadence.' Of this he was apparently proud.

And then quite soon after his encounter with his mother's grave Alyosha suddenly declared to him that he wished to enter the monastery and that the monks were prepared to admit him as a novice. In doing so he explained that this was his extreme desire and that he was asking his solemn permission as father. The old man was already aware that the Elder Zosima, who was living in the monastery hermitage, had made a particular impression on the 'quiet boy'.

'Of course, that Elder is the most honest monk they've got over there,' he said, having silently and reflectively heard Alyosha out, yet scarcely at all astonished by his request. 'Hm, so that's where you want to go, my quiet boy!' He was half drunk and suddenly smiled his long smile, a smile which though semi-intoxicated did not lack cunning and drunken slyness. 'Hm, I had a feeling you would end up doing something like this, do you know? This is exactly what you've been aiming for. Well, so be it, on you go, after all you've got your two little thousand, they'll do you for a dowry, and I, my angel, will never abandon you, and even now I shall contribute whatever the going rate is for you if they ask me. Though, of course, if they don't ask, why make a nuisance of ourselves, eh? After all, you're like a canary with your money, two pecks a week ... Hm. You know, there's one monastery at a place not far from here where they have a little colony, and it's common knowledge that it's only the 'monastery wives', as they call them, who live in it – about thirty pieces of wife I think there are ... I've been there and you know it's interesting, in its own way, of course, as a sort of variety. The only drawback is the terrible *russisme* of the place, they haven't any French girls at all as yet, but they could have, there's bags of money. When they find out about it – then they'll start arriving. Well, but there's none of that here, no monastery wives, but about two hundred monks instead. They're a decent bunch. Observe the fasts. I have to hand it to them ... Hm. So you want to be a monk, do you? You know, I'll miss you, Alyosha; believe you me, I really have grown fond of you ... But actually, you know, it's quite convenient: you'll be able to pray for us sinners, and we shall need it, for we've done rather a lot of sinning while we've been here. I've often wondered who would ever say a prayer for me. Is there such a person in the world? My dear boy, you know, I'm really horribly stupid on that account; or don't you believe me? Horribly. You see, I may be stupid, but I go on thinking and thinking about that – oh, now and again, of course, not all the time. I mean, I think it's out of the question that the devils will forget to drag me off with them when I kick the bucket. But then I think: what about those hooks?* Where do they get them from? What are they made of? Iron? Where do they make them? Is there some sort of factory down there? I mean, those fellows over in the monastery no doubt believe that hell has a ceiling. But you see I'm prepared to believe in hell, only it must be one that doesn't have a ceiling; it seems more refined, more enlightened that way – sort of Lutheran, really. But really, in the end it'll all be the same, won't it? Whether there's a ceiling or whether there isn't? Yes, that's the nub of the whole damned question! Well, and if there isn't a ceiling then there won't be any hooks either. And if there aren't any hooks, and that's the end of it, then I still find it hard to believe in: who'll drag me off on hooks, and if no one does, what will happen then, where will there be any justice? *Il faudrait les inventer*, those hooks, especially for me, for me alone, because if you only knew, Alyosha, what a shameless fellow I am! . . .'

'But there aren't any hooks there,' Alyosha said quietly and earnestly, giving his father a close scrutiny.

'Yes, yes, only the shadows of hooks. I know, I know. That is how a certain Frenchman described hell: *'J'ai vu l'ombre d'un cocher, qui avec l'ombre d'une brosse frottait l'ombre d'une carrosse'.** My dear lad, how do you know there aren't any hooks? Wait till you've been with the monks for a bit, then you'll be singing another tune. But anyway, off you go, work your way to the truth over there, and then come and tell me about it: whatever they say, a man would feel better about going to the next world if he knew what he'd find there. And as a matter of fact, it will be more suitable for you to be with those monks than with me, a drunken old man and his tarts . . . though you're like an angel, and none of it affects you. Well, and it's possible nothing will affect you there, either, and that is why I'm giving you my permission – because my hopes are pinned on the latter. The devil hasn't addled your brains. You'll burn up and cool down again, be cured and come back to me. And I shall be waiting for you: for after all, I feel you're the only person in the world who hasn't condemned me, my dear boy, I feel it, and I can't do other than feel it! . . .'

And he even burst into whimpering. He was sentimental. He was in a bad mood and sentimental.

5

The Elders

POSSIBLY some readers will suppose my young man to have been a morbid, ecstatic, poorly developed nature, a pallid dreamer, a consumptive

and haggard manikin. On the contrary, Alyosha was at that time a person-
able, red-cheeked youth of nineteen with a bright gaze and bursting with
health. He was in those days even very handsome – well-proportioned, of
average height, with dark-brown hair and a straight, though somewhat
elongated oval of a face, brilliant wide-spaced dark-grey eyes, most
reflective and to all appearance most calm. It will, perhaps, be said
that red cheeks are no obstacle to either fanaticism or mysticism; but it
seems to me that Alyosha was even more of a realist than anyone. Oh, it
cannot be denied that in the monastery he believed completely in miracles,
but in my experience miracles never bother a realist. It is not miracles
that incline a realist towards faith. The true realist, if he is not a believer,
will invariably find within himself the strength and the ability not to
believe in miracles either, and if a miracle stands before him as an
incontrovertible fact, he will sooner disbelieve his senses than admit that
fact. And even if he does admit it, it will be as a fact of nature, but one
that until now has been obscure to him. In the realist it is not faith that is
born of miracles, but miracles of faith. Once the realist believes, his
realism inexorably compels him to admit miracles too. The Apostle
Thomas declared that he would not believe until he saw, and when he
saw, said: 'My Lord and my God.' Was it the miracle that had made him
believe? The likeliest explanation is that it was not, and that he came to
believe for the sole reason that he wanted to believe and, perhaps, in the
inmost corners of his being already fully believed, even when he said:
'Except I shall see . . . I will not believe.'*

It will, perhaps, be said that Alyosha was dull-minded, undeveloped,
had not completed his course, and the like. That he had not completed
his course is true; but to say that he was dull-minded or stupid would be
to do him a great injustice. I shall merely reiterate what I have already
said above: he had entered upon this road simply because at that time it
alone had made a strong impression on him and presented itself to him at
once as an ideal of deliverance for his soul which was straining out of the
murk unto the light. Add to this that he was in part a youth of our most
recent times, that is to say honest by his very nature, demanding truth
and justice, seeking and striving to believe in them and, having come to
do so, demanding with all the power of his soul an immediate part in
them, demanding a quick deed, with the unbending desire to sacrifice
everything for that deed, even his life. Though it is unfortunately the
case that these youths fail to comprehend that the sacrifice of one's life is,
in a large number of such instances, possibly the easiest option, and that
to sacrifice, for example, five or six years of one's youth-inflamed life on

difficult, laborious study, on book-learning, even if only for the purpose of decupling within oneself the strength required in order to serve that same truth and that same deed which has become one's dearest aspiration and which one has set oneself the task of accomplishing – such a sacrifice is quite often almost entirely beyond many of them. All that Alyosha did was to select a road that ran contrary to all the others, but with the same thirst for a quick deed. No sooner, having given the matter some serious thought, had he been struck by the conviction that God and immortality existed, than he immediately, of course, said to himself: 'I want to live for immortality, and I will accept no half-way compromise.' By precisely the same lights, had he decided that God and immortality did not exist he would have immediately become an atheist and a socialist (for socialism is not only a problem of labour, or the so-called 'fourth estate', but is in the first instance a problem of atheism, of the contemporary embodiment of atheism, the problem of the Tower of Babel, constructed expressly without God, not for the attainment of heaven from earth, but for the abasement of heaven to earth). Alyosha found the prospect of continuing to live his life as before positively strange and even impossible. As the Scriptures say: 'If thou wilt be perfect, distribute all that thou hast and come, follow me.'* But Alyosha said to himself: 'I cannot give up two roubles instead of "all", and instead of "come, follow me" merely attend Mass.' It may have been that from the memories of his infancy there had remained some image of our local monastery, where his mother may have taken him to morning liturgy. Or again, it may have been the effect of the oblique rays of the setting sun before the icon towards which his 'wailer' mother had stretched him forth. He may only have come to us then in reflection in order to find out whether here too there were only two roubles and – in the monastery encountered this Elder . . .

This Elder, as I have already explained above, was the Elder Zosima; but here I must also say a few words about the general nature of the 'Elders' in our monasteries, and now declare my regret that upon this road I do not feel myself to be sufficiently competent or assured. I shall none the less endeavour to give a brief and superficial account. In the first place, then, those competent in the specialism assert that the Elders and the Elderhood have been with us in our Russian monasteries only since very recent times, even less than a century, while in the rest of the Orthodox East, in Sinai and on Mount Athos in particular, they have already existed for well over a thousand years. It is claimed that the Elderhood also existed among us in Russia in the most ancient times, or that it certainly must have existed, but that in consequence of Russia's tribulations – the Tatar invasions, the mass upheavals, the break in our former relations with the East after the subjugation of Constantinople – this institution became forgotten among us and the Elders died out. It was resuscitated among us at the end of the last century by one of the great *podvizhniki** (as he is known), Paisy Velichkovsky and his disciples, but even today, almost a hundred years later, it still exists in very few monasteries and has even on occasion been subjected to what almost amounts to persecution as an unprecedented novelty in Russia. It has thrived in particular among us here in the land of Rus at a certain renowned hermitage, the Kozelsk Optina.* When and how it became implanted in our own local monastery I cannot say, but within it there was already a third succession of Elders, of whom the Elder Zosima was the most recent; he too, however, was now almost at his last gasp from feebleness and illness, and no one even knew who was going to replace him. This was an important question for our monastery, as our monastery had not to this date acquired a positive reputation for anything in particular: it contained neither any sacred relics of the devout nor any revealed miracle-working icons, there were not even any glorious legends connected with our history, there were no historical achievements, or services to the Fatherland, against its name. It throve and became renowned all over Russia because of its Elders, to see and listen to whom the pilgrims thronged in their multitudes for thousands of versts from all across the land. So then, what is an Elder? An Elder is someone who takes your soul and your will into his soul and his will. Having chosen an Elder, you give up your own will and render it unto him in full obedience, with full self-abnegation. This test, this terrible school of life is accepted voluntarily by the one who dooms himself in the hope, after long ordeals, of conquering himself, of mastering himself to a degree where he may at last attain by dint of lifelong obedience a total freedom, that is to say, freedom from himself, and avoid the lot of those who live all their lives without ever finding the self within themselves. This invention – the Elderhood, that is – is not a theoretical one, but has been derived in the East from a practical experience that now stretches back for a thousand years. One's obligations to an Elder are of an order different from those associated with the ordinary 'vows of obedience' which there have always been in our Russian monasteries. Here it is a question of the perpetual confession of all who are working under the Elder, and of an indissoluble link between binder and bound. It is related,* for example, that once, in the most ancient period of Christendom, a certain novice who had not fulfilled a certain vow of obedience imposed on him by his

Elder left his monastery and arrived in another country, passing from Syria into Egypt. There, after long and great deeds he was considered worthy of suffering torture and a martyr's death for the Creed. But when the Church was burying his body, honouring him as a saint, quite suddenly, as the deacon was proclaiming: 'Ye learners, go forth!'* the coffin with the body of the martyr lying in it suddenly went shooting off and was cast out of the temple, and this as many as three times. And only then did they learn that this holy martyr had broken his vow and left his Elder, and so could not be absolved without his Elder's releasing him from it, even in spite of his great deeds. Not until the Elder had been summoned and had released him from his vow could the burial be performed. Of course, this is only an ancient legend, but here is a true story of much more recent date: one of our present-day monks* had gone to live on Mount Athos, and suddenly his Elder instructed him to leave Mount Athos, which he had come to love as a sacred shrine, a quiet refuge, to the depths of his soul, and to go first unto Jerusalem to worship at the holy places, and then back to Russia, to its northern part, Siberia: 'That is the place for you, not here.' Surprised, and crushed by grief, the monk went to Constantinople and appeared before the Oecumenical Patriarch, imploring him to release him from his vow of obedience, whereupon the Oecumenical Ruler answered him that not only was he, the Oecumenical Patriarch, unable to release him, but that there was not a man in all the world, nor could there be, who had the authority to release him from the vow that had been imposed on him by his Elder, excepting that Elder alone. In such manner is the Elderhood in certain cases invested with a limitless and inscrutable power. That is why in a large number of our Russian monasteries the Elderhood was initially met with what almost amounted to persecution. At the same time the Elders immediately began to acquire a high degree of respect among the common people. To the Elders of our monastery, for example, there thronged both plebeians and the most nobly born, with the purpose of submitting to them, of confessing before them their doubts, their sins, their sufferings, and of obtaining their counsel and teachings. Witnessing this, the adversaries of the Elders vociferated along with other complaints the one that here was an instance of the mystery of confession being autocratically and frivolously debased, in spite of the fact that the perpetual confession of one's soul to an Elder as his novice or secular is not at all conducted in the guise of a mystery. The end of it was, however, that the Elderhood held its ground and is now little by little establishing itself in the Russian monasteries. It should perhaps also be noted that there is probably some truth in the claim that this tried and tested, thousand-year-old implement for the moral regeneration of mankind from slavery into freedom and for his moral perfection may turn into a two-edged blade, as there are some whom it may lead not to humbleness and ultimate self-mastery, but rather to the most satanic pride – to fetters, that is to say, not freedom.

The Elder Zosima was about sixty-five, came of a landowning family, and had once in his very early youth been in the military, serving as an ober-officer* in the Caucasus. Without doubt, he had made an impression on Alyosha because of some especial quality of his soul. Alyosha lived in the very cell of the Elder, who had conceived a real liking for him and admitted him into his presence. It should be observed that Alyosha, living in the monastery at that time, was as yet not bound by anything, could go off wherever he wished for whole days, and if he wore his cassock he did it voluntarily, in order not to differ from others in the monastery. Though of course he also enjoyed wearing it for its own sake. It may have been that Alyosha's youthful imagination was strongly affected by the power and the glory by which his Elder was constantly surrounded. Of the Elder Zosima it was said by many that in admitting for so many years into his presence all those who came to him in order to confess their hearts and who thirsted for counsel and healing discourse, he had taken into his soul so many revelations, griefs and unbosomings that in the end he had acquired a perspicacity of such subtle depth as made the first glance at the face of a stranger who had come to him sufficient for him to be able to guess correctly the reason for his arrival, the object of his need, and even the nature of the torment that was racking his conscience, and that he would astonish, embarrass and sometimes almost frighten the newcomer by such intimacy with his secret before the latter had even uttered a word. In this context, however, Alyosha nearly always observed that many, indeed practically all of those who came to the Elder for the first time in order to have a private talk with him made their entrances in fear and trembling, but always came out radiant and joyful, and the blackest of countenances turned to happy ones. Alyosha was also singularly impressed by the fact that the Elder was in no wise stern; on the contrary, there was unfailingly what almost amounted to gaiety in his demeanour. The monks used to say of him that he formed close soul-attachments precisely to those who were more sinful, and that those who were most sinful, those too were most beloved by him. Of the monks there were some, even towards the very end of the Elder's life, who were his haters and enviers, but they were by this time growing few, and they kept silent, though there were among their number several persons very famous and important in the monastery, as for example one of the most ancient cenobites, a great observer of the vow of silence and an exceptional faster. But all the same it was now beyond question that the vast majority had taken the side of the Elder Zosima, and of these there were very many who positively loved him with all their hearts, ardently and sincerely; some were even attached to him with a kind of fanaticism. They used to say openly, though not quite out loud, that he was a saint, that of this there was no longer any doubt and, foreseeing his imminent decease, went in expectation from the departed of immediate miracles and great glory in the very nearest future for the monastery. In the miraculous powers of the Elder, Alyosha too believed unquestioningly, just as he believed unquestioningly the story of the coffin that flew out of the church. He saw that many of those who brought their sick infants or grown kinsfolk, imploring the Elder to lay his hands upon them and recite a prayer over them, soon returned a second time, some even on the very next day, and, falling down before the Elder in tears, thanked him for the healing of their sick. The question of whether this was really genuine healing or whether it was simply a natural amelioration brought about in the course of the illness did not exist for Alyosha, for by now he had complete faith in the spiritual powers of his teacher, and he experienced his teacher's glory almost as his own personal triumph. Especially did his heart quiver, and in his whole being did he almost seem to shine, when the Elder came out to the gates of the hermitage to greet the multitude of pilgrims from the common folk which was waiting there with the sole aim of seeing the Elder and being blessed by him, having gathered from all across Russia. They would fall down before him, weep, kiss his feet, kiss the earth on which he stood, and cry out; the women would stretch out to him their infants, and sick 'wailers' would be led before him. The Elder would talk to them, recite a short prayer over them, bless them and give them leave to depart. Sometimes of late he had become so weak from the attacks of his illness that he scarcely had the strength to come out from his cell, and the pilgrims sometimes had to wait several days in the monastery before he appeared. For Alyosha there was never any question as to why they all loved him so much, why they abased themselves before him and wept with tender emotion at the mere sight of his countenance. Oh, he understood all too well that for the humble soul of the common Russian peasant, exhausted by toil and woe, and even more by perpetual injustice and perpetual sin, both its own and that of the world, there was no more powerful need or consolation than to find a holy object or person and to fall down before it and worship it: 'Even if among us there is sin, untruth, injustice and temptation, at least in certain places, somewhere on the earth, there are men who are holy and exalted; to make up for it, those men have truth and justice, to make up for it, those men know truth and justice; so it has not been lost to the world, and one day it will come to us, too, and will reign in all the world, as was promised.' Alyosha was aware that precisely thus did the common folk feel and even think, and this he understood; but that the Elder was this very same holy man, this preserver of God's truth and justice in the eyes of the common folk – with regard to that he himself, in company with these weeping muzhiks and their sick women stretching out their infants to the Elder, was not in the slightest doubt. As for the conviction that upon his decease the Elder would afford the monastery exceptional glory, it is possible that it reigned within Alyosha's soul even more powerfully than in that of anyone else in the monastery. And indeed throughout all this most recent time a kind of deep, fiery, inner enthusiasm had begun to burn ever more violently within his heart. It troubled him not in the slightest that this Elder stood before him as an isolated instance: 'It makes no difference, he is holy, in his heart there is the secret of renewal for all, the power that will at last establish truth and justice upon earth, when all men shall be holy and love one another, and there shall be neither rich nor poor, neither self-exalters nor humiliated, but all shall be as the children of God and the true reign of Christ shall begin.' Such were the dreams of Alyosha's heart.

It appears that the arrival of his two brothers, whom he had earlier not known at all, made a very deep impression on Alyosha. Even though brother Dmitry Fyodorovich arrived the later of the two, he befriended him more quickly and more closely than he did brother Ivan Fyodorovich (with whom he shared the same mother). He was extremely interested in getting to know brother Ivan, but although Ivan had already been here for two months, and they had seen each other fairly often, they had as yet in no way struck up any sort of friendship: Alyosha himself had little in the way of conversation and seemed to be waiting for something, as if he were embarrassed about something, while brother Ivan, though Alyosha had initially noticed the long and curious gazes he directed upon him, soon appeared to have dismissed him from his thoughts altogether. Alyosha had observed this with a certain amount of personal confusion. He put his brother's lack of interest down to the difference in their ages and in particular to the unequal degree of their education. But Alyosha also had another idea: he thought such an almost non-existent curiosity and concern for him might possibly have its origins in some aspect of Ivan's life that was completely unknown to him, Alyosha. For some reason it always appeared to him as though Ivan were taken up with something, something inward and important, that he was striving towards some kind of goal, perhaps one very hard of attainment, so that he had no time for him, and that this was the sole reason why he viewed Alyosha with such absent-mindedness. Alyosha also pondered as to whether there were not here some element of contempt for him, the rather foolish novice, on the part of the intellectual atheist. He was in no doubt at all that his brother was an atheist. This contempt, if such it was, could not offend him, yet all the same it was with an uneasy sense of confusion obscure even to himself that he waited for his brother to make some closer approach to him. Brother Dmitry Fyodorovich always spoke of brother Ivan with the deepest respect and a kind of peculiar emotion. It was from him that Alyosha learned all the details of the important business matter which had of late united the two elder brothers in a close and remarkable bond. Dmitry's enthusiastic words about his brother Ivan seemed the more distinctive in Alyosha's eyes, as brother Dmitry was by comparison with Ivan almost entirely lacking in education, and placed side by side they appeared to constitute such a glaring opposition in terms of personality and character that it would perhaps have been impossible to imagine two men more dissimilar.

At this particular time it was, too, that there occurred a meeting, or, better put, a gathering of all the members of this disconsonant family in the cell of the Elder, a gathering that had an extraordinary impact on Alyosha. The excuse for this gathering was, if truth be told, a false one. Precisely at this time had the differences of opinion concerning the legacy and the evaluation of the estate between Dmitry Fyodorovich and his father, Fyodor Pavlovich, attained what evidently seemed to be a quite impossible pitch. The strain in their relations had come to a head and was now unendurable. It appears that it was Fyodor Pavlovich who first and, it also appears, in jest, mooted the idea that they should all assemble in the cell of the Elder Zosima and, while not having recourse to his direct mediation, should somehow contrive to reach an accommodation in a more decorous manner, towards which end the Elder's dignified bearing and person might be expected to make an uplifting and reconciliatory contribution. Dmitry Fyodorovich, who had never been to the Elder's cell and had never even set eyes on him, thought of course that the purpose of involving the Elder was in some way to frighten him, Dmitry; but as he himself had been nourishing a certain amount of hidden self-reproach for a great many particularly harsh things he had said in the course of an argument with his father of late, he accepted the challenge anyway. It is relevant to note that in contrast to Ivan he did not live in his father's house but separately, at the other end of the town. At this point it happened that Pyotr Aleksandrovich Miusov acquired a particular enthusiasm for this idea of Fyodor Pavlovich's. A 'forties-and-'fifties liberal, a free-thinker and an atheist, he, from boredom, perhaps, or perhaps for the sake of frivolous amusement, took a particular concern in this matter. He suddenly conceived a desire to take a look at the monastery and its 'holy man'. As his long-running disputes with the monastery still continued and his litigation concerning the land boundaries of their domains, certain wood-felling, fishing and other rights was still in process, he lost no time in exploiting this circumstance under the pretext of wishing to come to an agreement with the Father Superior: could not their disputes somehow be settled in more amicable fashion? There was no doubt that a visitor who came to the monastery with such good intentions stood much more chance of obtaining an attentive and courteous reception in the monastery than one who was merely inquisitive. As a result of all these considerations there might within the monastery be a certain amount of internal pressure on the sick Elder, who of late had scarcely left his cell at all and had even, on account of illness, been refusing to see his usual guests. The upshot of it was that the Elder gave his consent and the day was appointed. 'Who made me a judge or a divider over you?'* he declared to Alyosha with a smile.

On learning of the meeting, Alyosha was greatly troubled. If any of these litigators and altercators were able to view this conference with any degree of seriousness, it was without doubt brother Dmitry alone; the rest of them would all arrive for purposes that were frivolous and possibly, where the Elder was concerned, insulting – that was how Alyosha saw it. Miusov and brother Ivan would come out of curiosity, perhaps of the most vulgar sort, while his father would probably do so in order to create some buffoon-like and theatrical scene. Oh, though Alyosha refrained from saying anything, he knew his father deeply and well enough. I reiterate: this boy was not at all as ingenuous as everyone supposed him. With a sense of heavy foreboding he awaited the day that had been set. There can be no doubt that in his heart of hearts he cared very much that these family discords should be resolved. None the less, his principal care was for the Elder: he feared for him, for his glory, dreaded any insults that might come his way, particularly the subtle, polite sneers of Miusov and the lofty unspoken reservations of the intellectual Ivan, according to the way it all appeared to him in his imaginings. He even wanted to take the risk of warning the Elder, of telling him something about these men who were likely to arrive, but thought the better of it and kept silent. He confined himself to sending a message through a certain acquaintance of his to his brother Dmitry on the eve of the appointed day, saying that he loved him very much and that he expected him to fulfil what he had promised. This caused Dmitry to reflect, as he could not for the life of him remember what it was he had promised, and merely replied in a letter that he would exert every effort to restrain himself 'before baseness', and that although he deeply respected the Elder and brother Ivan, he was convinced that what lay in store for him was either some trap or an unworthy farce. 'Even so, I had sooner swallow my tongue than be found lacking in respect for the holy man of whom you think so much,' Dmitry wrote in the conclusion of his brief letter. It did little to raise Alyosha's spirits.

BOOK II

AN INAPPROPRIATE GATHERING

I

They Arrive at the Monastery

THE day turned out fine, warm and clear. It was the end of August. Their interview with the Elder had been set for immediately after late liturgy, at approximately half-past eleven. Our visitors to the monastery did not, however, visit the service, but arrived just as the show came to an end. They arrived in two carriages; in the first, a stylish landau harnessed to a pair of expensive horses, sat Pyotr Aleksandrovich Miusov with a distant kinsman of his, a very young man of about twenty, Pyotr Fomich Kalganov. This young man was preparing to go up to university; but Miusov, in whose home he was for some reason presently living, had been trying to tempt him abroad with him to Zurich or Jena in order to enter a university there and complete his studies. The young man had not yet made up his mind. He was pensive and seemed to be elsewhere. His features were pleasant, his constitution strong, his build rather tall. In his gaze there was from time to time a strange immobility: like all very absent people he would look at one long and steadily without seeing one at all. He had little to say for himself and was slightly awkward, but it would sometimes happen – though never except in a tête-à-tête with someone – that he became extremely talkative, vehement and risible, laughing on occasion at God only knows what. But his animation would fade just as swiftly and suddenly as it had begun. He was always well and even exquisitely attired: he already possessed an independent fortune and could expect to acquire much more. With Alyosha he was on terms of familiar companionship.

In a thoroughly decrepit, rattling, but spacious hackney carriage drawn by a pair of old grey-pink horses which had lagged badly behind Miusov's landau, sat Fyodor Pavlovich with the fruit of his loins, Ivan Fyodorovich. Dmitry Fyodorovich had been told the day before of the day and the hour, but he was late. The visitors left their carriages by the enclosure in the yard of the hotel and went on foot through the monastery gates. Apart from Fyodor Pavlovich, it appeared that none of the four had ever previously set foot in a monastery of any kind, and it was probably about thirty years since Miusov had been to church. He gazed about him with a certain curiosity that was not shorn of a certain affected free-and-easiness. His observant intellect, however, failed to be impressed by anything within the monastery except the ecclesiastical and agricultural structures, which were, it should be added, of the most ordinary kind. The last of the people were filing out of the church, taking their hats and crossing themselves. Among the common folk were also encountered guests of more elevated social station, two or three ladies, and one very old general; they were all putting up at the hotel. The beggars clustered round our visitors immediately, but no one gave them anything. Only Petrusha Kalganov produced a ten-copeck piece from his *porte-monnaie* and bustling about him, covered in embarrassment for God knows what reason, quickly slipped it to one of the peasant women, managing to get out: 'Divide it in equal amounts.' To this none of his fellow wayfarers made any comment, so there was no reason for him to be embarrassed; but, observing this, he grew even more so.

It was, however, strange; in the normal course of events their arrival would have been expected, even with some degree of ceremony: one of them had not long ago made an endowment of a thousand roubles, while another was a very rich landowner and, it would appear, a most progressively educated man, on whom all here were partially dependent with respect to the river fishing, in consequence of an eventual twist the legal proceedings were likely to take. Yet now, in spite of this, none of the official representatives had come out to meet them. Miusov absently surveyed the gravestones in the vicinity of the church and was on the point of commenting that these little plots must have gone for more than a rouble or two, entailing as they did the right of burial in such 'hallowed' ground, but thought the better of it: within him simple liberal irony was degenerating into something that nigh approached anger.

'The devil knows who to ask in this muddle . . . We must get the matter settled, for time is slipping away,' he said suddenly, as though he were talking to himself.

They were suddenly approached by a certain elderly, balding gentleman in a wide summer paletot, whose eyes had the sweetness of syrup. With a tilt of his hat and a honeyed lisp he introduced himself to them all as 'Maksimov, landowner, from Tula'. He instantly showed an eagerness to allay our wayfarers' concern.

'The Elder Zosima lives in the hermitage, shut up tight in the hermitage, about four hundred yards from the monastery, through the woods, through the woods . . .'

'Sir, even I know that the way lies through the woods,' Fyodor

Pavlovich replied. 'It's just that we can't quite remember the exact route, we haven't been here for a long time.'

'Well it's just through this gateway, and then straight through the woods ... the woods. Come along, would you like me to ... I myself ... I myself ... Through here, through here ...'

They emerged from the gateway and directed their steps through the wood. The landowner Maksimov, a man of some sixty years, did not so much walk as rather almost run at their side, examining them all with a convulsive, almost outlandish curiosity. There was something about his eyes that was reminiscent of a lobster.

'Look, we are going to see this Elder on some business of ours,' Miusov observed sternly. 'We have been given an audience with him *in camera*, and so although we are grateful to you for showing us the way, we cannot possibly invite you to come in with us.'

'I've been, I've been, I've already been ... *Un chevalier parfait!*' And the landowner gave a snap of his fingers.

'Who is a *chevalier*?' Miusov inquired.

'The Elder, the magnificent Elder, the Elder ... The monastery's pride and glory, Zosima. He's the sort of Elder who ...'

But his untidy flow of speech was interrupted by a rather short little monk who had caught the wayfarers up; he was very pale and emaciated, and he wore a hood. Fyodor Pavlovich and Miusov came to a halt. With an extremely polite, almost waist-low bow he pronounced:

'The Father Superior obediently summons you all to dine with him after your visit to the hermitage, gentlemen. In his chambers at one o'clock, no later. You too,' he said, addressing Maksimov.

'I shall most certainly comply!' Fyodor Pavlovich exclaimed, tremendously pleased by the invitation. 'Most certainly. And you know, we've all given our word that we'll behave ourselves while we're here ... How about you, Pyotr Aleksandrovich, will you come?'

'Oh, why ever not? What did I come here for, if not to see all their local customs. The only thing that gives me cause for hesitation is that I am with you, Fyodor Pavlovich ...'

'Yes, Dmitry Fyodorovich does not yet exist.'

'Well, and it would be an excellent thing if he were to be absent; do you suppose it appeals to me, all this muddle of yours, and with you thrown in as well? So yes, we shall come to dinner, you may convey our thanks to the Father Superior,' he said, turning to the little monk.

'But I'm to take you to the Elder first,' the monk replied.

'Well, if that is the case, then I shall go to the Father Superior, I shall in the meantime go directly to the Father Superior,' the landowner Maksimov began to chirrup.

'The Father Superior is occupied at the present moment, but as you wish . . .' the monk articulated hesitantly.

'What a horrible, intrusive old codger,' Miusov commented out loud, when the landowner Maksimov had trotted off back to the monastery.

'He looks like von Sohn,'* Fyodor Pavlovich said suddenly.

'Is that all you can think of . . . In what way does he look like von Sohn? Have you ever seen von Sohn?'

'I've seen a photograph of him. It's not his facial features, though, but something one can't explain. He's a perfect von Sohn number two. I can always tell things like that just by looking at a man's physiognomy.'

'Well, perhaps; you're a connoisseur of these matters. All I shall say, Fyodor Pavlovich, is this: you yourself were so good as to mention just now that we'd given our word to behave decently. I say to you: restrain yourself. And if you start to make a buffoon of yourself I do not intend to be put on the same level as you in this place . . . You see what sort of a man this is,' he said, addressing the monk. 'I'm even afraid to go among decent folk with him.'

To the pale, bloodless lips of the little monk there came a delicate, silent ghost of a smile, one not without cunning of a sort, but he made no answer, and it was only too clear that he was keeping quiet out of a sense of his own dignity. Miusov knit his brow even more deeply.

'Oh, the devil take them all, an external façade that's been developed over centuries, but in essence it's just rubbish and charlatanry!' flashed through his head.

'Here it is, the hermitage – we're there!' Fyodor Pavlovich shouted. 'It has an enclosure and locked gates.'

And he proceeded to make large crossing motions before the saints that were painted above the gates and to either side of them.

'A man goeth not to another monastery with the statutes of his own,' he observed. 'There are twenty-five holy men living in this hermitage, all staring at one another and eating cabbage. And not a single woman is allowed in through these gates, that's the most remarkable part. It really is true, you know. Except how is it I heard that the Elder receives ladies?' he said, suddenly turning to the little monk.

'Even now there are persons of the female gender from among the common people here, there they are, over there, in the small gallery, waiting. And for lady-persons of the higher sort, two little rooms have been appointed here on the main gallery, but outside the enclosure, look, those windows there, and the Elder comes out to them by an inner passage when he is well, that is to say, he comes over to the other side none the less. There's one lady there now, a Mrs Khokhlakova, a land-owner's wife from Kharkov, waiting with her enfeebled daughter. He's probably told them he'll come out to them, though of late he's grown so infirm that he hardly even appears to the commoners.'

'You see, even in a hermitage there's a little loophole to the lady kind. Holy Father, please don't think I'm trying to be funny, I'm simply making an observation. You know, on Mount Athos – perhaps you've heard? – not only are the monks forbidden to visit women, but women are forbidden altogether, along with all other creatures of female sex: hens, turkey-hens, heifers . . .'

'Fyodor Pavlovich, I shall go home and leave you here alone, and when I'm gone they'll march you out of here, that is my prophecy to you.'

'What am I doing to get in your way, Pyotr Aleksandrovich? I say, just look!' he exclaimed suddenly, as he stepped through to the other side of the hermitage enclosure. 'Look what a valley of roses they live in!'

It really was so: though there were no roses now, there was in every spot where they could have been planted a multitude of rare and splendid autumn flowers. They were, it was evident, cherished by a seasoned hand. Flower-beds had been arranged within the enclosures of the churches and between the graves. The small house in which the Elder's cell was to be found – wooden, single-storeyed, with a gallery before the entrance, had also been planted round with flowers.

'I wonder if there was any of this here in the days of the previous Elder, Varsonofy? They say he didn't take kindly to refinement, used to come rushing out and beat even the female sex with his stick,' Fyodor Pavlovich observed as he climbed the steps of the porch.

'The Elder Varsonofy did indeed on occasion appear like a holy fool, as it were, but there are also many stupid tales told about him. As for beating people with a stick, he certainly never did that,' the little monk replied. 'Now, gentlemen, if you will wait for a moment, I shall announce your presence.'

'Fyodor Pavlovich, this is the last time I shall say it: remember what you agreed. Behave yourself properly, or I shall pay you back,' Miusov had time to mutter once more.

'I really don't know what you're in such a lather about,' Fyodor Pavlovich commented, mockingly. 'Or is it that you're worried about your sins? After all, they do say he can tell by one's eyes what one's brought with one. Fancy a citizen of Paris and a progressive-minded gentleman like yourself valuing their opinion so highly – you've really given me something to marvel at!'

But Miusov did not have time to respond to this piece of sarcasm, for they were requested to go in. He made his entrance in a state of some irritation . . .

'Well, now I know how I'm going to behave; I'm irritated and I shall start arguing . . . I'll lose my temper – and degrade both myself and the cause,' flashed through his head.

2

The Old Buffoon

THEY came into the room almost simultaneously with the Elder, who on sight of them immediately appeared from his small bedchamber. In the cell sat two of the cloister's hieromonachs* who had arrived there before them and had been waiting for the Elder to come out. One of them was the Father Bibliothecary, and the other Father Paisy, a man ill though not old, but very – as was said of him – learned. In addition there stood, waiting in a corner (and continuing to stand throughout), a young fellow in an ordinary frock-coat, about twenty-two by the look of him, a seminarian and future divine who for some reason lived under the patronage of the monastery and the brotherhood. He was tall of stature, with fresh features, broad cheekbones and narrow little hazel-coloured eyes that displayed wit and attentiveness. His face expressed an utter deference but a proper one, in which there was no obvious fawning. To the guests who had entered he did not even bow in greeting, as one not their equal but, on the contrary, dependent and under the jurisdiction of others.

The Elder Zosima came out in the company of a novice and Alyosha. The two hieromonachs stood up and greeted him with the deepest of bows, touching the earth with their fingers, and then, having taken his blessing, kissed his hand. When he had blessed them, the Elder responded to each of them with the same very deep bow, touching the earth with his digits, and from each of them he requested blessing also for himself. The entire ceremony took place with great seriousness, not at all like some everyday ritual, but almost with a certain degree of emotion. To Miusov, however, it seemed that it was all done with the deliberate intention of producing an effect. He had been standing at the head of the group of his fellows who had entered. The proper thing to do – he had in fact thought this over the evening before – in spite of any causes, and solely out of plain courtesy (as such were the customs in this place), would be to approach the Elder and be blessed by him, at least be blessed by him, if not actually kiss his hand. Now, however, seeing the hieromonachs perform all these bowings and osculations, in a single second he altered his resolve: with an air of seriousness and importance he made a rather deep, but secular, bow and then retreated to a chair. Fyodor Pavlovich did exactly likewise, for once reproducing Miusov's every action like a monkey. Ivan Fyodorovich made his obeisances in a very solemn and courteous manner, but also standing to attention, while Kalganov was so smothered in embarrassment that he made no bow at all. The Elder let drop the hand that had been about to raise itself over them in blessing and, bowing to them a second time, requested them all to sit down. Blood leapt to Alyosha's cheeks; he felt shame. His ill misgivings had been realized.

The Elder seated himself on a small mahogany leather-covered sofa of very ancient construction, accommodating his guests, the hieromonachs excepted, all four of them in a row on four mahogany chairs upholstered in black, extremely frayed and tattered, leather. The hieromonachs found seats apart from the rest, one by the door, the other by the window. Alyosha, the seminarian and the novice remained standing. The whole cell was of very unassuming dimensions and had a somehow wilted look to it. The accoutrements and furnishings were primitive, poor and only the most necessary. Two pots of flowers stood on the window-ledge, and in one corner there were many icons – one of them of the Mother of God, enormous in size and probably painted long before the Schism.* In front of it glimmered an icon-lamp. Next to it there were two more icons in resplendent mountings, then next to them hand-carved cherubs, porcelain eggs, a Catholic crucifix of ivory with a Mater Dolorosa embracing it, and several foreign engravings from the work of great Italian painters of bygone centuries. Beside these elegant and expensive copperplates there was a jaunty display of a few sheets of the most plebeian Russian lithographic portraits depicting saints, martyrs, hierarchs and the like, which may be bought for a few copecks at any country fair. There were one or two lithographic portraits of present and former Russian bishops, but only on the other walls. Miusov glanced quickly round at all this 'official stuff' and surveyed the Elder with a fixed gaze. He respected his own gaze, had that weakness, one at any rate forgivable in him, taking into consideration the fact that he was now fifty years old – an age at which a prosperous man of the world always acquires more deference towards himself, sometimes even involuntarily.

He took an instant dislike to the Elder. Indeed, there was about the Elder's person something to which many people, and not only Miusov, might have taken a dislike. He was a short, hunched-up little man with very frail legs, only sixty-five years of age but whom illness made appear much older, at least by some ten years. The whole of his face, a very gaunt one, was peppered with little wrinkles, of which there were particularly many around his eyes. These eyes were small, of the clear variety, swift and brilliant, like two brilliant points of light. Grey wisps of hair remained only at his temples, he had a little, straggling, wedge-shaped beard, and his lips, which often bore an ironic smile, were as thin as two pieces of string. His nose could not have been described as long, but was rather sharp and watchful, like the beak of a bird.

'By all the signs a nasty, petty-arrogant little chappie,' flashed through Miusov's head. He was altogether very annoyed with himself.

The sound of a clock striking helped to set the conversation going. In quick tattoo a cheap little wall-clock with weights chimed out twelve o'clock precisely.

'Bang on time!' Fyodor Pavlovich exclaimed. 'But my son Dmitry Fyodorovich still isn't here yet. Please accept my apologies for him, Sacred Elder! (Alyosha fairly shuddered in all his being at the 'Sacred Elder'.) Personally I always try to be punctual, to the very minute, as I know that punctuality is the courtesy of kings.' *

'Except that you, at any rate, are not a king,' Miusov muttered, instantly unable to hold himself in check.

'No, I'm not, I'm not a king. And just fancy, Pyotr Aleksandrovich, why I even knew that myself, I swear to God I did! And there I go putting my foot in it as usual! Your Reverence!' he exclaimed with a kind of instantaneous, passionate fervour. 'You see before you a buffoon, verily a buffoon! Thus do I introduce myself. Alas, an inveterate habit! My occasionally putting my foot in it and saying things I shouldn't – I actually do it on purpose, the purpose of making people laugh and of being pleasant. One must be pleasant, mustn't one? About seven years ago I arrived in a certain horrible little town, I had a bit of business there, had started hanging out with some wretched merchant riff-raff. We went to see the *ispravnik*, the district chief of police, because we needed to invite him to a meal in order to ask him for certain permission we required. The chief of police came out, a big, fat man with white hair and a face like a funeral – the most dangerous types in such cases: it's their livers, their livers. I went straight up to him and said to him, you know the way one does it, with the casual air of a man of the world: "Now then,

Mr *ispravnik*, we should like you to be, so to speak, our Napravnik!"* "What's all this about Napravnik?" he said. I realized in the first half-second that my attempt had failed, he was standing there looking grim, staring at me. "Oh," I said, "I was just trying to make a joke to cheer us all up: Mr Napravnik is actually one of our most renowned orchestral conductors, and that is exactly what we require for the harmony of our enterprise: a sort of conductor . . ." And I mean, I'd explained it all to him sensibly with the right comparisons, hadn't I? "I'm sorry," he said, "I am the chief of police, the *ispravnik*, and I will not tolerate people making puns about my rank." He turned on his heel and went. I ran after him, shouting: "Yes, yes, you're the chief of police, the *ispravnik* not Napravnik!" "No," he said. "If you really must know, my name is Napravnik too." And just fancy, that was the end of our business plans! And you see, I'm always, always doing things like that. I unfailingly damage my prospects through my own good manners! Once, many years ago now, I even said to a certain influential person: "Your wife is a ticklish woman, sir" – meaning ticklish in the sense of her honour, of her moral qualities, as it were, yet he suddenly replied to me: "Have you been tickling her?"* I couldn't restrain myself, and suddenly I thought, I'll try a bit of courtesy: "Yes sir," I said, "I have." Well, at that point he gave *me* a tickle or two . . . But that was a long time ago, so I don't feel embarrassed about telling people; I am constantly doing myself harm that way!'

'You are doing it this very moment,' Miusov muttered with distaste. The Elder studied the one and the other without saying anything.

'Really? Just fancy, I even knew that, Pyotr Aleksandrovich; you know, I had a premonition that I would, as soon as I opened my mouth, and that you would be the first to point it out to me. At seconds like those, when I see that my joke's not turning out as I intended it, at seconds like those, your Reverence, both my cheeks begin to cleave to my lower gums, and I almost have a sort of a fit; it's something I've had since I was a lad and gained my daily bread by sponging and being a sponge in the homes of gentlefolk. I'm a buffoon of long standing, your Reverence, and have been so from birth, every bit the same as a holy fool; I won't argue that it may be there's an unclean spirit lurking in me, one of small proportions, as a matter of fact – a more significant one would have chosen a different abode, only not in you, Pyotr Aleksandrovich, for you are an insignificant abode. On the other hand I do believe, however, I believe in God. Only recently have I had a doubt or two, but to make up for it here I sit now awaiting great words. I, your

Reverence, am like the *philosophe* Diderot* (he pronounced the name to rhyme with 'rot'). Do you know the story, most holy Father, of how the *philosophe* Diderot appeared before Metropolitan Platon* in the reign of Catherine the Great? He went in and told him straight: "There is no God." Upon which the great hierarch raised his finger and replied: "The fool hath said in his heart, There is no God."* Without further ado, Diderot fell down at his feet: "I believe," he cried, "and will accept baptism." And so he was baptized right then and there. Princess Dashkova was his godmother, and Potyomkin* his godfather . . .'

'Fyodor Pavlovich, this is intolerable! I mean, you yourself know that you're talking nonsense and that that stupid anecdote is untrue, so why are you carrying on like this?' Miusov said in a trembling voice, by now completely unable to restrain himself.

'All my life I've had a suspicion it wasn't true!' Fyodor Pavlovich exclaimed with animation. 'And to make amends, gentlemen, I will tell you the whole truth: great Elder! Forgive me, that last bit about the baptism of Diderot I made up myself, on the spur of the moment, it just popped out, had never entered my mind before. I made it up to add a bit of piquancy. And I'm carrying on like this, Pyotr Aleksandrovich, in order to be pleasant. Though I must say I sometimes wonder why I bother. But as for Diderot, I must have heard that bit about "the fool hath said in his heart" at least two dozen times from the local landowners round here when I was a lad and lived in their homes; by the way, Pyotr Aleksandrovich, I also heard it from your aunt, Mavra Fominishna. They're all still convinced that the atheist Diderot went to argue with the Metropolitan Platon about God . . .'

Miusov rose, having lost not only his patience, but also, it appeared, his self-control. He was in a rabid fury, at the same time conscious that this made him seem absurd. For indeed, in the cell there was unravelling an event outrageous in the extreme. In this very cell, for perhaps some forty or fifty years now, even in the days of the previous Elders, visitors had gathered, but always with the deepest reverence, in no other wise. Almost all those who were admitted realized, upon entering the cell, that they were being shown an especial favour. Many fell to their knees and remained there throughout the entire meeting. Many of the 'higher-up' personages, even the most learned, positively free-thinking ones, who arrived either out of curiosity or for certain specific reasons, upon entering the cell with the others or upon receiving an audience *in camera*, had each and every one of them made it their primary obligation to maintain an attitude of the most profound veneration and delicacy throughout the entire interview, all the more so as here money was not involved, but only love and mercy on the one hand, and on the other – repentance and the urge to resolve some vexed question of the soul or vexed moment in the life of their own hearts. So that buffoonery of the kind now displayed by Fyodor Pavlovich, one lacking in veneration towards the place in which he found himself, produced in at least some of the witnesses a sense of bewilderment and surprise. The two hieromonachs, though in no way altering their physiognomies, had been listening with serious attention for what the Elder would say, but were now, it seemed, preparing to rise, like Miusov. Alyosha was on the point of tears, his head lowered. Stranger than anything else he found the fact that his brother, Ivan Fyodorovich, on whom he had placed his sole reliance and who alone had such influence on their father as would suffice to make him stop, was now sitting completely impassive on his chair, his eyes lowered as, with what was evidently the curiosity of the inquisitive, he waited to see how it would all end, as though in this matter he himself were a quite uninvolved bystander. At Rakitin (the seminarian), a man with whom he was also well-acquainted and nearly on close terms, Alyosha could not even bear to look: he knew what Rakitin was thinking (though he was the only person in the entire monastery who did).

'Forgive me . . .' Miusov began, turning to the Elder, 'for also possibly appearing to you as a participant in this unworthy jest. My error is in having believed that even a man such as Fyodor Pavlovich would understand his obligations in visiting such a venerable personage . . . I had no idea I should have to ask to be excused for having come in with him . . .'

Pyotr Aleksandrovich did not finish his sentence and, covered in utter embarrassment, began to make his exit from the room.

'Do not be anxious, I beg you,' the Elder said suddenly, getting up from his seat on his frail legs and, taking Pyotr Aleksandrovich by both hands, made him sit down in his armchair again. 'Please be calm, I beg you. I particularly beg you to be my guest.' And turning, with a bow, he sat down on his small sofa again.

'Great Elder, impart your pronouncement: do I offend you with my sprightliness or do I not?' Fyodor Pavlovich suddenly exclaimed, seizing both arms of his chair as though preparing to leap up out of it depending on the answer he received.

'I earnestly beg you also not to be anxious and not to be intimidated,' the Elder said to him, meaningfully. 'Do not be intimidated, be just as you are at home. And above all, do not be so ashamed of yourself, for it is from that that all the rest proceeds.'

'Just as I am at home? In my natural state, you mean? Oh, that's a lot, far too much, but — I accept with pious emotion. You know, blessed father, you shouldn't encourage me to assume my natural state, don't risk it . . . not even I want to go that far. I tell you that in advance in order to protect you. And as for the rest, sir — well, it's still subject to the murk of obscurity, even though some people would like to paint me in gaudy colours. I say that with you in mind, Pyotr Aleksandrovich; but where you, where you are concerned, most holy Being, all I can say is: I pour ecstasy!' He raised himself and, lifting his arms in the air, pronounced: 'Blessed is the womb that bare thee, and the paps which thou hast sucked* — especially the paps! You know, when you made that observation of yours just now — "do not be so ashamed of yourself, for it is from this that all the rest proceeds" — it was as if you'd penetrated right through me and read my insides. When I go among people I do indeed always feel that I'm more vile than any of them and that they all take me for a buffoon, and so I say to myself: "Very well, I really will play the buffoon, I'm not afraid of what you think of me, because you're all of you to a man more vile than I!" That's the reason I'm a buffoon, it's shame that makes me so, great Elder, shame. From pure mistrust do I play the lout. I mean, if only I were confident on entering that all would instantly accept me as a man of the utmost charm and intelligence — Lord! What a good person I should be then! Master!' he said, suddenly falling to his knees. 'What shall I do to inherit eternal life?'* Even now it was hard to know whether he was joking or whether he really was in a state of such pious emotion.

The Elder raised his eyes to him and with a smile pronounced:

'You yourself have long known what you must do, you have enough intelligence: renounce drunkenness and intemperance of tongue, renounce voluptuousness, and in particular the worship of money, and close your drinking houses, if not all, then at least two or three of them. And principally, above everything else: stop telling lies.'

'You mean the sort of things I was saying about Diderot?'

'No, it has nothing to do with that. The main thing is that you stop telling lies to yourself. The one who lies to himself and believes his own lies comes to a point where he can distinguish no truth either within himself or around him, and thus enters into a state of disrespect towards himself and others. Respecting no one, he loves no one, and to amuse and divert himself in the absence of love he gives himself up to his passions and to vulgar delights and becomes a complete animal in his vices, and all of it from perpetual lying to other people and himself. The one who lies to himself is often quick to take offence. After all, it is sometimes rather enjoyable to feel insulted, is it not? For the person knows that no one has insulted him, and that he himself has thought up the insult and told lies as an ornament, has exaggerated in order to create a certain impression, has seized on a word and made a mountain out of a molehill – is well aware of this, and yet is the very first to feel insulted, feel insulted to the point of pleasure, to the point of great satisfaction, and for that very reason ends up nurturing a sense of true animosity . . . But please get off the floor and sit down properly, I earnestly beg you; why, these are also nothing but false gestures . . .'

'Blessed man! Let me kiss your dear hand!' said Fyodor Pavlovich, leaping up and quickly implanting a smacking kiss on the Elder's slender hand. 'It is indeed, indeed enjoyable to feel insulted. That's the best way I've ever heard it put. I have indeed, indeed all my life felt insulted to the point of pleasure, felt insulted for the sake of aesthetics, for it is not only enjoyable but even sometimes beautiful to be the object of an insult; that's what you left out, great Elder: beautiful! I must write it down in my notebook! But I have lied, lied, all my life, really, each day and hour thereof. Truly, I am a liar, and the father of it! Actually, I'm not sure if that's quite right, I always get the Scriptures mixed up – well, the son of it, the son of a lie – even that will do. Only . . . angel mine . . . the occasional fib about Diderot's all right! Diderot won't do any harm, but certain little words will. Incidentally, Great Elder, there's something I nearly forgot; you see, the year before last I decided to come and get some information here, that's to say, make a visit here and really ask and find out about something. Only please don't let Pyotr Aleksandrovich interrupt. This is what it is: is it true, great Father, that in the *Chet'i-Minei** there's a story about a holy miracle-worker who was tortured for his creed and that when in the end his head was cut off he rose, picked it up and "kissed it sweetly", and walked for a long distance, bearing it in his arms, and still "kissing it sweetly"? Is that true or not, honest fathers?'

'No, it's not true,' said the Elder.

'There is nothing of that kind in any of the *Chet'i-Minei*. Which saint did you say the story concerned?' asked one of the hieromonachs, the Father Bibliothecary.

'I myself don't know which one it is. Haven't the foggiest. I was led into delusion, it was talk. I heard it, and do you know who told it to me? Pyotr Aleksandrovich Miusov here, the man who got so annoyed about Diderot just now, he told it to me.'

'I never told you that, I never talk to you at all.'

'It's true you didn't tell it to me personally; but you did tell it to a company in which I was present, about four years ago it will be now. I mention it because you shook my faith with that ridiculous story, Pyotr Aleksandrovich. You hadn't the faintest idea at the time, but I went home with that shaken faith of mine, and I've been shaking more and more ever since. Yes, Pyotr Aleksandrovich, you have been the cause of a great fall! That's in a different class from Diderot, sir!'

Fyodor Pavlovich had become violently worked up, though it was quite plain to everyone that he was once again pretending. In spite of this, Miusov was cut to the very core.

'What rubbish; in fact, all of this is rubbish,' he muttered. 'It's true that I might have told that story once . . . but not to you. I was told it myself. I heard it in Paris, from a certain Frenchman, who said he thought it was read from our *Chet'i-Minei* as part of our service . . . He's a man of great learning, who was making a special study of statistics about Russia . . . He'd lived a long time in Russia . . . I haven't read the *Chet'i-Minei* . . . and don't intend to . . . All manner of things get said over dinner, don't they? . . . We happened to be dining at the time . . .'

'Yes, that day you were dining, and I lost my faith!' Fyodor Pavlovich said, teasing him.

'What do I care about your faith?' Miusov nearly shouted, but suddenly restrained himself, saying with contempt: 'You literally soil everything you come into contact with.'

The Elder suddenly rose from his seat:

'Forgive me, gentlemen, if I leave you for just a few minutes,' he said, addressing all the visitors, 'but there are those who wait and who arrived earlier than you. Now don't go telling lies again,' he added, turning to Fyodor Pavlovich with a merry countenance.

He left the cell. Alyosha and the novice rushed to help him down the staircase. Alyosha had hardly been able to breathe, he was overjoyed to get out, but was also relieved that the Elder had not taken offence and was in good spirits. The Elder was headed in the direction of the gallery in order to bless the people who were waiting for him. But all the same, Fyodor Pavlovich stopped him at the door of the cell.

'Most blessed man!' he exclaimed with emotion. 'Permit me to kiss your dear hand once again! Nay, with you a man may talk, a man may live! Do you suppose I always lie thus, playing the buffoon? Know then that all the time I have been feigning in order to put you to the test. All the time I have been probing you in order to find out if a man may live

with you. To find out if there was room along with your pride for my
humbleness. I award you the testimonial of honour: a man may live
with you! But now I shall be silent, for all time I shall be silent. I shall sit
down in that armchair and be silent. Pyotr Aleksandrovich, you may
speak now, you are now the chief person here . . . for ten minutes.'

3
Women of Faith

DOWNSTAIRS, by the small wooden gallery which had been attached to
the outer wall of the enclosure there was on this occasion a crowd made
up solely of women, some twenty wives of the common folk. They had
been informed that the Elder was finally about to come out, and they had
assembled in expectation. Out on to the gallery also came the landowning
Khokhlakovas, who had also been awaiting the Elder, but in the accommodation reserved for upper-class female visitors. There were two of them:
mother and daughter. Mrs Khokhlakova, the mother, a rich lady who
always dressed with taste, was a person still quite young and very
pleasant to the gaze, somewhat pale, with eyes that were very lively and
almost completely black. She was no more than thirty-three, and she had
already been a widow for some five years. Her fourteen-year-old daughter
was afflicted by a palsy of the legs. The poor young girl had been unable
to walk for the past half-year, and she was wheeled about in a long bath
chair. She had a charming little face, somewhat thin from her illness, but
full of gaiety. Something frolicsome shone in her large dark eyes with
their long eyelashes. Ever since the spring her mother had planned to
take her abroad, but during the summer they had been held up by
arrangements connected with their estate. They had been staying the past
week in our town, more on business than on pilgrimage, but had already
once, three days before, visited the Elder. Now they had suddenly
returned, even though they knew that these days the Elder was hardly
ever able to receive anyone, and by dint of earnest supplication had
begged yet once again 'the fortune of beholding the great healer'.

As she waited for the Elder to come out the mother sat in a chair
beside her daughter's bath chair, and two paces from her stood an old
monk, not one from our local monastery, but visiting from an obscure
and remote northern cloister. He also desired to be blessed by the Elder.
But when the Elder appeared on the gallery he began by making straight
for the common folk. The crowd was pressed against the small porch-

way with three steps that connected the low gallery with the field. The Elder stood on the topmost step, put on his *epitrachilion** and began to bless the women who were crowding towards him. A certain 'wailer' was dragged towards him by both arms. As soon as this woman set eyes on the Elder she suddenly began in incoherent shrieking, hiccuping and shaking all over as in a puerperal fit. Placing his *epitrachilion* upon her head, the Elder recited a short prayer over her, and she at once stopped shrieking and grew calm. I know not how it is these days, but in my childhood I frequently chanced to see and hear these 'wailers' in villages and monasteries. They were brought to morning service, they used to make a dog-like yelping or barking all over the church, but when the holy gifts were brought forth and they were led before them the 'possession' would cease and the sick women would always grow quiet for a time. Child as I was, this struck and surprised me greatly. But then I heard from certain landowners and especially my teachers in the town, in response to my queries, that all this was a pretence adopted with the purpose of avoiding work, and that it could invariably be eradicated by means of a suitable rigour, in confirmation of which various anecdotes were cited. Subsequently, however, I learned with surprise from certain medical specialists that in these cases no pretence is involved, that this is a terrible female malady, especially prevalent, it would appear, among us here in the land of Rus, and testifying to the grievous fortunes of our rural womenfolk, a malady that proceeds from exhausting work undertaken too soon after difficult childbirth irregularly performed without any medical help; that proceeds, moreover, from desperate misfortune, from beatings and the like, which certain female natures are quite simply unable to tolerate according to the general example. The strange and momentary healing of such possessed and struggling women as soon as they were led before the holy gifts, something which had been explained to me as a pretence and even as a conjuring-trick doubtless arranged by those self-same 'clericals', probably also took place in a most natural manner, and the women who led her before the gifts and, more importantly, the sick woman herself, believed implicitly, as in an established truth, that the unclean spirit that had taken possession of the sick woman would never be able to endure it if she, the sick woman, as she was being led before the gifts, were to bow before them also. And for this reason it was (and could not be otherwise) that at the moment of their bowing before the gifts there invariably took place in these nervous and, of course, also mentally afflicted women a kind of unavoidable jolt to the entire organism, a jolt brought on by the expectation of a certain miracle of healing and by the most complete faith that it would be achieved. And achieved it was, if only for a single moment. In precisely such fashion was it achieved now, as soon as the Elder covered the sick woman with his *epitrachilion*.

Many of the women who had been crowding towards him burst into tears of ecstasy and tender emotion, induced by the effect of the moment; others strained to kiss at least the hem of his garments, and yet others recited some lament.* He blessed them all, and engaged some of them in conversation. He already knew the 'wailer'; she had been brought from nearby, from a village only about six versts from the monastery, and had been here previously.

'But here is a distant one,' he said, pointing to a woman who was not at all old yet, but was very thin and emaciated, with a face that was less burned than wholly blackened by the sun. She was on her knees, staring at the Elder with a motionless gaze. There was something almost frenzied in it.

'From far away, little father, from far away, three hundred versts from here. From far away, father, from far away,' the woman said in a sing-song voice, rocking her head smoothly from side to side and holding her cheek in her palm. She spoke as though she were reciting a lament. There is among the common folk a grief that is silent and long-suffering; it withdraws into itself and says nothing. But there is also a grief that is hysterical: eventually it breaks forth in tears and from that moment passes into reciting. This is particularly true of the women. But it is no easier than the silent kind of grief. The recitings and lamentings provide assuagement only by irritating the heart and causing it still greater hysterical anguish. Such grief desires no consolation, it nourishes itself upon its sense of unassuagability. The recitings are only the need to constantly rub salt in the wound.

'You must be from the tradesfolk?' the Elder continued, studying her with curiosity.

'We're townsfolk, father, townsfolk, from the peasantry, but we're townsfolk, we live in the city. I came here to see you, father. We'd heard about you, little father, heard about you. My poor little son is dead and buried, and I've gone as a pilgrim to pray. I've been to three monasteries, and they told me: "Go there, Nastasyushka, go there" – that's to you they meant, my darling, to you. So here I came; yesterday I was standing in church, and today I've come to see you.'

'Why are you crying?'

'It's my little son, dear father, he was two years old, and only three

months more and he'd have been three,* the little thing. It's my son
who's causing me such pain, father, my son. He was the last we had, we
had four, Nikitushka and I, but they don't stay with us, our children,
dear one, they don't stay with us. I saw the first three dead and buried,
and I wasn't that terrible sorry they went, but this last one's gone and
died, and I can't get him out of my mind. It's just as if he were standing
there before me, he won't go away. He's fair wrung my soul dry. If I see
his little clothes, his little shirt or his little boots I start to howl. I spread
out everything that's left of him, every single thing that was his, I look at
it and howl. I said to Nikitushka my husband: "Give me leave, master,
that I may go on a pilgrimage." He's a cabman, we're not poor, father,
not poor, we ply the cabman's trade on our own account, everything's
our own, the horses and the cab. But what good is our property to us
now? He'll have taken to the bottle in my absence, my Nikitushka, I
know he will, he's done it before: no sooner do I turn away than he
yields to weakness. But now I've stopped even thinking about him. This
is my third month away from home. I've forgotten, forgotten everything
and I don't want to remember; and anyway, what would I do with him
now? I've finished with him, finished with everyone. And I don't want to
see our house and our property now, I don't want to see anything at all!'

'Let me tell you something, mother,' the Elder said. 'Once upon a
time,* a great saint of antiquity saw in the temple one such as you, a
mother who was also weeping for her infant, her only child, whom the
Lord also had summoned. "Do you not know," the saint said to her,
"how daring such infants are before the throne of God? There are none
more daring than they in all the Kingdom of Heaven: 'You gave us life,
O Lord,' they say to God, 'yet no sooner had we beheld it than You
took it away from us again.' And with such daring do they ask and
demand that the Lord immediately accords them the rank of angels. And
therefore," said the holy man, "do you too rejoice, O woman, and weep
not, for your infant is now with the Lord in the assembly of His angels."
Thus did the holy saint address the weeping woman in those ancient
days. For he was a great saint and could not impart a falsehood unto her.
Therefore let me tell you also, mother, that your infant too of a certainty
now stands before the throne of the Lord, rejoicing and merry, and
saying his prayers for you. So weep, though, also, but rejoice.'

The woman listened to him, holding her cheek in her hand, her eyes
lowered. She gave a deep sigh.

'My Nikitushka consoled me that same way, in the very words you
used, he said: "You silly woman, why do you weep, our little son is sure

to be now with the Lord God singing glorias with the angels." He said that to me, though he was crying too, I could see, he was crying just like I was. "I know, Nikitushka, in what other place could he be if not with the Lord God, it's just that he isn't here, here with us now, Nikitushka, beside us, where he used to sit!" If I could only take one little peep at him, take one little look at him again, I wouldn't go up to him, I wouldn't say anything, I'd hide in a corner, just to see him for a single moment, hear him playing outside and coming in and shouting in his dear little voice: "Mamma, where are you?" If I could only hear him toddling about the room on his little feet just once, just once, making that "tuck-tuck" noise with his feet, so quickly, so quickly, I remember, when he'd run up to me, shouting and laughing, if only I could hear his little feet, if I heard them I'd recognize them! But he isn't there, little father, he isn't there, and I'll never hear him again! Here's his little sash, but he himself is gone, and now I'll never see him, never hear him again! . . .'

She produced from her bosom the small gold-embroidered braid sash that had been her little boy's and, at the mere sight of it, was shaken by sobbing, covering her eyes with her fingers, through which trickled the tears that had flooded forth.

'And that,' the Elder said, 'that is the ancient "Rachel weeping for her children, and would not be comforted, because they are not",* and such are the bounds placed upon earth for you, the mothers. And be not consoled, and feel no need to be consoled, be not consoled and weep, only each time you weep be sure to remember that your little son – he is one of God's angels – looks down at you from up there and can see you, and rejoices at your tears, and draws God's attention to them. And for a long time yet will this great motherly weeping be upon you, but in the end it will turn to quiet joy, and your bitter tears will simply be tears of quiet tenderness and heart-cleansing emotion, rescuing you from your sins. But I will pray for the repose of your infant's soul, what was his name?'

'Aleksey, little father.'

'There's a gracious name. After Alexis the Man of God?'*

'Yes, little father, yes, after Alexis the Man of God!'

'There was a saint! I shall pray, mother, I shall pray and in my prayer I shall mention your sorrow and pray for the health of your spouse. Only it is wrong of you to have left him. Go to your husband and cherish him. Your little boy will see from up there that you have abandoned his father, and he will weep for the two of you; why are you spoiling his beatitude? After all, he is alive, alive, for the soul liveth for ever; and though he be not in your house, he is invisibly with you. How will he enter in if you say that you hate your house? To whom will he enter if he does not find you together, father and mother? Now he comes to you in dreams, and you suffer, but then he will send you gentle dreams. Go to your husband, mother, go there this very day.'

'I will, my dear, for what you've said I will. You have mended my heart for me. Nikitushka, my Nikitushka, you wait for me, my darling, you wait for me!' the woman began to recite, but the Elder had already turned to a certain very *old* little old woman who was dressed not in pilgrim's garb, but in that of a town dweller. From her eyes it was plain that she had some purpose in coming and that there was something she wanted to say. She introduced herself as the widow of a non-commissioned officer, from not very far away — somewhere in our town, at any rate. Her son Vasenka worked in the commissariat and had gone to Siberia where he had been stationed in Irkutsk. He had sent her two letters from there, but it was now a year since she had heard anything from him. She had tried to obtain some information about him, but did not really know where to apply.

'You see, Stepanida Ilyinishna Bedryagina — she's a merchant's wife, a rich one — said to me the other day: "Now then, Prokhorovna, what you ought to do is write your son's name down for remembrance, take it to the church and have them say a prayer for the repose of his soul. His soul will start to fret," she said, "and he'll write you a letter. And this is a sure method," she said, "it's been tried many times." But well, I have my doubts . . . Dear light of ours, tell me if it's true or not, and if that would be a good thing to do?'

'Do not even think of it. You ought to be ashamed even to ask. And in any case how is it possible that a living soul be remembered for repose, and by the man's own mother, too? That is a great sin, not far removed from witchcraft, and it is forgiven unto you only because of your ignorance. You would do better to pray to the Queen of Heaven, swift helpmeet and intercessor, for his health, and that she forgive you your mistaken thoughts. I will say one other thing to you, Prokhorovna: either he will soon come back to you in person, your son, or he will most certainly send you a letter. So bear that in mind. Go now, and from this day forth be calm. I say to you, your son is alive.'

'Dear one of ours, may God reward you, benefactor of ours, supplicant for us all and for our sins . . .'

But the Elder had already observed in the throng two burning eyes

that strove towards him from the face of an exhausted, apparently consumptive, though still young peasant woman. She stared at him without
saying anything, her eyes were begging for something, but she seemed to
be afraid to make an approach.

'What brings you, my dear?'

'Absolve my soul, my darling,' she said quietly and without hurry, got
down on her knees and prostrated herself at his feet.

'I have sinned, darling father, and I am afraid of my sin.'

The Elder sat down on the bottom step, and the woman approached
him, still upon her knees.

'I've been a widow since the year before last,' she began in a half-
whisper, seeming to quiver all over. 'It was hard being married, my
husband was an old man, he'd given me a sore beating. He was ill in bed;
as I looked at him I thought: what if he recovers and gets up again, what
then? And then this idea came to me . . .'

'Wait a moment,' said the Elder, and he brought his ear right down to
her lips. The woman continued in a quiet whisper, so that almost nothing
could be overheard. This did not take her long.

'And this was the year before last?'

'Yes. To begin with I didn't think about it, but now I've begun to be
poorly and the misery has come upon me.'

'Are you from a long way off?'

'Five hundred versts from here.'

'Have you told it at confession?'

'Yes, twice.'

'And were you admitted to communion?'

'Yes. I'm afraid; I'm afraid to die.'

'Be not afraid, and never be afraid, and do not be in misery. Just as
long as repentance does not grow scarce within you – then God will
forgive anything. And indeed there is and can be no sin upon all the
earth that the Lord will not forgive the truly repentant. And there is no
sin that man could commit so great as would ever exhaust God's infinite
love. For could there ever be a sin that could exceed God's love? Care
only for repentance, unceasing repentance, but as for fear, drive it out
altogether. Have faith that God loves you in a way of which you cannot
dream, loves you even with your sin and in your sin. For it was said long
ago that there shall be more joy in heaven over one sinner that repenteth
than over ten just men.* Go now, and have no fear. Bear no ill-will
towards others, and no anger in the face of injury. In your heart forgive
your husband all the wrongs he did you, and truly make your peace with

him. As you repent, so will you love. And if you love, you will belong
to God ... With love all things may be redeemed, all things may be
rescued. If I, a sinful human being like yourself, have been moved by you
and taken pity on you, how much more so God. Love is such a priceless
treasure that the whole world may be purchased with it, and the sins not
only of oneself but also those of others be redeemed. Go now and have
no fear.'

He crossed her three times, took the miniature icon from around his
neck and placed it round hers. Without a word she bowed down to the
ground. He raised himself and cast a merry look at one robust woman
who bore a suckling infant in her arms.

'I'm from Vyshegorye, dear one.'

'But that's six versts you've had to struggle with your child. What
brings you here?'

'I've come to see how you are. I was here before, or have you
forgotten? Your memory can't be up to much if you've forgotten me.
They said in our village that you were poorly, so I thought to myself, I'll
go and see how he is for myself: but now I behold you and you don't
look poorly at all! You'll live another twenty years, sure you will, and
God be with you! And anyway, how could you be poorly with all those
supplicants you have praying for you?'

'Thank you for all of it, dear woman.'

'And my plea will only be a small one: here's sixty copecks — you take
it, dear father, and give it to a woman that's poorer than me. On my way
here I was thinking: "I'll do best to give the money to him, he'll know
who needs it."'

'Thank you, dear one, thank you, kind one. You have my love. I will
certainly fulfil your plea. Is that a little girl you have there?'

'Yes, dear light. Lizaveta's her name.'

'May the Lord bless you both, both yourself and the infant Lizaveta.
You have brought gladness to my heart, mother. Goodbye now, dear
ones, goodbye now, precious and kind.'

He blessed them all and to all deeply bowed.

4

A Lady of Little Faith

THE visiting lady landowner, as she beheld all this scene of discourse
with the common people and the blessing of them, shed quiet tears and

wiped them away with a handkerchief. She was a sentimental lady of society with inclinations that were in many respects sincerely good. When the Elder at last approached her, she greeted him with ecstasy:

'I experienced so many, many things as I watched all that moving scene . . .' she said, unable to finish her sentence from excitement. 'Oh, I understand why the common people love you, I myself love the people, I desire to love it, for how can one not love it, our fine Russian people, simple-souled in its greatness?'

'How is your daughter's health? You again wished to talk with me?'

'Oh, I have begged insistently, I have implored, I have been ready to go down on my knees and remain there for three days below your windows if necessary until you admitted me. We have come to you, great healer, in order to express all our ecstatic gratitude. Why, you have cured my Liza, you've completely cured her, and by what means? – by praying for her on Thursday and by the laying-on of your hands. We have come hurrying to kiss those hands, to pour out our feelings and our reverence.'

'How can that be, cured? She is still in a bath chair, is she not?'

'But the night fevers have completely gone, it's more than forty-eight hours since she had one, ever since Thursday,' the lady began to prattle nervously. 'And not only that: her legs have gained strength. This morning when she rose she was well, she had slept all night, look at the colour in her cheeks, look at her shining eyes. Before she was always crying, but now she laughs, she's gay, happy. Today she absolutely demanded to be allowed to stand, and she stood for a whole minute on her own, without anyone helping to support her. She's bet me that at the end of two weeks she'll be dancing the quadrille. I sent for a local doctor here, by the name of Herzenstube; he shrugged his shoulders and said: "I wonder; I am puzzled." And you suppose we could simply leave you alone, and not come winging our way here in order to thank you? Well, then, say thank you, *Lise*, say thank you!'

Lise's sweet, laughing little face suddenly grew more serious, she sat up in the bath chair as tall as she could and, looking at the Elder, clasped her little hands before him, but could not help herself and suddenly burst into laughter . . .

'It's him, it's him,' she said, pointing to Alyosha with childish annoyance at not having been able to prevent herself from laughter. Anyone who had taken a look at Alyosha, who was standing a pace back from the Elder, would have observed on his features a swift blush that in an instant suffused his cheeks. His eyes flashed, and he lowered them.

'She has an errand with you, Aleksey Fyodorovich . . . How are you?'

the mother continued, turning suddenly to Alyosha and extending towards him her charmingly gloved hand. The Elder looked round and gave Alyosha a quick, attentive look. Alyosha went over to Liza and, smiling a somewhat strange and awkward smile that contained more than a hint of irony, extended his hand to her, too. *Lise* made a solemn face.

'Katerina Ivanovna has sent this to you through me,' she said, handing him a small letter. 'She particularly asks you to visit her, but soon, soon, and you mustn't disappoint her but go and see her without fail.'

'She wants me to visit her? Me to go and see her . . . But why?' Alyosha muttered in deep astonishment. His face had suddenly acquired a look of thorough concern.

'Oh, it's all to do with Dmitry Fyodorovich and . . . all these recent happenings,' the mother explained fleetingly. 'Katerina Ivanovna has now arrived at a certain decision . . . but in order to go through with it she absolutely must see you . . . Why? Naturally I don't know, but she asked you to go and see her as soon as you possibly can. And you'll do it, I know you will – in this case Christian feeling positively demands it.'

'But I've only ever seen her once,' Alyosha continued in the same bewilderment.

'Oh, she is such an exalted, such an unfathomable being! By her sufferings alone, never mind the rest . . . Consider what she has endured, what she is enduring even now, consider what awaits her . . . All that is dreadful, dreadful!'

'Very well, I shall go,' Alyosha decided, having read through the brief and mysterious letter in which, apart from the earnest request that he arrive, there were no explanations at all.

'Oh, that would be sweet and magnificent of you,' said *Lise*. 'You see, I said to mamma, he won't come, not for anything in the world, he's living as a monk. What an excellent, excellent man you are! Why, I've always known you were an excellent man, and it gives me pleasure to say so now!'

'*Lise*!' her mother said imposingly, though she immediately smiled.

'You have forgotten us, too, Aleksey Fyodorovich, you never seem to feel like visiting us: yet *Lise* has told me on two occasions now that she only feels happy in your presence.'

Alyosha raised his lowered eyes, again blushed suddenly and again, himself now knowing why, smiled his ironic smile. By now, however, the Elder was no longer observing him. He had entered into conversation with the visiting monk who, as we have already said, had been waiting beside *Lise*'s bath chair for him to come out. This was plainly one of the most ordinary kind of monks, that is to say, of common rank, with a limited, inviolable view of the world, but a man of faith and in his way persistent. He declared that he had come from somewhere in the far north of Russia, from the monastery of St Sylvester in Obdorsk, a poor one with only nine monks. The Elder blessed him and invited him to visit him in his cell whenever he wished to do so.

'But how do you dare to perform such deeds?' the monk asked unexpectedly, pointing to *Lise* in a solemn, imposing manner. He was alluding to her 'cure'.

'Of that it is, of course, too early to speak as yet. The relief she has experienced is not a complete cure and may also have proceeded from other causes. But if anything has taken place, it is by no other power than that of God's volition. All is from God. Come and visit me, Father,' he added to the monk, 'for I cannot always receive guests: I am sick, and I know my days are counted.'

'Oh no, no, God won't take you from us, you're going to live for a long, long time yet,' the mother exclaimed. 'Any anyway, what illness can you have? You look so full of health and gaiety and happiness.'

'Today I feel unusually improved, but I know from past experience that it will only last a moment. I now understand my illness without error. But if I seem to you so full of gaiety, there is no way that you could ever delight me so much as to make such an observation. For human beings were created for happiness, and whosoever is completely happy is also worthy of saying to himself: "I have fulfilled the behest of God upon this earth." All the righteous, all the saints and all the holy martyrs were every one of them happy.'

'Oh, how you talk, what bold and elevated words,' the mother exclaimed. 'You speak and it's as if they pierced right through one. But even so, happiness, happiness – where is it? Who is able to say of himself that he is happy? Oh, since you were so kind as to admit us today yet one more time to see you, then hear all that I did not finish telling you upon the last occasion, did not dare to, all that from which I suffer so, and which began so long, so long ago! I suffer, forgive me, I suffer . . .' And in a hot rush of feeling she clasped her hands before him.

'From what in particular?'

'I suffer . . . from a lack of faith . . .'

'A lack of faith in God?'

'Oh no, no, of that I do not even dare to think, no, it's the life to come – that is such a riddle! And I mean, there is no one, no one who can answer it! Look, you are a healer, a connoisseur of the human soul: I, of course, cannot demand that you believe me entirely, but I assure you by the most solemn precept that not out of light-mindedness do I say to you now that this notion of a future life beyond the grave agitates me to the point of torture, of horror and of panic . . . And I do not know who to turn to, all my life I have not dared . . . and so now I am making so bold as to turn to you. Oh God, what sort of woman will you think me now?' She wrung her hands.

'Do not be troubled on account of my opinion,' the Elder replied. 'I fully believe in the sincerity of your anguish.'

'Oh, I am so grateful to you! You see, I close my eyes and think: if everyone else believes, then why do I feel all this? And now people say that it all stems in the first place from a fear of nature's frightening manifestations and that none of it is based in reality. But wait, I think: all my life I've believed that I shall die, and that suddenly there will be nothing there, only "burdock growing on a grave",* as I read in the work of a certain writer. That is dreadful! How, how am I to restore my faith? Though actually, I only had it when I was a little girl, it was something automatic, something I didn't even need to think about . . . How, how can it be proven? I have come now to abase myself before you and ask you for this. I mean, if I let this opportunity pass me by, then no one will give me an answer for the rest of my life. How can it be proven, how can one be convinced it is true? Oh, it's too unfortunate! I stand and look around me and see that no one could care less, or practically no one, no one worries about this any more, and I'm the only person who cannot endure it. It is murderous, murderous!'

'Without doubt, it is murderous. But here it is not possible to prove anything; it is, however, possible to be convinced.'

'How? By what means?'

'By the experience of active love. Try to love your fellow human beings actively and untiringly. In the degree to which you succeed in that love, you will also be convinced of God's existence, and of your soul's immortality. And if you attain complete self-renunciation in your love for your fellow creatures, then you will unfailingly come to believe, and no form of doubt will ever be able to visit your soul. That has been tested, that is precisely true.'

'Active love? But that is another question, and it is such a question, such a one! You see, my love for mankind is so great that, would you believe it, I sometimes dream of giving up all, all that I possess, of forsaking *Lise* and of joining the Sisters of Mercy. I close my eyes, I think and dream, and at those moments I sense within myself an overmastering strength. No wounds, no septic sores would be able to frighten me. I would dress them and bathe them with my own hands, I would be a sick-nurse to those sufferers, I am ready to kiss those sores . . .'

'It is already much and good that your mind should dream of this, and not of some other thing. One day suddenly by chance you really will perform some good work.'

'Yes, but would I last in such an existence for long?' the lady continued hotly, and almost in a kind of frenzy. 'That is the question! That is the question that torments me most of all. I close my eyes and ask myself: would you last long on such a path? And if the sick person whose sores you are washing does not at once respond with gratitude, but starts instead to torment you with caprices, failing either to cherish or even notice your philanthropic devotion, begins to shout at you, making rude demands, even complaining to someone in authority (the way that people in great physical suffering often do) – what then? Will your love survive, or will it not? And then, you see, I realized with a shudder that if there is one thing that would be capable of instantly cooling my "active" love for mankind, it is ingratitude. Quite simply, I am the kind of woman who works for a reward, and I want the reward at once, in the form of praise for myself and reciprocated love. I am incapable of loving anyone on any other terms!'

She was in an access of the most sincere self-flagellation and, when it was over, gave the Elder a look of challenging resolve.

'That is almost precisely what a certain medical man once told me, long ago now,' the Elder observed. 'The man was already quite advanced in years, and of unquestionable intelligence. He spoke just as frankly as you have done, though also with humour, a rueful kind of humour; "I love mankind," he said, "but I marvel at myself: the more I love mankind in general, the less I love human beings in particular, separately, that is, as individual persons. In my dreams," he said, "I would often arrive at fervent plans of devotion to mankind and might very possibly have gone to the Cross for human beings, had that been suddenly required of me, and yet I am unable to spend two days in the same room with someone else, and this I know from experience. No sooner is that someone else close to me than his personality crushes my self-esteem and hampers my freedom. In the space of a day and a night I am capable of coming to hate even the best of human beings: one because he takes too long over dinner, another because he has a cold and is perpetually blowing his nose. I become the enemy of others," he said, "very nearly as soon as they come into contact with me. To compensate for this, however, it has always happened that the more I have hated human beings in particular, the more ardent has become my love for mankind in general."'

'But then what is to be done? What is to be done in such a case? Is one to give oneself up to despair?'

'No, for it is sufficient that you grieve over it. Do what you are able, and it will be taken into consideration. In your case much of the work has already been done, for you have been able to understand yourself so deeply and sincerely! If, however, you have spoken so sincerely to me now only in order to receive the kind of praise I have just given you for your truthfulness, then you will, of course, get nowhere in your heroic attempts at active love; it will all merely remain in your dreams, and the whole of your life will flit by like a wraith. You will also, of course, forget about the life to come, and you will end by somehow acquiring a kind of calm.'

'You have overwhelmed me! It is only now, at this very moment, as you were speaking, that I realized I was indeed merely expecting you to praise me for my sincerity when I told you I could not tolerate ingratitude. You have pre-empted me, you have caught me out and explained me to myself!'

'Do you say so, indeed? Well now, after a confession like that from you, I believe that you are sincere and good-hearted. If you do not reach happiness, always remember that you are on the right road, and try not to deviate from it. The main thing is to shun lies, all forms of lies, lies to yourself in particular. Keep a watch on your lies and study them every hour, every minute. Also shun disdain, both for others and for yourself: that which appears to you foul within yourself is cleansed by the very fact of your having noticed it in you. Also shun fear, although fear is only the consequence of any kind of lying. Never be daunted by your own lack of courage in the attainment of love, nor be over-daunted even by your bad actions in this regard. I regret I can say nothing more cheerful to you, for in comparison to fanciful love, active love is a cruel and frightening thing. Fanciful love thirsts for a quick deed, swiftly accomplished, and that everyone should gaze upon it. In such cases the point really is reached where people are even willing to give their lives just as long as the whole thing does not last an eternity but is swiftly achieved, as on the stage, and as long as everyone is watching and praising. Active love, on the other hand, involves work and self-mastery, and for some it may even become a whole science. But I prophesy to you that at the very moment you behold with horror that in spite of all your efforts, not only have you failed to move towards your goal, but even seem to have grown more remote from it — at that very moment, I prophesy to you, you will suddenly reach that goal and discern clearly above you the miracle-working power of the Lord, who has loved you all along and has all along been mysteriously guiding you. Forgive me that I cannot stay longer with you, they are waiting for me. Until we meet again.'

The lady wept.

'But what about *Lise*, *Lise*? Give her your blessing, give her your blessing!' she said, suddenly a-flutter.

'It is not worth loving her. I saw the mischief she was up to all the time,' the Elder pronounced with humour. 'Why were you laughing at Aleksey all the time?'

Lise had indeed been amusing herself all the time with this trick of hers. She had long observed, even since the previous occasion, that Alyosha was embarrassed by her and tried not to look at her, and now this had begun to entertain her greatly. She would wait on the alert and catch his gaze: unable to tolerate the gaze so relentlessly directed upon him, Alyosha would suddenly, involuntarily, driven by some overmastering power, himself stare closely at her, and at once she would smile an ironic smile of triumph straight back into his eyes. Alyosha's embarrassment and annoyance would increase still further. At last he turned away from her completely and hid behind the Elder's back. After a few minutes he again, drawn by that same overmastering power, turned to ascertain whether anyone was looking at him or not, and saw that *Lise*, leaning over the edge of her bath chair so that she almost fell out, was studying him sideways and waiting with bated breath for him to look her way; and when she caught his gaze she burst into such peals of laughter that even the Elder lost patience, and said:

'Why are you embarrassing him like this, you mischievous girl?'

Lise suddenly, quite unexpectedly, blushed, flashed her eyes, her face grew terribly serious, and in a hotly indignant, complaining voice she suddenly said quickly and nervously:

'Well, why has he forgotten it all? He used to carry me in his arms when I was little, he and I used to play together. I mean, he used to come and give me reading lessons, did you know that? Two years ago, when he was saying goodbye, he said he'd never forget, that we were eternal friends, eternal, eternal! And now he's suddenly scared of me, does he think I'm going to eat him, or what? Why won't he come near me, why won't he talk to me? Why won't he come and visit us? It's not as though you wouldn't let him out: I mean, we know he goes visiting all over the place. It isn't right for me to invite him, he ought to have remembered it first, if he hadn't forgotten. Oh well, I suppose he's living as a monk now! Why have you made him wear that long cassock thing? ... If he tries to run he'll trip up and fall ...'

And suddenly, losing her self-control, she covered her face with one hand and burst into terrible, unrestrained fits of her long, nervous, quivering and inaudible laughter. The Elder smilingly heard her out and with tenderness blessed her; but as she began to kiss his hand, she suddenly pressed it to her eyes and broke into tears, saying:

'Please don't be angry with me, I'm a fool, I'm not worth anything ... and Alyosha is perhaps right, very right not to want to go visiting a silly girl like me.'

'I shall send him without fail,' the Elder decided.

5

May it Come to Pass, May it Come to Pass!

THE Elder's absence from the cell lasted for some twenty-five minutes. It was now past twelve-thirty, but Dmitry Fyodorovich for whose sake they had all gathered was still not there. He seemed, however, almost to have been forgotten by them, and when the Elder came back to the cell he found a most animated general conversation in progress among his guests. The chief participants in the conversation were Ivan Fyodorovich and the two hieromonachs. Miusov, too, was trying to join the fray, and very heatedly, it appeared, but once more he was out of luck; he was evidently running in second place, and his comments elicited little response, yet one more factor which merely served to increase the sense of irritability that had been building up in him. The fact was that even before this he had had one or two caustic exchanges of general knowledge with Ivan Fyodorovich and had found a certain careless disdain for himself quite intolerable, though he had borne it with sang-froid: 'Until now, at any rate, I have stood at the summit of all that is progressive in Europe, but this new generation really does ignore us,' he was thinking to himself. Fyodor Pavlovich, who had personally promised to sit in a chair and keep quiet, really had remained silent for some time, but was watching his neighbour Pyotr Aleksandrovich with a mocking little smile and was plainly gratified at his irritated condition. He had long been planning to settle a few old accounts and was now reluctant to miss his chance. At last he could bear it no longer, stooped forward over his neighbour's shoulder and again began to taunt him in a low voice:

'Why didn't you leave just now after my "kissing it sweetly" story, instead of consenting to stay in such disreputable company? Because you felt insulted and injured and stayed on in order to show off your intellect in revenge. Now you won't leave until you've given your show.'

'Are you starting on that again? On the contrary, I shall leave right now.'

'Last, last of all will you leave,' said Fyodor Pavlovich, inserting another thrust. This took place almost at the very moment the Elder made his return.

For a moment or two the argument died down, but the Elder, settling into his earlier place, surveyed them all as though affably bidding them continue. Alyosha, who was by now a skilled interpreter of almost every expression on the Elder's face, saw plainly that he was dreadfully tired and was overstraining himself. In the most recent phase of his illness he had begun to have fainting fits caused by the exhaustion of his energies. A pallor almost of the same kind as that which preceded a fainting fit was now spreading across his face, and his lips had turned white. But it was obvious that he did not wish to dismiss the assembly; he seemed, moreover, to have some purpose of his own – what could it be? Alyosha watched him fixedly.

'It is this most curious article of his we are discussing,' the hieromonach Iosif, the bibliothecary, pronounced, turning to the Elder and pointing towards Ivan Fyodorovich. 'He arrives at many fresh conclusions, and it seems that his idea is a two-edged sword. In connection with the question of the Ecclesiastical–Civil Court and the extent of its jurisdiction* he has published in one of the journals an article replying to a certain person of spiritual authority who wrote an entire book on the subject . . .'

'I regret that I have not read your article, but I have heard about it,' the Elder replied, studying Ivan Fyodorovich with a fixed and vigilant eye.

'He defends a most curious point of view,' the Father Bibliothecary continued, 'and in the question of the Ecclesiastical–Civil Court evidently quite rejects the separation of Church from State.'

'That does indeed arouse one's curiosity, but in what sense do you mean it?' the Elder asked Ivan Fyodorovich.

The latter finally replied to him, not, however, with the condescending politeness Alyosha had feared the day before, but modestly and reticently, with evident consideration and, it was plain, without the slightest ulterior motive.

'I proceed from the assumption that this merging of elements, that is to say the essences of Church and State, taken individually, will of course be endless, in spite of the fact that it cannot be achieved and that it will never be possible to bring it to any normal or in any way harmonious condition, as there is a lie at the very foundation of the matter. A compromise between Church and State in such questions, as for example at present in that of criminal justice, is to my mind impossible by its very nature. The person of spiritual authority to whom I was replying maintains that the Church has a precise and definite place in the State. I retorted to him, however, that, on the contrary, the Church must contain within it the whole of the State and not simply occupy a certain corner of it, and that if this is for some reason impossible at present, then by the very essence of things it must be set as the principal and direct goal of the entire further development of Christian society.'

'Quite correct!' Father Paisy, the taciturn and learned hieromonach, said firmly and nervously.

'The purest Ultramontanism!'* cried Miusov, crossing and recrossing his legs with impatience.

'Ah, but we have no mountains!' Father Iosif exclaimed and, turning to the Elder, went on: 'He replies, among other things, to the following "basic and essential" propositions of his opponent — a person of spiritual authority, please note. The first of these is that "no social body can or should appropriate to itself the power to order the civil and political rights of its members". The second is that "criminal and civic—legal authority should not be invested in the Church and is incompatible with its status both as a divine institution and as an alliance of human beings for religious ends." And finally, the third is that "the Church is a kingdom not of this world". . .'*

'A most unworthy play on words for a person of spiritual authority!' Father Paisy broke in again, unable to resist. 'I have read this book, the one you were replying to,' he said, turning to Ivan Fyodorovich, 'and was surprised by the person of spiritual authority's assertion that "the Church is a kingdom not of this world". If it is not of this world, then it follows that it cannot have its being upon earth at all. In the Holy Gospel the words "not of this world" are not employed with this meaning. To play with such words is impermissible. The Lord Our Jesus Christ came down to earth for the express purpose of establishing the Church upon it. The Kingdom of Heaven is, of course, not of this world, but in heaven; it cannot, however, be entered except through the Church, which has been founded and established upon earth. And so worldly puns of this sort are impermissible and unworthy. For the Church is indeed a kingdom and is appointed to rule and in its due course must indubitably manifest itself as a kingdom over all the earth – as it was promised to us . . .'

He suddenly fell silent, as though he were keeping himself in check. Ivan Fyodorovich, who had heard him out with deference and attention, then continued, with exceptional calm but obligingly and straightforwardly as before, turning to the Elder:

'All my article said was that in ancient days, the days of the first three centuries of Christianity, Christianity upon earth manifested itself only as a Church and was only a Church. But when the pagan Roman State conceived the desire to become Christian, it could not happen otherwise than that, having done so, it merely included the Church within itself, but continued to remain a pagan State in very many of its practices. If one views the matter objectively, one can see that this was bound to occur. There were in Rome, however, viewed as a State, too many vestiges of pagan civilization and wisdom, as for example even the very goals and fundamental principles of the State itself. Upon entering into the State, the Church of Christ could not of course surrender any of its own fundamental principles, hewn from the same rock on which it stood, and could not but pursue the very goals that once had been firmly set and prescribed for it by the Lord Himself, including the goal of converting the entire world, and thereby the whole of the ancient State and Church. Thus (in the interests of the future, that is to say), it is not the Church that must seek a fixed place within the State, like any other "social body" or "alliance of human beings for religious ends" (as the author to whom I replied describes the Church), but, on the contrary, every earthly State that will henceforth be obliged to convert itself fully into a Church and become nothing other than a Church, having now renounced all goals that are not concomitant with its Churchly status. But all this will in no wise degrade it, take away its honour or its glory as a mighty State, or the glory of its rulers, but will only turn it aside from a false, still pagan and mistaken path on to the true and genuine one that alone will lead it to the goals of eternity. That is why the author of the book about "The Principles of Ecclesiastical–Civil Justice" would have been more correct if, in investigating and setting forth those principles, he had viewed them as a temporary compromise, still necessary in our sinful and imperfect times, but no more than that. But as soon as the deviser of those principles has the temerity to declare that the principles he is now setting forth and a portion of which Father Iosif has just enumerated, are immoveable, primordial and eternal, he flies straight in the face of the

Church and its sacred, primordial and immovable destiny. That is all my article said, and there you have a complete résumé of it.'

'In short, then,' Father Paisy articulated again, laying emphasis on each word, 'according to certain theories which have been excessively elaborated in this nineteenth century of ours, the Church must evolve into a State, as from a lower species to a higher one, in order subsequently to vanish in it, yielding to science, the spirit of the times and civilization. But if the Church is unwilling to do this and resists there is set aside for it within the State a certain mere corner, as it were, one which is, moreover, kept under constant surveillance – and this is generally the case throughout all the lands of Europe in our day. According to Russian thinking and aspirations, however, the desirable outcome is not that the Church should evolve into a State, as from a lower type of existence to a higher one, but that, on the contrary, the State should end by being deemed worthy to become exclusively a Church and nothing other.* May it come to pass!'

'Well sir, I must admit that now you have encouraged me a little,' Miusov said with an ironic smile, recrossing his legs again. 'As I understand it, this is the realization of an ideal, one infinitely remote, in the Second Coming. You are welcome to it. A beautiful Utopian dream concerning the end of wars, diplomats, banks and the like. Something not all that unlike socialism. But you see, I thought all this was in earnest and that the Church intended *now*, for example, to try criminals and sentence them to the birch and penal servitude, and possibly even death.'

'Yes, but even if now there were only an Ecclesiastical–Civil Court, not even in that case would the Church send men to penal servitude or the scaffold. Crime and our view of it would then undoubtedly change, little by little, of course, not suddenly and not overnight, but rather quickly all the same . . .' Ivan Fyodorovich pronounced calmly, without the flicker of an eyelid.

'Are you in earnest?' said Miusov, giving him a fixed glance.

'If everything were to become the Church, the Church would excommunicate from itself those elements that were criminal and recalcitrant, and would then abstain from cutting off heads,' Ivan Fyodorovich continued. 'Where would an excommunicant go, I ask you? After all, then he would have to forsake not only his fellows, but Christ as well. You see, by his crime he would have risen in rebellion not only against his fellows, but against the Church of Christ. This is, of course, in the strict sense true even now, except that it is not publicly stated, and the conscience of the present-day criminal very often, exceedingly so, in fact, enters into bargains with itself, as if to say: "I may have committed theft, but I have no quarrel with the Church, I am no enemy of Christ." That is what the present-day criminal quite frequently says to himself; well, and when the Church will have supplanted the State, then it will be difficult for him to say this without going against the whole of the Church over all the earth, as though he were to declare: "Everyone is wrong, everyone has strayed, everyone is a part of the false Church, and I alone, the murderer and thief, am the true Christian Church." And, well, this is something that is very hard to say to oneself, it demands an enormous mass of preconditions, of circumstances that do not often occur. Now take, on the other hand, the view of the Church itself regarding crime: does it not have a duty to change in the face of the present almost pagan view of the matter, and move from being a mechanical amputation of infected limbs, such as takes place at present as a safeguard to society, towards transforming itself, completely this time and without falsehood, into an idea concerning the rebirth of man, his resurrection and salvation . . .'

'But what on earth are you talking about? Once again I cease to understand,' Miusov said, interrupting. 'This is another of your fantasies. It's shapeless stuff, and there's nothing one can get hold of. What excommunication is it that you mean, what kind of excommunication? I have my suspicions that you're simply making fun of us, Ivan Fyodorovich.'

'You know, if truth be told, it is thus even now,' the Elder said suddenly, and they all turned towards him at once. 'After all, if Christ's Church did not exist at present there would be nothing to restrain the criminal from his wrongdoing, nor even any punishment to follow it − genuine punishment, that is, not the mechanical sort of which you were speaking just now and which merely sours the heart in the majority of instances, genuine punishment, the only effective kind, that deters and pacifies, and is contained in an awareness of one's own conscience.'

'But how can that be, may one be permitted to know?' Miusov asked with the most animated curiosity.

'Like this,' the Elder began. 'All these deportations to forced labour, which were earlier accompanied by floggings, reform no one, and more importantly have no deterrent effect, either, and not only does the number of capital crimes fail to diminish, but the more time passes, the greater does it become. After all, you must surely agree that this is so. And it transpires that, consequently, society is not safeguarded at all, for though one unhealthy limb is mechanically amputated and deported far away, out of sight, in its place there at once appears another criminal, and possibly even two. If there is anything that will safeguard society even in a time such as ours and will reform the criminal, making him evolve into a new person, it is again solely the law of Christ, manifesting itself in an awareness of one's own conscience. Only in perceiving his guilt as a son of a Christian society — the Church, in other words — will he also perceive his guilt before society itself, before the Church, that is to say. Consequently the present-day criminal is capable of perceiving his guilt only before the Church, and not before the State. Now if justice were to be invested in a society-as-Church, society would know whom to bring back from excommunication and join to itself once more in communion. At present, however, the Church, possessing no active legal authority, but only the opportunity of making a certain moral condemnation, itself retreats from an active punishment of the criminal. It does not excommunicate him from itself, but makes do with issuing to him a fatherly admonishment. Not only that, it even tries to preserve with the criminal all the details of the Christian ecclesiastic communicacy: admits him to church services, to the holy gifts, gives him alms and treats him more as one in thrall than as a guilty person. But what would happen to the criminal — oh merciful Lord! — if Christian society too, the Church, that is to say, were to reject him in the way the civil law rejects and amputates him? What would happen if, instantly following the punishment meted out to him by the civil law, the Church were to punish him with excommunication? There could be no more desperate plight, at least for the Russian criminal, for Russian criminals retain their religious faith. Yet who can tell: perhaps a terrible thing would then take place — there might occur a loss of faith within the criminal's despairing heart, and then what might take place? But the Church, like a tender and loving mother, withholds herself from active punishment, as the guilty one has already been punished all too severely by the justice of the State without her intervention, and after all there must be someone to take pity on him. The Church does this principally because the justice of the Church is the only form of justice that accommodates within itself the truth and is consequently unable to join forces, morally or materially, with any other form of justice, even in a temporary compromise. Here no bargains may be struck. It is said that in Europe the criminal seldom repents, as the most recent theories confirm him in the notion that his crime is not a crime at all, but merely an act of revolt against an unjustly oppressive power. Society amputates him from itself by means of a power that triumphs over him quite mechanically, and accompanies this excommunication with hatred (such at least are the stories that they tell about themselves in Europe) – with hatred and the most complete indifference and neglect concerning his subsequent fate as a brother to the rest. Thus it all takes place without the slightest ecclesiastical compassion, for in many instances there are no longer any Churches there at all, and all that remain are churchmen and fine ecclesiastical buildings, as the Churches there have themselves long striven to evolve from the lower form of life – the Church – to the higher form – the State – in order to vanish in it completely. That, at any rate, appears to be the situation in the Lutheran lands. In Rome, however, a State has been proclaimed in place of a Church for a thousand years now. The result is that the criminal no longer perceives himself as a limb of the Church and, excommunicated, falls into despair. And if he does return to society, he does it not infrequently with such hatred that society excommunicates him, as it were, from itself. What the end of this is you may judge for yourselves. In many instances it would appear that the same thing takes place among us here in Russia; but the fact of the matter is that, in addition to the established courts, there is in our land also the Church, which never breaks off its communion with the criminal as one of its dear and beloved sons, and there exists, moreover, and is preserved, though only in thought, the justice of the Church which though it is no longer active is still alive for the future, even if only in a dream, and is unfailingly perceived as such by the criminal himself, by the instinct of his soul. What was said here just now is also true: to the effect that if the Church really were to be granted legal authority, in all its power, that is to say if the whole of society were simply to be converted into a Church, not only would the legal authority of the Church have an influence upon the reform of the criminal of a kind it never has at present, but the incidence of crime itself might start to diminish at a surprising rate. Indeed, there can be no doubt that the Church would view the criminal of the future and the crime of the future in many respects quite differently than it does at present and would be able to return the excommunicant, anticipate the schemer and regenerate the fallen. It is true,' the Elder smiled thinly, 'that Christian society is not yet ready for this and merely stands upon the shoulders of the seven men of honest report;* but as they never grow scarce, so it still firmly abides in the expectancy of its complete transformation from a society that is as yet little more than a pagan body into one Oecumenical and Sovereign Church. May it come to pass, even if only at the ends of the world, for it alone is predestined to be accomplished! And there is no reason to be perplexed by the times or the seasons,* for the secret of all times and seasons is in God's Wisdom, in his Providence and Love. And that which by human calculation may still seem far away indeed, may by God's predestiny already stand upon the eve of its fulfilment, at the very door. May this latter come to pass!'

'May it come to pass, may it come to pass!' Paisy repeated, sternly and reverentially.

'Extraordinary, quite extraordinary!' said Miusov, not so much with fervour as with a kind of suppressed indignation.

'What is it that appears to you so extraordinary?' Father Iosif inquired, cautiously.

'But what in reality *is* this?' Miusov exclaimed, as if he had suddenly broken free of some restraint. 'The State is to be abolished upon earth, and the Church is to be elevated to the rank of State! That is not Ultramontanism, it is Arch-Ultramontanism! Not even Gregory VII dreamed of it!'*

'I am afraid you have understood it in quite the wrong order!' Father Paisy said sternly. 'It is not the Church that is to turn itself into a State, be clear about that. That is Rome and her dream. That is the third temptation of Satan!* No, on the contrary — the State is to turn itself into a Church, ascend to the condition of a Church and become a Church over all the earth, something that is the complete opposite of Ultramontanism, and Rome, and your interpretation, and is simply the great predestination of Orthodoxy upon earth. From the East this star will shine.'*

Miusov preserved an imposing silence. His entire form expressed an unusual personal dignity. A haughtily condescending smile had appeared on his lips. Alyosha had been following the whole scene with a violently beating heart. The entire conversation had stirred him to the foundations. He took a casual glance at Rakitin; the latter stood motionlessly in his previous station by the door, attentively listening and watching, though with lowered eyes. From the lively flush in his cheeks, however, Alyosha guessed that Rakitin too was stirred, possibly no less than himself; Alyosha knew what had stirred him.

'Permit me to tell you a certain small anecdote, gentlemen,' Miusov said suddenly in an imposing voice and with an air of especial gravitas. 'In Paris, some years ago now, just after the December revolt,* I one day had occasion, while paying a social call to a certain extremely important person in authority at the time, a friend of mine, to encounter at his home a certain most curious gentleman. He was, this individual, not so much a police spy as a kind of director of an entire team of political police spies — in its own way a rather influential position. Seizing upon the chance out of exceptional curiosity, I engaged him in conversation;

but as he was there not in the capacity of an acquaintance, but as a subordinate functionary delivering a certain type of report, and as he, for his part, had observed the way in which I was received in the home of his superior, he deemed me worthy of a certain degree of candour — well, of course, only relatively so, that is to say he was more courteous than candid, with that particular courteousness at which the French are so good, and all the more so as he recognized me to be a foreigner. But I well understood the fellow. The theme of our deliberations had turned to the socialist revolutionaries who as a matter of fact were the subject of persecution at the time. Omitting the principal substance of the conversation I shall cite only one most curious observation that suddenly broke from this little gentleman: "Actually," he said, "all those socialists — the anarchists, atheists and revolutionaries — are not the ones who give us the headaches; we keep an eye on them, and their movements are well known to us. There are among them, however, though they are not many, a number of peculiar characters: these are people who believe in God and are Christians, yet are at the same time socialists. Now they are the ones who give us the worst headaches, they are a fearsome bunch! The socialist who is a Christian is more worthy of fear than the socialist who is an atheist." These words shocked me at the time, but now in your company, gentlemen, they have somehow unexpectedly recalled themselves to me again . . .'

'You mean that you apply them to us, and see in us socialists?' Father Paisy inquired bluntly and without circumlocution. But before Pyotr Aleksandrovich could think of a reply, the door opened and in walked the long-awaited Dmitry Fyodorovich. They had indeed almost given up waiting for him, and at that initial moment his sudden appearance even occasioned a certain surprise.

6

Why is a Man Like That Alive?

DMITRY Fyodorovich, a young man twenty-eight years old, of average height and pleasant face, looked nevertheless far older than his years. He was muscular, and in him one could detect formidable physical strength, yet even so there was about his face something almost morbid. His face was lean, its cheeks sunken, their complexion shot with a kind of sickly yellow. His rather large, dark eyes gazed bulgingly, and though they appeared to have a firm persistence, somehow lacked definition. Even when he got excited and spoke irritably his gaze seemed not to obey his inner mood but to express something else, something that was on occasion not at all in keeping with the moment in question. 'It's hard to guess what he's thinking about,' people who had engaged him in conversation would sometimes say. Others, perceiving in his eyes a morose, reflective look, would on occasion be suddenly shocked by his unexpected laughter, which bore testimony to the gay and playful thoughts that were within him at the very time he looked upon the world with such moroseness. As it happened, a certain morbidity of feature might have been understandable in him just then: everyone knew or had heard of the extremely disturbed and 'dissipated' existence into which among us he had recently thrown himself, just as everyone knew of the extraordinary states of irritation he attained in the quarrels with his father concerning the disputed money. About this several anecdotes were already circulating in the town. It is true that he was by nature irritable, 'of unsteady and irregular mind', as Semyon Ivanovich Kachalnikov, our local Justice of the Peace, had characteristically expressed himself on the subject at a certain gathering. Dmitry Fyodorovich made his entrance meticulously and stylishly dressed, in a buttoned-up frock-coat, black gloves and holding a top hat in his hands. As a military man in recent discharge from the service, he had a moustache and for the time being shaved only his beard. His dark-chestnut hair was cut short and combed casually across his temples. He strode broadly, decisively, officer-fashion. For an instant he paused on the threshold and surveying them all with a glance went straight up to the Elder, surmising him to be the host. He bowed deeply to him and asked for blessing. The Elder, raising himself, blessed him; Dmitry Fyodorovich reverently kissed his hand and with unusual agitation, almost irritation, pronounced:

'Please be so generous as to forgive me for making you wait so long. But in response to my insistent questions about the time of the audience, Smerdyakov, the manservant sent by my pater, told me twice in the most emphatic tone of voice that it was set for one o'clock. Now I suddenly discover . . .'

'Do not be anxious,' the Elder broke in. 'It is perfectly all right, you are a little late, but it matters not . . .'

'I am extremely grateful to you and could expect no less of your goodness.' Having snapped this out, Dmitry Fyodorovich bowed one more time and then, suddenly turning in the direction of his 'pater', made in his direction too the same deep, reverential bow. It was plain that he had considered this bow in advance and had devised it in all sincerity, viewing it as his duty to express by means of it his reverence and good intentions. Fyodor Pavlovich, though he had been caught napping, was quick to devise a response of his own: in answer to Dmitry Fyodorovich's bow he leapt out of his chair and replied to his son with an identical bow that was every bit as deep. His features had suddenly grown solemn and imposing, something that gave him, however, an air of decided nastiness. Then without saying anything, according everyone present in the room a general bow of greeting, with his large and decisive strides Dmitry Fyodorovich walked over to the window, sat down in the only remaining vacant chair not far from Father Paisy and, leaning forward in it with the whole of his mass, instantly made ready to listen to the sequel of the conversation he had interrupted.

The appearance of Dmitry Fyodorovich had taken up no more than some two minutes, and so the conversation could hardly fail to revive again. By now, however, Pyotr Aleksandrovich did not deem it necessary to reply to Father Paisy's nagging and almost irritating question.

'You must permit me to cast this subject aside,' he said with a certain worldly carelessness. 'It is, in any case, a complex one. Look, there's Ivan Fyodorovich giving us his ironic smile: that means he must have something interesting to tell us on this occasion, too. Why don't you ask him?'

'Nothing particular, except for one small comment,' Ivan Fyodorovich at once replied, 'and that is that European liberalism in general — even our Russian liberal dilettantism — frequently confuses the end results of socialism with those of Christianity, and has done so for a long time now. This wild deduction is of course a characteristic feature. Actually, as it turns out, it is not only the liberals and the dilettantes who confuse socialism with Christianity, but also the gendarmes — the foreign ones, of course. Your Paris anecdote is rather characteristic, Pyotr Aleksandrovich.'

'I really must again beg permission to leave this subject,' Pyotr Aleksandrovich said again, 'and shall instead relate to you, gentlemen, another anecdote concerning Ivan Fyodorovich, one that is most interesting and characteristic. No more than some five days ago, in a certain company, for the most part female, here in our town, he solemnly declared in the course of argument that in all the earth there is nothing whatever to compel human beings to love their fellows, and that a law of the type "man shall love mankind" is wholly non-existent, and that if hitherto there has been any love upon the earth it has proceeded not from a natural law but solely from the fact that human beings have believed in

their own immortality.* Ivan Fyodorovich added, moreover, the paren-
thetical observation that in this same circumstance rests the whole of the
natural law, and that if one were to destroy mankind's faith in its own
immortality, there would instantly grow enfeebled within it not only
love, but every vital force for the continuation of universal life. Not only
that: then nothing would be immoral, all things would be lawful, even
anthropophagy. But he went still further: he concluded with the assertion
that for every private individual – such as ourselves at present, for
example – who believes neither in God nor in his own immortality, the
moral law of nature must instantly be transformed into the complete
opposite of the old, religious law, and that selfish egoism even to the
point of evil-doing must not only be lawful to man, but must even be
acknowledged to be necessary, the most reasonable and indeed possibly
the most decent way out of his situation. From a paradox such as this,
gentlemen, you may draw your own conclusions regarding all the rest of
the things he considers it meet to proclaim and may intend to continue to
proclaim, our dear eccentric and paradoxalist, Ivan Fyodorovich.'

'Permit me,' Dmitry Fyodorovich suddenly exclaimed, 'just in order
to make sure my ears did not deceive me. The argument is as follows:
"Evil-doing must not only be lawful, but even recognized as being the
most necessary and most intelligent way out of the situation in which
every atheist finds himself"! Is that so, or is it not?'

'It is precisely so,' Father Paisy said.

'I shall remember.'

Having said this, Dmitry Fyodorovich just as abruptly fell silent
again. They all glanced at him with curiosity.

'Do you really hold such a conviction regarding the consequences of
the decline of men's faith in the immortality of their souls?' the Elder
suddenly inquired of Ivan Fyodorovich.

'Yes, that was what I said in my article. Without immortality there can
be no virtue.'

'Blessèd must you be, if thus you do believe – either that or thoroughly
unhappy.'

'Why unhappy?' Ivan Fyodorovich smiled.

'Because in all probability you yourself believe neither in the immortality of your soul nor even in the things you wrote about the Church and
the ecclesiastical question.'

'You may well be correct . . . Though actually, I spoke not entirely in
jest, either . . .' Ivan Fyodorovich suddenly confessed in a strange manner,
at the same time rapidly blushing.

'Truly said — you spoke not entirely in jest. That idea has not yet been resolved within your heart and is tormenting it. But even a martyr sometimes likes to keep himself amused with his despair, out of sheer despair, as it were. For the moment that is what you are doing: amusing yourself with your despair — in articles for journals and in worldly disputations, yourself not believing in your own dialectics and with pain in your heart smiling sceptically at them to yourself . . . This question has not been resolved within you, and therein lies your great unhappiness, for it insistently demands resolution . . .'

'But can it be resolved in me? Resolved in a positive direction?' Ivan Fyodorovich continued to inquire, strangely, still looking at the Elder with a vague, inexplicable smile.

'If it cannot be resolved in a positive direction, it will never be resolved in a negative one, either — you yourself know that property of your heart; and therein lies all its torment. But render thanks to the Creator who has given you an exalted heart that is able to experience such torment, to set its affection on things above "and seek those things which are above, for our conversation is in heaven". May God grant you that the resolution of your heart shall come upon you while you are yet on earth, and may God bless your path.'

The Elder raised his hand and was about to cross Ivan Fyodorovich from where he sat. But the latter suddenly rose from his chair, walked over to him, received his blessing and, having kissed his hand, returned silently to his place. His mien was firm and serious. This action, so unexpected in him, like all Ivan Fyodorovich's foregoing discourse with the Elder, seemed to strike them all with its quality of enigma and even solemnity, so that for a moment they all fell silent, and in Alyosha's face there was expressed something almost akin to fear. Miusov, however, suddenly shrugged his shoulders, and at that very same moment Fyodor Pavlovich leapt up from his chair.

'Divine and most holy Elder!' he exclaimed as he pointed to Ivan Fyodorovich. 'This is my son, the flesh of my flesh, the most beloved flesh of mine! He is my most respectful, as it were, Karl Moor, while this other son, Dmitry Fyodorovich, the one who has just come in and with regard to whom I seek justice here in your cell, is a most disrespectful Franz Moor — both of them straight out of Schiller's *The Robbers*,* while I, I myself am in that case *Regierender Graf von Moor*!* Be our arbiter and our salvation! We stand in need not only of your prayers, but also of your prophecies.'

'Speak without foolery and do not commence with insults to your kith and kin,' the Elder replied in a faint, exhausted voice. It was plain that he was growing tired, the more so the longer the audience continued, and his strength was visibly ebbing.

'An unworthy farce of which I had presentiment on my way here!' Dmitry Fyodorovich exclaimed in indignation, also leaping up from his chair. 'Forgive me, Reverend Father,' he said, turning to the Elder, 'I am an uneducated man and do not even know the correct way to address you, but you have been deceived, and you have been too kind in allowing us to congregate here. All pater wants is a scandal, and as to why – that's his calculation. He always has a calculation. But now I think I know what it is . . .'

'They all accuse me, all of them!' Fyodor Pavlovich shouted in his turn. 'Even Pyotr Aleksandrovich here accuses me. You have accused me, Pyotr Aleksandrovich, you have accused me!' he said, turning suddenly to face Miusov, though the latter would not have dreamed of interrupting him. 'They accuse me of snatching those legacies and pocketing them; but forgive me, exists there not justice? There in the courts of justice they will reckon it up for you, Dmitry Fyodorovich, according to your receipts, your letters and agreements, how much you have had, how much you have blown to the winds and how much remains to you! Why does Pyotr Aleksandrovich attempt to evade pronouncing judgement? Dmitry Fyodorovich is no stranger to him. Because they're all out to get me, and the fact of the matter is that Dmitry Fyodorovich is in debt to me, and it's not by some small amount but several thousands, sir, for which I have all the documents! Why, the town is a-babble and a-thunder with his debaucheries! And in that place where he was serving before he was paying out one and two thousand a time for the seduction of decent girls; that, Dmitry Fyodorovich, is known to us, sir, in the most secret and intimate detail, and I shall prove it, sir . . . Most holy Father, would you believe it: there was one girl he made fall in love with him, a most well-bred young thing, of good family, with a private fortune, the daughter of his former superior, a brave colonel, decorated with the St Anne's Ribbon on the neck with crossed swords;* he compromised the girl by offering her his hand, and now she's here, now she's an orphan, his fiancée, while he, before her very eyes, pays visits to one of our local seductresses. But though this seductress has been living, as it were, in a citizens' marriage with a certain respectable man, but is of independent character, a fortress unassailable to any, every bit as good as a lawfully wedded wife, for she is virtuous – yes, sir! Sainted fathers, she's virtuous, all right! But Dmitry Fyodorovich intends to unlock this fortress with a golden key, which is why he's strutting about in front of me now, he intends to rob me of my money when he's already squandered thousands on that seductress; he's been borrowing money incessantly for that purpose and, incidentally, from whom, do you suppose? Shall I tell them or not, Mitya?'

'Be silent!' Dmitry shouted. 'You can wait until I've gone, but do not presume to stain the honour of a most noble maiden while I am here ... Your even daring to mention her is sufficient disgrace for her ... I will not stand for it!'

His breath was choking.

'But Mitya! Mitya!' Fyodor Pavlovich exclaimed nervously, forcing a few tears. 'What about parental blessing? I mean, if I curse you, what will happen then?'

'You brazen-faced sham!' Dmitry Fyodorovich barked violently.

'That's his father, his father he's talking about! What do you suppose he's like with the rest? Gentlemen, imagine: there is here in our town a poor but respectable man, a retired captain in the army, down on his luck, was dismissed from the service, but not publicly, not by a court martial, retaining all his honour, saddled with a large family to feed. Well, three weeks ago, at an inn, this Dmitry Fyodorovich of ours grabbed him by the beard, and by that very same beard hauled him out on to the street, and in that very same street, in front of everyone, gave him a sound thrashing, and all because the fellow's a secret attorney in a certain little business venture of mine.'

'That's all lies! Truth on the outside, lies on the inside!' Dmitry said, quivering with anger in every limb. 'Pater! I do not seek to justify my actions; indeed, in front of everyone I confess: I acted like a wild beast with that captain and am now filled with remorse and self-loathing for my bestial anger, but your captain, that attorney of yours, went to see the lady whom you describe as a seductress and began to invite her in your name to take the promissory notes I signed with you and bring a summons against me, threatening to have me put in gaol if I pestered you too much about the settlement on the value of the property. Yet now you have reproached me with having a weakness for that lady, when you yourself drilled her to entrap me! I mean, she tells me that straight to my face, has told it to me herself, while she laughed at you! The only reason you want to have me put in gaol is because you're jealous of me with regard to her, because you yourself had begun to make approaches to that woman with your amorous feelings, and once again I was told all about it, and once again she laughed – do you hear? – laughed at you, making a story out of it. So there you have him, holy monks, this man, this father in reproach of his depraved son! Gentlemen of the witness, please forgive my wrath, but I already anticipated that this insidious old man had summoned you here in order to make a scandal. I came in order to forgive him if he would but give me his hand, to forgive him and to request his forgiveness! But since he has this very moment insulted not only myself but also a most noble maiden whose name I do not even dare to take in vain out of reverence for her, I have decided to expose his whole rotten game in public, even though he is my father! . . .'

He could continue no further. His eyes flashed, his breath came with difficulty. But everyone in the cell was agitated, too. All but the Elder had risen anxiously from their seats. The Father Hieromonachs gazed sternly but awaited the Elder's will nevertheless. The latter, however, sat looking pale; but his pallor was that not of agitation, but of the helplessness occasioned by infirmity. A beseeching smile glimmered on his lips; now and then he would raise his hand, as though in an attempt to stop the ravings of the possessed, and, of course, a single gesture from him would have been sufficient to curtail the scene; but he himself appeared to be waiting for something, and he would stare at them fixedly, as though trying to understand something still further, as though there were something he had not yet cleared up for himself. At last Pyotr Aleksandrovich felt himself to have been well and truly humiliated and disgraced.

'For the scandal that has occurred we must all bear the guilt,' he said hotly, 'but I must say that in coming here I did not anticipate it, even though I knew with whom I should be dealing . . . A stop must be put to this at once! Your Reverence, please believe me when I tell you that all the details that have come to light here were unknown to me in any precise manner, that I did not want to believe them and have learned them now for the first time . . . A father is jealous of his son over a woman of immoral conduct and himself plots with this brute creature to have his son put in prison . . . And this is the company I was pressed into coming here with . . . I have been tricked, I declare to you all that I have been tricked no less that the rest of you . . .'

'Dmitry Fyodorovich!' Fyodor Pavlovich howled suddenly in a strange voice that was not his own. 'Were you not my son I would this very instant have summoned you to a duel . . . with pistols, at a distance of three paces . . . Across a handkerchief! Across a handkerchief!'* he finished, stamping both feet.

There are with old liars who all their lives have played the actor moments when they begin to show off to such a degree that they of a truth quiver and weep with emotion, the fact notwithstanding that even at that very moment (or only a second thereafter) they may whisper to themselves: 'Why, are you lying, you old brazen-face, you're being an actor even now, in spite of all your "holy" anger and your "holy" moment of anger.'

Dmitry Fyodorovich frowned horribly and stared at his father with inexpressible contempt.

'I thought . . . I thought,' he articulated, almost quietly and with restraint, 'that I was coming home with the angel of my soul, my bride, to cherish him in his old age, but I see merely a depraved voluptuary and a most base farceur!'

'To a duel!' the little old man howled again, panting, and spraying himself with spittle at each word. 'And as for you, Pyotr Aleksandrovich Miusov, let me tell you, sirrah, that it may well be that in all your stock there has never been a woman more exalted or more honourable – honourable, do you hear – than this one who in your opinion is a "brute creature", as you had the unspeakable temerity to call her just now! And you, Dmitry Fyodorovich, have exchanged your bride for that very same "brute creature", so you must have decided that your bride wasn't worth the soles of your boots, that's the kind of "brute creature" she is!'

'Shameful!' The words suddenly burst from Father Iosif.

'Shameful and disgraceful!' in his adolescent voice, trembling with excitement and flushed red all over, Kalganov, who had remained silent all this time, suddenly exclaimed.

'Why is a man like that alive?' Dmitry Fyodorovich snarled hollowly, almost in a frenzy of choler, strangely raising his shoulders to an exceeding degree and growing almost hunchbacked as a result. 'No, tell me, can he really be permitted to go on defiling the earth with his person?' he said, looking round at them all, and pointing to the old man. He spoke slowly and measuredly.

'Do you hear, monks, do you hear him, the father-murderer?' said Fyodor Pavlovich, pouncing upon Father Iosif. 'There is the reply to your "Shameful"! What is shameful? It may be that this "brute creature", this "woman of immoral conduct" is more holy than you yourselves, resident gentlemen of the hieromonach status! It may be that she fell in her girlhood, a prey to her surroundings,* but she "loved much", and even Christ forgave the woman who loved much . . .'*

'It was not for that kind of love Christ forgave . . .' burst in impatience from the meek Father Iosif.

'Oh yes it was, it was, for that very same kind, dear monks, that very same kind! You live here on cabbage and think you're men of honest report! You eat gudgeons,* a gudgeon a day, and think you can purchase God with the stuff.'

'Impossible, impossible!' said voices from every corner of the cell.

But this entire scene, which had now attained the quality of outrage, was curtailed in a most unexpected manner. The Elder suddenly got up from where he had been sitting. Though Alyosha had almost completely lost his presence of mind out of terror for what might happen to the Elder and to everyone else, he managed to support him by the arm. The Elder took a step in the direction of Dmitry Fyodorovich and then, going right up to him, sank down in front of him on his knees. For a second Alyosha thought he had fallen because of weakness, but this was not the case. Having stationed himself on his knees, the Elder bowed at Dmitry Fyodorovich's feet in a full, clearly defined and conscious bow, even touching the floor with his forehead. Alyosha was so overcome by wonder that he did not even manage to support the Elder when the latter got up again. The merest smile gleamed faintly on the Elder's lips.

'Forgive me! All of you, forgive me!' he articulated, bowing a farewell greeting in all directions to his guests.

For a few instants Dmitry Fyodorovich stood there like one stricken: a bow at his feet − what was this? At last he suddenly exclaimed: 'Oh God!' − and, covering his face with his hands, rushed from the room. Behind him, flocking in a throng, went all the other guests too, in their confusion not even taking their leave or performing the customary bows. Only the hieromonachs went over again to be blessed.

'What was that foot-bowing business he was up to, was it some kind of emblem?' said Fyodor Pavlovich, now suddenly pacified again for some reason, in an attempt to restart the conversation, but not daring to to address any of them individually. At that moment they were all passing out through the enclosure of the hermitage.

'For a madhouse and for madmen I cannot answer,' Miusov instantly replied with malicious hostility, 'but at any rate I shall in future spare myself your company, Fyodor Pavlovich, and please believe me when I tell you that it will be for good. Where is that monk who was here earlier? . . .'

But 'that monk' − the one, this is to say, who had earlier invited them to dine with the Father Superior, did not keep them waiting. He was there to greet the guests as soon as they descended the porch from the cell of the Elder, as though he had been waiting for them all the time.

'Venerable Father, please be so good as to convey my deepest respects to the Father Superior and tell him that I, Miusov, must personally ask to be excused before His Reverence in connection with the fact that because of certain sudden and unforeseen circumstances I can on no account have the honour of taking part in his banquet, for all my most earnest desire to do so,' Pyotr Aleksandrovich said to the monk irritably.

'Actually, the unforeseen circumstance is me!' Fyodor Pavlovich immediately chimed in. 'You see, Father, Pyotr Aleksandrovich does not wish to remain in my company, otherwise he'd go like a shot. And go you shall, Pyotr Aleksandrovich, you shall grace the Father Superior with your presence, and – *bon appetit*! Please understand that it is I who shall refuse, not you. Let's home, let's home, at home we'll sup, but here I feel unable, Pyotr Aleksandrovich, my dear kinsman,'

'I am no kinsman of yours, nor have I ever been, you base man!'

'I said it especially to infuriate you, because it's our kinship you're avoiding, though you're a kinsman to me all the same, I can prove it by the holy calendar;* for you, Ivan Fyodorovich, I shall in time send horses, you may remain here if you wish, you too. But as for you, Pyotr Aleksandrovich, why, good manners positively demand that you now go to the Father Superior, for you must offer apologies for the commotion that you and I caused back there . . .'

'But are you really going to leave? Are you not lying?'

'Pyotr Aleksandrovich, how could I dare to after what has taken place? I got carried away, forgive me, gentlemen, I got carried away! Not only that, but I'm shaken. And ashamed, too. Gentlemen, some men have hearts like that of Alexander the Great, while others have hearts like that of little dog Fidelka. My heart is like that of little dog Fidelka. My tail is between my legs! I mean, how after an escapade like that can I possibly go to dinner and scoff down the monastery sauces? I am too ashamed, I cannot do it, you must excuse me!'

'The devil if I know; what if he's up to his tricks again?' Miusov thought, pausing in reflection as he watched the retreating buffoon with a bewildered gaze. The latter turned round as he went, and observing that Pyotr Aleksandrovich was watching him, blew him a kiss with one hand.

'What about you – will you go to the Father Superior's?' Miusov abruptly inquired of Ivan Fyodorovich.

'Well, why not? In any case, yesterday he particularly invited me to visit him.'

'It's too bad, I really feel almost positively obliged to attend this blasted dinner,' Miusov continued with the same sour irritability, not even paying any heed that the little monk was listening. 'I feel we ought to offer our apologies for the disturbance we have caused here and explain that it wasn't us . . . What is your opinion?'

'Yes, I think we ought to explain it wasn't us. What is more, pater will not be there,' Ivan Fyodorovich observed.

'Having your pater there would be all we need! This blasted dinner!'

And, in spite of everything, they all set off. The little monk kept silent and listened. On the way through the woods only once did he observe that the Father Superior had been expecting them for a long time and that they were more than half an hour late. No one said anything in reply. Miusov looked at Ivan Fyodorovich with hatred.

'Why, he's going to dinner as though nothing had taken place!' he thought. 'A brazen brow and a Karamazov conscience.'

7

A Seminarian—Careerist

ALYOSHA led his Elder to the little bedchamber and sat him down on the bed. It was a very small room with only the essentials of furniture; the bed was narrow and iron-framed, and on it instead of a mattress there was only a layer of thick felt. In one corner, near the icons, was a reading-stand with a cross and a New Testament on it. The Elder lowered himself helplessly on to the bed; his eyes were glistening and his breath came with difficulty. Having seated himself, fixedly and as though he were considering something, he looked at Alyosha.

'Off you go, dear fellow, off you go, Porfiry will suffice for me, and you ought to hurry. They need you there, off you go to the Father Superior's and serve at table.'

'Give me your blessing to remain here,' Alyosha said in a beseeching voice.

'You are needed more there. There there is discord. Go serve at table, and make yourself useful. If devils rise up, recite a prayer. And bear in mind, dear offspring (the Elder liked to call him this), that henceforth you do not belong here. Remember that, young man. As soon as God sees fit to let me pass away, you must leave the monastery. You must go away entirely.'

Alyosha shuddered.

'What is wrong? For the present you do not belong here. I give you my blessing for your great task of obedience in the world at large. You have much travelling yet to do. And you will have to get married, you will have to. You will have to endure everything before you return again. And there will be much work to do. But I have faith in you, and that is why I am sending you. With you is Christ. Cherish him and he will cherish you. You will behold great woe and in that woe you will be happy. Here is my behest to you: in woe seek happiness. Work, work untiringly. Remember what I have said to you from this day forth, for though I shall talk with you again, not only my days but my hours, too, are counted.'

On Alyosha's face there again appeared a powerful movement. The corners of his lips were trembling.

'What is it now?' the Elder asked, smiling quietly. 'Let the secular bid their deceased farewell with tears; here, however, we rejoice at the departing father. We rejoice and supplicate for him. But leave me now. Off you go, and hurry. Be close to your brothers. And close not to one, but to them both.'

The Elder raised his hand to bless. Protest was out of the question, though Alyosha had an extreme desire to stay. He also wanted to ask, and indeed the question was on the point of slipping from his tongue: what had been augured by that prostration to his brother Dmitry? – but he did not dare to ask it. He knew that the Elder would himself have explained it to him, had that been possible. But since he had not, that meant his will was not so inclined. That prostration had struck a terrible chord inside Alyosha; with blind faith he saw in it a mysterious significance. A mysterious one, and possibly one of dread. As he left the hermitage enclosure in order to get to the monastery in time for the start of dinner with the Father Superior (only to serve at table, of course), his heart was suddenly wrung painfully within him, and he stood still; before him once again he seemed to hear the words of the Elder prophesying his own so imminent decease. That which the Elder had prophesied, and with such exactitude, must surely take place. Alyosha piously believed that. But how could he manage without him, how could he live without seeing him, hearing his voice? And where would he go? Telling him not to weep and to leave the monastery, O Lord! It was a long time now since Alyosha had experienced such anguish. He walked quickly through the woods that separated the hermitage from the monastery and, without even the strength to endure his own thoughts, so heavily did they weigh upon him, began to look at the centuries-old pine trees on both sides of the woodland path. The distance was not very great, some five hundred paces, no more; at this hour one might not have expected to encounter anyone, but suddenly at the first bend of the path he noticed Rakitin. The latter was awaiting someone.

'Is it me you're waiting for?' Alyosha asked, drawing level with him.

'The very man,' said Rakitin, with an ironic smile. 'You're hurrying to get to the Father Superior's. I know; he's having a high table. There hasn't been a table like it since he had the Bishop and General Pakhatov to dinner, if you remember. I shan't be there, but you go and serve out the sauces. Aleksey, tell me one thing: what means this dream?* It's that that I wanted to ask you.'

'What dream?'

'The prostration to that fine brother of yours, Dmitry Fyodorovich. Why he even let his forehead hit the floor!'

'I take it you are referring to Father Zosima?'

'That's right, I am,'

'And the forehead hitting the floor?'

'Aha, I see I expressed myself with insufficient reverence! Well, never mind. So, what about this dream, then, what does it signify?'

'I don't know what it means, Misha.'

'I knew he wouldn't explain it to you. Not that there's anything particularly abstruse about it, of course — just the usual holy nonsense.* But the trick was performed on purpose. And now all the town's sanctimonious hypocrites will spread it through the province: "What," they'll say, "does this signify?" If you ask me, the old fellow has true perspicacity: he's caught a whiff of foul play. Your place reeks of it.'

'What kind of foul play?'

Rakitin was visibly eager to unburden himself of something.

'It's something that's going to happen in that little family of yours. It will take place between those fine brothers of yours and your pecunious pater. You see, Father Zosima let his forehead hit the floor just to be on the safe side. So that if something does take place, they'll all say: "Aha, why that's what the holy Elder predicted, he made a prophecy" — though what sort of a prophecy's involved in hitting your head on the floor? "No," they'll say, "it was an emblem, an allegory," and the devil only knows what! They'll sing his praises, they'll commit it all to memory: "He foresaw a crime," they'll say, "he marked the criminal." All that holy fools do is like that: they make the sign of the cross at the tavern and cast stones at the church. Your Elder isn't any different: the man of honest report is driven away with the stick, while the murderer receives a bow at his feet.'

'What crime? What murderer? What are you implying?' Alyosha stood as though rooted to the spot, and Rakitin also paused.

'What murderer? As if you didn't know! I'll wager you've thought of

A SEMINARIAN-CAREERIST

it before now. Actually, this is quite interesting. I say, Alyosha, you always tell the truth, even though you're always falling between two stools:* have you or haven't you thought of it before now? Tell me.'

'I have,' Alyosha replied quietly. Even Rakitin was troubled.

'What did you say? You mean you *have* thought of it?' he exclaimed.

'I . . . I haven't really,' Alyosha mumbled. 'It's just that when you began to talk so strangely about it all just now I felt I had.'

'You see (and how clearly you put it), you see? Today, as you gazed upon your dear papa and your fine brother Mitya, you thought of a crime. Well, it looks as though I'm not mistaken, am I?'

'But wait, wait,' Alyosha interrupted, with worry in his voice. 'From what do you deduce all this? . . . Why does it interest you so much? That's the first thing.'

'Two quite distinct but understandable questions. I shall reply to each of them individually. From what do I deduce it? I'd have deduced nothing if today I hadn't suddenly seen your brother Dmitry Fyodorovich, instantly and suddenly, exactly for what he is. It was as though in one single feature of his character I instantaneously caught the whole man. These very honest but passionate men have a line in them one should not try to cross. Otherwise — otherwise, he may stick a knife in your papa. And you papa's a drunken and intemperate libertine, never ever has he known moderation in anything — they'll neither of them be able to hold back, and down into the ditch they'll go. . .'

'No, Misha, no, if that is all it is you have put new courage in me. It will not get that far.'

'Then why are you shaking all over? Do you know something? He may be an honest man, that dear Mitya (he's stupid, but honest); but he's a voluptuary. That is his designation and his entire inner essence. He has it from his father, that base voluptuous lust. Why, I positively wonder at you, Alyosha: how is it you're such a virgin? I mean, you're a Karamazov! The voluptuary streak in your family has increased until it's become a raging inflammation. Well, and now these three voluptuaries are watching one another . . . with hidden knives. The three of them have knocked their foreheads together, and you may easily be the fourth . . .'

'You're wrong about that woman. Dmitry . . . despises her,' Alyosha said, almost shivering.

'Grushenka, you mean? No, brother, he doesn't despise her. Not if he can wittingly exchange his bride for her, he doesn't. In cases like that . . . in cases like that, brother, there's a principle involved that you won't understand as yet. In a case like that, if a man falls in love with some beauty, with a female body, or even with a mere part of a female body (a voluptuary may understand what I mean), and then for her sake he'll give up his own children, he'll sell his own father and mother, Russia and the fatherland; where he was honest, now he'll go thieving; where he was gentle, now he will kill, where he was faithful, now he'll betray. The bard of women's feet,* Pushkin, sang the praises of those feet in poetry; other men don't do that, but can't look at women's feet without going crazy. Though I mean, it's not only their feet . . . In such cases, brother, contempt's not a great deal of help, even if he did feel it for Grushenka. Even if he does despise her, he won't be able to tear himself away from her.'

'I understand that,' Alyosha blurted out suddenly.

'Do you, indeed? Yes, I expect you probably do, if it's the first thing you blurt out like that,' Rakitin said with malicious relish. 'You let that slip by accident, it just came out. It makes your confession all the more precious: it means it's already a familiar subject to you, it's something you've already thought about, voluptuous lust. Oh, you virgin! You're a dark horse, Alyosha, my lad, I agree that you're a saint, but you're a dark horse, and the devil only knows the things you've thought about, the things you know about! A virgin, yet you've already been to the depths – I know, I've been watching you for a long time. You're a Karamazov, too, a real Karamazov – and so species and selection aren't empty words after all. On your father's side a voluptuary, on your mother's a holy fool. What are you trembling for? Am I telling the truth, eh? Do you know that Grushenka got down on her knees to me? "You bring him to me," she said – that's you she was talking about – "and I'll pull the cassock off him." I mean, you have no idea how she begged and begged me to bring you! But it made me wonder why she finds you so interesting. She's not exactly an ordinary sort of woman herself, you know!'

'Please give her my regards and tell her that I shan't be coming,' Alyosha said with a crooked, ironic smile. 'But finish what you were saying, dear Mikhail, and then I shall tell you what is on my mind.'

'What is there to finish? It's all quite clear. All this is an old refrain, brother. If even you contain a voluptuary within you, then what of your brother Ivan, who's from the same womb? I mean, he's a Karamazov, too. There's the nub of your whole Karamazov question: you're either voluptuaries, money-grubbers or holy fools! Your brother Ivan is at present publishing theological articles, tongue-in-cheek, with some thoroughly stupid, unknown motive, though he himself is an atheist, and admits the baseness of what he is doing – that's your brother Ivan all over. Not only that, but he's in the process of taking Mitya's bride away from him for himself, and it looks as though he will achieve that aim as well. And how can he fail: he has the consent of dear Mitya himself, because Mitya is giving him his bride of his own accord in order to be free of her and be able to go off to Grushenka as quickly as possible. And this in spite of all his disinterestedness and nobility of character, note that. Such men are the most fatal. The devil only knows what to make of you all after that: he himself admits his baseness and yet makes a point of embroiling himself in it still further! But listen to what comes next: dear Mitya is now having his path crossed by his wretched old codger of a father. Why, the old fellow has positively lost his head over Grushenka, the mere sight of her is enough to bring the juices to his mouth. I mean, it was solely because of her and for her sake alone that he created that scandal in the cell just now, for the sole reason that Miusov had the effrontery to call her a licentious brute. He has fallen for her worse than a cat. Before she only used to do his bidding in connection with some shady bar-room business for a salary, but now he's suddenly woken up and realized what a treasure he's been ignoring, he's flown into a frenzy, keeps coming to her with propositions, none of them decent, of course. Well, and so they're on a collision course, the papa and dear son, on that pretty little path. But Grushenka doesn't go either to the one or to the other, for the time being she is hedging her bets and teasing them both, looking to see which one would be the more advantageous, for after all though it may be possible to snatch a lot of money from the papa, on the other hand he won't marry her, and may in the end turn Jew-mean and shut his purse. In that event Mitya too will be worth something; he hasn't any money, but on the other hand he's able to marry. Yes, sir, able to marry! To give up his bride, Katerina Ivanovna, a peerless beauty, rich, a noblewoman and a colonel's daughter, and to marry Grushenka, the former concubine of the filthy old merchant, lecherous muzhik and town mayor Samsonov. Out of all that combination there may indeed occur an act of foul play. And that's just what your brother Ivan's waiting for – then he'll be in clover: he'll acquire Katerina Ivanovna, for whom he's wasting away, and he'll grab her sixty-thousand-rouble dowry into the bargain. To a wee naked babe of a man like himself that's a rather enticing prospect for a beginning. And I mean, do take note: not only will he not cause Mitya any offence – he'll make him feel obliged to him till his dying day. Why, I know for a fact that only last week dear Mitya himself was drunkenly shouting to everyone out loud in an inn with some gypsy girls that he wasn't worthy of his bride, Katerina Ivanovna, but that his brother Ivan was. And Katerina Ivanovna herself, of course, won't turn away a charmer like Ivan Fyodorovich in the end; why, she's already swithering between the two of them. What is it about this Ivan that's bowled you all over and made you treat him with such reverence? For he's laughing at you: he's rolling in clover, as much as if to say, here I am, tasting the nectar at your expense.'

'How is it you know all this? How can you speak with such certainty?' Alyosha suddenly inquired, abruptly and frowning.

'And why are you asking those questions, yet are afraid of what I may answer? It can only mean that you yourself agree that I've spoken the truth.'

'You dislike Ivan. Ivan would not be tempted by money.'

'Oh, wouldn't he, indeed? And how about the beauty of Katerina Ivanovna? It's not money alone that's involved here, though sixty thousand is an enticing sum.'

'Ivan's sights are set higher than that. Ivan would not be tempted even by thousands. Ivan isn't in quest of money, or peace of mind. He may possibly be in quest of torment,'

'I say, what dream is *this*, now? Oh you . . . gentlefolk!'

'Oh, Misha, his soul is a wild and stormy one. His mind is in captivity. Inside him there is a great, unresolved idea. He's the sort of man who needs not millions but the resolution of his idea.'

'Literary stealing, Alyosha, old chap. You have just paraphrased your Elder. My, I do believe Ivan has presented you with a riddle!' Rakitin exclaimed with open malice. The expression of his face had even changed, and his lips had grown contorted. 'And it's a stupid kind of a riddle, there's nothing in it to fathom. Just give your brains a bit of a stir and you'll understand. That article of his is ridiculous and absurd. I mean, you heard his stupid theory just now: "If the soul's not immortal, there's no virtue, either, and that means all things are lawful." (And do you recall the way your dear brother Mitya shouted "I shall remember!"?) A seductive theory for scoundrels . . . I'm getting carried away, this is stupid . . . not scoundrels, but braggadocios with "ideas unresolved in their profundity". He's a nasty little boaster, and the essence of it is: "On the one hand it's impossible not to admit, and on the other it's impossible not to confess!" His entire theory is a piece of vileness! Mankind will find within it the strength to live for virtue, even if it doesn't believe in the immortality of the soul! It will find it in a love of liberty, equality and fraternity . . .'

Rakitin was worked up now and could scarcely hold himself in check. But suddenly, as though remembering something, he paused.

'Well, that's enough of that,' he said, smiling even more crookedly than before. 'What are you laughing at? Do you think I'm a tasteless clod?'

'No, that didn't even cross my mind. You're clever, but . . . Oh, let's forget it, it was stupid of me to make fun of you like that. I can understand you losing your temper, Misha. From your passion I could guess that you yourself are not indifferent to Katerina Ivanovna; I've suspected that for a long time, brother, and that's why you dislike Ivan. Are you jealous of him?'

'I suppose you think I'm jealous on account of her money, too? Go on, add that as well.'

'No, I'm not going to add anything about her money, I'm not out to insult you.'

'Well, if you say so, I believe you, but on the other hand, the devil take you and your brother Ivan! Neither one of you is capable of seeing that one could take a hearty dislike to him even without getting Katerina Ivanovna mixed up in it. And in any case, why *should* I like him, the devil take it? I mean, he apparently deems it fitting to shout names at me. So why shouldn't I have the right to shout names at him?'

'I have never heard him say one word about you, good or bad; he doesn't mention you at all.'

'Well, I heard that the day before last at Katerina Ivanovna's he was swearing at me like a trooper in my absence – that's how interested he was in your obedient servant. And after that, the question of who is jealous of whom is one to which I really don't have the answer, brother! He was so good as to express the notion that if I didn't assent to the career of an abbot in the very imminent future and take the step of having myself tonsured, I would without question depart for St Petersburg and attach myself to one of the "fat" journals, most likely in the critical section, write for a dozen years or so and end by transferring the journal to my ownership. Then I'd reissue it, most likely with a liberal, atheistic slant and a nuance of socialism, even a little out-and-out social-ism, but keeping my ears pricked up, or rather, to be more precise, running with the hare and hunting with the hounds and deceiving the fools.* The end of my career, according to your brother's interpretation, will consist in my dash of socialism not preventing me from putting the money raised from subscriptions into a current account and on occasion investing it in stocks and shares, under the guidance of some little Jew or other, until such time as I'm able to rustle up the resources to build myself a St Petersburg tenement into which I shall move the journal's editorial offices, letting the remaining floors to tenants. He even predicted the site of the tenement: near the New Kamenny Bridge over the Neva from Liteyny Prospect to the Vyborg Side, which they're planning to build in the capital . . .'*

'Oh, Misha, why I bet that's how it all works out, right to the very last word!' Alyosha suddenly exclaimed, unable to restrain himself and laughing a slight, merry laugh.

'You too are indulging in sarcastic remarks, Aleksey Fyodorovich.'

'No, no I'm only joking, please forgive me. I have something else on my mind. Only you must permit me to inquire: who could have given you such details, and from whom did you hear them? I mean, you couldn't have been at Katerina Ivanovna's in person when he spoke about you?'

'I wasn't, but Dmitry Fyodorovich was, and it was Dmitry Fyodorovich I heard it from, or rather, if you prefer, he didn't actually tell it to me but I overheard it, though I didn't have much choice in the matter, as I was in Grushenka's bedroom and couldn't come out while Dmitry Fyodorovich was in the next room.'

'Oh yes, I've forgotten, why, she's a relation of yours . . .'

'A relation? Are you calling Grushenka a relation of mine?' Rakitin exclaimed suddenly, turning red all over. 'Have you gone crazy, or something? Your brains must be addled.'

'Oh? She's not related to you? I heard that she was . . .'

'Where could you possibly have heard that? But what can one expect of you Karamazovs – posing as some sort of grand and ancient noblemen, when your father used to go trotting round other people's tables playing the buffoon and only got his seat in the kitchen out of charity. All right, I'm just the son of a priest, and a greenhorn compared to the likes of you, but don't think you can get away with those smiling insults. I too have my honour, Aleksey Fyodorovich. It's out of the question that I could be any relation of Grushenka, a public prostitute, and I'll have you understand that, sir!'

Rakitin was in a state of violent irritation.

'For God's sake, please forgive me, I had no idea, and anyway, how can you call her a public prostitute? Is she . . . that kind of a woman?' Alyosha said suddenly, blushing. 'I tell you again, I really did hear that she was related to you. You often go to see her, and you yourself told me that there is no amorous relation between you and her . . . So you see it never occurred to me that you despised her so much! Does she really merit it?'

'If I go to see her, then I must have my own reasons for it, and that will have to suffice you for an explanation. But as far as the question of our being related is concerned, then it's more probable that that fine brother of yours or even your pater himself would tie her to you as a relation rather than to me. Well, here we are. In you go, to the kitchen will be best. I say, what's going on here, what is this? Are we too late? Surely they can't have finished already? Or have the Karamazovs been up to their tricks again? Yes, that's no doubt what it is. Look, there's your pater, and there's Ivan Fyodorovich off after him. They've just come rushing out of the Father Superior's chambers. Look, there's Father Isidor shouting something after them from the porchway. And your pater's shouting too and waving his arms, he's probably using bad language. Hah! There's Miusov now, making off in his carriage, look, you see, there he goes. And there's landowner Maksimov running off – yes, there's been a scandal; that means the dinner never took place! What did they do, nail the Father Superior? Or have they themselves been nailed? That would be a job worth doing! . . .'

Rakitin's exclamations were not without point. There had indeed been a scandal, an unheard-of and unexpected one. It had all taken place 'by inspiration'.

8

A Scandal

As Miusov and Ivan Fyodorovich were already entering the Father Superior's chambers there took place within Pyotr Aleksandrovich, who was a man of sincere good manners and delicacy, a certain process also delicate of a kind: he began to feel shame at being angry. He sensed that he ought, in essence, to have such a lack of respect for Fyodor Pavlovich as would have made it impossible for him to have lost his sang-froid in the Elder's cell and thus himself be at a loss, as had transpired. 'At any rate, the monks themselves are not to blame for it,' he suddenly decided in the porchway of the Father Superior's chambers. 'And if these are men of respectability (this Father Nikolay, the Father Superior, is from the nobility, it appears), then why should one not be kind, friendly and polite with them? . . . I shall raise no dispute, I shall even agree with what they say, I shall lure them by kindness and . . . and . . . at last shall prove to them that I am no companion of that Aesop, that buffoon, that Pierrot and have been deceived just as surely as they all have been . . .'

On the vexed question of the wood-felling and the fishing (where all the said activities took place he himself did not know), he decided he would finally yield to the monks, once and for all, that very day, all the more so as it was all worth very little money, and that he would bring his legal action against the monastery to a close.

All these benevolent intentions were fortified still further when they entered the Father Superior's dining chamber. As a matter of fact, the latter did not possess a dining chamber proper, for really in the whole of the premises only two of the chambers were at his disposal, though these were, it was true, rather more spacious and better appointed than those of the Elder. But even here the garnishings of the chambers were not distinguished by any especial comfort; the furniture was of the leather type, mahogany-framed, in the old-fashioned style of the 1820s; even the floors were not painted; on the other hand everything glistened with cleanliness, and in the windows there were many expensive varieties of flowers; but the principal luxury at this moment was, of course, the luxuriously set table, though actually this too was a relative matter: the cloth was clean, the plates and glasses sparkled; there were three different sorts of bread, each magnificently baked, two bottles of wine, two bottles of noble monastery mead and a large glass jug of monastery *kvas*, renowned in the district. Vodka there was none at all. Rakitin later put it about that on this occasion the dinner was to have contained five courses: sterlet soup and fish *pirozhki*; then boiled fish in some rather rare and excellent recipe; then cutlets of salmon, ice cream and *compote* and, to end with, milk *kisel'** à la blancmange*. All this had been nosed out by Rakitin, who had been unable to resist a quick peep into the Father Superior's kitchen, where he had a few connections. Everywhere he had connections, and everywhere an informant. His heart was extremely restless and envious. Possessing a complete awareness of his own considerable abilities, he nervously exaggerated them in his self-conceit. He was not in the slightest doubt that he was going to be a doer and a man of action in his own way, but Alyosha, who was very attached to him, found it a source of torment that his friend Rakitin was dishonourable and completely unaware of it, and that on the contrary, knowing of himself that he would not steal money from the table, he firmly considered himself to be a man of the highest honour. There was nothing that Alyosha or, indeed, any other person could have done about this.

Rakitin, as a minor personage, could not be invited to the dinner, though invitations had been made to Father Iosif and Father Paisy, and to a certain other hieromonach as well. They were already waiting in the

Father Superior's dining chamber when Pyotr Aleksandrovich, Kalganov and Ivan Fyodorovich made their entrance. Waiting also slightly to one side was the landowner Maksimov. In order to greet his guests, the Father Superior came out in front into the centre of the room. He was a tall, rather meagre but still strong old man; his black hair was abundantly mingled with grey, and his face was long, solemn and funereal. He bowed to his guests without a word, though this time they went to him for blessing. Miusov even thought he would risk trying to kiss the Father Superior's hand, but the latter managed to tug it away in time and the kiss did not materialize. Ivan Fyodorovich and Kalganov, on the other hand, this time took full blessing, that is to say with the most straightforward and plebeian smack of the lips on the hand.

'We must truly ask your forgiveness, most exalted Reverence,' Pyotr Aleksandrovich began, grinning amiably but still in the same solemn and deferential tone, 'for appearing without our fellow-wayfarer Fyodor Pavlovich, whom you invited; he has been compelled to forego your table, and not without reason. In the cell of the Reverend Father Zosima, carried away by his unfortunate family dispute with his son, he uttered some quite inapposite words . . . words, indeed, that were quite improper . . . as, I believe' (he glanced at the hieromonachs), 'your most elevated Reverence is already aware. And thus, recognizing his guilt and sincerely repenting of it, he felt ashamed and, unable to master it, begged us, myself and his son, Ivan Fyodorovich, to declare before you all his sincere regret, repentance and contrition . . . In short, he hopes and intends to compensate for it all subsequently, but for the present, requesting your blessing, he begs you to forget about what has happened . . .'

Miusov stopped speaking. As he pronounced the final words of his tirade he felt completely happy, to such a degree that not even a vestige of his recent irritation remained within his soul. He now fully and sincerely loved mankind again. The Father Superior, having heard him out, inclined his head slightly and articulated in reply:

'I deeply regret the departure of the one who has absented himself. It might have been that at our table he would have come to like us, just as we might have come to like him. Welcome to our meal, gentlemen.'

He stood before the icon and began to say a prayer out loud. They all reverently bowed their heads, and the landowner Maksimov even pushed himself forward, clasping his hands before him in a show of especial reverence.

And now it was that Fyodor Pavlovich had his final fling. It should be observed that he really had intended to leave and really had sensed the impossibility, after his disgraceful conduct in the Elder's cell, of his going to dinner at the Father Superior's as though nothing had taken place. Not that he felt any great degree of shame or guilt; perhaps even the contrary; yet still he sensed that for him to attend the dinner would be improper. No sooner had his rattling carriage been driven to the porch of the hotel than he, upon climbing into it, suddenly paused for a moment. He recalled the words he had uttered in the Elder's cell: 'When I go among people I do indeed always feel that I'm more vile than any of them and that they all take me for a buffoon, and so I say to myself: "Very well, I really will play the buffoon, I'm not afraid of what you think of me, because you're all of you to a man more vile than I!"' He wanted to take his revenge on them all for his own dirty tricks. He suddenly remembered now in passing that once, in the old days, someone had asked him: 'Why do you hate such-and-such a person so?' And at the time he had replied, in a fit of his buffoon's lack of shame: 'For this reason: while it's true he has done me no harm, I once played a most unscrupulous dirty trick on him, and no sooner had I played it than I at once began to hate him.' Recalling this now in a moment's reflection, he ironically smiled a quiet and malicious smile to himself. His eyes flashed, and his lips even trembled. 'Now I've started I may as well see it through,' he decided suddenly. In that split second his most intimate sensation could have been expressed in words such as these: 'Well, I'm not going to rehabilitate myself now, so why don't I just brazenly spit upon them, as if to say, "I don't care what you think of me, so there!"' He instructed his coachman to wait, returned to the monastery with rapid steps and went straight to the Father Superior's chambers. He as yet had no real idea of what he was going to do, but knew he was no longer his own master and that it would need but the slightest push to bring him to the extreme limit of some filthy action — though only that, and not some crime or escapade for which he would have to answer in court. In the final account he was always able to hold himself in check and had even on occasion marvelled at this capacity of his. He showed himself in the Father Superior's dining chamber at the very instant the prayer had ended and they were all moving towards the table. Pausing on the threshold, he surveyed the company and began to laugh — a long, shameless, malicious laugh, looking them all valiantly in the eye.

'They all thought I'd left, but here I am!' he shouted to the whole chamber.

For one moment they all stared at him, uttering no word, and suddenly they all sensed that now something repulsive and absurd was about to happen, something that would undoubtedly end in scandal. Pyotr Aleksandrovich immediately passed from a most good-natured temper to one most truculent. All the things that had faded within his heart and died away at once revived and rose up again.

'No, this I cannot endure!' he exclaimed. 'Under no circumstances can I . . . and on no account can I!'

The blood had rushed to his head. His speech was even growing confused, but by now there was no need of eloquence, and he grabbed his hat.

'What is it he can't?' Fyodor Pavlovich let out. 'Under no circumstances can he and on no account can he what? Your Reverence, may I come in or not? Will you receive another table-guest?'

'I bid you welcome with all my heart,' the Father Superior replied. 'Gentlemen!' he added suddenly. 'May I be permitted to request from the bottom of my soul that, leaving behind your incidental disagreements, you come together in love and familial harmony, with a prayer to the Lord, at our humble table . . .'

'No, no, out of the question!' Pyotr Aleksandrovich shouted, almost beside himself.

'Well if it's out of the question for Pyotr Aleksandrovich, it's out of the question for me, too, and I'll not stay. That's why I came here. I shall now accompany Pyotr Aleksandrovich everywhere he goes; if you leave, Pyotr Aleksandrovich, then so shall I – if you remain, then so shall I. You really stung him in the worst place, Father Superior, with that remark about familial harmony: he doesn't recognize me as part of his family! Isn't that so, von Sohn? Look, there's von Sohn standing there. Hello, von Sohn.'

'You . . . are you talking to me, sir?' murmured the bewildered landowner Maksimov.

'Of course I am,' shouted Fyodor Pavlovich. 'Who else would I be talking to? A Father Superior could never be a von Sohn!'

'But, I mean, my name isn't von Sohn, it's Maksimov!'

'No, it's von Sohn, you're von Sohn. Your Reverence, do you know about von Sohn? It was one of those homicide cases: he was murdered in a place of harlotry – I believe that's what those locales are called among you – murdered and robbed and, for all his venerable years, hammered into a packing-case, sealed up tight and sent from St Petersburg to Moscow in a baggage car with a tag on. And while they were banging him in the harlot damsels sang songs and played the psaltery, or tickled the ivories, rather. Well, so this is that very same von Sohn. He's risen from the dead, haven't you, von Sohn?'

'What is this? How is it possible?' voices from among the group of hieromonachs said.

'Come along, we're going!' Pyotr Aleksandrovich shouted, turning to Kalganov.

'No, sir, with your permission!' cried Fyodor Pavlovich, shrilly interrupting, and taking another step into the room. 'With your permission I shall complete what I was about to say. Back there in the cell I was slandered with having behaved without due respect just because I shouted something about gudgeon. My kinsman, Pyotr Aleksandrovich Miusov, prefers that in discourse there be *plus de noblesse que de sincerité*, while I prefer it the other way round, I like my discourse to have *plus de sincerité que de noblesse*, and – a fig for *noblesse*! Don't you agree, von Sohn? With your permission, Father Superior, though I may be a buffoon and acting like one, I am a knight of honour, and I wish to speak my mind. Yes, sir, a knight of honour, and what is wrong with Pyotr Aleksandrovich is simply tweaked vanity, and nothing more. I may also have come here now in order to take a look and to express an opinion. A son of mine, Aleksey, is living here as a monk; as his father, I am concerned about his lot, and have a duty so to be. I have been listening and playing my role, and all the time watching on the sly, and now I want to play the final act of my performance for you, too. After all, how is it in our world? With us, what falls is left to lie. With us, what once has fallen, lie for ever shall. Methinks, sir, 'tis not meet! I will arise! Holy fathers, you exasperate me. Confession is a great and secret mystery, one before which I too bow in reverence and am ready to prostrate myself, yet back there in the cell just then they all of a sudden started getting down on their knees and confessing out loud. Is it permitted to confess out loud? The holy fathers established confession by ear, for only then can one's confession be a secret mystery, and this has been so since ancient days. For how could I explain to him in front of them all that I, for example, did this and that . . . Oh, that and this, you understand? Why, betimes 'twould be indecent even to describe it. I mean, that in itself would be a scandal! No, dear fathers, here among you a man is drawn into the ways of the flagellants . . . As soon as I have a chance I shall write a letter to the Holy Synod, and take Aleksey my son home with me . . .'

Here a *nota bene*. Fyodor Pavlovich had been listening to the church-bells. There had at one time been malicious rumours which had even reached the bishop (not only in our monastery, but also in others where the Elderhood had become established) that the Elders were acquiring too much respect, with a result even prejudicial to the dignity of the office of

Father Superior, and that, among other things, the Elders were abusing the mystery and secrecy of the confession, etcetera, etcetera. Preposterous accusations which had perished of their own accord among us and elsewhere. But the stupid devil that had caught up Fyodor Pavlovich and was bearing him upon his own nerves further and further into the shameful depths had also whispered to him this former accusation, of which Fyodor Pavlovich himself understood not even the first word. Indeed, he could not even express coherently, all the more so because on this occasion no one in the Elder's cell had been down on his knees confessing out loud, and Fyodor Pavlovich could not possibly have witnessed such a thing and was merely repeating old rumours and tittle-tattle that he had remembered from somewhere. Having delivered himself of his stupid remarks, however, he sensed that he had been spouting preposterous rubbish and suddenly conceived a desire to prove on the spot to his listeners, and even more to himself, that what he had said was not at all rubbish. And although he was very well aware that with each word he pronounced he would add an even greater quantity of even more absurd rubbish to what he had already delivered, he was unable to hold himself in check and went plummeting down as though over a precipice.

'What vileness!' Pyotr Aleksandrovich exclaimed.

'Forgive me,' the Father Superior said, suddenly. 'It was said in days of old: "And there began to speak many a one against me, saying of me foul things. Yet hearing them, I said within myself: this is the healing of the Lord Jesus who hath sent it to restore my soul in its vainglory." And so do we too thank you with obedience, precious guest!'

And he bowed from the waist before Fyodor Pavlovich.

'Tsk-tsk-tsk! Bigotry and old phrases! Old phrases and old gestures! Old falsehoods and the official posturing of low bows! Oh, we're well acquainted with those bows! "A kiss to the lips and a dagger to the heart", as in Schiller's *The Robbers*. I have no time for falsehood, fathers, I desire the truth! But the truth is not to be found in gudgeon, and that is what I have proposed! Father monks, why do you observe the fasts? Why do you expect a heavenly reward for it? Why, for a reward such as this I too would come here to observe the fasts! No, holy monk, what you ought to be doing is practising virtue in life and being of use to society, not locking yourself up in a monastery with all expenses paid and waiting for rewards from up there – you'd find that a little harder to achieve. You see, Father Superior, I too know how to mould my phrases. Now what have they got lined up here?' he said, going over to the table. 'Factori's Vintage Port, Médoc bottled by the Brothers Yeliseyev – why, holy fathers, this beats your gudgeon, doesn't it? Look at all the bottles the fathers have set up, heh, heh, heh! And who has supplied all this? The Russian muzhik, the toiler, with his calloused hands, brings hither his earned groat, snatching it from the bosom of his family and the state's requirements! Why holy fathers – you leech upon the common folk!'

'That is quite unworthy on your part,' said Father Iosif. Father Paisy remained stubbornly silent. Miusov fled in a headlong dash from the room, followed closely by Kalganov.

'Well, fathers, I think I too shall follow Pyotr Aleksandrovich. I shall not come to visit you again, not even though you implore me on bended knees. A thousand roubles I sent you, so you sharpened your eyes again, heh, heh, heh! No, there won't be any more where it came from. I shall take revenge for my vanished youth, for all my degradation!' he cried, banging his fist on the table in an access of manufactured emotion. 'Great has been the significance of this monastery in my life! And many the bitter tears I have shed because of it! You set my wife, the wailer, against me. You pronounced your anathema on me at all seven councils, spread stories about me all over the neighbourhood! It's time to call a halt, fathers, for now we live in a liberal age, an age of steamships and railroads. Not a thousand roubles, not a hundred roubles, not even a hundred copecks – nothing will you receive from me!'

Again a *nota bene*. Never had our monastery been of any particular significance in his life, and no bitter tears had he shed because of it. So carried away by his manufactured tears was he, however, that for a single moment he almost believed what he had said; he even began to weep with emotion; but at the same instant sensed that it was time to turn the cart around. In response to his malicious lie, the Father Superior inclined his head and again imposingly pronounced:

'For it is said in another place: "Suffer heedfully the dishonour that may befall thee with joy, and be not dismayed, nor hate the one that dishonoureth thee." So too shall we act.'

'Tsk, tsk, tsk! "They mused not on earthly things," and the rest of that mumbo-jumbo. Muse not on earthly things, fathers, but I'm going now. And, exercising my authority as a parent, I'm taking my son Aleksey with me for good. Ivan Fyodorovich, my most respectful son, you must allow me to request you to follow me! Von Sohn, what's the point of you staying here? Come to my house in town forthwith. I keep a jolly place. It's not more than a verst or so, and instead of lenten oil I'll serve you sucking-pig with kasha; we shall dine; I'll give you cognac, then a liqueur; there's cloudberry . . . I say, von Sohn, don't miss your lucky chance!'

He made his exit, shouting and gesticulating. This was the moment at which Rakitin had caught sight of him emerging from the house and had pointed him out to Alyosha.

'Aleksey!' his father hailed him from a distance, having sighted him. 'I want you to move back to my house altogether, bring your pillow and your mattress with you, and not show your face round here again.'

Alyosha stood rooted to the spot, silently and attentively observing the scene. Meanwhile, Fyodor Pavlovich got into his carriage, while behind him, not even turning to Alyosha in order to say goodbye, silently and morosely Ivan Fyodorovich began to climb in too. At this point, however, there took place a certain scene of comic buffoonery, almost defying belief, which completed the episode. Suddenly by the footboard of the carriage appeared the landowner Maksimov. He had come running up out of breath, anxious not to be too late. Rakitin and Alyosha had seen him running. In such haste was he that in his impatience he raised one foot on to the step on which Ivan Fyodorovich's left foot was still standing and, grabbing hold of the bodywork, began to try to jump into the vehicle.

'I want to come too, I want to come with you too!' he screamed out, as he tried to jump in, laughing a merry little laugh, with bliss on his features and ready for anything. 'Please take me too!'

'Now didn't I just say,' Fyodor Pavlovich cried enthusiastically, 'that this is von Sohn? That this is the real von Sohn, risen up from the dead? How on earth did you manage to get away from there? Tell us what von Sohn tricks you got up to and how you of all men could walk out of that dinner? I mean, one has to have a brazen brow to do that kind of thing! I've got one, but I'm surprised at you, old chap! Come on, jump in, jump in! Let him on, Vanya, he'll make it all the jollier. He can lie at our feet somewhere. Can't you, von Sohn? Or should we find a place for him up on the box with the driver? . . . Jump on to the box, von Sohn! . . .'

But suddenly Ivan Fyodorovich, who had already taken his seat, silently and with all his might elbowed Maksimov in the chest, so that the latter went flying several yards. That he did not fall flat on his face was a mere whim of chance.

'Let us be off!' Ivan Fyodorovich shouted to the driver in tones of spite.

'Now why did you do that? What's wrong with you? Why did you hit him like that?' said Fyodor Pavlovich, hurling himself round, but the carriage was already in motion. Ivan Fyodorovich made no reply.

'I don't know what to make of you,' Fyodor Pavlovich said after a pause that lasted some two minutes, squinting sideways at the fruit of his loins. 'I mean, it was your idea, all this business with the monastery, it was you who egged us on to it and gave your approval, so why are you losing your temper now?'

'You've spouted enough nonsense now; take a rest for a bit,' Ivan Fyodorovich replied in a curt, stern tone.

Fyodor Pavlovich was again silent for a couple of minutes.

'Some cognac wouldn't go amiss now,' he observed sententiously. But Ivan Fyodorovich made no reply.

'When we get home you can have some too.'

Ivan Fyodorovich continued to remain silent.

Fyodor Pavlovich waited another couple of minutes.

'And as for Alyosha-my-lad, I'm taking him out of that monastery, no matter how disagreeable you find it, most respectful Karl von Moor.'

Ivan Fyodorovich gave a contemptuous shrug of his shoulders and, turning away, began to look at the road. All the way home after that they spoke not another word.

Book III
Voluptuaries

I

In the Lackeys' Hall*

THE house of Fyodor Pavlovich Karamazov was far from standing in the centre of the town, but neither was it completely in the outskirts. It was rather decrepit, but had a pleasant exterior: one-storeyed, with an attic, lustreless grey paint and a red iron roof. As a matter of fact, it looked as though it might well continue to stand for a very long time yet, spacious and cosy. Within it there were many and various little storerooms, cubby-holes and unexpected little flights of stairs. It had rats, but Fyodor Pavlovich was not entirely displeased with them: 'Say what you like, they help to relieve the monotony of an evening when one's alone.' For indeed, it was his custom to release the servants for the night to their outbuilding, and to lock himself up in the house until morning. This outbuilding stood in the yard, and was of extensive and solid construction; Karamazov had had a kitchen put in there, even though there was a kitchen in his house: he was not fond of kitchen odours, and his meals were brought across the yard to him winter and summer. The fact was that the house had been built for a large family, and it could have accommodated five times as many people, masters and servants alike. At the time of our narrative, however, it contained only Fyodor Pavlovich and Ivan Fyodorovich, and in the servants' outbuilding only three members of domestic staff: the old man Grigory, his old wife Marfa and the servant Smerdyakov, a man still young. It is necessary to speak of these three official persons in somewhat more detail. Of old Grigory Vasilyevich Kutuzov we have, as a matter of fact, already said sufficient. He was a firm and unyielding man, stubbornly and in a straight line proceeding towards his goal, once that goal had for whatever reasons (often astonishingly illogical ones) established itself before him as an indisputable truth. Generally speaking he was honest and unsusceptible to bribes. His wife, Marfa Ignatyevna, in spite of having all her life unquestioningly bowed to her husband's will, had always nagged him horribly, as for example just after the emancipation of the serfs, when she had wanted him to leave Fyodor Pavlovich and go to Moscow, there to start up some little business (they had some pathetic little nest-egg); but Grigory had then decided once and for all that the woman was wrong, 'because all women are dishonourable,' and that they ought not to leave their master of long standing, whatever his defects, because that was now 'their duty bound'.

'Do you understand what duty is?' he had inquired of Marfa Ignatyevna, addressing himself to her.

'Yes I do, Grigory Vasilyevich, but what duty do we have to stay here? That's what I shall never understand,' Marfa Ignatyevna had replied firmly.

'Well, don't understand, then, but that is how it is going to be. And from now on you can hold your tongue.'

So it came to pass: they did not leave, and Fyodor Pavlovich granted them a salary, not a very large one, but he paid it whenever it was due. Grigory was also aware of the fact that he had an unquestionable influence on his master. He sensed this, and he was not mistaken: Fyodor Pavlovich, a cunning and stubborn buffoon, of very resolute character 'in certain of life's matters', as he himself expressed it, was, much to his own astonishment, of positively wishy-washy character in certain other 'matters of life'. He himself knew full well what these were, knew and went in fear of many things. In certain matters of life it was necessary to keep one's ears pricked up; this was hard to achieve without a faithful manservant, and Grigory was a most faithful manservant. It had even transpired that in the course of his career Fyodor Pavlovich had many times been actually beaten, quite badly so, and it had always been Grigory who had rescued him, not without on each occasion delivering a sermon afterwards. But beatings alone could not have frightened Fyodor Pavlovich: there were also instances of a more elevated sort, even very subtle, complex ones, when Fyodor Pavlovich himself would probably not have been capable of defining the extraordinary need of a faithful and intimate manservant he would now and then suddenly and inexplicably begin to sense within himself for the space of a moment. These were instances that almost seemed to involve some morbid condition: most depraved, and in his voluptuous lust often brutal, like an evil insect,* Fyodor Pavlovich would on occasion suddenly experience within himself, in his drunken moments, a sense of spiritual terror and moral concussion that echoed almost physically, as it were, within his soul. 'My soul seems to quiver in my throat at those times,' he would say now and again. It was at moments such as these that he liked there to be within reach, close to hand, though preferably not in the same room but in the outbuilding, a manservant, firm and devoted, not at all like himself, not prey to depravity, who though he saw all the libertinage that was taking place and knew all the secrets, would tolerate it none the less out of devotion, would not object and most importantly – would offer no reproach and raise no threat, either in this world or the world to come, and in emergencies might even shield him – against whom? Against someone who, though unknown, was dangerous and terrifying. The essence of it was that there should without fail be *someone else*, a person of long and friendly acquaintance, whom in moments of distress he could summon with the unique purpose of scrutinizing his features, possibly exchanging a brief word or two with him even on some quite unrelated subject, and who, if he seemed not to care, was at least not angry, would somehow lighten his heart, and if he were angry would, well, merely render it the sadder. It would sometimes happen (though as a matter of fact extremely seldom) that Fyodor Pavlovich would even go to the outbuilding during the night and wake Grigory, asking him to come and see him for a moment. Grigory would arrive, and Fyodor Pavlovich would talk of various trivial matters and quickly dismiss him, sometimes even with a little gibe and a little joke, and then, with a spit of devil-may-care, turn in for the night and sleep the slumber of the righteous. Something of this kind had also taken place in Fyodor Pavlovich upon Alyosha's arrival. Alyosha had 'stabbed his heart' by 'being there, seeing it all and not condemning any of it'. Not only that: he had brought with him an unprecedented thing: a complete absence of contempt for him, the old man, indeed quite the reverse – a constant affection and a wholly natural, straightforward attachment to him who so little deserved it. All this had been an utter surprise to the old womanizer and family exile, and quite unexpected to one who until now had loved only 'depravity'. After Alyosha's departure he confessed to himself that he now understood something he had hitherto been reluctant to understand.

I have already mentioned at the outset of my narrative how Grigory hated Adelaida Ivanovna, Fyodor Pavlovich's first spouse and the mother of his first son, Dmitry Fyodorovich, and how, on the contrary, he defended his second spouse, the 'wailer' Sofya Ivanovna, against his master and against all who might think to utter negative or frivolous remarks concerning her. His emotions of sympathy for that unfortunate creature had turned into something that was sacred to him, so that even twenty years on he would not tolerate, from no matter whom, even the slightest negative allusion to her and would at once administer short shrift to the offender. In outward appearance Grigory was a cold and solemn man, not talkative, and liable to utter words that were weighty and lacking in frivolous content. By exactly the same lights was it

impossible to tell at first glance whether he loved his meek and obedient
wife or not; yet love her he did, and she, of course, knew this. This
woman Marfa Ignatyevna was not only far from stupid — she was, if
anything, even more intelligent than her spouse, and was at any rate more
sensible than he with regard to everyday matters; yet even so she submitted
to him meekly and unmurmuringly from the very beginning of their
conjugal union, and undoubtedly respected him for his spiritual eminence.
It was remarkable that all their lives they each had spoken very little to
the other, even about the most basic and actual matters. The solemn and
majestic Grigory invariably considered all his affairs and concerns alone,
and Marfa Ignatyevna had long understood once and for all that he had
no need whatsoever of her counsels. She sensed that her husband valued
her silence and that he perceived in it a sign of intelligence. He never ever
beat her, with the exception of a single instance, and even then only
slightly. Once on the estate, in the first year of Adelaida Ivanovna's
marriage to Fyodor Pavlovich, the maids and women of the village, who
were then still serfs, were gathered into the master's yard to sing and
dance. They had just begun a rendering of 'In the Meadows'* when all of
a sudden Marfa Ignatyevna, then a woman still young, leapt out in front
of the chorus and flung herself into a performance of the 'Russkaya' in an
especial manner, not in the village style, the way the women danced it,
but as she herself had done as a servant girl in the home of the wealthy
Miusovs on the stage of their domestic landowners' theatre, the actors of
which were trained by a dancing-master specially ordered from Moscow.
Grigory had seen his wife dance, and back home in the outbuilding an
hour later gave her a talking-to, accompanied by some pulling of the
locks. But there the chastisements had ended once and for all, and were
never repeated not even a single time throughout all of their married life,
and Marfa Ignatyevna had abstained from dancing ever since.

God granted them no children; there had been one little mite, but he
had died. Grigory, it was plain, loved children, and made no secret of the
fact, that is to say he was not ashamed to make it manifest. When
Adelaida Ivanovna had run away he had assumed personal charge of
Dmitry Fyodorovich, a three-year-old boy, taking care of him for almost
a year, seeing that his hair was combed and even washing him in the
trough. Later he had also busied himself with Ivan Fyodorovich and
Alyosha, for which he had been given a slap in the face; but all this I
have already related. The only joy he had received from his own little
mite was the hope he had when Marfa Ignatyevna had been pregnant. But
when the mite was born, his heart had been stricken by grief and horror.

The fact was that the boy had been born six-fingered. On seeing this, Grigory was so overwhelmed by unhappiness that not only did he remain silent right up to the day of the baptism, but made a special point of going out into the garden to do so. It was spring, and he spent three whole days digging the beds in the garden's kitchen allotment. The third day was the day of the infant's baptism: by this time Grigory had managed to weigh the matter over. Going into the outbuilding where the clergy were assembling and the guests arriving, among them Fyodor Pavlovich, who had made a personal appearance in his capacity of god-father, he had suddenly declared that the child 'ought not to be baptized at all' – declared it softly, without enlargement, barely grinding out each word with set teeth, all the while staring dully and fixedly at the priest.

'Why so?' the priest inquired with jovial surprise.

'Because it's a . . . dragon . . .'* Grigory muttered.

'A dragon? What on earth do you mean?'

Grigory said nothing for a moment or two.

'There's been an adulteration of nature . . .' he muttered, very indistinctly but very firmly, and plainly reluctant to enlarge further.

Some laughter broke out and, needless to say, the poor little mite was baptized. Grigory prayed diligently at the font, but he did not alter his opinion of the newborn infant. As a matter of fact he did not interfere in any way, but for the whole two weeks in which the sickly boy lived he hardly once looked at him, seemed even reluctant to notice him and spent most of his time away from the outbuilding. But when two weeks later the boy died of thrush, he himself laid him in his little coffin, gazed at him with deep anguish and, as they were showering earth upon his shallow little grave, got down on his knees and bowed to it prostrate. From that day many years passed without him ever once mentioning his child; Marfa Ignatyevna never once referred to it in his presence either, and whenever she had occasion to speak of her 'little one' she did it in a whisper, even if Grigory Vasilyevich was not there. According to Marfa Ignatyevna as soon as he left that same little grave he began to occupy himself mainly with the 'divine', read the *Chet'i-Minei*, mostly to himself and alone, on each occasion donning his large round silver spectacles. Seldom did he read aloud, only during Lent. He loved the book of Job, had from somewhere procured a handwritten copy of the orations and sermons of 'the Godbearing Father St Isaac of Nineveh'* and read it assiduously for many years, understanding almost nothing of it, but perhaps for that very reason loving and cherishing that book more than any other. Most recently he had begun to study and lend an ear to the teachings of the flagellants,* an activity possible in various regions of our neighbourhood; they plainly made a tremendous impression on him, but he did not deem it necessary to go over to the new faith. The dogmaticism he acquired 'from the divine' naturally gave his physiognomy an even greater solemnity.

It is possible that he inclined towards mysticism. And then as fortune would have it the appearance in the world of his six-fingered infant, followed by its death, coincided with another highly strange, unexpected and original incident, one that left upon his soul, as once he subsequently expressed it, a 'seal'. It so transpired that on the very date the six-fingered mite was buried, Marfa Ignatyevna, waking in the night, thought she heard the wailing of a newborn child. She was afraid and woke her husband. He lent an ear and observed that he thought it was more like someone groaning, 'a woman, by the sound of it'. He got up and put his clothes on; it was quite a warm May night. Coming out on to the porch he clearly determined that the groans were coming from the garden. But the garden had been closed up for the night with lock and key from the side of the yard, and it was impossible to get into it except by that one entrance, as it was surrounded by a tall and massive fence. Returning home, Grigory lit a lantern, took the garden key and, paying no attention to the hysterical horror of his spouse who still said she could hear the crying of a child and that this must surely be her little boy who was calling her, silently entered the garden. At this point he clearly discerned that the groans were coming from the little bathhouse that stood in the garden not far from the gate, and that it was indeed a woman who was making them. Opening the door of the bathhouse he beheld a spectacle before which he stood dumbfounded; a girl, a holy fool of the town who wandered about its streets and was known to all its inhabitants by the sobriquet of Lizaveta Smerdyashchaya – 'Lizaveta the Stinker' – had managed to get into their bathhouse and had just given birth to an infant. The infant lay next to her, and she lay dying next to it. She spoke not, for the simple reason that she was unable to speak. But all this must be separately elucidated.

2

Lizaveta Smerdyashchaya

THERE was in all this a certain particular circumstance, one that deeply shook Grigory, confirming within him once and for all a certain loathsome

and unpleasant suspicion he had earlier had. This Lizaveta Smerdyashchaya, 'the Stinker', was a wench of most diminutive stature, 'nobbut
two arshins',* as many of the God-praying old crones of our little town
touchingly used to say of her in recollection after her death. Her twenty-
year-old countenance — broad, healthy and rosy-cheeked — was that of
the complete idiot; and the gaze of her eyes, though submissive, was
immobile and unpleasant. All her days, summer and winter alike, she
went barefoot and clad in nothing but a hempen shift. Her almost raven
locks, extremely thick and curly like a ram's, clung to her head in the
semblance of some enormous fur hat. They were, moreover, invariably
bespattered with earth and mud, and leaves, splinters and woodchips
adhered to them, as she invariably slept upon earth and mud. Her father
was a homeless, ruined and infirm artisan called Ilya, who had taken to
drink in a bad way and sponged a living as a kind of johnny-all-trades in
the households of some prosperous masters who were also local artisans.
As for Lizaveta's mother, she had long since passed away. The eternally
infirm and aggressively spiteful Ilya would administer inhuman beatings
to Lizaveta whenever she returned home. This she did seldom, however,
as she eked a parasitical living all over the town as a holy fool and a
woman of God. Even Ilya's masters and Ilya himself and even many of
the town's compassionate folk, who were mostly the shopkeepers and
their wives, on several occasions attempted to dress Lizaveta with more
decorum than was provided by her shift alone, and when winter came
along would invariably attire her in a sheepskin coat and make her put on
boots; but usually, although she meekly let them dress her in these
things, she would go away somewhere, preferably to the porch of the
parish church, and remove from herself all the donated garments —
kerchief, skirt, sheepskin coat and boots alike — leave them all on the spot
and depart barefoot and clad in nothing but her shift as before. It
happened once that the new governor of our province, on a flying visit
of inspection to our little town, felt his finer emotions to have been
insulted by the sight of Lizaveta, and although he understood that this
was a 'holy fool', as he had been apprised, he nevertheless issued the
reproof that a young wench wandering around in nothing but her shift
was a violation of public decency, and that henceforth it must cease. But
the governor went away, and they left Lizaveta as she was. At length her
father died, and by that very fact she became even more the darling of all
the town's more devout personages, as an orphan. Indeed, it seemed that
everyone was fond of her; even the little boys did not tease her or call
her names, and the little boys of our town, especially those at the school,

are a perky lot. She would enter the houses of strangers, yet no one ever chased her away — on the contrary, they would all of them treat her kindly and give her a coin or two. Given a coin, she would take it and at once dispose of it in one of the collection boxes, either at the church or the prison. Given a boublik or kalatch* at the market, she would unfailingly depart with it and give either boublik or kalatch to the first little mite she encountered, or else stop one of our wealthiest ladies and give it to her; and those ladies would receive it with positive joy. She herself lived solely on black bread and water. Calling in at a luxury shop she would sit down surrounded by all the expensive goods, the money within sight, yet the owners were never wary of her, knowing that even if one laid out thousands of roubles in her presence and forgot about them, she would take not a copeck. To church she went rarely, but slept either in the porch of a church or, climbing over someone's wicker fence (in our town there are still many such wicker fences in lieu of the wooden kind even to this day), in someone's kitchen garden. At home, that is to say in the house of those masters among whom her deceased father had lived, she would make an appearance on average twice a week, though in winter her visits were daily, but only overnight, and she would sleep either in the passage or the cowshed. It was marvelled that she was able to endure a life of this kind, but she had by this time grown accustomed to it; though she was small of stature, she was of unusually sound constitution. Some of the gentry in our town also used to assert that she did all this merely out of pride, but somehow this did not square: she could not even speak a word and only occasionally succeeded in moving her tongue and mumbling something — and what pride could there be in that? It had so transpired that once (this was rather a long time ago), on a warm, bright September night at the time of the full moon, very late by our local standards, a certain tipsy assemblage of our local gentlemen who had been out enjoying themselves, some five or six brave fellows, were returning from their club to their homes 'by way of the rears'. On either side of the lane there was a wicker fence behind which extended the kitchen gardens of the adjacent houses; the lane itself gave on to a boardwalk that led across the long and malodorous puddle which it is sometimes the custom among us to refer to as a river. By the fence, amidst the nettles and burdock, our company espied the sleeping Lizaveta. The somewhat over-refreshed gentlemen stopped above her with loud laughter and began to crack witticisms with every imaginable absence of censorship. To one young blood there suddenly occurred a quite eccentric question on an impermissible theme: whether, that is to say, anyone at all could consider such a brute to be a woman, and what if they were now to, etcetera. They all with proud repugnance determined that the negative was true. But in this little band Fyodor Pavlovich also happened to be present, and of an instant he leapt up and declared that of course she was a woman, even very much so, and that here there was even a special kind of piquancy to be had, etcetera, etcetera. It is true that at the period in question he was pushing his role of buffoon in an excessive and even artificial manner among us, fond of springing up to provide entertainment for the gentry, with a show of equality, of course, but really making himself look like a perfect boor before them. This was at the very time he received from St Petersburg the news of the death of his first spouse, Adelaida Ivanovna, and when with crape in his hat he was drinking and behaving so outrageously that some of the townsfolk, even the most dissipated among them, could not view him without wincing. The assemblage, of course, burst out laughing at the unexpected opinion; a certain individual among them even began to egg Fyodor Pavlovich to action, but the rest of them proceeded to affect an even greater degree of indifference, though still with the utmost merriment, and at last they all continued on their route. Afterwards Fyodor Pavlovich always solemnly swore that on that night he too had departed with the rest; perhaps this really was the case, for no one knows for certain and has never known, but some five or six months later everyone in the town began to talk with sincere and extreme indignation about the fact that Lizaveta was pregnant; questions were asked and inquiries were made as to whose was the sin, and who the offender. Then suddenly the terrible rumour passed round the town that the offender was indeed none other than Fyodor Pavlovich. Where had it arisen, this rumour? Of the assemblage of tipsy gentlemen there remained by now in the town but one participant, and this a respectable state councillor in advanced middle years with a family and grown-up daughters, who by no stretch of the imagination could have set about spreading anything, even had there been something to spread; as for the other participants, they had all five of them by this time gone their separate ways. But the rumour pointed to Fyodor Pavlovich and continued to point to him. Of course the latter was not even particularly miffed by it: he would not have considered it necessary to answer to a bunch of shopkeepers and artisans. At that period of his life he was proud and conversed solely with his company of gentlemen and civil servants, whom he provided with such entertainment. Now at this time it was that Grigory forcefully and with all his might stood up for his master, not only defending him against all these calumnies, but also engaging in verbal combat and altercation on his behalf, with the result that he changed many people's minds. 'It's she herself, the foul one, who's to blame,' he would say affirmatively, and the offender was none other than 'Karp the Screwbore' (as a certain fearsome convict, notorious in the town, was known, who at around this time had escaped from the local prison and was hiding out somewhere among us). This surmise appeared to have probability on its side, for Karp was remembered, and remembered in particular for having been at large in the town during those selfsame nights at the approach of autumn, when he had performed three burglaries. But not only did this event and all its attendant rumours fail to divert the public's sympathy from the poor holy fool – everyone began to guard and protect her even more. The shopowner Kondratyeva, a certain well-to-do widow, even made arrangements to have Lizaveta move into her house at the end of April, intending not to let her out again until she had borne the child. An unremitting watch was kept on her; but, unremitting watch or no, it came to pass that on the evening of the very last day Lizaveta suddenly left Kondratyeva in stealth and turned up in Fyodor Pavlovich's garden. How in her condition she had succeeded in climbing over the tall and massive garden fence, remained something of an enigma. Some asserted that she had been 'carried over', and others that she had been 'transported'. The most probable explanation is that it all took place in a natural, though most peculiar manner, and that Lizaveta, who was able to climb over wicker fences into other people's kitchen gardens in order to sleep the night there, also somehow managed to climb on top of Fyodor Pavlovich's fence, and from it had jumped, though with injury to herself, into his garden, in spite of her condition. Grigory rushed to Marfa Ignatyevna and sent her out to assist Lizaveta, himself running off to fetch the old midwife, one of the tradesfolk who happened to live nearby. The little mite was saved, but by break of day Lizaveta had died. Grigory took the infant, carried him to the house, sat his wife down and placed the baby boy upon her knees, right against her very breast: 'An orphaned child of God is kin to all, and to ourselves the more so. This one has been sent us by our little boy deceased, and is the offspring of a devil's son and a woman righteous. Feed him and henceforth weep no more.' And so Marfa Ignatyevna fostered the little mite. He was baptized and christened Pavel, and without being told to, everyone of their own accord began to add to this the patronymic 'Fyodorovich'. Fyodor Pavlovich received this without protest, even seeming to find it all amusing, though he still continued to disavow his role in it with all his might. The townsfolk approved of his having taken in a foundling. Subsequently, Fyodor Pavlovich even thought up a surname for the foundling: he named him Smerdyakov, after the sobriquet of his mother, Lizaveta Smerdyashchaya. This Smerdyakov it was who became Fyodor Pavlovich's second man-servant and was living, at the time of our story's beginning, in the outbuild-ing together with old Grigory and old Marfa. He was made use of as a cook. It would really be most helpful to append some special remarks about him here, but my conscience forbids me to divert the attention of my reader with such commonplace lackeys, and I shall therefore proceed with my narrative, in the sanguine trust that the details about Smerdyakov will come forth of themselves in the course of the tale's unfolding.

3

The Confession of an Ardent Heart. In Verse

ALYOSHA, upon hearing the injunction of his father hurled at him by the latter from his carriage as he left the monastery, stood still for some time in great bewilderment. Not that he stood dumbfounded, for that never happened to him. Rather it was the other way about: for all his concern, he at once made time to pay a visit to the Father Superior's kitchen in order to ascertain what excesses his papa had wrought upstairs. Then, however, he set upon his way, in the sanguine trust that on his route to the town he would somehow succeed in resolving the problem that tormented him. I should point out in advance that the shouts of his father and his injunctions that he move back home, and 'bring your pillow and your mattress with you', had intimidated him not in the least. He knew only too well that the injunction, issued out loud and with such ostenta-tious clamour, had been made 'in the heat of the moment', for the sake, as it were, even of aesthetic effect – in much the same way as recently an over-inebriated artisan of their little town who on his own name-day and in the presence of guests, losing his temper on being refused any more vodka, had suddenly begun to smash his own crockery, rend his own clothing and that of his wife, break his furniture and ultimately the windows of the house, and all of this for nothing but the sake of aesthetic effect; and the same thing was, of course, happening now to his papa. On the morrow, it need hardly be said, the over-inebriated artisan, having once more attained a sober condition, had regretted the cups and plates he had smashed. Alyosha knew that the old man too would the very next day most likely allow him to return to the monastery, and might even do

so today. And he was entirely sure that while his father might intend to
insult others, he had no such intention towards him. Alyosha was sure
that there was no one in the whole world who would ever wish to insult
him, and not only that, but that there was no one who would be capable
of such a thing. This as an axiom to him, something given once and for
always, without argument, and in this sense he moved forward without
ever wavering.

At that moment, however, there had surged up within him a certain
other fear, one of quite a different nature, made all the more tormenting
by the fact that he himself would have been unable to find a designation
for it, namely the fear of a woman, and the fear namely of Katerina
Ivanovna, who in her recent note, conveyed to him by Mrs Khokhlakova,
had so insistently beseeched him to go and see her for some purpose.
This urgent demand that he do so had at once implanted a sense of vague
torment within his heart, and as the morning wore on this nagging sense
had gripped him more and more acutely, in spite of all the scandalous
scenes and incidents that had ensued in the monastery and just now at the
Father Superior's, etcetera, etcetera. His fear had nothing to do with any
uncertainty as to what it was she wished to talk about with him or what
he would say in reply. Nor was it woman in general he feared in her: to
be sure, he was acquainted with few women, but even so he had spent all
his life, from his earliest infancy right up until the time he had entered
the monastery, alone and exclusively with them. It was this particular
woman, this Katerina Ivanovna, whom he feared. He had feared her right
from the very first time he had set eyes on her. He had seen her in all on
no more than one or two occasions, possibly three, and had once even
uttered a casual word or two to her. In his memory he had retained an
image of her as a beautiful, proud and imperious girl. It was not,
however, her beauty that tormented him, but something else. The inexplicable quality of his fear itself now rendered it ever more intense within
him. This girl's designs were of the most noble kind, he knew that; she
was striving to rescue his brother Dmitry, who was already guilty in her
regard, and her striving proceeded from nothing but sheer generosity.
And now, in spite of this awareness and the recognition he could not but
accord all these fine and generous emotions, the nearer he approached her
house, so a chill progressed along his spine.

He had concluded that at her house he would not find his brother Ivan
Fyodorovich, who was so close to her: brother Ivan was probably with
their father now. Even more certain was it that he would not find Dmitry
there, and he already fancied he knew why. So their conversation would

take place *tête-à-tête*. He would very much have liked to drop in to see brother Dmitry for a moment before this fateful conversation. Without showing him the letter, he could have exchanged a few words with him on the subject. But brother Dmitry lived far away and was probably not at home now, either. Standing still for a moment, he at last, finally, made up his mind. Making the sign of the cross over himself with a quick and habitual motion and smiling at something immediately after, he resolutely set off towards his formidable lady.

He knew where her house was. But if he were to go there by way of Main Street, then across the market-square, and so on, it would take him rather a long time. Our little town is exceedingly dispersed, and the distances in it rather large. Moreover, his father was expecting him, might possibly not yet have had time to forget his injunction, might revert to his old caprice, and so he would have to hurry if he were to attend both destinations. In consequence of all these factors he decided to abbreviate his route, proceeding 'by the rears', for he knew all these ins and outs of our little town like the back of his hand. To go 'by the rears' meant almost to dispense with roads altogether, passing along lonely enclosures, sometimes even climbing over other people's wicker fences and walking past other people's backyards where, however, all and sundry would recognize him and say hello to him. By such a route he could cut the distance to Main Street by half. In one spot on his way he even had to pass very close to his father's house, past the garden that lay next door to its own and belonged to a certain crooked and decrepit little pokehole of a house with four windows. The owner of this wretched little house, Alyosha knew, was a certain female of the town's lower middle classes, an old woman who had lost the use of her legs and lived with her daughter, formerly an 'improved' chambermaid in the capital, who until not long ago had lived in generals' households, and had now for the year since she arrived home on account of her mother's illness been flouncing about in fashionable dresses. This old woman and her daughter had, however, sunk into dire poverty and even made daily visits as neighbours to Fyodor Pavlovich's kitchen for soup and bread. Marfa Ignatyevna was glad to serve it up for them. But though the daughter made these visits for soup she had sold not one of her dresses, and one of them even had a very long train. This last circumstance Alyosha had learned, quite casually, of course, from his friend Rakitin, who was *au fait* with all the goings-on in their wretched little town without exception, and having learned it had quite naturally forgotten it at once. But now, as he drew level with the garden of his female neighbour, he suddenly remembered about that

train, quickly raised his downcast and reflective head and . . . suddenly
stumbled on a most unexpected encounter.

Frantically signalling to him with both hands, having clambered up on
to something on the other side of the neighbouring garden's wicker
fence, his brother Dmitry Fyodorovich was summoning and beckoning
him, evidently afraid not only to shout but even to utter a word out loud
in case he was heard. Alyosha immediately ran over to the fence.

'It's just as well you looked round, otherwise I think I'd have shouted
to you,' Dmitry Fyodorovich whispered to him in hurried delight.
'Climb over here! Quickly! Oh, how wonderful that you've come. I was
just thinking about you . . .'

Alyosha was also pleased, and was only at a loss as to how he should
climb over the fence. But Mitya caught his elbow with a Herculean arm
and assisted his leap. Tucking up his cassock, Alyosha jumped across
with the adroitness of a barefooted town urchin.

'Hurry up, now, come on!' The words burst from Mitya in an ecstatic
whisper.

'But where?' Alyosha asked, also in a whisper, gazing around him to
all sides and observing that he found himself in a completely empty
garden, in which apart from the two of them there was no one. The
garden was small, but there were at least some fifty yards between them
and the mistress's little house. 'Anyway, there's no one here, so why are
you whispering?'

'Why am I whispering? Oh, the devil confound it!' Dmitry Fyodorovich suddenly exclaimed in a most audible voice. 'Yes, why am I
whispering? Well, you see what chaos nature can suddenly bring about.
I'm here in secret and am guarding a secret. Explanations later, but as it's
a secret I suddenly started to talk in a secret way, whispering like an idiot
when it's not necessary. Come on! Over there! Don't say a word till we
get there. I could kiss you!

> Glory to on earth the highest,
> Glory to the highest in me! . . .

I was reciting that to myself as I sat here just now, before you arrived . . .'

The garden was no more than about a *desyatina** or so in size, but was
planted with trees only on its perimeter, along all four fences – with
apples, maples, limes and birches. The middle of the garden was empty,
turned over to a grass plot, which yielded a few poods* of hay in
summer. From springtime on the garden was rented out by the mistress
at a fee of a few roubles. There were also beds of raspberries, gooseberries

and currants, these too only along the fences; the vegetable beds close to the house itself were, however, a recent addition. Dmitry Fyodorovich took his guest to one of the corners of the garden most distant from the house. In that place there suddenly stood revealed, amidst the densely growing limes and the old bushes of currant and elder, guelder rose and lilacs, something that resembled the ruins of a most ancient green summer-house, blackened and lopsided, with trellised walls but with a covered top, and in which it was possible to shelter from the rain. This summer-house had been built God only knows when, some fifty years ago according to local legend, by the owner of the little house, Aleksandr Karlovich von Schmidt, a retired lieutenant-colonel. But it had fallen into thorough disrepair, the floor had rotted, all the floorboards were unsteady and the timber smelt of damp. In the summerhouse stood a green wooden table which had been dug into the ground, and around it there were benches, also green, on which one still might sit. Alyosha had immediately noticed his brother's ecstatic condition, and upon entering the summerhouse spotted on the little table a half-bottle of cognac and a liqueur glass.

'That's cognac!' Mitya laughed loudly. 'I bet you looked and thought "He's drinking again," didn't you? Never trust a phantom!

> Trust not the empty, lying throng,
> Forget the doubts that you have had . . .*

I'm not drinking, I'm merely "tasting the nectar" in the words of that pig Rakitin of yours who's going to be a state councillor and say "I'm tasting the nectar" for the rest of his days. Come and sit down. I could throw my arms around you, Alyosha, and press you to my bosom and crush you, for in all the world . . . I genu-ine-ly . . . genu-ine-ly . . . (do you realize? do you realize?) love only you!'

He delivered this last line in a state approaching frenzy.

'Only you, and a certain "low woman" I've fallen in love with and on account of whom I've gone to rack and ruin. But to fall in love is not the same as to love. One may fall in love and still hate. Mark what I say, while I'm still able to be cheerful about it! Sit down at the table here, and I'll sit beside you and look at you and tell you everything. You'll do all the listening, and I'll do all the talking, because it's high time. Though you know, I think the talking had best be done very quietly, because here . . . here . . . the most unexpected ears may come to light. I'll explain everything, in a word: the sequel follows shortly. Why else have I longed to see you, thirsted for you the way I have all these days, and as I do now? (I dropped anchor here five days ago.) Why, do you think? Because you're the only person I can tell it all to, because it's necessary, because you're necessary, because tomorrow I'll come down to earth with a bang, because tomorrow life will end and start again in earnest. Have you ever dreamed you were falling from a high place into a pit? Well, that's the way I'm falling now, and it's for real. And I'm not afraid, so don't you be. Well, I suppose I am really, but it's sweet to me. Or not so much sweet as ecstatic . . . Well, the devil take it, it's all the same, I don't care what it is. Strong wit, feeble wit, wit of womankind — I don't care! Let us render praise unto nature: look at all the sun, the heavens so cloudless, the leaves all green, it's still high summer, four in the afternoon and what silence! Where were you off to?'

'To father's, though first I was going to see Katerina Ivanovna.'

'To see her and father as well? Ha, what a coincidence! I mean, why do you think I asked you to come over here in the first place, what do you think I've been longing and thirsting and burning for in every crevice of my soul, even in the hollows of my ribs? To send you as a messenger from myself to father, and then to her, Katerina Ivanovna, and that way be shot of them both. To send them an angel. I could send anyone, I suppose, but I wanted to send them an angel. And now here you are, off to see her and father anyway.'

'Were you really going to send me?' The words broke from Alyosha in a rush, and his face bore an expression of pain.

'Wait, you knew I was. My eyes tell me that you grasped the whole thing at once. But don't say anything, just keep quiet for the moment. Don't pity me and don't burst into tears!'

Dmitry Fyodorovich got up, reflected, and placed a finger against his forehead:

'She's summoned you herself, she's sent you a letter or something, and that's why you're going to see her, isn't it? Otherwise you wouldn't be going?'

'This is her note,' Alyosha said, producing it from his pocket. Mitya quickly read it through.

'And you went by the rears! O gods! I thank you for sending him by the rears so that he fell into my lap like the golden fish the simple old fisherman caught in the fairy-tale.* Now you shall listen, Alyosha, now you shall listen, my brother. This time I'm going to tell you everything. For I must tell it to someone. I've already told it to the angel in the sky, but I must also tell it to the angel upon earth. You're the angel upon earth. You'll hear me out, you'll think it over and you'll forgive . . .

That's what I need — for someone to forgive me. Listen: if two beings suddenly tear themselves away from all earthly things and go flying off into the improbable, or at least one of them does, and before he goes flying off or goes to his death comes to the other and says: do for me such and such, the sort of thing that no one asks anyone to do, the sort of thing one could only request on one's deathbed — then do you really suppose that the other would not fulfil that request . . . if he was a friend, if he was a brother?'

'I'll fulfil it, but you must tell me what it is, and be quick about it,' said Alyosha.

'Be quick about it . . . Hm. Don't be in such a hurry, Alyosha: you're in a hurry and you're anxious. This is no time for haste. This time the world's come out on to a new street. Oh, Alyosha, what a pity you haven't hit upon ecstasy! Though actually, what am I saying to him? Someone like you not hit on it? What am I saying, booby that I am?

> Be thou noble, O man!*

What poet wrote that?'

Alyosha made up his mind to be patient. He understood that all the matters that affected him were now possibly bound up here, and only here. For a moment Mitya reflected, leaning his elbow on the table and resting his head on his palm. Neither spoke for a while.

'Lyosha,' said Mitya, 'you're the only person who won't laugh at this! I'd like to start . . . my confession . . . with Schiller's hymn to joy. *An die Freude!* But I don't know any German, all I know is *An die Freude*. And please don't think I'm talking rubbish because I'm drunk. I'm not drunk at all. Cognac is cognac, but I need two bottles in order to get drunk —

> And Silenus with his ruddy face
> Upon a stumbling ass*

but I haven't even drunk a quarter of a bottle and I'm not Silenus. I'm not Silenus but I have the strength in me,* for I've taken a decision that will last for ever. You must forgive me the pun; you'll have to forgive me a lot of things today, not just puns. Don't be uneasy, I'm not beating about the bush, I'm talking business and in a second I'll get down to it. I'm not going to pull the Jew from my bosom, as they say. Wait now, how does it go . . .'

He raised his head, thought for a moment and suddenly began in ecstasy:

Timid, naked, wild lurked hiding
Troglodyte in rocky caves,
O'er the fields went nomad striding
And the fields he laid to waste.
Hunter with his spear and arrows
Dreadful through the forests tore,
Woe to those left by the billows
On that harsh and hostile shore!

From Olympus' heights descended,
Mother Ceres goes in quest
Of Persephone, the ravished,
Wild before her lies the earth.
Neither nourishment nor lodging
Is there for the goddess there;
And no sign of godly worship,
Shrine or temple anywhere.

Fruit of fields and sweet grape-clusters
Do not glisten at the feasts;
Only reek remains of corpses
On the bloodstained altar-piece.
And with sad eye now wherever
Ceres now her gaze unrolls –
In deep degradation foundered
Everywhere man she beholds!*

Sobs suddenly broke from Mitya's breast. He gripped Alyosha by the hand.

'Friend, friend, in degradation, in degradation even now, man must endure a terrible number of things on earth, a terrible burden of misery! Don't get the idea that I'm just a boor with an officer's stripes who drinks cognac and runs after whores. Why, brother, I think of almost nothing else but that degraded man, when I'm not talking rubbish, that is. Please God let me not talk rubbish now and not start showing off. The reason I think about that man is that I myself am such a man.

That from baseness' vile dominion
Man may rise to soul's rebirth,
Man may rise to soul's rebirth,
He must join eternal union
With his ancient Mother Earth.*

But the only thing is, how am I to join eternal union with the earth? I don't kiss the earth, I don't churn up her breast:* what am I to do, become a muzhik or a shepherd? I go and know not whether I have landed in foulness and ignominy or in light and joy. I mean, that's where the trouble lies, for all the world is an enigma! And whenever I've had occasion to wallow in the very deepest ignominy of lust (and that's all I've had occasion to do), I've always read that poem about Ceres and man. Has it set me on the right road again? Never! Because I'm a Karamazov. Because if I throw myself into the abyss I do it straight, head first and heels last, and am even glad that I've fallen in such a degrading posture and consider it flattering to myself. And it's there, in that very ignominy, that I suddenly begin the hymn. I may be cursed, I may be base and vile, but I too shall kiss the hem of the robe in which my God enwraps Himself;* even though at the very same time I may still be following the Devil, I am Your son, O Lord, and I love You, and sense the joy without which the world cannot stand and be.

> To the soul of God's creation
> Joy eternal brings her draught,
> In strong secret fermentation
> Flames the cup of life aloft;
> Coaxing grassblades to the daylight
> Making chaos into suns,
> She in spaces never fathomed
> By the gazer pours her glance.

> At the breast of blessèd nature
> All that breathes now drinks of joy;
> Every nation, every creature
> She draws with her on her way;
> Gives us friends in our misfortunes,
> Charities' garlands and grapes' blood,
> Gives the insects — lust voluptuous . . .
> And an angel faces God.*

  'But enough of verses! I have shed tears, and you must let me weep. I know it may be a stupid thing, at which all will laugh, but you will not. Your dear, sweet eyes are burning too. Enough of verses. Now I want to speak to you on the "insects", the ones that God has endowed with voluptuous lust:

> Gives the insects — lust voluptuous . . .

'Brother, I am one of those insects, and that line was written specifically about me. All of us Karamazovs are the same, and that crawling insect dwells even in you, the angel, engendering storms within your blood. I say storms, because voluptuousness is a storm, and more than a storm! Beauty is a terrifying and a horrible thing! It's terrifying because it can't be defined, and it can't be defined because God has set nothing but riddles. Here the two banks of the river meet, and here all contradictions exist together. Brother, I'm very far from being a man of the new progressive education, but I've thought a lot about this. There are a terrible number of mysteries! There are too many riddles that weigh man down upon earth. Try to solve them and fall on your feet as best you can. Beauty! What is more, I find it intolerable that there should be men, even those with the loftiest hearts and with lofty intellects, too, who start out with the ideal of the Madonna and end up with the ideal of Sodom. Even more terrifying are those who even though they bear the ideal of Sodom within their souls do not reject the ideal of the Madonna, and whose hearts burn with it, truly, truly burn with it as they did in their young and unblemished years. No, man is broad, far too broad, even; I would narrow him. The devil only knows what's at stake here, that's the truth of it! Things that seem ignominy to the mind, to the heart are nothing but beauty. Beauty in Sodom – can that be true? You may be certain that it is precisely there that beauty resides for the vast major-ity of people – have you fathomed that secret? The horror of it is that beauty is not only a terrifying thing – it is also a mysterious one. In it the Devil struggles with God, and the field of battle is the hearts of men. And as a matter of fact, it's natural that those who are in pain should talk about it. Now listen, for I want to come to the matter in hand.'

4

The Confession of an Ardent Heart. In Anecdotes

'I led an extravagant life back there. Father said earlier that I paid out several thousand on seducing girls. That's a phantom, and a pig of one too, and there wasn't any of that, and as for what there was, for "that" in particular money was not necessary. Money to me is an accessory, the ardour of the soul, part of the furniture. Today here she is, my lady, tomorrow a little street girl might take her place. I'd give them both some fun, throwing money around in handfuls with music, noise, gypsy girls. If necessary I'd give money to her too, because they take it, they take it with alacrity, it can't be denied, and they're pleased and grateful. The upper-class ladies had a soft spot for me, not all of them, but some of them, some of them; but I always preferred the back alleys, the dark and lonely lanes behind the market-place — that's where you'll find the adventures, the surprises, the nuggets in the mire. I'm talking in allegories, brother. In that wretched little town where we were stationed there weren't any real back alleys, but there were moral ones. Oh, if you were the kind of man I am, you'd know what I mean. I loved depravity, I loved the shame of depravity. I loved cruelty: after all, I'm a bedbug, am I not, an evil insect? In a word — a Karamazov! One day there was a picnic involving the whole town, we travelled in seven *troikas*; in the winter darkness of the sleigh I began to press the dear little hand of a certain young girl who lived next door to me and forced her into kissing me, that girl, that daughter of a civil servant, poor, sweet, meek, and who wouldn't have said boo to a goose. She allowed it, she allowed a lot of things in the dark. She thought, poor wretch, that I would come for her the following day and make her a proposal (I was, you see, valued mainly as a potential bridegroom); but I didn't say a word to her for five months after that. When we had one of our town dances (we have them now and again) I'd see her watching me from a corner of the room with her little eyes, saw them burning with a light — a light of meek indignation. That game had merely gratified the voluptuous insect lust I nourished in myself. Five months later she married a civil servant and went away ... angry yet still loving me, perhaps. Now they live a happy life together. Note that I never told anyone, I didn't blacken her name; though I may be base in my desires and in love with baseness I'm not dishonourable. You're blushing, I saw your eyes flash fire just then. You've had enough of this filth. And it was all just so many flowers *à la* Paul de Kock,* even though the cruel insect was growing and swelling great within my soul. There's a whole album of reminiscences there, brother. May God send them health, the pretty darlings. When I broke with them I always preferred not to quarrel. I never gave them away, I never blackened the name of a single one of them. But that will do. I say, I hope you didn't think I asked you to come over here just for this rubbish, did you? No, what I want to tell you is rather more interesting than that; but please don't be surprised that I'm not embarrassed to tell you, but may even seem relieved to do so.'

'You're saying that because I blushed,' Alyosha remarked suddenly. 'I blushed not because of the things you were saying, the things you said you'd done, but because I am the same as you are.'

'You? Oh, I think that's going a bit far.'

'No, it's not,' Alyosha said with heat. (This idea had plainly been on his mind for a long time now.) 'They are the rungs of the same ladder. I'm on the very lowest rung, and you're somewhere up at the top, on the thirteenth. That's the way I see this matter, but it's all the same thing, it's absolutely one and the same story. Once a person has stepped on to the lowest rung he has absolutely no option but to climb up to the highest one.'

'You mean it's better not to get on the ladder at all?'

'Whoever is able had better not get on it at all.'

'And are you able?'

'Apparently not.'

'No more, Alyosha, no more, dear fellow; I could kiss your dear hand out of sheer tender emotion. That rogue Grushenka knows a thing or two about men, she once told me that one day she'd gobble you up. All right, all right, now I'm the one who'll say no more. From these loathsome things, from this margin besmirched by fly-blots, let us pass on to my tragedy, which is also set in a margin besmirched by fly-blots, that is to say by every form of baseness. You see, although the filthy old man was making up all that stuff about my seducing innocent young things, the fact is that in my tragedy something of the sort really did happen, though only once, and even that didn't come to anything. For all his upbraiding me with that figment of his imagination, the old man has no idea about that business: I've never told anyone about it, you're the first to hear of it from me now, apart from Ivan, of course, Ivan knows it all. He learned of it long before you did. But Ivan is a tomb.'

'Ivan – a tomb?'

'Yes.'

Alyosha was listening with extreme attention.

'You must understand that even though I was a lieutenant in that battalion, a line battalion,* I was under more or less constant surveillance, as though I were some kind of penal exile. But the wretched little town gave me a terrific reception. I was throwing a lot of money about, people believed I was rich, I myself believed it. Though as a matter of fact I must have satisfied them on some other account, as well. They'd shake their heads, but they were really fond of me. My lieutenant-colonel, who was already an old man, suddenly conceived a dislike of me. He kept seizing on my faults; though I had friends in the right places, and indeed the whole town was behind me, so he couldn't seize on my faults all that hard. Part of the blame was also my own — I purposely didn't show him the deference I ought to have. I was too proud. This stubborn old man, not at all a bad old chap and a most genial host, had had two wives, both of whom were now dead. One of them, the first, had come from some sort of ordinary folk and had left him a daughter who was equally ordinary. In my time she was already a spinster of twenty-four and she lived with her father and her aunt, the sister of her deceased mother. The aunt personified a blend of ordinariness with humility, while her niece, my lieutenant-colonel's elder daughter, personified ordinariness with *panache*. Whenever I bring her to mind I like to put in a good word for her: never, dear fellow, have I known a more charming example of the female character than that spinster. Agafya, she was called, just imagine, Agafya Ivanovna. And she wasn't at all bad-looking, either — in the Russian taste: tall, buxom, full-bodied, with beautiful eyes, though perhaps a bit coarse about the face. She'd never married, though two men had sought her hand; she'd said no and kept her good spirits. I got along rather well with her — no, not in the way you think, there was none of that, but simply as a friend. You must understand that I often took up with women in a completely innocent way, on friendly terms. I'd chatter away to her, saying the most outspoken things to her, you'd never believe — and she'd just laugh. A lot of women like outspokenness, take note of that, and there was also the fact that she was just a girl, and I found that hugely diverting. And there was another thing: on no account could one have referred to her as a young lady. She lived in her father's house with her aunt, somehow voluntarily belittling herself and making no attempt to be on equal terms with any other kind of society. Everyone was fond of her and she was much in demand, as she was a first-rate dressmaker: it was a talent she had — she asked no money for her services, performed them out of kindness, but whenever anyone did give her anything by way of payment she did not refuse. As for the lieutenant-colonel, now — what can one say? The lieutenant-colonel was one of the most important people in our locality. He lived in grand style, received the whole town at his dinners and dances. When I arrived and joined the battalion people all over the wretched little town began to say that soon we should be having a visit from the lieutenant-colonel's second daughter in St Petersburg, a peerless beauty among beauties who had apparently only just left one of the aristocratic institutes in the capital city. This second daughter was none other than Katerina Ivanovna, and she was born to him by his second wife. And this second wife, she's dead now, had come from some sort of large, prestigious general's family, though as a matter of fact, as I have been reliably informed, she never brought the lieutenant-colonel a copeck. What she had was relatives, but that was all; she may possibly have had some hopes, but ready cash she had none. And yet, when the "institute girl" arrived (only on a visit, and not permanently), the whole of our miserable little town seemed to acquire new life and its most noble and distinguished ladies – two engineers' wives and a lieutenant-colonel's widow – and indeed all the rest, all the rest taking their cue from them at once took a hand, whisked her away, began to organize entertainments for her, made her the tsarina of their balls and picnics, concocted *tableaux vivants* in aid of some governesses or other. I kept mum, went on throwing money about, and in fact at that time I pulled off a little trick that set the whole town buzzing. Once at a soirée I saw her measuring me with her gaze, this was at the home of the battery commander, but I didn't go up to her at the time, as if to say: "I don't think you're worth getting to know." When I did go up to her a bit later, also at a soirée, and began to talk to her, she hardly glanced at me and set her lips in a contemptuous smile; all right, I thought, just wait, I'll take my revenge! I behaved like a most horrible churl in the majority of such instances at the time, even I was aware of it. The main thing I was aware of was that this "Katenka" was no naïve institute girl but rather a woman of character, proud and possessed of real virtue, with, above all, intelligence and progressive education, two things that I myself lacked. You think I intended to propose to her? Not in the least, I intended simply to take my revenge for being such a fine fellow, and her not noticing it. And meanwhile, excess and atrocity. In the end the lieutenant-colonel placed me under arrest for three days. It was precisely at about this time that father sent me the six thousand, after which I sent him a formal renunciation of all and everything, declaring that, in other words, we were now "quits" and that I would make no further demands on him. At the time I understood nothing of what was going on; brother, until the time of my arrival here, even until these last few most recent days, until today, even, I understood nothing of all those financial wrangles I was conducting with father. But to the devil with all of that just now, that can wait. And then, having received that six thousand, from a certain little letter a friend wrote me I suddenly learned something of great interest to me, namely that our lieutenant-colonel was under a cloud with the powers that be, that they suspected him of being at fault in something, in brief, that his enemies were preparing a tasty tidbit for him. And indeed, the commander of our division arrived and just about blew his head off. Then, a short time later, he was ordered to hand in his papers and quit the service. I won't go into the details of how it all happened; he really did have enemies, but suddenly in the town there was an extreme cooling towards him and all his family, it was as if everyone had suddenly backed away from him. It was then that I pulled off my first little trick: I met Agafya Ivanovna, with whom I'd always maintained a friendship, and told her: "You know, your papa's missing some four and a half thousand roubles of public money." "What are you talking about, why are you saying that? The general was here just recently, the money was all there . . ." "It may have been there then, but it isn't now." She got horribly frightened: "Please don't try to intimidate me; from whom did you hear this?" "Don't be alarmed," I said, "I'm not going to tell anyone, and anyway you know that on that account I'm a tomb, and all I want to do is to add something on that account just 'in case', as it were: when they demand that four and half thousand from your papa and he turns out not to have it, he'll be had up in court, and then he'll be off to serve in the ranks in his old age, so I think you'd better send me your institute girl in secret, it just so happens that I was recently sent some money, and what I think I shall do is lavish four and a half thousand on her and keep our secret sacred." "Oh, what a scoundrel you are," she said (that was how she put it!), "what a wicked scoundrel you are! And in any case, how dare you!" She left in fearful indignation, and I shouted after her once again that the secret would be kept sacred and inviolate. I should say in advance that in this entire episode both these women, Agafya and her aunt, turned out to be pure angels, and they truly worshipped that sister of theirs, Katya, belittled themselves in her regard, served her as if they were her chambermaids . . . The only thing was that Agafya went and told her about my little trick — the conversation we'd had, I mean. I subsequently found that out as plain as my hand, and of course it was exactly what I had wanted.

'Suddenly a new major arrived to take over the battalion. And take it over he did. The old lieutenant-colonel just as suddenly fell ill, couldn't move a limb, stayed at home for two whole days, but didn't return the public sum. Kravchenko, one of our local doctors, swore he really was ill. But you see, there was something I knew and had known for a long time beyond all shadow of doubt, a secret I had discovered: that whenever the authorities had sent someone to inspect the sum, it had afterwards disappeared for a time, and this had been going on for some four years now. The lieutenant-colonel had loaned it out to a certain most loyal individual, one of our local merchants, an old greybeard of a widower called Trifonov who went around in gold-rimmed spectacles. This fellow would go to the fair, do whatever wheelings and dealings he had to do there and then immediately return the money to the lieutenant-colonel in its entirety, always with a present of sweets from the fair and together with the sweets some little percentage points of interest as well. But on this occasion (I happened to learn all this entirely by chance from Trifonov's slob of a son, his child and inheritor, one of the most depraved young louts the world has ever produced), on this occasion, as I say, Trifonov, having returned from the fair, brought no money with him. The lieutenant-colonel went rushing to accost him: "Never have I received anything from you, and nor could I have done," was his answer. Well, so our lieutenant-colonel stayed at home with his head wrapped in a towel, and all three of them put ice on his temples; suddenly an orderly showed up with the cash-book and the instruction that the public sum was to be surrendered at once, without delay, within two hours' time. He signed his name, I saw that signature in the cash-book later on – got up, said he was going to put on his uniform, ran off to his bedroom, picked up his double-barrelled fowling-piece, put in a charge, rolled in an army bullet, removed the boot from his right leg, propped the gun against his chest and began to seek the trigger with his toe. But Agafya already had her suspicions, had remembered what I'd said that time, went creeping up and spied on him in time: she burst inside, threw herself at him from behind, hurled her arms round him, and the gun went off at the ceiling; no one was hurt; the others came rushing in, seized him, took the rifle away, held his arms . . . All of this I subsequently learned right down to the last detail. I was in my lodgings at the time, it was getting dark and I was just on the point of going out, having dressed, groomed my hair, scented my handkerchief and taken my cap, when suddenly the door opened and there, facing me, right there in my quarters, stood Katerina Ivanovna.

'Strange things sometimes happen: I mean, no one saw her go up to my lodgings at the time, and so the town never knew anything about it. I rented my quarters from two most ancient ladies, civil servants' widows who provided me with meals and service, respectful old biddies they were, obeyed me in everything and at a word from me subsequently both remained as dumb as two lumps of cast-iron. Of course I understood the whole thing at once. She came in and looked straight at me; there was a determined, even cheeky look in her dark eyes, and only along her lips and around them could I detect a lack of resolve.

'"My sister said you'd give me four and a half thousand roubles if I came and asked you for it ... in person. Here I am ... so please give me the money! ..." she said, but she couldn't go on with it, she gasped and took fright, her voice choked and the corners of her lips and the lines around them began to quiver. Alyoshka, are you listening or have you fallen asleep?'

'Mitya, I know that what you're going to say will be nothing but the truth,' Alyosha got out in agitation.

'That's right, and you must let me tell it. And if it's to be the truth, then it must be exactly as it happened, and I shan't spare myself. The first thought that occurred to me was a Karamazov one. You know, brother, I was once bitten by a centipede and lay in a fever for two weeks afterwards; well, what I suddenly felt now was that my heart had been bitten by a centipede, by the evil insect, do you understand? I measured her with my eye. Have you seen her? She's a beautiful woman, you know. But it wasn't that kind of beauty she had then. What made her beautiful at that moment was that she was noble, while I was a scoundrel, that there she was in all the majesty of her generosity and sacrifice for her father, while I was a mere bedbug. And yet now she was *completely* dependent on me, bedbug and scoundrel, completely, the whole of her, body and soul alike. There you have her in outline. I'll tell you straight: this thought, this thought of the centipede, gripped my heart so violently that it almost bled to death from sheer agony. It seemed that even a struggle was out of the question: I had no alternative but to act like a bedbug, like a savage tarantula, without any compassion ... I nearly choked. Listen: you see, of course I could have gone the next day and asked for her hand, so as to bring it all to a decent, as it were, conclusion and so that no one would ever find out about this or have any chance of doing so. Because you see, though I may be a man of base desires, I am honest. But then suddenly at that very instant someone whispered in my ear: "You know, when you arrive with your proposal of marriage tomorrow that woman won't even come out and see you but will get her coachman to manhandle you off the premises, as if to blazon it all over town that she's not afraid of you!" I glanced at the girl and knew that my voice did not lie: that was it, of course that was how it would be. I'd be carted outside by the scruff of my neck, I could see that now by the look on her face. Malice seethed up inside me, I felt like pulling a really base, piggish, merchant's sort of trick on her: I wanted to look at her with a mocking snigger and then, while she was still there in front of me, discombobulate her in a tone of voice that only some merchant could produce:

' "This is about the four thousand? But that was simply a joke of mine, madam, whatever has got into you? You have been banking on dreams, madam. I might have been prepared to let you have a couple of hundred, and gladly, too, but four thousand — that's not the kind of sum one throws away on trifles of this kind, my lady. You have put yourself to needless trouble."

'Of course, I'd have lost everything and she'd have run away, but on the other hand it would have been an infernally vindictive thing to do, it would have been worth all the rest. I'd howl with remorse all the rest of my life, if only I could pull off this trick now! You must believe me when I tell you that never before had I looked at a woman with hatred at a moment like that, not with a single woman had it happened — and yet I swear by the cross that I looked at that woman for some three to five seconds with a terrible hatred — with the kind of hatred from which there's only a single hair's breadth of distance to love, the most reckless love! I went over to the window, placed my forehead against the frozen pane and I remember that the ice of it burned my forehead like a fire. I didn't keep her waiting long, don't worry, I turned round, went over to the table, opened its drawer and took out a five-thousand-rouble five per cent anonymous bond* (it lay between the pages of my French diction-ary). Then without saying anything I showed it to her, folded it, handed it to her, opened the door to the passage for her and, retreating one step, made her a deep, reverential and most heartfelt bow, believe you me! She shuddered all over, gave me a fixed look for a second, turned horribly pale, just like a white tablecloth, and suddenly, still without a word and without any rush but softly, deeply, slowly, got right down at my feet and leaned her forehead on the floor, not like an institute girl but like a real Russian! Then she leapt up and fled. When she ran out I was wearing my sword; I took it out and intended to run myself through with it right there and then — why, I don't know, it was of course a terribly stupid idea, but it must have been the ecstasy. There are some kinds of ecstasy, you know, that can make a man kill himself; but I didn't run myself through, just kissed the sword and put it back in its sheath again — a fact which, by the way, I might easily not have mentioned to you. And even now, in telling you about all these struggles, I've done a bit of decorative padding in order to make myself look more impressive. But very well, let it be so, and the devil confound all spies of the human heart! There you have the whole of that earlier "incident" of mine with Katerina Ivanovna. And that means that now brother Ivan knows about it, and you — and no one else!'

Dmitry Fyodorovich got up, strode a pace or two in agitation, produced a handkerchief, wiped the sweat from his brow and then sat down again, not in the place he had occupied before, however, but in another, on the bench opposite, against the other wall, so that Alyosha had to turn round completely to him.

5

The Confession of an Ardent Heart. 'Heels Last'

'Now,' said Alyosha, 'I know the first half of this affair.'

'The first half you understand: it's a drama, and it happened back there. The second half is a tragedy, and it's going to take place here.'

'Of the second half I don't yet understand anything,' Alyosha said.

'And what about me? Do I understand?'

'Wait, Dmitry, there's one central word here. Tell me: I mean, you're betrothed, you are betrothed to her even now, are you not?'

'I wasn't betrothed to her immediately, not until three months later. The day after it happened I said to myself that the incident was exhausted and at an end, there would be no follow-up. To go and propose to her seemed to me a base thing to do. As for her, I heard not so much as a peep out of her during all the subsequent six weeks or so she spent in our town. Apart, that is to say, for a certain occurrence: on the day after her visit her chambermaid slipped over to my quarters and, without saying anything, handed me a package. It had an address on it: to so-and-so. I opened it — and there was the change from the five-thousand-rouble bond. All she had wanted was four and a half thousand, but there had been a commission of over two hundred roubles on the sale of the bond. I think she had sent me only about two hundred and sixty roubles, I don't remember now properly, and there was just the money — no note, no word, no explanation. I searched the package for some pencil mark or other — n-nothing! Oh well, I made do with blowing the rest of the money on such a spree that the new major too was compelled to give me a dressing-down. And as for the lieutenant-colonel, well, he returned the public sum — in order and to everyone's astonishment, as no one had supposed he still had all that money tucked away. He returned it and then was taken ill, retired to bed, lay there for some three weeks, then suddenly there was a softening of the brain and within five days he'd packed it in. They buried him with military honours, as the order sacking him from the force hadn't yet come through. Katerina Ivanovna and her sister, having only just seen their father to his grave, some ten days later repaired to Moscow in the company of their aunt. And then right on the very day of their departure (I hadn't been visiting them and didn't see them off), I received a tiny little missive written on blue frilly notepaper and containing only a single pencilled line: "I shall write to you, please wait. K." That was all.

'I'll explain it for you now in a few words. In Moscow their lives were suddenly transformed with the speed of lightning and the unexpectedness of an Arab folk-tale. This general's widow, her principal female relative, had suddenly and at a single stroke lost her two most immediate inheritresses, her two closest nieces – both of them died of smallpox within the same week. The shocked old lady was overjoyed to see her Katya, received her like her own daughter, like a saving star, threw herself upon her and instantly rewrote the will in her favour, but with the comment that that was for the future and for now making her a straight gift of eighty thousand roubles, more or less saying: "Here's your dowry, do with it what you will." A hysterical woman, I had occasion to observe her in Moscow later on. Well, then suddenly I received four and half thousand roubles in the mail; I was naturally amazed, surprised as a man who has lost his tongue. Three days after that the promised letter also arrived. I've got it with me even now, it never leaves me, and I shall die with it on my person – would you like me to show it to you? Please read it, you must – in it she makes me an offer of her hand, she offers herself, saying things like: "I love you to distraction, and even if you don't love me it doesn't matter, you will merely be my husband. Please don't be afraid – I don't want to cause you any trouble, I want to be your domestic chattel, the very carpet you walk on . . . I want to love you to eternity, I want to rescue you from yourself." Alyosha, I am unworthy even to relate those lines in my scoundrel's words and my scoundrel's tone of voice, my customary scoundrel's tone of voice from which I've never been able to reform myself! This letter ran me through to the core and still does so, and do you really think I can possibly feel lighthearted now, today? At the time I wrote her an instant reply (there was no possible chance of my going to Moscow). In tears I wrote it; there was one thing in it of which I shall be eternally ashamed: I referred to the fact that now she was rich, with a dowry, while I was but a destitute churl – I referred to money! I should have endured it in silence, but my pen ran away with me. At the same time I immediately wrote to Ivan in Moscow, in my letter explaining it all to him as best I was able, six pages that letter ran to, and asking him to go and see her. What are you staring at, why are you looking at me like that? Yes, well, Ivan fell in love with her, and he still is, I know it, it was a stupid thing for me to do in the eyes of ordinary, worldly men, but perhaps that kind of stupidity alone can save us all now! Ha! Surely you must have noticed what respect she has for him, how she reveres him? Do you really suppose that having compared the two of us she could possibly love a man such as me, particularly after all that has happened?'

'Oh, I'm quite certain it's a man such as you she'd love, not one like him.'

'It's her virtue she loves, not me,' Dmitry Fyodorovich let out suddenly, in spite of himself, but with vicious hostility. He began to laugh, but a second later his eyes flashed, he turned crimson and brought his fist down violently on the table.

'I swear, Alyosha,' he exclaimed with a terrible and sincere wrath at himself, 'believe it or not, but as God is holy and as Christ is Lord I swear that I, though I made fun of her loftier emotions just now, know that I am a million times more spiritually insignificant than she, and that those loftier emotions of hers are as sincere as those of a heavenly angel! The tragedy of it is that I know that for a fact. What does it matter if a man does a spot of declaiming now and again? I'm declaiming myself just now, am I not? But I mean, I'm sincere about it, I'm sincere! And you see where Ivan's concerned I understand the malediction with which he must now look upon nature, even more so when one considers his intelligence! To whom, to what has preference been shown? It has been shown to a monster of cruelty, who even here, even though he's engaged to be married and everyone's eyes are on him, has been unable to contain his debauchery – and this in the presence of his bride, his bride! And so a man such as I is preferred, and he is refused. But for what reason? For the reason that a maiden wants to do violence to her own life and fortunes out of gratitude! Absurd! I have never said anything in this vein to Ivan. And Ivan, of course, has never breathed so much as half a word nor dropped even the slightest hint to me about it; but fate will be enacted, the worthy man will take his place and the unworthy man will slink away to the side-lane for ever – his own dirty side-lane, his beloved and appropriate side-lane, and there, in the filth and the stink, he'll perish voluntarily and with pleasure. I know I'm talking the most horrible nonsense, my words are all clapped out, I feel as though I were placing bets at random, but even so, the way I've described it is the way it will come to pass. I'll drown in the side-lane, and she'll get married to Ivan.'

'Brother, wait,' Alyosha again interrupted with extreme concern. 'Look, there's one thing you still haven't explained to me: I mean, you're betrothed, you're formally betrothed to her, aren't you? Then how will you break with her, if she, your bride-to-be, doesn't wish it?'

'Yes, I'm her betrothed, formal and blessed, it all took place in Moscow on my arrival, with all the religious pomp and ceremony and icons, in the finest manner. The general's wife performed the blessing and – can you imagine, even congratulated Katya: "You've chosen the right man," she said. "I can see right through him." And imagine, she took a dislike to Ivan and didn't congratulate him. While I was in Moscow I also managed to discuss a lot of things with Katya, I did the honourable thing and presented myself to her without hiding anything, in sincere detail. She heard it all through:

> There was dear abashment,
> There were tender words . . . *

Well, and there were proud words, too. It was then that she forced out of me a great promise that I'd reform my ways. I gave her the promise. And so now . . .'

'What, then?'

'And so now I have summoned you and hauled you over here today, on this particular date – remember it! – with the purpose of sending you, also this very day, to Katerina Ivanovna, and . . .'

'What?'

'Telling her that I'll no longer go to see her, and that I bow to her.'*

'But is that possible?'

'Well, that's why I'm sending you in my place, because it's impossible, and anyway how could I tell her it myself?'

'But where will you go?'

'To my side-lane.'

'So you're going to Grushenka!' Alyosha exclaimed sadly, wringing his hands. 'Was Rakitin really telling the truth, then? And I thought you'd simply paid her one or two visits and were now done with her.'

'Could a man who's betrothed do a thing like that? Is it possible, and with a bride like that, and for all to see? I mean, I do have some honour, I think. As soon as I began paying those visits to Grushenka I stopped being a betrothed and an honourable man. What are you staring at? Look, I went to see her in the first instance in order to give her a whipping. I'd discovered and now know for certain that Grushenka had been given a promissory note with my signature by that junior captain, my father's attorney, with the intention that she should take out exaction proceedings against me so I'd calm down and stop my pestering. They wanted to give me a fright. I was out to deal Grushenka a whipping. I'd noticed her vaguely before out of the corner of my eye. She's not much to look at. I knew about her old merchant, who's ill now into the bargain, lying in bed without the use of his limbs, but that won't stop him leaving her a pretty sum. I also knew that she liked to make a bit of dough and made it by lending at wicked rates of interest, the cunning vixen, the rogue, without mercy. I went to give her a whipping and stayed. The tempest raged, the pestilence struck, I succumbed to the taint, which I bear to this day, and knew it was all finished, that never would there be anything else. The cycle of the seasons was complete. That was the essence of my life. And then suddenly, as luck would have it, three thousand roubles turned up in my pocket, the pocket of a pauper. She and I set off for Mokroye, that's about twenty-five versts from here, I took some gypsies there, both men and women, and champagne, and got all the muzhiks there drunk, as well as all their wives and wenches, I flung thousands of roubles around. Three days later I was skint as a bald-headed falcon, but at least I was a falcon.* Do you suppose the falcon got anywhere? She didn't even show it to me from a distance. I tell you, it's a curve. Grushenka, the rogue, has a certain curve in her body, it's there even in her foot, there's even a trace of it in the small toe of her left foot. I've seen it and kissed it, but that's all – I swear! She would say: "If you like, I'll marry you, after all you're a pauper. If you'll say you won't whip me and will let me do anything I want, I might marry you" – and she laughed. She's laughing even now!'

Almost in a kind of rage Dmitry Fyodorovich got up from where he had been sitting, and suddenly he looked drunk. His eyes were now shot with blood.

'And do you really want to get married to her?'

'If she agrees, then I will, instantly, and if she doesn't then I still won't go away; I'll be the yardkeeper in her yard. Look . . . look, Alyosha . . .' he said, suddenly came to a halt in front of him and then, seizing him by the shoulders began to shake him violently. 'Do you not realize, you innocent boy, that all that is delirium, inconceivable delirium, for this is a tragedy! Listen, Alyosha, I may be a man of baseness, with base and reprobate passions, but a thief, a pickpocket, a cloakroom pilferer, that Dmitry Karamazov can never be. Well, but now listen to something else: I am indeed a pilferer, a thief of pocket and cloakroom! Just before I set off to give Grushenka a whipping, that very same morning, Katerina Ivanovna had summoned me in the most formidable secrecy, so that no one should find out about it for the present (why, I don't know, apparently that was the way she wanted it), and asked me to go to the main town of the province and there dispatch three thousand roubles by mail to Agafya Ivanovna in Moscow – it had to be done from the town so that no one would learn of it here. It was with those three thousand roubles in my pocket that I turned up at Grushenka's, and it was that money we spent on our trip to Mokroye. Subsequently I let on that I'd made a lightning visit to the town, but I didn't produce the postal receipt, told her I'd sent the money and would bring her the receipt, though I haven't done that yet, I "forgot". Now what do you think will happen when you go to her today and say: "He bows to you," and she asks you: "And the money?" You might still say to her: "He's a base voluptuary, an ignoble fellow who can't control his feelings. He didn't send your money but spent it, because he couldn't restrain himself, like an animal" – but you could add: "All the same, he's not a thief, here's your three thousand, he returns it to you, he wants you to send it to Agafya Ivanovna, and for himself bows to you." But the way it is now all she'll say is: "Where's the money?"'

'Mitya, I can understand that you're unhappy, but you're not as unhappy as you think you are – stop killing yourself with despair, don't do it!'

'What do you think I'm going to do, shoot myself because I can't return her three thousand? That is the whole point – I'm not going to shoot myself. I'm not up to it now – later, perhaps, but for now I'm going to Grushenka . . . It's my skin, after all.'

'And when you are with her?'

'I shall be her husband, I shall award myself the rank of spouse, and if a lover arrives I'll move into the next room. I shall scrub the dirty galoshes of her paramours, blow the coals in her samovar, run at her beck and call . . .'

'Katerina Ivanovna will understand it all,' Alyosha suddenly articulated, solemnly. 'She'll grasp the depth of all this unhappiness and will reconcile herself. She has a lofty intelligence, and she'll see that no one could be more unhappy than you.'

'She won't reconcile herself to it all,' Mitya said, grinning. 'There's something here, brother, that no woman in the world could ever reconcile herself to. And do you know what the best thing to do would be?'

'What?'

'Return the three thousand to her.'

'But where would you get it? Listen, I have two thousand. Ivan will give you another, there's your three, now take it and return it to her.'

'But when will it arrive, your three thousand? What's more, you're not twenty-one yet, and it is absolutely necessary without fail that you should bow to her for me today, with the money or without, because I cannot procrastinate any longer, that is the point this matter has reached. Tomorrow will be too late, too late. I am going to send you to father.'

'To father?'

'Yes, before you go and see her. I want you to ask him for three thousand.'

'But Mitya, why, he won't part with it.'

'Of course he won't, I know that. Aleksey, do you know what despair means?'

'Yes, I do.'

'Listen: he's not legally in debt to me in any way. I've had everything I'm owed by him, everything, I know. But I mean he's morally in debt to me, is he or isn't he? After all, he played a clever move with my mother's twenty-eight thousand and made a hundred thousand from it. So let him give me back just three thousand out of the twenty-eight to draw up my soul out of hell,* and may that settle the score for many a sin of his! And as for myself, when I get that three thousand I'll call it quits, that's a solemn promise, and he'll never hear from me ever again. I'm giving him one last chance to be a father. Tell him that God Himself has sent him this chance.'

'Mitya, there's no way that he'll part with it.'

'I know that, I know it inside out. Particularly now. Not only that, I now know something else as well: only the other day, perhaps as recently as yesterday, he discovered for the first time *seriously* (mark that word — "seriously") that Grushenka may really not be joking and may intend to jump into marriage with me. He knows her character, he knows the little she-cat. Well, is he really going to give me money, too, in order to facilitate that event, when he himself is out of his mind over her? But even that's not all, I have yet one more item of news to tell you: I know that about five days ago he went to the bank and took out three thousand roubles in one-hundred-rouble banknotes, packed them into a large envelope with five seals, and tied it across with red silk tape. You see the details I know? And on the envelope was written: "For my angel Grushenka, if she decides to come", scribbled by himself, in quiet, on the sly, and there's no one who knows he has the money there except his manservant Smerdyakov, in whose honesty he believes like his very own self. He's been waiting for Grushenka now for three or four days, hoping she'll come for the envelope — he sent word, telling her about it, and she sent word back, saying "perhaps I will". So I mean, if she goes to the old man, how can I marry her, eh? Do you understand now why I'm hiding here in secret, and what it is I'm on the lookout for?'

'Her?'

'You've got it. There's a fellow who rents a box of a room from one of those floozies of landladies we have around here, Foma's his name. Foma hails from our district, he's an ex-soldier from our outfit. He acts as their servant, by night he guards the place and by day he goes shooting grouse, and he makes a living by it. I've moved into his place; neither he nor the landladies know my secret, that I'm here on the lookout.'

'Is Smerdyakov the only person who knows?'

'Yes. He'll also let me know if either she or the old man puts in an appearance.'

'Was it Smerdyakov who told you about the envelope?'

'Yes. It's the most terrific secret. Not even Ivan knows about the money, or about any of it. And the old man's sending Ivan on a little drive to Chermashnya* for two or three days: a buyer's turned up who is prepared to pay eight thousand for the birch grove, cutting it down for timber, and so the old man turned to Ivan for help and said: "You lend a hand, and go there yourself" – for two or three days, that's to say. He wants Grushenka to come to him while Ivan's not there.'

'So he's waiting for Grushenka even today?'

'No, she won't come today, the omens are against it. She definitely won't come!' Mitya cried suddenly. 'Smerdyakov is of the same opinion. Father is drinking now, he's sitting at table with brother Ivan. Go there, Aleksey, and ask him for that three thousand . . .'

'Mitya, dear fellow, what is wrong with you?' Alyosha exclaimed, leaping up from his seat and staring intently at the ecstatic and entranced Dmitry Fyodorovich. For an instant he thought that the latter had lost his reason.

'Why do you say that? I haven't gone mad,' Dmitry Fyodorovich enunciated with a fixed and even somewhat solemn look. 'All I'm doing is sending you to father because I know it's the right thing to do: I have faith in a miracle.'

'A miracle?'

'A miracle of Divine Providence. God has knowledge of my heart, he sees the whole of my despair. He sees the whole of this scenario. Would he really help an atrocity to take place? Alyosha, I have faith in a miracle, go!'

'All right, I will. Tell me, are you going to wait here?'

'Yes, I know it won't be quick, that you can't just go there and get it bang, like that. He's drunk now. I am prepared to wait three hours, four hours, five, six or seven hours, as long as I know that today, even if it's not until midnight, you'll go to Katerina Ivanovna, *with the money or without the money*, and say: "He asks me to bow to you." I particularly want you to repeat that line: "He asks me to bow to you."'

'Mitya! But what if Grushenka arrives today . . . or if not today, then tomorrow or the day after?'

'Grushenka? I shall be watching on the sly, I shall burst in and stop them . . .'

'But what if . . .'

'Then I shall commit murder. I will not stand back and endure it.'

'Whom will you murder?'

'The old man. I won't kill her.'

'What are you saying, brother?'

'Oh, look, I don't know, I don't know . . . Perhaps I shall murder him and perhaps I shall not. My fear is that his face will suddenly grow hateful to me at that moment. I hate his Adam's apple, his nose, his eyes, his shameless snigger. I experience a personal loathing. That is what I fear, and then I will not be able to control myself . . .'

'I shall go, Mitya. I believe that God will see to it as he knows best that there is no atrocious happening of that kind.'

'And I shall sit here and wait for a miracle. But if it does not take place, then . . .'

Alyosha, reflective, set off for his father's house.

6

Smerdyakov

HE did indeed find his father still at table. The table had, according to customary habit, been laid in the reception room, even though the house had a proper dining room. This reception room was the largest room in the house, and had been furnished with a kind of old-fashioned pretension. The furniture was of the most ancient, white, with decrepit red semi-silk upholstery. Mounted in the piers between the windows were looking-glasses in mannered frames of antique fretwork, also white, with gold inlays. On walls that had been decorated with white wallpaper that had already cracked in many places swaggered two large portraits – one of some prince or other, who some thirty years before had been governor-general of the local territory, and the other of some bishop, now also long deceased. In the corner nearest the front of the room there were several icons, before which a lamp was kept burning all night . . . not so much out of piety as in order that the room should be illumined at night. Fyodor Pavlovich went to bed very late, at three or four in the morning, and until then would ceaselessly walk about the room or sit in an armchair, thinking. Such was the habit he had formed. He would not infrequently pass the night completely alone in the house, sending his servants to the outbuilding, though in general there remained with him at nights his manservant Smerdyakov, who slept on a bench in the vestibule. When Alyosha entered the meal had been wholly consumed, though coffee and fruit preserves had been brought. After dinner Fyodor Pavlovich was fond of sweets with cognac. Ivan Fyodorovich was right there at table, also having coffee. The manservants Grigory and Smerdyakov stood in attendance. Both masters and servants were plainly in a state of uncommonly cheerful animation. Fyodor Pavlovich was loudly guffawing and laughing; even from the passage Alyosha had caught his shrill laughter, so familiar to him from earlier days and had at once deduced by its sound that his father was as yet far from drunk, but was merely wallowing in good humour.

'Here he is, here he is!' Fyodor Pavlovich began to howl, all of a sudden hugely pleased to see Alyosha. 'Come and join us, sit down, have some coffee – why, it's lenten, lenten, and it's hot, and good! I shan't offer you cognac, you're a keeper of the fasts, but will you have some anyway – eh? No, I'd better give you a liqueur, a noble one! Smerdyakov, go to the cupboard, it's on the second shelf to the right, here are the keys, look lively, now!'

Alyosha made the initial gestures of refusing the liqueur.

'It will be served anyway, if not to you then to us,' Fyodor Pavlovich beamed. 'But wait, have you eaten or not?'

'Yes, I have,' said Alyosha, who to tell the truth had consumed no more than a hunk of bread and a glass of *kvas* in the Father Superior's kitchen. 'But I'd be glad of a cup of hot coffee.'

'That's the boy! There's a fine lad! He's going to have coffee. Does it need heating up? No, it's still on the boil. Noble coffee, Smerdyakov's brew. That Smerdyakov of mine is an artist at coffee and kulebiakis,* and at fish soup too, to be sure. Come and have fish soup some time, give me a bit of warning in advance . . . But wait, wait, why, I told you to move back here with your mattress and pillows earlier today, didn't I? Lugged your mattress with you, have you? Heh-heh-heh! . . .'

'No, I didn't bring it,' Alyosha said, also with an ironic grin.

'But were you frightened, were you frightened then, back there, were you frightened? Oh, my little pigeon, how could I possibly do anything to harm you? Listen, Ivan, I just can't sit here and see him gazing into my eyes like that and laughing, I can't! The whole of my insides start laughing along with him, I'm that fond of him! Now then, Alyosha my lad, let me give you my parental blessing.'

Alyosha stood up, but by that time Fyodor Pavlovich had changed his mind.

'No, no, I shall simply cross you for now, there, like that, now sit down again. Well, now you shall have some entertainment, and on your favourite theme, too. You'll laugh, and plenty. Balaam's ass has begun to talk,* and how she talks, sir, how she talks!'

Balaam's ass turned out to be the lackey Smerdyakov. Still only a young man of some twenty-four years, he was intensely unsociable and silent. It was not that he was shy or ashamed or anything – no, he was, on the contrary, of haughty temperament and seemed to view everyone with contempt. And now it is impossible to avoid saying at least a few words about him, especially at this point in the narrative. Although he had been reared by Marfa Ignatyevna and Grigory Vasilyevich, the boy had grown up 'without any gratitude', as Grigory expressed it, a strange boy who looked at the world from a corner. In his childhood he had been very fond of stringing up cats and then giving them ceremonial burials. He would on such occasions drape around him a sheet, which acted as a kind of surplice, chanting and waving something over the dead cat as though he were censing it. All this he did in stealth, with the greatest of secrecy. Grigory once caught him at this practice and administered harsh chastisement to him with the birch. The boy had withdrawn to a corner and for a week scowled from there, disapprovingly. 'He doesn't like you nor me, that cruel monster,' Grigory would say to Marfa Ignatyevna, 'and he doesn't like anyone else either. You're not human,' he would say, suddenly turning to Smerdyakov. 'You're not human, you came out of the steam on the bathhouse wall,* you did . . .' Smerdyakov, it subsequently transpired, was never able to pardon him these words. Grigory trained him in reading and writing and, when he had attained the age of about twelve, began to instruct him in biblical history. But the project instantly came to nothing. It appears that one day, at what can only have been his second or third lesson, the boy suddenly gave a derisive grin.

'What's the matter with you?' Grigory inquired, peering at him threateningly over his spectacles.

'Oh nothing, sir. The Lord God created the light on the first day, and the sun, moon and stars on the fourth day. So where did the light on the first day come from?'

Grigory was rendered speechless. The boy stared mockingly at his teacher. There was even something haughty in his stare. Grigory could not contain himself. 'This is where it came from!' he cried, and smote his disciple violently across the cheek. The boy endured the slap without a word of retort, but then skulked in his corner again for several days. Chance would have it that just one week later there became manifest in him, for the first time in his life, the falling sickness that was to remain with him for the rest of it. Having learned of this, Fyodor Pavlovich suddenly seemed to alter his view of the boy. Previously he had viewed him more or less with indifference, though he never rebuked him and on meeting him invariably gave him a copeck or two. In a good-natured frame of mind he would occasionally send the boy some sweet morsel from his table. Now, however, learning of his illness, he became positively concerned about him, summoned a doctor to effect a cure until it proved that no cure was possible. The fits arrived once a month on average, and varied in duration. The fits were also of varying intensity – some were insignificant, others very cruel. Fyodor Pavlovich forbade Grigory in the strictest terms to punish the boy physically, and began to admit him to his chambers upstairs. Instruction of him in whatever subject was also for the present something he forbade. Once, however, when the boy was about fifteen, Fyodor Pavlovich observed him hanging about near the book-cupboard and trying to read the titles of the books through the glass. Fyodor Pavlovich had rather a lot of books, some hundred or more volumes, but no one had ever seen him actually reading one. He instantly gave Smerdyakov the key to the book-cupboard: 'Very well then, read, you can be our librarian, it will do you more good than loafing around in the yard, go on, sit down and read. Here's one for you to get through.' And Fyodor Pavlovich took out *Evenings on a Farmstead near Dikanka* for him.*

The boy got through the book, but remained dissatisfied; never once during his reading did he smile, but on the contrary reached the end of the book with a frown.

'What's wrong? Didn't you find it funny?' asked Fyodor Pavlovich.

Smerdyakov was silent.

'Answer, fool.'

'It's all about things that aren't true,' Smerdyakov mumbled with a smirk.

'Oh, clear off and go to the devil, you soul of a lackey. Wait, here's Smaragdov's *General History** for you, everything in it's true, read that.'

But Smerdyakov read not even ten pages of Smaragdov, he found it tedious. And so the book-cupboard was locked up once again. Soon after this, Marfa and Grigory informed Fyodor Pavlovich that there had gradually begun to manifest itself in Smerdyakov a terrible finickiness: while eating his soup he would take the spoon and search about in the soup for all he was worth, bend forward, scrutinize it, draw up a spoonful and raise it to the light.

'What is it, a cockroach?' Grigory would inquire.

'Perhaps it's a fly,' Marfa would comment.

The cleanly youth never ventured a reply, but the same thing happened with bread, with meat and indeed with every kind of food: he would raise a piece on his fork, study it as though through a microscope, engage in long deliberation, and finally bring himself to dispatch it to his mouth. 'Will you look at the little lord he's turned into?' Grigory would mutter as he stared at him. Fyodor Pavlovich, upon learning of this new quality of Smerdyakov's, immediately decided that he should be a cook, and sent him off to Moscow for instruction. In the process of instruction he passed several years and returned with a face that was radically altered. He suddenly seemed to have put on an extraordinary number of years, he had acquired wrinkles that were quite incommensurate with his age, his skin had turned sallow, and he had begun to resemble a Skopets.* From a psychological point of view, however, he returned almost the same as he had been before his departure for Moscow: was still just as unsociable and felt not the slightest requirement for anyone else's company. Even in Moscow, as was subsequently related, he had said not a word; Moscow as such had interested him extremely little, and though he had discovered one or two things, to all the rest he paid no attention. He even visited the theatre once, but returned without a word, in displeasure. On the other hand he came back to us from Moscow in fine attire, a clean dress-coat and linen, very thoroughly cleaned his apparel twice a day with a brush without fail and in person, and was inordinately fond of polishing his own fashionable calf-leather boots with a special English blacking until they gleamed like mirrors. He proved to be a splendid cook. Fyodor Pavlovich granted him a salary and Smerdyakov spent it almost entirely on clothing, pomade, scent and the like. For the female sex, however, he appeared to have just as much contempt as for the male, conducting himself with them in a manner that was sedate and even inaccessible. Fyodor Pavlovich began to take a slightly different view of him. The crux of the matter was that his fits of the falling sickness had intensified, and on those days the meals were cooked by Marfa Ignatyevna, something that did not at all concur with Fyodor Pavlovich's designs.

'Why are you having so many of these fits?' he would sometimes ask, scowling at his new cook, studying his face. 'Perhaps you ought to marry some girl, do you want me to find you one?'

But this kind of talk would only make Smerdyakov turn pale with annoyance, and he would not reply. Fyodor Pavlovich would withdraw with a wave of the hand. The main thing was that he was convinced of Smerdyakov's honesty, and was definitely certain that he would never ever steal anything. If once transpired that Fyodor Pavlovich, when in a fine state of drunkenness, dropped in the mire of his own courtyard three 'rainbow' hundred-rouble notes* which he had only just received, noticing their absence only on the following day: no sooner had he frantically begun to search his pockets than the 'rainbows' suddenly appeared, all three of them, upon the table. Where had they come from? Smerdyakov had picked them up and brought them in the previous night. 'Well, brother, I've never come across a fellow like you before,' Fyodor Pavlovich had said brusquely, giving him ten roubles. It should be added that not only was he convinced of Smerdyakov's honesty — for some reason he even loved him, though the fellow looked at him with the same scowl he accorded the others, maintaining a constant silence. It was seldom that he opened his mouth to speak. If at this time anyone had thought to inquire, looking at him: 'What are the interests of this lad and what is it that most frequently preoccupies his mind?', it must be admitted that mere looking would not have suggested any answer. Yet on occasion, whether in the house, out in the courtyard or on the street, Smerdyakov would come to a halt, reflect and continue to stand thus for up to ten minutes at a stretch. A physiognomist submitting him to close scrutiny would have said that here there was at work no thought, no process of the intelligence, but rather some form of contemplation. There is by the artist Kramskoy a certain remarkable painting that goes under the title of *The Contemplator*:* depicted is a forest in winter, and there, all alone in the forest, on a roadway, in a ragged old caftan and bast shoes, stands a wretched little muzhik who has wandered there in deepest solitude, stands seemingly in reflection, yet is not thinking but is apparently 'contemplating'. Were you to jog his elbow he would start and look at you as though he had just awoken, but would take nothing in. To be sure, he would at once recover his wits, but were you to ask him what he had been standing there thinking about, he would doubtless be unable to remember any of it, but would on the other hand doubtless still harbour within him the impression to which he was subject during his contemplation. These impressions are dear to him, and he is probably saving them up, imperceptibly and even without being conscious of it — for what purpose and reason he also does not know: perhaps, having saved them for many years, he will suddenly turn his back on everything and go to Jerusalem to wander and live as a monk, or perhaps he will suddenly burn down his native village, or perhaps both the one and the other will occur at the same time. There is a sufficiency of contemplators among the common folk. And Smerdyakov was probably one of them and was probably likewise avidly saving up his impressions, almost without himself knowing why yet.

7

A Disputation

BUT Balaam's ass had suddenly begun to talk. A curious subject had arisen: that morning, while collecting some goods at the shop of the merchant Lukyanov, Grigory had heard from him the story of a certain Russian soldier* who, somewhere far away upon the frontiers of our land, among the Asiatics, where he had fallen captive and been coerced on pain of immediate and agonizing death to renounce Christianity and go over to Islam, had not consented to change his faith and instead accepted martyrdom, allowing the skin to be flayed from his back, and had died glorifying Christ and praising His name — which act of sacred heroism was reported in that day's newspaper. Of this it was that Grigory had begun to speak at table. Fyodor Pavlovich had on earlier occasions also invariably been fond, at the end of the table, over the dessert, of laughing and talking for a while, even if it were only with Grigory. On this particular occasion he was in a lighthearted and agreeably unconstrained mood. Hearing the item of news communicated as he slowly but steadily sipped his cognac, he made the observation that a soldier of that kind ought instantly to be promoted to the rank of saint and his flayed skin dispatched to some monastery or other: 'Then they'd fairly see the crowds and the money flow in.' Grigory frowned, aware of the fact that Fyodor Pavlovich had not been moved in the slightest by the story, but was, according to his customary habit, beginning to indulge in blasphemy. Then it was that Smerdyakov, who had been standing by the door, suddenly grinned. On previous occasions, too, Smerdyakov had very frequently been admitted to the dining table to stand in attendance, towards the end of the meal, that is. Indeed, from the time of Ivan Fyodorovich's arrival in our town he had begun to appear at dinner almost every day.

'What's up with you?' Fyodor Pavlovich inquired, observing the grin in a trice and realizing, of course, that it was directed at Grigory.

'Well, sir, it's regarding the fact,' Smerdyakov suddenly began loudly and unexpectedly, 'that if that soldier's heroism was so very great, sir, then there'd have been no sin in it if on that one occasion he'd have renounced Christ's, as it were, name and his own baptism, and thereby saved his life for good deeds with which over the years he might have atoned for his cowardice.'

'What do you mean, there'd have been no sin in it? That's balderdash, and for that they'll cast you straight into hell and roast you there like a side of mutton,' Fyodor Pavlovich had chimed in.

This was the very point at which Alyosha entered. Fyodor Pavlovich, as we have seen, was hugely pleased to see him.

'Your favourite subject, your favourite subject!' he giggled joyfully, making Alyosha sit down to listen.

'With regard to the side of mutton, sir, that is not so, and there'll be nothing of that kind, sir, nor is it probable that there would be, if the matter be viewed in all justice,' Smerdyakov observed solidly.

'What on earth does he mean – "in all justice"?' Fyodor Pavlovich exclaimed even more merrily, nudging Alyosha slightly with his knee.

'He's a scoundrel, that's what he is!' suddenly burst from Grigory. Wrathfully he looked Smerdyakov straight in the face.

'With regard to calling me a scoundrel I think you'd do better to wait a moment, Grigory Vasilyevich, sir,' Smerdyakov retorted calmly and discreetly, 'and reason it out for yourself, without resorting to abuse: once I'd fallen captive to the tormentors of the Christian race and they had demanded of me that I curse the name of God and renounce my own baptism, then I'd be fully empowered to do that by my own reason, for there'd be no sin in it.'

'But you've said that already; stop painting pictures and offer us some proof!' cried Fyodor Pavlovich.

'Bouillon-boy!' Grigory whispered, contemptuously.

'With regard to calling me a bouillon-boy I think you ought again to wait a moment and reason it out for yourself, without resorting to abuse, Grigory Vasilyevich, sir. For no sooner did I say to my tormentors: "No, I'm not a Christian and I curse my own God" – I'd instantly and especially become anathema and accursèd by the very highest Divine Justice, and I'd be excommunicated from the Holy Church just as surely as a pagan foreigner, so that even at that very moment, sir — not only when I'd said it, but even when I'd only had the notion of saying it, even before a quarter of a second had passed, sir, I'd be excommunicated — is that not so, Grigory Vasilyevich?'

It was with evident satisfaction that he said all this to Grigory, even though he was really only answering Fyodor Pavlovich's questions and was very well aware of this, maintaining all the while, however, the pretence that the questions were being put to him by Grigory.

'Ivan!' Fyodor Pavlovich exclaimed suddenly. 'Put your head down so I can whisper in your ear. He's acting like this in order to impress you, he wants you to say something nice about him. Go on now, do it.'

Ivan heard out his papa's ecstatic communication with perfect seriousness.

'Wait, Smerdyakov, be quiet for a bit,' Fyodor Pavlovich exclaimed again. 'Ivan, come here again and let me whisper in your ear.'

Once more, with an air of great seriousness, Ivan Fyodorovich put his head down.

'I love you just as much as I do old Alyosha. Don't ever think I don't love you. Cognac?'

'Yes, please.' 'But you yourself have taken a fair bit on board already,' Ivan Fyodorovich thought as he gave his father a flat look. Smerdyakov, on the other hand, he was observing with extreme curiosity.

'You're accursèd and anathemaed even now,' Grigory burst out suddenly. 'And how after that can you dare, you scoundrel, to argue, if . . .'

'Stop calling him names, Grigory, stop it!' Fyodor Pavlovich interrupted.

'I think you ought to wait, Grigory Vasilyevich, even if only for a very short time, sir, and listen further, because I haven't finished yet. Because at the same time as I became instantly accursèd of God, at that same, at that highest moment, sir, I would already have become a kind of foreign pagan, and my baptism would be removed from me and exchanged into nothing — isn't that at least so, sir?'

'Get to the point, brother, get to the point,' Fyodor Pavlovich said, hurrying him up, and taking a mouthful from his glass with enjoyment.

'And if I weren't a Christian no more, then that would mean that I wouldn't have lied to my tormentors when they asked me whether I was a Christian or not, for I'd already have had my Christianity annulled by God Himself, by reason of my mere intention and before I'd even managed to utter a word to my tormentors. And if I'd already been demoted, then by what manner of means and what kind of justice could I be called to account in the next world as a Christian for having renounced Christ, when for the mere intention, long before the renunciation itself, I'd had my Christianity cancelled? If I wasn't a Christian any more, then that would mean I couldn't renounce Christ neither, for I'd have nothing to renounce. Who's going to call a pagan Tartar to account, Grigory Vasilyevich, even in heaven, for not having been born a Christian, and who's going to punish him for it, seeing as how you can't flay two hides off of one ox? Why, even if Almighty God Himself were to call him to account when he died, I bet it would only be with some most minor punishment (as He couldn't very well let him go without being punished altogether), since He'd decide that it wasn't the chap's fault if from pagan parents he'd come pagan into the world. After all, the Lord God couldn't very well grab hold of the Tartar by force and say he too was a Christian, could he? I mean, if the Almighty Lord did that, He'd be telling a downright lie! And surely the Almighty Lord of heaven and earth couldn't utter a lie, even if it were only a single word, sir?'

Grigory, rendered speechless, stared at the orator, his eyes popping out of his head. Although he had no proper understanding of what was being said, he had suddenly grasped something of all this rubbish and paused with the air of a man who has suddenly struck his forehead against a wall. Fyodor Pavlovich finished his glass and burst into shrill laughter.

'Alyosha, my boy, Alyosha, my son – how do you like that? Ah, you casuist! He's been with the Jesuits somewhere, Ivan. Ah, you *smerdyashchiy* (stinking) Jesuit, who taught you all that? Only you're talking rot, you casuist, rot, rot, rot. Now don't you shed a tear, Grigory, we're going to blow him to smithereens this very minute. Very well, she-ass, now tell me this: you might be in the right where your tormentors were concerned, but after all you'd still have renounced your faith and you yourself said that in that instant you'd be accursèd and anathemaed; well, if it came to an anathema it's not something they'd pat you on the back for in hell now, is it? What's your answer to that, my splendid Jesuit?'

'There's no doubt, sir, that I'd have renounced my faith, yet all the same there'd be no special sin in it, sir, and even if there was just a little, it'd be of the very most ordinary kind, sir.'

'What on earth does he mean – "of the very most ordinary kind, sir?"'

'That's rot, you accur-r-r-sèd fiend!' Grigory spat.

'Reason it out for yourself, Grigory Vasilyevich,' Smerdyakov continued calmly and sedately, apprising victory, but as if he were being magnanimous to a defeated foe. 'Reason it out for yourself, Grigory Vasilyevich: why, it's written in the Scriptures that if one has even a grain of faith and says unto the mountain, remove hence into the sea, it'll go, without any delay, at one's first command. All right then, Grigory Vasilyevich, if I'm such an atheist and you're such a believer that you're for ever calling me names, why don't you try telling the mountain to remove hence, if not into the sea (because it's a long way from here to the sea, sir), then at least as far as that stinking little river of ours, the one that flows past the bottom of our garden, you'll see for yourself at that very moment that it hasn't removed at all, sir, but will stay in its previous condition and order, no matter how much you shout at it, sir. And what that means, Grigory Vasilyevich, is that you don't believe in the proper manner neither, but merely hurl all sorts of names at others. And besides, if it be a-taken into consideration that no one in our day, not only you, sir, but no one full stop, right from the very highest personages down to the very last muzhik, sir, is able to shove mountains into the sea, apart maybe from one single person in the whole world, or two at most, and they're probably living as anchorites in secret in the Egyptian desert somewhere, so you'd never be able to find them – then if that's so, sir, and all the others turn out to be atheists, then surely the Lord will place His curse upon all those others, the entire population of the earth apart, that is, from those two anchorites, and in His mercy, that's so renowned, pardon not a single one of them? And it's for that reason that I hope and trust that, once having doubted, I'll be pardoned if I shed the tears of repentance.'

'Wait!' Fyodor Pavlovich shrilled in an apotheosis of ecstasy. 'So you still suppose there are two men who are able to move mountains, you suppose their existence? Ivan, put that little detail in your pipe and smoke it, write it down: there you have the whole of the Russian character!'

'Your observation that that is a characteristic feature of Russian popular religious belief is a perfectly correct one,' Ivan Fyodorovich concurred with an approving smile.

'You agree! If you agree, it must be so! Alyosha, my boy, it's true, isn't it? I mean, a faith like that is wholly Russian, is it not?'

'No, what Smerdyakov has is not at all a Russian sort of faith,' Alyosha pronounced earnestly and firmly.

'I'm not talking about his faith, I'm talking about that feature of the story, about those two anchorites, that one little detail: I mean surely that's Russian, Russian?'

'Yes, that's a wholly Russian trait,' Alyosha smiled.

'Your remark is worth a gold sovereign, she-ass, and I shall send it to you this day, but even so, in the rest of it you're wrong, wrong, wrong; what you have to get into your head, fool, is that we all of us here are deficient in belief because of merely trivial reasons, because we haven't the time: for one thing, we're beset by practical matters, and for another, God hasn't given us enough time, having allotted a mere twenty-four hours to each day, making it impossible for us even to get enough sleep, never mind repent! But you, in that situation you were describing, would have renounced your faith when faith was all you had left to think about and when all that mattered was that you show your faith! I mean to say, brother, I think that would constitute a sin, would it not?'

'Yes, I suppose in a way it would, but reason it out for yourself, Grigory Vasilyevich: why, in a way it would mitifigate the sin rather than constitute it. What I mean is that if at the time I believed in the holy truth in the way that one's supposed to believe in it, then I really would be sinning if I didn't accept martyrdom for my own faith and instead went over to the pagan Mohammedan one. But I mean, then it wouldn't get as far as martyrdom, sir, because all I'd have to do at that instant would be to say to the mountain: remove hence and squash my tormentor, and at that same instant it would remove hence and squash him like a cockroach, and off I'd go as though nothing had happened, praising and glorifying God. But if at that very same moment I experientiated all that I cried to the mountain: "Squash those tormentors" – and it didn't, then how, tell me, could I fail at the same time to doubt, particularly at such a fearful hour of great and mortal terror? As it was, I'd already know that I wouldn't completely attain the Kingdom of Heaven (for the mountain hadn't moved at my word, and consequently they wouldn't put much credentiality in my faith up there in the next world and I wouldn't be able to expect much of a reward when I got there), so why should I in addition allow the skin to be flayed from my body without no purpose? For even if by that time they'd already flayed half the skin from my back, not even then would anything I said or shouted remove the mountain hence. Well, at a moment like that not only might doubt assail me, but I might even be decided of my reason out of fear, so that reasoning would be quite impossible, sir. And in that case how could I be held particularly guilty if, seeing neither here nor there reward nor vantage for myself, I at least saved my own skin? And so, trusting greatly in the mercy of the Lord, I hope that I may be completely forgiven, sir . . .'

8

Over Some Cognac

THE dispute had ended, but it was a strange thing: towards its conclusion the so cheerfully animated Fyodor Pavlovich had suddenly begun to frown. He frowned and knocked back another glass of cognac, one he could this time very well have done without.

'All right, you Jesuits, now clear off out of here,' he suddenly cried to the manservants. 'Off you go, Smerdyakov. Today I shall send you the gold sovereign I promised you, but now you must go. Don't you shed any tears, Grigory, go and see Marfa, she'll console you and make up your bed for you. The scum won't let us sit in quiet after our meal,' he suddenly snapped in annoyance after the servants had instantly withdrawn at his command. 'Smerdyakov comes prying to our table every dinnertime now, and it's you he's so curious about. What have you done to encourage him?' he added in Ivan Fyodorovich's direction.

'Nothing at all,' the latter replied. 'He has decided that I'm worthy of respect, that's all; he is a lackey and a boor. Progressive cannon fodder, though, when the time arrives.'

'Progressive?'

'Oh, there will be others and better, but there will also be those like him. To start with they'll all be like him, but later on there will be better.'

'And when will the time arrive?'

'Oh, when the rocket goes up, or doesn't go up, as the case may be. At present the common folk haven't much time for these bouillon-boys.'

'There you are, you see, dear fellow – that Balaam's ass will go on thinking and thinking, and the devil knows what she'll think herself to in the end.'

'She will have plenty of ideas to save up,' Ivan smiled, ironically.

'You see, I know he can't stand me, in the same way as he can't stand anyone else either, and he has exactly the same attitude towards you, too, even though you think he's decided that you're "worthy of respect". And as for dear boy Alyosha, oh, he's despised old Alyosha for a long time. But he doesn't steal anything, he's not a gossip-monger, he keeps quiet, doesn't go telling tales about us to all and sundry, makes splendid kulebiakis, and all in all, quite honestly, let him go to the devil – is there any need to discuss him?'

'Of course there isn't.'

'And as for the things he may get into his head, as a general rule what the Russian muzhik needs is the birch. That's something I've always maintained. Our muzhik is a knave, and not to be spared, and it's just as well he's still occasionally given a hiding even now. The Russian land is mighty in the birch. Destroy the forests and the Russian land will perish. What I want are intelligent men. We've stopped flogging our muzhiks because we're so darned clever, but they continue to flog themselves. And they do well too. "For with what measure ye mete it shall be measured to you again . . ."* or however it goes. In a word, it shall be measured. But Russia is pigwash. My friend, if you knew how I hate Russia . . . that is, not Russia, but all these flaws and vices . . . though perhaps Russia, too. *Tout cela c'est de la cochonnerie.* Do you know what I like? I like wit.'

'That's another glass you've downed. I think you've had enough.'

'Wait — I shall have one more, and one more after that, and there I shall leave it. Now wait a moment, you interrupted me. On my way through Mokroye I asked an old man a few questions on the subject, and he told me: "The thing we like best is birching the wenches after we've sentenced them,* and we always let the lads do it. The ones they give a birching today they takes as brides on the morrow, so it's become quite a custom among the wenches." How do you like those Marquis de Sades, eh? But, however you view it, it has some wit. Why don't you come over with me and take a look sometime? Alyosha, my boy, you're blushing! Don't be embarrassed, my child. It's a pity I never got to the point of sitting down to dinner at the Father Superior's back there and telling the monks about the wenches of Mokroye. Alyoshka, don't be angry with me for the way I outraged your Father Superior back there. My dear fellow, it's just how the wickedness takes me. I mean if there's a God, and He exists — well, then of course I shall be guilty and shall be held answerable for it, but if He doesn't exist at all then perhaps they need some more of that medicine, those fathers of yours! Why, they could probably do with having their heads cut off, as they're holding up the development of progress. Would you believe me, Ivan, if I told you that torments my emotions? No, you don't believe it, I can see by your eyes. You believe what people say, that all I am is a buffoon. Alyosha, do you believe that I am not just a buffoon?'

'I believe that you are not just a buffoon.'

'And I believe that you believe, and that you're speaking sincerely. You look sincere and you talk sincere. But Ivan doesn't. Ivan's so high and mighty ... But all the same. I'd like to put an end to that little monastery of yours. Take all that mysticism and abolish it throughout the lands of Russia until those idiots finally see the light. And what a mass of gold and silver the Mint would rake in!'

'But why abolish it?' said Ivan.

'To make the truth shine out sooner, that's why.'

'But I mean, if that truth does shine out, you'll be the first to be robbed and then ... abolished.'

'Ha! Why, you know, you may very well be right. Oh, what a donkey I am!' Fyodor Pavlovich said suddenly, throwing up his arms and giving his forehead a slight knock. 'Well, in that case, Alyoshka, let your little monastery stay where it is, while we, the clever people, stay in the warm and enjoy our cognac. Do you know, Ivan, that God Himself must have arranged it thus on purpose? Ivan, tell us: is there a God or is there not? Mind, now: tell us for certain, tell us in earnest! Why are you laughing again?'

'I'm laughing at that witty observation of yours just now about Smerdyakov's faith in the existence of two Elders who were able to move mountains.'

'You mean you're reminded of it now?'

'Very much so.'

'Well, I'm a Russian too and possess the Russian proclivity, and even if one scratches a philosopher like you one will probably find a proclivity of a similar kind underneath. If you like, I shall find it for you. Let us stake a bet that I'll have found it by tomorrow. But never mind – tell us: does God exist or doesn't He? Only speak in earnest! I want to know in earnest, now.'

'No, He doesn't.'

'Alyosha, my boy: does God exist?'

'Yes, He does.'

'Ivan, does immortality exist, of any kind, even just the smallest, tiniest kind?'

'No, there is no immortality, either.'

'None whatever?'

'None whatever.'

'In other words, either the most complete zero or else something. Perhaps there's something? At any rate not nothing!'

'Complete zero.'

'Alyosha, my boy: does immortality exist?'

'It does.'

'What about God and immortality?'

'Both God and immortality. Immortality is in God.'

'Hm. It is more probable that Ivan's right. Merciful Lord, just think how much faith, how much energy man has given in vain to that dream, and for how many thousands of years! Who is it laughs at man thus? Ivan! For the last time, and in definite terms: does God exist or doesn't He? For the last time, I ask the question!'

'And for the last time I say no.'

'Then who is laughing at man, Ivan?'

'The Devil, probably.' Ivan Fyodorovich smiled, ironically.

'And does the Devil exist?'

'No, the Devil doesn't exist, either.'

'What a pity. The devil confound it, when I think what I would do to the man who first invented God! Stringing him up on the bitter asp would be too good for him.'

'There would be no civilization at all if no one had invented God.'

'Wouldn't there? Without God, you mean?'

'No. And there wouldn't be any cognac, either. But all the same, I think we shall have to take your cognac away from you.'

'Wait, wait, wait, dear chap, just one more little glass. I've hurt Alyosha's feelings. You're not angry are you, Aleksey? My dear little Alekseychik, Alekseychik dear?'

'No, I'm not. I know your thoughts. Your heart is better than your head.'

'My heart is better than my head? Merciful Lord, and just think who's saying it! Ivan, do you love our Alyosha?'

'Yes, I love him.'

'Love him.' (Fyodor Pavlovich was growing very tipsy.) 'Listen, Alyosha, I behaved in a thoroughly gross manner towards that Elder of yours earlier today. But I was excited. And I mean, that Elder has wit, don't you think, Ivan?'

'Yes, he possibly has.'

'He has, he has, *il y a du Piron là-dedans*.* He's a Jesuit, a Russian one, that is. And he's a noble creature, within him seethes a hidden indignation at having to pretend . . . at having to put on holiness all the time.'

'But I mean to say, he believes in God.'

'Not one whit does he. Didn't you know? Why, he himself tells everyone that, or at least, not everyone, but all the clever people who come to see him. He actually interrupted Governor Shults straight to his face and said: "*Credo*, but I do not know what in."'

'Really?'

'Yes, really. But I have respect for him. He has about him something Mephistophelean, or better, perhaps, something out of *A Hero of Our Time* ... Arbenin, or whatever he's called* in the book ... in other words, you see, he's a voluptuary; he's such a voluptuary that even now I'd be afraid for my daughter or my wife if they'd gone to confess to him. You know, when he starts telling stories ... A couple of years ago he invited us to his cell for tea, with liqueurs, too (the ladies send him liqueurs), and he started to paint such a picture of the old days that we split our sides laughing ... There was one particular story about the way he'd cured a crippled woman. "If my legs were well I'd dance a certain dance with you," he said. How do you like that, eh? "I played a few of the old Mount Athos tricks in my time," he said. He fleeced the merchant Demidov of sixty thousand.'

'What, you mean he stole it?'

'Demidov brought the money to him as to someone he could trust, saying: "Keep it safe for me, old fellow, they're going to search my premises tomorrow." And keep it safe he did. "You've endowed it to the Church," he said. "You're a scoundrel," I said to him, but he said no, he wasn't a scoundrel, but he had a broad nature ... Though actually, that wasn't him ... It was somebody else. I've got him mixed up with somebody else ... without noticing. Well, I'll have one more glass and that will be enough: take the bottle away, Ivan. I've been talking through my hat, why didn't you stop me, Ivan ... and tell me I was?'

'I knew that you would stop of your own accord.'

'Now you're the one who's talking through his hat, you did it out of spite for me, out of nothing but spite. You despise me. You've come to my house and treat me in it with contempt.'

'And I shall leave it, too: the cognac has gone to your head.'

'I have implored you by Christ and all the angels to make that trip to Chermashnya ... for a day or two, but you do not do it.'

'I will go tomorrow, if it is that important to you.'

'I don't think you will. You want to stay here and spy on me, that's what you want to do, you bastard, and that's why you won't make the trip.'

There was no stopping the old man. He had attained the stage of intoxication at which certain drunkards, hitherto peaceful, suddenly feel an urge to lose their temper and prove their true mettle.

'Why are you staring at me? What sort of eyes are those? They're looking at me and saying: "You drunken slob!" Your eyes are suspicious, your eyes are contemptuous ... You've come here with some crafty purpose. See, there's my boy Alyosha looking at me, but his eyes are radiant. Alyosha doesn't view me with contempt. Aleksey – don't love Ivan ...'

'Don't be angry with my brother! Stop saying things to offend him,' Alyosha suddenly got out.

'Oh very well, perhaps I am in the wrong. Ha, my head hurts. Take the cognac away, Ivan, that's the third time I've said it.' He began to reflect and then suddenly smiled a long, cunning smile. 'Ivan, don't be angry with a senile old man. I know you don't like me, but even so, don't lose your temper. There's nothing to like me for. Off you go to Chermashnya, and I'll come and see you there, bring you something for your sweet tooth. I'll introduce you to a certain little girlie there, I picked her out a long time ago. For the moment she's still at the bare-legged stage. Don't be afraid of those little "bare-legged dancers",* don't turn up your nose at them – they're pearls!'

And he gave his own hand a smacking kiss.

'For me,' he said, growing suddenly animated in all his movements, almost appearing to sober up for an instant, now that he had landed on his favourite theme. 'For me ... Oh, you little boys! You babies, you little infant piglets, for me ... there has not been one ugly woman in the whole of my life, that's my principle! Are you able to comprehend that? No, how could you? You still have milk, not blood, in your veins, you've not yet hatched from your shells! According to my book, it is possible to find in every woman something extremely – the devil take it – interesting, something you'll never find in any other – only you have to know where to look, that is the tricky part! It's a talent! For me there has never been any such thing as a *mauvaise*: the simple fact of her being a woman, that simple fact alone is half the battle ... but how could you understand that? Even the *vieilles filles*, even in them you can sometimes find things that make you want to shake your head at the stupid idiots who let them get old and yet still haven't noticed them! The "bare-legged dancer", like the *mauvaise*, has to be surprised, straight away, first thing – that's how you take her. Didn't you know? She has to be surprised to the point of ravishment, transfixion, shame that such a *barin** should have fallen for a miserable little commoner like herself. It's truly marvellous that for as long as there are cads and *barins* in the world, there will also forever be a little Miss Mop and forever be her master, and I mean that's all that one requires for happiness in life! But wait a moment ... listen, Alyosha, my boy, I was continually surprising your dear dead mother, only it got expressed in rather a different vein. I was never normally affectionate towards her, but suddenly, when the moment arrived — suddenly I'd start fawning on her like the devil's business, go crawling to her on my knees, kiss her feet and send her unfailingly, unfailingly — I remember it as though it were today — into that little laugh of hers, brittle, resonant, not loud, but nervous and peculiar. It was the only one she had. I knew that that was the way her illness always began, that on the morrow she'd start wailing like a "wailer", and that this little laugh she had now was no token of delight; but you see, even though it was an illusion, it served as a kind of delight. That's what it means to be able to find one's little characteristic feature in the whole! Once Belyavsky — he was a certain handsome little fellow from round this way, rolling in money, he was — went running after her and took it into his head to drop in and see me, and he suddenly gave me a slap in the face, and in front of her, too. Then she, who had always been such a sheep — why, I thought she was going to beat me to death for that slap, the way she flew at me, saying: "Now you are beaten, beaten, you took a slap from him! You have sold me down the river to him," she said, "and how dare he hit you in front of me! Don't you ever, ever dare to come and see me again! Go this minute and challenge him to a duel! . . ." So then I carted her off to the monastery to have a bit of meekness put in her, and the holy fathers read her a lecture. But as God's my witness, Alyosha, never did I say or do anything to hurt my little wailer! Well, perhaps only once, and that was in the first year of our marriage: she did a great deal of praying then, made a point of observing all the feasts of the Mother of God and would always banish me to my study when they were on. All right, I thought, let's see if I can't thrash all that mystical stuff out of her! "Look," I said, "look, here's your icon, here it is, look, I'm taking it down from the wall. Now then: you believe it has the power to work miracles, but I'm going to spit on it before your very eyes, and nothing will happen to me afterwards!" When she saw it, O Lord, I thought: she's going to kill me now, but instead all she did was jump up, wring her hands and then suddenly cover her face with them; then she convulsed all over and fell to the floor . . . fairly collapsed, she did. Alyosha, Alyosha! What's wrong with you, what is it?'

The old man leapt up in alarm. From the very moment Fyodor Pavlovich had started to talk about his mother, Alyosha's face had gradually begun to alter. He turned red, his eyes began to burn, his lips to tremble . . . The drunken old codger continued to spray himself with spittle and did not notice anything until the very moment at which something very strange suddenly happened to Alyosha, and there occurred with him a precise repetition, in every detail similar, of what Fyodor Pavlovich had just related in connection with the wailer. Alyosha suddenly leapt up from the table, exactly in the way his mother had done in the story, wrung his hands, then covered his face with them, fell as though the legs had been cut from under him into his chair and began to convulse all over in a hysterical fit of sudden, shattering and inaudible tears. The extraordinary resemblance he bore to his mother made a particular impression on the old man.

'Ivan, Ivan! Bring him some water, quickly! It's what used to happen to her, exactly the same thing that used to happen to his mother in the old days! Spray him with water from your mouth, that's what I used to do with her. It's because of what I said about his mother, his mother . . .' he muttered to Ivan.

'I believe I am not wrong in supposing that his mother was my mother, too?' Ivan broke forth suddenly with ungovernable and wrathful contempt. The old man flinched in the lightning of his gaze. But at this point something very strange took place, only for one second, to be sure: it appeared that the old man really had let it slip his memory that Alyosha's mother was Ivan's mother, too . . .

'What do you mean, your mother?' he muttered, not taking it in. 'Why do you mention that? What mother are you talking about? She wasn't your . . . Ha, the devil! Why, of course she was! Ha, the devil! Well, that was some kind of mental blackout, brother, the worst I've ever had, I apologize, Ivan, there was I thinking . . . Heh-heh-heh!' He paused. A long, drunken, semi-vacant, grin drew his face apart. And then suddenly at that very instant a terrible clamour and thunder resounded in the passage, violent shouts were heard, the door flew open wide and into the reception room stormed Dmitry Fyodorovich. The old man threw himself towards Ivan in fear:

'He'll kill me, he'll kill me! Protect me, protect me!' he howled, clinging to the skirts of Ivan Fyodorovich's coat.

9

Voluptuaries

IMMEDIATELY after Dmitry Fyodorovich, Grigory and Smerdyakov came running into the reception room. They had already engaged in a tussle with him out in the passage in their attempts to keep him from entering (following an instruction issued by Fyodor Pavlovich himself a few days earlier). Availing himself of the fact that, upon bursting into the reception room, Dmitry Fyodorovich had paused for a moment in order to look around, Grigory swiftly circumnavigated the table, closed both halves of the double doors on the opposite side of the room that led through to the inner chambers, and stood before the barred doorway, both arms spread apart in a cross and ready to defend the entrance, as it were, to the last drop. Seeing this, Dmitry gave a sound that was more like a yelp than a shriek, and threw himself at Grigory.

'So she's in there! They've got her hidden in there! Away, scoundrel!' He tried to jerk Grigory aside, but the latter shoved him backwards. Out of himself with rage, Dmitry swung his arm and struck Grigory with all his might. The old man collapsed as though the legs had been cut from under him, and Dmitry, leaping over him, burst through the door. Smerdyakov remained in the reception room, at its opposite end, pale and quivering, pressing himself close to Fyodor Pavlovich.

'She's here!' Dmitry Fyodorovich shouted. 'I saw her myself, turning towards the house just now, only I couldn't catch up with her. Where is she? Where is she?'

This cry of: 'She's here!' produced an unfathomable effect upon Fyodor Pavlovich. All his fear vanished.

'Stop him, stop him!' he howled, rushing off in pursuit of Dmitry Fyodorovich. Grigory had meanwhile picked himself up off the floor, but he still seemed almost beside himself. Ivan Fyodorovich and Alyosha ran off to catch up their father. From the inner room came the sound of something falling to the floor, breaking and smashing: it was a large glass vase (not an expensive one) on a marble pedestal which Dmitry Fyodorovich had knocked against as he ran past.

'Run him to ground, fell him!' the old man howled. 'To my assistance!'

Ivan Fyodorovich and Alyosha finally managed to catch up with the old man and made him go back to the reception room by force.

'What are you up to, hounding after him like that? He will quite simply kill you!' Ivan Fyodorovich shouted at his father, wrathfully.

'Vanechka, Lyoshechka, she must be here, Grushenka's here, he says he saw her running through . . .'

He was choking for breath. He had not been expecting Grushenka on this occasion, and the sudden news that she was here instantly sent him out of his mind. He quivered all over, he almost went insane.

'But I mean, you have the evidence of your own eyes to prove that she has not been here!' shouted Ivan.

'What if she came in the back door?'

'But the back door is locked, and you have the key . . .'

Dmitry suddenly appeared back in the reception room. He had, of course, found the back door locked, and the key to the locked door was indeed in Fyodor Pavlovich's pocket. All the windows in each room were also locked; so there was nowhere that Grushenka could have got in, and nowhere she could have got out, either.

'Stop him!' Fyodor Pavlovich began to squeal, as soon as he caught sight of Dmitry again. 'He's stolen the money I had there in the bedroom!' And, tearing himself away from Ivan, he again lunged at Dmitry. The latter, however, raised both arms and suddenly grabbed the old man by the two last remaining matted locks of hair that grew at his temples, gave them a violent tug and sent him crashing to the floor. After that he struck the recumbent man two or three times about the face with his heel. The old fellow began a shrill and penetrating groan. Though he was not as strong as his brother Dmitry, Ivan Fyodorovich hurled both his arms about the latter and tore him away from the old man as hard as he could. Alyosha also helped him with all the meagre quantity of strength at his disposal, ringing his brother round with his arms from in front.

'You madman, why, you have killed him!' shouted Ivan.

'It's what he deserves!' Dmitry exclaimed, panting. 'And if I haven't, I'll come back again and do it another time. You won't be able to stop me.'

'Dmitry! You must go immediately – leave!' Alyosha shrieked imperiously.

'Aleksey! You alone shall tell me, you alone will I believe: was she here just now or wasn't she? I myself saw her coming out of the lane, slipping past the wicker fence and making in this direction. I shouted to her, but she ran away . . .'

'I swear to you, she hasn't been here, and no one here is expecting her!'

'But I saw her . . . That means she's . . . I'll find out presently where she is . . . Goodbye, Aleksey! Not a word to Aesop about the money now, you must go straight to Katerina Ivanovna this instant and tell her: "He asks me to bow to you, bow to you, bow to you! That's all – just to bow, and to bow farewell!" Describe the scene to her.'

In the meantime Ivan and Grigory had lifted up the old man and had sat him down in the armchair. His face was bloody, but he was conscious and he listened avidly to Dmitry's shouting. He still thought Grushenka really was somewhere in the house. On leaving, Dmitry Fyodorovich gave him a glance of hatred.

'I have no remorse about your blood!' he exclaimed. 'Beware, old man, look out for your dream, because I too have a dream! I place my curse on you and renounce you entirely . . .'

Then he ran from the room.

'She's here, she must be here! Smerdyakov, Smerdyakov,' the old man gasped hoarsely and almost inaudibly, beckoning to Smerdyakov with his little finger.

'She isn't here, I tell you, you crazy old man,' Ivan shouted at him, maliciously. 'Well, now he's passed out. Bring some water and a towel! Look lively, Smerdyakov!'

Smerdyakov went rushing off to fetch water. At last they managed to undress the old man, carry him into the bedroom and put him to bed. They bound his head in a wet towel. Enfeebled by cognac, violent emotion and physical blows he instantly, as soon as his head touched the pillow, closed his eyes and sank into oblivion. Ivan Fyodorovich and Alyosha went back to the reception room. Smerdyakov removed the fragments of shattered vase, and Grigory stood by the table, his eyes blackly lowered.

'Why don't you wet your head and lie down, too?' Alyosha said to Grigory. 'We shall look after him here; that was a horrible punch my brother gave you . . . on the head.'

'He dursed me!'* Grigory said blackly and distinctly.

'He "dursed" father, too, never mind about you!' Ivan Fyodorovich observed, twisting his mouth.

'I used to wash him in the trough . . . He dursed me!' Grigory said again.

'The devil take it, if I hadn't wrenched him away I think he'd have killed him, too. It wouldn't take much to put paid to Aesop, would it?' Ivan Fyodorovich whispered to Alyosha.

'May the Lord forbid!' Alyosha exclaimed.

'Why "forbid"?' Ivan continued in the same whisper, twisting his features in malice. 'One vile reptile may consume the other, and good riddance to them both.'

Alyosha gave a startled shudder.

'Oh don't worry, I shan't allow a murder to take place, any more than I did just now. You stay here, Alyosha; I'm going out for a stroll in the yard, my head is starting to ache.'

Alyosha went into his father's bedroom and sat by the head of the bed behind the screen for about an hour. The old man suddenly opened his eyes and looked at Alyosha for a long time without saying anything, apparently recalling and reflecting. Suddenly an uncommon agitation displayed itself in his features.

'Alyosha,' he began to whisper, cautiously, 'where is Ivan?'

'In the yard, he's got a headache. He's watching us.'

'Give me that mirror, look, that one over there, give it to me!'

Alyosha gave him the small, round, folding hand-mirror that stood on the chest of drawers. The old man glanced at himself in it: his nose had swollen up rather badly, and on his forehead above his left eyebrow there was a sizeable purple bruise.

'What is Ivan saying? Alyosha, my dear, my only son, I am scared of Ivan; I'm more scared of Ivan than I am of the other one. You are the only one I'm not scared of.'

'You shouldn't be afraid of Ivan, either. Ivan is angry, but he will protect you.'

'Yes, Alyosha, but what about the other one? Dear angel, speak the truth: was Grushenka here earlier or was she not?'

'No one has set eyes on her. It's an illusion, she hasn't been here!'

'But Mitka wants to marry her, marry her!'

'She won't take him as a husband.'

'She won't, won't, won't, not for anything will she!' the old man exclaimed, starting wide awake in delight, as though at that moment he could have heard no more joyous news. In ecstasy he grabbed hold of Alyosha's hand and firmly pressed it to his own heart. Tears had even begun to shine in his eyes. 'Look, that little icon, the one of the Mother of God I told you about before, I want you to take it, take it away with you. And I give you permission to go back to the monastery . . . I was joking earlier, please don't be angry. Alyosha, my head hurts . . . Lyosha, soothe my heart, be my angel, speak the truth!'

'Are you still trying to find out if she was here or not?' Alyosha said sadly.

'No, no, no, I believe you, but listen: go and see Grushenka yourself or arrange to meet her somehow; ask her soon, as soon as possible, use your eyes and make a guess which of us she wants to marry: me or him? Ah? Well? Can you do it or can't you?'

'If I see her I shall ask her,' Alyosha muttered in embarrassment.

'No, she won't tell you,' the old man broke in. 'She's a butterfly. She'll start kissing you and saying she wants to marry you. She's a deceiver, she's a shameless hussy, no, it's out of the question for you to go and see her, out of the question!'

'And anyway, pater, it would be wrong, it would be altogether wrong.'

'Where was it he was sending you just now, when he shouted "Go and see her" as he was running off?'

'He was sending me to Katerina Ivanovna.'

'For money? In order to ask for money?'

'No, not for that.'

'He hasn't got any money. Not a single drop. Listen, Alyosha, I'll sleep on it and think it over, and in the meantime off you go. Perhaps you may even meet her . . . Only you must come and see me tomorrow morning without fail; without fail. There's a certain little thing I have to tell you tomorrow; will you come?'

'Yes, I will.'

'If you come, make it look as though it's your own idea, as though you've come on a visit. Don't say to anyone that I told you to come. Don't say a word to Ivan.'

'Very well.'

'Goodbye, angel; just now you interceded on my behalf, I won't forget it, ever. Tomorrow I shall tell you a certain little thing . . . only first I must think a bit more . . .'

'And how are you feeling now?'

'Oh, tomorrow, tomorrow I shall be up and about, I shall be as right as rain, as right as rain, as right as rain! . . .'

As he was crossing the yard, Alyosha encountered brother Ivan on a bench by the gates: the latter was writing something in his notebook with a pencil. Alyosha conveyed to Ivan the news that the old man had woken up and was conscious, and that he had allowed him to go back to the monastery for the night.

'Alyosha, I'd be very happy if I could meet with you tomorrow morning,' Ivan said in a friendly tone, getting up – it was a friendliness that took Alyosha quite by surprise.

'I'm going to see the Khokhlakovas tomorrow,' Alyosha replied. 'I may also go and see Katerina Ivanovna tomorrow, if I don't find her in now . . .'

'Off to Katerina Ivanovna's in spite of everything, eh? Is it to do with that "bow to her, bow to her" business?' Ivan smiled, suddenly. Alyosha was embarrassed.

'I think I grasped it all from what he was shouting, and from one or two of the other things that happened. I expect Dmitry has asked you to go and see her and tell her that he . . . well . . . well, to put it briefly, "bows to her"?'

'Brother! Where is all this horror between father and Dmitry going to end?' Alyosha exclaimed.

'It's hard to be sure. Nowhere, probably: the whole thing may run out of steam. That woman is a wild beast. At any event, the old man must be kept in the house, and Dmitry must not be let in.'

'Brother, allow me to ask you something else: does any man really have the right to determine, just by looking at other people, which of them is worthy of living and which is unworthy?'

'Why introduce a test of worthiness into it? That question is more often than not decided in the hearts of men not at all on grounds of worthiness, but in connection with quite different causes, which are, moreover, far more natural. And as for the question of right – who does not possess the right to desire?'

'Surely not the death of another person?'

'Yes, even that. Why should one lie to oneself, when all men live like that and are probably unable to live in any other way? I suppose you're asking this in connection with my earlier remark about one vile reptile eating another? In that case, permit me to ask you: do you consider me too, like Dmitry, capable of shedding the blood of Aesop, well, and of killing him, eh?'

'What's got into you, Ivan? Never was there anything like that in my thoughts! Not even Dmitry do I consider . . .'

'Thank you for that, anyway,' Ivan smiled, ironically. 'Be assured that I shall always defend him. But where my desires are concerned, in the given instance I leave myself ample latitude. Goodbye until tomorrow. Don't condemn me, and don't look on me as an evil-doer,' he added with a smile.

They shook hands firmly, as never before. Alyosha sensed that his brother had acted first in taking a step towards him and that he had done this for some reason, quite certainly with some intention.

10

The Twain Together

ALYOSHA emerged from his father's house in a humour that was even more jaded and depressed than it had been earlier, when he had gone in. His mind was also as if fragmented and disconnected, while at the same time he felt afraid to connect the fragments together and draw the general conclusion from all the tormenting opposites he had experienced that day. It was almost something bordering on despair, an emotion previously foreign to Alyosha's heart. Above it all loomed, like a mountain, the central, fatal and unresolvable question of how his father and brother Dmitry would settle their differences with respect to this formidable woman. Now he himself was a witness. He himself had been present and seen them confront each other. As a matter of fact, it was only brother Dmitry who was likely to end up unhappy, wholly and horribly unhappy: a manifest calamity awaited him. There were also other people who were concerned in all this, concerned, perhaps, to a far greater degree than Alyosha had ever perceived before. There was even starting to be an element of mystery about it. Brother Ivan had taken towards him the step that Alyosha had long wished he would take, and yet now for some reason he felt scared by this step of *rapprochement*. And those women? It was a strange thing: a short time earlier he had set off for Katerina Ivanovna's in a state of extreme embarrassment, yet now he felt no such confusion; on the contrary, he was actually hurrying to get there, as though he expected to receive guidance from her. It would, however, obviously be more difficult to discharge his errand now than would have been the case earlier: the question of the three thousand had been finally resolved, and brother Dmitry, now feeling himself bereft of honour and without the slightest hope, would of course not stop at any degradation. What was more, he had instructed him to tell Katerina Ivanovna about the scene that had taken place at their father's house.

It was already seven o'clock and growing dark when Alyosha guided his steps towards Katerina Ivanovna, who occupied a certain very spacious and comfortable house on Main Street. Alyosha knew that she lived with two aunts. As a matter of fact, one of them was only the aunt of her sister Agafya Ivanovna; she was that unmurmuring person in the house of Katerina Ivanovna's father who had looked after Katerina and her sister when she had arrived there from her institute. As for the other aunt, she was a 'refined' and stately Moscow lady, though of the impoverished variety. Rumour had it that they both bowed to Katerina Ivanovna in everything and that their presence in her household was maintained exclusively for the sake of social etiquette. As for Katerina Ivanovna, she bowed only to her benefactress, the general's widow, who had remained in Moscow on account of her illness, and to whom she was twice a week duty bound to send a letter, containing a detailed bulletin of her activities.

When Alyosha entered the hallway and asked the housemaid who opened the door to announce his presence, it was plain that in the reception room his arrival was already known (he had, perhaps, been observed from the window), for he instantly heard a kind of commotion, the sound of skittering female footsteps and swishing dresses: two or three women had apparently come running out. Alyosha found it strange that he should by his arrival produce such excitement. He was, however, immediately conducted to the reception room. It was a large room, appointed with elegant and abundant furniture, not at all in the provincial manner. There was any number of sofas, couches and *chaises-longues*, of tables great and small; pictures hung upon the walls, vases and lamps stood on the tables, there was a multitude of flowers, and by the window even an aquarium. The twilight had made the room a little on the dark side. On one of the divans, where evidently ladies had just now been seated, Alyosha could discern a silken mantilla cape that had been cast aside, and on the table in front of the sofa two unfinished cups of chocolate, sponge cakes, a crystal plate of blue raisins and another of sweets. Guests were evidently being entertained. Alyosha realized that he had arrived during a social visit, and frowned. But at that very instant the door-curtain was raised and Katerina Ivanovna entered with swift, hurried steps, smiling a joyful, enravished smile, and stretching out both arms towards Alyosha. At that same moment a serving-maid brought in and placed upon the table two lighted candles.

'Thank God, at last you are here! All day I have prayed to Him only for you! Sit down.'

Katerina Ivanovna's beauty had already made a striking impression on Alyosha when, some three weeks earlier, brother Dmitry had brought him to her for the first time to be presented and introduced, at her own most pressing request. The conversation between them had not at that meeting, however, taken hold. On the supposition that Alyosha was simply very embarrassed, Katerina Ivanovna had, as it were, taken pity on him and had spent most of the time on that occasion talking to Dmitry Fyodorovich. Alyosha had kept silent, but discerned a great many things with great clarity. He had been struck by the imperiousness, the proud pertness, the self-assurance of this haughty girl. And all these qualities were beyond any doubt. Alyosha felt that he was not overestimating them. He found her large black burning eyes magnificent and thought they went particularly well with her pale, even slightly pale-yellow, oval face. But in those eyes, just as in the outline of her delightful lips, there was something that, though his brother might fall powerfully in love with it, could not be the object of such love for long. He almost spoke this thought out loud to Dmitry when the latter, after the visit, began pestering him and beseeching him to make no secret of the impression he had received from his first sight of the bride-to-be.

'You'll be happy with her, but perhaps . . . it won't be a very tranquil sort of happiness.'

'You're right there, brother; women like that don't change, they're never reconciled to fortune. So you don't think I'll love her for ever, do you?'

'No, it may be that you will, but you may not always be happy with her . . .'

At the time, Alyosha had uttered his opinion blushing and vexed at the fact that, having yielded to his brother's implorings, he had delivered himself of such 'stupid' thoughts. Because, no sooner had he uttered it than this opinion of his seemed to him quite dreadfully stupid. What was worse, he even began to feel shame at having expressed himself in such categorical terms about a woman. It was, therefore, with all the greater amazement that he sensed now at first sight of the approaching Katerina Ivanovna that he might on that earlier occasion have been thoroughly mistaken. This time her features radiated an unfeigned, straightforward goodness of disposition, a direct and ardent sincerity. Of all her earlier 'pride and haughtiness', which had made such an impression on Alyosha at the time, there was now visible only a bold, well-bred energy and a kind of serene and pillar-strong faith in herself. From his first glance at her, from the first word she spoke, Alyosha understood that the entire tragic nature of her situation in respect of the person she so loved was by no means a secret to her, and that it was indeed possible that she knew everything, decidedly everything. And yet, in spite of that, there was so much radiance in her features, so much confidence in the future. Alyosha suddenly felt that against her he had committed a serious and deliberate wrong. He was at once defeated and attracted. In addition to all this, he observed from her very first words that she was in a kind of violent agitation, one that was possibly most uncharacteristic in her – an agitation that was almost like ecstasy.

'I've been waiting and waiting for you, because it's from you that I can find out the whole truth – and from no one else!'

'I came . . .' Alyosha muttered, growing confused, 'I . . . He sent me . . .'

'Ah, he sent you, well, it is just as I thought. Now I know it all, all of it!' Katerina Ivanovna exclaimed, her eyes suddenly beginning to flash. 'Before you go any further, Aleksey Fyodorovich, I want to tell you why I have awaited your arrival with such eagerness. You see it is possible that I know far more than even you yourself do; it isn't news that I require from you. Rather, it is this: I need to know your own, personal and most recent opinion of him, I want you to tell me in the most direct, unadorned, even crude manner (oh, you may be as crude as you like!) — how you yourself view him just now and how you view his situation after your meeting with him today? That may perhaps be better than if I, whom he no longer wishes to visit, were to go and have the matter out with him in person. Have you understood what it is I want from you? Now why has he sent you to me? (I knew he would do it!) Tell me simply, tell me every last word of it!'

'He told me to . . . bow to you, and to say that he'll never come to see you again . . . but to bow to you.'

'Bow to me? Is that what he said, are those the words he used?'

'Yes.'

'Perhaps he made a slip and used the wrong phrase, a word he didn't intend?'

'No, he told me specifically to use that expression: "bow to you". He said it about three times, so I wouldn't forget.'

Katerina Ivanovna flared crimson.

'You must help me now, Aleksey Fyodorovich, for it is now that I require your assistance: I shall tell you the thought that is in my mind, and you shall simply tell me whether it's correct or not. Look: if he merely asked you to bow to me in passing, without insisting on the way it was phrased, without laying special emphasis on any of the words, that would be that . . . There would be an end of it! But if he insisted on that particular word, if he particularly requested you not to forget to convey to me that *bow* — then he must have been agitated, beside himself, perhaps! He had taken his resolve and panicked at it. He had left me not with a firm step, but as though he had fallen off a precipice. His emphasis on that word may merely be a sign of bravado . . .'

'That's right, that's right!' Alyosha confirmed, heatedly. 'That's the way I too see it now.'

'And if that is so, then he is not entirely ruined! He is simply in despair, but I may yet be able to save him. Just a moment: didn't he say anything to you about money, about three thousand?'

'Not only did he say it, but that was the thing that was making him more miserable than anything else. He said that now he was stripped of his honour and that nothing made any difference any more,' Alyosha replied with fervour, sensing with all his heart the hope that was returning to his heart, the hope that there really was perhaps a way out and a salvation for his brother. 'But how is it you . . . know about that money?' he added, and suddenly cut himself short.

'I have long known about it, and I know the truth. I sent a telegram inquiry to Moscow, and I have long known that the money did not come. He did not send the money, but I kept silent. Last week I discovered that he still needed money . . . In all this I have had only one object: that he should know to whom he can turn, and who his most faithful friend is. No, he does not want to believe that I am his most faithful friend, he will not recognize me, views me only as a woman. All week I've been racked by a terrible worry: what can I do to protect him from the shame he will feel when he knows I've found out about his having spent the three thousand? That is to say, I don't mind if he's ashamed about other people knowing, or if he's ashamed of himself, just as long as he's not ashamed with regard to me. After all, he tells it all to God without shame. Then why does he still to this day not realize how much I will tolerate for his sake? Why, why does he not know me, how can he dare not know me after all that has happened? I want to save him for ever. I don't mind if he forgets me as his bride! Yet here he is, afraid for his honour in my regard! I mean, he was not too afraid to unburden himself to you, Aleksey Fyodorovich, was he? So why have I still not deserved the same treatment?'

These last words were spoken in tears; the tears spurted from her eyes.

'I have to tell you,' Alyosha said, also in an unsteady voice, 'what happened just now with him and father.' And he related the entire scene, related how he had been sent for the money, how Dmitry had stormed in, beaten his father and then yet again repeated his particular and insistent request to him, Alyosha, that he should go and 'bow to her'. 'He went off to see that woman . . .' Alyosha added, quietly.

'And you think I won't tolerate that woman? Does he think I won't? But he won't marry her,' she said suddenly with a nervous laugh. 'A Karamazov would never burn with a passion like that for the rest of his days. It's a passion, not love. He won't marry, because she won't take him as a husband . . .' Katerina said again with a strange, mocking smile.

'I think he may,' Alyosha said sadly, lowering his eyes.

'He won't, I tell you. That girl's an angel, do you realize that? Do you?' Katerina Ivanovna suddenly exclaimed with uncommon fervour. 'She's the most fantastical of fantastical beings! I know how seductive she is, but I know too how kind, firm and noble she is. Why are you looking at me like that, Aleksey Fyodorovich. Does what I say surprise you, do you not believe me? Agrafena Aleksandrovna, my angel!' she suddenly cried to someone, looking into the adjoining room. 'Come in and see us, this is a dear, sweet man, this is Alyosha, he knows all about our concerns, come in and show yourself to him!'

'Oh, I was just waiting behind the curtain for you to call me,' a soft, even slightly sugary female voice pronounced.

The door-curtain lifted, and ... Grushenka herself, laughing and rejoicing, came over to the table. Something inside Alyosha gave a kind of flinch. He rooted his gaze on her, was unable to turn away his eyes. Here she was, that formidable woman – the 'wild beast', to use the epithet that half an hour earlier had escaped the lips of brother Ivan. And yet, before him stood, or so it seemed to the gaze, at any rate, a most ordinary and straightforward creature – a decent, charming woman, attractive, perhaps, but so similar to all other attractive but 'ordinary' women! To be sure, she was pretty, exceedingly so, even – a Russian beauty, of the type that is beloved of so many. She was a woman rather tall of stature – somewhat shorter, however, than Katerina Ivanovna (who was truly tall) – buxom, with body movements that were almost inaudible, as though they had also been pampered to some special, sugary manufacture, like her voice. She made her approach with a step that was quite unlike Katerina Ivanovna's brisk and powerful one; it was, on the contrary, inaudible. Her feet could not be heard at all against the floor. Softly she lowered herself into an armchair, softly she rustled her sumptuous black silk dress, pampering her buxom, white-as-foam neck and broad shoulders in a black woollen shawl. She was twenty-two years old, and her face expressed that age precisely. It was a very white face, with a high, pale-pink nuance of colouring. The outline of her features was almost too broad, and her lower jaw even jutted slightly forward. Her upper lip was thin and delicate, while her lower, which protruded a little, was twice as plump and almost swollen-looking. But her most wonderful, most abundant chestnut-coloured hair, her dark sable eyebrows and delightful blue-grey eyes with long eyelashes would unquestionably have compelled the most indifferent and preoccupied individual, even in a crowd somewhere, while out for a walk, amidst the crush, suddenly to stop before this face and long remember it. What made the strongest impression on Alyosha in this face was its child-like, ingenuous expression. Her gaze was like that of a child, she took happiness in things like a child, namely in the way she had come over to the table 'rejoicing' and as if she were expecting something with the most childish, impatient and trustful curiosity. Her gaze enlivened the soul – Alyosha could feel that. There was also something else in her, something he could not or would not fix with any certainty, but which had possibly suggested itself to him unconsciously, namely again that softness and gentleness of her body movements, their feline inaudibility. And yet this body was a powerful and generous one. Under the shawl one could guess at her broad, buxom shoulders, her high, still quite youthful breasts. This body held out the promise, perhaps, of a Venus de Milo's form, though by now unavoidably in somewhat exaggerated proportions – this was something that could already be anticipated. The connoisseurs of Russian female beauty could have predicted without error, just by looking at Grushenka, that this fresh, still youthful beauty would by the time she was thirty have lost its harmony and run to fat, that even her face would have grown fat and flabby, that very quickly small wrinkles would appear near her eyes and on her forehead, the complexion of her face coarsened, turned purple, perhaps – that this, in a word, was the beauty of a moment, a transient beauty of a kind that is so frequently encountered in the Russian woman. Alyosha was not, of course, thinking about this, but even though capti-vated, he found himself wondering with an unpleasant sensation that was almost one of regret: why does she draw out her words like that and why can't she speak naturally? It was plain that she did it because she found beauty in this lengthening and artificially sugary emphasis of the syllables and sounds she uttered. This was, of course, merely a bad habit of *mauvais ton*, one that bore witness to an inferior upbringing, a conception of propriety vulgarly acquired in childhood. And yet, this intonation and way of speaking struck Alyosha as an almost outrageous contradiction of that childishly joyful and simple-souled facial expression, that quiet, happy shining of her eyes, such as one might behold in a young babe! Within the space of an instant Katerina Ivanovna had sat her down in an armchair opposite Alyosha and kissed her with ecstasy several times upon her laughing lips. It was as though she were in love with her.

'We are meeting for the first time, Aleksey Fyodorovich,' she said in ecstasy. 'I wanted to get to know her, to see what she looked like, I had intended to go and visit her, but she came to see me at my first request. I had a feeling that we should sort it all out between us, she and I! My heart had a premonition of it . . . I was implored not to take this step, but I had a premonition of the outcome and I wasn't wrong. Grushenka has explained it all to me, all her intentions; like a good angel she has flown to my side and brought me tranquillity and joy . . .'

'You have not disdained me, dear and worthy young mistress,' Grush-enka said drawlingly in a voice that rose and fell, still with the same sweet, joyful smile.

'Do not even dare to say such words to me, you charmer, you en-chantress! How could I possibly disdain you? Look, I shall kiss your lower lip yet again. It looks as though it has swollen, so here is something to make it yet more swollen, and yet more, yet more . . . Look at the way she laughs, Aleksey Fyodorovich, the heart is enlivened at the sight of this angel . . .' Alyosha blushed and shook with a slight, imperceptible tremor.

'You spoil me, dear young mistress, but I may not be at all worthy of your tenderness.'

'Not worthy! She, not worthy!' Katerina Ivanovna exclaimed again with the same fervour. 'I think you ought to know, Aleksey Fyodorovich, that we are a fantastical little head, that we are a wilful but proud-as-proud little heart! We are noble, Aleksey Fyodorovich, we are magnanimous, do you know that? We have merely been unfortunate. We have been too quick to make all kinds of sacrifices to a man who is perhaps not worthy of them, or is frivolous. There was a certain man, an officer, too, and we gave him everything – this was a long time ago, five years back – and he forgot us and took a wife instead. Now he is a widower, he wrote us a letter, he is coming here – and you see, it is him alone, him alone that we love to this day and have loved all our life! When he gets here, Grushenka will be happy again, for all these five years she's been miserable. But who will reproach her, who can boast of her favour? Only that crippled old man, the merchant – but he has been more like her father, her friend, her guardian. At the time, he found her in despair, in torment, abandoned by the man she had so loved . . . I mean, she was going to drown herself, and that old man saved her, saved her!'

'So much do you say to defend me, dear young mistress, and such haste do you make with it all,' Grushenka drawled again.

'Defend? Is it for us to defend you, oh, how could we possibly dare? Grushenka, angel, give me your dear little hand; look at this plump, delightful little hand, Aleksey Fyodorovich. Do you see it? It has brought me happiness and brought me back to life, and now I shall kiss it, back and palm, there, there and there!' And three times, in near-ecstasy, she kissed the indeed delightful and possibly even too plump hand of Grushenka. The latter, meanwhile, watched her 'dear young mistress' with a nervous, resonant little laugh, and it was plain that she liked having her hand kissed in this fashion. 'Maybe there's just a bit too much of this ecstatic emotion,' flickered through Alyosha's head. He blushed. His heart all this time was somehow peculiarly uneasy.

'Why, do not shame me, dear young mistress, by kissing my hand so while Aleksey Fyodorovich is here.'

'You think I wanted to shame you by it?' said Katerina Ivanovna in some surprise. 'Oh, my dear, how little you understand me!'

'Well, it may be that you do not understand me quite, neither, dear young mistress, I may be far worse than you suppose. I have an evil heart, I am wilful. I ensnared Dmitry Fyodorovich, poor man, just because he mocked at me once upon a certain time.'

'But why, now you shall save him. You've given your word. You shall bring him to reason, you shall reveal to him that you love another, have long done so, and that this other now offers you his hand . . .'

'Oh no, I never gave you any such word. You yourself said all those things to me, but I never gave you any word.'

'Then I must not have understood you aright,' Katerina Ivanovna said quietly and almost with a tinge of pallor. 'You promised . . .'

'Oh no, young angel mistress, nothing did I promise you,' quietly and evenly, still with the same lively-spirited and innocent expression, Grushenka interrupted. 'Look, you can see even now, worthy young mistress, what a nasty, capricious creature I am beside yourself. Whatever I want to do, I do. Maybe I did promise you something back earlier, but you see, now I'm suddenly thinking again that I fancy him after all, that Mitya: I mean, there was one time when I fancied him a lot, nearly for a whole hour. So you see, perhaps I'll go and tell him now that he should stay with me from this day hence . . . That's the kind of fickle one I am . . .'

'That is not at all . . . what you were saying earlier . . .' Katerina Ivanovna barely managed to get out.

'Oh, earlier! But you see, I'm soft at heart, and stupid. I mean, just think what he's put up with because of me! And what if I go home and suddenly start feeling for him – then what?'

'I had no idea . . .'

'Oh, young mistress, how good and noble you are beside the likes of me. Well, now you will soon fall out of love with me, silly fool that I am, when you get to know my stubborn nature. Give me your dear little hand, young angel mistress,' she asked tenderly, and almost with reverence she took the hand of Katerina Ivanovna. 'Look, dear young mistress, I take your hand and kiss it as you kissed mine. You kissed me three times, and I'd need to kiss you three hundred times to draw even with you for it. But so it must be, and then let God's will be done, and it may come to pass that I'll be your total slave and wish to serve you slavishly in all things. As God disposes, so let it be, without any pacts or promises between us. Your hand, your dear little hand, your hand! Dear young mistress, my outrageous beauty!'

She quietly brought the 'dear little hand' to her lips, though to be sure with the strangest of purposes: to 'draw even' in terms of kisses. Katerina Ivanovna did not remove her hand: she had heard out in timid hope the latter, rather strangely expressed promise of Grushenka to 'slavishly' serve her in all things; she was staring intently into her eyes: in those eyes she saw the same ingenuous, trustful expression, the same serene, lively spirits ... 'Perhaps she's just very naïve!' flashed with hope through Katerina Ivanovna's heart. Grushenka, meanwhile, almost in ecstasy over the 'dear little hand', was slowly raising it to her lips. But right by her lips she suddenly held the hand there for two or three instants of time, as though she were reflecting on something.

'You know, young angel mistress,' she suddenly drawled in the most tender and sugary voice, 'you know, I think I shall just take your hand, and not kiss it.' And she broke into a little gleeful laugh.

'As you wish ... What's got into you?' Katerina Ivanovna suddenly said, with a start.

'Well, that way you shall remember that while you kissed my hand, I did not kiss yours.' Something in her eyes suddenly flashed. She stared at Katerina Ivanovna with horrible fixity.

'Brazen hussy!' Katerina Ivanovna said without warning, as though she had suddenly understood something; she flared scarlet and leapt up from her seat. Unhurriedly, Grushenka also got up.

'That's what I shall tell Mitya when he gets here – that you kissed my hand, but I kissed yours not at all. And oh, how he will laugh!'

'Dirty vixen, out!'

'Oh, how shameful, young mistress, oh, how shameful, 'tis not decent for you to say such things, dear young mistress.'

'Out, brute venal creature!' Katerina Ivanovna began to howl. Every feature of her utterly contorted face was a-quiver.

'Oh, so it's venal now, is it? You yourself used to go and sell your charms to the young gallants in the twilight for money when you were a young girl, why, I know you did.'

Katerina Ivanovna gave a scream and was on the point of throwing herself upon her, but Alyosha held her back with all his might:

'Don't move! Don't speak! Don't say anything, don't give her any reply – she's going, she'll be gone in a moment!'

At the sound of this hue and cry, into the room at that instant rushed both Katerina Ivanovna's two female kinsfolk, followed by the housemaid. They all dashed towards her.

'Yes, I am going,' Grushenka said, snatching up her mantilla from the sofa. 'Alyosha, please come with me, dear.'

'You must go now, go quickly!' Alyosha implored her, putting his hands together.

'Dear sweet Alyosha, come with me! I've a certain pretty, pretty little word to tell you on the way! Sweet Alyosha, it was for you I made this scene. Come with me, darling, you shall not regret it.'

Alyosha turned away, wringing his hands. Grushenka, laughing her resonant laugh, ran out of the house.

Katerina Ivanovna had succumbed to a fit. She was sobbing, and spasms were choking her. Everyone was fussing around her.

'I told you this would happen,' the elder of the aunts was saying. 'I tried to keep you from taking this step . . . you are too hot-headed . . . How could you bring yourself to take such a step? You do not know these brute creatures, and of that one they say she is worse than any of them . . . No, you are too self-willed!'

'She's a tiger!' Katerina Ivanovna howled. 'Why did you stop me, Aleksey Fyodorovich? I'd have beaten her black and blue, black and blue!'

She was unable to control herself in Alyosha's presence, and possibly did not even wish to do so.

'What she needs is the lash, on the scaffold, dealt by the public executioner, in front of the mob! . . .'

Alyosha backed away towards the door.

'But good God!' Katerina Ivanovna shrieked suddenly, clutching her hands together. 'That man! That he could be so dishonourable, so inhuman! Why, he told that brute creature what happened there that fatal day, that eternally cursed, cursed day! "You used to go and sell your charms, dear young mistress!" She knows! Your brother is a scoundrel, Aleksey Fyodorovich!'

Alyosha had an urge to say something, but could not find a single word. His heart was being wrung with pain.

'You must go, Aleksey Fyodorovich! I feel ashamed, I feel terrible! Tomorrow . . . I implore you on my knees, come back tomorrow. Please do not condemn me – forgive me, or I know not what else I may do to myself!'

Alyosha emerged almost reeling into the street. He had just as much desire to weep as she. Suddenly a serving-maid caught him up.

'The mistress forgot to give you this little letter from Mrs Khokhlakova, it's been lying there ever since dinner.'

In mechanical fashion Alyosha accepted the small pink envelope and, almost without being conscious of it, put it in his pocket.

11

Yet One More Ruined Reputation

FROM the town to the monastery it was not more than slightly over a
verst. Alyosha quickly walked along the road, which was empty at this
hour. It had almost become night, at thirty paces it was already difficult
to make out objects. Halfway along there was a crossroad. At the
crossroads, under a lonely broom willow, an unknown figure came into
sight. No sooner had Alyosha stepped on to the crossroads than the
figure leapt up, rushed at him and in a frantic voice shouted:

'*La bourse ou la vie!*'*

'Oh, it's you, Mitya!' Alyosha said, but with a violent shudder of
surprise.

'Ha-ha-ha! Not expecting me? I wondered: where should I wait for
you? Near her house? There are three ways from there, and I might have
missed you. In the end I decided to wait here, because I thought, well,
he's bound to come past here, there's no other way to get to the
monastery. Very well then – tell me the truth, squash me like a cockroach
. . . But what's wrong?'

'It's nothing, brother . . . I was scared, that's all. Oh, Dmitry! The
sight of father's blood today,' Alyosha wept. He had long desired to
weep, and now it was as if something suddenly gave way within his soul.
'You nearly murdered him . . . you cursed him . . . and I mean here you
are now . . . at a time like this . . . making jokes . . . *La bourse ou la vie!*'

'Ha, what of it? You think it's not proper, eh? Not suited to the
occasion?'

'Well no . . . It's just that . . .'

'Wait. Take a look at the night: do you see what a dark one it is, do
you see those clouds, what a wind there is now! I hid in there under that
broom willow to wait for you, and thought (I swear to God I did!):
what's the point of suffering any more, what's the point of waiting?
Here's a broom willow, I've a handkerchief, I've a shirt, I can make a
rope from them right now, there are my suspenders, too, and – let me
not burden the earth any longer, let me not dishonour it by my base
presence! And then just now I heard you coming – O Lord, it was as
though something had swooped down on me all of a sudden from on
high: why, I thought, there is someone whom I love after all, and look,
here he is, here is that very same beloved person, my own dear brother

whom I love more than anyone else in the world and alone in the world! And so much did I love you, so much at that moment did I love you, that I thought: I shall this instant throw myself on his neck! And then a stupid thought came to me: "I shall liven him up, and give him a fright." And like a Tom-Fool I shouted: "*la bourse!*" Please forgive my tomfoolery – that was just rubbish, but in my soul there's still some decency . . . Well then, to the devil with it, but tell me, what was going on there? What did she say? Go on – squash me, strike me down, don't have any mercy! Did she fly into a fury?'

'No, nothing like that . . . There was nothing of that kind at all, Mitya. What happened just now was . . . that I found both of them there.'

'What do you mean, both of them?'

'Grushenka visiting Katerina Ivanovna.'

Dmitry Fyodorovich went rigid.

'Impossible!' he exclaimed. 'You're raving! Grushenka at her house?'

Alyosha related everything that had happened to him right from the moment he had gone into Katerina Ivanovna's house. He talked for some ten minutes, and though it could not be said that he did so flowingly or well, he managed none the less to give a clear account, catching the principal words and actions and vividly communicating, often by means of a single detail, his own feelings. Brother Dmitry listened without saying anything, his stare fixed with a terrible, motionless quality, but it was plain to Alyosha that he had already understood everything, had assessed the whole of the evidence. But the further the story progressed, the more his face acquired a look that was one less of gloom than of menace. He frowned, he clenched his teeth, his motionless gaze became somehow even more motionless, more fixed, more dreadful . . . It was for this reason all the more unexpected when suddenly, with unfathomable rapidity, his entire face, which until now had been angry and truculent, altered at once, his compressed lips parted and Dmitry Fyodorovich dissolved in the most uncontrollable, the most unfeigned laughter. He literally dissolved in laughter, for a long time could not even speak for laughing.

'She didn't kiss her hand! She didn't kiss it, but ran away!' he screamed out in a kind of morbid ecstasy – a brazen ecstasy, one might even have said, had that ecstasy not been so lacking in affectation. 'And the other one shouted, "She's a tiger!" So she is! That she ought to be taken to the scaffold? Yes, yes, she ought, she ought, my sentiments exactly, and it should have happened long ago! Yes, brother, very well, to the scaffold let it be, but first I must get over her. I understand the Empress of

Brazenry, the whole of her is there, the whole of her is expressed in that hand, the infernaless! She's the empress of all the infernalesses the mind could conjure on the earth! An ecstasy all of her own! And she ran off home? Right then, now I'll ... hah ... run off after her! Alyosha old chap, don't blame me, I mean, I agree that strangling's too good for her ...'

'And what about Katerina Ivanovna?' Alyosha exclaimed sadly.

'I can see her too, I can see right through her, and see her as never before! It's positively a discovery of the four cardinal points, or the five,* rather! This is that same little Katenka, the institute girl, who wasn't afraid to run for succour to an absurd boor of an officer on a generous impulse in order to save her father, at the risk of being horribly insulted! Oh, but our pride, our need to take risks, our challenge to fortune, our infinite challenge! You say it was her aunt who tried to stop her? That aunt, you know, is herself a tyrant; after all, she's the sister of that Moscow general's widow. She used to put on airs even more, but then her husband was convicted of state embezzlement, and lost everything, his estate, the lot, and his proud spouse suddenly lowered her voice and from that day hasn't raised it again. So she tried to restrain Katya, and Katya wouldn't obey. It's as if she were saying: "I can conquer everything, everything is subject to me; if I want, I can put even Grushenka under a spell" – and – you see, she had faith in herself, believed in her own swagger, and so who's guilty? Do you suppose that she kissed Grushenka's hand first with some special design, some cunning calculation? No, she really, really had fallen in love with Grushenka, or rather not with Grushenka but with her own dream, her own delirium – "because", it's as if she were saying, "it's *my* dream, *my* delirium!" Alyosha, dear boy, how did you manage to get free of them, of women like those? Did you run away, tucking up your cassock? Ha-ha-ha!'

'But brother, I don't think you realize what offence you caused Katerina Ivanovna by telling Grushenka about that day, for Grushenka immediately threw in her face the accusation that she'd "gone to sell your charms in stealth to the young gallants"! Brother, what could be more offensive than an insult like that?' What tormented Alyosha more than anything was the thought that his brother seemed glad about Katerina Ivanovna's degradation, though that, of course, could not be.

'Damn!' Dmitry Fyodorovich suddenly exclaimed, frowning horribly and striking his forehead with the palm of one hand. The realization had dawned on him only now, even though Alyosha had just told him about it all at one stroke, both the insult and Katerina Ivanovna's shriek of

'Your brother is a scoundrel!' 'Yes, perhaps I did indeed tell Grushenka about that "fatal day", as Katya puts it. Yes, I did, I told her, I remember doing it! It was that day at Mokroye, I was drunk, the gypsy girls were singing . . . But I mean I was sobbing and in tears, I was down on my knees, I was praying to Katya by all the icons, and Grushenka knew that. She knew everything that day, and I remember that she herself wept . . . Oh, to the devil with it! But could it be any different now from the way it is? That day she wept, but now . . . now "a dagger to the heart"! Such is woman's way.'

He lowered his eyes and pondered.

'Yes, I'm a scoundrel! An uncontestable scoundrel!' he pronounced suddenly in a black voice. 'It's all the same whether I wept or not, I'm still a scoundrel! Go there and say I accept the title, if that will make her feel any better. Well, that's enough – farewell now, what's the point of wasting any more words? There's no joy in it. You must take your road, and I must take mine. And I don't want to meet with you again, until what will possibly be the very last moment. Farewell, Aleksey!' He powerfully shook Alyosha's hand and, still with his eyes lowered, not raising his head, as though tearing himself free, began to stride rapidly off towards the town. Alyosha watched him go, incredulous that he should have left so utterly without warning.

'Wait, Aleksey – one more confession, to you alone!' Dmitry Fyodorovich said, suddenly coming back again. 'Look at me, take a good look at me: see, here, right here – a terrible infamy is in preparation.' (As he said the words 'right here', Dmitry Fyodorovich smote his chest with his fist, and with such a strange air that it appeared the infamy was kept and secreted right there on his breast, in some definite place, in his pocket perhaps, or strung round his neck.) 'You already know me: a scoundrel, a confessed scoundrel! But let me tell you that whatever I may have done in the past, may do now, or in the future – nothing, nothing can compare in vileness with the infamy which now, at this very moment I bear here upon my breast, see, here, here, which is active and accomplishing itself and of which I am the complete master, to prevent or accomplish, note that! And let me tell you also that I shall accomplish, not prevent it. I told you everything just now, but did not tell you that, because not even I had enough of a brazen brow to do that! I could still prevent myself from my action; in doing so, I could tomorrow restore an entire half portion of my lost honour, but I shall not do so, I shall accomplish the vile design, and may you be an advance witness to the fact that I say so with malice aforethought! Murk and catastrophe! There's no point in explaining, you'll find out soon enough. The stinking side-lane and the infernaless! Farewell. Don't pray for me, I'm not worthy of it, and in any case it's quite unnecessary, quite unnecessary . . . I have no need of it at all. Go on, be off with you!'

And he suddenly moved away, this time for good. Alyosha set off towards the monastery. 'How can it be, how can it be that I shall never see him again, what is he trying to say?' he thought in a wild imagining. 'Well, tomorrow I shall certainly see him, I'll seek him out, I'll make quite sure I seek him out, what on earth is he trying to say?'

The monastery he avoided altogether, passing directly through the pine woods to the hermitage. There the gate was opened to him, even though no one was normally admitted at that hour. His heart quivered as he entered the Elder's cell: why, why had he come out, why had the Elder sent him 'into the world'? Here there was quiet, here there was holiness, while out there all was confusion and murk in which one was instantly lost and went astray . . .

In the cell were the novice Porfiry and the hieromonach Father Paisy, who had looked in every hour of the day to learn the condition of Father Zosima who, as Alyosha learned with panic, was growing ever weaker. Even his usual evening conversation with the brethren could not take place on this occasion. Normally, every evening, after the service, and just before going to bed, the monastery's brethren would come thronging into the Elder's cell, and each would confess aloud to him his transgressions of the day, his sinful dreams, his thoughts, temptations, even quarrels if such had transpired. Some of them made confession on their knees. The Elder would settle, reconcile, admonish, impose penance, deliver his blessing and dismiss them. These brotherly 'confessions' were what the Elderhood's opponents had protested against, saying that they were a profanation of the confession as secret mystery, that they almost amounted to blasphemy, though they were nothing of the kind. Representation had even been made to the eparchial see that not only did confessions of this kind fail to achieve any good purpose, but were actually and inherently conducive to sin and temptation. It was said that many of the brethren found it burdensome to go to the Elder, but went willy-nilly, because all the others went, and they did not wish to be considered proud and rebellious in thought. It was related that some of the brethren, before setting off for the evening confession, used to make prior arrangements among themselves, of the type 'I shall say that you got angry with me this morning, and you shall back me up' – this in order to have something to say and so be free of the nuisance. Alyosha knew that this really did sometimes happen. He also knew that there were among the brethren those who were highly indignant at the fact that, as a matter of custom, even letters from members of the hermits' families were taken first to the Elder, who opened them and perused their contents before the recipients did. It was, of course, supposed that all this must occur freely and sincerely, wholeheartedly, in the name of voluntary contrition and saving grace, but in actual fact it sometimes turned out to be most insincere, and even false and deceitful. The more senior and experienced of the brethren, however, stuck to their principles, arguing that 'for those who have come within these walls sincerely in order to live the monkish life, for them all these vows of obedience and endurance will beyond doubt prove salutary and will bring them great advantage; those who, on the other hand, find them a burden and complain about them are not really monks at all and have come to the monastery in vain – the place of such is in the world. From sin and the Devil there is no hiding-place, however, not only in the world, but also in the monastery, and there is no point in indulging sin.'

'He is grown enfeebled, the somnolence is on him,' Father Paisy told Alyosha in a whisper, having blessed him. 'It is even hard to wake him up. But he should not be roused. He woke up for about five minutes, asked that his blessing be given to the brethren, and asked the brethren to mention him in their nocturnal prayers. He intends to take Communion again at early-morning service. He mentioned you, Aleksey, he asked if you had left, and they replied that you were in the town. "To that end did I give him my blessing; he belongs there, not here, for the present" – that was his utterance regarding you. He remembered you with love, with concern, have you any idea of what an honour that is? Only why is it that he has determined you should spend a period of time in the world? It can only mean that he has foreseen something in your destiny! I hope you realize, Aleksey, that if you do return to the world it must be as a kind of vow of obedience imposed upon you by your Elder, and not for the sake of vain frivolity and worldly amusement.'

Father Paisy made his exit. That the Elder was departing, of that Alyosha had no doubt, though he might still live on for a day or two. With fiery resolve Alyosha decided that – in spite of the promise he had given that he would see his father, the Khokhlakovas, his brother and Katerina Ivanovna – tomorrow he would not go out of the monastery at all and would stay with his Elder right up to the very end. His heart was a-fire with love, and he bitterly reproached himself for having even for a moment back there in the town forgotten the person he had left in the

monastery on his deathbed, the person whom he honoured more than anyone else in the world. He walked through into the Elder's small bedchamber, got down on his knees and prostrated himself before the sleeping
figure. The Elder was sleeping quietly, unmoving, his scarce breathing
even and almost imperceptible. His features were tranquil.

Going back into the other room – the same room in which the Elder
had received his visitors that morning – Alyosha, almost without undressing and removing only his boots, settled down on the small leather sofa,
hard and narrow, on which he always slept now and had long done so,
every night, with the addition only of a pillow. As for the mattress, about
which his father had shouted to him earlier, he had long ceased to use it.
Of his clothes, he took off only his cassock, covering himself with it in
lieu of a blanket. Before he slept, however, he threw himself to his knees
and spent a long time in prayer. In his burning prayers he did not ask
God to explain his confusion to him, but merely expressed a thirst for
tender delight, the delight of old, which always visited his soul after the
praise and glory to God of which his bedtime prayers usually consisted.
This joy, when it visited him, brought with it a light and tranquil sleep.
Praying even now, he suddenly felt in his pocket the small pink envelope
that Katerina Ivanovna's serving-maid had given him after she had caught
him up out in the street. He felt uneasy, but finished his prayers. Then
after some hesitation he opened the envelope. Inside it there was a letter
to him signed by *Lise* – the very same young daughter of Mrs Khokhlakova, who had so laughed at him that morning in the Elder's presence.

'Aleksey Fyodorovich,' she had written,

I am writing to you in secret, not even mamma is aware of it, and I know it is
wrong. But I shall not be able to go on living if I do not tell you what has
come into being within my heart, though apart from us two, no one must
know it as yet. But how am I to tell you what I so much want to tell you?
Paper, it is said, does not blush; I assure you that that is not so, and that it
blushes every bit as red as I myself am now, all over. Darling Alyosha, I love
you, I have loved you ever since we were children, in Moscow, when you
were quite different from how you are now, and I shall love you all my life. I
have singled you out with my heart in order to join with you in unison, and
so we may complete our lives together in old age. On condition, of course,
that you leave the monastery. As for our years, we shall wait for as long as
the law commands. By then I am bound to be well, and be up on my feet and
dancing.

You can see that I have given it all careful thought; yet there is one thing that I cannot imagine, and that is what you will think of me when you read this. I know I am always laughing and making mischief, I made you lose your temper earlier today, but I swear to you that a moment or two ago, before I picked up my pen, I said a prayer to the image of the Mother of God, and even now I am praying and very nearly weeping.

My secret is in your hands; tomorrow, when you come, I don't know how I shall be able to look at you. Oh, Aleksey Fyodorovich, what if I cannot restrain myself again, like a silly idiot, and begin laughing as I did this morning at the sight of you? I mean, you will just think I'm a nasty mocker and you will not place any credence in my letter. And so I beseech you, darling, if you have any compassion for me, when you come in tomorrow not to look straight into my eyes, because I, in meeting yours, may suddenly burst out laughing, for there is also the fact that you will be wearing that long dress . . . Even now I run cold all over at the thought of it, and so when you come in please don't look at me at all for a while, just look at mamma or the window.

Now I have written you a love letter, O my God, what have I done? Alyosha, please do not treat me with contempt, and if I have done something really wicked and made you angry, then grant me pardon. Now the secret of my perhaps for ever ruined reputation is in your hands.

I shall weep today, I know it. Goodbye until our rendezvous, until our *dreadful* rendezvous. *Lise*.

P.S. Alyosha, only you must be sure, be sure, be sure to come! *Lise*.

Alyosha read this through with surprise, read it twice, reflected and suddenly began, quietly and pleasantly, to laugh. Then he started, for this laughter appeared to him sinful. A moment later, however, he again burst out laughing, just as quietly and just as happily. Slowly he put the letter back in its small envelope, made the sign of the cross over himself, and went to bed. The confusion within his soul had suddenly passed. 'O Lord, have mercy on them all, those people I met today, preserve them, unhappy, stormy ones, and guide them. Yours are the paths: by those same paths then save them. You are love, and You will send joy to all!' muttered, as he crossed himself and fell into a stormless slumber, Alyosha.

PART TWO

BOOK IV
CRACK-UPS*

I

Father Ferapont

EARLY in the morning, before it was even light, Alyosha was stirred from slumber. The Elder had awoken feeling much enfeebled, though he desired to move from his bed to an armchair. He was fully conscious; his face, though it was much fatigued, was none the less serene, almost joyful, and his gaze was merry, affable, inviting. 'It may be that I shall not survive this day that has begun,' he said to Alyosha; thereupon he declared a wish to take confession and Communion without delay. Father Paisy was his habitual confessor. Upon completion of the two sacraments, the *soborovanie*, or holy unction, began. The hieromonachs assembled together, and little by little the cell was filled with hermits. Meanwhile day had dawned. People also began to arrive from the monastery. When the service was at an end, the Elder desired to bid farewell to them all and kissed each one. Because of the cell's cramped confines, those who arrived ahead of the others went outside to make room for them. Alyosha stood beside the Elder, who had now moved back to his armchair. He spoke and taught to the best of his ability, and his voice, though enfeebled, was still firm enough. 'So many years have I taught you and, therefore, so many years have I spoken aloud, that I have almost acquired a habit of speaking, and of speaking in order to teach you, until it has come to the point where silence would almost be more difficult for me than speech, dear fathers and brothers, even now in my present enfeebled condition,' he said in jest, tenderly gazing upon the throng that crowded around him. Alyosha later remembered some of the things he said that day. But even though he spoke clearly, and in a voice that was rather firm, his discourse was somewhat incoherent. He spoke of many things, seemed anxious to say everything, to give utterance to it all again before the moment of his death, and say all that which he had not finished saying in the course of his life; and this not for the sake of teaching only, but almost from a thirst to share his joy and his ecstasy with all creatures and all things, once more in his life to pour out his heart . . .

'Love one another, fathers,' the Elder instructed them (or so, at least, Alyosha recalled it later on). 'Love the people of God. For we are no holier than the secular for having come here and retired into seclusion within these walls, but, on the contrary, each who comes here, by the very fact of his doing so, has perceived to himself that he is inferior to all the secular and to all creatures and all things upon the earth . . . And the longer the monk lives within his walls, the more keenly must he recognize this. For in the opposite instance there would have been no reason for him to come here. When, however, he perceives that not only is he inferior to all the secular, but that before all men he bears a guilt in respect of all creatures and all things, in respect of all men's sins, the sins of the world and the sins of the individual, then alone is it that the purpose of our union is attained. For know, dear ones, that each single one of us is indubitably guilty in respect of all creatures and all things upon the earth, not only with regard to general guilt, the guilt of the world, but also individually – each for all people and for each person on this earth. This realization is the crowning garland of the monkish path, and of each person upon earth. For monks are not different from the rest of men, but are only such as upon earth all men ought to be. Then alone will our hearts be tenderly embarked upon a love that is infinite, universal, knowing no satiety. Then each of you will have the strength to acquire the whole world by means of love and with your tears wash away the sins of the world. Let each go near his heart, let each make confession to himself unceasingly. Do not be afraid of your sin, even as you perceive it, but repent, and make no terms with God. Again I say – do not be proud. Do not be proud before the small, and do not be proud before the great, either. Do not hate those who reject you, defame you, revile you and slander you. Do not hate the atheists, the teachers of evil, the materialists, even the wicked among them, not only the good, for in their midst there are many that are good, especially in our time. Make mention of them in your prayers thus: "O Lord, save all of those for whom there is no one to pray, save even those who are unwilling to pray to You." And add at the same time: "Not out of pride do I pray for this, O Lord, for I myself am more vile than all men and all things . . ." Love God's simple Russian folk, do not let the flock be taken away by strangers, for if you fall asleep in laziness and in your fastidious pride, or worse, in self-interest, they will come from every side and take away your flock. Interpret the Gospel to the folk unceasingly . . . Do not practise usury

. . . Have no love of silver and gold, do not hoard . . . Believe, and hold fast the banner. Raise it high aloft . . .'

The Elder, it should be said, spoke more fragmentarily than has been reported here and as Alyosha recorded it later on. Sometimes the Elder's speech broke off altogether, as though he were gathering his energies and out of breath, yet even so he was almost in ecstasy. He was listened to with tender emotion, yet many marvelled at his words and thought them obscure . . . Later on all these words were remembered. When Alyosha had occasion to absent himself from the cell for a moment, he was struck by the universal excitement and expectation of the brethren who crowded the cell and the environs of the cell. Among some of them the expectation was almost uneasy, while in others it was solemn. They all expected something instant and great to take place at the time of the Elder's assumption. This expectation was from a certain point of view almost frivolous, but even the most severe of the Elders were subject to it. Most severe of all were the faces of the Elder and hieromonach Paisy. Alyosha only absented himself from the cell because he was mysteriously called outside by a certain monk on an errand from Rakitin, who had arrived from town with a strange letter to Alyosha from Mrs Khokhlakova. The latter had conveyed to Alyosha a certain curious item of news, one that arrived at an apposite moment. The fact was that among the female believers from the common folk who the day before had come to bow their greetings to the Elder and take blessing from him had been a certain old woman of the town, Prokhorovna, the NCO's widow. She was the one who had asked the Elder if her dear son Vasenka who had gone to Siberia on service to Irkutsk, and from whom she had had no news for a year, now could be included in the commemorations at the morning service as if he were one deceased, for the repose of whose soul prayers might be said? To which the Elder had offered her a stern reply, forbidding any such prayers and likening them to witchcraft. But then, forgiving her because of her ignorance, he had added, 'as though looking into the book of the future' (as Mrs Khokhlakova expressed it in her letter), the consolation that her son Vasya was 'without doubt alive' and that he would either 'come back to her in person, or send her a letter', and that she should go to her house and await him. 'And what do you suppose?' Mrs Khokhlakova added in ecstasy. 'The prophecy has been fulfilled, to the very letter, and even more than that.' No sooner had the old woman returned home than she was given a letter from Siberia that had been waiting for her. But there was more: in that letter, which he had written on his journey, from Yekaterinburg, Vasya made known to his mother that he was travelling to Russia, returning in the company of a certain civil servant, and that some three weeks after she received the letter he hoped to 'embrace his mother'. Mrs Khokhlakova hotly and insistently begged Alyosha to convey at once this newly accomplished 'miracle of prophecy' to the Father Superior and to all the brethren: 'This must be known to all, to all!' she exclaimed in the conclusion of her letter. Her letter had been written hurriedly, hastily, and the correspondent's excitement was reflected in each line of it. But there was no point in Alyosha conveying it to the brethren, for all were already aware of it: Rakitin, in sending the monk to him, had, moreover, instructed him also to 'most respectfully inform his high eminence the Father Paisy' that he, Rakitin, had a certain matter to discuss with him, one of such importance, however, that he did not 'dare to postpone its communication even for a moment', and 'bowed to the earth before him' to forgive him for his boldness. In view of the fact that the monk had communicated Rakitin's request to Father Paisy before doing so to Alyosha, when Alyosha arrived, there remained nothing for him to do, having read the letter, but to report its contents at once to Father Paisy merely in the function of a document. And now even this severe and distrustful man, as he frowningly read the news of the 'miracle', was unable to hold back a certain inner emotion. His eyes glittered and his lips suddenly smiled, solemnly and with deep sincerity.

'Shall we yet behold?'* suddenly almost burst from him.

'We shall yet behold, we shall yet behold!' the monks around him repeated, but Father Paisy, frowning again, requested them all at least for the time being not to inform anyone of the matter out loud, 'until it has received still further confirmation, for there is much frivolity among the secular, and after all this thing may have come to pass by natural means,' he added cautiously, as if to purge his conscience, but almost without confidence in his own reservation, something that the others could see and hear very well. That very same hour, of course, the 'miracle' became known to the whole monastery and even to many of the secular who had come to the monastery for the liturgy. Struck more than any in the cloister by the miracle that had been accomplished was the visiting little monk 'from St Sylvester', who hailed from a certain minor cloister at Obdorsk, in the far north of Russia. He was the one who had bowed to the Elder the day before as he stood near Mrs Khokhlakova and, drawing his attention to the 'healed' daughter of that lady, had asked him with deep emotion: 'How do you dare to perform such deeds?'

The fact was that by this time he had reached a state of some bewilderment, and almost did not know what he should believe. On the evening of the previous day he had already visited a father of the monastery, Ferapont, in his private cell behind the beehives, and had been struck by this encounter, which had produced an extreme and terrible impression on him. This Elder, the Father Ferapont, was that same most ancient cenobite, the great faster and observer of the vow of silence, whom we have already mentioned as an adversary of Father Zosima, and principally – of the Elderhood, which he considered a dangerous and light-minded novelty. He was an extremely dangerous adversary, even though as an observer of the vow of silence he hardly ever said a word to anyone. The danger he represented was principally that a large number of the brethren were in complete sympathy with him, and of the secular who came to the monastery very many revered him as a great man of righteousness and a *podvizhnik*, in spite of the fact that they also saw in him beyond question a holy fool. But it was this holy fool aspect of him that captivated them. To the Elder Zosima this Father Ferapont never went. Even though he lived inside the hermitage, they did not trouble him much with the hermitage rules, again because he conducted himself for all the world like a holy fool. He was about seventy-five, if not more, and he lived behind the hermitage's beehives, in a corner of the wall, in an old, wooden cell that was almost a ruin, and had been placed there back in the most ancient times, in the last century, for a certain other great faster and observer of the vow of silence, Father Iona, who had lived to the age of 105 and about whose heroic deeds many most curious stories circulated within the monastery and in its environs to this day. Father Ferapont had at last, some seven years earlier, achieved his goal of being settled in this same secluded little cell, which was simply an *izba*, though it bore a marked resemblance to a chapel, containing as it did an extremely great quantity of donative icons with donative icon-lamps that flickered everlastingly before them, with Father Ferapont there to look after them and light them as though he had been specially appointed to the task. He ate, it was said (and it was true), only two pounds of bread in three days, no more; they were brought to him every three days by the beekeeper who lived right there among the beehives, but even to this attendant beekeeper Father Ferapont seldom uttered a word. These four pounds of bread, together with the Sunday communion loaf, always punctually sent to the holy fool after late Mass by the Father Superior, constituted his entire weekly nourishment. The water in his pitcher was, however, changed daily. At Mass he seldom appeared. The worshippers who arrived would sometimes see him remain all day in prayer, never rising from his knees or looking around him. Or, if he sometimes did enter into discourse with them, he was short, abrupt, strange and almost always offensive. There were, however, very rare instances on which he would actually talk to those who arrived, but for the most part he would merely utter some strange remarks, which always presented the visitor with a great enigma, and would then, in spite of all and any entreaty, refuse to say anything further in explanation. He had no ecclesiastical title, but was simply an ordinary monk. There was current a very strange rumour, though only among the most benighted, that Father Ferapont was in communion with celestial spirits and that with them alone did he conduct his discourse, and that this was why he was silent among men. The little monk from Obdorsk, having picked his way to the beehives by following the instructions of the beekeeper, also an extremely morose and uncommunicative monk, went to the corner where Father Ferapont's cell was. 'He may talk to you as to a stranger, but on the other hand you may not get anything out of him at all,' the beekeeper had forewarned him. The little monk made his approach, as later he described, with the most intense fear. The hour was rather late. On this occasion Father Ferapont was sitting by the door of his cell, on a low bench. Above him there was the slight rustle of an old elm tree. The chill of evening was settling in. The little monk from Obdorsk prostrated himself before the holy fool and begged his blessing.

'Is it your idea that I should prostrate myself before you, monk?' Father Ferapont said. 'Arise now!'

The little monk got up.

'In blessing you will bless yourself, now sit down beside me. Where be you from?'

What startled the poor little monk most of all was that Father Ferapont, for all his undoubtedly great commitment to fasting and for all his very advanced years, none the less had the look of a strong, tall old man of erect deportment, was unstooping, and had a fresh-complexioned face that, albeit thin, was yet healthy. It was also beyond doubt that there also still remained in him a considerable physical strength. As to his build, it was of the athletic kind. In spite of his age being so great, he was not even completely grey, still possessing very thick and at one time jet-black hair upon his head and chin. His eyes were grey, large and glowing, but they protruded extremely, to a degree where they were positively unnerving. He spoke with a strong emphasis on the letter 'o'.* He wore a long fawn-coloured *armyak** of coarse 'convict' cloth, to give it its old appellation, tied at the waist with a thick rope. His neck and chest were exposed.

A very thick, almost completely blackened shirt, which for months on
end he never took off, showed through from under the *armyak*. Rumour
had it that under the *armyak* he wore chains that weighed thirty pounds.
Upon his feet he wore without hose a pair of old, almost disintegrated,
peasant shoes.

'From a little cloister at Obdorsk, the monastery of St Sel-i-vester,'
the visiting little monk replied meekly in his north Russian accent,
observing the recluse with his swift, curious eyes, which none the less
were somewhat frightened.

'I have been with your Selivester. I stayed there. Is he well, old
Selivester?'

The little monk faltered, and said nothing.

'What muddle-headed fellows you are! How do you observe the Fast?'

'Our table is ordered according to the old hermitage routine: for the
seven weeks of Lent, on Mondays, Wednesdays and Fridays no table is
served. On Tuesdays and Thursdays the brethren receive white loaves,
fruit broth with honey, cloudberries or pickled cabbage, and oat flour
mixed with water. On Saturdays we have plain cabbage soup, *lapsha**
with peas, and kasha, all with vegetable oil. On Sundays we have dried
fish and watered kasha with our cabbage soup. During Holy Week, from
Monday right up until Saturday evening, for six days, no food and drink
are prepared, and only bread and water may be consumed, and that with
abstemiousness; and if possible we do not even take that every day, but
rather as it is decreed for the first week of Lent. On Good Friday we eat
nothing, and on Easter Saturday we must also fast until the third hour of
the noon, whereupon we may partake of a small quantity of bread and
water and a single chalice of wine. On Maundy Thursday we eat cooked
food without oil, and drink wine with bread. For concerning Maundy
Thursday it is written in the statutes of the Council of Laodicea:* "Let
no one break ordinance on the Thursday of the final week, and thus
dishonour the whole of Lent." So it is with us. But what is that compared
to you, great Father?' the little monk added, his spirits reviving, 'for all
the year round, even at Holy Easter, you live only on bread and water,
and the bread which for us suffices for two days, you make last all seven.
This great abstemiousness on your part is a true glory.'

'And what about mushrooms, milk-agarics?' Father Ferapont inquired
suddenly, pronouncing the letter 'g' with aspiration, almost like a 'kh'.

'Milk-agarics?' the little monk echoed in surprise.

'Just so. I could renounce their bread, and not depend on it at all, go
away into the forest somewhere and live on milk-agarics or berries; but

they'll never renounce it, so they must be bound to the Devil. There's pagans among them nowadays who say there's no point in fasting so much. Their argument's a proud and pagan one.'

'Oh, how true,' the little monk sighed.

'And have you seen the devils with that other lot?' Father Ferapont inquired.

'Which other lot do you mean?' the little monk timidly desired to know.

'I went to the Father Superior's last year at Pentecost, but I haven't been back since. Some of them had devils sitting on their chests, hiding beneath their cassocks, you could almost see their little horns sticking out; there was one fellow who had a devil peeking out of his pocket, quick eyes it had, it fairly scared me; one chap had a devil in his belly, right in the most unclean part of him, and there was another who had one hanging round his neck, it had grabbed hold of him, and he was carrying it about with him, unable to see it.'

'You mean you . . . see them?' the little monk asked.

'That's right — I tell you, I know them inside out. As I was on my way out of the Father Superior's, I looked — there was one hiding behind the door, a great big one, an arshin and a half or more in height, with a great long thick brown tail; well, when the end of his tail got caught in the chink of the door, not being stupid, I suddenly banged the door shut and jammed that tail of his in it. He began to squeal and struggle, and I made the sign of the cross over him — three times I did it. He died right then and there, like a squashed spider. He must have rotted in that corner, and stunk, but they've never seen him, never smelt him. Not for a year have I been there now. I'm letting you in on it only because you're not from these parts.'

'Terrible are the words you speak! But say, O great and blessed Father,' said the little monk, his boldness increasing more and more, 'is it true what the great and glorious rumours about you say, spreading even unto the remote territories, that you're in constant communion with the Holy Ghost?'

'It descends. Just when, it depends.'

'What do you mean, it descends? In what guise?'

'A bird.'

'The Holy Ghost in the form of a dove?'

'The Holy Ghost is one thing, but the Holy Spirit is another. The Holy Spirit is different, it may come down as other birds, too: now as a swallow, now as a goldfinch, and now as a blue-tit.'

'How can you distinguish it from a blue-tit, then?'

'It speaks.'

'How does it speak, in what language?'

'The language of men.'

'And what does it say to you?'

'Oh, today it proclaimed that a fool would visit me and ask me base things. Much, O monk, do you desire to know.'

'Awesome are your words, O most blessed and most holy Father,' the little monk said, shaking his head from side to side. Though in his fearful eyes mistrust was also visible.

'Now do you see that tree?' Father Ferapont asked, after a certain silence.

'Yes, I see it, most blessed Father.'

'To you it's an elm, but to me it presents a different kind of spectacle.'

'What kind of spectacle?' the little monk said, after a pause of futile expectation.

'It takes place in the night. Do you see those two boughs there? In the night those are Christ's hands stretching out to me and seeking me, I see them clearly and I tremble. It's terrifying – oh, terrifying!'

'Why is it terrifying, if Christ is there?'

'Well, he may seize hold of me and bear me up on high.'

'Alive?'

'Haven't you heard of the spirit and power of Elias?* He'll embrace me and bear me hence . . .'

Although in the wake of this conversation the little monk from Obdorsk returned to the tiny cell he had been allotted in the quarters of one of the brethren in a state of rather intense bewilderment, there could be no doubt that even so his heart inclined more towards Father Ferapont than towards Father Zosima. The little monk from Obdorsk thought fasting the most important thing, and found nothing particularly surprising about the fact that a great faster like Father Ferapont should 'see wonders'. His words were, of course, somewhat absurd, but after all, the Lord only knew what was contained in them, those words, and all holy fools who went searching for alms in Christ's name had words and actions that were similarly strange. The part about the devil's tail being jammed in the door, for example, he was prepared to believe not only in an allegorical sense, but also in the direct one. There was, in addition, the fact that even earlier, before arriving at the monastery, he had had a violent prejudice against the Elderhood, which hitherto he had known only from stories, following the lead of many others in viewing it as a dangerous novelty. After taking a look round the monastery, he had succeeded in detecting the secret murmuring of several light-minded brethren who were not in accord with the Elderhood. He was, moreover, by nature an intrusive and quick-fingered monk with an inordinate curiosity about everything. That was why the great tidings of the new 'miracle' accomplished by Father Zosima had plunged him into extreme bewilderment. Alyosha later recalled that among the monks who had crowded around the Elder and near his cell there had many times darted before him, poking his nose into every group, the small figure of the inquisitive guest from Obdorsk, who lent an ear to everything and made inquiries of all. At the time, however, he had paid him little notice and only recalled it all later . . . And in any case, that was not what preoccupied him: the Elder Zosima, again feeling weariness and retiring once more to his bed suddenly, as his eyes were on the point of closing, called him to mind and summoned him to come to his side. Alyosha immediately came running. The only people with the Elder then were Father Paisy, the hieromonach Father Iosif and a novice, Porfiry. The Elder, opening his exhausted eyes and looking fixedly at Alyosha, had suddenly asked him:

'Are your family expecting you, dear offspring?'

Alyosha was hesitant.

'Do they not have need of you? Did you promise any of them that you would be there today?'

'I made promises . . . to my father . . . my brothers . . . other people as well.'

'You see? Go without fail. Do not be sad. Know that I shall not die without uttering in your presence my last word upon earth. To you will I utter that word, dear offspring, and to you will I bequeath it. To you, dear beloved offspring, for you love me. But now for the present go unto those to whom you have promised.'

Alyosha at once submitted, even though he found it difficult to leave. The promise that he would hear the Elder's last homily upon earth and, principally, that it would be bequeathed to him, Alyosha, shook his soul with ecstasy. He began to hurry in order that, having brought to a conclusion all that awaited him in the town, he might return the more quickly. None other than Father Paisy delivered the parting homily, and it was one that made an extremely strong and unexpected impression upon him. This was when they had both emerged from the Elder's cell.

'Remember, young one, untiringly' – thus did Father Paisy begin, directly and without any preamble – 'that secular learning, having united itself into a great power, has studied all the celestial things that were bequeathed to us in the Holy Books, and after the cruel analysis of the scholars of this world there remains of all the earlier holiness absolutely nothing at all. But their study was conducted piecemeal, and they missed the whole; indeed, such blindness is positively worthy of marvel. Whereas the whole stands right before their eyes immovably as ever, and the gates of hell* shall not prevail against it. Has it not lived for nineteen centuries, does it not live even now in the movements of individual souls and the movements of the popular masses? Even in the souls of those very atheists who have destroyed everything it lives, as ever, immovably! For even the disavowers of Christianity and those in mutiny against it are in their essence of the same Christian mould, and such they have remained, for to this day neither their wisdom, nor the fervour of their hearts has been vigorous enough to create a higher image of man and his dignity than the one indicated of old by Christ. Such attempts as there have been to do so have resulted only in monstrosities. Make particular note of that, young one, for into the world you are appointed by your departing Elder. It may be that, in remembering this great day, you will not forget my words either, words given you in cordial parting, for you are young, and the world's temptations are heavy and it is not in your power to bear them. Well now go, orphan.'

With this homily Father Paisy blessed him. On his way out of the monastery, as he pondered all these surprising words, Alyosha suddenly perceived that in this monk who hitherto had been so strict and stern towards him he had now encountered a new and unexpected friend, a new leader who warmly loved him – as though the Elder Zosima, in the time of his dying, had bequeathed him to him. 'And perhaps that really is what took place between them,' Alyosha thought suddenly. The unanticipated and scholarly reasoning he had listened to just then, precisely that and not some other, testified only to the ardency of Father Paisy's heart: he was already hurrying to arm, as quickly as possible, the youthful mind for conflict with temptations and to protect the youthful soul bequeathed to him with an engirdlement, a stronger one than which he himself could not conceive.

2

At His Father's

BEFORE doing anything else, Alyosha went to see his father. As he made his approach, he remembered that his father had been particularly insistent that he should somehow contrive to enter in stealth, unseen by brother Ivan. 'Why so?' Alyosha suddenly wondered now. 'If father has something to tell me alone, in stealth, then why must I enter in stealth? There must have been something else he wanted to tell me yesterday when he was so excited, but he didn't have time,' he determined. All the same, he was very relieved when, on opening the gate for him, Marfa Ignatyevna (Grigory, it turned out, had fallen ill and lay in bed in the outbuilding) conveyed to him in response to his query the information that it was 'two hours since Ivan Fyodorovich went out, sir'.

'And what about pater?'

'He's up, drinking his coffee,' Marfa Ignatyevna replied somewhat coldly.

Alyosha went inside. The old man sat alone at the table, in slippers and an old topcoat, looking over some sort of accounts, for the sake of diversion, though without great attentiveness. He was completely alone in the whole house (Smerdyakov had also left, in order to buy the provisions for dinner). But it was not the accounts that were on his mind. Though he had risen early that morning and had endeavoured to maintain his spirits, he none the less had a tired and enfeebled look. His brow, on which overnight enormous purple bruises had spread, was swathed in a red handkerchief. His nose had also swollen powerfully overnight, and on it there had also formed a number of blotchy bruises which, though inconsiderable, somehow nevertheless decidedly imparted to his entire countenance a particularly malign and irritable aspect. The old man knew this, and as Alyosha entered gave him an unfriendly glare.

'It's cold, the coffee,' he snapped curtly. 'I shan't ask you to have any. Look, my good fellow, I'm making do with the plainest of fish soups today and I'm not inviting any guests. Why have you called?'

'To find out how you are,' Alyosha said.

'Yes. And not only that, but yesterday I myself told you to come here. This whole thing's a lot of rot. You've put yourself out for nothing. As a matter of fact, I knew you'd instantly come trailing over here . . .'

This he articulated with the most hostile of feelings. In the meantime he had risen from his chair, taking a concerned look in the mirror (for what was possibly the fortieth time that morning) at his nose. Also, he began to adjust the red handkerchief on his brow to make it look more elegant.

'A red one's better, a white one would make the place look like a hospital,' he observed sententiously. 'All right, so how are things with you over there? How's that Elder of yours?'

'He is very ill; it is possible that he may die today,' Alyosha answered, but his father did not even catch what he said, and at once forgot his own question.

'Ivan has left,' he said suddenly. 'He's putting all his energy into trying to capture Mitka's bride from him, and that is why he is living here,' he added with venom and, with a twist of his mouth, looked at Alyosha.

'Did he really say that to you?' Alyosha asked.

'Yes, and it wasn't just recently either. I shall let you into a secret: it was three weeks ago. I wonder if he's come here in order to cut my throat by stealth? What's the purpose in his coming here?'

'What are you saying? Why are you talking like this?' Alyosha said, extremely perturbed.

'I have to admit he hasn't been asking me for money, but even so he's not going to get a bean out of me. I, my dearest Aleksey Fyodorovich, plan to live as long as possible in the world, I'd have you know, and so each copeck is necessary to me, and the longer I live, the more necessary it will become,' he continued, strolling about the room from corner to corner, keeping his hands in the pockets of his capacious, grease-stained topcoat of yellow summer linen. 'For the time being I'm still a man, and only fifty-five, but I intend to pursue the career of man for another twenty years or so, for I mean, when I get old I'll be disgusting, they won't come to me then of their own free will, well, and it's then that a bit of money will come in handy. So now I'm amassing more and more of it solely for my own use, my dear Aleksey Fyodorovich, sir, I'd have you know, because I intend to live out my mucky existence right to the end, I'd have you know. The mucky way is sweeter: everyone condemns it, but everyone goes down it, only they do it secretly, while I do it openly. And you see, it's because of my lack of dissembling that all the muck-dwellers have fallen upon me. But as for that paradise of yours, Aleksey Fyodorovich, I don't want to go there, I'd have you know, and indeed any decent man would be ashamed to go to that paradise of yours, that's always assuming it exists, of course. In my opinion I shall fall asleep and not wake up again, and there'll be nothing there. Remember me in your prayers if you want to, and if you don't, then the devil take your hide. There you have my philosophy. Ivan talked well when he was here yesterday, even though we were all drunk. Ivan is a braggadocio, and he has no real erudition at all ... He's not even particularly well-educated, either, keeps quiet and smiles that ironic smile at you as he does so – that's the only trick he knows.'

Alyosha listened to him and said nothing.

'Why doesn't he talk to me? And even when he does talk, he adopts that grand pose; he's a scoundrel, your Ivan! And as for Grushka, I shall marry her at once, if I wish it. Because with money behind one all one has to do is wish, Aleksey Fyodorovich, and it all comes true. That's the very thing Ivan is scared of and is on the watch for, that I'll marry her, and that's why he's pushing Mitka to marry her instead: he thinks he can keep that Grushka from me that way (as though I'd leave him money if I don't marry her!), but on the other hand, if Mitya marries Grushenka, then Ivan will take his rich bride for himself, that's the plan he's working on! He's a scoundrel, your Ivan!'

'How edgy you are. You're still suffering from the effects of yesterday; you ought to go back to bed,' said Alyosha.

'There you are, you see,' the old man suddenly observed, as though it were the first time it had entered his head, 'you can say that and it doesn't make me angry, yet if Ivan were to say the same thing to me, I should lose my temper. You are the only one with whom I've had some sort of kind moments; in other wise I'm a wicked man.'

'You're not a wicked man, but a corrupted one,' Alyosha smiled.

'Look, I was going to have that brigand Mitka put in prison today, and I still don't know what I'm going to do about him. Of course, in our present fashionable era it's the done thing to view fathers and mothers as a prejudice, but I mean to say, even in times like ours I don't think the law permits old fathers to be dragged about by the hair while one stamps their ugly mugs on the floor with one's heels, in their own home, and makes threatening boasts to come back and do them in properly – and all of it before witnesses, sir. I, if I felt like it, could settle his hash and have him put in prison for the things he did yesterday.'

'So you're not going to make a formal complaint?'

'Ivan has talked me out of it. Ordinarily, I should not give a spit for what Ivan tells me, but there's a certain little thing I happen to know . . .'

And, leaning down to Alyosha, he remarked further in a confidential semi-whisper:

'If I have him put in prison, the scoundrel, she will get to hear of it, and she will instantly run to his side. But if today she hears that the fellow beat me, a frail old man, half to death, she will probably want to have nothing more to do with him and will come to pay me a visit . . . That's the sort of temperament we're endowed with, you see – always do the contrary of what's expected. I know her inside out! I say, won't you have a little cognac? Have some of that cold coffee, and I'll add a quarter of a glassful to it – it makes a pleasant taste, dear boy.'

'No, I don't want it, thanks. Look, I shall take this bread with me, if you'll let me,' Alyosha said, and, picking up a three-copeck roll, put it in the pocket of his cassock. 'And you shouldn't be drinking cognac, either,' he advised cautiously, studying the old man's face.

'Your truth – it puts me on edge, gives me no peace. But I mean to say, just one small glass . . . Why, I shall fetch it from the little cupboard . . .'

He unlocked the 'little cupboard', poured out a small glassful, downed it, then locked the cupboard again and replaced the key in his pocket.

'That will suffice, one glass won't kill me.'

'There, now you're kinder,' Alyosha smiled.

'Hm! I don't need cognac in order to love you, but with scoundrels I'm a scoundrel too. Vanka hasn't gone to Chermashnya – why? Because he wants to spy on me: how much will I give Grushenka if she arrives? They're all scoundrels! And in any case, I don't really see Ivan as one of my own. Where did a fellow like that appear from? He's not a Russian type at all. As though I'd ever leave him anything! In fact, I'm not going to leave a will, and that's something else I'll have you know. And as for Mitka, I shall squash him like a cockroach. At night I often squash black cockroaches with my slippers: they fairly crack when one steps on them. Your Mitya will crack in similar fashion. I say *your* Mitya, because you love him. There – you love him, and I'm not scared by the fact that you love him. Now if Ivan were to love him, I'd be scared for my life. But Ivan doesn't love anyone, Ivan is not a Russian, men like Ivan are not Russians, they are stirred-up dust . . . The wind will blow and the dust will pass . . . Yesterday, when I told you to come here, it was because a stupid notion had occurred to me: I wanted to find out through you what I could do about Mitya-my-lad, whether if I were now to count out a thousand, or maybe two into his palm he'd agree, beggar and scoundrel that he is, to clear out of this place completely for five years or so, and preferably for thirty-five, without Grushka, relinquishing her for good – eh?'

'I . . . I shall ask him,' Alyosha muttered. 'If you were to let him have the whole three thousand, then perhaps he'd . . .'

'No, you are wrong! There is no need to ask him now, no need to do anything. I've thought the better of it. It was just a stupid notion that crept into my noddle yesterday. I won't give him anything, not so much as a bent copeck, I need my money for myself,' the old man said with a fling of his arm. 'I'll squash him like a cockroach without any of that. Say nothing to him, or else he'll go on hoping. And as for yourself, there's nothing for you to do here in my house, so off you go, now. What about that intended of his, Katerina Ivanovna, whom he's hidden from me all this time with such very great care – will she marry him or won't she? You visited her at her house yesterday, if I'm not mistaken?'

'She won't give him up on any account.'

'You see, it's men such as him that the tender young ladies are fond of, debauchees and scoundrels! I tell you, those pale young ladies are trash; how much better . . . But there we are! Had I his youth, and the looks I had in the old days (for I was handsomer than he at twenty-eight), I'd have made just as many conquests as he. The rascal! But he's not going to get Grushenka, sir, no sir, he's not. I'll turn him into muck!'

With these last words he again flew into a temper.

'Off you go, there's nothing for you to do in my house today,' he snapped, curtly.

Alyosha went over to him in order to take his leave and kissed him on the shoulder.

'What's that for?' the old man said, slightly astonished. 'I mean, we're going to meet again, aren't we? Or do you think we won't?'

'It was nothing like that, I just did it, with no other thought.'

'Well, I am the same, I had no other thought, either,' the old man said, staring at him. 'But listen, listen!' he shrilled after him. 'Come back again soon, and there will be a fish soup, a fish soup, I shall make it myself, a special one, not like today's! Tomorrow, do you hear, come back again tomorrow!'

And no sooner had Alyosha gone out through the doorway than he went over to the 'little cupboard' again and gulped down another half-glassful.

'I'll have no more now!' he muttered, with a grunt, locked up the cupboard again, again replaced the key in his pocket, then went into the bedroom, lay down on the bed in exhaustion and in a single instant fell asleep.

3

He Gets Mixed Up with Schoolboys

'THANK God that he didn't ask me about Grushenka,' it was Alyosha's turn to reflect as he emerged from his father's and set off in the direction of Mrs Khokhlakova's house. 'Otherwise I'd probably have had to tell him about the meeting I had with her yesterday.' Alyosha had a painful sense that overnight the warring parties had mustered new force, and that with the new day that had dawned their hearts had again turned to stone: 'Father's on edge, in a nasty mood, he's dreamed up some idea and taken a stand on it; and what of Dmitry? He has also dug himself in overnight, and has also, therefore, got himself on edge, in a nasty mood, and has also, of course, dreamed up some plan or other. Yes, I shall certainly have to track him down today, no matter what happens . . .'

But Alyosha did not succeed in deliberating for long: on his way he suddenly became caught up in an event which, though on the face of it not particularly important, struck him very forcibly. No sooner had he traversed the square and turned into a side-lane in order to attain Mikhailovsky Street, which runs parallel to Main Street, but is divided from it by a small ditch (the whole of our town is riddled with ditches), he espied in front of a little bridge below him a small flock of schoolboys, all of them quite young, aged from nine to twelve, no more. They were returning to their homes from class, with their little satchels on between both shoulders, some with small leather bags on straps over only one, some in jackets, others in wretched little coats and yet others in the sort of high boots with folded tops in which little boys whose wealthy fathers spoil them like to show off. The whole group was having a lively discussion about something, and was evidently in council. Alyosha was never able to walk past young boys in indifference; that had been the case with him in Moscow, too, and although he was fondest of children aged three or so, schoolboys of around ten or eleven also greatly appealed to him. For this reason it was then that, no matter how preoccupied he was now, he suddenly had an urge to turn their way and enter into conversation with them. As he made his approach, he looked intently at their ruddy, animated little faces and suddenly perceived that each of the boys had a stone in his hand, and some of them two. On the other side of the ditch, at approximately thirty yards from the group, there stood by a fence yet another boy, also a scholar, also with a schoolbag at his side, about ten years old, to guess by his height, no more, or even less than that – pale, sickly, with flashing black eyes. He was attentively and inquisitively watching the group of six schoolboys, who were obviously his companions, had just come out of school with him, but with whom he was evidently on hostile terms. Alyosha went over and, turning to one blond, curly headed, ruddy-faced boy in a black jacket, observed, looking him up and down:

'When I used to carry a schoolbag like the one you've got we wore them on our left side so we could instantly get at them with our right hand; but you're wearing yours on your right side, where it's hard for you to get at it.'

In beginning so directly with this down-to-earth comment, Alyosha had no premeditated cunning; it is, however, out of the question for an adult person to begin in any other way if he is to enter straight into the confidence of a child, and especially of a whole group of children. It is, in other words, necessary to begin in a serious and down-to-earth fashion and in such a way that one is on a completely equal footing; Alyosha knew this by instinct.

'But he's left-handed,' another boy, a sprightly and robust young fellow of about eleven, instantly replied. The other five boys all stared at Alyosha.

'He even throws stones left-handed,' a third boy commented. Just at that moment a stone hurtled into the group, slightly grazing the left-handed boy, but flew past, though it had been thrown with skill and energy. It had been thrown by the boy on the other side of the open ditch.

'Thrash him, plant one on him, Smurov!' they all shouted. But Smurov (the left-hander) required no prompting and delivered instant repayment: he cast a stone at the boy across the ditch, but missed: the stone struck the ground. Without a moment's delay the boy on the other side of the ditch threw another stone at the group, this time straight at Alyosha, striking him rather painfully on the shoulder. The pocket of the boy on the other side of the ditch was full of stones at the ready. This could be seen thirty yards away by the swelling pockets of his little coat.

'That one was meant for you, for you, he chucked it at you on purpose. Well, you're a Karamazov, a Karamazov, aren't you?' the boys cried, roaring with laughter. 'Right, now everyone let fly at him together – open fire!'

And six stones at once came hurtling from the group. One of them hit the boy on the head, and he fell, but instantly leapt up and in a frenzied fury began to reply to the group with stones. From both sides there ensued a constant fusillade: in the pockets of many in the group there were also stones at the ready.

'What is this you are doing? Are you not ashamed, gentlemen? Six of you to one, why, you will kill him!' Alyosha shouted.

He leapt up and stood in the path of the hurtling stones in order to protect with his girth the boy on the other side of the ditch. For a moment, three or four of the boys desisted.

'He's the one who started it!' a boy in a red shirt shouted in a voice of childish petulance. 'He's a rotter, he jabbed Krasotkin with his penknife at school this morning and made him bleed. Krasotkin didn't want to sneak on him, but this chap's got to be given a bashing . . .'

'But why? I bet you tease him, don't you?'

'Look, he threw another one at your back just now. He knows you,' the boys began to shout. 'It's you he's chucking them at now, not us. Right, everyone, let him have it again, and don't miss, Smurov!'

And again there began an exchange of fire, this time a very bitter one. One of the stones struck the chest of the boy on the other side of the ditch; he gave a shriek, burst into tears and went running uphill to Mikhailovsky Street. A hubbub arose from the group: 'Aha, he's got cold feet, he's run away, the loofah!'

'Karamazov, you don't know yet how rotten he is, killing him would be too good for him,' the boy in the jacket echoed with burning eyes; he was evidently older than the rest of them.

'What sort of a fellow is he?' Alyosha asked. 'Is he a sneak?'

The boys exchanged glances that were almost derisive.

'Are you going that way, up to Mikhailovsky Street?' the same boy continued. 'Then go and catch up with him . . . Look, you see, he's stopped again, he's waiting there, staring at you.'

'He's staring at you, staring at you!' the boys joined in.

'Look, go and ask him if he likes bathhouse loofahs – broken, hairy ones. Do you hear? Go on, ask him!'

A universal guffaw rang out. Alyosha looked at them, and they at him.

'Don't go, he'll bash you,' Smurov shouted in warning.

'Young gentlemen, I shan't ask him anything about loofahs, because I bet you're teasing him with that; I shall, however, find out from him why you dislike him so much . . .'

'Go on, find out, find out,' the boys laughed.

Alyosha walked across the little bridge, climbed the hill along past a fence, and went straight up to the boy who was in such disfavour.

'Be careful!' they shouted in warning. 'He won't be scared of you, he'll jab you suddenly, on the sly, the way he did Krasotkin.'

The boy was waiting for him, standing stock-still. Going right up to him, Alyosha saw before him a boy of not more than nine, a puny, stunted specimen with a long, thin, oblong little face, and large, dark eyes that gazed at him with malice. He was wearing a soiled and rather threadbare old coat that was now grotesquely too small for him. His bare arms stuck out of its sleeves. On the right knee of his trousers there was a large cloth patch, and in his right boot, at the cap, where his big toe was, gaped a large hole that, it was plain, had been heavily smeared with ink. Both the swelling pockets of his coat were stuffed with stones. Alyosha stopped two paces from him and gazed at him inquiringly. The boy, instantly guessing from Alyosha's eyes that the latter was not about to beat him, also dropped his swagger and actually deigned to speak.

'I'm on my own, and there's six of them . . . I'm going to kill the lot of them,' he said suddenly, his eyes glittering.

'That stone that hit you must have hurt very much,' Alyosha observed.

'But I got Smurov on the head!' the boy exclaimed.

'They said over there that you know me and that you threw a stone at me for something I'd done,' Alyosha said, inquiringly.

The boy gave him a black look.

'I don't know you. Do you know me?' Alyosha said, pursuing his inquiry.

'Stop bothering me!' the boy suddenly exclaimed in petulance, continuing, however, to stand stock-still, as though he were awaiting something and again with a malicious glitter of his eyes.

'All right, I shall go,' said Alyosha. 'Only I don't know you and I'm not teasing you. They told me their manner of teasing you, but I don't intend to tease you. Now farewell!'

'Monk, monk, in silken pants!'* the boy jeered, still following Alyosha with the same malicious and provocative stare, and also striking an attitude, going on the assumption that Alyosha would now certainly fall upon him; but Alyosha turned round, gave him a look and departed on his way. He had not gone three paces, however, when he was struck painfully in the back by the very largest cobblestone the boy had in his pocket.

'So you do it from behind? I suppose then it's true what they said about you, that you attack people on the sly?' Alyosha said, turning round again, but the boy threw another stone at Alyosha in frenzied fury, straight in the face this time, but Alyosha succeeded in protecting himself, and the stone hit his elbow.

'You ought to be ashamed! In what way have I harmed you?' he exclaimed.

The boy was waiting, silently and provocatively, for only one thing: that now Alyosha should certainly fall upon him. When he saw, however, that the latter even now was not about to do so, he grew completely enraged, like a small wild animal: he tore from the spot and instead hurled himself at Alyosha. Before the latter had succeeded in moving a muscle, the enraged boy, his head down, and grabbing Alyosha's left hand in both of his own, painfully bit Alyosha's middle finger. He sank his teeth into it and kept it between them for some ten seconds. Alyosha shouted with pain, tugging at his finger with all his might. The boy at last released it and leapt away to his previous distance. The finger had been severely bitten, right by the nail, deeply, to the bone; the blood was pouring out. Alyosha fetched out his handkerchief and wrapped it tightly around his wounded hand. This took him almost a whole minute. All the while the boy stood waiting. At last Alyosha lifted his quiet gaze to the boy.

'Very well,' he said. 'Do you see how badly you've bitten me? I think that's enough, isn't it? Now tell me – in what way have I harmed you?'

The boy stared in surprise.

'Even though I don't know you at all and have met you for the first time,' Alyosha continued just as calmly, 'it must certainly be that I have harmed you in some way – you would not have caused me such pain without reason. So what have I done and in what way am I guilty before you? Tell me.'

In lieu of a reply the boy suddenly began to cry loudly at the top of his voice, and fled from Alyosha at a run. Alyosha slowly followed him up to Mikhailovsky Street, and still for a long time, far away, he saw the boy running, never diminishing his pace, never looking round and, no doubt, still crying at the top of his voice. He determined that as soon as he could find a spare moment he would seek the boy out and resolve this enigma that occasioned him such extreme surprise. Now, however, he had no time.

4

At the Khokhlakovas'

QUICKLY did he approach the house of Mrs Khokhlakova; a handsome, two-storeyed, privately owned stone house, one of the finest in our little town. Although Mrs Khokhlakova lived for most of the time in another province, where she owned an estate, or in Moscow, where she had a private residence, in our town too she had a house of her own, which had been left to her by her fathers and predecessors. Indeed, her estate in our district was the largest of the three she owned, yet hitherto her visits to our province had been most infrequent. She came running out to Alyosha while he was still in the hallway.

'Did you get it, did you get my letter about the new miracle?' she said quickly and nervously.

'Yes, I got it.'

'Did you pass it around, show it to everyone? He's brought a mother back her son!'

'He's going to die today.'

'I know, I've heard — oh, how I want to talk to you! To you or at any rate someone, about all this. No, it's you, it's you I want to talk to! And how I regret that it is on no account possible for me to see him! The whole town is a-buzz, everyone is waiting. But now . . . Do you know that Katerina Ivanovna is visiting with us just now?'

'I say, that's fortunate!' Alyosha exclaimed. 'Now I shall be able to see her in your house. Yesterday she told me to come and see her today without fail.'

'I know it all, all of it. I have heard what took place at her house yesterday, every detail, and about all the outrageous things done by that . . . brute creature. C'est tragique, and if I'd been in her shoes I'd have — I don't know what I'd have done in her shoes! But what a fellow that brother of yours, Dmitry, is, too — O good God! Aleksey Fyodorovich, I'm so confused, imagine: your brother's in there now, no, not the dreadful one we had yesterday but the other one, Ivan Fyodorovich, he's with her in there talking: they're having such a solemn conversation . . . And you'd hardly believe what's taking place between them just now — it's dreadful, I tell you it's a crack-up, a horrid fairy-tale one mustn't believe, not on any account: they're both destroying each other for some unknown reason, they both know it and are taking pleasure in it. I have waited for you! I have yearned for you! The fact is that I can't endure this. I shall tell you all about it in a moment, but just now there's something else and it's really the most important thing — oh my, I'd almost forgotten all about it: tell me, why has Lise got herself into a hysterical state? No sooner did she hear you were here than she instantly began to go hysterical!'

'Maman, you're the one who's being hysterical now, not I,' the small voice of Lise suddenly twittered from the side room, through a little chink in the door. The chink was of the very tiniest, and the small voice contained a note of cracking, every bit the same as when one wants to laugh but is suppressing one's laughter with all one's might. Alyosha had immediately noticed this chink, and thought it probable that Lise was looking through it at him out of her bath chair, but he could not see enough to be certain.

'It's small wonder, *Lise*, small wonder . . . Your whims and fancies will drive me to hysterics, too, and as a matter of fact, Aleksey Fyodorovich, she's been well and truly ill all night, in a fever, moaning! I could hardly wait for morning and Herzenstube. He says that "nothing can he understand" and that we must wait for a little. That Herzenstube always comes and says that "nothing can he understand". As soon as you walked up to the house she uttered a scream and had a fit, and gave directions that she be moved back to her former room . . .'

'Mamma, I was quite unaware that he was walking up to the house, and my wanting to move back in here had absolutely nothing to do with him.'

'That isn't true, *Lise*, Yulia ran in to tell you that Aleksey Fyodorovich was coming, she was acting as your lookout.'

'Dear, darling mamma, all this is terribly unwitty of you. Now if you'd like to make amends and say something really intelligent, dear mamma, why don't you tell our esteemed Aleksey Fyodorovich who has just walked in that he has proved how lacking in wit he is by the sole fact of having taken it into his head to come and visit us today after yesterday's events, and even though we're all laughing at him.'

'*Lise*, you permit yourself too many liberties, and I warn you that eventually I shall resort to sterner measures. No one is laughing at him and I for one am delighted that he has come, he is necessary to me, quite indispensable. Oh, Aleksey Fyodorovich, I am so unhappy!'

'But what is it ails you, mamma, dear?'

'Oh, these whims and fancies of yours, *Lise*, your changeable nature, your illness, that dreadful night we've just had with your fever, that dreadful, eternal Dr Herzenstube, yes, that's what he is, eternal, eternal, eternal! Everything, in fact, everything . . . Even that miracle, even that! Oh, how it shocked me, how it shook me, that miracle, dear Aleksey Fyodorovich! And now this tragedy which is taking place in the drawing room, and which I cannot endure, I cannot, I declare to you in advance that I cannot. A comedy, possibly, but not a tragedy. Please say that the Elder Zosima will live until tomorrow, he will, won't he? O my God! What's happening to me, I keep closing my eyes and realizing that it's all nonsense, nonsense.'

'I wonder if I might ask you,' Alyosha suddenly broke in, 'whether you could let me have a clean scrap of cloth in order to tie up my finger. I've hurt it rather badly, and it's extremely painful.'

Alyosha unwrapped his bitten finger. The handkerchief was thickly smeared with blood. Mrs Khokhlakova gave a scream and shut her eyes for a moment.

'O God, what a wound, this is dreadful!'

But *Lise*, the instant she caught sight of Alyosha's finger through the chink, opened the door wide and hard.

'Come in, come in here to my room,' she shouted, urgently and commandingly. 'With no foolishness now! O merciful Lord, how could you all just stand there all this time and say nothing? He could have bled to death, mamma! Where did you do this, how did you do it? We must have water first, water! We must wash the wound, and you must simply put it in cold water until the pain stops, and hold it there, hold it. Quick, quick, mamma, we must have water, in the slop-basin. See to it quickly, I said,' she ended nervously. She was in a complete panic; Alyosha's wound had shocked her terribly.

'Don't you think we ought to send for Herzenstube?' Mrs Khokhlakova exclaimed.

'Mamma, you will kill me. Your Herzenstube would simply come and say that nothing can he understand! Fetch some water, water! Mamma, for heaven's sake, please go to the kitchen yourself and make Yulia hurry up, what's holding her up in there, why doesn't she come at once? Quickly, mamma, or I shall die . . .'

'But it's just a trivial matter!' Alyosha exclaimed, frightened by their fear.

Yulia came running with the water. Alyosha lowered his finger into it.

'Mamma, for the love of God, fetch some lint; some lint and that astringent, cloudy stuff for cuts, whatever it's called. We've got some, we've got some . . . Mamma, you know where the bottle is, in the medicine cupboard in your bedroom, on the right, there's a large bottle of it and some lint . . .'

'I'll bring it all in a moment, *Lise*, but you must stop shouting and not be so upset. Look how steadfastly Aleksey Fyodorovich is enduring his misfortune. But where could you possibly have hurt yourself so dreadfully, Aleksey Fyodorovich?'

Mrs Khokhlakova promptly went out of the room. This was the moment *Lise* had been waiting for.

'Before we go any further you must answer one question,' she said to Alyosha quickly. 'Where did you hurt yourself like that? When you have given me your answer we shall talk about something else altogether. Well, then?'

Alyosha, sensing by instinct that the interval of time before her mother came back was dear to her, hurriedly, omitting many things and abbreviating them, but none the less clearly and precisely gave her an account of his mysterious meeting with the schoolboys. Having heard him out, *Lise* clasped her hands in anguish:

'Is it possible, is it possible that you went getting mixed up with urchins, and in that dress, too?' she exclaimed angrily, every bit as though she possessed some right over him. 'Well, if you can do such a thing you're a boy yourself, the very smallest boy there could possibly be! But you must without fail do what you can to make inquiries about that nasty little urchin and give me all the details, because there's some sort of secret here. Now the second thing, but first a question: Aleksey Fyodorovich — are you able, in spite of the pain you are in, to talk about matters that are completely trivial, yet still with your wits about you?'

'Most certainly I can, and in any case I can't feel the pain all that much now.'

'That's because your finger is in the water. We'll have to change the water right now, for it will warm up instantly. Yulia, please go instantly to the cellar and bring us a piece of ice and another slop-basin full of water. Very well, now she has gone I shall tell you what I really want: dear Aleksey Fyodorovich, please return to me instantly the letter I sent you yesterday — instantly, because mamma may come in any moment and I don't want . . .'

'I don't have the letter on me.'

'Not true — you have. I had a feeling that would be your reply. It's in that pocket of yours. You've no idea how much I repented of that stupid practical joke all night. Please return the letter to me at once, give me it back!'

'It's at the place where I came from.'

'But you can't view me as a child any more, a tiny little child, after that letter I wrote you with such a stupid practical joke in it! I ask your forgiveness for the stupid practical joke, but you must bring me the letter without fail, if you really don't have it on you — and you must bring it today, you must, you must!'

'Today is out of the question, because I'm going to the monastery and I may not be back to see you for two, three, even four days, because the Elder Zosima . . .'

'Four days, what rubbish! Tell me, did you have a good laugh at me?'

'I didn't laugh one little bit.'

'Why not?'

'Because I completely believed it all.'

'You're saying that to offend me!'

'Not in the least. No sooner had I read it than it immediately occurred to me that that was how it would all work out, because the moment the Elder Zosima dies I shall have to leave the monastery. Then I'll continue my course of studies and take the exam, and when the time prescribed by law arrives, we shall be married. I will love you. Though I still haven't had time to think about it properly, it occurred to me that I couldn't possibly find a better wife than you, and the Elder has instructed me to marry . . .'

'Well, I mean, I'm a freak, I have to be wheeled around in a bath chair!' laughed Liza, a blush reddening her cheeks.

'I'll wheel you around myself, though I'm certain that by then you'll have recovered.'

'But you're mad,' Liza said nervously. 'A practical joke like that and you've suddenly manufactured all this nonsense out of it! Ah, here's dear mamma, perhaps it's just as well. Mamma, what a long time you always take over everything, really, I don't know! Look, here's Yulia bringing the ice now!'

'Oh, *Lise*, stop shouting, please do stop it. That shouting of yours makes me . . . What am I to do if you go and put the lint somewhere else. I had to hunt and hunt . . . I wouldn't put it past you to have done it intentionally.'

'But I mean to say, I couldn't very well have known he'd arrive with a bitten finger, could I? Though actually, if I had known, I might very well have done it intentionally. Angel mamma, you're beginning to say some extremely witty things.'

'They may be witty, but what an exhibition of yourself you've been making, *Lise*, all on account of Aleksey Fyodorovich's finger and the rest of it! Oh, dear Aleksey Fyodorovich, it's not the details that are making me despair, not that Herzenstube fellow, but all of it together, that's what I can't endure.'

'Enough, mamma, enough on the subject of Herzenstube,' Liza laughed merrily. 'Be quick now, and hand me the lint, mamma, and the stuff in the bottle. I remember what it's called now, Aleksey Fyodorovich, it's just lead foment, but it's a marvellously good one. Mamma, just imagine, he got into a fight with some urchins in the street on his way here, and one of them bit him; well, isn't he himself a little, little man, and could anyone marry him after that, mamma, because imagine, he wants to get married, mamma. Just imagine him married – wouldn't it be absurd, wouldn't it be dreadful?'

And all the while *Lise* laughed her nervous little laugh, slyly gazing at Alyosha.

'Now, what's all this about marrying, *Lise*, what's put that into your head? And in any case it's really quite unsuitable for you to be talking about it, when that boy might have rabies.'

'Oh, mamma! Are there such things as rabid boys?'

'Of course there are, *Lise*, anyone would think I'd said something stupid. If a rabid dog bit your boy, and he became a rabid boy, then he might go and bite someone in his turn. How well she's bound you up, Aleksey Fyodorovich, I'd never have been able to do it like that. Are you still in pain?'

'Only very slightly now.'

'And you're not scared of water?' *Lise* inquired.

'Now that's enough, *Lise*, it's possible that I spoke rather thoughtlessly about rabid boys, and you immediately made a song and dance out of it. Do you know, Aleksey Fyodorovich, that as soon as Katerina Ivanovna found out you were here, she fairly rushed over to my house, she yearns for you, yearns for you.'

'Oh, mamma! You ought to go there alone, he can't possibly go just now, he's suffering too much.'

'I'm not suffering at all, I'm perfectly able to go,' said Alyosha.

'What? You're leaving? Is that what you mean? Is that it?'

'What of it? I mean, when I'm through over there I shall return here and we can talk again as much as you please. I'd really like to see Katerina Ivanovna without too much delay, as I very much want to get back to the monastery today as soon as possible.'

'Mamma, take him and escort him out of here at once. Aleksey Fyodorovich, don't bother to call on me after you've been to see Katerina Ivanovna, just go straight back to your monastery, and good riddance to you! And as for me, I want to sleep, I didn't get any sleep last night!'

'Oh, *Lise*, these are only jokes on your part, but if only you really would fall asleep!' Mrs Khokhlakova exclaimed.

'I don't know in what way I can . . . I can stay for another three or four minutes – even five,' Alyosha mumbled.

'Even five! Oh, escort him out of here at once, mamma, he's a monster!'

'*Lise*, you have taken leave of your senses. Let us go, Aleksey Fyodorovich, she is far too whimsical today, I'm afraid of overexciting her. Oh, life with a nervous woman is a misery, Aleksey Fyodorovich! And yet perhaps she really means what she says, and felt she wanted to sleep while you were with us. How quickly you have made her sleepy, and how fortunate that is!'

'Oh, mamma, how charmingly you've begun to talk, I embrace you, mamma, for that.'

'And I you, *Lise*. Listen, Aleksey Fyodorovich,' Mrs Khokhlakova said solemnly and mysteriously, in a rapid whisper, as she and Alyosha set off. 'I don't want to put any ideas into your head, nor do I want to raise this curtain, but you must go in and see for yourself what is taking place in there, it is an outrage, it is the most fantastic comedy: she is in love with your brother Ivan Fyodorovich, yet she's trying to convince herself with all her might that it's your brother Dmitry Fyodorovich she loves. It is terrible! I shall come in with you and, if I am not banished from their presence, shall await the ending.'

5

Crack-up in the Drawing Room

BUT in the drawing room the talk was already at an end; Katerina Ivanovna was in great agitation, though she also had a resolute air. The moment Alyosha and Mrs Khokhlakova entered, Ivan Fyodorovich rose in order to depart. His face was somewhat pale, and Alyosha gave him a look of concern. The fact was that for Alyosha there had now been resolved a certain doubt he had harboured, a certain disturbing riddle that had for some time been tormenting him. About a month earlier he had on several occasions and from various quarters been prompted with the notion that brother Ivan was in love with Katerina Ivanovna and, this being the salient point, that he actually intended to 'capture' her from Mitya. Until the very most recent time this had struck Alyosha as a monstrous notion, though it had caused him much concern. He loved both brothers and was afraid of such rivalry between them. Yet only yesterday Dmitry Fyodorovich had suddenly and openly declared to him that he was positively delighted by the fact of Ivan's rivalry and he, Dmitry, would be greatly helped by it. Helped to what end? To marry Grushenka? Alyosha, however, viewed that marriage as a foul and desperate one. In spite of all this, Alyosha had believed right up until last night that Katerina Ivanovna herself loved his brother Dmitry unyieldingly and to the point of passion – but only until last night. On top of this, he had for some reason gone on imagining that she could not love one such as Ivan, and that she loved his brother Dmitry, just as he was, in spite of all the monstrousness of a love like that. Yesterday, however, in the scene with Grushenka he had suddenly thought he glimpsed something different. The word 'crack-up', uttered just then by Mrs Khokhlakova, had almost made him start, because that very night, half waking up at dawn, he had suddenly, no doubt in response to some dream, articulated: 'Crack-up, crack-up!' He had indeed dreamed all night of yesterday's scene at the house of Katerina Ivanovna. Now suddenly the open and stubborn assurance of Mrs Khokhlakova that Katerina Ivanovna was in love with brother Ivan and was simply being perverse, under the influence of freakish behaviour, of 'crack-up', in deceiving herself and torturing herself with an unnatural love for Dmitry that seemed to stem from some kind of gratitude – made a deep impression on Alyosha: 'Yes, perhaps the whole truth really is contained in those words!' But if that were the case, what sort of position was brother Ivan in? Alyosha sensed by a kind of instinct that a woman with a character like that of Katerina Ivanovna must wield power, and that she would be able to wield power only over a man such as Dmitry, and not on any account over one such as Ivan. For Dmitry only would (though presumably with a long delay) submit to her 'for his own happiness' (which Alyosha positively wished), but Ivan would not, Ivan was not capable of submitting to her, and indeed that submission would bring him no happiness. Such was the notion of Ivan's character that Alyosha had already, in spite of himself, for some reason formed. And now, at the instant he entered the drawing room, all these waverings and considerations darted and flickered through his mind. And there was yet another thought that flickered past – suddenly and uncontrollably: 'What if she doesn't love either of them?' I should note that Alyosha had been almost ashamed of such thoughts and had rebuked himself for having them on those occasions when in the course of the last month they had come to him. 'After all, what do I understand of women and love, and what right do I have to arrive at such conclusions?' he would think in silent rebuke to himself after every such thought or surmise. Yet at the same time it was impossible not to have these thoughts. He knew by instinct that now, for example, in the fate of his two brothers this rivalry was a horribly important question and one on which horribly much depended. 'One vile reptile may consume the other,' brother Ivan had pronounced yesterday, while talking irritably of father and brother Dmitry. So in Ivan's eyes brother Dmitry was a reptile, was he, and perhaps had long been one? Probably ever since brother Ivan had got to know Katerina Ivanovna? Those words had, of course, broken from Ivan yesterday in spite of himself, yet that increased their significance. If this were the case, then what sort of peace could one expect? Was this not, on the contrary, a fresh motive for hatred and enmity within their family? And most important of all, which of them was he, Alyosha, to feel sorry for? And what was he to wish for each one? He loved them both, but what was he to wish for each of them amidst such terrible contradictions? In all this muddle one might completely lose one's way, but Alyosha's heart could not tolerate the unknown, as the character of his love was forever active. A passive love was something of which he was not capable; the love conceived within him, he at once went to assist. For that it was necessary to set a goal, to have a firm knowledge of what was good and desirable for each of them and, having ascertained the correctness of the goal, to proceed towards the natural next step of helping them. In all this, however, there was in place of a firm goal nothing but vagueness and muddle. That word 'hysteria' that had been uttered just now! What did he understand even of that? Of all this muddle he did not comprehend even the first word!

On catching sight of Alyosha, Katerina Ivanovna quickly and in tones of joy said to Ivan Fyodorovich, who had already risen from his seat in order to depart:

'Just a moment! Stay just for another moment. I want to hear the opinion of someone here whom I trust with all my being. Katerina Osipovna, don't you leave either,' she added, turning to Mrs Khokhlakova. She made Alyosha sit down beside her, while Mrs Khokhlakova seated herself opposite, beside Ivan Fyodorovich.

'Here in this room are all my friends, all the friends I have in the world,' she began passionately in a voice that quivered with sincere and suffering-filled tears, and Alyosha's heart at once turned towards her again. 'Yesterday you, Aleksey Fyodorovich, were a witness to that . . . outrage and you saw the way I reacted. You didn't see that, Ivan Fyodorovich, but he did. What he thought of me yesterday I do not know, I know only that were the same thing to repeat itself today, just now, I would manifest the same emotions that I did yesterday – the same emotions, the same words and the same gestures. You recall my gestures, Aleksey Fyodorovich, you yourself restrained me from one of them . . .' (As she said this, she turned red in the face and her eyes began to glitter.) 'I declare to you, Aleksey Fyodorovich, that I cannot reconcile myself to any of it. You see, Aleksey Fyodorovich, I do not even know whether I love *him* now. He has become pitiable to me, and that is a poor testimony of love. If I loved him, continued to love him, I think I might not feel pity for him now, but on the contrary – hatred . . .'

Her voice began to shake, and teardrops glittered in her lashes. Alyosha felt an inward shock: 'This girl is truthful and sincere,' he thought, 'and . . . and she's not in love with Dmitry any more!'

'That's right! Quite right!' Mrs Khokhlakova burst out in an abrupt exclamation.

'Wait, dear Katerina Osipovna, I have not told you the principal, the final thing that I decided last night. I have a sense that the decision I have come to is a dreadful one – for me – but I already know that I will not alter it at any cost, and that it will remain valid for the rest of my life, so let it be. My dear, my good, my constant and magnanimous adviser, profound knower of the heart, and sole friend in all the world, Ivan Fyodorovich, approves of it and praises my decision . . . He knows what it is.'

'Yes, I approve of it,' Ivan Fyodorovich pronounced in a quiet but firm voice.

'But I desire that Alyosha too (oh, Aleksey Fyodorovich, please forgive me for calling you simply "Alyosha"), I desire that Aleksey Fyodorovich, too, should now tell me in the presence of these two friends of mine – am I right or am I not? I have an instinctive presentiment that you, Alyosha, my brother dear (for you are my brother dear),' she said in passionate ecstasy, gripping his cold hand in her own, which was hot, 'that your decision, your approval, all my torments notwithstanding, will give me peace of mind, because after what you have to say I shall grow calm and reconcile myself – I have a presentiment of it!'

'I don't know what it is you are asking me about,' Alyosha said with a flushed countenance, 'all I know is that I am fond of you and at this moment wish you more happiness than I wish myself! But you must understand that I know nothing of these matters . . .' he suddenly added hurriedly, though it was not clear why.

'In these matters, Aleksey Fyodorovich, in these matters what count most now are honour, duty and something else of which I am not sure, but it is something loftier, perhaps even loftier than duty itself. The heart within me tells of this overmastering emotion, and overmasteringly it draws me onwards. For briefly, in two words, I have already taken my decision: even if he marries that . . . brute creature,' she began majestically, 'that one I shall never, never be able to forgive, even then *I shall not give him up*! From this day forth I shall never, never give him up!' she uttered in a kind of hysteria of pale, forced ecstasy. 'Not, that is to say, that I shall go trailing after him, trying to make him notice me and pestering him – oh no, I shall go and live in another town, wherever you please, but all my life, all my life I shall shadow him relentlessly. When, on the other hand, he becomes unhappy with that creature, and that will certainly be very soon, then let him come to me, and he will encounter a friend, a sister ... Only a sister, of course, and that forever so, but in the end he will come round to the idea that I am truly his sister who loves him and has sacrificed her whole life for him. I shall attain a situation, I shall insist on it, where he will recognize me and give up everything to me, without embarrassment!' she exclaimed, almost in frenzy. 'I shall be his god, to whom he will say his prayers – and that is the least that he owes me for his betrayal and for what I endured on account of him yesterday. And may he perceive all his life that I shall be faithful to him and to the promise I gave him, even though he was unfaithful and false to me. I shall ... I shall turn myself into nothing more than a means for his happiness (oh, how shall I put it), the instrument, the mechanism of his happiness, and that for my whole life, my whole life, and that he shall perceive it henceforth for the rest of his life! There, that is my decision! Ivan Fyodorovich gives me his unqualified approval.'

She was gasping for breath. It was possible that she had intended to express what was in her mind with a far greater degree of propriety, elegance and naturalness, but it had all come out in an all too slapdash and blatant manner. There had been in it too much youthful absence of self-restraint, too much of the irritable excitement she had felt the previous day, of the need to look haughty, she felt it herself. Her face seemed suddenly to cloud over, her eyes assumed an ugly expression. Alyosha immediately noticed all this, and in his heart there was a stirring of compassion. And then brother Ivan, too, stepped in.

'All I did was to express my view,' he said. 'With any other woman all that would have come out in an overdone, forced sort of way, but in your case it did not. Another woman would not have been in the right, but you are. I do not know what motive to ascribe to it, but I perceive that you are extremely sincere, and for that very reason you are in the right.'

'But I mean, that is only how she is at this moment ... And what's in her at this moment? Nothing but the insult she received yesterday – that's all!' Mrs Khokhlakova suddenly burst out, unable to control herself; though plainly not wishing to become involved, she had lost the battle and come out with a very true perception.

'Indeed, indeed,' Ivan broke in, with a kind of sudden recklessness, evidently angry at having been interrupted. 'Indeed, but for another woman this moment would be only a memory of yesterday, and no more than a moment, while for a woman with a character like Katerina Ivanovna's it will extend throughout the whole of her life. That which for other women would only be a promise, for her is an everlasting, onerous, possibly gloomy, but tireless, duty. And she will derive sustenance from the sense of this completed duty! Your life, Katerina Ivanovna, will now pass in long-suffering contemplation of your own emotions, your own heroic self-sacrifice and your own misery but, in the time that follows, that suffering will ease, and your life will turn into the pleasurable contemplation of a firm and proud intention enacted once and for always, one truly proud, at any rate desperate, but established by you as a victory, and this awareness will at last afford you the most complete satisfaction and will reconcile you with all the rest of it . . .'

He said this resolutely, with a kind of spite, plainly in jest, and even, perhaps, not wishing to conceal his intention, that is to say, that he was speaking in mockery and jest.

'O good Lord, how wrong all this is!' Mrs Khokhlakova exclaimed again.

'Aleksey Fyodorovich, now you must speak! I excruciatingly want to know what you will say to me!' Katerina Ivanovna exclaimed, and then suddenly dissolved in tears. Alyosha rose from the sofa.

'This is nothing, nothing!' she continued in tears. 'It's because of the disorder I'm in, because of last night, but while I am near two such friends as you and your brother I still feel strength . . . because I know . . . neither of you will ever abandon me . . .'

'Unfortunately, as soon as tomorrow, perhaps, I shall have to return to Moscow and abandon you for a long time. And unfortunately it is something that cannot be altered . . .' Ivan Fyodorovich articulated suddenly.

'Tomorrow, you're going to Moscow?' said Katerina Ivanovna, her entire face suddenly wrenched out of shape. 'But . . . but good God, what a stroke of good luck!' she screamed, her voice completely changed in a single instant, her tears likewise instantly banished, not a shadow of them left. Quite literally in a single instant did this extraordinary change take place in her, dumbfounding Alyosha in the extreme: in the place of the poor, insulted girl who had been weeping just then in a kind of hysteria of emotion there now suddenly appeared a grown woman, one with complete self-mastery who seemed positively full of extreme satisfaction, as though she were overjoyed about something.

'Oh, it's not good luck that I must say farewell to you, of course not,' she said, suddenly correcting herself, as it were, with a sweet, worldly smile. 'A friend such as you could not think that; I am, on the contrary, only too miserable about being deprived of your company' (she suddenly threw herself towards Ivan Fyodorovich and, gripping him by both hands, squeezed them with ardent emotion); 'no, the lucky part of it is that you yourself, in person, will now be in a position to convey to my aunt and Agasha in Moscow the whole of my situation, the whole of my present horrible dilemma, in complete frankness with Agasha and sparing dear aunt in the way that only you know how. You can have no idea how miserable I was last night and this morning as I wondered in bewilderment how I should ever write them this dreadful letter, because there is simply no way, not by any stretch of the imagination, that this could be described in a letter . . . Now, however, it will be easy for me to write, because you will be there with them in person and be able to explain it all. Oh, how relieved I am! But my sense of relief concerns only that, please again believe me. For me you are, of course, irreplaceable . . . I shall run and write the letter immediately,' she said in sudden conclusion, already making a step in order to go out of the room.

'But what of Alyosha? The opinion of Aleksey Fyodorovich, which you so eagerly desired to hear?' Mrs Khokhlakova exclaimed. A biting and irate tone sounded in her words.

'I haven't forgotten about that,' Katerina Ivanovna said, suddenly coming to a halt. 'But in any case, why are you being so hostile to me at a moment like this, Katerina Osipovna?' she pronounced with bitter, passionate reproach. 'What I said, I confirm. I need his opinion, and more than that: I need his decision! Whatever he says, so shall it be — there, on the contrary, that is the degree to which I yearn for your words, Aleksey Fyodorovich . . . But what is wrong?'

'I never thought, I can't imagine it!' Alyosha exclaimed suddenly in tones of sorrow.

'What, what can't you imagine?'

'He's leaving for Moscow, and you screamed that you were relieved — you screamed it intentionally! And then you immediately began to explain that it wasn't that that you were relieved about, and that, on the contrary, you regretted . . . losing a friend — but even that was intentional play-acting. You acted it as though you were in a comedy at the theatre!'

'At the theatre? What? What on earth are you talking about?' Katerina Ivanovna exclaimed in profound bewilderment, flaring scarlet and knitting her brows.

'Well, no matter how much you keep assuring him that you regret his departure as that of a friend, you still keep insisting to his face that it's marvellous luck he's leaving . . .' Alyosha got out, almost totally out of breath. He stood overlooking the table, but did not sit down.

'What are you referring to, I don't understand . . .'

'Oh, I don't even know myself what it is. I suddenly had a kind of illumination . . . I know I'm not expressing this well, but I shall say it all the same,' Alyosha continued in the same trembling and failing voice. 'My illumination was that it's possible that you have never loved brother Dmitry at all . . . from the very beginning . . . And that brother Dmitry, too has never loved you at all. Not ever, right from the very beginning . . . But has only revered you. I truly do not know how I can dare to bring myself to this, but I must tell someone the truth, because no one here wants to tell it . . .'

'What truth?' Katerina Ivanovna screamed, and something hysterical resonated in her voice.

'This one,' Alyosha babbled, as though he had taken a leap from a rooftop. 'Summon Dmitry at once – I shall find him – and let him come here and take you by the hand, then take brother Ivan by the hand and unite your hands. Because you are tormenting Ivan for the sole reason that you love him . . . and are tormenting him with your love for Dmitry, which is a hysterical love . . . a false love . . . because you've convinced yourself that it's real . . .'

Alyosha broke off and fell silent.

'You . . . you . . . you're a little holy fool, that's what you are!' Katerina Ivanovna suddenly snapped, her face pale and her lips twisted with malice. Ivan Fyodorovich suddenly began to laugh and got up from his seat. He was holding his hat.

'You are wrong, my kind Alyosha,' he said with a facial expression that Alyosha had never oberved in him before, an expression that seemed to convey youthful sincerity and powerful, outspoken feeling that could not be checked. 'Never has Katerina Ivanovna loved me! She has known all along that I love her, even though I have never spoken a word to her of my love – has known it, but has not loved me. Neither have I been, even once, even for a single day, her friend; the proud woman did not require my friendship. She has maintained me in her presence for continuous revenge. She has taken her revenge on me for all the insults she has constantly and every moment endured throughout all this time from Dmitry, insults dating from their first encounter . . . Because even their first encounter stayed in her heart as an insult. That's the sort of heart she has! All I have done all this time is listen to her talk about her love for him. I shall now depart, but let me tell you, Katerina Ivanovna, that in reality he is the only one you love. And you love him increasingly the more he insults you. That is the form your hysteria takes. You love him exactly as he is, as he insults you, so do you love him. Were he to mend his ways you would instantly give him up and stop loving him altogether. But he is necessary to you, in order that you may ceaselessly observe your heroic sacrifice of faithfulness and reproach him for his unfaithfulness. And all of this stems from your pride. Oh, there's a lot of selfdisparagement and self-degradation mixed up in it, but it all stems from pride ... I am far too young, and have loved you far too intensely. I know that it would be better if I did not tell you that, that it would show more dignity on my part simply to leave your presence; that would be less insulting to you. But after all I am going far away and I shall never return. This is for ever, you see ... I don't want to sit next to a crack-up ... As a matter of fact, I can't say any more, I've said it all. Farewell, Katerina Ivanovna, you can't be angry with me, because I'm being punished a hundred times worse than you: punished by the mere fact that I shall never see you again. Farewell. I do not need your hand. You have tormented me too consciously for me to be able to forgive you at this moment. My forgiveness will come later, but for the moment your hand is not required.

Den Dank, Dame, begehr ich nicht,'*

he added with a crooked smile, proving, however, quite out of the blue, that he too was capable of reading Schiller, to a point where he even had lines off by memory, something with which Alyosha would never have credited him. Ivan stalked out of the room, not even pausing to pay his regards to Mrs Khokhlakova. Alyosha wrung his hands.

'Ivan,' he called after him, like a lost soul, 'come back, Ivan! Oh no, now he'll never come back, not for anything in the world!' he exclaimed again in an illumination of sorrow. 'But it's because of me, I'm the one who's at fault, I started it! Ivan was talking with malice, in an ugly way. He was being unfair, and there was malice in it ...' Alyosha clamoured like a halfwit.

Katerina Ivanovna suddenly went into the other room.

'You've done nothing wrong, you have acted charmingly, like an angel,' Mrs Khokhlakova whispered quickly and ecstatically to the mournful Alyosha. 'I shall make every effort to see that Ivan Fyodorovich doesn't leave.'

The joy was shining in her face, much to Alyosha's intense annoyance; but suddenly Katerina Ivanovna returned. She was holding two 'rainbow' banknotes.

'There is one great favour that I want to ask you, Aleksey Fyodorovich,' she began, addressing herself directly to Alyosha, in a voice that appeared calm and even, for all the world as though nothing at all had taken place just now. 'A week – yes, it was a week ago, I think – Dmitry Fyodorovich performed a certain intemperate and unfair action, a very disgraceful one. There is in our town a certain unsavoury place, a certain inn. In it he encountered that retired officer, that second-grade captain, whom your papa used to employ on some kind of business matters. Having lost his temper with that second-grade captain for some reason, Dmitry Fyodorovich caught him by the beard and in front of everyone led him out into the street in that degrading aspect and continued to lead him thus for rather a long way; it is said, too, that a boy, the son of that second-grade captain, who attends our local college, still but a child, having seen this kept running alongside and sobbing out loud, interceding for his father and rushing up to everyone to ask them to support him, but they all merely laughed. Forgive me, Aleksey Fyodorovich, but I cannot recall that shameful action of *his* without indignation . . . an action of a kind that only Dmitry Fyodorovich could have resolved upon in his anger . . . and his passions! I cannot even describe it, am incapable . . . my words become confused. I made inquiries about this fellow who was being so mistreated and learned that that he is a man of great poverty. His last name is Snegiryov. He was found guilty of some misdemeanour in the service, was dismissed, I do not know the whole story, and has now, together with his family, his wretched family of sick children and a wife who is a madwoman, apparently, fallen into terrible destitution. He has lived in our town for a long time, working in some capacity as a scribe somewhere, and now suddenly he receives no salary. I at once thought of you . . . that is to say, I wondered – I do not know, I am in something of a muddle – you see, I wanted to ask you, Aleksey Fyodorovich, my most kind Aleksey Fyodorovich, to go and see him, seek out a pretext, gain entrance to their lodgings, the lodgings of that second-grade captain, I mean – O Lord, how confused I am! – and tactfully, cautiously – as you alone are able to do it –' (Alyosha suddenly went red) 'and give him this grant-in-aid, look, two hundred roubles. He'll most likely accept them. That's to say, you must persuade him to accept it . . . Or no, how can I say it? Look, it's not a payment to him for keeping quiet and not filing a complaint (because it appears he was going to file a complaint), but simply one made out of sympathy, out of a desire to help, from me, from me, the bride of Dmitry Fyodorovich, and not from him himself. To put it briefly, you will be able . . . I would go there myself, but you will be able to do it far better than I. He lives on Ozyornaya Street, in the house of the artisan's widow Kalmykova. Please, in the name of God,

Aleksey Fyodorovich, do this for me; now, however, I feel slightly tired
... Goodbye ...'

Suddenly she turned around and disappeared again behind the portière
so quickly that Alyosha did not succeed in uttering a word – though he
wished to speak. He wished to ask for forgiveness, to take the blame upon
himself – to say at least something, because his heart was full, and to leave
the room without doing so seemed to him decidedly out of the question.
Mrs Khokhlakova, however, caught him by the arm and led him out
herself. In the hallway she again made him pause, as she had done earlier.

'She's a proud one, always fighting with herself, but she's lovely,
goodhearted, with a generous soul!' Mrs Khokhlakova exclaimed in a semi-
whisper. 'Oh, how I love her, especially on certain occasions, and how glad I
am once again, about all, all of it! Dear Aleksey Fyodorovich, you see, you
didn't know it, but I think I ought to tell you that we all, all of us – I, both of
her aunts – oh, all of us, even *Lise*, have for a whole month now done nothing
but wish and pray that she would turn her back on Dmitry Fyodorovich,
who has no time for her and does not love her, and that she would marry Ivan
Fyodorovich, a first-rate young man of progressive education, who loves
her more than anything else in the world. You see, we got together a whole
conspiracy, and it's even possibly the only thing that's keeping me here ...'

'But I mean, she was in tears, she'd been insulted again!' Alyosha cried.

'Have no faith in the tears of a woman, Aleksey Fyodorovich – in
these instances I'm always against the woman; I'm for the man.'

'Mamma, you're spoiling him and corrupting him,' the reedy little
voice of *Lise* was heard to say from the other side of the door.

'No, I'm the reason for it all, I'm horribly to blame!' the inconsolable
Alyosha repeated in a burst of agonized shame at his behaviour, even
covering his face with his hands from shame.

'Quite the opposite: you have acted like an angel, like an angel, I am
ready to repeat it thousands upon thousands of times.'

'Mamma, how has he acted like an angel?' the little voice of *Lise* was
again heard to say.

'For some reason I suddenly imagined as I watched all that,' Alyosha
continued, as if he had not heard Liza, 'that she loves Ivan, and so I said
that stupid thing ... and what will happen now?'

'To whom, to whom?' *Lise* exclaimed. 'Mamma, you must want to
destroy me. I ask you questions, but you don't answer them.'

At that moment the chambermaid ran in.

'Katerina Ivanovna's poorly, ma'am ... in tears ... it's the hysterics,
she's thrashing about something dreadful!'

'What on earth?' *Lise* cried in a voice that was anxious now. 'Mamma, I'm the one who's supposed to have hysterics, not her!'

'*Lise*, for goodness sake stop shouting, stop making my life such a misery. You're still at an age where it's out of the question for you to know all the things that grown-ups know; I shall come and tell you everything it's right to tell you. O good Lord! I must run, I must run . . . Hysterics are a good sign, Aleksey Fyodorovich, it's excellent that she's having hysterics. It's what she deserves. In these cases I'm always against women, against all these hysterics and female tears. Yulia, run and tell her I'm on my way. And tell her she herself is to blame for Ivan Fyodorovich walking out as he did. He won't leave, however. *Lise*, for goodness sake, stop shouting! All right, I know you're not shouting, it's I who am shouting, you must forgive your poor mamma, but I'm in ecstasy, ecstasy, ecstasy! And did you observe, Aleksey Fyodorovich, what a young man Ivan Fyodorovich looked just now as he walked out, said all those things and walked out? I thought he was so intellectual, such an academic, but there he was suddenly so fiery and passionate, so young and honest, so young and inexperienced, and how beautiful, beautiful it was, just like you . . . And he even recited that line of German poetry, just in the sort of way you would have done! But I must run, I must run. Aleksey Fyodorovich, please be quick about that errand and come back as soon as you can. *Lise*, is there anything you need? For goodness sake don't delay Aleksey Fyodorovich by even a minute, he'll be back again with you very soon . . .'

At last Mrs Khokhlakova made her departure. Before going, Alyosha tried to open *Lise*'s door.

'No you don't!' *Lise* exclaimed. 'Now not on any account! Speak from where you are, through the door. How did you ever get to be an angel? That's what I'd like to know.'

'Because of dreadful stupidity, *Lise*! Farewell.'

'Don't dare to leave like this!' *Lise* exclaimed.

'*Lise*, I'm seriously troubled! I'll be back in a moment, but I'm greatly, greatly troubled!'

And he ran out of the room.

6

Crack-up in the Izba*

HE really was seriously troubled, and in a way that he had hitherto seldom experienced. He had leapt into the fray and 'made a fool of himself' – and in what a matter: one of amorous feelings! 'After all, what do I understand of all that, what sense can I possibly make of such matters?' he repeated to himself for the hundredth time, as he blushed. 'Oh, the shame would be nothing, the shame is merely the punishment due to me, no, the real trouble is that now I shall without question be the cause of fresh unhappiness ... Yet the Elder sent me in order to bring reconciliation and unity. Was that any way to bring unity?' At that point he again suddenly recalled how he had 'united their hands', and again felt terribly ashamed. 'Even if I did it all sincerely, I ought to have been cleverer beforehand,' he suddenly concluded, not even smiling at his conclusion.

Katerina Ivanovna's errand was to be discharged at Ozyornaya Street, and brother Dmitry lived right there on the way to it, in a nearby side-lane. Alyosha decided at all events to call in on him before going to the quarters of the second-grade captain, though he had a premonition that he would not find his brother in. He suspected that the latter would now possibly make a point of trying to hide from him somehow – but whatever happened he would have to track him down. For time was running short: from the time he had left the monastery the thought of the departing Elder had not left him for a single minute, a single second.

In outlining her errand, Katerina Ivanovna had made fleeting allusion to another circumstance that was also of extreme interest to him: when Katerina Ivanovna had mentioned the little boy, a schoolboy, the second-grade captain's son, who had run, crying loudly, at his father's side, there had, even as she did so, suddenly flitted through Alyosha's mind the thought that this boy was probably that schoolboy of earlier that day who had bitten him on the finger when he, Alyosha, had asked him in what way he had offended him. Now Alyosha was almost certain of it, he knew not why. Thus distracted by extraneous considerations, he found diversion in it and decided 'not to think' about the 'blunder' he had made just now, not to torment himself with repentance, but to carry out his purpose, and then let come what may. With this thought his spirits definitely revived. At which prompting, having turned off into the side-lane in the direction brother Dmitry lived, he took from his pocket the bread roll he had taken at his father's house, and ate it as he went. This fortified his spirits.

Dmitry proved not to be at home. The landlords of the wretched little house – an old joiner, his son and aged wife – looked at Alyosha with positive suspicion. 'We haven't seen him for three nights, maybe he's quit for somewhere else,' the old man replied to Alyosha's earnest questioning. Alyosha perceived that his reply derived from some previously issued instructions. To his question: 'Isn't he at Grushenka's, or maybe at Foma's again?' (Alyosha deliberately gave these indiscretions an airing) all the housefolk looked at him with positive fear. 'They like him, so they're giving him their support,' Alyosha thought. 'That's good.'

Finally he tracked down in Ozyornaya Street the house of the artisan's widow Kalmykova, a miserable, rickety little house with warped timbers, only three windows looking on to the street, and a dirty yard, solitary in the midst of which stood a cow. The entrance was from the yard into the outside passage; to the left of the passage lived the old landlady with her daughter, also an old woman; both, it appeared, were deaf. In response to his question about the second-grade captain, several times repeated, one of them, having at last understood that the questioning concerned their tenants, jabbed a finger through the passage, pointing to the door that led into the *chistaya izba*, the 'good' room. The second-grade captain's quarters proved to be no more than an ordinary peasant *izba*. Alyosha was in the act of placing his hand on the iron bracket in order to open the door when he suddenly noted with surprise the odd silence on the other side of it. He knew from Katerina Ivanovna's remarks that the second-grade captain was a family man: 'Either they're all asleep or they know I've arrived and are waiting for me to open the door; I'd better knock first.' And he did. A reply was heard, not at once, however, but possibly as much as ten seconds later.

'Who's that?' someone shouted in a loud and intensely angry voice.

At this, Alyosha opened the door and stepped over the threshold. He found himself in an *izba* which, though it was quite roomy, was extremely encumbered both with people and with all sorts of domestic paraphernalia. On the left was a big Russian stove. From the stove to the left-hand window a length of cord had been stretched, and on it hung various ragged articles of clothing. Against each wall, left and right, there was a bed, covered with a crocheted bedspread. On one of them, the left-hand one, had been erected a pile of four cotton print pillows, in descending order of size. On the other bed only one very small pillow was visible. Further over in the corner by the door there was a small space, divided off by a curtain or sheet, which had also been slung over a cord stretched transversely across the corner. Behind this curtain there could also be observed on one side a bed that had been improvised from a bench and a chair placed against it. A simple rectangular wooden muzhik's table had been moved out of the door corner to the central window. All three windows, each with four small green mildewed panes, were very dim and were tightly closed, so that the room was rather stuffy and not all that light, either. On the table lay a frying pan that contained the remains of some fried eggs, and beside it a gnawed hunk of bread and, in addition, a half-*shtof** with only the feeble residues of earthly bliss at its bottom. On a chair beside the left-hand bed was stationed a woman who might have passed for a lady, attired in a cotton print dress. She was very thin in the face, and yellow; her extremely sunken cheeks bore instant witness to her morbid condition. But what struck Alyosha most of all was the gaze of the poor lady — a gaze at once intensely inquiring and horribly supercilious. And right up to the time the lady herself began to speak and all the while that Alyosha was talking to the landlord, in likewise inquiring and supercilious manner did she continue to transfer her large, hazel-coloured eyes from one speaker to the other. Beside this lady, by the left-hand window, stood a young girl with a rather unattractive face and scanty, rust-coloured hair, poorly, though very neatly dressed. She surveyed the newly arrived Alyosha with fastidious disdain. To the right, also by the bed, sat yet one more female creature. This was a very pathetic specimen, a girl also young, aged around twenty, but hunch-backed and lame, with withered legs, as Alyosha was subsequently informed. Her crutches stood nearby, in the corner, between the bed and the wall. The remarkably kind and beautiful eyes of the poor girl gazed at Alyosha with a sort of tranquil meekness. At the table, finishing his fried egg, sat a man of some forty-five years, short of stature, lean, of feeble constitution, reddish-haired, with a sparse, rust-coloured little beard that for all the world resembled a bedraggled loofah (this comparison and especially the word 'loofah' fairly sparked through Alyosha's mind for some reason at first sight of him, he remembered this later on). It was plain that this same gentleman it had been who had shouted 'Who's that?', as there was no other man in the room. When Alyosha had entered, however, the man had almost fallen off the bench on which he was sitting at table, and, hurriedly wiping himself with a napkin in which there were many holes, came running up to Alyosha.

'A monk out collecting for the monastery — picked the right house, didn't he!' the girl who was standing in the left-hand corner meanwhile said loudly.

But the gentleman who had come running up to Alyosha instantly turned round to her on his heels and in an agitated voice that verged on the unhinged replied to her:

'No, miss, Varvara Nikolayevna, that is not so, you guess wrongly, miss! Permit me, sir, to ask in my turn,' he said, suddenly turning to

Alyosha again, 'what has prompted you to visit us ... in these lower depths,* sir?'

Alyosha looked at him intently; it was the first time he had seen this man. There was about him something awkward, hurried and short-tempered. Though he had plainly had more than a drop to drink just now, he was not drunk. His face displayed a kind of extreme brazenry and at the same time – strange, this was – a visible cowardliness. He resembled a man who had long been submissive and endured much, but who had now conceived a desire to leap up and declare himself. Or, even better, like a man who would horribly like to deal you a blow, but who was horribly afraid that you would deal him one back. In the things he said and in the intonation of his rather penetrating voice one could sense a kind of cracked humour, now aggressive, now timid, unable to sustain the right note and becoming unhinged. He had asked the question about the 'lower depths' almost trembling all over, with staring eyes, leaping up to Alyosha with such intensity that the latter found himself taking a step backwards. This gentleman was dressed in a dark, thoroughly inferior nankeen overcoat of some kind, darned and with stains on it. The trousers he was wearing were extremely light in colour, of a kind that no one wears nowadays, checked and of some very thin material, rumpled below and therefore riding up, as though he had, like some small boy, grown out of them.

'I am ... Aleksey Karamazov ...' Alyosha started to get out in reply.

'I am excellently able to understand, sir,' the gentleman at once said sharply, letting it be known that he already had a good idea of who Alyosha was. 'Second-Grade Captain Snegiryov, sir, in my turn; but all the same, I should like to know just what has prompted you ...'

'Oh, I've simply dropped in to see you. You see, what I really want is to tell you something ... If you'll permit me, that is ...'

'In that case here is a chair, sir, be so good as to take a place, sir. That is what they used to say in the comedies of old: "Be so good as to take a place ..."' and with a swift gesture the second-grade captain snatched up a vacant chair (a plain muzhik one, made entirely of wood and with no upholstering) and placed it more or less in the centre of the room; then, snatching up another chair for himself, he sat down opposite Alyosha, staring at him intensely as before and in such a fashion that their knees almost came into contact.

'Nikolay Ilyich Snegiryov, sir, former second-grade captain in the Russian infantry, sir, though disgraced by my defects yet still a second-grade captain. I really ought to be called Second-Grade Captain

Slovoyersov,* not Snegiryov, for it's only in the second half of my life
that I've begun to employ that manner of speech. It's one that's acquired
in degradation, sir.'

'Yes,' Alyosha said with an ironic smile, 'only is it acquired deliberately
or against one's will?'

'As God is my witness, against one's will. I never used to use it, all
my life never used it, and then suddenly I fell and when I got up again,
there it was, the *slovoyers* – "sir" all the time. These things are ordered
by a higher power. I perceive that you have an interest in the questions
of our time. What, however, can have prompted such curiosity, for I live
in surroundings that render impossible the receiving of guests?'

'I've come . . . about that same matter . . .'

'About that same matter?' the second-grade captain said, interrupting
him with impatience.

'Apropos the meeting you had with my brother, Dmitry Fyodorovich,'
Alyosha said, sharply and uncomfortably.

'But which meeting, sir? Oh, that one, sir? You mean, concerning the
loofah, the bathhouse loofah?' he said, suddenly moving his chair so close
that this time his knees really did bump into Alyosha. His lips had
somehow peculiarly contracted until they formed no more than a thread.

'What loofah?' Alyosha muttered.

'Papa, he's come to you to complain about me!' from behind the
curtain in the corner shouted the little voice, now familiar to Alyosha, of
the boy he had encountered earlier. 'He's the man whose finger I bit
today!' The curtain was tugged aside, and in the corner, under the icons,
on the little bed that had been made up on the bench and chair, Alyosha
saw his erstwhile foe. The boy lay covered by his little coat and an old
and diminutive quilted bedspread. He was plainly unwell and, to judge
from his burning eyes, in a feverish heat. Now he gazed at Alyosha not
in his earlier manner, but fearlessly, as if to say: 'I'm at home, you can't
get me now!'

'What's this about biting fingers?' the second-grade captain said, starting up from his chair. 'Has he bitten your finger, sir?'

'Yes, he has. This afternoon he was throwing stones with some boys
out in the street; he was outnumbered six to one. I went over to him, and
he threw a stone at me, and then aimed another at my head. I asked him
what I'd done to offend him, and he suddenly rushed at me and severely
bit my finger, I don't know for what reason.'

'I shall flog him immediately, sir! I shall flog him this very minute, sir!'
the second-grade captain said, leaping up from his chair altogether now.

'But you see, I'm not making any sort of complaint, I simply wanted you to know . . . I really don't want you to flog him. In any case, he seems ill now . . .'

'And did you think I would, sir? Did you think I'd take my dear little Ilyusha and flog him in front of you for your complete satisfaction? Do you require it right away, sir?' the second-grade captain said, suddenly turning to Alyosha with a gesture as though he intended to throw himself upon him. 'I am sorry about your finger, sir, but would you not like it, before I flog my dear little Ilyusha, were I to chop off four of my own fingers, right now in front of your very eyes, for your righteous satisfaction, look, with this knife I have here? Four fingers, I think, sir, will be sufficient for the assuaging of your thirst for vengeance, sir, you will not demand the fifth?' He suddenly paused and seemed almost on the point of choking. Every smallest line of his face moved and twitched, and he stared with extreme provocation. He was almost in a frenzy.

'I believe that now I've understood it all,' Alyosha replied quietly and sadly, remaining seated. 'The truth is that your boy is a good little boy, he loves his father and he threw himself upon me as the brother of the man who harmed him. I understand that now,' he repeated, thinking it over. 'But my brother Dmitry Fyodorovich repents of his action, I know that, and if only it will be possible for him to come and see you, or, best of all, meet you again at the same place, he will ask your forgiveness in everyone's presence . . . if you desire.'

'In other words he's torn out my little beard and now asks forgiveness, as if to say: there, I've brought it to an end and given you satisfaction — is that it, sir?'

'Oh no, on the contrary, he will do whatever you like and however you like!'

'So that if I ask his highness to kneel down before me in that very inn, sir — the Capital City is its designation — or in the square, sir, then he'd do it?'

'Yes, he'd kneel down.'

'You transfix me, sir. Translacrimate me and transfix me, sir. I am too, too touched. Allow me to perform a complete introduction: my family, my two daughters and my son — my brood, sir. If I were to die, who would give them love, sir? And while I still live, who would give love to a nasty little fellow like myself apart from them? Great is this deed that the Lord has enacted for each human being of my kind, sir. For it needs must be that even a human being of my kind should be given love by someone, sir . . .'

'Oh, how very true!' Alyosha exclaimed.

'That's enough of your buffoonery, some fool comes visiting and you bring shame on us!' the girl by the window suddenly shrieked, addressing her father with an air of fastidious contempt.

'Stay a while, Varvara Nikolayevna, permit me to sustain the tenor of my thoughts,' her father shouted to her, doing so in commanding tones yet looking at her most approvingly. 'That's the sort of temperament we have, sir,' he said, turning once more to Alyosha –

> 'And nothing in all nature's realm
> Did he desire to bless.*

Well, actually it ought to be in the feminine form: "Did she desire to bless", sir. But allow me to present you to my spouse, too: here, sir, is Arina Petrovna, a lady with gammy legs, sir, some three-and-forty years of age, her legs do operate, but not very well, sir. From the simple folk, sir. Arina Petrovna, smooth out the wrinkles on your face: here is Aleksey Fyodorovich Karamazov. Stand up, Aleksey Fyodorovich,' he said, taking Alyosha by the arm, and with a strength one really would not have expected of him suddenly brought him to his feet. 'You are being presented to a lady, you must stand up, sir. Dear little mother, it's not that Karamazov who ... well, etcetera, etcetera, but his brother who resplends with humble virtue. Permit me, Arina Petrovna, permit me, dear little mother, permit me to kiss your dear sweet hand as a preliminary.'

And considerately, tenderly even, he kissed his spouse's dear sweet hand. The girl by the window turned her back on the scene with indignation, and the superciliously inquiring face of the spouse suddenly expressed a remarkable affection.

'How do you do? Please sit down, Mr Chernomazov,'* she said.

'Karamazov, little mother, Karamazov (we're simple folk, sir),' he supplied in a whisper again.

'Very well, Karamazov or however you say it, though Chernomazov is good enough for me ... Come, come, sit down – why has he brought you to your feet? A lady with gammy legs, he calls me, well, I can use them, but they've swollen up like three-gallon milk churns, while the rest of me's just withered away. Before I used to be as fat as anything, but now I look as though I'd swallowed a needle ...'

'We're simple folk, simple folk, sir,' the captain prompted yet once more.

'Oh, papa, oh, papa,' the hunchbacked girl, who had hitherto been silent, said suddenly from her chair, covering her eyes with her handker-chief.

'Buffoon!' the girl by the window snapped out.

'You see the kind of tales we have to tell,' the mother said, throwing her arms wide and pointing to her daughters. 'They blow like clouds; the clouds drift by, and it's back to the same old tune again. Before, when we were military folk, a lot of that class of person used to come and see us. I don't equate a person with his actions, dearie. If you like a person, then like 'em. The deacon's wife used to come and say: "Aleksandr Aleksan-drovich is a man with a most wonderful soul, while Nastasya Petrovna," she'd say, "is a fiend from hell." "Well," I'd reply, "let people worship them as they choose to, but you're a little pile, and you smell vile." "And you," she'd say, "ought to be kept in obedience." "Oh, you blackened steel," I'd say to her, "who have you come to give lessons to?" "I," she'd say, "let in clean air, while you let in the foul." "All right then," I'd reply, "you go and ask any of the gentlemen officers whether my air's clean or not." And so from that time onward that's preyed on my mind, and the other day I was sitting right here, as I am now, and lo and behold that very same general walked in, the one who came here at Holy Week: "Tell me, Your Excellency, is it done for a well-born lady to let in the air from outside?" "Yes," he replied, "you ought to open a window or a door, because your air's not fresh." Well, and that's what they all say! And why are they so interested in my air, anyway? A corpse would smell worse. "I," I said, "shan't pollute your air, I'll order clogs and off I'll jog!" Now then, darlings, now then, dearies, don't be so hard on your own mother! Nikolay Ilyich, dearie, have I not satisfied you, why, I've only dear little Ilyusha left, who comes home from his class at school and loves me. Yesterday he brought an apple. Forgive me, darlings, forgive me, dearies, forgive your own mother, forgive me, for I'm all alone, and why has my air grown loathsome to you?'

And the poor lady burst into tears that spurted in a torrent. The second-grade captain dashed headlong to her side.

'Dear little mother, dear little mother, little pigeon, enough, enough! You are *not* all alone. All of us love you, all of us worship you!' And he again began to kiss both her hands and to stroke her face tenderly with his palms; then, suddenly snatching up his napkin, he began to wipe the tears from her eyes. Alyosha even had the impression that tears had begun to flash in the eyes of the second-grade captain himself. 'Very well, sir! Do you see, sir, do you hear, sir?' said the second-grade captain, suddenly turning round to him in a kind of fury, pointing to the poor halfwitted woman.

'I see and I hear,' Alyosha muttered.

'Papa, papa! Surely you're not trying to . . . Let him be, papa!' the little boy suddenly shouted, raising himself on his bed and staring at his father with a burning gaze.

'And will you finally have done with your buffoonery, with showing off your stupid capers that never lead anywhere!' Varvara Nikolayevna shouted, really angry now, still from the same corner, even stamping her foot.

'With perfect justice do you lose your temper on this occasion, Varvara Nikolayevna, and I shall render you swift satisfaction. Don your cap, Aleksey Fyodorovich, and I shall take this peaked affair – and let us go, sir. It is necessary to have a serious word in your ear, only without these walls. That girl who sits there is my daughter, sir, Nina Nikolayevna, sir, I neglected to present her to you – an angel of God in fleshly form . . . flown down to mortal men . . . if you can grasp my meaning . . .'

'Why, he's shaking all over, as though he were having spasms!' Varvara Nikolayevna continued in indignation.

'And this one, the one who is stamping her foot at me and accused me just now of being a buffoon – she is also an angel of God in fleshly form, sir, and with justice did she call me one. Let us go, Aleksey Fyodorovich, it is necessary to conclude the matter, sir . . .'

And, seizing Alyosha by the arm, he led him out of the room directly into the street.

7

And Out in the Fresh Air

'Fresh air, sir – in my mansion the air is downright impure, in positively every sense. Let us, sir, betake us of a gentle promenade. I should very much like to engage your interest, sir.'

'I also have a certain pressing errand with you,' Alyosha observed, 'but the trouble is, I don't know how to start.'

'How could I have failed to perceive that you have an errand with me, sir? After all, without an errand you would never have called on me. Or did you really only come to complain about the boy, sir? Why, that is not probable, sir. And on the subject of the boy, sir: I couldn't go into all the ins and outs of it while we were back there, sir, but out here I shall describe that scene for you, sir. You see, that loofah was thicker, sir, no more than a week ago – I'm talking about my little beard, sir; you see, it was my little beard they called a loofah, the schoolboys principally, sir. Well sir, you see, sir, that day your dear brother Dmitry Fyodorovich took to pulling me about by my little beard, hauled me out of the inn on to the square, and just at that moment the schoolboys were coming out of the school, and Ilyusha was with them. When he saw me in that condition, sir, he threw himself towards me: "Papa!" he cried. "Papa!" He caught at me, embraced me, tried to tear me away, shouting at my insulter: "Let go, let go, this is my papa, my papa, forgive him" – I mean, that is what he shouted: "Forgive him!"; with those wretched little arms of his he embraced him, too, and his hand, that very same hand of his, he kissed it, sir . . . I remember that moment, and the expression on his little face, sir, I have not forgotten it, sir, and I shall not forget it, sir!'

'I vow it upon oath,' Alyosha exclaimed, 'my brother will convey to you his repentance in the most sincere, the most complete fashion, even though it be on his knees upon that very same square . . . I shall compel him, otherwise he is no brother to me!'

'Aha, so it still remains at the project stage. It proceeds not directly from him, but simply from the noble emotion of your fiery heart, sir. That is how you should have said it, sir. But in that case permit me to finish telling you about your dear brother's most elevated, knightly and officerly nobility too, for he displayed it on that occasion, sir. When he had had enough of hauling me about by my loofah, he set me at liberty, sir: "You," he said, "are an officer, and I am an officer, and if you can find a second, a respectable fellow, then send him to me – I shall give you satisfaction, even though you are a scoundrel!" That is what he said, sir. In truth, a knightly spirit! At that point Ilyusha and I beat a retreat, and that genealogical, familial scene was imprinted upon Ilyusha's memory for ever. But it is not for us to abide among the gentry, sir. Well, form your own opinion, sir, you yourself were so good as to step within my mansion just now – what did you see, sir? Three ladies, sir, one with gammy legs who is a halfwit, another with gammy legs who is a hunchback, and the third with legs that are in order but who is excessively brainy, a *coursiste*,* sir, yearning to get back to St Petersburg, there upon the banks of the Neva to search for the rights of Russian woman. I need hardly mention Ilyusha, sir, he is only nine years old, sir, as solitary as a thumb, for if I die – then what will become of all these lower depths, that is the principal question I ask you, sir? And if that is the case, then if I challenge him to a duel, and he kills me instantly and outright, what then? What will happen to them all, sir? Even worse than that would be if he doesn't kill me, but only maims me: I couldn't work, but my mouth would still be there, and who would feed it then, my mouth, and who would feed them, all of them, sir? Or should I have to send Ilyusha every day not to school, but out begging instead? Well, that is what it would entail for me to challenge him to a duel, sir, it's a stupid idea, sir, and there's an end to it, sir.'

'He shall beg you to forgive him, he shall bow down to your feet in the centre of the square,' Alyosha exclaimed again with a burning gaze.

'I was going to take him to court,' the second-grade captain continued, 'but unroll our legal code: do you suppose I should receive much satisfaction from my wronger for that wrong to my person, sir? And then all of a sudden Agrafena Aleksandrovna called me to her, and cried: "Do not even think of it! If you take him to court I'll bring forward enough evidence to make it plain in public to the whole world that he beat you for your crooked dealings, and then you'll be had up before the law yourself." But the Lord alone sees from whom the said crooked dealings arose, sir, and at whose bidding I acted in the said instance like a little stooge – wasn't it on her instructions, sir, and those of Fyodor Pavlovich? "And not only that," she added, "I'll give you the sack for good, and you'll never work for me again. And I'll tell my merchant too (that's her name for him, the old man: 'my merchant'), and he'll kick you out as well." Then I thought, if her "merchant" kicks me out too, what will I do then, who will give me work then? I mean, the two of them are all I have left, as not only has your dear father Fyodor Pavlovich given up having any trust in me, for a certain extraneous reason, sir, but himself, having got his hands on some receipts of mine, intends to haul me up before the courts. As a consequence of all this I have cut my cloth to suit my coat, sir, and you have seen the lower depths, sir. But now permit me to inquire: was it a bad bite he gave your finger earlier, Ilyusha, I mean? In my mansion just now I could not bring myself to enter into that particular detail.'

'Yes, a very bad one, and he was very worked up. He took it out on me, as a Karamazov, for the wrong that had been done to you, that is clear to me now. But if you had seen the way he and his schoolmates were flinging those stones at one another! It is most perilous, they might have killed him, they're children, without any sense, one of those stones might have gone and broken his head.'

'Oh, one did hit him, sir – not on the head but in the chest, sir, just above the heart, sir, it was one of those stones today, there's a bruise, sir, he came back groaning and in tears, and now he has fallen ill.'

'But I mean, are you aware that he attacks them all first? He lost his temper with them because of what had happened to you; they say that he recently stuck his penknife into one of the boys, Krasotkin.'

'I heard about that, as well, there is peril there, sir; Mr Krasotkin is a government official who lives in this town, and we may not have heard the last of it, sir . . .'

'My advice to you,' Alyosha continued with heat, 'is not to send him to school at all for a while, until he calms down, and this anger of his has passed . . .'

'Anger, sir!' the second-grade captain caught up. 'Yes, anger is what it is, sir. He may be just a scrap of a boy, but it's a great anger he has in him, sir. You don't know the half of it, sir. Permit me to throw some detailed light on this episode. The fact is that after the said event all the boys in the school began to tease him about the "loofah". In schools, children are a tribe without mercy: on their own they are heaven's own angels, but together, particularly in schools, they are very frequently without mercy. When they started to tease him, a spirit of decency quickened within Ilyusha. Your ordinary sort of boy, your spineless son – such a lad would have just put up with it, felt shame for his father, but this one entered the fray on his father's account, one against all. On his father's account, and on account of truth, sir, of justice, sir. For what he endured that day, when he kissed your dear brother's hands and cried to him: "Forgive my papa, forgive my papa," only God and I can know, sir. And that is the way that our young children – that is to say, not yours, but ours, sir, the children of contemptible but decent-living paupers, sir, discover justice upon earth at nine years of age, sir. How could the rich do that? All their lives they remain ignorant of such profundity, yet my little Ilyusha, at the very moment on the square when he kissed your brother's hands, sir, at that same moment passed through the whole truth, sir. That truth, sir, entered into him and smote him down for ever, sir,' the second-grade captain pronounced with ardour and again in a kind of frenzy and as he did so he struck his left palm with his right fist, as if desirous to express in living terms the manner in which his Ilyusha had been smitten down by 'the truth'. 'That same day he went into a fever on me, sir, all night he raved. All that day he had spoken little to me, been even completely silent, only I could see that he was looking, looking at me from the corner, though most of the time he kept his face near the window and pretended to be studying his lessons, but I could see that it wasn't his lessons that were on his mind. The next day I had a drop or two to drink, sir, and I don't recall much, sir, sinner that I am, I assuaged my grief, sir. Then little mother also began to cry, sir – I'm very fond of little mother, sir – and, well, to assuage my grief I took a drop on the last of my cash, sir. Oh, good sir, do not view me with contempt: among us here in Russia the drunken folk are the kindest and the best. The very kindest and best of men are those who are most drunk. The point was, I was on my back and Ilyusha wasn't in my thoughts very much that day, and yet that very day it was that the urchins had been making a laughing-stock of him at school all morning, sir: "Loofah!" they shouted at him. "Your father was hauled out of the inn by his loofah, and you ran alongside begging forgiveness." On the third day he again arrived back from school, and I gazed at him – he looked terrible, with no colour in his cheeks. "What's wrong with you?" I said. He made no reply. Well, in my mansion one has only to start a conversation and little mother and the girls join in immediately – in any case, the girls had already found out all about it, right back on the first day. Varvara Nikolayevna had already started to growl: "Buffoons, jack puddings, we can't have any sense around here, can we?" "Precisely so, Varvara Nikolayevna, we can't have any sense around here, can we?" And with that I managed to shake her off on that occasion. Well, sir, that evening I took the boy out for a stroll. I should tell you, sir, that every evening before that he and I had been in the habit of going out for a stroll, along exactly the same route that you and I are passing along now, all the way from our garden gate to that big milestone over there by the wicker fence at the side of the road, where the town's common pasture begins: a lonely and excellent place, sir. Ilyusha and I would walk there, his little hand in my own, as a rule; his hand is just a little bit of a hand, with thin little fingers that are cold – you see, he has gone and developed a weak chest on me. "Papa!" he said. "Papa!" "What?" I said to him, and I could see his eyes were glittering. "Papa, what he did to you that time, papa!" "But what can I do about it, Ilyusha?" I said. "Don't let him get away with it, papa, don't let him. The schoolboys say he gave you ten roubles for allowing him to do that." "No, Ilyusha," I said, "I wouldn't take money from him now, not for anything." Well, then he started to shake all over, took my hand in both his little ones, and kissed it again. "Papa," he said, "papa, challenge him to a duel, at school they tease me by saying you're a coward and that you'll take ten roubles from him instead of challenging him to a duel." "Ilyusha, it's out of the question for me to challenge him to a duel," I replied, and I set before him briefly all the things I have just explained to you on that account. He heard me through. "Papa," he said, "papa, all the same, don't let him get away with it: when I grow up I myself will challenge him, and I'll kill him!" His little eyes were glittering and burning. Well, but all the same I am his father, after all, and it behoved me to give him a word of truth. "Killing," I told him, "is a sin, even if it's in a duel." "Papa," he said, "papa, when I'm big I'll fell him to the ground, I'll smash the sword from his hands with my own sword, I'll rush at him, fell him to the ground, brandish my sword over him and say to him: 'I could kill you now, but I grant you forgiveness, so there!'" You see, you see, good sir, what a fine little process had been at work in that head of his during those two days, why, he'd been thinking about that revenge with a sword day and night, and that must have been what he was raving about in the night, sir. Only when he started coming home from school sorely and unmercifully beaten the day before yesterday did I find out what had been going on, and you are right, sir; further to that school I shall not send him, sir. I discovered that he'd been putting himself in opposition to the whole class and challenging them all, he'd become fuelled with anger, his heart was enkindled within him – and then I was afraid for him. Again we took a stroll. "Papa," he asked, "papa, why, it's true that rich people are the strongest people in the world, isn't it?" "Yes, Ilyusha," I said, "there is no one in the world who is stronger than a rich man." "Papa," he said, "I'll make myself rich, I'll join the officer corps and defeat them all, the Tsar will give me a medal, I'll come back here and then no one will dare touch you." After that he was silent for a bit, and then he said – his little lips were still quivering the way they'd been before – "Papa," he said, "what a nasty town ours is, papa!" "Yes, dear Ilyusha," I said, "our town is not very nice." "Papa, let's go and live in another town, a nice one," he said, "where people know nothing about us!" "We shall do that," I said, "we shall do that, Ilyusha – just as soon as I've saved up the money." I was glad of the chance to get his mind off those dark thoughts, and he and I began to dream of how we would go and live in another town. We'd buy our own horse and cart, put little mother and the sisters in it, cover them up, and we ourselves would walk alongside, from time to time I'd help him up top, but I'd go on walking alongside, because the horse must be attended to, we couldn't all sit in the back, after all – and so we'd set off. He was hugely taken with this, especially with the notion we should have a horse of our own and that he should ride it. Well, it's no secret that a Russian boy is born together with a horse. We talked idly for a long time; "Thank goodness," I thought, "I've got his mind off it, I've cheered him up." This was the evening before last, but then yesterday evening something else came along. He'd been to that school again in the morning, but he came home

looking black, very black again. In the evening I took him by his little
hand to accompany him on a stroll, but he was silent, didn't speak. A
breeze had sprung up, the sun had gone in, there was a breath of autumn,
and it was already getting dark – we walked, both of us sad. "Well, boy,
how shall you and I get ready for our journey?" I said, hoping to revive
our conversation of the evening before. He said nothing. But I felt his
little fingers give a shudder in my hand. "Aye," I thought, "it's bad,
there's something else now." We reached that milestone, just as you and
I have now, I sat down on it, and the sky was full of kites, hissing and
cracking, we could see about thirty of them. It's the kite season just now,
you see. "There, Ilyusha," I said, "it's time we had another go at flying
that kite we made last year. I'll have a go at repairing it, where have you
got it stowed away?" My little boy made no reply, just looked to one
side, stood with his back to me. And then the wind suddenly began to
howl, raising the sand . . . Suddenly he threw himself bodily towards me,
embraced me round the neck with both his little arms, squeezed me. You
know, if young children are proud and reticent and try to keep their tears
back for a long time, when those tears finally burst forth under the
pressure of some great unhappiness, they do not so much flow, sir, as
spurt in torrents, sir. It was with those warm torrents of tears that he
suddenly drenched my whole face, sir. He burst into convulsive sobbing,
shuddering and pressing me to him as I sat on the milestone. "Papa," he
screamed, "Papa, dear papa, how he humiliated you!" Then I broke out
sobbing, too, sir, and we sat there shaking with our arms around each
other. "Papa," he would say, "dear papa!" "Ilyusha," I'd reply, "dear
Ilyushechka!" No one saw us then, sir, God alone saw us, and maybe
he'll enter it on my service list, sir. Please thank your dear brother,
Aleksey Fyodorovich. No, sir, I will not flog my little boy for your
satisfaction, sir!'

Once more he concluded with his earlier aggressive, cracked eccentricity. Alyosha had a sense, though, that the man now trusted him and that
had some other person been in his place he would not have 'conversed' in
such a way, nor conveyed to him the things he had just conveyed. This
enlivened the spirits of Alyosha, whose soul was trembling with tears.

'Oh, how I should like to make it up with your boy!' he exclaimed. 'If
you would arrange it . . .'

'Quite so, sir,' the second-grade captain muttered.

'But now there's something else I want to talk to you about, something
else entirely,' Alyosha continued to vociferate. 'Listen! I have an errand
to discharge with you: that selfsame brother of mine, that Dmitry, has

also insulted the girl who is to be his bride, a girl of most noble bearing whom I expect you have heard about. I'm within my rights in conveying to you the insult she received, I am even duty-bound to do so, because she, having learned of the offence you suffered and of your whole unhappy situation, gave me the errand just now ... earlier today ... of delivering this relief to you ... though it is only from her, and not from Dmitry, who has abandoned her, in no way from him, and not from me, his brother, either, and not from anyone but her exclusively, from her alone! She implores you to accept her help ... You and she have both been insulted by the same person ... She only remembered about you when she had endured an insult from him similar to the one you had endured from him (similar in magnitude, that is)! So it's like a sister going to help her brother. She gave me the specific errand of persuading you to accept from her these two hundred roubles, as from a sister. No one will find out about it, there will be no unfounded tittle-tattle ... Look, here are two hundred roubles, and I swear to you, you must accept them, or else ... or else it means that everyone on earth must be the enemies of one another! But after all, there are brothers, too, upon earth ... You have a decent soul ... You must understand this, you must!'

And Alyosha offered him the two brand-new 'rainbow' banknotes. At that moment both men were in fact standing beside the large milestone, by the fence, and there was no one in the vicinity. The banknotes seemed to make a fearsome impression on the second-grade captain: he shuddered, but initially from almost pure surprise; nothing of the kind had ever visited his fancy, and such an outcome was totally unexpected. The notion that he might receive help from someone, and in such a substantial sum, had never occurred to him even in his wildest dreams. He took the banknotes and for a moment was almost unable to speak; some entirely new emotion flickered in his face.

'To me, to me, sir, that is so much money, two hundred roubles! Sainted fathers! Why, merciful Lord, I have not set eyes on that much money for the last four years! And she said she was doing it as a sister ... Is that really true, is it true?'

'I swear to you that everything I have told you is true!' Alyosha shouted. The second-grade captain turned red.

'Listen, sir, my dear fellow, listen, sir, I mean, if I accept it, shan't I be a scoundrel, eh? In your eyes, I mean, Aleksey Fyodorovich, shan't I, shan't I be a scoundrel? No, Aleksey Fyodorovich, sir, you must hear me to the end, sir, hear me to the end,' he said hurriedly, touching Alyosha with both hands. 'Look, here you are trying to make me accept it on the grounds that a "sister" has sent it, yet inwardly, privately to yourself, sir — won't you feel contempt for me if I accept it, sir, won't you, eh?'

'Why no, no, I tell you! I swear to you upon my own salvation that that is not the case! And no one shall ever find out about it, only we shall know: I, you, she and a certain lady who is her close friend . . .'

'A lady — whatever next? Listen, Aleksey Fyodorovich, hear me out, sir, you see, the moment has come for you to hear me to the end, sir, for you cannot even imagine what those two hundred roubles mean to me now,' the impoverished wretch continued, gradually attaining a kind of chaotic, almost savage ecstasy. He seemed to have been thrown off keel, and he spoke with extreme haste and hurry, as though he were afraid he would not be allowed to say everything. 'In addition to the fact that this money has been gained by honest means, from such a revered and sacred "sister", sir, do you realize that now I shall be able to obtain treatment for little mother and for Ninochka — my little hunchbacked angel, my daughter? Dr Herzenstube came out on a call to me, from the kindness of his heart, and he examined them both for a whole hour: "Nothing can I understand," he said, "nothing," but apparently the mineral water they sell in the local pharmacy here (he prescribed it for her) would be of indubitable benefit to her, and he also prescribed medicinal footbaths. That mineral water costs thirty copecks a pitcher, sir, and she might need to drink, say, forty of them. Well, anyway, I took the prescription and placed it on the shelf beneath the icons, and there it remains. And for Ninochka he prescribed bathing in some kind of solution, some sort of hot baths, every day, morning and evening, and how were we to dream up a course of treatment like that, in that mansion of ours, without servants, without help, without vessels and water, sir? And Ninochka is racked by rheumatism, I haven't told you about that yet, at night her whole right side aches, she goes through agonies and, would you believe it, the God's own angel, she puts up with it in order not to disturb us, she restrains herself from groaning in order not to wake us up. We eat whatever comes our way, whatever we can get hold of, and you see, she will only take the very last morsel, the scraps one would only throw to a dog, as if to say: "I'm not worthy of that morsel, I'm depriving you, I'm being a burden on you." That is what her angel's gaze is trying to make manifest. We wait on her, but she finds that distressing: "I don't deserve it, I don't deserve it, I'm an unworthy cripple, a useless cripple" — and how could she not deserve it, sir, when she has entreated God for us all with her angelic meekness, and without her, without her quiet words, our lives would be a hell, sir — why, she has even had a softening influence on Varya. But you mustn't condemn Varvara Nikolayevna either, sir, she is also an angel, an insulted one. She arrived on our doorstep in the summer, and she had sixteen roubles, she'd earned them by giving lessons and had put them aside for her departure, for September – now, that is, when she'd intended to use them in order to pay for her journey back to St Petersburg. But we took her bit of money and spent it all, and now she has no money to pay for her journey, that's what, sir. And she couldn't return there anyway, because she's working for us like a convict girl – you see, we've harnessed and saddled her like a jade, she looks after us all, mends, washes, sweeps the floor, puts little mother to bed, and little mother is capricious, sir, and little mother is tearful, sir, and little mother is insane, sir! . . . So you see, now with these two hundred roubles I can hire a servant-maid, do you realize, Aleksey Fyodorovich, I can undertake the treatment of those beloved creatures, sir, I shall send the *coursiste* to St Petersburg, sir, I shall purchase beef, sir, I shall arrange a new diet for us all, sir. Merciful Lord, why, this must be a dream!'

Alyosha was exceedingly pleased that he had given cause for such happiness and that the impoverished wretch had consented to be made happy.

'Wait, Aleksey Fyodorovich, wait,' the second-grade captain said, clutching at another dream that suddenly presented itself to him and again chattering on in a frenzied and accelerated outpouring: 'Do you understand, sir, that now Ilyushka and I may actually be able to realize our dream: to buy a horse and a *kibitka*,* and a raven-black horse it must be, he specifically asked for a raven-black horse, and we'll set off the way we imagined it the day before yesterday. There's a friend of mine who's a lawyer in the province of Kursk, sir, we were boys together, sir, and I was told by a reliable source that if I go there he'll give me the post of clerk in his office, sir, and I mean, who knows, perhaps he really will . . . Well, and little mother and Ninochka would go in the back, I'd set Ilyushechka up to drive, and I'd go on foot, on foot, and I'd get us all there, sir . . . Merciful Lord, and if I could reclaim just one of the bad debts I have here, there might even be enough for that, sir!'

'There will, there will be enough!' Alyosha exclaimed. 'Katerina Ivanovna will send you as much as you require, and I also have money, you know, you may borrow as much as you need, as from a brother, as from a friend, and give it back later. (You'll grow rich, you'll grow rich!) And you know, you could have thought up no better plan than this going to live in another province! It will be your salvation, and even more, of your boy – but look, you must do it now, quickly, before winter, before the cold weather, and write to us from there, and we shall remain brothers . . . It's not a dream at all!'

Alyosha was on the point of embracing him, so pleased was he. Taking a glance at him, however, he suddenly paused: the man stood, his neck craned forth, his lips craned forth, his features frenzied and pale, and his lips whispered something, as though he were trying to get something out; there were no sounds, but his lips kept whispering, there was something strange about it.

'What's wrong with you?' Alyosha said with a sudden start.

'Aleksey Fyodorovich . . . I . . . you . . .' the second-grade captain muttered and jerked, staring at him wildly and intently with the look of a man who has decided to throw himself from a mountain, and at the same time his lips seemed to smile. 'I, sir . . . You, sir . . . How would you like me to show you a certain little conjuring trick, sir?' he suddenly articulated in a firm, rapid whisper, his speech no longer jerky now.

'What conjuring trick?'

'A little conjuring trick, a little *hocus-pocus*,' the second-grade captain said, still in a whisper; his mouth had twisted to the left, his left eye had closed to a slit, while he, without faltering, continued to glare at Alyosha as though he were riveted to him.

'But what's wrong with you, what conjuring trick do you mean?' the latter cried, in complete panic now.

'This one, watch!' the second-grade captain suddenly screamed.

And, showing him the two 'rainbow' banknotes which all along, throughout the entire conversation, he had been holding by their corners in the thumb and index finger of his right hand, he suddenly clutched them with a kind of frenzied ecstasy of rage, crushed them together and squeezed them hard in his right hand.

'Did you see it, sir, did you see?' he screamed at Alyosha, pale and beside himself, and, suddenly raising his fist aloft, threw the two crushed banknotes with full force on the sand. 'Did you see it, sir?' he screamed again, pointing at them. 'Well, look then, sir!'

And, suddenly raising his right foot, with savage malice he hurled himself into stamping on them with his right heel, exclaiming and grunting with each blow of his foot.

'There is your money, sir! There is your money, sir! There is your money, sir! There is your money, sir!' Suddenly he took a leap backwards and straightened himself up in front of Alyosha. His entire demeanour expressed an ineffable pride.

'Please inform the persons who sent you, sir, that the loofah will not sell its honour, sir!' he let out, extending one arm into the air. Then quickly he turned and hurled himself into flight; he had not run five paces, however, when, turning round again full-face, he suddenly blew Alyosha a kiss. But then again, still not having gone five paces, he turned round one last time, but this time without the twisted laughter in his features, which, on the contrary, were now convulsed with tears. In a rapid, wailing, jerking, choking patter he managed to bark out:

'What would I be able to tell my little boy, if I took money from you for our disgrace?' – and, having said this, he threw himself into flight, this time not turning round any more. Alyosha stared after him with inexpressible sadness. Oh, he realized that right up to the last moment the man himself had not known he was going to crumple up the banknotes and fling them away. As he ran, he did not once turn round, as Alyosha knew he would not. Alyosha was reluctant to pursue the man and call after him, and he knew the reason. When the man had disappeared from sight, Alyosha retrieved the two banknotes. They were merely very crushed after their flattening and trampling in the sand, but were quite intact and even crackled like the brand-new ones they were when he uncreased them and smoothed them out. Having done this he folded them, stuffed them in his pocket and went off to see Katerina Ivanovna in order to report on the success of his mission.

BOOK V
PRO AND CONTRA

I
A Betrothal

MRS Khokhlakova again met Alyosha before anyone else did. She was in a hurry. Something important had happened: Katerina Ivanovna's hysterics had ended in a swoon, whereupon there had set in 'a dreadful, fearful asthenia:* she lay down, turned up her eyes and began to rave. Now she has a fever, we've sent for Herzenstube, we've sent for her aunts. Her aunts are here now, but Herzenstube hasn't shown up yet. Everyone is sitting waiting in her room. Something is going to happen, for she has lost consciousness. Oh, what if it's brain fever?'*

As she exclaimed this, Mrs Khokhlakova had about her an air of serious alarm: 'It's serious, serious!' she kept adding at every turn, as though all that had happened to her previously were lacking in seriousness. Alyosha heard her through with sorrow; he began to give her an account of his adventures, too, but at his very first words she interrupted him: she had no time, she wanted him to sit with *Lise* and with *Lise* to wait for her.

'And *Lise*, dearest Aleksey Fyodorovich,' she whispered almost into his ear, '*Lise* astonished me just now most strangely, but what she said also touched me, and therefore my heart forgives her everything. Imagine, no sooner had you left than she suddenly began to repent sincerely of having laughed at you today and yesterday. You see, she wasn't laughing, it was merely a joke she was playing. But she repented so seriously, almost to the point of tears, that I was astonished. Never, in all the times that she has laughed at me, has she ever repented seriously, but has always done so in fun. And you know, she laughs at me every minute of the day. Yet now she was acting seriously, now it was all serious. She values your opinion extremely, Aleksey Fyodorovich, and please, if you are able, do not take offence at her nor harbour any grudge against her. I myself am constantly being lenient with her, as she is such a clever little thing – would you credit it? She said just now that you were the friend of her childhood – "the most serious friend of my childhood" – imagine that, the most serious, and in that case what am I? She has on that account extremely serious emotions, and even reminiscences, but most often it is these phrases and little remarks, these most unexpected little remarks of a kind one would never anticipate, but which suddenly come shooting out. Take that thing she said about the pine tree, for example: when she was in her early childhood there used to be a pine tree in our garden, and perhaps it's still there, so there's no reason to talk about it in the past tense. Pine trees are not like human beings, they go for a long time without altering, Aleksey Fyodorovich. "Mamma," she said, "I remember that pine tree [*sosna*] as if I'd just awoken from a dream [*kak so sna*]" only she put it somewhat differently, because there's a confusion there, pine tree is a stupid word, and the point is that she said apropos of that something so original that I really would not trust myself to relate it to you. And anyway, I've forgotten it all. Well, goodbye, I'm suffering from bad nervous shock, and I shall probably go insane. Oh, Aleksey Fyodorovich, I've gone insane twice in the course of my life, and received treatment for it. Go to *Lise*. Cheer her up as you are always so charmingly able to. *Lise*!' she called, approaching the door of her room. 'Look, I've brought you Aleksey Fyodorovich, whom you have so insulted, and he's not at all angry with you, I assure you, on the contrary he's astonished you should think it!'

'*Merci, maman*, come in, Aleksey Fyodorovich.'

Alyosha went in. *Lise* looked somewhat embarrassed and suddenly flushed all over. It seemed she was ashamed of something, and as is always the case in such instances, began to talk with the utmost rapidity about another matter entirely, as though this other matter were the only thing that interested her at the present moment.

'Mamma has just related to me, Aleksey Fyodorovich, the entire story of those two hundred roubles and of this errand you were given . . . to go and see that poor officer . . . and she told me the whole of that dreadful story of how he was mistreated and, do you know, even though mamma is a very incoherent story-teller . . . she keeps missing bits out . . . I listened and wept. Well then, what happened, did you deliver that money, and how is the unfortunate man now?'

'That's just the point, I didn't deliver it, and there's an entire story there, too,' Alyosha replied, for his part, too, as though the thing that concerned him most was the fact that he had not delivered the money, while *Lise* could see perfectly well that he was avoiding her gaze and also quite plainly attempting to talk of another matter. Alyosha sat down at the table and began to relate what had happened, but right from his very first words he completely stopped being embarrassed, carrying *Lise* in her turn along with him. He spoke under the influence of powerful emotion and of the extraordinary impression made on him by what had just taken place, and he managed to tell the story well and in detail. Formerly too, back in Moscow, when *Lise* had been only a child, he had liked to go to her and tell her things, whether it was something that had just happened to him, or something he had read, or some memory from his childhood. Sometimes they had even dreamed together and composed whole tales *à deux*, for the most part cheerful and comical ones. Now it was as though they had somehow both suddenly been carried back to their Moscow days, two years earlier. *Lise* was extremely moved by his story. Alyosha was able to portray before her with ardent emotion the character of Ilyushechka. When, however, he concluded, giving all the details, the scene in which the unhappy man had stamped on the money, *Lise* wrung her hands and cried out in uncontainable emotion:

'So you didn't deliver the money, you let him run away! Good Lord, but you should have run after him and caught him up . . .'

'No, *Lise*, it's better that I didn't,' said Alyosha, getting up from his chair and pacing concernedly about the room.

'What do you mean, better? In what way better? Now they'll starve to death!'

'No they won't, because those two hundred roubles won't escape them after all. He'll take them tomorrow, even with all that's happened. Tomorrow he'll take them, there's no doubt of it,' Alyosha pronounced, striding about in reflection. 'You see, *Lise*,' he continued, suddenly coming to a halt before her, 'I myself made a certain mistake there, but even that mistake has turned out for the best.'

'What mistake, and why for the best?'

'Because he's a cowardly fellow, of weak character. He's been exhausted by suffering and he's very good-hearted. Why, even now I keep asking myself why he suddenly took offence and stamped on the money like that, because I do assure you that right up to the very last moment he didn't know he was going to do it. And now I can see that there were many things there at which he took offence . . . and indeed it could not be otherwise in his situation. In the first place, he took offence at the very fact of having shown too much joy at the money in my presence, and of not having concealed it from me. If he had simply been pleased, not excessively, without showing it, and had started to swagger and give himself airs as others do when they accept money, then he'd have been able to endure it and do the same, but he had shown too much unfeigned joy, and that was what he found so offensive. Oh, *Lise*, he's an unfeigning and good-hearted man, and that's the whole trouble in these cases! The whole time he spoke to me his voice was so weak, enfeebled, and he spoke so very fast, giggled with that odd little laugh of his, or just wept ... It's true, he wept, such was his delight ... talked about his daughters ... and about the post he would be given in another town ... And no sooner had he poured out his soul, than he suddenly grew ashamed at having shown me all his soul like that. Then he instantly conceived a hatred for me. For he's the kind of poor person who's extraordinarily shamefaced about being poor. The main reason he felt insulted was that he'd taken me for his friend too quickly and had yielded to me too soon; he started off by flying at me, trying to intimidate me, but then suddenly, as soon as he saw the money, he began to embrace me. Because he actually embraced me, kept touching me with his hands. In a state like that he could not fail to experience it all as a degradation, and then I made the mistake I spoke of, a very important one: I suddenly went and told him that if he didn't have enough money to move to another town, he'd receive some more, and that I myself would give him as much as he required out of my own funds. It was that which suddenly took him by surprise: why, he seemed to be saying, had I leapt to his assistance? You know, *Lise*, it's dreadfully hard for a man who's suffered harm when everyone starts to look upon him as though they were his benefactors. I've heard that said, the Elder told it to me. I don't know how to express it, but I've often witnessed that very thing. Why, I myself feel the same. The main thing was that even though he didn't know right up to the very last moment that he was going to stamp on the banknotes, he could feel it coming, that is beyond question. And that's why his ecstasy was so intense, because he could feel it coming. And so, even though all that was so horrible, it was none the less for the best. I even consider that it was for the very best, that no better outcome could be imagined ...'

'Why, why would no better outcome be imagined?' exclaimed *Lise*, looking at Alyosha in great astonishment.

'Because, *Lise*, had he not stamped on that money, but taken it instead, then, on arriving home, after an hour or so he would have started to weep over his degradation, that is quite certainly what would have transpired. He would have started to weep and, no doubt, tomorrow would have come to me at first light and thrown the banknotes at me and stamped them into the ground, as he did earlier. Yet now he has gone away full of pride and triumph, even though he knows that he's "done for himself". And from that it follows that now there will be nothing simpler than to compel him to accept those two hundred roubles no later than tomorrow, because he has already proved his honour, has flung the money away, stamped it into the ground. What's more, when he did so, he can never have dreamed that I'd take the money back to him tomorrow. And all the while there's the fact that he does need that money terribly. Even though he's proud just now, this very day he will start to reflect on the help he's deprived himself of. At night he will reflect even more deeply, he'll dream about it, and by tomorrow morning he'll very likely be prepared to come running to me and beg forgiveness. And that is when I shall present myself, saying: "Here, you are a proud man, you have demonstrated your merit, now take the money, and forgive us." And at that point he will take it!'

It was with a kind of rapture that Alyosha pronounced:

'And at that point he will take it!' *Lise* clapped her hands.

'Oh that is true, that is true, I've suddenly understood it so terribly well! Oh, Alyosha, how do you know all these things? You're so young yet you already know what is in people's souls. I would never have hit on that . . .'

'The main thing we have to do now is to make him see that he's on an equal footing with us all, in spite of the fact that he's borrowing money from us,' Alyosha continued in his rapture, 'and not only on an equal, but even on a higher footing . . .'

'"On a higher footing" – what a lovely expression, Aleksey Fyodorovich, but do go on, do go on!'

'Well, perhaps that wasn't the right way to phrase it . . . on a higher footing . . . but it doesn't matter, because . . .'

'Oh no, it doesn't matter, it doesn't matter at all! Forgive me, Alyosha, dear . . . You know, I don't think I've had a proper respect for you until now . . . that's to say, I've respected you on an equal footing, but now I shall do so on a higher one. Now don't be angry at me for "witticizing", dear,' she at once chimed in with powerful feeling. 'I'm small and ridiculous, but you, you . . . Listen, Aleksey Fyodorovich, is there not in all this reasoning of ours, or rather yours . . . no, I prefer ours . . . is there not in this an element of contempt for him, for that unfortunate man . . . in our taking apart his soul the way we're doing now, as though we were superior? Mm? In our predicting with such certainty that he'll accept the money? Mm?'

'No, *Lise*, there is no contempt in it,' Alyosha replied firmly, as though he had readied himself beforehand for that question. 'I thought about that myself, as I came here. Think about it: what contempt can there be, when we're just the same as he is, when everyone's the same as he is? For I mean, we're all like him, no better. And even if we were better, we'd still behave like him if we were in his position . . . I don't know what you think of yourself, *Lise*, but I consider that in many ways I have a petty soul. While he doesn't – on the contrary, his soul is full of tact and delicacy. No, *Lise*, there's no contempt for him involved! You know, *Lise*, my Elder once told me: "People must be looked after in every respect as though they were children, and some as though they were patients in hospital . . ."

'Oh, Aleksey Fyodorovich, oh, my dear man, let us look after people as though they were patients!'

'All right, *Lise*, I'm ready, only I'm not quite ready in myself; at some times I'm very impatient, and at others it's as though I were blind. Now with you it's another matter.'

'Oh, I don't believe it! Aleksey Fyodorovich, how happy I am!'

'How good of you that you should say that, *Lise*.'

'Aleksey Fyodorovich, you're a wonderfully good man, but you some-times seem like a pedant . . . and yet when one looks at you, you're not a pedant at all. Go and look outside the door, open it slowly and see if mamma's eavesdropping,' *Lise* whispered suddenly in a kind of nervous, hurried whisper.

Alyosha went and opened the door a little way, and reported that no one was eavesdropping.

'Come here, Aleksey Fyodorovich,' *Lise* went on, blushing redder and redder. 'Give me your hand, like this. Listen, I have an important confession to make to you: that letter I sent you yesterday was not written as a joke, but was serious . . .'

And with her hand she covered her eyes. It was plain that it cost her a great deal of embarrassment to make this confession. Suddenly she gripped his hand and kissed it fiercely three times.

'Oh, *Lise*, that's wonderful,' Alyosha exclaimed in delight. 'Why, I was quite certain it was serious.'

'Certain? Well I never!' She suddenly drew his hand aside, without, however, releasing it from hers, blushing dreadfully and letting out a happy little giggle. 'I kiss his hand and he says "that's wonderful".' But she reproached him unjustly: Alyosha, too, was in great confusion.

'My wish is that you should always like me, *Lise*, but I don't know how to bring that about,' he muttered with an effort, and also blushing.

'Alyosha, dear, you're cold and insolent. Do you see? He deigned to elect me as his spouse and was content to leave it at that! He was already certain that my letter was serious, have you ever heard the like? I mean to say, that is sheer insolence – that's what!'

'But is it bad, then, that I was certain?' Alyosha suddenly laughed.

'Oh no, Alyosha, on the contrary, it's most terribly good,' said *Lise*, looking at him tenderly and with happiness. Alyosha stood, holding her hand all the while in his. Suddenly he bent and kissed her right on the lips.

'What is this now? What has got into you?' *Lise* exclaimed. Alyosha was completely at a loss.

'Well, forgive me if it's wrong. Perhaps I'm behaving very stupidly. You said I was cold, so I went and gave you a kiss . . . Only I can see it was a stupid thing to do.'

Lise began to laugh and covered her face with her hands.

'And in that dress!' broke from her between bursts of laughter, but suddenly she stopped laughing and grew perfectly serious, almost severe.

'Well, Alyosha, I think we shall wait a while with our kisses, because neither of us is ready for that yet, and we still have a very long time to wait,' she concluded, suddenly. 'You'd do better to tell me why you want to take me, such a foolish girl, and a sick little foolish girl too, you who are so clever, so intellectual, so good at noticing things? Oh, Alyosha, I'm terribly lucky, because I don't deserve you at all.'

'Wait, *Lise*. In another few days' time I shall be coming out of the monastery altogether. When I come out into the world I shall have to take a wife, that I know. That is what *he* instructed me to do. Whom better could I take but you . . . and who but you would take me? I've already thought it over. For one thing, you've known me since you were a child, and for another, there are in you very many abilities which I lack altogether. Your soul has more gaiety than mine; above all, you are more innocent than I, for I have already come into contact with many, many things . . . Oh, you don't know — I mean, I am a Karamazov, too! What do I care if you laugh and make jokes at me too? On the contrary, please laugh away, I'm more than happy for you to do so. The only thing is that you laugh like a little girl, yet you think to yourself like a female martyr . . .'

'A female martyr? Whatever do you mean?'

'Yes, *Lise*, that question you asked just now about whether we felt scorn for that unfortunate man, performing an anatomy of his soul in the way we were doing — that's a martyr's question. You see, I don't know how to put this, but those in whom such questions arise are themselves capable of suffering. As you sit in your bath chair you must have time to reflect on many things . . .'

'Alyosha, give me your hand, why do you take it away?' *Lise* uttered in a strange, small voice that was weakened and feeble with happiness. 'Listen, Alyosha, what clothes will you wear when you come out of the monastery, what sort of outfit will it be? Don't laugh, don't be angry, it's very, very important for me.'

'As far as outfits are concerned, *Lise*, I have not yet given them much thought, but whatever you like, that is what I shall wear.'

'I want you to wear a dark-blue velvet coat, a white piqué waistcoat and a soft grey goatsfelt hat . . . Tell me, did you believe earlier that I didn't love you, when I disowned the letter I sent you yesterday?'

'No, I didn't.'

'Oh, insufferable, incorrigible man!'

'You see, I knew that you . . . as it were, loved me, but I made it seem as though I believed you didn't, so you'd feel more . . . comfortable . . .'

'Even worse! Worse, and yet better than ever. Alyosha, I love you terribly. Before you arrived I made a plan: I would ask you for the letter I sent you yesterday, and if you calmly took it out and gave it to me (something you might always be expected to do) then that meant that you didn't love me at all, felt nothing for me, but were just a stupid and unworthy boy, and I was lost. But you'd left the letter in your cell, and that gave me hope: the truth is, isn't it, that you left it in your cell because you knew I would ask for it back, so you wouldn't have to give me it back? Isn't that so? Isn't it?'

'Ah, *Lise*, no, it's not so at all, why, I have the letter with me just as I did earlier, it's in this pocket, here it is.'

Laughing, Alyosha produced the letter and showed it to her from a distance.

'Only I shan't let you have it back, you must read it from my hands.'

'What? So you were lying, you're a monk and you told a lie?'

'Perhaps I did,' Alyosha said, laughing too, 'so I wouldn't have to give you it back. It's very precious to me,' he added suddenly with powerful feeling and again blushing. 'This is for ever now, and I shall never let anyone else have it!'

Lise gazed at him in delight.

'Alyosha,' she babbled again, 'go and look outside the door and make sure that mamma is not eavesdropping!'

'Very well, *Lise*, I'll take a look, only wouldn't it be better not to — don't you think? Why should you suspect your mother of doing something so base?'

'What do you mean — base? What baseness is there in it? She's simply eavesdropping on her daughter, and it's her right, and not anything base,'

Lise said, flaring up. 'You may be certain, Aleksey Fyodorovich, that when I am a mother and have a daughter like myself I shall eavesdrop on her without fail.'

'Indeed, *Lise*? It's not a nice thing to do.'

'Oh, for goodness sake, what is base about it? If I were to eavesdrop on some ordinary social chit-chat that would be base, but here my own daughter has shut herself up with a young man ... Listen, Alyosha, you may as well know that I shall also keep an eye on you right from the day of our wedding, and you may as well also know that I shall open all your letters and read them. So don't say I haven't warned you ...'

'Yes, of course, if that's ...' Alyosha muttered. 'Only it's not very nice ...'

'Oh, what scorn! Alyosha, dear, let us not fall out from the very start – I'd better be entirely truthful with you: eavesdropping is, of course, a most beastly thing to do and of course I'm not right and you are, but I shall eavesdrop all the same.'

'Then do it. You won't find anything to spy on on my account,' Alyosha laughed.

'Alyosha, will you submit to me? That is also something we must first determine.'

'With all my inclination, *Lise*, and most certainly, but not in important matters. Where important matters are concerned, if you disagree with me I shall act as duty instructs me.'

'That is as it should be. Then you may as well know that I, too, am not only prepared to submit to you in important matters, but will yield to you in all the rest as well and give you my oath on that now – in all matters, and for the whole of my life,' *Lise* exclaimed fierily, 'and with happiness, with happiness! Not only that, I vow to you that I shall never eavesdrop on you, never once and never ever, and will never read a single one of your letters, because you are right, and I am not. And even though I may want dreadfully to eavesdrop, and I know that I will, all the same I shall not do so, because you consider it ignoble. You are now like my providence ... I say, Aleksey Fyodorovich, why have you been so sad all these days, both yesterday and today? I know that you have troubles and calamities, but I can see that you also have some kind of special sadness, a secret one, perhaps, mm?'

'Yes, *Lise*, I have a secret one, too,' Alyosha pronounced sadly. 'I can see that you must love me if you have guessed that.'

'But what kind of sadness is it? Concerning what? Can you tell me?' *Lise* got out, in a timid plea.

'I'll tell you later, *Lise* . . . afterwards . . .' Alyosha said in confusion. 'It would probably be incomprehensible to you now. Why, I don't think I could even tell you if I tried.'

'I also know that your brothers and your father are making you unhappy, aren't they?'

'Yes, there's my brothers, too,' Alyosha said, as if in reflection.

'I don't like your brother Ivan Fyodorovich, Alyosha,' *Lise* commented suddenly.

Alyosha noted this comment with some surprise, but did not take it up.

'The brothers are ruining themselves,' he continued, 'and so is my father. And they are ruining others along with them. It's the "earthen force of the Karamazovs", as Father Paisy expressed it the other day – earthen and violent, untrimmed . . . I don't even know whether the spirit of God moves upon the face of that force. All I know is that I myself am a Karamazov. Am I a monk, a monk? Am I a monk, *Lise*? Did I hear you say a moment ago that I was a monk?'

'Yes, I said that.'

'Well, it is possible that I do not even believe in God.'

'You don't believe? Whatever has happened to you?' *Lise* said quietly and cautiously. But Alyosha made no reply to this. There was in this, in these too sudden words of his something deeply mysterious and deeply subjective, something that was possibly obscure even to himself, but already without doubt tormenting him.

'And you see now, in addition to all that, my friend is departing, the finest man in all the world, he is forsaking the earth. If you but knew, *Lise*, if you but knew how I am bound, how I am welded heart and soul to that man! And now I shall be left alone . . . I'm coming to you, *Lise* . . . Henceforth let us be together . . .'

'Yes, together, together! From this day forth always together for the rest of our lives. Look, you may kiss me – I permit you to.'

Alyosha gave her a kiss.

'Well, now you must go, Christ be with you!' (And she crossed him.) 'Go quickly *to him*, while he still lives. I realize now that I have cruelly delayed you. I shall say prayers for him today, and for you. Alyosha, we shall be happy! Do you think we shall be happy, do you?'

'I think we shall, *Lise*.'

As he came out of *Lise*'s room, Alyosha did not deem it necessary to go through and see Mrs Khokhlakova and, without saying goodbye to her, began to make his way out of the house. But no sooner had he opened the door and emerged on to the staircase than suddenly before him there appeared Mrs Khokhlakova herself. From the first word she spoke Alyosha guessed that she had been waiting there for him on purpose.

'Aleksey Fyodorovich, this is dreadful. This is childish nonsense and sheer rubbish. I hope you won't dare even to think of ... It is folly, folly, folly!' she hurled at him.

'Well, but don't tell her that,' said Alyosha, 'or she'll get excited, and that will do her harm at present.'

'I hear the sensible words of a sensible young man. Am I to take them to mean that you yourself only went along with her because you were reluctant, out of compassion for her morbid state, to anger her by contradiction?'

'Oh no, absolutely not, I spoke to her in perfect seriousness,' Alyosha declared, resolutely.

'In this case seriousness is impossible, unthinkable, and for one thing, I shall forbid you to cross my threshold ever again, and for another, I shall travel away and take her with me.'

'But why?' Alyosha said. 'I mean, it's so far in the future – we may have to wait for perhaps another year and a half.'

'Oh, Aleksey Fyodorovich, that is, of course, true, and in the course of a year and a half you will quarrel and part company with her a thousand times. But I feel so unhappy, so unhappy about it! Even though I know it's all nonsense, it has still overwhelmed me. Now I am like Famusov in the final scene,* you are Chatsky, she is Sofya, and, imagine, I've come running out on to the staircase on purpose in order to catch you – I mean, all the fateful things happen on the staircase in the play, too. I heard it all, I could scarcely keep my balance. So that is the explanation of all last night's horrors and all today's hysterics! For the daughter, love, and for the mother, death. Into the coffin with her. And now the second and most important thing: what is this letter she has written you, show it to me at once, at once!'

'No, I'd better not. Tell me, how is Katerina Ivanovna's health, I very much need to know.'

'She continues to lie in a delirium, she has not recovered consciousness; her aunts are here and all they can do is to moan and behave to me in that stuck-up fashion of theirs, and Herzenstube came and got such a terrible fright that I didn't know what to do with him or how to save him and was even on the point of sending for a doctor. They took him away in my carriage. And suddenly to cap it all you come here with this letter. To be sure, it's all still a year and a half in the future. In the name of all that is great and holy, in the name of your dying Elder please give me that letter, Aleksey Fyodorovich, me, her mother! If you like you may hold on to it with your fingers while I read it from your hands.'

'No, I'm not going to show you it, Katerina Osipovna, even if she were to permit me to, I wouldn't. I shall come tomorrow and, if you like, I shall discuss many things with you, but for now – farewell!'

And Alyosha ran down the stairs and out into the street.

2

Smerdyakov with a Guitar

AND in any case, he had no time. A thought had flashed across his mind, even as he had been saying his farewell to *Lise*. The thought was: how to find the most cunning manner in which to waylay brother Dmitry, who was plainly hiding from him? It was by no means early in the day, the time was now three in the afternoon. With all his being Alyosha yearned to be back in the monastery with his 'great one' who was dying, but the need to see brother Dmitry had overpowered everything else: with each hour in Alyosha's mind grew the conviction that a terrible and unavoidable catastrophe was about to take place. What precisely the catastrophe was and what he wanted to say to his brother at that moment, he himself might possibly not have been able to determine. 'My benefactor may die in my absence, but at least I shall not reproach myself all my life with the thought that perhaps I might have saved him but did not, walked by on the other side, hurried off to my home. In acting thus, I shall be obeying his great word . . .'

His plan consisted in taking Dmitry by surprise, namely by climbing, as he had done the day before, over that wicker fence, entering the garden and lying in wait for him in the summerhouse. 'If he's not there,' thought Alyosha, 'then, without a word to either Foma or the mistresses, I'll hide and wait in the summerhouse until evening if I have to. If he's watching out for Grushenka to arrive then he may very well come to the summerhouse . . .' As a matter of fact, Alyosha had not thought out the details of his plan very carefully, but he had decided to put it into action, even though he would not get back to the monastery that day . . .

It all went off without a hitch: he climbed over the wicker fence in almost exactly the same place he had done the previous day, and secretly made his way to the summerhouse. He did not want anyone to observe him: both the mistress and Foma (if he was there) might take his brother's side and act in obedience to his commands, and might either not let Alyosha into the garden, or else give his brother advance warning that someone was looking and asking for him. In the summerhouse there was no one. Alyosha sat down in the seat he had occupied yesterday and proceeded to wait. He took a look round at the summerhouse; for some reason it seemed far more decrepit than it had done yesterday, and indeed this time it seemed positively dilapidated. The day was, however, just as bright and sunny as it had been yesterday. On the green table there was imprinted a circle from yesterday's glass of cognac, which must have spilt. Empty and irrelevant thoughts occurred to him, as they invariably do during spells of tedious waiting: for example, why, in coming here, had he sat in precisely the same place he had sat in yesterday, and not in some other? At last he became very downcast, downcast from anxious uncertainty. But he had not sat for a quarter of an hour when suddenly, somewhere very close at hand, the chord of a guitar was heard. Some people were sitting, or had just sat down, about twenty yards from him, at all events no more, somewhere among the bushes. Alyosha was suddenly visited by a fleeting memory that as he had been coming away from his brother in the summerhouse he had seen or quickly glimpsed before him on his left near the garden fence an old, low, green bench amidst the shrubs. On it, apparently, the visitors had now seated themselves. But who could they be? Suddenly the voice of a certain male person began to sing a verse of a song in a rather sweet falsetto, as he accompanied himself on the guitar:

> By power that can't be conquered
> To my true love I'm bonded.
> O Lord have mer—cy
> Upon her and me!
> Upon her and me!
> Upon her and me!

The voice stopped. It was a lackey's tenor, and the eccentricity of the song was also characteristic of a lackey's song. Another voice, a female one this time, suddenly pronounced fawningly and almost timidly, but with great affection:

'Why have you not paid us a visit for so long, Pavel Fyodorovich, why do you forever treat us with such scorn?'

'Not a bit of it, miss,' the male voice replied, politely enough, but above all with a firm and insistent dignity. It was plain that the man was

in the dominant role, while the woman was flirting with him. 'The man –
I think he's Smerdyakov,' Alyosha thought; 'at least, he sounds like him,
and the lady must be the daughter of the mistress of the cottage here, the
daughter who arrived from Moscow, wears dresses with trains and goes
to eat soup at Marfa Ignatyevna's . . .'

'I'm ever so fond of verses, if they be well-concorded,' the female
voice continued. 'Why do you not resume?'

The voice broke into song anew:

> A Tsar's crown I'd surrender
> Were my sweet's health mended.
> O Lord have mer–cy
> Upon her and me!
> Upon her and me!
> Upon her and me!

'It sounded even better the last time,' the female voice observed. 'Of
the crown, you sang: "Were my dear's health mended." It sounded more
loving that way; I expect you've simply forgotten the words today.'

'Verses are nonsense, miss,' Smerdyakov snapped.

'Oh no, I like a verse very much.'

'The essential of verses, miss, is that they're rubbish, miss. Judge for
yourself: who in the world talks in rhyme? And if we all began talking in
rhyme, even if it were at the instruction of the authorities, would we ever
get much said, miss? Verses are not important, Marya Kondratyevna.'

'How clever you are about everything, how is it you have penetrated
the secret of everything?' the female voice said, fawning more and more.

'I might have done more, miss, I might have known more, miss, had it
not been for the lot I have suffered since I were not no more than a brat,
miss. I'd have shot in a duel the man who said I was a scoundrel because
I issued from the Stinker fatherless, and in Moscow they rubbed my nose
in it, it spread over there by way of Grigory Vasilyevich, miss. Grigory
Vasilyevich tells me off for mutinying against my nativity: "You opened
her matrix,"* he says. Well, matrix or no, but I'd have let myself be
murthered in the womb in order not to issue into the world at all, miss.
At the market they used to say, and your dear mother also began telling
me, out of her great tactlessness, that the Stinker wore a Polish plait upon
her head, and that her height was "nought but two arshins". Why did it
have to be "nought but", when she could just have said "nobbut", the
way everybody else does? She wanted to make it sound tearful, and I
mean, them's muzhik's tears, miss, and a muzhik's feelings, too. Can the

Russian muzhik have feelings the way a person of progressive education can? Because of his lack of education he can't have no feelings. Ever since I were not no more than a brat, whenever I heard "nought but two arshins", I felt like banging my head on the wall. I hate all Russia, Marya Kondratyevna.'

'If you were a nice young military cadet or a nice young hussar you would not speak like that, but draw your sword and go off to defend all Russia.'

'Not only do I not want to be a nice young military hussar, Marya Kondratyevna – I actually, on the contrary, wish the destruction of all soldiers, miss.'

'And when the enemy arrives, who will defend us then?'

'Nobody needs to, miss. In 1812 there took place a great invasion by the Emperor of the French, Napoleon I, the father* of the one who reigns at present, and it would have been a good thing if those same French had conquered us: a clever nation would have conquered an entirely stupid one, miss, and joined it to itself. We'd have quite different manners and habits, miss.'

'Are they really so much better than our own? I would not exchange one of our nice young dandies, not even for three Englishmen,' Marya Kondratyevna said tenderly, doubtless accompanying her remark with the most languorous of eyes.

'That is as ladies have their adorations, miss.'

'Why, you yourself are like a foreigner, like a real well-born foreigner, though I tell you it in shame.'

'If you desire to know, where lechery's concerned the fellows over there are just the same as the fellows over here. They're all scoundrels, miss, and the only difference is that over there your villain walks about in patent-leather boots, while over here he just stinks in his poverty and don't see nothing wrong in it. The Russian people needs the whip, miss, as Fyodor Pavlovich so truly said yesterday, though he's a crazy fellow, miss, with all them brats of his.'

'You yourself said that you had such respect for Ivan Fyodorovich.'

'And his honour reported about me that I'm a stinking lackey. His consideration of me is that I may mutiny; and he is wrong there, miss. If I'd had a sum like that in my pocket I'd have quit here long ago. Dmitry Fyodorovich is worse than any lackey, whether one takes into account his behaviour, his intelligence or his poverty, miss, and of nothing is he able, but of all is he respected. I'm nothing but a bouillon-boy, but with a bit of luck I might be able to open a café-restaurant on the Petrovka.* Because I'm a professional cook, and not one of those fellows in Moscow, apart from the foreigners, can serve up professional cooked food. That Dmitry Fyodorovich is a bare-breeches, miss, and even though he may summon to a duel the most eminent son of a count, and the count accepts it, miss, in what way is he better than me, miss? Because he's a lot more stupid than me. All that money he's whistled away without no purpose, miss.'

'I think a duel must be a very fine thing,' Marya Kondratyevna suddenly observed.

'In what way, miss?'

'It's so fearfully brave, especially if the nice young officers with pistols in their hands fire them at one another for a certain she. Quite simply a picture. Oh, were girls allowed to watch, I should most terribly like to do so.'

'It's all right if you're the one who's pointing the thing, but if the other fellow's pointing it at your ugly mug, it's a pretty stupid feeling you get, miss. You runs away, Marya Kondratyevna.'

'Surely you wouldn't run away, would you?'

But Smerdyakov vouchsafed her no answer. After a moment's silence another chord rang out and the falsetto came flowing out again with the final verse:

> In spite of all my trying
> I shall end up by flying,
> I'll go with pleasure sigh–ing
> And in the city live!
> And I shall not grieve.
> I shall not, shall not grieve,
> I shall not, will not, don't intend to grieve!

Here something unexpected happened: Alyosha suddenly sneezed. The people on the bench at once grew quiet. Alyosha got up and walked in their direction. It was indeed Smerdyakov – wearing his Sunday best, his hair pomaded and very neatly curled, and shod in patent-leather shoes. A guitar lay on the bench. And the lady was Marya Kondratyevna, the mistress's daughter; her dress was a light blue one, with a train two arshins long; she was a girl still young and not bad-looking, though she had a very round face and terrible freckles.

'Will brother Dmitry return soon?' said Alyosha, as calmly as he could.

Smerdyakov slowly raised himself from the bench; so did Marya Kondratyevna.

'Why do you suppose that I should be privy to the whereabouts of Dmitry Fyodorovich? It would be another matter were I employed as his keeper,' Smerdyakov replied quietly, succinctly and disdainfully.

'Oh, I simply thought I'd ask you – don't you know?' Alyosha said by way of explanation.

'Nothing of his whereabouts do I know, nor do I wish to know, sir.'

'But my brother made a special point of telling me that it's you who tell him about everything that goes on in the house, and that you promised to give him the word when Agrafena Aleksandrovna comes.'

Slowly and imperturbably, Smerdyakov raised his eyes to him.

'And how were you so good as to enter on this occasion, as the gate here was padlocked just an hour ago?'

'Well, I entered from the side-lane by climbing the fence, and went straight to the summerhouse. You will, I hope, forgive me for that,' he said, turning to Marya Kondratyevna. 'I needed to get hold of my brother quickly.'

'Oh, how could you possibly do anything to offend us?' Marya Kondratyevna simpered, flattered by Alyosha's apology. 'Why, Dmitry Fyodorovich himself often goes to the summerhouse that way, and we don't even know that he's there.'

'I've been looking for him high and low, I very much want to see him or to find out from yourselves where he is now. Please believe me when I tell you it's a matter that affects him urgently.'

'He never tells us anything,' Marya Kondratyevna began to babble.

'Though in the past I have frequented these here parts in the capacity of an acquaintance,' Smerdyakov began again, 'even here he has mercilessly importuned me with constant inquiries concerning the master: what is happening at his house and how is he, who has arrived and who has left, and is there not something else I can report to him? Twice he has even threatened me with death.'

'Death?' Alyosha said in wonder.

'Well, would that constitute anything much to him, sir, with his kind of character, which you were so good as to observe with your own eyes yesterday, sir? If you let Agrafena Aleksandrovna in, he says, and she spends the night here, it's your life that will be forfeit. I'm afraid of him something dreadful, sir, and if I weren't so afraid I'd have to report him to the municipal authorities. God knows, even, what he may cause to happen, sir.'

'"I'll crush you in a mortar," he said to him the other day,' Marya Kondratyevna added.

'Well, those were possibly just high words . . .' Alyosha observed. 'If I could talk to him now I'd have something to say to him about that . . .'

'This is the sole intimation I can give you,' Smerdyakov said suddenly, as though he had made up his mind about something. 'I come here sometimes for old neighbourly acquaintance's sake, and why should I not do so, sir? On the other hand, Ivan Fyodorovich sent me today at first light to him at his lodgings in that Ozyornaya Street of his, without a letter, sir, to get Dmitry Fyodorovich by word to come to the inn on the square here, sir, so they could dine together. I went, sir, but Dmitry Fyodorovich wasn't at those lodgings of his, sir, and it was already eight o'clock. "He was here," they said, "but he's gone away and hasn't been back." Those were his landlords' very words. It was as if they were in some kind of conspiracy together, sir, a mutual one, sir. He and your dear brother Ivan Fyodorovich may be sitting in that inn at this very minute, as Ivan Fyodorovich didn't come back for dinner, and Fyodor Pavlovich had his alone an hour ago and has now lain down to take his rest. I do, however, most earnestly request that you say nothing to him of myself or of the things I have conveyed to you, sir, for his honour will kill me for nothing, sir.'

'Brother Ivan called Dmitry to an inn today?' Alyosha quickly asked.

'That is precisely so, sir.'

'To the Capital City, the inn on the market-square?'

'To the very same, sir.'

'That is very probable!' Alyosha exclaimed in great agitation. 'Thank you, Smerdyakov, you have given me some important news, I shall go there at once.'

'Please do not give me away, sir,' Smerdyakov said as he went.

'Oh no, I shall present myself at the inn as though by chance, you may rest easy.'

'But where are you off to? I shall unlock the gate for you,' Marya Kondratyevna cried.

'No, it's quicker this way. I'll go back over the fence again.'

Smerdyakov's news had shaken Alyosha terribly. He set off towards the inn. To enter the inn dressed as he was could hardly be contemplated, but it would be all right for him to inquire on the staircase and have them summoned out to him. No sooner had he approached the inn, however, than one of its windows opened and brother Ivan himself shouted down to him:

'Alyosha, can you come up here and sit with me? You'd be doing me a great favour.'

'Indeed I can, only I don't know what people will think of the way I'm dressed.'

'Well, I just so happen to be in a private room, go up to the front and I'll come down and meet you . . .'

A moment later Alyosha was sitting beside his brother. Ivan was alone and was dining.

3

The Brothers Become Acquainted

IVAN was not, however, in a private room. It was just a place by a window divided off by a folding screen; even so, those who sat behind the screen could not be seen by others. This room was the first one, an entrance chamber, with a counter along the side wall. Waiters ran to and fro through the room every moment. By way of clientele there was only one little old man, a retired army bureaucrat, drinking tea in a corner. In the other rooms, though, there was in progress all the usual hubbub of an inn: calls for service, the opening of beer bottles, the clack of billiard balls, the droning of a hurdy-gurdy. Alyosha knew that Ivan almost never went to this inn and was indeed no lover of inns in general; for precisely this reason, he reflected, Ivan must be here in order to meet brother Dmitry according to some arrangement. Of brother Dmitry, however, there was no sign.

'I'll order you some fish soup or something – not by tea alone shall you live, after all,' cried Ivan, by all the evidence hugely pleased to have lured Alyosha inside. He himself had finished eating and was drinking tea.

'Very well, fish soup and tea to follow – I'm starved,' Alyosha said cheerfully.

'And cherry preserves? They have them here. Do you remember how fond you were of cherry preserves as a little boy when you lived at Polyonov's?'

'Oh, do you remember that? All right, preserves, too – I'm still fond of them.'

Ivan rang the bell for the waiter and ordered fish soup, tea and preserves.

'I remember it all, Alyosha, I remember you when you were no more than eleven years old – I was in my fifteenth year then. Fifteen and eleven, there's a difference there that prevents brothers ever being friends at those ages. I don't even know if I liked you. During the first years when I went to live in Moscow I really didn't think about you at all. Later on, when you also landed up in Moscow, I think we met only on one occasion somewhere. And now this is the fourth month I've been living here, and until today you and I haven't said a word to each other. Tomorrow I'm leaving, and as I sat here just now I was wondering: how could I get to see him in order to say goodbye? And then there you were walking past.'

'Did you wish to see me very much, then?'

'Yes. I want to get to know you properly, once and for all, and for you to become properly acquainted with me. And with that to say goodbye. In my view, the best time to get to know someone is before a parting. I've seen the way you've looked at me all these three months, your eyes have had a sort of constant expectation in them, and that's what I can't stand, that's the reason why I've made no approach to you. But in the end I've learned to respect you: the little man, I said to myself, knows how to stand his ground. Observe that though I'm laughing now, I speak in seriousness. I mean, you do know how to stand your ground, don't you? I like such people, whatever the ground is that they're standing on, and even if they're dear little laddies like yourself. That expectant look of yours has finally lost all its repugnance for me . . . I think that for some reason you love me, don't you, Alyosha?'

'Yes, I do, Ivan. Brother Dmitry says of you: "Ivan is a tomb." I say of you: "Ivan is an enigma." Even now you're an enigma to me, but I have managed to figure out one thing about you, though it is only since this morning!'

'And what might that be?' Ivan asked, laughing.

'You won't lose your temper?' Alyosha said, laughing too.

'Well?'

'The fact that you're every bit as much a young man as all the other twenty-three-year-old young men, every bit as much a nice, young, pristine, fresh and − yes, yellow-beaked boy! Oh, I say, I hope I haven't really offended you!'

'Not at all, you have surprised me with the similarity of our thoughts!' Ivan exclaimed with mirth and fervour. 'Would you believe it: ever since our meeting at her house that time all I've been able to think of concerning myself has been that twenty-three-year-old yellow-beakedness of mine, and now it's suddenly as though you'd guessed that and started out with it right away. As I sat here just now, do you know what I was saying to myself? That even if I had no faith in life, had lost my faith in the woman who was dear to me, lost my faith in the order of things, even gained the conviction that everything was, on the contrary, a disorderly, accursed and, possibly, devilish chaos, even if I were overwhelmed by all the horrors of human disenchantment – I should still want to go on living and, having once put my lips to that cup, would not turn away from it until I had drained it to the end! Though actually, by the time I am thirty, I shall probably fling down the cup even though I haven't drained it all and go away . . . where, I don't know. But until I am thirty, I know this with assurance, my youth will prevail over everything – all disenchantment, all revulsion at life. Many times I have wondered whether there exists in the world a despair of a kind that would be able to vanquish within me this frenzied and possibly indecent thirst for life, and I have decided that it apparently does not exist, before the age of thirty, that is, and then I shall have had enough in any case, or so it seems to me. This thirst for life is often called base by certain consumptive milksop-moralists, especially the poets. It is a somewhat Karamazovian feature, to be sure, this thirst for life in spite of everything, and it also without question dwells in you – but why is it base? There's still an awful lot of centripetal force left on our planet, Alyosha. Life wants to be lived, and I live it, even though it goes against logic. Very well, so I don't believe in the order of things, but the sticky leaf-buds* that open in spring are dear to me, as is the blue sky, as are certain people whom, would you believe it, sometimes one loves one knows not why, and as are certain human achievements in which one may perhaps have ceased to have any faith, but which for old time's sake one treasures in one's heart. Look, now, they've brought your fish soup; eat, and may it do you good. It's wonderful soup, they have a good recipe. I want to take a trip to Europe, Alyosha, and hence I shall take it; yet I mean, I know it's a cemetery I shall be going to, but it's the dearest, dearest of cemeteries, that's all. Dear corpses lie there,* each stone laid over them speaks of such ardently lived past life, such passionate faith in one's achievements, the truth one has gained, one's struggle and one's learning, that I know in advance I shall fall to the ground and kiss those stones and weep over them – at the same time convinced with all my heart that all this has long been a cemetery and in no way any more than that. And not from despair will I weep, but simply because I shall be happy at the tears I shed. I shall grow drunk on the tenderness of my own emotion. The sticky leaf-buds of spring, the blue sky – I love them, that's what! Here there is no intellect, no logic, here it is a question of loving with one's insides, one's belly, of loving one's own young energies . . . Do you understand anything of the rot I'm talking, Alyosha?' Ivan laughed, suddenly.

'Too well do I understand, Ivan: one wants to live with one's insides, one's belly – that was well said, and I'm terribly glad that you want to live that way,' Alyosha exclaimed. 'I think that everyone has a duty to love life above all else in the world.'

'To love life more than its meaning?'

'Most certainly; to love it before logic, as you say, especially before logic, for only then will I understand its meaning. That is how it has seemed to me for a long time now. Half of your task is complete, Ivan, and won: you love life. Now you must apply yourself to its second half, and you will be saved.'

'You're already saving me, yet maybe I haven't perished! And what does it consist of, this second half of yours?'

'In having to raise up your dead, which may never perhaps have died.* Well, now I shall have some tea. I'm glad that we're having this talk, Ivan.'

'I perceive that you are in some kind of fit of inspiration. I'm terribly fond of such *professions de foi* from such . . . novices. You're a man of firmness, Alyosha. Is it true that you intend to leave the monastery?'

'Yes. My Elder is sending me into the world.'

'Well then, we shall be seeing each other in the world, we shall meet until I am thirty, until I start to turn away from that cup I mentioned. Father doesn't intend to turn away from his cup until he's seventy, he even dreams of it when he's eighty, he said so himself, and that is serious coming from him, even though he's a buffoon. He too has taken a stand, but on his voluptuary passion, and as though it were a rock . . . though to be sure, after the age of thirty one may have nothing much left to take a stand on except that . . . But to go on with it until one's seventy is base; until the age of thirty is the preferable thing: one may retain "a shade of decency"* while cheating oneself all the while. Have you seen Dmitry today?'

'No, I haven't, but I've seen Smerdyakov.' And Alyosha told his brother quickly and in detail of his encounter with Smerdyakov. Ivan suddenly began to listen with real concern, and even asked him to repeat certain things.

'Only he asked me not to tell brother Dmitry what he'd said about him,' Alyosha added.

Ivan frowned and began to ponder.

'Is it Smerdyakov that makes you frown?' Alyosha asked.

'Yes, it is. To the devil with him, I really did want to see Dmitry, but now it doesn't matter . . .' Ivan said, unwillingly.

'And are you really going away so soon, brother?'

'Yes.'

'But what of Dmitry and father? How will things end between them?'
Alyosha said uneasily.

'Oh, that endless refrain of yours! How should I know? Am I my
brother Dmitry's keeper?' Ivan snapped irritably, but then suddenly gave
a kind of bitter smile. 'What Cain replied to God concerning his murdered
brother, wasn't it? Perhaps that's what you're thinking at this moment?
But the devil take it, I can't really go on staying here as their keeper,
after all! I've finished my tasks and I'm going. Oh, you probably think
I'm jealous of Dmitry, that all these past three months I've been trying to
take his beautiful Katerina Ivanovna away from him. The devil I have —
I've had my own tasks to see to. I've finished my tasks and I'm going. I
finished them earlier today, you were a witness to it.'

'You mean earlier today at Katerina Ivanovna's?'

'Yes, that's right, and I had done with it in one go. And what is it all
about, in any case? What concern is Dmitry of mine? Dmitry has
nothing to do with me. I had my own tasks to accomplish with Katerina
Ivanovna. You yourself, on the other hand, know that Dmitry behaved
in a way that suggested there was a conspiracy between him and me. I
mean, I'd made absolutely no request that he do so, yet he himself
solemnly delivered her into my hands and imparted his blessing. It's all
so ridiculous. Yes, Alyosha, yes, if you but knew how lighthearted I feel
now! Why, I've been sitting here dining and, would you believe it, I was
almost on the point of asking for champagne in order to celebrate the
first hour of my freedom. Nearly half a year, confound it — and then
suddenly, in one go, in one go I got free of it. Well, I mean, did I ever
suspect even yesterday that if I wanted to finish it, it wouldn't be any
trouble?'

'It's your love you're talking about, Ivan!'

'Well, call it love if you want to, yes, I fell in love with a young lady,
an institute girl. I tormented myself with her, and she tormented me too.
I brooded over her ... and suddenly it all flew away. Earlier today I
spoke with inspiration, but when I got outside I burst into laughter —
would you believe that? Yes, I mean literally.'

'Even now you talk about it with such joviality,' Alyosha observed,
studying his brother's features, which had indeed grown suddenly jovial.

'And how could I have known I didn't love her at all? Heh-heh! And
now it's turned out — I don't. And why, how appealing I found her! How
appealing I found her even earlier today, when I recited that speech. And

you know, even now she appeals to me terribly, and yet it's so easy to travel away from her. Do you suppose I'm boasting?'

'No. Only perhaps it wasn't love.'

'Alyosha, old chap,' Ivan laughed, 'don't embark on discourses concerning love! It's not a proper thing for you to do. Earlier today, earlier today you simply went charging in – tut-tut! I've even forgotten to kiss you for it ... And how she tormented me! It was like living beside a perpetual crack-up. Oh, she was sure that I loved her! It was me she loved, not Dmitry,' Ivan jovially insisted. 'Dmitry is nothing but a crack-up. All the things that I said to her earlier today were the absolute truth. The only thing is that she may need some fifteen or twenty years in order to come to the realization that she doesn't love Dmitry at all, and loves only me, whom she torments. And, indeed, she may never come to that realization, even in spite of the lesson she had today. Well, I did it the best way: got up and left for ever. And speaking of that, how is she now? What happened after I left?'

Alyosha told him about the hysterics, and said she was apparently unconscious and in a delirium.

'And the Khokhlakova isn't making it up?'

'It seems not.'

'We must ask and find out. Though as a matter of fact, no one ever died of hysterics. Well, let her have her hysterics, God sent hysterics to womankind as a mark of His affection. I shan't go there at all. Why should I go poking my nose in there again?'

'But I mean, you told her earlier today that she had never loved you.'

'I did it on purpose. Come on, Alyosha old chap, I'm going to order some champagne, we shall drink to my freedom. Oh, if only you knew how relieved I feel!'

'No, brother, we had better not drink,' Alyosha said suddenly. 'Besides, I feel rather sad.'

'Yes, you've been that way for quite a while; I've noticed.'

'So you're definitely leaving tomorrow morning?'

'Who said anything about the morning? Though as a matter of fact, I might. I mean, would you believe it, I have dined here today for the sole purpose of not having to dine with the old man, so loathsome has he become to me. He alone is reason enough for me to have left long ago. Anyway, why does my leaving make you so worried? You and I still have God knows how much time before my departure. A whole eternity of time, an immortality!'

'If you are leaving tomorrow how can you talk of an eternity?'

'But how does it concern us, you and me?' Ivan laughed. 'I mean, we shall have enough time to discuss the things that matter to us, those things – why else did we come here? Why do you look so astonished? Answer me: why are we meeting here? To talk about my love for Katerina Ivanovna, about Dmitry and the old man? About life abroad? About Russia's fateful situation? About the Emperor Napoleon? Is that it, is that why we're here?'

'No, it isn't.'

'Then that means you understand the real reason. It's one thing for others, but for us yellow-beaks it's another, we must first solve the everlasting questions, that is our concern. All of young Russia is discussing the eternal questions just now, and nothing else. Precisely now, when the old men have all gone away to occupy themselves with practical affairs. Why have you been looking at me with such expectation all these past three months? In order to inquire of me: "Believest thou, or dost thou not believe?"* – why, that is what these three months of expectant looks boil down to, don't they, Aleksey Fyodorovich, eh?'

'Perhaps,' Alyosha smiled. 'I say, you're not laughing at me now, are you, brother?'

'I laugh at you? Oh, I shouldn't want to upset my dear little brother who has gazed at me for three months with such expectation. Alyosha, look me in the eye: I mean, I'm every bit as much of a little boy as you are, and the only difference is that I'm not a novice. After all, how have Russian boys run the show up till now – a certain kind of boy, that is? Take this fetid inn, for example, this is where they gather, huddled in corners. They have never seen each other in their lives before, and when they get out of the inn they'll never see each other again for forty years, well, but what of it, what are they going to talk about now that they've snatched a minute or two in this inn of theirs? About the questions of the universe, what else? Is there a God, is there such a thing as immortality? And as for those who don't believe in God, well, they begin to talk of socialism and anarchism, of the reorganization of the whole of mankind according to a new regime, so that in the end it's the same old devil that pokes his head out, the same old questions, only seen from the other end. And what we see these days in our country is a large, large number of the most uniquely talented Russian boys doing nothing but talk of the eternal questions. Don't you think so?'

'Yes, for real Russians the questions concerning the existence of God and immortality, or the questions posed "from the other end", as you call them, are of course the most important ones and dominate all others, and that is as it should be,' said Alyosha, still studying his brother with the same quiet and searching smile.

'It's like this, Alyosha: to be a Russian is sometimes not at all a sensible thing to be, but even so it would be hard to imagine anything more stupid than the things with which our Russian boys occupy themselves these days. There is, however, Alyosha old chap, one Russian boy of whom I'm terribly fond.'

'How famously you introduced that remark,' Alyosha suddenly laughed.

'Well then, where do you want to begin, you tell me – with God? With the question of God's existence?'

'Begin wherever you like, even if it's from the "other end". You see, you proclaimed at father's yesterday that there is no God,' Alyosha said, giving his brother a searching look.

'I teased you with that at the old man's house during dinner yesterday for fun, and I saw how those pretty eyes of yours had caught fire. Now, however, I've nothing at all against discussing things with you, and I say that very seriously. I want to get closer to you, Alyosha, because I have no friends, I want to make the attempt. Well, then, see how you like this: perhaps I do accept God.' Ivan laughed. 'Does that come as a surprise to you?'

'Yes, of course it does, that's if you're not joking now, as well.'

'"Joking." That's what they said at the Elder's yesterday – that I was joking. Look, my lad, there was a certain old sinner* who lived in the eighteenth century who once pronounced that if there were no God it would be necessary to invent him, *s'il n'existait pas Dieu il faudrait l'inventer*. And indeed man has invented God. And the strange thing, the wonderful thing, is not that God really does exist, but that an idea like that – the idea of God's necessity – could find its way into the head of a savage and vicious animal such as man, so sacred is it, that idea, so touching, so exceedingly wise and so greatly to his honour. As for myself, I long ago decided not to think about whether man created God or God man. I shall not, of course, bring up in that regard all the contemporary axioms of our Russian boys, all of which to the very last one are inferred from European hypotheses; because the things that are hypotheses over there instantly become axioms in the hands of our Russian boys, and not only of them, but doubtless also of their professors, because even our Russian professors nowadays are those very same Russian boys. And so I shall avoid all hypotheses. I mean, what is the task you and I have to perform now? It is for me to explain to you as quickly as possible what my essence is, or rather what kind of person I am, in what I believe and in what I place my hope, isn't it – eh? And for that reason I want to make it plain that I accept God directly and simply. There is, however, one thing that needs to be noted: if God exists and if he really did create the earth then, as common knowledge tells us, he created it according to Euclidean geometry, while he created the human mind with an awareness of only three spatial dimensions. Even so, there have been and still are even today geometers and philosophers of the most remarkable kind who doubt that the entire universe or, even more broadly, the entirety of being was created solely according to Euclidean geometry, and who even make so bold as to dream that the two parallel lines which according to Euclid can on no account converge upon earth may yet do so somewhere in infinity. And so, my lad, I've decided that if I can't even understand that, then how am I to understand about God? I meekly confess that I do not possess the faculties needed to solve such questions, the mind I have is a Euclidean, earthbound one, and so how are we to make inferences about that which is not of this world? And indeed I advise you never to think about that, Alyosha, and least of all concerning God and whether He exists or not. Those are all questions unsuited to a mind that has been created with an awareness of only three dimensions. So, I accept God, and not only do I do so willingly, I also accept His supreme wisdom and His purpose, both of which are completely unknown to us, I believe in the order, the meaning of life, I believe in eternal harmony – one in which we shall all as it were fuse together – I believe in the Word towards which the universe strives and which once "was with God" and which *is* God, well, and so on into infinity. Too many words have been wasted apropos of all that. It looks as though I'm already on the right track, doesn't it? So let me tell you that in the last analysis, this world of God's – I don't accept it, even though I know that it exists, and I don't admit its validity in any way. It isn't God I don't accept, you see; it's the world created by Him, the world of God I don't accept and cannot agree to accept. Let me qualify that: like a young babe, I am convinced that our sufferings will be healed and smoothed away, that the whole offensive comedy of human conflict will disappear like a pathetic mirage, like the infamous fabrication of the Euclidean human mind, as weak and undersized as an atom, and that ultimately, during the universal finale, at the moment of eternal harmony, there will occur and become manifest something so precious that it will be sufficient for all hearts, for the soothing of all indignation, the redemption of all men's evil-doings, all the blood that has been shed by them, will be sufficient not only to make it possible to forgive but even to justify all the things that have happened to men – and even if all that, all of it, makes itself manifest and becomes reality, I will not accept it and do not want to accept it! Even if the parallel lines converge and I actually witness it, I shall witness it and say they have converged, but all the same I shall not accept it. That is my essence, Alyosha, that is my thesis. Now I have expressed it to you seriously. I purposely began this conversation with you in as stupid a manner as possible, but I've led it up to my confession, because that is the only thing required. It wasn't necessary for you to hear about God, but simply to learn what your beloved brother lives by. And I have told it.'

Ivan suddenly ended his long tirade with a display of singular and unexpected emotion.

'And why did you begin "in as stupid a manner as possible"?' Alyosha asked, gazing at him reflectively.

'Well, in the first place, for the sake of *russisme*: Russian conversations on these subjects are invariably conducted in as stupid a manner as possible. And in the second place: the greater the stupidity, the closer to the matter in hand. The greater the stupidity, the greater the clarity. Stupidity is brief and guileless, while wit equivocates and hides. Wit is a scoundrel, while stupidity is honest and sincere. I led the conversation up to the subject of my despair, and the more stupidly I portrayed it, the greater was the advantage to myself.'

'Will you explain to me why you "don't accept" the world?' Alyosha said.

'Of course I will, it's no secret, it is what I have been leading up to. My dear little brother, it's not that I want to corrupt you or topple you from your foundations, but rather that I should, perhaps, like to be healed by you.' Ivan smiled suddenly, for all the world like a meek boy. Alyosha had never seen a smile like that on his features before.

4

Mutiny

'THERE is a certain confession I have to make to you,' Ivan began. 'I have never been able to understand how it is possible to love one's neighbour. In my opinion the people it is impossible to love are precisely those near to one, while one can really love only those who are far away. I once read somewhere concerning "Ioann the Almsgiver"* (a certain saint) that when a hungry and frozen itinerant came to him and asked him to warm him, he put him to bed in his own bed, got into it together with him, put his arms around him and began to breathe into his mouth, which was festering and foul with some terrible disease. I'm convinced that he did this in the grip of a hysterical lie, out of a love that was prescribed by duty, and because of the *epithymia** he had taken upon himself. In order to love a person it is necessary for him to be concealed from view; the moment he shows his face – love disappears.'

'The Elder Zosima spoke of that on several occasions,' Alyosha observed. 'He also said that a person's face often prevents many who are as yet unpractised in love from loving him. But after all, there is much love in mankind, and it almost resembles the love of Christ, I myself know that, Ivan . . .'

'Well I must say I *don't* at present know it, nor do I understand it, and there is a countless multitude of people who would go along with me there. The question is, of course, whether that's because of their inferior qualities, or whether it's just that their nature is so constituted. In my view, the love that Christ showed towards people is in its way a miracle impossible upon earth. It is true, he was God. But we are not gods. Let us assume, for example, that I suffer deeply – yet I mean, another person would never be able to perceive the degree to which I suffer, because he is another person, and not me, and on top of that it's seldom that a person will agree to recognize another as a sufferer (as though it were some kind of rank). Why won't he agree to it, do you suppose? Because, for example, I smell bad, or have a stupid expression on my face, or because I once trod on his toes. What's more, there is suffering and suffering: degrading suffering that degrades me – hunger, for example – is something that my benefactor will permit in me, but let the suffering be of ever such a slightly loftier sort, such as for an idea, for example, then no, only in very rare cases will he permit that, because he may, for example, look at me and suddenly perceive that the expression on my face is not at all like the one his fantasy supposes ought to be on the face of someone who is suffering for an idea. So he then at once deprives me of his beneficent deeds, though he does so not at all from any rancour of heart. Beggars, particularly beggars from good backgrounds, ought never to show themselves in public, but rather beg for alms through the medium of the newspapers. It's also possible to love one's neighbour in the abstract, and even sometimes from a distance, but almost never when he's close at hand. If things were always as they are on stage, at the ballet, where the beggars, when they appear, come on in silken rags and tattered lace and beg for alms while dancing gracefully, then one might still bring oneself to admire them. Admire, but not in any sense love. However, enough of that. I merely wanted to give you my point of view. I was going to go on to speak of the suffering of mankind in general, but let us rather concentrate on the sufferings of children. That will reduce the scope of my argument by some tenfold, but let us talk simply of children. Thus taking some of the wind out of my own sails, needless to say. Well, for one thing, young children may be loved even when they are close to, even when they are dirty, even when they have ugly faces (though I think that young children never have ugly faces). And for another thing, I refrain from talking about grown-ups because, in addition to the fact that they are loathsome and do not deserve love, they also have requital for that: they have eaten of the apple and have grown aware of good and evil and become "as gods". They continue to eat it even to this day. But young children have not eaten of it at all and are as yet guilty of nothing. Are you fond of young children, Alyosha? I know that you are, and so you will understand why it is I want to talk of them at present. If they also suffer horribly upon earth, it is, of course, for their fathers, they are punished for their fathers who have eaten the apple — but, I mean, that is an argument from another world, one incomprehensible to the human heart here upon earth. It is out of the question that the innocent one shall suffer for another, especially when it is such an innocent as that! You may find it surprising in me, Alyosha, but I also am terribly fond of young children. And please take note that people who are cruel, enslaved by passion, carnivorous, Karamazovian, are sometimes very fond of children. Children, while they are children, until the age of seven, for example, are terribly apart from other people: it's as though they were a different species with a different nature. I knew a certain robber in prison: during his career he had had occasion, while massacring entire households in their homes, into which he broke at night in order to commit burglary, at the same time to murder several children, too. Yet, as he sat in prison, he grew fond of them to a degree that was strange. From a window of the gaol the only thing he did was watch the children playing in the prison yard. One small boy he taught to come and stand under the window where he was, and the boy became great friends with him ... You don't know why I'm saying all this, Alyosha? I seem to have a headache, and I feel sad.'

'You talk with a strange look,' Alyosha observed uneasily. 'It's as if you were in a kind of madness.'

'Incidentally, a certain Bulgarian I met in Moscow told me not so long ago,' Ivan Fyodorovich continued, almost without listening to his brother, 'about the atrocities committed by the Turks and Circassians down there in Bulgaria* because of their fear of a mass uprising on the part of the Slavs – that is to say, burning, knifing, raping women and children, nailing convicts to fences by their ears and leaving them there until morning, when they hang them – and so on, it's not possible to imagine it all. Actually, people sometimes talk about man's "bestial" cruelty, but that is being terribly unjust and offensive to the beasts: a beast can never be as cruel as a human being, so artistically, so picturesquely cruel. The tiger simply gnaws and tears and that is the only thing it knows. It would never enter its head to nail people to fences by their ears and leave them like that all night, even were it able to do such a thing. Those Turks, by the way, even tormented children with voluptuous relish, from cutting them out of their mother's wombs with a dagger to throwing the babes in the air and catching them on bayonets before their mothers' eyes. The fact of it being before their mothers' eyes constituted the principal delight. There was, however, one small scene that interested me a great deal. Imagine: a mother stands trembling with an infant in her arms, around her the Turks who have entered. They contrive a merry little act: they fondle the infant, laugh in order to amuse it, they succeed, the infant laughs. At that moment a Turk points a pistol at it, four inches from its face. The baby boy laughs joyfully, stretches out his little hands to grab the pistol, and suddenly the artist pulls the trigger right in his face and smashes his little head to smithereens . . . Artistic, isn't it? As a matter of fact they say that Turks are very fond of sweet things.'

'Brother, where is all this leading?' Alyosha asked.

'I think that if the Devil doesn't exist and, consequently, man has created him, he has created him in his own image and likeness.'

'Just in the same way he created God, in that case.'

'Oh, you really do know how to turn the clever phrase, as Polonius says in Hamlet,'* Ivan laughed. 'You beat me at my own game, good, I'm glad. After all, your God must be rather fine if man created him according to his own image and likeness. You asked just now why I was saying all these things: well, you see, one of my hobbies is the collecting of certain little facts; what I do, if you can credit it, is to note down and cull together from newspapers and reports, whatever the source, little anecdotes of a certain sort, and I now have a fine collection. The Turks are, of course, part of the collection, but they're all foreigners. I also have home-bred items which are even better that the Turkish ones. You know, with us it takes the form of flogging, the birch and the lash, and that is a national phenomenon: in our country the nailing of ears is unthinkable, we are Europeans, after all, but the rod and the lash – they are Russian, and cannot be taken away from us. In Europe it looks as though they have given up flogging altogether as a method of punishment, whether it's because their morals and manners have undergone a process of purification, or whether it's because laws have been established of such a kind that man may no more dare to flog his fellow man, but they have compensated themselves for that with another, as in our case, also purely national phenomenon, so national indeed that I think for us it would be impossible, though as a matter of fact it appears to be catching on among us too, in particular ever since the religious movement* began to affect the higher levels of our society. I have in my possession a certain delightful little brochure, a translation from the French, which describes the execution in Geneva, by no means long ago, only some five years back, of a certain villain and murderer named Richard, a fellow of twenty-three, I think, who repented and converted to the Christian faith upon the very scaffold. This Richard was someone's illegitimate son, who while yet a babe, about six years old, had been "given away" by his parents to some Swiss mountain shepherds, and they had nurtured him in order to employ him in labour. He grew up in their home like a small wild animal, the shepherds gave him no form of education but, on the contrary, when he was only seven sent him out to graze the flock, in the rain and cold, almost without clothing and almost without food. And then of course, so doing, not one of them reflected nor repented but, on the contrary, believed themselves fully within their rights, for Richard had been given to them like an object, and they did not even deem it necessary to feed him. Richard himself gave testimony that in those years he, like the Prodigal Son in the New Testament, would fain have filled his belly with the mash given to the pigs that were being fattened for sale, but he was not even given that and was flogged when he stole from the pigs, and thus he passed the whole of his childhood and youth until such time as he gained his maturity and, his energies fortified, embarked upon a life of petty thieving. The savage began to earn money by doing day labour in Geneva; he drank what he earned, lived like an outcast and ended by murdering some old man and robbing him. He was caught, put on trial and condemned to death. They don't have time for sentimentality over there, you know. Well, in prison he was at once surrounded by pastors and members of various Christian brotherhoods, charitable ladies and the like. In prison he was taught to read and write, had the New Testament explained to him, was exhorted, persuaded, pressured, pestered and weighed upon, and then lo and behold, in the end he himself solemnly confessed to his crime. He underwent conversion, he himself wrote to the court that he was a monster of cruelty and that at last he had been deemed worthy of being illumined by God and of receiving His grace. The whole of Geneva was in turmoil, the whole of pious and charitable Geneva. All who were of elevated station and good breeding rushed to see him in prison; Richard was kissed, embraced: "You are our brother, grace has come upon you!" And Richard himself only piously wept: "Yes, grace has come upon me! Before, all my childhood and youth, I would fain have eaten of the husks that the swine did eat, yet now grace has come upon me, and I die in the Lord!" "Yes, yes, Richard, die now in the Lord, you have shed blood and must die in the Lord. Even though you are not to blame for being wholly ignorant of the Lord at all at the time when you envied the swine their husks and when you were flogged for stealing their husks from them (which was a very bad thing to do, for stealing is not permitted), you have shed blood and must die." And then his last day arrived. The unnerved Richard wept and could do nothing but repeat every moment: "This is the finest day of my life, I am going to the Lord!" "Yes," cried the pastors, the judges and the charitable ladies, "this is your happiest day, for you are going to the Lord!" All these people made their way to the scaffold behind the cart of shame in which Richard was being taken there, in carriages, on foot. Then they attained the scaffold: "Die now, brother," they cried to Richard, "die in the Lord, for grace has come upon you!" And then, covered in the kisses of his brothers, brother Richard was hauled to the scaffold, placed upon the guillotine and had his head lopped off in brotherly fashion, since grace had come upon him. Well, that's character-istic. This brochure was translated into Russian by some Russian Lutheran charity-mongers from the upper levels of society and distributed free of charge by the newspapers and other publishers for the enlightenment of the Russian people. The good thing about the Richard story is its national quality. Though in our country it seems to people absurd to cut off someone's head because he has become a brother to us and because grace has come upon him, we do none the less, I repeat, have our own such folly, one that is possibly even worse. In our country the torture of flogging is a historical, direct and most intimate source of pleasure. Nekrasov has some lines* about a muzhik lashing his horse with a knout on the eyes, "on its meek eyes". Who has not seen such a thing, it is a *russisme*. He describes a puny little horse, on whose cart too much has been piled, getting bogged down with its load, unable to haul it out. The muzhik flogs it, flogs it in a frenzy, flogs it, at last, not understanding what he is doing, in an intoxication of flogging lashes it viciously, countless times: "Though you are not strong enough, yet pull, even though it kills you, pull!" The wretched little jade strains, and then he starts to lash it, the defenceless creature, about its eyes, "its meek and weeping eyes". Beside itself it gives a jerk, hauls the cart out and sets off, trembling all over, not breathing, almost sideways, with a kind of hopping skitter, somehow unnaturally and ignominiously – in Nekrasov that is terrible. But after all, it is only a horse, and God gave horses unto man that he might flog them. Or so at any rate the Tartars would have had us understand, giving us the knout as a reminder of it. But after all, human beings may be flogged, too. And so here we have a cultured gentleman of progressive education and his lady wife flogging their own daughter, a babe of seven years, with the birch – I have a detailed account of it noted down. The dear papa is glad the twigs have knots in them, "it will sting more", he says, and then he begins to "sting" his own daughter. I know for a certainty that there are floggers of a kind who grow excited with each blow to the point of voluptuous pleasure, quite literally voluptuous pleasure, increasingly with each consecutive blow, progressively. They flog for a minute, they flog for five, they flog for ten, onward, harder, faster, more and more painfully. The child cries out, the child is, at last, unable to cry out, it gasps: "Papa, papa, my papa, my papa!" By some devilish piece of bad luck the case is brought to court. An advocate is hired. The advocate was long ago characterized by the Russian people in the saying "the *ablakat** is a hired conscience". The advocate cries out in defence of his client. "The case," he says, "is such a simple one, so ordinary and based in family life – a father gives his daughter a thrashing, and to the shame of the times we live in is taken to court!" Persuaded, the members of the jury retire and bring back a verdict of not guilty. The members of the public roar with happiness that the torturer has been acquitted. I wasn't there, damn it, or I'd have bellowed a proposal that a stipend be founded in the torturer's name! . . . Delightful little scenes. But I have even better ones concerning young children, I have a great, great many items about Russian children in my collection, Alyosha. The father and mother of a little five-year-old girl, "most respectable and high-ranking people, educated and of progressive views", conceived a hatred of her. Let me tell you, I once again positively assert that in many scions of mankind there is a curious property – the love of torturing children, but only children. To all other specimens of the human race these same torturers are even favourably and meekly inclined, as befitting humane men of European and progressive education, but they have a great love of torturing children, and their love for children is even based on that. It is the very unprotected aspect of these creatures that tempts the torturers, the angelic trustfulness of the child, which has nowhere to go and no one to turn to – this it is that excites the foul blood of the torturer. In every human being, of course, there lurks a beast, a beast of anger, a beast of voluptuous excitement derived from the cries of the tortured victim, a beast uncontrollable, unleashed from the chain, a beast of ailments contracted in debauchery – gout, cirrhosis and the like. Those progressively educated parents subjected that poor five-year-old girl to every torture one could think of. They beat her, flogged her, kicked her, themselves not knowing why, turned her whole body into a mass of bruises; at last they attained the highest degree of refinement: in the cold and freezing weather they locked her up for a whole night in the outside latrine because she did not ask to be relieved (as though a five-year-old child, sleeping its sound, angelic sleep, could learn to ask to be relieved at such an age) – what is more, they smeared her eyes, cheeks and mouth all over with faeces and compelled her to eat those faeces, and it was the mother, the mother who did the compelling! And that mother was able to sleep, hearing at night the moans of the poor little child, locked up in the foul latrine! So now do you understand, when a small creature that is not yet able to make sense of what is happening to it beats its hysterical breast in a foul latrine, in the dark and cold, with its tiny fist and wails with its bloody, meek, rancourless tears to "dear Father God" to protect it – now do you understand all that rot, my friend and my brother, my godly and humble lay brother, do you understand why all that rot is so necessary? Without it, they say, man would not be able to survive upon earth, for he would not know good from evil. Why recognize that devilish good-and-evil, when it costs so much? I mean, the entire universe of knowledge is not worth the tears of that little child addressed to "dear Father God". I say nothing of the sufferings of grown-ups – they have eaten the apple, and the devil with them, and the devil take them all, but the children, the children! I'm tormenting you, Alyosha, my lad, you look as though you were beside yourself. I shall stop, if you wish.'

'It's all right, I also want to suffer,' Alyosha muttered.

'Just one, just one more little scene, and that for curiosity's sake, a very characteristic one, and principally because I've just read about it in one of the symposia of our antiquities, either in the *Archive* or the *Antiquity*,* I think; I'd have to check up, I've even forgotten where I read it. It happened during the blackest period of serfdom, back at the start of the century, and all hail to the Liberator of the people!* Back then at the start of the century there was a certain general, a general with grand connections, a most prosperous landowner, but of the sort (to be sure, even then it appears very few in number) who upon retiring from the service were very nearly convinced that they had earned the right to dispose over the lives and deaths of their subjects. In those days there were such men. Well, so the general lived on his estate of two thousand souls, swaggered around, treating his lesser neighbours as though they were his retainers and buffoons. A kennel with hundreds of dogs and nearly a hundred huntsmen, all in uniforms, all on horseback. And then one day a serf boy, a little lad of only eight years old, while playing some game or other threw a stone and bruised the leg of the general's favourite beagle. "Why has my favourite dog gone lame?" "It was the boy," he was informed, "he threw a stone at it and bruised its leg." "Ah, so it was you," the general said, looking him over. "Seize him!" He was seized, taken from his mother, kept overnight in the lock-up, and at first light the next morning the general came driving out in full dress-uniform, mounted his horse, around him his retainers, dogs, huntsmen, stalkers, all on horseback. Around them the serf folk were gathered for the purpose of edification, and in front of them all the mother of the guilty boy.

'The boy was brought out from the lock-up. A cold, gloomy, misty autumn day, first-rate for hunting. The general ordered the boy to be undressed, he was stripped naked, shivering, out of his mind with terror, not daring to utter a sound . . . "Send him on his way!" the general ordered. "Run, run!" the huntsmen shouted to him, the boy set off at a run . . . "Tally ho!" the general howled and unleashed at him a whole pack of borzoi hounds. He hunted him down in front of his mother, and the dogs tore the child to little shreds! . . . I think the general was put in ward.* But . . . what should one have done with him? Shot him? Shot him in order to satisfy one's moral feelings? Tell me, Alyosha, my lad!'

'Shot him!' Alyosha said quietly, raising his eyes to his brother with a kind of pale, distorted smile.

'Bravo!' Ivan howled in a kind of ecstasy. 'Why, if you can say that, it means . . . A fine schemonach* you are! So that's the kind of little devil that crouches in your heart, Alyosha Karamazov, my lad!'

'It was a preposterous thing for me to say, but . . .'

'There you have it – but! . . .' Ivan shouted. 'You ought to realize, novice, that preposterous things are all too necessary upon earth. The world rests upon preposterous things, and indeed it's possible that without them absolutely nothing would ever have come into existence. We know that which we know!'

'What do you know?'

'That I don't understand anything,' Ivan continued in a kind of delirium. 'And that I don't want to understand anything now, either. I want to remain with the facts. I decided long ago not to understand. If I understand anything, I shall instantly be untrue to the facts, and I have decided to remain with the facts . . .'

'Why are you putting me to the test like this?' Alyosha exclaimed in hysterical sorrow. 'Will you please finally tell me?'

'Of course I will, to tell you is what I've been leading up to. You are dear to me, and I don't want to let you go and shall not yield to your Father Zosima.'

Ivan said nothing for a moment, and his face suddenly became very sad.

'Listen to me: I took the exclusive instance of young children in order to make it more obvious. Of the other human tears in which the earth is steeped from crust to core I have not said a word, I have purposely kept my subject narrow. I am a bedbug and I confess with all due self-disparagement that I am quite unable to understand why everything is ordered thus. So it must be the fault of people themselves: given paradise, they wanted freedom and stole fire from heaven, knowing the while that they would be unhappy, and so there is no reason to feel sorry for them. Oh, with my pathetic, earthly, Euclidean mind I only know that there is suffering, that "none does offend",* that one thing proceeds from another, quite plainly and simply, that everything flows and evens out – but after all, that is merely Euclidean rubbish, and after all, I know it, but I cannot agree to live by it! What is it to me that "none does offend" and that I know it? I want retribution, otherwise I shall destroy myself. And retribution not at some place and some time in infinity, but here upon earth, and in such a way that I see it for myself. I have believed in it, and I want to see it for myself, and if by that time I am already dead, then let me be raised up again, for if it all takes place when I am not there, it will be too hurtful. For I did not suffer in order with my villainous actions and my sufferings to manure a future harmony for someone else. I want with my own eyes to see the lion lie down beside the fallow deer and the one who has been slaughtered get up and embrace the one who has killed him. I want to be here when everyone suddenly discovers why it has all been the way it has. All the religions of the earth have been founded on that desire, and I believe. But here, however, are the children, and what am I going to do with them then? That is the question I am unable to resolve. For the hundredth time I repeat – there are a great number of questions, but I have taken the sole instance of young children for here it is irrefutably evident what I must say. Look: if everyone must suffer in order with their suffering to purchase eternal harmony, what do young children have to do with it, tell me, please? It is quite impossible to understand why they should have to suffer, and why should they have to purchase harmony with their sufferings? Why have they also ended up as raw material, to be the manure for someone else's future harmony? Solidarity in sin among human beings I understand; I even understand solidarity in retribution, but I mean to say, there can be no question of solidarity in sin among young children, and if it is indeed true that they are solidary with their fathers in all the villainous actions of their fathers, then it goes without saying that therein is a truth that is not of this world and is impossible for me to understand. Some wag will perhaps say that, like it or not, the child will grow up and in time commit sins — but here is one who has not grown up and yet at eight years old was hunted down by dogs. Oh, Alyosha, I do not blaspheme! And I understand what a shaking must rend the universe when all that is in heaven and under the earth flows together in one laudatory voice and all that liveth and hath lived exclaims: "Just and true art Thou, O Lord, for Thy ways are made plain!" And when the mother embraces the torturer who tore her son to pieces with his dogs, and all three of them proclaim in tears: "Just and true art Thou, O Lord," then, of course, the day of knowledge will have dawned and all will be explained. The only trouble is that it's precisely that I cannot accept. And for as long as I am on the earth I shall hasten to make arrangements of my own. You see, Alyosha, it may very well be, perhaps, that when I reach the moment in my life at which I see it, or rise up from the dead in order to do so, I myself may exclaim with all the rest, as I watch the mother embracing the torturer of her little child: "Just and true art Thou, O Lord!", but it is something I do not want to do. While there is still time I shall hasten to guard myself, and so I decline the offer of eternal harmony altogether. It is not worth one single small tear of even one tortured little child that beat its breast with its little fist and prayed in its foul-smelling dog-hole with its unredeemed tears addressed to "dear Father God"! It is not worth it because its tears have remained unredeemed. They must be redeemed, or there can be no harmony. But by what means, by what means will you redeem them? Is it even possible? Will you really do it by avenging them? But what use is vengeance to me, what use to me is hell for torturers, what can hell put right again, when those children have been tortured to death? And what harmony can there be where there is hell: I want to forgive and I want to embrace – I don't want anyone to suffer any more. And if the sufferings of children have gone to replenish the sum of suffering that was needed in order to purchase the truth, then I declare in advance that no truth, not even the whole truth, is worth such a price. And above all, I do not want the mother to embrace the torturer who tore her son to pieces with his dogs! Let her not dare to forgive him! If she wants, she may forgive him on her own account. She may forgive the torturer her limitless maternal suffering; but as for the sufferings of her dismembered child, those she has no right to forgive, she dare not forgive his torturer, even if her child himself forgave him! And if that is the case, if they dare not forgive, where is the harmony? Is there in all the world a being that could forgive and have the right to forgive? I do not want harmony, out of a love for mankind I do not want it. I want rather to be left with sufferings that are unavenged. Let me rather remain with my unavenged suffering and unassuaged indignation, *even though I am not right*. And in any case, harmony has been overestimated in value, we really don't have the money to pay so much to get in. And so I hasten to return my entry ticket.* And if I am at all an honest man, I am obliged to return it as soon as possible. That is what I am doing. It isn't God I don't accept, Alyosha, it's just his ticket that I most respectfully return to him.'

'That is mutiny,' Alyosha said quietly, his eyes lowered.

'Mutiny? I don't like to hear you say such a word,' Ivan said with emotion. 'One can't live in a state of mutiny, but I want to live. Tell me yourself directly, I challenge you – reply: imagine that you yourself are erecting the edifice of human fortune with the goal of, at the finale, making people happy, of at last giving them peace and quiet, but that in order to do it it would be necessary and unavoidable to torture to death only one tiny little creature, that same little child that beat its breast with its little fist, and on its unavenged tears to found that edifice, would you agree to be the architect on those conditions, tell me and tell me truly?'

'No, I would not agree,' Alyosha said quietly.

'And are you able to allow the idea that the people for whom you are constructing the edifice would themselves agree to accept their happiness being bought by the unwarranted blood of a small, tortured child and, having accepted it, remain happy for ever?'

'No, I cannot. Brother,' Alyosha said suddenly, his eyes flashing, 'just now you said: "Is there in all the world a Being that could forgive and have the right to forgive?" Well, that Being does exist, and It can forgive everything, everyone, man and woman alike, *and for everything*, because It gave its innocent blood for all things and all men. You have forgotten about It, but on It the edifice is founded, and this it is that people will exclaim to It: "Just and true art Thou, O Lord, for Thy ways are made plain." '

'Ah, you mean "the only sinless one"* and His blood! No, I haven't forgotten about Him and have, on the contrary, been amazed at how long it has taken you to introduce Him into the argument, for your kind usually wheel Him out right at the start. Listen, Alyosha, don't laugh, but I once composed a *poema** – I did it about a year ago. If you're able to waste another ten minutes or so with me, would you let me tell you what it says?'

'You've written a *poema*?'

'Oh, no, I didn't write it,' Ivan said, laughing, 'never in my life have I written down so much as two lines of verse. No, I dreamed this *poema* up and committed it to memory. I dreamed it up with passion. You shall be my first reader, or listener, rather,' Ivan said with an ironic smile. 'Shall I tell you what it says or not?'

'By all means,' Alyosha managed to get out.

'My *poema* is entitled "The Grand Inquisitor", a preposterous thing, but I feel like telling it to you.'

5

The Grand Inquisitor

'YOU see, even here we can't get by without a preface – a literary preface, that is, confound it!' Ivan said, laughing. 'And what kind of an author am I? Look, the action of my poem takes place in the sixteenth century, and back then – as a matter of fact, this ought still to be familiar to you from your days at school – back then it was the custom in works of poetry to bring the celestial powers down to earth. Dante I need hardly mention. In France the magistrates' clerks and also the monks in the monasteries used to give entire dramatic spectacles in which they brought on to the stage the Madonna, the angels, the saints, Christ and even God Himself. Back in those days it was all very unsophisticated. In Victor Hugo's *Nôtre Dame de Paris*,* under the reign of Louis XI, an edifying spectacle is given to the people free of charge in the auditorium of the Paris Town Hall, to celebrate the birthday of the French Dauphin,* under the title *Le bon jugement de la très sainte et gracieuse Vièrge Marie*, in which she herself appears in person and pronounces her *bon jugement*. In our own country, in the Moscow of pre-Petrine antiquity,* dramatic spectacles of almost the same kind, especially of stories from the

Old Testament, also took place from time to time; but, in addition to dramatic spectacles, there passed throughout all the world a large number of tales and "verses" in which when necessary the saints, the angels and all the powers of heaven wrought their influence. The monks in our monasteries also occupied themselves with the translation, copying and even the composition of such poems, and in such times, too: under the Tartar yoke. There is, for example, a certain little monastic poem (from the Greek, of course) entitled *The Journey of the Mother of God Through the Torments*,* with scenes and with a boldness that are not inferior to those of Dante. The Mother of God visits hell, and her guide through the "torments" is the Archangel Michael. She beholds the sinners and their sufferings. This hell, incidentally, contains a most entertaining category of sinners in a burning lake: those of them who sink into this lake so deep that they are unable to swim to its surface again are "forgotten by God" – a phrase of exceptional force and profundity. And lo, the shocked and weeping Mother of God falls down before God's throne and appeals to him to grant forgiveness to all who are in hell, all whom she has seen there, without distinction. Her entreaty with God is of colossal interest. She implores him, she will not depart, and when God draws her attention to the nailed hands and feet of His Son and asks her: "How can I forgive his torturers?" she commands all the saints, all the martyrs, all the angels and archangels to fall down together with her and pray for the forgiveness of all without discrimination. The upshot of it is that she coaxes from God a respite from the torments each year, from Good Friday to Whit Sunday, and out of hell the sinners at once thank the Lord and loudly cry unto Him: "Just and true art thou, O Lord, that thou hast judgèd thus." Well, my little poem would have been in similar vein, had it appeared in those days. He appears on my proscenium; to be sure, in my poem. He does not say anything, only makes his appearance and goes on his way. Fifteen centuries have now passed since He made his vow to come in his kingdom, fifteen centuries since his prophet wrote: "Behold, I come quickly."* "But of that day and that hour knoweth no man, not even the Son, but only my Father in heaven,"* as He himself prophesied while yet on the earth. But human kind awaits him with its earlier faith and its earlier tender emotion. Oh, with even greater faith, for fifteen centuries have now passed since the pledges have ceased to be lent to man from the heavens:

> Thou must have faith in what the heart saith,
> For the heavens no pledges lend.*

'And only faith in that which is said by the heart! To be sure, there were many miracles back in those days. There were saints who effected miraculous healings; to some righteous men, according to their life chronicles, the Queen of Heaven herself came down. But the Devil does not slumber, and in humankind there had already begun to grow a doubt in the genuineness of these miracles. Just at that time there appeared in the north, in Germany, a terrible new heresy.* An enormous star, "burning as it were a lamp" (that's the church, you see), "fell upon the fountains of the waters, and they were made bitter".* These heresies began blasphemously to contradict the miracles. But all the more ardent was the faith of those who remained true believers. The tears of humankind ascended to Him as before, He was awaited, loved, trusted in, people thirsted to suffer and die for him, as before . . . And for how many centuries had humankind prayed with faith and ardour: "O God the Lord, show us light",* for how many centuries had it appealed to Him that He, in His immeasurable compassion, should deign to come down among His supplicants. He had been known to condescend before and had visited certain men of righeousness, martyrs and holy cenobites while yet they lived on earth, as it is written in their "Lives". Among us Tyutchev, who believed profoundly in the truth of His words, announced that

> Weighed down by the Cross's burden,
> All of you, my native land,
> Heaven's Tsar in servile aspect
> Trudged while blessing, end to end.*

Which really was the case, I do assure you. And so it happens that He conceives the desire to manifest Himself, if only for an instant, to His people – to His struggling, suffering, stinkingly sinful people that none the less childishly love Him. My poem is set in Spain, at the most dreadful period of the Inquisition, when bonfires glowed throughout the land every day to the glory of God and

> In resplendent *autos-da-fé*
> Burned the wicked heretics.*

Oh, this is not, of course, that coming in which He will appear, according to His promise, at the end of days in the clouds of heaven with power and great glory and which will take place suddenly, "as the lightning cometh out of the east, and shineth even unto the west". No, He has conceived the desire to visit his children at least for an instant and precisely in those places where the bonfires of heretics had begun to crackle. In His boundless mercy He passes once more among men in that same human form in which for three years He walked among men fifteen centuries earlier. He comes down to the "hot streets and squares"* of the southern town in which only the previous day, in a "resplendent *auto-da-fé*", in the presence of the king, the court, the knights, the cardinals and the loveliest ladies of the court, in the presence of the numerous population of all Seville, there have been burned by the Cardinal Grand Inquisitor very nearly a good hundred heretics all in one go, *ad majorem gloriam Dei*.* He has appeared quietly, unostentatiously, and yet – strange, this – everyone recognizes Him. That could have been one of the best bits in my poem – I mean, the question of why it is that everyone recognizes him. The people rush towards him with invincible force, surround him, mass around him, follow him. Saying nothing, He passes among them with a quiet smile of infinite compassion. The sun of love burns in his heart, the beams of Light, Enlightenment and Power flow from his eyes and, as they stream over people, shake their hearts with answering love. He stretches out His arms to them, blesses them, and from one touch of Him, even of His garments, there issues a healing force. Then from the crowd an old man, blind since the years of his childhood, exclaims: "O Lord, heal me, that I may behold thee," and lo, it is as though the scales fall from the blind man's eyes, and he sees Him. The people weep and kiss the ground on which He walks. The children throw flowers in his path, singing and crying to Him: "Hosannah!" "It's Him, it's Him," they all repeat, "it must be Him, it can't be anyone but Him." He stops in the parvis of Seville Cathedral just at the moment a white, open child's coffin is being borne with weeping into the place of worship: in it is a seven-year-old girl, the only daughter of a certain noble and distinguished citizen. The dead child lies covered in flowers. "He will raise up your child," voices cry from the crowd to the weeping mother. The cathedral *pater* who has come out to meet the coffin looks bewildered and knits his brows. But then the mother of the dead child utters a resounding wail. She throws herself at his feet: "If it is You, then raise up my child!" she exclaims, stretching out her arms to him. The procession stops, the coffin is lowered to the parvis floor, to his feet. He gazes with compassion, and his lips softly pronounce again: *"Talitha cumi"** – "Damsel, I say unto thee, arise." The girl rises in her coffin, sits up and looks around her, smiling, with astonished, wide-open eyes. In her arms is the bouquet of white roses with which she had lain in the coffin. Among the people there are confusion, shouts, sobbing, and then suddenly, at that very moment, on his way past the cathedral comes the Cardinal Grand Inquisitor himself. He is an old man of almost ninety, tall and straight, with a withered face and sunken eyes, in which, however, there is still a fiery, spark-like gleam. Oh, he is not dressed in his resplendent cardinal's attire, the attire in which yesterday he showed himself off before the people as the enemies of the Roman faith were being burned — no, at this moment he wears only his old, coarse monkish cassock. Behind him at a certain distance follow his surly assistants and servants and the "Holy" Guard. He stops before the crowd and observes from a distance. He has seen it all, has seen the coffin being put down at His feet, has seen the damsel rise up, and a shadow has settled on his face. He knits his thick, grey brows, and his eyes flash with an ill-boding fire. He extends his index finger and orders the guards to arrest Him. And lo, such is his power and so accustomed, submissive and tremblingly obedient to him are the people that the crowd immediately parts before the guards, and they, amidst the sepulchral silence that has suddenly fallen, place their hands on Him and march Him away. Instantly, the crowd, almost as one man, bow their heads to the ground before the Elder—Inquisitor, and without uttering a word he blesses the people and passes on his way. The Guard conduct the Captive to a narrow and murky vaulted prison in the ancient building of the Ecclesiastical Court and lock Him up in it. The day goes by, and the dark, passionate and "unbreathing" Seville night begins. The air "of lemon and of laurel reeks."* In the midst of the deep murk the prison's iron door is suddenly opened and the old Grand Inquisitor himself slowly enters the prison with a lamp in his hand. He is alone, the door instantly locks again behind him. He pauses in the entrance and for a long time, a minute or two, studies His face. At last he quietly goes up to Him, places the lamp on the table and says to Him:

'"Is it you? You?" Receiving no answer, however, he quickly adds: "No, do not reply, keep silent. And in any case, what could you possibly say? I know only too well what you would say. And you have no right to add anything to what was said by you in former times. Why have you come to get in our way? For you have come to get in our way, and you yourself know it. But do you know what will happen tomorrow? I do not know who you are, and I do not want to know: you may be He or you may be only His likeness, but tomorrow I shall find you guilty and burn you at the stake as the most wicked of heretics, and those same people who today kissed your feet will tomorrow at one wave of my hand rush to rake up the embers on your bonfire, do you know that?

Yes, I dare say you do," he added in heartfelt reflection, not for one moment removing his gaze from his Captive.'

'I don't quite understand this part of it, Ivan,' Alyosha smiled; all the time he had listened in silence. 'Is it simply an immense fantasy, or is it some mistake on the part of an old man, some impossible *quiproquo*?'

'Why don't you assume it's the latter.' Ivan burst out laughing. 'If you've been so spoiled by contemporary realism that you can't endure anything fantastic and you want it to be a *quiproquo*, then so be it. It certainly can't be denied,' he laughed again, 'that the old man is ninety, and might easily have long ago been driven insane by the idea that is in his mind. On the other hand, the Captive might have struck him by His appearance. Or it might simply have been a hallucination, the vision of a ninety-year-old man on the threshold of death, given added feverish intensity by the previous day's *auto-da-fé* of a hundred burned heretics. Is it not, however, a matter of indifference to us whether it's a *quiproquo*, or whether it's a colossal fantasy? The point is merely that the old man wants to speak his mind, to finally say out loud the things he has kept silent about for ninety years.'

'And the Captive says nothing either? Gazes at him, but says no word?'

'But that is how it must be in all such instances,' Ivan laughed again. 'The old man himself remarks to Him that He has not the right to add anything to what has already been said by Him in former times. If one cares to, one can see in that statement the most basic characteristic of Roman Catholicism, in my opinion, at least; it's as if they were saying: "It was all told by you to the Pope and so it is now all of it in the Pope's possession, and now we should appreciate it if you would stay away altogether and refrain from interfering for the time being, at any rate." That is the sense in which they not only speak but also write, the Jesuits, at least. I've read such things in the works of their theologians. "Do you have the right to divulge to us so much as one of the mysteries of the world from which you have come?" my old man asks Him, supplying the answer himself: "No, you do not, lest you add anything to what has already been said by you, and lest you take away from people the freedom you so stood up for when you were upon the earth. Anything new that you divulge will encroach upon people's freedom to believe, for it will look like a miracle and their freedom to believe was what mattered to you most even back then, fifteen hundred years ago. Was it not you who so often used to say back then: 'I want to make you free'?* Well, but now you have seen those 'free' people," the old man suddenly adds with a thoughtful and ironic smile. "Yes, this task has cost us dearly," he continues, looking at him sternly, "but we have at last accomplished it in your name. For fifteen centuries we have struggled with that freedom, but now it is all over, and over for good. You don't believe that it is over for good? You look at me meekly and do not even consider me worthy of indignation? Well, I think you ought to be aware that now, and particularly in the days we are currently living through, those people are even more certain than ever that they are completely free, and indeed they themselves have brought us their freedom and have laid it humbly at our feet. But we were the ones who did that, and was that what you desired, that kind of freedom?"'

'Once again I don't understand,' Alyosha broke in. 'Is he being ironic, is he laughing?'

'Not at all. What he is doing is claiming the credit for himself and his kind for at last having conquered freedom and having done so in order to make people happy. "For only now" (he is talking about the Inquisition, of course) "has it become possible to think for the first time about people's happiness. Man is constituted as a mutineer; can mutineers ever be happy? You were given warnings," he says to Him, "you had plenty of warnings and instructions, but you did not obey them, you rejected the only path by which people could have been made happy, but fortunately when you left you handed over the task to us. You gave your promise, you sealed it with your word, you gave us the right to bind and loose,* and so of course you cannot even dream of taking that right from us now. So why have you come to get in our way?"'

'I wonder if you could explain the meaning of that phrase: "you had plenty of warnings and instructions"?' Alyosha asked.

'Yes, well, that is exactly the point on which the old man wants to speak his mind.'

'"The terrible and clever Spirit, the Spirit of self-annihilation and non-existence," the old man continues, "that great Spirit spoke with you in the wilderness, and we are told in the Scriptures that it 'tempted' you. Is that so? And would it be possible to say anything more true than those things which he made known to you in three questions and which you rejected, and which in the Scriptures are called 'temptations'? Yet at the same time, if ever there took place on the earth a truly thunderous miracle, it was on that day, the day of those three temptations. Precisely in the emergence of those three questions did the miracle lie. Were one to imagine, just for the sake of experiment and as an example, that those three questions put by the terrible Spirit had been lost without trace from the Scriptures and that it was necessary to reconstruct them, invent and compose them anew so they could again be entered in the Scriptures, and for this purpose to gather together all the sages of the earth – the rulers, the high priests, the scholars, the philosophers, the poets, and give them the task of inventing, composing three questions, but of such a kind that would not only correspond to the scale of the event but would also express, in three words, in but three human phrases, the entire future history of the world and mankind – then do you suppose that all the great wisdom of the earth, having united together, would be able to invent anything at all even remotely equivalent in power and depth to those three questions that were actually put to you that day by the mighty and clever Spirit in the wilderness? Why, by those very questions alone, by the sheer miracle of their emergence it is possible to gain the realization that one is dealing not with a fleeting human intelligence, but with one that is eternal and absolute. For it is as if in those three questions there is conjoined into a single whole and prophesied the entire subsequent history of mankind, there are manifested the three images in which all the unresolved historical contradictions of human nature throughout all the earth will coincide. Back then this was not as yet evident for the future was unknown, but now after the passage of fifteen centuries we can see that everything in those three questions was the product of such foresight and foreknowledge and was so reasonable that it is no longer possible to add anything to them or to remove anything from them.

'"Decide for yourself who was right: You or the One who questioned You that day? Remember the first question, though not in literal terms, its sense was this: 'You want to go into the world and are going there with empty hands, with a kind of promise of freedom which they in their simplicity and inborn turpitude are unable even to comprehend, which they go in fear and awe of – for nothing has ever been more unendurable to man and human society than freedom! Look, you see those stones in that naked, burning hot wilderness? Turn them into loaves and mankind will go trotting after you like a flock, grateful and obedient, though ever fearful that you may take away your hand and that your loaves may cease to come their way.' But you did not want to deprive man of freedom and rejected the offer, for what kind of freedom is it, you reasoned, if obedience is purchased with loaves? You retorted that man lives not by bread alone, but are you aware that in the name of that same earthly bread the Earth Spirit will rise up against you and fight with you and vanquish you, and everyone will follow it, crying: 'Who is like unto this beast, he has given us fire from heaven!'* Are you aware that centuries will pass, and mankind will proclaim with the lips of its wisdom and science that there is no crime and consequently no sin either, but only the hungry. 'Feed them, and then ask virtue of them!' – that is what will be inscribed upon the banner they will raise against you and before which your temple will come crashing down. In the place of your temple there will be erected a new edifice, once again a terrible Tower of Babel will be erected, and even though this one will no more be completed than was the previous one, but even so you would be able to avoid that new Tower and abbreviate the sufferings of the human beings by a thousand years, for after all, it is to us that they will come, when they have suffered for a thousand years with their Tower! Then they will track us down again under the ground, in the catacombs, hiding (for we shall again be persecuted and tortured), they will find us and cry to us: 'Feed us, for those who promised us fire from heaven have not granted it.' And then we shall complete their Tower, for it is he that feeds them who will complete it, and it is only we that shall feed them, in your name, and lie that we do it in your name. Oh, never, never will they feed themselves without us! No science will give them bread while yet they are free, but the end of it will be that they will bring us their freedom and place it at our feet and say to us: 'Enslave us if you will, but feed us.' At last they themselves will understand that freedom and earthly bread in sufficiency for all are unthinkable together, for never, never will they be able to share between themselves! They will also be persuaded that they will never be able to be free, because they are feeble, depraved, insignificant and mutinous. You promised them the bread of heaven, but, I repeat again, can it compare in the eyes of a weak, eternally depraved and eternally dishonourable human race with the earthly sort? And if in the name of the bread of heaven thousands and tens of thousands follow you, what will become of the millions and tens of thousand millions of creatures who are not strong enough to disdain the earthly bread for the heavenly sort? Or are the only ones you care about the tens of thousands of the great and the strong, while the remaining millions, numerous as the grains of sand in the sea, weak, but loving you, must serve as mere raw material for the great and the strong? No, we care about the weak, too. They are depraved and mutineers, but in the end they too will grow obedient. They will marvel at us and will consider us gods because we, in standing at their head, have consented to endure freedom and rule over them – so terrible will being free appear to them at last! But we shall say that we are obedient to you and that we rule in your name. We shall deceive them again, for we shall not let you near us any more. In that deception will be our suffering, for we shall be compelled to lie. That is the significance of the first question that was asked in the wilderness, and that is what you rejected in the name of freedom, which you placed higher than anything else. Yet in that question lay the great secret of this world. Had you accepted the 'loaves', you would have responded to the universal and age-old anguish of man, both as an individual creature and as the whole of mankind, namely the question: 'Before whom should one bow down?' There is for man no preoccupation more constant or more nagging than, while in a condition of freedom, quickly to find someone to bow down before. But man seeks to bow down before that which is already beyond dispute, so far beyond dispute that all human beings will instantly agree to a universal bowing-down before it. For the preoccupation of these miserable creatures consists not only in finding that before which I or another may bow down, but in finding something that everyone can come to believe in and bow down before, and that it should indeed be *everyone*, and that they should do it *all together*. It is this need for a *community* of bowing-down that has been the principal torment of each individual person and of mankind as a whole since the earliest ages. For the sake of a universal bowing-down they have destroyed one another with the sword. They have created gods and challenged one another: 'Give up your gods and come and worship ours or else death to you and to your gods!' And so it will be until the world's end, when even gods will vanish from the world: whatever happens, they will fall down before idols. You knew, you could not fail to know that peculiar secret of human nature, but you rejected the only absolute banner that was offered to you and that would have compelled everyone to bow down before you without dispute – the banner of earthly bread, and you rejected it in the name of freedom and the bread of heaven. Just take a look at what you did after that. And all of it again in the name of freedom! I tell you, man has no preoccupation more nagging than to find the person to whom that unhappy creature may surrender the gift of freedom with which he is born. But only he can take mastery of people's freedom who is able to set their consciences at rest. With bread you were given an undisputed banner: give bread and man will bow down, for nothing is more undisputed than bread, but if at the same time someone takes mastery of his conscience without your knowledge – oh, then he will even throw down your bread and follow the one who seduces his conscience. In that you were right. For the secret of human existence does not consist in living, merely, but in what one lives for. Without a firm idea of what he is to live for, man will not consent to live and will sooner destroy himself than remain on the earth, even though all around him there be loaves. That is so, but how has it worked out? Instead of taking mastery of people's freedom, you have increased that freedom even further! Or did you forget that peace of mind and even death are dearer to man than free choice and the cognition of good and evil? There is nothing more seductive for man than the freedom of his conscience, but there is nothing more tormenting for him, either. And so then in place of a firm foundation for the easing of the human conscience once and for all – you took everything that was exceptional, enigmatic and indeterminate, took everything that was beyond people's capacity to bear, and therefore acted as though you did not love them at all – and who was this? The one who had come to sacrifice his life for them! Instead of taking mastery of people's freedom, you augmented it and saddled the spiritual kingdom of man with it for ever. You desired that man's love should be free, that he should follow you freely, enticed and captivated by you. Henceforth, in place of the old, firm law, man was himself to decide with a free heart what is good and what is evil, with only your image before him to guide him – but surely you never dreamed that he would at last reject and call into question even your image and your truth were he to be oppressed by so terrible a burden as freedom of choice? They will exclaim at last that the truth is not in you, for it would have been impossible to leave them in more confusion and torment than you did when you left them so many worries and unsolvable problems. Thus, you yourself laid the foundation for the destruction of your own kingdom, and no one else should be blamed for it. And yet is that really what was offered you? There are three powers, only three powers on the earth that are capable of eternally vanquishing and ensnaring the consciences of those feeble mutineers, for their happiness – those powers are: miracle, mystery and authority. You rejected the first, the second and the third, and yourself gave the lead in doing so. When the wise and terrible Spirit set you on a pinnacle of the temple and said to you: 'If you would know whether you are the Son of God, then cast yourself down from hence, for it is written that the angels will take charge of him and bear him up, and he will not fall and dash himself to pieces – and then you will know if you are the Son of God, and will prove how much faith you have in your Father.'* But having heard him through, you rejected his offer and did not give way and did not cast yourself down. Oh, of course, in that you acted proudly and magnificently, like God, but people, that weak, mutiny-ing tribe – are they gods? Oh, that day you understood that by taking only one step, the step of casting yourself down, you would instantly have tempted the Lord and would have lost all faith in him, and would have dashed yourself to pieces against the earth which you had come to save, and the clever Spirit which had tempted you would rejoice. But, I repeat, are there many such as you? And could you really have supposed, even for a moment, that people would have the strength to resist such a temptation? Is human nature really of a kind as to be able to reject the miracle, and to make do, at such terrible moments of life, moments of the most terrible fundamental and tormenting spiritual questions, with only a free decision of the heart? Oh, you knew that your great deed* would be preserved in the Scriptures, would attain to the depth of the ages and to the outermost limits of the earth, and you hoped that, in following you, man too would make do with God, not requiring a miracle. But you did not know that no sooner did man reject the miracle than he would at once reject God also, for man does not seek God so much as miracles. And since man is not strong enough to get by without the miracle, he creates new miracles for himself, his own now, and bows down before the miracle of the quack and the witchcraft of the peasant woman, even though he is a mutineer, heretic and atheist a hundred times over. You did not come down from the Cross when they shouted to you, mocking and teasing you: 'Come down from the Cross and we will believe that it is You.'* You did not come down because again you did not want to enslave man with a miracle and because you thirsted for a faith that was free, not miraculous. You thirsted for a love that was free, not for the servile ecstasies of the slave before the might that has inspired him with dread once and for all. But even here you had too high an opinion of human beings, for of course, they are slaves, though they are created mutineers. Look around you and judge, now that fifteen centuries have passed, take a glance at them: which of them have you borne up to yourself? Upon my word, man is created weaker and more base than you supposed! Can he, can he perform the deeds of which you are capable? In respecting him so much you acted as though you had ceased to have compassion for him, because you demanded too much of him – and yet who was this? The very one you had loved more than yourself! Had you respected him less you would have demanded of him less, and that would have been closer to love, for his burden would have been lighter. He is weak and dishonourable. So what if now he mutinies against your power and is proud of his mutiny? This is the pride of a small boy, a schoolboy. These are little children, mutinying in class and driving out their teacher. But the ecstasy of the little boys will come to an end, it will cost them dearly. They will overthrow the temples and soak the earth in blood. But at last the stupid children will realize that even though they are mutineers, they are feeble mutineers, who are unable to sustain their mutiny. In floods of stupid tears they will at last recognize that the intention of the one who created them mutineers was undoubtedly to make fun of them. They will say this in despair, and their words will be blasphemy, which will make them even more unhappy, for human nature cannot endure blasphemy and in the end invariably takes revenge for it. Thus, restlessness, confusion and unhappiness – those are the lot of human beings now, after all that you underwent for the sake of their freedom! Your great prophet* says in an allegorical vision that he saw all those who took part in the first resurrection and that of each tribe there were twelve thousand. But if there were so many of them, they cannot have been human beings, but gods. They had borne your Cross, they had borne decades in the hungry and barren wilderness, living on roots and locusts – and of course, it goes without saying that you may point with pride to those children of freedom, of a love that is free, of the free and magnificent sacrifice they have made in your name. Remember, however, that there were only a few thousand of them, and those were gods – but what about the rest? And in what way are the other weak human beings to blame for not having been able to bear the same things as the mighty? In what way is the weak soul to blame for not having the strength to accommodate such terrible gifts? And indeed, did you really only come to the chosen ones and for the chosen ones? But if that is so, then there is a mystery there and it is not for us to comprehend it. And if there is a mystery, then we were within our rights to propagate that mystery and teach them that it was not the free decision of their hearts and not love that mattered, but the mystery, which they must obey blindly, even in opposition to their consciences. And that was what we did. We corrected your great deed and founded it upon *miracle, mystery* and *authority*. And people were glad that they had once been brought together into a flock and that at last from their hearts had been removed such a terrible gift, which had brought them so much torment. Were we right, to teach and act thus, would you say? Did we not love mankind, when we so humbly admitted his helplessness, lightening his burden with love and allowing his feeble nature even sin, but with our permission? Why have you come to get in our way now? And why do you gaze at me so silently and sincerely with those meek eyes of yours? Why do you not get angry? I do not want your love, because I myself do not love you. And what is there I can conceal from you? Do you think I don't know who I'm talking to? What I have to say to you is all familiar to you already, I can read it in your eyes. And do you think I would conceal our secret from you? Perhaps it is my own lips that you want to hear it from – then listen: we are not with you, but with *him*, there is our secret! We have long been not with you, but with *him*, eight centuries now. It is now just eight centuries* since we took from him that which you in indignation rejected, that final gift he offered you, when he showed you all the kingdoms of the world: we took from him Rome and the sword of Caesar and announced that we alone were the kings of the world, the only kings, even though to this day we have not succeeded in bringing our task to its complete fulfilment. But whose is the blame for that? Oh, this task is as yet only at its beginning, but it has begun. The world will have to wait for its accomplishment for a long time yet, and it will have to suffer much, but we shall reach our goal and shall be Caesars and then we shall give thought to the universal happiness of human beings. And yet even back then you could have taken the sword of Caesar. Why did you reject that final gift? Had you accepted that third counsel of the mighty Spirit, you would have supplied everything that man seeks in the world, that is: someone to bow down before, someone to entrust one's conscience to, and a way of at last uniting everyone into an undisputed, general and consensual ant-heap, for the need of universal union is the third and final torment of human beings. Invariably mankind as a whole has striven to organize itself on a universal basis. Many great peoples have there been, and peoples with great histories, but the loftier those peoples, the more unhappy, for more acutely than others have they been conscious of the need for a universal union of human beings. The great conquerors, the Tamburlaines and Genghis Khans, hurtled like a whirlwind through the world, striving to conquer the universe, but even they, though they did so unconsciously, expressed the same great need of mankind for universal and general union. Had you accepted the world and the purple of Caesar, you would have founded a universal kingdom and given men universal peace. For who shall reign over human beings if not those who reign over their consciences and in whose hands are their loaves? Well, we took the sword of Caesar, and, of course, in taking it rejected you and followed *him*. Oh, centuries yet will pass of the excesses of the free intellect, of their science and anthropophagy, because, having begun to erect their Tower of Babel without us, they will end in anthropophagy. But then the beast will come crawling to our feet* and lick them and sprinkle them with the bloody tears from his eyes. And we will sit upon the beast and raise the cup, and on it will be written: MYSTERY! But then and only then for human beings will begin the kingdom of peace and happiness. You are proud of your chosen ones, but all you have are chosen ones, and we shall bring rest to all. And there is more: how many of those chosen ones, of the mighty, who might have become chosen ones, at last grew tired of waiting for you, and have transferred and will yet transfer the energies of their spirits and the fervour of their hearts to a different sphere and end by raising their *free* banner against you. But it was you yourself who raised that banner. In our hands, though, everyone will be happy and will neither mutiny nor destroy one another any more, as they do in your freedom, wherever one turns. Oh, we shall persuade them that they will only become free when they renounce their freedom for us and submit to us. And what does it matter whether we are right or whether we are telling a lie? They themselves will be persuaded we are right, for they will remember to what horrors of slavery and confusion your freedom has brought them. Freedom, the free intellect and science will lead them into such labyrinths and bring them up against such miracles and unfathomable mysteries that some of them, the disobedient and ferocious ones, will destroy themselves; others, disobedient and feeble, will destroy one another, while a third group, those who are left, the feeble and unhappy ones, will come crawling to our feet, and will cry out to us: 'Yes, you were right, you alone were masters of his secret, and we are returning to you, save us from ourselves.' Receiving loaves from us, of course, they will clearly see that what we have done is to take from them the loaves they won with their own hands in order to distribute it to them without any miracles, they will see that we have not turned stones into loaves, but truly, more than of the bread, they will be glad of the fact that they are receiving it from our hands! For they will be only too aware that in former times, when we were not there, the very loaves they won used merely to turn to stones in their hands, and yet now they have returned to us those very same stones have turned back to loaves again. All too well, all too well will they appreciate what it means to subordinate themselves to us once and for all! And until human beings understand that, they will be unhappy. Who contributed most of all to that lack of understanding, tell me? Who split up the flock and scattered it over the unknown ways? But the flock will once more gather and once more submit and this time it will be for ever. Then we shall give them a quiet, reconciled happiness, the happiness of feeble creatures, such as they were created. Oh, we shall persuade them at last not to be proud, for you bore them up and by doing so taught them to be proud; we shall prove to them that they are feeble, that they are merely pathetic children, but that childish happiness is sweeter than all others. They will grow fearful

and look at us and press themselves to us in their fear, like nestlings to
their mother. They will marvel at us and regard us with awe and be
proud that we are so powerful and so clever as to be able to pacify such a
turbulent, thousand-million-headed flock. They will feebly tremble with
fright before our wrath, their minds will grow timid, their eyes will brim
with tears, like those of women and children, but just as lightly at a nod
from us will they pass over into cheerfulness and laughter, radiant joy
and happy children's songs. Yes, we shall make them work, but in their
hours of freedom from work we shall arrange their lives like a childish
game, with childish songs, in chorus, with innocent dances. Oh, we shall
permit them sin, too, they are weak and powerless, and they will love us
like children for letting them sin. We shall tell them that every sin can be
redeemed as long as it is committed with our leave; we are allowing them
to sin because we love them, and as for the punishment for those sins,
very well, we shall take it upon ourselves. And we shall take it upon
ourselves, and they will worship us as benefactors who have assumed
responsibility for their sins before God. And they shall have no secrets
from us. We shall permit them or forbid them to live with their wives or
paramours, to have or not to have children – all according to the degree
of their obedience – and they will submit to us with cheerfulness and joy.
The most agonizing secrets of their consciences – all, all will they bring
to us, and we shall resolve it all, and they will attend our decision with
joy, because it will deliver them from the great anxiety and fearsome
present torments of free and individual decision. And all will be happy,
all the millions of beings, except for the hundred thousand who govern
them. For only we, we, who preserve the mystery, only we shall be
unhappy. There will be thousands upon millions of happy babes, and a
hundred thousand martyrs who have taken upon themselves the curse of
the knowledge of good and evil. Quietly they will die, quietly they will
fade away in your name and beyond the tomb will find only death. But
we shall preserve the secret and for the sake of their happiness will lure
them with a heavenly and eternal reward. For if there were anything in
the other world, it goes without saying that it would not be for the likes
of them. It is said and prophesied* that you will come and prevail anew,
will come with your chosen, your proud and mighty ones, but we will
say that they have saved only themselves, while we have saved all. It is
said that the whore who sits on the beast holding her MYSTERY will be
disgraced, that the weak will rise up in mutiny again, that they will tear
her purple and render naked her 'desolate' body. But then I shall arise
and draw your attention to the thousands upon millions of happy babes,

who know not sin. And we, who for the sake of their happiness have taken their sins upon us, we shall stand before you and say: 'Judge us if you can and dare.' You may as well know that I am not afraid of you. You may as well know that I too was in the wilderness, that I too nourished myself on roots and locusts, that I too blessed the freedom with which you have blessed human beings, I too prepared myself to join the number of your chosen ones, the number of the strong and the mighty, with a yearning to 'fulfil the number'.* But I came to my senses again and was unwilling to serve madness. I returned and adhered to the crowd of those who have *corrected your great deed*. I left the proud and returned to the humble for the sake of their happiness. What I say to you will come to pass, and our kingdom shall be accomplished. I tell you again: tomorrow you will see that obedient flock, which at the first nod of my head will rush to rake up the hot embers to the bonfire on which I am going to burn you for having come to get in our way. For if there ever was one who deserved our bonfire more than anyone else, it is you. Tomorrow I am going to burn you. *Dixi*."'

Ivan paused. He had grown flushed from talking, and talking with passion; now that he had stopped, however, he suddenly smiled.

Alyosha, who had listened to him all this time without saying anything, though towards the end, in a state of extreme agitation, he had several times attempted to interrupt the flow of his brother's speech, but had evidently held himself in check, suddenly began to speak as though he had leapt into motion.

'But . . . that is preposterous!' he exclaimed, turning red. 'Your poem is a eulogy of Jesus, not a vilification of him, as you intended it. And who will listen to you on the subject of freedom? That is a fine way, a fine way to understand it! That is not how it's understood in the Orthodox faith. That's Rome, and not even Rome completely, either, that isn't true – it's the worst elements in Catholicism, the inquisitors, the Jesuits! . . . And in any case, a fantastic character like your Inquisitor could not possibly have existed. What are these sins of human beings that have been taken by others upon themselves? Who are these bearers of mystery who have taken upon themselves some kind of curse for the sake of human happiness? Whoever heard of such people? We know the Jesuits, bad things are said of them, but they're not as they appear in your poem, are they? They're not at all like that, in no way like that . . . They are simply a Roman army for a future universal earthly kingdom, with an emperor – the Pontiff of Rome at their head . . . That is their ideal, but without any mysteries or exalted melancholy . . . The most

straightforward desire for power, for sordid earthly blessings, for enslave-
ment ... like a future law of serf-ownership, with themselves as the
owners ... that's all they care about. Why, they probably don't even
believe in God. Your suffering Inquisitor is only a fantasy ...'

'Hold on, hold on,' Ivan said, laughing. 'What a temper you're in. A
fantasy, you say – very well! All right, it's a fantasy. But wait a moment:
do you really suppose that the whole of that Catholic movement of
recent centuries is nothing but a desire for power in order to attain
earthly comfort? That wouldn't be something Father Paisy taught you,
would it?'

'No, no, on the contrary, Father Paisy did actually once say something
that was slightly similar to your idea ... but of course it wasn't the same,
not the same at all,' Alyosha suddenly remembered.

'A valuable piece of information, nevertheless, in spite of your, "not
the same at all". The question I want to ask you is why have your Jesuits
and inquisitors joined together for the sole purpose of attaining wretched
material comfort? Why may there not be among them a single martyr,
tormented by a great *Weltschmerz* and loving mankind? Look: suppose
that out of all those who desire nothing but sordid material comfort there
is just one – just one, like my aged Inquisitor – who has himself eaten
roots in the wilderness and raged like one possessed as he conquered his
flesh in order to make himself free and perfect, though all his life he has
loved mankind and has suddenly had his eyes opened and seen that there
is not much moral beatitude in attaining perfect freedom if at the same
time one is convinced that millions of the rest of God's creatures have
been stitched together as a mere bad joke, that they will never have the
strength to cope with their freedom, that from pathetic mutineers there
will never grow giants to complete the building of the Tower, that not
for such geese did the great idealist dream of his harmony. Having
understood all that, he returned and joined forces with ... the clever
people. Could that really not happen?'

'A fine lot of people he joined! How can one call them clever?'
Alyosha exclaimed, almost reckless in his passion. 'They have no intelligence, nor do they have any mysteries or secrets ... Except perhaps
atheism – that is their only secret. Your Inquisitor doesn't believe in
God, that's his whole secret!'

'So what if even that is true? At last you've realized it! And indeed it is
true, that is indeed the only secret, but is that not suffering, even for a
man such as he, who has wasted his entire life on a heroic feat in the
wilderness, and has not been cured of his love for mankind? In the

decline of his days he becomes clearly persuaded that only the counsel of the terrible Spirit could in any way reconstitute in tolerable order the feeble mutineers, "imperfect, trial creatures, who were created as a bad joke". And lo, persuaded of this, he sees that it is necessary to proceed according to the indication of the clever Spirit, the terrible Spirit of death and destruction, and to such end accept deceit and falsehood and lead people consciously to death and destruction and deceive them moreover all of the way, so that they do not notice whither they are being led, so that at least on the way those pathetic blind creatures shall believe themselves happy. And note that it is deceit in the name of the One in whose ideal the old man had all his life so passionately believed! Is that not a misfortune? And even if there were only one such man at the head of this entire army, "thirsting for power for the sake of mere sordid earthly blessings", then would not one such man be enough to produce a tragedy? Not only that: one such man, standing at their head, would be enough in order to establish at last the whole guiding idea of the Roman cause with all its armies and Jesuits, the loftiest idea of that cause. I declare to you outright that I firmly believe that these unique men have never been hard to find among those who stand at the head of the movement. Who can say – perhaps there have been such unique men even among the Roman pontiffs? Who can say – perhaps that accursed old man who loved mankind with such a stubborn, original love exists even now in the form of a whole crowd of such unique old men and not by mere accident but as a secret alliance, formed long ago for the preservation of the mystery, for its preservation from feeble and unhappy human beings, in order to make them happy. That is certainly the case, and must be so. I fancy that even among the Masons there is something of the same sort of mystery at the basis of their movement and that the Catholics hate the Freemasons so much because they see them as rivals, a division of the unity of the idea, while there must be one flock and one shepherd ... As a matter of fact, in defending my thesis like this, I feel like an author who is unable to withstand your criticism. Enough of this.'

'I think you are a Freemason yourself!' Alyosha suddenly let out. 'You don't believe in God,' he added, this time with extreme sorrow. It seemed to him, moreover, that his brother was gazing at him with mockery. 'How does your poem end?' he asked suddenly, looking at the ground. 'Or have we already had the end?'

'I was going to end it like this: when the Inquisitor falls silent, he waits for a certain amount of time to hear what his Captive will say in response. He finds His silence difficult to bear. He has seen that the

Prisoner has listened to him all this time with quiet emotion, gazing straight into his eyes and evidently not wishing to raise any objection. The old man would like the Other to say something to him, even if it is bitter, terrible. But He suddenly draws near to the old man without saying anything and quietly kisses him on his bloodless, ninety-year-old lips. That is His only response. The old man shudders. Something has stirred at the corners of his mouth; he goes to the door, opens it and says to Him: "Go and do not come back . . . do not come back at all . . . ever . . . ever!" And he releases him into "the town's dark streets and squares."* The Captive departs.'

'And the old man?'

'The kiss burns within his heart, but the old man remains with his former idea.'

'And you along with him, you too?' Alyosha exclaimed sadly. Ivan laughed.

'Oh, Alyosha, why, you know, it's nonsense — it's just an incoherent *poema* by an incoherent student who has never so much as put two lines of verse to paper. Why are you taking it so seriously? Surely you don't think that now I shall go straight there, to the Jesuits, in order to join the crowd of people who are correcting His great deed? Oh Lord, what do I care about that? I mean, I told you: all I want to do is to hold out until I'm thirty, and then — dash the cup to the floor!'

'And the sticky leaf-buds, and the beloved tombs, and the blue sky, and the woman you love? How are you going to live, what are you going to love them with?' Alyosha exclaimed sadly. 'With a hell like that in your breast and your head, is it possible? No, of course you're going to join them . . . and if you don't, you'll kill yourself, you won't be able to endure!'

'There is a power that can endure everything!' Ivan said, with a cold, ironic smile now.

'What power?'

'The Karamazovian power . . . the power of Karamazovian baseness.'

'You mean, to drown in depravity, to crush the life from your soul in corruption, is that it, is that it?'

'Possibly that too . . . Only perhaps when I'm thirty, I shall escape, and then . . .'

'But how will you escape? With what means will you escape? With your ideas it's impossible.'

'Again, the Karamazovian way.'

'So that "all things are lawful"?* All things are lawful, is that what you mean, is that it?'

Ivan frowned and suddenly turned strangely pale.

'Ah, you've got hold of the little remark I made yesterday at which Miusov took such offence . . . and which brother Dmitry was so naïve as to butt in and repeat?' he said, smiling a crooked smile. 'Yes, perhaps: "all things are lawful", since the remark has been made. I do not disown it. And dear Mitya's version of it is not so bad, either.'

Alyosha stared at him without saying anything.

'In leaving, brother, I had imagined that in all the world I have only you,' Ivan said suddenly, with unexpected emotion, 'but now I see that in your heart there is no room for me, my dear hermit. I do not disown the formula "all things are lawful", but, I mean, are you going to disown me because of it – eh? eh?'

Alyosha rose, walked over to him, and without saying anything kissed him quietly on the lips.

'Literary thieving!' Ivan exclaimed, suddenly passing into a kind of ecstasy. 'You stole that from my *poema*! But never mind, I thank you. Come on, Alyosha, let us go, it is time both for you and for me.'

They went outside, but paused by the entrance to the inn.

'Look, Alyosha,' Ivan pronounced in a resolute voice. 'If I am indeed capable of loving the sticky leaf-buds, then I shall love them at the mere memory of you. It is enough for me that you are somewhere here, and I shan't yet lose my will to live. Is that enough for you? If you like, you may take it as a confession of love. But now you must go to the right, and I to the left – and enough, do you hear, enough. That is to say that if it proves that L do not leave tomorrow (though it seems to me that I most certainly shall) and we were again to meet somehow, then I want you not to say another word to me on all these subjects. I earnestly request you. And concerning brother Dmitry I also particularly request that you not even so much as mention him to me ever again,' he added in sudden irritation. 'It's all settled and decided, isn't it? And in exchange for that, I for my part will also give you a certain promise: when I attain the age of thirty and want to "dash the cup to the floor" then, wherever you are, I shall come once again to discuss things with you . . . even if it's from America, I shall have you know. I shall come specially. It will be very interesting to set eyes on you at that time: what will you be like? You see, it's quite a solemn sort of promise. And indeed it may well be that we are saying goodbye for seven, for ten years. Well, go to your *Pater Seraphicus** now, after all, he is dying; if he dies in your absence you may well be angry at me for having kept you back. Goodbye, kiss me once more – like that – and go . . .'

Ivan suddenly turned and went his way, without looking round this
time. It resembled the manner in which brother Dmitry had left Alyosha
the day before, though then the mood had been quite different. This
strange little observation flashed, like an arrow, through Alyosha's sad
mind, sad and sorrowful at that moment. He waited for a bit as he
watched his brother go. For some reason he suddenly noticed that
brother Ivan walked with a kind of sway and that, seen from behind, his
right shoulder looked lower than his left. Never had he observed this
previously. Suddenly, however, he also turned and set off almost at a run
in the direction of the monastery. It was by now getting very dark, and
he felt a sense that was almost one of fear; something new was growing
within him, something he was unable to account for. The wind rose
again, as it had done yesterday, and the ancient pine trees soughed darkly
around him as he entered the hermitage woods. He was almost running.
'Pater Seraphicus' – that name, he had taken it from somewhere – where?
– flashed through Alyosha's brain. 'Ivan, poor Ivan, and when will I see
you again . . . Here is the hermitage, O Lord! Yes, yes, it is him, it is
Pater Seraphicus, he will save me . . . from him and for ever!'

Later on, several times in his life, he recollected that moment with
great bewilderment, wondering how he could suddenly, having only just
parted with Ivan, so completely forget his brother Dmitry, who that
morning, only a few hours ago, he had determined to track down,
vowing not to return without having done so, even if it meant he could
not go back to the monastery that night.

6

One as Yet Very Indistinct

BUT Ivan Fyodorovich, having parted from Alyosha, went home, to
Fyodor Pavlovich's house. It was strange, however: he was suddenly
assailed by an unendurable anguish, one which, he could not help noting,
with each step he took in the direction of the house increased further and
further. The strangeness lay not in the anguish itself, but in the fact that
Ivan Fyodorovich could not for the life of him determine what it concerned. He had often suffered anguish before, and it would have been
surprising had it not arrived at such a moment, when the very next day,
making a sudden break with all that had drawn him here, he was going
once more to take a sharp turn to one side and enter upon a new,
completely unfamiliar path, again all on his own, as before, with many

hopes, though he knew not of what, expecting much, far too much, of life, but unable himself to determine anything, either of his expectations or his desires. And yet all the same at this moment, though the anguish of the new and the unfamiliar really was in his soul, it was anything but that which tormented him. 'Is it not the revulsion I feel towards my father's house?' he wondered to himself. 'Something like that – so repulsive has it become to me, and even though today is the last time I shall cross that loathsome threshold, yet still it's repulsive . . .' But no, that was not what it was, either. Was it his saying goodbye to Alyosha and his erstwhile conversation with him? 'How many years have I gone without deigning to say a word to anyone, and yet suddenly I blabbered all that rubbish.' Indeed, it might be a youthful annoyance at youthful inexperience and youthful vanity, an annoyance at not having been able to express himself properly, especially with someone like Alyosha, for whom his heart really did have significant plans. Of course, this too was only to be expected – the annoyance, that was to say; in fact, it could hardly be otherwise, but even that was not it, still not what the trouble was. 'Anguish to the point of nausea, yet I am unable to determine what it is I want. Perhaps I should not think at all . . .'

Ivan Fyodorovich proceeded to attempt 'not to think', but even that did not help. The main thing that annoyed him about this anguish, and the main reason that it irritated him, was that it possessed a sort of accidental, wholly external aspect; this he could feel. Some being or object stood constantly present somewhere, rather in the way something may on occasion constantly present itself to one's gaze, while for a long time, as one works or engages in heated conversation, one fails to notice it yet all the while grows visibly irritated, almost tormented, until at last it dawns on one to move aside the worthless object, frequently a very trivial and absurd one, some item that has been left where it does not belong: a handkerchief fallen to the floor, a book not returned to the bookcase, and so on and so forth. At last Ivan Fyodorovich, in a most foul and irritated condition of spirit, attained his parental home and suddenly, some fifteen paces from the wicket gate, as he glanced at the entrance way, realized in a flash what it was that had so tormented and disturbed him.

On the bench by the entrance sat the lackey Smerdyakov, and from a first glance at him Ivan Fyodorovich understood that the lackey Smerdyakov also sat in his soul and that it was precisely this person it was unable to endure. Everything was suddenly bathed in light and became clear. Earlier, as Alyosha had described his encounter with Smerdyakov, something dark and repulsive had suddenly penetrated his heart, instantly evoking within him a reciprocal malice. Later, during their conversation, Smerdyakov had been forgotten for a while, but had nevertheless remained in his soul, and no sooner had Ivan Fyodorovich parted from Alyosha and walked alone to the house, than the forgotten emotion had instantly begun to surface again. 'Can it really be true that this good-for-nothing scoundrel is able to upset me to such a degree?' he wondered with intolerable malice.

The fact was that Ivan Fyodorovich really had conceived a deep antipathy towards this man of late, particularly during the last few days. He had even himself begun to notice this mounting emotion in respect of this creature, an emotion akin almost to hatred. It was possible that the process of hatred had grown so intense for the initial reason that at the outset, when Ivan Fyodorovich had first come to live among us, things had been rather different. Then Ivan Fyodorovich had suddenly begun to take an especial interest in Smerdyakov, even finding him rather original. He had himself schooled him to talk to him, always, however, marvelling at a certain incoherence or, rather, a certain disturbance of his mind, and was unable to think what it might be that could so constantly and persistently disturb it. They would talk about philosophical questions and even about how there could have been light on the first day when the sun, moon and stars had only been brought into being on the fourth, and how this should be interpreted; but Ivan Fyodorovich soon grew convinced that the important point here had nothing whatever to do with the sun, moon and stars, that even though these were of interest to Smerdyakov they were entirely insignificant and that what he was after was something altogether different. This may or may not have been the case, but whatever the truth of the matter, he had begun to display and manifest a boundless vanity that was, moreover, a wounded one. This had not appealed to Ivan Fyodorovich at all. It was from this that his sense of revulsion had sprung. Subsequently there had been the disorderly scenes in the house, Grushenka had appeared, the episodes involving Dmitry Fyodorovich had begun, troubles had ensued — these things they spoke of, too, but although Smerdyakov invariably talked of them with great agitation, it was again quite impossible to discover what it was he wanted in this respect. One could even marvel at the illogicality and chaotic nature of some of his desires, which would involuntarily come to the surface and were always equally obscure. Smerdyakov kept pumping him with questions, which were always of an oblique, evidently prepared nature, but why he did so he would not explain, and usually at the most heated point of his questioning he would suddenly fall silent or pass to some other subject altogether. The thing that Ivan Fyodorovich found most irritating of all, however, and that had finally inspired him with such revulsion, was the singular and loathsome familiarity that Smerdyakov had begun in no small measure to display towards him, one that increased with the passage of time. It was not that he took the liberty of being discourteous; on the contrary, he always spoke with exceptional deference, but it came to the point where Smerdyakov evidently began to consider himself, heaven knows why, in some kind of solidarity with Ivan Fyodorovich, and invariably spoke in a tone that made it seem as though between the two of them there were now something agreed and secret, something that had once been spoken on both sides, was known only to the two of them and to the other mere mortals who pottered about them was quite simply incomprehensible. Even then, however, it had taken Ivan Fyodorovich a long time to understand the real reason for his mounting revulsion and it was only of late that he had realized its cause. With a sense of squeamish irritation he began now to pass through the wicket gate in silence, not looking at Smerdyakov, but Smerdyakov rose from the bench, and by this one gesture alone Ivan Fyodorovich in a flash realized that the man wanted to engage him in particular conversation. Ivan Fyodorovich gave him a look and paused, and the fact that he had suddenly paused and not gone past as he had intended to a moment earlier made him violently lose his temper. In anger and revulsion he stared at Smerdyakov's emaciated, *skopets*-like physiognomy with its hair combed at the temples and whipped up into a little topknot. His left eye, ever so slightly narrowed, winked and smiled ironically, as though he were saying: 'Where are you off to, you won't get past me, for you see, we two clever men have some business to discuss.' Ivan Fyodorovich began to tremble:

'Away, scoundrel, what company am I for you, fool?' was what was about to leap from his tongue, but, to his very great astonishment, what leapt from it was something quite different:

'How is pater, is he asleep or has he woken up?' he said in a quiet, meek voice that was unexpected even to himself, and suddenly, in a manner also entirely unexpected, sat down on the bench. For a split second he felt almost afraid – he remembered that later. Smerdyakov stood facing him, his hands behind his back, staring at him with confidence, almost sternly.

'His honour is still reposing, sir,' he articulated without hurry. (It was as if he were saying: 'You spoke first, and not I.') 'I'm surprised at you, sir,' he added, after a silence during which he lowered his eyes in an affected manner, advancing his right foot and fidgeting with the toecap of his patent-leather shoe.

'Why are you surprised at me?' Ivan Fyodorovich enunciated brusquely and sternly, restraining himself with all his might, and suddenly with revulsion it dawned on him that he felt the most intense curiosity, that not for anything in the world would he leave this place until he had satisfied it.

'Why haven't you gone to Chermashnya, sir?' Smerdyakov said, suddenly looking up and smiling familiarly. It was as if his narrowed left eye were saying: 'Well, if you're a clever man you will understand why I'm smiling.'

'Why should I go to Chermashnya?' Ivan Fyodorovich asked in astonishment.

Smerdyakov again said nothing.

'Well, sir, even Fyodor Pavlovich himself kept beseeching you to,' he said at last, not hurrying and almost as if he himself attached no value to his answer, as if to imply, 'I'm getting myself off the hook with a third-rate excuse, just in order to have something to say.'

'Ah, the devil, can't you be more precise, what is it you want?' Ivan Fyodorovich at last exclaimed wrathfully, from meekness passing over into vulgarity.

Smerdyakov brought his right foot in towards his left and drew himself up straighter, but continued to gaze with the same equanimity and the same little smile.

'It's nothing essential, sir . . . I were just making conversation, sir . . .'

Again, a silence ensued. For very nearly a minute neither of them said anything. Ivan Fyodorovich knew it was his duty to get up immediately and lose his temper, but Smerdyakov went on standing there, facing him, as if in expectation: 'I'm waiting to see if you'll lose your temper or not.' Thus, at any rate, did it appear to Ivan Fyodorovich. At last he began to stagger to his feet. It was as if Smerdyakov seized the moment as opportune.

'My position is a dreadful one, Ivan Fyodorovich, sir, and I really do not know where to turn,' he said suddenly, in a firm, clearly articulated voice, ending his last word with a sigh. Ivan Fyodorovich at once sank back on the bench again.

'They're both quite insane, sir, they've both gone right back to early childhood again, sir,' Smerdyakov continued. 'I'm talking about your parent and that fine brother of yours, sir, Dmitry Fyodorovich. He'll get up now, Fyodor Pavlovich will, and start pestering me every moment with: "Why hasn't she arrived? What's the reason for her not arriving?" – and so on all the way until midnight and even after. And if Agrafena Aleksandrovna doesn't arrive (because I think it may be that she doesn't ever intend to arrive, sir), he'll hurl himself on me again in the morning: "Why hasn't she arrived? What's the reason for her not arriving? When is she going to arrive?" – as though I were in some way to blame for it. On the other hand, sir, there's the matter of how, as soon as it gets dark now, or even before, that fine brother of yours will come to pay me a neighbourly visit with a weapon in his hands: "Watch out," he'll say, "blackguard, bouillon-boy: if you don't spot her and don't let me know she's arrived – you'll be the first one I'll kill." The night will pass, and tomorrow morning he too, like Fyodor Pavlovich, will start a-torturing me like a torturer, sir: "Why hasn't she arrived, when is she going to show her face?" – and again it will be as though I'm guilty before him because his lady hasn't turned up. And so angry are they getting with every day and every hour, worse and worse, the two of them, sir, that sometimes I could take my own life from terror, sir. Why, sir, I have no faith in them, sir.'

'Well, why did you get involved? Why did you start taking messages to Dmitry Fyodorovich?' Ivan Fyodorovich said, irritably.

'But how could I not get involved? And actually, I tried not to get involved in any way, if you want to know the whole truth, sir. Right from the very beginning I didn't say anything, didn't dare to make any objection, and it was he himself who made me act as his Licharda.* Ever since, all he's been able to say is: "I'll kill you, you blackguard, if you let her slip!" I most certainly suppose, sir, that tomorrow I shall have a long fit of the falling sickness.'

'What are you talking about?'

'One of them long fits, sir, an exceptionally long one, sir. They last for several hours, sir, or maybe even a day or two, sir. I once had one that lasted for about three days, I fell down from the garret that time. It stops and goes away, and then it starts up again; I could not gain my reason for three days. Fyodor Pavlovich sent for Herzenstube, the local doctor, sir, and he put ice on my temples, and employed some other remedy, as well . . . I could have died, sir.'

'But I thought it was supposed to be impossible to anticipate a fit of the falling sickness, and to say it will happen at such-and-such a time. Why do you say you're going to have one tomorrow?' Ivan Fyodorovich inquired with a peculiar and irritable curiosity.

'That's precisely so, sir, it's impossible to anticipate it.'

'What's more, you fell down from the garret that time.'

'I go up to the garret every day, sir, I could fall down from the garret tomorrow. And if not from the garret, then I'll fall into the cellar, sir, I go down to the cellar every day, too, sir, on my necessary business, sir.'

Ivan Fyodorovich gave him a long look.

'You're talking through your hat, I can tell, and I don't think I understand you,' he said quietly, but with a touch of menace. 'What are you going to do tomorrow — pretend to have a fit of the falling sickness for three days? Eh?'

Smerdyakov, who had again been looking at the ground and fidgeting with the toecap of his right shoe, now made his right foot still, advanced his left instead, raised his head and with a grin pronounced:

'Even if I played that very trick, sir, the trick of pretending, I mean, sir, which is very easy for a person with experience, why even then I'd be fully within my rights to employ such means in order to save my life from death; for when I am lying ill in bed, then even if Agrafena Aleksandrovna comes to see his parent, he can't ask a sick man: "Why didn't you report it?" Even he would be ashamed.'

'Ah, the devil!' Ivan Fyodorovich suddenly hurled at him, his face distorted with malicious anger. 'Why are you always so frightened for your life? All those threats made by brother Dmitry are simply hot air, nothing more. He won't kill you; he'll kill, but it won't be you!'

'He'll kill me like a fly, sir, and I'll be the first, sir. But what frightens me more is something else: that I shall be considered an accessory when he goes and does something stupid to his parent.'

'Why should you be considered an accessory?'

'I shall be considered an accessory because I let him into the signals, in great secret, sir.'

'What signals? To whom? The devil take you, speak more clearly!'

'It is my duty to confess to you in all entirety,' Smerdyakov drawled with pedantic composure, 'that I share a certain secret with Fyodor Pavlovich. He, as you are aware (if you are aware of it, sir), has for several days now immediately, as soon as it is night or even evening, taken to locking himself in. Of late you've begun going back up to your room early, and yesterday you didn't go out at all, sir, and so it may be that you are not aware how zealously he's now begun to lock himself up for the night. And even if Grigory Vasilyevich himself was to come, then he'd only unlock the door if he was convinced by his voice it was him, sir. But Grigory Vasilyevich doesn't come, sir, because I'm the only one who waits on him now in his rooms, sir — them were his orders right from the very moment he started this bit of fun with Agrafena Aleksandrovna, sir, but now, in accordance with his directions, even I make myself scarce at night, and spend it in the outbuilding, though I'm not allowed to sleep until midnight but have to stay on look-out, get up and make rounds of the yard, waiting for Agrafena Aleksandrovna to come, sir, as he's been waiting for her several days now, like a real madman. The way he talks is like this, sir: she, he says, is scared of him, of Dmitry Fyodorovich (his honour calls him Mitka, sir), "and so she'll come to me late at night by way of the rears; you", he says, "must watch out for her right until it's midnight and even after. And if she comes, you must run up and knock on my door — or window, from the garden — the first two times slowly, like this: one . . . two . . . and then immediately after three times quickly: rat-tat-tat. Then," he says, "I shall know at once that she's come, and I'll open the door for you without making any noise." There was another signal he told me, for in case there was an emergency — first two times quickly: "rat-tat", and then after a bit another one time, much louder. Then he'll know that something unforeseen's come up and that I need to see him urgently, and he'll open up for me and I'll go in and tell him what's happened. That one's for if Agrafena Aleksandrovna can't come herself but sends someone to notify him of something; or then again Dmitry Fyodorovich may arrive, so it may be to notify him that he's close at hand. He's terrible scared of Dmitry Fyodorovich, so that even if Agrafena Aleksandrovna's already arrived and she and he have locked themselves in, and meanwhile Dmitry Fyodorovich is somewhere close at hand, even then I'm sworn to go and let him know immediately, by knocking three times, and the first signal of five knocks means: "Agrafena Aleksandrovna has arrived," and the second signal of three knocks means — "it's very, very urgent"; he's taught me it and explained it to me by example several times. And since there's only him and me in the whole of the universe what knows about those signals, sir, he'll open up for me without any doubt and without calling out (he's awful scared of calling out loud). Well, now Dmitry Fyodorovich knows them signals, too.'

'What do you mean, he knows them? Did you tell him? How could you dare to tell him?'

'Because of this same very fear, sir. And how could I not mention it to him, sir? Every day Dmitry Fyodorovich keeps on at me, saying: "Are you trying to deceive me, are you trying to conceal something from me? I'll break both your legs!" Well it was then that I gave him access to those secret signals, so he would at least see my servility and therefore be sure that I'm not trying to deceive him but am reporting everything to him.'

'If you think he'll use those signals and try to get in, you must not admit him.'

'But when I'm lying in my fit, sir, how will I be able to stop him coming in, even if I had the courage to try, knowing how desperate he is, sir?'

'Ah, the devil take you! Why are you so certain that you're going to have a fit of the falling sickness, the devil take you? Are you making fun of me, or what?'

'How would I ever dare to make fun of you? Is fear like mine any occasion for fun? I can feel that I'm going to have the falling sickness, I have a sort of premonition, and it will come upon me out of pure fear, sir.'

'Ah, the devil! If you're going to be in bed then Grigory will keep watch. You must tell Grigory about it in advance and he won't let him in.'

'Without the *barin*'s instructions, sir, I don't dare to tell Grigory Vasilyevich about the signals, not on any account. And regarding the possibility that Grigory Vasilyevich may hear him and not let him in, well the fact is that ever since yesterday he's been taken poorly, and Marfa Ignatyevna is planning to get him over it tomorrow. They agreed about it earlier. It's a very peculiar treatment, sir: Marfa Ignatyevna knows how to make some kind of a liqueur and she keeps a ready stock of it, strong stuff it is, made from some herb or other — it's a secret of hers, sir. And she treats Grigory Vasilyevich with this secret medicine about three times a year, sir, when he gets all seized up with the lumbago, sir, like a palsy it is, sir, about three times a year, sir. Then Marfa Ignatyevna takes a towel, sir, soaks it in the liqueur stuff and rubs his back all over for half an hour, sir, until it's dry, sir, right until it's even red and swollen, sir, and then she makes him drink the rest of what's in the bottle, sir, with a certain prayer, sir, only it's never the whole lot, because on those rare occasions she keeps a little bit for herself and also has a tipple, sir. And I tell you, both of them, not being drinkers, immediately fall flat on their backs, sir, and sleep for a long time very soundly, sir; and when Grigory Vasilyevich wakes up he's nearly always completely recovered, sir, and when Marfa Ignatyevna wakes up she always has a sore head afterwards, sir. So that if Marfa Ignatyevna carries out her plan tomorrow, sir, they're not likely to hear anything, sir, or let Dmitry Fyodorovich in, sir. They'll be asleep, sir.'

'What a rigmarole! And it's all going to dovetail as if according to some design: you're going to have a fit, and those other two are going to be unconscious!' Ivan Fyodorovich shouted. 'I say, are you going to arrange it so it dovetails?' broke from him suddenly, and he knit his brows threateningly.

'How would I ever arrange such a thing, sir? And why should I bother, when it all depends on Dmitry Fyodorovich alone, sir, and on the thoughts that are in his head, sir . . . If he wants to commit anything, he will, sir, and if he doesn't commit it, well, I'm not likely to want to bring him here on purpose in order to shove him into your parent's room.'

'But why should he want to get in to see father, and on the sly, too, if, as you yourself say, Agrafena Aleksandrovna isn't going to show up at all?' Ivan Fyodorovich continued, turning pale with malicious anger. 'You yourself say, and indeed all the time I have lived here I have been quite certain that the old man has simply been indulging in fantasy and that that brute creature won't show up. Why would Dmitry break in on the old man, if she doesn't show up? Speak! I want to know your thoughts.'

'Why, sir, you know yourself why he'll come, so what good are my thoughts to you? He'll come solely because of his nasty temper or because of his suspicions about whether I'm really ill or not, he'll start having doubts and go hunting through the rooms in his impatience the way he did yesterday: as if to say, perhaps she's got away from him somewhere on the sly. He's also very well aware that Fyodor Pavlovich has a big envelope ready with three thousand roubles sealed inside it under three seals, sir, tied up with ribbon and inscribed in his own hand: "For my angel Grushenka, if she decides to come", and then, three days later, with the addition: "For my little chicken". That's the questionable part of it, sir.'

'Rubbish!' Ivan Fyodorovich shouted, almost in a frenzy. 'Dmitry isn't going to break in and steal the money, and murder father while he's about it. He might have murdered him yesterday because of Grushenka, like a frenzied, foul-tempered fool, but he's not a burglar!'

'He needs money very badly just now, sir, he needs it in the uttermost extremity, Ivan Fyodorovich. You just don't know how badly he needs it,' Smerdyakov declared with exceptional calm and remarkable succinctness. 'What's more, sir, he views that three thousand as his own, and he explained as much to me: "My parent still owes me the sum of three thousand," he said. And on top of all that consider, Ivan Fyodorovich, a certain undeniable truth, sir: I mean, it's practically certain that if she decides to, Agrafena Aleksandrovna will make him marry her, the *barin*, I mean, Fyodor Pavlovich, sir, if she decides to, sir — well, and you see, she may very well decide to, sir. I mean, I'm just saying she won't come, but she may decide she wants even more than that, sir, in other words quite simply to become the *barynya*, sir. I know that merchant of hers, Samsonov, told her in all frankness that a marriage like that would be not at all a stupid thing for her to undertake, and he laughed, too, when he said it. And she herself is far from stupid in her mind, sir. She doesn't stand to gain much from marrying a naked babe like Dmitry Fyodorovich, sir. So that taking that as given, now, Ivan Fyodorovich, you can see for yourself that after the death of your parent neither Dmitry Fyodorovich nor even that nice brother of yours Aleksey Fyodorovich will end up with anything, not so much as a rouble, sir, because Agrafena Aleksandrovna will marry him in order to have everything bequeathed to her and have whatever capital there is transferred to her own name, sir. But if your parent were to die now, while there's none of that going on, sir, then each of you would immediately get forty thousand of the readies, sir, even Dmitry Fyodorovich, whom he so hates, sir, as his will hasn't been made, you see, sir . . . Dmitry Fyodorovich is perfectly well aware of all that . . .'

Something seemed to distort and quiver in Ivan Fyodorovich's face. Suddenly he flushed.

'Then why after all that,' he said, interrupting Smerdyakov, 'do you advise me to go to Chermashnya? What did you mean by that? I shall go away, and look at what's going to happen among you here.' Ivan Fyodorovich took a breath with difficulty.

'That is quite correct, sir,' Smerdyakov said quietly and soberly, watching Ivan Fyodorovich fixedly, however.

'What do you mean, that is quite correct?' Ivan Fyodorovich interrogated him, restraining himself by force of effort, his eyes glittering with menace.

'I said it because I was sorry for you. If I were here in your place, I'd turn my back on it all . . . rather than sit through a business like this, sir . . .' Smerdyakov replied, with an air of utter frankness, gazing at Ivan Fyodorovich's glittering eyes,

'The way I see it, you're a massive idiot and, need one add . . . a horrible scoundrel!' said Ivan Fyodorovich, suddenly getting up from the bench. Thereupon he began to make his way through the wicket gate, but suddenly paused and turned round to face Smerdyakov. There occurred something strange: all of a sudden, as though in a convulsion, Ivan Fyodorovich bit his lip, clenched his fists and, given another instant, would certainly have thrown himself upon Smerdyakov. The latter had at any rate observed this and at the same moment started and jerked his whole body backwards. But the instant passed safely for Smerdyakov, and Ivan Fyodorovich turned towards the gate without saying anything, though in a kind of bewilderment.

'I am going to Moscow tomorrow, if you want to know – early tomorrow morning – that is all!' he said with malice, loudly and distinctly, afterwards surprised at himself, wondering why he had needed to say this to Smerdyakov at the time.

'That will be best, sir,' the latter supplied, as though he had been waiting for this. 'Though it's possible that you may be disturbed in Moscow by a telegram and have to return in the event of some incident, sir.'

Ivan Fyodorovich paused again, and again turned quickly round to face Smerdyakov. But something appeared to have happened to him. All his familiarity and casualness of manner had leapt from him in a trice; the whole of his face displayed extreme attention and expectation, though it was now of a timid and servile kind: 'Are you going to say anything more, are you going to add anything?' were the words that could be read in his fixed gaze that really seemed to be piercing its way into Ivan Fyodor-ovich.

'And would I also not be called from Chermashnya . . . in the event of something happening?' Ivan Fyodorovich suddenly howled, his voice for some unknown reason horribly raised.

'Yes, sir . . . you'd be disturbed in Chermashnya, too, sir . . .' Smerdya-kov muttered in a near-whisper, as though he were at a loss, but continu-ing fixedly, fixedly to stare Ivan Fyodorovich straight in the eye.

'Only Moscow is far away and Chermashnya is close at hand, so is it my travel expenses that you're worried about when you insist on Cher-mashnya, or are you simply worried that I'm taking such a long way round?'

'That is quite correct, sir . . .' Smerdyakov muttered in a voice by this time broken, smiling foully and again convulsively preparing to leap back in time. But much to Smerdyakov's astonishment, Ivan Fyodorovich suddenly began to laugh and quickly walked in through the wicket gate, still laughing. Anyone who had glanced at his face would have concluded beyond doubt that he had not begun to laugh from any promptings of good humour. Indeed, he himself could not on any account have said what were his feelings at that moment. He moved and walked as though in a convulsive spasm.

7

'It's Always Interesting to Talk to a Clever Man'

AND indeed spoke thus, too. Encountering Fyodor Pavlovich in the reception room, having only just entered, he suddenly shouted to him, waving his arms: 'I'm going upstairs to my room, not in to see you, goodbye,' and walked past, even trying to avoid looking at his father. It may very well have been that the old man was excessively hateful to him at that moment, but such an unceremonious manifestation of hostile feeling came as a surprise even to Fyodor Pavlovich. And the old man really had, it was plain, wanted to tell him something as soon as possible, to which end he had especially come out to meet him in the reception room; having absorbed this compliment, he said nothing, but with a mocking air followed the fruit of his loins with his gaze up the staircase to the attic until it disappeared from view.

'What's he behaving like that for?' he quickly asked Smerdyakov, who had followed Ivan Fyodorovich in.

'He must be angry about something, sir, who can tell with him?' the latter muttered evasively.

'The devil, then! Let him be angry! Bring in the samovar and then make yourself scarce, and be quick about it. Is there no news?'

At this point there ensued a bout of questions of precisely the kind that had caused Smerdyakov to complain to Ivan Fyodorovich just then, questions, that is to say, concerning the expected female visitor, and we shall omit them here. Within half an hour the house had been locked and bolted, and the demented old codger paced alone about the rooms in the anxious and imminent expectation of five prearranged knocks, staring out of the dark windows now and again and seeing through them nothing but the night.

It was by this time very late, but Ivan Fyodorovich was still awake, and weighing things over. Late it was before he went to bed that night – about two o'clock. We shall not, however, reproduce the entire current of his thoughts, and indeed now is not the time for us to enter into his soul: that soul shall have its turn. And even were we to attempt such reproduction, it would be very hard, because these were not thoughts, but rather something very ill-defined, and chiefly – all too ill-at-ease. He himself could feel that he had lost all his bearings. He was also tormented by various strange and almost entirely unexpected desires, such as the following: after midnight he suddenly felt an insistent and intolerable urge to go downstairs, unlock the door, go over to the outbuilding and beat Smerdyakov unmercifully, though had he been asked why, he himself would quite certainly have been unable to set forth one single reason with any accuracy, save perhaps that this lackey had become hateful to him as the most insufferable assailant of his honour it was possible to find upon the earth. On the other hand, several times that night his soul had been gripped by a kind of inexplicable and degrading cowardice, which – he could feel this – had even made him suddenly lose his physical powers. His head ached and whirled. Some emotion of hatred was pincering his soul, as though he were making ready to take his revenge on someone. He even hated Alyosha as he remembered the conversation he had had with him earlier, and at moments he also experienced an immeasurable hatred of himself. As for Katerina Ivanovna, she had almost gone out of his head, something he later found greatly astonishing, even more so when he himself retained a firm memory of having the previous morning, when he had so proudly boasted at her house that he would the following day depart for Moscow, at the same time whispered to himself: 'Why that's rubbish, you won't go, it will be far harder for you to tear yourself away than you're bragging now.' Recalling this night long afterwards, Ivan Fyodorovich brought to mind with particular revulsion how suddenly he would get up from the sofa and quietly, as though he were horribly afraid that someone might be spying on him, open the door, go out on to the staircase and listen to Fyodor Pavlovich moving about, pacing to and fro in the rooms downstairs – listen for a long time, some five minutes at a stretch, with a strange curiosity, holding his breath, his heart pounding, though why he did all this, why he listened – he, of course, himself did not know. This 'action' he dubbed all his life thereafter a 'loathsome' one and all his life considered it, deep within himself, in his soul of souls, as the basest action of his entire existence. At these moments he did not even feel any hatred towards Fyodor Pavlovich himself, but was only filled with a curiosity that consumed all his energies: was he walking about down there? What was he doing down there in his rooms? He divined and considered how he must be staring out of the dark windows and suddenly pausing in the midst of the room and waiting, waiting for someone to knock. Ivan Fyodorovich had gone out on to the staircase a couple of times to indulge in this pursuit. When all had grown quiet and Fyodor Pavlovich went to bed at around two o'clock, Ivan Fyodorovich also went to bed with the firm resolve of falling quickly asleep, as he felt horribly exhausted. And indeed: he suddenly fell into a sound, dreamless sleep, but awoke early, at about seven, when it was already light. Opening his eyes, he suddenly felt to his wonderment an access of unusual energy within himself, quickly leapt up and quickly put his clothes on, then hauled out his suitcase and without delay hurriedly began to pack it. It so happened that yesterday morning he had received his linen back from the washerwoman. Ivan Fyodorovich even smiled an ironic smile at the thought that everything had fitted together so well, that there was nothing to hold up his sudden departure. And sudden it certainly was. Though Ivan Fyodorovich had said yesterday (to Katerina Ivanovna, Alyosha and later Smerdyakov) that he would leave tomorrow, going to bed last night he remembered very well that at that moment he had not been thinking of going away, or at any rate had never dreamed that his first deed upon waking up that morning would be to rush to pack his suitcase. At last both suitcase and travelling-bag were ready; it was nearly nine o'clock when Marfa Ignatyevna came up to his room with her usual daily question: 'Where will you drink tea, in your room or will you come downstairs?' Ivan Fyodorovich went downstairs with a semblance almost of cheerfulness, though there was about him, in his words and gestures, something incoherent and hurried. Greeting his father affably and even venturing a particular inquiry as to his health, without awaiting the conclusion of his parent's reply he at once declared that in an hour's time he would be travelling to Moscow, for good, and asked him to send for some horses. The old man listened to this communication without the slightest astonishment, quite indecently forgetting to bemoan the departure of the fruit of his loins; instead, he suddenly began to fuss about in an extraordinary manner, having apropos remembered a certain urgent matter of his own.

'Oh, you annoying fellow! What a fellow you are! Why didn't you tell me yesterday? Oh well, never mind, we'll make it work all the same. Please do me a great favour, dear kindred father mine,* and look in at Chermashnya on your way. I mean, you only have to take a left turning at Volovya Station and go just twelve versts down the road, and there you are at Chermashnya.'

'For pity's sake, I can't: it is eighty versts to the railway, and the locomotive for Moscow departs from the station at seven o'clock in the evening – I shall only have just enough time to catch it.'

'You can catch it tomorrow, or the day after, but today I want you to take the turning to Chermashnya. What's it going to cost you to put a parent's mind at rest? If I hadn't had things to see to here, I'd have nipped down there long ago, because there's an exceptionally urgent bit of business there, but it's not the right time for me just now . . . You see, I've a birch grove down there in two lots – in Begichev, and in Dyachkino, in the waste ground. The Maslovs, an old man and his son, they're merchants, won't pay more than eight thousand for the timber, yet only last year a buyer turned up who was offering twelve, but he wasn't from round these parts, and there's the rub. Because our local bunch in town here have no commercial pull these days: the Maslovs lord it over everyone – father and son, they're worth a hundred thousand: what they want they get, and none of our local chaps dares to take them on. Well, I had a letter from the priest of Ilyinskoye last Thursday saying that Gorstkin had arrived – he's another of those rotten merchant fellows, I know him, only the precious thing about him is that he's not from around these parts, but from Pogrebovo, and that means he isn't scared of the Maslovs, because he's not from round here. Eleven thousand, he said, I'll give you for your grove, do you hear? But he'll only be here another week, the priest said in his letter. So now I want you to go there and come to an agreement with him . . .'

'Then write to the priest, let him do it for you.'

'He's not capable of it, that's the whole point. The priest hasn't an eye for such things. The man's pure gold, I'd have no qualms about letting him look after twenty thousand for me, and I wouldn't even ask him for a receipt, but he hasn't an eye in his head, as though he weren't even a grown man at all, and a crow could hoodwink him. And yet he's a man of learning, can you credit it? This Gorstkin looks like a muzhik, goes about in a blue *poddyovka*,* but where character's concerned he's an utter villain, and therein lies our common misfortune: he tells lies, that's the trouble with him. Sometimes he tells such stories that one can only wonder what the reason for it is. The year before last he told me that his wife had died and that he'd married another woman, and none of it was true, can you credit it? His wife hasn't died at all, she's still alive and gives him a beating every three days. So that's why we must find out now whether he's telling the truth when he says he wants to buy the grove and will pay eleven thousand for it.'

'Well, in that case I also shall be unable to make much of a contribution, for I have no eye for such things, either.'

'Wait, hang on a minute. You'll manage, because I'll tell you all the signs by which you may know him. This Gorstkin, I've been dealing

with him for a long time. Look: you need to keep an eye on his beard; he
has this little beard, a nasty, straggling, ginger one. If his beard's shaking
and he's talking in an angry fashion – that means it's all right, he's telling
the truth, he wants to do business; but if he's smoothing his beard with
his left hand, and chuckling to himself – well, that means he's out to
swindle you, he's cheating. Never look him in the eye, you won't be able
to tell anything from his eyes, the water's dark, he's a swindler – no,
look at his beard instead. I'll give you a letter, and you can show it to
him. He calls himself Gorstkin, only that isn't his real name: it's
Lyagavy* – but you mustn't address him by that name, he'll take it as an
insult. If you come to an agreement with him and can see that it's all
right, write to me immediately. All you need to put is "He isn't lying",
or words to that effect. Try to keep him to eleven thousand, you can
drop the price by a thousand, but not by any more. Think about it:
between eight and eleven there's a difference of three thousand. It's just
as if I'd had that three thousand as a windfall, it takes a long time to find
a buyer, and I need the money so badly I could cut someone's throat for
it. When you let me know that the deal is in earnest I'll nip down there
myself and round it off, I shall find the time somehow. But why should I
go galloping off there now, if it's all something the priest's made up?
Well, will you go or won't you?'

'Ah, I've no time, spare me the trouble.'

'Ach – you might at least oblige your father, I won't forget! None of
you has a heart, that's the trouble! What difference will a day or two
make to you? Where are you bound for now – Venice? That Venice of
yours isn't going to collapse in two days. I'd send dear Alyosha, but
what could dear Alyosha contribute to such matters? No, I want you to
go because you're a clever man, do you think I can't see it? You're no
timber merchant, but you've an eye in your head. The important thing
here is to see if the man's talking in earnest or not. Keep an eye on his
beard, I tell you: if it starts shaking – that means he's in earnest.'

'So you yourself are going to shove me off to that accursed Chermashnya in person, are you?' Ivan Fyodorovich exclaimed with a malicious
smile.

Fyodor Pavlovich either did not perceive the malice or did not wish to
perceive it, but he caught the smile:

'Then you'll go, you'll go? I'll write the letter for you in a jiffy.'

'I don't know whether I shall go, I don't know – I shall decide *en
route*.'

'Why does it have to be *en route*? Decide now. My dear fellow, decide!

Come to an agreement with him, write me a couple of lines, give them to the priest, and he will send me your missive in a flash. And after that I shan't detain you, you may embark for Venice. The priest will have you driven back to Volovya Station with his own horses . . .'

The old man was simply in an ecstasy; he wrote the letter, sent for the horses, *zakuski* were served, cognac. When the old man was happy about anything he always started to behave expansively, but on this occasion he seemed to hold himself in check. About Dmitry Fyodorovich, for example, he uttered not so much as a single word. As for the parting, it seemed to affect him not at all. It was even as though he could not find anything to talk about; and Ivan Fyodorovich took good note of this: 'I'm damned if he's not fed up with me!' he thought to himself. Only as he was accompanying his son down the steps of the porch did the old man begin to show any signs of agitation, and moved up close in order to kiss him. Ivan Fyodorovich, however, lost no time in offering him his hand to shake, plainly in an effort to ward off the kiss. The old man instantly understood and in a trice reined himself in.

'Well, God go with you, God go with you!' he said from the porch. 'Why, you'll come back again some time in your life, won't you? Well, see that you do, I'm always glad to see you. Well, Christ be with you!'

Ivan Fyodorovich climbed into the springless carriage.

'Farewell, Ivan, don't take it too badly!' his father cried for the last time.

All the menials came out to see him off: Smerdyakov, Marfa and Grigory. Ivan Fyodorovich made a present of ten roubles to each of them. When he was already seated inside the carriage, Smerdyakov leapt up to adjust the rug.

'You see . . . I'm going to Chermashnya . . .' broke suddenly from Ivan Fyodorovich; as they had done the previous day, the words leapt out of their own accord, this time with a kind of nervous laugh. He remembered this for a long time afterwards.

'So it's true what they say, then: that it's always interesting to talk to a clever man,' Smerdyakov answered resolutely, giving Ivan Fyodorovich a heartfelt glance.

The springless carriage rolled into motion and darted away. The traveller's soul was troubled, but he gazed avidly around him at the fields, the hills, the trees, at a flock of geese that was flying high above him over the clear sky. And suddenly he felt really happy. He attempted to engage the driver in conversation, and some of what the muzhik told him he found enormously interesting, but after a minute he realized that it had all gone in one ear and out the other and that he really had not understood anything of what the muzhik said. He fell silent, and that felt all right too: the air was pure, fresh, with an edge of chill, the sky clear. Images of Alyosha and Katerina Ivanovna began to flit through his mind; but he quietly smiled an ironic smile and quietly blew upon the dear shades, and they wafted away: 'Their time will come again,' he thought. Quickly covering the distance to the first station, they changed horses and darted off to Volovya. 'Why is it always interesting to talk to a clever man, what did he mean by that?' he thought, suddenly catching his breath. 'And why did I let him know I was going to Chermashnya?' They reached Volovya Station at a gallop. Ivan Fyodorovich got out of the springless carriage and was surrounded by coachmen. They haggled about the price of the journey to Chermashnya, twelve versts along a country road. He gave instructions that the horses be harnessed. He made his way inside the post-house, took a look round, glanced at the station-master's wife and suddenly went back out on to the porch again.

'Forget about Chermashnya. Shall I have time to get to the railway by seven this evening, brothers?'

'We'll just about make it. Do you want them harnessed up?'

'Do it this instant. Is there any one of you who may be in the town tomorrow?'

'How could there not be, sir — there's Mitry here, he'll be in town.'

'I wonder, Mitry, if you could do something for me? I want you to go and see my father, Fyodor Pavlovich Karamazov, and tell him I haven't gone to Chermashnya. Can you do that?'

'Why not, sir, I can go and see him: I've known Fyodor Pavlovich a long time.'

'And here's a tip for you, because I think he may not give you one . . .' said Ivan Fyodorovich, laughing with good spirit.

'Indeed he won't,' said Mitry, laughing too. 'Thank you, sir, I shall do it without fail.'

At seven o'clock that evening Ivan Fyodorovich boarded the train and darted off to Moscow. 'Away with all that went before, I'm finished with my old world for ever, and I don't want to hear so much as a peep out of it ever again; I am going to a new world and new places, and I shall not look back!' But instead of ecstatic bliss there suddenly descended upon his soul a terrible gloom, and his heart ached with an intense sorrow such as he had never experienced in his life before. All night he thought things over; the train sped on, and only at dawn, as it pulled into Moscow, did he suddenly seem to come awake.

'I'm a scoundrel' he whispered to himself.

But Fyodor Pavlovich, having seen off the fruit of his loins, remained well satisfied. For a whole two hours he felt almost happy and slowly imbibed much cognac; but suddenly in the house there occurred an event most vexatious and unpleasant to all, one that instantly cast Fyodor Pavlovich into great disarray: Smerdyakov, who had for some reason gone to the cellar, fell down into it from the uppermost step of the stairway. It was just as well that Marfa Ignatyevna happened to be out in the yard at the time and opportunely heard him. His fall she did not see, but she did hear the cry, a cry of a peculiar nature, strange, but one already long familiar to her – the cry of an epileptic falling in a fit. Whether he had had the fit at the moment he had begun his descent of the steps, which would of course mean that he had instantly plunged below insensible, or whether it was, on the other hand, that the fall and the shock had precipitated the fit in Smerdyakov, who was well known to have epilepsy – it was impossible to tell, but whatever the truth of the matter they found him at the bottom of the cellar, in writhings and convulsions, flailing about him and with foam at his mouth. Initially they thought he must have broken something, an arm or a leg, and caused injury to himself, but it appeared that 'The Lord had spared him' as Marfa Ignatyevna expressed it: their fears turned out to be groundless, and the only difficulty they had was in getting hold of him and carrying him out of the cellar into God's good day. Help was solicited from among the neighbours, however, and by various means the task was accomplished. Among those present throughout the whole of this cere- mony was Fyodor Pavlovich himself; he himself proffered assistance, evidently most alarmed and almost at the end of his tether. Yet the patient did not regain consciousness: the fits, though they subsided for a time, came back again with renewed vigour, and they all concluded that the same thing was about to happen as had happened last year, when he had likewise fallen, by accident, on that occasion from the garret. It was remembered that at that time they had applied ice to his temples. There was still some ice in the cellar, and Marfa Ignatyevna made the necessary arrangements; as for Fyodor Pavlovich, towards evening he sent for Dr Herzenstube, who arrived at once. Having examined the patient thoroughly (he was the most thorough and careful doctor in all the province, an ageing and most venerable old fellow), he concluded that the fit was an acute one and might, 'prove dangerous', that he, Herzenstube, it all did not yet understand, but that the following evening, were the present remedies to prove inefficacious, he would most certainly apply some

others. The patient was put to bed in the outbuilding, in a little room
next to the chamber of Grigory and Marfa Ignatyevna. All day thereafter
Fyodor Pavlovich suffered one mishap after another: that dinner was
cooked by Marfa Ignatyevna, the soup, in comparison with that normally
prepared by Smerdyakov, was 'like slop-water', and the fowl turned out
to be so deprived of moisture that even to chew it was quite beyond the
realms of possibility. To her master's bitter, though justified, reproaches,
Marfa Ignatyevna retorted that the fowl was in any case a very old one,
and that as for herself, she had never trained to be a cook. Towards
evening there presented itself yet another cause for concern: it was
brought to Fyodor Pavlovich's notice that Grigory, who had been poorly
ever since the day before yesterday, was now almost completely incapacitated by lumbago. Fyodor Pavlovich finished his tea as early as possible
and locked himself up alone in the house. He was in an intense and
troubled state of expectation. The fact was that precisely this evening did
he expect the arrival of Grushenka almost as a matter of certainty; at any
rate he had received from Smerdyakov, early that morning, what
amounted to a categorical assurance that 'she promises to come without
fail, sir'. The heart of the unquiet old fellow beat anxiously, he paced
about his empty rooms and listened. It was essential that he keep his ears
pricked: Dmitry Fyodorovich might be on the look-out for her somewhere, and as soon as she knocked on the window (Smerdyakov had the
day before yesterday assured Fyodor Pavlovich that he had told her
where and in what manner she should knock), he must unlock the door
as quickly as possible and under no circumstances detain her in the
passage a second longer than was necessary, lest – God forbid – she take
fright at something and run away. Fyodor Pavlovich had his work cut
out for him, but never before had his heart been suffused with such sweet
hope: after all, it was now almost certainly possible to predict that on this
occasion she would arrive without fail! . . .

Book VI

The Russian Monk

I

The Elder Zosima and His Guests

WHEN Alyosha, with anxiety and pain in his heart, went inside the Elder's cell, he paused in near amazement: instead of a man ill and passing away, and possibly already unconscious, such as he had feared to find him, he suddenly caught sight of him sitting in his armchair, with a face which, although it was exhausted from debility, was none the less merry and cheerful, surrounded by guests and conducting with them a quiet and radiant discourse. He had, as a matter of fact, risen from his bed no more than a quarter of an hour before Alyosha's arrival; the guests had already gathered in his cell earlier, waiting for him to wake up, after a firm assurance from Father Paisy that 'the master will undoubtedly rise in order once more to discourse with those dear to his heart, as he himself spake and as he himself promised this morning.' This promise, like every other remark of the departing Elder, Father Paisy had believed firmly, to the point that if he had seen him already quite without consciousness and even without breath, but had his promise that he would yet once more arise and say farewell to him, he would quite possibly have not believed that he had died at all, still in the constant expectation that the dying man would regain consciousness and fulfil what had been promised by him. That morning the Elder Zosima had uttered to him in affirmative tones, as he passed into slumber: 'I shall not die before I once more know the intoxication of discoursing with you, beloved ones of my heart; I shall look upon your dear countenances, I shall pour out my soul to you yet one more time.' Those who had gathered for this, probably the last discourse of the Elder were his most devoted friends of long years' standing. They were four: the hieromonachs Iosif and Father Paisy, the hieromonach Father Mikhail, the Father Superior of the hermitage, a man not yet all that old, far from being particularly learned, of humble station yet firm in spirit, an unshakeable and plain believer, stern of aspect but permeated by a deep religious tenderness within his heart, though it was a tenderness which he concealed to the point almost of shame. The fourth guest was a little monk, plain and unpretentious and quite old, of the poorest peasant station, Brother

Anfim, who was very nearly illiterate, a taciturn and quiet man who very seldom spoke to anyone, the meekest of the meek, someone who gave the impression of being perpetually frightened by something great and terrible that was beyond his mental grasp. This, as it were, trembling individual was a favourite of the Elder Zosima, and all his life he had accorded him an unusual respect, though it was possible that there was no one to whom all his life he had spoken fewer words than to him, notwithstanding the fact that he had at one time spent many years with him, wandering the length and breadth of Holy Rus'. This had been very long ago, some forty years earlier, when the Elder Zosima had just begun his monastic endeavour in a certain poor and little-known Kostroman monastery* and when soon after that he had gone to accompany Father Anfim on his wanderings for the collection of alms with which to sustain their poor Kostroman monastery. All, guests and host alike, had made themselves comfortable in the Elder's second room, which contained his bed, a room, as was indicated earlier, exceedingly confined, so that all four (Porfiry the novice, who was also present, remained standing) were scarcely able to accommodate themselves around the armchair of the Elder on the chairs that had been brought in from the first room. Darkness had already begun to fall, and the room was lit by the lamps and wax candles in front of the icons. Catching sight of Alyosha, who had been embarrassed upon entering and was standing in the doorway, the Elder smiled to him joyfully and stretched forth his hand:

'Hail, quiet one, hail, dear one, here you are. I knew that you would come.'

Alyosha approached him, bowed to the earth before him and began to weep. Something burst from within his heart, his soul trembled, he wanted to sob.

'What is it? No, you must wait with your mourning,' the Elder smiled, placing his right hand on Alyosha's head. 'You see, here I sit in discourse, and perhaps I shall live another twenty years yet, as that good, dear woman from Vyshegorye wished me yesterday, she that hath charge of the infant Lizaveta. Remember, O Lord, the mother and the infant Lizaveta!' (He crossed himself.) 'Porfiry, did you take her gift where I told you?'

This was a reference to the six ten-copeck pieces that had been contributed by his cheerful female admirer for 'a woman that's poorer than me'. Contributions of this kind are made as an *epithymia* imposed voluntarily upon oneself for whatever reason, and must always consist of money that has been earned by one's own effort. The evening before, the

Elder had sent Porfiry to a certain artisan's widow of our town who had children, lost all her possessions in a fire and subsequently took to begging. Porfiry hastened to report that the errand had been accomplished and that he had given her the money, telling her, as he had been instructed, that it came 'from an unknown benefactress'.

'Arise, dear one,' the Elder continued, addressing Alyosha. 'Let me look at you. Did you go to your family and did you see your brother?'

Alyosha thought it strange that he should ask so firmly and specifically about only one of his brothers — but which one was it? This might mean that it was for the sake of that brother he had sent him away both yesterday and today.

'I saw one of my brothers,' Alyosha replied.

'I speak of the brother who was here yesterday, the older one, to whom I bowed down to the ground.'

'I only saw him yesterday, and today I haven't been able to find him,' said Alyosha.

'You must hurry to find him, tomorrow again you must hurry and go there, leave everything and hurry. It may be that you can still prevent something dreadful. Yesterday I bowed down to his great future suffering.'

He suddenly fell silent and appeared to reflect. His words had been strange. Father Iosif, who had been a witness of yesterday's prostration by the Elder, exchanged looks with Father Paisy. Alyosha's endurance ran out.

'Father and teacher,' he said in extreme agitation, 'your words are too obscure . . . What is this suffering that awaits him?'

'Do not be curious. Yesterday something terrible presented itself to me, as though the whole of his destiny were expressed in his gaze. His eyes bore a certain expression . . . so that in my heart for an instant I sensed horror at what that man is preparing for himself. On one or two occasions in my life I have seen a similar expression on the faces of a few . . . It seemed to portray the entire destiny of those men, and their destinies, alas, were accomplished. I sent you to him, Aleksey, for I thought that your brotherly countenance would aid him. But even our destinies are from the Lord. "Except a corn of wheat fall into the ground and die, it abideth alone: but if it die, it bringeth forth much fruit." Remember this saying. And as for you, Aleksey, many times in the course of my life have I blessed you in my thoughts for your countenance, I should like you to know that,' the Elder said with a quiet smile. 'I think of you like this: you will go out beyond these walls, but in the world you will abide as a monk. Many are the adversaries you will face, but even your enemies will love you. Many are the misfortunes that life will bring you, but even with them you will be happy, and you will bless life, and make others bless it with you — which is the most important thing. For that is your nature. My fathers and teachers,' he said in a moved voice, turning to his guests, 'never until this day have I told, even to this youth himself, why his countenance has been so dear to my soul. Only now will I say it: his countenance has been to me as a reminder and a prophecy. At the dawning of my days, when I was still a small child, I had an older brother who died as a youth, before my eyes, at the age of only seventeen. And later, as I lived my life, I gradually attained the conviction that this brother of mine had been in my destiny a kind of indication and preordination from above, for had he not appeared in my life, had he not existed at all, never, perhaps, I think now, would I have taken monastic orders or entered upon this precious path. That first manifestation took place in my childhood, and now upon the decline of my path there has manifested itself before my very eyes what seems like its repetition. The wondrous thing, fathers and teachers, is that, though he does not really resemble him in feature, or only a little, Aleksey has seemed so spiritually akin to him that on many occasions I have quite simply seen him as that youth, my brother, who has come to me at the end of my path mysteriously, as a kind of memory and emotion, making me wonder even at myself and at my strange dream. Do you hear these words, Porfiry?' he said, turning to the novice who attended him. 'On many occasions I have seen on your face an expression almost of grief that I love Aleksey more than I do you. Now you know why it was so, but I do love you, please know that, and on many occasions I have grieved at your grief. As for you, dear guests, I want to tell you about this youth, my brother, for there has not been in all my life a manifestation more precious than this, more prophetic and more touching. My heart has been moved, and I contemplate my life at this moment as though I were living it all over again . . .'

Here I must observe that a partial record of this final discourse of the Elder with the guests who visited him on the last day of his life has been retained. It was written down by Aleksey Fyodorovich Karamazov from memory some time after the Elder's death. But whether it consists entirely of that evening's discourse, or whether he had appended to his record earlier discourses with his teacher, this I cannot now determine; in the record, moreover, the whole of the Elder's side of the discourse is presented in a continuous fashion, as though he were describing his life in the form of a narrative tale addressed to his friends, whereas there can be no doubt from subsequent reports that what actually took place was somewhat different, for the discourse that evening was conducted in general fashion, and though the guests interrupted their host but little, they none the less spoke on their own account, intervening in the conversation and possibly even telling and narrating certain things of their own; then again, the Elder's narration could not have possessed such a continuous quality, for he sometimes gasped for breath, lost his voice and even lay down to rest on his bed, though he did not fall asleep, and his guests did not go away. On one or two occasions the discourse was broken by readings from the New Testament, given by Father Paisy. It is also worthy of note that not one of the guests supposed that the Elder would die that very same night, all the more so since on this last evening of his life, having slept deeply during the day, he suddenly seemed to acquire a new strength which sustained him throughout the whole of this long discourse with his friends. This was, as it were, a final surge of tender and pious feeling which sustained within him an incredible animation, but only for a short time, for his life was suddenly cut short ... But more of this anon. For the present I wish only to inform the reader that it has been my preference to avoid giving all the details of the discourse, confining myself to the Elder's narrative as it is presented in the manuscript of Aleksey Fyodorovich Karamazov. That way it will be more concise and less wearisome, though of course, I repeat, Alyosha derived much of the material from earlier discourses and combined it all together.

2

From the Life of the Departed in God
the Hieroschemonach the Elder Zosima, Collated
from His Own Words by Aleksey Fyodorovich
Karamazov

BIOGRAPHICAL INFORMATION

(a) Concerning the Youth Who was the Elder Zosima's Brother

BELOVED fathers and teachers: I was born in a far-off northern province, in the town of V—, of a father who was of the gentry, but not aristocratic or of any particularly high official grade. He died when I was but two years old, and I have no memory of him at all. He left my dear mother a small wooden house and a certain amount of capital, not great but sufficient to enable her to live with her children in a state removed from penury. There were in the care of my dear mother but two of us: myself – Zinovy, and my elder brother – Markel. He was some eight years older than me, of hot and irritable temper, but good at heart, not given to mocking and strangely taciturn, particularly in his own home, with me, with mother and the servants. He was a good gymnasium scholar, but did not mix with his companions, though he did not quarrel with them either; thus, at any rate, did my mother remember him. Some six months before his decease, when he had already passed his seventeenth birthday, he got into the habit of visiting a certain man who led a retired existence among us, some sort of political exile who had been banished to our town from Moscow for freethinking. This exile was a man of not inconsiderable learning and was an eminent philosopher in the university. For some reason he took a liking to Markel and began to encourage visits from him. The youth would spend whole evenings with him, and this went on all winter, until the exile was recalled to government service in St Petersburg – at his own request, for he had protectors and patrons. Lent began, but Markel would not fast, heaping abuse and ridicule on it: 'It is all mere nonsense, and there is no God, either,' he would say, horrifying my mother and the servants, and even me, small as I was, for though I was only nine years old, I too was very alarmed. All our servants were bondsmen and bondswomen; there were four of them, and they had all been purchased on behalf of a landowner of our acquaintance. I can still recall how dear mother sold one of the four, the cook Afimya, who was lame and getting on in years, for sixty paper roubles,* and engaged a freedwoman in her place. And then in the sixth week of Lent my brother suddenly got worse, for he was always unwell – chesty, of weak constitution and disposed towards consumption; he was tall enough, but thin and puny, with a face that was, however, of most goodly form. Whether he had caught cold I do not remember, but the doctor arrived and quickly whispered to dear mother that it was galloping consumption and that he would not survive the spring. Mother began to weep, began to ask my brother with circumspection (mainly in order not to frighten him) to fast for a little and then attend communion with God's holy mysteries, for he was at that time still up and about. Upon hearing this, he lost his temper and gave God's temple a good rating, but then grew meditative: he had guessed at once that he was dangerously ill and that this was why his mother was sending him, while still he had the strength, to fast and attend communion. As a matter of fact, he himself already knew that he had long been unwell, and even a year previously had once announced to mother and me at table with sang-froid: 'I am not long for this world among you, and I may not live one more year,' and now it was as if that had been a prophecy. Some three days went by, and Holy Week began. And then, from the Tuesday evening, my brother went to fast and take communion. 'I am doing this, properly speaking, for you, dear mother, in order to please you and to calm your fears,' he told her. Mother wept from happiness, and also from grief: 'It means his end must be near, if there is such a sudden change in him.' But not for long did he go to church; he took to his bed, and so was given confession and communion at home. The days were starting to be bright, serene and fragrant – it was a late Easter. All night he would cough, I recall; he slept badly, and in the mornings would always get dressed and try to sit in a soft armchair. That is how I shall remember him: sitting there quietly, meekly, smiling, in reality ill, but with a countenance of cheerfulness and joy. He had undergone a complete spiritual alteration – such a wondrous change had suddenly begun within him! Our old nurse would enter his room: 'Let me light the lamp before your icon, dearie,' she would say. And previously he had not allowed it, would even blow it out. 'Light it, dear nurse, light it, I was a cruel monster to forbid you earlier. As you light the lamp you say your prayers, and I, in rejoicing for your sake, say mine also. That means we pray to the same God.' Strange did those words seem to us, and mother would go away to her room and weep and weep, though when she came in again to him she would wipe her eyes and assume an air of cheerfulness. 'Dear mother, don't cry, my darling,' he used to say. 'I have much time to live yet, I shall make merry with you both, and my life, my life will be joyful and merry!' 'Oh, dear boy, what kind of merriment can there be for you, when all night you burn in a fever and cough till your chest nearly bursts apart?' 'Mamma,' he replied to her, 'do not weep, life is paradise, and we are all in paradise, but we don't want to realize it, and if we did care to realize it, paradise would be established in all the world tomorrow.' And we all wondered at his words, so strangely and so resolutely did he say this; we felt tender emotion and we wept. Friends would come to visit us: 'My beloved, my dear ones,' he would say, 'what have I done to deserve your love, why do you love such a one as me, and why did I not know it and value it earlier?' To the servants who came in he would say every moment: 'My beloved, my dear ones, why do you serve me, am I worthy of it? If God would have mercy on me and let me stay among the living, I would serve you, for all must serve one another.' Kind mother, when she heard this, shook her head: 'My dear one, it's your illness that's making you talk like this.' 'Mamma, joy of my life,' he said, 'it's impossible that there be no masters and no servants, but let me be the servant of my servants, and let me be to them what they are to me. And I say to you also, dear mother, that each of us is guilty before the other for everything, and I more than any.' Dear mother smiled wryly at this, she wept and smiled, saying: 'But why are you more guilty before all than anyone else? What about the murderers and brigands? What offences have you committed, that you should blame yourself more than anyone else?' 'Dear mother, droplet of my blood,' he said (at that time he had begun to use endearments of this kind, unexpected ones), 'beloved droplet of my blood, joyful one, you must learn that of a truth each of us is guilty before all for everyone and everything. I do not know how to explain this to you, but I feel that it is so, to the point of torment. And how could we have lived all this time being angry with one another and knowing nothing of this?' Thus did he arise from slumber, each day growing more and more full of tender piety and joy, and trembling all over with love. The doctor used to come – old Eisenschmidt, the German, on his rounds: 'Well, doctor, will I live another day upon the earth?' he would ask – he used to like to play the clown with him. 'Not only will you live another day, you will live many days yet,' the doctor used to reply to him, 'you will live for months and even years.' 'Oh, what use are months and years!' he would exclaim. 'Why count the days, when one is enough for a man to know all of happiness? My dear ones, why do we quarrel, boast in front of one another, remember wrongs against one another? We should go straight into the garden and make merry and romp, love and praise and kiss one another, and bless our lives.' 'He is not long for the world, your son,' the doctor told dear mother as she was seeing him off from the porch, 'he is lapsing from illness into madness.' The windows of his room overlooked the garden, and our garden was a shady one, with old trees on which the springtime buds were forming, and where the early birds came to rest, twittering and singing through his windows. And suddenly, as he looked at them, lost in wonder at them, he began to ask them for forgiveness: 'Birds of God, birds of joy, you must forgive me too, for against you too I have sinned.' No one was able to understand this at the time, but he wept with joy: 'Yes,' he said, 'all around me there has been such divine glory: birds, trees, meadows, sky, and I alone have lived in disgrace, I alone have dishonoured it all, completely ignoring its beauty and glory.'

'You take too many sins upon yourself,' dear mother would say, weeping. 'But dear mother, joy of my life, I am crying from joy, and not from grief; why, I myself want to be guilty before them, only I cannot explain it to you, for I do not know how to love them. Let me be culpable before all, and then all will forgive me, and that will be paradise. Am I not in paradise now?'

And there was much more, which I cannot remember and cannot enter here. I recall that I once went in to see him alone, when there was no one attending him. The hour was vesperal, serene, the sun was going down, illuminating all his room with an oblique ray. At the sight of me he motioned me towards him, I went across to him and he took me around the shoulders with both hands, looked into my face tenderly, lovingly: 'Well,' he said, 'off you go now and play and live for me!' I left then, and went off to play. But many times in my life I have remembered with tears how he told me to live for him. Many more wondrous and beautiful things did he say, though they were incomprehensible to us at the time. He died during the third week after Easter, conscious, and though by that time he had stopped talking, he did not change right up to his very last hour: looked joyful, with good cheer in his eyes, kept seeking us with his gaze, smiling to us, calling us. Even in the town people talked much about his death. All this affected me deeply at the time, but not too much, though I wept a great deal at his burial. I was a youngster, a child, but in my heart it all remained ineradicably, the emotion was preserved. It would all, inevitably, in its own time, rise up and answer like an echo. And so indeed it came to pass.

(b) Concerning Holy Scripture in the Life of Father Zosima

Then dear mother and I were left alone. It was not long before good acquaintances began to counsel her, saying: 'Look, now you have only one son left, and you are not poor, you have capital, so why not follow the example of others and send your son to St Petersburg? If he stays here you may deprive him of a noble destiny.' And they advised dear mother to take me to St Petersburg and have me enrolled in the Cadet Corps, in order that I might subsequently enter the Imperial Guard. For a long time dear mother hesitated: how was she to part with the last of her sons? In the end, however, she made her decision, though not without many tears, in the hope of contributing towards my happiness. She took me to St Petersburg, secured me a place in the Corps and after that I never saw her again: for at the end of three years she too died, having all three of them grieved and trembled for us both. Of my parental home I have retained only precious memories, for a person can have no memories more precious than those of his earliest childhood in his parental home, and this is nearly always so, if there is in the family even the slightest degree of love and union. Indeed, precious memories may be retained even from the very worst of families, if only your soul is capable of seeking that which is precious. Among my domestic memories I also include my memories of biblical history, which in my parental home, though only a child, I was very curious to learn. In those days I had a book, a biblical history, with beautiful pictures and the title *One Hundred and Four Sacred Tales of the Old and New Testaments*,* and using it I also learned to read. Even now it sits upon my shelf here, and I guard it like a precious memory. But I recall that even before I learned to read, there visited me a certain spiritual awakening, when I was only eight years of age. On the Monday of Holy Week dear mother took me alone (I do not recall where my brother was at that time) to the temple of the Lord, for morning Mass. It was a sunny day, and as I remember it now I seem to see once again the incense rising from the censer and quietly floating aloft, and up in the cupola, through the narrow little window, God's rays fairly streaming into the church down upon us, and, as it rose towards them in waves, how the incense appeared to dissolve in them. I watched in tender emotion, and for the first time in my life I accepted with understanding the first seed of God's word into my soul. Out into the midst of the temple came a young lad bearing a large book, so large that it seemed to me he could hardly carry it, and placed it upon the lectern, opened it and began to read, and suddenly for the first time I understood some of it — for the first time in my life I understood what was read in the temple of God. There was a man in the land of Uz,* perfect and upright, and his substance was such-and-such, so-and-so many camels, so-and-so many sheep and she-asses, and his sons went and feasted in their houses, and he loved them greatly and said prayers for them to God: for perhaps they had sinned in feasting. And then when the sons of God went to present themselves before the Lord, Satan came along with them, and said he had come from going to and fro in the earth and from walking up and down in it. 'Hast thou considered my servant Job?'* God asked him. And God boasted to Satan, pointing to his great and perfect servant. And Satan smiled mockingly at God's words: 'Deliver him unto me and you will see that your servant will raise his voice against you and curse your name.' And God delivered his righteous one, whom he so loved, unto Satan, and Satan smote his sons and his daughters and cattle, and scattered his wealth, suddenly, as by one of God's thunder-bolts, and Job rent his mantle, and fell down upon the ground, and began to wail: 'Naked came I out of my mother's womb, and naked shall I return thither: the Lord gave, and the Lord hath taken away: blessed be the name of the Lord from this day hence and ever more!' Fathers and teachers, look leniently upon my tears now – for all my youth seems to rise up before me once again and I seem to breathe now as I breathed then with my paltry lungs of an eight-year-old boy, and feel, as I did then, surprise, confusion and joy. And those camels so engaged my imagination then, and Satan, who could talk to God in such a manner, and God, delivering his servant to ruin, and his servant, exclaiming: 'Blessed be your name, in spite of that you punish me!' – and afterwards the sweet and quiet singing in the temple: 'Let my prayer arise',* and again the incense from the priest's censer and the kneeling prayer! Ever since that day – why, only yesterday I took it into my hands again – I have been unable to read that most biblical of tales without tears. What unimaginable greatness and mystery it contains! Later on I heard the words of the mockers and blasphemers, proud words: how could the Lord deliver the most beloved of his saints to the idle ploys of Satan, take his children from him, smite him with illness and sore boils, so that he took him a potsherd to scrape the pus from his wounds, and for what? – merely in order to be able to boast to Satan: 'There, that is what my perfect servant is able to endure for my sake!' But the greatness of it is that here there is a mystery – that here the earth's transitory countenance and eternal truth have come into contact with each other. In the face of earthly truth an act of eternal truth is accomplished. Here the Creator, as in the first days of Creation, completing each day with an utterance of praise – 'That which I have made is good' – looks at Job and again praises one of his creations. But Job, in praising the Lord, serves not only him, but also the whole of his creation from generation to generation and from age to age, ever more, for to that he has been preordained. Lord, what a book this is, and what lessons there are in it! What a book is Holy Scripture, what a miracle and what a strength is given to man with it! Like a sculpture composed of the world, of man and human characters, and it has all been named and explained for the ages, ever more. And how many mysteries are resolved and revealed: God gives Job back his well-being, grants him wealth anew, again many years go by, and lo, he has more children, new children, and he loves them – Lord, but how can he love these new children, one might think, when the ones he had before are no more living, when he has lost them? Remembering them, how can he be truly happy as he was before, with new ones, however dear those new ones are to him? But he can, he can: the old grief of the great mystery of human life gradually passes into a quiet, tender joy; in place of the boiling blood of youth there comes a meek, serene old age: I bless the daily rising of the sun, and my heart sings to it as it did of old, but now I am more enamoured of its setting, its long, oblique rays, and the quiet, gentle, tender memories that accompany them, the dear images from the whole of a long and blessed life – and above it all the truth of God, moving, reconciling, all-forgiving! My life is approaching its end, I know that and sense it, but with each day of mine that remains now I can feel my earthly life coming into contact with a new, infinite, unknown but closely approaching life, whose premonition makes my soul tremble with ecstasy, my mind flood with light, and my heart weep joyfully . . . Friends and teachers, I have heard on several occasions, and it is a call that in recent times has become even more audible, our Russian priests, especially the rural ones, complaining tearfully and universally about their small stipends and the degradation of their position, and declaring bluntly, even in print – I myself have read such things – that they cannot interpret the Scriptures to the people any longer now, for their stipends are too small, and if the Lutherans and heretics are now arriving and beginning to lure away their flocks, then let it be so, for their stipends are too small. Lord! I think, may God grant them an increase in those stipends that are so precious to them (for their complaint is justified), but verily I say: if anyone is guilty in this regard, then half the guilt is our own! For though it may be true that he has no time, though he may be justified in claiming that he is all the time oppressed by work and religious ceremonies, why, even so, it is not *all* the time, and he does after all have an hour or so in all the week in which he can also remember God. Then again, his work is not performed the year round. Were he to assemble in his home once a week, at the evening hour, at first only the small children – their fathers would come to hear of it, and the fathers, too, would start to arrive. And it would not be necessary to build a mansion for this undertaking, but merely to receive some guests in one's *izba*; have no fear, I say to him, they will not make a mess of your *izba*, after all it is only for a single hour that you will hold your assembly. Come then, I say to him, open this book before them and begin to read without long words and without self-conceit, not putting yourself above them, but tenderly and gently, yourself taking delight in what you read to them and so that they listen to you and understand you, who love those words yourself, stopping only occasionally in order to explain some word incomprehensible to the common folk; do not worry, they will understand it all, their Orthodox hearts will understand it all. Read to them of Abraham and Sarah, of Isaac and Rebecca, of how Jacob went to Laban and wrestled in a dream with the Lord and said: 'How dreadful is this place',* and you will make an impression on the devout minds of the common folk. Read to them, and to the little children especially, of how the brothers sold into slavery their own brother, the sweet boy Joseph, the dreamer and great prophet, telling their father that his son had been devoured by an evil beast, and showing him his bloodied coat. Read how then the brothers went down to buy corn in Egypt, and Joseph, by now a great courtier, unrecognized by them, tormented them, accused them, detained his brother Benjamin, yet loving them all the while: 'I love you and, loving, torment you.' For after all, throughout the whole of his life he had remembered ceaselessly how they had sold him somewhere in the hot steppe, by a well, to some merchants, and how, wringing his hands, he had wept and begged his brothers not to sell him as a slave into a strange land, and now, setting eyes on them again after so many years, loved them again immeasurably, but tormented and tortured them, loving them all the while. At last he withdrew from them, unable to endure the torment of his own heart, threw himself upon his couch and wept; then he wiped his face and came out to them bright and radiant and announced to them: 'Brethren, I am Joseph your brother!' Then I say to him: you may read further of how the Elder Jacob rejoiced upon learning that his beloved son was still alive and went into Egypt, forsaking his native land, and died in a strange country, uttering in his testament the very great pronouncement,* which had lodged mysteriously within his meek and fearful heart throughout the whole of his life, that from among his tribe, the tribe of Judah, would come the great hope of the world, its Reconciler and Saviour. Fathers and teachers, forgive me and do not be angry that like a little child I prattle on about things with which you have long been familiar and concerning which you could instruct me a hundred times more cleverly and more elegantly. It is from enthusiasm that I say these things, and you must forgive my tears, for I love this book! Let him also weep, the priest of God, and he will see that the hearts of his listeners tremble in answer to him. All that is required is a little seed, a tiny one: if he throws it into the soul of the common folk, it will not die, it will live on in his soul for the rest of his life, concealed in him amidst the darkness, amidst the stench of his sins, like a point of light, like a great reminder. And it is not necessary, not necessary to do much explaining or instruction, he will understand it all without that. Do you suppose the common folk will not understand? Try reading to them also the tale, and a touching and moving one it is, of the fair Esther and the haughty Vashti; or the wondrous legend of the prophet Jonah in the belly of the whale. Do not forget, either, the parables of Our Lord, especially those in the Gospel According to St Luke (such was my practice), and then Saul's conversion of the Jews* from the Acts of the Apostles (that is indispensable, indispensable!), and finally perhaps, from the *Chet'i-Minei*, the Lives of Aleksey the Man of God and of the sublimely great and joyous martyr and mother, the God-seer and Christ-bearer Mary of Egypt* – and you will pierce their hearts with these simple legends, and all of it for only one hour each week, regardless of your small stipend, one single little hour. And, I say to him, you will see for yourself that our common folk are gracious and ready to give thanks, they will return your kindness a hundredfold; remembering the zealous efforts of their priest and his moving words, they will help him voluntarily upon his field,* and will also help him in his home, and will accord him greater respect than before – thus will his stipend already be made larger. A matter so straightforward that on occasion we have even been afraid to speak of it out loud, for they may laugh at you, and yet how true it is! Whoever has no faith in God will have no faith in God's people, either. But whoever acquires faith in God's people will also behold His holiness, even though previously he has had no faith in it at all. Only the people and its coming spiritual strength will convert the atheists among us, who have uprooted themselves from their native soil. And what is the word of Christ without example? Ruin awaits the people without the word of God, for the people's soul thirsts for His word and every beautiful perception. In our youth, a long time past now, very nearly forty years ago, Father Anfim and I walked the length and breadth of Rus', gathering alms for the monastery, and on one occasion we stayed the night near a large river accessible to shipping, on the bank, with fishermen, and down with us had sat a certain youth of comely aspect, a peasant, some eighteen years of age by the look of him, who was hurrying back to his locality in order the following day to haul a merchant's barge in a towing-gang. And I saw him looking ahead of him with a moved, clear gaze. It was a light night in July, quiet and warm, the river was wide, a vapour rose from it, refreshing us, a fish jumped here and there with a splash, the birds had fallen silent, all was quiet and fair of form, all was immersed in prayer. And only the two of us, the youth and I, did not sleep, but talked together about the beauty of this world that God has created, and about its great mystery. Each stalk of grass, each little insect, each ant and golden bee, they all to a bewildering extent know the paths they must follow; having no intellect, they testify to God's mystery, incessantly accomplishing it in themselves, and I could see that the heart of the charming youth was fired. He confided to me that he loved the forest, the birds of the forest; he was a bird-catcher, understood each of their calls, knew how to lure any bird. 'I know of no better thing than to be in the forest,' he said, 'and indeed it is all good.' 'Verily,' I replied to him, 'all is good and magnificent, because all is truth. Look,' I said to him, 'upon the horse, that great animal that stands close to man, or at the ox that nourishes him and works for him, thoughtful and with hanging head, look upon their countenances: what meekness, what devotion to man, who often flogs them without pity, what lack of malice, what trust and what beauty there is in their countenances. It is most moving to realize that they bear no sin, for all things and all creatures universally, all except for man, are without sin, and Christ is with them first, before he is with us.' 'What?' the youth inquired. 'Is Christ with them, as well?' 'How can it be otherwise?' I said to him. 'For his word is for all, and all creation and all creatures, each little leaf is striving towards the word, singing praise to God, weeping to Christ, unknown to itself, accomplishing this by the mystery of its sinless life. Yonder in the forest,' I said to him, 'roams the fearsome bear, menacing and truculent, and yet in no wise guilty because of it.' And I told him the story of how once a bear came to a great saint* who was living as a hermit in the forest, in a little cell, and how the great saint was moved to compassion for it, fearlessly went out to it and gave it a piece of bread, saying: 'Off you go now, Christ is with you,' and how the truculent beast withdrew, obediently and meekly, causing him no harm. And the youth was moved at the notion that the bear had withdrawn without causing any harm, and that Christ was with him, too. 'Oh,' he said, 'how good that is, how all God's things are good and wondrous!' He sat in sweet and quiet reflection. I could see he had understood. And beside me he fell into a light and sinless slumber. The Lord bless youth! And then, when I too retired to sleep, I prayed for him. Lord, send peace and light unto thy people!'

(c) A Reminiscence of the Youth and Early Manhood of the Elder Zosima While Yet in the Secular World. A Duel

At St Petersburg, enrolled in the Cadet Corps, I remained for a long time, almost eight years, and with the new training I closed off many of my childhood impressions, though I forgot nothing. In their stead did I absorb so many new habits and even opinions that I became transformed into a creature almost savage – cruel and preposterous. I acquired a gloss of politeness and worldly manners together with a knowledge of the French language, while at the same time we all of us viewed the common soldiers who served us in the Corps as not much better than cattle, and I was no exception in this regard. Indeed, I was perhaps worse than the rest, for of all my companions I was the most receptive to outside influences. When we graduated as officers we were ready to shed our blood if anyone offended the honour of our regiment, while of genuine honour none of us had the slightest conception, and had any of us had one, he himself would have been the first to laugh it to scorn. Drunkenness, debauchery and reckless behaviour were things of which we were very nearly proud. I will not say that we were wicked; all these young men were good at heart, but conducted themselves in a wicked fashion, and I in the wickedest of all. The point was that some capital of my own had come into my hands, and so I proceeded to live for my own enjoyment, with all my youthful headlong desire – free of restraint, I set forth at full sail. But here is the wondrous part: at that time I read books and did so with positively great enjoyment; only the Bible did I almost never open, though I never parted with it either, but took it with me everywhere: in truth, I was cherishing that book, without myself being aware of the fact, 'for an hour, and a day, and a month, and a year'.* Having served thus for some four years, I found myself at length in the town of K—, where our regiment was at that time stationed. The social life of the town was diverse, crowded and merry, welcoming and opulent, and everywhere I was received well, for I had been born with a cheerful disposition, and was moreover reputed to be not exactly a pauper, which in society counts for more than a little. It was at this juncture that there occurred a certain circumstance that was to serve as the start of it all. I became attached to a certain young and attractive maiden, intelligent and deserving, of radiant and noble character, the daughter of respected parents. These were people of no small consequence: they had wealth, influence and power, and they received me cordially and with affection. And then I suddenly took it into my head that the girl was tenderly disposed towards me – my heart caught fire at such a dream. I later perceived and fully realized that it was possible I had loved her with such passion not at all, but had simply revered her exalted intellect and character, something I could hardly have failed to do. At the time, however, love of self prevented me from offering my hand to her: wretched and dreadful did it seem to have to say goodbye to the temptations of a lewd, untrammelled, bachelor existence at such young years, given, to boot, the possession of money. Though I did drop certain hints. At any rate, for a short while I postponed taking any decisive step. Then without notice I had to undertake a special assignment in another district for two months. When the two months were up I returned and suddenly discovered that the girl was now married, to a rich local landowner, a man who though older than myself in years was still young, with connections in the capital and in the best society, something I did not have, a man of great kindness who was, moreover, progressively educated, and that kind of education I did not possess at all. So shocked was I by this unexpected occurrence that I almost lost my reason. My principal distress lay in at the same time discovering that this young landowner had long been her fiancé and in the fact that on a number of occasions I had met him at her parents' home, but, blinded by the virtues of my character, had failed to notice anything. This it was, however, that I found hardest of all to take: how could it be that everyone had known about it, yet I alone had not? And I suddenly felt an intolerable surge of malice. With colour in my face, I began to recall how many times I had almost declared my love to her, and as she had not stopped me or warned me, I concluded that she had been laughing at me. Later, of course, I thought the better of this, recollecting that she had in no way laughed at me; on the contrary, she herself had playfully cut short such conversations, substituting other topics in their place – but at the time I was unable to perceive this and blazed with vengefulness. I remember that this vengefulness and this anger of mine were wretched and abhorrent to me in the extreme as, being of an easygoing nature, I was unable to be angry with anyone for long, and so I fanned the flames myself, as it were, artificially, in the end behaving in a manner that was preposterous and morally deformed. I bided my time, and on one occasion I suddenly managed to insult my 'rival' on what was apparently the most irrelevant of pretexts, making fun of a certain opinion he expressed concerning a certain important event then – this took place in the year 1826* – and succeeded in doing so wittily and with finesse, so people said. Then I forced him to call me to account, and during our discussion I behaved so offensively that he accepted my challenge, in spite of the enormous difference between us, for I was younger than he, insignificant and of lowly rank. I subsequently gained reliable knowledge that he had accepted my challenge also out of some kind of jealous feeling towards me: he had been a little jealous of me even earlier, in respect of his wife, whom then he had only been engaged to; now he thought that if she were to learn that he had endured an insult from me but had not challenged me to a duel, she would begin involuntarily to despise him and her love for him would grow uncertain. I quickly obtained a second, a companion who was a lieutenant in our regiment. Although at that time duels were savagely punished, there was what amounted to a kind of vogue for them among the servicemen – so widespread and ingrained do barbarous prejudices on occasion grow. The end of June was approaching, and now our meeting had been appointed for the morrow, outside town, at seven o'clock in the morning – and in truth, there then befell me something that was in a way to seal my fate. That evening, upon returning home, in a state of truculence and moral deformity, I became angry with my batman Afanasy and struck him twice about the face with all my strength, drawing blood. He had been in my employ but a short time, and I had had occasion to strike him previously, but never with such brutal savagery. And perhaps you will credit it, dear ones, if I tell you that forty years have passed since that day, yet even now I remember it with shame and torment. I went to bed and fell asleep for some three hours; when I raised my head again the day was already beginning. I suddenly got to my feet, did not feel like sleeping any more, walked over to the window, opened it – it looked on to the garden – and saw the sun rising, everything warm and beautiful, the calls of the birds beginning to resound. 'Why does my soul feel as though there were something shameful and base in it?' I wondered. 'Is it not perhaps because I am going to spill blood?' No, I thought, it did not seem to be that. Well then, was it not because I was afraid of death, afraid of being killed? No, not that at all, not even that ... And suddenly I realized what it was: it was because the evening before I had mercilessly beaten Afanasy! And suddenly I saw it all again, as though it were being repeated: he stood before me, and I struck him with all my might, directly in the face, while he kept his hands at his sides, his head held erect, his eyes staring as though he were standing to attention on the parade ground, quivering with each blow and not even daring to raise an arm in order to shield himself – and this was what a human being had been reduced to, this was one man beating another! Ach, what a crime! It was as though a sharp needle had passed right through my soul. I stood there like a crazy man, and the sun was shining, the leaves were rejoicing, sparkling, and the birds, the birds were singing their praise to God ... I covered my face with the palms of both hands, collapsed on to the bed and broke into violent sobbing. And then I remembered my brother Markel and the words he had spoken to our servants before his death: 'My beloved, my dear ones, why do you serve me, am I worthy of it?'

'Yes, am I worthy of it?' suddenly leapt through my head. Indeed, why should I be worthy of having another man, the same as I was, the image and likeness of God, serve me? Thus it was that this question thrust itself into my mind for the first time. 'Dear mother, beloved droplet of my blood, in truth each of us is guilty before the others for everyone, only people don't realize it, but if they did, we should all instantly be in paradise!' 'O Lord, is that not true also?' I wept, and I thought – in truth I am perhaps more guilty than all, and worse than all the other people in the world! And suddenly the whole truth presented itself to me in all its enlightenment: what was I going to do? I was going to kill a good and clever man of noble spirit, who was in no way culpable in my regard, and thereby deprive his spouse of happiness for ever, torture her and kill her. With these thoughts did I lie prone upon the bed, my face pressed to the pillow, marking not at all the onward flux of time. Suddenly my companion, the lieutenant, came in to fetch me, with the pistols. 'Aha,' he said, 'that's good, you're up – come on now, it's time, let us be on our way!' At that, I began to rush to and fro, completely lost my head, but nevertheless we went outside to get into the landau. 'Wait here,' I said to him, 'I shall be back in an instant, I have left my purse inside.' And I ran back alone into my quarters, and went straight to Afanasy's little cupboard of a room: 'Afanasy,' I said, 'yesterday I struck you twice in the face, please forgive me,' I said. He fairly started, as though he had taken fright, staring at me – and I perceived that this was not enough, not nearly enough, and suddenly, just as I was, in my epaulettes, I bumped my forehead to the ground, right at his feet: 'Forgive me!' I said. At that point he froze in complete stupefaction: 'Your honour, father, *barin*, how can you . . . am I worthy of it? . . .' and he suddenly began to weep, just as I had done earlier, covered his face with the palms of both hands, turned to the window and shook violently all over with tears, while I ran out to my companion and sprang into the landau with a shout of 'Drive on!' 'If you want to see a victor,' I cried to him, 'there is one sitting before you now.' I was in a kind of ecstasy, laughing and talking, talking all the way – I do not remember now what I talked about. He looked at me: 'Well, brother, you're a brave fellow, I can see you'll be a credit to the uniform.' Thus did we arrive at the place, and they were already there, waiting for us. We were placed apart, at twelve paces' distance from each other, he had the first shot – I stood before him cheerfully, face to face, direct, not blinking an eyelid, gazing at him pleasantly, knowing what I was about to do. When he fired, the shot only grazed my cheek, brushing past my ear. 'Thank God,' I cried, 'no one has been killed!' – and I seized my pistol, turned behind me and threw it up into the air, over into the forest. 'There,' I cried, 'good riddance to you!' I turned round to face my antagonist: 'Dear sir,' I said, 'I ask your forgiveness, a stupid young man, for having through my own fault caused you great offence and having now compelled you to shoot at me. I am ten times your inferior, and possibly even more. Please convey that to the lady whom you honour more than anyone else in the world.' No sooner were the words out of my mouth when all three of them began to shout and clamour. 'Excuse me,' said my antagonist, really losing his temper, 'if you had no intention of fighting, why did you put me to all this trouble?' 'Yesterday I was still stupid,' I said, 'but today I have acquired a bit of sense.' I made my reply sound cheerful. 'I believe you about yesterday,' he said, 'but about today it is difficult to concur with your opinion.' 'Bravo!' I cried to him, clapping my hands. 'I agree with you on that, too – I deserve it!' 'Are you going to shoot, dear sir, or not?' 'No, I am not,' I said, 'but if you wish you may fire again, though it would be better if you refrained from doing so.' The seconds, too, raised a cry of protest, especially my own, who shouted: 'What do you mean by bringing shame upon the regiment, asking for forgiveness while on the firing-line? If only I had known!' I stood there facing them all, but I was no longer laughing: 'Gentlemen,' I said, 'is it really such an astonishing thing in our time to encounter a man who is willing to show remorse for his stupidity and to publicly apologize for that of which he is guilty?' 'But not on the firing-line, surely?' my second shouted again. 'That is the whole point,' I replied to him. 'That is the astonishing thing, because I ought to have apologized when first we arrived, even before his shot, in order not to lead him into great and mortal sin; but we have established ourselves in the world,' I said, 'in a manner so morally deformed that to act thus was well nigh impossible, for only after I had faced his shot at twelves paces could my words mean anything to him now, and had I spoken them before his shot, when first we arrived, he would simply have said I was a coward, frightened of his pistol and not worth listening to. Gentlemen!' I suddenly exclaimed with all my heart, 'take a look around you at God's gifts: the sunny sky, the pure air, the gentle grass, the birds, a nature that is beautiful and without sin, while we, we alone, are godless and stupid and do not realize that life is paradise, for all that we have to do is to want to understand, and at once it will begin in all its beauty, and we shall embrace one another and weep . . .' I wanted to go on, but I could not, I was even out of breath, in a delightfully pleasant, youthful sort of way, and in my heart there was such happiness as I had never experienced in all my life. 'All that is very sensible and devout,' my antagonist said to me, 'and, at any rate, you are a man of originality.' 'You may laugh,' I said to him, laughing, 'but later you will praise me.' 'But I am ready to praise you now, by all means, I give you my hand, for you seem like a man who is really sincere.' 'No,' I said, 'don't do it just now, but later, when I have made myself better and deserve your respect, then you may give it to me – and you will do well to do so.' We returned home, my second showered me with abuse all the way home, but I kept embracing him. My companions instantly got to hear of what had happened, and they gathered together in order to court-martial me that very day: 'He's besmirched the uniform,' they said. 'He ought to leave the service.' Voices for the defence were also heard: 'He faced one shot, after all,' they said. 'Yes, but he was afraid of the other shots and asked for forgiveness on the firing-line.' 'If he'd been afraid of being shot,' retorted the voices for the defence, 'he'd have fired his pistol first, before asking forgiveness, but he threw it into the forest fully loaded, no, it was something else, something original.' I listened, it amused me to look at them. 'My dearest friends and companions,' I said, 'please do not be anxious about my leaving the service, because I have already taken the necessary steps, I have handed in my application and did so this morning, at the chancery; when I receive my discharge I shall at once go and join a monastery, and as a matter of fact, that is why I have made my application.' As soon as I said this, they all of them to a man burst into loud laughter: 'Oh, you should have told us in the first place, that explains it all, we can't court-martial a monk,' they said, laughing, and would not quieten down, yet their laughter was not at all derisive but rather affectionate and merry, they all suddenly grew fond of me, even those who had been my most fervid accusers, and thereafter, throughout that whole month, until my discharge came through, it was as if they carried me around on their shoulders: 'Oh, you monk,' they would say. And each of them had an affectionate word for me, they began to try to talk me out of it, felt really sorry for me: 'What are you doing to yourself?' 'No,' they would say, 'he's one of us, and he's brave, he faced that shot but couldn't fire his own pistol; he must have had a dream the night before about becoming a monk, and that's why he couldn't do it.' In the town's social circles the reaction was almost the same. Whereas previously I had not been noticed much there, but merely received with cordiality, now all of a sudden they all started vying with one another to get to know me and invite me to their houses: and while they laughed at me, they also treated me with affection. I should observe here that although people talked about our duel quite openly at the time, the military authorities covered up the affair, for my antagonist was a close relative of the general, and as the whole thing had passed off without any blood being spilt and seemed almost to have been done in jest, and as, moreover, I had applied for a discharge, they did indeed turn it into a jest. And then I began to talk out loud and without fear, in spite of their laughter, because it was not malicious but good-natured. These conversations took place for the most part at soirées, in the company of ladies; at that time it was mostly the women who were fond of listening to me, compelling their menfolk to do likewise. 'But how can it be that I am guilty before everyone?' each of them would say, laughing in my face. 'Well, how can I be guilty before you, for example?' 'Oh,' I replied to them, 'how can you hope to understand that, when the whole world has long been progressing along another road, and when downright falsehood is considered by us as truth, and when we expect and demand similar falsehood from others. What I did, you see, was to go and act sincerely for once in my life, and what was the result? That I became a kind of holy fool to you all: even though you have taken a liking to me, you still laugh at me,' I said. 'But how could one not take a liking to you?' the hostess said to me laughing aloud in my presence, though the gathering in her house was a numerous one. Suddenly I saw arising from the midst of the ladies that same young female person for whose sake I had issued the challenge to the duel and whom so recently I had intended to make my bride; I had not observed her arrival at the soirée. She got to her feet, came over to me and extended her hand: 'Please allow me to make it clear to you,' she said, 'that I am the first to refrain from laughing at you, and that, on the contrary, I thank you with tears and declare my respect for you concerning the action you took.' At that point her husband, too, came over, and then suddenly they were all reaching out their hands to me, practically embracing me. I was filled with gladness, but most of all I suddenly noticed a certain gentleman, a man already advanced in years, who was also coming up to me; though I knew him by name, I had never made his acquaintance, and until that evening we had not even exchanged so much as a word.

(d) The Mysterious Visitor

He had been in government service in our town for a long time, and occupied an eminent position, was a man looked up to by all, rich, with a reputation for philanthropy, donated significant sums of capital to the almshouse and the orphanage and, in addition to this, performed many good deeds in secret, without publicity, all of which was subsequently discovered after his death. He was about fifty years of age and had an air about him almost of severity, said little; he had, on the other hand, been married for no more than ten years to a spouse still young, from whom he had had three children as yet still in their infancy. The following evening I sat alone at home, when suddenly my door opened and this same gentleman entered my lodgings.

I should observe that I was not then living in my previous quarters, having, as soon as I had handed in my application for a discharge, vacated them for others in the home of an old woman, a civil servant's widow, and her maid; my removal to these new lodgings took place solely because on the very same day I returned from my duel I had dispatched Afanasy back to his company, for I was ashamed to look him in the eye after the action I had taken towards him earlier – so inclined is the unprepared secular to be ashamed of even those deeds of his that are most just.

'I . . .' the gentleman who had entered my lodgings said to me, 'I have been listening to you in various homes with great curiosity for several days now and have at last conceived a desire to become personally acquainted with you in order to talk with you in more detail. Can you, dear sir, perform for me such a great favour?' 'I can,' I said, 'with the greatest of pleasure, and shall consider it a particular honour.' As I said this, I felt almost afraid, such a striking impression had he made on me from the very first moment. For although people had listened to me and had shown curiosity, no man had yet approached me with such an earnest and severe inward demeanour. And this one had actually come into my own lodgings. He sat down. 'Great,' he continued, 'is the strength of character that I discern in you, for you were not afraid to serve the truth in such an affair, where you ran the risk of bearing, for the sake of your sense of what is right, the general contempt of all.' 'I think you possibly exaggerate your praise of me,' I said to him. 'No, I do not exaggerate,' he replied to me. 'Believe me, it is far more difficult to accomplish such an action than you suppose. In fact,' he continued, 'that was the thing that struck me so greatly, and is the real reason why I have come to see you. Please describe for me, if you do not shrink from my curiosity as being possibly indecent, what it was you felt at that moment when in the course of a duel you resolved to ask for forgiveness, if you remember? Please do not construe my question as a frivolous one; on the contrary, in asking it I have a secret purpose of my own, one which I shall certainly explain to you later, if it shall please God to bring us more intimately together.'

All the time he was saying this, I looked him straight in the eye and suddenly experienced towards him a most powerful sense of trust, added to which there was a curiosity unusual in myself, for I could feel that there was within his soul a secret of some peculiar nature.

'You ask what it was I felt at the moment I asked forgiveness of my opponent,' I replied to him, 'but I would do best to tell you right at the outset what I have not yet told to others.' And I told him all that had taken place with Afanasy at my quarters and how I had bowed to the earth before him. 'From that you may see for yourself,' I concluded, 'that by the time it came to the duel I already felt easier, for I had begun my progress at home, and once I had embarked upon that road, all that followed later was not only without difficulty, but even joyous and merry.'

He heard me through, watching me in such a pleasant manner: 'All this,' he said, 'is exceedingly curious, and I shall come and see you again not once, but many times.' And from that day hence he began to drop in on me practically every evening. And we should have become great friends, had he also told me about himself. On that subject, however, he said almost not a word, keeping up a constant flow of questions about me, instead. In spite of this, I grew very fond of him and with perfect trust confided to him all my feelings, for I thought: 'Why do I require to know his secrets? I do not need them in order to see that the man is righteous. What is more, he is such an earnest fellow and unequal to me in years, yet he comes to visit me, a youth, and does not show disdain for me.' And many useful things did I learn from him, for he was a man of lofty intellect. 'That life is paradise,' he told me one day, 'is something I have long thought about,' adding suddenly: 'It is all that I think about.' He looked at me, smiling. 'I am more convinced of it than you, and later you shall discover why.' Hearing this, I thought to myself: 'It sounds as though he wants to divulge something to me.' 'Paradise,' he said, 'is concealed in each one of us, and now it is contained within myself, and I want it to begin for me tomorrow and to last for the rest of my life.' I looked: he spoke with tender piety, watching me mysteriously, as though he were questioning me. 'And as for what you said,' he continued, 'about each person being guilty for all creatures and for all things, as well as his own sins, there your reasoning was perfectly correct, and it is remarkable that you were suddenly able to embrace this idea in such completeness. And indeed it is true that when people understand this idea the Kingdom of Heaven will begin for them, not in a dream but in actual fact.' 'But when,' I exclaimed to him then with sorrow, 'will that come true, and will it ever come true? Is it not only a dream and nothing else?' 'There,' he said, 'you have no faith, you preach to others yet have no faith yourself. Know then that this dream will come true, as you put it, have faith in that, only it will not be now, for every process has its law. This is a matter of the soul and of psychology. In order for the world to be transformed into a new mould it is necessary that human beings themselves shall psychically turn on to another path. Until you really make yourself the brother to all, brotherhood will not arrive. Never, prompted by science or self-interest alone, will human beings be able to share their property and their privileges in harmless fashion. None will consider that he has enough, and all will grumble, envying and destroying one another. You ask when what I describe will come true. It will come true, but first there must be a period of human *solitariness*.' 'What kind of solitariness do you mean?' I asked him. 'The kind that reigns everywhere now, particularly in our own time, though it has not yet established itself universally, and its hour has not yet come. For each now strives to isolate his person as much as possible from the others, wishing to experience within himself life's completeness, yet from all his efforts there results not life's completeness but a complete suicide, for instead of discovering the true nature of their being they lapse into total solitariness. For in our era all are isolated into individuals, each retires solitary within his burrow, each withdraws from the other, conceals himself and that which he possesses, and ends by being rejected of men and by rejecting them. He amasses wealth in solitariness, thinking: how strong I am now and how secure, yet he does not know, the witless one, that the more he amasses, the further he will sink into suicidal impotence. For he has become accustomed to relying upon himself alone and has isolated himself from the whole as an individual, has trained his soul not to trust in help from others, in human beings and mankind, and is fearful only of losing his money and the privileges he has acquired. In every place today the human mind is mockingly starting to lose its awareness of the fact that a person's true security consists not in his own personal, solitary effort, but in the common integrity of human kind. But it will certainly be the case that this terrible solitariness will come to an end, and all will comprehend at once how unnaturally they have divided themselves one from the other. Such will be the spirit of the age, and they will be astonished that they have sat in darkness for so long without seeing the light. And then shall appear the sign of the Son of Man in heaven* . . . But until that day we must nevertheless cherish the banner from time to time, and even though he does it individually, a man must suddenly show an example and lead his soul out of solitariness to a heroic deed of brotherly and loving communion, even though he does it in the capacity of a holy fool . . . This, in order that the great idea shall not die . . .'

In such ardent and enraptured colloquies did our evenings pass, one after the other. I even gave up my rounds of society and began to appear less and less frequently as a visitor in people's homes; the fashion surrounding me had, moreover, begun to pass. I say this not in condemnation, for I continued to receive affection and a cheerful welcome; but of the circumstance that in the social world fashion is a not inconsiderable empress, of that one must also take cognizance. Upon my mysterious visitor, on the other hand, I began to gaze at last in admiration, for, in addition to the pleasure I experienced in the face of his intellect, I began to sense that he was nourishing within himself a certain project and was preparing himself for what might possibly be a great heroic deed. It may also have been that he was pleased I did not show any outward curiosity about his secret, that neither directly nor by allusion did I question him about it. At length, however, I perceived that he had almost begun to live in an agony of wishing to divulge something to me. At any rate, this became quite plain approximately a month after he had taken to visiting me. 'Are you aware,' he asked me one day, 'that there is in the town a great deal of curiosity concerning us both? People find it strange that I come to see you so often. But let them, for *soon all will be explained*.' At times he was suddenly assailed by an extreme agitation, and almost invariably in such cases he would get up and leave. At other times, however, he would stare at me long and penetratingly, and I would think: 'He is going to say something in a moment,' but he would suddenly interrupt his thoughts and begin to talk of something ordinary and of common knowledge. He also began frequently to complain of headaches. And then one day, quite unexpectedly, after he had spoken long and ardently, I saw him turn suddenly pale, his face completely twisted and distorted, staring at me.

'What ails you?' I said. 'Do you feel unwell?'

For he had indeed complained of a headache.

'I . . . do you know . . . I . . . killed a person.'

He said it smiling, but he was white as chalk. 'Why does he smile?' was the thought that suddenly transfixed my heart, before I had time to make any sense of it. I too had turned pale.

'What is this you say?' I cried to him.

'You see,' he replied to me, still with a pale, ironic smile, 'how much it has cost me to say the first word. Now that I have said it I think I have started along the road. I shall travel it.'

Long did I not believe him, and indeed I came to it not at once but only after he had been to see me for three days in a row and narrated it all to me in detail. I had considered him deranged, but ended at last by being convinced, with the greatest sorrow and surprise, which I took no pains to conceal. There had been committed by him a great and terrible crime, fourteen years before, against a certain wealthy lady, a young and attractive person, the widow of a landowner, who owned a house in our town for when she made visits there. Having conceived a great love for her, he made her a declaration of love and began to try to persuade her to marry him. She had, however, already given her heart to another, a certain aristocratic military man of considerable rank who was at that time on a campaign,* but whom she soon expected to return to her. She rejected his proposal and asked him not to pay her visits. Having ceased to do so, but being familiar with the disposition of her house, one night he stole into her chambers from the garden by way of the roof, with the greatest of boldness, risking discovery. But as very often is the case, it is precisely those crimes committed with uncommon boldness that are most frequently successful. Entering the garret of the house through a dormer window, he descended to her accommodations by means of the stepladder, being aware that the door at its foot was not always secured by lock and key, thanks to the negligence of the servants. He had been relying upon this inadvertence on the present occasion, too, and found it to be so. Making his way to the living apartments, he passed in the darkness into her bedchamber, in which a lamp was burning. And, as if by design, both of her maidservants had gone out on the sly, without asking permission, to a name-day celebration that was taking place in a house on that same street. The rest of the servants and serving-maids were asleep in the servants' rooms and the kitchen, on the ground floor. At the sight of the sleeping woman his passion flared up, and then his heart was seized by vengeful, jealous hatred and, beside himself, like a man intoxicated, he went over to her and plunged a knife straight into her heart, so that she did not even cry out. Then with infernal and most criminal calculation he arranged things so as to suggest that the servants had done it: did not disdain to take her purse, unlocked her chest of drawers with the keys which he fished out from under her pillow and took several items from inside it, in precisely the way an ignorant male servant would have done, that is to say, leaving the securities and taking only the money, taking a few of the larger gold articles and neglecting the small ones that were ten times more valuable. He also pocketed some other things as keepsakes, but of this later. Having accomplished this dreadful deed, he left by his earlier route. Neither on the following day, when the alarm was raised, nor subsequently throughout all the rest of his life did it ever enter anyone's head to suspect the true villain! Even concerning his love for her no one knew anything, for he had always been of a taciturn and uncommunicative disposition and had no friend to whom he might have confided his soul. He was thought merely to have been an acquaintance of the murdered woman and not even a particularly close one, for during the past two weeks he had not paid her an open visit. Her bondsman-servant Pyotr was instantly suspected, and indeed all the circumstances fitted together in order to confirm this suspicion, for this servant had known, and the deceased lady had not concealed it from him, that she intended to send him away to the army as payment of the recruit-debt* owed by her, as he was single and moreover of reprobate conduct. He had been heard in a drinking-house, angry and intoxicated, threatening to kill her. And two days before her death he had run off to the town where he had stayed at some unknown address. The day after the murder he had been found on the road near the town gate, mortally drunk, with a knife in his pocket, the palm of his right hand oddly stained with blood. He asserted that the blood had come from his nose, but he was not believed. As for the two serving-maids, they owned up to having been out at the celebration and apologized for having left the front door unlocked until their return. And indeed there were a great number of other similar indications by means of which the innocent servant was ensnared. He was arrested and a process at law was begun, but no more than a week later the arrested man fell sick of a fever and died unconscious in hospital. With that the matter was closed, abandoned to the will of God, and all, judges, police and society alike, remained convinced that the crime had been committed by no one but the deceased servant. And thereupon began the punishment.

The mysterious visitor, who was now my friend, informed me that at first he had not even been tormented by the gnawings of conscience at all. He suffered long torments, but not of that kind, only those of regret at having killed the woman he loved, at the fact that she was no more, and that, having killed her, he had killed his love, while the fire of passion remained within his blood. To the innocent blood he had spilt, however, and to the fact that he had murdered another human being, he almost never devoted any thought at the time. As for the notion that his victim might have become another man's spouse, it seemed to him impossible, and so for a long time he was persuaded in his conscience that he could not have acted any differently. He was initially somewhat perturbed by the arrest of the servant, but the sudden illness and ensuing death of the accused man had the effect of calming him, for in manifest probability the man had died (so he reasoned at the time), not because of his arrest or his fear, but by reason of a catarrhal ague incurred during the days of his flight when, mortally drunk, he had wallowed for an entire night upon the ground. Concerning the articles and money he was little troubled, for (thus did he continue to deliberate) the theft had been committed not for any motive of self-interest, but in order to divert suspicion elsewhere. The value of the stolen things was insignificant, and he soon donated a sum equivalent to its whole and even slightly greater to the almshouse that had been founded in our town. He did this with the especial purpose of stilling his conscience on account of the theft, and it was a remarkable fact that for a time, even quite a long one, he really did experience a sense of calm – he himself told me this. In those days he had embarked upon a period of intense activity in government service, angling for himself a difficult and troublesome assignment which kept him busy for about two years, and, being of strong character, he almost began to forget what had taken place; and whenever he did remember it, he tried not to think about it at all. He also embarked upon philanthropy, establishing many institutions and making many charitable donations in our town, announced himself in the capitals, and was elected in Moscow and St Petersburg as a member of the philanthropic societies there. But nevertheless, in the end he began to reflect, and did so with a torment that was beyond his strength to bear. At this point his fancy was engaged by a certain beautiful and sensible young lady, and he quickly married her, hoping that marriage might dispel his solitary anguish, and that by entering upon a new path and zealously fulfilling his duty in respect of wife and children he would leave his old memories behind once and for all. Instead, what happened was quite contrary to this expectation. Even in the first month of his marriage the ceaseless thought began to trouble him: 'My wife there – she loves me, but what if she were to find out?' When she became pregnant with their first child and announced this to him, he was suddenly troubled: 'I am giving life, but have taken it away.' As his children were born, he thought: 'How can I dare to love, instruct and educate them in the ways of man, how can I talk to them of virtue: I have spilt blood.' His children grew up and were beautiful, he wanted to caress them, and he thought: 'But I cannot look upon their serene and innocent countenances; I am not worthy of it.' At last he began to see cruel and menacing visions of the blood of his murdered victim, of her young life that had been destroyed, of her blood that cried out to be avenged. He began to have horrible dreams. Being resolute of heart, however, he endured the torment long: 'By my secret torment I shall redeem it all,' he thought. But even this hope was in vain: the longer his suffering continued, the more intense did it grow. His philanthropic activity had begun to earn him respect in society, though all were intimidated by his severe and gloomy character; but the more respect he acquired, the more unendurable to him did it become. He confessed to me that he had thought of killing himself. But instead another dream began to visit him – a dream which he at first considered impossible and crazy, but which leeched his heart so greedily that it could not be wrenched away. He dreamed thus: of getting up, going out before the people and declaring to all that he had murdered someone. For some three years did he go around with this dream inside him, and it visited him constantly in different aspects. At last he attained the belief with all his heart that, having declared his crime, he would of a certainty heal his soul and be at rest once and for all. Having attained it, however, he felt a sense of horror in his heart, for how could he bring himself to execute this deed? And suddenly there had occurred that incident in the course of my duel. 'As I gazed at you, I took my resolve.' I looked at him.

'And can it really be,' I exclaimed to him, lifting my hands, 'that a little incident like that was capable of engendering in you such resolution?'

'My resolution has been three years in the engendering,' he replied to me. 'The incident at your duel merely gave it a spur. As I gazed at you I reproached myself and envied you.' He announced this to me with positive severity.

'In any case, no one will believe you,' I observed to him. 'Fourteen years have passed.'

'I have proof, formidable proof. I shall submit it.'

And then I began to weep, and kissed him.

'One thing decide for me, one thing!' he said to me (as though now all depended on myself). 'My wife, my children! My wife may die from grief, and though my children will not be deprived of lands and title, they will be the children of an exiled convict, and for aye. And the memory, the memory that I shall leave behind me in their hearts!'

I was silent.

'And to part with them, to leave them for eternity? For it will be for aye, for aye!'

I sat there, silently whispering a prayer to myself. At last I arose, filled with dread.

'What is it?' he said, looking at me.

'Go,' I said, 'declare what you have done. It will all pass, the truth alone will remain. Your children will understand when they grow up how much magnanimity there was in your great resolution.'

That day he left me as though he had indeed taken his resolve. This notwithstanding, he kept coming back to see me almost every evening for more than two weeks, in a state of constant preparation, but still unable to take the final step. He had worn my heart out. Sometimes he would arrive with an air of firmness and say with tender piety:

'I know that paradise will begin for me, will begin immediately I declare what I have done. For fourteen years I have been in hell. I want to suffer. I shall accept suffering and start to live. One can pass one's life in falsehood, but one cannot go back. Now it is not only my neighbour whom I dare not love, but even my own children. O Lord, but after all my children will perhaps understand what my suffering has cost me, and they will not condemn me! The Lord is not in strength, but in truth.'

'All will comprehend the heroic deed you have accomplished,' I said to him, 'if not now, then later, for you have served truth, a truth that is higher and not of this world . . .'

And he would leave me like a man consoled, and on the morrow would arrive once more, rancorous and pale, and say mockingly:

'Every time I come to see you you look at me with such curiosity, as if to say: "Have you not declared it yet?" Wait, do not be too contemptuous of me. It is, after all, not as easy as it appears to you. It may yet be that I cannot bring myself to do it at all. Perhaps then you will go and inform on me – eh?'

But not only was I too afraid to look at him with rash curiosity – I even feared to glance at him at all. I was worn out to the point of illness, and my soul was full of tears. I even lost sleep at nights.

'I have just come,' he continued, 'from my wife. Have you any idea of what a wife is? As I was leaving my children cried to me: "Goodbye, papa, come back soon and read the *Children's Reader** with us." No, you have no idea! No man gains wisdom from another's woe.'

As he said this, his eyes began to glitter and his lips to twitch. Suddenly he brought his fist down hard on the table, making the objects on it jump – he was such a gentle man, it was the first time such a thing had happened.

'But is it necessary?' he exclaimed, 'is it incumbent upon me? After all, no one has been convicted, no one has been sent into penal exile because of me, the servant died of his illness. And for the blood I spilt I have been punished with torments. And in any case, they won't believe me, no proof that I could ever bring will ever make them believe me. Is it necessary to declare my deed, is it incumbent upon me, is it? For the blood I have spilt I am prepared to suffer for the rest of my life, if only my wife and children are not affected. Would it be just to drag them down along with me? Are we not in error? Where is justice in this case? And will others perceive that justice, will they value it, respect it?'

'O Lord,' I thought to myself, 'he thinks of the respect of others at a time like this!' And so sorry then did I begin to feel for him that I think I myself would have shared his partage, had that been any way to bring him alleviation. I saw that he was in a frenzy. I felt horror, grasping now not with my mind alone, but with my living soul, the cost of such resolve.

'Decide my fate!' he exclaimed again.

'Go and declare your deed,' I whispered to him. My voice was shaky, but I whispered the words firmly. Then I picked up from the table my copy of the New Testament, in a Russian translation, and showed him St John, chapter 12, verse 24:

'Verily, verily, I say unto you. Except a corn of wheat fall into the ground and die, it abideth alone: but if it die, it bringeth forth much fruit.' I had read that verse immediately before his arrival.

He read it. 'True,' he said, but with a bitter, ironic smile. 'Yes,' he said after a pause, 'terrible are the things one comes across in those books. To shove them under someone's nose is easy enough. But who wrote them? Surely not human beings?'

'The Holy Ghost did,' I said.

'It is easy for you to talk,' he said, again smiling ironically at me, but this time almost with hatred. I picked up the book again, opened it at another passage and showed him Hebrews, chapter 10, verse 31. He read:

'It is a fearful thing to fall into the hands of the living God.'

He read it, and fairly threw the book from him. He had even begun to tremble all over.

'A terrible verse,' he said, 'you have chosen, indeed.' He got up from his chair. 'Well,' he said, 'goodbye, it may be that I shall not come again ... We shall see each other in paradise. So it is fourteen years since I "fell into the hands of the living God" – and that is how those fourteen years had best be described. Tomorrow I shall ask those hands to release me ...'

I was on the point of embracing him and kissing him, but I did not dare – so distorted were his features and so heavy his look. He went out.

'O Lord,' I thought, 'where has the fellow gone?' I threw myself to my knees before the icon and began to weep for him to the Most Holy Mother of God, swift Intercessor and Helper. Half an hour went by as I knelt there in tears and prayer; it was by this time late at night, around twelve o'clock. Suddenly, I looked: the door opened and he came in again. I was dumbfounded.

'But where have you been?' I asked him.

'I . . .' he said. 'I . . . it would seem, have forgotten something . . . my handkerchief, it would seem. Well, even if I have not, let me at least sit down . . .'

He took a chair and sat down. I was standing over him. 'You sit down too,' he said. I did so. We continued to sit there for some two minutes, and he looked at me fixedly; then suddenly he smiled his ironic smile — I remember that — then rose to his feet, embraced me tightly and gave me a kiss . . .

'Remember,' he said, 'how I came to see thee a second time. Remember it, dost thou hear?'

For the first time he addressed me as *thou*. And departed. 'Tomorrow,' I thought.

So it proved to be. I did not know that evening that the morrow was his birthday. I had not been out of my lodgings for the past few days, and so there was no one from whom I could have discovered it. Annually upon this day he held a large gathering at his home, at which the whole town assembled. Such was the case even now. And lo, after the prandial feast he walked into the centre of the room, holding in his hands a document — a formal report to the police. And since the chief of police, his superior, was present, he at once read out the document to all the assembled people, and in it was a full description of his crime in all its details: 'As an outcast I cast myself out* from the midst of men,' the document concluded. 'God has visited me, and I want to suffer!' With that, he produced and displayed upon the table all the evidence by which he thought to prove his crime and which he had preserved for fourteen years: the gold articles which had belonged to the murdered woman and which he had stolen with the motive of diverting suspicion from himself, her medallion and cross, which he had removed from around her neck — in the medallion there was a portrait of her betrothed — her notebook, and, finally, two letters: one from her betrothed to her, announcing his imminent arrival and her reply to this letter, which she had begun but not concluded, leaving it upon the table with the aim of posting it the following day. Both letters he had taken with him — to what end? To what end had he preserved them, instead of destroying them as incriminating evidence? And lo, what should happen: all were assailed by surprise and horror, and none would believe, though they had all listened to what he had to say with extreme curiosity, but as from a man who was sick, and several days later the matter was finally settled and verdict pronounced in every household – the unhappy man was deranged. The police and the court could hardly let the case rest there, but even they drew up short: though the articles and letters that had been submitted certainly made them reflect, here too it was decided that even if these documents turned out to be genuine it would none the less be hard to make a charge of murder stick on the basis of them alone. And then again, he might have received the gold articles from her as her friend and for safekeeping. As a matter of fact, I have heard it said that the authenticity of the gold articles was subsequently established by means of consultation with many friends and relatives of the murdered woman and that there were no doubts on the matter. But these proceedings too were fated to be left without completion. Some five days later they all discovered that the sufferer had fallen ill and that there were fears for his life. With what illness he was affected I am unable to determine, it was said to be a tachycardiac disorder, but it became known that the council of doctors had, at his wife's insistence, testified as to his mental condition also, and that they had drawn the conclusion that derangement had set in. I gave nothing away, even though everyone rushed to question me, but when I expressed a wish to visit him, I received lengthy abuse from them all, particularly his spouse: 'It is you,' she said to me, 'who have upset him, he was gloomy enough before, but during this last year we have all noticed that he has been unusually agitated and has been doing strange things, and it is you who are at the bottom of it all, no one else; he has not been out of your lodgings for a whole month.' And lo, not only his spouse but everyone in the town hurled themselves upon me and accused me: 'It is all your doing,' they said. I remained silent, and indeed I felt rejoicing within my soul, for I beheld the unfailing mercy of God towards the one who turns up against himself and takes the punishment upon himself. As for his derangement, I was unable to believe in it. I too was at last allowed to see him, for he himself had insistently demanded to say farewell to me. I entered, and saw immediately that not only his days but also his hours were numbered. He was weak and sallow of feature, his hands trembled, and he gasped for breath, but looked at me with tender piety and joy.

'It is accomplished!' he said to me. 'Long have I thirsted to see you, why did you not come?'

I did not explain to him that I had not been allowed to see him.

'God has taken compassion on me and is calling me unto him. I know that I am dying, but for the first time in so many years I feel joy and peace. As soon as I had done what was incumbent on me I at once felt paradise within my soul. Now I dare to love my children and to kiss them. I am not believed, and no one has believed me, neither my wife, nor my judges; never will my children believe me, either. In this I see God's mercy towards my children. I shall die, and my name will be unsullied for them. But now I sense the nearness of God, and my heart rejoices as in paradise . . . I have performed my duty . . .'

He could not speak, he gasped for breath, squeezed my hand warmly, gazed at me ardently. But our conversation did not last long, for his spouse kept looking in to keep a watchful eye upon us. Even so, he managed to whisper to me:

'But do you remember how I came to see you that evening a second time, at midnight? How I told you to remember it? Do you know why I came? You see, I came to kill you!'

I fairly started.

'That evening I emerged from your lodgings into the darkness and set off wandering through the streets, struggling with myself. And suddenly I conceived such a hatred of you that my heart could barely endure it. "Now," I thought, "he alone binds me and is my judge, now I cannot renounce the punishment I shall receive tomorrow, for he knows all." And it was not that I feared you would inform on me (I had no thought of that), but rather that I thought: "How shall I be able to look him in the eye if I do not inform on myself?" And though you had been at the other end of the world, but living, it would have been all the same: the thought that you were alive, and knew all, and were judging me — that thought would have been unendurable. I began to hate you, as though you were the cause of it all and bore the guilt for it all. That night I went back to your lodgings again, I remembered that there was a dagger lying on your table. I sat down and asked you also to be seated, and for a whole minute reflected. Had I killed you, I should have perished for that murder all the same, even though I had not declared my earlier crime. But at that moment I did not think of that, and did not want to think of it. I simply hated you and desired to be avenged on you with all my might for everything. But My Lord conquered the devil in my heart. Know, however, that never in your life were you more close to death.'

At the end of a week he died. The whole town walked with his coffin to the grave. The archpriest delivered a short and heartfelt oration. They lamented the terrible illness that had cut short his days. But after he had been buried the whole town rose up against me and even stopped receiving me as a visitor in their homes. To be sure, some of them, at first only a few, but subsequently more and more, started to believe the truth of his testimony, and they began to come and see me in order to ply me with questions, which they did with great curiosity and glee: for men like to see the fall of a righteous man and to witness his disgrace. But I told them nothing and soon got out of town altogether, and five months later the Lord God saw fit to embark me upon a firm and well-apportioned path, and I blessed the invisible finger that had so plainly pointed it to me. As for Mikhail, the long-suffering servant of God,* I have remembered him in my prayers each day unto this day.

3

*From the Discourses and Teachings of
the Elder Zosima*

(e) Something Concerning the Russian Monk and His Possible Significance

FATHERS and teachers, what is a monk? In the enlightened world this word is pronounced in our day by some with mockery, and by some even as an expletive. And the more time passes, the more this is so. It is true, oh, it is true, that there are in the monkhood also many parasites, lovers of the flesh, voluptuaries and brazen vagabonds. Worldly men of progressive education point to this: 'You are,' they say, 'idlers and useless members of society; shameless beggars, you live upon the efforts of others.' Yet even so how many meek and humble ones there are in the monkhood, thirsting for seclusion and ardent prayer in silence. These are pointed to less and are even passed over without comment altogether, and how surprised would the same worldly men be if I told them that from these meek souls who thirst for secluded prayer may once again issue the salvation of the Russian land! For verily they are being prepared in silence 'for an hour, and a day, and a month, and a year.' Meanwhile in their seclusion they are preserving the image of Christ in well-apportioned and undistorted form, in the purity of God's truth, as it was handed down to them by the most ancient fathers, apostles and martyrs, and when the need arrives they will show that image to the wavering truth of the world. Great is this thought. This star will shine in the east.

Such is my opinion concerning the monk, and is there any falseness in it, or pride? Go, look among the secular and at all the world that exalts itself above God's people: have not God's image and his truth become distorted therein? What they have is science, and in science only that which is subject to the senses. The spiritual world, on the other hand, the loftier half of man's being, is rejected altogether, cast out with a certain triumph, hatred even. The world has proclaimed freedom, particularly of late, and yet what do we see in this freedom of theirs: nothing but servitude and suicide! For the world says: 'You have needs, so satisfy them, for you have the same rights as the wealthiest and most highly placed of men. Do not be afraid to satisfy them, but even multiply them' – that is the present-day teaching of the world. In that, too, they see freedom. And what is the result of this right to the multiplication of needs? Among the rich *solitariness* and spiritual suicide, and among the poor – envy and murder, for while they have been given rights, they have not yet been afforded the means with which to satisfy their needs. Assurance is offered that as time goes by the world will become more united, that it will form itself into a brotherly communion by shortening distance and transmitting thoughts through the air. Alas, do not believe in such a unification of men. In construing freedom as the multiplication and speedy satisfaction of needs, they distort their own nature, for they engender within themselves many senseless and stupid desires, habits and most absurd inventions. They live solely for envy, for love of the flesh and for self-conceit. To have dinners, horses and carriages, rank, and attendants who are slaves is already considered such a necessity that they will even sacrifice their lives, their honour and philanthropy in order to satisfy that necessity, and will even kill themselves if they cannot do so. Among those who are not rich we see the same thing, and among the poor envy and the frustration of needs are at present dulled by drunkenness. But soon in place of alcohol it will be blood upon which they grow intoxicated – to that they are being led. I ask you: is such a man free? I knew one 'fighter for the cause' who himself told me that when in prison he was deprived of tabacco so tormented was he by this deprivation that he almost went and betrayed his 'cause' in order that he should be given some tobacco. And after all, it is a man such as this who says: 'I am going to fight for mankind.' Well, where can such a man go and of what is he capable? Of a quick action perhaps, but he will not endure long. And it is small wonder that in place of freedom they have found slavery, and in place of service to brotherly love and the unity of mankind they have found *isolation* and solitariness, as my mysterious visitor and teacher told me in my youth. And so it is that in the world the idea of service to mankind, of the brotherhood and inclusiveness of men, is fading more and more, and in truth this thought is now encountered with mockery, for how can he desist from his habits, this slave, where can he go, if he is so accustomed to satisfying his countless needs, which he himself has invented? Solitary is he, and what concern can he have for the whole? And they have reached a point where the quantity of objects they amass is ever greater, and their joy is ever smaller.

The monkish path is a different matter. Obedience, fasting and prayer are even the objects of laughter, and yet it is only in them that the path to true and genuine freedom is contained: I cut off from myself my superfluous and unnecessary needs, humble and scourge my vain and proud will with obedience and thereby attain, with God's help, freedom of spirit, and together with it spiritual gaiety! Which of them is more capable of raising aloft a great idea and of going to serve it – the isolated rich man, or this *freed one* – freed from the tyranny of objects and habits? The monk is reproached for his solitariness: 'You have withdrawn into solitariness in order to save yourself, living the life of a monk within monastery walls, and have forgotten the brotherly service of mankind.' But we shall see which of them will be more diligent in the matter of brotherly love. For the solitariness is not ours, but theirs, only they do not see it. And from our midst since olden days have come leaders of the people, so why should they not exist now? The same meek and humble fasters and vowers of silence will rise up and go to accomplish the great task. From the people is the salvation of Russia. As for the Russian monastery, it has from time immemorial been with the people. And if the people are in solitariness, then we too are in solitariness. The people believe in our way, and the unbelieving activist will achieve nothing among us here in Russia, even though he be sincere of heart and genius-endowed of mind. Remember this. The people will go to meet the atheist and will conquer him, and there will arise a united Orthodox Russia. Then cherish the people and stand guard over their hearts. In silence, educate them. That is your monkish task, for this people is a Bearer of God.

(f) Something Concerning Masters and Servants and Whether it is Possible for Masters and Servants to become in Spirit Mutually Brothers

Lord, it cannot be denied, there is sin among the people, too. And the flame of corruption is multiplying even visibly, hourly, making its way from above. Solitariness is coming upon the people also: there begin kulaks and extortioners; already the merchant desires more and more honours, is eager to show himself progressively educated, though he possesses no such education whatsoever, and to this end vilely disdains ancient custom and is even ashamed of the faith of his fathers. He drives out to call on princes, yet is himself but a muzhik gone rotten. The people have festered in drunkenness and can no longer desist from it. And how much cruelty towards their families, their wives, their children, even; all because of drunkenness. In factories I have even seen children of ten years: unhealthy-looking, stunted, bent and already depraved. An airless hall, clattering machinery, work all God's day, depraved words and vodka, vodka – is that what is needed by the soul of a child still so young? He needs the sun, childish games and everywhere a radiant example and at least a drop of love. This shall not be, O monks, this torture of children shall not be, rise up and preach this quickly, quickly! But God will save Russia, for though the common man is depraved and cannot renounce his stinking sins, he knows all the same that his stinking sin is cursed of God and that he doth badly, sinning. So tirelessly still does our people believe in the truth, recognizing God and weeping in tender piety. Things are otherwise with those who are higher up. They, led by science, want to establish themselves in truth and justice with their minds alone, but now without Christ, as formerly, and they have already proclaimed that crime does not exist, that sin does not exist. And they are right in their way: for if one has not God, then what crime can there be? In Europe the people are already rising up against the rich with force, and popular leaders everywhere lead it to bloodshed and teach that its anger is right. But 'cursed be their anger, for it is cruel'.* And the Lord will save Russia, as he has already saved her many times. From the people salvation will come, from its faith and humility. Fathers and teachers, cherish the faith of the people, and this is not a dream: all my life what has struck me about our great people is its genuine and well-apportioned dignity, I myself have seen it, myself can testify to it, have seen it and wondered, seen it in spite of the stench of the sins and the beggarly aspect of our people. It is not servile, our people, and this after the servitude of two centuries. Free in aspect and behaviour, but without any sense of injury. And neither vengeful nor envious. 'You are noble, you are rich, you are clever and talented – and so be it, may God bless you. I honour you, but I know that I too am a human being. By honouring you without envy I display my human dignity before you.' Verily, if they do not actually say this (for they are not able yet to say it), thus do they *act* – I myself have seen it, I myself have experienced it, and you may believe:

the poorer and lowlier our Russian, the more noticeable in him is this well-apportioned truth, for the rich kulaks and exploiters among them are for the most part already depraved, and much, much of this has stemmed from our own negligence and lack of alertness. But God will save his people, for Russia is great in her humility. I dream of seeing and indeed already seem to clearly see our future: for it will be that even the most depraved of our wealthy men will end by being ashamed of his wealth before the poor, and the poor man, seeing this humility, will understand and yield to him with joy and with affection respond to his well-apportioned shame. Believe me, this is how it will end: all things are moving towards it. Only in the dignity of the human spirit can there be equality, and this will be understood by our country alone. Were we brothers, there would be brotherhood, but until there is brotherhood never will there be an equal sharing. We preserve the image of Christ, and it shines like a precious diamond to the whole world . . . May it come to pass, may it come to pass!

Fathers and teachers, once something happened to me that I found deeply affecting. One day while on my wanderings I met, in the provincial capital K——, my former batman Afanasy, at which time eight years had gone by since I parted from him. He caught sight of me by chance at the market, recognized me, ran up to me, and, O God, how glad he was to see me, he fairly hurled himself upon me: 'Little father, sire, is it you? Do I really see you again?' He took me back to where he lived. Now he was no longer in the army and was married, with two young children. He and his spouse earned a living as hawkers at the market. His little room was poor, but neat and joyful. He sat me down, heated the samovar, sent for his wife, as though I had made the day into some kind of festival for him by visiting him. He brought his young children over to me: 'Bless them, little father,' he said. 'Is it for me to bless them?' I replied to him. 'I am a simple, humble monk, I shall pray for them, and as for you, Afanasy Pavlovich, always, every day since that day have I prayed for you, for it all began with you.' And I explained this to him, as best I was able. The man was taken aback, stared at me and simply could not comprehend that I, his former 'sire', an officer, stood before him now in such an aspect and in such garb: he even wept. 'Why do you weep?' I said. 'You unforgettable man, you ought rather to rejoice for me in your soul, dear fellow, for my path is joyous and bright.' He did not say a great deal, just kept sighing and shaking his head at me in tender emotion. 'Where is all your wealth?' he inquired. I replied to him: 'I have given it to the monastery, for we live in a community together.' After we had drunk tea

I began to say goodbye to him, and suddenly he gave me a fifty-copeck piece, and then I looked and he was giving me another fifty-copeck piece, slipping it into my hand, in a hurry: 'That one is for you,' he said, 'as a man of wandering and travel, perhaps it will stand you in good stead, little father.' I accepted his coin, bowed to him and his spouse and went on my way cheered and thinking: 'There, now the two of us — he in his room and I as I walk — sigh and smile joyfully, in the gaiety of our hearts shaking our heads and remembering how God led us to our encounter.' And since that day I have never seen him again. I was his master and he my servant, yet now that he and I had exchanged kisses lovingly and in spiritual tenderness, between us a great act of human unity had taken place. I thought about this a great deal, and the way I see it now is like this: is it really so beyond the mind to suppose that this great and simple-hearted act of unity may in its own time everywhere take place among our Russian people? I have faith that it will take place and the appointed season is drawing nigh.

But of servants I will add the following: formerly, as a youth, I was often angry with my servants — 'the cook has served the food too hot, my batman has not cleaned my uniform'. Then, however, there suddenly dawned on me the thought expressed by my dear brother, which I had heard from him in my childhood: 'Am I really worthy of having another person serve me, and do I have the right to order him about because of his poverty and ignorance?' And then I also experienced wonder at how the very most simple thoughts, which are quite clear and self-evident, take such a long time to appear in our minds. Life without servants is impossible in the secular world, but act in such a manner that your servant is freer in spirit than if he were not a servant.* And why should I not be a servant to my servant, in such a way that he should even be aware of it, and without any pride on my part or lack of credence on his? Why should my servant not be to me as one of my own flesh and blood, so that at last I accept him into my family and rejoice in this? Even at the present time this is something that may be accomplished in such a fashion, but it will serve as the foundation of a future glorious unity of men, when servants are not what a man will seek for himself nor what he will desire to make of those who are his like, as he does now but, on the contrary, with all his might will himself desire to become the servant to all, in the manner described in the Gospels.* And is this really a dream, that at last man shall find his joys alone in deeds of enlightenment and mercy, and not in cruel delights, as he does now — in gluttony, lechery, self-conceit, boasting and the envious exaltation of one above the other? I firmly believe that it is not, and that the time is nigh. People laugh and ask when this time will begin and whether it is probable that it will begin. I, on the other hand, am of the opinion that with Christ we shall resolve this great matter. And how many ideas have there been upon earth, in human history, which only ten years earlier were unimaginable and which suddenly appeared when their mysteriously appointed season arrived, to go spreading all over the earth? So among us, too, shall it be, and our people shall shine like a light to the world, and all shall say: 'The stone which the builders rejected, the same is become the head stone of the corner.'* And the mockers shall themselves be asked: 'If what we have is a dream, then when will you build up your edifice and establish yourselves in truth and justice with your minds alone, without Christ?' And if they themselves declare that, on the contrary, they are moving towards unity, then verily this will be believed only by the most simple-hearted of them, so that one may even marvel at this simple-heartedness. Verily, they possess more dreamlike fantasy than we do. They think to establish themselves in truth and justice, but, having rejected Christ, they end by bathing the world in blood, for blood seeketh blood, and they that take the sword shall perish with it too.* And were it not for the covenant of Christ, they should destroy one another even unto the last two men upon the earth.* And in their pride those last two would not be able to stay each other's hands, but the last would slay the one before the last, and then himself as well. And this would be accomplished, were it not for the covenant of Christ, that for the sake of the meek and the humble those days shall be shortened.* In the time after my duel, when still I wore my officer's uniform, I began to talk about servants when I went into society, and I recall that everyone marvelled at me: 'What do you want us to do?' they said, 'sit our servants down on the sofa and bring them cups of tea?' And then I said to them in answer: 'Well, why not, if at least only on occasion?' Then they all laughed. Their question was a frivolous one, and my reply unclear, but I think that it contained a certain amount of truth.

(g) Concerning Prayer, Love and the Contiguity with Other Worlds

Young one, do not forget prayer. Each time in your prayer, if it be sincere, a new emotion will make itself fleetingly glimpsed, and in it a new thought with which you were previously unfamiliar and which will give you courage again; and you will realize that prayer is an education. Remember also: each day and whenever you are able, say to yourself over and over again: 'O Lord, have mercy on all those who have appeared before you this day.' For at each hour and each moment thousands of human beings forsake their life upon this earth and their souls present themselves before the Lord – and no one knows how many of them have parted from the earth in solitariness, in sadness and in the anguish that no one will regret their passing nor even knows anything of them at all: whether they have lived or not. And lo, from the other end of the earth, perhaps, your prayer for the repose of his soul will rise up to the Lord, even though you did not know that man at all, nor he you. How deeply affecting it is for his soul, at the moment it appears itself in terror before the Lord, to feel that for him too there is a supplicant, that there is still upon earth a human creature that loves him, too. And indeed God will look upon the two of you more kindly, for if you have had such compassion for that man, how much more will God, who is infinitely more merciful and loving than you, take compassion on you. And for your sake will he forgive him.

Brothers, do not be afraid of human sin, love man in his sin, also, for this likeness of Divine Love is indeed the summit of love upon earth. Love the whole of God's creation, both the whole and each grain of sand. Each leaf, each sunbeam of God, love it. Love the animals, love the plants, love every object. If you love each object you will also perceive the mystery of God that is in things. Once you have perceived it, you will begin untiringly to be more conscious of it with each day that passes. And at last you will love the whole world with an all-inclusive, universal love. Love the animals: God has given them the basis of thought and an untroubled joy. So do not disturb it, do not torment them, do not take away their joy, do not put yourself in opposition to God's intent. Man, exalt not yourself above the animals: they are sinless, and you in your grandeur fester the earth with your appearance on it and leave your festering footprints after you – alas, almost every one of us! Love young children especially, for they are also sinless as angels, and live in order to affect us with tender emotion, to purify our hearts, and as a certain indication to us. Woe unto the man who offendeth a babe. But Father Anfim taught me to love young children: he, sweet and silent in our wanderings, would take the half-copeck pieces we received as alms and buy them, the children, honey-cakes and fruit-drops, and distribute them among them: he could not pass children without a tremor of the soul: such is the man.

Before certain thoughts one stands in bewilderment, especially at the sight of human sin, and one asks oneself: 'Should I take it by force, or by humble love?' Always determine: 'I shall take it by humble love.' If thus you determine once and for all, you will be able to subdue the whole world. Loving humility is a terrible force, the most powerful of all, the like of which there is none. Each day and hour, each minute walk close to yourself and take care that your inward form is well-apportioned.* Perhaps you have walked past a little child, walked past him angry, with a foul remark, with a wrathful soul; it may be that you did not notice him, the child, but he saw you, and your inward form, unattractive and impious, may have remained within his unprotected little heart. You were not even aware of this, but by that very fact it may be that you have sown a bad seed in him, and it may grow, and all because you did not guard yourself in the presence of a young child, because you had not tutored in yourself a love circumspect and active. O brothers, love is an instructress, but one must know how to acquire her, for she is acquired with effort, purchased dearly, by long labour and over a long season, for it is not simply for a casual moment that one must love, but for the whole of the appointed season. After all, anyone is capable of loving casually, even the doer of evil. The youth who was my brother asked forgiveness of the birds; that might seem foolish, and yet it is true, for all is like an ocean, all flows and is contiguous, and if you touch it in one place it will reverberate at the other end of the world. Though it may be insanity to ask forgiveness of the birds, after all, both birds and child and indeed all animals around you would feel easier if you yourself were inwardly better-apportioned than you are now, even if they felt so only by a single drop. All is like an ocean, I say to you. Then you would start to pray to the birds, too, tormented by an all-inclusive love, as in some kind of ecstasy, and pray that they release you from your sin. Hold such ecstasy dear, however foolish it may seem to men.

My friends, ask God for gaiety. Be gay as children, as the birds of the sky. And let not human sin confound you in your deeds, do not be afraid that it will frustrate your task and not allow it to be accomplished, do not say: 'Strong is sin, strong is impiety, strong is the vicious world in which men live, and we are alone and helpless, that vicious world will frustrate us and not allow us to accomplish our good deeds.' Avoid, O children, this melancholy! There is but one salvation from it: take yourself and make yourself a respondent for all human sin. Friend, this is indeed truly so, for no sooner do you sincerely make yourself the respondent of all creatures and all things than you will immediately see that it is in reality thus and that it is you who are guilty for all creatures and all things. But by foisting your own laziness and helplessness on to other people, you will end by partaking of satanic pride and by murmuring against God. My view of satanic pride is like this: it is hard for us on earth to grasp it, but for this reason it is so easy to fall into error and to partake of it, while yet supposing we are doing something great and beautiful. And indeed while yet we are upon earth there are many of the most powerful emotions and movements of our nature that we cannot as yet grasp; do not be tempted by this and do not suppose that this may serve you as an excuse for anything, for the Eternal Judge will ask of you what you have been able to grasp and not what you have failed to — you yourself will be persuaded of this, for then you will behold things in their correct light and will argue no more. Verily, upon earth we are, in a manner of speaking, out wandering, and were it not for the precious image of Christ before us we should have perished and wandered astray for good, like the human race before the Flood. Much upon earth is concealed from us, but in recompense for that we have been gifted with a mysterious, sacred sense of our living connection with another world, with a celestial and higher world, and indeed the roots of our thoughts and emotions are not here, but in other worlds. That is why the philosophers say that it is impossible to grasp the essence of things upon earth. God took seeds from other worlds and sowed them upon this earth and cultivated his garden, and all that could come up, did so, but that which has grown lives and has its life only in the sense of its mysterious contiguity with other worlds, and if that sense weakens or is destroyed in you, then what has grown dies within you. Then you become indifferent to life and even conceive a hatred of it. Thus do I think.

(h) Is it Possible to be a Judge of One's Fellow Men? Of Faith Unto the End

Bear in mind particularly that you can be no man's judge. For a criminal can have no judge upon the earth until that judge himself has perceived that he is every bit as much a criminal as the man who stands before him, and that for the crime of the man who stands before him he himself may well be more guilty than anyone else. Only when he grasps this may he become a judge. However insane this sounds, it is true. For were I myself righteous, it is possible that there would be no criminal standing before me. If you are able to take upon yourself the crime of the man who stands before you and is judged by your heart, then lose no time, but do so and suffer for him yourself, while letting him go without reproach. And even if the law itself appoints you as his judge, then act even then to

the best of your ability in this same spirit, for he will go away and
condemn himself even more harshly than your judgement. But if with
your kiss he departs unfeeling and laughing at you, then do not be
tempted by this: it means that his season has not yet arrived, but it will
arrive in its own good time; and if it does not arrive, it matters not: if not
he, then another will do it instead of him, suffer, and condemn, and take
the blame upon himself, and the truth will be accomplished. Believe this,
believe it without doubt, for in this lies all hope and all the faith of the
saints.

Work untiringly. If you remember in the night as you retire to sleep:
'I have not done what was incumbent upon me,' then rise at once and do
it. If around you men are malicious and unfeeling and unwilling to listen
to you, then fall down before them and beg them for forgiveness, for
verily you are guilty of the fact that they do not want to listen to you.
And if you cannot speak to the malicious ones, then serve them silently
and in humility, without ever losing hope. If, on the other hand, all
forsake you and even drive you away with force, then, remaining alone,
fall to the earth and kiss her,* moisten her with your tears and the earth
will bear fruit of your tears, even though no one has seen or heard you in
your solitariness. Have faith unto the end, even though it should happen
that all upon earth are led astray and you are the only faithful one
remaining; even then make sacrifice and extol God — you, the only one
remaining. And if two such as you should meet, then there you have the
entire world, a world of living love, embrace one another in tender piety
and extol the Lord: for though it is only in the two of you, His truth has
none the less been replenished.

If you yourself should sin and be sorrowful, even unto death,* about
your sins, or about one inadvertently committed by you, then rejoice for
the other, rejoice for the righteous man, rejoice in the fact that even
though you may have sinned, he is none the less righteous and has not
sinned.

If on the other hand men's evil-doing should arouse you to indignation
and sorrow that is now not to be mastered and even amounts to a desire
for vengeance upon the evil-doers, then fear this emotion more than any
other; instantly go and seek for yourself such torments as though you
yourself had been guilty of that evil-doing of men. Accept those torments
and endure them, and your heart will be assuaged, and you will realize
that you yourself are guilty, for you might have brought light to the
evil-doers, as the only sinless one, and you did not shine. If you had
shone, then with your light you would have illumined the path for

others, too, and he that committed the evil deed might not have committed it in your light. And though you shine, but see that human beings are not saved even by that, stay resolute and do not doubt in the power of the heavenly light; have faith that even if they have not been saved now, they shall be saved hereafter. And if they are not saved even hereafter, then their sons will be saved, for your light shall not die, though you are now dead. The righteous man shall depart, but his light remains. Men are always saved after the death of the one who saves. The human race fails to accept its prophets and does them to death, but men love their martyrs and honour those whom they have martyred. You, on the other hand, must work for the sake of the whole, you must act for the sake of the future. Never seek any reward, for you already have a great reward upon this earth: your spiritual joy, which only the righteous man acquires. Be afraid neither of the highly placed nor of the strong, but be sage and always inwardly well-apportioned. Know the limit, know the seasons, learn these things. And remaining in solitariness, pray. Love to bow down to the earth and kiss her. Kiss the earth and untiringly, insatiably, love, love all creatures, love all things, seek this ecstasy and this frenzy. Moisten the earth with the tears of your joy and love those tears of yours. As for this frenzy, be not ashamed of it, cherish it, for it is the gift of God, a great gift that is vouchsafed not to the many, but to the chosen.

(i) Concerning Hell and the Fire of Hell, a Mystical Argument

Fathers and teachers, I think: 'What is hell?' I argue thus: 'The suffering of no longer being able to love.' Once, in infinite existence, immeasurable either by time or by space, a certain spiritual being was given, upon visiting the earth, the ability to say to itself: 'I am, and I love.' Once, only once, was it given a moment of love that was active, *alive*, and for the sake of that moment it was given earthly life, and with it the terms and the seasons, and what should befall: that happy being rejected the priceless gift, did not appreciate it, conceived no love for it, gave it a mocking glance and remained without feeling. Such a one, having already departed from the earth, saw Abraham's bosom, and spoke with Abraham, as it is related to us in the parable of Dives and Lazarus,* and contemplated paradise, and could ascend unto the Lord, but was tormented precisely by this, that if he ascended unto the Lord without having loved, those who had disdained love would attain contiguity with those who had loved. For he beheld clearly and said to himself: 'This day I have knowledge, and though I have conceived a thirst to love there will be no heroism in my love, no sacrifice, for earthly life is ended and Abraham will not bring me even a drop of living water (that is to say again, the gift of earthly life, the former and active) to cool the flame of thirst for spiritual love with which I am now afire, having disdained it upon earth; life does not exist now, and there shall be time no longer!* Even though I should be glad to give my life away for others, it is no longer possible, for that life has passed which could be sacrificed to love, and now between that life and this existence there is a great gulf fixed.' One hears talk of a hell-flame that is material: I shall not go into this mystery and do indeed fear to, but I think that if there were a material flame, then verily men would be glad of it, for, thus do I dream, at least for a second in this material torment their most terrible spiritual agony would be forgotten by them. And indeed, to remove this spiritual agony from them is impossible, for this torment is not an outward one, but is within them. And even were it possible to remove it, I think that then they would be even more bitterly unhappy. For though from paradise the righteous, contemplating their agonies, would forgive them and would summon them to them, loving them infinitely, by that very fact they would augment their sufferings even more, for they would quicken in them even more powerfully the flame of the thirst for an answering, active and grateful love, which was now impossible. In my heart of hearts I think, however, that the very cognizance of this impossibility would in the end serve to relieve them, for, having accepted the love of the righteous together with the impossibility of making requital for it, in this compliance and in the action of this humility, they will at last acquire a certain image of that active love which they disdained upon earth, and, as it were, a certain action that resembles it . . . I regret, my brothers and friends, that I am unable to say this clearly. But woe unto those who annihilate themselves while yet they are on the earth, woe to the suicides! I think there can be none more unhappy than these. It is a sin, we are informed, to say prayers for such as these, and outwardly the Church more or less rejects them, but in the secrecy of my heart I think that one might say a few prayers for them, too. After all, Christ will not be angered in the face of love. For such as these I have prayed inwardly all my life, I confess it to you, fathers and teachers, and even now I pray for them each day.

O, there are even in hell those who are proud and truculent, in spite of their undisputed knowledge and their contemplation of the irrefutable truth; there are those, frightening ones, who have communed with Satan and his proud spirit to the exclusion of all else. For them hell is already voluntary and insatiable; they are already willing martyrs. For in cursing God and life they have cursed themselves. They nourish themselves on their malicious pride like a hungry man in the wilderness who starts to suck the blood from his own body.* But they will be insatiable until the end of time and they will reject forgiveness; the God who calls them, they curse. They are unable to contemplate the living God without hatred and they demand that life shall have no God, that God shall destroy himself and all his creation. And they will burn in the fire of their anger eternally, thirsting for death and non-existence. But they shall not receive death . . .

Here the manuscript of Aleksey Fyodorovich Karamazov comes to an end. I say again: it is not complete and it is fragmentary. The biographical information, for example, goes up no further than to the Elder's early manhood. From his teachings and opinions there have been brought together as if into a unified whole things which he obviously said at different times and as a result of different promptings. Then again, all of what was spoken by the Elder during those last hours of his life is not defined exactly, and one is simply given an idea of the spirit and character of this discourse, if one compares it with what Aleksey Fyodorovich cites in his manuscript of earlier teachings. As for the death of the Elder, it took place, of a truth, quite unexpectedly. For though all those who gathered in his cell on that last evening were quite aware that his death was near, it was nevertheless impossible to imagine that it would ensue so suddenly; on the contrary, his friends, as I have observed above, seeing him that night so, it appeared, cheerful and eager to talk, were even persuaded that in his health there had occurred a notable improvement, if only for a little while. Even five minutes before his end, as was reported later on with wonder, nothing could have been predicted. He suddenly felt what must have been a most violent pain in his chest, turned pale and pressed his hands tightly to his heart. At that moment they all rose from their seats and rushed towards him; but he, though suffering, yet nevertheless gazing upon them with a smile, quietly lowered himself from his armchair to the floor and got to his knees, then bowed his face to the earth, spread wide his arms and, as if in joyful ecstasy, kissing the earth and praying (as he himself had taught), quietly and joyfully gave up his soul to God. The news of his death immediately passed round the hermitage and reached the monastery. Those who had been closest to the newly departed and those whose official duty it was, began to adorn his dead body according to ancient ritual, and all the brotherhood went off to assemble in the cathedral. And even before daybreak, as it was said later according to the rumours, the tidings of the newly departed reached the town. By morning practically the whole town was talking about the event, and many of its citizens poured into the monastery. But of this we shall speak in the book that follows, and for now we shall merely add in advance that before a day had passed there was accomplished something so unexpected to all, and if the impression it made in the surroundings of the monastery and in the town is anything to go by, so strange, alarming and disconcerting, that even now, after so many years, there is retained in our town the most lively memory of that day so alarming to many . . .

PART THREE

BOOK VII
ALYOSHA

I
*A Putrid Smell**

THE body of the sleeping* hieroschemonach Father Zosima was prepared for burial according to the established rite.* Dead monks and schemonachs are, as is well-known, not washed. 'When any of the monks departeth unto the Lord (it is written in the Great Book of Occasional Prayer), the enchargèd monk (that is, the one to whom this task has been appointed) spongeth his body with warm water, first describing with the *guba* (that is, the Greek sponge) a cross upon the forehead of the departed, upon his fingers, arms, feet and knees, but more than that naught.' All this was performed over the one who had fallen asleep by Father Paisy himself. After the sponging he dressed him in monkish attire and wound him round with a robe; to which end, according to statute, he slit it somewhat, in order to make the winding follow the shape of a cross. On his head he put a cuculus* with an eight-pointed cross. The cuculus was left open, while the sleeper's countenance was covered by a black aer.* In his hands was placed an icon of the Saviour. In such aspect towards morning was he transferred to his coffin (prepared already long before). It was, however, determined that the coffin be left in the cell (in the first large room, the same in which the departed Elder had used to receive brethren and seculars). As the sleeper was by rank a hieroschemonach, the hieromonachs and hierodeacons were to read over him not the Psalter but the Gospel. Immediately after the *panikhida** the reading was begun by Father Iosif; Father Paisy, who intended in the time that followed to read all day and all night, was as yet still very busy and preoccupied, together with the Father Superior of the hermitage, for there had suddenly begun to manifest itself, the more powerfully with each moment that passed, both among the monastery's brethren and among the seculars who had arrived from the monastery hotels and from the town in throngs, an unheard-of and even 'unseemly' excitement and impatient expectation.

Both the Father Superior and Father Paisy applied all their efforts to the calming of so frivolously excited a multitude. When it was sufficiently light there even began to arrive from the town some who had brought with them their sick, especially the children – as though they had been awaiting just this moment, evidently trusting in the instant power of healing* which, it was their belief, could not be long in manifesting itself. And now only was revealed the extent to which we all of us had become accustomed to view the now-sleeping Elder in his lifetime as a great and indubitable saint. For among the arrivals there were those who could in no way be considered simple plebeians. This great expectation of the faithful, so hastily and nakedly displayed with positive impatience, well-nigh insistence, even, struck Father Paisy as an unquestionable temptation,* one which, though it had been sensed by him long in advance, now verily exceeded his anticipation. Upon encountering the more agitated of the brethren, Father Paisy even began to reprimand them: 'Such instant expectation of something great,' he would say, 'is a frivolity, permissible only among the secular, and unseemly in ourselves.' But he was paid scant heed, and Father Paisy took note of this with concern, in spite of the fact that even he himself (if all be recollected truthfully), though he had been indignant at the overly impatient expectations, discerning in them frivolity and vanity, secretly to himself, in the depths of his soul, had been awaiting almost the same thing as these excited ones, a circumstance he could not but own up to himself was so. Certain encounters were none the less particularly galling to him, awakening in him as they did, by virtue of a certain presentiment, formidable doubts. Among the throng that pressed within the sleeper's cell he noted with a sense of inward repugnance (for which he at once upbraided himself) the presence of Rakitin, for example, or that far-travelled guest the brother from Obdorsk, who was still in the monastery, and both of them Father Paisy suddenly considered suspicious – though they were not the only ones who might have been noted in that sense. Of all the agitated monks, the brother from Obdorsk stood out as the greatest fusser and bustler; he could be observed universally, in every place; everywhere he made inquiries, everywhere he lent an ear, everywhere he whispered with a kind of special, mysterious air. As for the expression on his face, it was most impatient and seemed almost irritated that the expected event was taking such a long time to be accomplished. And when it came to Rakitin, then he, as it proved subsequently, had gone to the hermitage so early at the especial behest of Mrs Khokhlakova. That good-natured but spineless woman, who herself could not be admitted to the hermitage, no sooner had she woken up and learned of the one who had passed away, was suddenly inspired with such headlong curiosity that she had instantly dispatched Rakitin to the hermitage in her place, that the latter might observe everything and at once report to her by letter, approximately each half-hour, *all that took place*. As for Rakitin himself, she considered him the most devout and religious of young men – to such a degree was he able to manage everyone and present himself to each according to the other's desire, if he perceived even the least advantage to himself. The day was bright and cloudless, and many of the pilgrims who had arrived were crowding around the hermitage's tombs, which were most heavily concentrated around the church, as well as being scattered about the entire hermitage. As he wandered about the grounds, Father Paisy suddenly remembered Alyosha and the fact that it was a long time since he had seen him, since the previous night almost. And no sooner had he remembered him than at once he spotted him in the most remote corner of the hermitage, by the enclosure, sitting on the tombstone of a certain monk who had long lain there and had been famed for his great acts of pious heroism. He sat with his back to the hermitage, his face to the enclosure and seemed almost to be hiding behind the monument. Going right up to him, Father Paisy saw that, covering his face with both hands, he was silently but bitterly weeping, his whole body quaking with sobs. Father Paisy stood over him for a while.

'Enough, O dear son, enough, friend,' he pronounced at last with emotion. 'What is the meaning of this? You must rejoice, not weep. Or are you unaware that this day is the greatest of *his* days? Where is he now, at this moment, just remember that!'

Alyosha took a quick glance at him, uncovering his face which was swollen with tears, like that of a small boy, but at once, without getting a word out, turned away and again covered his features with both hands.

'Perhaps it is best so,' Father Paisy pronounced reflectively. 'Perhaps it is best that you weep, for Christ has sent you these tears.

'Those sweet, affecting tears of yours are but a rest unto your soul and will serve to restore gaiety to your dear heart,' he added, to himself now, as he walked away from Alyosha and thought about him lovingly. As a matter of fact, he walked away rather quickly, for he felt that at the sight of him even he might begin to weep. Meanwhile time passed, and the monastery services and requiems for the sleeper continued in proper order. Father Paisy again took the place of Father Iosif by the coffin and again took over the reading of the Gospel from him. But before three o'clock in the afternoon had passed there befell something of which I made mention at the end of the previous book, something so unexpected by any one of us and so contrary to the universal hope that, I repeat, a detailed and vain narrative concerning this event is still called to mind in our town and in all the surrounding neighbourhood with exceptional vividness even to this very day. Here let me add once more my own personal comment: the recollection of this vain and tempting event, in essence the most trivial and natural, fills me almost with repugnance, and it goes without saying that I should have omitted it from my tale altogether without mention, had it not in a most powerful and proverbial manner influenced the heart and the soul of the principal, *though also future*, hero of my tale, Alyosha, constituting within his soul a kind of turning-point and indeed an overturn that shook but definitively fortified his reason, guiding it throughout the rest of his life in the direction of a certain goal.

And so, to the tale. When still before dawn the body of the Elder, now prepared for burial, was placed within the coffin and borne out into the first room, in which formerly guests had been received, there arose among those tending the coffin the question: should the windows of the room be opened? But this question, uttered by someone fleetingly and in passing, remained without answer and almost unnoticed — and indeed, the only ones who noticed it, and then only to themselves, were a few of those present who reflected that to expect putrefaction and a putrid smell from the body of such a sleeper was a truly preposterous notion, worthy even of pity (if not mocking irony) with regard to the frivolousness and lack of faith of anyone who could deliver himself of this question. For quite the opposite was expected. And then soon after midday there began something which was at first perceived by those who came and went only in silence and to themselves and even with the evident fear of each of betraying to anyone his incipient thought, but which by three o'clock in the afternoon had manifested itself so clearly and incontrovertibly that in the twinkling of an eye the tidings of it flashed around the entire hermit-age and the entire assembly of pilgrims and visitors thereto, instantly found its way into the monastery, plunging into wonderment the entire corpus of monastics, and, at length, within the most inconsiderable space of time, also attained the town, where it perturbed every one of its inhabitants, believers and unbelievers alike. The unbelievers rejoiced, and when it came to the believers, some there were who rejoiced even more than the unbelievers, for 'men like to see the fall of a righteous man and

to witness his disgrace', as the departed Elder had himself given utterance
in one of his lessons. The fact was that there had begun to issue from the
coffin, little by little, but more noticeably with every hour that passed, a
putrid smell which by three o'clock had manifested itself all too distinctly
and was still by degrees becoming more intense. And long it was, and
hardly could there be recalled a time in all the past life of our monastery
since there had been a temptation so coarsely unbridled and in any other
instance even scandalous, such as displayed itself immediately after this
event among the very monks themselves. Subsequently, and even after
many years, certain level-headed of our monks, remembering all that day
in detail, marvelled and experienced horror as they wondered in what
manner the temptation could have attained such a degree at the time. For
even before this there had on occasion died monks who had led most
righteous lives, fearless Elders whose righteousness had been plain for all
to see, and from whose meek coffins had issued a putrid smell, appearing
naturally, as from all corpses, but this had produced no temptation, nor
even the slightest commotion. There had, of course, been in our monastery too certain monks of old who had passed away, whose memory was
still freshly retained within the monastery and whose remains, according
to legend, had not manifested putrefaction, a circumstance that had an
affecting and mysterious influence upon the brotherhood and was retained
within its memory as something spiritually well-apportioned and miraculous, a kind of covenant that in the future even greater glory would issue
from their sepulchres, if only by the will of God its time should come.
Of such brethren there was particularly retained the memory of the Elder
Iov, or Job, a renowned *podvizhnik*, great faster and observer of the vow
of silence who had lived to the age of a hundred and five, had passed
away long ago, back in the second decade of the present century, and
whose tomb was shown with especial and extreme veneration to every
pilgrim immediately upon his arrival, mysterious allusion being made the
while to certain great hopes and expectations. (This was the same tomb
upon which Father Paisy had found Alyosha sitting that morning.) In
addition to this long-recumbent Elder, there was freshly retained a similar
memory of a great Father Hieroschemonach who had died comparatively
recently, the Elder Varsonofy – the same from whom Father Zosima had
taken the Elderhood and whom, while he had been alive, all the pilgrims
who came to the monastery had considered an outright holy fool. Concerning both of these, legend recorded that they had lain in their coffins like
living men, had been buried quite unputrefied, and that even their countenances had seemed filled with radiance in the tomb. And some even

insisted on remembering that from their bodies had come a distinct and palpable fragrance. But even in spite of these memories so imposing, it would have been hard to explain the direct cause as a result of which there could at the coffin of the Elder Zosima have occurred such a frivolous, preposterous and malicious phenomenon. As for my own personal opinion, I believe that here much else was at work, a simultaneous conflux of many different causes exerting their influence at the same time. One of these, for example, was even that same old ingrained hostility to the Elderhood as being a harmful innovation, a hostility still deeply rooted in the minds of many brethren in the cloister. And then, of course, principally, there was a sense of envy for the sleeper's holiness so powerfully established in his lifetime that even to contest it seemed forbidden. For although the departed Elder had drawn many to his side, and not so much by miracles as by love, and had erected around him almost an entire world of those who loved him, he had nevertheless and even perhaps because of this brought into being those who envied him, and in the time that followed also bitter enemies, both open and concealed, and not among the monastics only, but even among the secular. Never, for example, had he done anyone any harm, but one would hear the question: 'Why is he considered so holy?' And this one question, repeated by degrees, at last engendered a veritable abyss of the most insatiable malice. That is why I also consider that many, having smelt the putrid smell that came from his body, and so soon — for not a day had passed since his death — felt boundless glee; in the same way as among those loyal to the Elder who had hitherto revered him there at once appeared those who very nearly felt a sense of outrage and personal insult at this event. As for the graduality of the affair, it proceeded in the following manner.

No sooner had the putrefaction begun to manifest itself than one could conclude from the mere aspect of the monks who entered the sleeper's cell the reason for their arrival. One would come in, stand there for a short time and go out again in order to repeat the news to the others, who would be waiting outside in a crowd, as quickly as possible. Some of those who were waiting would shake their heads dolefully, but others did not even try to conceal their glee, which shone openly in their malice-filled eyes. And no one bothered to reproach them any more, no one put in a good word, which was positively strange, as the Elder's devoted followers were after all in the majority within the cloister; but it seemed that on this occasion the Lord Himself had permitted the minority temporarily to gain the upper hand. It was not long before secular persons, too, began to appear in the cell in the same role of spy, mostly from among those visitors who had progressive education. As for the simple common folk, they entered in meagre numbers, though many of them had gathered in a throng outside the hermitage gates. There is, however, no doubt that as soon as three o'clock had passed the flood of secular visitors markedly increased, and precisely as a consequence of the tempting news. Those who might possibly not have arrived that day at all and had no plans to arrive now made a special point of arriving, among them several persons of considerable rank. As a matter of fact, though, the rules of proper ceremony had not yet outwardly, at least, been infringed, and Father Paisy, firmly, and enunciating every syllable, with stern demeanour, continued to read the Gospel aloud as if he had not noticed what was taking place, though he had long observed that there was something unusual. Soon, however, voices began to reach even his ears, at first very quiet, but gradually acquiring firmness and assurance. 'Evidently God's judgement is not the same as man's!' Father Paisy suddenly heard. These words were uttered in advance of all by a certain secular person, one of our municipal functionaries, a man already well on in years and, so far as anyone knew, thoroughly devout, but who, in speaking out loud, was merely repeating what the monks had long been echoing in one another's ears. They had long been uttering that hope-bereft remark, and what made it even worse was that every time it was uttered, with almost each minute that passed, it betrayed a certain new and more intense degree of triumph. But soon even the rules of proper ceremony began to be infringed, and then it was as though they all felt somehow entitled to infringe them. 'And how can *that* have happened?' certain of the monks said, initially as though they deplored it. 'His body was not large, it was dry, and had grown fast to his bones, so where can the smell be coming from?' 'It can only mean that it is a sign from God,' others were quick to add, and their opinion was accepted at once and without demur, for again they pointed out that had the smell been a natural one, the kind that might come from any sleeping sinner, it would have issued more slowly, and not with such undisguised rapidity, at least after a day and a night had passed, but 'this one' had 'got ahead of nature', and so what was involved here was nothing other than God and His deliberate finger. It was a sign from Him. This opinion made an irresistible impression. The meek Father Hieromonach Iosif, the bibliothecary, a favourite of the departed, began to retort to one or two of the scandal-mongers that it was 'not universally the case' and that in Orthodoxy this required non-putrefaction of the bodies of the righteous was by no means any sort of dogma, but merely an opinion, and that even in the most Orthodox parts of the world, on Mount Athos, for example, the putrid smell of a corpse gave rise to less embarrassment, and that there it was not non-putrefaction that was considered the principal indicator of the glorification of the saved, but the colour of their bones, after their bodies had lain in the ground many years and had even decomposed in it entirely, 'and if the bones be yellow as wax, then this is a most principal sign that the Lord has glorified the sleeping righteous; but if they be not yellow, but rather black, this signifies that the Lord deemed not the sleeper worthy of His glory – that is how it is on Mount Athos, that great and holy place, where Orthodoxy has been preserved from ancient times inviolable and in the most radiant purity,' Father Iosif concluded. But the words of the meek father floated by without making any impression and even provoked a mocking rebuff: 'That is all dry erudition and novelty for novelty's sake, there is no point in listening to it,' the monks decided to themselves. 'We view things in the old way; there is no shortage of new-fangled ideas at present – are we to imitate them all?' others added. 'Our monastery has had as many holy fathers as theirs. They sit down there under the Turks and have forgotten everything. Their Orthodoxy has long ago become muddy, and they don't even have any bells,' the most mocking of the brethren rejoined. Father Iosif went away in sorrow, all the more so since he had uttered his opinion rather irresolutely, as though he himself had little faith in it. But he foresaw with embarrassment that something very unseemly was beginning and that even disobedience was rearing its ugly head. Little by little, following Father Iosif, all the voices of reason were stilled. And somehow it befell that all those who had loved the departed Elder and had accepted the establishment of the Elderhood with pious and tender obedience suddenly seemed terribly afraid of something and upon encountering one another would merely glance timidly at one another's faces. As for those who were hostile to the Elderhood, viewing it as a dangerous novelty, they proudly held their heads high. 'Not only was there no bad smell from the body of the Elder Varsonofy, there oozed a fragrance from it,' they reminisced with malicious glee, 'and he earned it not by his Elderhood but because he himself was a righteous man.' And after that, a shower of condemnation and even accusation rained down upon the Elder newly passed away: 'He taught incorrectly; he taught that life is a great joy, and not a tearful humbling,' some, who belonged to the least intelligent of the brethren, said. 'His faith was of the fashionable kind, he refused to admit the existence of a material fire in hell,' others, who were even less intelligent, said. 'He did not take his fasting seriously, he permitted himself sweet things, mixed cherry preserves with his tea, he was very fond of them, the ladies used to send them to him. Shall a schemonach go drinking tea in company?' was heard from some envious ones. 'He had a swollen head,' the most gleefully malicious ones remembered with cruelty. 'He thought he was a saint, and if anyone went down on his knees before him he took it as his due.' 'He abused the sacrament of confession,' the most ferocious opponents of the Elderhood added in a malicious whisper, and these were of the oldest monks, the ones who took their pilgrimages and prayers to holy reliquaries most seriously, true fasters and observers of the vow of silence, who had said nothing during the sleeper's lifetime, but now suddenly opened their lips, which was a dreadful thing, for what they said had a powerful effect on the younger brethren and on those who had not yet become set in their ideas. One of the most attentive listeners was the guest from Obdorsk, the little monk from the monastery of St Sylvester, who kept sighing deeply and nodding his head. 'Yes, one can see, Father Ferapont was right in what he said yesterday,' he was thinking to himself, and then at that moment who should appear but Father Ferapont himself, coming out as though especially to aggravate the shock.

I have already made allusion to the fact that he emerged seldom from his small wooden cell behind the beehives, and did not even attend church for long periods of time, something to which everyone turned a blind eye, treating him as though he were a holy fool, and releasing him from the statutes incumbent upon the rest. Though if the truth be told, the real reason for this was a certain necessity. For it somehow seemed positively dishonourable that so great a faster and observer of the vow of silence, who prayed both by night and by day (he even slept on his knees), should be forever burdened with the common statutes if he himself were unwilling to submit to them. 'After all, he is more holy than any of us, and his observation of the faith is more rigorous than anything demanded by the statutes,' the monks would have said, 'and if he does not attend church that must mean that he himself knows when he must attend, he has his own statutes.' And so on account of these probable murmurs and temptations Father Ferapont was left undisturbed. The Elder Zosima, as everyone knew by now, was the object of an exceptional dislike on the part of Father Ferapont; and now to his little cell too had suddenly come the tidings that 'God's judgement is apparently not the same as man's', and that 'nature' had been 'got ahead of'. It may be assumed that one of the first to come running to him in order to convey the news was the guest from Obdorsk, who had visited him the day before and had gone away from him in a state of consternation. I also made allusion to the fact that Father Paisy, who stood, firm and resolute, reading aloud over the coffin, though he was unable to see or hear what was taking place outside the cell, had none the less flawlessly predicted most of it in his heart, for he knew his surroundings through and through. He was not embarrassed, but awaited all that might transpire without fear, tracing with a penetrating gaze the future outcome of the agitation which had already presented itself to his mental vision. Then suddenly an extraordinary crash, one that plainly now infringed all the rules of proper ceremony, struck his ears. The door had opened wide, and into view on the threshold came Father Ferapont. Behind him, down at the foot of the entrance porch, as could be perceived from the cell, and was even clearly visible from it, thronged a large number of monks who were accompanying him, with secular persons here and there in their midst. The accompaniers did not actually come inside, but remained at the foot of the porch; in doing so, however, they waited to observe what Father Ferapont would say or do, for in spite of all their boldness they sensed with a certain trepidation that he had not arrived without purpose. Pausing on the threshold, Father Ferapont uplifted his arms, from beneath the right one of which peeped out the keen and inquisitive little eyes of the guest from Obdorsk, who alone had been unable to restrain his impatience and had come running up the wooden steps after Father Ferapont, impelled by an overwhelming curiosity. But apart from him the others, no sooner had the door flown wide open with a crash, shrank even further back out of sudden trepidation. Raising his arms unto heaven, Father Ferapont suddenly howled:

'Exorcising shall I exorcise!',* and at once began, turning to all four quarters alternately, to make the sign of the Cross over all four corners of the cell with his hand. This action of Father Ferapont's was at once understood by those who had accompanied him; for they knew that wherever he made his entrance he invariably did this, and that he would not sit down or say a word until he had driven out the unclean force.

'Satan, go hence, Satan, go hence!' he repeated with each sign of the Cross. 'Exorcising shall I exorcise!' he howled again. He was in his coarse cassock, belted with a rope. From under his hempen shirt peeped his exposed chest, which was covered in grey hairs. His feet were completely bare. As soon as he began to wave his arms the cruel chains* he wore under his cassock began to shake and jangle. Father Paisy broke off his reading, came over to the door and stood before him in expectancy.

'Why have you come here, O honourable Father? Why do you infringe the rules of proper ceremony? Why do you disturb the gentle flock?' he said at last, looking sternly upon him.

'Wherefore I be i-cumen? Thou askest wherefore I be i-cumen? Dost thou believe?'* cried Father Ferapont, playing the holy fool for all he was worth. 'I have come hither in order to drive out the guests you have here, the filthy devils! I'm looking to see how many you've gathered while I've been away. I'm going to sweep them out with a birch besom, that's what I'm going to do.'

'You want to drive out the unclean one, but you may very well be serving him yourself,' Father Paisy continued without trepidation, 'and who can say of himself: "I am holy"? Surely not you, Father?'

'I'm filthy, not holy. I'm not going to sit down in a fine comfortable chair and have folk bow down to me like I were an idol!' Father Ferapont thundered. 'Nowadays people are destroying the holy creed. That departed Elder, that holy man of yours,' he said, turning to the throng and pointing to the coffin, 'rejected the devils. He used to give folk purgatives to keep the devils away. So now they've bred and multiplied among you like spiders in the corners. And even he himself has gone and stunk the place out. In this we see a great sign from the Lord.'

Now this was something that had actually taken place during the lifetime of Father Zosima. A certain one of the brethren had begun to dream, and ultimately to see waking visions of the unclean force. When in the greatest terror he had revealed this to the Elder, the latter had counselled him to observe ceaseless prayer and increased fasting. But when not even this had proved to be of any help, he had counselled him, while still maintaining his fasting and his prayers, to take a certain medicine. Many at the time had been tempted by this and had spoken of it among themselves, nodding their heads – most of all Father Ferapont, to whom a few of the revilers had instantly hurried in order to communicate to him this 'unusual' disposition of the Elder in so singular a case.

'Go hence, Father!' Father Paisy enunciated peremptorily. 'It is not for men to judge, but God. It may well be that we see here a "sign" of a kind which neither you, nor I, nor anyone is able to comprehend. Go hence, Father, and do not disturb the flock!' he repeated meaningfully.

'He didn't observe the fasts according to the rank of his habit, and that's why the sign has arrived. It's plain to see, and it's a sin to try to cover it up!' the wild zealot said, refusing to be quietened, and because of his fervour losing his self-control beyond all reason. 'He had a weakness for sweets, he did, the ladies used to bring them to him in their pockets, he indulged in tea-drinking, he made sacrifice to his belly, filling it with sweet things, and his mind with high-faluting thoughts . . . That is why he has suffered disgrace . . .'

'Frivolous are your words, O Father!' said Father Paisy, also raising his voice. 'I admire your fasting and your life of a *podvizhnik*, but frivolous are your words, which are like those of a youth in the secular world, inconstant and immature of mind. Go hence, O Father, I command you,' Father Paisy thundered in conclusion.

'All right then, I'll go hence!' said Father Ferapont, as though with a slight loss of countenance, but not abandoning his bitter tirade. 'You learned lot! Because you're so clever you have exalted yourselves above my insignificance. I couldn't hardly read nor write when first I trod hither, and in my time here I've forgotten what I did know, for the Lord God Himself has protected me, His little one, from your great wisdom . . .'

Father Paisy stood over him, waiting with firmness. Father Ferapont was silent for a moment and then suddenly, growing sad and putting his right hand to his cheek, pronounced in a voice that rose and fell lamentingly, while gazing at the coffin of the Elder:

'Tomorrow they will sing "The Helper and Protector" over him – a glorious canon, but over me, when I have breathed my last, all they will sing is "What Earthly Sweetness" – a little *stikhira*,'*[1] he said tearfully and with vexation. 'You have grown conceited and have exalted yourselves, empty is this place!' he howled suddenly like a madman, and, with a gesture of his arm, quickly turned away and quickly made his passage down the steps to the foot of the porch. The throng that was waiting below appeared to hesitate; some immediately departed in his wake, but others were slower to do so, for the entrance to the cell was still unbarred, and Father Paisy, who had followed Father Ferapont out on to the porch, stood there observing. But the old man with his loss of self-control had not yet quite finished: having gone some twenty yards, he suddenly turned towards the setting sun, uplifted both his arms and – as though someone had mown him down – toppled to the earth with a most formidable shriek:

1 During the carrying-out of the body (from the cell to the church and after the funeral service from the church to the cemetery) of a monk or schemonach the *stikhiry* 'What Earthly Sweetness . . .' are sung. If, on the other hand, the sleeper was a hieroschemonach, the canon 'The Helper and Protector . . .' is sung instead.

Dostoyevsky's Note.

'My Lord hath vanquished! Christ hath vanquished at the going-down of the sun!' he trumpeted violently, uplifting his arms to the sun, and, falling prone to the earth, began to sob out loud, like a small child, shaking all over with his tears and stretching out his arms across the ground. At that point they all rushed towards him, loud exclamations were heard, and answering sobs ... Some kind of frenzy had gripped them all.

'There is the holy one! There is the righteous one!' cries resounded, without trepidation now. 'There is the one who ought to be Elder,' others added with malice.

'He doesn't want to be an Elder ... He himself would refuse ... He doesn't want any part in all that accursed new-fangled business ... He doesn't want to imitate their tomfooleries,' other voices at once caught up, and it is difficult to imagine what it might have come to if at precisely that moment the bell had not begun to toll, summoning them to divine service. They all suddenly began to cross themselves. Father Ferapont, too, got up again and, protecting himself with the sign of the Cross, went back to his cell without looking round, continuing to exclaim all the while, though now something quite incoherent. Some monks trickled after him, but they were few in number, and the majority began to go their separate ways, hurrying to service. Father Paisy handed over the reading to Father Iosif and went down the steps. The frenzied shriekings of zealots could not make him waver, but his heart was suddenly saddened and anguished by something peculiar, and he felt this. He paused, and suddenly asked himself: 'Whence this sadness of mine, even unto loss of spirit?' – and with astonishment perceived at once that this sadness of his evidently proceeded from a most minor and particular cause: the fact was that among the other agitated brethren in the multitude that had been thronging just then outside the entrance to the cell, he had spotted Alyosha, and he remembered that, having caught sight of him, he had at once felt within his heart what almost amounted to a sensation of pain. 'Does that young fellow really mean so much to my heart now?' he suddenly inquired of himself with wonderment. And then just at that moment Alyosha walked past him, as though he were hurrying off somewhere, but not in the direction of the church. Their gazes met. Alyosha quickly averted his eyes, looking down at the ground, and from his appearance alone Father Paisy surmised what a powerful alteration was occurring within him at that moment.

'Or have you also succumbed to temptation?' Father Paisy suddenly exclaimed. 'Are you really one of the sceptics, too?' he added sorrowfully.

Alyosha paused and gave Father Paisy an indeterminate glance, but then quickly averted his eyes again and again looked down at the ground. He stood, moreover, sideways and did not turn to face his questioner. Father Paisy observed him attentively.

'Where are you hurrying off to?' he asked again. 'They are ringing the church bells for the service.' But Alyosha again made no reply.

'You're not leaving the hermitage, are you? Without asking permission, and without taking blessing?'

Alyosha suddenly gave a crooked smile, looked up very strangely at the inquiring father, the one to whom he had been entrusted by his former guide, the former lord of his heart and intellect, his beloved Elder, as the latter had lain dying, and suddenly, still as before without answer, but with a wave of his arm, as though he had not even any concern for proper deference, with swift steps walked towards the exit gates and out of the hermitage.

'You will be back again!' Father Paisy whispered, watching him go in sorrowful surprise.

2

The Right Moment

FATHER Paisy had, of course, not been mistaken in deciding that his 'dear boy' would be back again, and had even possibly (if not completely, then at least with a certain intuitive perspicacity) divined in its true significance the mood of Alyosha's soul. None the less, I openly admit that I myself should find it difficult now to convey clearly the exact significance of this strange and ill-determined moment in the life of my so beloved and still so youthful hero. To the sorrowful question directed by Father Paisy at Alyosha: 'Or are you one of the sceptics, too?' I could, of course, reply for Alyosha with firmness: 'No, he is not.' Not only that, but what was at work here was something quite the opposite: all his embarrassment proceeded from the circumstance that his faith was so strong. But embarrassment there was, it proceeded none the less, and was so tormenting that even subsequently, long after, Alyosha considered this sorrowful day one of the most distressing and fateful of his life. Were I, on the other hand, to be asked directly: 'Did all this anguish and unease proceed in him solely because the body of his Elder, instead of at once beginning to exert a healing influence, became subject, on the contrary, to an early putrefaction?', I should answer straight away: 'Yes, it really was so.' I would merely ask the reader not to be too hasty in laughing at my youth's pure heart. Not only do I myself not intend to ask forgiveness for him or to excuse and justify his simple faith on the grounds of his youthful age, for example, or his lack of advancement in the studies he had undertaken hitherto, etcetera, etcetera, but shall even do the opposite, and firmly declare that I feel a sincere respect for the nature of his heart. Without doubt, another youth, one who greeted the heart's impressions cautiously, already knowing how to love not with heat, but only warmth, with a mind which though sure was too reasonable for his age (and therefore too cheap), such a youth, I say, would have steered clear of what happened to my youth, but in certain instances it is, undeniably, more worthy of respect to give oneself up to an enthusiasm, even though it be an irrational one, which none the less proceeds from a great love, than not to give oneself up to it at all. And in one's young years all the more so, for a youth who is always reasonable is not to be relied upon and too cheap is his price – that is my opinion! 'Ah yes, but!' people of discretion will exclaim, perhaps, 'it is impossible for every youth to believe in a prejudice of that kind, and your youth is no rule for the others to follow.' To that I will reply again: 'Yes, my youth believed, believed sacredly and inviolably, but even so I shall not ask forgiveness for him.'

You see: though I announced above (and, possibly, in too much haste) that I did not intend to explain myself, excuse myself or justify my hero, I perceive that it is none the less incumbent upon me to clarify one or two things in order that the further development of the tale be understood. This is what I will say: miracles are not involved here. There was no expectation here of miracles, frivolous in its impatience. And not for the triumph of any convictions did Alyosha require miracles at the time (of that there was none whatsoever), nor for the sake of some previously acquired, preconceived idea, which might quickly have triumphed over another – oh no, not at all: in all this, before anything else, first and foremost, there stood before him a person, alone and no other – the person of his beloved Elder, of the righteous one whom he had revered to the point of worship. The fact was that all the love for 'all creatures and all things' which had concealed itself within his pure, young heart, both at that time and throughout the whole preceding year, seemed to have focused itself entirely, and possibly incorrectly, on one being alone, in the most powerful transports of his heart, at any rate – on his beloved Elder, now departed. To be sure, so long had this being stood before him as an unquestioned ideal that all his youthful energies and all their striving could not fail to be directed exclusively towards that ideal, and at moments even to the point where he forgot 'all creatures and all things'. (He himself remembered subsequently that upon that grief-laden day he had completely forgotten about brother Dmitry, concerning whom the day before he had experienced such anguish and concern; he had also forgotten to take Ilyushechka's father the two hundred roubles, a thing he had also passionately determined to do the day before.) But there again, it was not miracles he required but merely 'higher justice' which had, according to his lights, been infringed and by which so cruelly and suddenly his heart had been wounded. And what of it if that 'justice' had, in Alyosha's expectations, by the very course events had taken, assumed the form of miracles that might be imminently anticipated from the earthly remains of his former worshipped guide and leader? After all, everyone in the monastery had thoughts and expectations of that kind, even those before whose intellect Alyosha bowed, Father Paisy himself, for example, and so Alyosha, not troubling himself with any doubts, moulded his dreams too in the same form as that which all the others did. In any case, this had already been established in his heart by a whole year of monastery life, and his heart had already acquired a habit of such expectation. But justice did he thirst for, justice, and not simply miracles! And now here was the one who should have been, according to his hopes, exalted higher than anyone else in the whole world – here was that same one, instead of being crowned with the glory that befitted him, suddenly overthrown and disgraced! For what? Who had passed judgement on him? Who was capable of being such an arbiter? These were the questions that instantly exhausted his untried, virgin heart. He could not without a sense of personal outrage, of embittered and deep-seated animosity, even, face the fact that the most righteous of righteous ones had been delivered up to the mocking and malicious jeers of such a frivolous multitude, so clearly his inferiors. Nay, had there been no miracles at all, had there been manifested nothing miraculous nor any of the expectations been fulfilled, that he could have tolerated – but why had there come into being this defamation, this disgrace, this swift putrefaction which had 'got ahead of nature', as the more malicious of the brethren liked to say? Why this 'sign', which they were now in the process of interpreting together with Father Ferapont, and whence did they even derive the right to so interpret it? For where was Providence and its finger? Why had it concealed its finger 'at the most essential moment' (so Alyosha thought), almost as if it itself wished to subordinate itself to blind, dumb and merciless natural laws?

This was the reason why Alyosha's heart so oozed with blood, and then of course, as I have already said, there stood before him now the person whom he loved more than all in the world, and yet that person had been 'disgraced', had been 'defamed'! Well may it be that this grumble of my youth was a frivolous and unreflecting one, but again, for a third time, I repeat (and concede in advance that I also may be frivolous in doing so): I am glad that my youth did not prove himself so very reasonable at such a moment, for reason will always have its day in a man who is not stupid, and if at such an exceptional moment no love appears in the heart of a youth, then when will it ever arrive? I do not intend, however, to pass over in silence on this occasion a certain other strange phenomenon, which though only momentarily, none the less manifested itself within his mind at this fateful and confusing moment for Alyosha. This newly manifested phenomenon and fleeting *something* consisted of a certain tormenting mental image of the conversation, now untiringly recalled by him, he had had the day before with brother Ivan. Oh, it was not that there had within his soul been shaken any of the basic, spontaneous, as it were, religious beliefs. With regard to his God, he loved Him and believed in Him unshakeably, even though he had suddenly begun to grumble against Him. All the same, however, a kind of clouded, but tormenting and malicious, image retained from the memory of yesterday's conversation with brother Ivan now suddenly began to stir again within his soul, begging with ever-increasing intensity to emerge upon its surface. When darkness had begun to fall in earnest, Rakitin, who had been walking through the pine woods from the hermitage to the monastery suddenly spotted Alyosha, who was lying under a tree with his face to the ground, motionless and as if he were asleep. Rakitin went over to him and called his name.

'What, is it you, Aleksey? I say, have you really . . .' he began to get out, astonished, but stopped without finishing his sentence. He had intended to say: 'Have you really *come to this*?' Alyosha did not give him a glance, but by a certain movement he made Rakitin at once realized that he could hear and understand.

'But what is wrong with you?' he continued in astonishment, but it was an astonishment that had begun to yield upon his features to a smile that acquired an ever more mocking expression.

'Listen, I mean, I've been looking for you for more than two hours now. You suddenly vanished from over there. But what are you doing here? What holy nonsense are you up to now? I say, you might at least look at me . . .'

Alyosha lifted his head and sat up, leaning his back against the tree. He was not crying, but his features displayed suffering, and irritation was visible in his gaze. He was looking, though, not at Rakitin, but somewhere to the side.

'You know, your face has completely changed. There's none of that notorious meekness of yours in it that there usually is. Have you lost your temper with someone, eh? Has someone offended you?'

'Oh, give it a rest, will you?' Alyosha got out suddenly, still as before looking past him and making a weary gesture with his arm.

'Aha, so that's the way we are! We've started to raise our voice just like other mortals! And from one who used to be an angel, too! Well, my dear Alyosha, you have astonished me, do you know that? I speak in all sincerity. It's a long time since anything astonished me in this place. I mean to say, I always thought you were a man of progressive education . . .'

At last Alyosha looked at him, but somehow distractedly, as though he were still taking in little of what Rakitin said.

'Is all this really just because your old fellow's gone and stunk the place out? Did you really seriously believe that he'd start pulling off miracles?' Rakitin exclaimed, once more passing into a state of the most sincere amazement.

'I believed, I believe, and I intend to go on believing, so what more do you want?' Alyosha trumpeted irritably.

'Nothing, dear chap, nothing whatsoever. Ugh, the devil, why, not even a thirteen-year-old schoolboy would believe that nowadays. But anyway, the devil . . . So you've gone and got angry at your God now, have you, you've gone and mutinied against him; he's passed your Elder over for promotion, hasn't given him a medal for the big day! Oh, you poor sod!'

Alyosha looked at Rakitin for a long time, his eyes screwed up in a peculiar kind of way, and in his eyes something suddenly sparked . . . but it was not animosity towards Rakitin.

'I'm not mutinying against my God, I simply "do not accept his world"', Alyosha said suddenly with a crooked and ironic smile.

'What do you mean, you don't accept his world?' Rakitin said, having reflected the merest iota on his reply. 'What balderdash is this?'

Alyosha made no reply.

'Well that's enough nonsense, now let's get down to business: have you eaten anything today?'

'I can't remember . . . Yes, I think so.'

'Judging by the way you look, I'd say you need to fortify your energies. I mean to say, one feels sorry for you just at the sight of you. Why, you didn't even get any sleep last night, I heard, you had a meeting there. And then all that fussing and mussing afterwards ... I bet all you had to chew was a bit of the Antidoron.* I've got a piece of sausage in my pocket, I took it along with me from the town today just in case, when I was setting off for here, only I have a feeling sausage is something you won't ...'

'Let me have some sausage.'

'Aha! So that's the way you are! So it's a real mutiny, with barricades and all. Well, brother, we can't let slip a chance like this. Come on, let's go to my place ... I wouldn't mind downing a drop or two of vodka there, I'm dead beat. I suppose you wouldn't agree to having some vodka ... or would you?'

'Let me have vodka, too.'

'There we are! Wonderful, brother!' Rakitin said, his eyes staring wildly. 'Well, whether it's the one or the other, vodka or sausage, this is an incredible, fantastic opportunity, and we're not going to miss it for the world. Come on!'

Without saying anything, Alyosha got up off the ground and set off after Rakitin.

'If that brother Vanechka of yours could see this, how he'd be amazed! Oh, incidentally, your fine brother Ivan Fyodorovich went rolling off to Moscow this morning, did you know that?'

'Yes, I know,' Alyosha mouthed indifferently, and suddenly there fleeted through his mind the image of his brother Dmitry, but it was only a fleeting image, and though it reminded him of something, some urgent matter which would not brook an instant's delay, some kind of duty or fearsome obligation, this memory had no effect on him, did not attain his heart, in that same split second flew out of his memory and was forgotten. But Alyosha remembered it long after.

'That fine brother of yours Vanechka once pronounced concerning me that I was an "ungifted liberal lump". And you yourself on one nice little occasion also could not restrain yourself and gave me to understand that I was "dishonourable" ... So be it! Anyway, now I'm going to take a look at your giftedness and honourability' (Rakitin concluded to himself, in a whisper now). 'Oh, confound it, listen!' he said again, loudly. 'Let's avoid the monastery and follow this path straight to the town ... Hm. Actually, I ought to drop in and see Mrs Khokhlakova, too. Imagine: I wrote her a line or two about all that had happened and, just fancy, she replied to me instantly with a note, in pencil (that lady's inordinately fond of writing notes), in which she said that "never would I have expected from such a venerable Elder as Father Zosima *an action like that*!" She really did use that word: "action"! She also lost her temper, you see; oh, I don't know what to make of you all! Wait!' he exclaimed again, suddenly stood still and, catching hold of Alyosha by the shoulder, made him stand still too.

'You know, Alyosha, my lad,' he said looking inquisitively into his eyes, completely under the influence of a new thought which had suddenly illuminated him, and, though outwardly he was laughing, it was plain that he felt afraid to utter aloud this new, sudden thought of his, so little was he able to believe in this wondrous and totally unexpected mood in which he now beheld Alyosha. 'Alyosha, my lad, do you know where the best place for us to go now would be?' he got out at last, timidly and fawningly.

'It's all the same to me . . . wherever you like.'

'Then let's go and see Grushenka, shall we, eh? Will you come?' spake the good Rakitin, positively trembling all over with timid expectation.

'Yes, all right, let's,' Alyosha replied calmly and at once, and so unexpected was this to Rakitin, such swift and calm consent, that is to say, that he very nearly leapt out of his skin.

'W-well! . . . I never!' he began to exclaim in amazement, but then suddenly, firmly grasping Alyosha by the arm, quickly drew him off along the path, still dreadfully apprehensive that Alyosha might lose his determination. They walked in silence, for Rakitin was afraid even to open his mouth.

'And how pleased she'll be, how pleased she'll be,' he started to mutter, but again trailed away. For it was not at all for the sake of Grushenka's satisfaction that he was dragging Alyosha off to see her; he was a serious man and never undertook anything unless it held some advantageous purpose for himself. His purpose now was twofold: in the first instance, a vengeful one, that is to say, to see 'the disgrace of a righteous man' and Alyosha's probable 'fall' 'from saint to sinner', which he had already been savouring in advance, and in the second instance, he had in mind a certain material purpose, thoroughly advantageous to him, of which we shall speak in what follows.

'So the right moment has arrived,' he thought to himself gaily and full of malice. 'Very well, we shall grab it by the collar, this moment, for it couldn't have come at a better time.'

3
The Onion

GRUSHENKA lived in the most animated quarter of the town, near Cathedral Square, in the house of the merchant's widow Morozova, from whom she rented a small wooden outbuilding in the yard. Morozova's house, on the other hand, was large, constructed of stone, two-storeyed, old and very unprepossessing to the eye; in it, secluded from the world, lived the owner herself, an old woman, with her two nieces, who were also spinsters of most advanced years. She did not need to let her outbuilding in the yard, but it was common knowledge that she had admitted Grushenka as a tenant (some four years earlier) solely in order to gratify the wishes of a kinsman of hers, the merchant Samsonov, Grushenka's openly-avowed protector. It was said that the jealous old man, in accommodating his 'favourite' in the home of Morozova, had originally had in mind the old woman's vigilant eye, which might have been expected to keep a close watch on the behaviour of her new lodger. But the vigilant eye soon turned out to be unnecessary, and the upshot of it was that Morozova seldom even met Grushenka and in the end did not importune her with any surveillance whatsoever. To be sure, four years had now passed since the day the old man had brought from the provincial capital into this house an eighteen-year-old girl, timid, shy, thin, slender, broody and sad, and since that day much water had flowed under the bridge. The biography of this girl was unfamiliar to most people in our town, and what was known of it was inconsistent and confusing; more had not been discovered even of late, and this at a time when very many people had started to show an interest in the 'raving beauty' Agrafena Aleksandrovna had turned into over the space of four years. It was rumoured, though only rumoured, that as a mere child of seventeen she had been deceived by some officer or other, who had thereupon instantly abandoned her. The officer was supposed to have gone away and got married somewhere, while Grushenka had been left in poverty and disgrace. As a matter of fact, it was said that although Grushenka had indeed been rescued from poverty by her aged protector, she came of a decent family and apparently had her origins among the priesthood, being the daughter of some supernumerary deacon, or something of that kind. And lo, within the space of four years there had emerged from the sensitive, deceived and pathetic little orphan a rounded and rubicund

Russian beauty, a woman of bold and decisive character, proud and unblushing, who knew a thing or two about money, an acquirer, tight-fisted and careful, who by hook or by crook had already succeeded, as was said of her, in 'knocking together her own bit of capital'. Of one thing only were all convinced: that access to Grushenka was difficult and that, apart from her aged protector, there was not a man who in all those four years had yet been able to boast of her good graces. This was a firmly established fact, because to the acquisition of those good graces there had leapt forth a not inconsiderable number of volunteers, particularly during the past two months. But all attempts had proved to be in vain, and certain of the seekers had been compelled to beat a retreat in a manner that was even comic and shameful, thanks to a firm and mocking rebuff on the part of the spirited young lady. They also knew, in addition, that the young lady, particularly during the past year, had embarked upon what is called *gesheft*,* and that in this respect she had proved herself to have exceptional abilities, so that in the end many dubbed her a regular Jewess. Not that she ever lent money on interest, but it was known, for example, that as an associate of Fyodor Pavlovich Karamazov she really had for a time engaged in the buying-up of promissory notes for next to nothing, ten copecks to a rouble, subsequently receiving on certain of those promissory notes a rate of a rouble to ten copecks. The ill Samsonov, who in the course of the past year had lost the use of his swollen legs, a widower, the tyrant of his grown-up sons, a big-shot with hundreds of thousands tucked away, tight-fisted and implacable, had fallen, alas, under the powerful influence of his protégée, whom at first he had ruled with a rod of iron and had treated like dirt – 'on Lenten oil', as the scoffers used to say at the time. But Grushenka had succeeded in achieving her emancipation, not, however, without inspiring in him a limitless confidence regarding her fidelity. This old man, a smart dealer in the grand style (but now long since a corpse), was also of remarkable character, meaning principally that he was miserly and hard as flint, and though Grushenka had affected him deeply, so that he was unable to live without her (for the last two years, for example, this had been the case), he none the less did not allot her any large, significant amount of capital, and even had she threatened to abandon him altogether, even then would he have remained implacable. But he did, on the other hand, allot her a small amount of capital, and when this was discovered it, too, became a pretext of wonderment for everyone. 'You're a lass who knows what's what,' he told her as he allotted her some eight thousand roubles, 'so be the boss of your own show, but also be aware that, apart from your annual maintenance allowance which you will continue to draw as before, until my death you will receive nothing more from me, and not even in my will shall I allot you any more.' And indeed he kept his word: died and left everything to his sons, whom all his life he had kept around him more or less like servants, with their wives and children, and in his will he did not even mention Grushenka at all. All this later became known. On the other hand, with his advice on 'how to be the boss of one's own show with the aid of one's own capital', he helped Grushenka not a little and explained to her the workings of 'business'. When Fyodor Pavlovich Karamazov, who had originally come into contact with Grushenka in connection with a certain fortuitous piece of *gesheft*, ended quite unexpectedly to himself by falling blindly, even madly, in love with her, old Samsonov, who already had one foot in the grave, poked savage fun. It is worthy of note that throughout the entire period of their acquaintance Grushenka was completely and even cordially frank with her aged protector, and he, it appears, was the only person in the world to whom she accorded such treatment. Of very recent date, when Dmitry Fyodorovich, too, had suddenly appeared with his enamourment, the old man had stopped laughing. On the contrary, one day he earnestly and sternly counselled Grushenka: 'If you must choose between the two of them, the father and the son, then choose the father, but see to it that the old scoundrel marries you without fail and bequeaths you a decent sum of capital in advance. But don't hob-nob with that captain, there's no point in it.' Such were the actual words addressed to Grushenka by the old lecher, who already had a premonition that his death was near and did indeed, five months after delivering this advice, pass away. I shall additionally and cursorily observe that even though many people in our town knew about the preposterous and abnormal rivalry of the Karamazovs, father and son, the object of which was Grushenka, the true implications of her attitude to them both, the old man and his son, were understood by few at the time. Even Grushenka's two female servants (after the catastrophe, an account of which is yet to follow, had broken) subsequently testified in court that Dmitry Fyodorovich had been received by Grushenka out of sheer terror, because it appeared he had 'threatened to kill her'. Female servants she had two: one very aged, infirm and nearly deaf cook who dated from her family years at home, and the aged cook's granddaughter, a pert young girl of about twenty who was Grushenka's housemaid. But Grushenka lived very sparingly and in surroundings that were altogether modest. There were in her outbuilding only three rooms, which had been furnished by her landlady with ancient mahogany furniture in the style of the 1820s. When Rakitin and Alyosha went in to see her it was already deep twilight, but the rooms had not yet been lit. Grushenka herself lay in her sitting-room on her large, ungainly sofa with its back of red mahogany, hard and upholstered in leather that had long since worn away and gathered holes. Under her head she had the two white down pillows from her bed. She was lying supine, stretched out motionlessly, both arms placed together behind her head. She was dressed up, as though she were expecting someone, in a black silk dress and a thin lace *nakolka*,* which thoroughly suited her; over her shoulders was thrown a lace scarf that was pinned in place with a massive gold brooch. She was indeed waiting for someone, lay almost in anguish and impatience, her face slightly pale, with hot lips and eyes, as she tapped the tip of her right foot impatiently against the sofa's arm. No sooner did Rakitin and Alyosha appear than there occurred a minor commotion: from the hallway Grushenka could be heard quickly leaping up from the sofa and exclaiming in a frightened voice: 'Who is it?' But the visitors were met by the housemaid, who at once responded to her mistress:

'It's not him, miss, it's some others, they're all right.'

'What on earth's the matter with her?' Rakitin muttered, as he led Alyosha by the arm into the sitting-room. Grushenka stood by her sofa, apparently still in a state of fright. A thick strand of the dark chestnut braid in which her hair was set suddenly escaped from under the *nakolka* and fell on to her right shoulder, but she did not notice and did not set it right until she had given her visitors a close look, and saw who they were.

'Oh, it's you, Rakitka! What a fright you gave me. Who are you with? Who's this you've got with you? Merciful Lord, look who you've brought!' she exclaimed, having discerned Alyosha.

'Why don't you tell them to bring in some candles!' Rakitin said with the free and easy air of a most intimate acquaintance and close companion, who even had the right to give orders in the house.

'Candles . . . oh yes, of course, candles . . . Fenya, get him a candle . . . Well, you've picked a moment to bring him!' she exclaimed again, nodding at Alyosha, and, turning towards the mirror, quickly began to reset her braid. She did not seem exactly pleased.

'Done something wrong, have I?' asked Rakitin, in an instant almost taking offence.

'You gave me a fright, Rakitka, that's what,' Grushenka said, turning to Alyosha with a smile. 'Now don't you be afraid of me, Alyosha, my young dove, I'm fair delighted to see you, my unexpected guest. But Rakitka, you did give me a fright: for I mean, I thought Mitya had forced his way in. You see, I pulled the wool over his eyes a bit earlier and made him swear on his word of honour to believe me, but I told him lies. I told him I was going to see Kuzma Kuzmich, my old man, and that I was going to sit up counting money with him until late at night. I go to him every week you see, and we spend the whole evening doing the accounts. We lock the door: he clicks away on the abacus, and I sit entering it in the books – there's no one else he trusts. Mitya thinks I'm there, but I've shut myself up here at home – sitting here waiting for a message. How could Fenya have let you in? Fenya, Fenya! Run down to the front gate, open it and take a look round and see if the captain is anywhere about. He may be hiding and watching in secret, I'm terribly frightened!'

'There isn't anyone there, Agrafena Aleksandrovna, I went down and had a look round just now, and I go and look through the spyhole every minute, for I'm terrible a-feared myself!'

'Make sure the shutters are closed, Fenya, and the curtains ought to be drawn down – like this!' She herself drew down the heavy curtains. 'For if he sees a light he'll come rushing in. You see, Alyosha, I'm frightened of Mitya, that fine brother of yours, today.' Grushenka spoke loudly, and though she was anxious she seemed to be in a state that almost approached ecstasy.

'Why are you so afraid of Mitya today?' Rakitin wanted to know. 'You never seem shy with him, he dances to your pipe.'

'I tell you, I'm waiting for a message, a certain little golden message, that will make dear Mitya quite unnecessary now. And anyway, he didn't believe me when I told him I was going to see Kuzma Kuzmich, I can feel that. He's probably over there at home in the back of Fyodor Pavlovich's orchard, waiting to see if I'll come. And if he has settled down there that means he won't come here – so much the better. And yet I mean, I really did go down and see Kuzma Kuzmich, Mitya went with me, I told him I'd be there until midnight and that he was to come and take me home at midnight without fail. He left, I stayed at the old man's place for about ten minutes and then came back here again – oh, how frightened I was, I ran all the way in case I bumped into him.'

'And what have you got yourself all dressed up for like this? What's this curious thing you're wearing on your head?'

'You're the one who's curious, Rakitin! I tell you, I'm waiting for a certain little message. When it arrives I shall leap up and fly, and that's all you will see of me. That's why I'm all dressed up, so I shall be ready.'

'And where will you fly to?'

'Much knowledge soon makes one old.'

'I mean, just look at you. As pleased as the cat's whiskers . . . Never before have I seen you like this. You're all decked out as though you were off to a ball,' Rakitin said, looking her over.

'Much do you know of balls.'

'Oh, so you know much, do you?'

'I've seen a ball, too. The year before last Kuzma Kuzmich gave his son away in wedlock, and I watched from the gallery. And anyway, Rakitka, why should I stand here talking to you when a prince like this is here? A proper visitor, and no mistake! Alyosha, my young dove, I look at you and don't believe my eyes; merciful Lord, how ever have you popped up in my place? To tell you the truth, I never thought nor guessed I aught, nor would I ever have believed that you might come here. Even though now's not the right moment, I'm fair delighted to see you! Sit down on the sofa, here, look, that's right, my young moon. Truly, I can't get over it . . . Oh, Rakitka, if only you'd brought him yesterday or the day before! . . . But even so, I'm still delighted. Perhaps it's even better that it's now, at a moment like this, and not the day before yesterday . . .'

She sat down playfully on the sofa next to Alyosha, side by side with him, gazing at him with what could only be described as rapturous admiration. For she really was delighted, and had not been lying when she said this. Her eyes burned, her lips laughed, but did so with good-natured gaiety. Alyosha had not really expected her to have such a kindly expression on her face . . . Until yesterday he had met her hardly at all, had formed an intimidating notion of her, and had yesterday been so terribly shaken by the malicious and insidious trick she had played on Katerina Ivanovna and so very astonished that now he suddenly saw in her, as it were, a completely different and unexpected creature. And weighed down as he was by his own grief, his eyes none the less involuntarily paused on her with attention. All her manners seemed also to have changed since yesterday, altogether for the better: the sugary tone of her delivery was almost entirely absent now, as were those pampered and mannered movements . . . All was now simple, simple-souled, her movements were swift, direct, trustful, but she was very excited.

'Merciful Lord, such things are coming to pass today, to be sure,' she started to babble again. 'I don't even know why I am so delighted to see you, Alyosha. You may ask me, but I don't know.'

'Well, if you don't know, what are you delighted for?' Rakitin asked with an ironic smile. 'Before you were always going on at me: "bring him, bring him" — you must have had some aim in mind.'

'Oh, before I had a different aim, but that's all over now, this is not the right moment. I'm going to treat you to something nice, that's what I'm going to do. I'm in a better mood now, Rakitka. But sit down, Rakitka, why are you standing up? Oh, you've found a seat for yourself. Trust Rakitushka not to neglect himself. Look, Alyosha, there he is sitting opposite us, and he's taken offence, thinking why didn't I ask him to sit down first, before I asked you? Oh, he's so touchy, that Rakitka of mine, so touchy!' Grushenka laughed. 'Don't lose your temper, Rakitka, I'm in a good mood today. But why are you sitting there looking so mopey, Alyoshechka, are you frightened of me?' she asked, looking him in the eye with a merry, mocking laugh.

'He's miserable. There wasn't any promotion,' Rakitin said in a deep voice.

'What promotion?'

'His Elder developed a bad smell.'

'What do you mean, a bad smell? Spouting rubbish, that's what you are, trying to say something nasty. Be quiet, fool. Alyosha, let me sit on your knee, like this!' And suddenly, within the space of an instant, she leapt up and jumped, laughing, on to his knee like a small, affectionate she-cat, tenderly seizing him around the neck with her right arm. 'I'll cheer you up, my devout little boy! No, seriously, is it really all right if I sit on your knees like this, you won't get angry? If you tell me to, I shall jump off.'

Alyosha said nothing. He sat, afraid to move a muscle, he heard her words: 'If you tell me to, I shall jump off,' but did not reply, as though he had frozen. But there was in him nothing of that which might have been expected and which might have been imagined in him now, for example, by Rakitin, who was observing him carnivorously from where he sat. The great grief of his soul was swallowing all the sensations that might have been engendered within his heart, and had he been able in that moment to be fully aware of what was taking place, he himself would have realized that he was now by the strongest armour protected against any kind of seduction or temptation. Even so, in spite of all his confused unawareness of the state of his soul and of all the grief that was weighing him down, he still wondered at a certain new and strange sensation that was in the process of being born within his heart: this woman, this 'formidable' woman not only did not intimidate him now with the old fear, the fear that formerly had been engendered in him at any thought of womankind, had any such flickered within his soul, but, on the contrary, this woman, whom he had feared more than any, as she sat on his knees and embraced him, suddenly began to arouse in him a quite different, unexpected and peculiar emotion, a feeling of extraordinary, immense and most pure-hearted curiosity, and all this now without any fear, without the slightest trace of his former dread — that was what was foremost in his consciousness and what caused him an involuntary sense of surprise.

'That's enough of your nonsense, the two of you!' Rakitin exclaimed. 'Come on, Grushenka, why don't you pour us some champagne, it's your obligation, and you know it!'

'Indeed it is my obligation. You see, Alyosha, to crown it all I promised him champagne if he'd bring you here. Roll out the champagne, and I too will drink! Fenya, Fenya, bring us the champagne, that bottle that Mitya left, go on, quick, run and get it. And though I may have a tight fist, I shall give you the bottle — not you, Rakitin, you are a toadstool, but he is a prince! And though that is not what fills my soul at this hour, so let it be, I too will drink with you, I feel like a bit of debauchery!'

'But what's this you keep saying about a "moment", and what's the "message" you're waiting for, may one ask, or is that a secret?' Rakitin put in, trying with all his might to pretend that he did not notice the flicks and fillips that flew in his direction constantly.

'Oh, it's not a secret, and you yourself know only too well,' Grushenka suddenly said worriedly, turning her head towards Rakitin and leaning away a little from Alyosha, though she still continued to sit on his knees with her arm around his neck. 'The officer's coming, Rakitin, my officer's coming!'

'So I've heard, but is he really so close?'

'He's in Mokroye now, he's sending an estafette* here, he told me so in a letter I got earlier today. I'm sitting here waiting for the estafette.'

'You don't say! Why Mokroye?'

'It would take too long to tell you, and in any case you know enough.'

'I'd like to see Mitenka's face now — oh my! Does he know or not?'

'He doesn't know anything! Nothing at all! If he did, he'd kill me. But I'm not at all afraid of that now, I'm not afraid of his knife now. Be quiet, Rakitka, stop reminding me about Dmitry Fyodorovich: he's fairly brained my heart. In fact, I don't even want to think about that at this moment. Instead I can think about Alyoshechka, I shall look at Alyoshechka . . . I say, you might at least smile a bit at me, my young dove, cheer up, smile at stupid, happy old me . . . I say, he smiled, he smiled! Oh, what a nice look he's giving me. You know, Alyosha, I've kept thinking that you were angry with me about what happened the other day, at the lady's house. I behaved like a she-dog, that's what . . . Only it's just as well that it happened that way. It was both good and bad at the same time,' Grushenka smiled thinly and reflectively all of a sudden, and a small line of cruelty suddenly flickered in her smile. 'Mitya said that she shouted: "She ought to be whipped!" I really put her back up. She invited me there, she wanted to get the better of me, to seduce me with that chocolate of hers . . . Yes, it's just as well it happened like that,' she smiled again, thinly. 'But what I'm still afraid of is that you may be angry . . .'

'She's telling the truth, you know,' Rakitin put in suddenly with serious astonishment. 'You see, Alyosha, she really is afraid of you, a little chicken like you.'

'He may be a little chicken to you, Rakitka, but that's . . . because you've no conscience, that's what! You see, I love him with all my soul, I do, too! Do you believe me, Alyosha, do you believe that I love you with all my soul?'

'Oh, you shameless girl! Aleksey, this is a declaration of love she's making to you!'

'So what? I do love him.'

'And the officer? And the golden message from Mokroye?'

'That is one thing, but this is another.'

'A woman's reasoning, and no mistake!'

'Now don't you make me cross, Rakitka,' Grushenka said, hotly picking up the thread of the argument. 'That is one thing, but this is another. I love Alyosha differently. It's true, Alyosha, that I had a cunning plan for you before. You see, I'm base and I am wild, yet at certain moments I have looked on you as my conscience, Alyosha. I have thought: "My goodness, how a man like that must despise a woman like me." I thought that the other day, too, when I fled back here from the lady's house. I've noticed you for a long time like that, Alyosha, and Mitya knows it, too, I've talked to him about it. And Mitya understands what I mean. Would you believe it, Alyosha, but sometimes, truly, I look at you and feel ashamed, really ashamed of myself . . . But how it came to be that I began to think of you that way and when it started, I do not know and do not remember . . .'

Fenya entered the room and placed a tray on the table, containing an uncorked bottle and three glasses already poured.

'The champagne has arrived!' Rakitin exclaimed. 'Agrafena Aleksandrovna, you're all worked up, beside yourself. If you drink a glass you'll start dancing. A-ach! They couldn't even do this properly,' he added, examining the champagne. 'The old woman has poured it out in the kitchen, and the bottle has arrived without its cork, and the stuff's warm. Oh well, let's have it all the same.'

He approached the table, took a glass, drained it in one go and poured himself another.

'Champagne is something one doesn't come across every day,' he said, licking his lips. 'Right, now, Alyosha, take a glass, let's see what you're made of. What shall we drink to? The gates of paradise? Take a glass, Grusha, you too shall drink to the gates of paradise.'

'What gates of paradise are those?'

She took a glass. Alyosha took his, drank a mouthful, and put the glass back on the tray.

'No, I don't think I'd better!' he smiled quietly.

'But you boasted you would!' Rakitin exclaimed.

'Well if that's how it is, I shan't have any either,' Grushenka chimed in. 'Anyway, I don't feel like it. Rakitka, you can drink the whole bottle on your own. I'll only have some if Alyosha does.'

'The maudlin endearments have begun!' Rakitin said, teasing them. 'And she's sitting on his knees, too! He has, let us assume, a misfortune to contend with, but what have you? He has mutinied against his God, was on the point of wolfing sausage . . .'

'What did you say?'

'His Elder died today, the Elder Zosima, the holy man.'

'So the Elder Zosima has died!' Grushenka exclaimed. 'Merciful Lord, I did not know!' She crossed herself devoutly. 'Merciful Lord, oh, what am I doing, sitting on his knees at a time like this?' she said suddenly, jerking upright as in panic, and in an instant leapt from his knees and transferred herself to the sofa. Alyosha gave her a long look of astonishment and something in his face seemed to light up.

'Rakitin,' he said all of a sudden, loudly and firmly, 'do not tease me about mutinying against my God. I don't want to feel any rancour towards you, and so please try to be more kind. I have lost a treasure such as you have never possessed, and you cannot judge me now. You would do better to look over here, at her: did you see how she spared me? I came here in order to find an evil soul – that was why I was so drawn to come here, because I was feeling base and evil-tempered – and instead I found a sincere sister, I found a treasure, a loving soul . . . She spared me just now ... Agrafena Aleksandrovna, it is you I am talking about. You have just resurrected my soul.'

Alyosha's lips began to tremble and his breathing grew constricted. He stopped.

'Anyone would think she'd saved you!' Rakitin laughed, maliciously. 'And she was going to swallow you whole, do you realize that?'

'Wait, Rakitka!' Grushenka said, suddenly leaping up. 'Be quiet, the two of you. Now I shall say everything: you, Alyosha, be quiet because your words make me feel ashamed of myself, because I'm wicked and not good — that's what I am. And you, Rakitka, be quiet because you're telling lies. I did have a base idea of swallowing him whole, but now you're telling lies, it's all quite different now and don't let me hear you say any more, Rakitka!' Grushenka said all this with extraordinary agitation.

'Look at those two, they're possessed!' Rakitin hissed, examining them both with surprise. 'You're like crazy folk, it's as though I'd landed in a madhouse. You've softened each other's brains, you'll start weeping in a moment!'

'I will start weeping, I will start weeping!' Grushenka said several times. 'He called me his sister, and I shall never ever forget that! Only you see, Rakitka, though I may be wicked, I've still given my onion.'

'What onion? Fie, the devil, they really have gone mad!'

Rakitin was astonished at their exaltation and had touchily lost his temper, even though he might have fathomed that for both there had coincided all the elements necessary to shake their souls in the way that this infrequently occurs in life. But Rakitin, who possessed a remarkable sensitivity to all that concerned himself, only had a very crude grasp of the feelings and sensations of his fellow human beings — partly because of his youthful inexperience, and partly because of his great egoism.

'You see, Alyoshechka,' Grushenka laughed nervously all of a sudden, turning towards him, 'I boasted to Rakitka that I'd given my onion, but I shall not boast of it to you — I shall tell you about it with a different end in view. It's only a fable, but it's a good fable, I heard it when I was a little girl from my Matryona, who now works as my cook. Well then, it goes like this: "Once upon a time there was a wicked-wicked woman, who died. And she left behind her not one single good deed. The devils seized her and threw her into the fiery lake. But her guardian angel stood, and thought: 'What good deed of hers might I remember, in order to tell God?' He remembered, and told God: 'She pulled up an onion in the kitchen garden,' he said, 'and gave it to a beggarwoman.' And God replied to him: 'Very well,' he said, 'take that very same onion and offer it to her in the lake, let her reach for it and hold on to it, and if you can pull her out of the lake, then let her go to heaven, but if the onion breaks then let the woman remain where she is now.' The angel ran over to the woman and offered her the onion: 'Here you are, woman,' he said, 'reach for it, and hold on!' And then carefully he began to pull her, and soon she was nearly right out; but then the other sinners in the lake, when they saw that she was being pulled out, all began to catch hold of her, so that they should be pulled out together with her. But the woman was a wicked-wicked woman, and she began to kick them with her feet: 'I'm the one who's being pulled out, not you. The onion's mine, not yours.' And no sooner had she said that than the onion broke. And the woman fell back into the lake and burns there to this very day. As for the angel, he began to weep and left the spot." There, that's how that fable goes, Alyosha, I know it off by heart, for I am that wicked woman. I boasted to Rakitka that I'd given my onion, but to you I shall put it differently: that onion is *all* I have ever given in all my life, and it is the only good deed I've ever done. And do not praise me after this, Alyosha, do not think I am good, for I am wicked, wicked-wicked, and if you praise me you will lead to shame. Oh, I shall confess it all now. Listen, Alyosha: I so much wanted to get you to come to my place and kept bothering Rakitin so much about it, that I promised him twenty-five roubles if he'd bring you to me. Wait, Rakitka, just a moment!' With swift footsteps she approached the table, opened its drawer, took out a *porte-monnaie*, and from it a twenty-five-rouble banknote.

'What nonsense! What nonsense!' the perplexed Rakitin exclaimed.

'Accept the return of my obligation, Rakitin, I don't think you'll turn it down, for you requested it yourself.' And she tossed the note in his direction.

'I'd like to see me turn it down,' Rakitin said in a deep voice, plainly embarrassed, but bravely covering up his shame. 'That will come in very handy, fools exist for the profit of the clever man.'

'And now be quiet, Rakitin, now all that I shall say is for other ears than yours. Go and sit over there in the corner and keep quiet, if you don't like us, you can keep quiet.'

'Why should I like you?' Rakitin bit off, no longer trying to conceal his malice now. The twenty-five-rouble note he put in his pocket, and before Alyosha he really did feel ashamed. He had been counting on receiving his payment afterwards, so that the other should not learn of it, and now his shame made him lose his temper. Until that moment he had thought it most politic not to contradict Grushenka too much, in spite of all her flicks and fillips, for it was plain that she had a kind of power over him. Now, however, he too became angry:

'If you like someone you do so for something they've done, but what have you two ever done for me?'

'Well, you should like other people for nothing, the way Alyosha does.'

'How do you know he likes you? What sign has he ever shown you, that you make such a fuss of him?'

Grushenka stood in the middle of the room and spoke with ardour; her voice contained a note of hysteria.

'Be quiet, Rakitka, you don't understand a thing about us! And from now on do not dare to address me as *thou*, I will not permit it, and where did you get such boldness from, that's what I'd like to know! Sit in the corner and be quiet, like my lackey. And now, Alyosha, I shall tell you alone the plain truth, so you may see what a brute creature I am! I'm not talking to Rakitka, but to you. I wanted to destroy you, Alyosha, that is the whole truth of the matter, I had completely made up my mind to do it; I so much wanted to do it that I even bribed Rakitka with money to bring you here. And why did I want such a thing so much? You, Alyosha, were not even aware of anything, you would turn away from me, when you passed me you would lower your eyes, but I had watched you a hundred times before then, had begun to make inquiries about you from everyone. Your face had remained in my heart: "He despises me," I thought, "he doesn't even want to look at me." And in the end I was taken by such a degree of feeling that I surprised even myself: why was I so afraid of a little boy like that? I would swallow him whole and laugh. My spite had really been aroused. I don't know if you realize it, but no man in this town even dares to talk or even think of coming to Agrafena Aleksandrovna for that wicked business; the old man here is the only man I have, I am bound to him and sold to him, Satan wedded us, and I see none of the others. But when I saw you, I decided: I shall swallow him whole. I shall swallow him whole and laugh. You see what a wicked she-dog is the woman you called your sister! Well, now this assailant of my honour has arrived, and I am sitting here waiting for a message. Do you realize what he has been to me, this assailant of my honour? Five years ago, when Kuzma brought me here — I used to sit here, burying myself away from other people, hoping that no one would see me or get to hear of me, I was thin and stupid and I used to sit and sob, didn't sleep for nights on end, thinking: "And where is he now, the assailant of my honour? He's probably laughing with the other girl about me, and if I ever see him or meet him some time I know what I shall do: I shall pay him back, that's what I'll do, I shall pay him back!" At night in the darkness I would sob into my pillow, thinking all this over, tearing my heart on purpose, assuaging it with malice: "Oh, I shall pay him back, I shall pay him back!" That was what I used to cry aloud in the darkness. And when I would suddenly remember that there was nothing I could do to him, nothing at all, and that he must be laughing at me now, and might very easily have forgotten me altogether and dismissed me from his thoughts, I would throw myself from my bed to the floor, burst into impotent tears and lie there, shaking and shaking, until dawn. In the morning I would get up more vicious than a dog, and would gladly have swallowed whole the entire world. Then, what do you suppose? I began to save up capital, became hard and without mercy, put on flesh – I'd acquired some sense, you think, eh? Not a bit of it: no one in the whole world sees it and no one in the whole world knows it, but when the murk of night comes down I sometimes lie here, just like the little girl I was five years ago, grinding my teeth and wailing all night: "Oh, I shall pay him back, I shall pay him back!", and that is what is in my thoughts. Did you hear all that? Well then, now you understand me: a month ago this letter suddenly arrived: he was coming here, had lost his wife who had died, he wanted to see me. At the time I could scarcely breathe for shock, and then merciful Lord, I suddenly thought: "He'll come and whistle to me, call me, and like a little she-dog I'll go creeping to him, cowed and guilty!" As I thought that I could not believe it: "Am I base or am I not, will I run after him or will I not?" And now all this month I have been so angry with myself that it's even worse than it was five years ago. You see now, Alyosha, how wild and savage I am? Now I have told you the whole truth! I was playing with Mitya so that I wouldn't go running after that other. Keep quiet, Rakitka, it's not for you to judge me, I have not been talking to you. Just now, before you arrived, I was lying here, waiting, thinking, deciding the whole of my future fortune, and you will never know what things there were in my heart. No, Alyosha, tell your lady that she must not take offence at what happened the other day! . . . And no one in the whole world knows what I am going through now, and cannot know . . . Because today I may go there with a knife, I have not decided yet . . .'

And, having delivered herself of this 'pathetic' remark, Grushenka suddenly lost her self-control, did not finish her sentence, covered her face with her hands, threw herself upon the sofa and began to sob like a small child. Alyosha rose from his seat and approached Rakitin.

'Misha,' he said, 'please don't be angry. I know you resent what she said, but don't be angry. Did you hear what she said just now? One cannot ask so much of a human soul, one must be more merciful . . .'

Alyosha got this out in an uncontainable rush of heartfelt emotion. He needed to express himself, and he had turned to Rakitin. Had Rakitin not been there, he would have uttered his exclamations alone. But Rakitin gave him a mocking look, and Alyosha suddenly stopped.

'They spent all last night and this morning charging you up with that Elder of yours, and now you've let fly at me with him, Alyoshenka, man of God,' Rakitin said with a hate-filled smile.

'Do not laugh, Rakitin, do not smirk like that, do not speak of the departed: he is loftier than any man there has ever been on earth!' Alyosha cried out with a wail in his voice. 'I speak to you not as a judge, but as the least of the judged. What am I before her? I came here in order to be destroyed, saying: "Go on, go on!" – and that was because of my cowardice, while she, after five years of suffering, no sooner did someone come and say a sincere word to her, forgave everything, forgot everything and cried! The assailant of her honour has returned, is summoning her, and yet she forgives him everything and hurries to him in joy and she will not take the knife, she will not take it! Oh, I am not like that! I do not know whether you are like that, Misha, but I am not like that! Today, the moment I received this lesson, I . . . She loves in a way that is loftier than yours or mine . . . Have you heard her say this earlier, what she said just now? No, you have not; if you had, you would have understood everything long ago . . . And let the other woman, whom she offended the other day, let her, too, forgive her! And she will forgive her, if she learns of this . . . and she shall learn of it . . . This soul has not yet been reconciled, we must spare it . . . This soul may contain a treasure . . .'

Alyosha stopped speaking, for his breathing had been cut short. Rakitin, in spite of all his malicious anger, stared at him in astonishment. Never had he expected from the quiet Alyosha a tirade like this.

'Upon my word, we have an advocate among us! Have you gone and fallen in love with her, or something? Agrafena Aleksandrovna, I say, our keeper of the fasts has damn well gone and fallen in love with you, you have a conquest!' he exclaimed with brazen laughter.

Grushenka raised her head from the pillow and looked at Alyosha with a smile of tender emotion, which shone in her face that was now somehow suddenly swollen from the tears she had just shed.

'Leave him alone, Alyosha, my cherub; you see the kind of fellow he is, he's no one for you to talk to. You know, Mikhail Osipovich,' she said, turning to Rakitin, 'I was going to ask your pardon for having shouted at you, but now I don't feel like it any more. Alyosha, come over to me and sit down here,' she said, beckoning him with a joyful smile, 'there, yes, sit down here, and tell me' (she took him by the hand and peered, smiling, into his eyes) ' – tell me: do I love that man or do I not? The assailant of my honour, do I love him or not? Before you arrived I was lying here in the darkness, asking that question of my heart over and over again: do I love that man or do I not? You decide it for me, Alyosha, the time has come, and whatever you decide, so shall it be. Shall I forgive him or not?'

'But you've already forgiven him,' Alyosha got out, smiling.

'Yes, I suppose I have,' Grushenka said, reflectively. 'Oh, what a base heart! To my base heart!' she said as she suddenly snatched her glass from the table, drank it down in one, raised it and hurled it to the ground with a flourish. The glass smashed, its fragments tinkling. A thin line of cruelty flickered in her smile.

'Though perhaps I haven't forgiven him yet,' she said in a voice that was somehow stern, looking down at the ground, as though it were herself she was talking to. 'Perhaps my heart is only preparing itself to forgive him. I shall have to struggle some more with that heart of mine. You see, Alyosha, I've grown awfully fond of my five-year-old tears . . . It may be that I'm fond only of the assault upon my honour, and not of him at all!'

'Well I wouldn't like to be in his skin!' Rakitin hissed.

'No, and you won't be, Rakitka, never will you be in his skin. You shall stitch my shoes for me, Rakitka, that is the task I shall use you for, but one such as I you will never get your hands on . . . And neither, perhaps, may he . . .'

'Oh, really? Then why have you got yourself all dressed up like that?' Rakitin said, venomously taunting her.

'Don't you go criticizing the way I'm dressed, Rakitka, you do not yet know all that is in my heart! If I feel like it, I shall tear off this finery, right this very minute,' she exclaimed resonantly. 'You don't know what the purpose of this finery is, Rakitka! Perhaps I'll come out to him and say: "Have you ever seen me like this, eh?" After all, I was a thin, consumptive, seventeen-year-old cry-baby when he abandoned me. And I'll sit down close to him and seduce him and fan his passion: "Have you ever seen me as I am now?" I'll say. "Well then, that's all you're getting, my dear gentleman, for there's many a slip 'twixt cup and lip!"– perhaps

that's why I'm all dressed up like this, Rakitka,' Grushenka concluded
with a malicious little laugh. 'I'm wild, Alyosha, I'm savage. If I tear off
my finery I shall mutilate myself and my beauty, I shall burn my face and
lay it open with a knife, I shall go and beg for alms. If I don't feel like it,
I shan't go anywhere now or visit anyone, and if I want to I shall send
back to Kuzma everything he's given me, including all his money, and
shall go and work all my life as a daily drudge! ... Do you think I
wouldn't do that, Rakitka, do you think I wouldn't dare to do that? I
would, I would, in fact I'll do it right now, so just don't irritate me ...
and as for the other, I'll pull a long nose at him, and he won't get his
hands on me!'

These last words she shouted hysterically, but again lost her self-
control, covered her face with her hands, threw herself on the pillow and
again shook with sobs. Rakitin got up from his seat.

'It's time we were going,' he said. 'It's late, they won't let us in to the
monastery.'

Grushenka fairly leapt to her feet.

'Oh Alyosha, are you really going to leave?' she exclaimed in sorrowful
amazement. 'Oh, what is it you're doing to me now? You've got me all
worked up, all tormented to death, and now this night again, again I'm to
be left on my own!'

'You don't expect him to spend the night with you, do you? Though
if he wants to – let him! I shall go alone!' Rakitin chaffed with caustic
relish.

'Be quiet, wicked soul!' Grushenka shouted at him savagely. 'Never
have you spoken to me the kind of words that he came to speak to me.'

'What were they?' Rakitin muttered in irritation.

'I don't know, I've no idea, I've absolutely no idea what they were,
those words, it was my heart they spoke to, he turned my heart upside-
down ... He is the first and only man to have taken pity on me, so there!
Why did you not come earlier, cherub?' she said, suddenly falling on her
knees before him, almost in a frenzy. 'All my life I have waited for one
such as you, have known that someone like you would come and forgive
me. I had faith that someone would love even a filthy woman like me,
and not for the sake of mere shame ...'

'You ask what I've done to you?' Alyosha replied with tender emotion,
bending down to her and taking her by the hands. 'I've given you an
onion, just one very small onion, no more, no more ...'

And, having got this out, he himself began to weep. At that moment
there was a sudden clatter and commotion in the passage, and someone

entered the anteroom: Grushenka leapt up in what appeared to be extreme panic. Into the room, clattering and shouting, ran Fenya.

'Lady, my dear lady, the estafette has arrived!' she exclaimed merrily and out of breath. 'They're sending a tarantas from Mokroye for you, Timofey the coachman, with a *troika* of horses, they're putting on the new relay now ... The letter, the letter, dear lady, here's the letter!' In one hand she was holding a letter, and all the time she was shouting she waved it about in the air. Grushenka whipped the letter out of her hand and brought it up to the candle. It was no more than a small note, just a few lines, and she read it in a split second.

'He has called me!' she shouted, pale all over, her features distorted by a painful smile. 'He has whistled! Go creeping to him, little she-dog!'

But only for one split second did she stand in what looked like hesitation; suddenly the blood rushed to her head, suffusing her cheeks with fire.

'I shall go!' she exclaimed suddenly. 'Five years of my life! Farewell! Farewell, Alyosha, my fate is decided ... Go, go, go from me all of you now, and let me never see you again! ... Grushenka has flown off to her new life ... You too must think kindly of me, Rakitka. It may be that I am going to my death! Bang! Like a drunk woman!'

Suddenly she turned her back on them and ran into her bedroom.

'Well, she's not interested in us now!' Rakitin muttered. 'Come on, let's be off, or else that female shouting will start again, I'm fed up with all that shouting and tears!'

Alyosha, in mechanical fashion, allowed himself to be conducted outside. In the yard stood the tarantas, from which the horses were being unharnessed; people walked to and fro with a lantern, bustling about. A fresh *troika*, a team of three horses, was being led in through the open gateway. But no sooner had Alyosha and Rakitin come down the steps of the porchway than Grushenka's bedroom window suddenly opened, and she shouted after Alyosha in a resonant voice:

'Alyoshechka, bow to your brother Mitenka for me, and tell him to think kindly of me, his wicked girl. And also repeat these words of mine to him: "Grushenka has gone to a scoundrel, and not to you, who are a noble man!" And tell him, too, that Grushenka loved him for one small hour of time, only one small hour did she love him — and that he must remember that small hour all the rest of his life — tell him that Grushenka commands him to remember it all the rest of his life!'

She concluded in a voice that was full of sobbing. The window banged shut.

'Hm, hm!' Rakitin mumbled, laughing. 'She cuts your brother

Mitenka's throat, and then orders him to remember it all the rest of his life. Such carnivorousness!'

Alyosha made no reply, as though he had not even heard; he walked quickly beside Rakitin, as though he were in a dreadful hurry; he was in a kind of oblivion, his steps mechanical. Something suddenly stabbed at Rakitin, as though his fresh wound had been touched by a finger. This was not at all what he had expected when he had brought Alyosha together with Grushenka; it had all worked out quite differently, and in a way that was not as he wanted.

'He's a Pole, this officer of hers,' he said, breaking the silence again, and holding himself in check. 'And he's not really an officer at all now, he's been working as a customs official somewhere on the Chinese border, he's probably some creepy, effeminate little Pole. They say he was fired. Now he's got wind that Grushenka's got some capital to spend, so here he is back again – there's your explanation of all the miracles.'

Again Alyosha seemed not to hear. Rakitin could not restrain himself:

'So, converted a sinner, have you?' he said, laughing at Alyosha maliciously. 'Put the fornicatress back on the right road again? Cast out the seven devils, eh? So this is where they are, the miracles we've been expecting today, they've come to pass!'

'Stop it, Rakitin,' Alyosha said in response, with suffering in his soul.

'It's those twenty-five roubles, isn't it? That's why you "despise" me now! I've gone and sold a true friend down the river. But I mean to say, you're not Christ, and I'm not Judas.'

'Oh, Rakitin, honestly, I'd forgotten about that,' Alyosha exclaimed. 'It's you yourself who've reminded me . . .'

But Rakitin had now flown into a complete fury.

'The devil take your hides, each and every one of you!' he howled suddenly. 'And what the devil am I doing associating with someone like you? I don't want to know you any more after today. Off you go on your own, there's your way!'

And he turned sharply down another street, leaving Alyosha alone in the murk. Alyosha walked out of the town and crossed the fields to the monastery.

4
Cana of Galilee*

IT was already very late by monastery standards when Alyosha reached the hermitage; the gatekeeper let him in by a special route. Nine o'clock had already struck – the hour of common rest and repose after a day that had been so trying for them all. Alyosha timidly opened the door and stepped into the Elder's cell, in which his coffin now stood. Apart from Father Paisy, who was solitarily reading the Gospel over the coffin, and the novice youth Porfiry, worn out by the previous night's discourse and by the fuss and bustle of that day and now in the other room on the floor sleeping a sound, youthful sleep, there was no one in the cell. Father Paisy, though he heard Alyosha enter, did not even look in his direction. Having passed through the doorway, Alyosha turned to the right and made for a corner, got down on his knees and began to pray. His soul was full to overflowing, but in a manner troubled and unclear, and not a single sensation made itself plainly discerned, but, on the contrary, with all too great an effect, each kept ousting the last in a kind of quiet, even revolution. But there was a sweetness in his heart, and it was strange, but Alyosha was not surprised by this. Again he saw before him that coffin, that shut-up corpse so precious to him, but now the weeping, aching, agonizing sorrow there had been in his soul that morning was not there. Before the coffin, immediately upon entering, he fell as before a holy shrine, but joy, joy shone in his mind and in his heart. One of the cell's windows was open, the air was fresh and touched with cold – 'If they've taken the step of opening a window that means the smell must have got worse,' Alyosha thought. But even this reflection on the putrid smell, which only a little time before had seemed to him so dreadful and so inglorious, did not now open up in him the previous anguish and the previous indignation. He quietly began to pray, but soon himself sensed that he was praying almost mechanically. Scraps of thoughts fleeted through his soul, caught fire like little stars and instantly expired, replaced by others, and yet there reigned within his soul something whole, firm, assuaging, and he himself was conscious of it. At times he would ardently begin a prayer, so much did he want to render thanks and love . . . But, having begun it, he would suddenly pass over into something else, reflect, forgetting both the prayer and that which had interrupted it. He started to listen to what Father Paisy was reading, but, exceedingly fatigued, little by little he began to nod . . .

'*And the third day there was a marriage in Cana of Galilee*'; Father Paisy read, '*and the mother of Jesus was there: And both Jesus was called, and his disciples, to the marriage.*'

'A marriage? What's this? . . . A marriage?' rushed, like a whirlwind, through Alyosha's mind. 'She also has good fortune . . . has gone to a feast . . . No, she hasn't taken the knife, she hasn't taken the knife . . .

That was only a "pathetic" remark ... Well ... pathetic remarks must be forgiven, that's certain. Pathetic remarks bring comfort to the soul ... without them people would find their grief too hard to bear. Rakitin walked down a side-lane. For as long as he broods on the insults he thinks he has received he will always walk down a side-lane ... But the true way ... the true way is wide, straight, bright, made of crystal, and the sun is at its end ... Eh? What's that he's reading?'

'... *And when they wanted wine, the mother of Jesus saith unto him, They have no wine* ...' floated to Alyosha's ears.

'Oh yes, I've missed this part, and I didn't want to miss it, I love this passage: it's Cana of Galilee, the first miracle ... Oh, that miracle, oh, that dear miracle! It was not the grief of human beings but their joy that Jesus visited, and when for the first time he performed a miracle, he did it in order to contribute to human joy ... "Whoever loves human beings, loves their joy ..." That was what the deceased repeated every minute, that was one of his principal ideas ... "Without joy one cannot live," says Mitya ... Yes, Mitya ... All that is true and beautiful is always full of universal forgiveness — that's another thing he used to say ...'

'... *Jesus saith unto her, Woman, what have I to do with thee? mine hour is not yet come. His mother saith unto the servants, Whatsoever he saith unto you, do it.*'

'Do it ... Bring it about ... The joy, the joy of some poor folk, some very poor folk ... Of course they're poor, if they haven't even got any wine for their wedding ... The historians say that at that time the population settled around the lake of Gennesaret was of the very poorest one can possibly imagine ... And another great heart of another great being who was also there, his mother, knew that not only for the sake of his great and terrible deed had he come down to earth, and that his heart was also open to the simple, unsophisticated gaiety of certain dark, dark and guileless beings, who had affectionately invited him to their poor wedding. "Mine hour is not yet come," he says with a quiet smile (I am sure that he smiled to her meekly) ... Indeed, was it really in order to provide wine for the weddings of the poor that he came down to earth? And he went and did according to her request ... Oh, he's reading some more now ...'

'*Jesus saith unto them, Fill the waterpots with water. And they filled them up to the brim.*

'*And he saith unto them, Draw out now, and bear unto the governor of the feast. And they bare it.*

'*When the ruler of the feast had tasted the water that was made wine, and knew not whence it was: (but the servants which drew the water knew:) the governor of the feast called the bridegroom.*

'*And saith unto him, Every man at the beginning doth set forth good wine: and when men have well drunk, then that which is worse: but thou hast kept the good wine until now.*'

'But what's this? What's this? Why is the room expanding? ... Oh yes ... after all, it's a marriage, a wedding ... yes, of course. Here are the guests, here is the young couple sitting together, and the merry throng, and ... where is the wise architricline? But who is this? Who? The room has expanded again ... Who's that rising to his feet behind that big table over there? How ... Is he here too? Why, he is in his coffin ... But he too is here ... He has risen to his feet, has seen me, is coming over here ... O merciful Lord!'

Yes, him, him did he approach, the little, wizened old man, with fine wrinkles on his face, joyful and quietly laughing. The coffin was nowhere to be seen now, and he was wearing the same clothes he had worn yesterday when he had sat with them, when guests had gathered in his cell. His face was entirely uncovered, his eyes shone. How could this be? He, too, was at the feast, had also been called to the wedding in Cana of Galilee ...

'I, too, dear fellow, have been called, called and summoned,' the quiet voice said clearly above him. 'Why have you buried yourself away here, where no one can see you ... You too must come and be with us!'

His voice, the voice of the Elder Zosima ... And how could it not be him if he was calling him? The Elder helped Alyosha to his feet with one hand, and the latter got up off his knees.

'Let us be merry and gay,' the little, wizened old man continued. 'Let us drink the new wine, the wine of new and great joy; you see how many guests there are? Here are the bride and bridegroom, here is the wise architricline, he too is trying the new wine. Why do you marvel at me? I gave my onion, and so I am here. Many here have given only one onion, just one little onion ... What do our other deeds matter? And you too, my quiet fellow, you too, my meek boy, you too have given this day an onion to a woman who hungered for it. Begin, dear fellow, begin, meek one, your task! ... And do you see our sun, do you see it?'

'I'm afraid ... I dare not look ...' Alyosha whispered.

'Do not be afraid of it. It is terrible in its greatness before us, dreadful in its loftiness, but it is infinitely merciful, has assumed our likeness and with us is merry and gay, turns water into wine, that the joy of the guests be not broken off, awaits new guests, calls ever new ones and will do so until the end of the ages. Here they come, bring new wine, you see, they are bringing the vessels . . .'

Something was burning in Alyosha's heart, something suddenly filled him to the point of physical pain, tears of ecstasy burst from his soul . . . He stretched out his arms, uttered a scream and awoke . . .

Again the coffin, the open window and the quiet, solemn, distinct reading of the Gospel. But by now Alyosha no longer heard what was being read. Strange, but he had fallen asleep while kneeling, and now he was standing up, and suddenly, as though he had been uprooted from the spot, with three firm, rapid strides he walked right up to the coffin. He even knocked his shoulder against Father Paisy without noticing. The latter raised his eyes from his book for a moment, but immediately drew them away again, having grasped that something strange had taken place in the youth. Alyosha stared at the coffin for some thirty seconds, at the uncovered, immobile corpse that lay stretched out in it, with the icon on its breast and the cucula with its eight-pointed cross upon its head. Only just now had he heard its voice, and that voice still resounded in his ears. He still strained to hear, he still expected to hear more sounds . . . But suddenly, turning sharply away, he walked out of the cell.

He did not even stop in the porchway, but swiftly went down the steps. His soul, filled with ecstasy, thirsted for freedom, space, latitude. Above him wide and boundless keeled the cupola of the heavens, full of quiet, brilliant stars. Doubled from zenith to horizon ran the Milky Way, as yet unclear. The cool night, quiet to the point of fixity, enveloped the earth. The white towers and golden domes of the cathedral sparkled in the sapphire sky. In the flowerbeds luxuriant autumn flowers had fallen asleep until morning. The earth's silence seemed to fuse with that of the heavens, the earth's mystery came into contact with that of the stars . . . Alyosha stood, looked and suddenly cast himself down upon the earth like one who has had the legs cut from under him.

Why he embraced it he did not know, he did not try to explain to himself why he so desperately wanted to kiss it, kiss it, all of it, but weeping he kissed it, sobbing and drenching it with his tears, and frenziedly he swore to love it, love it until the end of the ages. 'Drench the earth with the tears of your joy and love those tears of yours . . .' resounded in his soul. What did he weep about? Oh, he wept in his ecstasy even about those stars that shone to him out of the abyss, and 'was not ashamed of this frenzy'. As though threads from all these countless of God's worlds had all coincided within his soul at once, and it trembled all over, in 'the contiguity with other worlds'. He wanted to forgive all creatures for all things and to ask forgiveness, oh, not for himself, but for all persons, all creatures and all things, while 'others asked the same for me' — resounded again in his soul. But with each moment that passed he felt plainly and almost palpably that something as firm and unshakeable as this celestial vault was descending into his soul. Something that was almost an idea took mastery of his intellect — and now for the rest of his life and until the end of the ages. A feeble youth had he fallen to the earth, yet now he arose a resolute warrior for the rest of his life and knew and felt this suddenly, at that same moment of his ecstasy. And never, never for all the rest of his life would Alyosha be able to forget that moment. 'Someone visited my soul in that hour,' he would say later with resolute faith in his words . . .

Three days later he left the monastery, something that was also in concordance with the precept of his deceased Elder, who had commanded him to 'abide in the world'.

BOOK VIII
MITYA

I

Kuzma Samsonov

BUT Dmitry Fyodorovich, to whom Grushenka, in flying off to a new life, had 'commanded' Alyosha to impart her final greeting and whom she had ordered to remember for ever the short hour of her love, was at that moment, though quite unaware of what had happened to her, also in a fearful state of trouble and commotion. In such an unimaginable condition had he been during the past two days that he might easily have suffered an inflammation of the brain, as he himself said later. Alyosha had not been able to track him down the previous day, nor on that same day had brother Ivan been able to arrange a meeting with him at the inn. The landlords of the little room he rented had, on his instructions, covered up his traces. During those two days he had literally hurled himself about in all directions, 'struggling with my fate and trying to save myself', as he put it later, and had even for several hours made a flying visit on a certain burning matter out of town, in spite of the fact that he was afraid to go away leaving Grushenka unwatched for so much as a moment. All this subsequently came to light in the most detailed and documentary fashion, but at the present time we shall sketch out in factual terms only the most essential particulars appertaining to the story of those dreadful two days in his life, which preceded the terrible catastrophe that burst so suddenly upon his fortunes.

Grushenka, though she had indeed loved him for a small hour or so truly and sincerely — that could not be denied — had at the same time, however, on occasion tormented him cruelly and without mercy. The principal thing was that he was unable to discover anything of her intentions; to coax them out of her with a caress or by force was likewise out of the question: not on any account would she have yielded, would merely have lost her temper and turned her back on him altogether, that he clearly understood at the time. He had a suspicion, a most correct one, that she herself was caught up in some kind of struggle, some kind of extraordinary indecision, was determining to do something yet could not make her determination final, and consequently not without grounds did he suppose, his heart dying within him, that at moments she must simply hate him and his passion. Such was, perhaps, indeed the case, but for all that just what it was that caused Grushenka such anguish he did not understand. Really, for him the whole question that tormented him could be summed up in a conflict between two alternatives: either himself, Mitya; or Fyodor Pavlovich. Here, incidentally, it is necessary to draw attention to a certain established fact: quite convinced was he that Fyodor Pavlovich was now definitely about to propose (if already he had not done so) to Grushenka a pact of lawful matrimony, and he did not believe for one moment that the old voluptuary had any expectation of acquitting himself for only three thousand roubles. This Mitya had deduced, knowing Grushenka and her character. That was why it could also appear to him at times that all Grushenka's torment and all her indecision likewise proceeded merely from the fact that she did not know which of them to choose and which of them would bring her more advantage. Of the imminent return of the 'officer', that is, of that man so fateful in Grushenka's life, whose arrival she awaited with such fear and agitation, he, strangely, in those days had not even thought to think. It was true that Grushenka had in the very most recent days been thoroughly silent with him on that subject. He was, however, fully aware, from her own mouth, of the letter she had received a month ago from her former seducer, and was even aware of a portion of its contents. That day, in a certain moment of ill-temper, Grushenka had shown him that letter, but to her astonishment he had attached to it almost no value whatsoever. And it would have been very difficult to explain why: it was, perhaps, for the simple reason that he himself, weighed down by all the monstrousness and horror of his struggle with his own father for this woman, could envision nothing more terrible and hazardous for himself than this, at the time, at least. In this bridegroom, who had suddenly sprung from nowhere after a disappearance of five years, he simply and positively did not believe, and this was particularly the case with regard to the latter's imminent arrival. Indeed, in this first letter of the 'officer', which Mitya had seen, the advent of the new rival was discussed in terms that were far from precise: the letter was very nebulous, very high-flown and filled with naught but the expression of sentiment. It should be noted that Grushenka had on that occasion concealed from him the letter's final lines, in which the return was discussed with somewhat greater precision. What was more, Mitenka later remembered having at that moment caught a certain involuntary and proud contempt for this epistle from Siberia* on the face of Grushenka herself. Thereafter Grushenka communicated nothing to Mitenka concerning her subsequent relations with the new rival.

Thus little by little did he actually forget about the officer altogether. His only thought was that no matter how it worked out over there and no matter what turn the affair might take, his approaching final collision with Fyodor Pavlovich was all too close and must be resolved as a matter of priority. His soul dying inwardly, he awaited at each moment Grushenka's decision and persisted in believing that it would be delivered in some sudden manner, by inspiration, as it were. Suddenly she would say to him: 'Take me, I am yours for ever,' and it would all be at an end: he would grab her and carry her off to the end of the world at once. Oh, at once would he carry her off, as far, as far as possible, if not to the end of the world, then to somewhere at the end of Russia, marry her and settle down with her incognito, so that no one should ever learn of them here, there or anywhere else. Then, oh then, a completely new life would at once commence! Of this other, renewed and indeed 'virtuous' life ('without fail, without fail virtuous') he dreamed by the minute and in frenzy. He thirsted for that resurrection and renewal. The foul cesspool in which he himself had become enmired by his own will had grown all too noisome to him, and he, like very many others in such instances, put faith more than anything else in a change of place: if only it were not for these people, if only it were not for this situation, if only he could fly away out of this cursed place and then – all would be regenerated, would take a new turn! That was where he put his faith and what he languished for.

But this was only in the first, *happy* resolution of the question. There was also another resolution, there presented itself another but indeed dreadful outcome. Suddenly she would say to him: 'Be off with you, I've just made up my mind together with Fyodor Pavlovich and am going to marry him, I don't need you any more,' and then ... but then ... As a matter of fact, Mitya did not know what would happen then, right up to the very last moment he did not know, and one must give him credit for that. He had no definite plans, the crime had not been deliberated. He only watched, spied and tormented himself, but none the less made himself ready for the first, happy outcome of his fate. He even drove away all other thoughts. But here already lay in its inception quite another torment, and there arose a certain completely new and irrelevant, but also fateful and irresoluble circumstance.

Namely, if she were to say to him: 'I am yours, carry me off,' then whither would he do so? What means, what money did he have with which to do it? It so happened that precisely at this juncture all the income he had managed to put together from Fyodor Pavlovich's hand-

outs, which had continued without cease for so many years, had dried up.
Of course, Grushenka had money, but on this score there suddenly
displayed itself within Mitya a terrible pride: he wanted to carry her off
and begin a new life with her on his resources, not on hers; he could not
even imagine taking her money, and suffered from this thought to the
point of tormented loathing. I shall not expatiate upon this fact, nor shall
I analyse it, but shall merely note: such was the cast of his soul at that
moment. All this might have proceeded obliquely and, as it were, unconsciously from the secret torments endured by his conscience because of
the money he had thievishly appropriated from Katerina Ivanovna: 'Before
the one I am a scoundrel and before the other I shall again immediately
appear as a scoundrel,' he later admitted to thinking at the time, 'and if
Grushenka finds out about it, she will not want such a scoundrel, either.'
And so, where was he to procure the means, how was he to get his hands
on the fateful money? If he did not do so, all would be lost and nothing
would be achieved, 'and solely because I didn't have enough money, oh,
the disgrace!'

I run ahead: the fact is that he may indeed have known where he could
get that money, and may also have known its precise whereabouts. At
present I shall not enter into further detail on this account, for it will all
be explained subsequently; but his principal misfortune resided in this
circumstance – and though it be somewhat vaguely, let me nevertheless
bring this into the open: that in order to get his hands on those financial
means of certain whereabouts, in order to *have the right* to get his hands
on them, it was first necessary for him to return the three thousand
roubles to Katerina Ivanovna – otherwise 'I'll be a pickpocket thief, and a
scoundrel, and I don't want to begin my new life as a scoundrel,' Mitya
decided, and so he determined to overturn the whole world if necessary
in order to return those three thousand roubles to Katerina Ivanovna at
all costs and as a matter of the *first priority*. The final process of this
decision had taken place in him during, so to speak, the very most recent
hours of his life, namely since his most recent meeting with Alyosha, two
days previously, in the evening, on the road, after Grushenka's insulting
behaviour towards Katerina Ivanovna, and Mitya, having heard an account
of it from Alyosha, had confessed to being a scoundrel, and instructed
that it be conveyed to Katerina Ivanovna, 'if that will make her feel any
better'. At that same time, during that same night, after parting from his
brother, he had felt in his frenzy that it would even be better 'to murder
and rob someone, as long as I repay my debt to Katya'. 'Let me sooner
appear as a murderer and a thief before the one whom I have murdered

and robbed, and before all men, and go to Siberia, than make it justifiable for Katya to say that I have betrayed her and stolen her money and used it to elope with Grushenka in order to begin a life of virtue! That I cannot do!' Thus with a grinding of teeth did Mitya give utterance, and indeed he might well have imagined at times that he would end by suffering an inflammation of the brain. For the present, however, he continued to struggle . . .

It was a strange thing: one might have supposed that, beyond despair, in the face of such a decision there remained to him nothing further; for where could he suddenly get his hands on that kind of money, particularly a naked babe such as himself? And yet all that time he persisted to the end in hoping that he would succeed in obtaining that three thousand, that it would arrive, come floating down to him somehow of its own accord, even though it were from heaven. Such, however, is the case of those who, like Dmitry Fyodorovich, prove themselves capable all their lives of doing no more than waste and squander the money they have obtained by inheritance in vain, while of the methods of making money they possess no conception. A most fantastic whirlwind had arisen within his head immediately after parting from Alyosha the day before yesterday, and had confused all his thoughts. The upshot of it was that he embarked upon a most preposterous undertaking. Yes, it is perhaps precisely in situations of this kind encountered by men of this kind that the most impossible and fantastic undertakings first appear possible. He suddenly made up his mind to go and see Grushenka's protector, the merchant Samsonov, propose to him a certain 'plan', and obtain from him under the terms of this 'plan' the whole of the necessary sum; from a commercial point of view he had no doubts of his plan whatsoever, doubted only as to the manner in which Samsonov himself might look upon his man-oeuvre, if it should occur to him to do so not merely from the said commercial point of view. Although Mitya knew this merchant by sight, he had never made his acquaintance, nor even once spoken to him. For some reason, however, and even for some considerable time now, there had grounded itself within him the conviction that this aged whore-monger, who now had one foot in the grave, might not at the present moment say nay were Grushenka to put her life in some sort of decent order and marry a 'dependable man'. And that not only might he not say nay, but might even actually wish such a thing and, were only a suitable occasion to arise, might himself facilitate it. Whether it was by rumour or from some remark passed by Grushenka, he also had reason to believe that the old man might very possibly prefer him as a suitor to Fyodor

Pavlovich. It may be that many of the readers of our tale will consider such a calculated expectation of assistance and a plan to take one's bride, as it were, from the very arms of her protector, as being in excessively bad taste and undiscriminating on the part of Dmitry Fyodorovich. The only observation I am able to tender is that Grushenka's past appeared to Mitya now to lie very definitely in the past. He gazed upon that past with infinite compassion and determined with all his passion's fiery glow that as soon as Grushenka might tell him that she loved him and would marry him, at once an entirely new Grushenka would come into being, and together with her an entirely new Dmitry Fyodorovich, without a single defect, and with every virtue: they would both forgive each other and would begin their lives in a wholly new fashion. As for Kuzma Samsonov, he considered him, in this previous, played-out past of Grushenka's, as a human being who had performed a fateful role in her life but whom she had never loved and who, most importantly, had already 'passed', gone to termination, so that he was no longer in existence. And indeed, and in addition, Mitya could not even bring himself to view him as a human being at all, for each and every person in the town knew that this was a mere sick ruin, whose relations with Grushenka were now only, as it were, paternal, and not at all upon the same foundation as before, and that this had long already been the case, for almost a year, in fact. At any rate, there was here not a little ingenuousness on Mitya's part, for in spite of all his defects he was a very ingenuous man. In consequence of this ingenuousness, he was, among other things, earnestly convinced that the aged Kuzma, as he prepared to pass away to the other world, felt sincere repentance for his past with Grushenka, and that she now possessed no protector or friend more devoted than this by now innocuous old man.

The day after his conversation with Alyosha in the open country, after which Mitya had hardly slept all night, at around ten o'clock in the morning he presented himself at Samsonov's house and gave instructions that his arrival be announced. This house was an old one – gloomy, very extensive, with two storeys, barns and sheds in the yard, and an outbuilding. On the lower floor lived Samsonov's two married sons with their families, his extremely aged sister and one unmarried daughter. In the outbuilding were accommodated his two estate managers, one of whom was also large of family. Both offspring and estate managers were cramped for space in their accommodations, but the upper storey was occupied solely by the old man, who would not allow even his daughter to share it with him, his daughter who tended to his needs and who at certain predetermined hours and in response to certain predetermined calls from

him was obliged on each occasion to go running up the stairs to him
from below, her long-ago contracted emphysema notwithstanding. This
upper storey was composed of a number of large state-rooms furnished
according to the taste of antique merchantdom, with long, dreary rows of
ungainly mahogany chairs and armchairs along the walls, crystal chandeliers in dustcovers, and gloomy mirrors in the piers between the windows.
All these rooms were completely empty and uninhabited, because the sick
old man skulked away in only one small room, his diminutive and remote
bedroom, where he was waited upon by an old serving-woman with her
hair in a kerchief, and a 'lad', whose abode was the top of a long, low
cupboard in the hallway. On account of his swollen legs the old man
could now hardly walk at all and only occasionally rose from his leather
armchair, when the old woman, supporting him by the arms, would
escort him once or twice about the room. He was stern and uncommunicative even with this old woman. On being informed of the arrival of the
'captain', he at once instructed that the man be denied admittance. But
Mitya kept up the pressure and had himself announced yet one more
time. Kuzma Kuzmich interrogated the lad in detail as to the appearance
of the man, whether he was drunk, whether he was likely to cause
trouble. And received the answer that 'he's sober all right, but he don't
want to go away'. The old man again instructed that the man be denied
admittance. Then Mitya, who had foreseen all this and had brought with
him paper and pencil for just such an eventuality, wrote in clear letters on
a scrap of paper one single line: 'On a most urgent matter that closely
concerns Agrafena Aleksandrovna' – and sent it in to the old man.
Having thought for a while, the old man instructed the lad to take the
visitor into the reception room, sending the old woman below with a
command to his younger son to come upstairs and present himself to him
forthwith. This younger son, a man well over six feet tall and of excessive strength, who shaved his features and dressed in the German style
(Samsonov himself went around in a caftan and beard), presented himself
immediately and without a word. They all shivered in their shoes before
the father. The father had invited this young blood less out of fear of the
captain, for he was of thoroughly intrepid character, than rather just in
case, mainly in order to have a witness should anything occur. Escorted
by his son, who took him by the arm, and the lad, he at last came sailing
out into the reception room. It must be supposed that he also entertained
a certain rather powerful curiosity. This reception room, in which Mitya
was waiting, was an enormous, gloomy chamber that murdered the soul
with dismal anguish, possessing two lights, a gallery, walls *en style de*

marbre and three enormous crystal chandeliers in dustcovers. Mitya sat on a tiny chair near the entrance door, with nervous impatience awaiting his lot. When the old man appeared at the opposite entrance, some ten sagenes from where Mitya sat, the latter suddenly leapt up and with his firm officer's arshin-wide steps strode towards him. Mitya was tolerably well-dressed, in a buttoned-up frock-coat, holding a top hat in black gloves, exactly as he had been dressed three days ago at the monastery, in the Elder's cell, at the family gathering with Fyodor Pavlovich and his brothers. The old man, with solemn severity, waited for him standing, and Mitya instantly sensed that, as he made his approach, the old fellow scrutinized him through and through. Mitya was also shocked by Kuzma Kuzmich's face, which had of late become exceptionally swollen: his lower lip, normally thick enough at the best of times, now had the appearance of a kind of loose and flabby pancake. In severe silence he bowed to his guest, directed him to an armchair beside the sofa, and himself, supporting himself on the arm of his son and groaning pain-fully all the while, slowly began to subside on to the sofa facing Mitya, so that the latter, seeing his painful efforts, instantly felt within his heart both remorse and a sense of delicate embarrassment at his own present insignificance before such an important person, whom he had disturbed.

'What is it, good sir, that you desire of me?' said the old man, who had now finally settled down; his words were slow, distinct, severe, but polite.

Mitya started, leapt up, but then sat down again. Then immediately he began to speak loudly, rapidly, nervously, with gestures and in a state of positive frenzy. It was evident that the man had come to his limit, was lost and in search of a final way out, and that if he did not find one then he would throw himself in the lake then and there. Old Samsonov doubtless understood this in a single flash, though his face remained as cold and inscrutable as that of a graven image.

'The most honourable Kuzma Kuzmich has doubtless already heard on more than one occasion of the series of *contretemps* I have been having with my father, Fyodor Pavlovich Karamazov, who has robbed me of the inheritance I was left by my very own mother . . . as the whole town is by now a-crackle with that which would be better left alone . . . Though actually, it might also have come to your attention by way of Grushenka . . . for that I bear the guilt: by way of Agrafena Aleksandrovna . . . of my much-respected and much-esteemed Agrafena Aleksandrovna . . .' thus did Mitya begin, only to break off almost at the first word. We shall not cite the whole of his remarks word for word, however, but shall merely offer them *en précis*. The nub of the matter, then, may be summarized by saying that he, Mitya, three months back had deliberately taken advice ('deliberately' was the word he used, not 'purposely') from a lawyer in the local provincial capital, 'a famous lawyer, Kuzma Kuzmich, Pavel Pavlovich Korneplodov – I expect you have heard of him? A roomy brow, a mind of almost statesman-like proportions ... He also knows you ... said the most glowing things about you ...' Mitya said, and broke off a second time. But these hiatuses did not deter him; he at once bounded over them and went leaping further and further. The said Korneplodov, having performed a detailed cross-examination and having scrutinized the documents Mitya was able to show him (concerning the documents Mitya expressed himself unclearly and with particular haste when he came to this part), delivered himself of the opinion that as far as the Chermashnya estate, which ought to belong to him, Mitya, by his mother's bequest, was concerned, it would indeed be possible to bring an action at law and thereby give the old hooligan something to think about ... 'because not all the doors are closed, and justice knows the way to get through'. In a word, there was even a hope of a supplementary payment of some six thousand from Fyodor Pavlovich, of seven, even, as Chermashnya was certainly worth no less than twenty-five thousand, in other words more like twenty-eight thousand – 'thirty, thirty, Kuzma Kuzmich, and just think, I didn't even pull in seventeen from that cruel man! ...' So that 'I' – Mitya – 'gave up that matter, for I don't know my way around the institutions of justice, but then having arrived here, was knocked senseless by a counter-action' (there Mitya again went astray and again nimbly leapt across): 'so look, most honourable Kuzma Kuzmich, would you not be willing to take all my rights against that monster of cruelty and give me in return for them just three thousand, that's all ... After all, there's no way in which you can possibly lose on the deal, I swear to you on my honour, on my honour, in fact quite the contrary – you might gain some six or seven thousand for only three ... But what is most important is that it must be done "this very day". I'll swear it to you before a notary, or however it's done ... In a word, I'm ready for anything, I'll give you all the documents you need, I'll sign whatever must be signed ... and we could clinch the written agreement at once, and if it's possible, if only it may be possible, we could do it right now, this morning ... You would let me have that three thousand ... for what man in this wretched little town is a capitalist if not you ... and thereby you would save me from ... in a word, you would save my poor head for a most noble deed, a most exalted deed, one might say ...

for I entertain the most noble feelings for a certain lady, whom you know all too well and whom you care for as a father. I would not have come to you if I did not know that your care for her is a fatherly one. And one might even say that in this business three men have banged their foreheads together, for fate is a scary thing, Kuzma Kuzmich! It's realism, Kuzma Kuzmich, realism! And since you ought to have been ruled out of the contest long ago, there remain but two foreheads, as I expressed it, perhaps not very adroitly, but then I am no *littérateur*. That is to say, one of the foreheads is my own, and the other belongs to – that monster of cruelty. And so you shall choose: is it to be me, or the monster of cruelty? It is all now in your hands – three fates and two destinies ... I'm sorry, I've got mixed up, but you understand ... I see by your honourable eyes that you have grasped it ... And if you have not, then into the lake with me, this very day, that's what!'

Mitya broke off his preposterous oration with this 'that's what' and, leaping up from where he sat, awaited a reply to his foolish proposal. Having uttered that last phrase he had suddenly sensed, with a feeling of hopelessness, that the whole thing had fallen through, and that all he had done was to talk the most dreadful gibberish. 'It's strange: while I was on my way here everything seemed fine, but now I'm spouting all this gibberish!' suddenly rushed through his hopeless head. During all the time he had spoken the old man had sat immobile, watching his every movement with an icy expression in his gaze. Then, however, having sustained him in expectation for a moment or two, Kuzma Kuzmich at last gave utterance in a most resolute and joyless tone:

'I'm sorry, sir, we do not involve ourselves in business of that kind.'

Mitya suddenly felt his legs turning to jelly.

'So what am I going to do now, Kuzma Kuzmich?' he muttered, smiling wanly. 'I mean, it's all up with me now, wouldn't you agree?'

'I'm sorry, sir ...'

Mitya continued to stand there, staring rigidly in front of him, and then suddenly noticed something flicker in the old man's face. He shuddered.

'You see, good sir, such business is not convenient for us,' the old man said, slowly. 'There would be hearings, lawyers, nothing but trouble! But if you wish, there is someone here in town, and you could apply to him ...'

'O my God, who can it be? You resurrect me, Kuzma Kuzmich,' Mitya suddenly began to babble.

'He's not from these parts, this man, and he isn't here just now. He's from the peasantry, makes a living in the timber trade, Lyagavy, they call him, "The Setter". He's been bargaining with Fyodor Pavlovich over that birch grove of yours in Chermashnya for a year now, and they keep falling out over the price, perhaps you've heard about it. It just so happens that he's turned up here again and is staying just now at the home of the priest of Ilyinskoye, oh, about twelve versts from Volovya Station, it will be, in the village of Ilyinskoye. He also sent me a letter on that same piece of business, on account of that birch grove, I mean, asking for advice. Fyodor Pavlovich intends to go and visit him there himself. So if you were able to get there first, before Fyodor Pavlovich, and were to suggest to Lyagavy the same proposal you told me about, it's quite possible that he . . .'

'A thought of genius!' Mitya said, interrupting in ecstasy. 'Let it be him, let him deal with it! He's in the process of bargaining, the price he's being asked to pay is too high, and here is the document that gives him the deeds of ownership, ha-ha-ha!' And Mitya suddenly broke into his short, wooden laugh, one quite unexpected, so that even Samsonov's head moved.

'How can I thank you, Kuzma Kuzmich?' Mitya bubbled.

'It is nothing, sir,' Samsonov replied, inclining his head.

'But you don't know, you have saved me, oh, a premonition drew me to you . . . Very well, to this country pope let me go!'

'It merits no gratitude, sir.'

'I hasten and I fly. I have abused your health. Never shall I forget, a Russian man says this to you, Kuzma Kuzmich, a R-russian man!'

'Quite, quite, sir.'

Mitya moved to grasp the old man's hand, in order to shake it, but a trace of malice flickered in the latter's eyes. Mitya took his hand away, but immediately reproached himself for his suspicion. 'It's because he's tired . . .' fleeted through his mind.

'For her! For her, Kuzma Kuzmich! Do you understand, it is for her!' he bellowed suddenly all over the entire reception-room, made a bow, a steep turn, and with those same swift, arshin-wide steps, not turning round, leapt towards the exit door. He was quivering with ecstasy. 'Why, all was going to ruin, and then this guardian angel saved me,' rushed through his mind. 'And if a smart dealer such as that old man (a most honourable old man, and what a bearing!) has pointed out this path to me, then . . . then, of course, the path is won. I must fly this instant. Whether I return before nightfall, or whether I return in the night, it matters not, for the cause is won. Could the old man really have been laughing at me?' Thus did Mitya exclaim as he strode into his lodging, and, of course, the matter could not present itself to him otherwise than it did, that is to say: either the advice was smart (coming as it did from a smart dealer), based on a knowledge of this Lyagavy (a strange surname!), or – or the old man had been laughing at him! Alas! That latter notion was the only correct one. Later, long afterwards, when the entire catastrophe had been enacted, old Samsonov himself would admit, laughing, that he had indeed exposed the 'captain' to ridicule. This was a malicious, cold and mocking individual, who was, moreover, possessed of certain morbid antipathies. It may have been the captain's look of ecstasy, or the foolish conviction of this 'prodigal and waster' that he, Samsonov, might fall for such rubbish as his 'plan', or it may have been an emotion of jealousy on account of Grushenka, in whose name 'that terror' had come to him with some kind of rubbish for money – I do not know exactly what it was that prompted the old man at the time, but at the moment Mitya stood before him, feeling his legs turn to jelly, and inanely exclaiming that he was lost – at that moment the old man looked at him with infinite malice and took it into his head to make fun of him. When Mitya had left, Kuzma Kuzmich, pale with malice, turned to his son and instructed him to see to it that in future 'that ragamuffin' never set foot in his house again nor even his yard, or he would . . .

He did not actually say what he threatened to do, but even his son, who had frequently witnessed his wrath, started with fear. For a whole hour thereafter the old man positively shook all over with malice, and when evening came he fell ill and sent for the 'leech'.

2

Lyagavy

So there it was: he must go 'post-haste', yet for horses he had not a copeck, or rather, he had two twenty-copeck pieces, and that was all, all that remained of all those years of his earlier prosperity! There lay in his room, however, an old silver watch of his which had long since stopped working. He snatched it up and bore it off to the Jewish watchmaker who was to be found in his wretched little shop at the bazaar. The latter gave him six roubles for it. 'I didn't even expect to get that!' cried the enraptured Mitya (he continued all the while to be in a state of rapture), snatched up his six roubles and ran off back to his lodgings. Once there he added to the sum, borrowing three roubles from his landlords, who lent him the money with pleasure, in spite of the fact that this was the last of their money they were parting with, so fond were they of him. In his ecstatic condition Mitya confided to them there and then that his fate was in the process of being decided, and informed them, in a dreadful hurry, of course, of almost the whole of the 'plan' he had just presented to Samsonov, then of Samsonov's decision, of his hopes for the future, and so on, and so forth. The landlords had even before now been initiated into many of his secrets, because they looked upon him as 'one of their own kind', and not at all as a proud *barin*. Having in such wise amassed nine roubles, Mitya sent for post-horses to take him to Volovya Station. It was in this fashion, however, that there appeared and was remembered the material fact that 'On the day before a certain event, at noon, Mitya had not a copeck and, in order to obtain money, sold his watch and borrowed three roubles from his landlords, and all of this before witnesses.'

I mention this fact in advance; later on my reasons for doing so will become clear.

As he drove post-haste to Volovya Station, Mitya, though radiant with the joyful anticipation that at last he was about to conclude and unravel 'all this business', trembled no less from fear: what would become of Grushenka now in his absence? Well, what if she were to decide that very day, at last, to go to Fyodor Pavlovich? That was why he had left without giving her any report of his actions, and why he had instructed his landlords on no account to reveal his whereabouts if anyone should come asking for him. 'I must, I must without fail return by this evening,' he kept saying to himself, as he sat in the jolting wagon – 'and I'll probably have to drag that Lyagavy back here ... to complete that document ...' – thus, his soul dying inwardly, did Mitya dream, but alas, his reveries were fated all too decisively not to be accomplished in harmony with his 'plan'.

For one thing, he was late, for he left Volovya Station by the cart-track. This cart-track turned out to be not twelve, but fifteen versts long. For another thing, he did not find the priest of Ilyinskoye at home, as the latter was away on a visit to a neighbouring estate. By the time Mitya tracked him down, setting out for that neighbouring estate still with the same by now exhausted horses, it was already almost dark. The priest, a shy and kindly looking little man, at once explained to him that this Lyagavy, though he had originally been staying with him, was now at Sukhoy Posyolok, and would be staying overnight at the *izba* of the forest warden, as he was also engaged in a timber deal over there. In response to Mitya's earnest request that he be taken to see Lyagavy at once — 'and so, as it were, be saved' — the priest, though at first he hesitated, consented to take him to Sukhoy Posyolok, evidently with a sense of curiosity; as bad luck would have it, however, he recommended that they go there 'on shanks's pony' as the distance involved was only about a verst 'and a little bit more'. Mitya, of course, agreed and began to lope along with his arshin-wide steps, so that the poor priest almost had to follow him at a run. The little fellow was not yet old, and endowed with extreme caution. Mitya at once began to talk to him of his plans, heatedly and nervously demanded counsel regarding Lyagavy, and went on talking all the way. The priest listened attentively, but offered little by way of counsel. To Mitya's questions he gave evasive answers: 'I don't know, oh, I don't know, how ever could I know such a thing?' etcetera. When Mitya began to talk about the series of *contretemps* he had been having with his father on the subject of his inheritance, the priest well and truly took fright, because he was in some kind of dependent relation to Fyodor Pavlovich. With astonishment, in fact, did he inquire why Mitya called this peasant businessman Gorstkin Lyagavy, and urged him to observe that even though the latter was indeed Lyagavy, he was not Lyagavy, because this name was violently offensive to him, and that Mitya must without fail address him as Gorstkin, 'otherwise you will accomplish nothing with him, and he will not listen' — the priest concluded. Mitya was somewhat suddenly surprised at this, explaining that thus did Samsonov himself refer to the man. Having learned of this circumstance, the priest at once killed the conversation, though he would have done well at the same time to explain to Dmitry Fyodorovich his conjecture: that if Samsonov had sent him to a muzhik like Lyagavy, had he not done so in order for some reason to make fun of him, and was there not something amiss here? Mitya, however, had no time to pause 'over such trivial matters'. He was in a hurry, strode onwards and, no sooner had he arrived in Sukhoy Posyolok, realized that they had walked not a verst, nor one and a half, but in all likelihood three; this vexed him, but he endured. They entered the *izba*. The forest warden, who was a friend of the priest's, was accommodated in one half of the *izba*, while in the other half, the living-room, through the passage, Gorstkin was to be found. They entered this living-room and lit a tallow candle. The room was heated to excess. On a deal table stood an extinguished samovar, next to it a tray with cups, an empty bottle of rum, a not-quite-empty *shtof* of vodka and the remains of a wheaten loaf. The guest himself lay stretched out on a bench, with his street-clothes bunched up together under his head instead of a pillow, snoring massively. Mitya stood in bewilderment. 'There's nothing for it, we shall have to rouse him: the matter I'm here on is far too important, I hurried all the way here and I'm in a hurry to get back by this evening,' Mitya said, beginning to grow anxious. But the priest and the forest warden stood in silence, keeping their opinion to themselves. Mitya went over and set about doing some rousing himself, set about it energetically, but the sleeper did not awake. 'He's drunk,' decided Mitya, 'but then what am I going to do, O Lord, what am I going to do!' And suddenly in a state of terrible impatience he set about tugging the sleeper by the arms, by the legs, shaking him by the head, lifting him up and sitting him down on the bench, and yet after long and strenuous efforts attained no more than that the latter began inanely to mumble and saltily, though with words that were unclear, to curse.

'No, I really think you had better wait a little,' the priest uttered at last, 'for he is plainly not up to it.'

'He's been drinking all day,' the forest warden responded.

'O God!' Mitya kept screaming. 'If you only knew how much I need to talk to him and in what despair I am now!'

'No, you had better wait a little, until morning,' the priest repeated.

'Until morning? For mercy's sake, that is impossible!' And in his despair he very nearly threw himself back into rousing the drunkard, but at once abandoned the attempt, having grasped the full pointlessness of such efforts. The priest said nothing, the sleepy forest warden was morose.

'What terrible tragedies realism arranges with human beings!' Mitya said in total despair. The sweat was pouring down his face. Taking advantage of the opportune moment, the priest very reasonably explained that though it might be possible to rouse the sleeper, being drunk he would nevertheless be incapable of any form of conversation, 'and you have an important matter to discuss with him, so you would be better to leave it until the morn . . .' Mitya threw up his hands and consented.

'Well, father, I shall stay here with a candle and await the right moment. When he wakes up, I shall begin . . . I'll pay you for the candle,' he said, turning to the forest warden, 'and for my lodging, too, you shall remember Dmitry Karamazov. The only problem is yourself, father, for I don't know what we're going to do with you: where will you sleep?'

'Oh, I shall go home, sir. I shall get there on his filly,' he said, indicating the warden. 'Whereupon I shall say farewell to you, sir, and wish you every joy in your endeavour.'

So it was determined. The priest set off on the filly, relieved to have got away at last, still, however, shaking his head in perturbation, as he reflected whether it might not be necessary tomorrow to inform his benefactor Fyodor Pavlovich in good time of this curious incident, 'for one can never be too sure, if I do not he may find out for himself, lose his temper and withdraw his charity'. The warden, having scratched himself, went off to his half of the *izba* in silence, and Mitya sat down on the bench in order, as he had expressed it, to 'await the right moment'. A deep anguish had, like a heavy mist, enshrouded his soul. A deep, terrible anguish! He sat, thought, but could think nothing through. The candle burned down, a cricket scraped, the heated room became stifling beyond endurance. He suddenly saw the garden, the path at the bottom of the garden, the door of his father's house opening, and Grushenka running in through it . . . He leapt up from the bench.

'A tragedy!' he said, grinding his teeth, mechanically walked over to the sleeper and began to look at his face. This was a lean, not-yet-old muzhik, with a very oblong face, light brown curls and a long, thin, reddish little beard; he was wearing a cotton shirt and a black waistcoat, from the pocket of which there peeped the chain of a silver watch. Mitya studied this physiognomy with terrible hatred, and for some reason it was the curls he found particularly hateful. Above all, it was unendurably offensive to him that here he, Mitya, was, standing over him with his business that would brook no delay, having sacrificed so much, having given up so much, totally exhausted, while this parasite, 'on whom my entire fate now depends, snores there as though nothing of all that existed, as though he were from another planet'. 'Oh, irony of fate!' Mitya exclaimed and all of a sudden, completely losing his head, he threw himself once again into rousing the drunken muzhik. He did so with a kind of rabid frenzy, tearing at him, shoving him, even beating him, but, continuing the process for some five minutes and again attaining nothing, in helpless despair he returned to his bench and sat down.

'Stupid, stupid!' Mitya kept exclaiming, 'and . . . how dishonourable this all is!' he suddenly added for some reason. His head had begun to ache horribly: 'Perhaps I should give up? Get away from this place altogether,' fleeted through his mind. 'No, I must wait till the morning. I shall stay here specially, specially! Why else did I come here, after all? And in any case I've no money to pay for the journey, so how can I get away – oh, how senseless!'

His head, however, was aching more and more. Motionlessly he sat and did not remember nodding off, having suddenly fallen asleep where he sat. He had evidently slept for a couple of hours or more. But had woken up because of the unendurable pain in his head, unendurable to the point of crying aloud. His temples hammered, the crown of his head hurt; having woken up, it took him a long time before he could completely regain his wits and make sense of what had happened to him. At last he realized that the heated room was full of terrible carbon-monoxide fumes, and that he could easily have died. But the drunken muzhik still lay there, snoring; the candle had guttered, and was on the point of going out. Mitya began to shout and rushed, stumbling and swaying, through the passage to the warden's half of the *izba*. The latter soon woke up, but, having heard that there were fumes in the other room, though he went to make the necessary dispositions, greeted the fact in a manner indifferent to the point of strangeness, which Mitya found both surprising and offensive.

'But he's dead, he's dead, and then . . . what then?' Mitya kept exclaiming before him in a frenzy.

They drew wide the doors, opened the window, cleared the chimney, Mitya hauled in a bucket of water from the passage, first wetting his own head and then, having found some rag or other, dipped it in the water and applied it to the head of Lyagavy. As for the warden, he continued to treat the whole event with a measure even of contempt and, having opened the window, pronounced morosely: 'It'll do like that'— and went back to resume his slumber, leaving Mitya a lighted iron lantern. Mitya continued to minister to the monoxide-fumed drunkard for about half an hour, constantly wetting his head, and was by now seriously intent upon staying awake all night, but, exhausted, sat down for just one moment in order to get his breath back, for an instant closed his eyes, then at once, without being aware of it, stretched out on the bench and fell asleep like a dead man.

He awoke horribly late. It was already about nine o'clock in the morning. The sun was shining brightly through the two small windows of the *izba*. Yesterday's curly-headed muzhik was sitting on the bench, already dressed in his *poddyovka*. Before him stood a fresh samovar and a fresh *shtof* of vodka. The old one of yesterday was now finished, and the new one was already more than half empty. Mitya leapt up and in a flash realized that the accursed muzhik was drunk again, drunk profoundly and beyond the brink of no return. He stared at him for a moment, his eyes bulging out of his head. As for the muzhik, he stared back silently and slyly, with a kind of offensive calm, a kind of contemptuous arrogance even, or so it appeared to Mitya. He rushed over to the man.

'Look, I'm sorry, you see . . . I . . . you've probably heard about me from the forest warden in the other part of the *izba*: I'm Lieutenant Dmitry Karamazov, the son of the old Karamazov with whom you're currently bargaining over his birch grove . . .'

'You're telling lies!' the muzhik suddenly rapped out firmly and calmly.

'What do you mean, lies? You are pleased to know Fyodor Pavlovich, are you not?'

'I'm not pleased to know any Fyodor Pavlovich,' the muzhik pronounced, shifting his tongue somehow heavily.

'The birch grove, the birch grove, the one you're bargaining with him about; I say, please wake up and come to your senses. Father Pavel of Ilyinskoye accompanied me here. You also wrote to Samsonov, and he sent me to you . . .' Mitya said, panting.

'L-lies!' Lyagavy rapped out again.

Mitya's legs turned cold.

'For heaven's sake, I mean, this isn't a joke, you know! I think you must be tipsy. But you might at least speak and show that you understand . . . otherwise . . . otherwise I really don't understand!'

'You're the decorator!'

'For heaven's sake, I'm Karamazov, Dmitry Karamazov, and I have a proposal to make to you . . . An advantageous proposal . . . highly . . . advantageous . . . on the very subject of the birch grove.'

The muzhik smoothed his beard with a consequential air.

'No, you took the contract for that job and turned out to be a scoundrel. You're a scoundrel!'

'And I assure you that you are mistaken!' Mitya exclaimed, wringing his hands in despair. The muzhik continued to smooth his beard and then suddenly narrowed his eyes in a sly manner.

'No, I tell you what you can show me: show me the clause in your contract that allows you to go plotting filthy mischief, do you hear? You're a scoundrel, do you know that?'

In gloom, Mitya withdrew, and suddenly it was as though something 'smote him on the brow', as he expressed it later on. In a single flash a kind of illumination took place within his mind, 'the torch was lit, and I perceived it all'. In stupefaction did he stand, marvelling at how he, a man of intelligence, after all, could have fallen for such a stupid trick, let himself get bogged down in an adventure of this kind and carry on with all this for a whole twenty-four hours, almost, fussing over this Lyagavy, wetting his head . . . 'Well, the man's drunk, drunk to the very devil, and he's going to continue his bout for another week yet — what's the point in waiting here? And what if Samsonov sent me here deliberately? And what if she . . . O God, what have I gone and done?'

The muzhik sat looking at him, laughing quietly to himself. On another occasion, Mitya might very well have killed the fool out of malicious hatred, but now he merely turned to jelly all over, like a young child. Quietly he went over to the bench, took his coat, silently put it on and went out of the room. In the other half of the *izba* he did not find the forest warden, there was no one there. From his pocket he took fifty copecks in change and placed it on the table, as payment for his night's stay, his candle and the inconvenience he had caused. As he came out of the *izba* he saw that around it there was only forest, and nothing else. He walked at random, unable even to remember which way to turn when he left the *izba* – to right or to left; the previous night, hurrying there with the priest, he had not observed the route. There was no feeling of vengeance towards anyone in his soul, not even towards Samsonov. He strode along the narrow forest track vacantly, perplexed, with a sense of having 'lost his cause' and quite unconcerned as to where he was headed for. Any child he met along his way could have got the better of him, so helpless had he suddenly become in soul and body. But somehow, one way or the other, he managed to get out of the forest: suddenly there appeared before him bare, harvested fields on a boundless expanse of space: 'What despair, what death all around!' he kept saying, as he strode onwards and onwards.

He was saved by some travellers: a cabman was driving an old merchant along the country road. When they drew even, Mitya asked them the way, and it proved that they were also headed for Volovya. They entered into parley, and Mitya was taken along as a fellow traveller. Some three hours later they arrived. At Volovya Station Mitya at once ordered post-horses to take him to town, and then suddenly realized that he was atrociously hungry. While the horses were being harnessed, an omelette was rustled up for him. He ate it all in a flash, ate the whole of a large hunk of bread, ate a sausage that happened to be to hand, and downed three large glasses of vodka. Having fortified himself, he felt more cheerful, and his soul brightened up. He flew on his way, urging the coachman on, and suddenly drew up a new and 'unalterable' plan, by means of which he would by the evening of that very day obtain 'that accursed money'. 'And to think, oh, to think that because of that miserable three thousand a human fate is perishing!' he exclaimed contemptuously. 'Today I shall settle the matter!' And had it not been for the constant thought of Grushenka and of whether or not something might have happened to her, he might have become thoroughly cheerful again. But the thought of her kept stabbing into his soul every moment like a sharp knife. At last they reached their destination, and Mitya at once went running off to Grushenka.

3

The Gold-mines

THIS was that same visit by Mitya of which Grushenka had given an account with such terror to Rakitin. At the time she had been expecting her estafette, and was thoroughly relieved that Mitya neither the day before nor that day had been to see her, hoping that God might grant he did not arrive until she had left, but then suddenly he had descended on her. The rest is known to us: in order to get him off her hands she had instantly persuaded him to take her to the house of Kuzma Samsonov, where she said she must with dreadful urgency go in order to 'count money', and when Mitya had at once done so, in parting from him outside the gates of Kuzma's house, had taken from him the promise that he would come to fetch her at twelve o'clock midnight, in order to escort her home again. Mitya was also relieved at this arrangement: 'If she's sitting over there with Kuzma, that means she won't be able to go and see Fyodor Pavlovich ... that's as long as she isn't lying, of course,' he appended at once. In his estimation, however, she was not lying. He was indeed of that type of jealous man who, in parting from the beloved woman, at once proceed to imagine God only knows what all kinds of horrors concerning what she may be up to and how she may be 'being unfaithful' to him, but – upon running back to her again, shaken, crushed, irrevocably persuaded that she really has managed to be unfaithful to him, from his first glance at her features, at the laughing, cheerful and affectionate features of that woman – is at once reborn in spirit, at once loses all suspicion and with joyful shame curses himself for his jealousy. Having taken Grushenka to Kuzma's house, he rushed back home to his lodgings. Oh, so much did there still remain for him to do that day! But, at any rate, his heart felt lighter now. 'Only now I must find out from Smerdyakov if anything came to pass there yesterday evening, for she may have gone there to see Fyodor Pavlovich for all I know – O God!' rushed through his head. The result was that even before he had had time to run back to his lodgings, the jealousy was once more beginning to swarm within his restless heart.

Jealousy! 'Othello is not jealous, he is trusting,'* Pushkin observed, and that single observation alone bears witness to the extraordinary depth of intellect possessed by our great poet. All that has happened to Othello is that his soul has had the brains beaten out of it, thereby muddying his whole world-outlook, because *his ideal has perished*. But Othello will not conceal himself, peep or spy: he is trusting. On the contrary, he must be influenced by suggestion, led on, aroused by dint of exceptional effort before he even so much as suspects unfaithfulness. Of different mettle is the truly jealous man. It is impossible to imagine the entire degree of disgrace and moral downfall to which the jealous man is capable of accommodating himself without the slightest pang of conscience. And in fact, it is not as if these were exclusively vulgar and sordid souls. On the contrary, though they may possess a lofty heart, a love that is pure and full of self-sacrifice, at the same time they may conceal themselves beneath tables, suborn with money the most base individuals, and accommodate themselves to a most loathsome, sordid swill of spying and eavesdropping. On no account would Othello ever be able to reconcile himself to unfaithfulness — forgive it, yes, he could not fail to do that, but reconcile himself to it, never, not even though his soul is free of rancour and innocent as the soul of a young babe. Not so with the truly jealous man: it is hard to imagine the things to which certain jealous men are able to acclimatize and reconcile themselves, and the things they are able to forgive! Jealous men are the first to forgive, and all women are aware of this. The jealous man may extremely quickly (after, of course, a fearful scene initially) be capable of forgiving, for example, an infidelity that has, more or less, already been proved, embraces and kisses he has already seen with his own eyes, if, for example, he has at the same time somehow been able to persuade himself that this was 'the last time' and that from this hour on his rival will disappear, travel away to the ends of the earth, or that he himself will now take her away to a location such as shall no longer be accessible to this dreaded rival. Of course, the reconciliation will be of temporary effect, because even were the rival indeed to disappear, tomorrow he will invent another, new one and be jealous of the new one, instead. And indeed, one might ask oneself what there could be in a love that required such spying, and what a love could be worth, that necessitated such energetic surveillance? But precisely this the truly jealous man will never understand, yet even so among them, truly, are on occasion to be found men of positively lofty heart. Remarkable, too, is the fact that these very men of lofty heart, as they stand in some small cupboard of a room, spying and eavesdropping, though they clearly understand with their 'lofty hearts' the enormity of the shame into which they themselves have crawled of their own volition, yet do not, at the moment, anyway, at which they stand in that cupboard of a room, ever feel a pang of conscience. In Mitya's case, at the sight of Grushenka his jealousy vanished, and for an instant he became trusting and noble, even despising himself for his evil emotions. But this merely signified that in his love for this woman there was something far loftier than he himself had supposed, and not only sensuality, not only the 'curve in the body' of which he had talked to Alyosha. On the other hand, however, no sooner had Grushenka disappeared than Mitya at once began to suspect her of every base and perfidious deed of unfaithfulness. In doing so, he experienced not one pang of conscience.

So it was that jealousy began to bubble up within him once again. Whatever happened, he had to hurry. The first thing was to obtain at least a driblet of money on loan. Yesterday's nine roubles had almost all been used up on travel, and without any money at all, of course, he could take not a step anywhere. But together with his new plan he had also, as he sat in the wagon the day before, deliberated on how he might obtain money on loan. He had a pair of good duelling pistols with cartridges, and if until now he had not pawned them, it was because he loved these heirlooms more than anything else he possessed. In the Capital City inn he had long ago become slightly acquainted with a certain young civil servant and had somehow learned at the inn that this young, unmarried and thoroughly well-to-do civil servant was passionately fond of weaponry, bought pistols, revolvers, daggers, hung them on the walls of his apartment, showed them off to friends, boasting, a master of explaining the system of the revolver, how to load it, how to fire it and so on. Without thinking for long, Mitya at once set off to see him and proposed that he pawn the pistols for ten roubles. The civil servant gleefully began to try to persuade him to sell them straight off, but Mitya would not consent, and the civil servant gave him ten roubles, declaring that he would on no account take interest. They parted on a friend-to-friend basis. Mitya made haste, he was desperate to get to Fyodor Pavlovich's house by way of the rears, to his summerhouse, in order to call out Smerdyakov as soon as possible. In such wise, however, was there once again established the fact that only three or four hours before a certain occurrence, of which I shall speak more below, Mitya had not a copeck of ready cash and had pawned an heirloom he loved, when suddenly, three hours later, he turned out to be in possession of thousands . . . But I run ahead.

At the home of Marya Kondratyevna (Fyodor Pavlovich's female neighbour) there awaited him a piece of news that shocked him and disturbed him in the extreme − it concerned the fact of Smerdyakov's illness. He heard a complete account of Smerdyakov's fall into the cellar, then of his epileptic attack, the doctor's arrival, the worries of Fyodor Pavlovich; with curiosity did he also discover that brother Ivan Fyodorovich had already rolled off to Moscow that morning. 'He must have gone through Volovya before I did,' thought Dmitry Fyodorovich, but the news about Smerdyakov upset him horribly.'What will I do now? Who will keep watch? Who will tell me what is going on?' With avidity did he begin to question these women: had they noticed anything yesterday evening? They knew all too well what he was endeavouring to find out, and tried to put his mind completely at rest: no one had come to the house, Ivan Fyodorovich had spent the night there, 'everything was completely as normal'. Mitya fell to thinking. There were no two ways around it, tonight he would have to stand sentry as well, but where? Here or outside Samsonov's gates? He decided that it would have to be both here and there, at discretion, but for the time being, for the time being . . . The fact was that now there stood before him that 'plan' of the day before, the new and this time sure-fire plan he had thought up in the wagon and any delay in the execution of which was now out of the question. Mitya decided to give up an hour to it: 'in an hour's time I shall decide the whole thing, discover everything and then, then, to start with, I shall go to Samsonov's house, find out if Grushenka is there, and in a flash return here, and stay here until eleven o'clock, and then go back to fetch her at Samsonov's and take her home.' This was how he determined to resolve the matter.

He flew off back to his lodgings, washed, combed his hair, brushed his clothes, got dressed and set out for the home of Mrs Khokhlakova. Alas, his 'plan' lay there. He had determined to borrow three thousand from this lady. And the principal gist of the matter was that somehow there had suddenly formed within him an extraordinary sense of conviction that she would not refuse him. It may perhaps be wondered why, if his sense of conviction were so great, he had not gone there earlier, to the society of his peers, as it were, rather than direct his steps to Samsonov, a man of alien disposition with whom he did not even know how to converse. The fact was, however, that in the course of the last month he had almost entirely severed his acquaintance with Mrs Khokhlakova, had indeed scarcely had acquaintance with her before that and knew very well, in addition, that she herself could not abide him. This lady had from the very beginning conceived a detestation of him simply for the fact that he

was Katerina Ivanovna's betrothed, while she for some reason had suddenly begun to wish that Katerina Ivanovna would give him up and
marry instead 'the charming Ivan Fyodorovich, who is educated in the
ways of chivalry and has such beautiful manners'. Mitya's manners, on
the other hand, she detested. Mitya even made fun of her and had on one
occasion managed to express the opinion that this lady was 'as lively and
over-familiar as she is lacking in education'. And then that morning, in
the wagon, he had suddenly been illuminated by a brilliant idea: 'But if she's
so against my marrying Katerina Ivanovna, against it to such a degree'
(he knew that it almost attained the point of hysterics), 'then how could
she now refuse me that three thousand were she to realize that I would
use it for the express purpose of leaving her Katya alone and clearing out
of this town for good? Once these spoilt upper-class ladies conceive the
whim of a desire for something, they will spare nothing in order that
everything shall turn out as they wish it. What's more, she is rich,' Mitya
thought to himself. As for the 'plan' itself, it was still the same as it had
been earlier, that is to say, an offer of his rights to the Chermashnya
estate – not, however, with a commercial end in view, the way he had
presented it to Samsonov the day before, not with any attempt to entice
the lady, as in the case of Samsonov the day before, with the opportunity
of doubling his money, making six or seven thousand out of three, but
simply as an honourable guarantee against a debt. As he developed this
new idea Mitya passed into ecstasy, but this was invariably the case with
all his undertakings, all his sudden decisions. Every time he had a new
idea, he abandoned himself to it with passion. Nevertheless, when he
stepped on to the porch of Mrs Khokhlakova's house he suddenly experienced a chill of horror along his spine: only at this second did he clearly
cognize, with mathematical clarity that this was, after all, his last hope,
that if he fell into one of his hiatuses this time there would remain to him
nothing in the world but 'to murder and rob someone for the sake of that
three thousand, no more and no less . . .' It was close on seven-thirty
when he rang the doorbell.

At first the matter seemed to go well: no sooner did he announce his
presence than he was instantly received with extraordinary swiftness.
'Why, it's as though she'd been waiting for me,' flickered through
Mitya's head, and then suddenly, no sooner had he been led into the
drawing room, the mistress of the chambers came in almost at a run and
declared to him bluntly that she had been waiting for him . . .

'I have waited, waited! Why, I could hardly even think that you
would come to see me, you yourself will agree, and yet all the same I have

waited for you – wonder at my instinct, Dmitry Fyodorovich, all morning I have been certain that you would come today.'

'That, madam, is indeed cause for wonder,' Mitya pronounced, sitting down rather clumsily, 'but . . . I have come on an extremely important matter . . . the most important of important matters, for myself, that is, madam, solely for myself, and I am in haste . . .'

'I know that you have come on a most important matter, Dmitry Fyodorovich, and here it is not a question of premonitions or retrograde hankerings after miracles (have you heard about the Elder Zosima?) here, here, there is mathematics: you could not fail to come after all that took place with Katerina Ivanovna, you could not, could not possibly fail to come – that is mathematics.'

'The realism of real life, madam, that is what it is! Permit me, however, to explain . . .'

'Precisely, Dmitry Fyodorovich – realism. I am now entirely in favour of realism, where miracles are concerned I am all too sorely instructed. Did you hear that the Elder Zosima has died?'

'No, madam, this is the first I have heard of it,' Mitya said with a certain degree of astonishment. The image of Alyosha fleeted through his mind.

'It happened last night, and can you imagine . . .'

'Madam,' Mitya said, breaking her off, 'I can imagine only one thing, and that is that I am in a most desperate plight and that if you do not help me, then everything will go to hang, and I shall be the first to do so. Forgive me for the triviality of the expression, but I am in an ague, in a fever . . .'

'I know, I know that you are, I know it all, and you cannot possibly be in any other condition of spirit, and whatever you say, I know it all already. I long ago took your fate into consideration, Dmitry Fyodorovich, I have been watching it and studying it . . . Oh, be assured that I am an experienced doctor of the soul, Dmitry Fyodorovich.'

'Madam, if you are an experienced doctor, then I on the other hand am an experienced patient,' Mitya said, forcing himself to adopt a courtly tone, 'and I have a presentiment that if you have been watching my fate in this way you will be able to assist it, faced as it is with downfall, but in order that this may be so you must at last permit me to explain to you the plan with which I have taken the risk of appearing before you . . . and explain to you what it is I expect to obtain from you . . . I have come, madam . . .'

'Do not explain, that is a secondary matter. But as regards help, Dmitry Fyodorovich, you would not be the first man I have helped. I expect you have heard of my cousin Belmesova, her husband was facing ruin, "going to hang" as you so characteristically expressed it, Dmitry Fyodorovich, but what of it, I directed him into horse-breeding, and now he prospers. Do you have a grasp of horse-breeding, Dmitry Fyodorovich?'

'Not the slightest, madam — oh, madam, not the slightest!' Mitya shouted in nervous impatience, even starting to get up from his seat. 'I only beseech you, madam, to hear me out, give me only two minutes of free discourse, that first I may explain to you everything, the whole of the project with which I have come to you. What is more, time presses on me, I am in dreadful haste! . . .' Mitya cried hysterically, sensing that she was again about to speak, and in the hope of shouting her down. 'I have come in despair . . . in the last extremity of despair, in order to beg you to lend me three thousand roubles, lend, I stress, and on a reliable pledge, madam, on terms of the most reliable security! Only permit me to explain . . .'

'You may tell me all that later, later!' Mrs Khokhlakova said, in her turn making an impatient gesture, 'and in any case all that you say I know already, I have told you that. You are asking for a specific sum, you need three thousand, but I shall give you immeasurably more, I shall save you, Dmitry Fyodorovich, but it is necessary that you obey me!'

Mitya fairly sprang up from his seat again.

'Madam, would you really be so kind?' he let out with extreme emotion. 'O Lord, you have saved me. Madam, you are saving a man from a violent death, from the pistol . . . My eternal gratitude . . .'

'I will give you infinitely, infinitely more than three thousand!' Mrs Khokhlakova cried, gazing with a radiant smile upon Mitya's ecstasy.

'Infinitely more? But so much I do not need. All that is essential to me is that three thousand, so fateful for me, and I for my part have come to guarantee you that sum with infinite gratitude, and offer you my plan, which . . .'

'Enough, Dmitry Fyodorovich, no sooner said than done,' Mrs Khokhlakova said in clipped tones, with the chaste solemnity of a benefactress. 'I promised to save you and I shall save you. I shall save you as I saved Belmesov. What think you of the gold-mines, Dmitry Fyodorovich?'

'The gold-mines, madam? I have never given them any thought.'

'Well, I have done so for you! I have thought of them, and thought of them again! For a whole month now I have been watching you with this goal in mind. A hundred times I have looked at you as you were passing, and have said to myself: there is a man of energy who ought to travel to the gold-mines. I even studied your walk and decided: that man will discover many gold-mines.'

'You decided it by my walk, madam?' Mitya asked, smiling.

'What? Yes, by your walk. Come now, surely you will not deny that it is possible to detect a person's character from the way he walks, Dmitry Fyodorovich? The natural sciences confirm it. Oh, now I am a realist, Dmitry Fyodorovich. Starting from this very day, in the wake of *toute cette histoire* at the monastery, which has upset me greatly, I am an outright realist and intend to throw myself into practical activity. I have been cured. "Enough!" as Turgenev said.'*

'But madam, the three thousand you so generously promised to lend me . . .'

'It shall not pass you by, Dmitry Fyodorovich,' Mrs Khokhlakova at once interrupted him. 'That three thousand is as good as in your pocket, and it will be not three thousand but three million, Dmitry Fyodorovich, in the very shortest of time! I shall tell you your mission: you shall discover gold-mines, amass millions, return and become a leader of men, moving us forward and directing us towards the common weal. Are we really to leave it all to the Jews? You shall construct buildings and various factories. You shall assist the poor, and they shall bless you. Now is the age of the railroad, Dmitry Fyodorovich. You shall become known and indispensable to the Ministry of Finance, which is at present in such dire straits. The fall in the value of our paper rouble keeps me awake at nights, Dmitry Fyodorovich, that side of me is little known . . .'

'Madam, madam!' Dmitry Fyodorovich interrupted again with an uneasy sense of anticipation, 'I shall most, most possibly follow your counsel, your wise counsel, madam, and shall perhaps set off yonder . . . to those gold-mines . . . and come back again and tell you about them . . . Come back many times, even . . . But at present that three thousand, which you so generously . . . Oh, it would unbind me, and if it were possible that today . . . That is to say, do you see, that I have at present not a moment, not a moment to lose . . .'

'Enough, Dmitry Fyodorovich, enough!' Mrs Khokhlakova broke in insistently. 'The question is: will you travel to the gold-mines or will you not, have you quite made your decision, answer mathematically.'

'I shall go, madam, later . . . I shall go wherever you wish, madam . . . but at present . . .'

'Oh, wait a moment, then!' cried Mrs Khokhlakova, jumping up and rushing towards her magnificent writing desk with its numerous small drawers, and beginning to open one drawer after another, searching for something in a dreadful hurry.

'The three thousand!' Mitya thought, dying inwardly, 'and right now, without any documents, without a formal agreement . . . oh, that is the way gentlemen do business! A magnificent woman, and if only she were not such a babble-box . . .'

'Here it is!' Mrs Khokhlakova exclaimed in joy, returning to Mitya, 'This is what I was looking for!'

It was a tiny silver icon on a necklet, of the kind that is sometimes worn together with a cross next to the skin.

'This is from Kiev, Dmitry Fyodorovich,' she continued with reverence, 'from the relics of the Great Martyr Varvara. Permit me to place it around your neck myself and thereby bless you for a new life and for new deeds.'

And she did indeed throw the icon about his neck and began to make the motions of putting it in its proper place. In great embarrassment Mitya bent down and began to assist her and, at last, succeeded in pushing the icon between his tie and the collar of his shirt and on to his chest.

'There, now you can go!' Mrs Khokhlakova pronounced, solemnly sitting down in her chair again.

'Madam, I am so touched . . . and I do not even know how I can thank you . . . for such emotions, but . . . if only you knew how precious time is to me now! . . . That sum, which I await so dearly from your generosity . . .

'O madam, if you can be so kind, so touchingly generous to me,' Mitya exclaimed suddenly in a fit of inspiration, 'then permit me to disclose to you . . . though as a matter of fact, it is something you have long known . . . that I love in this town a certain creature . . . I have been unfaithful to Katya . . . Katerina Ivanovna, I mean. Oh, I have been inhuman and dishonourable in her regard, but I have come to love another in this town . . . a certain woman, madam, whom you may very well despise, for you know it all already, but whom I cannot possibly abandon, not possibly, and so now, that three thousand . . .'

'Abandon everything, Dmitry Fyodorovich!' Mrs Khokhlakova interrupted in a most resolute tone. 'Abandon everything, and especially women. Your mission is the gold-mines, and you have no business taking women there. Later, when you return in wealth and glory, you will find yourself a companion for your heart in the very highest of society. She will be a contemporary girl, with knowledge and no prejudices. By then the woman question, which now is only beginning, will have attained fruition, and the new woman will have appeared . . .'

'Madam, it is not the right thing, not the right thing . . .' Dmitry Fyodorovich said imploringly, beginning to clasp his hands.

'It is the very thing, Dmitry Fyodorovich, the very thing you need, the thing for which you are thirsting, while yet unaware of it. I am a great enthusiast for the present-day woman question, Dmitry Fyodorovich. The development of woman and even a political role for woman in the very nearest future – that is my ideal. I myself have a daughter, Dmitry Fyodorovich, and that side of me is little known. I sent a letter to the writer Shchedrin* in that connection. That writer has explained to me so much, so much concerning the destiny of woman, that last year I sent him an anonymous letter consisting of two lines: "I embrace and kiss you, my writer, for the contemporary woman – continue." And I signed it: "A mother". I was going to sign it "A contemporary mother", but I wasn't confident enough, and made do simply with "A mother": that has more moral beauty, Dmitry Fyodorovich, and in any case the word "contemporary" would have reminded him of *The Contemporary** – a bitter memory for him in view of the censorship nowadays . . . O, Good Lord, whatever is the matter with you?'

'Madam,' Mitya said, leaping up at last, clasping his hands before her in helpless supplication, 'you will compel me to weep, madam, if you postpone any longer that which you so generously . . .'

'And you shall weep, Dmitry Fyodorovich, you shall weep! Those are fine emotions . . . Such is the path that lies before you! Your tears will relieve you, later you shall return and rejoice. Be sure to come back from Siberia post-haste and expressly to me, that you may rejoice with me . . .'

'But I am sorry,' Mitya suddenly howled, 'for the last time I beseech you, tell me, may I expect to receive the promised sum from you today? And if not, then when may I present myself in order to receive it?'

'What sum, Dmitry Fyodorovich?'

'The three thousand that you promised . . . that you so generously . . .'

'Three thousand? Roubles, you mean? Oh, no, I don't have three thousand,' Mrs Khokhlakova enunciated with a kind of calm surprise. Mitya froze.

'But you . . . just now . . . you said . . . you even used the expression "it is as good as in your pocket". . .'

'Oh no, you did not understand me, Dmitry Fyodorovich. If that is what you thought, then you did not understand me. I was talking about the gold-mines. To be sure, I promised you more, infinitely more, than three thousand, I remember it all now, but all I had in mind was the gold-mines.'

'And the money? The three thousand?' Dmitry Fyodorovich exclaimed, absurdly.

'Oh, if it's money you meant, then I have none. I have no money at all now, Dmitry Fyodorovich, and in fact I am at present waging a war with my estate-manager and myself borrowed five hundred roubles from Miusov the other day. No, no, money I have none. And you know, Dmitry Fyodorovich, even if I had, I should not let you have any. For one thing, I do not lend to anyone. To lend means to quarrel. But to you, to you I particularly would not lend, my fondness for you would preclude that, in order to save you I would not lend it to you, because all you need is one thing: the gold-mines, the gold-mines and the gold-mines!'

'Oh, to the devil! . . .' Mitya cried, emitting a sudden roar, and striking his fist on the table with all his might.

'Ah-h!' Mrs Khokhlakova screamed in fright, flying off to the opposite end of the drawing room.

Mitya spat and with rapid strides made an exit from the room, from the house, out into the street, into the dark! He strode like a man insane, smiting himself upon the breast, in that very same place on his breast where he had smitten himself two days earlier in front of Alyosha, at his last meeting with him in the evening, in the dark, on the road. The true significance of this beating of his breast *in that place* and what it was he wished to indicate thereby – that was as yet a secret which no one in the world yet knew, one which he had not even revealed to Alyosha, but that secret contained for him more than mere disgrace, it contained destruction and suicide, for thus had he determined, if he could not obtain that three thousand in order to pay back Katerina Ivanovna and thereby remove from his breast, 'from that place on his breast', the disgrace which he had borne upon it and which had so oppressed his conscience. This will all be fully explained to the reader in what follows, but for the present let him note only that this man, having seen his last hope vanish, had no sooner taken a few steps away from Mrs Khokhlakova's house than this man, who was physically so strong, suddenly dissolved in tears like a little boy. As he walked, blind to all else he wiped the tears away with his fist. Thus did he emerge on to the square, and then suddenly felt that he had bumped into something with the whole of his body. There resounded the squeaky wail of some wretched little old woman, whom he had very nearly knocked over.

'Lord-a-mercy, you nearly murdered me! Why don't you look where you're going, you terror?'

'What, is it you?' Mitya exclaimed, having discerned the features of the old woman in the darkness. It was the old serving-woman from Kuzma Samsonov's whom yesterday Mitya had noticed all too well.

'And who would you be, little father?' the old woman said in quite a different voice. 'I can't make you out in the dark.'

'You live at Kuzma Kuzmich's house, don't you? You're one of his servants?'

'That's right, little father, only just now I've been out at Prokhorych's . . . But can I still not make out who you are?'

'Tell me, old mother, is Agrafena Aleksandrovna with you now?' Mitya got out, beside himself with anticipation. 'I myself escorted her there earlier this evening.'

'She was here, little father, she came, stayed for a bit and then left.'

'What? She left?' Mitya exclaimed. 'When did she leave?'

'Oh, she came and she left almost at the same time, she was only with us for a minute or so. She told Kuzma Kuzmich some sort of story, it made him laugh, and then she went running off.'

'You're lying, accursed one!' Mitya howled.

'Ah-h!' the old woman cried, but Mitya had already gone; he ran as fast as he could to the house of Mrs Morozova. This was precisely at the time that Grushenka had gone off to Mokroye, no more than a quarter of an hour had passed since her departure. When the 'captain' suddenly ran in, Fenya was sitting with her grandmother, the cook Matryona, in the kitchen. At the sight of him Fenya began to yell blue murder.

'What are you yelling for?' Mitya howled. 'Where is she?' But without even letting the terror-frozen Fenya reply so much as a single word, he suddenly collapsed at her feet:

'Fenya, in the name of the Lord our Christ, tell me where she is!'

'I don't know anything, Dmitry Fyodorovich, little father, I don't know anything, little dove, you can kill me, but I don't know anything,' Fenya said, vowing and swearing. 'You yourself went off with her earlier . . .'

'She came back again!'

'No, she didn't, little dove, I swear to God, she didn't!'

'You're lying!' Mitya exclaimed. 'The very fact that you're so frightened tells me where she is!'

He rushed for the door. The frightened Fenya was relieved at having acquitted herself so cheaply, but she was very well aware that this was only because he had had no time and that otherwise things might have turned out badly for her. In rushing for the door, however, he none the less astonished both Fenya and old Matryona by a certain most unexpected manoeuvre: on the table stood a brass mortar, and in it a pestle, a small, brass pestle no more than one quarter of an arshin in length. Mitya, running out and already having opened the door with one hand, with the other suddenly as he passed snatched the pestle from the mortar and stuffed it in his side pocket, and that was the last that was seen of him.

'Oh, Lord-a-mercy, he's going to kill somebody!' Fenya shouted, wringing her hands.

4

In the Dark

WHERE had he gone running to? The answer was simple: 'Where could she be, but at the house of Fyodor Pavlovich? From Samsonov's house she must have run straight to his, that's quite clear now. The whole of the intrigue, the whole of the deceit are now plain . . .' All this flew round like a whirlwind inside his head. At the yard of Marya Kondratyevna's house he did not drop in: 'I mustn't go there, on no account must I go there . . . I mustn't raise the slightest suspicion . . . Marya Kondratyevna is obviously in the conspiracy, Smerdyakov also, also, they've all been bribed!' Another purpose had formed itself within him: circumventing the house of Fyodor Pavlovich in a wide detour, by way of the lane, he ran along Dmitrovsky Street, then crossed the little bridge and landed straight in the secluded lane that gave on to the rears, empty and uninhabited, with the wicker fencing of the neighbours' kitchen garden on the one side, and on the other – the strong, high fence that surrounded Fyodor Pavlovich's garden. Here he selected a place, and it appears to have been the same one where, according to the legend that was known to him, Lizaveta Smerdyashchaya had once climbed across. 'If she could do it,' fleeted through his mind, God only knows for what reason, 'then why shouldn't I?' And indeed, he jumped up and in an instant managed to grip the top of the fence with one hand, then with great energy stood on tiptoe, climbed up all in one go, and sat down astride of it. Nearby in the garden was the bathhouse, but from the top of the fence the illuminated windows of the house were also visible. 'It's true enough, there's light in the old man's bedroom, she's there!' – and he leapt down from the fence into the garden. Even though he knew that

Grigory was ill, and possibly Smerdyakov as well, and that there was no one who might hear him, he instinctively kept quiet, froze on the spot and began to listen. But all around there was dead silence and, as if by special design, the air was completely still, with not the slightest zephyr of a breeze.

'And only silence whispereth',* – that line of verse fleeted through his mind for some reason. 'Just as long as no one heard me jump across; I don't think anyone did.' Having stood still for a moment, he slowly walked through the garden, through the grass; avoiding the trees and the bushes he walked for a long time, masking every step, himself listening to every step he took. It took him about five minutes to make his way to the illumined windows. He remembered that there, beneath those very windows, there were several large, tall, thick bushes of elder and guelder rose. The door of the house that gave on to the garden on the left side of the façade was closed, and as he passed he made a special point of thoroughly checking this fact. At last he attained the bushes and concealed himself behind them. He scarcely breathed. 'Now I must wait,' he thought. 'If they've heard my footsteps and are listening now, then they'll need time to be reassured . . . If only I don't cough or sneeze.'

He waited for a couple of minutes, but his heart was beating horribly, and at moments he was almost out of breath. 'No, my heartbeat's not going to quiet down,' he thought, 'I can't wait any longer.' He was standing behind a bush in the shadow; the front half of the bush was illuminated by the window. 'The guelder, the hips, how red they are!' he whispered, not knowing why he did it. Quietly, with distinct, inaudible steps he approached the window and stood on tiptoe. The whole of Fyodor Pavlovich's bedroom appeared before him, as if it were in the palm of his hand. It was a small room, and the whole of it was divided transversely by a folding screen, a 'Chinese' one, as Fyodor Pavlovich called it. 'Chinese,' rushed through Mitya's head, 'and Grushenka's behind it.' He began to study Fyodor Pavlovich. The latter was attired in a new striped silk dressing-gown which Mitya had never seen him in before, belted by a silk cord with tassels. From beneath the collar of the dressing-gown peeped clean and stylish linen, a fine Holland shirt with gold studs. On Fyodor Pavlovich's head was the same red bandage that Alyosha had observed. 'Got himself dressed up,' Mitya thought. Fyodor Pavlovich stood close to the window, evidently in reflection; suddenly he jerked his head up, cocked his ear the merest shadow and then, having heard nothing, went over to the table, poured from a decanter half a liqueur-glass of cognac and drank it. Then he sighed with a great heave

of his chest, stood still again for a moment, absent-mindedly walked over
to the mirror in the pier between the windows, with his right hand lifted
the red bandage from his forehead slightly and began to study his bruises
and sores, which had not yet healed. 'He's on his own,' Mitya thought,
'the most probable thing is that he's on his own.' Fyodor Pavlovich
walked away from the mirror, turned suddenly to the window and looked
out of it. In a split second, Mitya leapt back into the shadow.

'Perhaps she's behind the screen, perhaps she's asleep now,' stabbed
like a dagger to his heart. Fyodor Pavlovich withdrew from the window.
'He was looking out of the window for her, that means she isn't here:
why would he be looking out into the dark? His impatience must be
wearing him down . . .' Mitya instantly leapt up and again began to stare
at the window. The old man was sitting at the table now, apparently
down in the dumps. At last he leaned one elbow on the table and placed
the palm of his right hand on his cheek. Mitya peered at him avidly.

'He's on his own, on his own!' he repeated again. 'If she were here,
he'd have a different expression on his face.' It was strange: in his heart
there had suddenly begun to seethe an absurd and peculiar annoyance at
the fact that she was not here. 'It's not because she isn't here,' Mitya said
to himself, interpreting, and furnishing his own reply at once, 'it's
because there's absolutely no way for me to find out for certain whether
she is here or not.' Mitya later recalled that his mind at that moment was
extraordinarily clear and that he understood everything right down to the
last detail, caught every smallest nuance. But anguish, the anguish of
ignorance and irresolution, was growing inside his heart with excessive
swiftness. 'Is she here, or isn't she?' began to seethe viciously within his
heart. And suddenly he mustered his determination, stretched forth his
hand and softly tapped the window-frame. He tapped the signal the old
man had prearranged with Smerdyakov: the first two taps slowly, and
then three times more quickly: 'rat-rat-rat' – the sound which denoted
that 'Grushenka has arrived'. The old man started, jerked his head up,
quickly sprang to his feet and rushed to the window. Mitya leapt back
into the shadow. Fyodor Pavlovich undid the window and stuck his head
out all the way.

'Grushenka, is it you? Is it you, is it?' he got out in a kind of
trembling semi-whisper. 'Where are you, little mother, little angel, where
are you?' He was in a state of terrible agitation, he was gasping for
breath.

'He's on his own!' Mitya decided.

'Where are you, then?' the old man shouted again, and he stuck his head out even further, stuck his shoulders out too, looking round in every direction, to right and to left. 'Come here; I've got a little present for you, come here, I'll show you! . . .'

'That's the envelope with the three thousand he means,' flickered through Mitya's consciousness.

'But where are you, then? Are you at the door? Wait a moment, I'll open it . . .'

And the old man very nearly clambered out of the window as he peered to the right, in the direction of the door that led into the garden, trying to see in the dark. Within a second he would certainly have gone running to unbar the door, not waiting for Grushenka to reply. Mitya observed from the side and did not stir a muscle. The entire profile of the old man, which so revolted him, the pendular Adam's apple, the crooked nose, the lips, smiling in lecherous expectation, all of this was brilliantly illuminated by the oblique ray of the lamp that shone from the left, from the room. A terrible, violent hatred suddenly seethed in Mitya's heart: 'There he is, my rival, my tormentor, the tormentor of my life!' This was an access of that same sudden, vengeful and violent hatred to which, as though in premonition, he had informed Alyosha in his conversation with him in the summerhouse four days ago, in reply to Alyosha's question: 'How can you say that you will kill father?'

'Oh, you see, I don't know, I don't know . . . Perhaps I'll murder him and perhaps I won't. My fear is that his face will suddenly grow hateful to me at that very moment. I hate his Adam's apple, his nose, his eyes, his shameless snigger. I experience a personal loathing. That is what I fear, and then I shall not be able to control myself . . .'

The personal loathing was mounting unendurably. Mitya was beside himself now and suddenly snatched the brass pestle from his pocket . . .

God, as Mitya said later, was keeping watch over him that night: at that very same time Grigory Vasilyevich awoke upon his sickbed. Towards the evening of that same day he had applied to himself a certain treatment, the one Smerdyakov had described to Ivan Fyodorovich, that is to say with the help of his spouse he had rubbed himself all over with vodka that contained some kind of secret and most strong infusion, had drunk the rest down with 'a certain prayer' whispered over him by his spouse, and lain down to sleep. Marfa Ignatyevna had also partaken and, being of sober habits, had fallen asleep beside her husband in a dead slumber. But then quite unexpectedly Grigory had suddenly woken up in the night, considered for a moment and, though he again at once felt a burning pain in the small of his back, raised himself from the bed. Then he again pondered on something, got up and quickly put his clothes on. It may have been that he had had a prick of conscience at having been asleep, leaving the house without a watchman 'at such a dangerous time'. The epilepsy-incapacitated Smerdyakov lay in the other little room without movement. Marfa Ignatyevna did not stir a limb. 'The woman's a-weak and a-wither,' he thought, having taken a look at her, and groaning went out on to the little porch. He intended, of course, merely to take a look from the porch, for he had not the strength to walk, and the pain in the small of his back and in his right leg was unendurable. But just at that moment he suddenly remembered that earlier that evening he had not locked the wicket gate that led into the garden. This was a man most punctual and precise, a man of long established routine and the habits of many years. Limping and writhing with pain, he descended the steps of the porch and set off for the garden. True enough, the gate was wide open. In mechanical fashion he stepped into the garden: it may have been that he thought he had seen something, or perhaps he had heard some sound, but, looking to the left, he caught sight of the *barin*'s open window; the window was empty now, and no one was looking out of it. 'Why is it open? It isn't summer now!' Grigory thought, and suddenly, just at that very moment, something unusual fleeted directly before him in the garden. Some forty paces ahead of him he thought he saw someone running along in the darkness, a shadow moving very swiftly. 'Good Lord!' said Grigory, and, beside himself, oblivious now to the pain in the small of his back, he dashed to intercept the runner. He took the shortest route, for the garden was evidently more familiar to him than it was to the runner; the latter set off towards the bathhouse, and then, having passed beyond it, rushed towards the enclosure . . . Grigory kept a watch on him, not losing him from sight, and ran in oblivion of all else. He attained the fence just at the very same moment as the fugitive was clambering over the fence. Transported beyond himself, Grigory uttered a howl, threw himself forward and with both hands seized hold of one of his legs.

So it was, his premonition had not let him down; he recognized him, it was he – the 'monster and father-murderer'.

'Father-murderer!' the old man shouted to the whole neighbourhood, but that was all he succeeded in shouting; he suddenly fell like a man struck by lightning. Mitya leapt back down into the garden and bent down over the prostrate man. In Mitya's hands was the brass pestle, and like an automaton he threw it into the grass. The pestle fell two paces from Grigory, not in the grass, however, but on the path, where it was most clearly visible. For a few seconds he studied the person who lay before him. The head of the old man was covered in blood; Mitya stretched forth his arm and began to feel that head. Later on he clearly recalled that he had a terrible desire to 'be completely sure' whether he had broken the old man's skull or only 'discombobulated' him with the pestle on the temple. But there was blood, a horrible amount of blood, and in a flash it had soaked Mitya's trembling fingers in a hot stream. He recalled that he snatched from his pocket his new white handkerchief, the one with which he had furbished himself upon setting out to see Mrs Khokhlakova, and placed it against the old man's head, in an absurd effort to wipe the blood from his face and forehead. But in a flash the handkerchief, too, was entirely saturated in blood. 'O Lord, but why am I doing this?' Mitya thought, suddenly coming to his senses. 'How can I find out now if I've broken his skull . . . And in any case, isn't it all the same?' he suddenly added hopelessly. 'If I've done him in, I've done him in . . . You've made your bed, old fellow, so now you must lie in it!' he said loudly and suddenly bolted for the fence, leapt over it into the lane and set off at a run. The handkerchief, drenched in blood, was crumpled in his right fist, and as he ran he stuffed it into the rear pocket of his dress coat. He ran headlong, and a few rare passers-by who encountered him in the dark, on the streets of the town, later recalled having met that night a man who was violently running. He was flying again to the house of Mrs Morozova. Earlier that evening, as soon as he had left, Fenya had rushed to Nazar Ivanovich, the senior yardkeeper, and had begun to implore him by 'Lordy Jesus' not to let the captain in — 'not never again, not today nor tomorrow neither'. Nazar Ivanovich, having listened to her plea, agreed to fulfil it, but as bad luck would have it he then absented himself upstairs to the accommodations of the *barynya*, whither he had been summoned unexpectedly, and on the upwards journey, encountering his nephew, a lad of some twenty years who had only very recently arrived from the country, instructed him to remain in the yard, but forgot to give any instructions concerning the captain. Having run up to the front gate, Mitya knocked. The lad recognized him instantly: Mitya had given him a tip on several occasions. At once the lad opened the side-gate for him, let him through and, with a merry smile obligingly hastened to inform him that 'you see, sir Agrafena Aleksandrovna bain't at home, sir.'

'Then where is she, Prokhor?' Mitya asked, stopping suddenly.

'A while ago she went away, about two hours it were, with Timofey, to Mokroye.'

'Why?' Mitya shouted.

'Oh, I wouldn't know that, sir – some officer it were she went to see; somebody called her over there and sent some horses . . .'

Mitya turned his back on him and went running in like a man half-insane to see Fenya.

5

A Sudden Resolve

THE latter was sitting in the kitchen with her grandmother, and they were both preparing to go to bed. Putting their trust in Nazar Ivanovich, they had, what was more, not barred the door from inside. Mitya came running in, rushed at Fenya and seized her tightly by the throat.

'Tell me this instant, where is she, who is she with at Mokroye now?' he howled in frenzy.

Both women uttered shrieks.

'Ah, I'll tell you, ah, dear Dmitry Fyodorovich, I'll tell you everything in a moment, nothing will I hide,' Fenya shouted in a rapid babble, frightened to death. 'She's gone to Mokroye to see the officer.'

'What officer?' Mitya howled.

'Her former officer, the same one, her former one, the one she had five years ago, who gave her up and then went away,' Fenya jabbered on in the same rapid babble.

Dmitry Fyodorovich released his hands from their vice-like grip around her throat. He stood facing her, pale as a corpse and mute, but from his eyes it was plain that he had taken it all in at one go, had understood everything, everything without even so much as a sentence being uttered, right down to the last detail, and had guessed his way to the truth. Not that poor Fenya, need it be added, was in any condition to observe in that second whether he had understood or not. Sitting on a clothes-trunk, just as she had been when he had run in, so she remained now, a-tremble all over and, her arms held out in front of her, as though in an attempt to shield herself, had frozen rigid in that position. With the frightened, terror-distended pupils of her eyes she fixed him motionlessly. While he, as if on purpose to intensify the effect, had both hands stained with blood. He must, *en route* and in running, have put them to his forehead as he wiped the sweat from his face, and upon his forehead and right cheek there had remained red patches of smeared blood. Fenya was on the point of hysterics, while the old cook had leapt up and was staring like a madwoman, having almost lost her wits. Dmitry Fyodorovich continued to stand still for a moment and then suddenly, in mechanical fashion, lowered himself on to a chair next to Fenya.

He sat, in a state less of consideration than in one almost of panic, a kind of stupor. Why, it was all as clear as daylight: this officer – he knew about him, knew everything about him, after all, knew about him from Grushenka herself, knew that a month ago he had sent her a letter. That meant that for a month, a whole month, this affair had been conducted in deep secret, kept from him, right up to the present appearance of this new arrival, and yet he had never thought of him! But how was it possible, how could he have failed to think of him? Why, really, had he forgotten about this officer at the time, forgotten about him the instant he had learned of him? This was the question that faced him now, like some kind of monster. And he contemplated this monster in true panic, his blood running cold with panic.

But suddenly, quietly and meekly, like a quiet and loving child, he began to talk to Fenya as though he had completely forgotten the manner in which he had just terrified, outraged and exhausted her. Suddenly, with an extreme precision that was positively astonishing for one in his position, he began to question Fenya. And Fenya, though she gazed wildly at his bloodstained hands, began to reply to each question he asked with astonishing readiness and haste, positively hurrying to place before him 'all the truthful truth of it'. Little by little, with a certain pleasure, even, she began to explain all the details, not at all out of any desire to cause him torment, but as if she were in a hurry to do with cordial sincerity all she could to be of service to him. Right down to the last detail she narrated to him the events of the whole of that day, the visit of Rakitin and Alyosha, how she, Fenya, had stood watch, how the *barynya* had gone and that she had shouted to Alyosha from the window a greeting to him, Mitenka, saying that he should 'remember for ever how she had loved him for one small hour'. On hearing of the greeting, Mitya suddenly smiled a bleak smile, and on his pale cheeks the colour flared. At that same moment Fenya said to him, without a shadow of fear now at her own inquisitiveness:

'What hands you have, Dmitry Fyodorovich, all covered in blood!'

'Yes,' Mitya replied in mechanical fashion, took an absent-minded glance at his hands and at once forgot about them and about Fenya's question. He again subsided into silence. From the time he had run in, some twenty minutes had now elapsed. His recent panic had passed, but it was now evident that he was completely in the power of some new and inexorable resolve. He suddenly rose from his seat and smiled reflectively.

'*Barin*, what is this that has happened to you?' Fenya said, again directing his attention to his hands; she spoke with commiseration, as though she were now the being closest to him in his misfortune.

Mitya again took a look at his hands.

'It's blood, Fenya,' he said, looking at her with a strange expression, 'it's human blood and, O God, why was it shed? But . . . Fenya . . . there is a certain fence here' (he gazed at her as though he were setting a riddle for her to answer), 'a certain fence that is high, and terrible to behold, but . . . tomorrow at dawn, when "the sun ascendeth in the heavens", Mitenka will leap over that fence . . . You don't know which fence I mean, Fenya? Well, never mind . . . it doesn't matter, tomorrow you will hear and know everything . . . but now farewell! I shan't get in the way and I shall keep myself to myself, I'm good at doing that. Live well, my joy . . . If you loved me for one small hour, then remember Mitenka Karamazov for ever . . . I mean, she used to call me Mitenka, don't you remember?'

And with these words he suddenly left the kitchen. As for Fenya, this exit frightened her if possible even more than when he had run in just then and hurled himself upon her.

Exactly ten minutes later Mitya entered the apartment of the young civil servant, Pyotr Ilyich Perkhotin, with whom he had pawned his pistols the day before. It was already half-past eight, and Pyotr Ilyich, having had his evening tea at home, had just enveloped himself once more in his dress coat as a preliminary to setting off for the Capital City inn to play billiards. Mitya caught him on his way out. The latter, setting eyes on him and on his bloodstained face, fairly yelped:

'Good Lord! What on earth has happened to you?'

'Look,' Mitya said quickly, 'I've come for my pistols and have brought you the money. I'd be most grateful. I'm in a hurry, Pyotr Ilyich, please, get them for me as quickly as you can.'

Pyotr Ilyich was growing more and more astonished: he had suddenly perceived that in Mitya's hand there was a large amount of money, and what astonished him most was that Mitya was holding this money and had entered with it in a manner in which no one holds money and no one enters with it; he was holding all the credit bills in his right hand, as though to show them off, his arm extended directly in front of him. The boy, Perkhotin's servant, who received Mitya in the antechamber, said later that he had walked into the antechamber like that, holding the money, and that consequently he must have had it in his right hand, holding it before him, even while he had been out on the street. The banknotes were all hundred-rouble ones, 'rainbows', and he was holding them in bloodstained fingers. Later, in response to subsequent questioning by interested persons as to how much money there had been, Pyotr Ilyich declared that at the time it was difficult to count it by eye; perhaps two thousand, perhaps three, but at any rate the wad had been a large one, 'fat enough'. As for Dmitry Fyodorovich himself, he, as Perkhotin also testified later, had been 'not at all himself, but not drunk, rather instead as if he were in some kind of ecstasy, very distracted, and yet at the same time almost focused, too, as though he were thinking about something and trying to reach some decision but not succeeding. He was in a great hurry, his replies were brusque, it was very strange, at moments he seemed not upset at all but even cheerful.'

'But I say, I say, what on earth has happened to you?' Pyotr Ilyich shouted again, studying his guest wildly. 'How did you get all that blood on you? Did you fall, or what – look!'

He seized him by the elbow and made him look in the mirror. Mitya, catching sight of his own bloodstained face, shuddered and knit his brows wrathfully.

'Hah, the devil! That's all I needed!' he muttered with vicious rage, quickly transferred the credit bills from his right hand to his left and convulsively tugged his handkerchief from his pocket. But the handkerchief too proved to be covered in blood (with this same handkerchief he had wiped the head and face of Grigory): it contained not one tiny patch of white, and it had less begun to dry than stiffened into a kind of lump which could not be unfolded. Mitya viciously hurled it to the floor.

'Hah, the devil! Have you a rag of some kind . . . I could wipe myself with . . .'

'So you are only stained, and are not injured? Then you had better wash,' Pyotr Ilyich replied. 'Look, here is the wash-hand basin, I shall fetch water.'

'A wash-hand basin? That's good . . . Only where shall I put this?' he said, in a kind of now truly strange bewilderment, directing Pyotr Ilyich's attention to his wad of hundred-rouble notes, staring at him inquiringly, as though the latter were to decide where he should put his own money.

'Stow it away in your pocket or put it on the table here, it won't get lost.'

'My pocket? Yes, my pocket. That's good . . . Oh, look, this is all a lot of rubbish!' he began to exclaim, as though suddenly snapping out of his distracted state of mind. 'Look, let's get this matter settled first, the pistols, please let me have them back, and here is your money . . . because I need them very, very urgently . . . and I have no time, not a drop of time to lose . . .'

And, removing the top hundred-rouble note from the wad, he proffered it to the civil servant.

'Why, I don't even think I have change,' the latter observed. 'Don't you have anything smaller?'

'No,' Mitya said, taking another glance at the wad and, as though he were unsure of the truth of his words, tested with his fingers two or three notes at the top. 'No, they're all the same,' he added and again looked inquiringly at Pyotr Ilyich.

'I say, how is it you've come into all these riches?' the latter asked. 'Wait, I'll get my boy to run over to Plotnikovs'.* They stay open late – we'll see if they can change it. Hey, Misha!' he shouted into the ante-chamber.

'Plotnikovs' delicatessen – a most magnificent idea!' Mitya also shouted, as though he had been visited by some thought. 'Misha,' he said, turning to the boy as he came in, 'look, run over to Plotnikovs' and say that Dmitry Fyodorovich sends his greetings and will be over there himself presently . . . And listen, listen: tell them that when I get there I want them to have some bottles of champagne ready for me, three dozen or so, packed up in the same way as the ones I took to Mokroye . . . I bought four dozen from them that time,' he said, suddenly addressing Pyotr Ilyich. 'They know how it was that time, you don't have to worry, Misha,' he went on, turning back to the boy again. 'And listen: get them to put in some cheese, and some Strasbourg pies, and some smoked *sig*,* and some ham, and some caviare – oh, everything, everything they have, a hundred or a hundred and twenty roubles' worth, like before . . . And listen: see that they don't forget the sweet things – candies, pears, a watermelon or two or three – no, I suppose one will be enough – and chocolate, boiled sweets, lozenges, *tyagushki** – oh, all the stuff they packed up for me when I went to Mokroye, three hundred roubles, it came to, with the champagne . . . Well, get them to do exactly the same for me now. And remember, Misha, if that's your name . . . I say, his name is Misha, isn't it?' he said again, addressing Pyotr Ilyich.

'But wait,' Pyotr Ilyich interrupted, listening to him and studying him with unease. 'It would be better if you went yourself, and then you'll be able to give the instructions yourself, whereas he'll only get them wrong.'

'Oh yes, you're right, you're right, I can see that he will! Ah, Misha, and I was going to give you a kiss for your trouble ... If you don't get it wrong there's ten roubles for you, now dash off as quick as you can ... The main thing is the champagne, get them to roll out the champagne, and the cognac, and the white and the red wine, and all of it as it was that time ...'

'I say, will you listen!' Pyotr Ilyich interrupted, with impatience now. 'What I said was: let him just run and change the note and tell them not to close shop, and then you can go and give the instructions yourself ... Give him your banknote. Quick march, Misha, put your best foot forward!' It seemed likely that Pyotr Ilyich was chasing Misha away because the latter was standing in front of the guest, his eyes a-goggle at his bloody face and bloodstained hands with their wad of money in shaking fingers, and continued to stand there, his mouth agape with fear and astonishment, in all probability grasping little of what Mitya was bidding him do.

'Well, now let us go and get you washed,' Pyotr Ilyich said, severely. 'Put the money on the table or stow it away in your pocket ... That's right, like that. Now come along. And take off your coat.'

And he began to assist him in removing his dress coat, and then once more suddenly yelped:

'Look! Even your coat has blood on it!'

'It's ... it's not on the coat. There's only a little bit on the sleeve here ... and this bit here, where the handkerchief was. It must have seeped through from my pocket. When I was with Fenya I sat on my handkerchief, that was when the blood seeped through,' Mitya instantly explained with a strange and astonishing trustfulness that this was so. Pyotr Ilyich heard him out, frowning.

'Well, you've managed to land up in some kind of scrape; you must have got into a fight with someone,' he muttered.

They began the process of washing. Pyotr Ilyich held the pitcher and poured out the water as required. Mitya hurried, using hardly any soap on his hands. (His hands were shaking, as Pyotr Ilyich recalled later.) Pyotr Ilyich at once urged him to use more soap and to rub harder. It was as though at that moment he had acquired a sort of superiority over Mitya, and this was increasingly so as time passed. Let us observe, apropos: the young man was of untimid character.

'Look, you haven't washed under your nails; well, now rub your face, look, here: on your temples, by your ear ... Are you going to go out wearing that shirt? Where is it you're going, anyway? Look, the whole cuff of your right sleeve has blood on it.'

'Yes, it has blood on it,' Mitya observed, examining the cuff.

'Then you must change your linen.'

'There isn't any time. But it's all right, I'll just do this, you see ...' Mitya went on in the same trusting tone of voice, drying his face and hands with the towel now and putting his coat back on again. 'Look, I shall just fold the edge of the cuff, it won't be visible under my coat ... You see?'

'Now tell me: where did you manage to end up in a scrape like this? Did you get into a fight? Eh? With whom? Not at the inn again, like last time? You haven't been going for the captain again, have you, beating him and pulling him by his beard?' Pyotr Ilyich asked reminiscingly, almost with a kind of reproach. 'And if it was not he, then whom have you beaten this time ... or killed, maybe?'

'Rubbish!' Mitya said.

'What do you mean – rubbish?'

'Oh, forget it,' said Mitya, and suddenly he smiled an ironic smile. 'I knocked down a little old woman on the square as I was running here just now.'

'You knocked her down? A little old woman?'

'An old man!' Mitya shouted, looking Pyotr Ilyich straight in the face, laughing and shouting at him as if the latter were deaf.

'Ah, the devil take it, an old man, a little old woman ... Have you killed someone, or haven't you?'

'We made it up with one another. We had a bit of a tussle – and made it up. In a certain place. We parted as friends. A certain fool of a chap – he forgave me ... by now he's definitely forgiven me ... though if he'd managed to get up again, he wouldn't have forgiven me,' Mitya winked suddenly. 'But you know, to the devil with him, do you hear, Pyotr Ilyich, to the devil, forget it! Just at this moment I don't want to bother with it!' Mitya positively snapped.

'Oh, it's just that I really don't know what makes you go getting mixed up with all and sundry ... Like that time you got involved with that second-grade captain, for no reason at all ... You've had a fight and now you're rushing off to spend far too much money – that's your character in a nutshell. Three dozen bottles of champagne – why do you need so much?'

'Bravo! Now let me have the pistols. I swear to you, honestly, I haven't any time. I'd like to talk to you, dear chap, but I haven't any time. And in any case forget it, it's too late for talking. Ah! Now where is my money, what did I do with it?' he screamed, and began to jab his hands in and out of his pockets.

'You put it on the table ... You put it there yourself ... Here it is. Did you forget? Really, you treat money as though it were water or litter. Here are your pistols. That's strange: at six o'clock this evening you pawned them with me for ten roubles, and now look at all that money you've got there, thousands. Two or three, I'll wager?'

'Three, I'll wager,' Mitya laughed, stuffing the money into the side pocket of his trousers.

'You'll lose it that way. I say, have you got gold-mines?'

'Gold-mines? Did you say gold-mines?' Mitya shouted with all his might, and rolled with laughter. 'Perkhotin, how would you like to go on a trip to the gold-mines? There's a certain lady in this town who'll dole out three thousand just to see you go. She did it for me, such is her love for those gold-mines! Mrs Khokhlakova, do you know her?'

'No, but I've heard of her and have seen her about. Did she really give you three thousand? Just doled it out like that?' Pyotr Ilyich said, staring mistrustfully.

'Well, tomorrow, when the sun, when Phoebus, eternally young, ascendeth in the heavens, glorifying and praising God, tomorrow go to her, to Khokhlakova, and ask her yourself: did she or did she not dole out three thousand to me? Go on, make your inquiries.'

'I don't know what your relationship with her is ... If you say it so affirmatively then I suppose she must have given you it ... And you've got the money in your hands, yet you're not off to Siberia, but are about to blow the whole three thousand ... Just where is it you *are* off to now?'

'Mokroye.'

'Mokroye? But I mean, it's night-time!'

'Mastryuk was dressed up rich, but now he has not a stitch!'*

'What do you mean, not a stitch? You've got all those thousands, yet you talk of not having a stitch?'

'It's not the thousands I'm referring to. To the devil with them! It's the ways of woman I mean:

> Easy led is woman's heart,
> Wanton and deceiving.*

I'm in agreement with Ulysses, those are his words in the poem.'

'I don't know, I can't make you out.'

'Am I drunk, do you suppose?'

'No, not drunk, but worse than that.'

'I'm drunk in spirit, Pyotr Ilyich, drunk in spirit, and now that's enough, that's enough ...'

'What are you doing with that pistol – loading it?'

'Yes, I'm loading the pistol . . .'

It was indeed so: Mitya, having opened the case that contained the pistols, had unlocked the powder horn from its fastening, carefully poured in the powder and inserted the charge. Then he took a bullet and, before rolling it in, raised it before him in two fingers above the candle.

'Why are you looking at the bullet?' Pyotr Ilyich inquired with uneasy curiosity as he followed this process.

'I just am. Imagination. Well, if you had decided to plant this bullet in your brain, then, as you loaded the pistol, wouldn't you look at it?'

'Why look at it?'

'If it's going into my brain, I'm interested to take a look at it, see what it looks like . . . Oh, but that's just rubbish, the rubbish of a moment. There, that's done,' he added, having rolled in the bullet and packed it with oakum. 'Pyotr Ilyich, my dear chap, it's rubbish, all rubbish, if only you knew what rubbish it is! Now give me a piece of paper.'

'Here you are.'

'No, I mean a smooth, clean piece of paper, writing paper. That's right.' And Mitya, snatching a pen from the table, quickly wrote on the scrap of paper two lines, folded the paper in four and stuffed it in his waistcoat pocket. He replaced the pistols in their case, locked it with its small key and picked up the case. Then he looked at Pyotr Ilyich and smiled a long, reflective smile.

'Now let us be on our way,' he said.

'Where are we on our way to? No, wait . . . I say, you're not really going to put that bullet through your brain, are you? . . .' Pyotr Ilyich got out uneasily.

'Oh, forget the bullet, that was just rubbish! I want to live, I love life! Bear that in mind. I love golden-curled Phoebus and his intemperate light . . . Dear Pyotr Ilyich, do you know how to step aside?'

'What do you mean?'

'How to make way. To make way for a dear being and for one who is hateful. So that the hateful one, too, becomes dear – to make way in that sense! And to say to them: well, God be with you, off you go then, pass by, while I . . .'

'While you?'

'That's enough, let us go.'

'As God is my witness, I shall tell someone,' said Pyotr Ilyich, staring at him, 'and get them to stop you from going there. Why are you going to Mokroye now?'

'There's a woman, there, a woman, and let that be enough for you, Pyotr Ilyich, and will you now please drop it!'

'You know, you may be a savage, but for some reason I've always rather liked . . . That's why I'm worried.'

'I thank you, brother. I'm a savage, you say. Savages, savages! That word is never off my lips: savages! Ah yes, here is Misha, I had almost forgotten him.'

Misha entered hurriedly with a wad of banknotes in small denominations and reported that at Plotnikovs' 'they're all on the go', and that bottles were being dragged out, and fish, and tea – very soon it would all be ready. Mitya snatched a ten-rouble note from the wad and gave it to Pyotr Ilyich, while another he threw to Misha.

'Do not dare!' Pyotr Ilyich exclaimed. 'I do not allow it in my home, and in any case it is morally wrong and will spoil him. Put your money away, look, put it here, why squander it? Tomorrow you may have good use for it, yet you'll be coming to me to ask for another ten roubles. Why do you keep stuffing it in your side pocket? You'll lose it, you know!'

'Listen, my dear fellow, what about going to Mokroye together?'

'Why should I go there?'

'Listen, if you like I shall uncork a bottle straight away, and we shall drink to life! I feel like a drink, and especially one with you. That's something we've never done together before, is it?'

'Well, we may possibly do so at the inn. Come along then, I myself am bound there now.'

'There's no time for the inn, let us go to Plotnikovs' delicatessen, to the snuggery at the back. Would you like me to ask you a certain riddle I have here?'

'Go on, then.'

Mitya took the scrap of paper from his waistcoat, unfolded it and showed it to Pyotr Ilyich. In large, clear handwriting it said:

'I punish myself for the whole of my life, the whole of my life I punish!'

'Why truly, I shall have a word with someone, I shall go this instant and have a word with someone,' Pyotr Ilyich said, having read what was on the scrap of paper.

'You won't have time, dear chap, now come along and let us drink, quick march!'

Plotnikovs' delicatessen was situated virtually no more than one house along from where Pyotr Ilyich lived, on the corner of the street. It was the principal delicatessen of our town, run by wealthy wholesalers, and in its own way not at all bad. It stocked everything one might find in any such store, any such delicatessen in the capital: wines 'bottled by the Brothers Yeliseyev', fruit, cigars, tea, sugar, coffee and so on. Three shopmen sat there constantly on duty, and two errand boys delivered the goods. Even though our part of the country had grown impoverished, its landowners dispersed, its trade become quiet, yet did the delicatessen prosper as before, and indeed better and better than before, with every year that passed: for these items there was a steady abundance of purchasers. Mitya's arrival was awaited at the store with impatience. It was vividly recalled how, some three or four weeks earlier, he had arrived in just such a sudden manner and bought all kinds of victuals and wines to the tune of several hundred roubles in straight money (they would never of course have entrusted anything to him on credit), it was recalled that then, as now, in his hands there had flashed an entire wad of rainbow notes and that he had thrown them around at random, without haggling, without considering or even wishing to consider to what end he required all those victuals and wines and the rest. Throughout all the town it had later been said that at the time, having rolled off to Mokroye with Grushenka, 'he blew in a single night and the day that followed three thousand in one fell swoop, and returned from the spree without the groat on which his mother bare him.' On that occasion he had raised an entire camp of gypsies (at that time passing through our locality in search of pasture), who, it was said, in the space of two days stole from him, the drunkard, countless sums of money and drank countless quantities of expensive wine. People related, laughing at Mitya, that in Mokroye he had plied the clodhopping muzhiks with champagne and stuffed the country maidens and wives with chocolates and Strasbourg pies. People in our town, especially down at the inn, also laughed at the open and public confession Mitya had made at the time (they did not laugh in his face, for to do so was somewhat dangerous), that from Grushenka all he had received for the whole of this 'escapade' was her letting him 'kiss her foot, and more than that she would not let me do'.

When Mitya and Pyotr Ilyich walked up to the store, they found by the entrance a *troika* of horses already prepared, and harnessed to a wagon, covered with a rug, with bells and jingles and the *yamshchik** Andrey, waiting for Mitya. Inside the store they had already almost completely managed to 'furbish' one hamper of victuals and were only awaiting Mitya's appearance in order to hammer it shut and load it into the wagon. Pyotr Ilyich was astonished.

'But where did you manage to get a *troika* from?' he asked Mitya.

'As I was running to your place, I met Andrey and told him to drive straight here to the store. There's no time to lose! Last time I drove there with Timofey, but Timofey is nowhere to be seen now, he's rolled off with a certain enchantress ahead of me. Andrey, are we going to be very late?'

'Their wagon will probably get there only an hour before ours, if that even, they've got an hour's start at most!' Andrey responded hurriedly. 'I harnessed Timofey's horses myself, so I know how they'll travel. Their ride won't be the same as our ride, Dmitry Fyodorovich, how could it be. They won't even get there an hour before us!' Andrey said again heatedly, before Dmitry could open his mouth. Andrey was a *yamshchik* not yet old, a lean, reddish-haired fellow in a *poddyovka*, with an *armyak* over his left arm.

'There's fifty roubles' vodka-money for you if you can get there no more than an hour after they do.'

'I'll guarantee you that, Dmitry Fyodorovich! Why, they won't even get there half an hour ahead of us, never mind an hour!'

Though Mitya had begun to bustle about, making arrangements, his words and instructions were somehow strange — haphazard, and not in sequence. He would begin one thing and forget its conclusion. Pyotr Ilyich decided he would have to engage and assist the matter.

'Four hundred roubles' worth, no less than four hundred, it must be exactly, exactly the same as last time,' Mitya commanded. 'Four dozen bottles of champagne, not a single bottle less.'

'Why do you want so much, what is it for? Wait!' Pyotr Ilyich began to howl. 'Do you call this a hamper? What does it have in it? Surely not four hundred roubles' worth?'

It was at once explained to him by the bustling shopmen in dulcet tones that in this first hamper there were only a half-a-dozen bottles of champagne and 'all kinds of items necessary for the preliminaries', consisting of *zakuski*, chocolates, fruit-drops, and so on. But that the main 'commission' would be packed and dispatched this very instant separately, as on the last occasion, in a special wagon also drawn by a *troika* and that it would get there on time, 'and arrive at the spot perhaps only an hour after Dmitry Fyodorovich'.

'No more than an hour, no more than an hour, and put in as many fruit-drops and *tyagushki* as you can; that's what the wenches down there like,' Mitya insisted with heat.

'The *tyagushki* are all very well. But four dozen bottles of champagne, what do you need them for? One dozen would be sufficient,' Pyotr Ilyich said, nearly losing his temper. He began to haggle, demanded to see the bill, refused to be fobbed off. The end of it was that no more than three hundred roubles' worth of victuals was procured.

'Ah, the devil have your hide!' Pyotr Ilyich cried, as though he had suddenly changed his mind. 'What business is it of mine? Throw your money away, if you obtained it for nothing!'

'This way, my thrifty steward, step this way, and don't be angry,' said Mitya, hauling him off to the snuggery at the back of the store. 'Look, they'll serve us a bottle right now, and we'll have a sip or two. Oh, I say, Pyotr Ilyich, let's go together, for you're a dear fellow, I like a man like yourself.'

Mitya sat down on a little wicker chair at a tiny table that was covered with a most filthy cloth. Pyotr Ilyich found a place for himself opposite him, and in a flash the champagne appeared. The gentlemen were asked whether they would like some oysters, 'first-class oysters, fresh today'.

'To the devil with your oysters, I shan't have any, and we don't need anything else either,' Pyotr Ilyich snapped with something approaching hatred.

'There's no time for oysters,' Mitya observed, 'and in any case I've no appetite. You know, my friend,' he said suddenly with feeling, 'I have never cared for all this disorder.'

'Well, who does? But three dozen bottles of champagne poured down the throats of muzhiks – that would surely make anyone's blood boil.'

'That's not what I'm talking about. I'm talking about the higher order. There is no order in me, no higher order . . . But . . . all that is finished, and there's no point in moaning about it. It's too late, and to the devil with it! All my life has been disorder, and now I must bring some order into it. I'm punning, eh?'

'You're raving, not punning.'

> 'Glory to on earth the highest,
> Glory to the highest in me!

That little verse broke from my soul once upon a time, not a verse, but a tear . . . composed it myself . . . though not the day I hauled the second-grade captain by his beard . . .'

'Why do you suddenly mention him?'

'Why do I suddenly mention him? Rubbish! Everything is coming to an end, everything is being equalled out, a line – and the balance is drawn!'

'Yes, I must say I do still keep thinking about those pistols of yours.'

'The pistols are rubbish, too! Drink and stop fantasizing. I love life, I have loved life too much, so much that it's positively loathsome. Enough! To life, my dear fellow, to life let us drink, to life do I propose a toast! Why am I so pleased with myself? I am base, but am pleased with myself. And yet, I'm tormented by the fact that I am base, but pleased with myself. I bless creation, am this moment ready to bless God and his creation, but ... I must exterminate a certain stinking insect, so that it does not go creeping about, does not spoil life for others ... Let us drink to life, friend brother! What can be more dear than life? Nothing, nothing! To life and to a certain empress of empresses!'

'Let us drink to life, and, I suppose, to your empress too.'

They each downed a glass. Though Mitya was both ecstatic and incoherent, he was also somehow sad. It was as though some insuperable and heavy concern were standing behind him.

'Misha ... is that your Misha come in? Misha, lad, Misha, come here, drink this glass for me, to golden-curled Phoebus, who will come tomorrow ...'

'I say, what are you giving him that for?' Pyotr Ilyich shouted in irritation.

'Oh go on, let me, I want him to have some.'

'A-achh!'

Misha downed the glass, bowed and ran away.

'He'll remember it longer,' Mitya observed. 'It's a woman I love, a woman! What is woman? The empress of the earth! Do you remember Hamlet? I feel sad, sad, Pyotr Ilyich. "I am so sad, I am so sad, Horatio ... Alas, poor Yorick!" Perhaps I am Yorick, too. Yes, just now I am Yorick, and shall be the skull later.'

Pyotr Ilyich listened and was silent, and Mitya said nothing either.

'What sort of a dog is that you have there?' he suddenly inquired absent-mindedly of one of the shopmen, having noticed in the corner a pretty little Bolognese with black eyes.

'That is the Bolognese of Varvara Alekseyevna, our mistress,' the shopman replied. 'She brought it with her and left it here with us. It will have to be taken back to her.'

'I once saw a dog like that ... in my regiment ...' Mitya said reflectively. 'Only, one of its hindlegs was broken ... Oh, by the way, Pyotr Ilyich, I meant to ask you: have you ever in your life stolen anything?'

'What kind of a question is that?'

'Oh, I just wanted to ask. You know, taken money from someone else's pocket? I'm not talking about the public coffers, everyone has a finger in those, and I'm sure you are no exception . . .'

'Go to the devil.'

'No, I mean something else: taking it straight from someone's pocket, from his purse, eh?'

'I once stole a twenty-copeck piece from my mother, I was nine years old, and I took it from the table. I took it on the sly and pocketed it.'

'Well – and then?'

'Well then nothing. I kept it for three days, then I grew ashamed, owned up and gave it back.'

Well – and then?'

'I received a thrashing, of course. What about you, didn't you ever steal anything?'

'Oh yes,' Mitya winked, slyly.

'What?' Pyotr Ilyich asked, becoming curious.

'A twenty-copeck piece from my mother, when I was nine, three days later I gave it back.' Having said this, Mitya suddenly got up from his seat.

'Dmitry Fyodorovich, we're in a hurry, aren't we?' Andrey suddenly shouted from the door of the delicatessen.

'Ready? Then let's be off!' Mitya cried in a burst of frantic movement. 'One final tale* and . . . Give Andrey a glass of vodka for the road this instant! And give him a large glass of cognac as well! Put this case (the one with the pistols) under the seat for me. Farewell, Pyotr Ilyich, think kindly of me.'

'But I say, you're coming back tomorrow, aren't you?'

'Oh, certainly.'

'Will you do so good as to settle our small account now?' the shopman asked, leaping to Mitya's side.

'Ah, yes, the account! Certainly!'

He again snatched from his pocket his wad of credit bills, removed from it three 'rainbows', threw them on the counter and quickly went out of the store. They all followed him and, bowing, saw him off with salutations and good wishes. Andrey grunted after the cognac he just downed and leapt on to the seat. But hardly had Mitya begun to sit down, than Fenya appeared before him quite unexpectedly. She came running up quite out of breath, with a scream clasped her hands before him and fell heavily to his feet.

'Little father, Dmitry Fyodorovich, little dove, please don't hurt the *barynya*! I've told you everything, I have! . . . And please don't hurt him either, for he was her former one! He's going to take Agrafena Aleksandrovna in marriage, that's why he's come back from Siberia . . . Little father, Dmitry Fyodorovich, do not ruin other people's lives.'

'Tsk-tsk-tsk, so that's it! I see, you're going to do some business down there,' Pyotr Ilyich muttered to himself. 'Now it all makes sense, now it all makes perfect sense. Dmitry Fyodorovich, if you want to be a man you must return the pistols to me at once!' he exclaimed loudly at Mitya. 'Do you hear, Dmitry?'

'The pistols? Just wait, dear fellow, I shall throw them in a puddle *en route*,' Mitya replied. 'Fenya, get up, you mustn't lie in front of me like that. Mitya isn't going to do any ruining, from now on that stupid man isn't going to ruin anyone. And listen, Fenya,' he shouted to her, already seated now, 'I insulted you before, so please forgive me and if you can, forgive a scoundrel . . . And if you can't, then it's all the same! Because now everything is all the same! Let's be off, Andrey, drive swiftly!'

Andrey made the wagon move off; the wagon-bell began its tintinnabulation.

'Farewell, Pyotr Ilyich! To you the final tear! . . .'

'Why, he's not even drunk, yet what rot he spouts!' Pyotr Ilyich thought as Mitya left. He had almost been of a mind to stay and oversee the loading of the wagon (pulled, too, by a *troika*) with the rest of the comestibles and wines, suspecting in advance that Mitya would be cheated and overcharged, but suddenly, growing angry with himself, he spat in indifference and went on to his inn to play billiards.

'A fool, even though he's a good fellow . . .' Pyotr Ilyich muttered to himself on the way. 'I've heard of this "former" officer of Grushenka's. Well, if he's arrived, then . . . Oh, those pistols! But the devil, what am I, his uncle, or something? Never mind about them! And anyway, nothing will happen. They're loud-mouths, and that's all. They'll get drunk and fight, they'll fight and make it up. Are those men of action? What about all those "I step aside" 's and "I punish myself" 's? Nothing will happen! A thousand times he's shouted things in that style when he was drunk at the inn. But now he isn't drunk. "Drunk in spirit" – that's the style scoundrels favour. Am I his uncle, or what? And he must certainly have been in a fight – his ugly mug was covered in blood. With whom, now? I shall find out at the inn. And his handkerchief had blood on it too . . . Fie, the devil, he left it on my floor . . . I don't give a spit!'

He arrived at the inn in a most foul condition of spirit and at once began a game. The game cheered him up. He played another and suddenly

began to talk to one of his partners of the fact that Dmitry Fyodorovich
had again come into some money, three thousand no more and no less,
he had seen it himself, and that he had once more rolled off on a spree to
Mokroye with Grushenka. This was greeted by his listeners with something approaching unusual curiosity. And they all began to talk, not
laughing, but somehow with a strange degree of seriousness. They even
interrupted their game.

'Three thousand? But where could he have got three thousand?'

They began to question him further. The information concerning Mrs
Khokhlakova was greeted with dubious looks.

'More likely he robbed the old man, that's what!'

'Three thousand! There's something not right there.'

'He was boasting out loud that he was going to kill his father,
everyone here heard him. And he was talking about three thousand then,
too . . .'

Pyotr Ilyich listened and suddenly began to reply to their questioning
in a dry manner, without giving much away. Concerning the blood there
had been on Mitya's face and hands he mentioned not a word, though
while he had been on his way to the inn he had intended to tell them
about it. A third game was begun, and little by little the talk about Mitya
subsided; when the third game was ended, however, Pyotr Ilyich desired
to play no more, put away his billiard cue and, without having supper, as
he had planned to, walked out of the inn. Emerging on to the square, he
stood still in bewilderment, positively marvelling at himself. He had
suddenly realized that what he intended to do now was to go to Fyodor
Pavlovich's house in order to find out whether anything had taken place.
'On account of some rubbish, which it's bound to be, I intend to wake
up someone else's household and make a scandal! Fie, the devil, am I
their uncle, or what?'

In a most foul condition of spirit he set off straight for his home and
then suddenly remembered about Fenya: 'Hah, the devil, I should have
questioned her earlier,' he thought in annoyance, 'I'd know everything
now.' And to such a degree did there suddenly flare up within him a
most impatient and stubborn desire to talk to her and discover everything,
that halfway there he took a sharp turn in the direction of Mrs Morozova's
house, in which Grushenka had her lodgings. Going up to the gate, he
knocked, and the sound of his knock, resounding in the silence of the
night, again appeared suddenly to sober and enrage him. To make
matters worse, there was no response – all in the house were asleep.
'Here too I shall make a scandal!' he thought with a kind of suffering in

his soul now, but instead of giving up and going away, he suddenly began to knock again, with all his might this time. The noise of it filled the whole street. 'But no – I shall knock until they respond, I shall knock until they respond!' he muttered, his rage at himself increasing with each boom to the point of rabid frenzy, this merely redoubling the violence of his blows at the gate.

6

'Here I Come!'

BUT Dmitry Fyodorovich was flying on his way. To Mokroye it was twenty odd versts, but Andrey's *troika* galloped so hard that they might be there in an hour and a quarter. The swift passage suddenly seemed to revive Mitya. The air was fresh and rather cold, large stars shone in the clear sky. This was the same night, and possibly the same hour on which Alyosha, having fallen to the earth, 'frenziedly swore to love it until the end of the ages'. But troubled, very troubled was Mitya's soul, and though many things tormented his soul now, at this moment his entire being was swooping irresistably towards her alone, his empress, to whom he was flying in order to catch one final glimpse of her. I shall say only one thing: his heart did not argue even for a moment. I may perhaps not be credited if I say that this jealous fellow felt for that young man, the new rival who had sprung out of the earth from nowhere, for that officer, not the slightest jealousy. Of any other man, had such a one appeared, he would have instantly been jealous and would, perhaps, once more have soaked his terrible hands in blood, but towards this one, this 'first one of hers', he felt now as he flew on his *troika*, not only an absence of jealous hatred, but even of any hostile feeling at all – though, to be sure, he had not yet set eyes upon him. 'Here there can be no argument, here it is a question of his right and hers; here is her first love, whom in five years she has not forgotten: that means that for these five years she has loved only him, so what am I, what am I poking my nose in for? What place have I in it? Step aside, Mitya, and give way! And in any case, what am I now? Now even if the officer were not there it would all be finished, even had he never come along at all, even then it would all be finished . . .'

Such were the words in which he might approximately have expressed his feelings, if he had been able to think rationally. But now he was past thinking rationally. The whole of his present resolution had come into

being without rational thought, in a single flash, had been experienced
and taken in its entirety and with all its consequences earlier, with Fenya,
at the first words she had uttered. Yet none the less, in spite of all the
resolution he had taken, his soul was troubled, troubled to the point of
suffering: not even his resolution gave him tranquillity. Too much stood
behind him, tormenting him. At moments he found this strange, too:
after all, he had already written his own sentence with pen and paper: 'I
punish myself and punish'; and the scrap of paper lay there, in his pocket,
prepared; after all, the pistol was loaded, after all, he had decided how on
the morrow he would greet the first intemperate ray of 'golden-curled
Phoebus', and yet with what had gone formerly, with all that stood
behind him and tormented him, he could not settle his score, he felt that
to the point of torment, and the thought of it dug the fangs of despair
into his soul. There was one moment on the way when he suddenly
wanted to tell Andrey to stop, to leap out of the wagon, take his loaded
pistol and finish it all, without even waiting for daybreak. But that
moment had flown by like a spark. And the *troika* also flew, 'devouring
space', and the closer the goal approached, so also did the thought of her,
of her alone, more violently and violently wrench the breath from him,
driving away all the other terrible spectres from his heart. Oh, he wanted
so much to look at her, even if only fleetingly, even from afar! 'Now she
is with *him*, well, now I shall see how she is with him, with her former
sweetheart, and that is all that I require.' And never yet had there arisen
in his breast so much love towards this woman who had sealed his fate,
so much emotion that was new, and had never been experienced by him
before, emotion that was surprising even to himself, emotion tender to
the point of prayer, of disappearance before her. 'And I shall disappear!'
he said suddenly in a fit of a kind of hysterical ecstasy.

They had galloped now for almost an hour. Mitya said nothing, while
Andrey, though he was a talkative muzhik, did not utter a word either, as
though he were afraid to open his mouth, and merely drove his 'jades',
his skinny but speedy bay-horse *troika*. When suddenly Mitya exclaimed
in terrible anguish:

'Andrey! But what if they're asleep?'

This had suddenly flashed into his mind; before it had never occurred
to him.

'I dare say they will be by now, Dmitry Fyodorovich.'

Mitya frowned painfully: here he was, flying to see them . . . with
emotions like these . . . and they were asleep . . . perhaps she was sleeping
with him . . . A shiver of hatred seethed within his heart.

'Make haste, Andrey, more speed, Andrey, faster!' he shouted in a frenzy.

'But perhaps they won't be asleep yet,' Andrey said, after a pause for thought. 'Timofey said earlier there was a lot of people gathered there . . .'

'At the station?'

'Not at the station but at Plastunov's, the inn, it's a private posting station, as well.'

'I know; and you say there are a lot of people there? Why? Who are they?' Mitya asked, jerking his head up in terrible anguish at the unexpected news.

'Well, Timofey said they was all gentry; two from the town, who they are I don't know, and another two, from out of town, apparently, and who else is there I didn't ask him in so many words. He said they'd started playing cards.'

'Playing cards?'

'So you see, they may not have gone to bed yet, if they've started playing cards. I dare say it's not more than nigh on eleven o'clock yet, no more.'

'Make haste, Andrey, make haste!' Mitya exclaimed again nervously.

'Sir, there's something I want to ask you,' Andrey began again, after another pause, 'only I don't want to make you angry, *barin*, I'm frightened, sir.'

'What do you want to ask me?'

'Just now Fedosya Markovna lay down at your feet, begging you not to hurt the *barynya* and someone else . . . so you see, sir, now that I'm driving you there . . . Forgive me, sir, it's just my conscience talking, perhaps I've said something stupid.'

Mitya suddenly seized hold of him from behind, by the shoulders.

'Are you a *yamshchik*? A *yamshchik*?' he began frenziedly.

'Yes, sir . . . a *yamshchik* . . .'

'Then you know that one has to give way. What kind of a *yamshchik* is it who never gives way, but just tramples others under his wheels, saying "Here I come!" No, a *yamshchik* does not trample others down. One must not trample human beings, spoil their lives; and if you have — then punish yourself . . . As soon as you have spoiled or ruined another man's life — punish yourself and depart.'

All this seemed to burst from Mitya as though in a fit of complete hysteria. Andrey, though he marvelled at the *barin*, none the less kept the conversation going.

'That's true, little father, Dmitry Fyodorovich, you're right there, it isn't good to trample other people, nor to go tormenting them, neither, just the same as it isn't good to go tormenting any other creatures, for all brute creatures are a part of God's creation, whether it be the horse, just because somebody wants to break his way through, or whether it be us *yamshchiks* . . . There's no holding them back, they just keep charging on, they just keep charging straight on.'

'Into hell?' Mitya broke in suddenly, and burst into his short, unexpected laugh. 'Andrey, you simple soul,' he said again, seizing him firmly by the shoulders, 'tell me: will Dmitry Fyodorovich end up in hell or not, what's your opinion?'

'I don't know, my little dove, it depends on you, because to us you're a . . . You see, sir, when the Son of God* were crucified on the Cross and died, he went straight down from the Cross into hell and freed all the sinners who were in torment there. And hell began to moan because it thought that now nobody would come to it any more, no sinners, that's to say. And then the Lord said to hell: "Stop moaning, hell, for from this day on there will come to you all kinds of powerful men, rulers, big judges and men of wealth, and you will be just as full as you've ever been until the end of the ages, when I shall come again." That is true, there's a story that goes like that . . .'

'A popular legend! Splendid! Give the left one more of the lash, Andrey!'

'So those are the folk for whom hell is ordained,' Andrey said, giving the left horse more of the lash, 'but for us, sir, you're naught but a little boy . . . That's how we consider you . . . And though you're the angry sort, sir, the Lord will forgive you for the simpleness of your soul.'

'And you, will you forgive me, Andrey?'

'What should I forgive you for, you have done me no harm.'

'No, for all men, for all men you alone, right now, this moment, here, on the road, will you forgive me for all men? Speak, soul of the simple folk!'

'Oh, sir! It makes me scared to drive you, such a strange way it is you talk . . .'

But Mitya did not catch this. In frenzy he prayed, wildly whispering to himself: 'O Lord, take me in all my lawlessness, but do not judge me. Let me pass without your judgement . . . Do not judge, for I myself have condemned myself; do not judge, for I love you, Lord! I myself am loathsome, but I love you: if you send me to hell, even there I will love you and will cry from there that I love you until the end of the ages . . .

But let me love to the end ... Here, now, let me love to the end, only five hours before your intemperate ray ... For I love the empress of my soul. I love and I cannot but love. You yourself see the whole of me. I shall fly to her, fall down before her: you were right to walk past me ... Farewell and forget your victim, never trouble yourself more!'

'Mokroye!' Andrey shouted, pointing forward with his knout.

Through the pale gloom of the night a firm mass of buildings suddenly showed black, scattered over an enormous expanse. The village of Mokroye had two thousand souls, but at this hour they were all already asleep, and only here and there through the gloom occasional lights still flickered.

'Make haste, make haste, Andrey, here I come!' Mitya exclaimed almost in a fever.

'They're not asleep!' Andrey said again, pointing with his knout at Plastunov's inn which stood right at the entrance to the village, and all six windows of which were brightly illumined.

'They're not asleep!' Mitya caught up, joyfully. 'Make thunder and lightning, Andrey, make haste at the gallop, roll up with a crash and a rattle! I'm on my way! Here I come!' Mitya exclaimed in a frenzy.

Andrey launched his exhausted *troika* into a gallop and did indeed roll up with a crash and a rattle at the tall porchway, and reined in his steaming, half-throttled steeds. Mitya leapt down from the wagon, and just at that moment the landlord of the inn, who really had been on his way to bed, took a curious glance from the porch at who this might be who had rolled up in such a fashion.

'Trifon Borisych, is it you?'

The landlord bent forward, had a good look, and then ran headlong down the steps of the porch and in servile ecstasy rushed towards the guest.

'Little father, Dmitry Fyodorovich! Do we see you again?'

This Trifon Borisych was a thickset and robust muzhik of average height, with a somewhat corpulent face, of stern and implacable aspect, particularly when faced by the muzhiks of Mokroye, but possessing the gift of swiftly altering his features into a most servile expression when he sensed an advantage to be had. He went around dressed in Russian style, in a side-fastening shirt and a *poddyovka*, had a considerable store of the lucre, but also dreamed incessantly of a higher role. Over half of the muzhiks were in his clutches, all were heavily in debt to him. He held land on lease from the local landowners and bought land himself, and the muzhiks worked this land for him in payment of debts from which they could never escape. He was a widower and had four grown-up daughters; one was already a widow, lived on his premises with her two young girls, his granddaughters, and worked for him like a charwoman. The second of this muzhik's daughters were married to a government clerk, some petty scribe who had worked his way up in the service, and on the wall of one of the inn's rooms there could be seen among the family photographs one, of miniature dimensions, of this petty clerk in his uniform and civil service epaulettes. The two younger daughters would, on church holidays or when setting off somewhere to pay a social visit, put on blue or green dresses, sewn in fashionable style, close-fitting at the rear and with trains an arshin long, but would on the following morn, as on any other day, rise at first light and with birch brooms in their hands sweep the chambers, bear out the slops and clear up the litter the guests had left behind. In spite of the dear little thousands he had already acquired, Trifon Borisych was very fond of emptying the coffers of a guest who was on a spree and, recalling that a month had not yet passed since in a single twenty-four hours he had, thanks to Dmitry Fyodorovich, during his spree with Grushenka, enriched himself to the tune of two hundred or so dear little roubles, if not an entire three, greeted him now joyfully and with alacrity just because of the very way that Mitya had rolled up to his porch, sniffing his plunder once more.

'Little father, Dmitry Fyodorovich, do we acquire you again?'

'Wait, Trifon Borisych,' Mitya began, 'the important thing first: where is she?'

'Agrafena Aleksandrovna?' the landlord said, understanding at once, and peering nervously at Mitya's face. 'Why she is . . . present here, too . . .'

'With whom? With whom?'

'Some guests who are travelling through, sir . . . One of them's a civil servant, a Pole apparently, to judge by the way he talks, it was him who sent the horses over for her from here; and the other fellow with him is either his companion or his fellow traveller, who can tell; they're dressed in civilian clothes . . .'

'What are they doing, are they on a spree?'

'What spree? They're not much of a quantity, Dmitry Fyodorovich.'

'No? Well, and what about the others?'

'The other two are from the town, gents, the both of them . . . They were on their way back from Cherni* and stayed. One of them, a young fellow, is a kinsman of Mr Miusov, apparently, only I can't remember his name . . . And the other one I expect you also know: the landowner

Maksimov, he says he was on a pilgrimage, visited that monastery of yours over there, and now he's travelling with this young kinsman of Mr Miusov . . .'

'And that's all of them?'

'That's all of them.'

'Wait, be quiet, Trifon Borisych, now tell me the most important thing: what of her — how is she?'

'Well, she arrived a while ago and she sits with them.'

'Is she cheerful? Laughing?'

'No, she doesn't seem to laugh much. Completely bored more like, I'd say she was, she's been combing the young fellow's hair.'

'You mean the Pole, the officer?'

'Why, he's not young, and he's certainly no officer; no, sir, not him, but that nephew of Mr Miusov's, the young one . . . only I can't remember his name.'

'Kalganov?'

'That's it — Kalganov.'

'Very well, I shall settle the matter myself. Are they at cards?'

'They were, but they've stopped now, they had tea and then the civil servant asked for liqueurs.'

'Wait, Trifon Borisych, wait, dear soul, I shall settle the matter myself. Now tell me the most important thing: are there any gypsies?'

'There's nary a trace of the gypsies, Dmitry Fyodorovich, they got chased out by the police, but there's Jews, who play dulcimers and violins, they're in Rozhdhestvenskaya, so you could send for them if you like. They'll come.'

'Send for them, send for them without fail!' Mitya screamed. 'And you can raise some wenches, too, like last time, Marya particularly, Stepanida too, Arina. Two hundred roubles for a chorus!'

'Why, for money like that I can raise the whole village for you, though they've gone off to snooze now. But little father, Dmitry Fyodorovich, are our local muzhiks worthy of such kindness, or our wenches either? Fancy allotting a sum like that to such villainy and coarseness! Is it for him, our muzhik, to smoke cigars, yet you gave him them. Why, after all, he stinks, the brigand. And even though we have ever so many wenches, they all have lice. Why, I will raise my own daughters for you for free, never mind a great big sum like that, only they've gone to bed now, so I'll have to give them a kick in the back and get them to sing for you. Last time you were here you plied the muzhiks with champagne, e-ech!'

Trifon Borisych's commiseration with Mitya was not genuine: on the previous occasion he had kept back half a dozen bottles of champagne for himself, and had picked up a hundred-rouble note from under the table and clutched it in his fist. There it had remained.

'Trifon Borisych, I threw away a certain little thousand here, didn't I? Do you remember?'

'You did, my dove, how could I not remember, I should think you left us with three.'

'Well, I've brought the same amount with me this time, too.'

And he took out his wad of credit bills and held them right under the landlord's nose.

'Now listen and understand: in an hour's time wine will arrive, *ʒakuski*, pies and sweetmeats – I want you to take it all upstairs as soon as it gets here. This hamper Andrey has, I want you to take it upstairs immediately, open it and serve the champagne at once ... And the most important thing, the most important thing is the wenches, the wenches, and make sure that Marya is there ...'

He turned towards the wagon and hauled his case of pistols out from under the seat.

'In settlement, Andrey, accept! Here's fifteen roubles for the *troika*, and here's fifty for vodka ... in recognition of your readiness, your love! Remember *barin* Karamazov!'

'I'm frightened, *barin* ...' Andrey began hesitantly. 'I'll take five roubles for tea, but more I won't accept. Trifon Borisych can be my witness. Forgive the stupid things I say ...'

'What are you frightened of?' Mitya said, measuring him with his glance. 'Well, the devil with you, if that's how it is!' he shouted, throwing him five roubles. 'Now then, Trifon Borisych, take me up there quietly and let me first of all get an eyeful of them, but so that they don't notice me. Where are they, in the blue room?'

Trifon Borisych looked at Mitya warily, but at once obediently fulfilled what was demanded: carefully he led him into the passage, entered the first large room, which adjoined the one in which the guests were sitting, and brought the candle out of it. Then on the sly he led Mitya in and stationed him in a corner, in the dark, from where he might freely discern the interlocutors, while remaining unseen by them. But Mitya did not look for long, and indeed could do no discerning: he caught sight of her, and his heart began to hammer, his eyes grew dim. She sat at the table, on one side, in an an armchair, and beside her, on the sofa, sat the rather pretty and still very young Kalganov; she was holding his hand and, it seemed, laughing, while the latter, without looking at her, was saying something loudly, as though in vexation, to Maksimov, who sat on the other side of the table facing Grushenka. As for Maksimov, something was making him laugh a great deal. On the sofa sat *he*, and beside the sofa, on a chair by the wall, sat another stranger. The one who was lounging on the sofa smoked a pipe, and Mitya had only a fleeting impression that this was some kind of rather fat and broad-faced little man who could not be very tall and who seemed to be angry about something. As for his companion, the other stranger, Mitya thought he looked rather exceptionally tall; more than this, however, Mitya was unable to discern. His breath choked. He was unable to endure it for even another moment, he put his case on a chest of drawers and directly, turning cold and dying inwardly, led his steps towards the interlocutors in the blue room.

'Ah!' Grushenka, who had been the first to notice him, shrieked in fright.

7

The Former and Beyond Dispute

MITYA, with his long, swift strides, stepped right up to the table.

'Gentlemen,' he began loudly, almost shouting, but stammering with every word, 'I . . . I mean you no harm! Do not be afraid,' he exclaimed, 'I mean you no harm, no harm,' he said suddenly, turning to Grushenka, who in her armchair had moved away towards Kalganov and had firmly seized his hand. 'I . . . I too am travelling. I shall stay here until morning. Gentlemen, may a passing traveller . . . join you until morning? Only until morning for the last time, in this very room?'

He concluded this by turning to the rather fat little man who sat on the sofa with his pipe. The man took the pipe out of his mouth rather grandly and in a stern voice pronounced:

'*Panie*,* we are private here. There are other chambers.'

'Why, is it you, Dmitry Fyodorovich? What are you doing here?' Kalganov responded suddenly. 'Please, sit down with us, greetings.'

'Greetings, dear man . . . and beloved one! I have always respected you . . .' Mitya replied joyfully and with alacrity, at once extending his hand to him over the table.

'I say, what a handshake! A regular finger-crusher!' Kalganov laughed.

'He always shakes hands like that,' Grushenka said brightly, with a timid smile, suddenly, it seemed, persuaded by Mitya's appearance that he was not going to start any trouble, studying him with intense curiosity and still with unease. There was something about him that she found extraordinarily striking, and indeed she had never expected that at such a moment he would enter and talk like this.

'Greetings, sir,' the landowner Maksimov sweetly echoed from the left. Mitya rushed over to him.

'Greetings, you are here, too, how relieved I am that you too are here! Gentlemen, gentlemen, I . . .' He again turned towards the *pan* with the pipe, evidently assuming him to be the principal personage here. 'I flew post-haste . . . I wanted to spend my last day and my last hour in this room, in this very room . . . where I too worshipped . . . my empress! Forgive me, *panie*!' he shouted in frenzy, 'I flew post-haste and swore a vow . . . Oh, do not be afraid, it is my final night! *Panie*, let us drink a peaceful settlement! Wine will be served in a moment . . . Look, I have brought this with me.' For some reason he suddenly whipped out his wad of credit bills. 'Permit me, *panie*! I want music, thunder, noise, all of what there was last time . . . But the worm, the needless worm shall crawl upon the earth, and be no more! The day of my joy I shall commemorate upon my final night! . . .'

He had almost lost his breath; many, many were the things he wanted to say, but all that came out were strange exclamations. The *pan* looked motionlessly at him, at his wad of credit bills, looked at Grushenka and was in evident bewilderment.

'If my *królewa* will permit . . .' he began.

'*Królewa*, is that a *koroleva*, a queen?' Grushenka broke in suddenly. 'I keep wanting to laugh, the funny way you talk. Sit down, Mitya, what are you going on about? Please don't frighten me. You won't, will you, you won't frighten me? If you promise not to, then I'm glad to see you . . .'

'Would I, would I frighten you?' Mitya exclaimed suddenly, throwing his arms in the air. 'Oh, go past, be upon your way, I shall not interfere! . . .' And suddenly, quite unexpectedly to all of them and, it need hardly be said, to himself as well, he threw himself on to a chair and burst into tears, turning his head towards the opposite wall, and with his hands tightly encircling the back of the chair, as though he were embracing it.

'Now, now, what a fellow you are!' Grushenka exclaimed, reproach-fully. 'That's just how he used to come to me – he would suddenly start talking, and I wouldn't understand any of it. And one time he'd burst into tears like that, and the next – oh, the shame there would be! What are you crying for? *And would there be any reason for you to?*' she suddenly added mysteriously, her irritation giving her little remark a special emphasis.

'I . . . I'm not crying . . . Well, greetings!' he said, turning round in a single instant on his chair, and suddenly laughed, not, however, with his jerky, wooden laugh but with one that was strangely long and inaudible, nervous and quaking.

'Well, here we are again. Well, cheer up, cheer up!' Grushenka said, coaxingly. 'I am very glad you have come, very glad, Mitya, do you hear what I say, I am very glad. I want him to sit here with us,' she said imperiously, as if she were addressing all of them, though her words were plainly intended for the sitter on the sofa. 'That is what I want, do you hear? And if he leaves, then I shall leave too, so there!' she added with eyes that suddenly flashed with light.

'What my empress wishes – that is the law!' the *pan* pronounced, with gallantry kissing Grushenka's small hand. 'I ask the *pan* into our company!' he said, addressing Mitya courteously. Mitya again leapt up with the plain intention of once again bursting into a tirade, but something else came out.

'Let us drink, *panie*!' he said, breaking off abruptly instead of continuing to talk. They all burst out laughing.

'Lord! And I thought he was going so start talking again,' Grushenka exclaimed nervously. 'Listen, Mitya,' she added, pressingly, 'stop jumping up and down now, and as for your having brought champagne, that is marvellous. I myself shall have some, for I cannot abide liqueurs. But what is best is that you yourself should have rolled along here, otherwise I think I should have died of boredom . . . I say, have you come on a spree again? But put that money away in your pocket! Where did you get all that?'

Mitya, in whose hand the banknotes were still crumpled together, attracting the notice of all and especially of the two *panowie*, swiftly and in embarrassment stuffed them into his pocket. He reddened. At that same moment the innkeeper brought an uncorked bottle of champagne on a tray with glasses. Mitya moved to snatch up the bottle, but was so confused that he forgot what he was supposed to do with it. Kalganov took it from him and poured the wine out for him.

'And another bottle, another one!' Mitya shouted to the innkeeper and, forgetting to touch glasses with the *pan* whom he had so solemnly invited to drink a peaceful settlement, he suddenly downed his entire glass alone, without waiting for anyone. His entire face suddenly altered. Instead of the solemn and tragic expression with which he had come in, there now appeared in it something that was almost infant-like. He suddenly seemed wholly meekened and humbled. He looked at them all timidly and joyfully, with a frequent nervous giggle and the grateful look of a guilty stray dog that has again been fondled and again been admitted to the house. He seemed to have forgotten everything and kept looking round at them all with a childish smile. At Grushenka he looked constantly laughing, and moved his chair right up to her armchair. Little by little he also became aware of the two *panowie*, though as yet he could make little sense of them. The *pan* on the sofa struck him with his bearing, his Polish accent, and principally – his pipe. 'What on earth? Well, I suppose it's all right if he smokes a pipe,' Mitya thought in contemplation. The somewhat podgy, almost forty-year-old face of the *pan* with its very small nose, under which two very thin sharp moustaches, dyed and insolent, could be seen, likewise did not arouse in Mitya the slightest of questions for the meantime. Even the *pan*'s very wretched little wig, manufactured in Siberia, with most stupidly combed-forward temple-locks, made no particular impression on Mitya: 'Well, I suppose if he wears a wig then that is as it should be, too,' he said to himself, continuing his blissful contemplation. As for the other *pan*, who was sitting over by the wall, younger than the *pan* on the sofa, surveying the entire company insolently and challengingly and listening to the general conversation with contempt, again Mitya was struck only by his tall stature, which was grossly disproportionate to that of the *pan* who sat on the sofa. 'If he stood up he'd be nearly seven feet tall,' flickered through Mitya's head. It also flickeringly occurred to him that this tall *pan* was probably the friend and myrmidon of the *pan* on the sofa, something in the order of his 'bodyguard', and that the little *pan* with the pipe was of course issuing the orders to the tall *pan*. But to Mitya all this seemed quite terribly good and indisputable. In the little dog there had died all trace of rivalry. Of Grushenka and the mysterious tone of some of her remarks he as yet understood nothing; all he could grasp, with a quaking of his whole heart, was that she was being affectionate to him, that she had 'forgiven' him and that she had sat him down beside her. He nearly went wild with delight when he saw that she had taken a sip of wine from her glass. The silence of the company suddenly, however, seemed to make an impression on him, and he began to look round at them with eyes that were in expectation of something: 'But why are we sitting here, why don't you begin, gentlemen?' his grinning gaze seemed to say.

'Well, he keeps talking nonsense, and we've been sitting here laughing,' Kalganov began suddenly, as if he had guessed what Mitya was thinking, and pointing to Maksimov.

'Nonsense?' Mitya said, breaking into his short, wooden laugh, instantly for some reason pleased. 'Ha, ha!'

'Yes. Imagine, he asserts that in the 1820s the whole of our cavalry married Polish girls; but that is the most dreadful rubbish, is it not?'

'Polish girls?' Mitya caught up again, in positive delight this time.

Kalganov was very well aware of Mitya's relation to Grushenka, and he had a hunch about the *pan* as well, but all this did not interest him much, indeed possibly did not interest him at all, for his interest lay most of all with Maksimov. He had ended up here with Maksimov by chance and had encountered the *panowie* here at the inn for the first time in his life. As for Grushenka, he had known her formerly and had once even visited her with someone; at the time she had not cared for him. Here, however, she was giving him very affectionate looks; before Mitya had got there she had given him a fondle or two, but he had somehow remained insensible to them. This was a young man, not more than twenty years old, stylishly dressed, with a very charming white little face and with beautiful, thick, chestnut-coloured hair. But in this white little face there were delightful light-blue eyes, with a clever, and sometimes even profound expression, not commensurate with his age even, in spite of the fact that the young man sometimes spoke and looked just like a child and was in no way shy about this, even being aware of it himself. In general he was very original, even capricious, though always affectionate. Sometimes in the expression of his face there flickered something fixed and stubborn; he would stare at you, listen, all the while, it would seem, obstinately dreaming of something all his own. Now he would become languid and lazy, now he would suddenly begin to grow excited, sometimes, it appeared, on the very vainest of pretexts.

'Imagine, I have been leading him around for four days now,' he continued, drawling the words, as it were, somewhat lazily, but without any foppishness, and completely naturally. 'You remember – ever since your brother pushed him out of the hackney carriage that day, and he went flying. At the time I found his behaviour very interesting, and I took him to my estate, but now he keeps spouting rubbish all the time, so that one really feels embarrassed to be with him. I am going to take him back . . .'

'The *pan* has never seen a Polish *pani*, and says what can never have been,' the *pan* with the pipe observed to Maksimov.

The *pan* with the pipe spoke decent Russian, at any rate far better than he pretended. If he used a Russian word he would twist it into a Polish form.

'But I mean to say, I myself was married to a Polish *pani*, sir,' Maksimov tittered in reply.

'I see, so you served in the cavalry then, did you? After all, you're the one who was talking about the cavalry. So you're a cavalry officer, are you?' Kalganov said, at once entering the fray.

'Yes, of course, is he a cavalry officer? Ha-ha!' Mitya shouted, avidly listening and quickly transferring his questioning gaze to anyone who said anything, as though God only knew what he expected to hear.

'No, sir, you see, sir ...' Maksimov said, turning to him, 'what I mean, sir, is that those *panienki* over there ... the pretty ones, sir ... when they dance the mazurka with our Uhlans ... when she's danced the mazurka with him she jumps up on to his lap like a kitten, sir ... a white one, sir ... and the gentleman-father and the lady-mother see it and permit it ... they permit it, sir ... and on the morrow the Uhlan goes and offers his hand ... You see, sir ... he offers his hand, hee-hee!' Maksimov tittered, in conclusion.

'*Pan lajdak*, the gentleman is a scoundrel!' the tall Pole on the chair growled suddenly, placing one leg across the other. Mitya could not help being struck by his enormous grease-blacked boot with its thick and dirty sole. Indeed, both *panowie* were dressed in rather grease-stained fashion.

'Oh, it's *lajdak* now! Why the abuse?' Grushenka said, growing suddenly angry.

'Pani Agrippina, the gentleman saw peasant women in Poland, not noble ladies,' the *pan* with the pipe observed to Grushenka.

'You may count on that!' the tall *pan* snapped contemptuously.

'There, that's more of it! Let him speak! If people want to speak, why interfere? We're enjoying ourselves!' Grushenka bit off.

'I do not interfere, *pani*,' the *pan* in the wig observed meaningfully, casting a long look towards Grushenka and, after a solemn pause, began to suck his pipe again.

'But I say, I say, the *pan* was speaking the truth just now,' Kalganov said, flaring up again, as though God only knew what the subject of conversation was. 'After all, he has never been in Poland, so how can he talk about it? It's true, isn't it, you didn't get married in Poland, did you?'

'No, sir, in the province of Smolensk, sir. Only an Uhlan had brought her there before that, sir, my spouse, sir, future, sir, with her lady-mother and her *tante*, and another female relative with a grown-up son, from Poland itself, from Poland itself ... and he ceded her to me. One of our lieutenants, he was, a very good young man. At first he himself had intended to marry her, but he did not, as she proved to be lame . . .'

'So you married a girl who was lame?' Kalganov exclaimed.

'That is correct, sir. They both hid it from me at the time, deceived me a little, they did. I thought she was jumping up and down . . . She kept jumping up and down, and I thought it was because she was so happy . . .'

'From joy at marrying you?' Kalganov howled in a kind of childish, ringing voice.

'Yes, sir, from joy, sir. But it proved to be for quite a different reason, sir. Later, when we had been wed, she came to me after the service and confessed and asked forgiveness with exquisite sentiment, sir, she said that as a little girl she had once jumped over a puddle and had injured her little foot, hee-hee!'

Kalganov fairly dissolved in the most childish laughter and almost fell on to the sofa. Grushenka too burst out laughing. As for Mitya, he was at the summit of happiness.

'You know, you know, he was speaking the truth just now, he wasn't lying!' Kalganov exclaimed, addressing Mitya. 'And you know, after all he's been married twice — it's his first wife he is talking about — his second wife, you know, ran away and is still alive, do you realize that?'

'Really?' Mitya said, swiftly turning towards Maksimov, an expression of extraordinary bewilderment on his face.

'Yes, sir, she ran away, sir, I had that misfortune,' Maksimov confirmed modestly. 'With a certain *monsieur*, sir. And the real trouble was that the first thing she did was to transfer the whole of my little estate into her own name. "You", she said, "are a man of education, you will be able to find a crust of bread for yourself." And with that she settled my hash. A most venerable bishop once observed to me: "One of your wives was lame, and the other was far too nimble on her feet." Hee-hee!'

'Listen, listen!' Kalganov fairly bubbled. 'If he's lying — and he often lies — then he is doing it solely in order to provide everyone with pleasure: and that, after all, is not base, now, is it? You know, sometimes I love him. He is very base, but he is naturally base — hm? What do you think? Another man may act basely because of some reason, in order to gain an advantage, but he does it simply, he does it by nature . . . Imagine, for example: he claims (yesterday he argued this throughout the whole of our day's journey) that Gogol wrote about him in *Dead Souls*.* If you remember, there is in that book a landowner Maksimov who has been flogged by Nozdryov; Nozdryov is brought before the law: "for the

infliction upon the landowner Maksimov of a personal insult by means of
the birch while intoxicated" – well, you remember? So there, imagine, he
claims that that was him and that it was he who received the
flogging! Well, I mean, can that be true? Chichikov undertook his travels
at the beginning of the 1820s at the very latest, so the years really do not
tally. He could not have been flogged at that time. I mean, surely he
could not, he could not?'

It was hard to understand why Kalganov was getting so worked up,
but he was getting sincerely worked up. Mitya selflessly entered into his
interests.

'Well, what if he *was* flogged?' he shouted, laughing.

'It was not that I was exactly flogged, sir, but it is so,' Maksimov
suddenly inserted.

'What do you mean – it is so? Were you flogged, or weren't you?'

'What time is it, sir?' the *pan* with the pipe said, turning to the tall *pan*
on the chair with an air of boredom. The latter shrugged his shoulders in
reply: neither of them had a watch.

'Why shouldn't we do a bit of talking? You must let others talk, too.
If you're bored then let others talk, and be quiet,' Grushenka said,
throwing up her head again, her involvement plainly calculated with
purpose. At that moment something seemed to flicker through Mitya's
mind for the first time. On this occasion the *pan* replied, with evident
irritation now:

'Sir, I do not contradict, I did not say anything.'

'Oh, very well, but now you must tell us this story,' Grushenka
shouted to Maksimov. 'Why are you all so quiet?'

'But there is no point in relating it, madam, for it is all mere stupidity,'
Maksimov caught up at once with evident satisfaction and a drop of
affectation, 'and even in Gogol all that is merely in allegorical form, for
he gave all the characters allegorical surnames: you see, Nozdryov was
not Nozdryov, but Nosov, and as for Kuvshinnikov – that is completely
different, because his real name was Shkvornyov. But Fenardi really was
Fenardi, only not an Italian but a Russian, Petrov, madam, and Mlle
Fenardi was pretty, madam, with her feet in *bas en tricot*, pretty ones,
madam, and a short little skirt with spangles, and she did indeed spin
round and round, only not for four hours, but only for four little
minutes, madam . . . and won everyone over . . .'

'But what were you flogged for, what was the reason for your being
flogged?' Kalganov howled.

'Because of Piron,* sir,' Maksimov replied.

'And who might he be?' shouted Mitya.

'Piron — the famous French writer, sir. At the time we were all drinking wine in high society, at an inn, at that very same fair. They had invited me along, and the first thing I did was to start quoting epigrams: "Is't thou Boileau? What comic travesty!"* And Boileau replies that he is going to a masked ball, or rather to the bathhouse, sir, hee-hee, and they took it as applying to them. And then I quoted another epigram, one that is very well-known to all educated men, a cutting one, sir:

> Thou'rt Sappho, Phaon I, from that no dispute flow,
> But to my everlasting woe
> The seaward path thou dost not know.*

They took offence even more at that and began to call me quite indecent names because of it, and in an attempt to set things right again I chose to tell a very educated anecdote about Piron, about how he was refused admission to the French Academy, and how he, in order to take his revenge, wrote his own epitaph for his own gravestone:

> *Ci-gît Piron qui ne fut rien*
> *Pas même académicien.*

Well, at that they went and flogged me.'

'But why? What for?'

'Because of my education. Many are the reasons for which people may flog a man,' Maksimov concluded, meekly and moralizingly.

'Oh, that's enough, how nasty all that is, I don't want to listen, I thought it would be something amusing,' Grushenka said, breaking him off suddenly. Mitya started up and at once stopped laughing. The tall *pan* got up from his seat and with the haughty air of one who is bored in company not his own began to pace about the room from corner to corner, his hands held behind his back.

'Will you look at him and his pacing!' Grushenka said, giving him a look of contempt. Mitya began to grow restless; moreover, he had observed that the *pan* on the sofa was looking at him with an air of irritation.

'*Pan,*' Mitya shouted, 'Let us drink, *panie*! The other *pan*, too: let us drink, *panowie*!' In a trice he had moved up three glasses and filled them with champagne.

'To Poland, *panowie*, I drink to your Poland, to the Polish land!' Mitya exclaimed.

'With the greatest of pleasure, *panie*, let us drink,' solemnly and benignly pronounced the *pan* on the sofa and took his glass.

'And the other *pan*, what's his name, *hej, jasnie wielmoźny* (your Excellency), take a glass!' Mitya said, in a fluster.

'Pan Wróblewski,' prompted the *pan* on the sofa.

'To Poland, *panowie*, hurrah!' Mitya shouted, raising his glass.

All three drank. Mitya seized hold of the bottle and at once poured another three glasses.

'Now to Russia, *panowie*, and let us be brothers!'

'Pour some for us,' said Grushenka, 'I too want to drink to Russia.'

'I, too,' said Kalganov.

'And I shall, also ... to dear little Russia, the dear old granny,'* Maksimov tittered.

'Everyone, everyone!' Mitya exclaimed. 'Landlord, more bottles!'

The three bottles that remained of those that Mitya had brought with him were brought. Mitya did the pouring.

'To Russia, hurrah!' he proposed, again. They all, apart from the *panowie*, drank, and Grushenka downed the whole of her glass in one. The *panowie* did not even touch theirs.

'Well now, *panowie*?' Mitya exclaimed. 'Will you follow us?'

Pan Wróblewski picked up his glass, raised it and said in a stentorian voice: 'To Russia within the frontiers of before 1772!'*

'That is much better!' the other *pan* shouted, and both at once drained their glasses dry.

'You're being silly, *panowie*!' broke suddenly from Mitya.

'*Pa-nie!!*' both *panowie* cried with menace, staring at Mitya like a pair of cockerels. Pan Wróblewski was particularly incensed.

'May one not have a soft spot for one's own country?' he proclaimed.

'Be quiet! Stop quarrelling! There must be no quarrels!' Grushenka shouted imperiously, stamping her foot on the floor. Her face was aflame, her eyes glittered. The glass she had just drunk had had its effect. Mitya was horribly alarmed.

'*Panowie*, forgive me! I was the guilty one, I shall not do it again. Wróblewski, Pan Wróblewski, I shall not do it again ...'

'And please will you sit down and be quiet, you stupid fellow!' Grushenka bit off at him with malicious vexation.

They all settled down in their seats again, they all fell silent, they all looked at one another.

'Gentlemen, I am the cause of it all,' Mitya began again, having taken in nothing of Grushenka's intervention. 'Well, what are we all sitting around for? Well, what shall we do ... to cheer things up, make things more cheerful again?'

'Indeed, they are truly lacking in cheer,' Kalganov drawled lazily.

'What about a little game of faro again, sir, like earlier . . .' Maksimov tittered suddenly.

'Faro? Splendid!' Mitya caught up, 'that is, if the *panowie* . . .'

'*Później, panie!*' the *pan* on the sofa replied, somewhat reluctantly.

'That is true,' Pan Wróblewski said, in confirmation of this.

'Pooz-no? What does pooz-no mean?' Grushenka asked.

'It means *później* – late, *pani*, the hour is late,' the *pan* on the sofa explained.

'With them it's always late, and their answer to everything is always no!' Grushenka almost screamed in vexation. 'They sit looking bored and make everyone else bored, too. To you, Mitya, they've said nothing all the time, and they've puffed themselves up over me . . .'

'My goddess!' the *pan* on the sofa exclaimed. 'As you say, so it shall be. I see your ill disposition, and therefore I am sad. I am ready, *panie*,' he concluded, addressing Mitya.

'Begin then, *panie*!' Mitya said, whipping his banknotes out of his pocket and placing two hundred-rouble bills on the table.

'I want to lose a lot to you, *pan*. Take your cards, make up the bank.'

'The cards ought to be supplied by the landlord, *panie*,' the little *pan* declared insistently and seriously.

'That is the best way,' Pan Wróblewski said in confirmation.

'By the landlord? Very well, I understand, let it be the landlord who supplies them, that was a good idea of yours, *panowie*! Bring us cards!' Mitya commanded the landlord.

The landlord brought in a fresh, unopened pack of cards and announced to Mitya that the wenches were getting ready, that the dulcimer-playing Jews would no doubt also be there shortly, but that the *troika* with the provisions had not yet arrived. Mitya leapt up from the table and ran into the next room in order to make the necessary arrangements at once. Only three wenches had arrived, however, and of Marya there was as yet no sign. And indeed, he did not know what arrangements to make, or why he had run in: he merely gave instructions that the fruit, boiled sweets and *tyagushki* be fetched from the hamper and distributed to the wenches. 'And vodka for Andrey, vodka for Andrey!' he ordered quickly, 'I offended Andrey!' Just then Maksimov, who had run in after him, suddenly touched him on the shoulder.

'I say, I wonder if you could lend me five roubles,' he whispered to Mitya. 'I should also like to take a risk at faro, hee-hee!'

'Marvellous, splendid! Here, have ten!' He again pulled all the credit bills out of his pocket and found a ten-rouble one. 'And if you lose, come to me again, come again . . .'

'Yes, sir,' Maksimov whispered delightedly, and scuttled back into the main room. Mitya also returned at once and tendered his excuses for having made them wait. The *panowie* had already sat down and had opened the pack of cards. Now the *panowie* wore a much more cordial look, one that was almost kindly. The *pan* on the sofa had lit a fresh pipe and had prepared the bank; his features even displayed a certain festive solemnity.

'To your chairs, gentlemen!' Pan Wróblewski proclaimed.

'No, I shan't play any more,' Kalganov responded. 'I lost fifty roubles to them earlier on.'

'The *pan* had no chance, the *pan* may have chance again,' the *pan* on the sofa observed in his direction.

'How much is in the bank? Will it cover any stake?' Mitya asked, heatedly.

'Listen, *panie*, you may stake hundred, you may stake two hundred, as much as you desire.'

'A million!' Mitya roared, laughing.

'Perhaps the *pan kapitan* has heard of Pan Podwysocki?'

'Now which Podwysocki would that be?'

'In Warsaw he kept an unlimited bank, would cover any stake that was made. Comes Podwysocki, sees thousand zlotys, lays his stake: *va banque*. The banker says: "Panie Podwysocki, do you stake zlotys or is it on your *honor*?" "On my *honor*, *panie*," says Podwysocki. "All the better, *panie*." The banker deals the round, and Podwysocki takes thousand zlotys. "Wait, *panie*," says banker, pulls out the drawer and gives him a million, saying, "Here, *panie*, these are your winnings! The bank had a million in it. "I didn't know that," says Podwysocki. "Panie Podwysocki," says banker, "you staked on your *honor*, and we on ours." Podwysocki took million.'

'That is not true,' said Kalganov.

'Panie Kalganow, in decent society such things are not said.'

'So a Polish gambler would give you a million, would he?' Mitya exclaimed, but at once caught himself up. 'Forgive me, *panie*, I am guilty, I am guilty again, he would, he would give you a million, on his *honor*, on Polish honour! You see how I speak Polish, ha-ha! Here, I will stake ten roubles, the knave leads.'

'And I will stake a little rouble on the queen, the queen of hearts, the pretty one, the *panienochka*, hee-hee!' Maksimov tittered, moving out his queen, and as if he desired to hide it from all, he came right up and quickly crossed himself under the table. Mitya won. The 'little rouble' won, too.

'Corner!'* cried Mitya.

'And I shall again stake a little rouble, a *simple*, a little, little *simple*,' Maksimov murmured blissfully, in tremendous joy that his little rouble had won.

'Trumps!' cried Mitya. 'A *double* on the seven!'

The *double*, too, was trumped.

'Stop now,' Kalganov said suddenly.

'A *double*, a *double*,' cried Mitya, doubling his stakes, yet whenever he did so, the card was trumped. But the 'little roubles' went on winning.

'A *double*!' Mitya barked in fury.

'Two hundred you have lost, *panie*. Will you stake another two hundred?' the *pan* on the sofa inquired.

'What, lost two hundred, have I? Then here's another two hundred! The whole two hundred on a *double*!' And, whipping the money out of his pocket, Mitya was about to throw two hundred roubles on the queen when Kalganov suddenly covered the notes with his hand.

'Enough!' he cried in his resonant voice.

'Why did you do that?' Mitya said, staring at him.

'Enough, I don't wish it! You shall play no more.'

'Why?'

'Just because. Spit and leave, that's why. I won't let you play any more!'

Mitya gazed at him in astonishment.

'Leave it now, Mitya, he's probably right; and anyway you've lost enough already as it is,' Grushenka, too, chimed in, a strange little note in her voice. Both *panowie* rose from their seats with an air of tremendous offence.

'Is this a joke, *panie*?' said the little *pan*, looking Kalganov up and down, severely.

'How dare you do this, *panie*?' Pan Wróblewski, too, barked at Kalganov.

'Do not dare, do not dare to shout!' cried Grushenka. 'Oh, you turkey-cocks!'

Mitya looked at them all in turn; but something in Grushenka's face suddenly struck him and at that same instant something completely new flickered in his mind – a strange new thought!

'Pani Agrippina!' the little *pan* began, completely red with insolent challenge, when suddenly Mitya, going up to him, clapped him on the shoulder.

'*Jasnie wielmożny*, two words with you.'

'What do you want, *panie*?'

'Into the other room, into the other chamber, I want to say two nice little words to you, of the very best, you will be pleased with them.'

The little *pan* was astonished and looked at Mitya warily. At once, however, he consented, though on the sole condition that Pan Wróblewski accompany him.

'The bodyguard, is it? Very well, let him come too, we need him as well!' Mitya exclaimed. 'Quick march, *panowie*!'

'Where are you off to?' Grushenka asked uneasily.

'We shall be back in one instant,' Mitya replied. A kind of boldness, a kind of unexpected cheerfulness had begun to sparkle in his face; quite different was it from the face with which he had entered that room an hour ago. He led the *panowie* into a small room on the right, not the other, large one, in which the chorus of wenches was getting ready and the table being laid, but into a bedroom in which there were trunks, chests and two large beds with a small mountain of cotton pillows on each. Here on a small plank table right in the furthest corner a candle burned. The *pan* and Mitya accommodated themselves at this table facing each other, while the enormous Pan Wróblewski stood at their side, his hands clasped behind his back. The *panowie* looked stern, but plainly curious.

'How may I serve the gentleman?' the little *pan* began to babble.

'This way, *panie*, I will not beat about the bush: here is some money for you.' He pulled out his credit bills. 'If you want three thousand, then take it and go you know where.'

The *pan* looked searchingly, staring with all his might, his gaze fairly boring into Mitya's face.

'*Trzy* thousand, *panie*?' He exchanged looks with Wróblewski.

'*Trzy, panowie, trzy!* Listen, *panie*, I can see you're a reasonable man. Take the three thousand and clear off to all the devils in hell, and take Wróblewski with you – do you hear? But I want you to do it right now, this very minute, and for ever, do you understand, *panie*, for ever march out of this door. What do you have in there: an overcoat, a fur? I shall bring them out for you. They'll harness a *troika* for you this very second and – *au revoir, panie!* Eh?'

Mitya awaited the reply with confidence. He had no doubts. Something exceptionally resolute flickered in the *pan*'s features.

'And the roubles, *panie?*'

'The roubles we shall do this way, *panie*: five hundred roubles this minute for you in order to hire a cab and as earnest money, and 2,500 tomorrow in the town – I swear on my honour, the money will be there, I will get it from under the ground if I have to!' Mitya shouted.

Again the Poles exchanged looks. The face of the *pan* began to alter for the worse.

'Seven hundred, seven hundred, not five hundred, right now, this moment, in your hands!' Mitya said, increasing the offer, and sensing that something unpleasant was afoot. 'What's wrong, *pan*, don't you believe me? I can't give you the whole three thousand at once. If I do, you may come back to her tomorrow ... And in any case, I don't have the whole three thousand on me just now, some of it's back in my lodgings in the town,' Mitya babbled, getting cold feet and losing his resolve with each word he spoke. 'I swear to God it's true, the money's over there, hidden away.'

In one instant an emotion of extraordinary personal dignity began to radiate in the features of the little *pan*:

'Is there anything else you would like?' he asked ironically. 'Fie, fie, for shame!' And he spat. Pan Wróblewski spat, too.

'You are spitting, *panie*,' Mitya said like a man in despair, realizing that the game was up, 'because you think you can get more out of Grushenka. You're a couple of castrated cockerels, the two of you, that's what you are!'

'I am offended to the last degree,' the little *pan* said, suddenly turning as red as a crayfish, and quickly, in the most terrible indignation, as if he desired to listen no further, made an exit from the room. After him, swaying from side to side, went Wróblewski, and after them both went Mitya, embarrassed and taken aback. He was afraid of Grushenka, he sensed that the *pan* was about to raise a hue and cry. So it happened. The *pan* entered the large room and stood theatrically in front of Grushenka.

'Pani Agrippina, I am offended to the last degree!' he exclaimed, but Grushenka suddenly seemed to lose all patience, as though she had been touched on her most tender spot.

'Russian, speak Russian, let there be not another word of Polish!' she shouted at him. 'You used to speak Russian in the old days, have you really forgotten it in five years?' She was red all over with anger.

'Pani Agrippina ...'

'My name is Agrafena, Grushenka, speak Russian, or I won't listen to you!' The *pan* began to puff and pant with *honor* and, murdering the Russian tongue, quickly and pompously pronounced:

'Pani Agrafena, I haff come here to forget old times and to forgiff them, to forget what wass before today . . .'

'What do you mean, forgive? Do you come here to forgive me?' Grushenka broke in, leaping up from her seat.

'Just so, *pani*, I am not small of soul but great of soul. But I wass surprissed, when I saw your loverss. Pan Mitya in this chamber gave me *trzy* thousands, so I should depart. I spat *pan* in the fiz.'

'What? He gave you money for me?' Grushenka shrieked hysterically. 'Is that true, Mitya? But how could you dare? Am I a venal creature and for sale?'

'*Panie, panie,*' Mitya howled, 'she is pure and radiant, and never have I been her lover! That is something you've made up! . . .'

'How dare you defend me in front of him?' Grushenka howled back, 'not from virtue have I been pure and not because I was afraid of Kuzma, but so I could be proud before him and so I could have the right to say "scoundrel" to him, when I met him. And did he really refuse to take the money from you?'

'No, he took it, he took it!' Mitya exclaimed, 'except that he wanted the whole three thousand at once, but I would only give him seven hundred as earnest money.'

'Ah, now I understand: he'd heard that I had money, and that's why he came to wed me!'

'Pani Agrippina,' the *pan* shouted, 'I am chevalier, I am aristocrat, and not *lajdak*! I haff come to take you as my spouse, but I see new *pani*, not she who wass before, but capricious and without shame.'

'Oh, clear off to wherever you came from! I shall order them to kick you out of here, and kick you out they will!' Grushenka screamed in a frenzy. 'Fool, fool was I, to have tortured myself for five years! And not because of him did I torture myself, I tortured myself out of spite! And in any case this isn't him! Was he ever like this? This is father, or someone! Where did you get that wig? The other was a falcon, but this is a drake! The other laughed and sang songs to me . . . And I, I, spent five years drowned in tears, cursed fool that I am, base and shameless one!'

She collapsed on her armchair and covered her face with her hands. At that moment there suddenly resounded from the neighbouring room on the left the choir of the now at last assembled Mokroye wenches — a devil-may-care dance song.

'This is Sodom!' Pan Wróblewski suddenly roared. 'Landlord, drive out shameless hussies!'

The landlord, who had been peeping round the door with curiosity for some time now, hearing the shouting and realizing that the guests were quarrelling among themselves, at once appeared in the room.

'You, what are you shouting about, yelling your mouth off like that?' he said, addressing Wróblewski with a lack of courtesy that was almost beyond the latter's comprehension.

'Filthy brute!' Pan Wróblewski began to bawl.

'Filthy brute? And what kind of cards were you using to play with just now? I brought you a pack, but you hid it! You were playing with fake cards! I could have you sent to Siberia for playing with fake cards, do you know that, because it's the same as using fake banknotes . . .' And, going up to the sofa, he stuck his fingers between the back and the cushion, and extracted from them the unopened pack of cards.

'Here it is, my pack and it hasn't been opened!' He raised it up and showed it all around. 'You see, I saw him putting my pack in there, and switching it for his own – you are a cheat, sir, not a *pan*!'

'And I saw the other *pan* cheating twice,' Kalganov shouted.

'Oh, now shameful, oh, how shameful!' Grushenka exclaimed, throwing up her hands, and in truth blushing for shame. 'Merciful Lord, what a terrible man, what a terrible man he's become!'

'I thought as much, too!' Mitya cried. But hardly had he managed to get this out than Pan Wróblewski, taken aback and brought to the point of rabid fury, turning to Grushenka and threatening her with his fist, shouted:

'Public harlot!' Hardly was this exclamation out of his mouth, however, than Mitya threw himself upon him, seized him with both arms, raised him aloft and in a single instant bore him out of the large room into the one on the right into which he had just led them both.

'I've put him on the floor in there!' he announced, returning at once, panting with excitement. 'He's a fighter, the villain, but I don't think he'll come back! . . .' He shut one half of the double doors and, holding the other wide open, bellowed out to the little *pan*:

'*Jasnie wielmożny*, won't you come back and join us? I beg you!'

'Little father, Mitry Fyodorovich,' Trifon Borisych piped up, 'why don't you take back the money you lost to them? After all, it's the same as if they'd stolen it from you.'

'I shall not reclaim my fifty roubles,' Kalganov suddenly responded.

'And I shan't take my two hundred back, either!' Mitya exclaimed, 'not for anything will I take it back, let him keep it as a consolation prize.'

'Bravo, Mitya! There's a good fellow!' Grushenka cried, and a note of terrible malice sounded in her cry. The little *pan*, who was purple with

rage, but had in no wise lost any of his dignified bearing, approached the
door, but stopped and suddenly said, addressing himself to Grushenka:

'*Pani*, if you want to follow me – then let us go, but if not, then farewell!'

And solemnly, huffing and puffing with indignation and umbrage, he
passed through the doorway. He was a man of character: even after all
that had happened he still had not lost hope that the *pani* might follow
them – to such a degree did he value himself. Mitya slammed the door
after him.

'Lock it,' said Kalganov. But the lock sprang to on the *panowie*'s side
of the door – they had locked themselves in.

'Bravo!' Grushenka cried again, with malice and no mercy. 'Bravo!
We're well rid of them!'

8

Delirium

THERE began something approaching an orgy, a cornucopia of a feast.
Grushenka was the first to shout that she be served with wine: 'I want to
drink, I want to drink myself completely drunk, like last time, do you
remember, Mitya, do you remember how well we got along together
then?' As for Mitya, he was in a kind of delirium, sensing that 'his
happiness' was nigh. In fact, though, Grushenka kept constantly chasing
him away: 'Off you go, make merry, tell them to dance, tell them all to
make merry, "hie thee, *izba*, and hie thee, stove",* like last time, like last
time!' she continued to exclaim. She was horribly roused. And Mitya
would rush off to make the arrangements. The chorus had assembled in
the neighbouring room. The room in which until now they had sat was
in any case too confined, being partitioned by a cotton curtain, behind
which there was again appointed an enormous bed with a plump feather
mattress and the same small mountain of cotton pillows. Indeed, in all
four 'guest' rooms of this inn there were beds everywhere. Grushenka
had made herself comfortable right in the doorway, Mitya had brought
her an armchair there; precisely thus had she sat 'last time', on the day
of their first spree here, from this vantage-point watching the chorus and
dancing. All the same wenches as had been there on that occasion were
together here now; the Jews with violins and zithers had also arrived, and
at last arrived too the so long-awaited wagon and *troika* with the wines
and provisions. Mitya bustled about. People who had no direct business

to be there were also entering the room, muzhiks and peasant wives who had been asleep but had woken up, sensing that a fabulous regalement was about to begin, as it had done a month back. Mitya hailed and embraced those he knew, remembered faces, uncorked bottles and poured out glasses for all who came. A particular eye for the champagne was shown only by the wenches; the muzhiks preferred rum and cognac and, more than anything else, hot punch. Mitya had hot chocolate prepared for all the wenches and saw to it that three samovars, which were to be kept bubbling all night and were not to be moved, were available for tea and punch for anyone who came along: whoever wished could treat himself. In a word, there began something disorderly and preposterous, but Mitya was as if in his native element, and the more preposterous things became, the more animated grew his spirits. Had one or other of the muzhiks come and asked him for money in these moments he would have instantly hauled out his entire wad and would have distributed it to right and to left without keeping count of it. It was no doubt for this reason, in order to guard Mitya, that the landlord, Trifon Borisych, who had by now, it appeared, given up all thought of retiring to bed for the night, kept scurrying around him almost continuously, drinking little, however (he only consumed one small tumbler of punch), and vigilantly supervising in his own way Mitya's interests. At the necessary moments he would with affection and servility stop him and endeavour to talk him out of handing out 'cigars and Rhine wine' or, God forbid, money to the muzhiks like 'last time', and was particularly indignant at the fact that the wenches were drinking liqueurs and eating chocolates: 'There's nothing but lice in those girls, Mitry Fyodorovich,' he would say. 'I kick them in the backside with my knee and tell them to consider it an honour – that's the sort they are!' Mitya once again called Andrey to mind and instructed that punch be sent out to him. 'I offended him earlier,' he kept saying in a voice that was slackened and filled with tender emotion. Kalganov had not intended to drink, and the chorus of wenches had not appealed to him much initially, but, having downed another two goblets of champagne, he grew fearfully mirthful, striding about the rooms, laughing and praising everything and everyone, both singers and orchestra. Maksimov, blissful and – yes, drunk, never left his side. Grushenka, who was also beginning to grow intoxicated, drew Mitya's attention to Kalganov: 'What a nice boy, what a wonderful boy he is!' And Mitya ran with ecstasy to exchange kisses with Kalganov and Maksimov. Oh, much did he anticipate; as yet she had said nothing of this kind to him and had even, plainly, been holding herself back from saying it, merely giving him a glance from time to time with an affectionate, but intemperate eye. At last she suddenly seized him tightly by the hand and drew him to her with force. She was at this time sitting in her armchair by the door.

'What was the idea, coming in like that the way you did just now, eh? The way you came in! . . . I was quite terrified. So you were going to let him have me, were you? Were you really?'

'I did not want to spoil your happiness!' Mitya babbled to her in bliss. His reply was, however, superfluous to her.

'Well, off you go . . . enjoy yourself,' she said, chasing him away again, 'and don't cry, I shall call you over again.'

And off he ran, and once again she proceeded to listen to the songs and watch the dancing, following him with her gaze, wherever he went, but within a quarter of an hour she again summoned him back, and again he came running.

'Well, now sit down beside me, and tell me how you knew I had come here yesterday; who did you hear it from first?'

And Mitya began to tell her everything, in an incoherent, disorderly, intemperate fashion, but the way in which he told it was strange, and he often frowned and lost his way in what he was saying.

'Why are you frowning?' she asked.

'It's nothing . . . I left a man who was ill back there. If only he'd get better, if only I knew he'd get better, I would give up ten years of my life right now!'

'Well, God will look after him, if he's ill. So did you really mean to shoot yourself tomorrow, you stupid fellow – and why? Actually, I like reckless men like you,' she prattled to him with a slightly heavy tongue. 'So you'll go to any lengths for my sake, will you? Eh? And did you really mean to shoot yourself tomorrow, you foolish man? No, stay a while, tomorrow I may have a certain little word to say to you . . . not today, but tomorrow. But you'd like me to say it today? No, I don't want to today . . . Well, off you go, off you go now, enjoy yourself.'

On one occasion, however, she beckoned him over in a kind of bewilderment and as if she were worried.

'What are you sad about? I can see that you're sad . . . Yes, I can see that you are,' she added, peering vigilantly into his eyes. 'Though you're over there kissing muzhiks and shouting, I can see there's something. No, you must make merry, for I am merry, and so must you be . . . There is someone here whom I love, can you guess who it is? Ah there, will you look: my boy has fallen asleep, he's had a drink too many, the poor dear.'

She spoke of Kalganov: the latter had indeed had a drink too many, and had fallen asleep for a moment as he sat on the sofa. Not from drink alone had he fallen asleep, though, for he had suddenly for some reason grown melancholy or, as he said, 'fed up'. He had also, moreover, been thoroughly depressed by the songs of the wenches, which had begun to pass, during the gradual progress of the drinking, into something all too unlenten and unbridled. And the same was true of their dancing: two wenches had dressed up as bears, and Stepanida, a pert little thing with a stick in her hand, playing the bearman, began to 'put them through their paces'. 'Let's have a bit more life in it, Marya,' she would shout, 'or else I'll give you the stick!' At last the bears collapsed on the floor in a manner that was really now quite indecent, to the loud laughter of the densely assembled and multifarious audience of muzhiks and women. 'Well, let them laugh, let them,' Grushenka said sententiously with a look of bliss on her face, 'if a day comes along when they can make merry for once, why should people not rejoice?' As for Kalganov, he looked as though someone had spattered something on his clothes. 'It is mere swinishness, all this national folk stuff,' he observed, as he walked away, 'It's like those springtime games of theirs, when they cherish the sun for the whole of a summer night.' But he had particularly not liked a certain 'new' ditty set to a sprightly dance melody, which described how a *barin* came riding and sounded out the girls:

> The *barin* sounded out the girls,
> Did they love him, did they not?

But the girls' opinion was that the *barin* could not be loved:

> The *barin* he will whip me sore,
> And I will love him never more.

Then a gypsy (*tsygan*, only they pronounced it *tsýgan*, with the stress on the first syllable) came riding, and he too did the same:

> The gypsy sounded out the girls,
> Did they love him, did they not?

But the gypsy could not be loved, either:

> The gypsy he will thieving go
> And he'll bring me naught but woe.

And many were the men who came thus riding, to sound out the girls, even a soldier:

> The soldier sounded out the girls,
> Did they love him, did they not?

But the soldier was turned away with contempt:

> The soldier'll wear his bag of kit
> While I behind him wade through . . .

Here there had followed a line of most uncensored character, which was sung quite openly and produced a furore among the listening audience. At last the matter was settled with a merchant:

> The merchant sounded out the girls,
> Did they love him, did they not?

And it turned out that they loved him very much, because, as they said:

> The merchant he will deal and trade,
> And I, the queen, will have it made.

Kalganov had even lost his temper:

'That song can really only have been written yesterday,' he observed out loud, 'and who is it writes things like that for them, anyway? All that's needed is for a Jew or a railway official to come riding through and sound out the girls: the Jew and the railway official would conquer them all.' And, with something approaching a sense of personal injury, he announced then and there that he was 'fed up', sat down on the sofa and suddenly fell into a drowse. His pretty little face had grown slightly pale and had settled back against the cushion of the sofa.

'Look how pretty he is,' Grushenka said, leading Mitya over to him. 'I was combing his sweet little head of hair earlier – it's like flax, his hair, so thick . . .'

And, stooping over him in tender emotion, she implanted a kiss on his forehead. In a single instant, Kalganov opened his eyes, glanced at her, got to his feet and with a look of the utmost worry inquired: 'Where is Maksimov?'

'So that's who he wants,' Grushenka laughed. 'But sit with me for a moment. Mitya, run and get his Maksimov.'

Maksimov turned out to be firmly ensconced with the wenches, only occasionally running back to pour himself a liqueur; he had had two cups of hot chocolate. His little face had flushed red, his nose had turned purple, and his eyes had become moist and sugary. He came running over and announced that now, 'to the accompaniment of a certain little *motif*' he was going to dance the *sabotière*.

'You see, sir, when I was small I was instructed in all these well-bred high-society dances . . .'

'Well, Mitya, off you go, off you go with him, and I shall watch him dance from here.'

'No, I too, I too shall come and watch,' exclaimed Kalganov, refusing Grushenka's offer to sit with him in most unsophisticated fashion. And so they all directed their steps across the room in order to watch. Maksimov did indeed perform his dance, but it failed to provoke any particular admiration in anyone apart from Mitya. The entire dance consisted of some kind of bobbings up and down with wrigglings of the feet to one side and the other, soles uppermost, and with each bob Maksimov would strike the palm of his hand against his sole. Kalganov did not like it at all, but Mitya positively showered the dancer with kisses.

'Well, thank you, perhaps you are tired now, what would you like from over here? A sweetmeat, eh? Or maybe a cigar?'

'A cigarette, sir.'

'What about a drink?'

'I'll have a drop of this liqueur here, sir . . . I say, have you any chocolates, sir?'

'Why, there's a whole wagonload of them on the table here, pick any one you please, my dove-like soul!'

'No, sir, I mean the kind that are made with vanilla . . . for old folk, sir . . . hee-hee!'

'No, brother, such special ones we do not have.'

'Listen!' the old man said suddenly, stooping right down to Mitya's ear. 'This girl here, Maryushka, sir, hee, hee, how would it be if it were possible for me to get to know her, by your kind graces? . . .'

'Well I'll be . . . that's what you want, is it? No, brother, you're talking nonsense.'

'After all, I am not doing anyone any harm, sir,' Maksimov whispered mournfully.

'Oh, very well, very well. All they're doing here, brother, is singing and dancing, but come to think of it, the devil! You'll have to wait for a bit . . . In the meanwhile have some of what there is, eat, drink, make merry. Do you need money?'

'Perhaps later, sir,' Maksimov smiled.

'Very well, very well . . .'

Mitya's head was burning. He went out into the passage on to the small wooden upstairs gallery that ran round a part of the whole building on the inside, overlooking the yard. The fresh air revived him. He stood alone, in the dark, in one corner, and suddenly clutched his head in both hands. His scattered thoughts suddenly united, his sensations fused into one, and it all gave light. A ghastly, horrible light! 'Well, if I'm going to shoot myself, then when shall I do it, if not now?' rushed through his mind. 'Go down and fetch the pistol, bring it up here and make an end of it all in this same dark and dirty corner.' Almost for a minute did he stand in irresolution. Earlier, as he had flown here, behind him had stood disgrace, the utter thievery he had already committed, and that blood, blood! . . . But then it had been easier, oh, easier! After all, then it had all been finished: he had lost her, given her up to another, as far as he was concerned she had perished, disappeared – oh, the sentence of doom had been easier for him then, had at least seemed unavoidable, necessary, for what reason was there left to remain in the world? But now! Was now the same as then? Now at least he was finished with one of the spectres, the scarecrow: that 'former' one, her indisputable, that fatal man had disappeared without leaving a trace. The terrible spectre had suddenly turned into something so small, so comical; it had been carried into the bedroom and locked in. Never would it return. She was ashamed, and from her eyes he could now clearly see whom it was she loved. Well, now all he had to do was live and . . . and yet it was impossible to live, impossible, oh, a curse on it! 'O God, give life again to the man cast down by the fence! Let this terrible cup pass from me!* After all, it was for sinners such as me that you performed your miracles, O Lord! But what, what if the old man is alive? Oh, then I shall destroy the shame of the rest of my disgrace, I shall return the stolen money, I shall return it, even if I have to dig up from under the earth . . . No vestiges of my disgrace will remain, except in my heart for ever! But no, no, oh, impossible, cowardly dreams! Oh, a curse on it!'

But even so a ray of some bright hope seemed to flash towards him in the dark. He leapt up and rushed back to the rooms – to her, to her again, to his empress for ever! 'Is not one hour, one single minute of her love worth all the rest of life, though it be in the torments of disgrace?' This wild question seized hold of his heart. 'To her, to her alone, to see her, hear her and not to think of anything, to forget everything, though it be only for this night, for an hour, a moment!' Right outside the entrance to the passage, still on the gallery, he collided with the landlord, Trifon Borisych. The latter appeared gloomy and concerned about something and, it appeared, had come out to look for him.

'What is it, Borisych, are you looking for me?'

'Oh no, not you, sir,' the landlord said suddenly, as if taken aback. 'Why would I be looking for you? But . . . where have you been, sir?'

'Why are you looking so fed up? Are you annoyed, or something? Just wait a bit, soon you'll be able to go to bed . . . What time is it now?'

'Well, it must be all of three o'clock. Or even getting on for four.'

'We shall finish, we shall finish.'

'Upon my word, it doesn't matter sir. In fact you may be as late as you please, sir . . .'

'What is wrong with him?' Mitya wondered fleetingly, and ran into the room where the wenches were dancing. But she was not there. She was not in the blue room, either; only Kalganov was there, asleep on the sofa. Mitya looked behind the curtain – she was there. She sat in a corner, on a clothes-chest, and, bent forward with her hands and head on the bed alongside, was bitterly weeping, restraining herself with all her might and suppressing her voice so as not to be heard. On catching sight of Mitya, she beckoned him to her, and, when he had run over to her, seized him tightly by the hand.

'Mitya, Mitya, I loved him, you see!' she said to him in a whisper. 'I loved him so much, all these five years, all, all this time! Was it him I loved or only my own spite? No, it was him! Oh, it was him! You see, I am lying when I say I loved only my own spite, and not him! Mitya, look, I was only seventeen then, he was so affectionate to me, so full of fun, he used to sing songs for me . . . Or at least that was how he seemed to the foolish little girl I was then . . . But now, O Lord, he is not like that, he is not like that at all. He doesn't even have the same face, it isn't him at all. I did not recognize him by his face. I rode here with Timofey and kept thinking, all the way I kept thinking: "How will I greet him, what will I say, how will we look at each other? . . ." The whole of my soul was dying inwardly, and then it was just as if he had poured a tub of slop-water over me. He spoke like a teacher: all of it so learned, so solemn, he greeted me so solemnly that I was quite nonplussed. There was no way I could get a word in. At first I thought he was embarrassed by that long Pole of his. I sat looking at them and thought: why is it I'm unable to say anything to him now? You know, it was his wife who had spoiled him, the one for whom he abandoned me that time and got married . . . It was she who had changed him. Mitya, the shame of it! Oh, I'm ashamed, Mitya, ashamed, oh, for the whole of my life I'm ashamed!

A curse, a curse on those five years, a curse on them! . . .' And again she dissolved in tears, without, however, releasing Mitya's hand, holding it tightly in her own.

'Mitya, little dove, wait, don't go away, I want to say one little word to you,' she whispered, suddenly raising her face to him. 'Listen, you tell me, who is it I love? There is someone here whom I love. Who is he? That is what you must tell me.' On her tear-swollen face a smile began to light up, her eyes were shining in the semi-dark. 'A certain falcon came in a while ago, so that my heart dropped. "Fool that you are, why, there is the one you love," my heart whispered at once. When you came in you filled everything with light. "But what's he afraid of?" I wondered. For I mean, you were afraid, completely afraid, you couldn't speak. "It isn't them he's afraid of," I thought. For could you ever be frightened of anyone? "It's me he's afraid of," I thought, "only me." For after all, Fenya had told you, you little fool, that I'd shouted out of the window to Alyosha that I loved Mitenka for one small hour, and that now I was off to love . . . another. Mitya, Mitya, how could I ever think, fool that I was, that I loved another after you? Do you forgive me, Mitya? Do you forgive me, or not? Do you love me? Do you love me?'

She leapt up and seized him by the shoulders with both arms. Mitya, speechless with ecstasy, stared into her eyes, her face, at her smile, and suddenly, embracing her tightly, hurled himself to kiss her.

'But will you forgive me for tormenting you? Why, I have worn you all out with torment because of my spite. I mean, I purposely drove that old codger out of his mind because of spite . . . Do you remember how you once drank a goblet at my house and then smashed it? I remembered that, and today I too smashed a goblet, to my "base heart" I drank. Mitya, my falcon, why don't you kiss me? Kiss me, kiss me harder, there, like that. If you love, then love! Now I shall be your slave, all my life your slave! 'Tis sweet to be a slave! Kiss me! Beat me, be rough with me, do what you will with me . . . Oh, indeed I deserve rough treatment . . . Wait! Wait a while, later, I do not want it like this . . .' she said, suddenly pushing him away. 'Off you go, Mitka, now I shall go and drink more wine, I want to be drunk, now I'm going to dance while I'm drunk, I want to, I want to!'

She tore herself from him and went out through the curtain. Mitya went out after her, like one who is drunk. 'Let it be, then, let it be, whatever happens now — for one single moment I will give up the world,' flickered through his head. Grushenka had indeed drunk down in one gulp another glass of champagne and had suddenly grown very intoxicated. She sat down in her armchair, in her previous place, with a blissful smile. Her cheeks had begun to blaze, her lips were aflame, her flashing eyes had acquired a light sheen, her passionate gaze beckoned. Something even seemed to have taken hold of Kalganov's heart, and he went over to her.

'Well, did you feel me kiss you just now as you slept?' she whispered to him. 'I'm drunk now, so there ... But are you not drunk? And why is Mitya not drinking? Why aren't you drinking, Mitya, I have had lots, but you've hardly had any ...'

'I'm drunk! Drunk already ... from you, but now I want to be drunk on wine as well.' He downed another glass and — strange did it seem to him — only from his most recent glass grew intoxicated, suddenly intoxicated, whereas all the time until now he had been sober, he himself remembered that. From that moment everything began to spin around him as in a delirium. He walked, laughed, talked to everyone and all of it almost as though he were not conscious. Only one fixed and burning emotion affected him every moment, 'like a burning coal in my soul', as he remembered it later. He would go up to her, sit down beside her, stare at her, listen to her ... As for her, she became tremendously talkative, called everyone over to her, would suddenly beckon to her some wench from the chorus who would approach, while she would either kiss her and let her depart, or else sometimes make the sign of the cross over her with one hand. One more moment or two, and she might have begun to cry. The 'old codger', as she called Maksimov, cheered her up no end. At every moment he kept running up to kiss her dear hand, 'and every dear finger of it', and finally performed yet one more dance to a certain old ditty which he himself sang. With especial ardour did he dance to the song's refrain:

> Little pig groo-groo, groo-groo,
> Little calf moo-moo, moo-moo,
> Little duck kwa-kwa, kwa-kwa,
> Little goose ga-ga, ga-ga.
> Little hen walked in the passageway,
> Tyuryoo-ryoo, ryoo-ryoo she did say,
> Ah, ah, she did say!

'Give him something, Mitya,' Grushenka said. 'Make him a present, after all, he is poor. Oh, the poor, the insulted! ... You know Mitya, I shall go to a nunnery. No, really, some day I shall go to one. Alyosha said some words to me today that I shall remember all my life ... Yes

. . . But today at least let us dance. Tomorrow the nunnery, but today let us dance. I want to be naughty, good people, and what if I do, God will forgive me. If I were God, I'd forgive everyone: "My dear little sinners, from this day hence I forgive you all." And I will go and ask forgiveness: "Forgive a stupid woman, good people, so there." A wild beast, that is what I am, so there. And I want to pray. I have given my onion. An evil-doer such as I, and she wants to pray! Mitya, let them dance, don't stop them. All the people on the earth are good, each single one of them. The world is a good place. Even though we are bad, the world is a good place. We are good and bad, both good and bad . . . No, tell me, I want to ask you: come close all of you, and I shall ask you: tell me this: why am I so good? For you see, I am good, I am very good . . . Well then: why am I so good?' Thus did Grushenka babble, growing more and more intoxicated, and finally announced straight out that now she too wished to dance. She rose from her armchair, and fell, staggering, to one side. 'Mitya, don't let me have any more wine, if I ask for it — don't let me have it. Wine doesn't give any peace. And everything spins round, even the stove, everything spins round. I want to dance. Let everyone watch me dance . . . how well and beautifully I dance . . .'

The intention was a serious one: she took a white cambric handkerchief out of her pocket and took it by one end, in her right hand, in order to wave it as she danced. Mitya began to bustle about, the wenches fell quiet, preparing to break into a dance song in chorus at the first nod. Maksimov, upon learning that Grushenka, too, wished to dance, squealed with ecstasy and began to bob up and down in front of her, crooning:

> Legs so slim, sides so plump,
> And a tail so curly.

But Grushenka waved her handkerchief at him and chased him away:

'Shoo, shoo! Mitya, why isn't anyone coming? Let everyone come . . . and watch . . . Call those others, too, the ones who are locked out . . . Why did you lock them out? Tell them I'm dancing, let them also see me dancing . . .'

'Hey you . . . Podwysockis! Come out, she's going to dance, she wants you to come in and watch.'

'*Lajdak!*' one of the *panowie* shouted in reply.

'And you're a sub-*lajdak*! You're a little sub-*lajdak*;* that's what you are.'

'I do wish you would stop making fun of Poland,' came the sententious observation of Kalganov, also now intoxicated beyond the limits of his capacity.

'Be quiet, boy! If I called him a scoundrel, that doesn't mean that I was calling the whole of Poland scoundrels. One *lajdak* does not make a Poland. Be quiet, my pretty boy, and have a chocolate.'

'Oh, what men! It's as though they weren't human beings at all. Why won't they make it up with one another?' said Grushenka, going out to dance. The chorus broke into: 'Oh, you passage, my passage'.* Grushenka began to go through the motions of throwing back her head, half-opening her lips, smiling, starting to wave her handkerchief and then suddenly, swaying violently on the spot, stood amidst the room in bewilderment.

'I'm too weak . . .' she said in a strange, exhausted voice. 'Forgive me, I'm too weak, I can't . . . I'm sorry . . .'

She bowed to the chorus, and then proceeded to bow to all four corners of the room in turn:

'I'm sorry . . . Forgive me . . .'

'You're tipsy, *baryn'ka*, tipsy, pretty *baryn'ka*,' voices were heard to say.

'Her ladyship is tight,' Maksimov explained, tittering, to the girls.

'Mitya, take me away . . . take me, Mitya,' Grushenka said, helplessly. Mitya rushed over to her, seized her in his arms and ran off behind the curtain with his precious prey. 'Well, I'm off now,' Kalganov thought and he left the blue room, closing both halves of the door behind him. But the feast in the main room thunderously continued, thundering even louder. Mitya put Grushenka down on the bed and bit into her lips with a kiss.

'Do not touch me . . .' she murmured to him in an imploring voice. 'Do not touch me until I am yours . . . I said I was yours, but you must not touch me . . . have mercy . . . In their presence, while they are here it's impossible. He is here. It's horrible here . . .'

'I shall obey! I would not dream of . . . I adore you! . . .' Mitya muttered. 'Yes, it is horrible here, oh, despicable.' And, without releasing her from his embrace, he lowered himself on to the floor beside the bed, on his knees.

'I know that even though you may be a wild beast, you are a noble one,' Grushenka enunciated heavily. 'It must be honest . . . henceforth it must be honest . . . and that we too should be honest, that we should be good and kind, not beasts, but good and kind . . . Take me away, take me far away, do you hear . . . I don't want to be here, I want to be far, far away . . .'

'Oh yes, yes, that is certain!' Mitya said as he pressed her in his embrace. 'I shall take you away, we shall fly . . . Oh, all my life for one year I would give away now, only to know about that blood!'

'What blood?' Grushenka interposed in bewilderment.

'Never mind!' Mitya said, grinding his teeth. 'Grusha, you want it to be honest, but I am a thief. I stole money from Katka . . . The disgrace, the disgrace!'

'From Katka? The young mistress, you mean? No, you did not. Give the money back to her, take some from me . . . Why are you shouting? Now all that is mine is yours. What do we need money for? We shall squander it all in any case . . . we're the kind of people who can't help squandering it. But you and I would do better to go and plough the earth. I want to scrape the earth with these hands of mine. We must work, do you hear? Alyosha has commanded it. I shall not be your lover, I shall be faithful to you, I shall be your slave, I shall work for you. We shall go to the young mistress and both bow to her, ask her to forgive us, and we shall go away. And even if she does not forgive us, we shall still go away. You must take the money to her, and love me . . . And not love her. Not love her any more. And if you do, I shall strangle her . . . I shall stab both her eyes out with a needle . . .'

'It is you I love, you alone, in Siberia I will love you . . .'

'Why Siberia? Though what of it, even Siberia will do, if that is what you want, it is all the same . . . We shall work . . . There is snow in Siberia . . . I love to drive over the snow . . . and there must be a sleighbell . . . Can you hear the bell ringing . . . Where is that bell ringing? People must be coming . . . There, now it has stopped ringing.'

In exhaustion she closed her eyes and suddenly seemed to fall asleep for a single moment. Somewhere in the distance a coachbell really had been ringing and had then suddenly ceased. Mitya inclined his head on to her breast. He had not noticed the ceasing of the bell, but then neither had he noticed that the singing too had ceased, and that in place of it and the drunken clamour that had filled the whole house dead silence suddenly reigned. Grushenka opened her eyes.

'What happened, was I asleep? Yes . . . the bell . . . I slept and had a dream: I dreamed I was riding over the snow . . . the sleighbell was ringing, and I was drowsing. With the man who was dear to me, it must have been you. And we went far away, far away . . . I embraced you and kissed you, pressed you to me, I was cold, and the snow was gleaming . . . You know, when the snow gleams at night, and the moon stares down, and it's as if I were not on the earth . . . I woke up, and my dear one was at my side, and how good that was . . .'

'At your side,' Mitya muttered, kissing her dress, her bosom, her arms. And suddenly he fancied something strange: it seemed to him that she was gazing straight in front of her, but not at him, not into his face, but above his head, fixedly and strangely motionless. Surprise suddenly displayed itself in her face, fear almost.

'Mitya, who is that staring at us?' she whispered suddenly. Mitya turned round and saw that indeed someone seemed to have moved the curtain apart and was watching them. And whoever it was, it seemed, was not alone. He leapt up and quickly strode towards the watcher.

'Through here, come through here to where we are, if you please,' someone's voice said, not loudly, but firmly and insistently.

Mitya came in through the curtain and stood motionless. The entire room was full of people, not, however, those who had been here earlier, but people who were completely new. A momentary chill ran along his spine, and he shuddered. He recognized all these men, in a single flash. There was that big, plump old man, in a paletot and a cap with a cockade — that was the *ispravnik*, the district chief of police, Mikhail Makarych. And that 'consumptive' type, the neatly dressed dandy, who always wore 'such shiningly polished boots' — that was his colleague the public procurator. 'He has a chronometer that cost four hundred roubles, he showed it to me.' And that rather young little man in glasses . . . his surname had just slipped Mitya's mind for a moment, but he knew him too, had seen him before: that was the investigator, the local state investigator, who had recently arrived 'from Jurisprudence'.* And there was the local police-inspector, Mavriky Mavrikich, him he knew without question, he was an acquaintance. Yes, and what about those men with metal badges, what were they doing here? And those two, muzhiks, they looked like . . . And there in the doorway were Kalganov and Trifon Borisych . . .

'Gentlemen . . . What is this about, gentlemen?' Mitya started to say, but suddenly, almost beside himself, almost not himself at all, exclaimed loudly, at the top of his voice:

'I un-der-stand!'

The young man in glasses suddenly moved forward and, stepping up to Mitya, began, though with dignity, yet almost hurrying slightly:

'We have with you . . . in short, I must ask you to step this way, over here, to the sofa . . . There exists a pressing need to have a talk with you.'

'The old man!' Mitya cried in a frenzy. 'The old man and his blood! . . . I un-der-stand!'

And as though the legs had been cut from under him he sat down as though he had fallen there, on a chair that stood near by.

'You understand? He understands! Parricide and monster of cruelty, the blood of your aged father cries out against you!' the old chief of police roared suddenly, stepping up to Mitya. He was beside himself, had turned purple and was shaking all over.

'But this is impossible!' the small young man exclaimed. 'Mikhail Makarych! Mikhail Makarych! This is not right, not right, sir! . . . I ask that I alone be permitted to speak . . . I would never have anticipated from you an episode of this kind . . .'

'But this is delirium, gentlemen, delirium!' howled the chief of police. 'Look at him: at night, drunk, with a licentious whore and covered in the blood of his father . . . Delirium!'

'I beg you with all my might, Mikhail Makarych, dear fellow, for once to restrain your emotions,' the public procurator who was his colleague began to whisper, 'otherwise I shall be compelled to take . . .'

But the little investigator did not let him finish; he turned to Mitya and firmly, loudly and solemnly pronounced:

'Mr Retired Lieutenant Karamazov, it is my duty to inform you that you are accused of the murder of your father, Fyodor Pavlovich Karamazov, which took place last night . . .'

He said a few other things as well, and the public procurator also seemed to put in something, but though Mitya was listening to them, he no longer understood what they were saying. With a wild gaze he looked round at them all . . .

BOOK IX
THE PRELIMINARY INVESTIGATION

I

The Beginning of the Civil Servant Perkhotin's Career

PYOTR Ilyich Perkhotin, whom we left knocking with all his might at the massive barred front gate of the house of the shop-owner Morozova, eventually, of course, succeeded in eliciting a response. On hearing such a violent battering at the gate, Fenya, who two hours earlier had been so frightened and who because of agitation and 'a-thinking' still could not bring herself to go to bed, was now afraid again almost to the point of hysterics: she fancied that this was Dmitry Fyodorovich knocking again (even though she herself had seen him leave), because only he could knock so 'brazen-like'. She rushed out to the yardkeeper, who had already upon being roused from slumber by the sound of the knocking gone out to the gate, and began to beg him not to let him in. But the yardkeeper questioned the knocker and, having learned who he was and that he wanted to see Fedosya Markovna concerning a very important matter, decided at last to unbar the gate for him. On entering the same said kitchen of Fedosya Markovna, its occupant, 'a-doubting and a-feared', imploring Pyotr Ilyich to let the yardkeeper come in too, Pyotr Ilyich began to interrogate her and in an instant landed on the very pith of the matter: that is to say, that Dmitry Fyodorovich, in running off to look for Grushenka, had snatched a pestle from a mortar, and had returned without the pestle, but with his hands covered in blood: 'And the blood it were still dripping, still dripping from them, fair dripping!' Fenya howled, having apparently created this dreadful piece of evidence within her own distraught imagination. The bloody hands had, however, been seen by Pyotr Ilyich himself, though by then they had not been dripping, and he himself had assisted in the process of washing them, and in any case the question was not how quickly the blood had dried, but where precisely Dmitry Fyodorovich had gone running off to with the pestle, whether it had really been to the house of Fyodor Pavlovich, and on what grounds it might so resolutely be affirmed that this was so? On this point Pyotr Ilyich thoroughly insisted and though in the last result he discovered no firm proof, he none the less nurtured what almost amounted to a conviction that Dmitry Fyodorovich could have gone running nowhere but to the house of his parent, and that consequently *something* must without question have taken place there. 'And when he came back,' Fenya added with agitation, 'and I told him everything I knew, I began to ask him: why, Dmitry Fyodorovich, little dove, are your hands covered in blood?' It appeared that he had replied to her that this was human blood and that he had just killed a man – 'admitted it, he did, confessed his guilt to me, and then suddenly he went rushing off like a madman. I sat down, and began to wonder: where had he gone rushing off like a madman to? He'll go to Mokroye, I thought, and he'll murder the *barynya* there. At that I ran off to beg him not to murder the *barynya*, to his lodgings I went, and on the way I was passing Plotnikov's shop and I saw he was already leaving and that his hands didn't have any blood on them now.' (Fenya had observed and remembered this). The old woman, Fenya's grandmother, confirmed all her granddaughter's testimony. Having asked her a further question or two, Pyotr Ilyich left the house in an even greater state of agitation and anxiety than that in which he had entered it.

One might have thought that the simplest and most direct thing for him to have done would be to go now to Fyodor Pavlovich's house and find out if anything had taken place there, and, if it had, then what exactly, and then, having thus attained a conviction beyond all dispute, only then to go to the chief of police, as Pyotr Ilyich had already firmly decided to do. But the night was dark, the gate of Fyodor Pavlovich's house a massive one, again he would have to knock, there was also the fact that Fyodor Pavlovich was only a remote acquaintance – and then, when he obtained a response and the gate was opened to him, and it suddenly became clear that nothing had happened there, tomorrow the derisive Fyodor Pavlovich would go around town relating the anecdote of how the civil servant Perkhotin, whom he did not know, had forced his way into his house in order to find out if someone had killed him. A scandal! And a scandal was what Pyotr Ilyich was afraid of more than anything else in the world. Even so, the emotion that swept him up was so powerful that, having stamped his foot on the ground and again roundly cursed himself, he at once rushed off in a new direction, not to Fyodor Pavlovich's house now, but to that of Mrs Khokhlakova. If, he thought, she would answer the question: had she lent three thousand, at such-and-such a time, to Dmitry Fyodorovich, then in the event of a negative reply he would at once go to the chief of police, without dropping in on Fyodor Pavlovich; but in the event of her reply being positive, he would postpone the whole thing until the morrow and return to his home. Here, of course, one is directly faced with the consideration that in the young man's decision to enter at night, almost at eleven o'clock, the house of a society lady with whom he was not at all upon terms of acquaintance, quite possibly raising her from her bed in order to ask her a question astonishing in consequence of its surroundings, carried with it perhaps an even greater chance of producing a scandal than were he to have gone to Fyodor Pavlovich. Such is, however, sometimes the case in situations like the present one, with the decisions of the most efficient and phlegmatic of men. For Pyotr Ilyich, at that moment, was anything but a phlegmatic man! All his life thereafter he recalled how an unmasterable sense of anxiety, which had by degrees taken control of him, had at last attained within him the quality of torment and had carried him away against his will. It goes without saying that all the way there he none the less continued to rail at himself for the fact that he was going to the house of this lady, but 'I shall follow this through, I shall follow this through to the end!' he repeated for the tenth time, grinding his teeth, and fulfilled his intention – through he did follow.

It was just on eleven o'clock when he entered the precincts of Mrs Khokhlakova's house. Admittance to the yard was granted to him without much delay, but to the question: was the *barynya* asleep or had she not retired, the yardkeeper was unable to give a precise reply, beyond saying that normally by this time she had retired. 'You'll have to go upstairs and have yourself announced; if the *barynya* wants to receive you she'll receive you, and if she doesn't – she won't.' Pyotr Ilyich ascended the stairs, but here things went with rather more difficulty. The manservant was unwilling to announce him, and at last summoned out the maid. Pyotr Ilyich politely but insistently requested her to announce to the *barynya* 'the arrival of a certain local civil servant named Perkhotin, on a matter of particular significance', and to tell her that 'were not the matter so very important he should never have dared to arrive' – 'there, announce it to her in precisely those words, precisely those words,' he requested the maid. The maid withdrew. He remained waiting in the vestibule. In fact, Mrs Khokhlakova, though she was not yet asleep, had already retired to her bedroom. She had been unsettled by Mitya's most recent visit and already sensed that tonight she would not escape the migraine she customarily suffered after such occasions. Upon hearing the maid's announcement and greeting it with astonishment, she irritably gave instructions that the man be turned away, in spite of the fact that this unexpected visit from a 'local civil servant' whom she did not know had interested her lady's heart in the extreme. This time, however, Pyotr Ilyich dug in his heels with the stubbornness of a mule: having heard that he was to be turned away, he requested with extreme insistence that he be announced to her once again and that she be informed 'in precisely those words' that he was here 'on a matter of extreme importance' and that the lady would 'possibly herself regret it if she did not receive him now.' 'It felt like tumbling over a precipice', was how he himself related it subsequently. The chambermaid, looking him up and down with surprise, went to announce him a second time. Mrs Khokhlakova was taken aback, thought for a moment, questioned the maid, asking what the man looked like, and learned that he was 'very proper dressed, ma'am, young and polite-like'. Let us observe in parenthesis and in passing that Perkhotin was, after all, a rather handsome young man, and was himself aware of this. Mrs Khokhlakova decided to come out. She was already in her dressing-gown and slippers, but over her shoulders she threw a black shawl. The 'civil servant' was requested to enter the drawing room, the very same one in which she had earlier received Mitya. Mrs Khokhlakova came out to greet her visitor with a sternly inquiring air and, without inviting him to sit down, began directly with the question: 'What can I do for you?'

'I have taken it upon myself to disturb you, madam, on the matter of our common acquaintance, Dmitry Fyodorovich Karamazov,' Perkhotin began; no sooner had he pronounced this name, however, than there suddenly manifested itself in the features of the mistress of the house an expression of the most intense irritation. She very nearly uttered a shriek and with fury broke into his words.

'How much longer, how much longer am I to be tormented with this dreadful man?' she exclaimed in a frenzy. 'How dare you, my dear sir, take it upon yourself to disturb a lady you do not know in her own home and at such an hour . . . and to present yourself to her in order to speak of a man who here, in this very room, only three hours ago, came to kill me, stamping his feet and leaving in a manner no one leaves a respectable house. I think you ought to know, dear sir, that I shall file a complaint with the authorities against you, that I shall make you pay for this, now be so good as to leave me this very instant . . . I am a mother, I shall this very moment . . . I . . . I . . .'

'Kill you, did you say? So he intended to kill you too, did he?'

'Why, has he killed someone already?' Mrs Khokhlakova asked, impetuously.

'If you will have the good inclination to hear me out, madam, for only half a minute, I shall in two words explain everything to you,' Perkhotin replied with firmness. 'This day, at five o'clock of the afternoon, Mr Karamazov borrowed from me, on comradely terms, the sum of ten roubles, and I know as a matter of positive fact that at that time he had no money, yet at nine o'clock this evening he entered my home bearing in his hand what looked like a wad of one-hundred-rouble banknotes, to a total, I should say, of two or even three thousand roubles. His hands and face were, moreover, covered in blood, and he himself appeared like a man almost demented. To my question, where had he got so much money from, he replied most precisely that he had just the moment before got it from you, that you had lent him the sum of three thousand so that he could travel to the goldfields . . .'

In Mrs Khokhlakova's features there was suddenly expressed an extraordinary and morbid agitation.

'O God! He has killed his old father!' she exclaimed, throwing up her hands. 'Never did I lend him any money, never! Oh, you must run, you must run! . . . Do not say another word! Save his old father, run to him, run to him!'

'Let me be clear about this, madam: so you lent him no money? You definitely recall that you lent him no sum whatsoever?'

'I did not, I did not! I refused him, because he was unable to appreciate it. He left in a rabid fury, stamping his feet. He charged at me, but I leapt out of the way . . . And I will also tell you, as one from whom I no longer intend to conceal anything, that he even spat at me, can you imagine? But why are we standing up like this? Oh, please sit down . . . Forgive me, I . . . Or perhaps it is better if you run, yes run, you must run and save the unhappy old man from a dreadful death!'

'But what if he has already killed him?'

'Oh good heavens, yes indeed! Then what shall we do now? What do you suppose, what ought one to do now?'

In the meantime she had made Pyotr Ilyich sit down and herself sat down opposite him. Pyotr Ilyich briefly but rather clearly set before her the history of the case, or at any rate that part of its history to which he himself had that day been a witness, and also related to her what he had learned during his recent visit to Fenya, including the news about the pestle. All these details shook the excited lady to an impossible degree, and she would scream and cover her eyes with her hands . . .

'Can you imagine, I had a presentiment of all this! I am endowed with this quality, that anything I imagine to myself does in fact take place. How many, many times have I gazed upon that dreadful man and thought: there is the man who will one day kill me. And so indeed it has happened ... that is to say, if he has not now killed me, but only his father, then that is probably because the hand of the Lord is at work protecting me, and on top of that he was too ashamed to kill me, because I myself, here, in this very place, who hung around his neck a little icon from the holy relics of St Varvara the Great Martyr ... And how near I was to death at that moment, after all, I went right up to him, right up close, and he stretched out the whole of his neck to me! You know, Pyotr Ilyich (forgive me, I think you said your name was Pyotr Ilyich) ... you know, I do not believe in miracles, but that little icon and this outright miracle that has happened to me now – that overwhelms me, and I again begin to believe in anything. Did you hear about the Elder Zosima? ... Though as a matter of fact, I do not know what I am saying ... And can you imagine, why, even with that little icon around his neck he spat at me ... that is to say, he only spat at me, did not kill me, and ... and then went galloping off over there! But where are we to go, where are we to go now, what do you suppose?'

Pyotr Ilyich got up and announced that he would now go straight to the chief of police and tell him everything, and let him do as he thought fit.

'Oh, he is a wonderful, wonderful man, I know Mikhail Makarovich. You must most certainly go to him. How resourceful you are, Pyotr Ilyich, and how well you have thought all this out; you know, in your place I should never have thought of that!'

'All the more so since I myself am a good friend of the chief of police,' Pyotr Ilyich observed, still standing and, apparently, wishing somehow to tear himself away as soon as possible from the clutches of this impetuous lady who on no account would allow him to make his farewells and be on his way.

'And you know, you know,' she babbled on, 'you must come and tell me what you see there and find out ... and what is discovered ... and how they deal with him and what they sentence him to. I say, we don't have the death sentence, do we? But you must come without fail, even if it is at three o'clock in the morning, even at four, even at half past four ... You must have me woken, shaken awake if I won't get up ... O God, in any case I shall not even be able to sleep. You know, don't you think I ought to go with you? ...'

'N-no, madam, but if you were to write three lines right now in your own hand, just in case, saying that you never lent Dmitry Fyodorovich any money, that would, I believe, not be superfluous ... just in case ...'

'Certainly!' Mrs Khokhlakova darted off in ecstasy to her writing desk. 'And you know, you astonish me, you simply overwhelm me with your resourcefulness and your ability in these matters . . . Do you work in the service here? How pleasant to hear that you work here . . .'

And, as she was still saying this, she rapidly inscribed in large handwriting on a half-sheet of notepaper the following lines:

Never in my life did I lend the unhappy Dmitry Fyodorovich Karamazov (as whatever else he may be, he is now unhappy) three thousand roubles, and never have I lent him any other money either, never, never! To this I swear by all that is holy in our world.

Khokhlakova

'Here is that note!' she said, quickly turning to Pyotr Ilyich. 'Now go, and save. It is a great *podvig*, a great deed of piety, on your part.'

And three times she made the sign of the Cross over him. She even came running out as far as the vestibule in order to see him off.

'How grateful I am to you! You will not believe how grateful I am to you now for having come to see me first. How is it that we have not met before? I should be very charmed to receive you in my house in future. And how pleasant it is to hear that you are in our local civil service . . . and so efficient, so resourceful . . . But they must value you, must come to understand you, and if there is anything I can do for you, then please believe me . . . Oh, I am so fond of youth! I am in love with youth. Young men – they are the foundation of all our present-day suffering Russia, all her hope . . . Oh, go, go! . . .'

But Pyotr Ilyich had already gone running off, for otherwise she would not have released him so soon. As a matter of fact, Mrs Khokhlakova had struck him rather agreeably, and this had even allayed somewhat his uneasiness at having been dragged into such a nasty business. Tastes may vary extremely – that is well known. 'And she's not really all that old at all,' he thought with an agreeable sensation, 'on the contrary, I would have taken her for her daughter.'

As for Mrs Khokhlakova, she was simply enchanted with the young man. 'So much ability, so much conscientiousness, and in such a young man in our time, and all of it with such manners and outward elegance. Why, it is said of our contemporary young men that they are not capable of anything, well, here is an example for you of one who is,' etcetera, etcetera. As a result, she even quite forgot about the 'dreadful happening' and, no sooner had she gone to bed, she suddenly recalled once more how 'near to death' she had been, and said: 'Oh, this is dreadful, dreadful!' At once, however, she sank into a most sweet, sound slumber. As a matter of fact, I should not have devoted so much space to such trivial and episodic details, had not this eccentric encounter I have just described between a young civil servant and a widow woman not at all yet old, had not served in days that followed as the foundation of the entire life career of this prompt and efficient young man, a fact which even to this day is remembered with amazement in our little town and concerning which we may perhaps add a special remark or two when we conclude our long narrative concerning the brothers Karamazov.

2

The Alarm

OUR local police chief Mikhail Makarovich Makarov, a retired lieutenant-colonel who had been renamed a court councillor, was a good and widowed man. He had first honoured us with his presence only three years previously, but had already earned general sympathy for the principal reason that he 'knew how to unite society'. There were always plenty of guests at his house, and without them, it appeared, he would have been unable to continue his residence. Someone dined with him every day without fail, whether it was two guests or even only one; without guests, however, no one sat down at table. There were also dinner parties, arranged on all kinds of pretexts, sometimes even the most unexpected ones. The food that was served, though it was not exquisite, was nevertheless abundant, the kulebiakis were magnificent, while the wines, though they did not excel in quality, made up for this in quantity. In the lobby stood a billiard table in a most respectable setting, that is to say, even with pictures of English racehorses in black frames along the walls, which, as is well known, constitute the essential ornament of any billiard-room in the home of a bachelor. Every evening there was a game of cards, even if only on a single table. But very frequently there also gathered there all the best society of our town, with mammas and daughters, to dance. Mikhail Makarovich, though in a widowed condition, nevertheless kept a family household, retaining in his home his long since widowed daughter, in her turn a mother with two unmarried girls, Mikhail Makarovich's granddaughters. These girls were by now grown-up and had finished their education, were of not unpleasing appearance and of merry disposition, and though everyone knew that no dowry

would ever accrue to either of them, they none the less managed to draw
into their grandfather's house the young men of our society. In affairs of
business Mikhail Makarovich was not particularly clever, but he executed
his duties no worse than many other men. To put it bluntly, he was, after
all, a rather uneducated man and was even somewhat carefree when it
came to a clear understanding of the limits of his administrative authority.
There were certain reforms passed during the present reign which he less
completely failed to make sense of than comprehended with certain
errors, sometimes highly noticeable ones, and not at all because of any
particular incapacity on his own part, but simply because of the carefree
nature of his character, because there was simply not time to go into the
details of it all. 'I am, gentlemen, more of a military soul than a civilian
one,' was how he would describe himself. Even concerning the precise
foundations of the peasant reform he had still not apparently formed any
definite or firm conception and learned of them, as it were, from year to
year, augmenting his knowledge in practical, involuntary fashion, yet all
the while he was a landowner. Pyotr Ilyich knew with precise certainty
that this evening he would encounter some of Mikhail Makarovich's
guests, though he did not know who they would be. And meanwhile
who should be sitting with him at a game of *yeralash** than the public
procurator and our *zemstvo** doctor, Varvinsky, a young man who had
only recently arrived among us from St Petersburg, one of those who
had brilliantly completed his course of studies at the St Petersburg Medical
Academy. As for the public procurator, or rather the deputy public
procurator, though everyone in our town called him the public procurator, Ippolit Kirillovich, he was one of our more singular individuals:
still on the young side, only thirty-five, but with a strong consumptive
tendency, and yet married to a very fat and childless lady; vain and
irritable, with a mind that was very solid, however, and a soul that was
even good. It appeared that the entire problem with his character was that
he had a somewhat higher opinion of himself than his real merits would
permit. And this was why he forever appeared uneasy. There were within
him, moreover, certain feeble impulses of a higher and even an artistic
sort, towards psychologism, for example, a special knowledge of the
human soul, a special gift for the analysis of the criminal and of his
crime. In this regard he considered himself to have been somewhat
discriminated against and passed over at work and was invariably certain
that there, in the higher spheres, he had been insufficiently appreciated
and that he had enemies. At moments of gloom he would even threaten
to defect to the advocacy, and take up criminal cases. The unexpected

parricide case concerning the Karamazovs seemed to have stirred him to the roots of his being: 'It's a case of a kind that could become famous all over Russia.' But this I insert myself, and run ahead.

In the neighbouring room, with the young ladies, sat also our young state investigator, Nikolay Parfenovich Nelyudov, who only two months previously had arrived among us from St Petersburg. Later on it was said, even with some surprise, that all these persons seemed to have assembled together as if by special design on the evening of the 'crime' in the house of the executive authority. Yet the truth of the matter was far more straightforward and involved an extremely natural course of events: for two days now the spouse of Ippolit Kirillovich had had toothache, and he was compelled to go somewhere in order to escape from her groans; and the doctor by his very nature could spend the evening nowhere other than at cards. As for Nikolay Parfenovich, he had even for three days now been planning to arrive on this evening at the house of Mikhail Makarovich, as it were, by chance, in order suddenly and insidiously to spring on his elder daughter Olga Mikhailovna the fact that he was privy to her secret, that today was her birthday and that she especially desired to conceal it from our society, so as not to have to invite the town to a ball. There lay ahead the prospect of much laughter and many hints as to her age, that she was afraid to make it known, that now he was the master of her secret he would on the morrow tell it to everyone, etcetera, etcetera. The charming young manikin was on this account an arrant knave, and indeed the ladies of our town had christened him 'the knave', something that apparently pleased him no end. As a matter of fact, he was of very good society, good family, good upbringing and good feelings, and though a *bon viveur*, a very innocent and always decent one. In respect of outward appearance, he was small of stature, weak and delicate in constitution. On his pale and slender little fingers there invariably sparkled several extremely large rings. When, however, he was discharging his duty, he would become extraordinarily solemn, as though construing his significance and his obligations to a point where these to him were as a sacred shrine. He was particularly good at pulling the rug from under the feet of murderers and other villains of the common folk during interrogations, and really did inspire in them if not respect then at any rate a certain wonder.

Pyotr Ilyich, as he entered the house of the police chief, was simply stunned: he suddenly saw that everything was already known there. Indeed, the cards had been abandoned, all were on their feet and arguing, and even Nikolay Parfenovich had come running over from the young ladies with a most pugnacious and impetuous air. Pyotr Ilyich was greeted by the astounding news that old Fyodor Pavlovich had indeed and in reality been murdered that evening in his own home, murdered and robbed. This had been discovered only an instant before, in the following manner.

Marfa Ignatyevna, the spouse of Grigory the cast-down-by-the-fence, though she had been fast asleep in her bed and might easily have continued to slumber there until morn, suddenly, however, woke up. This was promoted by a fearful epileptic howl from Smerdyakov, who was lying unconscious in the neighbouring small room – the howl with which his fits of the falling sickness always began and which always, all her life, terribly frightened Marfa Ignatyevna and had a morbid effect upon her. Never had she been able to accustom herself to them. Still with the sleep in her eyes, she leapt up and almost beside herself rushed into Smerdyakov's little closet of a room. In there, however, it was dark, and all she could discern were the sounds of the sick man beginning to snort and thrash about in fearsome manner. At this point Marfa Ignatyevna herself screamed aloud and began to call to her husband, when she suddenly realized that Grigory had not seemed to be in the bed when she had risen from it. She ran back to the bed and felt about in it again, but the bed really was empty. That meant he must have gone off somewhere – but where? She went running out on to the porch and timidly called him from the top of the steps. No answer, of course, did she receive, but on the other hand amid the still of night she heard from somewhere, far away in the garden, it seemed, the sound of moans. She listened closely; the moans were repeated again, and it became clear that they were indeed coming from the garden. 'Merciful Lord, 'tis like that time with Lizaveta Smerdyashchaya!' rushed through her distraught head. Timidly she descended the steps and managed to make out that the wicket gate that led into the garden was open. 'He must be in there, poor thing,' she thought, went over to the gate and then all of a sudden clearly heard Grigory calling her, calling her name: 'Marfa, Marfa!' in a feeble, moaning, terrible voice. 'Merciful Lord, preserve us from harm,' Marfa Ignatyevna whispered, rushed in the direction of the call and in such manner found Grigory. Found him, however, not by the fence, where he had been cast down, but some twenty paces therefrom. It later transpired that, having come to, he had crawled, and, doubtless, crawled long, losing consciousness several times and once again sinking into oblivion. She instantly noticed that he was covered all over in blood and began to scream at the top of her voice. As for Grigory, he babbled softly and incoherently: 'He's killed him ... killed his father ... what are you screaming for, you silly idiot ... run and call for help ...' But Marfa Ignatyevna would not be quietened and continued her screaming, and suddenly, having seen that the *barin*'s window was open and that there was light in it, she ran over to it and began to call Fyodor Pavlovich. Taking a glance through the window, however, she saw a terrible sight: the *barin* lay supine and motionless on the floor. His light-coloured dressing-gown and the front of his white shirt were drenched in blood. The candle on the table brightly illuminated the blood and the motionless, dead face of Fyodor Pavlovich. In the last stages of horror now, Marfa Ignatyevna rushed away from the window, fled from the garden, unbarred the front gate and went running by way of the rears to her neighbour Marya Kondratyevna. Both neighbours, mother and daughter, were by this time in bed, but in response to Marfa Ignatyevna's urgent and violent knocking at the shutters and to her screams they woke up and leapt to the window. Incoherently, shrieking and screaming, Marfa Ignatyevna managed, however, to inform them of the salient facts and called them to assist. It so happened that the wandering Foma was passing that night under their roof. In a flash they had him up, and all three went running to the place of the crime. On the way Marya Kondratyevna succeeded in recalling that earlier, at nine o'clock, she had heard a fearsome and penetrating howl that had been audible all over the neighbourhood, coming from their garden – and this must of course have been that very same cry uttered by Grigory when, having seized hold of the leg of Dmitry Fyodorovich, who had by then been sitting astride the fence, he had shouted: 'Father-murderer!' 'Someone on his own howled something and then suddenly stopped,' Marya Kondratyevna testified, as she ran. Arriving at the place where Grigory lay, the two women, with Foma's assistance, carried him over to the outbuilding. A candle was lit and they saw that Smerdyakov had not quietened down but was still thrashing about in his closet, his eyes squinting, and foam trickling from his lips. They bathed Grigory's head in water and vinegar, and at the touch of the water he completely regained consciousness and instantly asked: 'Is the *barin* killed or is he not?' At that, the two women and Foma went over to the *barin*'s house and, entering the garden, saw this time that not only the window but also the door that led from the house into the garden stood wide open, when all week the *barin* had locked himself up tight as tight every evening, not even permitting Grigory to knock at his door on any pretext whatsoever. At the sight of this open door, they all of them, the two women and Foma, were instantly afraid to enter the *barin*'s house, 'in case there's trouble later on'. But when they came back, Grigory instructed them to run at once to the chief of police himself. It was at that point that Marya Kondratyevna had run off and startled everyone at the police chief's house. Her arrival had preceded that of Pyotr Ilyich by only five minutes, so that the latter presented himself not merely with his conjectures and deductions, but as an obvious witness, who by the tale he had to tell confirmed even more the general conjecture as to the identity of the criminal (something which, as a matter of fact, in the depths of his soul, right up until that final moment, he had still refused to believe).

They decided to deal with the matter energetically. The assistant chief constable was at once encharged with the selection of four official witnesses, and with observance of all the legal regulations, which I shall not describe here, gained entry to the house of Fyodor Pavlovich and performed an investigation on the spot. The *zemstvo* doctor, a man of eager enthusiasm, new to his task, almost fell over his feet to be allowed to accompany the police chief, public procurator and state investigator. I shall merely note in brief: Fyodor Pavlovich proved to have been murdered beyond all question, his skull broken, but with what? Most probably, the very same weapon with which Grigory, too, had subsequently been struck down. And lo and behold, the weapon too was tracked down after Grigory, to whom what possible medical assistance had been administered, fairly coherently, though in a feeble and jerky voice conveyed to them the story of how he had been cast to the ground. A lantern search was begun by the fence and there, where it had been thrown down right on the garden path, in full open view, lay the brass pestle. In the room where Fyodor Pavlovich had lain no particular disorder was observed, but behind the screen, by his bed, a large envelope of thick paper, manufactured to government office specifications, was picked up from the floor; it bore the inscription: 'A little present of three thousand roubles for my angel Grushenka, if she decides to come,' and below had been added, probably later, by Fyodor Pavlovich himself: 'and for my little chicken'. The envelope bore three large red wax seals, but it had already been opened and was empty: the money had been taken out of it. They also found on the floor a slender pink ribbon, which had been used to tie up the envelope. In the testimony of Pyotr Ilyich there was one circumstance, among others, which produced an exceptional impression upon the public procurator and the state investigator, and this was his conjecture that Dmitry Fyodorovich was most certainly going to shoot himself at dawn, that he himself had determined to do this, had talked to Pyotr Ilyich of it, had loaded a pistol in front of him, had written a note, put it in his pocket, etcetera, etcetera. That when Pyotr Ilyich, still reluctant to believe him, had threatened to go and tell someone in order to avert the suicide, Mitya had said, baring his teeth in a grin: 'You won't have time.' This meant that it was necessary to hurry to the spot, to Mokroye, in order to catch the criminal while the crime was still fresh and before he really did take it into his head to shoot himself. 'It's self-evident, self-evident!' the public procurator kept saying in extreme excitement. 'That is exactly the way that madcaps like him think: "Tomorrow I shall kill myself, but a spree before I die!"' The story of how Mitya had bought wines and provisions at the delicatessen only got the public procurator even more worked up. 'Remember that young fellow, gentlemen, the one who killed the merchant Olsufyev, robbed him of one and a half thousand, went straight off and had his hair curled, and then, without even bothering to hide the money properly, almost carrying it about in his hand like this fellow's been doing, set off to visit the girls.' A delay was, however, imposed upon them all by the investigation, the search of Fyodor Pavlovich's house, the formal procedures, etcetera. All of that required time, and so some two hours ahead of them they dispatched to Mokroye the district superintendent Mavriky Mavrikiyevich Schmertzov, who just so happened to have arrived in town on the morning of the previous day to collect his salary. Mavriky Mavrikiyevich was given special instructions that upon his arrival in Mokroye he was, without raising any sort of alarm, to shadow the 'criminal' untiringly until the proper authorities arrived, as well as to appoint official witnesses, village police auxiliaries, etcetera, etcetera. Thus did Mavriky Mavrikiyevich act, preserving his incognito, the only person whom he, only partially, initiated into the secret of the affair being Trifon Borisovich, who was an old acquaintance of his. This period of time coincided with that during which Mitya had encountered the landlord out in the dark on the gallery looking for him, and when he had noticed a sudden change in Trifon Borisovich's features and manner of talking. Thus neither Mitya nor anyone else knew that he was being observed; as for his case of pistols, it had long ago been appropriated by Trifon Borisovich and hidden away in a secluded spot. And only at five in the morning, at dawn, almost, did the authorities arrive: the chief of police, the public procurator and the state investigator, in two carriages and with two *troikas* of horses. As for the doctor, he remained in Fyodor Pavlovich's house, his object being to conduct on the morrow an autopsy of the murdered man's corpse, but finding his interest principally drawn by the condition of the sick manservant Smerdyakov: 'Such long and violent fits of the falling sickness, being constantly repeated over a period of two days, are rarely encountered, and are a matter for scientific analysis,' he pronounced in excitement to his departing colleagues, and they congratulated him, laughingly, on his discovery. Moreover, the public procurator and the state investigator recalled very clearly that the doctor had added in the firmest tone of voice that Smerdyakov would not live until morning.

Now, after this long, but apparently necessary explanation, we have returned to precisely that point in our narrative where we interrupted it in the preceding book.

3

The Passage of a Soul Through the Torments.
Torment the First

AND SO, Mitya sat looking round at those present with a wild gaze, not comprehending that which was said to him. Suddenly he rose, threw his arms aloft and shouted loudly:

'Not guilty! Of this blood I am not guilty! Of the blood of my father I am not guilty . . . I wanted to murder him, but I am not guilty! Not I!'

No sooner had he managed to shout this, however, than in from behind the curtains leapt Grushenka, and fairly collapsed in a heap at the police chief's feet.

'It is I, I, accursed that I am, it is I who am the guilty one!' she shouted in a wail that rent the soul, tears pouring down her cheeks, and stretching her arms out to all. 'It was because of me that he killed! . . . It was I who drove him to the end of his tether and brought him to that! I also drove that poor little old man who is dead now to the end of his tether, I did it because of my malice, and brought him to that! I am the guilty one, I am the first, I am the principal, I am the guilty one!'

'Yes, you are the guilty one! You are the principal culprit! You are violent, depraved, the principal culprit!' the police chief howled, threatening her with his fist, but at that point he was swiftly and firmly put in check. The public procurator even circled him with his arms.

'This is going to turn into complete mayhem, Mikhail Makarovich,' he exclaimed. 'You are positively obstructing the investigation . . . ruining the case . . .' he almost choked.

'Take measures, take measures, take measures!' Nikolay Parfenovich bubbled in fearful agitation also. 'Otherwise it positively will not do! . . .'

'Together judge us!' Grushenka continued to wail in frenzy, still on her knees. 'Together punish us, I will go with him now even to the scaffold!'

'Grusha, my life, my blood, my sacred shrine!' Mitya said, throwing himself on his knees beside her and pressing her tightly in his embrace. 'Do not believe her,' he shouted. 'She bears no guilt for anything, neither for blood nor for anything!'

He later recalled that several people had dragged him away from her by force, but that she had suddenly been led away, and that he had regained his senses while sitting at the table. Beside him and behind him stood the men with metal badges. On the other side of the table from him, on the sofa, sat Nikolay Parfenovich, the state investigator, who kept trying to persuade him to drink a little water from a glass that stood on the table: 'It will refresh you, it will calm you, do not be afraid, do not be worried,' he added with extreme politeness. As for Mitya, he suddenly, this he recalled, acquired an intense curiosity regarding the investigator's large rings, the one set with amethyst, and the other with some bright-yellow, transparent stone that had a wonderful sheen. And long thereafter he remembered with astonishment that those rings had held an irresistible attraction for his gaze even during those terrible hours of interrogation, so that he was somehow unable to tear himself away from them and forget them as objects that bore no relevance to his situation. At Mitya's left, to one side of him, in the chair where Maksimov had sat at the onset of the evening, the public procurator had now made himself comfortable, while on Mitya's right, in the chair where Grushenka had sat then, there was a certain young man of ruddy complexion dressed in some kind of very threadbare hunting jacket, before whom were an inkwell and paper. It turned out that this was the investigator's clerk, whom he had brought with him. As for the chief of police, he now stood over by the window, at the other end of the room, beside Kalganov, who had also made himself comfortable on a chair by that very same window.

'Take a drink of water!' the investigator repeated gently for the umpteenth time.

'I have taken one, gentlemen, I have taken one . . . but . . . go on, gentlemen, squash me, punish me, decide my fate!' Mitya exclaimed, turning upon the investigator a bulging gaze of terrible fixity.

'So, you positively assert that you are not guilty of the murder of Fyodor Pavlovich, your father?' the investigator asked gently, but insistently.

'Yes! I am guilty of other blood, the blood of another old man, but not of my father's. And I mourn it! I killed, I killed an old man, I killed him and cast him down . . . But it is hard to answer for that blood with another blood, a terrible blood, of which I am not guilty! . . . A terrible accusation, gentlemen, as though I had been discombobulated on the forehead! But who *did* kill my father, who? Who could have killed him, if not I? A miracle, preposterous, impossible! . . .'

'Yes, now who could have killed him . . .' the investigator began, but Ippolit Kirillovich the public procurator (really the deputy public procurator, but we too for the sake of brevity shall call him public procurator), having exchanged glances with the investigator, pronounced, turning to Mitya:

'In vain do you trouble yourself on account of the old manservant Grigory Vasilyev. Know that he is alive, has recovered consciousness and will, it appears, in spite of the grievous beating you administered to him, according to his own testimony and that which you have just supplied, most certainly remain alive, at any rate according to the doctor's report.'

'Alive? So he is alive!' Mitya suddenly cried out, throwing his hands in the air. His whole face beamed and shone. 'O Lord, I thank You for this very great miracle which You have worked with me, a sinner and evil-doer, in answer to my prayers! . . . Yes, yes, this is in answer to my prayers, all night I have prayed! . . .' And three times he made the sign of the cross over himself. He was almost choking.

'So you see, from this same Grigory we have obtained such significant testimony concerning you, that . . .' the public procurator began to resume, but Mitya suddenly leapt up from his chair.

'One moment, gentlemen, in the name of God, just one small moment; let me go and see her . . .'

'Permit me! At this moment that is on no account possible!' Nikolay Parfenovich even very nearly shrieked, also leaping to his feet. Mitya was circled round by the men with metal badges on their fronts, but in the end he sat back down on the chair of his own accord.

'Gentlemen, what a pity! I was only going to see her for a single instant . . . in order to tell her that it has been washed away, has disappeared, that blood which all night has sucked at my heart, and that I am not a murderer now! Gentlemen, why, she is my bride!' he said suddenly, in ecstasy and reverence, scanning them all with his eyes. 'Oh, I thank you, gentlemen! Oh, how you have regenerated, resurrected me in one single instant! . . . That old man – why, he bore me in his arms, gentlemen, washed me in the trough, when as a child of three years old I had been abandoned by everyone, was my kindred father! . . .'

'So, you . . .' the investigator began.

'Permit me, gentlemen, permit me just one little minute more,' Mitya broke off, placing both elbows on the table and covering his face with the palms of his hands. 'Let me gather my thoughts just a little, let me draw breath, gentlemen. All of this is a terrible shock, a terrible shock, after all a man is not a drumskin, gentlemen!'

'You'd better have another drink of water . . .' Nikolay Parfenovich babbled.

Mitya took his hands away from his face and burst out laughing. His gaze was cheerful, he seemed to have wholly altered in a single instant. The whole tone of his demeanour had likewise altered: the man who sat here was again the equal of all these people, all these old acquaintances of his, every bit as much as if they had all assembled yesterday, when nothing had yet taken place, somewhere in the town's society. Let us, however, observe in passing that in the early days that followed his arrival among us, Mitya had been cordially received in the police chief's home, but that later, particularly over the last month, Mitya had hardly visited him at all, while the police chief, whenever he had encountered him, out in the street, for example, had frowned intensely and returned his bow merely out of politeness, something that Mitya had noted all too well. His acquaintance with the public procurator was even more remote, but to the public procurator's spouse, a nervous and fantastic lady, he sometimes paid visits, of the most respectable kind, it should be said, without even really knowing why he did so, and she would invariably receive him kindly, for some reason having taken an interest in him of recent time. As for the investigator, with him he had not yet succeeded in striking up an acquaintance, though he had met him too and had even spoken with him once or twice, on both occasions concerning the female sex.

'Nikolay Parfenych, I can see that you are a most skilful investigator,' Mitya said suddenly, breaking into cheerful laughter again, 'but now I am going to assist you of my own accord. Oh, gentlemen, I am resurrected . . . and please do not complain at my addressing you so simply and so bluntly. What is more, I am slightly drunk, I tell you that frankly. Nikolay Parfenych, I believe I have had the honour . . . the honour and the pleasure of meeting you in the home of my relative Mr Miusov . . . Gentlemen, gentlemen, I make no claim to be your equal, after all, I understand in what capacity I sit before you now. There is concerning me . . . if Grigory has given testimony against me . . . there is concerning me – oh, of course there is – a terrible suspicion! A horrible, horrible thing – you see, I understand it! But let us set to work, gentlemen, I am ready, and we shall settle the matter in a single instant now, because, well, listen, listen, gentlemen. You see, if I know that I am not guilty, then of course we can settle the matter in a single instant! Is that not so? Is it not?'

Mitya spoke swiftly and volubly, nervously and expansively, and as if he decidedly thought his listeners were his best friends.

'So, we shall for the moment put down that you categorically reject the accusation that has been brought against you,' Nikolay Parfenovich said imposingly and, turning to the scribe, dictated to him in an undertone the necessary form of what was to be set down.

'Put down? You're going to put this down in writing? Very well, go ahead, I consent, I give my complete consent, gentlemen ... But look ... Wait, wait, put it down like this: "He is guilty of violent and disorderly conduct, of having inflicted grievous bodily harm on a poor old man." Well, and I am also guilty inside myself, in the depths of my heart – but you do not need to put that down,' he said, suddenly turning to the scribe, 'they are my inward life, gentlemen, they do not really concern you, those depths of my heart, that is ... But of the murder of my old father – I am not guilty! That is an outlandish idea! That is a perfectly outlandish idea! ... I shall prove it to you, and you will be instantly persuaded. You will laugh, gentlemen, you yourselves will roar with laughter at your own suspicion! ...'

'Please calm yourself, Dmitry Fyodorovich,' the investigator reminded him, apparently, it seemed, desiring to calm the frenzied fellow with his own equanimity. 'Before we continue with the interrogation, I should like, if you will agree to reply, to hear from you a confirmation of the fact submitted in evidence that you apparently did not like the deceased Fyodor Pavlovich, were engaged in some kind of perpetual quarrel with him ... Here at least, a quarter of an hour ago, you apparently were so good as to state that you even wanted to kill him: "I did not kill him," you exclaimed, "but I wanted to!"'

'Did I say that? Oh, that may well be so, gentlemen. Yes, I am afraid that I did want to kill him, many times wanted to ... Unfortunately, unfortunately!'

'You wanted to. Will you not consent to explain what precisely were the principles that guided you in such hatred of the person of your father?'

'What is there to explain, gentlemen?' Mitya said, morosely shrugging his shoulders and lowering his eyes. 'After all, I have never hidden my feelings, the whole town knows of this – everyone at the inn knows of it. Only recently at the monastery I declared it, in the cell of the Elder Zosima . . . That same day, in the evening, I beat my father and nearly killed him, and swore that I would return and murder him, in the presence of witnesses . . . Oh, a thousand witnesses! For a whole month I have shouted it, everyone is a witness! . . . The evidence is at hand, the evidence speaks, shouts, but – feelings, gentlemen, feelings, they are something else. You see, gentlemen,' Mitya said, frowning, 'it seems to me that you have no right to ask me questions about feelings. Though you may be invested with power, that I understand, they are none the less my affair, my own inward, intimate affair, but . . . as I did not conceal my feelings before . . . in the inn, for example, and spoke them to each and all, then . . . then I shall make no secret of them now. You see, gentlemen, after all, I understand that in this case there is fearsome evidence against me: I told everyone that I would kill him, and suddenly he was killed: so how could it not be me, in that case? Ha-ha! I excuse you, gentlemen, I completely excuse you. After all, I myself have been struck to the epidermis, because who could have killed him, in the end, if not I? That is true, is it not? If not I, then who, who? Gentlemen,' he suddenly exclaimed, 'I want to know, I even demand of you, gentlemen: where was he killed? How was he killed, with what and how? Tell me,' he asked quickly, scanning the public procurator and the investigator with his eyes.

'We found him lying supine on the floor of his study, with his skull broken,' the public procurator said.

'That is terrible, gentlemen!' Mitya said suddenly with a shudder and, leaning his elbows on the table, covered his face with his right hand.

'We shall continue,' Nikolay Parfenovich broke in. 'So, what was it that guided you in your feelings of hatred? I believe that you publicly declared it was an emotion of jealousy?'

'Well, yes, jealousy, and not jealousy alone.'

'Arguments about money?'

'Yes, those too.'

'I believe there was an argument about the three thousand you claimed had not been paid to you according to your inheritance.'

'What do you mean, three thousand? It was more, more,' Mitya said, jerking up, 'more than six, more than ten, perhaps. I told it to everyone, shouted it to everyone! But I made up my mind that I would accept it, would reconcile myself to three thousand. I needed that three thousand to the point of murder . . . so that the envelope containing the three thousand

I knew was under his pillow, ready for Grushenka, I really considered as having been stolen from me, there you have it, gentlemen, I considered it my own, just as though it were my own property . . .'

The public procurator exchanged a significant look with the investigator and succeeded in passing him an imperceptible wink.

'We shall come back to this topic again,' the investigator said at once, 'but for now you must permit us to note and record precisely that small point: that you considered that money, in that envelope, more or less your own property.'

'Record away, gentlemen; after all, I understand that that is another piece of evidence against me, but I am not afraid of the evidence and speak against myself of my own accord. Of my own accord, do you hear? You see, gentlemen, I believe you think I am quite a different person from the one I am,' he suddenly added blackly and with melancholy. 'It is a noble man who speaks with you, a person of the noblest kind, and above all — please do not lose sight of this — a man who has committed a huge number of villainous acts, but who has always been and has remained a most noble creature, a creature, inwardly, in the depths, well, in short, I am unable to express myself . . . That is what I have struggled for in torment all my life, thirsting for nobility, I have been, as it were, a martyr to nobility and its seeker with a lamp, the lamp of Diogenes, and yet all my life I have committed nothing but base actions, like all of us, gentlemen . . . that is to say, like myself alone, gentlemen, not all of us, but myself alone, I have erred, alone, alone! Gentlemen, I have a headache,' he frowned with a martyred look. 'You see, gentlemen, I did not like his outward appearance, there was something dishonourable about it, his boasting and his flouting of every sacred thing, his mockery and unbelief, loathsome, loathsome! But now that he is dead, I think otherwise.'

'What do you mean — otherwise?'

'Well, perhaps not otherwise, but I regret that I so hated him.'

'You feel remorse?'

'No, not remorse, please do not write that down. I myself am not a good man, gentlemen, that is what. I myself am none too attractive, and so I had no right to consider him repulsive either, that is what I mean! That is what I should like you to record.'

Having got this out, Mitya suddenly became extremely sad. For some time now, gradually, as he gave his answers to the questions of the investigator, his mood had been growing blacker and blacker. And suddenly, just at that moment, an unexpected scene again broke out. The fact was that although Grushenka had been removed, she had not been taken very far, only as far as the third room along from the blue one in which the interrogation was now in progress. It was a small room with only one window, right behind the large room in which all night there had been dancing and sumptuous feasting. There she sat, and with her for the moment only Maksimov, terribly startled, terribly frightened and sticking close to her as though in her proximity he sought salvation. At their door stood some kind of muzhik with a metal badge on his front. Grushenka had been weeping, and then suddenly, when misery had approached her soul too nearly, she leapt up, threw her arms in the air and, shouting in a loud wail: 'Misery, misery me!', rushed out of the room to him, to her Mitya, and so unexpectedly that no one had time to stop her. As for Mitya, at the sound of her wail he shook all over, leapt up, uttered a howl and rushed headlong to meet her, as though he were beside himself. Once again, however, they were not permitted to consort, even though they had caught sight of each other. He was seized firmly by the arms: he struggled, tried to tear himself free, and three or four men were needed in order to restrain him. She too was seized, and he saw her stretching her arms out towards him as she was dragged away. When the scene was over, he came to his senses again in his previous seat, at the table, facing the investigator, and he shouted, addressing him:

'What do you want with her? Why are you tormenting her? She is innocent, innocent! . . .'

The public procurator and the state investigator attempted to talk him to reason. In this fashion a certain period of time went by, some ten minutes; at last into the room in a hurry came Mikhail Makarovich who had until now been kept outside, and loudly, in agitation, said to the public procurator:

'She has been removed, she is downstairs, will you not permit me, gentlemen, to say just one word to this unhappy man? In your presence, gentlemen, in your presence?'

'You are welcome to do so, Mikhail Makarovich,' the investigator replied, 'in the present instance we have no objection to it.'

'Dmitry Fyodorovich, listen, good fellow,' Mikhail Makarovich began, turning to Mitya, and the whole of his agitated face expressed a warm, almost fatherly compassion for the unhappy man. 'I myself took your Agrafena Aleksandrovna downstairs and entrusted her to the landlord's daughters, and that old chap Maksimov is with her now, won't leave her side, and I have made her see reason, do you hear? I have made her see reason and I have made her calm down, have got it into her head that what matters is to free you from suspicion, and so she must not interfere, must not make you miserable, otherwise you may become confused and make the wrong kind of depositions concerning yourself, do you understand? Well, in short, I have told her, and she has understood. She's a clever woman, brother, she's a good woman, she made to kiss the hands of an old man like me, she interceded with me for you. It is she who has sent me here to tell you not to worry about her, and I must, dear fellow, I must go back and tell her that you are not worried and are consoled regarding her. So – you must calm down, please grasp that. I am guilty before her, she is a Christian soul, yes, gentlemen, this is a meek soul that is guilty of nothing. So what am I to tell her, Dmitry Fyodorovich, will you sit quietly or will you not?'

The kindly fellow had said much that was superfluous, but Grushenka's grief, the grief of humankind, had penetrated his kindly soul, and the tears even stood in his eyes. Mitya leapt up and rushed to him.

'Forgive me, gentlemen, permit me, oh, permit me!' he cried. 'Angelic, angelic soul that you are, Mikhail Makarovich, I thank you for her! I shall, I shall sit quietly, I shall be of good cheer, please, from the limitless bounty of your soul tell her that I am of good cheer, of good cheer, that I shall even begin to laugh in a moment, knowing that with her there is such a guardian angel as yourself. In a moment I shall bring all this to an end and as soon as I am set free I shall go straight to her, she will see, let her but wait! Gentlemen,' he said, suddenly turning round to the public procurator and the state investigator, 'now I shall reveal to you all of my soul, I shall pour it all out, we shall bring this to an end in an instant, bring it to an end with good cheer – for at last we shall laugh, shall we not? But, gentlemen, this woman is the empress of my soul! Oh, permit me to say this, this is what I shall reveal to you ... For after all, I see that I am with men of the most noble sort: she is my light, she is my sacred shrine, if you only knew! You have heard her cries: "I will go with you even to the scaffold!" Yet what have I given her, I, a beggar, a bare-breeches, why does she show me such love, do I deserve it, clumsy, shameful brute with a shameful face that I am, such love that she will go into penal servitude with me? For my sake she threw herself at your feet just now, she, a proud woman and one who is guilty of nothing! How can I fail to worship her, to cry out, to strive to her, as I did just now? O gentlemen, forgive me! But now, now I am consoled! Consoled!'

And he fell back on to his chair and, covering his face with the palms of both hands, burst into sobs. But these were now the tears of happiness. In a flash he recovered himself. The old police chief was very satisfied, as were, it seemed, the jurists, too: they had a sense that the interrogation was just on the point of entering upon a new phase. When he saw the police chief leave the room, Mitya grew positively euphoric.

'Well, gentlemen, now I am yours, entirely yours. And . . . were it not for all these trivial matters, we should right now be able to come to an agreement. I again speak of trivial matters. I am yours, gentlemen, but I swear that what is needed is mutual trust – yours of me and mine of you – or else we shall never bring the matter to an end. It is for yourselves that I speak. Let us set to work, gentlemen, let us set to work, and, above all, please do not rummage so in my soul, do not torment it with trivia, but ask only concerning the facts of the case, and I shall at once render you satisfaction. And to the devil with trivial matters!'

Thus did Mitya vociferate. The interrogation began anew.

4

Torment the Second

'YOU will not believe how you restore our spirits, Dmitry Fyodorovich, by this readiness of yours . . .' said Nikolay Parfenovich with a lively air and with evident satisfaction, which shone in his large, light-grey protuberant, though, as a matter of fact, very short-sighted eyes, from which a moment earlier he had removed his spectacles. 'And that was a true remark you made just now with regard to this mutual confidentiality of ours, without which sometimes it is impossible to make any headway in cases of such importance, in the sense and instance that the person under suspicion really desires, hopes and is able to free himself from it. We for our part shall make every effort to do what it behoves us, and you yourself can see even now how we are going to conduct this case . . . Do you approve, Ippolit Kirillovich?' he said, turning to the public procurator suddenly.

'Oh, indubitably,' the public procurator said in assent, though somewhat coldly in comparison with Nikolay Parfenovich's transport of emotion.

I shall observe once and for all: our new arrival Nikolay Parfenovich had, from the very beginning of his career with us, felt towards our public procurator, Ippolit Kirillovich, an uncommon degree of respect and had almost united with him in heart. This was almost the only person who had an unconditional faith in the extraordinary psychological and oratorical talent of our 'discriminated-against-in-the-service' Ippolit

Kirillovich and who fully believed that the latter had indeed suffered discrimination. He had heard of him while he had still been in St Petersburg. What was more, the in his turn somewhat youngish Nikolay Parfenovich also turned out to be the only person in the entire world to acquire a sincere liking for our 'discriminated-against' public procurator. On their journey hither they had had time to make certain agreements and arrangements concerning the impending case, and now, at the table, the rather sharpish intellect of Nikolay Parfenovich caught in flight and decoded every indication, every movement in the features of his elder colleague, with hardly a word being uttered, from a mere glance alone, from the merest wink of an eye.

'Gentlemen, just let me tell it all alone, do not interrupt with trivia, and I shall in an instant set it all before you,' Mitya bubbled.

'Very well, sir. I thank you. But before we pass to the audition of your statement, I think you must permit me to confirm just one small fact, one that is very interesting to us, namely that concerning those ten roubles which yesterday, at around five o'clock you borrowed against the pledge of your pistols from your friend Pyotr Ilyich Perkhotin.'

'I pawned them, gentlemen, I pawned them for ten roubles, and what more can I say? That is all there was to it: as soon as I returned to the town from my journey, I pawned them.'

'So you had returned from a journey? You had been out of town?'

'Yes, gentlemen, I had made a journey of forty versts – did you not know?'

The public procurator exchanged a glance with Nikolay Parfenovich.

'And in any case, how about beginning your story with a systematic description of the whole of the way you spent yesterday, starting from the morning? Permit us, for example, to know: why did you absent yourself from town and when precisely did you leave and when return . . . and all the rest of those facts . . .'

'Well, you should have asked me for the story from the very beginning,' Mitya said, bursting into laughter, 'and, if you like, I shall begin not yesterday but with the day before, and from its morning, and then you too will understand where, how and why I walked and travelled. On the morning of the day before yesterday, gentlemen, I went to see a local merchant here named Samsonov in order to borrow three thousand in cash from him on the most reliable security – it was a sudden necessity, gentlemen, a sudden necessity . . .'

'Permit me to interrupt you,' the public procurator broke in courteously, 'but why did you suddenly need it, and why precisely that sum, three thousand roubles, that is to say?'

'Oh really, gentlemen, not more trivia: how, when and why, and why precisely that amount of money, and not some other, and all that rigmarole? . . . I mean, if you go on like that it will fill at least three volumes, and you'll need an epilogue as well!'

All this Mitya said with the good-natured but impatient familiarity of a man who desires to speak the whole truth and is filled with the best intentions.

'Gentlemen,' he said, as if suddenly reflecting on something, 'you must not complain of my being recalcitrant, again I ask you: once more have faith that I have complete respect for you and that I understand the present position of the case. Do not suppose that I am drunk. I have now sobered up. And even were I drunk, it would not be the slightest obstacle. After all, with me it's like in the saying:

> Sobered up, got wise – became stupid.
> Got drunk, became stupid – got wise.

Ha-ha! But as a matter of fact, gentlemen, I see that it is as yet unseemly for me to crack witticisms before you, while we have not yet explained ourselves to one another, that is. Permit me also to observe the demands of my own dignity. For I understand the present difference between us: after all, whatever the rights and wrongs of it, I sit before you as a criminal, and therefore as one in the highest degree not your equal, and you have been entrusted with the task of watching over me: for you are not going to pat me on the head for my treatment of Grigory, after all, it really is not possible to go breaking the skulls of old men and not be punished for it, after all because of him you are going to put me away in the house of correction for six months, say, or a year, I don't know what sentence you have for that, though I think it may be without disfranchisement, is that not so, public procurator? Well, so you see, gentlemen, I understand this difference . . . But you will also agree that you could put the Almighty himself off balance with questions like "Where did you go, how did you go, when did you go, and into what did you go?" You will set me off balance if you go on like that, and then you will weave it all into the pattern against me, and what will be the result? Nothing will be the result! And finally, if I have begun to talk nonsense now, then I shall conclude, and you, gentlemen, being men of the highest education and of most noble character, will forgive me. And in fact, I shall conclude with a plea: please, gentlemen, unlearn this red-tape manner of interrogation, that is to say this business of beginning with some wretched, insignificant details concerning what I felt like when I got up, what I had to eat, the way in which I spat, and, "having distracted the attention of the criminal", suddenly catching him out with a dumbfounding question: "Whom did you kill, whom did you rob?" Ha-ha! Why, that is your red tape for you, that is the way it's prescribed in your textbooks, that is what all your cunning is builded upon! But I mean, it is muzhiks you will distract with such cunning tricks, not me. After all, I understand what is what, I myself have been in the service, ha-ha-ha! You are not angry, gentlemen, you forgive my impudence?' he shouted, looking at them with a good-nature that was almost astonishing. 'After all, Mitka Karamazov said it, and so it may be excused, for in any man of wisdom it would be inexcusable, but in Mitka it is excusable! Ha-ha!'

Nikolay Parfenovich listened and also laughed. The public procurator, though he did not laugh, studied Mitya keenly, without lowering his eyes, as though he did not wish to miss either his slightest word, his slightest movement, or the slightest quiver of the slightest line upon his face.

'But that is how we began with you originally,' Nikolay Parfenovich retorted, still continuing to laugh, 'by not attempting to throw you off balance with questions about how you felt when you got up in the morning or about what you had to eat, but by even beginning with matters that are all too essential.'

'I understand, I have understood it and appreciated it, and even more do I appreciate your present kindness to me, a kindness that is unparalleled, and worthy of most noble souls. The three of us are gathered here as men of noble intention, and let everything between us be founded on the mutual trust of men of education and society who are bound together by gentle birth and honour. At any rate, permit me to consider you at this moment the best friends I have ever had in my life, at this moment of the degradation of my honour! Now that does not offend you, gentlemen, that does not offend you?'

'On the contrary, you have expressed it all most satisfactorily, Dmitry Fyodorovich,' Nikolay Parfenovich agreed solemnly and approvingly.

'And the trivia, gentlemen, away with all these pettifogging trivia,' Mitya exclaimed ecstatically, 'or the devil knows what may come of it, do you not agree?'

'I shall entirely follow your sensible counsel,' the public procurator intervened suddenly, turning to Mitya, 'but shall none the less persist with my question. It is too vitally essential for us to discover why precisely you required such a sum of money, that is to say, why precisely three thousand?'

'Why I required it? Well, in order to . . . well, to pay off a debt.'

'To whom, precisely?'

'That I positively refuse to say, gentlemen! Look, it is not because I cannot, or dare not, or am afraid to, for all of this is not worth talking about, it's a completely trivial matter. No, I refuse to say because here a principle is involved: this is my private life, and I shall not permit you to invade my private life. There is my principle. Your question is not material to the case, and all that is not material to the case is my private life! I wanted to pay off a debt, I wanted to pay off a debt of honour, but to whom — I shall not say.'

'Permit us to record that,' said the public procurator.

'Please do. Record it as follows: that I absolutely refuse to say. You may write, gentlemen, that I even consider it dishonourable to reveal the identity of the person concerned. Good heavens, what a lot of time you use up with your recording!'

'Permit me to warn you, dear sir, and once again remind you, if you were not aware of it,' the public procurator said in tones of especial and most severe reprimand, 'that you have a perfect right not to answer the questions that are being put to you now, while we, on the other hand, have no right to force answers from you, if you yourself decline to answer for one reason or another. That is a matter for your own personal consideration. In instances like the present one, however, our task also consists in explaining and drawing your attention to the degree of harm that you may incur to yourself by refusing to make this deposition or that. And now I request you to continue.'

'Gentlemen, why, I am not angry . . . I . . .' Mitya began to mutter, slightly embarrassed by the reprimand. 'Look, sir, you see, gentlemen, that same Samsonov whom I went to visit that day . . .'

We shall not, of course, adduce the details of his narrative, for they are already familiar to the reader. In his impatience, the narrator wished to tell everything right down to the last little nuance and at the same time do it as swiftly as possible. But as the depositions were made, so were they recorded, and thus it was inevitable that from time to time he was stopped. Dmitry Fyodorovich took a dim view of this, but submitted, was angry, but for the moment at least in a good-humoured sort of way. It was true that he would sometimes scream: 'Gentlemen, this would infuriate the Lord Almighty himself,' or: 'Gentlemen, do you realize that you are merely irritating me to no purpose?', but even so, as he exclaimed these things did not for the present alter his amicably expansive mood. Thus he narrated how two days before Samsonov had 'duped' him. (He had by this time fully realized that he had been duped that day.) The sale of his watch for six roubles in order to obtain money for his journey, a fact hitherto completely unknown to the investigator and the public procurator, at once aroused their extreme attention and this time to Mitya's boundless indignation: they thought it necessary to record this fact in detail, in the form of a secondary confirmation of the circumstance that even the day before he had scarcely a groat of money upon him. Little by little Mitya began to grow morose. Then, having described his journey to see Lyagavy and the night he had passed in the fume-filled *izba*, etcetera, he led his narrative up to his return to town and at that point began, without being particularly requested, to give a detailed description of the torments of jealousy he had suffered with Grushenka. He was listened to with silent attention, and particular scrutiny was given to the circumstance that he had long had an observation post for watching Grushenka in Fyodor Pavlovich's garden 'at the rears' of the house of Marya Kondratyevna, and that Smerdyakov brought him information: this was noted and recorded in much detail. Of his jealousy he spoke hotly and at length, and though he was inwardly ashamed at exhibiting his most intimate emotions, as it were, to 'public disgrace', he plainly made an effort to overcome his shame in order to be truthful. The fixity and impersonal sternness of the way in which the investigator and the public procurator looked at him during the delivery of his narrative at last troubled him rather intensely: 'This boy Nikolay Parfenovich, with whom only a few days ago I was passing stupid remarks about women, and this invalid of a public procurator, they don't deserve my telling them this,' flickered sadly through his mind, 'and I'm exposing myself to disgrace! "Endure, resign thyself, and silent be",' he thought, concluding his reflections with a line of poetry,* but again mustered his energies in order to continue further. Passing to the tale of Mrs Khokhlakova, he even recovered his cheerfulness again and even wanted to tell concerning that dear lady a certain recent small anecdote not material to the case, but the investigator stopped him and politely suggested to him that he proceed to 'things of a more essential nature'. At last, having described his despair and having told of that moment when, upon leaving Mrs Khokhlakova's house, he had even thought 'of cutting someone's throat as soon as possible and obtaining three thousand that way', he was again stopped, and the fact that he had 'wanted to cut someone's throat' recorded. Mitya let them write it without saying a word. At last he reached the point in his narrative when he had suddenly learned that Grushenka had deceived him and had left Samsonov's house as soon as he had brought her there, while she herself had said that she would stay with the old man until midnight: 'If I did not kill Fenya then, gentlemen, it was only because I had not the time,' suddenly burst from him at that juncture in the story. This too was thoroughly recorded. Mitya gloomily continued and began to tell of how he had run to his father in the garden, when the investigator suddenly stopped him and, opening his large briefcase that lay beside him on the sofa, took from it a brass pestle.

'Is this object familiar to you?' he asked, showing it to Mitya.

'Oh yes!' he smiled blackly, 'how could I fail to recognize it? Here, let me take a look at it . . . Or rather, the devil, I don't want to!'

'You forgot to mention it,' the investigator observed.

'The devil! I would not have concealed it from you, for I don't think we could have managed without it — what do you suppose? It just flew out of my memory.'

'Be so good as to tell us in detail how you came into possession of the weapon.'

'Certainly, I shall oblige you, gentlemen.'

And Mitya described how he had taken the pestle and gone running off.

'But what purpose did you have in view when you furnished yourself with a weapon of this kind?'

'What purpose? None! I just grabbed it and ran off.'

'But why, if you had no purpose?'

Within Mitya vexation was seething. He gave the 'boy' a fixed look and thinly smiled a smile of black hatred. The fact was that he had been growing more and more ashamed of having just then so sincerely and with such outpourings told 'men like these' the story of his jealousy.

'A fig for the pestle!' suddenly burst from him.

'But, sir.'

'Oh, I took it with me to fend off dogs. You know, the darkness . . . Just in case . . .'

'And previously, were you also in the habit of taking some weapon with you when you went out at night, if you have always been so afraid of the dark?'

'Hah, the devil, fie! Gentlemen, it really is literally impossible to talk to you!' Mitya screamed in the last degree of irritation and, turning to the scribe, red all over with hatred, quickly said to him with a note in his voice that was almost one of frenzy:

'Write this down at once . . . at once . . . "I took the pestle with me in order to go and kill my father . . . Fyodor Pavlovich . . . with a blow on the head!" Well, now are you satisfied, gentlemen? Worked it all out of your system now?' he said, staring with provocative challenge at the investigator and the public procurator.

'We understand all too well that your deposition just now was made because you were irritated with us and vexed by the questions we have been putting to you, questions which you consider trivial but which, in essence, are most essential,' the public procurator said to him in reply.

'Oh, for pity's sake, gentlemen! All right, I took the pestle ... Well, why do people usually take something with them in such cases? I don't know why. I just grabbed it and ran. That is all. For shame, gentlemen, *passons*, or else I swear I shall bring my story to a halt!'

He leaned his elbows on the table and propped his head in his hand. He was sitting sideways to them, looking at the wall, trying to keep a check on the evil surge of emotion within him. In actual fact, he horribly wanted to get up and declare that he would not say another word, 'not even if you take me to the scaffold'.

'You see, gentlemen,' he said suddenly, mastering himself with difficulty, 'you see, I hear what you are saying, and it seems to me ... you see, I sometimes have a certain dream ... a certain kind of dream, and I have it often, it repeats itself, that someone is chasing me, someone of whom I am horribly afraid, chasing me in the dark, at night, looking for me, and I hide somewhere from him, behind a door or a cupboard, I hide in a degrading way, and above all in such a way that he knows perfectly well my whereabouts, but seems to pretend on purpose not to know where I am, in order to torment me longer, in order to take pleasure in my terror ... That is what you are doing now! It's the same sort of thing!'

'So that's the kind of dream you have?' the public procurator inquired.

'Yes, that's the kind of dream I have. Don't you want to write it down in the record?' Mitya smiled crookedly.

'No, sir, it's not anything for the record, but all the same those are interesting dreams you have.'

'But now it is not a dream! It is realism, gentlemen, the realism of real life! I am the wolf and you are the hunters, well, and you are running the wolf to ground.'

'You should not make such a comparison ...' Nikolay Parfenovich began extremely gently.

'I should gentlemen, I should!' Mitya seethed again, even though, having plainly relieved his soul by this manifestation of sudden wrath, he had again begun to grow more mellow with each word. 'You may not believe every criminal or suspect whom you torture with your questions, but a man of the most noble inclinations, gentlemen, a man whose soul knows the most noble impulses (boldly do I cry it!) — no! Such a man you cannot fail to believe ... you do not even have a right not to ... but —

> be silent, heart,
> Endure, resign thyself, and silent be!

Well, what then, shall I continue?' he broke off, blackly.

'Very well, by all means,' Nikolay Parfenovich replied.

5

The Third Torment

MITYA, though he had spoken with severity, had apparently begun to try more and more neither to forget nor to omit one single small detail from his account. He described how he had jumped across the fence into his father's garden, how he had walked up to the window and then described all that had taken place as he had stood below it. Clearly, precisely, almost rapping out the words, he rendered an account of the feelings that had agitated him during those moments in the garden when he had so horribly wanted to know whether Grushenka was with his father or not. But it was a strange thing: this time both public procurator and investigator seemed to listen with the utmost restraint, their gazes shorn of emotion, their questions far less numerous. From their faces Mitya could deduce nothing. 'They've lost their temper and I've put their backs up,' he thought. 'Well, to the devil!' And when he described how he had at last determined to give his father the 'signal' that Grushenka had arrived and that he was to open the window, the public procurator and the investigator paid no attention whatsoever to the word 'signal', as though they had not grasped at all the significance this word possessed, and even Mitya noticed it. When at last he reached the moment when, having caught sight of his father leaning his head out of the window, he had begun to boil with hatred and had snatched the pestle from his pocket, he suddenly paused, as though by design. He sat staring at the wall and was aware that the eyes of the other two men were fairly boring into him.

'Well sir,' the investigator said, 'so you snatched out the weapon and ... and what happened after that?'

'After that? After that I killed him ... bashed him on the temple and opened his skull . . . At any rate, that is your version of it!' he said with a sudden flash of his eyes. All his suppressed wrath suddenly rose with extraordinary violence within his soul.

'Our version of it,' Nikolay Parfenovich said, talking him down. 'Well, and what is your version?'

Mitya lowered his eyes and for a long time said nothing.

'In my opinion, gentlemen, in my opinion it was like this,' he began quietly. 'Whether someone had shed tears for me, or whether it was my mother who had beseeched God for me, or whether some radiant spirit had kissed me in that moment − I do not know, but the Devil was vanquished. I rushed away from the window and ran towards the fence . . . My father took fright and for the first time made me out in the dark, screamed and leapt away from the window − I remember that very well. And I ran through the garden towards the fence . . . it was then that Grigory caught me up, when I was already sitting astride the fence . . .'

At this point he at last raised his eyes to his listeners. They, it appeared, were staring at him with an attention that was quite untroubled. A kind of convulsion of indignation passed through Mitya's soul.

'Why, gentlemen, I do declare that at this moment you are mocking me!' he burst out suddenly.

'What makes you think that?' Nikolay Parfenovich observed.

'Not one word do you believe, that is what makes me think it! You see, I realize that I have reached the principal point of my story: there the old man lies with a broken skull, while I − having tragically described how I wanted to kill him and had already snatched out a pestle in order to do it, suddenly run away from the window . . . A poem! In verse! One may take the fine fellow at his word! Ha-ha! Mockers is what you are, gentlemen!'

And with his whole body he swung round on the chair, making it creak.

'But did you not notice,' the public procurator began suddenly, as though he had paid no heed to Mitya's agitation, 'did you not notice as you ran away from the window whether the door, the one that leads into the garden and is situated at the other end of the outbuilding, was open or not?'

'No, it was not open.'

'Are you sure?'

'On the contrary, it was closed, and who could have opened it? Hah, the door, wait!' he said, as if suddenly coming to his senses, and very nearly started. 'Did you find the door open?'

'Yes, we did.'

'So who could have opened it, if not yourselves?' Mitya asked suddenly in fearful astonishment.

'The door was open, and there can be no doubt that your parent's murderer entered by that door and, having committed the murder, left by it also,' the public procurator articulated, almost rapping out the words, slowly and distinctly. 'That is quite clear to us. The murder obviously took place in the room, *and not through the window*, something that is unquestionably clear from the report that has been made, from the position of the body, and from all the other evidence. There can be absolutely no doubt of that circumstance.'

Mitya was horribly shocked.

'But that cannot be, gentlemen!' he exclaimed, totally at a loss. 'I . . . I did not go in . . . I tell you categorically, I am absolutely certain that the door was closed all the time I was in the garden and when I fled from it. All I did was stand under the window and see him through the window, and that is all, that is all . . . I remember it all right up to the very last moment. And even if I did not, I would still be certain, for the *signals* were only known to me, to Smerdyakov and to him, the deceased, and he, without signals, would never in the world have opened the door to anyone!'

'Signals? What signals are those?' the public procurator said with avid, almost hysterical curiosity, losing in a flash all his dignified restraint. He asked in a manner of timid, creeping approach. He had smelt an important piece of evidence, one hitherto unknown to him, and at once felt an intense fear that Mitya might possibly refuse to reveal it in its entirety.

'Oh, didn't you know?' Mitya said, winking at him and smiling a smile of mockery and hatred. 'And what if I refuse to tell you? Who will you learn it from then? For after all, the signals were known to the deceased, myself and Smerdyakov, and no one else, unless one includes heaven, which also knows them, but it is not going to tell you. It's an interesting little piece of evidence, the devil knows what one might build on it, ha-ha! It's all right, gentlemen, be comforted, I'll tell you it, your minds are full of stupid thoughts. You do not know with whom you are dealing! You are dealing with a suspect who is prepared to make depositions against himself, to his own detriment! Yes, sir, for I am a knight of honour, and you are not!'

The public procurator had swallowed all the pills, and now he merely trembled with impatience to learn the new piece of evidence. Mitya set before them in lengthy detail all that concerned the signals Fyodor

Pavlovich had devised for Smerdyakov, described for them the precise significance of each knock at the window, even making the knocks on the table and in response to Nikolay Parfenovich's question as to whether he, Mitya, in knocking at the old man's window, had also used the signal which denoted that 'Grushenka had arrived', he replied unambiguously that he had indeed used precisely that signal.

'There, now you may build your tower!' Mitya said, breaking off, and turning away from them again in contempt.

'And the only people who knew these signals were your deceased parent, yourself and the manservant Smerdyakov? No one else?' Nikolay Parfenovich inquired once more.

'Yes, the manservant Smerdyakov and also heaven. You must make a note of heaven, too, in your record; that would not be superfluous. And you yourselves will require the assistance of God.'

And of course, they began to enter all this in the record, but as they were doing so, the public procurator suddenly, as though he had quite unexpectedly stumbled upon a fresh idea, said:

'But I mean, if Smerdyakov also knew about these signals, and you categorically reject any accusation against you of responsibility for the death of your father, then was it not he who, having delivered the prearranged signals, caused your father to open the door to him, and then . . . committed the crime?'

With eyes that were deeply mocking but at the same time also filled with terrible hatred, Mitya gave him a stare. He stared long and silently, until the public procurator's eyes began to blink.

'You've caught the fox again!' Mitya said at last. 'You've tweaked the little scoundrel by his tail, heh-heh! I can see through you, public procurator! Why, you thought I was going to leap up straight away, seize hold of what you're suggesting to me, and shout at the top of my voice: "Yes, it was Smerdyakov, he is the murderer!" Come on, own up that that is what you thought, own up and then I shall continue.'

But the public procurator did not own up. He spoke no word, and waited.

'You're wrong, I'm not going to put the blame on Smerdyakov!' said Mitya.

'You do not even suspect him at all?'

'Do you?'

'We have had our suspicions of him, too.'

Mitya set his gaze upon the floor.

'Let us leave joking aside,' he said, blackly. 'Listen: right from the start, almost from the time when I came out to you from behind that curtain, that thought flickered through my mind: "It was Smerdyakov!" Here I have sat at the table, shouting my innocence of this blood, yet all the while I have been thinking: "It was Smerdyakov!" And Smerdyakov would not leave my soul alone. Now, a moment ago, I suddenly thought the same thing again: "It was Smerdyakov!", but only for a second: my instant, my very next thought was: "No, it was not Smerdyakov!" This is not his work, gentlemen!'

'Do you in that case suspect some other person?' Nikolay Parfenovich cautiously inquired.

'I know not who nor what the person, whether it be the hand of heaven or the hand of Satan, but it is not ... Smerdyakov!' Mitya snapped, decisively.

'But why do you so firmly and with such insistence assert that it is not he?'

'Because I am convinced. Because that is my impression. Because Smerdyakov is a man of the basest nature, and a coward. Or rather, not a coward but a combination of all the manifestations of cowardliness in the world taken together, walking on two legs. He was born of a hen. When he spoke to me, on each occasion he trembled lest I kill him, while I never even raised a finger against him. He fell at my feet and wept, he kissed these very boots, literally, begging me not to "frighten him" – what kind of a remark is that? And I even tried to give him money. He is a sickly hen with the falling sickness and a weak mind, a fellow whom an eight-year-old schoolboy could flatten to the ground. Is that a human being? No, gentlemen, it was not Smerdyakov, and in any case he has no love of money, has never taken any presents from me whatsoever ... And why should he kill the old man? After all, he may possibly be his son, his natural son, do you know that?'

'We have heard that legend. But then you too are the son of your father, and you yourself had been telling everyone you wanted to kill him.'

'A thrust! And a mean and nasty one! I am not afraid! Oh, gentlemen, perhaps you think it too vile to say it to my face! Vile, because I myself told you it. Not only did I want to kill him, I could have killed him, and indeed I voluntarily confessed that I very nearly *did* kill him! But you see, I didn't do it, my guardian angel rescued me – that is what you have not taken into consideration ... And that is why it seems vile to you, vile! Because I did not kill him, I did not, I did not! Do you hear, public procurator; I did not kill him!'

He very nearly choked. This was the first time in the course of the entire interrogation that he had been in a state of such excitement.

'And what did he tell you, gentlemen, that Smerdyakov?' he said in sudden conclusion, after a pause. 'May I ask you that?'

'You may ask us about anything,' the public procurator replied with a mien of cold severity, 'about anything connected with the factual aspect of the case, and we, I repeat this, are even obliged to satisfy you on every point. We found the manservant Smerdyakov, about whom you ask, lying unconscious in his bed in an extremely intense fit of the falling sickness, possibly the tenth he had suffered in a row. The medic who was with us, having witnessed the condition of the patient, even told us that he might not live until morning.'

'Well, in that case it was the Devil who killed my father!' suddenly burst from Mitya, as though until that moment he had all the time been wondering: 'Was it Smerdyakov or was it not?'

'We shall return to this part of the evidence again,' Nikolay Parfenovich decided. 'But for the present please be so good as to continue with your deposition.'

Mitya asked to take a rest. This he was courteously permitted. Having taken his rest he began to continue. But he was plainly in a bad way. He was at the end of his tether, morally outraged and shaken. To make matters worse, the public procurator now seemed as if on purpose to be playing on his nerves more and more each minute by his relentless fastening upon 'trivia'. Barely had Mitya described how, sitting on the fence, he had struck Grigory, who had gripped him by the left leg, over the head with the pestle and then immediately jumped down to the injured man's side, than the public procurator made him stop and asked him to describe in greater detail the manner in which he had sat on the fence. Mitya was astonished.

'Why, like this, astride it, one leg here and one leg there . . .'

'And the pestle?'

'I was holding it.'

'It wasn't in your pocket? Do you really remember that so clearly? Tell me, did you swing your arm down hard?'

'I must have done – why do you ask that?'

'I wonder if you would mind sitting on your chair in the manner you sat then on the fence, and demonstrating visually to us, for purposes of clarification, how and in what direction you swung your arm?'

'You're mocking me again, aren't you?' Mitya said, giving his interrogator a disdainful look; but the latter did not even blink. Mitya turned round convulsively, sat down astride the chair and swung his arm:

'Look, that's how I struck him! That's how I killed him! What more do you want?'

'I thank you. Now I wonder if you would be so good as to explain precisely why you jumped down, with what purpose and with what precise intention in view?'

'Oh, the devil . . . I jumped down because the man was injured . . . I don't know why . . .'

'Even though you were in a state of such agitation? And on the run?'

'Yes, even though I was both of those things.'

'Did you want to help him?'

'What do you mean . . . Yes, possibly I wanted to help him, I don't remember.'

'You were not in control of your thoughts? In other words, you were even in a certain state of oblivion?'

'Oh no, certainly not oblivion, I remember everything. Everything right down to the last little detail. I jumped down to take a look and I wiped the blood from his head with my handkerchief.'

'We saw your handkerchief. Did you hope to return the victim to life?'

'I don't know. I simply wanted to ascertain whether he was alive or not.'

'Ah, so you wanted to ascertain it, did you? Well, and what did you decide?'

'I am not a medic, I couldn't tell. I ran away, thinking I had killed him, and yet now he has recovered consciousness.'

'That will do admirably, sir,' the public procurator said in conclusion. 'I thank you. That is all I required. Now please be so good as to continue.'

Alas, it never even crossed Mitya's mind to tell them, even though he remembered it, that he had jumped down out of pity, and, standing over the man he believed he had murdered, had even uttered a few pathetic words: 'You've made your bed, old fellow, there's naught to be done, so now you must lie in it!' The public procurator, on the other hand, merely drew the conclusion that the man had jumped down 'at a moment like that and in a state of agitation like that', only in order to ascertain beyond all doubt whether or not the *sole* witness to his crime was alive. And that, consequently, what must have been the strength, determination, sang-froid and calculation of the man, if, even at a moment like that . . . etcetera, etcetera. The public procurator was satisfied, reflecting that he had 'played on the nerves of the sickly fellow, and he went and let the cat out of the bag'.

Mitya continued, in torment. But at once he was again made to stop by Nikolay Parfenovich.

'How could you have gone in to see the serving-maid Fedosya Markova, if your hands were so covered in blood and, as it subsequently appears, your face also?'

'But I had not noticed I was covered in blood at the time!' Mitya replied.

'He may have a point there, that does sometimes happen,' the public procurator said, exchanging a glance with Nikolay Parfenovich.

'Exactly – I had not noticed, that was an admirable contribution of yours, public procurator,' Mitya said in sudden approval. But now followed the story of Mitya's sudden decision to 'step aside' and 'let the fortunate ones pass'. And now he could no longer, as before, bring himself to divulge the contents of his heart and tell them of 'the empress of his soul'. The thought of speaking of her to these cold men who were 'leeching on him like bedbugs' made him feel sick. And so to their repeated questions he declared curtly and sharply:

'Well, I had decided to kill myself. What was there left to live for? That question came up of its own accord. Her lover, former and beyond dispute, who had outraged her honour but who at the end of five years had come galloping back with his love in order to complete the outrage by means of lawful wedlock. Well, then I understood that as far as I was concerned it was all lost . . . Behind me was disgrace, and now this blood, the blood of Grigory . . . What did I have to live for? Well, I went to redeem the pistols I had pawned, in order to load one and put a bullet through my noddle at dawn . . .'

'And in the night you had an extravagant feast?'

'That is correct. Hah, the devil, gentlemen, let us get this over with quickly. I quite certainly intended to shoot myself, not far from here, on the outskirts of town, I would have dispatched myself at five o'clock in the morning, I even had a note in my pocket, I wrote it at Perkhotin's, when I loaded the pistol. Here is the note, you may read it. What I am telling is not intended for you!' he suddenly added in contempt. He took the note from his waistcoat pocket and threw it in front of them on the table; the investigators read it with interest and, according to procedure, filed it away.

'And you never thought of washing your hands, even when you entered the home of Mr Perkhotin? Consequently you were not afraid of attracting suspicion?'

'What suspicion? It wouldn't have made any difference whether anyone had suspected me or not – I would have come out here at the gallop and shot myself at five o'clock, and you could have done nothing about it. After all, had it not been for what happened to my father you would never have discovered anything and would never have come here. Oh, this is the Devil's work, it was the Devil who killed my father, and it was through the Devil that you learned of it so quickly! How did you manage to get here so quickly? It's a marvel, a fantasy!'

'Mr Perkhotin told us that when you entered his home you were holding in your bloodied hands . . . your money . . . a large sum of money . . . a wad of one-hundred-rouble banknotes, and that this was also observed by the lad who works as his servant!'

'Yes, gentlemen, I seem to remember that that was so.'

'Well, now a certain little question is encountered. I wonder if you would mind telling us,' Nikolay Parfenovich began, extremely gently, 'where you could suddenly have obtained such a large sum of money, when the facts of the case demonstrate, even when calculations of time are taken into account, that you did not visit your lodgings?'

The public procurator frowned slightly at this question, put as it was in such point-blank manner, but did not interrupt Nikolay Parfenovich.

'No, I did not visit them,' Mitya replied, to all appearances with the utmost calm, but looking at the floor.

'In that case permit me to repeat the question,' Nikolay Parfenovich continued, with a kind of creeping approach. 'From where could you have obtained such a large sum, when by your own confession, at five o'clock on the evening of that day . . .'

'I needed ten roubles and pawned my pistols with Perkhotin, then I went to ask Mrs Khokhlakova for three thousand, but she wouldn't lend me them,' Mitya interrupted suddenly, 'yes, there, gentlemen, I needed the money, and there I was suddenly with three thousand in my hands, eh? You know, gentlemen, why, you are both now afraid that I'm not going to tell you where I got it. And you're right to be afraid, for I shall not tell you, gentlemen, your guess is correct, you shall not discover it,' Mitya rapped out suddenly with extreme resolve. For a second or two the investigators fell silent.

'You must realize, Mr Karamazov, that it is absolutely essential for us to know this fact,' Nikolay Parfenovich said softly and meekly.

'I do, but still I shall not tell you.'

The public procurator, too, added his voice and again reminded Mitya that a person under interrogation was permitted not to answer questions if he considered this the most advantageous course for him to take, etcetera, but that in view of the prejudice the suspected person might inflict upon himself by his silence and especially in view of the fact that the questions were of such an importance as to . . .

'And so on, gentlemen, and so forth! Enough, I have heard this rigmarole before!' Mitya said, again interrupting. 'I am perfectly aware of the importance of the matter at stake and of the fact that here is the most essential point, but even so I shall not tell you.'

'You see, sir, that is not our affair, but yours, and you will do damage to yourself,' Nikolay Parfenovich commented nervously.

'Look, gentlemen, let us leave joking aside,' Mitya said, raising his eyes quickly and looking at them both with firmness. 'From the very outset I knew that we were going to lock horns on this point. But at first, when I began to make my depositions earlier, all this was in the remotest fog, it was all in flux, and I was even so naïve as to begin by proposing "mutual trust" between us. Now I myself see that such trust could not possibly have existed, because we should, willy-nilly, have arrived at this accursed fence! Well, and so here we are! I cannot tell you, and that is all! As a matter of fact, I do not attach any blame to you, it is impossible for you to take me at my word, I understand that!'

He lapsed into black silence.

'But could you not, without in any way violating your resolve to remain silent about the most important point, could you not at the same time give us at least one little hint as to what were the powerful motives that could have led you to silence at a juncture in your present testimony so fraught with risk to yourself?'

Mitya smiled a sad, ironic, almost reflective smile.

'I am far kinder than you give me credit for, gentlemen, I shall tell you why, and shall give you your hint, even though you do not deserve it. I remain silent, gentlemen, because here I am involved in disgrace. Were I to reply to the question concerning where I obtained that money I should bring upon myself disgrace of such magnitude that it could not stand comparison with even the murder and robbery of my father, had I indeed murdered him and robbed him. That is why I cannot speak. Because of the disgrace. Well, gentlemen, are you not going to take that down?'

'Yes, we are,' Nikolay Parfenovich babbled.

'You ought not really to take down the part about "disgrace". I only told you that out of the kindness of my heart, and I could have with-held it – it was, so to say, a gift, and there you go, weaving it into the pattern! Oh well, write it down then, write what you will,' he concluded in disdainful contempt, 'I am not afraid of you and . . . am proud before you.'

'But will you not tell us the nature of this disgrace?' Nikolay Parfenovich began to babble.

The public procurator frowned horribly.

'Absolutely not, *c'est fini*, you're wasting your time. And in any case, there is no point in my soiling my hands. I've already soiled them enough with you. You do not deserve it, neither you nor anyone else . . . Enough, gentlemen, I rest my case.'

This was said too decisively. Nikolay Parfenovich ceased to press, but from Ippolit Kirillovich's glances he saw in a flash that the latter had not yet given up hope.

'Will you not at least tell us what the sum was you were holding when you entered the home of Mr Perkhotin, that is to say, precisely how many roubles?'

'I am unable to tell you that, either.'

'It appears that you told Mr Perkhotin about three thousand you had received from Mrs Khokhlakova?'

'Perhaps I did. Enough gentlemen: I shall not tell you how much money I had.'

'In that case will you please be so good as to describe how you travelled here, and all that you did when you reached here?'

'Oh, you can ask any of the local people here about that. Though I suppose, if you like, I can tell you.'

He told the story, but we shall not go over it again. He told it cursorily, without emotion. Of the ecstasies of his love he did not speak at all. He did, however, tell how his resolve to shoot himself had passed 'in view of the new facts'. He gave his account without offering reasons or going into detail. And indeed the investigators themselves were not particularly troubled on this occasion: it was clear that for them, too, the principal point did not now lie there.

'We shall check all this, we shall return to it all again during the interrogation of the witnesses, which will, of course, take place in your presence,' Nikolay Parfenovich said, concluding the interrogation. 'And now we must ask you to put on the table all the items in your possession, and particularly all the money you now have upon your person.'

'Money, gentlemen? By all means, I understand what is required. I am even astonished that you did not show an interest earlier. To be sure, there is nowhere I could have slipped away to, for here I sit for all to see. Well then, here is my money, here, count it, take it, that's it all, I think.'

He took all the money out of his pockets, even the small change, fishing out two twenty-copeck pieces from the side pocket of his waistcoat. The money was counted and found to total 836 roubles and forty copecks.

'And is that all?' the investigator asked.

'Yes.'

'You were so good as to say just now, in giving your evidence, that you left three hundred roubles at Plotnikov's delicatessen, gave ten to Mr Perkhotin, twenty to the *yamshchik*, lost two hundred at cards here, then . . .'

Nikolay Parfenovich re-counted it all. Mitya helped with alacrity. Every copeck was remembered and accounted for. Nikolay Parfenovich quickly did a sum.

'If we include the eight hundred you have here, that means you must originally have had only about fifteen hundred?'

'I suppose I must,' Mitya snapped.

'Then why does everyone assert that you had far more?'

'Let them.'

'But you yourself have asserted it.'

'Yes, I have.'

'We shall check all this against the testimony of the other persons who have not yet been questioned; please do not be concerned about your money, it will be kept in a proper place and will be at your disposal at the end of the . . . proceedings . . . if it proves, or, as it were, is proven, that you have an undisputable right to it. Well, sir, and now . . .'

Nikolay Parfenovich suddenly got up and firmly announced to Mitya that he was 'compelled and duty-bound' to institute a most detailed and thorough examination 'both of your garments and of all the rest . . .'

'By all means, gentlemen, I shall turn out all my pockets for you, if you wish.'

And he really did begin to turn out his pockets.

'We shall also have to ask you to remove your clothing.'

'What? Must I undress? Fie, the devil! Search me as I am! Can I not be as I am?'

'I am afraid you can't, Dmitry Fyodorovich, there is no way round it. You must take off your clothes.'

'As you wish,' Mitya said, blackly submitting. 'Only, please, not here, but behind the curtain. Who is going to conduct the examination?'

'Very well, naturally, behind the curtain,' Nikolay Parfenovich replied, inclining his head in token of consent. His little face displayed an even quite especial solemnity.

6

The Public Procurator Catches Mitya

WHAT now began was something Mitya found totally unexpected and astonishing. He would never on any account, even a moment earlier, have supposed that anyone might behave towards him, Mitya Karamazov, in such a fashion! Above all, a certain element of degradation had manifested itself, and on their part a 'disdainful' attitude, 'contemptuous' of him. He would not have minded taking off his coat, but he had been asked to undress further, too. And he had not really been asked either, but rather ordered to do so; he understood that very well. Out of pride and contempt he submitted completely, without a word. Behind the curtain, in addition to Nikolay Parfenovich, went the public procurator, and several muzhiks were also present, 'to provide manpower', Mitya thought, 'and perhaps for some other purpose as well'.

'Well, do I also have to take off my shirt?' he began sharply, but Nikolay Parfenovich did not reply to him: together with the public procurator he was immersed in the examination of Mitya's coat, trousers, waistcoat and cap, and it was plain that they had both now taken a lively interest in the examination: 'There is no ceremony at all in their behaviour,' flitted through Mitya's mind. 'They are not even observing common courtesy.'

'I ask you a second time: do I or do I not have to take off my shirt?' he said even more sharply and on edge.

'Don't worry, we shall inform you,' Nikolay Parfenovich replied, even somewhat domineeringly. Or so, at any rate, it appeared to Mitya.

Between the investigator and the public prosecutor a worried conference was meanwhile in progress, held in an undertone. There had proved to be, on the coat, and especially on its left skirt, at the back, some enormous patches of blood, which had dried, caked and not yet loosened to any great degree. The same was true of the trousers. Nikolay Parfenovich, had, moreover, with his own hands, in the presence of the witnesses, passed his fingers along the collar, the cuffs and all the seams of the coat and trousers, evidently searching for something – money, of course. Above all, to Mitya they made no secret of their suspicions that he might have sewn, and was capable of sewing, money into the garments. 'This is simply the way they would deal with a thief, not an officer,' he muttered to himself. They were also exchanging their ideas about him with one another in a strangely unconcealed manner, in his presence. For example the clerk, who was also behind the curtain, fussing about and providing his services, drew Nikolay Parfenovich's attention to the cap, which they also felt about in. 'Remember Gridenko the scribe, sir,' the clerk observed, 'last summer he went to collect the salaries of the whole office, but when he came back he said he'd lost them while drunk – and where do you think they found them? Right in that very same edging, on his cap, sir, he had hundred-rouble notes rolled up into little cylinders and sewn into the edging, sir.' The public procurator and the investigator recalled the case of Gridenko only too well, and so Mitya's cap, too, was placed to one side, while they decided that all this would have to be seriously looked at later on, and indeed a special examination made of all Mitya's garments.

'Permit me,' Nikolay Parfenovich suddenly yelped, having observed the rolled-up right cuff of the right sleeve of Mitya's shirt, and seen that it was entirely saturated in blood, 'permit me, but what is that – blood?'

'Yes,' Mitya snapped.

'But where has it come from, sir . . . and why is the cuff rolled back into the sleeve?'

Mitya told how he had got blood on the cuff while tending to Grigory, and had rolled it up at Perkhotin's when he had washed his hands there.

'We shall also have to take your shirt, it is highly important . . . as material evidence.' Mitya reddened and flew into a violent rage.

'What am I supposed to do, stand naked?' he cried.

'Don't worry . . . we shall find a way of setting it right, but for the moment please be so good as to remove your socks, too.'

'Is this some kind of joke you are playing on me? Do I really have to do that?' Mitya asked, his eyes flashing.

'We have no time for jokes,' Nikolay Parfenovich parried sternly.

'Well, if I have to . . . I . . .' Mitya muttered and, sitting down on the bed, began to take off his socks. He felt intolerably embarrassed: everyone else was dressed except he, and it was a strange thing – without his clothes on he himself felt guilty before them, and, above all, was himself almost ready to agree that he had suddenly become inferior to all of them and that now they had a perfect right to treat him with contempt. 'If everyone were undressed I should not be so ashamed, but to be the only one without my clothes while all the rest look on – that is dishonour!' flickered again and again through his mind. 'It is as though I were dreaming, I have sometimes had dreams in which I suffered dishonour like this.' But he found taking his socks off a positive torture: they were not very clean, and neither was his linen, and now everyone could see this. Above all, he did not like his feet, for all his life he had considered the big toes on both of them to be deformed, especially a certain coarse, flat, inward-turned toenail on the right foot, and now all of them could see it. His unendurable shame suddenly made him even more uncouth, even intentionally so. He himself tore the shirt from his body.

'Would you not care to search in a few other places as well, if you are not too embarrassed?'

'No, sir, for the present that will not be required.'

'Well, am I to remain naked?' he added in rage.

'Yes, for the time being that will be necessary . . . Please be so good as to sit down here, you may take a blanket from the bed and wrap yourself in it, while I . . . make all the necessary arrangements.'

All the items and articles were shown to the witnesses, a report was compiled, and at last Nikolay Parfenovich went out of the room, the garments being taken out after him. Ippolit Kirillovich also went out. With Mitya only the muzhiks remained; they stood without saying anything, never lowering their eyes from him. Mitya wrapped himself in a blanket, for he had begun to feel cold. His bare feet stuck out, and no matter how hard he tried he could not manage to pull the blanket over them and cover them up. It was for some reason a long time before Nikolay Parfenovich returned, 'a torturingly long time', Mitya ground through his teeth – 'he considers me a young whelp. That no-good public procurator has also gone out, doubtless because he feels contempt for me, he finds it too loathsome to gaze upon a naked man.' In spite of all this, Mitya still supposed that his garments would be examined somewhere and then brought back again. But what was his indignation when Nikolay Parfenovich suddenly returned with some quite different garments, borne by a muzhik who followed behind him.

'Well, here are some clothes for you,' he said casually, evidently very pleased with the success of his foray. 'Mr Kalganov has contributed these for this curious eventuality, as well as a clean shirt for you. He fortunately happened to have all these things in his trunk. As for socks and underwear, you may keep your own.'

Mitya boiled with terrible rage.

'I don't want someone else's clothes!' he shouted threateningly. 'Give me my own!'

'That is not possible.'

'Give me my own, to the devil with Kalganov, and his clothes, and with him himself!'

It took a long time for them to talk him round. Somehow, however, they managed to calm him. It was impressed upon him that his garments, being stained with blood, must be 'added to the body of material evidence', and that they 'had not even any right' to let him wear them . . . 'in view of how the case might end'. Somehow, Mitya at last managed to grasp this. He lapsed into gloomy silence and began hurriedly to dress. His only observation in putting the garments on was that they were of better quality than his own and that he did not want it to be thought he was 'taking advantage' of this. Moreover, he said that they were 'degradingly tight' for him: 'What am I supposed to do – play the buffoon in them for you . . . for your enjoyment?'

It was again impressed upon him that here too he was exaggerating, that Mr Kalganov, though taller than him in stature, was only slightly so, and that perhaps only the trousers might possibly be a little too long for him. The coat, however, really was too tight in the shoulders.

'The devil take it, I can't even button it up properly,' Mitya muttered again. 'Please be so good as to tell Mr Kalganov that I did not ask him for his garments and that I have been made to dress up as a buffoon.'

'He understands that very well, and tenders his regrets . . . not about his garments, of course, but rather about this whole case . . .' Nikolay Parfenovich began to mumble.

'A fig for his regrets! Well, where are we going now? Or are we going to go on sitting here?'

He was requested to go back into 'the other room'. Mitya went, sullen with hatred, and trying not to look at anyone. Wearing someone else's clothes he felt totally disgraced, even before these muzhiks and Trifon Borisovich, whose face had for some reason suddenly flickered in the doorway and then disappeared: 'He's come to take a look at the mummer,' thought Mitya. He sat back down on the chair he had occupied earlier. Something nightmarish and preposterous seemed to fill his consciousness, and he had a sense of not being in his right mind.

'Well, what are you going to do now, start to give me a birching? That must surely be the next step,' he ground out, addressing the procurator. To Nikolay Parfenovich he was reluctant to turn, as though he did not consider him worthy of being spoken to. 'He's been staring at my socks far too closely, and he even had them turned inside out, the scoundrel, he did that on purpose in order to show everyone what dirty linen I have!'

'Now we must proceed to the interrogation of the witnesses,' Nikolay Parfenovich announced, as though in reply to Dmitry Fyodorovich's question.

'Yes, sir,' the public procurator said reflectively, as if he too had something on his mind.

'Dmitry Fyodorovich, we have done what we could to protect your interests,' Nikolay Parfenovich continued, 'but, having received such a categorical refusal on your part to give us an explanation of the source of the sum that has been found upon your person, at the present moment we . . .'

'What is that stone in your ring?' Mitya interrupted suddenly, as though he were emerging from some kind of reverie, and pointing at one of the three large rings that adorned Nikolay Parfenovich's dainty right hand.

'In my ring?' Nikolay Parfenovich asked in astonishment.

'Yes, that one . . . the one on your middle finger, with those little veins in it, what kind of stone is it?' Mitya insisted with a kind of nervous irritation, like a stubborn child.

'It's a smoky topaz,' Nikolay Parfenovich smiled, 'would you like to take a look, I'll remove it . . .'

'No, no, don't remove it!' Mitya shouted ferociously, suddenly coming to his senses and getting angry at himself. 'Don't remove it, don't bother . . . The devil . . . Gentlemen, you have besmirched my soul! Do you really suppose that if I really had murdered my father I would try to conceal it from you, that I would prevaricate, lie, and hide? No, Dmitry Karamazov is not that sort, he would not be able to endure that, and were I guilty, I swear that I would not have awaited your arrival and the rising of the sun, as I originally intended, I would have exterminated myself before then, without even waiting for the dawn! I feel that now in my being. In twenty years of life I could not have learned as much as I have learned in this accursed night! . . . And do you suppose that during this night and at this moment now I would have been like this, like this sitting here with you now – do you suppose I would have spoken like this, behaved like this, looked at you like this, and at the world, if I really were a parricide, when not even the idea that I had unintentionally murdered Grigory has given me any peace all night – but not because of fear, oh, not simply because of fear of your punishment! No, because of the disgrace! And yet you want me also to reveal to you and tell you, mockers like yourselves who see nothing and believe in nothing, blind moles and mockers, yet one more villainy, one more disgrace, even though it might save me from your accusation? No, I would rather go into penal servitude! Whoever it was who unlocked the door to my father's house and entered by that door, that person was his murderer, and that person robbed him. As to his identity I am at a loss and in torment, but it is not Dmitry Karamazov, let me tell you that – and that is all that I can tell you, and now enough, and press me no more ... Send me into exile, have me flogged, but do not play upon my nerves any longer. I opt for silence. Summon in your witnesses!'

Mitya delivered his sudden monologue as though he had in advance quite decided to opt for total silence. The public procurator had been keeping an eye on him, and no sooner did he stop talking than, with an air of utter coldness and calm, he suddenly said, as though it were the most ordinary thing in the world:

'Well, you see, in connection with that open door which you have just mentioned, we are as it so happens now in a position to inform you, and precisely now, at the present juncture, of a certain extremely curious deposition, one highly significant, both to you and to ourselves, made by the old man whom you injured, Grigory Vasilyev. In response to our inquiries, upon regaining consciousness, he has insisted quite unambiguously that at the time when, coming out on to the porch and hearing a certain sound in the garden, he determined to enter the garden through the wicket gate, which was open, and that, having done so, even before he observed you running away in the darkness, as you have informed us, from the open window through which you had seen your parent, he, Grigory, taking a glance to the left and observing that the window was indeed open, at the same time noticed, far closer to him, that the door which you maintain was closed all the time you were in the garden was in fact wide open. I shall not conceal from you that Vasilyev himself firmly concludes and testifies that you must have run out of the door, though, of course he did not see you do so with his own eyes, having espied you for the first time only when you were at some distance from him, in the middle of the garden, running to the side of the fence ...'

Before this discourse was halfway at an end, Mitya leapt up from his chair.

'Rubbish!' he howled in sudden frenzy. 'Brazen deceit! He could not possibly have seen the door open, for it was closed ... He is lying! ...'

'I consider it my duty to repeat to you that his deposition is unambiguous. He is in no doubt. He stands by it. We have questioned him several times.'

'Indeed, we have questioned him several times!' Nikolay Parfenovich confirmed with heat.

'It is not true! Not true! It is either a slander upon my person or the hallucination of a madman,' Mitya continued to shout. 'It's quite simply

because he was in a delirium, bleeding from his injury, when he came to
he must have thought . . . He is raving.'

'Yes, sir, but after all, he noticed that the door was open not when he
came to, but before that, when he had gone into the garden from the outbuilding.'

'But it is not true, it is not true, it cannot be! He is making it up in
order to slander me, out of malice . . . He could not have seen that . . . I
did not run out of the door,' Mitya choked.

The public procurator turned to Nikolay Parfenovich and said to him
imposingly:

'Show it to him.'

'Is this object familiar to you?' Nikolay Parfenovich said, suddenly
placing on the table a large envelope of government office dimensions,
made of thick paper, on which three torn seals were still visible. The
envelope was empty and torn open at one side. Mitya's eyes bulged at it.

'That . . . that must be father's envelope,' he muttered, 'the one with
the three thousand . . . and let me see, if the inscription is there, permit
me: "for my little chicken" . . . yes, there it is: it's the three thousand,' he
exclaimed, 'the three thousand, do you see?'

'Naturally we see, sir, but we did not find the money in it, it was
empty, lying on the floor next to the bed, behind the screen.'

For several seconds Mitya stood like a man dumbfounded.

'Gentlemen, it was Smerdyakov!' he suddenly exclaimed with all his
might. 'He is the murderer, he the robber! He alone knew where the old
man kept the envelope . . . It was he, that is clear now!'

'But after all, you too knew about the envelope and that it was under
the pillow.'

'No I didn't: I never saw it at all, this is the first time I have seen it,
before I had only heard about it from Smerdyakov . . . He alone knew
where the old man kept it, I did not . . .' Mitya said, completely choked
for breath.

'Yet you yourself testified to us earlier than the envelope was under
your parent's pillow. You said in so many words that it was under the
pillow, so consequently you knew where it was.'

'We have a written record of it!' Nikolay Parfenovich confirmed.

'Rubbish, preposterous! I had absolutely no knowledge that it was
under the pillow. Why, it may not even have been under the pillow at all
. . . That was a random guess of mine, about its being under the pillow
. . . What does Smerdyakov say? That is the principal thing . . . For I
purposely exposed myself to doubt . . . When I told you it was under the

pillow I lied to you without thinking, and now you . . . Oh, you know how it is, a word slips from one's tongue, and one says something that is not true. No, only Smerdyakov knew, Smerdyakov alone, and no one else! . . . He did not even tell me where it was! But it was he, it was he; it is beyond all doubt that he is the murderer, that is as clear as daylight to me now,' Mitya howled in a frenzy that grew more and more intense, incoherently repeating himself in a passion of bitter rage. 'You ought to get that into your heads, and arrest him as soon, as soon as possible . . . He did the murder after I had run away and while Grigory still lay unconscious, that is clear now . . . He gave the signals, and father unlocked the door for him . . . Because he alone knew the signals, and without the signals father would never have unlocked the door for anyone . . .'

'But again you forget the circumstance,' still with the same restraint, but with a kind of triumph now, the public procurator observed, 'that if the door was already open there would have been no need to give the signals, while you were still present, while you were still in the garden . . .'

'The door, the door,' Mitya muttered, then stared at the public procurator without a word and helplessly sagged back on to the chair. They all fell silent.

'Yes, the door! . . . It is a phantom! God is against me!' he exclaimed, staring in front of him quite without thought now.

'So see,' the public procurator said solemnly, 'and judge for yourself, Dmitry Fyodorovich: on the one hand there is this deposition concerning the open door, out of which you ran, and which overwhelms both you and ourselves. On the other hand there is your incomprehensible, stubborn and almost embittered silence concerning the source of the money which had suddenly appeared in your hands, while only three hours earlier you had, by your own testimony, pawned your pistols in order to obtain a mere ten roubles! In view of all this you may determine for yourself whom we are to believe and on what we are to dwell. And please do not complain of us that we are "cold cynics and men of mockery", who are constitutionally unable to believe the noble impulses of your soul . . . Try instead to see the matter from our point of view . . .'

Mitya was in a state of unimaginable agitation, and had turned pale.

'Very well!' he suddenly exclaimed. 'I shall reveal to you my secret, I shall reveal from where I obtained the money! . . . I shall reveal the disgrace, in order that later no blame may attach either to you or to myself . . .'

'And do be assured, Dmitry Fyodorovich,' Nikolay Parfenovich chimed in in a little voice of what sounded like blissful joy, 'that every sincere and complete admission from you, made now, at this present moment, may subsequently contribute towards an immeasurable mitigation of your lot and may even, moreover . . .'

But the public procurator gave him a slight nudge under the table, and he managed to pull up in time. To be sure, Mitya was not even listening to him.

7

Mitya's Great Secret. Hissed Off the Stage

'GENTLEMEN,' he began, still in the same agitation, 'that money . . . I want to confess completely . . . that money was *my own*.'

The faces of the public procurator and the investigator positively dropped, so little was this what they had been expecting.

'How can it have been your own?' Nikolay Parfenovich babbled. 'Why, even at five o'clock that afternoon, by your own admission . . .'

'Hah, to the devil with five o'clock that afternoon and my own admission, that is not important now! That money was my own, my own . . . or rather not my own, but stolen, stolen by me, and it amounted to fifteen hundred, and I had it on me, had it on me all the time . . .'

'But where did you get it?'

'From around my neck, gentlemen, I got it from around my neck, this very neck of mine . . . I had it here, around my neck, sewn up in a rag and hanging from my neck. I had been carrying it there for a long time, a month, to my shame and disgrace!'

'But from whom did you . . . appropriate it?'

'"Steal it", you mean, don't you? Let us call things by their proper names. Yes, I consider that I more or less stole it, or, if you like, did indeed "appropriate" it. Though in my opinion I stole it. And yesterday evening I stole it beyond all doubt.'

'Yesterday evening? But you have just said that it was a month ago that you . . . obtained it!'

'Yes, but not from my father, not from my father, do not worry, I stole it not from my father, but from her. Let me tell you and please do not interrupt. You see, it is painful. Look: a month ago Katerina Ivanovna Verkhovtseva, my former betrothed, summoned me to her house . . . Do you know her?'

'Yes, sir, naturally we do.'

'And I can well understand that you do. She is a most noble soul, the most noble of noble souls, but she has long hated me, oh, long, long . . . and deservedly, deservedly has she hated me!'

'Katerina Ivanovna?' the investigator asked in astonishment. The public procurator also stared horribly.

'Oh, do not take her name in vain! I am a scoundrel for bringing her into this. Yes, I have seen that she hates me . . . I saw it long ago . . . from the very first time, when she came to see me at my lodgings that day . . . But enough, enough, you are not even worthy of knowing that, let us leave that entirely alone . . . And merely note instead that a month ago she summoned me to her house, gave me three thousand to pass on to her sister and another female relative in Moscow (as though she could not have sent it to them herself!), and I . . . this was precisely at that fateful moment of my life when I . . . well, in short, when I had just fallen in love with another, with *her*, my present betrothed, the woman whom you have downstairs in your custody, Grushenka . . . That day I spirited her off here to Mokroye and within the space of two days blew half of that cursed three thousand, keeping the other half for myself. Well, here is the fifteen hundred I kept back, I have been carrying it around on my neck instead of an incense-bag, and yesterday I unsealed the wad and blew it. What you hold in your hands now is the change, Nikolay Parfenovich, the eight hundred roubles' change that is left from the fifteen hundred I had yesterday.'

'Permit me, but how can that be? After all, it was three thousand that you squandered here a month ago, not fifteen hundred — everyone knows that.'

'Who knows it? Who has counted it? Whom have I allowed to count it?'

'But my dear sir why, you yourself told everyone that at that time you spent exactly three thousand.'

'To be sure, I did, I told the whole town and everyone thought that was so, even here, in Mokroye, they thought it was three thousand. The thing is, though, that I blew not three thousand, but only fifteen hundred, and sewed the rest of the money into an incense-bag; that is what happened, gentlemen, and that is where the money I had on me yesterday came from . . .'

'This is almost miraculous . . .' Nikolay Parfenovich babbled.

'Permit me to ask,' the public procurator said at last, 'if you have told anyone else of this circumstance . . . That is to say, that a month ago you retained this three thousand in your keeping?'

'No one.'

'That is strange. Are you quite sure?'

'Absolutely no one. Not a soul.'

'But then why such silence? What has prompted you to make such a secret of this fact? Let me explain myself more precisely: you have, at last, told us your secret, which in your own words is so "disgraceful", though in essence – only relatively speaking, of course, that is to say – that action, namely, the appropriation of three thousand roubles belonging to another person, an appropriation doubtless only temporary – that action was, in my view at any rate, merely one of highly flippant nature, but not so disgraceful, when, moreover, your character is taken into account ... Why, I will even concede that it was a highly dishonourable action, but a dishonourable, not a disgraceful one ... What I am leading up to, really, is that during the course of this month many people had already guessed, without your having to admit it, that it was Miss Verkhovtseva's money you had been spending – I myself have heard this legend ... Mikhail Makarovich, for example, has also heard it. So that, at last, it became almost more than a legend: a rumour that passed about the entire town. What is more, there is evidence that you yourself, if I am not mistaken, admitted the truth to someone, namely that the money belonged to Miss Verkhovtseva ... But what surprises me greatly is that you should until now, until this very moment, that is to say, have been so extraordinarily secretive about this fifteen hundred you say you put aside for yourself, there being combined with your secrecy something that even approaches terror ... It is improbable that a secret of that nature could cause you such torments in its confession ... for you yourself shouted just now that you had rather go into penal servitude than confess ...'

The public procurator fell silent. He was flushed. He had not attempted to conceal his vexation, which amounted almost to malicious hostility, and had delivered himself of all that had amassed within him, not even troubling about beauty of phrase, without coherence, that is, and almost without consistency.

'The disgrace was not in the fifteen hundred, but in the fact that I divided that fifteen hundred from the three thousand,' Mitya articulated firmly.

'But I mean to say,' the public procurator smiled with dry irritation, 'what is so disgraceful in your having used your own discretion and divided half of the three thousand you took dishonestly, or as you will have it, dishonourably? The more important thing is that you appropriated the three thousand, and not how you disposed of it. By the way, in any case, why did you dispose of the money in just that way, by dividing off that half? Why did you do it, for what purpose, can you explain that to us?'

'Ah, gentlemen, in the purpose lies the very pith of the matter!' Mitya exclaimed. 'I divided it off out of villainy, that is to say, out of calculation, for in this instance calculation is equivalent to villainy ... And that villainy continued for an entire month!'

'I do not understand.'

'You surprise me. However, I shall explain further, as it may indeed be difficult for you to understand. Look, follow my thread now: I appropriate three thousand which has been entrusted to my honour, I blow it on a spree until it is all spent, and then on the following morning present myself to her and say: "Katya, I am guilty, I have spent your three thousand" – well, is that a good way to behave? No, it is not – it is dishonourable and cowardly, the action of a wild beast and of a man who is bestially unable to control himself, is it not, is it not? But even so, not the action of a thief? Not the action of an outright thief, not that, do you agree? I squandered the money, but I did not steal it! Now the second, even more favourable instance: follow my thread carefully now, or I may lose it again – my head seems to be spinning – so, the second instance: I spend here only fifteen hundred out of the three, half of it, in other words. The following day I take her that half: "Katya, take from me blackguard and light-minded scoundrel that I am, this half, for I have squandered the other, and may squander this one too, so keep it out of harm's way!" Well, what if that instance were true? You might call me anything you like, a wild beast and scoundrel, but not a thief, most certainly not a thief, for were I a thief I should certainly not have brought back half the change, but would have appropriated it, too. At that point she would see that if I had returned half the money so quickly, I would return the rest, too, the money I had squandered, all my life I would strive for it, work for it, but find it and give it back. In that case I would be a scoundrel, but not a thief, not a thief, whatever else you like, but not a thief!'

'I suppose there is a certain difference,' the public procurator smiled coldly. 'But all the same, it is strange that you should perceive there to be such a fateful difference.'

'Yes, I do see such a fateful difference! Anyone may be a scoundrel, and probably everyone is, but not everyone, only an arch-scoundrel, may be a thief. Well, but I'm out of my depth in these subtleties ... Except that a thief is more vile than a scoundrel, that is my conviction. Listen: say I have carried the money about with me for an entire month, why, tomorrow I may decide to give it back, and then I shall be a scoundrel no more, but I cannot bring myself to take that decision, that is the problem, even though each day I try to do it, even though each day I keep pressing myself: "Go on, give it back, you scoundrel!", and yet a whole month goes by without my doing so! Well, is that a good way to behave, do you suppose, eh?'

'I suppose it is not very good, I understand that perfectly and will not argue with you,' the public procurator answered, reticently. 'But let us not quibble over these subtle points and differences; instead, please be so good as to allow us to return to the matter in hand. And the matter in hand is that you still have not explained to us, though we have questioned you, why in the first place you made that division of that three thousand, that is to say, spent one half of it, but hid away the other? For what precise purpose did you hide it away, what did you intend to use it for? I. insist upon receiving an answer to this question, Dmitry Fyodorovich.'

'Oh, why, of course!' Mitya exclaimed, smiting his brow. 'Forgive me, I have been causing you needless trouble by not explaining the principal point, otherwise you would have grasped it instantly, for it is in that purpose, in that purpose that the disgrace lies! You see that old man, the deceased, kept harassing Agrafena Aleksandrovna, and I was jealous, at the time I thought she was swithering between him and me; each day I would think: what if she suddenly takes a decision, what if she grows tired of tormenting me and suddenly says to me: "It is you I love, not him, take me away to the ends of the earth"? For all I had was two twenty-copeck pieces; how could I take her away, what would I do then – I would be lost. You see, I did not know her then and did not understand her, I thought that money was what she wanted and that she would not forgive me if I turned out to be poor. And so I insidiously counted out half of the three thousand and cold-bloodedly sewed it up with a needle, did it with calculation, before my drunken binge, and then, when I had finished, went to get drunk on the remaining half! No, sir, that is villainy! Have you grasped it now?'

The public procurator burst into loud laughter, as did the investigator.

'In my opinion, by restraining yourself and not blowing the lot you acted with positive good sense and moral propriety,' Nikolay Parfenovich giggled. 'For what was so very special about it all, sir?'

'Why, the fact that I had stolen the money, that is what! Oh my God, you horrify me with your lack of comprehension! Each and every day of the time during which I have carried that fifteen hundred around with me on my breast I have said to myself: "You're a thief, you're a thief!" And that, too, is why I have been behaving with such ferocious violence all month, that is why I picked a fight at the inn, why I gave father such a merciless beating, because I have felt I was a thief! I could not even bring myself, for I dared not, to tell my own brother Alyosha about that fifteen hundred: so deeply did I feel I was a scoundrel and a cheat! Let me tell you, however, that at the same time as I was carrying it around, each day and each hour I have said to myself: "No, Dmitry Fyodorovich, you may not yet be a thief." Why? For the simple reason that tomorrow you may go and return that fifteen hundred to Katya. And only yesterday, on my way from Fenya's kitchen to the home of Perkhotin, did I determine to tear my incense-bag from my neck, whereas before that moment I had not been able to take that step, and as soon as I done it, in that same moment I became a genuine and incontestable thief, a thief and a man of dishonour for the rest of my life. Why? Because together with the incense-bag I had torn away my dream of going to Katya and saying to her: "I am a scoundrel, but not a thief"! Now do you understand it, now do you understand?'

'But why did you determine to do this yesterday evening, in particular?' Nikolay Parfenovich began to interrupt.

'Why? It is ridiculous to ask: because I had sentenced myself to death, at five o'clock in the morning, here at dawn: "After all, it matters not," I thought, "whether I die a scoundrel or a man of noble quality!" But now it turns out that that is wrong, that it does matter! Will you believe me, gentlemen, when I tell you that what tormented me more than anything else during this night that is past was not, was not that I had killed the old manservant and that I faced Siberia, and when? When my love had been crowned with fulfilment and heaven had revealed itself to me again! Oh, it caused me torment, but not so much; not as much as that cursed awareness that I had finally torn that cursed money from my breast and spent it, and was consequently now a genuine thief! Oh, gentlemen, I repeat to you with the blood of my heart: much have I learned in this night! I have learned that not only is it impossible to live as a scoundrel, it is impossible to die a scoundrel, too ... No, gentlemen, one must die honourably! ...'

Mitya was pale. His face had an emaciated and exhausted look, in spite of the fact that he was extremely worked up.

'I begin to understand you, Dmitry Fyodorovich,' the public procurator drawled gently and even with something that resembled compassion.

'But all that is, if you please, in my opinion, merely nerves ... your sickly nerves, that is what I think, sir. And why, for example, in order to deliver yourself from all these torments, which have lasted almost an entire month, did you not go and return that fifteen hundred to the lady who entrusted it to you, and, having attained an understanding with her, why did you not, in view of your position, at the time so dreadful, as you have portrayed it, assay the combination which so naturally presents itself to the mind, that is to say, after making to her a noble confession of your errors, why did you not ask her for the sum you required, and which she, possessing as she does a generous heart, and beholding your distress, would of course have granted you, particularly if it were covered by a document or, let us say, by at least a security of the kind you offered to the merchant Samsonov and to Mrs Khokhlakova? After all, you do still consider that security valid even now, do you not?'

Mitya suddenly flushed red.

'Do you really consider me to that degree a scoundrel? It cannot be that you intend it seriously! ...' he said with indignation, looking the public procurator in the eye and almost unable to believe what he had heard him say.

'I assure you that I do intend it so ... Why do you suppose the contrary?' the public procurator said, astonished in his turn.

'Oh, how vile that would have been! Gentlemen, are you aware that you are tormenting me? With your permission I shall tell you everything, so let it be, I shall now in all my infernality confess to you, but in order to bring you to shame, and to astonish you with the villainy a combination of human feelings may attain. I think you should know that I already possessed that combination, the very one you spoke of just now, public procurator! Yes, gentlemen, I too have had that idea during this cursed month, to the point where I had almost made up my mind to go to Katya, so vile was I! But to go to her, to tell her of my betrayal and, for that same betrayal, for the execution of that betrayal, for the forthcoming expenses necessary for that betrayal, to ask her, Katya, to ask her for money (to ask, do you hear, to ask!) and at once to flee from her with another woman, with her rival, with the one who hated her and had insulted her — forgive me, but I think you must have lost your reason, public procurator!'

'That may or may not be so, but of course in the heat of the moment I did not think ... of this element of female jealousy ... if indeed there really was such jealousy as you assert ... Yes, perhaps there is something of that sort there,' the public procurator smiled, thinly.

'But what a filthy deed that would have been,' Mitya said, ferociously striking his fist on the table, 'it would almost have stunk so badly, that I do not even know! And you know, she might have given me that money, given me it out of the sweetness of revenge, out of her contempt for me, because she is also an infernal soul and a woman of great wrath! Then I would have taken the money, oh, I would have taken it, and then all the rest of my life . . . O God! Forgive me, gentlemen, I shout because I had that idea not long ago at all, only the day before yesterday, when I was wasting my time with Lyagavy, and then yesterday, yes, yesterday, all day yesterday, I remember it, until this thing happened . . .'

'What thing?' Nikolay Parfenovich inserted with curiosity, but Mitya did not hear him.

'I have made you a terrible confession,' he concluded, blackly. 'Please appreciate it, gentlemen. And indeed that is too little, to appreciate it is too little, you must value it, and if you do not, if that too evades your souls, then the plain fact is that you do not respect me, gentlemen, that is what I say to you, and I shall die of shame for having confessed to men such as yourselves! Oh, I shall shoot myself! And indeed, I see, I see already that you do not believe me! What, are you going to enter that in the record, too?' he exclaimed, in fear now.

'And what you said just now,' Nikolay Parfenovich said, looking at him in astonishment, 'that is to say, about your still thinking of going to see Miss Verkhovtseva in order to ask her for that sum right up to the very last moment . . . that, I assure you, is a very important piece of testimony for us, Dmitry Fyodorovich, and in fact it has a bearing on this whole case . . . and it is particularly important for you, particularly important for yourself.'

'In the name of mercy, gentlemen!' Mitya exclaimed, throwing up his hands, 'at least do not add that to your record, have some shame! After all, I have, as it were, torn my soul in half before you, and you have taken advantage of it and are rummaging with your fingers in both halves along the torn place . . . O God!'

He covered his face with his hands in despair.

'Please do not be so anxious, Dmitry Fyodorovich,' the public procurator said in conclusion. 'All that we have taken down just now you will yourself have read back to you later on, and anything you do not agree with we shall change according to your instructions. For the moment, however, I repeat for the third time this one small question: is it really true that you told no one, that is to say absolutely no one at all, of this money you had sewn into an incense-bag? That, I put it to you, is almost impossible to imagine.'

'No one, no one, and I only told you because otherwise you would have understood nothing! Now leave me in peace.'

'As you wish, sir: this matter must be explained, and we have plenty of time ahead of us for that, but meanwhile reflect: we have possibly dozens of testified statements that you yourself spread it around and even shouted to everyone that you had spent three thousand, three, and not fifteen hundred, and even now, following the appearance of the money you had last night, you have succeeded in telling many people that it was three thousand you brought with you here . . .'

'Not dozens, but hundreds of testified statements do you possess, two hundred statements, two hundred people have heard it, a thousand have heard it! . . .' Mitya exclaimed.

'Well, sir, you see that everyone, everyone testifies to it. So would you not agree that the word *everyone* carries some weight?'

'No I would not, for I was lying, and everyone else began lying after me.'

'But why did you need so badly to "lie", as you express it?'

'The devil knows. Out of a wish to brag, perhaps . . . yes . . . that I had spent so much money just like that . . . perhaps in order to forget about that cursed money . . . yes, that was the reason why . . . the devil . . . How many times are you going to ask that question? Well, so I told a lie, and of course once I had told it I didn't feel like correcting it. What makes a man lie on occasion, anyway?'

'It is very hard to be sure, Dmitry Fyodorovich, what makes a man lie,' the public procurator said, imposingly. 'However, tell me: was it large, this incense-bag, as you call it, which you had around your neck?'

'No, it wasn't large.'

'Of what size then, approximately?'

'The size of a hundred-rouble banknote folded in half – that size.'

'I think you had better show us the remnants of it. After all, you must have them somewhere.'

'Hah, the devil . . . what stupid things . . . I don't know where they are.'

'Permit me, however, to inquire: where were you when you removed it from your neck? After all, as you yourself have testified, you did not visit your lodgings.'

'When I had left Fenya and was on my way to Perkhotin, I tore it from my neck and took the money out of it.'

'In the dark?'

'I'd hardly need a candle, would I? I did it with my finger in a single flash.'

'Without using scissors, out in the street?'

'I think it was on the market-square; what would I have wanted scissors for? It was an ancient old rag, it fell apart instantly.'

'Where did you put it afterwards?'

'I threw it away right there.'

'Where, precisely?'

'On the market-square, somewhere on the square! The devil knows where. Why do you need to know that?'

'It is extremely important, Dmitry Fyodorovich: it constitutes material evidence in your favour, how can you not see that? Who helped you to do the sewing a month ago?'

'No one helped me, I did it myself.'

'Do you know how to sew?'

'A soldier must be able to sew, but in any case no particular skill was required.'

'And where did you obtain the material, the rag, that is to say, in which you sewed up the money?'

'Are you sure you're not laughing at me?'

'In no way, and in any case we have no time at all for laughter, Dmitry Fyodorovich.'

'I can't remember where I got the rag from, I just found it somewhere.'

'I would not have thought it the sort of thing one would forget.'

'Well, I swear to God, I can't remember, perhaps I tore it off some of my linen.'

'That is very interesting: perhaps tomorrow in your lodgings we might succeed in tracking down the shirt, or whatever it was, from which you tore a piece. What was it made of, the rag: of coarse cloth, of linen?'

'The devil knows what it was made of. Wait . . . I don't think I tore it off anything. It was made of calico . . . I believe I sewed the money into one of my landlady's bonnets.'

'One of your landlady's bonnets?'

'Yes, I lifted it from her.'

'Lifted it?'

'You see, I remember I once took one of her bonnets, possibly to wipe my pen on. I'd taken it without mentioning it to her, because it was a worthless rag, the remnants of it were lying about in my room, and here was this fifteen hundred, I took them and sewed it up in them . . . I'm sure I did. It was a wretched old calico thing, had been washed a thousand times . . .'

'And you remember that definitely?'

'I don't know about definitely. I think it was a bonnet. Well, but a fig for it!'

'In that case your landlady might at least recall that this item had gone missing?'

'Of course she wouldn't, she never noticed it was gone. It was an old rag, I tell you, an old rag, not worth a groat.'

'And where did you get the needle and thread?'

'That does it. I'm not going on with this. Enough!' Mitya said, finally losing his temper.

'And again, it is strange that you have so completely forgotten exactly where on the square you threw away this . . . incense-bag.'

'Well, why don't you have the square swept clean tomorrow, perhaps you will find it,' Mitya said with a thin smile. 'Enough, gentlemen, enough,' he said, making up his mind in a voice of exhaustion. 'I see clearly: you have not believed me! Not one word of it, and not one groat! The guilt is mine, not yours, I should never have stuck my neck out. Why, why did I defile myself by confessing my secret to you? For you think it is funny, I can see it by your eyes. It is you who have led me to this, public procurator! Sing a hymn to yourself, if you can . . . Oh, a curse on you, torturers!'

He inclined his head and covered his face with his hands. The public procurator and the investigator said nothing. After a moment he raised his head and stared at them as though without seeing. His face expressed an already accomplished and now irrevocable despair, and he had slowly fallen silent, now sitting there as though he were not even conscious. Meanwhile the business had to be completed: it was now necessary to proceed to the interrogation of the witnesses without delay. By now it was about eight o'clock in the morning. The candles had long ago been extinguished. Mikhail Makarovich and Kalganov, who all the time during the interrogation had been going in and out of the room, now both went out again. The public procurator and the investigator also looked extremely tired. The morning that had dawned was a wet one, the heavens were entirely covered in clouds and the rain was pouring down in bucketfuls. Mitya stared out of the window without thought.

'Is it all right if I look out of the window?' he suddenly asked Nikolay Parfenovich.

'Oh, as much as you wish,' the latter replied.

Mitya got up and went over to one of the windows. The rain was fairly lashing against the small, greenish panes. Directly below the window a muddy road was visible, and there, further away, in the rainy gloom, some rows of black, impoverished and unsightly *izbas*, which the rain seemed to have rendered even blacker and more impoverished. Mitya remembered 'golden-curled Phoebus' and how he had intended to shoot himself at his first ray. 'Probably a morning like this would have been better,' he smiled drily to himself, and then suddenly, swinging his arm down, turned to the 'torturers':

'Gentlemen!' he exclaimed, 'why, I see I am lost. But she? Tell me about her, I implore you, is she really to perish with me? After all, she is innocent, last night she shouted when she was not in her right mind that she was "guilty of everything". She is guilty of nothing, nothing! All night I have grieved as I sat here with you ... Can you not, may you not tell me: what will you do with her now?'

'You may decidedly set your mind to rest on that account, Dmitry Fyodorovich,' the public procurator replied at once, and with evident haste. 'We have for the moment no significant motives for troubling the lady in whom you are so interested. As the case proceeds, so, I hope, the same will prove to be true ... On the contrary, we for our part shall in this regard do all that is possible. Please be completely reassured.'

'Gentlemen, I thank you, why, I knew all along that you were men of honour and fairness, in spite of everything. You have lifted a burden from my soul ... Well, what are we going to do now? I am ready.'

'Well, sir, we must make haste. We must proceed to the interrogation of the witnesses without delay. It is essential that it all take place in your presence, and so ...'

'But will you not have a glass of tea first?' Nikolay Parfenovich interrupted. 'Why, I believe it has now been served!'

It was decided that if tea was ready downstairs (in view of the fact that Mikhail Makarovich had certainly gone away to 'have a bit of tea'), they should all have a glass and then 'continue and continue', proper tea, with snacks, to be deferred until a more leisurely hour. Tea was indeed discovered downstairs, and was swiftly delivered aloft. Mitya at first refused the glass which Nikolay Parfenovich graciously offered him, but then asked for one himself and drank it greedily. He really did have about him a look of exhaustion that was even astonishing. With his robust energies, one might have supposed that a single night of drinking would not have had much effect, even when combined with experiences of a most intense nature. Yet he himself felt that he could hardly sit upright, and from time to time all the objects in the room seemed to swerve and spin before his eyes. 'If this goes on much longer I shall probably start raving,' he thought to himself.

8

The Testimony of the Witnesses. The Bairn

THE interrogation of the witnesses commenced. We shall not, however, continue our narrative in the kind of detail we have hitherto employed. And so we shall leave out the manner in which Nikolay Parfenovich made it imposingly clear to all the summoned witnesses that they must testify according to both conscience and the truth and that they would later have to repeat their depositions upon oath. How, at last, it was required of the witnesses that they each sign the protocol of their depositions, etcetera, etcetera. Let us merely observe that the principal point to which the entire attention of the interrogatees was addressed was that very same question of the three thousand, that is to say, whether the sum Dmitry Fyodorovich had had upon him during his first spree at Mokroye a month back was three thousand or only fifteen hundred, the same thing being asked concerning his second spree, of the night before. Alas, all of the testimony, right to the last, was against Mitya, and not one piece of it spoke in his favour, while some of it even introduced new, almost stupefying evidence in contradiction of his statements. The first person to be questioned was Trifon Borisych. He appeared before the interrogators without the slightest trepidation, and wore instead an air of stern and severe indignation towards the accused, thereby undoubtedly imparting to himself an aspect of exceptional truthfulness and personal dignity. He spoke little, with reticence, waited for each question, gave replies that were precise and considered. Firmly and without a moment's hesitation, he asserted that a month ago there could have been no question of less than three thousand having been spent, that all the muzhiks could testify that they had heard about the three thousand from 'Mitry Fyodorovich' himself: 'To the gypsies alone he threw an awful lot of money. I should think he spent more than a thousand on them alone.'

'Not even five hundred, perhaps, did I give them,' was Mitya's gloomy comment to this, 'only I didn't count it, I was drunk, what a pity . . .'

This time Mitya sat sideways, his back to the curtain, listening in gloom, with an air of sadness and tiredness, as though to say: 'Hah, you may testify whatever you like, now it is all the same!'

'More than a thousand was spent on them, Mitry Fyodorovich,' Trifon Borisovich contradicted, firmly. 'You threw it away for nothing, and they picked it up. After all, these folk are thieves and swindlers, horse-stealers they are, they've been chased out of the village, otherwise they themselves would doubtless have given evidence of how much they made off you. I myself saw the amount you were holding then − I didn't manage to count it, you wouldn't let me that's true − but even by just looking I could see there was far more than fifteen hundred . . . Get away with your fifteen hundred! We've seen money before, and we can judge . . .'

With regard to the sum spent the night before Trifon Borisovich bluntly testified that Dmitry Fyodorovich had told him, immediately upon descending from his cart, that he had brought three thousand.

'Come now, Trifon Borisych, is that really so?' Mitya began to protest. 'Did I really tell you so categorically that I had brought three thousand with me?'

'You did, Mitry Fyodorovich. You said it when Andrey was there. Look, he's still here, Andrey, he hasn't gone yet, why don't you call him in? And in there, in the big room, when you were standing the wenches all those sweets and champagne, you shouted straight out that this would be the sixth thousand you'd left here − added to the previous ones, that is, that was the sense of it. Stepan and Semyon heard it, and Pyotr Fomich Kalganov was standing beside you at the time, perhaps he remembers, too . . .'

The testimony concerning a sixth thousand was received by the questioners with extraordinary interest. This new version appealed to them: three and three made six, so that meant there must have been three thousand on the first occasion, and three thousand now, making six thousand in all, it was clear now.

They questioned all the muzhiks Trifon Borisovich had referred to, Stepan and Semyon, the *yamshchik* Andrey and Pyotr Fomich Kalganov. Without a flicker of hesitation the muzhiks and the *yamshchik* confirmed Trifon Borisych's testimony. What was more, a particular record had been made, from the words of Andrey, concerning the latter's conversation with Mitya on the way, and Mitya's having supposedly asked 'whether he would end up in heaven or in hell', and 'whether he would be pardoned in the next world or not'. Ippolit Kirillovich, the 'psychologist', listened to all this with a thin smile and finally recommended that this testimony concerning where Dmitry Fyodorovich would end up also 'be appended to the case'.

The witness Kalganov entered reluctantly, in fretful gloom, and spoke to Nikolay Parfenovich and the public procurator as if he were seeing them for the first time in his life, though he had long been a daily acquaintance of theirs. He began by saying that he knew 'nothing of all this', 'nor do I wish to'. It turned out, however, that of the sixth thousand he too had heard, and he admitted that he had been standing nearby at the time. In his view, the sum of money Mitya had been holding was 'impossible to calculate'. With regard to the question of whether the Poles had cheated at cards, he testified in the affirmative. He also explained, to repeated inquiries, that after the Poles had been thrown out things had indeed started to go better for Mitya with Agrafena Aleksandrovna, and that she herself had said she loved him. Of Agrafena Aleksandrovna he spoke with reticence and veneration, as though she were a lady of the very best society, and never even once did he even permit himself to call her 'Grushenka'. In spite of the young man's evident revulsion at testifying, Ippolit Kirillovich spent a long time questioning him and learned from him all the details of what had constituted, as it were, Mitya's 'romance' during that night. Never once did Mitya stop Kalganov. At last the youth was dismissed, and he left in unconcealed indignation.

The Poles, too, were interrogated. Though they had lain down on the bed in their little room, they had not slept all night, and with the arrival of the authorities they had quickly dressed and tidied themselves, aware that they would certainly be sent for. They made their appearance with dignity, though not without a certain trepidation. The principal, that is to say the little *pan*, turned out to be a retired civil servant of the twelfth grade* who had worked in Siberia as a state veterinary surgeon, and his surname was Musialowicz. As for Pan Wróblewski, he turned out to be a privately practising *dentiste*, in Russian a plain 'tooth-doctor'. As soon as they entered the room they both at once, in spite of the fact that it was Nikolay Parfenovich who was asking the questions, began to direct their replies towards Mikhail Makarovich, who was standing at one side, in their ignorance assuming him to be the chief in rank and the person in authority here, calling him practically with every word they uttered: *'panie* Colonel'. And only after several slaps in the face and an admonition from Mikhail Makarovich himself did they realize that they must address their replies solely to Nikolay Parfenovich. It turned out that they were able to speak Russian even very very correctly, apart from the pronunciation of certain words. Of his relations with Grushenka, former and present, Pan Musialowicz began to speak with passion and with pride, the result being that Mitya instantly flew into a rage and shouted that he would not permit 'a scoundrel' to speak thus in his presence. Pan Musialowicz at once pricked up his ears at the word 'scoundrel' and requested that it be entered in the protocol. Mitya began to seethe with fury.

'Yes, a scoundrel, a scoundrel! You may enter that, and you may also enter that in spite of the protocol I none the less shouted that he was a scoundrel!'

Although Nikolay Parfenovich did in fact enter this in the protocol, he displayed as he did so on this unpleasant occasion a most praiseworthy efficiency and organizing skill: after delivering a severe reprimand to Mitya he at once cut short all further inquiries concerning the *roman*-esque side of the case and swiftly passed to the fundamentals. Among the fundamentals there manifested itself a certain deposition of the *panowie* that aroused an extraordinary interest on the part of the investigators: this was none other than the assertion that Mitya had, in that very room, attempted to bribe Pan Musialowicz and had offered him three thousand smart-money, the terms being seven hundred roubles in hand, and the remaining 2,300 'tomorrow morning in town', the verbal bribe being accompanied by a sworn declaration of honour to the effect that here in Mokroye he had not so much money at present, the bulk of it being in the town. Mitya rashly began to protest that he had never said for certain that he would give them the money in the town, but Pan Wróblewski confirmed the testimony, and Mitya himself, having thought for a moment, frowningly agreed that it was as the *panowie* stated, that he had been worked up at the time and might therefore indeed have said such a thing. The public procurator fairly sank his teeth into the deposition: it was becoming clear to the investigation (and was plainly deduced later on), that a half or a part of the three thousand which Mitya had got his hands on really could have been hidden away in the town somewhere, and possibly even somewhere here in Mokroye, this explaining the circumstance, so ticklish for the investigation, that Mitya had only eight hundred roubles on his person — a circumstance which had until now, though the only one of its kind and a rather insignificant one at that, served as a form of testimony in Mitya's favour. But now even this unique piece of testimony in his favour had been destroyed. To the public procurator's question as to where he could have obtained the remaining 2,300 to give to the *pan* on the morrow if, as he himself asserted, he had had only fifteen hundred in his room, and had yet given the *pan* his word of honour, Mitya firmly replied that he had on the morrow intended to offer the 'filthy Pope' not money, but a formal deed of his rights to the estate at Chermashnya, the same rights he had offered to Samsonov and Mrs Khokhlakova. The public procurator even smiled at 'the innocence of the gambit'.

'And do you suppose that he would have agreed to take these "rights" instead of 2,300 roubles in cash?'

'Of course he would,' Mitya snapped hotly. 'For pity's sake, that way he could have snaffled not only two, but four, or even six thousand! He'd at once have got together all his dirty advocates and Poles and Yids, and never mind three thousand — it would have been the whole of Chermashnya they'd have gotten out of the lawsuit.'

Pan Musialowicz's deposition was of course entered into the protocol in the fullest detail. With that, the *panowie* were dismissed. The fact of their having cheated at cards had hardly been mentioned; Nikolay Parfenovich was far too grateful to them to inconvenience them with such trivial matters, all the more so because all that had been a frivolous quarrel while they had been drunk at cards, and nothing more. As though there had not been enough drunken extravagance and outrageous behaviour in the course of that night . . . The result was that the money, the two hundred roubles, remained in the *panowie's* pockets.

Old Maksimov was the next witness to be summoned. He entered timidly and made his approach with little steps, looking unkempt and very melancholy. All this time he had been huddled away next to Grushenka, sitting in silence with her and 'every so often starting to whimper over her, wiping his eyes with his blue checked handkerchief', as Mikhail Makarovich later described it. In consequence of this she had herself calmed and comforted him. The little old fellow at once and in tears confessed that he was guilty, that he had borrowed 'ten roubles from Dmitry Fyodorovich, sir, because of my poverty, sir', and that he was ready to give it back . . . In response to a direct inquiry from Nikolay Parfenovich as to whether he noticed how much money Dmitry Fyodorovich had been holding as, having being closer to him than anyone else he could have actually seen the money in his hands when he had received the loan, Maksimov replied in the most decisive manner that there had been 'twenty thousand in cash, sir.'

'And had you ever seen twenty thousand in cash before?' Nikolay Parfenovich inquired with a smile.

'Oh yes of course, sir, I had, sir, only it wasn't twenty, sir, but seven, sir, when my lady spouse mortgaged my little estate. She only let me look at it from afar, boasted of it to me. It was a very large wad, sir, and all the notes in it were rainbows. Dmitry Fyodorovich's were all rainbows, too . . .'

He was soon dismissed. At last it was Grushenka's turn. The investigators were plainly concerned about the effect her appearance might have upon Dmitry Fyodorovich, and Nikolay Parfenovich even muttered a few words of admonition to him, but Mitya, in reply to him, silently inclined his head, thereby assuring him that there would 'be no impropriety'. Grushenka was ushered in by Mikhail Makarovich himself. She came into the room with a set, severe look on her features and an air that was almost one of calm, and quietly sat down on the chair that was indicated to her, facing Nikolay Parfenovich. She was very pale, seemed to be feeling cold, and had wrapped herself tightly in her magnificent black shawl. Indeed, she had begun to suffer from a slight, feverish ague – the onset of a long illness, which she subsequently endured after that night. Her severe mien, her direct and serious gaze and her calm manner produced a very favourable impression on everyone. Nikolay Parfenovich was at once even somewhat 'taken'. He himself confessed, when relating the matter somewhere subsequently, that only since that occasion had he perceived how 'handsome' this woman was, whereas previously though he had seen her now and again, he had always considered her some sort of 'local hetaera'. 'She has the manners of the very highest society,' he said enthusiastically, without thinking, at some ladies' circle or other. His words were, however, greeted with the most consummate indignation and for this he was at once dubbed a 'rascal', with which he was well pleased. As she had entered the room, Grushenka had seemed to cast a fleeting glance at Mitya, who in his turn had stared at her in anxiety, but her aspect at that moment had calmed him, too. After the first essential questions and admonitions, Nikolay Parfenovich, though somewhat stumblingly, yet managing to retain a most courteous demeanour, asked her: 'What is your relation to the retired lieutenant Dmitry Fyodorovich Karamazov?' To which Grushenka quietly and firmly declared:

'He is my friend, and it has been as a friend that I have received him during the past month.'

In response to further inquisitive questioning she declared with complete lack of equivocation that although 'at times' she had found him appealing, she did not love him, but had led him on 'out of my loathsome malice', just as she had led on that 'little old man', had seen that Mitya was very jealous of Fyodor Pavlovich and of all other men in her regard, but had merely found that amusing. She had never had any intention of going to live with Fyodor Pavlovich, but had merely been making fun of him. 'I was not interested in either of them, for during the whole of that month I was waiting for another man, one who was guilty before me . . . Only the way I see it,' she concluded, 'is that you have no business to be so inquisitive about that, and I have no need to reply to you, because it is my private affair.'

Thus instantly did Nikolay Parfenovich comply: on the '*roman*-esque' points he again ceased to insist, but passed straight to matters more earnest, that is to say, to the same, most crucial question of the three thousand. Grushenka confirmed that in Mokroye, a month ago, there really had been spent three thousand roubles, and though she herself had not counted the money, she had heard from Dmitry Fyodorovich himself that it had amounted to three thousand roubles.

'Did he tell you this in private or in someone else's presence, or did you only hear him talking of it to others while you were there?' the public procurator at once inquired.

To which Grushenka declared that she had both heard him say it in company and in private with her.

'Did you hear it from him in private on one occasion or several times?' the public procurator inquired again, and learned that Grushenka had heard it several times.

Ippolit Kirillych was well pleased with this deposition. From further questioning it also emerged that Grushenka knew the source of money and that Dmitry Fyodorovich had acquired it from Katerina Ivanovna.

'And did you not hear on even one occasion that the money that was squandered a month ago amounted not to three thousand, but to a lesser sum, and that Dmitry Fyodorovich had kept back an entire half of it for himself?'

'No, never did I hear that,' Grushenka testified.

It even further emerged that Mitya, on the contrary, often told her all that month that he had not a copeck of cash. 'He was always waiting to get some from his parent,' Grushenka said in conclusion.

'And did he ever in your presence . . . either in passing, or when in a temper,' Nikolay Parfenovich said suddenly, seizing at this, 'say that he intended to make an attempt on his father's life?'

'Oh yes, he did!' Grushenka said, taking a breath.

'On one occasion or on several?'

'He mentioned it several times, always when he was angry.'

'And did you believe he would carry out this threat?'

'No, I never did!' she replied firmly. 'I relied on his sense of noble honour.'

'Gentlemen, permit me,' Mitya exclaimed suddenly. 'Permit me to say just one word in the presence of you, Agrafena Aleksandrovna.'

'The permission is granted,' Nikolay Parfenovich said.

'Agrafena Aleksandrovna,' Mitya said, getting up from his chair, 'you must believe God and me: of the blood of my father, who last night was murdered, I am innocent!'

Uttering this, Mitya sat down on his chair again. Grushenka rose and devoutly crossed himself before the icon.

'Glory to Thee, O Lord!' she said in a passionate, heartfelt voice, and without yet sitting back in her place and addressing herself to Nikolay Parfenovich, added: 'Please believe what he said just now! I know him: he will go and say all kinds of things without thinking, either out of merriment or out of stubbornness, but if it's against his conscience he will never practise deceit. He will tell the truth straight out, please believe it!'

'Thank you Agrafena Aleksandrovna, you have lent succour to my soul!' Mitya responded in a trembling voice.

To questions concerning the money of the night before she declared that she did not know how much there had been, but had heard him many times tell people the night before that he had brought three thousand with him. And as for where he had got the money, he had told her alone that he had 'stolen' it from Katerina Ivanovna, and that she had replied to him that he had not stolen it and that he must give the money back on the morrow. To the public procurator's insistent question as to which money it was he said he had stolen from Katerina Ivanovna – the money he had last night or the three thousand which had been spent here a month ago – she declared that he had spoken of the money he had spent a month ago, and that that was what she had understood him to mean.

Grushenka was, at last, dismissed, and Nikolay Parfenovich impetuously declared to her that she might return to the town forthwith and that if there was anything he could do to facilitate this, with regard to horses, for example, or should she wish an escort, then he . . . for his part . . .

'I thank you humbly,' Grushenka said, bowing to him, 'but I shall travel with that little old man, the landowner, I shall take him back to town. For the present, however, I shall wait downstairs, if you will permit, to see what you decide to do with Dmitry Fyodorovich.'

She went out. Mitya was calm and even looked as though his spirits had been quite restored, but only for a moment. A strange, physical exhaustion was gaining mastery over him, growing as the time went by. His eyes were closing with weariness. At last the interrogation of the witnesses was over. They proceeded to the final drafting of the protocol. Mitya stood up, left his chair and went into the corner, over by the curtain, lay down on a large, rug-covered trunk that belonged to the landlord and in an instant fell asleep. He dreamed a strange dream, one quite inappropriate to the place and to the time. There he was, travelling in the steppes somewhere, in the place where he had served in the army long ago, in former days, and he was sitting in a cart, drawn by a pair of horses, which a muzhik was driving into the sleet. Only Mitya was cold, it was the beginning of November, and the snow was falling in large wet flakes and falling to earth, instantly melting. And the muzhik was driving him cheerfully, brandishing his whip in marvellous style, his beard long and chestnut-coloured, not really an old man, but perhaps about fifty, and wearing a grey muzhik *zipun*.* And there not far away was a peasant village, one could see the *izbas*, black as black, and half of them had burned to the ground, only charred timbers stuck up here and there. And at the entry barrier there were peasant women standing along the road, many of them, an entire row, all of them thin and emaciated, with faces that looked somehow brownish. There, in particular, at the end of the row was one, a tall and bony woman who looked about forty, but might easily be no more than twenty, with a long, thin face and a baby crying in her arms, for her breasts must have withered and there was not a drop of milk in them. And the baby cried and cried, stretching out its bare little arms with pathetic, small fists that were a kind of bluish colour all over from the cold.

'Why are they crying? What are they crying for?' Mitya asked as they flew past the women in dashing style.

'It's a bairn,' the *yamshchik* answered him, 'it's a bairn crying.' And Mitya was struck by the fact that the man had said it in his own, muzhik way: 'a bairn', not 'a baby'. And he liked it that the muzhik had said 'bairn': there seemed more pity in it.

'But why is it crying?' Mitya kept pressing, like one inane. 'Why are its little arms bare, why is it not covered up?'

'Why, the bairn is chilled to the bone, it's little clothes have frozen through, and don't keep it warm.'

'But why has it happened? Why?' Mitya kept asking inanely.

'Why, they're poor, burned out of everything, they've no bread, they're begging for their burned-down site.'

'No, no,' Mitya said, still appearing not to understand. 'What I want you to tell me is: why are those homeless mothers standing there, why is everyone poor, why is the bairn wretched, why is the steppe barren, why do they not embrace one another, kiss one another, why do they not sing songs of joy, why are they blackened so by black misfortune, why is the bairn not fed?'

And he felt to himself that although he was asking these questions wildly, without rhyme or reason, he could not prevent himself asking them in just that form, and that that was the form in which they must be asked. And he also felt rising within his heart a tender piety he had never experienced before, felt that he wanted to weep, that he wanted to do something for them all, so that the bairn should not cry any more, so that the bairn's withered, poverty-blackened mother should not weep, so that no one should have any tears at all from that moment on, and to do this immediately, without delay and without regard to any obstacle, with all the impetuosity of the Karamazovs.

'And I shall come with you, I shall never leave you now, I shall walk with you all my life,' the dear, heartfelt words of Grushenka sounded beside him.

'What is it you say? Walk where?' he exclaimed, opening his eyes and sitting up on his trunk, every bit like someone who has recovered from a swoon, and smiling radiantly. Over him stood Nikolay Parfenovich, inviting him to attend the reading of the protocol, and sign it. Mitya realized that he had slept for an hour or more, but he paid no attention to Nikolay Parfenovich. He was suddenly struck by the fact that beneath his head there was a pillow that had not been there when he had subsided in exhaustion upon the trunk.

'Who put a pillow under my head? Who was that kind person?' he exclaimed with a kind of ecstatic, grateful emotion and in a voice that almost wept, as though God only knew what boon had been accorded him. The kind person remained unknown even later, though it was possibly one of the muzhiks, or possibly Nikolay Parfenovich's little scribe who had found him a pillow out of compassion, but Mitya's entire soul was as if shaken by sobs and tears. He approached the table and declared that he would sign whatever was required.

'I had a good dream, gentlemen,' he declared somehow strangely, with a face somehow new, as though illumined by joy.

9

Mitya is Taken Away

WHEN the protocol had been signed, Nikolay Parfenovich turned solemnly to the accused and read him a 'Decision', which stated that on such-and-such a day of such-and-such a year, in such-and-such a place, the state investigator of such-and-such a circuit court, having interrogated such-and-such a person (Mitya, in other words) as being charged with such-and-such and such-and-such an offence (all the charges were carefully listed), and taking account of the fact that the accused, admitting no guilt in respect of the crimes that were imputed to him, had offered nothing in his own acquittal, while both witnesses (all were named) and material circumstances (so were these) fully indicated him to be the guilty party, had, being guided by such-and-such and such-and-such articles of the Penal Code, etcetera, decided: that in order to deny such-and-such a person (Mitya) access to the means whereby he might seek to evade investigation and trial, he be confined in such-and-such a prison fortress, the accused to be notified thereof and a copy of this decision to be delivered to the deputy public procurator, etcetera, etcetera. In a word, Mitya was informed that he was from this moment on a prisoner, and that he would at once be taken to the town, where he would be confined in a certain very unpleasant place. Mitya, having listened to it all attentively, simply shrugged his shoulders.

'Very well, gentlemen, I do not blame you, I am ready ... I realize that there is no other course open to you.'

Nikolay Parfenovich gently explained to him that he would at once be taken to the prison by the district superintendent, Mavriky Mavrikiyevich, who just so happened now to be present ...

'Wait,' Mitya said, interrupting suddenly, and then in an apparent surge of unmasterable emotion pronounced, addressing all in the room: 'Gentlemen, we are all of us cruel, we are all of us monsters of cruelty, we all of us drive men, mothers and babes at the breast to tears, but of us all – so let it be decided now – of us all I am the most villainous reptile! So be it! Each day of my life, beating my breast, I have promised to mend my ways and each day of it I have committed the same loathsome deeds. I understand now that what a man such as I requires is a blow, a blow of fate, that will seize him as in a lasso and bind him by external force. Never, never would I have picked myself up of my own accord! But the thunder has spoken.* I accept the torment of the charge and of my disgrace before the nation, I wish to suffer and to purify myself through suffering! For perhaps I may purify myself, gentlemen, how would that be – eh? But listen, for the last time: I am innocent of my father's blood! I accept punishment not for having killed my father, but for having wanted to kill him and for the possible likelihood that I would actually have done so ... All the same, however, I intend to fight you, and I announce that to you now. I shall fight you to the bitter end, and then may God decide! Farewell, gentlemen, please do not take amiss my having shouted at you during the interrogation, oh, I was then as yet so stupid . . . In a moment I shall be a prisoner, and now, for the last time, Dmitry Fyodorovich, as a man still free, extends to you his hand. In saying farewell to you, I say farewell to men! . . .'

His voice had begun to tremble and he actually did begin to extend his hand, but Nikolay Parfenovich, who was nearest to him, suddenly managed, with a kind of almost convulsive gesture, to hide his hands behind his back. Mitya noticed this in a flash, and started. He at once lowered his extended hand.

'The investigation is not yet concluded,' Nikolay Parfenovich began to babble, somewhat embarrassed. 'We shall continue in the town, and I, of course, for my part, am ready to wish you every success . . . in your acquittal . . . I personally, Dmitry Fyodorovich, have always considered you a man, as it were, more unfortunate than guilty . . . We all of us here, if I may be so bold as to speak in the name of those present, we all of us are ready to acknowledge you as a young man of fundamentally noble character, but one, alas, carried away by certain passions to a degree somewhat excessive . . .'

The small figure of Nikolay Parfenovich expressed towards the end of his discourse a most complete and utter stateliness of manner. Through Mitya's brain suddenly flickered the notion that in a moment this 'boy' would take him by the arm, lead him into a corner and there resume with him their recent conversation about 'girls'. But many are the quite irrelevant and inapposite thoughts which on occasion flicker even through the brain of a criminal being led to his death upon the scaffold.

'Gentlemen, you are kind, you are humane – may I see her, say farewell to her for the last time?'

'Without hesitation, but in the interests of . . . in short, you must now do so in the presence . . .'

'But please, be present! . . .'

Grushenka was led in, but the farewell was a short one, of few words, and Nikolay Parfenovich thought it unsatisfactory. Grushenka made a deep bow to Mitya.

'I told you that I am yours, and I shall be yours, I shall go with you for ever, wherever you are sent. Farewell, man who has guiltlessly brought ruin on himself!'

Her lips trembled and the tears flowed from her eyes.

'Forgive me, Grusha, for my love, for having brought ruin on you also with my love!'

Mitya had intended to say something more, but suddenly he interrupted his own words, and went out. Around him people at once materialized, who did not take their eyes from him. At the foot of the stairs, outside the porch to which he had rolled up with such thunder on Andrey's *troika*, stood two carts all ready to go. Mavriky Mavrikiyevich, a stocky, thickset man with a fat and flabby face, was irritated about something, some confusion that had suddenly arisen, had lost his temper and was shouting. In tones that were really excessively stern he told Mitya to get into one of the carts. 'Before, when I stood him drinks at the inn, there was quite a different expression on the man's face,' Mitya thought, as he climbed in. From the porch Trifon Borisovich, too, came down. People were crowding by the gate, muzhiks, peasant wives, *yamshchiks*, and all were staring at Mitya.

'Farewell, God's people!' Mitya shouted to them suddenly from the cart.

'Forgive us, too,'* two or three voices sounded.

'Farewell to you too, Trifon Borisych!'

But Trifon Borisych did not even turn round, perhaps because he was simply too busy. He was also shouting and fussing over something. It turned out that in the second cart, in which two village policemen were to accompany Mavriky Mavrikiyevich, not all was yet in running order. The little muzhik who had been detailed to drive the second *troika* was pulling on his *zipun* and violently arguing that the driver should not be he, but Akim. But Akim was not to be found; people ran off to look for him; the little muzhik insisted and implored them to wait.

'You know, Mavriky Mavrikiyevich, this common folk of ours is quite without shame!' Trifon Borisych exclaimed. Turning to the little muzhik he said: 'The day before yesterday Akim gave you twenty-five copecks, you drank it, and now you're shouting.' And to Mavriky Mavrikiyevich: 'I'm really surprised at your kindness to our scoundrelly common folk, sir, let me tell you that!'

'But why do you need a second *troika*?' Mitya began to intervene. 'Let us travel in one, Mavriky Mavrikiyevich — after all, I shall not run riot, I shall not try to escape from thee, so why is a convoy needed?'

'Sir, I must kindly ask you to learn to address me properly, if you do not know yet: I am not "thou" to you, kindly do not address me as "thou", sir, and please save your advice for another occasion . . .' Mavriky Mavrikiyevich suddenly snapped ferociously at Mitya, as though he were glad of this opportunity to vent his spite.

Mitya fell silent. He had flushed red all over. A split-second later he suddenly began to feel very cold. The rain had stopped, but the turbid sky was completely overcast with cloud, and a biting wind was blowing straight in his face. 'What is wrong with me, the ague?' thought Mitya, shrugging his shoulders convulsively. At last Mavriky Mavrikiyevich, too, climbed into the wagon, settled himself down heavily and broadly and, as though he had not noticed, squeezed Mitya tightly against the edge. To be sure, he was in a bad mood, and found the task with which he had been encharged thoroughly unappealing.

'Farewell, Trifon Borisych!' Mitya shouted again, this time with a sense that it was not from good-nature that he had shouted, but from malice, that he had shouted against his will. But Trifon Borisych stood proudly, both hands clasped behind his back and, fixing his eyes on Mitya, stared sternly and angrily at him, uttering not a word in reply.

'Farewell, Dmitry Fyodorovich, farewell!' the voice of Kalganov, who had suddenly appeared from somewhere, rang out. Running up to the wagon, he extended his hand to Mitya. He was wearing no cap. Mitya managed to seize his hand and shake it.

'Farewell, dear man, I shall not forget your generosity!' he exclaimed hotly. But the wagon had started to move, and their hands were parted asunder. The wagon bell began to ring – Mitya was taken away.

And Kalganov ran off into the passage, sat down in a corner, bent his head down, covered his face with his hands and wept – wept, as though he were still a small boy and not a young man of twenty. Oh, he believed almost completely in Mitya's guilt! 'What kind of people are these, what kind of people can there be after this?' he sobbed incoherently in bitter despondency, despair almost. He did not even want to live in the world at that moment. 'Is it worth it? Is it worth it?' sobbed the grieved youth.

PART FOUR

BOOK X
THE BOYS

I

Kolya Krasotkin

IT is early November. We have a frost of about eleven degrees, and it is accompanied by black ice. In the course of the night a small quantity of dry snow has fallen on the frozen earth, and a 'dry and whetted'* wind is lifting it and sweeping it about the dreary streets of our little town, and especially about the market-square. The morning is overcast, but it has stopped snowing. Not far from the square, in the near vicinity of Plotnikov's delicatessen, there stands a small house, very clean, both outside and in, which belongs to the widow of the civil servant Krasotkin. Mr Krasotkin himself, the provincial secretary, died a very long time back, almost fourteen years ago, but his widow, in her thirties now and still to this day a most decorative little lady, lives and thrives in her most clean little house 'on her own capital'. She lives decently and timidly, and is of delicate, but rather cheerful character. Her husband left her for the grave when she was only about eighteen, had lived with him only about a year, and had just borne him a son. Ever since, from the very day of his death, she had consecrated herself entirely to the education of this precious boy of hers, Kolya, and although she had loved him to distraction all these fourteen years, she had, of course, experienced on account of him incomparably more suffering than happiness, trembling and dying inwardly of terror almost every day lest he fall ill, catch cold, do something naughty, climb on to a chair and fall over, etcetera, etcetera. Then, when Kolya had started going to school, and subsequently to our progymnasium,* his mother had rushed together with him into the study of all the branches of learning, in order to assist him and rehearse with him his lessons, rushed, too, into making the acquaintance of the schoolmasters and their wives, had even buttered up Kolya's classmates, cunningly flattering them so that they should leave Kolya alone, not make fun of him, and give him no thrashings. She brought it to the point where because of her the little

brats did indeed begin to make fun of him and started to to tease him
with being a mother's boy. But the boy knew how to defend his patch.
He was a bold little fellow, 'incredibly strong', as the rumour of him
spread about his class, swiftly to be confirmed; was agile, of stubborn
character and a spirit of both enterprise and daring. He was a good
scholar, and there was even a rumour that both in arithmetic and in
world history he could 'stymie' even their teacher, Mr Dardanelov. But
although the boy viewed them from above, turning his nose up at them,
he was a good classmate and did not go around extolling his own virtues.
He accepted the respect of the other boys as his due, but conducted
himself in an amicable manner. Above all, he had a sense of moderation,
was able to restrain himself when necessary, and in his relations with
authority never overstepped a certain ultimate and sacred limit on the
other side of which a misdemeanour could not be tolerated, becoming
disorder, mutiny and lawlessness. And yet he was not at all, in any way,
averse to playing pranks on every suitable occasion, playing pranks like
the very least of boys, and not so much for the sake of playing pranks as
in order to make subtle points, perform strange wonders, inject some
'extra pepper', some style, and do some showing-off. Above all, he was
very vain. He even knew how to place his own mother in a subordinate
relation to him, wielding an influence over her that was almost despotic.
She did indeed subordinate herself, oh, long had she done so, and the
only thing she was unable to endure was the thought that her boy 'did
not love her very much'. It unceasingly appeared to her that Kolya was
'unfeeling' to her, and there had been instances when, dissolving in
hysterical tears, she had begun to reproach him for coldness. The boy did
not find this to his liking, and the more that outpourings of the heart
were demanded of him, the more, as it were, deliberately unyielding did
he become. Not deliberately, however, but involuntarily did this take
place in him – such was the character he possessed. His mother was
mistaken: he loved her very much, and what he did not like was only the
'milk-calf mush', as he expressed it in his schoolboy jargon. His father
had left behind him a book-cupboard in which there was a number of
books; Kolya was fond of reading and had already read some of them on
his own. His mother was not concerned by this, and was only occasionally
surprised when the boy, instead of going out to play, would kneel by the
cupboard for hours on end over some book or other. It was in this
manner that Kolya read certain things which he ought never really to
have been allowed to read at his age. As a matter of fact, though the boy
did not like to take his pranks beyond a certain limit, there had of late

begun some at which his mother had grown seriously alarmed – pranks, to be sure, not immoral in any way, but for all that of a desperate, daredevil nature. It just so happened that during the past summer, in July, in the course of the school holidays, the mother and her dearly beloved son had gone to spend a week in another district, some seventy versts away, as guests in the home of a certain distant female relative whose husband worked as an official at the local railway station (the very same station, the nearest to our town, from which Ivan Fyodorovich Karamazov set off for Moscow a month later). There Kolya had begun by conducting a detailed examination of the railway, studying the arrangements in an awareness that upon his return home he would, with his newly acquired knowledge, be able to shine among the scholars of his progymnasium. But at that time there just so happened to be several boys there, too, with whom he struck up an acquaintance; some of them lived at the station, others nearby – young lads of from twelve to fifteen, six or seven of them in all, two of them happening also to be from our little town. The boys played together, organized pranks, and then, on the fourth or the fifth day of the visit to the station the stupid young fellows got up a most impossible two-rouble wager, namely: Kolya, being practically the youngest of them all, and therefore somewhat despised by the older boys, out of either vanity or unpardonable valour, proposed that at night, when the eleven o'clock train arrived, he should lie down on his back between the rails and remain there without moving as the train passed over him at full steam. To be sure, a preliminary study had first been made, from which it had transpired that it really was possible to stretch oneself out and flatten oneself between the rails in such a manner that the train would hurtle overhead without touching the person below, though it would take some nerve to lie there! Kolya insisted firmly that he would lie there. The boys began to laugh at him, calling him a rotten little liar and a braggart, but only succeeded in egging him on still further. The thing that really riled him was that these fifteen-year-olds gave themselves excessive airs in front of him and had at first been unwilling even to accept him as their companion on the grounds that he was 'too young', which he had found quite intolerably offensive. And so they determined to go that evening a verst up the track from the station, so that the train, having left it, would have time to get up full speed. The boys set off. The night had turned out moonless, not only dark but almost pitch-black. At the appointed time Kolya lay down between the rails. The five other boys, who had made the wager, at first with a sinking of the heart, and then in fear and remorse, waited at the foot of

the embankment in the bushes beside the track. At last came the clanking
of the train in the distance as it left the station. Two red lamps flashed
out of the darkness, and the approaching monster began to rumble. 'Go
on, go on, get off the rails!' the boys began to shout to Kolya from the
bushes, dying inwardly with fear, but it was now too late: the train came
hurtling along and swept past. The boys rushed over to Kolya: he lay
motionless. They began to pull at him, began to lift him up. Suddenly, he
got up of his own accord and walked down the embankment without
saying a word. When he reached the foot he declared that he had lain
there as though unconscious on purpose, in order to give them a fright,
but the truth was that he really had lost consciousness, as he himself
confessed, only a long time later, to his mother. In this fashion, his
reputation as a 'desperate fellow' was consolidated for ever. He returned
home to the station as white as a sheet. On the following day he fell
slightly ill with a nervous fever, but was incredibly lively of spirit,
cheerful and at ease. The event that had taken place did not become
public knowledge at once, but when it reached our town it filtered
through to the progymnasium and came to the ears of its authorities. At
this point, however, Kolya's mother had rushed to entreat with the
authorities for the sake of her boy, the eventual upshot being that the
respected and influential schoolmaster Mr Dardanelov had prevailed upon
them and succeeded in defending Kolya's case with them, the matter
being dropped as though it had never taken place at all. This Dardanelov,
a man single and not by any means old, had been passionately and for
many years in love with Mrs Krasotkina and had already once, about a
year ago, most reverentially and dying inwardly with fear and tactful
scruple, ventured upon the risk of offering her his hand; but she had
flatly refused, viewing consent as a betrayal of her son, though Dardanelov, were certain enigmatic signs anything to go by, might even
possibly have had a certain right to hope that he was not entirely
repugnant to the charming, but all too chaste and delicate widow-woman.
Kolya's crazy prank had, it appears, broken the ice, and in return for his
intercession Dardanelov received a hint, albeit a remote one, that he
might yet entertain some hope; but Dardanelov was himself a positive
phenomenon of purity and tactful scruple, and so for the present that was
sufficient to ensure the plenitude of his happiness. He liked the boy,
though he would have thought it degrading to try to make him return
the sentiment, and dealt with him sternly and demandingly in class. But
Kolya himself kept him at a respectful distance, did his homework
impeccably, was second in his class, adopted a cold manner with Darda-

nelov, and the whole class firmly believed that Kolya was so good at world history that he could 'stymie' Dardanelov himself. And indeed, Kolya once asked him the question: 'Who were the founders of Troy?' – to which Dardanelov gave only a general reply concerning the peoples, their movements and migrations, the depths of the ages, mythology, but as to who had actually founded Troy, that is to say, which precise persons, he was unable to say, and even appeared for some reason to find the question idle and lacking in substance. But the boys remained in the conviction that Dardanelov did not know who had founded Troy. As for Kolya, he had read the section dealing with the founders of Troy in Smaragdov's *History*,* which was kept in the bookcase his parent had left after his decease. The upshot was that all the boys acquired a positive interest in the question of precisely who had founded Troy, but Krasotkin did not reveal his secret, and his reputation for knowledge was firmly established.

After the railway incident Kolya's relation to his mother underwent a certain change. When Anna Fyodorovna (Mr Krasotkin's widow) learned of her dear son's exploit she almost went out of her mind with horror. Such terrible fits of hysteria, lasting with intervals for several days, did she suffer that Kolya, by now seriously frightened, gave her his word of gentlemanly honour that such a prank would never again be repeated. He vowed on his knees before the icon and vowed by the memory of his father, as Mrs Krasotkina herself demanded, and as he did so the 'manly' Kolya himself broke into tears, like a six-year-old, from 'tender-heartedness', and all that day mother and son kept rushing into each other's embraces, weeping fit to burst. On the following morning Kolya awoke his old 'hard-hearted' self, except that he had now become less talk-ative, more modest, severe and reflective. To be sure, some six weeks later he again landed up in a certain prank, and his name even became known to our local justice of the peace, but it was a prank of quite a different kind, one even comical and hairbrained, and in any case it turned out to have been played not by him in person, but had only involved his connivance. Of this, however, later. The mother continued in her trembling and torment, but to the degree in which her anguish grew, so did Dardanelov experience a hope that grew likewise. It should be observed that Kolya had understood and unravelled Dardanelov's emotions in this regard and, of course, held him in profound contempt for his 'tender-heartedness'; he had previously even had the lack of tact to display this contempt in front of his mother, remotely hinting that he understood what Dardanelov was after. But after the railway incident he had changed his conduct on this account, too: permitted himself no more hints, even the most remote ones, and in his mother's presence had begun to utter more respectful opinions concerning Dardanelov, something which the sensitive Anna Fyodorovna at once understood in her heart with boundless gratitude, although at the slightest, most casual remark about Dardanelov uttered even by some outside visitor, were Kolya to be present at the time, she would suddenly flare crimson as a rose with embarrassment. Kolya would at these moments either look frowningly out of the window, or look to see if his boots were yawning at the toes yet, or furiously summon Perezvon,* the shaggy-coated, rather large and mangy dog he had suddenly procured from somewhere about a month ago, bringing it into the house and keeping it somewhere inside in secret, never showing him to any of his companions. He tyrannized the dog dreadfully, teaching it all sorts of tricks and artifices, and brought the poor creature to a point where it howled for him when he was out at school, and when he came home yelped with ecstasy, rushing around like a mad thing, begging, rolling over on the floor and pretending to be dead, etcetera, in a word, demonstrating all the tricks it had been taught, now, however, not on demand, but solely out of the ardency of its own ecstatic feelings and its grateful heart.

One thing occurs to me: I have forgotten to mention that Kolya Krasotkin was the same boy whom the boy Ilyusha, who is already familiar to the reader and was the son of the retired second-grade captain Snegirov, stabbed with his penknife in the hip when standing up for his father, whom the schoolboys had teasingly called a 'loofah'.

2

Youngsters

AND SO, on that frosty, cold, damp November morning the boy Kolya Krasotkin was at home. It was Sunday, and there were no classes. But it had already chimed eleven o'clock, and he absolutely had to go outside 'on a certain very important piece of business', and all the while there he was the only person in the house and decidedly in the capacity of its guardian, for it so transpired that all its more senior inhabitants had, because of a certain urgent and unusual circumstance, absented themselves from the premises. In the house of the widow Krasotkina, across the passage from the rooms she herself occupied, there was yet another set of living quarters, consisting of two small rooms, which were rented out to lodgers, and were occupied by a doctor's wife with her two young children. This doctor's wife was the same age as Anna Fyodorovna and her close friend, while the doctor himself had over a year ago now gone off somewhere first to Orenburg and then to Tashkent, it being some six months now since anything at all had been heard of him, so that were it not for the friendship of Mrs Krasotkina, which had somewhat mitigated the unhappiness of the abandoned doctor's wife, she would most certainly have expired in tears from that unhappiness. And then, as though on purpose to crown all these oppressive machinations of fate, it had also transpired that in the course of that very night, from Saturday to Sunday, Katerina, the only serving-maid the doctor's wife possessed, had suddenly and unexpectedly announced to her mistress that in the morning she intended to give birth to a child. How it had come to pass that no one had ever noticed this earlier was almost a miracle to them all. In shock, the doctor's wife thought it would be best, while still there was time, to take Katerina to a certain establishment designed to accommodate such cases in our little town at the home of a local midwife. As she valued this serving-maid greatly, she lost no time in fulfilling her project, took her there and, moreover, stayed with her there. Later, when morning came, there was for some reason a constant requirement for the friendly sympathy and assistance of Mrs Krasotkina, who was in this instance able to ask certain people for certain things and to afford a certain degree of patronage. Thus, both ladies were absent, while Mrs Krasotkina's serving-maid, the peasant woman Agafya, had gone to the market, and Kolya found himself the temporary guardian and sentinel of the 'little ones', that is to say the small son and daughter of the doctor's wife, who had been left all on their very own. Kolya was not afraid of guarding the house, and in any case he had Perezvon, who had been instructed to lie prone under the bench in the vestibule 'without moving' and who therefore each time Kolya entered the vestibule, on his way from room to room, twitched his head and gave two firm and ingratiating thuds of his tail on the floor, but, alas, the summoning whistle did not resound. Kolya would give the unhappy hound a threatening stare, and it would again sink into obedient torpor. No, if there was anything that Kolya found troubling, it was the 'little ones'. The unexpected thing that had happened to Katerina he viewed, of course, with the deepest contempt, but he was very fond of the fatherless little ones and had already taken them in a children's book. Nastya, the elder child, a girl who was now eight, was able to read, while the younger little one, the seven-year-old boy Kostya, very much liked to listen to his sister read. Of course, Krasotkin could have occupied them in more interesting fashion, that is to say, made them both stand side by side and begin to play soldiers with them, or hide-and-seek about the whole house. This he had done on several previous occasions and was not too snobbish to do so, so that even in his class the rumour had once begun to spread that Krasotkin played at horses with his diminutive lodgers, prancing like a trace-horse and bending his head to one side, but Krasotkin had proudly foisted off this accusation, with the reproving comment that with boys who were his contemporaries, thirteen-year-olds, it would indeed have been disgraceful to play at horses 'in our age', but that he had done it for the sake of the 'little ones', because he was fond of them, and let no one dare to ask him to render account of his feelings. In return, both 'little ones' worshipped him. On this occasion, however, he had no time for games. There lay ahead of him to be dealt with a certain very important matter of his own, one that even apparently contained what almost mounted to an element of secrecy, and all the while the time was going by, and Agafya, with whom he could have left the children, had still not returned from the market. Already several times he had crossed the passage, opened the door to the rooms of the doctor's wife and anxiously surveyed the 'little ones' who, on his orders, were reading the book he had given them, and each time he opened the door they silently smiled at him from ear to ear, in the expectation that he would come in and do something wonderful to make them laugh. But Kolya was in a state of mental anxiety, and did not go in. At last it had chimed eleven, and he had decided firmly and finally that if at the end of ten minutes the 'cursed' Agafya had not returned, he would leave the house without waiting for her, first, of course, making the 'little ones' give him their word of honour that they would not get cold feet, would not be naughty and would not be afraid and cry. With these thoughts he got into his wadded winter coat with the sealskin collar, put his satchel over his shoulder and, in spite of earlier repeated pleas from his mother that when he went out 'in such cold weather' he should always wear galoshes, merely glanced at them with contempt on his way through the vestibule and left the house in boots alone. Perezvon, seeing him dressed to go out, began to thud his tail on the floor with redoubled vigour, twitching all over with the whole of his body, and even started to let out a plaintive whine, but Kolya, at the sight of such passionate impetuosity on the part of his hound, decided that this was prejudicial to discipline and, even though only for a moment, made him stay under the bench and only when he had opened the door into the passage suddenly whistled him out. The hound leapt up like a mad creature and rushed to gallop before him in ecstasy. Crossing the passage, Kolya opened the door to the 'little ones'' room. Both were still sitting at the table as before, but were no longer reading, but hotly arguing about something. These children frequently had disputes with each other about various challenging day-to-day topics, and in them Nastya, being the elder, always had the upper hand; as for Kostya, if he did not agree with her, he nearly always went to appeal to Kolya Krasotkin, and if the latter delivered a verdict, it remained in categorical force for all parties. On this occasion the 'little ones'' dispute had engaged Krasotkin's interest somewhat, and he remained in the doorway to listen. The children had seen he was listening, and therefore began their altercation with even greater verve than usual.

'Never, never will I believe,' Nastya was babbling hotly, 'that little children are found by midwives in the cabbage-patches in kitchen gardens. It's winter now, and there aren't any cabbage-patches, and the midwife couldn't bring Katerina her daughter.'

'Phew!' Kolya whistled to himself.

'Or else it's like this: they do bring them from somewhere, but only to the women who get married.'

Kostya stared at Nastya, listened in deep thought and pondered.

'Nastya, what a silly girl you are,' he pronounced at last, firmly and remaining cool. 'How could Katerina possibly have a little child unless she was married?'

Nastya flew into a dreadful passion.

'You don't understand anything,' she said irritably, cutting him short. 'Perhaps she had a husband, only he's in prison, and now she's given birth.'

'Is her husband in prison?' the staid Kostya inquired with a consequential air.

'Or else it's like this,' Nastya broke in again, impetuously, having completely abandoned and forgotten her first hypothesis, 'she doesn't have a husband, you're right about that, but she wants to get married, and she's been thinking of getting married, thinking and thinking of it and she's still thinking of it, and now what she's got is not a husband but a little child.'

'Yes, that will be it,' Kostya agreed, completely vanquished. 'But you didn't say that before, so how could I have known?'

'Now then, youngsters,' Kolya said, taking a stride into their room. 'you're a dangerous bunch, I can see.'

'Have you got Perezvon with you?' Kostya grinned, and he began to snap his fingers and call Perezvon.

'Little ones, I'm in a difficult situation,' Krasotkin began grandly, 'and you must help me: I think Agafya must have fallen and broken her leg, for she hasn't come home yet, that is sure as signed and seal, and I have to go out. Will you let me go?'

The children gave each other worried looks, and their laughing faces began to display uneasiness. As a matter of fact, they had not yet fully understood what was being required of them.

'You won't be naughty when I'm gone? You won't climb up on the cupboard and break your legs? You won't start crying because you're on your own?'

The children's faces expressed deep dismay.

'In return I could show you a certain small item, a little copper cannon that can be fired using real gunpowder.'

The children's faces instantly brightened up.

'Show it to us,' Kostya said, beaming all over.

Krasotkin put his hand in his satchel, took from it a miniature bronze cannon and placed it on the table.

'You bet I will! Look, it has wheels,' he said, rolling the cannon across the table. 'And it can be fired. You can load it with lead shot and fire it.'

'And can it kill people?'

'It can kill anyone, all you have to do is aim.' And Krasotkin explained where the gunpowder went and where the piece of shot was rolled in, pointed to the little aperture that served as a touch hole and told them there was a recoil. The children listened with huge interest. They were particularly taken with the fact that there was a recoil.

'And have you got gunpowder?' Nastya wanted to know.

'Yes, I have.'

'Show it to us, too,' she said slowly, with a beaming smile.

Krasotkin again felt in his satchel and took from it a small glass phial that did indeed contain some real gunpowder, and in a screw of paper there proved to be some grains of lead shot. He even unstopped the phial and poured a little of the powder on to the palm of his hand.

'There, only we must be sure there is no naked flame anywhere, or else it will blow up and kill us all,' Krasotkin warned them for effect.

The children examined the gunpowder with reverential fear, which increased their pleasure even further. Kostya, however, was more drawn to the gunpowder.

'But doesn't the lead shot burn?' he wanted to know.

'No, it doesn't.'

'Let me have a little of the lead shot,' he said in a small, beseeching voice.

'I'll give you a little, here, take it, only please don't show it to your mother until I come back, or else she will think it's gunpowder, and she'll be horrified out of her wits and give you a taste of the birch.'

'Mamma never uses the birch on us,' Nastya observed at once.

'I know, I only said it for the sake of rhetorical style. And you must never deceive your mother, but on this occasion you may – until I get back. So, little ones, may I go? You won't be afraid and cry when I am gone?'

'Yes – we – will,' Kostya said slowly, already preparing to cry.

'We will cry, we're sure to!' Nastya echoed in a frightened babble.

'Oh, children, children, how dangerous are your years.* There's nothing for it, my chickadees, I shall just have to sit with you I know not how long. But the time, the time, my goodness!'

'Tell Perezvon to play dead,' Kostya requested.

'Oh, there is nothing for it, I shall have to resort to Perezvon. *Ici*, Perezvon!' And Kolya began to issue instructions to the dog, and the dog began to perform what he knew. He was a shaggy-coated dog, the size of an ordinary mongrel, with hair that was a kind of grey-lilac colour. His right eye was blind, and his left ear for some reason had a tear in it. He yelped and jumped, begged, walked on his hindlegs, threw himself on his back with all four paws in the air and lay without motion, as though he were dead. During this last trick the door opened, and Agafya, Mrs Krasotkina's fat serving-maid, a pockmarked peasant woman of about forty, appeared on the threshold, having returned from the market with a bag of the provisions she had bought in her hand. She stood and, holding the bag perpendicularly in her left hand, began to stare at the dog. Kolya, in spite of all his waiting for Agafya to arrive, did not interrupt the performance and, making Perezvon remain 'dead' for a certain length of time, at last whistled to him: the dog leapt up and began to jump with joy at having fulfilled his duty.

'Will you look at that hound?' Agafya said, for their edification.

'And what about you, female sex, why are you so late?' Krasotkin asked sternly.

'Female sex, indeed, will you listen to the little upstart?'

'Little upstart?'

'Yes, little upstart. What is it to you if I'm late. If I'm late, it's because I have my business to be late,' Agafya muttered, starting to occupy herself around the stove, in a voice that, however, was not at all displeased or angry, but, on the contrary, one of positive pleasure, as though she were glad of the chance of passing a word or two of playful tit-for-tat with the lively young *barin*.

'Listen, frivolous old woman,' Krasotkin began, getting up from the sofa, 'will you swear to me by all that is holy in this world, and beyond that by something else as well, that you will keep an unwearying eye on the little ones in my absence? I am going out.'

'Why do I need to swear to you?' Agafya laughed. 'I'll look after them well enough without that.'

'No, not unless you swear by the eternal salvation of your soul. Otherwise I shall not leave.'

'Well, don't then. What do I care, it's freezing outside, stay at home.'

'Little ones,' Kolya said, addressing the children, 'this woman is going to stay with you until I come back or until your mother comes back, because she too ought to have been back a long time ago. What is more, she will give you lunch. Will you do that, Agafya?'

'I will.'

'Goodbye, my chickadees, now I can leave with a tranquil heart. And listen, granny,' he said in a solemn undertone, as he passed Agafya, 'I hope you won't start telling them your usual old wives' tales about Katerina, please spare their childish years. *Ici*, Perezvon!'

'Oh, off you go,' Agafya snapped, with anger now. 'Think you're funny! You ought to get a good birching for saying things like that.'

3

A Schoolboy

BUT Kolya was no longer listening. At last he was able to go out. As he went out through the front gate he looked round, gave a tight shrug of his shoulders and, saying, 'It's frosty!', set off straight up the street and then right along the lane that led to the market-square. Upon reaching the last house before the square he stopped outside the gate, took a whistle from his pocket and blew it with all his might, as though giving some signal that had been arranged in advance. He had to wait no more than a minute, and then suddenly towards him from the wicket gate ran a ruddy-faced boy of about eleven, also clad in a warm, clean and even stylish little topcoat. This was the boy Smurov, who was in the preparatory form (while Kolya Krasotkin was now two forms higher), the son of a prosperous civil servant who with his wife had apparently forbidden him to play with Krasotkin as being a most notorious and desperate prankster, with the result that Smurov had now apparently run out on the sly. This Smurov, if the reader has not forgotten, was one of that group of boys who two months previously had thrown stones across the ditch at Ilyusha and who that day had told Alyosha Karamazov about him.

'I've been waiting for you a whole hour, Krasotkin,' Smurov said with a resolute air, and the boys began to stride towards the square.

'I was delayed,' Krasotkin replied. 'There were certain circumstances. Are you sure you won't get a thrashing for being with me?'

'Oh, for goodness' sake, do you suppose my parents thrash me? Have you got Perezvon with you?'

'Yes, Perezvon's here too!'

'Are you going to take him there?'

'Yes.'

'Oh, if only we had Zhuchka!'

'We can't take Zhuchka. Zhuchka does not exist. Zhuchka has disappeared in the murk of obscurity.'

'Oh, couldn't we do this?' Smurov said, stopping suddenly. 'I mean, Ilyusha says that Zhuchka also had a shaggy coat and was also that grey, smoky colour Perezvon is — so couldn't we just tell him this is Zhuchka, and perhaps he'll believe it?'

'Schoolboy, abominate lies, that is number one; even in a good cause, number two. Though the main thing is that I hope you didn't tell anyone about my coming here.'

'God forbid, why, I mean, I understand the situation. But Perezvon won't cheer him up,' Smurov sighed. 'Do you know what? That father of his, the captain, the loofah, told us that today he was going to bring him a puppy, a real Medelyansky hound,* with a black nose; he thinks that will cheer Ilyusha up, but I doubt it, don't you?'

'How is he, anyway — Ilyusha, I mean?'

'Oh, bad, bad! I think he's got consumption. He's fully conscious, only he breathes and breathes in this funny way, it's not a good way to breathe. The other day he asked to be helped to walk, we put his boots on for him, and he did walk a bit, but then he fell down. "There, papa," he said, "I told you my old boots were no good, I've never been able to walk in them." You see, he thought he'd fallen down because of his boots, and it was really because of his weakness. He won't live out the week. Herzenstube calls. They're rich again now, they've got lots of money.'

'The scoundrels.'

'Who are?'

'Doctors and all that medical riff-raff, generally speaking, and, of course, particularly speaking, too. I reject medicine. It's a useless institution. As a matter of fact, I am conducting an investigation into it all. But tell me, what is all this sentimental business you've started over there? I believe your whole class goes there now?'

'Not the whole of it, but about a dozen of us do, always, every day. It's nothing.'

'What surprises me is the role played by Aleksey Karamazov in it all: his brother is to be tried tomorrow or the day after for a crime like that, and yet he can spend so much time on sentimental business with some boys!'

'It isn't sentimental business at all. Anyway, you yourself are going to see Ilyusha now in order to make it up with him.'

'Make it up with him? A ridiculous expression. As a matter of fact, I permit no one to analyse my actions.'

'But how glad Ilyusha will be to see you! He does not even imagine that you will come. Why, why has it taken you so long to decide to come and see him?' Smurov exclaimed suddenly, with heat.

'Dear boy, that is my affair, not yours. I am going of my own accord, because such is my will, while you were all dragged over there by Aleksey Karamazov, so there is a difference. And how do you know I'm going there in order to make it up with him? I may have quite different reasons. It's a stupid expression.'

'It wasn't Karamazov at all, it had nothing to do with him. It was simply that our fellows started going there, at first with Karamazov, it's true. And there's been nothing of that kind, no stupid business at all. First one of us went, and then another, and so it went on. His father was incredibly glad to see us. You know, he'll simply go mad if Ilyusha dies. He can see that Ilyusha's going to die. And how glad he is that we've made it up with Ilyusha. Ilyusha asked about you, he didn't add any more. He just asked and was silent. But his father will either go mad or hang himself. I mean, he already behaves like a crazy fellow. You know, he is a man of noble intent, and we made a mistake that day. It was all the fault of that father-murderer who gave him the beating then.'

'All the same, Karamazov is a mystery to me. I could have made his acquaintance long ago, but in certain cases I like to be proud. Moreover, I have formed a certain opinion about him, one which I shall have to check and elucidate further.'

Kolya fell gravely silent; Smurov, too. Smurov was, of course, in reverential awe of Kolya Krasotkin and did not dare even to think of addressing him as an equal. Now, however, he was all agog with interest, as Kolya had explained that he was going 'by himself', and so there must certainly be some mystery involved here in the fact that Kolya had suddenly taken it into his head to go now and particularly today. They walked across the market-square, where on this occasion there were a large number of carts in from the country and a large number of domestic fowls. Under their awnings the women of the town were selling boubliks,* thread and the like. In our little town Sunday gatherings of this kind are in unsophisticated manner termed 'fairs', and there are many of them in the course of the year. Perezvon ran about in most animated spirits, swerving constantly to right and to left in order to sniff things here and there. When he met other little dogs he exchanged sniffs with them with extraordinary pleasure, according to all the doggy rules.

'I like to observe realism, Smurov,' Kolya said suddenly. 'Have you noticed the way dogs greet and sniff each other? It is a kind of general law of nature with them.'

'Yes, a ridiculous one.'

'Actually, no, it isn't ridiculous, you are wrong there. In nature there is nothing that is ridiculous, however much it may seem so to man and his prejudices. If dogs were able to reason and think critically, they would doubtless find just as much that was ridiculous, if not far more, in the social relations of the human beings who are their sovereigns – if not far more; that I repeat because I am firmly convinced that there is a far greater degree of folly among ourselves. That is a notion of Rakitin's, a first-rate one. I am a socialist, Smurov.'

'And what's a socialist?' asked Smurov.

'It's when all men are equal, when everyone owns the same common property, when there is no marriage and religion and all the laws are for each to pick and choose,* well, and all the rest of it. You're not old enough for that yet, it's too early for you to be thinking about it. I say, though, isn't it frosty?'

'Yes. It's twelve degrees below zero. Father looked at the thermometer today.'

'And have you observed, Smurov, that in the middle of winter, if it is fifteen or even eighteen degrees below zero, it seems not as cold as, for example, now, at the beginning of winter, when the freezing weather strikes suddenly, as now, with twelve degrees below, and there is not yet much snow. It's because people have not yet got used to it. With human beings habit is all, in everything, even in matters of nationhood and politics. Habit is the principal driving force. I say, though, what a ridiculous muzhik.'

Kolya pointed to a tall, strapping muzhik in a sheepskin coat, with a good-natured physiognomy, who was clapping his hands together in their sleeves beside his cart because of the cold. His long, chestnut-coloured beard was covered all over with hoar-frost.

'The muzhik's beard has frozen!' Kolya shouted in a loud, teasing voice as he walked past him.

'So have the beards of many,' the muzhik said, calmly and sententiously, in reply.

'Don't tease him,' Smurov observed.

'It's all right, he won't get angry, he is a good fellow. Hail and greetings, Matvey.'

'Hail.'

'Is your name really Matvey?'

'Yes, it is. Did you not know?'

'No, I didn't; I just called you that at random.'

'Would you credit it. I expect you're one of them schoolboys.'

'That's right, I am.'

'Well, do they thrash you?'

'Oh, now and again.'

'Hard?'

'Now and then.'

'Ach, life!' the muzhik sighed with all his heart.

'Hail and farewell, Matvey.'

'Farewell. You're a nice little lad, I'll say that.'

The boys continued on their way.

'That is a good muzhik,' Kolya said to Smurov. 'I like to talk with the common folk and am always pleased to render them their due.'

'Why did you tell him that lie about your getting thrashed?' asked Smurov.

'Well, it was necessary to keep him happy, wasn't it?'

'In what way?'

'Look, Smurov, I don't like being repeatedly questioned by someone who hasn't understood straight away. There are some things that cannot be explained. The way a muzhik sees it, schoolboys are thrashed and ought to be thrashed: what kind of a schoolboy is it who isn't thrashed, they think. And if I were suddenly to go and tell him that we aren't thrashed, well, it would upset him. However, I suppose you can't understand that. One has to know the art of talking to the common folk.'

'Only please don't tease them, or else there'll be another bit of trouble like the one with that goose.'

'Are you afraid, then?'

'Don't laugh, Kolya, but yes, I swear to God I'm afraid. My father would be terribly angry. He's strictly forbidden me to play with you.'

'Do not worry, on this occasion nothing will happen. Hello, Natasha,' he cried to one of the market women under an awning.

'What do you mean, Natasha? My name is Marya,' replied the clamorous voice of the market woman, who was by no means old.

'That is just as well. Hail and greetings, Marya.'

'Oh, the little beast, his head's hardly risen above the ground, and will you listen to him?'

'I've no time, no time to talk to you now, you may tell me about it on Sunday,' Kolya said, waving his arms as though it were she who was pestering him, and not the other way about.

'What will I tell you on Sunday? It was you who came up to me, and not the other way round, you bundle of tricks!' Marya began to shout. 'You need a good thrashing, that's what, it's well known you're a rude little troublemaker!'

Among the other market women who were selling things on their trays beside Marya laughter resounded, when suddenly, for no apparent reason, out from behind the arcade of the town shops leapt a certain vexed and irritated individual, who looked as though he might be a merchant's assistant, and not one of our own tradesmen, but from out of town, in a long blue caftan, a cap with a peak, and still young, with dark chestnut curls and a long, pale, pockmarked face. He was in a state of inane agitation, and at once began to threaten Kolya with his fist.

'I know you,' he exclaimed irritably, 'I know you!'

Kolya stared at him fixedly. He could not for the life of him remember having ever had any kind of skirmish with this man. But then, he had rather a lot of skirmishes with people in the street, and to remember them all was impossible.

'Oh, really?' he said, ironically.

'I know you! I know you!' the artisan kept repeating like a simpleton.

'So much the better for you. But I'm afraid I have no time, hail and farewell!'

'What tricks are you up to?' the artisan shouted. 'Are you up to your tricks again? I know you! Are you up to your tricks again?'

'Whether I am up to my tricks or not, brother, is none of your business,' Kolya said, coming to a halt and continuing to study the man.

'What do you mean, none of my business?'

'Just that — none of your business.'

'But whose is it, then? Whose? Tell me, whose is it?'

'Well, brother, it's Trifon Nikitich's business now, and not yours.'

'Who's Trifon Nikitich?' the young man said with foolish astonishment, though still worked up, and stared at Kolya. Kolya gravely measured him with this gaze.

'Have you been to the Church of the Ascension?' he suddenly asked him, sternly and insistently.

'What church is that? Why do you ask? No, I haven't been there,' the young man said, somewhat taken aback.

'Do you know Sabaneyev?' Kolya went on, even more sternly and more insistently.

'What Sabaneyev are you talking about? No, I don't know him.'

'Well, to the devil with you, then!' Kolya snapped suddenly and, taking a sharp turn to the right, quickly strode upon his way as though he viewed as being well beneath contempt the prospect of talking to a blockhead who did not even know Sabaneyev.

'Hey you, wait! What Sabaneyev do you mean?' the young man said, having recovered himself, and again in a pitch of furious excitement. 'Why did he say that?' he said, turning suddenly to the market women, looking at them stupidly.

The market women burst out laughing.

'He's a queer one, that boy,' one of them said.

'But who is he, who is he, this Sabaneyev?' the young man kept repeating violently, waving his right arm.

'He'll be the Sabaneyev who used to work for the Kuzmichevs, that's who he'll be,' one of the other market women suddenly guessed.

The young man stared at her wildly.

'Kuz-mi-chev?' a second woman broke in. 'But why are you calling him Trifon? His first name's Kuzma, not Trifon, and the name the little fellow used was Trifon Nikitich, so it can't be him.'

'His first name's not Trifon, and his last name is not Sabaneyev, it's Chizhov,' a third woman said, joining the fray. Until now she had been silent, listening gravely. 'Aleksey Ivanych he is by name and patronymic. Chizhov, Aleksey Ivanovich.'

'That's right, it's Chizhov,' a fourth woman insistently confirmed.

The utterly bewildered young man stared now at one, now at another.

'But why did he ask the question, why did he ask it, good women?' he kept exclaiming almost in despair. '"Do you know Sabaneyev?" when the devil only knows who Sabaneyev is?'

'No, you silly man, we've told you – his name's not Sabaneyev, but Chizhov, Aleksey Ivanovich Chizhov, that's who he is!' one of the women shouted at him sternly.

'Who is Chizhov? Well, who is he? Tell me, if you know.'

'That tall chap with the runny nose who used to sit in the market last summer.'

'And what would I be wanting with your Chizhov, good people, eh?'

'How would I know what you want with him?'

'Who knows what business you may have with him?' another chimed in. 'You yourself must know what you wants with him, if you keep on ranting away like that. After all it's you he would have told, not us, you stupid man. Do you really not know him?'

'Who?'

'Chizhov.'

'The devil takes his hide, this Chizhov, and yours too! I'll beat him black and blue, that I will! He's been making fun of me!'

'Is it Chizhov you're going to beat black and blue? More likely he'll do it to you! You're a silly fool, that's what you are!'

'No, you nasty, vicious woman, not Chizhov, not Chizhov, it's the boy I'm going to beat black and blue, that I am! Bring him, bring him here to me, he's been making fun of me!'

The women laughed loudly. As for Kolya, he was by now striding away in the distance with a triumphant expression on his face. Smurov walked beside him, looking round at the shouting group far away. He was also in very high spirits, though he was still worried about ending up in an escapade with Kolya.

'Who was this Sabaneyev you asked him about?' he asked Kolya, sensing in advance what the reply would be.

'How would I know? Now they'll carry on shouting until evening. I like to shake up fools, whatever their stratum of society. Look, there's another blockhead, that muzhik there. Take note: there's a saying that goes "there is nothing more stupid than a stupid Frenchman", but the Russian physiognomy, too, belies itself. Well, is it not written on the face of that muzhik that he's a fool, eh?'

'Leave him alone, Kolya, let us go past.'

'Not on any account will I leave him alone, now that I'm getting into my stride. Hey! Greetings, muzhik!'

The hefty muzhik, who was slowly walking past and must already have had a drink or two, his face round and rather simple-looking, his beard showing streaks of grey, raised his head and looked at the little fellow.

'Well, greetings, if you're not playing jokes, that is,' he said unhurriedly in reply.

'And what if I am?' Kolya laughed.

'If you are, then play them, and God be with you. It's all right, that is allowed. It is always allowed to play jokes.'

'Then I am guilty, brother, for I was joking.'

'Well, and may God forgive you.'

'What about you? Do you forgive me?'

'I forgive you very much. Now off you go.'

'I say, you really do seem to be a muzhik with some brains.'

'More brains than you,' the muzhik suddenly replied, his voice as solemn as before.

'I wonder,' Kolya said, rather taken aback.

'What I say is true.'

'Well, you may be right.'

'Indeed I may, brother.'

'Hail and farewell, muzhik.'

'Farewell.'

'There are different kinds of muzhik,' Kolya observed to Smurov after a certain silence. 'How could I have known I would hit upon a clever one? I am always prepared to recognize intelligence among the common folk.'

In the distance the cathedral clock tolled half past eleven. The boys began to hurry, and the rest of the still quite considerable way to the abode of Second-Grade Captain Snegiryov they traversed quickly and almost without conversation. Twenty yards from the house Kolya came to a halt and told Smurov to go on ahead and summon Karamazov out to him.

'One must have a preliminary sniff around,' he observed to Smurov.

'But why summon him out?' Smurov began to object. 'Just go inside, they'll be incredibly glad to see you. Why make your introductions out here in the cold?'

'I know very well why I want him out here in the cold,' Kolya snapped, despotically cutting him short (something he was inordinately fond of doing to these 'juniors'), and Smurov ran off to fulfil the command.

4
*Zhuchka**

WITH an important look upon his features Kolya leaned against the fence and began to wait for Alyosha to appear. Indeed, he had long wanted to meet him. He had heard a great deal about him from the boys, but until now had always displayed an outward air of contemptuous indifference whenever he had been talked of, and had even expressed himself 'critically' about Alyosha upon hearing the things he had been told concerning him. Privately, however, he was very, very keen to make his acquaintance: there was something in all the stories he had heard about Alyosha that was sympathetic and attractive. Thus the present moment was an important one; for one thing, he must not be found wanting, must demonstrate his independence: 'Or else he will think I am thirteen and take me for another of those junior boys. And what are those junior boys to him? I shall ask him when I meet him. It's a pity I'm so small, though. Tuzikov is younger than me, but he's half a head taller. However, I have an intelligent face; I'm not good-looking, I know my face is rotten to look at, but it's an intelligent one. I must also not talk too much, or else we'll start off with embraces straight away, and he'll think ... Pah, what a horrible thing it will be if he thinks that! . . .'

Thus did Kolya agonize, as with all the forces at his command he tried to assume a most independent air. Above all he was tormented by his inferior height, less by his 'rotten' face than by his height. The year before, on the wall of his room at home, in a corner, he had drawn a line in pencil that showed his height, and every two months since then he had gone there to measure himself again in excitement to see by how much he had managed to grow. But alas, he had not grown much at all, and this had at times driven him simply to despair. As for his face, it was not at all 'rotten'; it was, on the contrary, rather pleasant to look at – light-complexioned and pale, with freckles. His small, grey but lively eyes had a bold gaze and were often illuminated by emotion. His cheekbones were rather broad, his lips small, not very thick but very red; his nose was small and resolutely turned up: 'A real snub nose, a real snub nose!' Kolya would mutter to himself whenever he looked at himself in the mirror, and he always walked away from the mirror in indignation. 'And it's not even really an intelligent face, either, is it?' he would sometimes think, having doubts even about that. Though, as a matter of fact, it should not be supposed that worry about his face and height swallowed his soul entirely. On the contrary, no matter how painful were his moments before the mirror, he quickly forgot them, and even for a long time, 'in complete devotion to ideas and real life', as he himself defined his activity.

Alyosha soon appeared and hurriedly came over to Kolya; even at a distance of several yards Kolya could see that Alyosha's face was filled with joy. 'Is he really so glad to see me?' Kolya wondered with pleasure. Here let us observe in passing that Alyosha had greatly changed since the time we left him: he had forsaken his cassock, now wore a finely tailored frock-coat and a soft, round hat, and had had his hair cut short. All this lent him a great deal of added charm, and he looked thoroughly handsome. His pleasant face always had a cheerful look, but it was a cheerfulness that was quiet and tranquil. To Kolya's astonishment, Alyosha came out to him dressed just as he had been inside, without his topcoat on, and it was plain that he was in a hurry. Without preliminaries, he extended his hand to Kolya.

'Here you are at last, how we have all been waiting for you.'

'There are reasons why it has taken me so long, reasons of which you shall learn in a moment. I have long awaited this opportunity and have heard much about you,' Kolya muttered, slightly out of breath.

'But you and I should have met in any case, I have also heard much about you; here, however, here your arrival is belated.'

'Tell me, how are things here?'

'Ilyusha is very poorly, he is most certainly about to die.'

'Never! You cannot deny that medicine is a vile profession, Karamazov,' Kolya exclaimed with heat.

'Ilyusha has often, very often mentioned you, even, you know, in his sleep, when he was delirious. It is plain that you were very, very dear to him before ... until that incident ... with the penknife. And there is also another cause ... I say, is that dog yours?'

'Yes. He's called Perezvon.'

'And you haven't got Zhuchka?' Alyosha asked, looking dolefully into Kolya's eyes. 'He is lost, then?'

'I know you all want Zhuchka back, I have heard about it, sir,' Kolya smiled mysteriously, with faint irony. 'Listen, Karamazov, I shall explain the whole thing to you; indeed, that is the main reason why I have come here, and why I summoned you out, in order to give you a preliminary explanation of the whole *passage* before we go inside,' he began animatedly. 'You see, Karamazov, last spring Ilyusha entered the preparatory form. Well, everyone knows what our preparatory form consists of: junior boys, youngsters. They immediately began to tease Ilyusha. I am two forms higher up, and so, of course, I only saw it from a distance, from one side. What I saw was a small boy of feeble constitution who none the less refused to submit, who even fought back, proud, his eyes burning. I like boys like that. But they kept on and on at him. Above all I remember that at the time his clothes were terrible, his trousers rode up on his legs because they were too small, and his boots had dropped their soles. They made his life a misery because of that, too. They humiliated him. Well, that I won't stand for, so I stepped in and injected some extra pepper. You see, I beat them but they worship me, do you know that, Karamazov?' Kolya boasted expansively. 'As a matter of fact, in general I'm very fond of youngsters. I have two little chickadees around my neck at home just now, and it was they who held me up today. So anyway, they stopped beating Ilyusha and I took him under my protection. I could see he was a proud boy, and let me tell you, he was proud, but in the end he grew slavishly devoted to me, would carry out my slightest command, obeyed me as though I were a god, strained to imitate me. In the breaks between classes he would come to see me at once and we would stroll around together. It was the same on Sundays. The boys in our gymnasium laugh if a senior boy associates with a junior in such a way, but that is merely prejudice. Such is my caprice, and *basta* – don't you think? I was teaching him, developing him – why, tell me, may I not develop him, if he appeals to me? After all, here you are, Karamazov, getting together with all these little chickadees; that must mean that you want to have an effect on the younger generation, develop it, be of use to it, mustn't it? And I must confess that it was this feature of your character, which I learned of by hearsay, that interested me most of all. However, to the matter in hand: I noted the fact that within the boy there appeared to be developing a certain tender-skinned, sentimental quality, and I, you know, have been a resolute foe of all milk-calf mush from the very day of my birth. And moreover, there were contradictions: he was proud, yet he was slavishly devoted to me – slavishly devoted, yet suddenly his eyes would flash and he would even refuse to agree with me, argue, climb up and down the walls with rage. I would sometimes proclaim my adherence to various ideas: it was not so much that he did not agree with my ideas as that he rose in personal mutiny against me because I responded with indifference to his mushy talk. And then, in order to season him, the mushier his talk became, the more indifferent did I grow; I did it on purpose, for such was my conviction. My aim was to school his character, set it into line, create a human being . . . that sort of thing . . . well, I hardly need to tell someone like you, do I? Suddenly I noticed that for three days in a row he was troubled, upset, not about mushy things now, but about something else, something more powerful and lofty. What's the tragedy, I wondered. I accosted him and discovered what it was all about: somehow he had entered into contact with the lackey of your deceased father (who was then still alive), Smerdyakov, who had gone and taught the little fool a stupid trick, that is to say a brutal trick, a vile trick – to take a piece of bread, from the soft part of the loaf, stick a pin in it and throw it to some yard dog, the kind of dog that is always hungry and will swallow anything without chewing, and see what happens. So they made up a piece of bread like that and then threw it to that same shaggy-coated dog Zhuchka, about which there is now such a fuss, a yard dog from some yard where the simple fact was that no one fed it and it spent all day barking to the wind. (Are you fond of that stupid barking, Karamazov? I cannot abide it.) Well, it rushed at the bread, swallowed it and then began to yelp, went round in circles and at last threw itself into flight, fled, yelping all the while, and disappeared – that was how Ilyusha himself described it to me. He confessed to me what had happened, wept and wept, put his arms round me, shaking all over, and saying: "He yelped as he ran, he yelped as he ran" – that was all he could say, so deeply had that scene appalled him. Well, I could see there were pangs of conscience there all right. I took them seriously. Above all, I wanted to give him a lesson in discipline because of the things he had been saying and doing previously, so that, I confess, I used cunning, pretended to be in a state of indignation I probably was not in at all: "You have committed a dastardly deed, you are a scoundrel, and I shall not of course spread it around, but shall break off relations with you for the time being. I shall give this matter some thought and inform you through Smurov (the boy I was with when I arrived just now and who has always been devoted to me) whether I shall continue relations with you in the future or whether I shall shun you for ever as a scoundrel." That had a terrible effect on him. I confess that even at the time I felt I might have been too severe with him, but there was nothing for it, as such was my intention. The following day I sent Smurov to him with the message that I was "not speaking" to him any more, well, that's the expression we use when two companions sever relations with each other. The secret of it was that I intended to keep him on terms of banishment for only a few days, and then, witnessing his remorse, to extend the hand of friendship to him once again. That was my firm intention. But what do you suppose: he listened to what Smurov had to say, and suddenly his eyes flashed. "You may tell Krasotkin from me," he shouted, "that now I shall throw pieces of bread containing pins to all the dogs, all of them!" Aha, I thought, some private initiative showing through, we shall have to nip this in the bud, and I began to display complete contempt towards him, turning away every time I met him, or smiling ironically. And then suddenly there was this incident with his father, the loofah, do you remember? You have to understand that because of that he was already likely to be easy to provoke to the most terrible anger. When they saw that I had dropped him, the boys pounced upon him, teasing him with "Loofah, loofah!" It was at that point that the battles began, something I regret terribly, because it appears that on one occasion he received a very bad and painful beating. And then once he rushed at all the boys in the yard, as they came out of their classes, and it happened that I was standing a dozen yards away from him, and was able to watch him. And I swear that I do not recall laughing at the time; on the contrary, I felt very, very sorry for him, and in another moment I would have rushed to defend him. But suddenly he met my gaze: what he thought I had done, I do not know, but he whipped out his penknife, threw himself upon me and stuck it into my hip, look, here, near the top of my right leg. I did not move a muscle, I will admit to occasional bravery, Karamazov, and all I did was look at him with contempt, as though saying with my eyes: "If you wish to do it again, in exchange for all my friendship, then I am at your service." But he did not stab me a second time, his nerve failed him, he took fright, threw down his knife, began to sob out loud and set off at a run. Of course I didn't squeal on him and told all the other boys to keep it quiet so it did not reach the ears of the authorities, and did not even tell my mother until the wound had healed and the scar was insignificant, just a scratch. Later on I heard that that same day he got into a stone-hurling fight and bit your finger — but you must understand the state of mind he was in that day! Well, but what is to be done, I acted stupidly: when he fell ill I did not go and pardon him, or make it up with him, rather, I rue that now. But for that I had certain special reasons. Well, that is the whole story . . . only I believe I acted stupidly . . .'

'Oh, what a shame it is,' Alyosha exclaimed with emotion, 'that I did not know of this relation between you earlier, otherwise I myself would long ago have come and asked you to go and see him together with me. Why, in his fever, in his delirum he has raved about you. I did not know you were so dear to him! And have you really, really been unable to find this Zhuchka? His father and all the boys have been

hunting for it all over town. Why, the poor sick boy has already told his
father three times while I have been here: "I am sick, papa, because I
killed Zhuchka that day, and this is my punishment from God" – he
cannot be budged from that idea! And if only now you had been able to
find this Zhuchka and to demonstrate that it was not dead, but alive, then
I think his joy would have resurrected him. We had all pinned our hopes
on you.'

'Tell me, what made you hope that I would find Zhuchka, that it
would be I who would find him?' Kolya asked with extreme curiosity.
'Why was it me you counted on, and not someone else?'

'There was some sort of rumour that you were looking for him and
that when you had found him you would bring him here. Smurov said
something of that kind. Above all, what we are trying to do is to make
him believe that Zhuchka is alive, that he has been seen somewhere. The
boys procured him a live hare from somewhere, but as soon as he saw it,
he gave the merest smile and asked that it be set free in the fields. So that
was what we did. At that moment his father came home with a Medelyansky pup for him, he had also procured it from somewhere, thinking to
console him with it, but it only seemed to make matters worse . . .'

'Karamazov, tell me this, also: what kind of a man is this father? I
know him, but how would you describe him: a buffoon, a clown?'

'Oh no. There are people who feel very deeply, but are somehow held
down by force of weight. Their buffoonery is a kind of malicious irony
directed against those to whose faces they dare not speak the truth
because of their longstanding and degrading fear of them. Believe me,
Krasotkin, when I tell you that buffoonery of that kind can sometimes be
extremely tragic. Now everything, everything in the world for him has
concentrated itself in Ilyusha, and if Ilyusha dies he will either go mad
with grief or take his own life. I am almost convinced of that when I
look at him now!'

'I understand what you say, Karamazov, I can see that you know
human beings,' Kolya said with sincere emotion.

'And so, when I saw you with that dog, I thought it was Zhuchka you
had brought.'

'Wait for a bit, Karamazov. It may be that we shall find him yet. This
dog, however, is called Perezvon. I shall let him into the room now, and
it may be that by doing so I shall cheer Ilyusha up a bit more than his
father did with the Medelyansky pup. Wait, Karamazov, you are about to
discover something in a moment. Oh, my goodness, but how I am
keeping you!' Kolya suddenly exclaimed, in a rush. 'You are only wearing

a thin frock-coat in this cold, and I am keeping you out here; you see, you see what an egoist I am? Oh, we are all of us egoists, Karamazov!'

'Do not worry, to be sure, it is cold, but I am not prone to catch colds. Let us, however, go inside. Incidentally, what is your name? As far as your first name goes, I know you're called Kolya, but what is your proper, full name?'

'Nikolay, Nikolay Ivanovich Krasotkin, or, as they say in official talk: "Krasotkin son",' Kolya laughed for some reason, suddenly adding, however: 'I, of course, hate my first name, Nikolay.'

'Why is that?'

'Because it sounds so trivial, so official . . .'

'And you're thirteen?' Alyosha inquired.

'Fourteen, actually, I'll be fourteen in two weeks' time, very soon now. I will confess to you in advance a certain weakness, Karamazov, something for your ears alone, on our first meeting, so that you may instantly behold my true nature: I hate it when people ask me my age, I more than hate it . . . and, well . . . There is, for example, a slanderous rumour about me going around just now that says that last week I played robbers with the boys of the preparatory form. That I played with them is true, but that I played with them in order to provide myself with enjoyment, that is most certainly a slander. I have reason to believe that this rumour reached your ears; I assure you, however, that I played not for my own sake but for the sake of the youngsters, because had I not been there they would never have been able to think up anything. And you see, the boys in our school are always spreading nonsense around. This is a town of gossip, let me tell you.'

'But what if you had played for your own enjoyment, what would be so bad in that?'

'If I had done it for my own enjoyment, I'd . . . After all, you wouldn't play horses, would you?'

'Why don't you look at it like this?' Alyosha smiled. 'Take the example of adults who go to the theatre: at the theatre the adventures of all kinds of heroes are also represented, sometimes with robbers and scenes of martial conflict – so is not that really the same thing, in its own way, as it were? Young people who play at martial conflict in their hours of recreation, or who play at robbers, as you did – they are, after all, also engendering a kind of art, and a need for art is being engendered in their young souls, and these games are sometimes even more harmoniously composed than the spectacles one may see at the theatre, the only difference being that people go to the theatre to see actors, while here the young folk are themselves the actors. But that is only natural.'

'Do you really think so? Is that your conviction?' Kolya asked, gazing at him fixedly. 'You know, that is a rather interesting thought you have uttered; I shall now go home and bestir my brains in that regard. I will confess that I had been expecting to learn a few things from you. I came here in order to learn from you, Karamazov,' Kolya said finally in a voice of heartfelt and expansive emotion.

'And I from you,' Alyosha smiled, pressing his hand.

Kolya was extremely well-satisfied with Alyosha. He was struck by the fact that with him he was to the highest degree on an equal footing and that Alyosha spoke to him as to one of the 'very biggest'.

'In a moment I shall show you a certain stunt, Karamazov, one that is also a theatrical performance,' he laughed nervously. 'I came here to show you it.'

'Let us first go in here to the left, where the owners of the house live, all your friends have left their topcoats in there, as the room is so crowded and hot.'

'Oh, but I am only coming in for a moment, I shall go in and sit in my topcoat. Perezvon will stay out here in the passage and play dead: *Ici*, Perezvon, *couche* and die! – look, he is playing dead. And I shall first go in and spy out the lie of the land and then later, when it's time, I shall whistle "*Ici*, Perezvon" – and you'll see, he'll immediately come charging in like a scalded thing. Only we must see to it that Smurov does not forget to open the door at that moment. Now I shall make the necessary arrangements, and you shall see a stunt . . .'

5
By Ilyusha's Little Bed

THE room, already familiar to us, in which the family of our friend the retired Second-Grade Captain Snegiryov had its abode, was at that moment both airless and crowded because of the large audience that had assembled there. Several boys were sitting with Ilyusha on this occasion, and though they were all, like Smurov, eager to deny that it had been Alyosha who had got them to make it up with Ilyusha and had brought them together with him, this was none the less the case. The entire extent of his skill in this instance had been to bring them together with Ilyusha, one after the other, without any 'milk-calf mush' and quite as though unintentionally and by chance. But this had brought enormous relief to Ilyusha in his sufferings. Witnessing the almost tender friendship and concern that was offered to him by each one of these boys, his previous foes, he was very moved. Only Krasotkin had failed to turn up, and this lay on his heart like a heavy yoke. If there was in little Ilyusha's bitter memories one that was the bitterest of all, then it was that entire episode with Krasotkin, who had been his sole friend and defender, and at whom he had rushed with his penknife that day. This was also the view of the rather intelligent Smurov (who had been the first to come and make it up with Ilyusha). But Krasotkin, when Smurov had obliquely informed him that Alyosha would like to come and see him 'on a certain matter', had immediately cut him short and rebuffed the approach, instructing Smurov to inform 'Karamazov' without delay that he himself knew how to act, that he did not require advice from anyone and that if he were to go and see the sick boy then he himself would know best when to do it, as he had 'his own considerations'. This had been some two weeks before the present Sunday, and it was why Alyosha had not gone to see him as he had intended. As a matter of fact, though he had bided his time, he had none the less sent Smurov to Krasotkin once more, and then once more again. On both those occasions he had, however, responded with the most impatient and abrupt refusal, telling Alyosha that if he were to come for him he would never go and see Ilyusha, and would not want to be bothered again. Even until the very day before, Smurov did not know that Kolya had decided to visit Ilyusha this morning, and only the previous evening, while saying goodbye to Smurov, Kolya had suddenly abruptly told him to wait for him on the morrow at home, as they would both be going to see the Snegiryovs together, but that he must not dare to let anyone else know about his intended arrival there, as he wished it to be a surprise. Smurov had obeyed. But the hope that he might bring with him the lost Zhuchka had established itself within Smurov on the foundation of some words thrown away in passing once by Krasotkin to the effect that 'they're all a lot of asses if they can't find the dog, assuming it's alive'. But when Smurov had timidly, having waited for a suitable occasion, dropped an allusion to Krasotkin as to his guess concerning the dog, Krasotkin had suddenly flown into a dreadful temper, saying: 'What kind of an ass do you think I am, to go looking for other people's dogs all over town when I have my own Perezvon? And is it reasonable to hope that a dog that has swallowed a pin can still be alive? Milk-calf mush, that's all it is!'

And all the while, for some two weeks now, Ilyusha had lain on his little bed in the corner, near the icons. He had not attended classes ever since the time he had encountered Alyosha and bitten his finger. As a

matter of fact, his illness had begun that day, even though he had
managed to walk about the room and in the passage now and again
on the rare occasions when he had risen from his bed. In the end he
had become completely helpless, unable to move without his father's
help. His father trembled with concern over him, even stopped drinking
altogether, almost went out of his mind with fear that his son would die,
and often − especially after he had led him about the room by the arm
and put him back in his bed again − would suddenly run out into a dark
corner of the passage and, leaning his forehead against the wall, begin to
sob in a kind of shuddering, overflowing lamentation, stifling his voice
so that little Ilyusha should not hear his sobs.

Re-entering the room, he usually began to try to find something with
which to divert and console his dear son, telling him stories or comical
anecdotes, or mimicking various comical people he had chanced to meet,
even imitating animals and their comical howls and cries. But Ilyusha did
not like it at all when his father put on affected airs and made a buffoon
of himself. Though the boy tried not to show that he found it unpleasant,
he realized with pain in his heart that his father had been humiliated in
the eyes of society, and constantly, persistently, recalled the 'loofah' and
that 'terrible day'. Ninochka, the lame, meek and quiet sister of little
Ilyusha, also did not like it when her father put on affected airs (as for
Varvara Nikolayevna, she had long ago departed for St Petersburg to
attend courses at the university there), while the half-witted mother was
always immensely amused, laughing with all her might whenever her
spouse mimicked someone or affected certain comic gestures. This alone
could make her happy; all the rest of the time she spent constantly
grumbling and complaining that now everyone had forgotten her, that no
one had any respect for her, that people insulted her, etcetera, etcetera. In
the most recent days, however, she too seemed to have undergone a
complete change. She frequently began to gaze at Ilyusha in the corner
and would start to brood. She became much more reticent and subdued,
and if she did start crying she did it quietly, so that no one should hear.
The second-grade captain noticed this change in her with bitter bewilderment. At first the visits of the boys did not appeal to her and only made
her angry, but after a while the merry cries and stories of the children
began to entertain her, too, and in the end she enjoyed it all so much that
if those boys had ceased to visit she would have grown dreadfully
melancholy. Whenever the children told stories or began to play games,
she would laugh and clap her hands. Some she would call to her side, and
kiss. She took a particular liking to Smurov. And as for the second-grade

captain, the appearance in his quarters of children who had come to cheer Ilyusha up filled his soul from the very outset with ecstatic joy and even the hope that Ilyusha would now cease to be melancholy and therefore, perhaps, quickly recover. Never had he doubted, not even for one minute, right up to the most recent time, and in spite of all his fear about Ilyusha, that his son would suddenly recover. He greeted the young guests with reverence, never left their side, obliged them in everything, was prepared to carry them about on his back, and even began to do so, but Ilyusha did not like such games and they were forsworn. He began buying them little presents of honey-cakes or nuts, made tea for them and buttered slices of bread for them. It should be noted that throughout the whole of this time he was always in funds. Exactly as Alyosha had predicted, he had accepted the two hundred roubles from Katerina Ivanovna. Then Katerina Ivanovna, having learned in more detail of their circumstances and of Ilyusha's illness, had herself visited their quarters, made the acquaintance of the whole family and had even succeeded in charming the second-grade captain's half-witted wife. From that day on her hand had not stinted its generosity, and the second-grade captain himself, crushed with horror at the thought that his son might die, forgot his earlier *honor* and meekly accepted her alms. Throughout all this time Dr Herzenstube, at Katerina Ivanovna's request, had called to visit the sick boy every second day, punctually and promptly, but little had come of his visits, and he had stuffed the boy with medicines something dreadful. On this particular day, however, that is to say, on the present Sunday morning, a certain new doctor was awaited at the home of the second-grade captain, a doctor who had arrived from Moscow and was there considered a celebrity. He had been specially ordered and sent for from Moscow by Katerina Ivanovna at great expense — not for little Ilyusha, but for a certain other purpose which shall later be described in its proper place, but since he had arrived she asked him to visit little Ilyusha, too, of which the second-grade captain had been informed in advance. But as for the arrival of Kolya Krasotkin, he had had no presentiment of that at all, though he had long wished that this boy for whom his little Ilyusha so languished would indeed finally come to see them. At the same moment that Krasotkin opened the door and appeared in the room they were all, the second-grade captain and the boys, crowding around the sick boy's little bed, examining a tiny Medelyansky pup which had just been brought and had been born only the day before, though ordered a week previously by the second-grade captain in order to divert and console Ilyusha, who was still pining for his vanished and, of course, now deceased Zhuchka. But though Ilyusha, who had already heard of it and had known for the past three days that he was to be given a puppy, and not an ordinary one, but a real Medelyansky (which, of course, was terribly important), tried to show by his tact and sensitivity that he was glad of the gift, it was none the less plain to them all, his father and the boys, that the new puppy had probably only stirred up even more profoundly within his little heart the memory of the unhappy Zhuchka whom he had tortured to death. The puppy lay fidgeting about beside him, while he, smiling wanly, stroked it with his thin, pale, withered little hand; one could even see that he liked the pup, but . . . it was not Zhuchka, and if only he could have Zhuchka and the puppy together, how happy he would be!

'Krasotkin!' one of the boys shouted suddenly, having been the first to spot the newly entered Kolya. A visible commotion ensued, as the boys drew apart and stood at both sides of the little bed, thus suddenly exposing little Ilyusha entirely to view. The second-grade captain impetuously rushed to greet Kolya.

'Welcome, welcome . . . dear guest!' he babbled to him. 'Ilyusha, Mr Krasotkin has come to visit you . . .'

But Krasotkin, quickly giving him his hand, demonstrated in a flash his exceptional grasp of the social niceties. He instantly and before all else turned to the second-grade captain's spouse who was sitting in her armchair (and at that moment happened to be particularly displeased, grumbling that the boys were standing in the way of Ilyusha's bed, obstructing her view of the new puppy), very courteously bowed and scraped before her and then, turning to Ninochka, performed to her, as the other lady present, a similar bow. This courteous action produced upon the invalid lady an uncommonly pleasant impression.

'Well, one can see he's a well brought up young man,' she declared loudly, spreading her arms. 'But what about the rest of our guests? They arrive one on top of the other.'

'Now then, little mother: "one on top of the other"? What's that supposed to mean?' the second-grade captain babbled affectionately enough, though somewhat in fear of 'little mother's' reaction.

'Well, that's the way they come in. They get up on one another's shoulders out in the passage and then they come into a decent household like that, piggy-back style! What sort of guests are they?'

'But which boy, little mother, which boy did that, which one?'

'Why, that boy there did, today, sitting on that boy there, and that one sitting on that one . . .'

But Kolya was already standing by Ilyusha's little bed. The sick boy had turned visibly pale. He raised himself in the cot and stared at Kolya, fixedly, fixedly. The latter had not seen his former small friend for some two months now, and suddenly came to a halt before him, completely thunderstruck: he had had no idea that he would see such a thin and yellow little face, such eyes that burned with feverish heat and seemed to have grown horribly enlarged, such thin little arms. With astonished grief he studied Ilyusha's deep and rapid breathing, and his dried-up lips. He took a step towards him, gave him his hand and, almost completely at a loss for words, said:

'Well, old geezer . . . how are you getting along?'

But his voice failed, he lacked the proper casualness of manner, his face seemed to tug suddenly, and something began to quiver near his lips. Ilyusha smiled wanly at him, still not strong enough to utter a word. Kolya suddenly raised his arm and for some reason ruffled his hand through Ilyusha's hair.

'Ne-ver mind,' he murmured to him softly, partly in order to reassure him and partly because the words had come out without him really knowing why.

'What's this you've got — a new puppy?' Kolya inquired in a most dispassionate voice.

'Ye-e-es!' Ilyusha replied in a long, choking whisper.

'He has a black muzzle, that means he is one of the ferocious breed, a watchdog,' Kolya observed in a firm, grand tone, as if the whole purpose of his visit were connected with this puppy and its black muzzle. What was really at stake, however, was that he was trying with all his might to keep control of the emotion within himself, so as not to burst into tears like a 'junior', yet was none the less unable to do so. 'When he gets bigger you will have to put him on a chain, I can tell already.'

'He'll be huge!' one of the boys in the crowd exclaimed.

'It's plain to see, he's a Medelyansky, they're huge, like this, the size of a bull calf,' several small voices suddenly chimed.

'The size of a bull calf, a real bull calf, sir,' the second-grade captain said, leaping up. 'I especially found one of the ferocious, the most ferocious kind, and his parents are also huge and highly ferocious, standing this high off the floor . . . Please be seated, sir, look, here on Ilyusha's cot, or else over here on the bench. We welcome you, dear and long-awaited guest . . . Were you so good as to arrive together with Aleksey Fyodorovich, sir?'

Krasotkin sat down on the little bed, at Ilyusha's feet. Though it was possible that on his way he had prepared a casual beginning to the conversation, he now decidedly lost his thread.

'No . . . I came with Perezvon . . . That's the name of the dog I have now, Perezvon. It's a Slavic name. He's waiting out there . . . When I blow my whistle he will come charging in. I have a dog, too,' he said, turning to Ilyusha suddenly. 'I say, old geezer, do you remember Zhuchka?' striking him suddenly with the question, as with a physical blow.

Ilyushechka's little face suddenly creased and folded. He gazed at Kolya with an air of martyrdom. Alyosha, who was standing by the door, frowned and began to nod furtive signals to Kolya not to talk about Zhuchka, but Kolya either did not notice them or did not want to notice them.

'Where is . . . Zhuchka?' Ilyusha asked in a strained little voice.

'Well now, brother, your Zhuchka has gone — phut! Your Zhuchka has kicked the bucket!'

Ilyusha held his tongue, but gave Kolya one more long, fixed look. Alyosha, catching Kolya's eye, began again with all his might to nod to him, but Kolya averted his gaze once more, pretending that even this time he had not noticed.

'He's run off somewhere far away and kicked the bucket. How could he not kick the bucket after a titbit like that,' Kolya snapped mercilessly, yet as he did so he also seemed to start choking on something. 'But I've got Perezvon with me . . . It's a Slavic name . . . I've brought him for you . . .'

'Don't bo-ther!' little Ilyusha suddenly said.

'Oh, but yes, we must bother, you absolutely have to see him . . . You will find him very entertaining. I've brought him here especially . . . He's shaggy-coated, just like the other one . . . Madam, will you permit me to summon in my dog?' he said, turning suddenly to Mrs Snegiryova, in a state of excitement that was now quite unfathomable.

'Don't bother, don't bother!' Ilyusha exclaimed, with a grief-laden crack of strain in his little voice. Reproach had begun to burn in his eyes.

'I say, sir, I think you ought to . . .' burst suddenly from the second-grade captain from the trunk by the wall, where he had just begun to sit down again. 'I think you ought to . . . leave it for another time, sir . . .' he mouthed, but Kolya, in complete insistence and in a hurry now, suddenly called to Smurov: 'Smurov, open the door!' — and as soon as the latter opened it, Kolya blew his whistle. Perezvon came charging impetuously into the room.

'Up, Perezvon! Beg, beg!' Kolya roared, leaping up from his seat, and the dog, standing on its hindlegs, drew itself up right in front of Ilyusha's little bed. Something that no one had expected took place: Ilyusha gave a start and all of a sudden leaned violently forward, bent down to Perezvon and, as if dying with inward rapture, stared at him.

'This is . . . Zhuchka!' he shouted suddenly in a little voice that was cracked with suffering and happiness.

'And you thought it wasn't?' Krasotkin sang in a happy, resonant voice and, stooping down to the dog, picked him up and raised him to a level with Ilyusha.

'Look, old geezer, you see? He's blind in one eye, and his left ear has a tear in it, exactly the same distinctive marks you told me about. It was those distinctive marks that made it possible for me to track him down! I found him that very same day, practically, in no time at all. You see, he didn't have a proper owner, he didn't have an owner at all!' he exclaimed, turning round quickly to the second-grade captain, to the second-grade captain's spouse, to Alyosha, and then back to Ilyusha again. 'He was in the Fedotovs' backyard, he'd started to make that his home, but the Fedotovs weren't feeding him, he's a stray, a runaway from the country . . . And I found him . . . You see, old geezer, he must not have swallowed your titbit after all. If he had swallowed it, of course he'd have died, that's absolutely certain! He must have managed to spit it out, since he's still alive. And you can't have noticed him doing it. He must have spat it out, but pricked his tongue all the same, and that was why he had begun to yelp at the time. He yelped as he ran, and you thought it was because he had actually swallowed the pin. He could not have helped it, as dogs have very sensitive skin inside their mouths . . . more sensitive than that of human beings, far more sensitive!' Kolya exclaimed violently, his face flushed and radiant with ecstasy.

But Ilyusha was unable to say anything at all. He stared at Kolya with his large and somehow horribly bulging eyes, his mouth agape, and white as a sheet. Indeed, had the unsuspecting Krasotkin only known what an agonizing, murderous effect such a moment would have on the health of the sick boy, he would never on any account have pulled a trick of the kind he had just done. Alyosha was, however, probably the only person in the room who understood this. As for the second-grade captain, he seemed to have turned into the very smallest of small boys.

'Zhuchka! So this is Zhuchka?' he cried in a blissful voice. 'My dear

Ilyusha, why, this is Zhuchka, your Zhuchka! Little mother, why, it is Zhuchka!' He was very nearly in tears.

'And I never even guessed!' Smurov exclaimed ruefully. 'Bravo, Krasotkin, I always said he would find Zhuchka, and he has!'

'Yes, he has found him!' one of the others responded joyfully.

'Good fellow, Krasotkin!' a third little voice rang out.

'Good fellow, good fellow!' shouted all the boys, and they began to applaud.

'Wait, wait!' Krasotkin cried, trying to shout louder than any of them. 'I shall tell you how it happened, the whole of the trick lies in that, and not in anything else! You see, I tracked him down, took him back to my place and immediately hid him, kept him under lock and key, and didn't let anyone know he was there, right up until today. Smurov was the only person who knew anything, he found out two weeks ago, but I told him it was Perezvon, and he did not guess the truth; meanwhile, in the *entr'acte*, I taught Zhuchka a whole bag of tricks, and you shall see, you shall see what tricks he knows! I taught them to him, old geezer, so I could bring him to you trained and fluent in what he knows: as much as to say – "Look, old geezer, look at your Zhuchka now!" I say, have you a little piece of beef? He'll show you such a trick that you'll fall down with laughter – just a little piece of beef, oh come, surely you have one?'

The second-grade captain rushed impetuously out through the passage into the landladies' living quarters, where the second-grade captain's meals were also cooked. But Kolya, in order not to waste precious time, in a desperate hurry, cried to Perezvon: 'Die!' And the dog suddenly rolled over, lay on it's back and froze motionless with all its four legs pointing upwards. The boys laughed, Ilyusha gazed on with his former martyred smile, but the person who derived the greatest delight from Perezvon's feigned death was 'little mother'. She burst into peals of loud laughter at the dog, and began to snap her fingers and call:

'Perezvon! Perezvon!'

'He'll never get up, not for anything,' Kolya crowed in triumph and justifiable pride, 'though you shout to all the corners of the earth. Yet if I shout, he'll leap up in a flash! *Ici*, Perezvon!'

The dog leapt up and began to jump in the air, yelping with joy. The second-grade captain came running in with a piece of boiled beef.

'It's not too hot, is it?' Kolya inquired in a hurried, businesslike tone, taking the piece of beef. 'No, it's all right; dogs don't like hot food. Look, Ilyusha old chum, look, come on, old geezer, look, why aren't you looking? I bring him his dog and he doesn't want to look!'

The new trick consisted in placing the tasty morsel of beef on the outstretched muzzle of the motionlessly standing dog. The unhappy hound had to stand without moving with the morsel on his nose for as long as his master commanded, and to stay there, never budging, for up to half an hour. Perezvon, however, was sustained in his position for only the very briefest of brief moments.

'Take it!' Kolya shouted, and in a single flash the morsel flew from the muzzle to the mouth of Perezvon. It went without saying that the audience gave cries of ecstatic wonder.

'And did you really, did you really put off coming here all this time merely in order to train the dog?' Alyosha exclaimed with involuntary reproach.

'Only because of that,' Kolya shouted in a most ingenuous manner. 'I wanted to show him off in all his glory!'

'Perezvon! Perezvon!' cried Ilyusha, who had suddenly started to snap his thin little fingers, beckoning the dog.

'You don't need to do that! Just let him jump up on to your bed himself. *Ici*, Perezvon!' Kolya gave the bed a slap, and Perezvon flew like an arrow up to Ilyusha. The latter impetuously embraced the dog's head in both arms, and in a flash Perezvon was licking him all over one side of his face. Ilyusha pressed himself against him, stretched out on his little bed and hid his face from them all in the dog's shaggy coat.

'Merciful Lord, merciful Lord!' the second-grade captain exclaimed.

Kolya squatted down on Ilyusha's bed again.

'Ilyusha, I have one more trick to show you. I've brought you a toy cannon. Do you remember, I told you about it that day, and you said: "Oh, if only I could see it!" Well, I've got it with me now.'

And Kolya, hurrying now, took the miniature bronze cannon out of his satchel. The reason for his hurry was because he, too, was very happy: on another occasion he would have waited for the effect produced by Perezvon to pass away, but now he was in haste, disdaining all restraint: 'So you are happy, are you? Well, here is some more happiness!' He himself was thoroughly intoxicated with it.

'I had my eye on this little contraption for a long time when it belonged to the civil servant Morozov — for you, old geezer, for you. It wasn't doing anything in his home, he'd got it from his brother, and I swapped it with him for a book from papa's book-cupboard called *A Kinsman of Mahomet, or Salutary Folly*.* A hundred years old it was, dissolute stuff, published in Moscow in the days when there wasn't any censorship, and Morozov is a great reader of such things. You should have seen the way he thanked me . . .'

Kolya held the cannon up so that everyone could see it and take pleasure in it. Ilyusha raised himself on one elbow and, continuing to hug Perezvon with his right arm, studied the toy with admiration. The effect attained a high degree when Kolya announced that he had gunpowder, too, and that the cannon might be fired right away, 'if that will not alarm the ladies'. 'Little mother' at once asked to be allowed to examine the toy at closer range, and her request was immediately granted. The small bronze cannon on wheels appealed to her greatly, and she began to roll it to and fro across her knees. In response to the request for permission to fire she replied with the most complete consent, though failing to understand the import of the question. Kolya exhibited the gunpowder and the lead shot. The second-grade captain, as a former military man, took charge of the loading arrangements himself, pouring out the very smallest portion of powder, and requesting that the lead shot be postponed to another occasion. The cannon was placed upon the floor, pointing into empty air, three grains of powder were crammed into the touch hole and were lit with a match. There was a most magnificent report. Little mother gave an initial start, but then at once began to laugh with joy. The boys gazed on in blissful exultation, but more blissful than any of them, as he gazed at Ilyusha, was the second-grade captain. Kolya lifted up the cannon and immediately presented it to Ilyusha, along with the shot and powder.

'I brought this for you, for you! I've been keeping it for you for ages,' he said again, completely happy now.

'Oh, why don't you give it to me? Yes, I think you ought to give it to me!' little mother began to entreat suddenly, like a little girl. Her face displayed a pitiful expression of fear that she would not be given the toy. Kolya was embarrassed. The second-grade captain began to grow uneasily excited.

'Little mother, little mother!' he said, leaping to her side, 'the cannon is yours, is yours, but let Ilyusha look after it, as it has been given to him, but it is as good as yours, Ilyusha will always let you play with it, it will belong to you both, to you both . . .'

'No, I don't want it to belong to us both, no, I want it to be all mine, not Ilyusha's,' little mother continued, on the verge of genuine tears now.

'Mamma, please take it, here, take it!' Ilyusha cried suddenly. 'Krasotkin, would it be all right if I gave it to mamma?' he said, suddenly turning to Krasotkin with imploring features, as though fearing that the latter might take offence because he had given his present to someone else.

'Perfectly, all right!' Krasotkin consented at once and, taking the cannon out of Ilyusha's hands, gave it to little mother with a most courteous bow. Little mother actually burst into tears with emotion.

'Dear Ilyusha, there, there's a dear boy who loves his mother!' she exclaimed tenderly, and at once began again to roll the cannon to and fro across her knees.

'Little mother, let me kiss your dear hand too,' said her spouse, leaping over to her, and at once carrying out his intention.

'And if there's a dearest young man in all the world it is that kind boy!' said the grateful lady, pointing to Krasotkin.

'And I can bring you as much gunpowder as you need, Ilyusha. We make our own now. Borovikov found out how to do it: you take twenty-four parts of saltpetre, ten parts of sulphur and six parts of birchwood charcoal, pound them all together, pour on some water, mix the whole thing to a paste and sieve it through a drumskin – and then one has gunpowder.'

'Smurov has already told me about your gunpowder, but papa says that it's not the real thing,' Ilyusha responded.

'What do you mean?' said Kolya, blushing. 'Ours burns all right. Though of course, I don't really know . . .'

'No, sir, what I said was not important, sir,' said the second-grade captain suddenly, jumping up with a guilty look. 'I did, to be sure, say that that is not how real gunpowder is constituted, but it is not important, sir, one may also make gunpowder your way, sir.'

'I don't know, you have a better knowledge of it. We lit some in a stone pomade jar and it burned wonderfully, burned up entirely, leaving only a tiny patch of soot. But I mean, that was only the paste, and if one were to sieve it through a drumskin . . . No, really, you have a better knowledge of it, and I don't know . . . But Bulkin's father gave him a hiding because of our powder, did you hear?' he said suddenly, addressing Ilyusha.

'Yes, I did,' Ilyusha replied. He had been listening to Kolya with boundless interest and pleasure.

'We'd made up a bottle full of powder, and he was keeping it under his bed. His father saw it. It could explode, he said. And he gave him a thrashing right there and then. He said he was going to make a complaint to the gymnasium about me. He's not allowed to play with me now, none of the boys is. Not even Smurov's allowed to play with me, I've got a bad reputation with everyone; they say I'm a "desperate character",' Kolya smiled contemptuously. 'It all began with that business on the railway here.'

'Ah, we heard about that *passage* of yours!' the second-grade captain exclaimed. 'How on earth could you lie there? Were you really not afraid at all when the train passed over you? Surely you must have been terrified, sir?'

The second-grade captain was using cunning flattery on Kolya to a degree that was truly dreadful.

'N-not especially!' Kolya responded carelessly. 'It was that cursed goose that did my reputation most of the harm around here,' he said, turning back to Ilyusha again. But though he tried to affect a careless air as he talked, he was none the less unable to gain mastery over himself and continued, as it were, to lose the proper tone.

'Ah, I heard about the goose, too!' Ilyusha began to laugh, beaming all over. 'They told me, but I did not understand, were you really tried by a judge?'

'It was a most brainless episode, a most insignificant one, out of which, as is customary, our school concocted an entire elephant,' Kolya began casually. 'I was crossing the square one day, and a herd of geese happened to have been brought in by a herdsman. I stopped to look at the geese. Suddenly a certain young fellow who lives in town, Vishnya-kov, he works as an errand-man for Plotnikovs', gazed at me and said: "Why are you looking at the geese?" I looked at him: a stupid, round mug, the fellow must be twenty, but you know, I never turn away the common folk. I like to talk with the folk ... We have fallen behind the common folk — that is an axiom — you appear to be laughing, Karamazov?'

'No, God forbid, I am all ears for what you have to say,' Alyosha retorted with a most ingenuous air, and the suspicious Kolya was of an instant reassured.

'My theory, Karamazov, is a clear and simple one,' he at once began to hurry on again, joyfully. 'I believe in the common folk and am always glad to render them justice, but without on any account indulging them, that is *sine qua* ... Yes, but well, I was talking about the goose. Well, I turned to this foolish fellow and replied to him: "You see, I am thinking about what that goose is thinking about." He stared at me in complete stupidity: "And what is the goose thinking about?" he said. "Look," I said, "there is a cart laden with oats. Some oats are falling out of one of the sacks, and that goose has stretched his neck right under the wheel and is pecking the grain – do you see?" "I see it very well," he said. "Well then," I said, "if one were to move that very same cart a trifle forwards now – would the wheel cut through the goose's neck or would it not?" "Sure as apples," he said, "it would and all," and he grinned a smirky grin from ear to ear, fairly melted to a jelly. "Well then, let us to it," I said, "come along then, my good fellow." "Right you are," he said. And it did not take us long to rustle up a plan of action: he stood unobtrusively beside the bridle, and I to one side, in order to make the goose go in the right direction. The muzhik who was in charge of the geese happened to have let his attention wander just then, was talking to someone, so I did not have to do anything at all to make the goose go the right way; it stretched out its neck for the oats under the cart of its own accord, right under the wheel. I winked to the young fellow, he gave the bridle a jerk, and – c-crack, the goose's neck split in half! And then it just had to happen that at that same second all the muzhiks spotted us, well, and they all began to bawl together: "You did that on purpose!" "No, I didn't!" "Yes, you did!" Well, then they bawled: "Off to the *mirovoy** with him!", and they grabbed hold of me, too: "You were involved in it, too!" they said. "You helped him, the whole of the market knows you!" It's quite true, actually, the whole of the market does know me, for some reason,' Kolya added, with vanity. 'So we all traipsed off to the house of the *mirovoy*, and the goose was taken along too. The next thing I saw was that my young fellow had got scared and started to blub, blub like a woman. But the herdsman shouted: "Using that method a man could slaughter as many geese as he wanted!" Well, of course, there were witnesses. The *mirovoy* settled it all in a flash: the herdsman to receive a rouble for his goose, and the young fellow to be allowed to keep the goose. And for him not to indulge in jokes of that kind again in future. But the young fellow kept on blubbing like a woman: "It's wasn't my idea," he said, "it was him that put me up to it" – and he pointed at me. I replied with complete sang-froid that I had in no way put him up to it, that all I had done was to expound the basic idea, and had spoken merely in terms of a project. *Mirovoy* Nefedov smiled drily, and then at once got angry with himself for having smiled: "I am going to recommend to the authorities of your school," he said, "that you should not embark upon such projects in future, and concentrate instead upon your books and lessons." He didn't actually do that, it was just an idle threat, but the incident did get spread around and came to the ears of the school authorities: the people in our school have long ears, you know! Our classics teacher, Kolbasnikov,* got particularly waxy, but Dardanelov stuck up for me again. But now Kolbasnikov is as vicious as a donkey with stomach-ache at us all. Have you heard, Ilyusha, I mean, he's got married, taken a dowry of a thousand roubles from the Mikhailovs, and his bride is a mug-whirler* of the first order and the last degree. The chaps in the third form immediately composed an epigram:

> The third formers thought the news odd enough:
> He has married, our messy old Kolbasnikov.

Well, and it goes on like that, it's really funny, I shall bring you the whole of it later. I've no objection to Dardanelov, however: he's a man of knowledge, solid knowledge. Men like him I have respect for, though it's not because he stuck up for me . . .'

'Anyway, you stymied him on that question of who founded Troy!' Smurov suddenly inserted, decidedly proud of Krasotkin at this moment. He had found the tale about the goose most appealing.

'So you really did?' the second-grade captain chimed in, flattery in his voice. 'On the question of who founded Troy, sir? We have already heard about it, sir. Ilyusha told me about it at the time, sir . . .'

'Papa, he knows everything, he knows more than all of us put together!' little Ilyusha chimed in, too. 'I mean, the rest of it is just pretending, he is really our best pupil in every subject . . .'

Ilyusha gazed at Kolya with boundless happiness.

'Oh, that stuff about Troy was just rubbish, trivial nonsense. I personally consider that question a trivial one,' Kolya retorted with haughty modesty. By now he had completely succeeded in establishing the proper tone, though he was, as a matter of fact, somewhat uneasy: he sensed that he was in a state of high excitement and that concerning the goose, for example, he had embarked upon a narrative all too obviously from the heart; throughout its entire duration Alyosha had remained silent and serious, and the vain young boy had little by little begun to feel a clawing sensation at his heart: 'Is not the real reason for his silence because he views me with contempt, thinking that I seek his praise? If he dares to think such a thing, then I . . .'

'I consider that question a decidedly trivial one,' he said brusquely and haughtily, a second time.

'Well, I know who founded Troy,' suddenly and quite unexpectedly said one of the boys, one who had scarcely uttered a word until now, taciturn, and apparently shy, very good-looking, about eleven, by the name of Kartashov. He was sitting right over by the door. Kolya gave him a look of surprise and gravity. The fact was that the question: 'Who founded Troy?' had in every form acquired the status of a positive secret, to penetrate which it was necessary to read the relevant passage in Smaragdov. But none of the boys, except Kolya, possessed a copy of Smaragdov. And then on one occasion, when Kolya's back was turned, Kartashov had quickly and in stealth opened Kolya's copy, which lay among his other books, and hit directly upon the passage concerning the founders of Troy. This had happened quite a long time ago, but he had been too embarrassed to reveal publicly that he too knew who had founded Troy, fearing that something unpleasant might come of it and that Kolya might embarrass him in front of the others because of it. But now he had suddenly lost his reticence and had told them. It was something he had long wanted to do.

'Well, then, who did?' Kolya said, turning to him in supercilious condescension, having already guessed by Kartashov's features that the latter really did know and, of course, having prepared himself at once for all the consequences. In the general mood there occurred what is termed a dissonance.

'Troy was founded by Teucer, Dardanus, Ilius and Tros,' the boy trotted out in a flash, and immediately blushed to the roots of his hair, so terribly that one felt quite sorry to look at him. But all the boys stared at him fixedly, stared at him for a whole minute, and suddenly all those fixedly staring eyes turned simultaneously to Kolya. The latter still continued to measure the impudent boy with his gaze, a gaze of contemptuous sang-froid.

'The point is, however, how did they found it?' he deigned to say at last. 'And in general, what does it mean to found a city or a state? What did they do: turn up and each lay a brick, or what?'

Laughter resounded. The guilty boy turned from pink to crimson. He said nothing, he was on the point of tears. Kolya kept him like that for another moment or so.

'In order to speak of historical events like the founding of a national identity, one must first of all understand what this means,' he rapped out sternly for the boy's edification. 'As a matter of fact, I personally do not attach much importance to those old wives' tales, and in general I have very little respect for world history,' he suddenly added in a casual tone, addressing everyone in the room.

'World history, sir?' the second-grade captain inquired with a vague and sudden alarm.

'Yes, world history. It is the study of a series of human follies, and that is all. I respect only mathematics and the naturals,'* Kolya swaggered, taking a quick look at Alyosha: in this room, Alyosha's was the only opinion he feared. But Alyosha continued to say nothing and was serious, the way he had been all along. If Alyosha had said anything now, that would have been the end of the matter, but Alyosha preserved his silence, and "his silence might be contemptuous", and Kolya now became thoroughly irritated.

'Or again, these ancient languages we have at school now: they are sheer insanity, nothing more . . . I suppose you do not agree with me again, Karamazov?'

'No, I do not,' Alyosha smiled with restraint.

'If you want to know my opinion, I think ancient languages are something thought up by the police as a restrictive measure, and that is the sole reason why they have been introduced,' Kolya said, beginning little by little to grow out of breath again. 'They have been introduced because they are tedious, and because they blunt one's faculties. Things were tedious, so what could they do to make them even more tedious? Things were confused, so what could they do to make them even more confused? Well, they dreamed up ancient languages. That is my confirmed opinion of them, and I hope that I shall never change it,' Kolya finished abruptly. On both his cheeks there had appeared a flushed spot of red.

'It's true,' Smurov, who had been listening diligently, suddenly agreed in a small, resonant voice of conviction.

'And he's our best Latin scholar!' one of the boys suddenly exclaimed from the crowd.

'Yes, papa, he says that, and he is top of our class in Latin,' Ilyusha also retorted.

'So what if I am?' Kolya said, considering it necessary to defend himself, though he had thoroughly enjoyed the praise. 'I swot at Latin because I have to, because I promised my mother to get the diploma, and because the way I see it, what I have begun I might as well do properly, even though in the depths of my soul I despise classical antiquity and all of that villainy . . . Are you not of the same opinion, Karamazov?'

'But why is it "villainy"?' Alyosha smiled drily again.

'Oh, for heaven's sake: look – the classics have all been translated into every conceivable language, so it follows that it's not for the sake of studying the classics that they need Latin, but rather solely as a restrictive police measure, in order to blunt our faculties. What is that if not a villainy?'

'But who has taught you this?' Alyosha exclaimed at last in astonishment.

'Well, for one thing, I myself am perfectly able to deduce it without having to think very hard, and for another, let me tell you that what I just told you about the classics having been translated was said out loud to the whole third form by our teacher, Mr Kolbasnikov, himself . . .'

'The doctor is here!' Ninochka, who had said nothing all this time, suddenly exclaimed.

Indeed, up to the front gate of the house had driven the carriage that belonged to Mrs Khokhlakova. The second-grade captain, who had been waiting for the doctor all morning, rushed out to the gate at full tilt to greet him. Little mother gathered herself up and assumed an air of importance. Alyosha went over to Ilyusha and began to adjust his pillow for him. From her armchair Ninochka anxiously watched him as he set the little bed in order. The boys began hurriedly to say goodbye; some of them promised to return that evening. Kolya called Perezvon, and the latter jumped down from the bed.

'I shall stay here, I shall stay here!' Kolya said to Ilyusha in a flurry. 'I'll wait out in the passage and come back in again when the doctor has left, and I'll bring Perezvon, too.'

But the doctor was already on his way in – an important figure in a bear-fur overcoat, with long, dark side-whiskers and a shinily clean-shaven chin. Having stepped across the threshold, he suddenly came to a halt, as though taken aback: 'What is this? Where am I?' he muttered, keeping his coat on and not removing his sealskin cap with its sealskin peak from his head. The crowd, the impoverished look of the room, the washing hung out in one corner on a line, had thrown him off balance. The second-grade captain doubled up before him.

'You are here, sir, you are here, sir,' he muttered obsequiously. 'You are here, sir, in my quarters, sir, you have come to visit me, sir . . .'

'Sne-gi-ryov?' the doctor pronounced in a loud, important voice. 'Mr Snegiryov – is that you?'

'Oh yes it is, sir!'

'Ah!'

The doctor gave the room another fastidious sweep of his gaze and threw off his fur overcoat. The important medal at his neck flashed them all in the face. The second-grade captain caught the fur overcoat in flight, and the doctor removed his cap.

'Where is the *Paʒient*?' he inquired loudly and pressingly.

6

Precocious Development

'How do you suppose, what will the doctor tell him?' Kolya said in a quick patter. 'I say, though, what an ugly mug, don't you think? I cannot abide medicine!'

'Ilyusha will die. I think that is already certain,' Alyosha replied sadly.

'The scoundrels! Medicine is a scoundrel! I am, however, glad that I have got to know you, Karamazov. I have long wished to make your acquaintance. It is only a shame that we have met in such sorry circumstances . . .'

Kolya felt a great urge to say something even more impassioned, even more expansive, but something seemed to make him shiver inwardly. Alyosha noticed this, smiled and gave his hand a squeeze.

'I have long learned to respect in you a being of rare quality,' Kolya muttered again, losing his thread and unsure of his words. 'I have heard that you are a mystic and have lived in the monastery. I am aware that you are a mystic, but . . . that did not stop me. Contact with reality will cure you . . . With natures such as yours it cannot be otherwise.'

'What do you mean, "mystic"? Cure me of what?' Alyosha inquired, somewhat astonished.

'Oh, God and all that sort of thing.'

'Surely you do not mean to tell that you do not believe in God?'

'On the contrary, I have nothing against God. Of course, God is merely a hypothesis . . . but . . . I recognize his necessity, for the sake of order . . . for the sake of universal order and so on . . . and if he did not exist, it would be necessary to invent him,' Kolya added, beginning to redden. It had suddenly occurred to him that Alyosha might think he was anxious to exhibit his knowledge and to show what a 'big boy' he was. 'But that is not what I want to do at all,' Kolya thought with indignation. And he suddenly felt bitterly vexed.

'I confess that I cannot endure entering into all these wrangles,' he snapped. 'After all, surely it is possible to love mankind without believing in God, would you not agree? Why, Voltaire did not believe in God, yet he loved mankind, did he not?' ('Again, again,' he thought to himself.)

'Voltaire did believe in God, but I doubt if it was very much, and I doubt if he loved mankind very much either,' Alyosha said in a quiet, restrained and perfectly natural voice, as though he were talking to someone who was his equal in years or even his senior. Kolya was surprised by this lack of certainty in Alyosha about his own opinion of Voltaire and by the fact that he seemed to be giving him, little Kolya, this question to solve.

'So you have read Voltaire, have you?' Alyosha said in conclusion.

'Well, not really . . . Though I have read *Candide*, in Russian translation . . . an old, outlandish translation, a comical one . . .' (Again, again!)

'And you understood it?'

'Oh yes, all of it . . . or at least . . . but why do you suppose I would not understand it? It does, of course, contain many indecencies . . . But of course, I am capable of understanding that it is a philosophical novel and that it was written in order to advance an idea . . .' Kolya said, now quite confused. 'I am a socialist, Karamazov, I am a dyed-in-the-wool socialist,' he said, breaking off suddenly for no apparent reason.

'A socialist?' Alyosha began to laugh. 'And where did you find time for that? After all, you are only thirteen, are you not?'

Kolya doubled up with rage.

'For one thing, not thirteen but fourteen, fourteen in two weeks' time,' he said, positively blazing, 'and for another, I really fail to understand what my age has to do with it. The point at issue is the nature of my convictions, not the number of years I possess, is it not?'

'When that number is greater you yourself will realize the importance of age where convictions are concerned. I also had the impression that you were not using your own words,' Alyosha replied with modest calm, but Kolya broke him off passionately.

'Oh, for pity's sake! You want obedience and mysticism. Agree at least that, for example, the Christian faith has served the interests of only the rich and the élite, in order to keep the lower classes in slavery, is that not so?'

'Aha, I know where you read that, and someone must certainly have taught you it!' Alyosha exclaimed.

'For pity's sake! Why must I have read it? And precisely no one taught me it. I am perfectly capable myself . . . And you may as well know that I am not opposed to Christ. He was a thoroughly humane individual, and had he lived in our own times he would quite certainly have adhered to the revolutionary cause and might even have played a prominent role in it . . . That is quite certain.'

'But where, where have you got all this from? With what fool of a man have you been hobnobbing?' Alyosha exclaimed.

'Oh, for pity's sake, the truth cannot be hidden. Of course it is true that I often talk with Mr Rakitin apropos of a certain matter, but . . . They say that old Belinsky* said the same thing.'

'Belinsky? I do not recall it. He did not write that anywhere.'

'Even if he did not write it, they say that he said it. I heard it from a certain . . . though, actually, the devil . . .'

'And you have read Belinsky?'

'Well, you see . . . no . . . not exactly, but . . . I have read the part about Tatyana, and why she did not go with Onegin.'

'What do you mean, did not go with Onegin? Do you . . . understand that?'

'Oh, for pity's sake, I think you must take me for that junior Smurov,' Kolya said, grinning irritably. 'As a matter of fact, though, please do not think that I am such a revolutionary as all that. I very often do not agree with Mr Rakitin. If I mentioned Tatyana, it was not all because I am for the emancipation of women. I recognize that woman is a subordinate being and must obey. *Les femmes tricottent*, as Napoleon said,' Kolya said with an ironic grin, for some reason, 'and at least in that I completely share the conviction of that pseudo-great man. I also, for example, consider that to flee the fatherland for America is an act of baseness – worse, of stupidity. Why go to America when here too one may bring much advantage to mankind? Particularly now. A whole mass of fruitful activity. That is what I replied.'

'What do you mean, replied? To whom? Has someone asked you to go to America, then?'

'I will confess that I was urged to go, but I refused. This is, of course, between ourselves, Karamazov, do you hear, not a word to a soul. This is for your ears alone. I have no wish to fall into the paws of the Third Department* and take lessons beside the Chain Bridge.

> You will remember the building
> Beside the Chain Bridge!*

Do you remember? Is it not magnificent? What are you laughing at? You don't think I've been making it all up, do you?' ('And what if he discovers that that issue of *The Bell** is the only one there is in father's book-cupboard and that that is the only thing in it I have read?' Kolya thought fleetingly, but with a shudder.)

'My goodness, no I am not laughing,. nor do I for one moment suppose that you have been telling me stories. In fact, that is the very reason why I do *not* suppose it, because it is all of it, alas, the precise truth! But tell me, what about Pushkin, have you read anything by him? How about *Onegin*? ... After all, you were talking about Tatyana just now?'

'No, I have not read anything by him yet, but I intend to. I am without prejudices, Karamazov. I wish to hear both sides of the argument. Why do you ask?'

'I was simply curious.'

'Tell me, Karamazov, do you despise me dreadfully?' Kolya suddenly snapped, drawing himself up to his full height in front of Alyosha, as though taking up a position in battle. 'Please be so good as not to beat about the bush.'

'Despise you?' Alyosha said, looking at him in astonishment. 'But why should I do that? I am only sad that a charming nature such as yours, which has not yet even begun to live, should already have been corrupted by all this vulgar nonsense.'

'Please have no concern about my nature,' Kolya said, interrupting not without self-satisfaction. 'But that I am suspicious, that is so. I am stupidly suspicious, vulgarly suspicious. You smiled just now, and I thought it was because you ...'

'Oh, I was smiling at something else entirely. Look, I will tell you what I was smiling about: I recently read the remark of a certain European German who had lived in Russia concerning our present-day scholastic youth: "Show a Russian schoolboy a map of the stellar heavens," he wrote, "concerning which he has until now had no conception, and he will return it to you on the morrow with corrections." A total absence of knowledge and a wholeheartedly inflated opinion of himself – that was the German's view of the Russian schoolboy.'

'Oh, but that is absolutely true!' Kolya began to laugh loudly all of a sudden. 'Trueissimo, bang on the nail! Bravo, German! Except that the stupid fellow didn't see the good side, don't you think? An inflated opinion of oneself – that is all right, that is the result of youth, that may be corrected, if corrected it must be, but to make up for it there is an independence of spirit that begins in early childhood, practically, there is a boldness of thought and conviction, something quite different from their sausage-makers' cringing before authority ... Even so, though, the German put his finger on it! Bravo, German! Though I still say the Germans ought to be throttled. They may be brilliant at science, but I still say they ought to be throttled ...'

'Why must they be throttled?' Alyosha smiled.

'Well, perhaps I'm talking nonsense, I will admit it. I am sometimes a terrible baby, and when I am pleased about something I'm unable to hold myself back and may easily spout nonsense. Listen, though – you and I are chatting here about trivia, but that doctor has been in there for an awfully long time. Though actually, I suppose he may be examining "little mother" and that poor lame Ninochka. You know, I rather like that Ninochka. When I was on my way out she whispered to me: "Why did you not come before?" And in such a voice, with such reproach! I think she is incredibly kind and deserving of pity.'

'Yes, yes! Well, now you will be visiting often and you will see what a fine person she is. It is very good for you to get to know people like her, in order that you may learn to appreciate many other things, which you will discover only from an acquaintance with people like her,' Alyosha observed with heat. 'That will re-educate you better than anything else.'

'Oh, how sorry I am, how I curse myself for not having come before!' Kolya exclaimed with bitter emotion.

'Yes, it is a great shame. You yourself saw what a joyous impression you made on the poor young lad! And how he suffered as he waited for you!'

'Do not say it! You are rubbing salt on the wound. As a matter of fact, it serves me right: the reason I did not come was my vanity, my egotistical vanity and villainous despotism, of which all my life I have never been able to cure myself, though all my life I have cudgelled myself. I see it now. I am in many respects a scoundrel, Karamazov!'

'No, you have a charming nature, though it has been corrupted, and I understand all too well how you could have had such an influence on that noble boy whom illness has rendered so impressionable!' Alyosha replied hotly.

'To hear you say that to me!' Kolya exclaimed. 'And yet, imagine, I have thought – I have several times thought while I have been here, that you despised me! If you only knew how I treasure your opinion!'

'But is it really true that you are so suspicious, then? At such young years! Why, imagine, out there in the room as I watched you while you were talking I thought that very same thing – that you must be very suspicious.'

'Did you, indeed? What a sharp eye you have. Well, I never! I will lay a wager that it was when I told the story about the goose. It was precisely at that point that I felt you despised me deeply for being in a hurry to show myself off as a fine fellow, and I even suddenly conceived a hatred of you for that and launched into all that silly rigmarole. Then later, when I came to the bit (this was here, just now) where I said "If there were no God, one would have to invent him", I thought that I was in too much of a hurry to show off my education, especially since I read that saying in a book. But I swear to you, I was in such a hurry to show off not because of vanity, but just, oh, I don't know, because of joy, yes, I swear to God that's what it was, because of joy . . . although that is a deeply shameful character trait, when a man throws himself on everyone's neck because of joy. I am aware of that. On the other hand, however, I am now convinced that you do not despise me, and that it was all a figment of my imagination. Oh, Karamazov, I am deeply unhappy. I sometimes imagine God only knows what, that everyone is laughing at me, the entire world, and at such moments, at such moments I am quite simply ready to annihilate the entire order of things.'

'And worry the daylights out of everyone around you,' Alyosha smiled.

'And do that – especially to mother. Karamazov, tell me, am I being dreadfully ridiculous just now?'

'But do not think of that, do not think of that at all!' Alyosha exclaimed. 'And in any case, what does ridiculous mean? Are they few, those occasions on which a man is or may seem ridiculous? Besides, nowadays practically all men of ability are horribly scared of being ridiculous, and are so much the more miserable because of it. I am merely astonished that you should have begun to feel this, though, as a matter of fact, I have long observed it, and not in you alone. Nowadays even those who are still almost children have begun to suffer from this. It is almost a form of madness. In this vanity the Devil has assumed fleshly form and has crept into an entire generation, yes, the Devil,' Alyosha added, without a trace of the mocking smile that Kolya, who was staring at him intently, supposed would follow. 'It applies to you, as it does to all the rest,' Alyosha concluded, 'that is to say, as it does to very many of the rest, only you must not be like all the rest, that is what I will say to you.'

'Even in spite of the fact that all are like that?'

'Yes, even in spite of that. You alone must be different. And indeed you are different from the rest: just now you were not ashamed to confess to things that are bad and even ridiculous. And nowdays who will confess to such things? No one, and even the need for self-condemnation has ceased to be felt. Do not be like all the rest; even though you are the only one who is not, even then do not be like them.'

'Magnificent! I was not wrong about you. You are able to bring consolation. Oh, how I have striven towards you, Karamazov, how long I have sought to meet you! Have you really also thought about me?'

'Yes, I have heard about you and have also thought about you . . . and even if it is in part vanity that has impelled you to ask it, that does not matter.'

'You know, Karamazov, this mutual declaration of ours is rather like a declaration of love,' Kolya said in a voice that had somehow lost its firmness with bashfulness. 'Is that not ridiculous, is it not?'

'Not at all, and even if it were, it would not matter, because it is good,' Alyosha smiled radiantly.

'But you know, Karamazov, I think you will agree that you too are slightly ashamed with me . . . I see it in your eyes,' Kolya smiled somehow cunningly, but almost with something approaching happiness.

'But what is there to be ashamed about?'

'Well, why have you gone red in the face, then?'

'Why, that is your doing!' Alyosha laughed; he really had gone quite red in the face. 'Well, yes, it is a little shame-making, God knows why, I certainly do not . . .' he muttered, almost flustered, even.

'Oh, how I love you and treasure this moment, precisely because you too are ashamed about something with me! Because you are just like I am!' Kolya exclaimed in positive ecstasy. His cheeks were afire, his eyes glittered.

'Listen, Kolya, among other things, you are going to be very unhappy in life,' Alyosha said suddenly for some reason.

'I know, I know. How good you are at predicting things in advance!' Kolya said in immediate confirmation of this.

'But even so, life on the whole you will bless.'

'That's right! Hurrah! You are a prophet! Oh, we shall get along together, Karamazov. You know, what I think is most terrific of all is that you treat me entirely as an equal. Yet we are not equals, no, not equals — you are superior! But we shall get along. You know, all this past month I have kept saying to myself: "Either he and I will instantly get along with one another as friends for ever, or from our very first meeting we shall part mortal foes to the tomb!"'

'And of course in saying that you already loved me!' Alyosha laughed merrily.

'Yes I did, I loved you dreadfully, I loved you and dreamed of you! And how can you tell all these things, anyway? But I say, here's the doctor. O Lord, what is he going to say, look at his face!'

7
Ilyusha

THE doctor emerged from the living-room swathed in his fur coat once again and wearing his cap now. His face was almost angry and bore a fastidious expression, as though he were constantly afraid of getting himself dirty on something. He fleetingly cast his eyes about the passage and in doing so gave Alyosha and Kolya a stern look. Alyosha waved to the coachman from the doorway, and the carriage which had brought the doctor drove up to the front entrance. The second-grade captain ran out impetuously after the doctor and, bent double, almost cringing before him, stopped him for a last word. The face of the poor man bore a crushed appearance, his gaze frightened:

'Your Excellency, Your Excellency . . . is there really no . . .?' he began, but did not conclude, merely wringing his hands in despair, though still gazing at the doctor with a final plea, as though any word the doctor said now might really modify the sentence that had been pronounced on the poor boy.

'What is to be done? I am not God,' the doctor replied in a voice that, while offhand, none the less had the imposing grandeur of habit.

'Doctor . . . Your Excellency . . . will it be soon, soon?'

'Pre-pare yourself for anything,' the doctor rapped out, laying emphasis on each syllable and, lowering his gaze, himself prepared to step beyond the threshold in the direction of the carriage.

'Your Excellency, in the name of Christ!' the second-grade captain said, stopping him again in fear. 'Your Excellency . . . Then is there really nothing, nothing at all that will save him now? . . .'

'It does not de-pend on me now,' the doctor said impatiently. 'Although, in fact, ahem,' he said, pausing suddenly in his tracks, 'if, for example, you were able . . . to ex-pe-dite . . . your *Paʒient* . . . right now and without a moment's delay' (the words 'right now' and 'without a moment's delay' the doctor uttered not so much with sternness now, as with something approaching wrath, so that the second-grade captain even started) 'to Sy-ra-cuse, then . . . in con-se-quence of the new and favour-able cli-mat-ic con-dit-i-ons . . . there might, per-haps, oc-cur . . .'

'Syracuse!' the second-grade captain exclaimed, seeming as yet to take none of this in.

'Syracuse — that's in Sicily,' Kolya suddenly snapped out, by way of explanation. The doctor gave him a look.

'Sicily! But sir, Your Excellency,' the second-grade captain said, at a loss, 'why, you have seen!' And he cast his arms around, indicating his surroundings. 'And what about little mother . . . and the family?'

'N-no, family not to Sicily, you must send your family to the Caucasus, early in the spring . . . Your daughter should go to the Caucasus, and your spouse . . . having undergone the water cure also in the Cau-ca-sus in view of her rheumatisms . . . immediately after to be ex-pe-dit-ed to Paris, to the clinic of the *doc-teur psy-chi-atre Le-pel-letier*, I could give you the letter of introduction, and then . . . there might perhaps occur . . .'

'But doctor, doctor! Why, you see!' the second-grade captain cried suddenly with a wave of his arms again, indicating in despair the bare timbered walls of the passage.

'Well, that is not my affair,' the doctor said with a sardonic smile. 'I have only said what sci-ence can say to your question of the last resorts, but as for the rest . . . to my regret . . .'

'Do not be anxious, leech, my dog will not bite you,' Kolya snapped out loudly, having noticed the somewhat uneasy gaze the doctor was directing at Perezvon, who was standing in the doorway. A note of anger had begun to sound in Kolya's voice. He had used the word 'leech', instead of 'doctor', *on purpose* and, as he declared later, 'in order to give offence'.

'What did you say?' the doctor said, jerking up his head and staring at Kolya in astonishment. 'Who is this?' he said, turning to Alyosha suddenly, as though he were asking the latter to account for him.

'This is the master of Perezvon, leech, do not trouble yourself as to my identity,' Kolya rapped out again.

'*Zvon?*' the doctor echoed, failing to understand what 'Perezvon' referred to.

'But knows not where he's gone. Goodbye, leech, I shall see you in Syracuse.'

'Who is this? Who, who?' the doctor said, seething up dreadfully all of a sudden.

'He is one of our local schoolboys, doctor, he is a prankster, pay no attention to him,' Alyosha said quickly, frowning. 'Kolya, be quiet!' he exclaimed at Krasotkin. 'One must not pay any attention to him, doctor,' he said again, a little more impatiently now.

'A thrash-ing, he needs a thrash-ing, a thrash-ing!' shouted the doctor who was by now for some reason in a quite excessive lather, and had begun to stamp his foot.

'Why, you know, leech, my Perezvon may bite after all,' Kolya said in a trembling voice, his face pale and his eyes flashing. '*Ici*, Perezvon!'

'Kolya, if you say one more word I shall break with you for ever!' Alyosha exclaimed in a commanding voice.

'Leech, there is only one person in the whole world who can tell Nikolay Krasotkin what to do, and it is this man here,' Kolya said, pointing to Alyosha. 'Him do I obey, and now farewell!'

He darted away and, opening the door, quickly went back through into the room. Perezvon went rushing after him. The doctor began to stare at Alyosha, standing still as if stupefied for some five seconds more, then suddenly spat and walked quickly to the carriage, loudly repeating: 'This, this, this, I do not know what this is!' The second-grade captain rushed to help him in. Alyosha went back through into the room after Kolya. The latter was already standing by Ilyusha's little bed. Ilyusha was holding him by the hand and calling for his papa. After a moment the second-grade captain, too, returned.

'Papa, papa, come here . . . we . . .' Ilyusha began to babble in extreme excitement, but, evidently without the strength to continue, suddenly threw forward both his emaciated little arms and, as tightly as he possibly could, embraced them both at once, both Kolya and his papa, uniting them in one embrace and pressing himself towards them. The second-grade captain suddenly shook all over with speechless sobs, and Kolya's mouth and chin began to tremble.

'Papa, papa! Oh, how sorry for you I am!' Ilyusha groaned bitterly.

'Dear little Ilyusha . . . little dove . . . the doctor said . . . you will be well . . . we shall be happy . . . the doctor . . .' the second-grade captain began.

'Oh, papa! I mean, I know what the new doctor told you about me . . . I mean, I saw him!' Ilyusha exclaimed and again tightly, with all the strength he had, pressed them both towards him, hiding his face in his father's shoulder.

'Papa, don't cry . . . and when I die you must get a good boy, another boy . . . you must choose him from among all the rest, a good boy, and call him Ilyusha and love him instead of me . . .'

'That will do, old geezer, you're going to recover!' Krasotkin exclaimed all of a sudden, almost as though he were angry.

'But papa, you must never forget me, ever,' Ilyusha continued. 'You must visit my grave . . . and listen, papa, you must bury me beside that big stone of ours, the one you and I used to walk to, and you must take Krasotkin with you, in the evening . . . And Perezvon . . . And I will be waiting for you . . . Papa, papa!'

His voice broke off, and all three stood there embracing, silent now. Ninochka wept softly in her armchair, and suddenly, at the sight of everyone crying, little mother too burst into tears.

'Ilyushechka! Ilyushechka!' she howled.

Krasotkin suddenly freed himself from Ilyusha's embraces.

'Farewell now, old geezer, my mother is expecting me for dinner,' he said quickly. 'What a pity I did not warn her in advance! She will be very anxious ... But after dinner I shall come straight back to see you again, all afternoon, and all evening, and just wait till you hear all the things I have to tell you, just wait! I shall bring Perezvon, too, though I shall take him with me now, for without me he will only start to howl and be a nuisance to you. Goodbye until later!'

And he ran out into the passage. He had not wanted to burst into tears, but in the passage he began to cry after all. In this condition he was discovered by Alyosha.

'Kolya, you must be certain to keep your word and come back again, or else he will be dreadfully miserable,' Alyosha said with urgency.

'Certainly! Oh, how I curse myself for not having come before now,' weeping, and by now without embarrassment at doing so, Kolya muttered. At that moment the second-grade captain suddenly more or less leapt out of the room, instantly closing the door behind him. His face was frenzied, his lips quivered. He stood before the two young men and flung both arms aloft.

'I do not want a good boy! I do not want another boy!' he said in a wild whisper, grinding his teeth together. 'If I forget thee, O Jerusalem, let my tongue cleave . . .'*

He did not finish, as though he had swallowed something the wrong way, and sank helplessly on to his knees in front of the wooden bench. Clenching his head in both fists, he began to sob, with preposterous yelping sounds, exerting every effort, however, to prevent these yelps being heard in the living-room. Kolya ran out into the street.

'Goodbye, Karamazov! What about you – will you be back?' he cried brusquely and angrily to Alyosha.

'I shall come back this evening, for certain.'

'What was that he was saying about Jerusalem? . . . What was that all about?'

'It is from the Bible: "If I forget thee, O Jerusalem", in other words, if I forget all that is most precious to me, if I exchange it for anything, then may I be struck . . .'

'I understand, enough! Be sure that you come, too! *Ici*, Perezvon!' he shouted to the dog with perfect ferocity now, and began to stride off home with long, swift strides.

BOOK XI
BROTHER IVAN FYODOROVICH

I

At Grushenka's

ALYOSHA set off towards Cathedral Square and the house of the shopowner Mrs Morozova, where Grushenka lived. Grushenka had early that morning sent Fenya to him with the urgent request that he visit her. On subjecting Fenya to questioning, Alyosha discovered that the *barynya* had been in a state of considerable and particular anguish ever since the previous afternoon. Throughout the whole of the two months since Mitya's arrest Alyosha had been a frequent visitor to Mrs Morozova's house both on his own initiative and on errands for Mitya. Some three days after Mitya's arrest Grushenka had fallen seriously ill and had been ill for very nearly five weeks. For one week of those five she had lain unconscious. She had altered much about the face, grown thinner and sallow, though for almost two weeks now she could have gone out had she so desired. In the view of Alyosha, however, her face had become even more attractive, and he liked, when entering her room, to meet her gaze. Something firm and intelligent seemed to have consolidated itself within it. There were the telltale signs of some spiritual upheaval, and there had manifested itself a kind of immutable, humble, but benign and irreversible determination. Between her eyebrows there had appeared upon her forehead a small, vertical wrinkle, which lent her charming face an air of reflection concentrated in itself, which at a first glance could seem positively severe. Of her previous giddy headedness, for example, there remained not a trace. Alyosha also found it strange that, in spite of all the misfortune that had overtaken the poor woman, the bride of a groom who had been arrested for a terrible crime almost at the very moment she had become his bride, in spite of her subsequent illness and the almost inevitable decision of the court that loomed ahead of her, Grushenka had none the less not lost her previous youthful gaiety. In her eyes that earlier had been proud there had now begun to shine a kind of quietness, although ... although, as a matter of fact, those eyes again from time to time flamed with a certain ill-boding spark of light, whenever she was visited by a certain previous concern, which not only had not died away but had even grown magnified within her heart. The object of that concern was still the same: Katerina Ivanovna, whom Grushenka had while ill made mention of even in her delirium. Alyosha had come to understand that she was horribly jealous of her because of Mitya, in spite of the fact that Katerina Ivanovna had not once visited him in his confinement, though she could have done so whenever she had wished. All this had for Alyosha turned into a rather difficult problem, for he was the only person to whom Grushenka would confide her heart and she was constantly asking him for advice, advice which it was, however, sometimes quite beyond his power to give.

In concern he entered her lodgings. By now she was home; a half an hour earlier she had returned from Mitya, and from the quick movement with which she leapt up from her armchair to greet him, he concluded that she had been awaiting him with great impatience. Cards lay on the table, and a game of *durachki** had been dealt. On the leather sofa at the other side of the sofa a bed had been made, and on it reclined, in a dressing-gown and a cotton nightcap, Maksimov, plainly ill and enfeebled, though sweetly smiling. On returning with Grushenka from Mokroye that day some two months earlier, the homeless old fellow had stayed with her and had been inseparable from her ever since. Arriving back that day with her through the rain and slushy mire, wet through and frightened, he had sat down on the sofa and stared at her silently, with a timid, imploring smile. Grushenka, who had been in a state of terrible misery and already incipient fever, having almost forgotten about him during the first half hour of her arrival back because of various practical concerns, had suddenly given him a vague, fixed look: he had tittered in her face, a pathetic, lost titter. She had summoned Fenya and told her to give him something to eat. All that afternoon he had sat in his place almost without stirring; and when it had grown dark and the shutters were closed, Fenya had asked the *barynya*:

'If you please, *barynya*, is the gentleman going to stay the night?'

'Yes, make him a bed on the sofa,' Grushenka had replied.

On subjecting him to more detailed questioning, Grushenka had discovered that he really did at the moment, as it happened, have nowhere at all to go and that 'Mr Kalganov, my benefactor, declared to me outright that he would no longer have me as a guest in his house, and gave me five roubles.' 'Well, all right then, you may remain here,' Grushenka decided in her melancholy, giving him a compassionate smile. The old man had been convulsed with joy at her smile, and his lips had begun to tremble with grateful tears. Thus from that day the wandering sponge had remained with her. Not even during her illness had he once left the house. Fenya and her mother, Grushenka's cook, had not shooed him away but had continued to feed him and make his bed on the sofa. In the time that followed, Grushenka had even grown accustomed to him and, arriving back from Mitya (whom, her strength barely restored, she had at once begun to visit, even though she had not yet had time to recover properly), in order to drive away her melancholy, she would sit down and begin to talk to 'Maksimushka' about various trivial matters, anything, just so long as she kept her mind off her misery. It had turned out that the little old fellow was sometimes able to tell her things that were interesting, and in the end he had even become indispensible to her. Apart from Alyosha, who did not, however, visit her every day and who never stayed long, Grushenka had almost no guests at all. As for her old protector, the merchant, he had at this time been gravely ill, 'on the way out', as was said in the town, and he really did die only a week after Mitya's trial. Three weeks before his death, sensing that the *finale* was imminent, he summoned upstairs, at last, his sons with their wives and children, and instructed them not to leave his side. As for Grushenka, from that moment on he ordered the servants not to allow her into the house at all, and told them that if she came to the door they were to say that he hoped she would live a long life and a merry one, but that she should forget him altogether. Grushenka, however, sent almost every day to inquire about his health.

'At last you are here!' she cried, leaving her cards and greeting Alyosha joyfully. 'Maksimushka had me so worried that I thought you might not come at all. Oh, how I need to see you! Sit down at the table; well, what will you have – coffee?'

'Yes, perhaps I will,' said Alyosha, sitting down at the table. 'I'm truly famished.'

'I thought as much; Fenya, Fenya, bring the coffee!' Grushenka cried. 'I've had it on the boil for such a long time, it is waiting for you. And bring some *pirozhki*, and make sure that they are hot! Oh, Alyosha, before you go on, thunder and lightning struck me with these pies today. I took them to the prison for him, and would you believe it? He threw them back in my face, would not eat them. One of them he actually threw on the floor and stamped on. And I said: "I shall give them to the guard; if you have not eaten them by this evening it means that you are living off malicious spite!" – and with that I left. Why, we have quarrelled again, would you believe it? Every time I go there we quarrel.'

Grushenka rattled all this off in a single, excited salvo. Maksimov, who had instantly turned shy, lowered his eyes and smiled.

'And what was the subject of your quarrel this time?' Alyosha inquired.

'Why, I had certainly never expected it! Imagine, he'd grown jealous of my "former one": "Why are you keeping him?" he said. "So you've started to keep him, have you?" And now he's jealous all the time, nothing but jealous, jealous! He even sleeps and eats being jealous. He even got jealous of Kuzma last week.'

'But I mean, he knew about your "former one" already, did he not?'

'I shouldn't wonder. Yes, he knew about him right from the very beginning until today, but only today did he suddenly get up and start shouting foulmouthed things at me. I'm ashamed even to repeat the things he said. The silly fool! Rakitka had come to see him, I met him as I was on my way out. Maybe it was Rakitka who put him up to it, eh? What do you suppose?' she added, almost absent-mindedly.

'He loves you, that is what it is, he loves you very much. And he happens to be on edge at the moment.'

'I don't wonder that he's on edge, his trial is tomorrow. The reason I went there was in order to speak my mind to him about tomorrow, because, Alyosha, I am afraid even to think about what may happen tomorrow! You say he's on edge, well, so am I. Yet all he could talk about was the Pole! What a silly fool! Why, I expect he is even jealous of Maksimushka.'

'My spouse was also very jealous of me, madam,' Maksimov said, making his own contribution to the discussion.

'Oh, was she?' Grushenka burst out in reluctant laughter. 'Jealous because of whom?'

'The housemaids, madam.'

'Oh, that's enough, Maksimushka, I'm not in the mood to laugh just now, I feel positively furious. Now don't you go popping your eyes out at the *pirozhki*, they're bad for you, and I'm not going to give you any balsam either. Oh, the time I spend fussing over him, too; it's as though I were running an almshouse, really it is,' she said, breaking into laughter.

'I am not worthy of your beneficences, madam, I am an insignificant wretch, madam,' Maksimov got out in a tearful voice. 'You had better lavish your beneficences on those who are more necessary than I, madam.'

'Oh, Maksimushka, everyone is necessary, and how is one to know who is more necessary than another? You know, Alyosha, I could really do without that Pole altogether, he's gone and taken it into his head to fall ill today, too. I also went to visit him. Well, now I am going to make a special point of sending him some pies, I wasn't going to do it, but Mitya accused me of sending them, so now I shall make a special point of sending them, yes, I shall! Ah, here is Fenya with a letter! Well, it is as I supposed, from the Poles again, they are asking for money again!'

Pan Musialowicz had indeed sent an exceptionally long, but customarily flowery letter, in which he requested a loan of three roubles. Enclosed with the letter was a receipt with a note of liability, promising that the sum would be repaid within three months; the receipt had also been signed by Pan Wróblewski. Similar letters, all of them with similar receipts, had already been received by Grushenka from her 'former one' in rather large numbers. They had begun to arrive from the very day of Grushenka's recovery, some two weeks earlier. She was, however, aware that even during the time of her illness the two Poles had made calls to inquire as to her health. The first letter Grushenka had received had been a long one, on large-format notepaper, sealed with a large family seal and quite extraordinarily obscure and flowery in its rhetoric, so that Grushenka had read only half way through it and then set it down, having understood of it precisely nothing. She had, in any case, been hardly in a mood to attend to letters at the time. This first letter had on the subsequent day been followed by a second, in which Pan Musialowicz had requested a loan of two thousand roubles for the very briefest of terms. Grushenka had left this letter, too, without reply. There had then followed an entire series of letters, one each day, all of them equally pompous and flowerily rhetorical, except that with each one the sum requested had by degrees diminished, first to a hundred roubles, then to twenty-five, then to ten, and then, all of a sudden, finally, Grushenka had received a letter in which the two *panowie* requested from her only one rouble, enclosing a receipt signed by them both. At the time, Grushenka had suddenly taken pity on them, and had herself, in the gathering darkness, run to the *panowie*'s lodgings. She had found the two Poles in fearful poverty, destitution almost, without food, without firewood, without cigarettes, in debt to the landlady. The two hundred roubles they had won from Mitya at Mokroye had quickly vanished somewhere. Grushenka was, however, astonished when the two *panowie* greeted her with an overbearing pomposity and air of independence, according to all the prescriptions of etiquette and with bombastic speeches. Grushenka merely laughed and gave her 'former one' ten roubles. That same day, laughing, she had told Mitya about this, and he had not been jealous at all. From then on, however, the *panowie* had refused to let go of Grushenka, each day bombarding her with letters asking for money, in response to each of which she had sent a small amount. And then suddenly today Mitya had taken it into his head to become cruelly jealous.

'Silly fool that I am, I also dropped in to see him as I was going to see Mitya, for he is also very ill, my former *pan*,' Grushenka began again, in a hurried flutter. 'I tried to make a joke of it and told Mitya about it: "Imagine," I said, "my Pole took it into his head to play his guitar and sing me the songs he used to sing, he thought I would be touched and that I would marry him." But Mitya just leapt to his feet and started shouting abuse at me . . . So all right then, I shall send the *panowie* some pies! Fenya, have they sent the little girl over there yet? Look, give her three roubles and wrap up a dozen *pirozhki* in paper for them and tell her to take it all to them, and I want you, Alyosha, to make sure and tell Mitya that I've done it.'

'On no account will I tell him,' Alyosha said, smiling.

'Ach, you think he is miserable; why, I tell you, he made himself jealous on purpose, whereas really he does not care at all,' Grushenka said bitterly.

'What do you mean, on purpose?' Alyosha inquired.

'Oh, Alyoshenka, you are stupid, yes, you are, for all your cleverness you understand nothing, let me tell you that. I am not hurt that he should be jealous because of me, a woman like me, no, I would be hurt if he were *not* jealous. That is what I am like. I am not hurt by jealousy, I myself have a cruel heart, I myself can be jealous. No, what I find hurtful is that he does not love me at all, and is now being jealous *on purpose*, that is the point. Am I blind, after all, not to see? He suddenly started talking to me just now about that other woman, that Katka, saying she was this and that, that she'd ordered a doctor from Moscow for him for the trial in order to save him, that she'd ordered an advocate, too, one of the very best, the most learned ones. Well, so that means he must love her, if he has begun to praise her to my face, with those shameless eyes of his! He is guilty before me, so he has latched on to me in order to make me the one who bears the guilt, and unload it all on to me, saying, "You had the Pole before me, so it's all right for me to have Katya now." That's what he is up to! He wants to unload all the guilt on to me. He has latched on to me on purpose, on purpose, I tell you, but I will . . .'

But instead of saying what she would do, Grushenka covered her face with her handkerchief and burst into terrible sobs.

'He does not love Katerina Ivanovna,' Alyosha said firmly.

'Well, whether he does or whether he doesn't, that I shall soon find out for myself,' Grushenka said with a threatening note in her voice, removing the handkerchief from her face. It was a face that had grown distorted. With sorrow, Alyosha saw how suddenly its expression had altered from one of meekness and quiet cheerfulness to one of sullen malice.

'Enough of this stupid nonsense!' she blurted out suddenly. 'This is not at all why I asked you to come here. Alyosha, little dove, what will happen tomorrow, tomorrow? You see, that is what torments me! And I am the only person whom it torments! I look at everyone, and no one is thinking about it, no one is concerned with it in any way at all. Are you, at least, thinking about it? After all, it is his trial tomorrow! You tell me – what will the verdict be? After all, it was the lackey, the lackey who was the killer, it was the lackey who did it! Oh God! Will they really find him guilty, and not the manservant, and will no one intercede for him? After all, they haven't troubled the lackey at all, have they?'

'He has been subjected to strict interrogation,' Alyosha observed reflectively, 'but they all decided it was not he. Now he is ill, in bed. He has been ill ever since that day, when he had that fit of the falling sickness. He really is ill,' Alyosha added.

'O God, I wish you would go and see that advocate yourself and tell him everything in confidence. After all, they say he was ordered from St Petersburg at a cost of three thousand.'

'The three of us, I, brother Ivan and Katerina Ivanovna, raised the three thousand, and she ordered the doctor from Moscow herself for two. Fetyukovich, the advocate, would normally have charged more, but this case has become known throughout all of Russia, it is written about in all the newspapers and journals, and so Fetyukovich agreed to come more for the sake of the publicity, because the case has achieved a truly extraordinary notoriety. I saw him yesterday.'

'Well? And did you tell him?' Grushenka said hurriedly, jerking her head up.

'He heard what I had to say and made no reply. He said he had already formed a definite opinion. But he promised to take what I had said into consideration.'

'What does it mean – into consideration? Ah, the swindlers! They will destroy him! Well, and what about the doctor, what did she order him for?'

'In the capacity of an expert. The intention is to demonstrate that my brother is mad and that he killed while not in possession of his faculties,' Alyosha smiled quietly. 'Only my brother will not agree to that.'

'Ah, why, that is true, if it were he who had done it!' Grushenka exclaimed. 'He was crazy then, completely crazy, and it is I, I, villainess, who am guilty for that! Only you see, he did not do it, he did not! And yet everyone thinks he did, the whole town does. Even Fenya testified in such a way as to make it sound as though he had done it. And what happened in the delicatessen, and that civil servant, and the things that people had previously heard at the inn! Everyone, everyone is against him, they are all fairly baying for his blood.'

'Yes, there is an awful lot of evidence against him now,' Alyosha observed morosely.

'And that Grigory, Grigory Vasilyich, I mean, he keeps on insisting that the door was open, swears point blank that he saw it, one cannot budge him from it, I went to see him and talked to him myself. He gave me an earful, too!'

'Yes, that was perhaps the most powerful piece of testimony against my brother,' said Alyosha.

'And as for Mitya being crazy, well, that is indeed how he seems now,' Grushenka began suddenly, with a strange and particular air of mystery and concern. 'You know, Alyoshenka, I have been meaning to tell you about this for a long time: I go to see him every day and simply marvel. Tell me what you think: what are these things he has started to talk of all the time now? He talks and talks — I can't understand any of it, at first I thought it was something clever he was talking about, well, I am stupid, so that's why I don't understand, I thought; then he suddenly started to tell me about a "bairn", some baby or other, that is, saying "Why must the bairn be wretched?" "Because of that bairn I must go to Siberia now, I committed no murder, but I must go to Siberia now!" What was he talking about? What "bairn"? I couldn't understand a single word of it. Only I burst into tears when he said it, because he said it in such a good way, he was crying himself, and so I did too, and then he suddenly kissed me and made the sign of the cross over me with his hand. What was he talking about, Alyosha? Can you tell me what this "bairn" is?'

'Well, Rakitin has got into the habit of paying him visits for some reason,' Alyosha smiled. 'Though as a matter of fact ... this is not Rakitin's doing. I did not visit him yesterday, but I shall do so today.'

'No, it isn't Rakitka who has been upsetting him, it is his brother Ivan Fyodorovich, he is the one who has been paying him visits, let me tell you ...' Grushenka said, and her voice suddenly broke off. Alyosha stared at her like a man thunderstruck.

'Paying him visits? Has Ivan been paying him visits? Mitya himself told me that Ivan had not been to see him once.'

'Oh ... oh, that is typical of me! I have given away the secret!' Grushenka exclaimed in embarrassment, suddenly blushing crimson all over. 'Wait, Alyosha, do not say anything, now that I have given it away, so let it be, I shall tell you the whole truth: he has been to see him twice, the first time was when he had only just arrived – you see, that day he had just come post-haste from Moscow, when I had not yet taken to my bed, and the second time was when he came a week ago. He told Mitya not to let you know about it, not to let you know about it on any account, nor to let anyone else know either, he came in secret.'

Alyosha sat in deep reflection, trying to figure something out. The news had evidently given him a shock.

'Brother Ivan does not talk to me about Mitya's case,' he said slowly, 'and indeed in general these past two months he has spoken very little to me, and whenever I went to see him he was always annoyed that I had come, so I haven't been to see him for three weeks now. Hm ... If he was there a week ago, then ... during this week there really has been a kind of change in Mitya ...'

'That's right, a change, a change!' Grushenka swiftly caught up. 'There is a secret between them, they hatched a secret! Mitya told me himself there was a secret, and that it was such a one that he could not rest easy. And I mean, before he was cheerful, and he is cheerful now, only, you know, when he starts shaking his head about like that and pacing up and down the room, and rubbing the hair on his temple with the little finger of his right hand, then I know that he has something restless on his soul ... I know it! And yet he has been cheerful; even today he was cheerful!'

'But I thought you said he was on edge?'

'Yes, he was, but he was cheerful, too. He's on edge all the time, but at moments he cheers up, and then he suddenly goes back to being on edge again. And you know, Alyosha, I marvel at him constantly: ahead of him is such terror, yet sometimes he roars with laughter at such trivial things that one would think he was a baby himself.'

'And is it true that he told you not to tell me about Ivan? Were those his actual words: "don't tell him"?'

'Yes, those were his actual words. You are the person he is most afraid of, Mitya, I mean. That is why there is a secret, he himself said there was a secret ... Alyosha, little dove, go there, find out what secret it is they have, and come and tell me,' Grushenka said, jerking her head up in sudden entreaty. 'Settle it for me, poor woman, that I may know my accursed lot! That is why I called you here.'

'Do you think it is something to do with you, then? But then surely he would not have spoken of the secret in your presence.'

'I do not know. Perhaps he wants to tell me, but does not dare. Perhaps he is warning me. Telling me that there is a secret, but not what it is.'

'What do you yourself think it is?'

'What do I think it is? That my end has come, that is what I think. All three of them have been preparing my end, because Katka is involved here. All of this is Katka, it all comes from her. "She is this and she is that", meaning that I am not like her. He is telling me in advance, warning me in advance. He has decided to give me up, and that is the whole of the secret! The three of them have thought it up together — Mitka, Katka and Ivan Fyodorovich. Alyosha, I have long wanted to ask you: a week ago he suddenly disclosed to me that Ivan is in love with Katka, he said he must be, because he often goes to visit her. Was that the truth he told me? Speak according to your conscience, cut me to the quick.'

'I will not lie to you. Ivan is not in love with Katerina Ivanovna, that is what I think.'

'Well, and it is what I thought too that day! He is lying to me, the shameless one, that is what he is doing! And he has made himself jealous of me now so that he can unload the guilt on to me later on. I mean, he is a fool, he does not know how to cover up the traces, he is so open, so honest . . . Only I will give him his due, oh yes, I will! "You think I killed him," he said. He said that to me, he reproached me with that! Oh, to hell with him! But just wait, that Katka will have a hard time from me at the trial! There I shall say a certain little word or two . . . There I shall say it all!'

And again she began to weep bitterly.

'Look, Grushenka, this at least I can tell you definitely,' Alyosha said, getting up from his seat. 'For one thing, he loves you, loves you more than anyone else in the world, and only you, please believe me when I tell you that. I know. Oh, how I know. For another thing, I will tell you that I do not want to force the secret out of him, but if he tells me it himself today, then I will tell him straight that I have promised to tell you it. Then I will come back to you today and tell you. Only . . . the way I see it . . . Katerina Ivanovna is not mixed up in it at all, and the secret concerns something different. That is certainly the case. And it's really quite improbable that Katerina Ivanovna has anything to do with it, that is how it seems to me. Well, goodbye for now!'

Alyosha pressed her hand. Grushenka was still weeping. He could see that she had very little faith in his reassurances, but at least she felt better for having given vent to her unhappiness and having spoken her mind. He felt sorry to leave her in such a condition, but he had to hurry. Many tasks still lay ahead of him.

2

An Ailing Foot

THE first of those tasks lay at the house of Mrs Khokhlakova, and he hurried there in order to complete it as soon as possible and not be too late in order to see Mitya. Mrs Khokhlakova had been indisposed for three weeks now: for some reason she had developed a swollen foot, and though she had not taken to her bed entirely, she spent the afternoons reclining on a couch in her boudoir dressed in an attractive but proper *déshabillé*. Alyosha had once observed to himself with a wry but innocent smile that in spite of her illness Mrs Khokhlakova had almost begun to play the fashionable lady: there had appeared certain items of headwear, certain bow-ribbons and matinee jackets, and he had dimly begun to realize why this was so, though he drove these thoughts away as being idle. During the past two months she had begun to receive visits from, among other guests, the young man Perkhotin. It was some four days since Alyosha had been to see her and, as he entered the house, he was in a hurry to pass straight through to Liza's room, for his task lay with her, as Liza had yesterday sent a maid to him with the urgent plea that he come to see her at once 'on a certain very important matter', a plea which for several reasons had engaged Alyosha's interest. As the maid went in to announce Alyosha's presence to Liza, however, Mrs Khokhlakova, who had already learned from someone of his arrival, immediately sent out a request that he go in to see her 'just for one little moment'. Alyosha reasoned that it would be best to satisfy the mother's plea first, as otherwise she would keep sending her maid to Liza's room all the time he was there. Mrs Khokhlakova was reclining on her couch, dressed in particularly ceremonial fashion and evidently in a state of extreme nervous excitement. Alyosha she greeted with cries of ecstasy.

'It is aeons, aeons, whole aeons since I have seen you! A whole week, for mercy's sake – oh, though actually you were here only four days ago, on Wednesday, were you not? You have come to see *Lise*, and I am sure that you intended to pass straight through to her room on tiptoe without my hearing. My dear, dear Aleksey Fyodorovich, if only you knew how she worries me! But that is for later. Though it is the most important thing, it is none the less for later. My dear Aleksey Fyodorovich, I entrust my Liza to you completely. After the death of the Elder Zosima – the Lord rest his soul!' (she made the sign of the cross over herself) '– after him I look upon you as a schemonach, even though you are wearing that charming new suit of yours. Where did you find such a tailor in our town? But no, no, that is not important, that is for later. Forgive me if I sometimes call you Alyosha, I am an old woman, and all is permitted to me,' she smiled coquettishly, 'but that is also for later. The important thing, I must not forget the important thing. Please, remind me of it yourself, if I start to talk you must say: "And the important thing?" Oh, how can I tell what the important thing is now? Since the time that *Lise* took back her promise – her childish promise, Aleksey Fyodorovich – to marry you, you will have understood that all that was merely the playful childish fantasy of a sick young girl who has long been chairbound – thank God, now she can walk again. This new doctor whom Katya has ordered from Moscow for that unfortunate brother of yours, who tomorrow ... Well, what of the morrow! I expire at the mere thought of the morrow! From curiosity, mainly ... In a word, that doctor came to see us again yesterday and saw *Lise* ... I paid him fifty roubles for the visit. But all of this is not the important thing, it is again not it ... You see, I have completely lost the thread now. I am hurrying. Why am I hurrying? I do not know. I have dreadfully ceased to know anything now. Everything in my head has got all mixed up into a kind of lump. I'm afraid that you'll go and hop out of my hands from boredom, when I've only just set eyes on you. Oh, my goodness! What are we doing sitting here, and above all – coffee! Yulia, Glafira, coffee!'

Alyosha quickly thanked her and said he had only just had some coffee.

'At whose house?'

'Agrafena Aleksandrovna's.'

'That ... that is the house of that woman! Oh, she has brought ruin on everyone, although, as a matter of fact, they say she has taken to religion, though it is a little late. She would have done better to do it earlier, when it was needed, why do it now, what is the use of it? No, don't say anything, Aleksey Fyodorovich, for I have so much to say that I think I may say nothing to you at all. This dreadful trial ... I shall certainly go, I am preparing myself, I shall be carried in on a chair, I can sit up, you know, there will be people with me, and you know, after all, I am a witness. How shall I ever be able to speak, how shall I do it? I do not even know what to say. I mean, I shall have to take an oath, shall I not, shall I not?'

'Yes, but I do not think it will be possible for you to attend.'

'I can sit up; ah, you are making me lose my thread again! This trial, this wild act, and afterwards they will all go off to Siberia, others will marry, and all of it so quickly, so quickly, and everything will change, and finally, nothing, they will all be old men staring into their coffins. Well, so let it be, I am tired. This Katya — *cette charmante personne*, she has shattered all my hopes: now she will follow one of your brothers to Siberia, and your other brother will follow her, too, and live in the next town, and they will all torment one another. It is simply driving me out of my mind, and what is worse, the publicity: it has been written about in all the St Petersburg and Moscow newspapers a million times. Oh, and yes, imagine, there was an article that mentioned me, too, and said I had been the 'dear friend' of your brother, I do not want to say the ugly word, imagine, imagine!'

'That cannot be! Where was this article?'

'I will show you it in a moment. I received it yesterday — and read it then, too. Look, here, it's in *Hearsay*, that's a St Petersburg paper. It only started publication this year, I am so fond of hearsay, so I took out a subscription, and now it has all come down about my head: this is the kind of hearsay they publish. Look, here, in this column, read it.'

And she proffered to Alyosha a page of a newspaper which had been lying under her pillow.

She seemed less distraught than completely defeated, and it was possible that everything in her head really had turned into a tangled mass. The newspaper article was of a thoroughly characteristic nature and must, of course, have had a very ticklish effect on her; but to her good fortune, perhaps, she was at this moment incapable of concentrating on any one thing for long, and so a moment later had managed even to forget about the newspaper and to skip to another subject entirely. Of the fact that the fame of the dreadful trial had spread universally throughout all Russia, Alyosha had long known, and, Lord, what wild reports and correspondence he had read during the course of those two months, among other more reliable reports concerning his brother, the Karamazovs in general and even himself. One newspaper had even said that in terror following his brother's crime he had become a schemonach and shut himself up in the monastery; in another this theory had been refuted, the correspondent suggesting instead that together with his Elder, Zosima, he had broken open the monastery's safe-box and 'done a bunk'. This most recent *Hearsay* story was headed: 'From Skotoprigonyevsk'* (such, alas, is the name of our little town, I have long kept it concealed), 'on the occasion of the Karamazov Trial'. It was a short item, and of Mrs Khokhlakova there was no mention; indeed, all the names concerned had been cut out. Readers were merely notified that the criminal, whose trial was now about to take place with such a lot of fuss and ballyhoo, a retired army captain of insolent manner, a lazy fellow who was a landowner in favour of serfdom, engaged now and then in *amours* and exercised a particular influence on certain 'ladies pining in solitude'. That one of these 'pining widows', who tried to look younger than her age, though she already had a grown-up daughter, had been so taken in by him that only two hours before the crime had taken place she had offered him three thousand roubles on condition that he run away with her instantly to the gold-mines. But that the evil fellow had preferred to murder his own father, rob him of three thousand and get the money that way, thinking to do it with impunity, rather than go traipsing off to Siberia with the forty-year-old charms of his pining lady. This playful correspondence ended, as is proper, with an expression of noble indignation regarding the immorality of parricide and of the former laws of serfdom. Reading the article with curiosity, Alyosha folded the page and gave it back to Mrs Khokhlakova.

'Well, it cannot be anyone but me, can it?' she began to prattle again. 'Yes, it is me, why, I suggested that plan about the gold-mines to him only an hour before it happened, and now here they are writing about "forty-year-old charms"! But was that why I suggested it to him? He put that in on purpose! May the Eternal Judge forgive him those "forty-year-old charms", as I forgive him, but really . . . really, do you know who it is? It is your friend Rakitin.'

'Perhaps,' Alyosha said. 'Though I have heard nothing of it.'

'It is he, it is he, and no perhaps about it! I mean, I had him thrown out . . . Why, you know the whole of that story, do you not?'

'I know that you asked him not to visit you in future, but precisely why – that I . . . from you, at any rate, have not heard.'

'In that case you must have heard it from him! Well, does he vilify me? Does he vilify me greatly?'

'Yes, he does, but then he vilifies everyone. However, the reason why you showed him the door – that I did not hear from him, either. And anyway in general I meet with him very seldom. We are not friends.'

'Well, then I shall disclose to you the whole story and, it can't be avoided, I will confess, there is a certain detail of it for which I myself possibly bear the guilt. Only one small, small detail, the very smallest one, so small that perhaps it does not exist at all. Look, Alyosha, my little dove' – Mrs Khokhlakova suddenly assumed an air of playfulness, and at her lips there flickered a charming, though mysterious smile – 'you see, I have my suspicions . . . you must forgive me, Alyosha, I am as a mother to you . . . oh, no, no, on the contrary, I speak to you now as to my father . . . because a mother would be quite unsuitable here . . . Well, just as I might have done to the Elder Zosima at confession, and that is the most certain analogy, that is entirely suitable: after all, I called you a schemonach earlier – well, you see, that poor young man, your friend Rakitin (O Lord, I simply cannot make myself be angry with him! I do get vexed and irritated with him, but not very), in a word, that frivolous young man, seems suddenly, imagine, to have taken it into his head to fall in love with me. I only noticed it after a while, after a while, but at first, about a month ago, that's to say, he began to visit me often, every day, nearly, though we had been acquainted before. I was not aware of anything . . . and then suddenly I had a kind of illumination, and I began, to my astonishment, to notice what was happening. You know that two months ago I began to receive that modest, charming and deserving young man, Pyotr Ilyich Perkhotin, who works in the service here. You yourself have met him any number of times. And do you not agree, he is so deserving, serious. He comes to see me three times a day, but not every day (though that would be perfectly all right) and always so nicely dressed, and in general I like young men, Alyosha, talented, modest ones, like you, but he has an intellect that is almost statesman-like, he talks so charmingly, and I shall most certainly, most certainly intercede for him. He is a future diplomat. He almost rescued me from death by coming to my house that dreadful night. Well, and your friend Rakitin always arrives in such boots and stretches them out on the carpet . . . Well, in a word, he actually began to pass me certain hints, and then suddenly one day, as he was on his way out, he squeezed my hand dreadfully hard. No sooner had he done it than my foot began to ail. He had met Pyotr Ilyich at my house before and, would you believe it, he kept needling him, needling him, going on at him about something. I just looked at them both, the way they were behaving towards each other, and I laughed inwardly. Then suddenly one day I was sitting alone, or rather, no, I was lying down at the time, and Mikhail Ivanovich arrived, and imagine, he had brought with him a poem he had written, the very

shortest of poems, about my ailing foot, that's to say, he had described
my ailing foot in verse. Wait now, what was it again,

> That foot, that foot, that little foot,
> So ailing and so fair . . .

or how did it go — you know, I can never remember poems — I've got it
lying around here somewhere — well, I shall show it to you afterwards, it
is a gem, a gem, and you know, it is not just about my foot, it has a
moral message, with a gem of an idea, only I've forgotten it, in a word,
fit straight for an album. Well, of course, I thanked him, and he was
visibly flattered. Hardly had I finished thanking him than Pyotr Ilyich
came in, and Mikhail Ivanovich suddenly scowled as black as night. I
realize now that Pyotr Ilyich was hindering him in some object, because
Mikhail Ivanovich quite certainly intended to say something after he had
read the poem, I could feel that, and then Pyotr Ilyich walked in. I
suddenly showed Pyotr Ilyich the poem, without telling him who had
written it. But I am certain, I am certain that he guessed at once, even
though he will not admit it even now, but says he did not guess; but he
does that on purpose. Pyotr Ilyich immediately burst into roars of
laughter and began to criticize: it was a wretched little poem, he said,
which must have been written by some seminarian or other — and, you
know, with such vehemence, such vehemence! At that point your friend,
instead of bursting into laughter, suddenly flew into a complete fury . . .
O Lord, I thought, they are going to start fighting: "I wrote it," he said.
"I wrote it as a joke," he said, "for I consider the writing of verses to be
an unworthy occupation . . . But my poem is a good one. They want to
put up a monument* to your Pushkin for his women's feet, but my poem
has a tendency, and you," he said, "are in favour of serfdom"; "You," he
said, "possess no humane sympathies, you feel none of the present-day
enlightened emotions, you have not been touched by culture, you are,"
he said, "a bureaucrat, and you take bribes!" Well, then I began to raise
my voice and entreat them to stop. But Pyotr Ilyich, you know, is quite
a bold fellow really, and he suddenly assumed a tone of the utmost
nobility: he looked at him mockingly, listened and then made an apology:
"I did not know . . . " he said. "If I had known, I would have praised it
. . . Poets are so touchy," he said. In a word, it was mockery delivered in
a tone of the utmost nobility. He explained that to me afterwards, that it
had all been mockery, but at the time I thought he was being sincere.
Only suddenly one day when I was reclining, as I am now before you, I
thought: would it or would it not be an acceptable thing to do if I were

to show Mikhail Ivanovich the door for having in such an unseemly manner shouted at a guest in my own home? And then, would you believe it: as I lay there, I closed my eyes and thought, would it or would it not be acceptable, I could not decide, and I tortured myself, tortured myself, and my heart was beating: ought I to scream or ought I not to? One voice said: "Scream!" and another said: "Don't!" But no sooner had that second voice spoken than I screamed and suddenly fell into a dead swoon. Well, of course there was uproar. Suddenly, I got up and told Mikhail Ivanovich that I was sorry to have to tell him that I did not wish to receive him in my house any more. And then I had him thrown out. Oh, Aleksey Fyodorovich! I am well aware that it was a nasty thing to do, for after all I had been lying to him all the time, I was not really angry with him at all, but it suddenly — that is the important thing, suddenly — seemed to me that it would be such a nice thing, that scene . . . Only, would you believe it, that scene was quite natural all the same, because I even burst into tears and wept for several days afterwards, and then suddenly after dinner one day I forgot about it all. Well, now it is two weeks since he last came to see me, and I thought: is he really never going to come back? That was yesterday, and then suddenly towards evening this issue of *Hearsay* arrived. I read it and gasped, well, who could have written that about me, it must have been him, he must have gone home that day, sat down and — written it; he sent it to them — and it was published. For I mean, that was two weeks ago. But Alyosha, heaven only knows the things I am saying, everything but what I ought to be talking about. Oh, it's as though the words just came out of their own accord!'

'It is really dreadfully important that I get to the prison in time to see my brother today,' Alyosha began to mutter.

'That's it, that's it! You have reminded me of it all! Listen, what is an affect?'

'What kind of an affect?' Alyosha said in astonishment.

'A judicial affect.* The kind of affect for which one may obtain a full pardon. Whatever one may have done — one receives an instant pardon.'

'But what are you talking about?'

'Well, you see: this Katya . . . Oh, she is a dear, dear creature, only I really do not know whom she is in love with. Not long ago she was sitting with me, and I could get nothing out of her. All the more so since the way she talks to me now is so superficial, in a word, all about my health and nothing more, and she even adopts a certain tone of voice, but anyway, I said to myself: very well, have it your own way . . . But oh yes, about this affect, now: this doctor has arrived. You know about that, do you not? Oh, how could you not know, the one who knows about madmen, why, I mean, you ordered him, or rather, not you, but Katya. Katya again! Well, so you see: a man may be not mad at all, but then suddenly he has an affect. He may have all his wits about him and know what he is doing, yet all the while he is having an affect. Well, that is probably what happened to Dmitry Fyodorovich: he had an affect. It was when the new courts opened that people discovered about affects. That is the beneficent influence of the new courts. This doctor came to see me and asked me about that evening, well, about the gold-mines, and so forth: "What was he like then?" he said. There can be no question that he was in a state of affect – as soon as he walked in, he shouted "money, money, three thousand, give me three thousand", and then he suddenly went away and committed murder. "I did not want to do it," he said, but he did it all the same. And that is why they will pardon him, for that very same reason, that he tried not to do it, but did it.'

'But he did not do it,' Alyosha cut in rather brusquely. Worry and impatience were gaining an increasing hold over him.

'I know, it was that old man Grigory who did it . . . '

'Grigory?' Alyosha exclaimed.

'Yes, it was him, him, Grigory. After Dmitry Fyodorovich hit him he lay on the ground, and then he got up, saw that the door was open, went in and murdered Fyodor Pavlovich.'

'But why, why?'

'He had had an affect. After Dmitry Fyodorovich had hit him over the head he came to and had an affect, went in and committed the murder. And as for the fact of him saying that he did not do it, well, it may be that he simply does not remember. Only, you see: it would be better, far better if Dmitry Fyodorovich had done it. And indeed, he actually did, even though I say it was Grigory – I am quite sure that it was Dmitry Fyodorovich who did it, and that is far, far better! Oh, not better because a son killed his father, I am not advocating that, on the contrary, children ought to respect their parents, no, it is simply that it would be better if it were he, for then you would have no reason to weep, as he committed the murder without being conscious, or rather quite conscious, but without being aware of how it had happened to him. No, let them pardon him; that would be so humane, and would let people see the beneficent influence of the new courts, and you see I did not know, but they say it was decided long ago, and yesterday when I found out about it, I got such a shock that I immediately wanted to send for you; and later on, when they've pardoned him, to have him come straight from the court over to my house to have dinner, and I shall invite friends, and we shall drink to the new courts. I don't think he would be dangerous, and in any case I shall invite a very large number of guests, so they could always escort him out if he did anything, and later on he could be a *mirovoy* in another town, or something, because those who have themselves endured misfortune make the best judges. But above all, which of us now is not in a state of affect? You, I, we are all in a state of affect, and there are so many examples: a man sits there, singing a romance, and suddenly he takes a dislike to something, picks up a pistol and kills anyone who happens to be in the way, and then afterwards he is pardoned. I read about it recently, and all the doctors have confirmed it. Nowadays doctors do a lot of confirming, they confirm everything. For heaven's sake — even my *Lise* is in a state of affect, yesterday and the day before she was driving me to tears, and only today did I realize that she is simply in a state of affect. Oh, *Lise* does distress me so! I thought she had gone completely mad. Why has she asked you to call? Did she ask you herself or have you come to see her of your own accord?'

'Yes, she asked me to come, and I am just on my way in to see her,' Alyosha said, starting to get to his feet in resolute fashion.

'Ah, dear, dear Aleksey Fyodorovich, here, here is perhaps the most important thing,' Mrs Khokhlakova said with a little scream, suddenly beginning to weep. 'As the Lord is my witness, I sincerely trust you with my *Lise*, and it does not matter that she has asked you to come here without telling her mother. But forgive me, I cannot similarly trust your brother, Ivan Fyodorovich, with her so easily, though I continue to see in him a young man of the utmost chivalry. Imagine, he suddenly came in and visited *Lise*, and I knew nothing about it.'

'He did what? How? When?' Alyosha said in extreme astonishment. He did not sit back down again but listened standing.

'I shall tell you, that is possibly why I asked you in, for you see, I do not know now why I asked you in. You see, Ivan Fyodorovich has only been to see me twice since he returned from Moscow, the first time as a friend on a social visit, and the second time, well, that was quite recently, Katya was with me, and he dropped in, having found out that she was here. I certainly had not been counting on frequent visits from him, as I was aware of how busy he was already, *vous comprenez, cette affaire et la mort terrible de votre papa*, only I suddenly discovered that he had been again, only not to see me, but *Lise*, this was about six days ago, he had arrived, stayed for five minutes and left again. But I only found out about this a whole three days later from Glafira, so I was really quite *frappée*. I immediately summoned *Lise*, and she laughed: "He thought you were asleep," she said, "and so he looked in to see me and inquire about your health." Of course, that really was what had happened. Only *Lise*, *Lise*, O Lord, how she distresses me! Imagine, one night – this was four days ago, just after you left last time you were here – she suddenly had a fit, with shouting and screaming and hysterics! Then the following day she had another fit, and then the next day another, and then yesterday, yesterday she had this affect. And she suddenly shouted at me: "I hate Ivan Fyodorovich, I demand that you never receive him again, that you forbid him to enter the house!" I was stupefied at such an unexpected utterance and I retorted to her: "Why should I do that to such a deserving young man who is, moreover, possessed of such knowledge and such misfortune, for, after all, they are all a misfortune, *toutes ces histoires*, are they not?" She suddenly burst into laughter at my words, and in a way that was, you know, so insulting. Well, I was actually relieved, for I thought I had cheered her up and that her fits would now pass, all the more so as I myself wanted to banish Ivan Fyodorovich from the house for his strange visits without my consent, and demand an explanation from him. Only suddenly this morning Liza woke up and lost her temper with Yulia and, imagine, gave her a slap in the face. Why I mean, that was *monstrueux*, I am on *vous* terms with my maids. And then suddenly an hour later she was on her knees, embracing Yulia and kissing her feet. As for me, she sent a maid in to tell me that she would not come to see me at all and would never come to see me again, and when I myself managed to make myself hobble in to see her, she rushed to kiss me and started weeping and, as she kissed me, she fairly heaved me out of the room without saying a word, with the result that I never discovered anything. And now, my dear Aleksey Fyodorovich, all my hopes are fastened upon you and, of course, the fate of my entire life rests in your hands. I want you simply to go to *Lise*, find out from her everything, in the way that you alone are able to do, and come and tell me, me, her mother, for, you realize, I shall die, I shall simply die if all this goes on much longer, either die or flee the house. I am at the end of my endurance, I possess endurance, but I may lose it, and then . . . and then dreadful things will happen. Oh, good Lord, here is Pyotr Ilyich at last!' Mrs Khokhlakova screamed, suddenly radiant all over, as she caught sight of Pyotr Ilyich Perkhotin on his way in. 'You are late, you are late! Well, sit down, now, speak, decide my fate, what did that advocate say? Where are you going, Aleksey Fyodorovich?'

'I am going in to see *Lise*.'

'Oh yes! Then you will not forget, you will not forget what I requested of you? My fate, my fate hangs in the balance!'

'Of course I shall not forget, if I can manage to ... but I am so behind time,' Alyosha muttered, quickly withdrawing.

'No, you must be sure, be sure to come back and see me, and no "if I can manage to", or I shall die!' Mrs Khokhlakova shouted after him, but Alyosha had already gone out of the room.

3

A Little Demon

WHEN he went into Liza's room, he found her reclining in her old bath chair, the one in which she had been wheeled about when unable to walk. She made no move to greet him, but her sharp, observant gaze fairly drilled into him. Her eyes were slightly inflamed, her features pale and sallow. Alyosha was amazed at how she had changed in the course of three days, had even grown thinner. She did not extend her hand to him. He himself touched her long, thin fingers that lay immobile on her dress, then without saying anything sat down facing her.

'I know that you are in a hurry to get to the prison,' Liza said sharply, 'but mamma has detained you in there for two hours — she has just been telling you about me and Yulia.'

'How did you learn that?' Alyosha inquired.

'I eavesdropped. Why are you staring at me like that? If I feel like eavesdropping and do so, there is nothing wrong in that. I do not request your pardon.'

'Has something upset you?'

'On the contrary, I could not be happier. I was just thinking just now for the three-dozenth time what a good thing it is that I refused you and that I shall not be your wife. You are not worthy to be a husband: if I married you, and suddenly gave you a letter to take to the one whom I loved after you, you would take it and unfailingly deliver it, and bring the reply back, too. And when you were forty, you would still be delivering my letters for me.'

She suddenly began to laugh.

'There is malice in you and yet at the same time there is also a simple-heartedness,' Alyosha said to her, smiling.

'That is because I feel no shame in your presence, and indeed I do not want to feel shame in your presence, yours, that is, please note. Alyosha, why is it that I do not respect you? If I respected you, I should not be able to talk to you without feeling shame, after all, should I?'

'No, you would not.'

'And do you believe that I feel no shame in your presence?'

'No, I do not.'

Liza again gave a nervous laugh; she spoke swiftly, in haste.

'I have sent your brother Dmitry Fyodorovich some sweets in prison. Alyosha, you know, you are really quite handsome! I shall always love you dreadfully for having so quickly allowed me not to love you.'

'Why did you ask me to come here today, *Lise*?'

'I felt like telling you a certain wish I have. I wish that some man would torment me, marry me, and then torment me, deceive me and leave me. I do not want to be happy!'

'You have fallen in love with disorder?'

'Oh, disorder is what I want. I keep wanting to set the house on fire. I see myself going up to it and setting light to it on the sly, it absolutely must be on the sly. They try to put out the flames, but it keeps on burning. And all the while I know who did it, but I say nothing. Oh, such stupid nonsense! And it's so boring!'

She waved her slender hand in revulsion.

'You live a wealthy life,' Alyosha said quietly.

'Well, is it better to be poor, then?'

'Yes, it is.'

'That is something that monk of yours who died told you. It isn't true. Let me be rich, and all the rest poor, and I shall eat sweets and sup cream, and not let anyone else have any. Oh, don't say anything, don't say anything at all,' she said waving her hand again, though Alyosha had not even opened his mouth, 'you have said all this to me before, I know it off by heart. It's boring. If I am poor I shall murder someone – and if I am rich I may murder someone, too – why sit still? And you know, I want to go cutting, go cutting the rye. I shall marry you, and you will become a muzhik, a real muzhik, we shall have a little foal, how would you like that? Do you know Kalganov?'

'Yes, I do.'

'He goes everywhere in a dream. He says: "Why live in reality? It's better to dream." One may dream the most amusing things, but life is boring. He is going to marry me soon, you know, he has already made me a declaration of love. Do you know how to spin a top?'

'Yes, I do.'

'Well, he is like a top: you twirl him round and let him go and then whip him, whip him, whip him with a little whip: if I marry him, I shall spend all my life letting him go. Do you feel no shame sitting here with me?'

'No.'

'You are dreadfully angry because I am not talking about religious things. I do not want to be religious. What will be the punishment in the other world for the very greatest sin? You ought to know the exact details of that.'

'You will earn the condemnation of God,' Alyosha said, studying her fixedly.

'Well, that is what I want. I shall arrive and be condemned, and then I shall suddenly laugh in their faces. I do dreadfully want to burn the house down, Alyosha, our house, do you still not believe me?'

'But why? There are even children, of twelve years old or thereabouts, who have a terrible hankering to set fire to something, and set fire to it they do. It's a kind of illness.'

'Not true, not true; anyway, I don't care if there are children like that, that is not what I am talking about.'

'You are mistaking bad things for good ones: it's a passing crisis, and your old illness may be to blame for it.'

'Ah, so you do despise me, then! The plain fact is that I don't want to do good things, I want to do bad ones, and there is no illness involved in it.'

'Why do you want to do bad things?'

'So that nothing should be left anywhere. Oh, good it would be if nothing were to be left anywhere! You know, Alyosha, I sometimes think of doing a dreadful amount of bad things, really nasty ones, of doing them for a long time on the sly, and then suddenly everyone will find out. They will all stand round me and point their fingers at me, and I will look back at them. I like that idea. Why do I like it so much, Alyosha?'

'Well, it is the desire to crush something good, or else, as you said, set fire to it. That also happens.'

'But, I mean, I was not simply saying it, I am going to do it.'

'I believe it.'

'Oh, how I love you for saying that: "I believe it." After all, you never, never lie. But perhaps you think that I have told you all this on purpose, in order to tease you?'

'No, I do not . . . though there is possibly a little of that desire, too.'

'Yes, there is. I would never lie to you,' she continued with a kind of flashing glint in her eyes.

Alyosha was more and more astonished by her seriousness of manner: there was not a shadow of risibility or facetiousness in her features now, though formerly a certain gaiety and jocularity had never left her even in her most 'serious' moments.

'There are moments when people actually like crime,' Alyosha said, reflectively.

'Yes, yes! You have spoken my thoughts, they like it, they all like it, always, and not just at "moments". You know, it's as if everyone had once agreed to lie about it, and has been lying about it ever since. Everyone says they hate immorality, yet secretly they all like it.'

'And are you still reading immoral books, as you were before?'

'Yes. I am. Mamma reads them and hides them under her pillow, and I steal them.'

'Do you feel no shame at destroying yourself?'

'I want to destroy myself. There is a boy who lives near here, he lay down under the rails and let the train go by on top of him. Lucky boy! Listen, your brother is to be tried now for having murdered his father, and yet everyone likes the idea that he murdered his father.'

'They like it?'

'Yes, they like it, they all like it! They all say it is dreadful, but secretly they like it very much. And I am first among them.'

'In your words about other people there is a certain amount of truth,' Alyosha said quietly.

'Oh, what thoughts you have in your head!' Liza shrieked in ecstasy. 'And in a monk's, too! You would not believe how I respect you, Alyosha, for the fact that you never lie. Oh, let me tell you a funny dream I had: I sometimes have dreams about devils, it's night, and I'm in my room with a candle, and suddenly there are devils everywhere, in every corner, and under the table, and they open the doors, and outside the doors there is a crowd of them, and they want to come in and catch hold of me. And then they come up to me and seize me. But I suddenly make the sign of the cross over myself, and they all shrink back, afraid, only they don't go away altogether, but stand by the doors and in the corners, waiting. And suddenly I feel a terrible urge to start cursing God out loud, and then I do, and they suddenly come up to me in a crowd again, they're so delighted, well, and then they seize hold of me again, and then I suddenly make the sign of the cross over myself again – and they all shrink back. It's terribly jolly, it quite takes one's breath away.'

'I myself have had that very same dream,' Alyosha said suddenly.

'Really?' Liza screamed in surprise. 'Listen, Alyosha, do not laugh, this is terribly important: is it possible that two different people could have the same dream?'

'Certainly it is possible.'

'Alyosha, I tell you, this is terribly important,' Liza continued in a kind of extreme astonishment. 'It's not the dream that is important, but the fact that you could have had the very same dream as I. You never lie to me, so do not lie now: is it true? You are not making fun?'

'It is true.'

Liza was dreadfully struck by something, and fell silent for some thirty seconds or so.

'Alyosha, visit me, visit me more often,' she said suddenly in an imploring voice.

'I shall always, all my life come and visit you,' Alyosha replied firmly.

'Look, I am saying all this only to you,' Liza began again. 'I am saying it to myself, and also to you. You alone, of all the people in the world. I like talking to you better than talking to myself. And I feel no shame at all in your presence. Alyosha, why do I feel no shame at all in your presence? Alyosha, is it true that the Jews steal little children at Passover and kill them with knives?'

'I do not know.'

'Well, I have a book in which I read about a trial somewhere, where a Jew had first cut off all the fingers of both hands belonging to a child of four years old, and then crucified him against a wall, hammered in nails and crucified him, and then at his trial he said that the boy died quickly, within four hours. That was quick! He said that the boy had groaned and groaned and that he had stood feasting his eyes on him. That is good!'

'Good?'

'Yes, good. I sometimes think that I myself crucified him. He hung on the wall, groaning, and I sat down opposite him and ate pineapple *compôte*. I'm very fond of pineapple *compôte*. Are you?'

Alyosha said nothing and looked at her. Her pale and sallow features were suddenly distorted, her eyes began to burn:

'You know, after I had read about that Jew I shook all night with weeping. I kept seeing that little boy screaming and groaning (boys of four realize what is happening to them, after all), and all the time that thought of the *compôte* never left me. In the morning I sent a letter to a certain person, asking him to come and see me *without fail*. He arrived, I suddenly told him about the boy and the *compôte*, told him *all*, *all*, and said that it was "good". He suddenly began to laugh, and said it really was good. Then he got up and left. He was with me for only five minutes. Did he despise me, did he? Tell me, tell me, Alyosha, did he despise me?' she said, straightening up in the chair, her eyes flashing now.

'Tell me,' Alyosha said in agitation, 'did you yourself invite him, this man?'

'Yes, I did.'

'Did you send him a letter?'

'Yes.'

'Solely in order to ask him about this, about the boy?'

'No, it had nothing to do with that, nothing at all. But when he came in, I immediately asked him about that. He made his reply, laughed, got up and left.'

'He certainly did the honourable thing as far you were concerned,' Alyosha said quietly.

'But did he despise me? Was he laughing at me?'

'No, because it may be that he himself believes in *compôte*. He, too, is rather ill now, *Lise*.'

'Yes, he does believe in it!' Liza exclaimed, her eyes flashing.

'He despises no one,' Alyosha went on. 'It is simply that he trusts no one. And if he has no trust, then naturally there is contempt there, too.'

'For me, as well? For me?'

'For you, as well.'

'That is good,' said Liza, almost grinding her teeth. 'When he went out, laughing, I felt it was good to be held in contempt. They were both good – the boy with his severed fingers, and to be held in contempt . . .'

And with eyes that were somehow inflamed with malice she laughed in Alyosha's face.

'You know, Alyosha, you know, what I would like is . . . Alyosha, please save me!' she said, suddenly darting up from her chair, rushed towards him and embraced him tightly in her arms. 'Save me,' she said, almost in a moan. 'Do you think I would ever have told anyone else in the whole world what I have told you? But you see, it is the truth, the truth! I am going to kill myself, for everything is so loathsome to me! I do not want to live, for everything is so loathsome to me! Everything, everything is loathsome to me! Alyosha, why do you not love me, why have you absolutely no love for me?' she ended in a frenzy.

'But I do love you!' Alyosha replied, hotly.

'And will you weep for me, will you?'

'Yes, I will.'

'Not because I have refused to be your wife, but simply for me, will you weep, will you weep?'

'Yes, I will.'

'Thank you! Yours are the only tears I need. Let all the other people punish me and crush me with their heels, all, all of them, with the exception of *no one*! Because there is no one whom I love. Do you hear? No one! On the contrary, I hate everyone! Off you go, Alyosha, it's time you went to see your brother!' she said, suddenly tearing herself free of him.

'But you cannot be left like this!' Alyosha said, in fear, almost.

'Off you go to your brother, or the prison will be closed, off you go, here is your hat! Give Mitya a kiss from me, off you go, off you go!'

And she practically heaved Alyosha out through the door by force. Alyosha gazed at her in sorrowful bewilderment, and then suddenly felt in his right hand a letter, a tiny little letter, firmly folded and sealed. Glancing at it, he instantly read the name on it: 'To Ivan Fyodorovich Karamazov'. He gave Liza a quick look. Her features had grown almost menacing.

'Give it to him, see that you give it to him without fail!' she commanded him in a frenzy, shaking all over. 'Today, immediately! Otherwise I will poison myself! This is why I asked you to come here!'

And quickly she slammed the door. The latch clicked. Alyosha put the letter in his pocket and went straight down the stairs without looking in to see Mrs Khokhlakova, forgetting about her, even. As for Liza, no sooner had Alyosha made his retreat than she at once released the latch, opened the door a little way, inserted her finger into the crack and, slamming the door shut with all her might, crushed that finger. Some ten seconds later, freeing her hand, she quietly, slowly, returned to her bath chair, sat down, straightening up completely, and began fixedly to look at her blackened finger and at the blood that was welling up from under the nail. Her lips trembled, and quickly, quickly she whispered to herself:

'I am vile, vile, vile, vile!'

4

A Hymn and a Secret

IT was already quite late (and in any case a November day is hardly very long) when Alyosha rang at the gates of the prison. It was even beginning to get dark. Alyosha knew, however, that he would be let through to see Mitya without obstacle. These things are arranged in our town as they are everywhere else. To start with, of course, upon the conclusion of the preliminary investigation, access to Mitya for relatives and certain other persons was proscribed by certain necessary formalities; but subsequently the formalities were, if not actually slackened, then somehow of their own accord made subject to certain established exceptions for one or two of Mitya's visitors. This was true to such a degree that on occasion meetings with the prisoner in the room appointed for that purpose took place very nearly *entre quatre yeux*. As a matter of fact, such people were very few: only Grushenka, Alyosha and Rakitin. Grushenka was, however, regarded with much favour by none other than Mikhail Makarovich, the chief of police himself. His shouting at her in Mokroye had lain upon the old fellow's conscience. Subsequently, having learned the true gist of the case, he had entirely altered his opinion of her. And it was a strange thing: though he was resolutely convinced of Mitya's guilt in the crime, from the time of Mitya's imprisonment he had somehow begun to look upon him with a greater and greater degree of mildness: 'The fellow may have had a good soul, but he went to ruin, like the Swede,* from drunkenness and disorder!' His earlier horror was supplanted by a kind of pity. As for Alyosha, the police chief was very fond of him and had long been friendly with him, while Rakitin, who had in the time that followed taken to visiting the prisoner very often, was one of the closest acquaintances of the 'police chief's young ladies', as he called them, and was to be found in their house every day, hanging about. In the home of the prison's supervisor, a good-natured old man, though a seasoned and tireless sweat in the cause of duty, nevertheless, he also gave private lessons. Alyosha was also a particular and long-established friend of the supervisor, who liked to talk to him of 'wisdom' in general. Ivan Fyodorovich, for example, the supervisor viewed not so much with respect as with positive fear, this being inspired principally by his opinions, though the supervisor was himself a great philosopher, having got there 'with his own intellect', of course. For Alyosha, though, he seemed to experience a kind of irresistible fellow-feeling. During the last year the old man happened to have begun the study of the Apocryphal Gospels* and was constantly telling his young friend about his impressions. Earlier he had even come to see him at the monastery, talking to him and to the hieromonachs for whole hours on end. In a word, Alyosha, even though he were to arrive late at the prison, needed only to go through and see the supervisor, and the matter was always arranged for him. Moreover, everyone who worked at the prison, right down to the lowest guard, was accustomed to seeing him there. As for the sentries, they, of course, made no difficulties for him as long as he had the authorization of the powers-that-be. Mitya, when called out from his cell, always went downstairs to the place that was appointed for visits. Entering this room, Alyosha bumped into Rakitin, who was just leaving Mitya. Both Rakitin and Mitya were talking in loud voices. Mitya, while seeing him off, was laughing greatly at something, while Rakitin seemed to be muttering some reply. Rakitin, especially of late, seemed very averse to encountering Alyosha, would hardly speak to him, almost, and even bowed to him only with effort. Seeing Alyosha enter now, he suddenly frowned and moved his eyes to the side, as though he were entirely preoccupied with the buttoning of his large, thick overcoat with its fur collar. After that, he at once proceeded to look for his umbrella.

'I don't want to forget anything that belongs to me,' he muttered, solely in order to have something to say.

'See that you don't forget anything that belongs to others!' Mitya quipped, and immediately burst into loud laughter at his own wit. Rakitin blazed up in a flash.

'Save that advice for your Karamazovs, your serf-owning spawn, not for Rakitin!' he shouted suddenly, fairly shaking with fury.

'Hey, what's got into you? It was a joke!' Mitya exclaimed. 'Fie, the devil! They are all like that,' he said turning to Alyosha, nodding towards the swiftly exiting Rakitin. 'He was sitting here, laughing and pleased as punch, and then suddenly he goes and boils over! He didn't even give you a nod, nothing at all, have you and he fallen out over something? Why are you so late? I've not so much been waiting for you as yearning for you all morning. Oh well, it doesn't matter! We shall make up for it.'

'Why has he taken to visiting you so often? Have you and he become friends, or something?' asked Alyosha, also nodding in the direction of the door through which Rakitin had made himself scarce.

'Made friends with Mikhail? No, not really. And in any case, the fellow is a swine! He thinks I'm a . . . scoundrel. Like the others of his kind, he doesn't understand jokes, either − that's the worst thing about them, those fellows. They will never understand jokes. And anyway, their souls are arid, flat and arid, they remind me of when I was driving up to the prison and looked at the prison walls. But he is a clever man, a clever one. Well, Aleksey, my head is for the chop!'

He sat down on the bench and made Alyosha sit down beside him.

'Yes, your trial is tomorrow. I say, have you really so completely given up hope, brother?' Alyosha said with shy emotion.

'Why do you ask that?' Mitya said, glancing at him in a way that somehow lacked focus. 'Oh, it's to do with the trial! Well, the devil! Until now you and I have spoken together of nothing but trivial stuff, this trial, for example, while I have said nothing to you of the most important thing. Yes, my trial is tomorrow, but it was not in connection with my trial that I said that my head is for the chop. It is not my head, but what has been in my head that is for the chop. Why do you look at me with such criticism in your face?'

'What are you talking about, Mitya?'

'Ideas, ideas, that's what! Ethics. What is ethics?'

'Ethics?' Alyosha said, in surprise.

'Yes, is it some kind of science?'

'Yes, it is . . . only . . . I confess that I am unable to tell you precisely what kind of science it is.'

'Rakitin knows. Rakitin knows a lot of things, the devil take his hide! He's not going to be a monk. He plans to go to St Petersburg. He says he wants a job in the critical section of a journal, only it must be one that is graced by a progressive tendency. Well, that way he can both be of use to society and arrange a career for himself. Oh, they're masters at arranging careers for themselves! The devil with ethics! I'm for the chop, Aleksey, yes I am, you man of God! I love you more than anyone else. My heart trembles for you, I love you so much. Who was Carl Bernard?'

'Carl Bernard?' Alyosha said, again in surprise.

'No, not Carl, wait, I've got it wrong: Claude Bernard.* What's he to do with? Chemistry, or what?'

'He must be a scientist,' Alyosha replied, 'only I confess to you that I cannot tell you much about him. All I have heard is that he is a scientist, but of what kind I do not know.'

'Well, the devil take his hide, I don't know either,' Mitya said, swearing. 'Some scoundrel or other, most probably; anyway, they're all scoundrels, the lot of them. But Rakitin will make it, Rakitin will make it through the crack, another Bernard. Oh, those Bernards! They breed like rabbits!'

'But what is the matter?' Alyosha asked insistently.

'He wants to write about me, to write an article about my case and thus inaugurate his role in literature, that's why he's been visiting me, he explained it to me himself. He wants to write something with a progressive tendency, that says something like: "He couldn't help committing murder, he'd fallen prey to his environment," and so on, and so forth, he's explained it to me. "It will have a touch of socialism," he says. Well, the devil take his hide, if it's to have a touch of that, then so let it be, it's all the same to me. He doesn't like brother Ivan, hates him, and he hasn't got much mercy for you, either. Well, I don't tell him to go away, because he is a clever man. It's just that he gives himself these high and mighty airs. I said to him only just now: "The Karamazovs are not scoundrels but philosophers, because all real Russian people are philosophers, but you, though you've done some studying, are not a philosopher, you are a shit." He laughed, in a nasty sort of way. And I told him: "*De* thought*ibus non est disputandum*,"* do you like the witticism? At any rate, I, too, entered the world of classical scholarship,' Mitya suddenly burst out in loud laughter.

'Why are you for the chop? In the sense you meant just now?' Alyosha cut in.

'Why am I for the chop? Hm! Well, what it boils down to . . . if one takes it as a whole, is that — I'm sorry for God, there, that is why!'

'What do you mean, you're sorry for God?'

'Look, imagine: in there, in the nerves inside my head, or rather they're inside my brain, those nerves (oh, the devil take them!) . . . there are these little tails, well, and as soon as they start to tremble . . . that is to say, you see, I fix my eyes on something, like this, and they start to tremble, the little tails . . . and when they start to tremble, an image appears, and it does not appear at once, but after the passage of an instant, a second, and then there appears an aspect, that's to say, rather, not an aspect — the devil take its hide, the aspect — no, an image, that's to say, an object or an event, well, the devil take their hides — and that is why I contemplate first, and think later . . . because of the little tails, and not at all because I have a soul or because I am any kind of "image and likeness", all that is mere foolery. You see, brother, Mikhail explained it to me yesterday, and it was like a scorching blast in my face. It is magnificent, Alyosha, this science! The new man is coming, that I understand . . . But all the same, I'm sorry for God!'

'Well, that is good,' said Alyosha.

'That I'm sorry for God? It's chemistry, brother, chemistry. There is nothing for it, Your Reverence, you must move over a little, chemistry is coming! And Rakitin does not like God, oh no, he does not like him! That is the most sensitive spot in all of them! But they conceal it. They lie. Pretend. "Well, are you going to expound these ideas in a critical section?" I asked. "No, obviously they wouldn't let me," he said, laughing. "Only how," I asked, "is man to fare after that? Without God and without a life to come? After all, that would mean that now all things are lawful, that one may do anything one likes." "Were you not aware of it?" he said. He laughed. "A clever man," he said, "may do anything he likes, a clever man knows a thing or two, but you," he said, "have gone and killed a man and got yourself into hot water, and now you're rotting in prison!" He said that, to me he said it. A real swine! In the old days I used to throw chaps like him out, but now I listen to them. I mean, he says much that is sensible. He also writes cleverly. He started reading me one of his articles a week ago, and I actually went and copied out a few lines of it – wait, I've got it here.'

In haste, Mitya fished out a piece of paper from the pocket of his waistcoat and read:

'"In order to resolve this question it is first of all necessary to align one's personality with one's reality." Do you understand that?'

'No, I do not,' said Alyosha.

He was studying Mitya with curiosity, and listening to him.

'Neither do I. It's vague and obscure, but it's clever. "Everyone writes like that nowadays," he told me, "because that's what the intellectual climate is like . . ." They're afraid of the intellectual climate. He also writes poetry, the scoundrel. He has sung the praises of Mrs Khokhlakova's foot, ha-ha-ha!'

'So I heard,' said Alyosha.

'Did you? And have you heard the wretched little poem?'

'No.'

'I have it here, look, I shall read it to you. You don't know about it, I haven't told you, there is a whole tail that hangs thereby. The scoundrel! Three weeks ago he took it into his head to pull my leg: "Look," he said, "you have gone and got into hot water like a silly idiot because of a mere three thousand, but I am going to get my hands on a hundred and fifty thousand, I shall marry a certain little widow and buy a stone property in St Petersburg." And he told me he was flirting with Mrs Khokhlakova, a woman who was not very clever even when she was young and has now at forty completely lost her reason. "And she is very sentimental," he said, "so that is how I shall get her. I shall marry her, take her off to St Petersburg, and there I shall begin publishing a newspaper." Well, and he had that nasty, voluptuary spittle on his lips – not because of Mrs Khokhlakova, but because of the hundred and fifty thousand. And he convinced me, he really convinced me; kept coming to see me, every day: "She's yielding," he would say. His face was all beaming with joy. And then suddenly he was shown the door: Pyotr Ilyich Perkhotin gained the upper hand, brave fellow! Why, I could fairly smother that silly idiot of a woman with kisses for turfing him out! Yes, you see, it was during the time when he was coming to see me that he composed these wretched verses. "For the first time I have sullied my hands," he said, "have written a poem, for the purpose of seduction, that is to say, for a useful end. Once I have got my hands on the silly woman's capital I shall then be in a position to benefit the civic weal later on." Why, they have a civic excuse for all kinds of villainy! "Anyway," he said, "I have done better than your Pushkin, for I have managed to put some civic concern into a humorous little poem." I can see his point about Pushkin. Why, if he really were a capable fellow, but had merely indulged in versifying about pretty feet! But I mean, he was so proud of his wretched little poem! The vanity of them, the vanity! "Upon the Convalescence of the Fair and Ailing Foot of My Love's Object" — that was the title he had invented for it — the frisky fellow!'

> Oh, this little foot so fair,
> Swollen just a little, there!
> Doctors call on it with cures,
> Bandage it and make it worse.

> 'Tis not feet, though, make me pine —
> Poet Pushkin sing their praise:
> For the head I grieve and pine,
> And it cannot grasp ideas.

> It had grasped a little bit,
> But fair foot got in the way!
> Let the foot be healed and fit,
> So that comprehend head may.*

'A swine, a pure swine, but the blackguard cut a playful measure! And he really did put some "civic concern" into it. And how angry he got when he was shown the door. He ground his teeth!'

'He has already had his revenge,' said Alyosha. 'He wrote a newspaper story about Mrs Khokhlakova.'

And Alyosha quickly told him about the story in the newspaper *Hearsay*.

'Yes, that's him, that's him!' Mitya confirmed, frowning. 'These newspaper stories ... I mean, I know ... why, the rascally things that have already appeared about Grusha, for example! ... And about the other woman, Katya, as well ... Hm!'

He took a few worried paces round the room.

'Brother, I cannot stay long,' Alyosha said, after a pause. 'Tomorrow is a great and dreadful day for you: God's judgement will be accomplished over you . . . and that is why I am surprised that you can be like this, and instead of considering the matter in hand keep talking about God only knows what . . .'

'Well, you needn't be surprised,' Mitya cut in, hotly. 'Why should I talk about that stinking cur all the time, anyway? That murderer? We have talked about that long enough, you and I. I don't want to talk about that stinking son of Smerdyashchaya any more! God will slay him, you will see, now hold your tongue!'

In agitation he went over to Alyosha and suddenly kissed him. His eyes had begun to burn with light.

'Rakitin would not understand this,' he began, wholly in the grip of a kind of ecstasy, 'but you, you will understand it all. That is why I have yearned for you to come. You see, there are many things that I have long wanted to express to you here, within these shabby walls, but about the principal thing I have said nothing: it was as though the time had not yet come for it. I have waited until this final hour in order to pour out my soul to you. Brother, during these last two months I have felt a new man in myself, a new man has been resurrected within me! He was imprisoned within me, but he would never have appeared had it not been for this lightning bolt. I am afraid! Oh, what do I care if I have to chip out ore in the mines for twenty years with a hammer – of that I am not afraid at all; no, it is something else I am afraid of now: that the resurrected man may leave me! It is possible there, too, in the mines, under the earth, beside one, in another convict and murderer like oneself to find a human heart and to consort with him, for there, too, it is possible to live, and love, and suffer! It is possible to resuscitate and resurrect in that convict the heart that has stopped beating, it is possible to nurse him for years and bring out, at last, from the den of thieves into the light a soul that is lofty now, a consciousness that is that of a martyr, resuscitate an angel, resurrect a hero! And after all, there are many of them now, hundreds, and we all bear the guilt for them! Why did I have that dream of the "bairn" at such a moment? "Why is the bairn wretched?" That was a prophecy to me at that moment! It is for the sake of the "bairn" that I shall go. Because all of us are guilty for all the rest. For all the "bairns", for there are little children and grown-up children. All the "bairns". I shall go for all, for it is necessary that someone shall go for them. I did not kill my father, but I must go. I accept! This all came to me here . . . here within these shabby walls. And there are many of them, after all, there are hundreds of them, the subterranean folk, with hammers in their hands. Oh yes, we shall be in fetters, and shall have no freedom, but then, in our great misery, we shall again rise up in the joy without which it is impossible for a man to live, or God to exist, for God gives joy, that is his privilege, a great one . . . O Lord, let man melt away in prayer! How is it possible that I shall be down there under the earth without God? Rakitin is wrong: if God is driven from the face of the earth, we shall meet him under the earth! It is impossible for a convict to be without God, even more impossible than for someone who is not a convict! And then we, the subterranean folk, will sing out of the bowels of the earth a tragic hymn to God, with whom is joy! All hail to God and his joy! I love him!'

Mitya, as he uttered his wild speech, was almost choking. He had turned pale, his lips were trembling, and tears were rolling from his eyes.

'No, life is full, there is life under the earth, too!' he began again. 'You would not believe, Aleksey, how much I want to live now, what a thirst to exist and to experience, within these same shabby walls, there has been born in me! Rakitin does not understand it, all he wants is to build a property and fill it with tenants, but I waited for you, instead. In any case, what is suffering? I am not afraid of it, even though it be numberless. Now I am not afraid, though before I was. You know, I may not even answer at my trial . . . And it seems to me that there is so much of this strength in me now that I shall vanquish everything, all of the suffering, only so that I may keep saying to myself constantly: "I am!" I may endure a thousand torments — yet I am, I may writhe under torture — but I am! I may sit in a tower, but I exist, I can see the sun, but even if I cannot see the sun, I know that it exists. And to know that the sun is there — that is already the whole of life. Alyosha, my cherub, the different philosophies are leading me to despair, the devil take their hides! Brother Ivan . . '

'What about brother Ivan?' Alyosha tried to cut in, but Mitya did not hear.

'You see, before I did not have any of these doubts, but this was all concealed inside me. Perhaps it was precisely because unknown ideas were seething within me that I went drinking and getting into fights and behaving like a madman. I got into fights in order to quench them in myself, to calm them, constrain them. Brother Ivan is no Rakitin, he is hiding an idea. Brother Ivan is a sphinx, and he says nothing, forever says nothing. While I am tormented by the question of God. That alone

torments me. For what if he does not exist? What if Rakitin is right, and
he is an artificial idea dreamed up by mankind? Then, if he does not exist,
man is the boss of the earth, of creation. Magnificent! Only how will he
be virtuous without God? That is the question. I think about it all the
time. For whom will he love then, whom will man love? To whom will
he render gratitude, to whom will he sing his hymn? Rakitin just laughs.
Rakitin says that it is possible to love mankind without God. I mean,
only a snotty-nosed shrimp could state such a thing to be true, but as for
me I can't make any sense of it. Life comes easily to Rakitin: "You
know," he said to me today, "you would do better to concern yourself
with the broadening of man's civic rights, or at any rate with trying to
keep down the price of beef; by doing that you will demonstrate a plainer
and more intimate love for mankind than you ever will by your philosophies." In response to which I fired back: "Without God," I said, "you
yourself would push up the price of beef by a hundred per cent and make
a rouble out of every copeck." That made him lose his temper. For what
is virtue? Answer me that, Aleksey. To me virtue means one thing, while
to a Chinaman it means another – it is, in other words, a thing that is
relative. Or am I wrong! Is it not relative? A perfidious question! Please do
not laugh when I tell you that it has kept me awake for two nights
without sleep. Now the only thing that astonishes me is that people can
live and yet never think about that. Such idle vanity! Ivan does not have
a God. He has an idea. One that's too big for me. But he says nothing. I
think he is a Freemason. I have asked him, but he says nothing. I have
told him that I would like to taste the waters of his well, but he says
nothing. Only once has he uttered one little remark.'

'What was it?' Alyosha caught up quickly.

'I had said to him: "Well, if that is how it is, then are all things
lawful?" He frowned: "Our dear papa, Fyodor Pavlovich," he said, "was
a sucking-pig, but he had the right ideas." I mean, that was what he fired
off at me. That was the only thing he said. It was niftier than what
Rakitin had to say.'

'Yes,' Alyosha confirmed with bitterness. 'When did he come to see
you?'

'Of that later, but now something else. About Ivan I have until now
told you almost nothing. I have delayed it until the end. When this stunt
of mine here is over and the sentence is pronounced, then I shall have
something to tell you, then I shall tell you it all. There is a certain
terrible matter here ... And of that matter you shall be judge for me. But
do not start asking me about it at present, at present I want you to say

nothing. You were talking just now about tomorrow, about my trial, but you see, I don't know anything about it.'

'Have you spoken to this advocate?'

'Oh, the advocate! I have told him everything. He is a soft-spoken scoundrel from the capital. A Bernard! Except that he believes me about as much as a bent half copeck. He believes I'm the murderer, fancy that – oh, I can tell. "Then why," I asked, "have you come to defend me in such a case?" I don't give a spit for them. They have also ordered a doctor, they want to make out that I am mad. I will not allow it! Katerina Ivanovna intends to fulfil "her duty" to the end. Even if it kills her!' Mitya said, smiling a thin and bitter smile. 'The she-cat! The cruel heart! And I mean, she knows that I said of her in Mokroye that day that she was "a woman of great wrath"! She has been told of it. Yes, the evidence has piled up like the sand of the sea! Grigory insists on his version of the facts. Grigory is honest, but a fool. Many people are honest thanks to the fact that they are fools. That is a thought of Rakitin. Grigory is an enemy of mine. Some people are better to have as enemies than as friends. I say that with reference to Katerina Ivanovna. I fear, oh, I fear that at my trial she will tell the story about the earthly prostration after the four and a half thousand! She will pay it back to the very end, right to the uttermost farthing.* I do not want her sacrifice! At my trial they will put me to shame! Somehow I shall endure it. Go and see her, Alyosha, ask her not to talk of that at my trial. Or is it impossible? Well, the devil, it matters not, I shall endure! I am not sorry for her, though. She herself desires it. The thief deserves to suffer. I shall conduct my own defence, Aleksey . . .' Again he smiled his thin and bitter smile. 'Only . . . only Grusha, O God! Why must she take so much suffering upon herself now?' he suddenly exclaimed, with tears. 'Grusha is killing me, the thought of her is killing me, killing me! She was here with me just a while ago . . '

'She told me. She has been very upset by you today.'

'I know. For my character the devil take my hide. I got jealous! As I was letting her go I felt remorse, I kissed her. Did not ask her forgiveness.'

'Why not?' Alyosha exclaimed.

Mitya suddenly burst out laughing in a manner that was almost cheerful.

'God preserve you, dear boy, from ever asking a woman you love to grant you forgiveness for your guilt! Especially, especially a woman you love, no matter how guilty you are before her! Because women, women, brother, are the devil only knows what, and after all they, at least, are something I know about! Well, just try admitting to a woman your guilt, say something like: "I am guilty, please forgive me, I'm sorry" – immediately you will receive a hail of rebukes! On no account will she forgive you in a simple, straightforward manner, no, she will degrade you to the level of a floor-cloth, she will find things that never even happened, will take everything, forget nothing, add things of her own, and only then forgive. And I speak of the best, the best of them! She will scrape out the last scrapings and empty them all on your head – such, I will tell you, is the soul-flaying character that sits in all of them, all to the last one, those angels without whom it is impossible for us to live! You see, my little dove, I will tell you simply and straightforwardly: any respectable man has a duty to be under the thumb of at least some woman or other. Such is my conviction: though it is not so much a conviction as a feeling. A man has a duty to be magnanimous, and that will not blemish a man. It will not even blemish a hero, it will not blemish a Caesar! Well, but do not ask her to grant you forgiveness, never do that, not on any account. Remember the rule: it was taught to you by your brother Mitya, who went to his ruin through women. No, I had better oblige Grusha in some way without her forgiveness. I venerate her, Aleksey, venerate her! Only she does not see it, no, for her there is never enough love. And she torments me, torments me with love. It is not like before! Before she merely tormented me with her infernal curves, but now I have accepted the whole of her soul into my own and through her have myself become a human being! Will they marry us? For without that I will die of jealousy. Every day I think I notice something . . . What has she told you about me?'

Alyosha gave an account of all the things that Grushenka had said earlier. Mitya listened to it all in detail, asking for certain things to be repeated, and was content.

'So she is not angry that I am jealous,' he exclaimed. 'A true woman! "I myself have a cruel heart." Oh, I like that kind, the cruel kind, though I cannot endure it when they are jealous on my account, I cannot endure it! We will fight each other. But I shall love her – love her infinitely. Will they marry us? Can convicts be married? That is the question. But without her I cannot live . . .'

Mitya paced frowningly up and down the room. The room was now almost in darkness. He suddenly became extremely preoccupied.

'So there is a secret, she says, a secret? I have started a conspiracy of three against her, and "Katka" is involved in it – is that what she thinks?

No, sister Grushenka, that is not so. There you have missed the mark, in your woman's way! Alyosha, my little dove, very well, come what may! I shall reveal to you our secret!'

He took a look round in all directions, quickly went right up to Alyosha who was standing before him, and began to whisper to him with an air of secrecy, though really no one could have heard them: the old guard was drowsing on the bench in the corner, and not a word could have slipped through to the ears of the sentries.

'I shall reveal to you the whole of our secret!' Mitya whispered quickly. 'I intended to do it later, because what could I possibly decide without you? You are everything to me. And though I say that Ivan is the loftiest one of us, for me you are a cherub. Only your decision will decide. Perhaps it is you who are the loftiest one, and not Ivan. You see, this is a matter of conscience, a matter of the loftiest conscience – a secret so important that I myself am unable to cope with it and have postponed it all for you to deal with. And yet at present it is too early to decide, because we must await the sentence: when the sentence is pronounced, then you shall decide my fate. Do not try to decide it now; I shall tell you very soon, you will hear it, but do not try to decide anything now. Wait and do not say anything. I shall not reveal everything to you. I shall merely tell you the general idea, without the details, and you must not say anything. No questions, no movements, are you agreed? Though as a matter of fact, O Lord, what shall I do with your eyes? I fear that your eyes will speak your decision, even though you say nothing. Hah, I fear it! Alyosha, listen: brother Ivan proposes that I *escape*. I will not tell you the details: it has all been thought out in advance, it can all be arranged. But please say nothing, do not try to decide anything. My plan is to go to America with Grusha. I mean, I cannot live without Grusha! For what if they will not let her join me in Siberia? Can convicts be married? Brother Ivan says they cannot. And without Grusha what will I do under the earth with my hammer? I will merely smash my own head in with it! And what about from the other point of view, that of conscience? After all, I will have run away from suffering! There was a sign, but I rejected the sign, there was a path of cleansing, but I turned about and went to the left. Ivan says that "with the right attitude" one can be of much more use in America than one can be under the earth. Well, but where will our subterranean hymn be sung? What is America, America is just more vanity! And I think that in America, too, there is a lot of swindling. I will have run away from crucifixion! For I mean, Aleksey, I tell you that you alone are able to understand this and no one

else, for others it is stupid nonsense, ravings, all that I have told you
about the hymn. They will say I have gone mad or am a fool. But I have
not gone mad, and I am not a fool, either. Ivan, too, understands about
the hymn, oh, how he understands, only he makes no response to it, he
says nothing. He does not believe in the hymn. Do not speak, do not
speak: I mean, I can see the look in your eyes: you have already decided!
Do not decide anything, have mercy on me, I cannot live without
Grusha, wait until the trial!'

Mitya ended like a man in frenzy. He held Alyosha by the shoulders
with both hands and drilled into his eyes with his thirsting, inflamed
gaze.

'Can convicts be married?' he repeated a third time, in an imploring
voice.

Alyosha listened with extreme astonishment; deeply shocked.

'Tell me one thing,' he said. 'Does Ivan absolutely insist on it, and
who had the idea first?'

'It was Ivan, he had the idea, and he insists on it! For a long time he
did not come to see me and then suddenly a week ago he did, and that
was the first thing he said. He insists on it dreadfully. He does not
request it, he commands it. In my obedience he does not doubt, even
though I have turned my heart inside out for him, as I have for you, and
spoken of the hymn. He told me how he was going to arrange it, he had
gathered all the information, but I'll tell you about that later. He wants it
to the point of hysteria. The main thing is money: "Ten thousand in
order to get you out of prison," he said, "and twenty thousand in order
to get you to America, and on ten thousand," he said, "we shall arrange a
magnificent escape for you."'

'And he instructed you absolutely not to tell me?'

'To tell absolutely no one, and above all you: on no account were you
to be told! He doubtless fears that you will act as my conscience. Please
do not tell him that I have told you. Hah, no, do not tell him!'

'You are right,' Alyosha decided, 'it is impossible to decide until the
court has passed its sentence. After the trial you yourself will decide; then
you yourself will find the new man within you, and he will take the
decision.'

'The new man or the Bernard, who will decide in Bernardian fashion!
For it seems that I myself am a contemptible Bernard!' Mitya said
bitterly, baring his teeth in a grin.

'But brother, have you really, really given up all hope of acquitting
yourself?'

Mitya jerked his shoulders up convulsively and gave a negative sign with his head.

'Alyosha, little dove, it's time you were going!' he said in a sudden hurry. 'The supervisor shouted in the yard, he'll be here in a moment. It's past visiting time, and we're breaking the regulations. Give me a quick hug, and a kiss, and cross me, little dove, cross me for the cross I shall carry tomorrow . . .'

They hugged and gave each other a kiss.

'You know,' Mitya said suddenly, 'Ivan proposes that I flee, yet I mean, he himself believes that I committed the murder!'

A sad and ironic smile forced itself to his lips.

'Have you asked him whether he does?' Alyosha inquired.

'No, I haven't. I wanted to, but I could not do it, I did not have the courage. But it doesn't matter, after all, I can see it in his eyes. Well, good-bye!'

Once again they quickly exchanged kisses, and Alyosha had already started to move towards the door when suddenly Mitya called to him again:

'Stand still so I can look at you, like that.'

And again he seized Alyosha tightly by the shoulders. His face had suddenly gone quite pale, and in the near-dark this was terribly conspic-uous. His lips were contorted, his gaze drilled into Alyosha.

'Alyosha, tell me the complete truth, as before the Lord God: do you believe that I did it? You, you yourself, do you believe it? The complete truth, and do not lie!' he cried to him in frenzy.

Everything seemed to sway before Alyosha, and into his heart – he felt it – there passed a kind of stab.

'No, what are you . . .' he began to murmur like one lost.

'The whole truth, all of it, and do not lie!' Mitya said again.

'Never for one moment have I believed you to be a murderer,' suddenly tore from Alyosha's breast in a trembling voice, and he raised his right arm aloft, as though invoking God as a witness to what he had said. In one split second the whole of Mitya's face was illuminated with beatitude.

'Thank you!' he got out in a long, drawn-out breath, as though uttering a sigh after coming round from a dead swoon. 'You have given me new life . . . Would you believe it: until now I have been afraid to ask you – you, that is, you! Well, off you go, off you go! You have strengthened me for tomorrow, and may God bless you! Yes, go now, and love Ivan!' were the last words that burst from Mitya.

Alyosha went outside completely in tears. Such a degree of suspicion on Mitya's part, such a degree of mistrust felt even for him, Alyosha — all of that suddenly uncovered before Alyosha an abyss of hopeless misery and despair within the soul of his unhappy brother such as he had had no inkling of before. A deep, infinite compassion suddenly seized hold of him, momentarily exhausting him. His stabbed heart ached horribly. 'Love Ivan!' — he suddenly remembered the words Mitya had uttered just then. And he was on his way to see Ivan. Even that morning he had felt a terrible need to see Ivan. Ivan had tormented him no less than he had tormented Mitya, and now, after this meeting with his brother, he tormented him more than ever.

5

Not You, Not You!

ON his way to see Ivan he had to walk past the house in which Katerina Ivanovna lodged. There was light in the windows. He suddenly came to a halt and decided to go in. It was more than a week since he had seen Katerina Ivanovna. But it had now occurred to him that Ivan might possibly be with her at this very moment, particularly on the eve of such a day. Ringing the bell and starting to climb the staircase, which was dimly lit by a Chinese lamp, he saw a man coming down, in whom as they drew level he recognized his brother. The latter, it appeared, was on his way out after visiting Katerina Ivanovna.

'Ah, it is only you,' Ivan Fyodorovich said, coldly. 'Well, goodbye. Are you on your way up to see her?'

'Yes.'

'I do not advise it, she is "in agitation", and you will only upset her even further.'

'No, no!' a voice suddenly cried from above, out of a door that had been opened in a flash. 'Aleksey Fyodorovich, have you come from him?'

'Yes, I went to see him.'

'Was there anything he asked you to tell me? Please come in, Alyosha, and Ivan Fyodorovich, you must come back in again, too, you must, you must. Do you hear me?'

In Katya's voice there had begun to resonate a tone of such command that Ivan Fyodorovich, after a moment's procrastination, resolved nevertheless to climb the stairs again together with Alyosha.

'She was eavesdropping!' he whispered to himself in annoyance, but Alyosha caught his words.

'You will forgive me if I do not remove my coat,' said Ivan Fyodorovich, entering the reception room. 'I shall not sit down. I shall not stay for more than a minute.'

'Sit down, Aleksey Fyodorovich,' said Katerina Ivanovna, herself remaining on her feet. She had altered little of late, but her dark eyes flashed with an ominous fire. Alyosha later recalled that she had seemed to him exceptionally beautiful at that moment.

'What was his message for me?'

'It consisted of only one thing,' said Alyosha, looking her straight in the face. 'That you should be merciful to yourself and not say anything at the trial about . . .' – he faltered slightly – 'what happened between you . . . at the time you first made each other's acquaintance . . . in that town . . .'

'Ah, it's about the earthly prostration for that money!' she caught up, breaking into bitter laughter. 'Well, is it himself he fears for or is it for me – eh? He said I should be merciful, did he? Merciful to whom? To him, or to myself? Tell me, Aleksey Fyodorovich.'

Alyosha studied her fixedly, trying to understand her.

'Both to him and to yourself,' he said quietly.

'Indeed,' she rapped in a voice that somehow conveyed malice, and then suddenly blushed. 'You do not know me yet, Aleksey Fyodorovich,' she said grimly, 'and neither do I know myself yet. Perhaps you will be coming here to trample me under your feet after my questioning tomorrow.'

'Your testimony will be honourable,' said Alyosha, 'and that is all that counts.'

'A woman is frequently dishonourable,' she ground out. 'Only an hour ago I was thinking that I was afraid to touch that monster of cruelty . . . as though he were a poisonous reptile . . . and yet no, to me he is still a human being! But was he the murderer? Was he?' she suddenly exclaimed hysterically, quickly turning to Ivan Fyodorovich. In a flash Alyosha understood that she had already put this very same question to Ivan Fyodorovich, perhaps only a minute before his arrival, and not for the first time, either, but for the hundredth, and that it had ended in a quarrel.

'I went to see Smerdyakov . . . It was thou, thou who convinced me that he was the father-murderer. I believed only thee!' she continued, still addressing Ivan Fyodorovich. The latter, as though constraining himself, smiled sardonically. Alyosha started at the sound of this 'thou'. He had never even suspected the existence of such relations between them.

'Well, in any case, that will do,' Ivan cut in. 'I am going now. I shall return tomorrow.' And, immediately turning on his heel, he walked out of the room and without further ado descended the stairs. With a kind of commanding gesture, Katerina Ivanovna suddenly seized Alyosha by both hands.

'Please go after him! Catch up with him! Do not leave him alone for a single moment,' she whispered rapidly. 'He is mad. Do you not know that he has gone mad? He has a fever, a nerve fever! The doctor told me, now go, run after him . . .'

Alyosha sprang up and rushed out after Ivan Fyodorovich. The latter had not yet managed to go fifty paces.

'What do you want?' he said, turning round to face Alyosha suddenly, aware that the latter was trying to catch him up. 'She has told you to run after me because I'm mad. I know it all by heart,' he added vexedly.

'In that she is wrong, but she is right that you are ill,' said Alyosha. 'I was looking at your face when we were with her just now: you have a very ill face, very, Ivan!'

Ivan kept walking on without a pause. Alyosha went after him.

'I say, Aleksey Fyodorovich, do you know the manner in which people go mad?' Ivan asked quite suddenly in a quiet voice in which there was no longer any annoyance, but rather a most simple-hearted curiosity.

'No, I don't; I suppose that there are many different kinds of madness.'

'And can one observe in oneself that one is going mad?'

'In my opinion it is impossible to do such a thing with any clarity,' Alyosha replied in surprise. Ivan fell silent for a little while.

'If there is something you want to talk to me about, then please change the subject,' he said suddenly.

'Oh, in case I forget, I have a letter for you,' Alyosha said timidly and, taking Liza's letter out of his pocket, he handed it to him. They happened just to have reached a lamp-post. Ivan recognized the hand at once.

'Ah, it is from that little demon!' he said, breaking into malicious laughter and, without bothering to open the envelope, suddenly tore it into several pieces and threw them to the winds. The scraps of paper went fluttering away.

'Not yet sixteen, it seems, yet already she offers herself!' he said contemptuously, again beginning to stride along the street.

'What do you mean, offers herself?' Alyosha exclaimed.

'It is well known how depraved women offer themselves.'

'What is wrong with you, Ivan, what is wrong with you?' Alyosha said, taking Liza's part with angry sorrow. 'She is a child, you are insulting a child. She is ill, she is herself very ill, and perhaps she is also losing her reason . . . I could not refuse to give you her letter . . . In fact I hoped I might hear something from you . . . that would save her.'

'There is nothing to be heard from me. If she is a child, then I am not her nurse. Be silent, Aleksey. Do not continue. I would not even think of such a thing.'

They both said nothing again for a while.

'Now she will be up all night imploring the Mother of God to tell her how to behave at the trial tomorrow,' he said again suddenly, with brusque malice.

'Is it . . . is it Katerina Ivanovna you mean?'

'Yes. Whether she should appear as Mitenka's rescuer or as his destroyer. She will be praying for light to be granted to her soul. As yet she still does not know, you see, she has not had time to prepare herself. She also thinks I am a nanny, wants me to lull her to sleep!'

'Katerina Ivanovna loves you, brother,' Alyosha said with a feeling of sadness.

'Possibly. Only I am no admirer of hers.'

'She suffers. Why then do you say things to her . . . sometimes . . . things that make her have hope?' Alyosha continued with timid reproach. 'You see, I know that you have given her hope. Please forgive me for speaking in this way,' he added.

'I am unable to do what is necessary in this case, to break off relations with her and tell her plainly that I am doing it!' Ivan declared in irritation. 'It will have to wait until sentence has been pronounced on the murderer. If I break with her now, she will send that good-for-nothing to his ruin at the trial tomorrow, because she hates him and knows she does. It is all lies, lies upon lies! And now, until I have broken with her, she will go on hoping and will not destroy that cruel monster, knowing that I want to help him out of trouble. I wish that cursed sentence would hurry up and come!'

The words 'murderer' and 'cruel monster' provoked a painful response within Alyosha's heart.

'But what can she say that will destroy our brother?' he asked, considering the import of Ivan's words. 'What testimony can she give that could send Mitya to his ruin?'

'You don't know that yet. She possesses a document, in Mitya's own hand, which mathematically proves that he killed Fyodor Pavlovich.'

'Impossible!' Alyosha exclaimed.

'Why not? I have read it myself.'

'There can be no question of such a document!' Alyosha said again, with heat. 'There cannot be, for he is not the murderer. It was not he who killed father, it was not he!'

Ivan Fyodorovich suddenly stood still.

'Then who is the murderer, in your opinion?' he asked somehow coldly, or such was the impression he gave, and a note that was almost one of haughtiness sounded in the tone of his question.

'You yourself know who it is,' Alyosha said quietly and with sincere emotion.

'Who? You mean that fairy-tale about the crazy idiot, the epileptic? Smerdyakov?'

Alyosha suddenly felt himself trembling all over.

'You know who it is,' burst from him helplessly. He was choking.

'But who, then, who?' Ivan exclaimed, almost in fury now. All his restraint had suddenly disappeared.

'I only know one thing,' Alyosha said, still almost in a whisper. 'Whoever murdered father, *it was not you.*'

'"It was not you"? What do you mean – "it was not you"?' Ivan said, dumbfounded.

'It was not you who murdered father, not you!' Alyosha repeated with firm conviction.

The silence lasted for half a minute.

'I know that it was not. What is the matter, are you delirious?' Ivan said, smiling crookedly and palely. His eyes were virtually boring into Alyosha. They were again standing near a lamp-post.

'No, Ivan, the fact is that you yourself have said several times that you are the murderer.'

'When did I say it? . . . I have been in Moscow . . . When did I say it?' Ivan stammered, completely at a loss.

'You have said it to yourself many times, when you were alone during these terrible two months,' Alyosha continued, quietly and clearly as before. He spoke, however, as though he were beside himself, as though not of his own will, as though in obedience to some overpowering call. 'You have accused yourself and have confessed to yourself that the murderer is no one but you. But it was not you who did it, you are wrong, the murderer is not you, do you hear, not you! God sent me to you in order to tell you this.'

They both fell silent. For one whole long minute this silence endured. Both stood staring into each other's eyes. Both were pale. Suddenly Ivan began to tremble, and he gripped Alyosha tightly by the shoulder.

'You have been in my room!' he said in a grinding whisper. 'You have been in my room at night, when he came . . . Confess . . . you have seen him, haven't you? You have seen him!'

'To whom are you referring? Mitya?' Alyosha asked in bewilderment.

'No, not Mitya, to the devil with the cruel monster!' Ivan howled in frenzy. 'Do you know about his visits to me? How did you find out? Tell me!'

'Who is *he*? I don't know to whom you're referring,' Alyosha stammered, in fear now.

'Yes, you do . . . otherwise how could you . . . there can be no question that you know . . .'

Suddenly, however, he seemed to check himself. He stood as though he were thinking something over. A strange, sardonic smile twisted his lips.

'Brother,' Alyosha began again in a trembling voice. 'I have said this to you because you will believe my words, I know that. I spoke those words to you for your whole life: *it was not you*! For your whole life, do you hear! And it was God who charged my soul with the task of saying them to you, even though you may hate me now forever from this day forth . . .'

But Ivan Fyodorovich, it seemed, had now entirely managed to regain his self-mastery.

'Aleksey Fyodorovich,' he said with a cold smile, 'prophets and epileptics I cannot endure; and above all, emissaries of God, you know that all too well. From this moment I sever my relations with you, and I think that it will be for good. I request you to leave me now, at this crossroads we have reached, this very moment. This lane here will take you to your lodgings. Take particular care not to come and visit me today. Do you hear?'

He turned on his heel and, striding resolutely, walked straight off, without turning round.

'Brother,' Alyosha shouted after him, 'if anything should happen to you today, please, before anything else, think of me! . . .'

But Ivan did not reply. Alyosha stood at the crossroads near the lamp-post until Ivan had completely disappeared in the gloom. Then he turned and slowly set off along the lane for where he lived. Both he and Ivan Fyodorovich lived on their own, in different lodgings: neither of them had wished to go on living in Fyodor Pavlovich's deserted house. Alyosha rented a furnished room in the household of some artisans; while Ivan Fyodorovich lived rather far from him and occupied a spacious and rather comfortable apartment in a wing of a certain pleasant house that belonged to a certain civil servant's widow who was far from poor. His only servant in the entire wing was, however, a certain ancient and entirely deaf old woman who suffered from rheumatism in every joint, went to bed at six o'clock in the evening and rose at six o'clock in the morning. Ivan Fyodorovich had during these past two months acquired strangely simple tastes, and was very fond of being completely alone. He even kept tidy himself the room he occupied, and rarely entered the other rooms of his apartment. Arriving at his house's front gate, already grasping the handle of the doorbell, he paused. He felt himself still quivering with rancorous tremor. Suddenly he took his hand away from the bell-handle, spat, turned back and quickly walked all the way to the other, opposite end of the town, some two versts' distance from his lodgings, to a certain tiny, lopsided timber house in which Marya Kondratyevna, Fyodor Pavlovich's former neighbour, who had gone to his kitchen for soup, and to whom Smerdyakov had sung his songs and played the guitar that day, lodged. Her former house she had sold, and now she and her mother lived in what was little more than an *izba*, the ill and almost dying Smerdyakov having moved in with them on the very day of Fyodor Pavlovich's death. It was to him that Ivan Fyodorovich had now directed his steps, drawn by a certain sudden and invincible thought.

6

The First Visit to Smerdyakov

THIS was now the third time since his return from Moscow that Ivan Fyodorovich had gone to talk to Smerdyakov. He had seen him and talked to him, for the first time after the catastrophe, on the first day of his arrival, and had then visited him again two weeks later. After this second occasion he had, however, ceased his meetings with Smerdyakov, so that it was now more than a month since he had seen him or heard anything much about him. Ivan Fyodorovich had returned from Moscow only on the fifth day after the death of his parent, with the result that he had not even managed to see his coffin; the burial had taken place on the very eve of his arrival. The cause of Ivan Fyodorovich's delay lay in the fact that Alyosha, not knowing his precise address in Moscow, had had recourse, for the sending of his telegram, to Katerina Ivanovna, and the latter, being also in ignorance of his present address, had telegraphed her sister and aunt, reckoning that Ivan Fyodorovich would have visited them immediately upon his arrival in Moscow. He had visited them, however, only on the fourth day after his arrival and, reading the telegram, had at once, of course, flown headlong to our town. The first person he had met in our town was Alyosha, but, having discussed things with him, was thoroughly amazed that Alyosha was not willing even to suspect Mitya, but pointed his finger straight at Smerdyakov as being the murderer, something that ran directly counter to all the other opinions held by people in our town. After a subsequent interview with the chief of police and the public procurator at which he learned the details of the charge and the arrest, he was even more surprised at Alyosha, ascribing his opinion simply to brotherly feeling aroused to the ultimate degree and to Alyosha's feeling of compassion for Mitya whom, as Ivan knew, Alyosha loved dearly. In passing, let us insert, once and for all, just a couple of words concerning Ivan's feelings for his brother Dmitry Fyodorovich: he really did not like him at all and at the very most felt for him an occasional sense of compassion, this tempered, however, with a large measure of contempt that had attained the quality of loathing. Mitya's whole being, even his external appearance, was extremely uncongenial to him. As for Katerina Ivanovna's love for Mitya, Ivan viewed it with indignation. He had, however, also gone to see Mitya in prison on the first day of his arrival, and not only had this meeting failed to weaken his conviction as to Mitya's guilt – it had actually strengthened it. That day he had found his brother in a state of unease, of morbid excitement. Mitya had been loquacious, but distracted and incoherent, his remarks extremely brusque, had accused Smerdyakov and got dreadfully confused. Above all he kept talking of the three thousand which the deceased had 'stolen' from him. 'The money is mine, it was mine,' Mitya kept repeating. 'Even if I had stolen it, I would have been right.' The whole body of evidence against him was something he almost did not try to refute, and if he did try to interpret the facts in his favour, then he did it in a manner that was thoroughly inconsistent and preposterous – rather as if he did not even want to defend himself at all before Ivan or anyone else, but on the contrary lost his temper, proudly disdained the charges against him, cursed and boiled over. His reaction to the testimony of Grigory concerning the open door was merely one of contemptuous laughter, and he claimed that it had been 'the Devil who opened it'. He could, however, present no coherent explanation of that fact. At that first meeting he had even managed to offend Ivan Fyodorovich, telling him brusquely that those who themselves asserted that 'all things are lawful' were in no position to suspect or question him. He was in general on this occasion extremely hostile to Ivan Fyodorovich. It had been immediately after this rendezvous with Mitya that Ivan Fyodorovich had set off that day to Smerdyakov.

While yet still on the train, speeding back from Moscow, he had thought constantly of Smerdyakov and of his most recent conversation with him on the eve of his outward journey. There was much in it that troubled him, much that seemed to him suspicious. In making his depositions to the state investigator, however, Ivan Fyodorovich had for the time being said nothing of that conversation. He had postponed it all until his meeting with Smerdyakov. The latter was at that time in the town's hospital. Dr Herzenstube, and also Dr Varvinsky, whom Ivan Fyodorovich encountered at the hospital, both firmly stated in response to Ivan Fyodorovich's insistent questions that Smerdyakov's attack of falling sickness was indubitably genuine, and reacted with positive astonishment to the question as to whether he might not have been pretending on the day of the catastrophe. They had given him to understand that this attack was even an unusual one, having continued and repeated itself over a period of several days, with the result that the life of the *Patient* was decidedly at risk, and that only now, after the application of the remedies that had been undertaken, was it possible to state with positive assurance that the sick man would remain alive, though it was very possible (Dr Herzenstube added) that his reason would remain partially deranged 'if not for the whole of his life, then at any rate for a rather considerable time'. In response to Ivan Fyodorovich's impatient demand as to whether this meant that consequently Smerdyakov was now insane, they vouchsafed the reply that while this was not as yet the case, 'certain abnormalities could be observed'. Ivan Fyodorovich had determined to find out for himself what these abnormalities were. At the hospital he was at once admitted as a visitor. Smerdyakov was in a separate ward, where he lay upon a bed. Near him was another bed, occupied by a certain enfeebled artisan of the town who was swollen in every part of his body with the dropsy and was evidently going to die either tomorrow or the day after; he was in no condition to impede the conversation. At the sight of Ivan Fyodorovich, Smerdyakov exposed his teeth in a distrustful grin, and for an initial moment even seemed to quail. So, at least, it fleetingly appeared to Ivan Fyodorovich. It was, however, only a moment, and on the contrary for all the rest of the time Smerdyakov almost shocked him with his composure. From his very first glance at him, Ivan Fyodorovich was unquestionably convinced that Smerdyakov was in a state of complete

and extreme morbidity: he was very weak and spoke slowly, almost as
though it were difficult for him to move his tongue; he had lost a great
deal of weight and his skin had a yellow appearance. Throughout the
entire twenty minutes or thereabouts for which the visit lasted, he kept
complaining of headache and pain in all his limbs. His *skopets*-like, dried-
up face seemed to have become much smaller, his sidewhiskers were
matted, and instead of a topknot there jutted aloft only one thin little
strand of hair. But his screwed-up left eye that appeared to be somehow
hinting at something gave away the earlier Smerdyakov. 'It's always
interesting to talk to a clever man,' Ivan immediately remembered. He sat
down on a stool at Smerdyakov's feet. Smerdyakov moved his whole
body on the bed in pain, but did not speak first, said nothing, and indeed
looked as though he were no longer particularly interested in any case.

'Can you talk to me?' Ivan Fyodorovich inquired. 'I shall not greatly
tire you.'

'Indeed I can, sir,' Smerdyakov mumbled in a weak voice. 'Is it long
since your honour was pleased to arrive?' he added indulgently, as
though encouraging a disconcerted visitor.

'I only got here today . . . to try to sort out the mess you seem to have
got yourselves into here.'

Smerdyakov gave a sigh.

'Why the sighing? After all, you knew, did you not?' Ivan Fyodorovich
barked straight out.

Smerdyakov maintained a stolid silence.

'How could I not have known, sir? It was all clear in advance. Only
how could I have known, sir, that I would be led into this?'

'Led into what? Stop prevaricating! After all, it was you yourself who
predicted you would have an attack of the falling sickness if you went
down into the cellar, was it not? You referred quite specifically to the
cellar.'

'Have you mentioned that to the investigation?' Smerdyakov asked
with calm curiosity.

Ivan Fyodorovich suddenly lost his temper.

'No, not yet, but I shall do so without fail. You, brother, are going to
have to do a lot of explaining to me now, and I think you ought to
know, my little dove, that I will not allow myself to be played around
with!'

'But why would I do that, sir, when all my hope and trust is in you,
just like in the Lord God, sir?' Smerdyakov said, still with complete
calm, and only closing his little eyes for a moment.

'For one thing,' Ivan said, proceeding to business, 'I know that one cannot predict an attack of the falling sickness in advance. I have made inquiries, so do not try to prevaricate. The day and the hour are impossible to predict. So how that day were you able to predict to me the day and the hour, even mentioning the cellar? How could you have known in advance that you were going to fall into that particular cellar in a fit, if your falling sickness was not feigned on purpose?'

'It was a part of my duties to go down to that cellar in any case, sir, even several times a day, sir,' Smerdyakov drawled slowly. 'And it was in just the same way that I fell down from the garret a year ago, sir. It's sure and certain that one cannot predict the falling sickness in advance to the day and the hour, but one may always have the feeling that it's coming.'

'But you predicted the day and the hour!'

'As regards my falling sickness, sir, you would do best, good sir, to consult the doctors here, concerning the question of whether it was a real attack or not a real one, but as for myself I have nothing more to tell you on that subject.'

'And what about the cellar? How did you know it would happen in the cellar?'

'You have that cellar on the brain! When I went down into the cellar that day I was a-feared and a-frit with doubt, and even more a-feared because I was deprivated of your company and could expect no protection from anyone in the whole world. I went down into that cellar that day and I thought: "It's going to come now, it's going to smite me, will I fall down or not?", and because I was so a-frit with doubt that undevoidable spasm suddenly came and grabbed me by the throat, sir . . . well, and so down I went flying. All that, and all the previous conversation between you and me, sir, on the eve of that day in the evening by the gates, sir, when I told you about my fear and about the cellar, sir — all that I have told in detail to Mr Dr Herzenstube and Investigator Nikolay Parfenovich, and they have written it all down in their protocol, sir. And the other doctor here, Mr Varvinsky insisted to everybody as a special point that it happened because of the thought I had, because of my very same worrying about whether I was going to fall or not. And so it came and grabbed me. That's what they wrote down, sir, and sure and certain it must have happened like that, exclusively because of my fear, sir.'

Having said this, Smerdyakov, as though exhausted by weariness, took a deep breath.

'So you said all that in your deposition, did you?' Ivan Fyodorovich asked, slightly taken aback. The fact was that he had been planning to frighten Smerdyakov by saying he intended to tell the investigation about their conversation that day, and now it turned out that Smerdyakov had told it himself.

'What do I have to fear? Let them write down the whole of the veritable truth,' Smerdyakov pronounced firmly.

'And did you describe for them the whole of our conversation by the gates, word for word?'

'No, I could not say that it was word for word, sir.'

'And what about your being able to feign the falling sickness, as you boasted to me you could that day? Did you also tell them that?'

'No, I didn't tell them that, either, sir.'

'Now tell me: why did you send me to Chermashnya that day?'

'I was scared you'd go away to Moscow, sir. Chermashnya is nearer, after all, sir.'

'You are lying: you yourself asked me to go: "Off you go," you said, "out of harm's way!"'

'Oh, I said that exclusively out of friendship for you and because of the devotion of my heart, foresensing trouble in the house, sir, and being a-sorry for you. Only I was more sorry for myself than I was for you, sir. "Off you go, out of harm's way," I said, so you would realize that things were going to get rough at home, and so you would stay to protect your parent.'

'Then you should have said it more directly, fool!' said Ivan Fyodor-ovich, suddenly flaring up.

'But how could I have done, sir? It was the fear in me alone that made me speak, sir, and anyway you might have been angry with me. I ought, of course, to have apprehended lest Dmitry Fyodorovich make that scandal and carry off that money, for he saw as his own, but who could have known that it would end with such a murder? I thought his honour was only simply going to steal that three thousand roubles that the *barin* kept under his mattress, sir, in an envelope, sir, but his honour went and murdered him, sir. How could I have guessed that, good sir?'

'Well, if you yourself say that it was impossible to guess it, then how could I have surmised it and remained? What tangled web are you weaving now?' Ivan Fyodorovich said, pondering.

'You could have surmised it, sir, because I was telling you to go to Chermashnya instead of Moscow, sir.'

'But how could I have surmised it from that?'

Smerdyakov appeared to be very tired and was again silent for a while.

'You could have surmised it, sir, by that very same fact, sir, that if I was deflecting you to Chermashnya, that that would mean I desired your most intimate presence here, for Moscow is far away, and Dmitry Fyodorovich, a-knowing that you were not far off, would not be so encouraged. And then at very short notice, in case anything happened, you could have come and protected me, for I myself had drawn your attention to Grigory Vasilyevich's illness, and also that I was a-feared of the falling sickness. And whenupon I had explained to you about those knocks, by the use of which it were possible to enter the room of the deceased, and that they were already known to Dmitry Fyodorovich through me, I thought that you would then surmise that his honour was unquestionably going to do something that day, and that never mind about Chermashnya, you would stay here altogether.'

'He speaks very coherently,' thought Ivan Fyodorovich, 'even though he is mumbling; why did Herzenstube speak of a derangement of the faculties?' Aloud, he exclaimed in anger: 'You are trying to play cunning tricks on me, the devil take your hide!'

'Well, I must confess that I thought that day you had surmised everything,' Smerdyakov countered with an air of the utmost ingenuousness.

'If I had, then I would have remained!' Ivan Fyodorovich let out, flaring up again.

'Well, sir, you see, I thought that you, having surmised, would get yourself out of harm's way as soon as possible, even if it were only by running away somewhere to save yourself from a fearful end, sir.'

'You mean you thought that everyone is a coward like you?'

'Forgive me, sir, I thought that as I am, so were you.'

'Of course, I should have surmised,' Ivan said in agitation, 'and indeed I did surmise something vile on your part . . . Only you are lying, you are lying again,' he exclaimed, as he suddenly remembered something. 'Do you remember how you came up to my carriage that day and said to me: "It's always interesting to talk to a clever man"? In other words, you were relieved that I was going, were you not, if you praised me like that?'

Smerdyakov sighed again, and then yet again. Colour seemed to appear in his face.

'If I was,' he said, gasping slightly, 'it was exclusively because you had agreed to go, not to Moscow, but to Chermashnya. Because you'd be nearer then; only I said those very same words to you not in praise but in reproach, sir. You did not understand that, sir.'

'Reproach for what?'

'For the fact that, even though you foresensed trouble, you were abandoning your own parent, sir, and were unwilling to protect us, because they could always have hauled me in for that three thousand, and say that I had stolen it, sir.'

'The devil take your hide!' Ivan shouted again. 'Wait: did you tell the state investigator and the public procurator about those knocks?'

'I told it all as it is, sir.'

Once again, Ivan Fyodorovich was privately astonished.

'If I thought of anything that day,' he began again, 'then it was about some vile action solely on your part. Dmitry Fyodorovich was capable of murder, but that he would steal — that I did not believe at the time . . . While on your part I expected any manner of vile action. Yet you yourself told me that you were able to feign the falling sickness — why did you tell me that?'

'Exclusively because of my simple-heartedness. And anyway, never in all my life have I pretended to have a fit of the falling sickness on purpose, and I only said it to you as a boast. It were sheer stupidity, sir. I had grown very fond of you and was treating you with complete simplicity.'

'My brother makes against you the straight accusation that you committed the murder and that you were the thief.'

'Well, what else is left to him now?' Smerdyakov said, exposing his teeth in a bitter smile. 'And who will believe him after all the evidence there's been? The open door was seen by Grigory Vasilyevich, sir, so how can he say such things after that, sir. And anyway, let God dispose of him. He trembles, does his honour, as he tries to save himself . . .'

Softly he fell silent and then all of a sudden, as though it had just occurred to him, added:

'I mean, look, sir, it's the same thing again: his honour wishes to unload it all on me and make out that it was the work of my hands, sir — I've already heard that, sir — and I mean, it's the same with this business about me being a master at feigning the falling sickness: well, would I have told you in advance that I was able to feign it if I had really had such a design on the life of your parent? If I had been planning a murder of that kind, would I have been such a fool as to incriminate myself like that in advance, and to one of his own sons, for pity's sake, sir? Does that resemble probability? I mean, in order for that to be, sir, well, on the contrary, it never ever could, sir. Like this conversation between you and I, nobody hears it excepting Providence alone, sir, and if you was to tell

Nikolay Parfenovich and the public procurator, by doing so you might in actual fact protect me, sir; for what kind of an evil-doer is it who can be so simple-hearted in advance of having done it? That would make them all think a lot.'

'Listen,' said Ivan Fyodorovich, getting up from his seat, deeply struck by this last argument of Smerdyakov's and breaking off the conversation, 'I do not suspect you at all and even consider it ridiculous to do so ... On the contrary, I am grateful to you for having set my mind at rest. Now I shall go, but I shall come to see you again. For the moment goodbye, and please recover. Is there anything you would like me to get you?'

'I am grateful for everything, sir. Marfa Ignatyevna does not forget me, sir, and assists me if there is anything I need, out of her customary kindness. I receive daily visits from kind people.'

'Then goodbye for now. I shall, of course, say nothing about your ability to feign the illness ... and I would advise you, too, to tell nothing of it to the investigation,' Ivan suddenly said for some reason.

'I understand very well, sir. And if you tell nothing of it, then I shall not tell all the conversation we had by the gates that day, either ...'

Here it happened that Ivan Fyodorovich quickly went out and then, when he had only gone about a dozen paces down the corridor, suddenly felt that in the last sentence Smerdyakov had uttered there lay some kind of offensive meaning. He was about to turn back, but it had only been a fleeting thought, and saying 'Foolishness!' to himself, he left the hospital even more quickly. The main thing was that he really did feel his mind had been set at rest, and by the very fact that the guilty person was not Smerdyakov but his brother Mitya, even though one might have thought the opposite would turn out to be true. Why this was he was reluctant to analyse at the time, even feeling a revulsion at digging about in his feelings. For some reason he wanted to forget about it all as quickly as possible. Subsequently, during the days that followed, when he became acquainted with all the evidence that weighed against Mitya, he grew entirely convinced of Mitya's guilt. There were the depositions of the most insignificant people, which were none the less almost shocking in their import – such as, for example, those of Fenya and her mother. To say nothing of those of Perkhotin, the people at the inn and at Plotnikovs' delicatessen, and the witnesses at Mokroye. The most crushing weight of evidence was contained in the details. The revelation concerning the secret 'knocks' had surprised the state investigator and the public procurator almost as much as Grigory's statement concerning the open door.

Grigory's wife, Marfa Ignatyevna, declared bluntly in response to Ivan Fyodorovich's demand that Smerdyakov had lain all night in the room through the partition, 'not more than three yards from our bed, it were', and that even though she herself slept soundly, she had woken up many times, hearing his moans: 'He kept moaning all the time, constantly moaning.' When he had a word with Herzenstube and conveyed to him his doubt that Smerdyakov was in any way insane, but was merely enfeebled, all he got out of the old man was a thin little smile. 'Well, do you know what he is making a special study of at present?' he asked Ivan Fyodorovich. 'He is learning French vocabulary; he has an exercise book under his pillow in which there are French words written out in Russian characters, heh-heh-heh!' Ivan Fyodorovich at last abandoned every doubt. Of brother `Dmitry he could not even think without a sense of loathing. One thing was, however, strange: that Alyosha stubbornly continued to insist that Dmitry had not committed the murder, but that it had 'in all probability' been Smerdyakov. Ivan had always felt that Alyosha's opinion was something he valued highly, and it was for that reason that he was now so very bewildered by it. He also found it strange that Alyosha did not seek to engage him in conversation about Mitya, never raised the subject himself but merely replied to Ivan's questions. Ivan Fyodorovich also noticed this very forcibly. As a matter of fact, he was at this time distracted by a certain quite irrelevant matter: during the first days after his arrival from Moscow he had given himself up wholly and irrevocably to his fiery and reckless passion for Katerina Ivanovna. This is not the place to raise the subject of this new passion of Ivan Fyodorovich, one which was subsequently to have an effect on his whole life: that might áll serve as a canvas for another narrative, another novel which I do not know whether I shall ever undertake. All the same, however, I cannot even now remain silent concerning the fact that when Ivan Fyodorovich, walking with Alyosha as I have described from the house where Katerina Ivanovna lived, said to him: 'I am no admirer of hers', he had at that moment been lying dreadfully: he loved her to distraction, though it was also true that at times he hated her to a point where he might even have killed her. Here many causes had come together: deeply shaken by what had happened to Mitya, she had rushed to Ivan Fyodorovich, who had now come back to her again, as to her saviour. She had been offended, wounded, degraded in her emotions. And now here again had appeared the man who had formerly loved her so much – oh, she knew it all too well, and whose mind and heart she always placed so far above herself. But the stern girl had not given herself up entirely in sacrifice, in spite of all the Karamazovian lack of restraint in the desires of her beloved and in spite of all the charm he exercised over her. At the same time she was ceaselessly tormented by remorse at having betrayed Mitya, and in terrible, quarrelsome moments with Ivan (and they were many) she would tell this to him straight out. This it was that he had, in talking to Alyosha, called 'lies upon lies'. There was, of course, contained in it a good deal of falsehood, and this above all was what Ivan Fyodorovich had found so vexing . . . but of all this later. In a word, he had for a time almost forgotten about Smerdyakov. And yet, two weeks later, after his first visit to him, there had again begun to torment him the same strange thoughts as before. Enough be it to say that he had ceaselessly begun to ask himself: why, that last night in Fyodor Pavlovich's house before his departure, had he gone out on the staircase like a thief and listened to what his father was doing downstairs? Why with revulsion had he remembered this later, when on his journey on that morning of the following day he had suddenly fallen into a state of such anguish and, as he arrived in Moscow, said to himself: 'I am a scoundrel!'? And now it suddenly occurred to him that it was possibly because of all these tormenting thoughts that he was now ready to forget even Katerina Ivanovna, so intensely had they all of a sudden taken possession of him again! With this thought in his head, he happened to encounter Alyosha in the street. He at once stopped him and suddenly asked him a question:

'Do you remember that day when Dmitry burst into the house after dinner and beat up father, and when outside afterwards I told you that I reserved for myself "the right to desire"? Tell me, did you think that day that I desired father's death?'

'Yes, I did,' Alyosha replied quietly.

'Well, as a matter of fact, it really was the case, and there is no great mystery about it. But did it not also occur to you at the time that I really did want "one vile reptile to consume the other", that's to say, that Dmitry should murder father, and as soon as possible . . . and that I myself would even be quite willing to help bring it about?'

Alyosha turned slightly pale and looked into his brother's eyes without saying anything.

'Go on, then, tell me!' Ivan exclaimed. 'I want with all my being to know what you thought that day. I must know; the truth, the truth!' He took a heavy breath, already looking at Alyosha with a kind of hatred in advance.

'Please forgive me, I did think that at the time,' Alyosha whispered and fell silent, without adding a single 'mitigating circumstance'.

'Thank you!' Ivan rapped out and, turning his back on Alyosha, quickly went on his way. From that time on Alyosha noticed that brother Ivan began to steer clear of him and even to treat him with hostility, with the subsequent result that he stopped calling on him. But it was at that moment, just after the encounter with him, that instead of going home. Ivan Fyodorovich suddenly set off to see Smerdyakov again.

7

The Second Visit to Smerdyakov

SMERDYAKOV had by this time already been discharged from the hospital. Ivan Fyodorovich was familiar with his new abode: in that very same small and wretched, lopsided timber house consisting of two rooms divided by an outside passage. In one of the rooms lodged Marya Kondratyevna and her mother, and in the other Smerdyakov, on his own. God only knows on what basis he had moved in with them, gratis or for money. It was subsequently thought that he had moved in with them in the capacity of Marya Kondratyevna's betrothed, and for the time being was living with them gratis. Both mother and daughter respected him greatly and looked on him as someone who stood above them. Having knocked and gained entrance, Ivan Fyodorovich stepped into the passage and, following Marya Kondratyevna's direction, turned straight left into the 'white room',* which was occupied by Smerdyakov. This room contained a tiled stove, and was fiercely heated. The walls were resplendent with blue wallpaper, all of it torn, it was true, and in the cracks behind it there swarmed a terrible quantity of brown cockroaches which made an incessant rustling. The furniture was hardly worth speaking of: two benches, one along each wall, and two chairs beside a table. This table, though a plain wooden one, was, however, covered by a tablecloth with pink designs on it. At each of the two small windows stood a pot of geraniums. In the corner was an icon-case containing icons. On the table stood a small, badly battered copper samovar and a tray on which there were two cups. But Smerdyakov had already finished drinking tea, and the samovar had gone out. He was sitting at the table on one of the benches and, looking at an exercise book, was scrawling something with a pen. A bottle of ink stood alongside, together with a low, cast-iron candlestick which, however, contained a stearin candle. Ivan Fyodorovich at once concluded by the look of Smerdyakov's face that he had made a complete recovery from his illness. His face was fresher in complexion, more rounded, his topknot back in place and his sidewhiskers sleeked down. He was wearing a stripy quilted dressing-gown which was, however, very threadbare and pretty well worn to rags. On his nose was a pair of spectacles, which Ivan Fyodorovich had not seen him wearing previously. This most trivial circumstance suddenly even seemed doubly to incense Ivan Fyodorovich: 'A brute like that, yet he wears spectacles!' Smerdyakov slowly raised his head and stared fixedly at the newcomer through them; then slowly he took them off and got up from the bench, though not at all respectfully, but even lazily, solely in order to observe merely the most essential courtesy, without which it is almost impossible to get by. All this fleeted through Ivan's head within the space of a split second, and all this he at once took in and observed, and above all — the way Smerdyakov was looking at him, decidedly angry, unwelcoming and even supercilious, as if to say: 'Why have you come poking your nose in here, we made our agreement that day, so why have you come back again?' Ivan Fyodorovich could scarcely hold himself in check:

'Your room is hot,' he said, still standing, and undoing his coat.

'Take it off, sir,' Smerdyakov consented.

Ivan Fyodorovich took off his coat and threw it on the bench, with trembling hands took a chair, quickly moved it up to the table and sat down. Smerdyakov had succeeded in lowering himself on to his bench first.

'Before we go any further: are we alone?' Ivan Fyodorovich asked, sternly and impetuously. 'Will they not hear us from over there?'

'No one will hear anything, sir. You saw for yourself: there is a passage.'

'Listen, my little dove: what was that remark you let slip as I was on my way out from seeing you at the hospital, to the effect that if I were to keep silent about you being a master of feigning the falling sickness, then you would not tell the state investigator all our conversation by the gates? What was the meaning of that "all"? What were you implying then? Were you trying to threaten me? With the idea that I had entered into some kind of association with you, was afraid of you, was that it?'

Ivan Fyodorovich said this in a complete fury, visibly and on purpose letting it be known that he viewed any beating about the bush or veiled approach with contempt and was playing with an open hand. Smerdyakov's eyes flashed with malice, his left one began to blink, and immediately, though with customary measure and restraint, he gave his reply, as if to say: 'You want it pure and straight? Then here it is, pure and straight.'

'Well, what I was implying, and the reason why I said it, was that even though you were a-knowledgeable in advance about that murder of your kindred parent, you left him to his fate that day, so that people should not make evil conclusions about your feelings, and perhaps also about something else – that was what I was promising not to tell the authorities that day.'

Though Smerdyakov spoke without hurry and to all appearance in control of himself, his voice now even contained something firm and insistent, a note of menacing and brazen challenge. Insolently he fixed his eyes upon Ivan Fyodorovich, and for an initial moment the latter was even dazzled:

'What? What did you say? Are you in your right mind?'

'Perfectly in my right, full mind, sir.'

'But do you suppose that I *knew* about the murder that day?' Ivan Fyodorovich exclaimed at last, and he banged his fist hard on the table. 'What do you mean – "and perhaps also about something else"? Speak, scoundrel!'

Smerdyakov said nothing and continued to study Ivan Fyodorovich with the same insolent look.

'Speak, foul and stinking villain – what is this "something else"?' the latter howled.

'Well, by that "something else" I was that moment implying that you yourself was possibly very much desirous of the death of your parent that day.'

Ivan Fyodorovich leapt up and struck him on the shoulder with all his might, making him sway aside towards the wall. In a single flash Smerdyakov's face was wet with tears, and, saying: 'For shame, good sir, to strike a weak man,' he suddenly put his blue-checked cotton handkerchief, which was completely covered in snot, to his eyes and embarked on a quiet and tearful sobbing. About a minute went by.

'Enough! Stop!' Ivan Fyodorovich said at last, commandingly, sitting down on his chair again. 'Do not exhaust the last of my patience!'

Smerdyakov took the filthy rag away from his eyes. Each tiny feature of his wrinkled face was expressive of the insult he had just endured.

'So then, scoundrel, you thought that day that I was at one with Dmitry in wishing to kill father?'

'Your thoughts that day I did not know, sir,' Smerdyakov said in an injured voice, 'and the reason I stopped you that day, as you were going out through the gates, was to try you on that very point, sir.'

'Try me on what point? What?'

'Well, on that very same circumstance: did you or did you not wish that your parent would be a-murdered as soon as possible?'

Ivan Fyodorovich's indignation was more than anything else aroused by this insistent, brazen tone, which Smerdyakov obstinately refused to drop.

'It was you who killed him!' he exclaimed, suddenly.

Smerdyakov smiled a thin, contemptuous smile.

'You yourself know very well that it was not me who killed him. And I thought that a clever man would have nothing more to say about that.'

'But why, why did there appear in you such suspicion of me that day?'

'As you already know, exclusively from fear, sir. For in such a position was I that day that, a-shaking in fear, I suspected everyone. I decided to try you out, too, sir, for I thought that if you, too, desired the same thing as that fine brother of yours, then that was the end of this whole business, and I myself would perish also, like a fly.'

'Listen, this is not what you were saying two weeks ago.'

'When I spoke to you in the hospital it was the same thing I was implying, only I supposed that you would understand without superfluous words and would yourself not wish me to talk of it directly, being the very clever man you are, sir.'

'Will you listen to him? But reply, reply, I insist: how, tell me, and by what manner of means could I have implanted within your villainous soul such a wretched suspicion in my regard?'

'The actual killing of him, that you yourself could on no account have done, sir, but the wanting of it, that someone else should kill him, that you wanted.'

'And how calmly, how calmly he says it, too! And for what reason did I want it, what point was there in my wanting it?'

'What point, sir? Well, what about the inheritance, sir?' Smerdyakov caught up with venom and even a kind of vengefulness. 'After all, each of the three brothers could expect to receive nearly forty thousand after the death of your parent, and maybe even more, sir, and yet if Fyodor Pavlovich was to have married that lady, Agrafena Aleksandrovna, sir, then after the altar she would immediately have transferred the whole of the capital to her own name, for her honour is not at all stupid, sir, and then all you three fine brothers would not have got so much as two roubles between you after the death of your parent. Well, and was there much between them and the altar, sir? Just a hair's breadth, sir: that *barynya* would only have had to wave her pinky at him and his honour would have gone running off to the church after her honour with his tongue hanging out.'

With suffering, Ivan Fyodorovich held himself in check.

'All right,' he said at last. 'You see, I have not leapt up, have not beaten you to a pulp, have not murdered you. Now go on, and tell me: according to you, I had put Dmitry up to it, was relying on him to do it?'

'How could you not have done, sir? After all, if his honour was to do it, then he would lose all his rights as a gentleman, all his rank and property, and he'd have to go into exile, sir. And then, I mean, sir, his allotted portion would remain to you and your fine brother Aleksey Fyodorovich, in equal parts, sir, that's to say you would each get not forty but sixty thousand, sir. It's sure and certain that you were relying on Dmitry Fyodorovich that day!'

'I will not tolerate this from you! Listen, scoundrel: if I had relied on anyone that day to do it, then it would of course have been on you, not Dmitry, and, I swear, I even sensed some kind of villainy on your part . . . that day . . . I remember the impression I had!'

'And I also thought that day, just for a moment, that you were relying on me,' Smerdyakov said with a mocking grin, 'and by that very same thing you exposed yourself to me even more, for if you sensed something in me and at the same time left the town, that meant you were more or less saying: "You may kill my parent, and I will not prevent you."'

'Scoundrel! That is how you understood it!'

'And all because of that very same Chermashnya, sir. For mercy's sake! There you were getting all ready to go off to Moscow, and every time your parent asked you to go to Chermashnya, you refused, sir! And then just because of a stupid remark I made you suddenly changed your mind and agreed, sir! And why should you have agreed to go to Chermashnya? If you went not to Moscow but to Chermashnya, without cause, exclusively because of a remark of mine, then that means you must have been expecting I was going to do something.'

'No, I swear it, no!' Ivan howled, grinding his teeth.

'But how can that be, sir? You should, on the contrary, as the son of your parent, have made it your first duty to have taken me down to the police station that day for those words of mine, and had the hide taken off me, sir . . . or at any rate given me a beating right there and then, but you, for pity's sake, sir, on the contrary, not being angry in the least, immediately obliged and acted exactly according to my stupid remark and went away, sir, which was a really silly thing for you to do, for you ought to have stayed behind to preserve the life of your parent . . . How could I help putting two and two together?'

Ivan sat with knitted brows, convulsively leaning on his knees with both fists.

'Yes, it's a pity I didn't give you a beating,' he smiled bitterly. 'I could not have hauled you down to the police station that day: for who would have believed me and what evidence could I have produced, well, but if I had given you a beating . . . pity I did not think of it; even though beating servants is forbidden, I'd have made a fine mess of your ugly mug all the same.'

Smerdyakov looked at him almost with pleasure.

'In the normal instances of life,' he said in that complacently doctrinaire tone of voice with which he had once argued with Grigory Vasilyevich about religious faith, teasing him as he stood at Fyodor Pavlovich's table, 'in the normal instances of life beating servants is indeed forbidden by the law nowadays, and the masters have all stopped beating us, sir, well, but in the distinctual instances of life, and not only in Russia, but in all the world, even though it be the very French Republic itself, they continue to beat us, just as they did in the time of Adam and Eve, sir, and they will never stop it, sir, and yet you even in a distinctual instance did not dare, sir.'

'What are you learning French vocabulary for?' Ivan said nodding towards the exercise book that lay on the table.

'Well, why should I not be learning it, sir, in order to further my education a-considering that it may one day beneed me to reside in those happy provinces of Europe?'

'Listen, monster,' Ivan said, shaking all over, his eyes flashing, 'I do not fear your accusations, no matter what you tell the authorities, and if I did not beat you to death just now, it was solely because I suspect you of this crime and am going to have you up before the law. And you may be sure that I will find you out!'

'Well, in my opinion you would do better not to say anything, sir. For what could you testify against me in my complete innocence, and who would believe you? Only if you do start testifying, then I will tell everything, sir, for why should I not defend myself?'

'Do you suppose I fear you now?'

'Even if the court does not believe all the things I have told you just now, the public will believe them, sir, and you will be covered with shame, sir.'

'So what you mean is "it's always interesting to talk to a clever man" again, is it?' Ivan ground out.

'Your honour has hit the mark exactly, sir. Be clever, sir.'

Ivan Fyodorovich rose, trembling all over with indignation, put on his coat and, without making any further reply to Smerdyakov, without looking at him, even, quickly walked out of the room. Cool evening air refreshed him. The moon was shining brightly in the sky. A terrible nightmare of thoughts and feelings seethed within his soul. 'Should I go right now and testify against Smerdyakov? But what shall I say in my testimony? He is innocent, after all. On the contrary, it will be he who accuses me. Indeed, why did I go to Chermashnya that day? Why, Why?' Ivan Fyodorovich wondered. 'Yes, of course, I expected something, and he is right . . .' And again for the hundredth time he recalled how on that last night in his father's house he had eavesdropped on his father from the staircase, recalled it with such suffering now, however, that he even stood still on the spot as though he had been run through by a knife: 'Yes, I expected it that day, it is true! I wanted, I truly wanted there to be that murder! But did I want it, did I? . . . I must kill Smerdyakov! . . . If I do not dare to kill Smerdyakov now, then it is not worth my living any longer! . . .' Then Ivan Fyodorovich, without returning to his lodgings, walked straight to the house where Katerina Ivanovna lived and frightened her by his appearance: he was like a man who had lost his mind. He related to her the whole of the conversation he had had with Smerdyakov, right down to the last small detail. He could not calm himself down, no matter how much she tried to make him, kept pacing about the room and talking in a strange, jerky manner. At last he sat down, leaned his elbows on the table, rested his head in both hands and delivered a strange aphorism:

'If it was not Dmitry but Smerdyakov who committed the murder, then I, of course, am an accomplice, for I put him up to it. Whether I did put him up to it, I do not yet know. But if he, and not Dmitry, committed the murder then, of course, I, too, am a murderer.'

On hearing this, Katerina Ivanovna rose in silence from where she was sitting, walked over to her writing table, unlocked a casket that stood upon it, took out a sheet of paper and placed it before Ivan. This sheet of paper was the very same document of which Ivan Fyodorovich later informed Alyosha as being the 'mathematical proof' that brother Dmitry had killed their father. It was a letter Mitya had written to Katerina Ivanovna while drunk, on the very same evening he had met Alyosha out on the open road as the latter was on his way back to the monastery after the scene at Katerina Ivanovna's house, when Grushenka insulted her. That day, on parting from Alyosha, Mitya had gone rushing off to Grushenka's; it is not known whether he actually saw her, but by nightfall he was in the Capital City inn, where he got well and properly drunk. In his intoxicated state he demanded pen and paper and scrawled a document that was to have important consequences for him. It was a frenzied, verbose and incoherent letter, truly 'drunken'. Its effect was similar to when a drunk man, returning home, starts with extraordinary fervour to tell his wife or some other member of his household the manner in which he had just been insulted, what a scoundrel his insulter is and, on the contrary, what a fine fellow he himself is and the come-uppance he will deliver to that scoundrel – and all of it at excessive length, incoherent and excited, with a banging of fists on the table and with drunken tears. The paper he had been given for the letter at the inn was a grimy scrap of ordinary writing paper, of inferior quality and on the reverse of which someone had written a sum. For drunken verbosity there had evidently been insufficient room, and not only had Mitya used up all the margins, but the final lines were actually written on top of what was already there. The contents of the letter were as follows:

Fateful Katya!
Tomorrow I shall obtain the money and will return your three thousand to you, and farewell – woman of great wrath, but farewell also my love! Let us end! Tomorrow I will obtain it from all men, and if I do not, then I give you my word of honour that I will go to father and break his skull and take the money from under his pillow, if only Ivan has gone away. I will go into penal servitude, but I will return the three thousand. And to yourself farewell. I bow down to the earth, for before you I am a scoundrel. Forgive me. No, you had better not forgive me: it will be easier both for me and for you! Better to penal servitude than your love, for I love another, and today you have come to know her all too well, so how can you forgive? I shall kill the man who is my thief! I shall go away from you all, to the East, so that I may know no one. *Her* neither, for you alone are not my tormentress, but she is, also. Farewell!

ps   I write a curse, but you I worship! I hear it within my breast. A string is left there, vibrating. Better that my heart be rent asunder! I shall kill myself, but first that cur. I shall tear the three out of him and throw them to you. Though I am a scoundrel before you, I am not a thief! Await the three thousand. Under the cur's mattress, tied with a pink ribbon. It is not I who am a thief, but I shall kill my thief! Katya, do not view me with contempt: Dmitry is not a thief, but a murderer! He has killed his father and brought ruin to himself, in order to stand and not endure your pride. And in order not to love you.

PPS   I kiss your feet, farewell!

PPPS   Katya, pray God that men will give me the money. Then I shall not bear blood upon me, but if they do not – then I shall! Kill me!

your slave and foe
D. Karamazov

When Ivan had read the 'document', he stood up, convinced. This meant that his brother had committed the murder, and not Smerdyakov. And if it was not Smerdyakov, then consequently it was not he, Ivan, either. This letter suddenly acquired in his eyes a mathematical significance. For him there could now be no more doubts as to Mitya's guilt. Incidentally, Ivan had never had any suspicion that Mitya could have committed the murder together with Smerdyakov, and indeed this was not commensurate with the evidence. Ivan's mind was set completely at rest. The following morning he recalled Smerdyakov and his gibes merely with contempt. A few days later he was positively astonished that he could have let his suspicions cause him such agonizing personal torment. He determined to treat him with contempt and to forget him. In this fashion a month went by. Concerning Smerdyakov he asked no more questions of anyone, but heard in passing a couple of times that the latter was very ill and not in possession of his reason. 'It will end with insanity,' young Dr Varvinsky said of him on one occasion, and Ivan remembered this. In the last week of that month Ivan himself began to feel very unwell. He had already been to consult the doctor whom Katerina Ivanovna had ordered from Moscow and who had arrived just before the trial. And it was precisely at this time that his relations with Katerina Ivanovna became aggravated in the extreme. They were like two foes who were in love with each other. Katerina Ivanovna's *retours d'opinion*, of momentary duration, but intense, in Mitya's favour, now drove Ivan to the point of frenzy. It is a strange fact that right up to the last scene described by us, at Katerina Ivanovna's, when Alyosha came to see her, sent by Mitya, he, Ivan, had not once in all that month heard her express any doubts as to Mitya's guilt, in spite of all her *retours* to him, which he so hated. Another remarkable thing is that he, feeling that he hated Mitya more and more with each day that passed, at the same time understood that it was not for Katya's *retours* to him that he hated him, but for the fact that *he had killed their father*! He fully sensed and was aware of this. None the less, some ten days before the trial he went to Mitya and proposed to him a plan of escape – a plan which had evidently been thought up long before. Here, besides the principal motive that had prompted him to such a step, a responsible factor was also a certain unhealed scar within his heart left by a certain little remark of Smerdyakov's to the effect that it was to his, Ivan's advantage for his brother to face the charge, for the sum received by Alyosha and him in inheritance from their father would then be raised from forty to sixty thousand. He had determined to sacrifice thirty thousand solely from his own side in order to arrange Mitya's escape. Returning from seeing him at the prison that day, he was terribly sad and troubled: he had suddenly begun to have a sense that the reason he wanted the escape was not only in order to sacrifice thirty thousand on it and thus heal his scar, but also for some other reason. 'Is it because within my soul I am a murderer, too?' he had started to wonder. Something distant but burning had stung his soul. Above all, throughout that entire month it had been his pride that had suffered terribly, but of that later . . . When, with his hand on the bellpull of his lodgings after his conversation with Alyosha, Ivan Fyodorovich had taken a sudden decision to go and see Smerdyakov, he had acted in obedience to nothing but the peculiar indignation that had suddenly boiled up within his breast. He suddenly remembered how Katerina Ivanovna had exclaimed to him in Alyosha's presence only a short time earlier: 'It was you, you alone, who convinced me that he (Mitya, that is) was the murderer!' At this memory, Ivan positively froze: never in his life had he tried to convince her that the murderer was Mitya; on the contrary, upon his return from Smerdyakov he had still suspected himself. On the contrary, it was *she*, she who had set that 'document' before him and proved his brother's innocence! And suddenly there she had been, exclaiming now: 'I myself have been to see Smerdyakov!' When had she been? Ivan knew nothing of it. It could only mean that she was far from being convinced of Mitya's guilt! And what could Smerdyakov have told her? What, what precisely had he told her? A terrible anger caught light within his heart. He could not understand how half an hour earlier he could have let her say those words and yet not cried out. He had taken his hand away from the bellpull and set off to see Smerdyakov. 'This time I may kill him,' he thought as he went.

8

The Third, and Final, Visit to Smerdyakov

WHEN he had still covered only half of his route there arose a dry, biting wind of the same kind there had been early in the morning of that day,

and a powdery, thick, dry snow began to descend. It fell to the earth
without clinging to it, the wind whirled it around, and soon a proper
snowstorm had begun. In that part of our town where Smerdyakov lived
there are almost no lamp-posts at all. Ivan Fyodorovich strode along in
the gloom, not noticing the snowstorm, finding the way by instinct. His
head was aching and there was an agonizing throbbing in his temples. In
his wrists, he could feel this, there were convulsions. Somewhat before he
reached Marya Kondratyevna's wretched little house, he encountered a
solitary drunken muzhik, small of stature, in a little patched *zipun*,
walking in zigzags, grumbling and cursing; suddenly, the man stopped
cursing and in a hoarse, drunken voice began to sing:

> Oh, now Vanka's gone to *Piter*,
> And for him I shall not wait!*

But each time he broke off at this second line and again began to curse
someone, then again suddenly launched into the same song again. Ivan
Fyodorovich had long felt a terrible hatred for him, without thinking
about him at all, and now suddenly realized what he was singing. He
instantly had an overmastering urge to strike dead the little muzhik from
above with his fist. It so happened that just at that moment they drew
level, and the little muzhik, with a violent sway, suddenly knocked
against Ivan at full force. The latter pushed him away in rabid fury. The
little muzhik went flying and thudded like a block of wood to the frozen
earth, moaned with pain only once: 'Oh-oh', and fell silent. Ivan walked
over to him. The man lay supine, completely without movement, and
unconscious.

'He will freeze to death,' thought Ivan, and he strode off again to see
Smerdyakov.

When he was still out in the passage, Marya Kondratyevna, who had
run to open the door with a candle in her hands, began to whisper to him
that 'Pavel Fyodorovich' (Smerdyakov, that is) was 'very ill, sir, not that
he's a-bed, sir, but almost as if he'd lost his reason, sir, told me to clear
the tea away, he didn't want any.'

'Acting rough, is he?' Ivan Fyodorovich asked coarsely.

'Oh no, he's very quiet, sir, only you mustn't talk to him for very
long . . .' Marya Kondratyevna requested.

Ivan Fyodorovich opened the door and stepped into the room.

It was heated just as fiercely as it had been on the previous occasion,
but several changes were noticeable: one of the lateral benches had been
carried outside and in its place there had appeared a large, old, leather-

covered sofa made of mahogany. On it a bed had been made up with rather clean, white pillows. On the bedding sat Smerdyakov, still wearing his former dressing-gown. The table had been drawn up to the sofa, so that there was very little room. On the table lay a fat book in a yellow cover, but Smerdyakov was not reading it; he seemed, instead, to be sitting doing nothing. Ivan Fyodorovich he greeted with a long, silent look, evidently not in the slightest astonished by his arrival. He had changed greatly about the face, was much thinner and sallower. His eyes were sunken, and their lower lids were blue.

'So you really are ill, are you?' Ivan Fyodorovich said, coming to a halt. 'I shall not detain you long and shall not even remove my coat. Where may I sit down?'

He went round to the other side of the table, moved a chair up to the table and sat down.

'Why the silent look? I only have one question to ask you, and I swear I shall not leave until you have replied to it: has the *barynya* Katerina Ivanovna been to see you?'

For a long time Smerdyakov continued his silence, still staring quietly at Ivan in his previous manner; then, however, he suddenly made a wave of his arm and turned his face away.

'What is wrong?' Ivan exclaimed.

'Never mind.'

'What do you mean, never mind?'

'Well, she was here, but it's no concern of yours. Leave me alone, sir.'

'No, I will not leave you alone! Now tell me: when was she here?'

'Oh, I have forgotten to remember her,' Smerdyakov said with a contemptuous smile, and again suddenly, turning his face back towards Ivan, fixed him with a kind of frenziedly hateful stare, the same stare he had given him at his last visit a month before. 'You are ill yourself, I'd warrant, sir, look how pinched your face is, you look terrible,' he said to Ivan.

'Never mind about my health, answer the question.'

'And why have your eyes gone yellow? The whites are completely yellow! Are you very unhappy then?'

He smiled contemptuously, then suddenly burst into outright laughter.

'Listen, I told you I shall not leave you until you have given me a reply!' Ivan let out in terrible irritation.

'Why are you pestering me, sir? Why are you tormenting me?' Smerdyakov said with suffering in his voice.

'Hah, the devil! What do I care about you. Answer the question, and I shall leave you at once.'

'There is no answer I can give you!' Smerdyakov said, lowering his eyes again.

'I assure you that I shall compel you to reply!'

'What are you so worried about all the time?' Smerdyakov said suddenly, fixing him in a stare, this time not of contempt, however, but almost with a kind of disgust. 'Is it because the trial is starting tomorrow? Look, nothing is going to happen to you, be convinced of that! Go home, go to bed and sleep peacefully, you need have no apprehension.'

'I do not understand you . . . What have I to fear tomorrow?' Ivan said in astonishment, and suddenly a kind of fear did indeed put a breath of chill into his soul. Smerdyakov gave him an appraising look.

'You don't un-der-stand?' he said in a slow, reproachful voice. 'A fine thing for a clever man to make such a comedy out of himself, and no mistake!'

Ivan stared at him without a word. Even this unexpected tone, some-how quite unprecedentedly arrogant, in which this former lackey of his was now addressing him, was extraordinary. Such a tone he had not adopted even on their last encounter.

'You have nothing to fear, I tell you. I won't give any evidence against you, there isn't any. My, how your hands do shake. Why are your fingers a-jerking like that? Go home, *it was not you who killed him.*'

Ivan gave a shudder of recognition. He remembered Alyosha.

'I am aware that it was not I . . .' he began to stammer.

'A-ware, are you?' Smerdyakov caught up again.

Ivan sprang up and seized him by the shoulder.

'Tell all, reptile! Tell all!'

Smerdyakov was not in the slightest alarmed. He only riveted his eyes on him with insane hatred.

'Well, if that is how it is, then it were you who killed him,' he whispered to him in fury.

Ivan sank on to his chair as though he had just fathomed something.

'You mean the thing you said last time? When we met on the last occasion?'

'Well, last time you stood before me and understood it all, and so you will understand it now.'

'All I understand is that you are a madman.'

'The man does not grow tired of it! Here we sit face to face, so what is the purpose of playing the fool, acting comedies with each other? Or are you still trying to unload it all on to me alone, and to my face, what is more? You did the murder, you are the principal murderer, and I was only your minion, your faithful servant Licharda,* and fulfilled that task in compliance with your instructions.'

'Fulfilled it? So it was you who murdered him, then?' Ivan said, turning cold.

A shock seemed to pass through his brain, and he began to quiver all over with a cold and shallow trembling. Now it was Smerdyakov's turn to look at him with astonishment: he had probably at last been struck by the sincerity of Ivan's fear.

'But did you really not know?' he murmured suspiciously, smiling crookedly in his face.

Ivan kept staring at him, as though his tongue had been paralysed.

> Oh, now Vanka's gone to *Piter*,
> And for him I shall not wait! . . .

suddenly went ringing through his head.

'Do you know something? I fear that you are a dream, a ghost that sits before me!' he murmured.

'There are no ghosts here, sir, apart from the two of us, sir, and a certain third party as well. Without doubt he is here, that third party, he is present, between the two of us.'

'Who is he? Who is present? Who is the third party?' Ivan Fyodorovich said in fear, looking around him and hastily seeking someone with his eyes in all the corners.

'The third party is God, sir, Providence itself, sir, it is here beside us now, sir, only it's no good your looking for it, you will not find it.'

'You are lying! You did not murder him!' Ivan howled in a rabid frenzy. 'You are either a madman or you are teasing me as you did last time!'

Smerdyakov, as he had done all along, kept watching him inquisitively, without any fear at all. He was still quite unable to master his suspicion, and still believed that Ivan 'knew everything', but was trying to 'unload it all on to him alone', 'and to his face, what is more'.

'Wait a moment, sir,' he said at last in a faint voice and suddenly, drawing his left leg out from underneath the table, he began to turn up the trouser on it. The leg proved to be clad in a long white stocking, and shod in a slipper. Without hurrying, Smerdyakov removed the garter and put his fingers deep inside the stocking. Ivan Fyodorovich stared at him and suddenly began to shake with convulsive fear.

'Madman!' he howled and, quickly springing up from his seat, staggered back, knocking his back against the wall and seeming to adhere to it, the whole of him stiffened up into a straight line. In insane horror he stared at Smerdyakov. The latter, not in the slightest troubled by his fear, kept digging about inside the stocking as though he were straining with his fingers to catch hold of something and pull it out. At last he caught hold of whatever it was, and began to pull. Ivan Fyodorovich saw that it was some kind of papers, or perhaps a packet of papers. Smerdyakov pulled it out and placed it on the table.

'There, sir!' he said, quietly.

'What?' Ivan replied, shaking.

'Be so good as to take a look, sir,' Smerdyakov articulated, just as quietly.

Ivan stepped towards the table, began to seize hold of the packet and undo it, but suddenly jerked his fingers away as though from contact with some repulsive, fearsome reptile.

'Your fingers are still a-trembling, sir, in convulsions, sir,' Smerdyakov observed, and then, without haste, undid the paper. Under the wrapper there turned out to be three wads of hundred-rouble rainbow credit bills.

'It's all here, sir, all three thousand of it, you don't need to count it. Here, take it, sir,' he invited Ivan, nodding towards the money. Ivan sank on to his chair. He was as white as a sheet.

'You gave me a fright ... with that stocking ...' he said, somehow strangely grinning.

'Did you really, really not know until now?' Smerdyakov asked again.

'No, I did not. I thought it was Dmitry. Brother! Brother! Ah!' He suddenly gripped his head with both hands. 'Listen: did you kill him on your own? With my brother, or without him?'

'I did it with you alone, sir; you and I together murdered him, sir, and Dmitry Fyodorovich is innocent, sir.'

'Very well, very well ... Of myself we shall speak later. Why am I trembling all the time ... I cannot get the words out.'

'You were ever the bold one, sir, "all things are lawful", you used to say, and now look how a-feared you are!' Smerdyakov mouthed in wonder. 'Would you not like some lemonade, I shall order it now, sir. It may refresh you greatly. Only we ought to cover this up first, sir.'

And again he nodded at the wads of bills. He began to get up in order to shout through the door to Marya Kondratyevna that she make some lemonade and bring it in, but looking for something with which to cover up the money so she should not see it, first started to take out his handkerchief, but as it proved to be quite covered in snot, picked up from the table the only book that lay on it, the fat one in the yellow cover, which Ivan had noticed on his way in, and sat it on top of the money. The title of the book was *The Sermons of Our Holy Father Isaac of Nineveh*. Ivan Fyodorovich had time to read the lettering in mechanical fashion.

'I do not want any lemonade,' he said. 'Of myself we shall speak later. Sit down and tell me: how did you do it? Tell everything . . .'

'You should at least take your coat off, sir, or you will stew.'

Ivan Fyodorovich, as though it had only just occurred to him now, tore off his coat and threw it, without rising from his chair, on the bench.

'Tell me, then, please. Tell me.'

He had almost calmed down. He was quite sure that Smerdyakov would tell him *everything* now.

'You want to know how it was done, sir?' Smerdyakov sighed. 'It was done in the most natural manner, sir, from your very own instructions . . .'

'Of my instructions we shall speak later,' Ivan Fyodorovich cut in again, but this time not shouting as before but articulating his words firmly and almost as though he were in complete control of himself. 'Just tell me in detail how you did it. The whole of it in sequence. Leave out nothing. The details, above all, the details. I request you.'

'You went away, and that day I fell down into the cellar, sir . . .'

'With the falling sickness or only feigning it?'

'Feigning it, of course, sir. I feigned it all. I walked down the staircase calm as you please, sir, right to the bottom, sir, and calmly I lay down, sir, and when I'd lain down I started a-howling. I thrashed about until they carried me upstairs.'

'Just a moment! Were you feigning all the time, even afterwards, in the hospital?'

'Oh no, sir. The next day, in the morning it was, I had an attack of the real thing, and it were stronger than any I'd had for years. Two days I lay completely unconscious.'

'Very well, very well. Continue.'

'They put me on this bunk, sir, I knew they would, behind the partition, sir, because whenever I was ill Marfa Ignatyevna always made me sleep behind that partition in their room, sir. They have always been kind to me, right from the time I was born, sir. At night I groaned, sir, only quietly. I was waiting for Dmitry Fyodorovich to come.'

'To your room, you mean?'

'Why would he come to my room? I was waiting for him to come to the house, because I already had no doubt at all that his honour would arrive that very night, for a-deprivated of my presence and a-having no information he would sure and certain come and climb over the fence and get into the house, sir, as he were able, sir, and do it no matter what.'

'And if he had not come?'

'Then nothing would have happened, sir. Without him I would never have dared.'

'Very well, very well . . . try to speak more clearly, take your time, and above all — leave nothing out!'

'I expected he was going to murder Fyodor Pavlovich, sir . . . that was for certain, sir . . . Because I had already prepared him . . . in the latter days, sir . . . and more than anything because now he knew those signals. With all his honour's rage and suspicion, which had been ac-cumulating in the latter days, it was sure and certain that by means of the signals he would get into the house, sir. It was sure and certain. So I was waiting for him, sir.'

'Just a moment,' Ivan cut in. 'After all, if he had murdered him, he would have taken the money and carried it off; I mean, you must have realized that, must you not? So what would there have been for you in it afterwards? I do not see it.'

'Well, you see, he would never have discovered where the money was, sir. You see, that were just something I told him, about the money being under the mattress. Only it wasn't true, sir. Before it was always kept in a box, and so it was, sir. But later on I told Fyodor Pavlovich, as his honour trusted me exclusively in the whole of mankind, to transfer that envelope with the money to the corner behind the icons, because no one would ever think of looking there, especially if he were in a hurry. So it lay, that envelope did, behind the icons in his honour's room, sir. It would have been a silly thing to do to keep it under the mattress, sir, for in the box at least it would have been under lock and key. But now everyone believed that it were under the mattress. A stupid way of reasoning, sir. So if Dmitry Fyodorovich was to have done the murder, then, finding nothing, he would either have run away, sir, quickly, a-fearing any whisper, as is always the case with murderers, or he would have been arrested, sir. So then, sir, I could always, the next day or even that very same night, sir, have crawled behind the icons and carried off the money, sir, and all the guilt would have been unloaded on to Dmitry Fyodorovich. I could always rely on that.'

'Well, and what if he had not killed him, but only beaten him?'

'If he had not killed him, then of course I would not have dared to take the money and the whole thing would have been in vain. But I was in the calculation that his honour would beat his honour senseless, and I'd have time to take the money, and then report to Fyodor Pavlovich that it were none other than Dmitry Fyodorovich, having a-beaten his honour, who'd made off with the money.'

'Wait . . . I am confused. So it was Dmitry who did the murder, and you only took the money?'

'No, it wasn't his honour who did it, sir. Why, I could say even now that it was him . . . but I do not want to lie to you, because . . . because if it really is true, as I see it is, then you have understood nothing until now, and have not been feigning towards me, so as to unload all your obvious guilt on to me, before my very eyes, then even so you are guilty of the whole thing, sir, for you knew about the murder and instructed me to do it, sir, while you yourself, a-knowing of it, went away. So I want this evening to provide to you and to your face that the principal murderer in it all is exclusively you, sir, and I am only the less principal one, even though it was I who did the murder. But you are the main murderer before the law!'

'Why? Why am I the murderer? O God!' Ivan said, losing his endurance at last, and forgetting that he had said he would put off talking of himself until the end of the conversation. 'Is it still that business about my going to Chermashnya? Just a moment, tell me, why did you require my agreement, if you had already taken my going to Chermashnya as such? How do you interpret it now?'

'Certain of your agreement, I would have known that when you returned you would not raise a big howl about that lost three thousand, if for some reason the authorities were to suspect me instead of Dmitry Fyodorovich, or to suspect that I was in league with Dmitry Fyodorovich; on the contrary, you would have defended me against others . . . And having obtained your inheritance, later on you would be able to reward me now and then, for all the rest of your life, because it would be after all through me that you had obtained your inheritance, for otherwise, had he a-married Agrafena Aleksandrovna, all you'd have got would have been a long nose!'

'Ah! So you intended to torment me later, too, all my life, did you?' Ivan ground out. 'And what if I had not gone away that day, but had testified against you?'

'What could you have testified? That I was trying to get you to go away to Chermashnya? Well, I mean to say, that is nonsense, sir. What is more, after the conversation we had had you would either have gone away or stayed behind. If you had stayed, then nothing would have happened that day, I would have known that you did not want that deed to be done, and would have undertaken nothing. And if you'd gone, then that would mean you were assuring me that you did not dare to testify against me at the trial and that you'd turn a blind eye to my having that three thousand. And afterwards you would not be able to chase me up at all, because then I would tell it all to the authorities, sir, that is to say, not that I had done a robbery or murder – that I would not have said, sir – but that you yourself had put me up to robbing and murdering, only I had not agreed. It was for that reason that I needed your agreement, so that there would be no means by which you could bring me to bay later on, sir, for where would you have had the proof of it, and I on the other hand would always be able to bring you to bay by revealing the craving your honour had for the death of your parent, and mark my words – in the public gallery they would have believed it and you would have been covered in shame for all the rest of your life.'

'So I had it, I had that craving, did I?' Ivan ground out again.

'Beyond a doubt you had it, sir, and by agreeing as you did that day in silence you determined me upon that deed, sir,' Smerdyakov said, giving Ivan a resolute stare. He was very weak and spoke quietly and wearily, but something inward and concealed was firing him, and he plainly had some ultimate resolve. Ivan could sense this.

'Continue,' he said. 'Continue on the subject of that night.'

'Very well, sir, to continue! There I was, a-lying and a-listening, when I thought I heard the *barin* give a yell. And before that Grigory Vasilyevich had suddenly got up and gone outside and then gave an howl, and then all was quiet, darkness. I lay there waiting, my heart was a-hammering, I could not endure it. At last I got up and went, sir – I could see that the window of the *barin*'s room on the left was open on to the garden, and I took another step to the left, sir, so as to try and hear whether he was alive or not, and I could hear the *barin* rushing about in there and groaning, so that meant he was alive, sir. Ach, I thought! I went up to the window and shouted to the *barin*: "It's me!" And he shouted to me: "He was here, he was here, he's got away!" Dmitry Fyodorovich he meant, that was, sir. "He's killed Grigory!" "Where is Grigory?" I whispered to him. "Over there, in the corner," he said, pointing, and he was whispering, too. "Wait there a minute," I said. I walked over to the corner to look, and stumbled on Grigory Vasilyevich; he was lying down, covered in blood, and unconscious. So it seemed it was right enough, then, Dmitry Fyodorovich had been there, was what immediately jumped into my head, and immediately I decided to get it all over with sudden, sir, since even if Grigory Vasilyevich was still alive, he wouldn't see anything for the time being, since he was lying there unconscious. There was only one risk, sir, and that was Marfa Ignatyevna might wake up all of a sudden. I was quite aware of that at that moment, only you see the craving to do it had taken a hold of me, and my breath was fair choking. I went back under the *barin*'s window and said: "She's here, she's arrived, Agrafena Aleksandrovna has come, she's asking for you." Well, at that he fairly shivered like a babe in arms: "Where is she? Where?" he kept groaning, though he still didn't believe it. "She's standing there," I said. "Open up!" He stared through the window at me, not sure whether to believe me or not, but he was a-feared of unlocking the door, and that was because he was a-feared of me, I thought. And it was funny: all of a sudden then I took it into my head to tap out those very same signals to him on the window-frame, the ones that meant Grushenka had arrived, right in front of him, to his face: my words he did not seem to believe, but when I tapped out the signals he immediately ran to open the door. He opened it. I started to go in, but he blocked my way with his body. "Where is she, where is she?" he kept saying, looking at me and trembling. Well, I thought: if he's that a-feared of me, it's bad! And then my legs even went weak from that very same fear that he wouldn't let me into the rooms, or start shouting, or that Marfa Ignatyevna would come running, or that anything at all might happen, I don't remember now, at the time I must have been white as a sheet as I stood before his honour. I whispered to him: "But she's there, there, under the window, how is it you haven't seen her?" "Well, bring her over here, then, bring her over here!" "But she's a-feared," I said, "she got frightened by your yelling, she went and hid in the bushes, go and call her from your study." He ran off, went up to the window, and put a candle in the window. "Grushenka," he shouted, "Grushenka, are you here?" He shouted it, he didn't want to lean out of the window, didn't want to leave my side, because of that very same fear, because he was very a-feared of me, and so he did not dare to leave my side. "But there she is," I said (I went up to the window, and stuck my head and shoulders right out of it), "there she is in that bush, she's laughing at you, don't you see?" Suddenly he believed me, and he fair shook, terrible in love he was with her, sir, and he stuck himself right out of the window. Then I snatched up that very same cast-iron paperweight that sat on his honour's table, you remember, sir, about three pounds I should think it weighed, swung it up and then hit him right on the temple with one corner of it. He didn't even utter a squeak. Only

suddenly he sank down, and I had a second go at him, and a third. At the
third go I could feel I'd a-broken his skull. He suddenly rolled over on
his back, with his face up, all covered in blood. I had a look: there was
no blood on me, it hadn't splashed, I wiped the paperweight, put it back
on the table, went behind the icons, took the money out of the envelope,
and threw the envelope on the floor and that very same pink ribbon
beside it. I went down into the garden, shaking all over. Right up to that
apple tree, the one with the hollow inside it — you know that hollow, and
I'd had my eye on it for a long time, there was a rag and a piece of paper
inside it I'd put there a long time ago; I wrapped the entire sum in the
paper, and then in the rag, and stuffed it deep inside. So it stayed there
for more than two weeks, that very same sum, sir, and I only took it out
again after I'd left the hospital. I returned to my bed, lay down and
thought in fear: "Now, if Grigory Vasilyevich is completely dead, then
by that very same fact it may turn out very bad, and if he is not dead and
recovers, it may turn out very well, because then he may be a witness
that Dmitry Fyodorovich came to the house, and so he was the one who
did the murder and carried off the money," sir. Then I started to groan
with doubt and impatience, so as to waken Marfa Ignatyevna the more
quickly. She got up at last, rushed over to me, but when she suddenly
saw that Grigory Vasilyevich was not there, she ran outside and I could
hear her starting to wail in the garden. Well and then it all went on all
night, and by then my mind was calm about everything.'

The narrator paused. Ivan had listened to him all the while in deathly
silence, never moving a muscle, never releasing him from his gaze.
Smerdyakov, on the other hand, had merely glanced at him from time to
time, for the most part averting his eyes, as he delivered his narrative.
Upon its conclusion he seemed himself to be in a state of agitation and
was breathing heavily. Sweat had appeared on his face. It was, however,
impossible to tell whether the emotion he felt was one of remorse or not.

'Wait,' Ivan caught up, reflecting. 'What about the door? If he only
opened the door to you, then how could Grigory have seen it open
before you arrived on the scene? For after all, Grigory saw it before you,
did he not?'

It was remarkable that Ivan asked these questions in a most calm tone
of voice, one that even seemed quite different, quite without menace, so
that if someone had opened the door now and glanced in at the two of
them from the doorway, he would have certainly concluded that they sat
peaceably engaged in a conversation about some commonplace, though
interesting, subject.

'On account of that door and Grigory Vasilyevich's saying that he saw it open, he only thought he did,' Smerdyakov smiled crookedly. 'For I mean to say, sir, I tell you, that is not a man, sir, but a stubborn gelding: and he did not see the door open, he only thought he did – but you won't ever make him think otherwise, sir. It is a stroke of good fortune for you and me that he got this idea into his head, for it means that Dmitry Fyodorovich will definitely be convicted.'

'Listen,' Ivan Fyodorovich said, as though he were beginning to grow flustered again and were making an effort to piece something together, 'listen . . . There is much more that I wanted to ask you, but I have forgotten . . . I keep forgetting and becoming confused . . . Yes! Simply tell me this one thing: why did you unseal the envelope and leave it lying on the floor? Why did you not just take the money away in the envelope . . . When you were telling me what happened, I had the impression from the way you talked about that envelope that you were describing what you were supposed to do with it . . . But why that was what you were supposed to do with it, I can't work out . . .'

'Oh, I acted that way with it on account of a certain reason, sir. For if the man were knowledgeable and habitual, like me, for example, had seen that money before and might very well have put it in that envelope himself and watched his honour seal it and write the inscription on it, then for what purpose would such a man, sir, assuming that he'd done the murder, have unsealed that envelope again after it, and in such a hurry-scurry, too, a-knowing as he did that the money was sure and for certain in that envelope, sir? On the contrary, if this thief was like me, for example, he would just have stuck that envelope in his pocket, never bothering to unseal it, and made himself scarce with it as quickly as possible, sir. Dmitry Fyodorovich would have done it quite different, sir: his honour only knew about the envelope from hearsay, he'd never actually seen it, and and when he got hold of it, say from under the mattress, for example, he'd have unsealed it right there and then, in order to find out if the money was in it or not. After that he'd have thrown the envelope itself away, never thinking that it might remain as incriminating evidence against him, because his honour is not an habitual thief, sir, and had obviously never stolen anything before, for his family is all gentlefolk, sir, and if he'd now dared to steal something, he'd see it not as stealing, but as just coming to take back what was really his, as he'd told the whole town beforehand and even boasted to everyone out loud about how he was going to go and get back what was rightfully his from Fyodor Pavlovich. I told that idea of mine to the public procurator during the inquiry, only not so clearly, but rather sort of as a hint, sir, as though I myself was not understanding of it, and as though the public procurator had thought of it himself, and not me put it into his head, sir – oh, the public procurator fairly began to drool at the mouth when I gave him that very same hint, sir . . .'

'Is that really so? Did you really think it all out on the spot there that night?' Ivan Fyodorovich exclaimed, almost speechless with surprise. He again looked at Smerdyakov in fear.

'For the love of mercy, how could I have thought it all up in such a hurry-scurry, sir? It was all thought out in advance.'

'Well . . . well, if that is so, then the devil himself must have helped you!' Ivan Fyodorovich exclaimed again. 'No, you are not stupid, you are far more clever than I thought . . .'

He rose to his feet with the obvious intention of pacing about the room. He was in a terrible state of anguish. But since the table was blocking his way and he would almost have had to wriggle his way between it and the wall, he merely turned round where he stood and then sat down again. Not being able to pace up and down suddenly, perhaps, irritated him, and in his former frenzy he suddenly howled:

'Listen, you wretched, contemptible man! Do you really not understand that if I have not yet killed you, it is only because I am saving you until you have given your answer at the trial tomorrow? As God is my witness' – Ivan raised his arm aloft – 'perhaps I too was guilty, perhaps I really did have a secret desire for . . . father's death, but, I swear to you, I was not as guilty as you think, and it is possible that I did not put you up to anything at all. No, no, I did not! But even so, I shall testify against you myself, tomorrow, at the trial, I have decided! I shall tell everything, everything. But you and I shall go to court together! And whatever you say against me at the trial, whatever the testimony you give – I shall accept it and not be afraid of you; I shall myself confirm it all! But you too have a duty to confess before the court! You have, you have, and we shall go to court together! So it shall be!'

Ivan said this solemnly and with energy, and it was already apparent from his glittering gaze alone that so it would be.

'You are ill, I see, sir, altogether ill, sir. Your eyes are completely yellow, sir,' Smerdyakov declared, quite without mockery, however, and even with a kind of commiseration.

'We shall go to court together!' Ivan repeated, 'and if you refuse, then no matter – I shall confess alone.'

Smerdyakov was silent for a moment, as though he were pondering.

'That will not be, sir, not on any account, and neither will you go, sir,' he resolved at last, in a categorical manner that allowed of no appeal.

'You do not understand me!' Ivan exclaimed in a voice of rebuke.

'You will be too ashamed, sir, if you confess it all on yourself. Even worse, it will be completely useless, sir, because you see I shall just say straight out that I never ever said anything of the kind to you, sir, and that you are either in some kind of illness (and I dare say you are, sir), or that you are so sorry for that fine brother of yours that you are sacrificing yourself, and have thought all this up to incriminate me, since whatever you may say all your life you have considered me a marsh-fly, and not a man. Well, and who will believe you, and what single piece of proof have you got?'

'But look here, what about that money you showed me just now? Surely that was to persuade me you were telling the truth?'

Smerdyakov removed St Isaac of Nineveh from the wads of banknotes and put him to one side.

'You will take that money with you when you go, sir,' Smerdyakov sighed.

'Of course I shall! But why are you returning it to me if you committed murder in order to obtain it?' Ivan said, giving him a look of great astonishment.

'I have no need of it whatever, sir,' Smerdyakov said quakily, with a wave of his hand. 'I did have a thought previously, sir, that with that kind of money I could begin a new life, in Moscow or even abroad, that was the dream I had, sir, all the more so because I thought that "all things are lawful". It was true what you taught me, sir, for you told me a lot about that then: for if there is no infinite God, then there is no virtue, either, and there is no need of it whatever. That was true, what you said. And that was how I thought, too.'

'You came to it with your own mind?' Ivan said with a crooked smile.

'With your guidance, sir.'

'And now I suppose you have come to believe in God, if you are returning the money to me?'

'No, sir, I have not, sir,' Smerdyakov whispered.

'Then why are you returning it?'

'That's enough ... never mind, sir!' Smerdyakov said with another wave of his hand. 'Why, you yourself were always saying then that "all things are lawful", so now why are you so a-worried, you yourself, sir? You even want to go to court and testify against yourself ... Only that will not be! You will not go and testify!' Smerdyakov decided again, resolutely and with conviction.

'You will see!' Ivan said.

'It cannot be. You are very clever, sir. You like money, I know that, sir, you like esteem also, because you are very proud, you like the charms of the fair sex an inordinate amount, and most of all you like living in peaceful prosperity and not having to bow to anyone – that more than anything, sir. You will not want to spoil your life for ever by accepting such shame at the trial. You are like Fyodor Pavlovich, more than any of them sir, more than any of his other children you have turned out like him, with the same soul as his honour had, sir.'

'You are not stupid,' said Ivan, as if struck; the blood leapt to his face. 'I used to think you were stupid. You are a serious fellow now!' he observed, somehow all of a sudden looking at Smerdyakov in a new way.

'It was your pride that made you think I was stupid. Take the money, sir.'

Ivan took all three wads of credit bills and put them in his pocket without wrapping them in anything.

'I shall show them in court tomorrow,' he said.

'No one will believe you, sir, seeing that now you have enough money of your own, they will think you took it from a box and brought it along, sir.'

Ivan stood up from his chair.

'I say to you again that if I have not killed you it is solely because you are necessary to me for tomorrow, remember that, do not forget it!'

'All right then, kill me, sir. Kill me now,' Smerdyakov said strangely all of a sudden, strangely looking at Ivan. 'You wouldn't even dare to do that,' he added, with a bitter smile, 'you wouldn't dare to do anything, bold man that you once were, sir!'

'Until tomorrow!' Ivan barked, as he moved to go.

'Wait . . . show me the money one more time.'

Ivan took out the credit bills and showed them to him. Smerdyakov looked at them for about ten seconds.

'Well, off you go, then,' he said, with a wave of his hand. 'Ivan Fyodorovich!' he suddenly called after him.

'What is it?' Ivan Fyodorovich said turning round, already on his way out.

'Farewell, sir!'

'Until tomorrow!' Ivan barked again, and went outside.

The snowstorm was still continuing. He took his first strides briskly, but suddenly seemed to begin to stagger. 'This is something physical,' he thought with a smile. Something that almost resembled joy had entered his soul. He felt within himself a kind of infinite resolve: an end to the hesitations that had caused him such dreadful torment all this last time! His decision had been taken 'and now it will not alter', he thought with happiness. At that instant he suddenly tripped on something and very nearly fell. Coming to a halt, he discerned at his feet the little muzhik he had knocked down, still lying in the same place, without consciousness or movement. The snowstorm had almost buried his entire face. Ivan suddenly seized hold of him and carried him on his shoulders. Having glimpsed a light in a little house to the right, he knocked on its shutters and asked the artisan who responded and to whom the little house belonged for assistance in carrying the muzhik to the police station, promising to give him three roubles in return. The artisan made himself ready and came outside. I shall not describe in detail the manner in which Ivan Fyodorovich then succeeded in attaining his goal and installing the muzhik at the police station, so that it might at once be arranged for him to be examined by a doctor, something on which he again made generous disbursement 'for expenses'. I will merely say that the task occupied almost a whole hour. But Ivan Fyodorovich was very well satisfied. His thoughts rambled and went to work. 'If my decision concerning tomorrow had not been taken with such resolve,' he thought suddenly with pleasure, 'I would not have stopped to spend a whole hour in seeing to the little muzhik, but would have walked on past him and not cared a spit that he was going to freeze to death . . . But I say, how well I am able to observe myself!' he thought at that same moment with even greater pleasure. 'And yet there they have decided that I am going mad!' As he reached the house where he lived, he suddenly came to a halt as an unexpected question occurred to him: 'Well, should I not simply go to the public procurator right now and tell him everything?' Turning again towards the house, he resolved the question: 'Tomorrow I shall do it all together!' he whispered to himself, and strangely, almost all his joy and all his satisfaction passed in a single flash. And when he stepped into his room, his heart was suddenly touched by something icy, that seemed to be a reminiscence, or more precisely, a reminder of something tormenting and repulsive that was to be found in that very room now, at that moment, and had been there earlier. He wearily lowered himself on to his sofa. The old woman brought him a samovar, he made tea but did not touch it; he dismissed the old woman until the following morning. He sat on the sofa and felt his head go round. He felt ill and powerless. He began to fall asleep, but then got up in agitation and paced about the room in order to drive sleep away. At moments it seemed to him that he was raving. But it was not his illness that preoccupied him most; sitting down again, he began to gaze around him from time to time, as though he were looking out for something. This happened several times. At last his gaze directed itself fixedly at a single point. Ivan smiled, but a colouring of anger flooded his face. For a long time he sat where he was, propping his head hard in both hands and yet also squinting over at the previous point, at the sofa that stood against the opposite wall. It seemed that there was something there that irritated him, some object, agitating, tormenting him.

9

The Devil. Ivan Fyodorovich's Nightmare

I am not a doctor, yet even so I feel that the moment has arrived when I decidedly must explain to the reader at least something of the character of Ivan Fyodorovich's illness.* Running ahead, I shall say but one thing: he was now, this night, on the very eve of a *delirium tremens* which had at last completely taken possession of his organism, long deranged but until now stubbornly resistant to the illness. Knowing nothing of medicine, I shall risk expressing the supposition that he really had perhaps, by a fearsome exertion of his will, managed to ward off the illness for a time, hoping of course to surmount it altogether. He knew that he was not well, but he felt a loathing reluctance to be ill at this time, at these approaching moments that were so fateful in his life, when it was necessary for him to be present, to express his opinion boldly and decisively and to 'defend himself against himself'. He had, as a matter of fact, gone one day to see the new doctor who had arrived from Moscow, ordered from there by Katerina Ivanovna in consequence of a certain fantasy of hers, which I have already mentioned in the foregoing. The doctor, having heard what he had to say and having examined him, had concluded that he was suffering from something almost akin to a disorder of the brain, and was not in the slightest astonished by a certain confession which the other, with revulsion, made to him. 'Hallucinations in your condition are very possible,' the doctor determined, 'though they ought to be verified ... and in general you will have to begin serious treatment without losing a minute, otherwise it will go badly.' Upon leaving the consulting chamber, however, Ivan Fyodorovich had not followed his sensible advice and had neglected to enter hospital for a cure: 'After all, I can walk, I still have strength for the time being, when I collapse it will be a different matter, then let anyone administer treatment who cares to,' he decided, with a wave of his hand. And thus he sat now, almost aware himself that he was in a delirium, and, as I have already said, staring fixedly at some object on the sofa against the opposite wall. Someone, God knew how he had entered, for he had not been in the room when Ivan Fyodorovich, returning from his visit to Smerdyakov, had entered it, had suddenly turned out to be sitting there. He was some kind of *gospodin*,* or rather, a certain kind of Russian 'gentleman', no longer young in years, *'qui frisait la cinquantaine'*, as the French say, with a not so very noticeable trace of grey in his hair that still was long and thick, and in his short and wedge-shaped beard. He was dressed in a brown jacket, evidently from a good tailor, but now rather shabby, having been made the year before last and now quite out of fashion, of a kind that no man of society and means had worn for the past two years. His shirt and collar, his long, scarf-like necktie were all in the manner affected by every smartish gentleman, but if one looked closer one could see that the shirt and collar were rather dirty, and the broad scarf very threadbare. The checked trousers of the guest were of an excellent fit, but were again too light in colour and somehow tighter than anyone wore now; the soft, white goatsfelt hat which the guest had brought along with him, quite out of keeping with the season, produced the same effect. It was, in a word, one of respectability maintained on very slender pecuniary means. The gentleman looked as though he belonged to the class of former lily-fingered landowners who flourished in the days of serfdom; having plainly seen something of the world and of respectable society, having once had connections and having retained them, possibly,· even to this day, but gradually, with impoverishment consequent upon a merry life lived in youth and the recent abolition of serfdom, having turned, as it were, into a kind of sponge *du bon ton*, roaming among his good old friends, who would allow him to stay in their homes because of his easy, pliant character, and also in view of the fact that he was all the same a man of respectability, whom it was even possible to sit down at one's table, though, of course, in a modest place. Sponges of this kind, gentlemen of pliant character, who are able to tell stories, make up a hand at cards and are decidedly not fond of any assignments that may be foisted upon them, are generally bachelors or widowers, possibly with children, but children who are invariably being brought up somewhere far away, by some aunts or other, to whom the gentleman will almost never allude in polite society, as though slightly ashamed of such kinship. With his children he will gradually lose the habit of consorting altogether, from time to time

receiving from them letters of greeting upon his name-day or at Christ-
mas, and will sometimes even write replies to them. The physiognomy of
the unexpected guest was not so much good-natured as again pliant and
ready, depending on the circumstances, to deliver any pleasant remark
that was required. He wore no watch, but had a tortoiseshell lorgnette
on a black ribbon. On the middle finger of his right hand there was a
massive gold ring set with an inexpensive opal. Ivan Fyodorovich preserved a hostile silence and made no move to speak. The guest waited
and sat precisely like a sponge who has just come down from the room
that has been allotted him upstairs to keep his host company at tea, but is
meekly silent in view of the fact that his host is busy and considering
something with a frown; ready, however, to embark upon any pleasant
conversation as soon as his host should initiate it. Suddenly his face
seemed to express a certain sudden concern.

'Look,' he began to Ivan Fyodorovich, 'do forgive me, but I simply
wanted to remind you: I mean, you went to visit Smerdyakov in order to
find out about Katerina Ivanovna, but you left without doing so. I
daresay you must have forgotten . . .'

'Ah, yes!' suddenly broke from Ivan, and his face was clouded with
concern. 'Yes, I forgot . . . As a matter of fact, though, it does not matter
now, it can all wait until tomorrow,' he muttered to himself. 'And let me
tell you,' he said irritably, addressing the guest, 'I myself would have
been bound to remember it, because it is precisely that which has been
causing me all this anguish! Why did you come out with that remark? So
I would believe that you had put the idea into my head, and that I had
not remembered it myself?'

'Well, do not believe it, then,' the gentleman said with a dry but
kindly smile. 'What kind of belief is it that is forced upon a man? What
is more, in the matter of belief no proof is of any avail, especially the
material sort. Thomas believed* not because he saw the risen Christ, but
because he already desired to believe. Look at the spiritualists, for example
. . . I am very fond of them . . . Imagine, they suppose that they are
conducive to religious faith because the devils from the world to come
show them their horns. "That is already material proof," they say, "that
the world to come exists." The world to come and material proof,
whatever next! And I mean, it is one thing to prove the existence of the
Devil, but surely the existence of God demands another proof entirely? I
intend to join an idealist society and form an opposition movement
within it: "I am a realist," I'll say, "not a materialist, heh-heh!"'

'Look,' Ivan Fyodorovich said, suddenly getting up from behind the table. 'I now feel as though I am in a delirium . . . and, of course, I am . . . talk all the nonsense you wish, it is all the same to me! You will not drive me to frenzy like last time. I am merely ashamed of something . . . I want to pace about the room . . . I sometimes do not see you and do not even hear your voice, like last time, but I always divine the nonsense you talk, because *it is I, it is I myself who am speaking, not you*! The only thing I do not know is whether I was asleep last time or whether I was awake when I saw you. Well, now I am going to wet a towel in cold water and put it to my head, and perhaps you will vanish.'

'I am pleased that you and I have passed straight to addressing each other as *"tu"*,' the guest began.

'Fool,' Ivan laughed, 'do you suppose I would address you as *"vous"*? I am cheerful now, and I only have a pain in my temple . . . and in the crown of my head . . . only please do not philosophize the way you did last time. If you cannot take yourself off, then at least talk some cheerful rubbish. Tell me some gossip, after all, you are a sponge, so tell me some gossip. A nightmare like this is too much of a burden! But I am not afraid of you. I shall overcome you. They will not take me to the madhouse!'

'*C'est charmant*, a sponge. Why there I am, cold sober. What on earth am I, if not a sponge? Incidentally, you know, I have been listening to you and have marvelled slightly: I do declare that little by little you are beginning to take me for something real and not just something in your fantasy, as you insisted I was on the last occasion . . .'

'Not for one moment do I take you for a truth that is real,' Ivan exclaimed in what even amounted to fury. 'You are a falsehood, you are my illness, you are a ghost. Only I do not know how to destroy you, and perceive that for a certain time I must suffer you. You are a hallucination I am having. You are the embodiment of myself, but only of one side of me . . . of my thoughts and emotions, though only those that are most loathsome and stupid. In that regard you might even be of interest to me, if only I had time to throw away on you . . .'

'With your permission, with your permission, I shall expose your guilt: back there by the lamp-post, when you turned on Alyosha and shouted at him: "You discovered it from *him*! How did you know that *he* comes to visit me?" I mean, that was me you were referring to, was it not? So you see, for just one teensy little moment you believed, believed that I really do exist,' the gentleman laughed mildly.

'Yes, that was due to a weakness of nature . . . but it is out of the question that I believed in your existence. I am unsure whether I was asleep or on my feet last time. It is possible that I dreamed of you then, but I certainly did not see you when I was awake . . .'

'But then why were you so stern with him today, with Alyosha, I mean? He is such a dear fellow; I bear the guilt before him for the Elder Zosima.'

'Be silent about Alyosha! How dare you, lackey!' Ivan laughed again.

'You call me names, yet at the same time you laugh – a good sign. Actually, you know, you are far more pleasant with me today than you were last time, and I can understand why: this great decision . . .'

'Be silent about my decision!' Ivan exclaimed with ferocity.

'I understand, understand, *c'est noble, c'est charmant*, tomorrow you are going to go to court and defend your brother, making a sacrifice of yourself . . . *c'est chevalieresque.*'

'Be silent, or I will give you a kicking!'

'I shall in part be relieved, for then my goal will be accomplished: if you give me a kicking it will mean that you believe in my reality, for ghosts are never kicked. However, joking apart: you see, I do not mind, you may call me names if you wish, but I think you might do better to be a drop more civil, even with me. "Fool" and "lackey" – well, what kind of words are those?'

'In calling you names, I apply them to myself!' Ivan laughed again. 'You are I, my very self, only with a different phiz. You say the very things that are already in my head . . . and are quite powerless to tell me anything new!'

'If I concord with you in ideas, that only redounds to my honour,' the gentleman said with tact and dignity.

'Only you take all my foul ideas – and above all, my stupid ones. You are stupid and vulgar. You are horribly stupid. No, I cannot tolerate you! What am I to do, what am I to do?' Ivan ground out.

'*Mon ami*, I none the less wish to be a gentleman and to be treated thus,' the guest began, in a fit of a certain purely sponge-like and already, in advance, yielding and good-natured ambition. 'I am poor, but . . . I will not say that I am particularly honest, but . . . usually in society it is accepted as an axiom that I'm a fallen angel. Though I swear to God, it beats me how I could ever have been an angel. If I ever was one, it must have been so long ago that to have forgotten it is no sin. Nowadays I cherish only the reputation of a man of respectability and get by somehow, trying to be pleasant. I love human beings sincerely – oh, I have in many things been slandered! Here, when from time to time I change my place of residence and stay among you, my life seems to pass in a way that is almost real, and that appeals to me most of all. You see, I too, like you yourself, suffer from the fantastic, and so I like your earthly reality. Here among you everything is mapped out, here everything is formula, geometry, while among ourselves there is nothing but indeterminate equations! Here, I wander and dream. I am fond of dreaming. What is more, on the earth I become superstitious; no, please don't laugh: it is precisely that which appeals to me — that I become superstitious. I adopt all your customs: I have grown fond of going to the Russian baths, can you credit it, and I like to steam myself with priests and merchants. My dream is to take fleshly form, but finally, irrevocably, in some fat, seven-pood* merchant's wife and to believe in all the things she believes in. The ideal I strive for is to go into a church and with pure heart to set up a candle, I swear to God it is. Then there would be a limit to my sufferings. And you know, I have grown fond of sampling the medical arrangements here among you, too: this spring there was smallpox about, and I took the inoculation at the foundling hospital — if you only knew how pleased with myself I was that day: I gave ten roubles to the Brother Slavs! . . . But you aren't listening. You know, I really don't think you're yourself today,' the gentleman said, after a slight pause. 'I know that you went to see that doctor yesterday . . . Well, how is your health? What did the doctor say to you?'

'Fool!' Ivan snapped out.

'While you, on the other hand, are so clever. Are you calling me names again? Oh, but I did not ask out of concern, merely for the sake of conversation. Don't answer if you'd rather not. Now there is this rheumatism going around again . . .'

'Fool,' Ivan repeated.

'You may say what you like, but last year I caught such a rheumatism that I recall it to this day,'

'The Devil has rheumatism?'

'But why not, if sometimes I take fleshly form? When I do that, I accept the consequences. Satan *sum et nihil humanum a me alienum puto.*'*

'What, what? Satana *sum et nihil humanum* . . . that is quite intelligent for the Devil!'

'I am glad to oblige at last.'

'But look here, you did not borrow that from me,' Ivan said, pausing suddenly, almost shocked. 'That is not something that has ever entered my head — strange . . .'

'*C'est du nouveau, n'est-ce pas?* This time I shall do the honest thing, and explain to you. Listen: in dreams, and especially nightmares, oh, the kind that are caused by indigestion or whatever, a man sometimes witnesses such artistic conceits, such complex and realistic scenes, such events or even whole worlds of events, connected by such intrigues to such unexpected details, all the way from your higher manifestations to the very last button on a dicky as, I swear to you, Lev Tolstoy could never write, and yet the people who have such dreams are often not writers at all, but the most run-of-the-mill people, civil servants, journalists, priests . . . Apropos of that, there is even a problem *tout entier*: one government minister has even confessed to me himself that all his best ideas come to him while he is asleep. Well, and so it is even now. Though I am a hallucination you are having, I say things that are original, just as I would in one of your nightmares, things that have never entered your head until now, and in no sense do I repeat your own ideas — yet all the same I am merely a nightmare you are having, and nothing more.'

'You lie. Your aim is precisely to convince me that you exist in your own right, and are not one of my nightmares, yet you yourself assert that you are a dream.'

'*Mon ami*, today I chose a particular method, I shall elucidate it to you later on. Wait, now, where was I? Yes, well and so that day I caught a cold, only not here among you, but there . . .'

'What do you mean, there? Tell me, are you going to be with me much longer, might you not possibly leave?' Ivan exclaimed almost in despair. He stopped pacing about, sat down on the sofa, again leaned his elbows on the table and clutched his head in both hands. He tore the wet towel from his forehead and threw it aside in vexation: it had plainly not worked.

'Your nerves are upset,' the gentleman said with a familiarly casual, but perfectly friendly air. 'You are even angry with me for catching cold, yet it happened in the most natural manner. That day I was hurrying to a certain diplomatic *soirée* at the home of a certain St Petersburg lady of high society who aspired to influence with the ministers of the cabinet. Well, I was wearing evening dress, a white tie, gloves, and yet I was God only knows where and, in order to get down to earth among you I still had a certain distance to fly through space . . . of course, it's no distance at all, really, but you know even a ray of light from the sun takes eight minutes to get there, and there I was, imagine, in evening dress and an open waistcoat. Spirits do not freeze, but when I took fleshly form, well . . . in a word, I did not think properly, but set off, and I mean, out there in those open expanses, in space, in those waters "which were above the firmament"* — I mean, it is so cold . . . so cold that "cold" is not really the right word for it, can you imagine: one hundred and fifty degrees below zero! You know that pastime favoured by village girls: when it's thirty below they tell the new girl to lick the axe: her tongue freezes to it in an instant, and the silly blockhead tears the skin off it, and it bleeds; and I mean, that is only when it's thirty below — at a hundred and fifty below I should think one would only have to put one's finger to the axe and it would drop off, as long as . . . as long as it were possible for there to be an axe there . . .'

'And would it be possible for there to be one?' Ivan Fyodorovich suddenly interrupted, absent-mindedly and with loathing. He was trying with all his might to resist believing in his delirium and thus lapsing finally into insanity.

'An axe?' the guest asked in his turn, astonished.

'Well, yes, what would happen to an axe there?' Ivan Fyodorovich suddenly exclaimed with a kind of ferocious and insistent stubbornness.

'What would happen to an axe in space? *Quelle idée!* If it went far enough it would, I think, begin to orbit the earth, itself not knowing why, in the form of a satellite. Astronomers would compute the rising and the setting of the axe, Gattsuk* would enter it in the calendar, and that is all.'

'You are stupid, you are horribly stupid!' Ivan said, obstinately. 'Please talk some cleverer rot, or I shall not listen. You are trying to overwhelm me with realism, convince me that you exist, but I do not intend to believe that you exist! I shall not believe it!'

'But I'm not talking rot, it is all true; the truth, alas, is nearly always lacking in cleverness. You really do, I perceive, expect of me something great and possibly even beautiful.* That is much to be regretted, for I can only give what I am able . . .'

'Stop philosophizing, ass!'

'What philosophy can there be, when the whole of my right side is paralysed, and I groan and bellow? I have been to all the doctors: they are excellent at providing you with a diagnosis, will run over all the symptoms of your illness on the tips of their fingers — well, but when it actually comes to a cure, that they are unable to effect. I ran across one enthusiastic student chappie here: "Even if you die," he said, "at least you will know what illness you have died of"! Or again, there is this manner they have when sending you to a specialist, as if to say: "We only do the diagnosis, now off you go and see such-and-such a specialist, he will cure you." The old kind of doctor, the kind who used to treat any kind of illness, has quite, quite disappeared, let me tell you, nowadays they're all specialists, and they all advertise in the newspapers. If it's your nose there's something wrong with, they will send you to Paris, saying: "There is a European specialist there who treats noses." When you go to Paris, he examines your nose: "I can only cure your right nostril,"* he says, "because I do not treat left nostrils, that is not my specialism, but if you will go next to Vienna, there you will find a special specialist who will cure your left nostril." What would you do? I resorted to folk medicine. One German doctor advised me to go to the Russian baths, sit on the ledge and rub myself with salt and honey. Solely in order to pay a visit to the baths again, I went: smeared the stuff all over myself, but it didn't have any effect. In despair I wrote to Count Mattei in Milan: he sent me his book and the drops, well, the less said the better. And imagine: it was Hoff's Malt Extract that worked! I bought it quite by accident, drank down one and a half bottles of it, and I could have danced, the pain all vanished as if by magic. I decided I would definitely have a "thank you" message to him published in the newspapers, a sense of gratitude was prompting me, and imagine, another difficulty came along: not a single newspaper would take my message. "It would look very reactionary," they said, "no one would believe it, *le diable n'existe point*." They advised me to have it published anonymously. Well, but what sort of "thank you" message would it be if it were anonymous? I laughed with the fellows in the office: "I know that it's reactionary to believe in God in our day," I said, "but after all, I'm the Devil, it's all right to believe in me." "We understand what you mean," they said, "after all, who doesn't believe in the Devil, but all the same it's impossible, it could harm our progressive image. What about publishing it as a joke?" Well, I thought that would be too banal. So it wasn't published. And you know, I still feel annoyed about it. My best emotions, such as gratitude, for example, are formally forbidden me solely on account of my social position.'

'You're embarking on philosophy again!' Ivan ground out with hatred.

'May God preserve me, but you know, it is impossible not to complain sometimes. I am a man who has suffered calumny. Take your constant allegation that I am stupid, for example. There one may perceive your youth. *Mon ami*, the matter lies not in intelligence alone! I have a good and cheerful heart, "you see, I also write various little *vaudevilles*".* You really do, it seems, take me for a Khlestakov grown grey and yet, you know, my destiny is a far more serious one. In accordance with some pre-temporal disposition of which I have never been able to make head nor tail, it is my function to "negate", yet really I am of sincere good heart and am quite incapable of negation. "No, off you go and negate," they say, "without negation there will be no criticism, and what kind of a journal would it be that had no 'critical section'? Without criticism there will be nothing but a 'hosannah'. But in order to create life a 'hosannah' alone is not enough, the 'hosannah' must pass through the crucible of doubt," well, and so on, in that vein. As a matter of fact, I do not involve myself with all that, it was not I who created it, and I am not responsible. Well, and so they chose their scapegoat, compelled me to write in the critical section, and the result was life. *Nous comprenons cette comédie*: I, for example, quite plainly and simply insist upon annihilation for myself. "No," they say, "you must go on living, for without you there would be nothing. If everything on earth were reasonable, nothing would ever happen. Without you there would be no events, and it is necessary that there should be events." Well, and so on I drudge with unwilling heart so that there may be events, and bring about unreason by command. People think *toute cette comédie* is something serious, all their unquestionable intelligence notwithstanding. There lies their tragedy. Well, and they suffer, of course, but . . . all the same they live, they live in reality, not in fantasy; for suffering is also life. Without suffering what pleasure would there be in it? Everything would turn into one single, endless church service: much holy soaring, but rather boring. Well, and I? I suffer, but even so I do not live. I am the "x" in an indeterminate equation. I am one of life's ghosts, who has lost all the ends and the beginnings, and even at last forgotten what to call myself. You are laughing . . . No, you are not laughing, you are angry again. You are eternally angry, you would like there to be nothing but intelligence, but I will tell you again that I would renounce all this empyrean existence, all these honours and ranks just in order to be able to take fleshly form in the person of a seven-pood merchant's wife and set up candles to God in church.'

'So you don't believe in God either?' Ivan said, smiling with hatred.

'Well, how can I explain it to you, if you are serious, that is . . .'

'Does God exist or not?' Ivan barked, again with ferocious insistence.

'Ah, so you are serious? My dear little dove, I swear to God I do not know, *pour vous dire le grand mot.*'

'You do not know, yet you see God? No, in yourself you do not exist, you are *me*, all you are is *myself*, and nothing more! You are rubbish, you are my imagination!'

'Well, if you like, I am of the same philosophy as you, now that it

would be true to say. *Je pense, donc je suis*, that is the one thing I know
for sure, and as for all the rest of what surrounds me, all these worlds,
God and even Satan himself — for me it remains unproven whether all
that exists in itself or is merely a certain emanation of mine, the logical
development of my *I*, which has a pre-temporal and individual existence
. . . in a word, I break off in haste, for you look as though you are about
to jump up and box my ears.'

'I had rather hear you tell some anecdote!' Ivan said, with painful
effort.

'I have an anecdote, and one precisely on your theme, only it is not so
much an anecdote as, well, a legend. Just now you reproached me for my
unbelief: "You see God," you said, "and yet you do not believe." But,
mon ami, why, after all, I am not the only one, everyone among us there
has grown confused, and all because of your science. While still there
were atoms, the five senses, the four elements, well, it all held together
somehow. There were atoms even in the ancient world, after all. But
when it was learned among us that you had discovered the "chemical
molecule" and "protoplasm", and the devil only knows what else — well,
our tails really fell between our legs. A proper old muddle ensued; above
all, there was superstition, gossip; you know, we have just as much
gossip as you do, even a bit more, and finally there were denunciations to
the authorities, for you know we also have a certain department* where
"information" of a certain kind is received. Well, then there appeared this
légende sauvage, which dates from our Middle Ages — not yours, but ours
— and even among us no one believes it except seven-pood merchants'
wives, again not yours, but ours. Everything you have, we have, too,
that is one of our secrets which I shall let you into out of friendship, even
though it is forbidden. The legend concerns heaven. There was, it is said,
among you here upon earth, a certain thinker and philosopher who
"rejected everything, laws, conscience, faith",* and, above all, the life to
come. He died, thinking that he would go straight into darkness and
death, yet there before him was the life to come. He was amazed and
indignant: "This runs counter to my convictions," he said. Well, for that
he received a sentence . . . though, of course, you must forgive me, you
see I am only telling you what I have heard, it is only a legend . . . He
was sentenced, you see, to walk a quadrillion kilometres (we have gone
over to kilometres now, you know) in darkness, and when he had
finished that quadrillion the gates of heaven would be opened to him and
all would be pardoned him . . .'

'And what other torments do you have in the other world apart from walking a quadrillion kilometres?' Ivan cut in with a kind of strange animation.

'What torments do we have? Ah, do not even inquire: before we had all sorts of things, but nowadays they are mostly of a moral sort, "pangs of conscience" and all that rubbish. That is also something we have acquired from you, from the "softening of your ways".* Well, and who have been the gainers? Those without conscience, for what are pangs of conscience to him who has no conscience whatsoever? In fact, it has been the decent folk who have suffered, those who still have a conscience and a sense of honour ... That is what reforms can do on soil that is unprepared, especially when they have been copied from foreign institutions – nothing but harm! A touch of the old fire and brimstone would be better. Well, so this fellow who had been sentenced to a quadrillion stood still, had a look round, and then lay down across the road: "I shall not go, out of principle I shall not go!" Take the soul of an enlightened Russian atheist and mix it with the soul of the prophet Jonah* who sulked in the belly of the whale for three days and three nights – there you have the character of this road-recumbent thinker.'

'What was he recumbent on?'

'Oh, no doubt there was something. Are you laughing again?'

'The staunch fellow!' Ivan exclaimed, still with the same strange animation. Now he was listening with a kind of unexpected interest. 'Well, and is he still lying there?'

'There's the rub – no, he isn't. He lay there for almost a thousand years, but then got up and went.'

'The ass!' Ivan exclaimed with a loud, nervous laugh, still apparently trying to figure something out with intense effort. 'Surely it would be all the same, whether he lay there for eternity or walked a quadrillion versts? Why, that would be a billion years of walking, would it not?'

'Even more – much more, only I don't have a pencil and paper to do the calculation. And in any case, you see, he got there long ago, and that is where the anecdote begins.'

'Got there? Where did he get a billion years from?'

'But you see, you are still thinking in terms of the earth we have at present! Why, the earth we have at present may have repeated itself a billion times; you know – become extinct, frozen over, cracked, crumbled to pieces, disintegrated into its constituent origins, becoming the waters again, "which were above the firmament", then a comet again, then a sun, then another earth produced from that sun – I mean, this process of development may already have repeated itself an infinite number of times, and always in the same form, right down to the very last small detail. A most indecently tedious monstrosity . . .'

'Very well, very well, but what happened when he got there?'

'Well, as soon as the gates of heaven had been opened to him and he had gone inside, after he had been there no more than two seconds – and by his watch, by his watch (though I should think his watch must long ago have disintegrated into its constituent elements), he exclaimed that in the course of those two seconds it would be possible to walk not only a quadrillion, but a quadrillion quadrillion, and even raised to the quadrillionth power! In a word, he sang a "hosannah", and overdid it, too, with the result that there were some there, of a nobler cast of thought, who were even unwilling to shake hands with him at first: he'd been rather too enthusiastic about hopping over to the conservatives, they said. The Russian character. I repeat: it is a legend. I sell it to you at the value for which I purchased it. So you see, those are the sort of ideas that still circulate there among us concerning all those matters.'

'I've caught you!' Ivan exclaimed with a kind of almost childish joy, as though he had finally remembered something. 'That anecdote about the quadrillion years – I composed it myself! I was seventeen at the time, attending the gymnasium . . . I composed that anecdote and told it to one of my schoolfriends, Korovkin, his name was, it was in Moscow . . . That anecdote is so typical that I could not have borrowed it from anywhere. I had begun to forget it . . . but now it has come back to me unconsciously – to me, and it was not you who told it! In the way that thousands of things sometimes come back to one unconsciously, even when one is being driven to the scaffold . . . It came back to me in a dream. And you are that dream! You are a dream and do not exist!'

'By the passion with which you repudiate me,' the gentleman said, laughing, 'I am convinced that you do believe in me none the less.'

'In no way! I do not believe in one hundredth part of you!'

'But in a thousandth part of me you do. After all, homoeopathic doses may often be the most effective. Admit that you believe, at least in a ten thousandth part . . .'

'Not for a single minute!' Ivan exclaimed in fury. 'Though as a matter of fact I wouldn't mind believing in you,' he added strangely, all of a sudden.

'Aha! Now there is a confession! But I am kind, and I shall help you. Listen: it is I who have caught you, and not the other way round! I purposely told you your anecdote, which you had already forgotten, so that you would finally lose faith in my existence altogether.'

'You lie! The purpose of your appearance is to persuade me that you exist.'

'Indeed. But vacillations, anxiety, the struggle between belief and disbelief — after all, those are sometimes such a torment to a man of conscience like yourself, that he would rather hang himself. Indeed, knowing that you believe in me a tiny bit, I allowed you to disbelieve in me altogether by telling you that anecdote. I have been leading you between belief and disbelief alternately, and in so doing I have had my own purpose. It is a new method, sir: you see, if you completely lose faith in my existence, then you will instantly begin to assure me to my very face that I am not a dream, but really do exist, I know you; and then I shall attain my purpose. But my purpose is a noble one. I shall implant in you but a tiny seed of faith, and from it shall grow an oak — and indeed, such an oak that as you sit upon it you will wish to join "the father anchorites and dames immaculate";* for that you secretly very, very much desire, you will eat locusts, drag yourself off into the wilderness to live as a monk!'

'So you, a scoundrel, are endeavouring to bring about the salvation of my soul, are you?'

'Well, one must do a good deed some time, after all. You are losing your temper, you are losing your temper, I can see it!'

'Buffoon! Have you ever tempted those who eat locusts and pray in the barren wilderness for seventeen years, overgrown with moss?'

'My little dove, that is all I have ever done. One may forget the world and all the worlds beyond it, but to one such man one will adhere, for a diamond is, when all is said and done, a very precious thing; you see, one such soul is on occasion worth an entire constellation — we have our own arithmetic, you know. Victory is a precious thing! And you know, some of them, I swear to God, are not in any way inferior to you in development, though you may not believe it: they are able to contemplate such abysses of belief and disbelief at one and the same moment that, truly, it sometimes seems that were he to advance one hair's-breadth further, the fellow would go flying "arsy-versy", as the actor Gorbunov* would say.'

'Well, so you have been led by the nose?'

'*Mon ami*,' the guest observed sententiously, 'it is better to be led by the nose on occasion than to find oneself quite without a nose at all, as a certain ailing marquis pronounced quite recently (a specialist must have been treating him) during confession to his holy Jesuit father. I was there, it was simply charming. "Return to me," he said, "my nose!" And beat his breast. "My son," the *pater* prevaricated, "all is accomplished according to the unknowable destinies of Providence and an apparent disaster sometimes brings in its wake an exceptional, though invisible advantage. If stern fortune has deprived you of your nose, then your advantage is that all the rest of your life no one will ever dare to tell you that you have been led by the nose." "Holy father, that is no consolation!" the despairing marquis exclaimed, "on the contrary, I would be only too delighted to be led by the nose every day for the rest of my life, if only it were in its proper place!" "My son," the *pater* sighed, "it is wrong to demand all blessings at once, and this is already a complaint against Providence, which even now has not forgotten you; for if you cry, as you cried just now, that you would be ready to be led by the nose all the rest of your life, then even now your desire has been fulfilled, though obliquely: for, having lost your nose, you are by that very fact being led by it . . ."'

'Ugh, how stupid!' Ivan barked.

'*Mon ami*, my intention was simply to make you laugh, but I swear to you that that is authentic Jesuit casuistry, and I also swear that it happened letter for letter as I have described it to you. This recent incident caused me a great deal of trouble. That very same night, upon returning home, the unhappy young man shot himself; I was with him constantly until the very last moment . . . But as for those Jesuit confession boxes, they really are the sweetest diversion I know in the melancholy minutes of life. Here is another instance for you, from just the other day. To an old *pater* there came a little *blondine*, a Norman girl of about twenty. Beauty, curves, a perfect pose — enough to make one's mouth water. She stooped down and whispered her sin through the speak-hole. "My goodness, daughter of mine, have you fallen again already? . . ." the *pater* exclaimed. "O, Sancta Maria, what do I hear: with another man this time? But how long is this to continue, and have you no shame?" "*Ah mon père*," the peccatrix replied, the tears of penitence rolling down her cheeks, "*Ça lui fait tant de plaisir et à moi si peu de peine!*"* Well, imagine such a reply! At that point I withdrew: that was the cry of nature herself, that, if you will, was better than any innocence! I absolved her of her sin right there and then, and was on the point of turning to leave, but was at once constrained to go back again: I could hear the *pater* making a rendezvous with her through the speak-hole for that evening — I mean, he was an old man — a heart of stone, yet he fell in a single instant! It was nature, it was the truth of nature claiming its own! What, are you turning up your nose again, angry again? I really don't know how to oblige you . . .'

'Let me alone, you chatter in my brain like a nightmare that will not stop,' Ivan groaned in pain, helpless before his vision. 'I am sick of you, unendurably and agonizingly sick of you! I would give much to be able to drive you away!'

'I repeat, moderate your demands, do not demand of me "all that is great and beautiful"* and you will see how amicably you and I can get along together,' the gentleman said, imposingly. 'If truth be told, you are losing your temper with me because I have not manifested myself to you in some red glow or other, "a-thunder and a-glitter",* with singed wings, but have appeared before you in such modest guise. In the first place, your aesthetic sense is offended, and, in the second, your pride: how, you say, could such a vulgar devil come calling on a great man such as you? No, I am afraid that there is still in you that romantic vein, so derided by Belinsky in his day. What is to be done, young man? Earlier, you know, as I was preparing to come and see you, I had the notion of appearing to you as a retired State Councillor with a record of service in the Caucasus and the Star of the Lion and Sun* on my evening coat, but felt positively apprehensive about doing so, as you would have given me a thorough trouncing just for having the Lion and Sun on my evening coat and not, at the very least, the Pole Star* or the Sirius*. And yet you keep telling me I am stupid. But, as the Lord is mine, I lay no claim to be your equal in intelligence. When Mephistopheles appeared to Faust,* he testified concerning himself that while wishing evil, he did only good. Well, that is as he likes, but I am quite the contrary. I may be the only person in all nature who loves truth and sincerely desires good. I was there when the Word who died upon the cross ascended into heaven, bearing at his bosom the soul of the crucified thief who was on his right hand, I heard the joyful squeals of the cherubim, as they sang and cried "Hosannah!", and the thunderous howl of ecstasy from the seraphim that shook heaven and all the universe. And lo, I swear by all that is holy, I wanted to join in the chorus and cry with them all: "Hosannah!" It was already on the tip of my tongue, breaking from my bosom ... I am, after all, you know, very sensitive and artistically impressionable. But common sense — oh, a most unfortunate property of my nature — restrained me even there within the proper limits, and I let the moment slip! For what — I thought at that same moment — what would have transpired after my "Hosannah"? In an instant everything in the world would have become extinct and no more events would have taken place. And so you see, solely because of the call of duty and my social position, I was compelled to crush the moment of goodness within myself and remain with my loathsome deeds.

Someone else appropriates all the honour for being good, while only loathsome deeds were left me to my lot. But I do not envy him the honour of living by trickery, I am not ambitious for honour. Why out of all the beings in the world have I alone been doomed to the curses of all respectable men and even to the kicks of their boots? For, in taking fleshly form, I must on occasion also take such consequences. I mean, I know there is a secret there, but on no account will they let me in on that secret, for then, having realized what it was all about, I might bellow "Hosannah!", and instantly the essential minus would disappear and reason would dawn in all the world, and along with it, of course, would come the end of everything, even of newspapers and journals, because who would subscribe to them then? I mean, I know that in the end I shall knuckle under, walk my quadrillion, I too, and discover the secret. But until that happens I shall sulk and with unwilling heart fulfil my appointed purpose: to destroy thousands so that one may be saved. How many, for example, were the souls that had to be destroyed and the honourable reputations that had to be defamed in order to obtain even one righteous Job, about whom they used to tease me so cruelly in those bygone days! No, until I am let in upon the secret there are two truths that exist for me: one that is of that place and is theirs, as yet quite unknown to me, and another that is mine. And it is still uncertain as to which of them will be better . . . Have you fallen asleep?'

'It would be no wonder if I had,' Ivan groaned menacingly. 'All that is stupid in my nature, all that I have long ago lived through, ground through the mill of my intellect and thrown aside like offal, you serve up to me as some novelty!'

'Even now I fail to please you! And I thought you might be seduced by my literary mode of exposition: that "Hosannah" in heaven – that wasn't a bad little invention of mine, was it? And then that sarcastic tone *à la* Heine just now, eh? Don't you think?'

'No, never have I been such a lackey! And how could my soul have engendered such a lackey as you?'

'*Mon ami*, I know a certain most charming and lovable young Russian *barin*: a young thinker and great lover of literature and exquisite objects, the author of a *poema* of promise, with the title "The Grand Inquisitor" . . . He was the only audience I had in mind!'

'I forbid you to speak of "The Grand Inquisitor"!' Ivan exclaimed, blushing all over in shame.

'Well then, what about "The Geological Revolution"?* Do you remember? Now there was a fine little *poema*!'

'Be silent, or I shall kill you!'

'Is it me you will kill? No, you must forgive me, I wish to speak my mind. Indeed, I came here in order to accord myself that satisfaction. Oh, I love the dreams of my young and ardent friends a-tremble with the thirst for life! "Those new men," you said to yourself last spring, as you prepared to come here, "they think they can destroy everything and start off with anthropophagy. The stupid fools, they never asked me! In my view it is not necessary to destroy anything, all that need be destroyed in mankind is the idea of God, that is what one must proceed from! It is with that, with that one must begin – O, blind ones, who understand nothing! Once mankind, each and individually, has repudiated God (and I believe that that period, in a fashion parallel to the geological periods, will arrive), then of its own accord, and without the need of anthropophagy, the whole of the former world-outlook and, above all, the whole of the former morality, will collapse, and all will begin anew. People will unite together in order to take from life all that it is able to give, but only for the sake of happiness and joy in this world. Man will exalt himself with a spirit of divine, titanic pride, and the man-god will appear. Vanquishing nature hour by hour, already without limits, by his will and science, man will thereby experience, hour by hour, a pleasure so elevated that it will replace all his former hopes of celestial pleasures. Every man will discover that he is wholly mortal, without the possibility of resurrection, and will accept death proudly and calmly, like a god. Out of pride he will grasp that there is no point in him complaining that life is a moment, and he will come to love his brother without any need of recompense. The love will only be sufficient for the moment of life, but the very consciousness of life's momentariness will intensify its fire just as much as it formerly ran to fat in hopes of an infinite love beyond the grave" . . . well and so on, etcetera, etcetera, in the same genre. Most charming!'

Ivan sat with his hands pressed to his ears and looked at the floor, but began to tremble in all his body. The voice continued:

'Now the question, my youthful thinker thought, was as follows: is it possible that such a period may ever arrive? If it does, then all is decided, and mankind will finally establish itself. But since, in view of man's deep-rooted stupidity, this may not happen for another thousand years, it is lawful that everyone who now recognizes the truth should establish himself exactly as he pleases, on the new principles. It is in this sense that "all things are lawful" to him. Not only that: even if that period never arrives, in view of the fact that God and immortality do not exist it is

lawful for the new man to become a man-god, even though he is the only
one in the entire world, and, of course, in his new rank, for him to jump
over, with a light heart, every former moral hurdle set by the former
man-slave, if need be. For God there exists no law! Where God is — that
place is holy! The place where I am will at once be the foremost place of
all ... "all things are lawful", and *basta*! All that is very charming;
except that if he intends to play the swindler why does he also, apparently,
require the sanction of the truth? But such is our modern Russian
manikin: without sanction he will not dare even to play the swindler, to
such a degree has he come to love the truth ...'

The guest spoke, evidently carried off by his own eloquence, increasingly raising his voice and casting mocking looks at his host; but he did
not succeed in concluding: Ivan suddenly seized a tea-glass from the table
and threw it at the orator with all his might.

'*Ah, mais c'est bête enfin!*' the latter exclaimed, leaping up from the
sofa and brushing away the splashes of tea from himself with his fingers.
'He's remembered Luther's inkwell! He thinks I'm a dream and throws
tea-glasses at it! It's the way a woman would behave! You know, I
suspected all along that you were only pretending to stop your ears,
while really you were listening ...'

At the frame of the window there suddenly resounded from outside a
firm and insistent knocking. Ivan Fyodorovich sprang up from the sofa.

'I say, you had better go and open up,' the guest exclaimed, 'it is your
brother Alyosha, and he has a most unexpected and interesting message, I
guarantee you!'

'Be silent, deceiver, I knew it was Alyosha before you told me, I had a
premonition that he would come, and of course he has come with a
reason, a "message"! ...' Ivan exclaimed in a frenzy.

'Then open up, go and open up for him. There is a snowstorm
outside, and he is your brother. *Monsieur, sait-il le temps qu'il fait? C'est
à ne pas mettre un chien dehors ...*'*

The knocking continued. Ivan was on the point of lunging towards
the window; but something suddenly seemed to bind his arms and legs.
With all his might he strained to burst his trammels, but it was no good.
The knocking at the window was growing increasingly louder and faster.
At last the trammels suddenly burst, and Ivan Fyodorovich sprang up on
the sofa. Both candles had almost burned to nothing, the tea-glass he had
just thrown at his guest stood before him on the table, but on the sofa
opposite there was no one. The knocking at the window frame, though
it continued insistently, was not at all as loud as it had seemed to him

only a few moments before in his dream, but was, on the contrary, very restrained.

'It is not a dream! No, I swear it, it was not a dream, it has all just happened!' Ivan Fyodorovich exclaimed, rushed to the window and opened the *fortochka*.*

'Alyosha, I thought I told you not to come here!' he cried to his brother, ferociously. 'In two words: what do you want? In two words, do you hear?'

'Smerdyakov hanged himself an hour ago,' Alyosha replied from outside.

'Come round to the porch, I'll open the door for you,' Ivan Fyodorovich said, and he went to open the door to Alyosha.

10

'He Said That'

As he entered, Alyosha told Ivan Fyodorovich that slightly over an hour previously Marya Kondratyevna had come running to his lodgings and announced that Smerdyakov had taken his own life. 'I went in to take away his samovar, and there he was, hanging from a nail on the wall.' To Alyosha's question as to whether she had reported it in the proper quarters, she replied that she had reported it to no one, but 'came rushing straight to you first, and ran as hard as I could all the way'. She had been like a madwoman, Alyosha related, and had been trembling all over like a leaf. And when Alyosha had run together with her to their *izba*, he had found Smerdyakov still hanging there. On the table lay a note: 'I exterminate my life by my own will and inclination, in order to blame no one.' Alyosha left the note on the table where it was, and went straight to the house of the chief of police, to whom he reported everything, 'and then I came straight to you', Alyosha concluded, staring fixedly into Ivan's face. Indeed, all the time he had spoken, he had not taken his eyes off him, as though he were very shocked by something in the expression of his face.

'Brother,' he exclaimed suddenly, 'I think you must be dreadfully ill! You gaze at me and it's as if you don't understand what I am saying.'

'It is good that you have come,' Ivan said, almost reflectively, and as though he had not heard Alyosha's exclamations at all. 'You see, I knew he had hanged himself.'

'But from whom?'

'I do not know. But I knew it. Did I? Yes, he told me. He told me just now . . .'

Ivan stood in the middle of the room, still speaking in the same reflective way and gazing at the floor.

'Who is *he*?' Alyosha asked, and found himself looking round the room.

'He has slipped away.'

Ivan raised his head and quietly smiled:

'He was frightened of you, of you, the dove. You are the "pure cherub".* Dmitry's name for you is a cherub. A cherub ... The thunderous howl of ecstasy from the seraphim! What is a seraph? Possibly an entire constellation. And possibly that entire constellation is only some chemical molecule ... Is there a constellation of the Lion and the Sun, do you know?'

'Brother, sit down!' Alyosha said in alarm. 'Sit down, for the love of God, here, on the sofa. You are in delirium, rest on the cushion, there, like that. Would you like me to put a wet towel round your head? Perhaps that might make it better?'

'Yes, give me a towel, there is one on the chair, I threw it there earlier.'

'It isn't there. Don't be anxious, I know where it is; look, it's here,' Alyosha said, running to earth at the other end of the room, beside Ivan's toilet table, a clean, still folded and unused towel. Ivan looked strangely at the towel; for a split second, his memory seemed to return to him.

'Wait,' he said, half getting up from the sofa. 'Earlier, an hour ago, I took that very same towel from over there and soaked it in water. I put it to my head and then threw it over here ... so how can it be dry? There wasn't another one.'

'You put this towel to your head?' Alyosha asked.

'Yes, and I was pacing about the room, an hour ago ... How can the candles have burned out already? What time is it?'

'It will soon be twelve.'

'No, no, no!' Ivan exclaimed suddenly. 'It wasn't a dream! He was here, he was sitting over there, on that sofa. While you were knocking at the window I threw a tea-glass at him ... look, this one ... Wait. I was asleep before, but this was not a dream. And it has happened before. I have dreams now, Alyosha ... only they are not dreams, but things I see when I am awake: I walk about, I can talk and see ... yet I'm asleep. But he was sitting there, he was there, right there on that sofa ... He is horribly stupid, Alyosha, horribly stupid,' Ivan laughed suddenly, starting to pace about the room.

'Who is stupid? Who is it you are talking about, Ivan?' Alyosha asked again, unhappily.

'The Devil! He has got into the habit of paying me visits. Twice he has been now, even three times, I think. He teased me by telling me I was angry that he looked like an ordinary devil and not a Satan with singed wings, in thunder and glittering glory. But he is not Satan, that is a lie of his. He is a false pretender. He is just a devil, a rubbishy, petty devil. He goes to the Russian baths. If you took his clothes off you would probably find a tail underneath, a long, smooth one like that of a Great Dane, an arshin in length, and brown . . . Alyosha, you're freezing, you've been out in the snow, would you like some tea? Well? You're cold, aren't you? Would you like me to order some tea? *C'est à ne pas mettre un chien dehors* . . .'

Alyosha quickly ran over to the wash-stand, soaked the towel, persuaded Ivan to sit down again and put the wet towel round his head. He sat down next to him.

'What was it you were saying to me about Liza earlier?' Ivan began again. (He was growing very anxious to talk.) 'I like Liza. I said something nasty to you about her. And I was not expressing my true feelings, for I like her . . . I am afraid about what Katya may do tomorrow, more afraid about that than anything else. About the future. Tomorrow she will turn her back on me and crush me under her feet. She thinks I am destroying Mitya out of jealousy towards her! Yes, that is what she thinks! But it is not so! Tomorrow is a cross, but not a gallows. No, I shall not hang myself. Do you know, Alyosha, I could never take my own life! Do you think it's because of baseness? I am not a coward. No, it is because of my thirst for life! How did I know that Smerdyakov had hanged himself? Yes, it was *he* who told me . . .'

'And you are absolutely sure that someone was sitting here?' Alyosha inquired.

'He was there, on that sofa in the corner. You would have made him go away. And indeed you did make him go away: he vanished when you appeared. I love your face, Alyosha. Did you know that I love your face? But *he* – he is I, Alyosha, I myself. All that is base in me, all that is vile and to be despised! Yes, I am a romantic, he has noticed that . . . though that too is a slander. He is horribly stupid, but he puts it to his advantage. He is cunning, bestially cunning, he knows how to drive me to rabid fury. He has kept teasing me by telling me I believed in him, and thereby compelled me to listen to him. He has pulled the wool over my eyes as though I were a little boy. As a matter of fact, he has told me many things that are true about myself. I could never have said those things to myself. You know, Alyosha, you know,' Ivan added, intensely serious and a tone that was almost confidential, 'I should very much like it if he really were *he* and not me!'

'He has driven you to exhaustion,' Alyosha said, looking at his brother with compassion.

'He teased and provoked me! And you know, he did it with such skill, such skill: "Conscience! What is conscience? I make it myself. Why am I tormenting myself, then? Out of habit. Out of a universal human habit that has been acquired over seven thousand years. So then, if we drop the habit we shall be gods." He said that, he said that!'

'And not you, not you?' Alyosha could not keep himself from exclaiming. 'Well, let him say it, turn your back on him and forget him! Let him carry off with him all that you are cursing now, and let him never return!'

'Yes, but he is wicked. He was laughing at me. He was insolent, Alyosha,' Ivan said with a shudder of outrage. 'But he said about me things that are not true, many things that are not true. In fact, he slandered me to my face. "Oh, you are going to testify and perform a heroic act of virtue, you are going to tell the court that it was you who murdered your father, that the lackey killed him on your instigation . . ."'

'Brother,' Alyosha cut in, 'control yourself: it was not you who killed him. That is a falsehood!'

'He says it, he, and he knows this: "You are going to perform a heroic act of virtue, yet in virtue you do not believe — that is what torments you and angers you, that is why you are so vengeful." That was what he has been saying about me, and he knows what he is saying . . .'

'It is you that says it, not he!' Alyosha exclaimed sorrowfully, 'and you say it in delirium, tormenting yourself!'

'No, he knows what he is saying. "You are going to testify out of pride, you will stand there and say: 'It was I who murdered him, and why do you squirm with horror, you are lying! I despise your opinion, I despise your horror.'" He says that about me, and then he suddenly says: "And you know, you want them to praise you: 'He is a criminal, a murderer, but what magnanimous emotions, he wants to save his brother and has confessed!'" I mean, that is a lie, Alyosha!' Ivan exclaimed suddenly, his eyes beginning to flash. 'I do not want stinking shits to praise me! That was a slander, Alyosha, a slander, I swear it to you! For that I threw the tea-glass at him, and it smashed against his ugly snout.'

'Brother, please calm yourself — stop it!' Alyosha begged him.

'Yes, he knows how to torment, he is cruel,' Ivan continued, not listening. 'I always had a presentiment of why it was he came. "Even if it is true," he said, "that you were going to testify out of pride, you still hoped that Smerdyakov would be found guilty and sent to do penal servitude, that Mitya would be acquitted and that you will be condemned only *morally* (you know, he laughed at that point!), while other people would praise you. But now Smerdyakov is dead, has hanged himself — well, but now who at the trial will believe you alone? Yet you are going to testify, you are going to, going to all the same, you have decided that you will. Why, after this?" That is terrible, Alyosha, I cannot endure such questions. Who dares to ask me such questions?'

'Brother,' Alyosha broke in, stock-still with terror, yet in spite of it as though he had some hope of bringing Ivan to reason, 'how could he have told you that Smerdyakov was dead before I got here, when no one yet knew of it and indeed there had been no time for anyone to learn of it?'

'He told me,' Ivan pronounced firmly, permitting no doubt. 'That was all he spoke of, if you like. "One could understand it," he said, "if you believed in virtue: 'I don't care if they don't believe me, I am going to testify out of principle.' But I mean, you are a sucking-pig, like Fyodor Pavlovich, and what is virtue to you? Why are you going to drag yourself off to that court, if your sacrifice will serve no purpose? Because you yourself do not know why you are going there! Oh, you would give a lot to know why you are going there! You think you have taken a decision to? No, you have not yet taken any decision. You are going to sit up all night trying to decide whether you should go or not. But in the end you will go and will know that you are going, you know that whatever you try to decide, the decision does not depend on you. You will go because you do not dare not to. Why you do not dare — fathom that for yourself, there is a riddle for you!" And he got up and left. You arrived, and he left. He called me a coward, Alyosha! *Le mot de l'énigme*, that I am a coward! "It is not for such eagles to go soaring above the earth!" He added that, he added that! And Smerdyakov said the same thing, too. He ought to be killed! Katya views me with contempt, I have noticed it for a month now, and Liza will soon be the same! "You are going to testify so that people will praise you" — that is a bestial lie! You also have contempt for me, Alyosha. Now I am beginning to hate you again. And I hate that vicious monster, too, I hate the monster, too! I don't want to rescue the monster, let him rot in penal servitude! He struck up the hymn, so let him sing it! Oh, tomorrow I will go and testify, I will stand before them all and spit in their faces!'

He leapt up in a frenzy, threw the towel from his head and began again to pace about the room. Alyosha recalled his brother's earlier words: 'It is as though I were asleep and yet awake . . . I walk about, I can talk and see . . . yet I'm asleep.' Precisely the same thing seemed to be taking place right now. Alyosha stayed with him. He had at first had the notion of running to fetch the doctor, but he was afraid to leave his brother on his own: there was no one at all to whom he could entrust him. At last Ivan gradually began to lose consciousness altogether. He continued to speak, spoke incessantly, but now with complete incoherence. His words were even slurred, and then suddenly where he stood he gave a violent lurch. Alyosha was, however, in time to support him. Ivan allowed himself to be led over to the bed, Alyosha somehow managed to get his clothes off and make him lie down. He remained sitting over him for another hour or two. The sick man slept deeply, without movement, his breath coming quietly and evenly. Alyosha picked up a pillow and lay down on the sofa without undressing. As he fell asleep he prayed for Mitya and for Ivan. Ivan's illness was becoming comprehensible to him: 'The torments of a proud decision; a conscience that is deep!' The God in whom he did not believe, together with the truth, had conquered his heart, which still did not want to submit. 'Yes,' rushed through Alyosha's head, which was by now resting on the pillow, 'yes, if Smerdyakov is dead, then no one will believe Ivan's testimony; but he will go and testify all the same!' Alyosha smiled quietly: 'God will prevail!' he thought. 'Either he will rise up in the light of truth, or . . . perish in hatred, taking vengeance on himself and on everyone else for his having served that in which he does not believe,' Alyosha added bitterly, and again he said a prayer for Ivan.

Book XII

A Judicial Error

I

The Fateful Day

At ten o'clock in the morning of the day that followed the events I have described, the session of our circuit court was opened, and there began the trial of Dmitry Karamazov.

I shall say in advance, and say it with insistence: I consider it far from being within my powers to relate everything that took place at the trial, and not only with due completeness, but even in due sequence. It appears to me, none the less, that were I to recollect everything and elucidate it all in proper fashion, an entire book would be required, and even an exceedingly large one. Let not, therefore, the complaint be made against me that I relate only that which struck me personally and was the object of my particular recollection. It is possible that I have mistaken the secondary for the primary, have even totally omitted the most clear-cut and most essential details . . . As a matter of fact, however, I perceive that it is better not to make excuses. I shall do what I am able, and readers themselves will realize that I have done only that.

And in the first place, before we enter the court chamber, I shall mention the thing that particularly struck me that day. As a matter of fact, it struck not only me but, as it subsequently turned out, everyone else as well. Namely: everyone knew that this case had begun to interest all too many people, that everyone was burning with impatience for the trial to start, that within the social circles of our town much had already been said, supposed, exclaimed and dreamed for a whole two months now. Everyone also knew that this case had received publicity throughout all Russia, yet even so no one had imagined that it could have shaken each and everyone to such a burning, such an irritable degree, and not only in our town, but universally, as it turned out at the trial itself on that day. Guests had come travelling to us especially for this day not only from our local provincial capital, but from several other towns of Russia as well, and also from Moscow and St Petersburg. Legal experts arrived, as did even one or two persons of the aristocracy, and also ladies. All the tickets had been snapped up. For the particularly honoured and aristocratic male visitors seats of quite an extraordinary kind had even been especially provided at the very table where the members of the tribunal sat: there had appeared an entire row of armchairs occupied by various personages, something which had never been permitted among us before. There turned out to be particularly many ladies, both from our town and from elsewhere, constituting, I believe, not less than half of the entire public. Of visiting legal experts alone there proved to be so many that the authorities were positively at a loss as to where to put them, as all the tickets had long ago been begged, dispensed and solicited. I myself saw a special enclosure which had been erected in hasty and temporary fashion behind the platform at the end of the chamber, and into which all the visiting legal experts were admitted, considering themselves fortunate to be able to stand there, for in order to save space the chairs had been entirely removed from the said enclosure, and the entire assembled multitude stood throughout the whole 'case' in a densely packed mass, shoulder to shoulder. Some of the ladies, particularly the ones who had come from elsewhere, appeared in the gallery of the chamber dressed in exceptional finery, but the majority of the ladies had even forgotten about finery. On their faces one could read a hysterical, avid, almost morbid curiosity. One of the most characteristic peculiarities of all this company that had assembled in the chamber, and one which it is essential to note, was that, as was later confirmed by many observations, almost all the ladies, at any rate a most enormous majority of them, supported Mitya and favoured his acquittal. The principal reason for this was possibly the fact that there had been formed about him the notion that he was a conqueror of female hearts. It was known that two women who were rivals were to appear. One of them, Katerina Ivanovna, was of particular interest to them all: concerning her there were exceptionally many unusual stories, and about her passion for Mitya, even in spite of his crime, astonishing anecdotes were related. Particular mention was made of her pride (she had made social visits to practically no one in our town), of her 'aristocratic connections'. It was said that she planned to ask the government to permit her to accompany the criminal into penal servitude and be married to him somewhere in the mines, underground. With no less excitement did they await the appearance in the court of Grushenka, in her capacity of Katerina Ivanovna's rival. With agonizing curiosity did they await the meeting, before the court, of the two rivals – the proud, aristocratic girl and the 'hetaera'; Grushenka was, as a matter of fact, better known to our ladies than Katerina Ivanovna. She, 'the destructress of Fyodor Pavlovich and his unhappy son', our ladies had seen before, and all of them, almost to a woman, were astonished that father and son could have become to such a degree enamoured of such 'a very ordinary, even quite unattractive Russian artisan's daughter'. In a word, there were many rumours. I have positive knowledge that in our town alone there even occurred some serious family quarrels because of Mitya. Many ladies quarrelled violently with their spouses because of a difference of views about this dreadful case, and it was natural that thereafter all the husbands of these ladies appeared in the chamber of the court not only ill-disposed towards the defendant, but even boiling with resentment towards him. Indeed, it can on the whole be positively stated that, in contradistinction to the lady element, the entire male element was inclined against the defendant. Stern, frowning faces were seen, others even openly hostile, and these in large numbers. It is also true that Mitya had succeeded in offending many of them personally during his sojourn among us. Of course, some of the visitors were almost even prone to levity and were really quite indifferent to Mitya's fate, though not, it should be said, to the case under examination; all were preoccupied with its outcome, and the majority of the men unequivocally desired retribution for the criminal, except perhaps the legal experts, who cherished not the moral side of the case, but only, as it were, its relevance in terms of contemporary jurisprudence. All were excited by the arrival of the celebrated Fetyukovich. His talent was universally known, and this was not the first occasion on which he had appeared in the provinces to defend a much-bruited criminal case. After he had defended them, such cases invariably became famous all over Russia and were remembered long afterwards. Several anecdotes concerning our public procurator and the chairman of the court were also in circulation. It was related that our public procurator trembled before his meeting with Fetyukovich, that they had been old enemies ever since their St Petersburg days, and the beginning of their careers, that our vain Ippolit Kirillovich, who had constantly believed himself to be discriminated against by someone ever since his time in St Petersburg, on the grounds that his talents had not been properly appreciated, had found his spirits resurrected in connection with the Karamazov case and even hoped to resurrect his faded career by means of that case, except that Fetyukovich was intimidating him. With regard to his trembling before Fetyukovich, however, these opinions were not quite correct. Our public procurator was not by character one of those whose spirits fail them in the face of danger, but on the contrary one of those whose vanity increases and takes wing precisely to the extent of the increasing danger. In general it should be noted that by nature our public procurator was excessively hot-tempered and morbidly susceptible. Into certain cases he put his entire soul, conducting them as though upon his decision the whole of his fate and the whole of his fortune depended. In the world of jurisprudence this attracted some mirth, for by this very quality of his our public procurator had even earned a certain renown, if far from universal, then yet far greater than might have been supposed in view of his modest position in our court. Especial mirth was aroused by his passion for psychology. In my opinion, all were mistaken: it seems to me that both as man and as character our public procurator was far more serious than many people thought. The trouble was that he had failed to establish himself as such, this morbidly afflicted man, with his very first steps at the very beginning of his career, and thereupon subsequently for the whole of the rest of his life. As for the chairman of our court, I can say of him no more than that he was a man of progressive education and humanity, who was familiar with the practical aspects of his office and the most contemporary ideas. He was rather vain, but did not lose much sleep over his career. His principal aim in life was to be a man of progress. Anyway, he had connections and a private fortune. Of the Karamazov case he took, as it subsequently proved, a rather excitable view, but only in a general sense. What engaged him was the phenomenon as such, its classification, the view of it as a product of our social principles, as a characterization of the Russian *Element*, etcetera, etcetera. Towards the personal character of the case, towards its tragic nature, as well as towards the personalities of the individuals who were involved, especially the defendant, his attitude was one of a rather abstract indifference – as, indeed, was perhaps proper.

Long before the appearance of the tribunal, the chamber was crammed to overflowing. Our chamber of sessions is the best auditorium to be found in our town, being spacious, high-ceilinged and endowed with a good resonance. To the right of the members of the tribunal, who were accommodated at a certain elevation, a table and two rows of armed wooden chairs had been provided for the jury. To the left were the places of the defendant and his counsel. In the centre of the chamber, near the location of the tribunal, stood a table of 'material evidence'. On it lay the bloodied white silk dressing-gown of Fyodor Pavlovich, the fateful brass pestle with which the presumed murder had been accomplished, Mitya's shirt with its blood-bespattered sleeve, the frock-coat, entirely covered in bloody stains behind at the site of the pocket into which that day he had stuffed his handkerchief, sopping wet with blood, the handkerchief itself, now quite stiff with blood that had turned brown, the pistol which Mitya had loaded at the home of Perkhotin for the purpose of his suicide and which Trifon Borisovich had taken from him on the sly in Mokroye, the envelope with the inscription in which Grushenka's three thousand had been kept in readiness, the slender pink ribbon in which it had been tied, and various other objects I do not recall. At some remove, further off into the depths of the chamber, began the seating for the public, though in front of the balustrade there were also some armed chairs for those witnesses who, after they had given their testimony, would be kept within the chamber. At ten o'clock the tribunal appeared, consisting of the chairman, a magistrate and an honorary Justice of the Peace. At once the public procurator also naturally appeared. The chairman was a stocky, thick-set man, of less than average height, with a haemorrhoidal complexion; he was aged about fifty, had dark hair, cut short, in which there were streaks of grey, and wore a red ribbon − of which decoration I now forget. As for the public procurator, it seemed to me, and not only to me, but to everyone else as well, that he was somehow very pale, his face almost green in colour, apparently as though he had lost a great deal of weight in the space of a single night, for I had seen him only two days earlier, and then he had been every bit his normal self. The chairman began by asking the bailiff whether all the members of the jury were present . . . I perceive, however, that I am unable to continue in this fashion, for the reason that there were many things that I simply could not hear, while others I missed or failed to grasp, and yet others I have forgotten to mention; the principal reason, though, being that, as I earlier observed, were I to recollect everything that was said and took place, I should quite literally have an insufficiency both of time and of space. All I know for certain is that neither by the one side nor the other, those, that is to say, of the defence counsel and the public procurator respectively, were many of the jurymen challenged. I do, however, recall the composition of the jury: four of our local civil servants, two merchants and six peasants and artisans of our town. There were in our social circles, particularly among the ladies, those who long before the trial had asked with a certain astonishment: 'Can it really be that such a sensitive, complex and psychologically involved case is to be given up to the decision of some government clerks and, when all is said and done, muzhiks, and what will a government clerk understand of it all, let alone a muzhik?' Indeed, all four civil servants who had ended up in the jury were minor functionaries, of lowly rank and grizzled hair − only one of them was somewhat younger − little-known in our social circles, having vegetated on meagre salaries, doubtless with aged wives with whom it would be impossible for them to appear in public, and each with a whole heap of children who were even quite possibly barefoot louts who at the very most passed their leisure hours with wretched games of cards and had, of course, never read a single book. As for the two merchants, though they had a sedate look, they were somehow strangely silent and unmoving; one of them was shaven and dressed in German style; the other, with a small, greying beard, wore round his neck some kind of medal on a red ribbon. Of the artisans and peasants there is not much that need be said. Our Skotoprigonyevsk artisans are practically the same as peasants, and even drive the plough. Two of them were also dressed in German style and perhaps for that very reason looked dirtier and more unprepossessing than the other four. As a result, it was indeed all too easy to be visited by the thought, as I myself was visited by it as soon as I had had a proper look at them: 'What can men like those comprehend of a case like this?' Even so, their faces produced a strangely imposing and almost menacing impression, stern and frowning.

At last the chairman opened the hearing of the case of the murder of the retired titular councillor Fyodor Pavlovich Karamazov – I do not remember quite how he put it that day. The bailiff was instructed to bring in the defendant, and then Mitya appeared. A hush descended on the chamber, one could have heard a fly. I do not know how others reacted, but the sight of Mitya impressed me most disagreeably. Above all, he arrived looking the most dreadful dandy, wearing a brand-new frock-coat. I later discovered that he had ordered the frock-coat especially for this day from his old tailor in Moscow, who still had his size. He wore brand-new kid gloves and a dandified shirt, collar and cuffs. With his long, arshin-spaced strides he marched in, looking directly, almost fixedly, before him, and sat down in his place with a most dauntless air. At once and without delay his defence counsel, the celebrated Fetyukovich, also came in, and a kind of suppressed rumble passed through the chamber. This was a long, dried-up man with long, thin legs, exceedingly long, pale, thin fingers, his face clean-shaven, with hair that was modestly brushed and rather short, and thin lips that were from time distorted by something halfway between a jeer and a smile. He must, by the look of him, have been about forty. His face would have been pleasant enough, had it not been for his eyes, which, though small and inexpressive in themselves, were set extraordinarily close to one another, separated only by the thin bone of his thin, oblong nose. In a word, this physiognomy had about it something sharply bird-like, that struck one. He was in coat and tails, and wore a white tie. I recall the chairman's opening interrogation of Mitya, concerning his name, rank, etcetera. Mitya delivered his replies in a voice that was curt, but somehow unexpectedly loud, so that the chairman even jerked his head up and looked at him almost with surprise. After that a list of the persons who had been summoned to the judicial proceedings was read out – the witnesses and experts, in other words. The list was a long one; four of the witnesses were not present: Miusov, who was by now in Paris, but whose deposition had been obtained at the time of the preliminary investigation, Mrs Khokhlakova and the landowner Maksimov because of illness and Smerdyakov because of his sudden death, concerning which a police report was submitted. The news about Smerdyakov provoked a violent commotion and whispering in the chamber. There were of course many in the public who as yet knew nothing at all of this sudden episode that had involved his suicide. What they found particularly shocking, however, was Mitya's sudden outlandish behaviour: no sooner had the news concerning Smerdyakov been announced than he suddenly from his place exclaimed to the whole chamber:

'To a dog the death of a dog!'

I recall that his defence counsel went rushing to his side and that the chairman addressed him with a warning that severe measures would be taken were outlandishness of this kind to be repeated. Mitya nodded his head and abruptly told his defence counsel several times, though not at all as though he felt the slightest contrition:

'I won't do it again, I won't do it again! It just came out! I won't do it again!'

And, I need hardly add, this brief episode did not work in his favour with the opinion of the jury and the public. His character had declared itself and provided its own introduction. It was under the influence of this impression that the referring clerk read out the bill of indictment.

It was rather brief, but thorough. Only the principal reasons why the said person had been brought to court, why he was to be tried, and so on, were listed. None the less, it made a strong impression on me. The referring clerk read out the document clearly, resonantly and distinctly. The whole of that tragedy seemed once again to appear before all present in vivid, concentrated manner, illumined by a fateful and inexorable light. I recall that immediately after the document had been read out the chairman of the court asked Mitya loudly and imposingly:

'Prisoner at the bar, do you or do you not plead guilty?'

Mitya suddenly rose from his seat:

'I plead guilty to drunkenness and depravity,' he exclaimed, again in a voice that was somehow unexpectedly loud, almost frenzied, 'to laziness and debauchery. I wanted to become an honourable man for ever at the very second I was cut down by fate! But of the death of the old man, my enemy and father – I am not guilty! Of having robbed him – no, no, I am not guilty, and I cannot be: Dmitry Karamazov is a scoundrel, but not a thief!'

Having shouted this out, he sat down again, apparently shaking all over. The chairman again addressed him with a brief but admonitory exhortation to reply only to the questions, and not to launch upon irrelevant and frenzied exclamations; whereupon he ordered that the proceedings should begin. All the witnesses were brought in to take the oath. At this point I had a view of them all together. As a matter of fact, the brothers of the defendant were permitted to give testimony without taking the oath. Following an exhortation by the chairman and a priest, the witnesses were led away and kept separate from one another as far as was possible. After that they began to be summoned out one by one.

2

Dangerous Witnesses

I do not know whether the public procurator's witnesses and those for the defence had been divided by the chairman into any kind of groups, nor whether there was any precise order in which it was proposed to call them. Such arrangements must, I think, have existed. All I know is that the public procurator's witnesses were the first to be called. I repeat: I do not intend to describe the whole of the questioning, step by step. In any case, my description would prove to be in part superfluous, for in the speeches of the public procurator and the defence, when they began their pleadings, the entire trend and implication of all the facts and heard testimony became, as it were, focused upon a single point with brilliant and characteristic illumination, and those two remarkable speeches I, at least in places, noted down in completeness, and shall relate them in due course, together with a certain extraordinary and quite unexpected episode in the course of the hearing which broke out suddenly even before the judicial pleadings and undoubtedly influenced its grim and fateful outcome. I shall observe only that from the very first moments of the trial there emerged a peculiar characteristic of this 'case', one that was observed by all, to wit: the unusual strength of the prosecution by comparison with the resources available to the defence. Everyone realized this at the very first instant the facts began, by a process of concentration, to marshal themselves in this grim court chamber and by degrees all that horror and all that blood started to come to light. It is possible that everyone began to realize from the very first steps that this was not even in any way a case about which there was any dispute, that here there could be no doubts, that, in essence, no pleadings were really necessary, that the pleadings would be only a formality and that the defendant was guilty, manifestly and irrevocably guilty. I even think that all the ladies, every single one of them, a-thirst as they were with such impatience for the acquittal of the 'interesting' defendant, were at the same time quite convinced of his complete and utter guilt. Not only that: it seems to me that they would even have been upset were his guilt not to have been so confirmed, for then the denouement, when the defendant was actually acquitted, would lose much of its effect. That he would be acquitted – of that, strange to relate, all the ladies were irrevocably convinced almost until the very last moment: 'He is guilty, but he will be acquitted on grounds of humanity, of the new ideas, the new emotions that are now about,' etcetera, etcetera. It was for that very reason that they had come running here with such impatience. As for the men, they were mainly interested in the battle between the public procurator and the renowned Fetyukovich. They all felt astonishment, wondering what even a celebrated talent like Fetyukovich could make of such a hopeless case, of such a scooped-out egg, and therefore followed his heroic endeavours with strained attention, every step of the way. But right to the end, until his speech, Fetyukovich kept them all guessing. Those with some experience in these matters had a feeling that he possessed some system, that some predetermined notion had already formed within his brain, that before him lay a purpose, but what it was – that was almost impossible to divine. His assurance and extreme self-confidence were, however, blatantly obvious. What was more, all instantly noticed with satisfaction that in the course of his brief sojourn among us, a mere matter of some three days, perhaps, he had familiarized himself with the case to an astonishing degree and had 'studied it in the most slender detail'. It was, for example, afterwards related with pleasure how at opportune moments he had succeeded in leading all the public procurator's witnesses 'up the garden path', doing all that was possible to confuse them, and above all to tarnish their moral reputations, thereby automatically tarnishing their evidence. It was, as a matter of fact, supposed that he did this at the very most as a kind of game, for the sake, as it were, of a certain juridical virtuosity, in order to leave out none of the accepted methods of advocacy: for all were convinced that by all these 'tarnishings' he could obtain no great or lasting advantage and that he probably realized this better than any of them, having some idea in reserve, some as yet concealed weapon of defence which he would suddenly reveal when the moment arrived. For the time being, however, conscious of his strength, he was, as it were, playing games and enjoying himself. Thus, for example, when Grigory Vasilyevich, Fyodor Pavlovich's erstwhile valet, who had given the most capital testimony concerning the 'open door into the garden', the defence counsel fairly battened on to him when it was his turn to put questions. It should be noted that Grigory Vasilyevich made his appearance in the chamber without being in the slightest intimidated by the grandeur of the proceedings or the presence of the enormous public that was listening to him, and wore an aspect that was calm and very nearly majestic. He gave his testimony with the same confidence with which he might have talked to his Marfa Ignatyevna when they were alone, only with more reverence. To confuse him was impossible. He was initially questioned for a long time by the public procurator concerning all the details of the Karamazov household. A picture of the family emerged with vivid clarity. It could be seen and heard that the witness was ingenuous and impartial. For all his most profound reverence for the memory of his former *barin*, he none the less declared, for example, that the latter had been unfair to Mitya and had 'brought his children up wrong. If it had not been for me the young boy would have had lice,' he added, while giving an account of Mitya's childhood years. 'It was also not right of the father to treat the son badly over the mother's family estate.' With regard to the public procurator's question as to what grounds he had for asserting that Fyodor Pavlovich had treated his son badly over the settlement, Grigory Vasilyevich, much to everyone's surprise, presented almost no firm evidence worth speaking of, yet none the less insisted that the settlement had been 'wrong' and that Fyodor Pavlovich 'ought to have given him a few thousand more'. I should observe, incidentally, that this question of whether Fyodor Pavlovich really had short-changed Mitya was later put by the public procurator with especial insistence to all those witnesses to whom he was able to put it, excluding neither Alyosha nor Ivan Fyodorovich, but not from a single one of them was any precise information obtained; all asserted it to be a fact, yet none was able to furnish definite proof of any kind. After Grigory had described the scene at table, when Dmitry Fyodorovich had burst in and beaten his father, threatening to return and kill him, a gloomy impression passed through the chamber, particularly as the old manservant described the event calmly and without superfluous words, in his own curious idiom, and the effect was one of extraordinary eloquence.

Concerning the injury done him by Mitya, who had struck him on the face and knocked him to the ground, he observed that he felt no anger over it and had long forgiven it. Of the deceased Smerdyakov he expressed the opinion, crossing himself as he did so, that he had been a fellow of some ability, but stupid and plagued by illness, and an atheist, moreover, the atheism having been bred in him by Fyodor Pavlovich and his eldest son. Concerning Smerdyakov's honesty, however, he confirmed at once and almost with heat that Smerdyakov, at that 'certain time' when he had found the money the *barin* had dropped, had not hidden it away but taken it to the *barin*, who had 'given him a gold 'un' and henceforth began to trust him in everything. As to the door into the garden, he confirmed with stubborn insistence that it had been open. As a matter of fact, so many questions were put to him that I am unable to recollect them all. At last the questioning passed to the defence counsel, and he began as a matter of the first priority to inquire about the envelope in which 'it would appear' Fyodor Pavlovich had kept three thousand roubles for 'a certain lady person'. 'Did you see it yourself – you, a servant who were so close to your *barin* for so many years?' Grigory replied that he had not, and had not even heard anyone mention such money 'until the very time when all did start to speak of it'. This question about the envelope Fetyukovich for his part also put to all those witnesses to whom he was able to put it, with the same insistence that the public procurator had put his question concerning the division of the estate, and likewise received from them all the reply that none had seen the envelope, though very many had heard of it. The defence counsel's insistence on this question was noticed by everyone right from the outset.

'May I now, with your permission, put to you the following question?' Fetyukovich said suddenly and quite unexpectedly. 'Of what did that balsam or, so to speak, liqueur consist, with which, as is clear from the preliminary investigation, you rubbed your afflicted back that evening before you went to sleep, hoping thereby to make it better?'

Grigory looked at his questioner dully and then, after remaining silent for a time, muttered:

'There was sage in it.'

'Only sage? Can you remember if there was anything else?'

'There was plantain, too.'

'And pepper, perhaps?' Fetyukovich asked with curiosity.

'Yes, pepper as well.'

'And so on, etcetera. And all of it in vodka?'

'No, in raw spirit.'

A barely perceptible titter passed through the chamber.

'You see – in raw spirit, even. Having rubbed your back, you were then, I believe, so inclined as to drink the remaining contents of the bottle, while a certain devout prayer, known only to your spouse, was said?'

'That is correct.'

'How much did you drink, would you say, at a guess? A liqueur-glass or two?'

'I must have had a tumbler of it.'

'A tumbler of it, even. Perhaps even a tumbler and a half?'

Grigory fell silent. It was as if he had realized something.

'A tumbler and a half of pure raw spirit – now, that is a rather handsome thing, would you not agree? One might behold "doors opened on heaven",* never mind one into a garden, might one not?'

Grigory remained silent. Another titter passed through the chamber. The chairman made a slight movement.

'Can you say for certain,' said Fetyukovich, sinking his claws deeper and deeper, 'whether you were asleep or not at the moment you saw the open door into the garden?'

'I was on my feet.'

'That is not quite proof that you were not asleep' (more and more tittering in the chamber). 'Would you, for example, have been capable of answering if someone had asked you a question – well, for example, what year it is now?'

'That I do not know.'

'Oh come – what year is it now, Anno Domini, since the birth of Christ, do you not know?'

Grigory stood with a bewildered look, gazing steadily at his tormentor. It evidently did seem strange that he did not know what year it was.

'Well, perhaps you know how many fingers you have?'

'I am a dependant,' Grigory said suddenly in a loud, distinct voice, 'and if the powers that be wish to make mock of me, then I must endure it.'

This seemed to cause Fetyukovich to backstep slightly, but the chairman, too, joined in the fray and delivered an exhortatory reminder to the defence counsel that he ought to ask questions that were more appropriate. Fetyukovich listened, bowed with dignity, and announced that his questioning of the witness was at an end. It was, of course, possible that both among the jury and the members of the public there had remained a tiny worm of doubt concerning the testimony of a man who had had the opportunity of 'beholding a door into heaven' while in a certain condition of medical treatment and who was, moreover, even ignorant of what year it was since the birth of Christ, with the result that the defence counsel attained his purpose all the same. Before Grigory withdrew, however, another episode took place. The chairman, turning to the defendant, inquired if he had any comments to make concerning the testimony that had just been given.

'Apart from the bit about the door, everything he said was true,' Mitya exclaimed loudly. 'For combing away my lice – I thank him, for forgiving me the blows I gave him – I thank him; the old man has been honest all his life and as faithful to my father as seven hundred poodles.'

'Prisoner, choose your words with more caution,' the chairman said sternly.

'I am not a poodle,' Grigory, too, complained.

'If anyone is a poodle, it is I!' cried Mitya. 'If that is an insult, then I take it upon myself, and I ask his forgiveness: I behaved like a wild beast and treated him cruelly! I was also cruel to Aesop.'

'Who is Aesop?' the chairman again raised sternly.

'Oh, that Pierrot . . . my father, Fyodor Pavlovich.'

The chairman once more and in no uncertain terms told Mitya, most sternly and imposingly, that he should choose his expressions with more care.

'By behaving this way you are harming yourself in the opinion of your judges.'

In his questioning of the witness Rakitin, the defence counsel also deployed his resources with precisely the same considerable skill. I should observe that Rakitin was a most important witness, and one whom the public procurator undoubtedly valued greatly. It turned out that Rakitin knew everything, knew an extraordinary amount, had been to visit everyone, seen everything, spoken to everyone, and possessed a most detailed knowledge of the biography of Fyodor Pavlovich and all the Karamazovs. To be sure, he had also heard about the envelope containing the three thousand only from Mitya. On the other hand, he gave a detailed account of Mitya's exploits in the Capital City inn, described all his compromising words and gestures, and related the story of the 'loofah' of Second-Grade Captain Snegiryov. With regard to the particular point concerning whether Fyodor Pavlovich owed anything to Mitya on the settlement of the estate, not even Rakitin was able to provide any indication and merely talked himself out of it with general remarks of a contemptuous nature, such as: 'Who could have fathomed which of them was guilty or which of them owed the other anything, in the face of all that crazy Karamazov behaviour, of which no one could make any sense whatsoever?' The entire tragedy of the case being tried he depicted merely as the product of the inveterate usages of serfdom and of a Russia that was sunk in disorder, suffering in the absence of proper institutions. In a word, he was given an opportunity to express a number of opinions. It was with this trial that Mr Rakitin for the first time announced his presence and came to public notice; the public procurator knew that the witness was writing an article for a journal concerning the present case and later on, in his speech (as we shall see in what follows), adduced several of the ideas in that article, showing that he was already familiar with it. The picture painted by the witness was a dire and gloomy one, and it lent great support to the case of 'the prosecution'. On the whole, indeed, Rakitin's arguments captivated the public with their independence of thought and the unusual nobility of their flight. There were even two or three bursts of sudden clapping, these being heard at the point where mention was made of serfdom and of Russia's suffering because of a lack of social discipline. But Rakitin, being still, after all, a young man, made a small error of judgement which the defence counsel at once turned to excellent advantage. While replying to certain questions concerning Grushenka, still carried away by his success of which, naturally, he himself was aware, and by that elevation of noble feeling at which he had soared, he took the liberty of referring to Agrafena Aleksandrovna somewhat contemptuously as 'the merchant Samsonov's kept woman'. He would subsequently have given much in order to take back that small remark, for Fetyukovich at once caught him out over it. And all because Rakitin had never dreamed that the latter could within such a short time have managed to acquire a familiarity with the case that took in such intimate details.

'Permit me to know,' the defence counsel began with a most cordial and even deferential smile, when it came to his turn to put questions. 'You are, are you not, that same Mr Rakitin whose booklet, *The Life of the Sleeping in God the Elder the Father Zosima*, published by the Eparchial See, full of profound, religious ideas and containing an excellent and pious dedication to His Grace, which I recently read with such pleasure?'

'I did not write it to be published . . . it was published later,' Rakitin muttered, as though suddenly caught off guard and almost in shame.

'Oh, that is wonderful! A thinker such as yourself is able, and even duty-bound, to address all social phenomena on the very broadest footing. With the patronage of His Grace your most useful booklet has sold out, and has been of unquestionable benefit . . . But now there is one thing which, above all, I should be curious to learn from you: I believe you said just now that you have been very closely acquainted with Miss Svetlova?' (*Nota bene*: Grushenka's last name turned out to be 'Svetlova'. This I discovered for the first time only that day, during the progress of the trial.)

'I cannot answer for all my acquaintances . . . I am a young man . . . and who can answer for all the people he encounters?' Rakitin said, blushing scarlet all over.

'I understand, I understand only too well!' Fetyukovich exclaimed, as though he were himself embarrassed and were hurrying to make an impetuous apology. 'You, just like any other man, might in your turn be interested in the acquaintance of a young and attractive woman who was readily willing to receive the flower of our local youth, but . . . I merely wished to inquire: you see, we know that about two months ago Svetlova had very much wished to make the acquaintance of the youngest Karamazov, Aleksey Fyodorovich, and simply for bringing him to her, and namely in the monk's attire which he wore at the time, she promised to give you twenty-five roubles as soon as you delivered him. This, as we know, took place on the evening of the day that ended with the tragic catastrophe that has served as the grounds for the present case. Did you take Aleksey Karamazov to Miss Svetlova – and did you then receive a payment of twenty-five roubles from her? That is what I should like to hear from you.'

'It was a joke . . . I do not see why you should be interested in that. I took the money in jest . . . intending to pay it back later . . .'

'So you did take it, then. Yet as far as we are aware, you have not yet given it back . . . or have you?'

'This is a triviality . . .' Rakitin muttered. 'I cannot answer such questions . . . Of course I shall give it back.'

At this point the chairman stepped in, but the defence counsel announced that he had finished his questions to Mr Rakitin. Mr Rakitin left the stage somewhat tarnished. The effect produced by the most lofty nobility of his speech had, after all, been spoiled, and Fetyukovich, as he followed him with his eyes, seemed to be saying, as he pointed him out to the public: 'There, such are your noble accusers!' I recall that even this stage of the proceedings did not pass without an episode on Mitya's part: driven to wild fury by the tone in which Rakitin had spoken of Grushenka, he suddenly shouted from his place: 'Bernard!' And when the chairman, upon the conclusion of Rakitin's questioning, turned to the defendant and asked him whether he wished to make any comments of his own, Mitya shouted in a booming voice:

'He's been trying to borrow money from me even while I've been in prison! He's a despicable Bernard and a careerist and he doesn't believe in God, he tricked His Grace!'

Mitya was, of course, again brought to reason on account of the violence of his expressions, but Mr Rakitin had been dealt the final blow. The testimony of Second-Grade Captain Snegiryov fared little better, but for quite another reason. He appeared before the court dressed in dirty clothing that was worn to tatters, dirty boots and, in spite of all the precautions and preliminary 'expert medical examination', suddenly turned out to be completely and utterly drunk. To the questions concerning the insult that had been wrought on him by Mitya, he suddenly refused to answer.

'God be with him, sir. My little Ilyusha forbade me to. God will grant me recompense there yonder, sir.'

'Who has forbidden you to speak? To whom are you referring?'

'Ilyushechka, my little son: "Papa, papa, how he humiliated you!" By the stone he said it. Now he is dying, sir . . .'

The second-grade captain suddenly began to sob, and fell heavily to his knees before the chairman. He was quickly ushered away, to the laughter of the public. The impression the public procurator had worked to create did not materialize at all.

The defence counsel, on the other hand, continued to deploy all the resources at his disposal and caused greater and greater astonishment by his familiarity with the very finest details of the case. Thus, for example, the testimony of Trifon Borisovich began to produce a most powerful effect and was, of course, extremely inauspicious for Mitya. For he calculated, very nearly on his fingers, that during his first visit to Mokroye a month before the catastrophe, Mitya had spent no less than three thousand or 'very, very near it. On those gypsy girls alone how much he threw away! And as for our louse-ridden muzhiks, it wasn't "fifty copecks on the street" he had thrown them, but at least twenty-five-rouble notes. And how much they quite simply stole from him that night, sir! And I mean, them that stole, they didn't leave their hands behind, and how could they be caught, the thieves, sir, when his honour himself was throwing all that money around? I mean, our folk are robbers, they've no concern for their souls. And how much went on our wenches, our village wenches! I tell you, sir, folk have gotten rich here since that night — before there was naught but poverty.' In a word, he recollected each expenditure and totted it all up as on a counting-frame. Thus the notion that only fifteen hundred roubles had been spent, the rest having been put away in the incense-bag, became inconceivable. 'I saw it myself, I saw him holding three thousand as if it was a single copeck piece, with my own eyes I beheld it, and surely I should know how much it was, sir!' Trifon Borisovich exclaimed, trying with all his might to oblige the 'powers that be'. But when the questioning passed to the defence counsel, the latter, almost without attempting to refute the man's testimony, suddenly brought up the subject of how in Mokroye, during that first spree, a month before the arrest, the *yamshchik* Timofey and another muzhik, Akim, had, on the floor of the outside passage, found a hundred roubles which Mitya had dropped while in a state of intoxication, and had presented it to Trifon Borisovich, who had given them each a rouble reward. 'Well, so did you return that hundred roubles to Mr Karamazov that night, or did you not?' No matter how Trifon Borisovich tried to get out of it, after the muzhiks had been questioned he confessed to having taken the hundred roubles, merely adding that he had scrupulously returned and entrusted all the money to Dmitry Fyodorovich that night 'out of pure honesty, though I doubt if his honour, being so drunk at the time, sir, would be able to remember it now'. But as before the muzhiks had been summoned as witnesses he had denied the existence of the hundred roubles' windfall, his statement that he had returned the sum to the intoxicated Mitya was naturally laid open to grave doubt. Thus again, one of the most dangerous witnesses put forward by the procurator's office left the stand under a cloud of suspicion and with his reputation badly tarnished. The same thing also happened with the Poles: they appeared in court proud and independent. They loudly testified that, in the first place, they both 'served the Crown', that 'Pan Mitya' had offered them three thousand in an attempt to buy their honour, and that they themselves had seen a large sum of money in his hands. Pan Musialowicz inserted a fearful number of Polish words into his sentences and, when he perceived that this only elevated him in the eyes of the chairman and the public procurator, at length felt his spirits elevated to such a degree that he began to speak entirely in Polish. But Fetyukovich caught them, too, in his snare: no matter how much the witness Trifon Borisovich tried to get out of it, he had to admit that the pack of cards he had supplied had been substituted by Pan Wróblewski with his own, and the Pan Musialow- icz, while keeping the bank, had put in a false card. This was confirmed by Kalganov, who testified in his turn, and both *panowie* withdrew in a certain disgrace, even to laughter from the public.

Much the same thing subsequently occurred with nearly all the most dangerous witnesses. Fetyukovich was able to cast a moral smear upon them and dismiss them with a certain degree of indignity. The amateurs and legal experts merely gazed on in admiration and were again simply at a loss to understand what good and final purpose could be served by it all, for, I repeat, they all sensed the irrefutable nature of the charge, which increased more tragically with each moment. But from the self-confidence of the 'great wizard' they could see that he was calm, and waited: not in vain, after all, had 'such a man' come all the way from St Petersburg, and being 'such a man' he was not going to return there with nothing to show for it.

3

The Expert Medical Examination and One Pound of Nuts

THE expert medical examination was likewise not of much help to the defendant. Indeed, Fetyukovich himself, it seems, had not placed much reliance on it, as it proved subsequently. In essence it took place solely upon the insistence of Katerina Ivanovna, who had summoned the celebrated doctor especially from Moscow. The defence had, of course, nothing to lose by it, and in the best instance might even possibly gain by it. As a matter of fact, it resulted in an upshot that was even almost somewhat comic, because of a certain discordance of opinion among the doctors. The experts were the celebrated doctor from out of town, then our own Dr Herzenstube and, finally, the young physician Varvinsky. Both the latter also figured in the trial as ordinary witnesses called by the public procurator. The first to be questioned in the capacity of expert was Dr Herzenstube. He was an old man in his seventies, grey-haired and balding, of average height and sturdy constitution. Everyone in our town valued and respected him greatly. He was a conscientious physician, an excellent and pious man, some kind of Herrnhuter or 'Moravian Brother'* – I do not really know for certain. He had lived in our town for a very long time and comported himself with extreme dignity. He was kind and philanthropic, treated the poor who were sick and the peasants gratis, went into their hovels and *izbas* and left money for medicine, but was at the same time as stubborn as a mule. To get an idea out of his head once it had taken root there was impossible. Incidentally, nearly everybody in our town already knew that the famous visiting physician had during the two or three days of his sojourn among us permitted himself several extremely offensive remarks concerning the talents of Dr Herzenstube.

The fact was that though the Moscow physician charged for his visits no less than twenty-five roubles a time, several people in our town had been delighted at the opportunity afforded by his arrival, had not stinted with their money and gone rushing to consult him for advice. All these patients had, of course, been previously treated by Dr Herzenstube, and now the famous physician subjected his treatment, with extreme severity, to a universal criticism. At length, when presenting himself to these patients, he would bluntly inquire: 'Well, who's been making a mess of you here, then – Herzenstube? Heh-heh!' Dr Herzenstube had, of course, learned of all this. And now all three doctors appeared one after the other for questioning. Dr Herzenstube declared bluntly that 'the abnormality of the defendant's mental faculties lets itself be perceived of itself'. Subsequently, having presented his deliberations, which I shall omit here, he added that this abnormality chiefly let itself be perceived not only in many of the defendant's previous actions, but even now, at that very moment, and when he was asked to explain in what it could be perceived, at that very moment, the old doctor with all his bluntness of character indicated the fact that the defendant, when entering the chamber, 'had an unusual air, strange for the circumstances, strode forwards like a soldier, and kept his eyes in front of him fixed, while it would have been more correct for him to look to the left, where the ladies of the public were sitting, for he is a great admirer of the fair sex and must have been very much thinking about what the ladies would say of him now', the old fellow concluded in his original idiom. It should be added that he spoke the Russian language much and willingly, but somehow each sentence he uttered came out in the German manner, something which, as a matter of fact, caused him no embarrassment, for all his life it had been one of his foibles to consider the Russian he spoke as model in character, 'better than even the Russians speak', and was even very fond of resorting to Russian proverbs, asserting every time he did so that Russian proverbs were the best and most expressive of all the proverbs in the world. I should observe that in conversation, perhaps from some kind of absent-mindedness, he frequently forgot the most ordinary words, which he really knew perfectly well, but which for some reason would suddenly slip out of his mind. In fact, though, the same thing happened when he spoke German, and then he would wave his hand in front of his face as though seeking to catch hold of the lost word, and no one could have made him continue with what he had started to say until he had found it, that lost word. His observation regarding the idea that the defendant might have been expected, upon entering, to have looked at the ladies aroused a frivolous whisper in the public. Our old doctor was very well-liked by all the ladies in our town, and they also knew that he, a bachelor all his life, pious and chaste, looked upon women as ideal beings of a higher kind. This was why his unexpected observation seemed terribly strange to them all.

The doctor from Moscow, when in his turn he was questioned, brusquely and insistently confirmed that he believed the mental condition of the defendant to be abnormal, 'even in the highest degree'. He spoke much and cleverly of 'affect' and 'mania' and came to the conclusion that to judge by all the information that had been gathered the defendant had for several days before his arrest undoubtedly been in a state of morbid affect and that if he had committed the crime, though he might have been conscious of doing so, had nevertheless performed it almost involuntarily, being quite without strength to resist the morbid psychological inclination that had taken mastery of him. In addition to 'affect', however, the doctor also perceived mania, which already prophesied in advance, in his words, the straight road to complete insanity. (NB: I give my account in my own words; the doctor expressed himself in very learned and specialized language.) 'All his actions ran counter to logic and common sense,' he continued. 'I cannot speak of what I did not see, namely the crime itself and *toute cette catastrophe*, but even the day before yesterday, in the course of his conversation with me, his eyes had an unaccountable fixity in their gaze. His unexpected laughter, when it was quite out of place. His constant and incomprehensible irritation, the strange words he used: "Bernard", "ethics", and others similarly inapposite.' Especially did the doctor perceive this mania, however, in the fact that the defendant was even unable to speak of the three thousand roubles of which he considered himself to have been cheated without a kind of extraordinary irritation, while describing and recalling all his other failures and resentments quite easily. Indeed, according to certain information, he had on earlier occasions invariably, in precisely similar fashion, flown into a kind of frenzy whenever the subject of that three thousand had been raised; yet everyone testified of him that as a man he was without self-interest or money-grubbing. 'With regard to the opinion of my learned colleague,' the doctor from Moscow added ironically, bringing his speech to an end, 'that the defendant, upon entering the chamber, might have been expected to look at the ladies and not straight in front of him, I shall merely say that, quite apart from the frivolous nature of such a conclusion, it is also radically flawed; for, though I entirely agree that the defendant, upon entering the chamber of the court in which his fate was to be decided, might not have been expected to look so fixedly in front of him and that this might indeed be viewed as a symptom of his abnormal mental condition at that given moment, I none the less on the contrary assert that he might have been expected to look, not leftwards, at the ladies, but rather to the right, seeking the eyes of his defence counsel, in whose assistance his only hope now lies and on whose protection his entire fate now depends.' The doctor expressed his opinion decisively and insistently. But the discordance of opinion between the two learned experts was lent an especial comic pathos by the unexpected conclusion of the physician Varvinsky, who was questioned last of all. In his view, the defendant, now as earlier, was in a state that was completely normal, and though indeed he must before his arrest have been in a nervous and extremely agitated condition, the causes of this could have been many, and of the most obvious: jealousy, anger, a constantly drunken condition, etcetera. It was, however, impossible that this nervous state could have contained any particular element of the 'affect' that had just been mentioned. As for the question of whether the defendant might have been expected to look to the left or to the right upon entering the chamber, then, in his 'modest opinion', the defendant might have been expected, upon entering the chamber, to look straight before him, as indeed he had, for straight before him sat the chairman and the judges of the tribunal on whom his entire fate now depended, 'so that, by looking straight before him, he also proved the completely normal state of his mind at that given moment', the young physician said, concluding his 'modest' testimony with a certain degree of heat.

'Bravo, leech!' Mitya cried from his place. 'Precisely so!'

Mitya was, of course, silenced, but the opinion of the young physician had a most decisive influence on tribunal and public alike, for, as it proved subsequently, everyone agreed with him. As a matter of fact, Dr Herzenstube, questioned this time as a witness, suddenly and quite unexpectedly served Mitya's advantage. As an old resident of the town who had long known the Karamazov household, he gave several pieces of evidence that were of great interest to the 'prosecution' and suddenly, as though he had just realized something, added:

'Yet, you know, the poor young man might have had an incomparably better fate, for he was good of heart both in his boyhood and afterward, for I know that. The Russian proverb says, however: "If someone has one mind, then that is good, but if another clever man comes visiting, that is even better, for then there will be two minds, and not merely one . . ."'

'Yes, yes, two heads are better than one,' impatiently supplied the public procurator, who was long familiar with the old fellow's habit of talking slowly and at inordinate length, unembarrassed by the impression he made or by compelling everyone to wait for him but, on the contrary, greatly savouring his own slow, potato-like and always joyfully self-satisfied German wit. For the old fellow liked to coin witticisms.

'Oh, y-yes, that is what I am saying,' he continued stubbornly, 'one mind is good, but two are far better. But to him another mind did not come, and he sent his own mind . . . Now wait, where did he send it? That word – where did he send his mind, I have forgotten,' he continued, agitating his hand before his eyes. 'Ah yes, *spazieren*.'

'For a walk?'

'Yes, for a walk, that is what I am saying. Well, his mind went off for a walk and reached such a far-off place that it got lost. And yet he was a youth of sensitivity and gratitude, oh, I remember him very well when he was an urchin so high, left in the backyard of his father's house, running around without any boots on and with his little trousers held up by a single button . . .'

A kind of sensitive and emotional note suddenly sounded in the voice of the honest old fellow. Fetyukovich fairly gave a start, as though he had had a premonition of something, and instantly fastened on to it.

'Oh yes, I myself was still a young man then . . . I was . . . let me see, yet, I was forty-five then, and I had only just arrived here. And I felt sorry for the boy, and I asked myself: why do I not buy him one pound . . . Now let me see, yes, a pound of what? I have forgotten what they are called . . . A pound of the things that children are very fond of, what are they called – oh, what are they called . . .' the doctor said, beginning to wave his hands about again. 'They grow on trees, and then are picked and given to everyone as presents . . .'

'Apples?'

'Oh, n-n-o-o! A pound, a pound, apples come in dozens, not pounds . . . No, there are many of them, and they are all small, one puts them in the mouth and *Kr-r-rach*! . . .'

'Nuts?'

'Yes, nuts, that is what I am saying,' the doctor confirmed in the calmest fashion, as though he had not been searching for the word at all, 'and I took him a pound of nuts, for no one had ever brought him a pound of nuts, and I raised my finger and said to him: "Boy! *Gott der Vater!*" He laughed and said: "*Gott der Vater – Gott der Sohn.*" He laughed again and babbled: "*Gott der Sohn – Gott der heilige Geist.*" Then he again laughed, and said as best he could: "*Gott der heilige Geist.*" And I went away. Two days after that I was walking by and he himself shouted to me: "Uncle, *Gott der Vater, Gott der Sohn*", and forgot only the "*Gott der heilige Geist*", but I reminded him, and I again felt very sorry for him. But then he was taken away, and I did not see him any more. And then twenty-three years passed, and one morning I was sitting in my study, already with a white head, and suddenly a blooming young man walked in, whom I could not recognize for the life of me, but he raised his finger and, laughing, said: "*Gott der Vater, Gott der Sohn und Gott der heilige Geist!* I have just arrived and have come in order to thank you for the pound of nuts: for no one had ever bought me a pound of nuts, and you alone bought me a pound of nuts." And then I remembered the happy days of my youth and the poor little boy in the yard with no boots, and my heart gave a turn, and I said: "You are a young man of gratitude, for all your life you have remembered that pound of nuts which I brought you when you were a little boy." And I embraced him and blessed him. And I began to weep. He laughed, but he wept, too . . . for the Russian very often laughs when he ought to weep. But he wept, too, I could see it. And now, oh, lackaday! . . .'

'I weep even now, German, I weep even now, thou man of God!' Mitya cried suddenly from his place.

Whatever one might think, this little anecdote produced a certain favourable impression upon the public. The principal effect in Mitya's favour was, however, produced by the testimony of Katerina Ivanovna, of which I shall speak in a moment. And indeed in general, when the witnesses *à décharge*, those, that is to say, called by the defence counsel, began to testify, it was as if fate suddenly and even seriously began to smile upon Mitya, and as if — something even more remarkable — this were contrary to the expectation of even the defence counsel himself. Before Katerina Ivanovna, however, Alyosha was questioned, and he suddenly remembered a certain fact that possessed the aspect of something that was even tantamount to positive testimony in contradiction of one of the most important points of the case for the prosecution.

4

Fortune Smiles Upon Mitya

THIS was something that occurred quite unexpectedly, even to Alyosha himself. He was called without oath, and I recall that from the very first words of his questioning all sides took an exceptionally mild and sympathetic attitude towards him. It was evident that good renown had gone before him. Alyosha testified modestly and with restraint, but through his statements one could plainly detect an ardent sympathy for his unhappy brother. In replying to one question he outlined the character of his brother as that of a man who might indeed be violent and swept along by his passions, but one also noble, proud and magnanimous, even ready to make sacrifice, should such be required of him. He confessed, though, that in the latter days his brother had, because of his passion for Grushenka and his rivalry with his father, been in an intolerable plight. Indignantly did he reject even the supposition that his brother might have committed murder with the purpose of robbery, though he also confessed that that three thousand had turned within Mitya's mind into something almost approaching a mania, that he viewed them as the inheritance that had not been paid to him because of the deception of his father and that, being quite without self-interest, he could not even speak of that three thousand without frenzy and rabid fury. Concerning the rivalry of the two 'lady persons', as the public procurator called them – Grushenka and Katya, in other words – he gave replies that were evasive and was even reluctant to answer one or two of the questions altogether.

'At least will you say whether your brother told you that he intended to kill his father?' the public procurator inquired. 'You may refuse to answer if you consider it necessary,' he added.

'Not in so many words,' Alyosha replied.

'How, then? Obliquely?'

'He once told me of his personal hatred for father and that he was afraid that . . . in a desperate moment . . . a moment of physical loathing . . . he might even kill him.'

'And hearing him say this, did you believe him?'

'I'm afraid to say that I did. But I was always convinced that some higher feeling would always save him at the fateful moment, as indeed it did save him, for *it was not he* who killed my father,' Alyosha concluded firmly in a loud voice and to the whole chamber. The public procurator started like a warhorse hearing a bugle call.

'Be assured that I have complete faith in the most total sincerity of your conviction, neither regarding it as conditional upon nor assimilating it in any way to your love for your unhappy brother. Your curious view of the entire tragic episode that was enacted in your household is already known to us from the preliminary investigation. I will not conceal from you that I find it unusual and believe that it contradicts all the other testimony that has been obtained by the public procurator's office. I therefore consider it necessary to ask you with insistence: what precisely were the facts that guided your thoughts and led to your being so wholly convinced of your brother's innocence and, conversely, of the guilt of another person whom you named directly at the preliminary investigation?'

'At the preliminary investigation I merely answered the questions that were put to me,' Alyosha said, 'and made no accusation of my own against Smerdyakov.'

'Yet you did name him, did you not?'

'I named him because of what my brother Dmitry had said. Even before my interrogation I was told what took place at his arrest and that he himself had testified against Smerdyakov. I am quite certain that my brother is not guilty. And if he is not the murderer, then . . .'

'Then it must be Smerdyakov? Why must it be Smerdyakov? And why are you so definitively convinced of your brother's innocence?'

'I could not possibly have disbelieved my brother. I know that he would never lie to me. I could see by his face that he was not lying to me.'

'Only by his face? And that is all your proof?'

'More proof than that I have none.'

'And concerning the guilt of Smerdyakov you also found your conviction on no other proof than your brother's words and the expression on his face?'

'No, I have no other proof.'

With this the public procurator discontinued his questions. Alyosha's answers had produced upon the public an impression of deep disappointment. Of Smerdyakov there had been talk in our town even before the trial: some had heard this or that, some had alluded to certain things; it had been said of Alyosha that he had gathered some extraordinary proof in favour of his brother and prejudicial to the lackey, and yet now there was nothing, no proof at all apart from some moral convictions, so greatly to be expected in the natural brother of the accused.

But Fetyukovich, too, began to examine Alyosha. To the question as to when precisely the defendant had told him, Alyosha, of his hatred for their father and of the possibility that he might murder him, and as to whether he had heard him say this at, for example, their last encounter before the catastrophe, Alyosha, in giving his reply, suddenly seemed to start, as though he had only just recalled something and realized its significance:

'I have now remembered a certain event which I had begun completely to forget, and the meaning of which was not at all clear to me at the time, yet now . . .'

And with enthusiasm, it being apparent that he had only now hit suddenly upon the idea, Alyosha recollected how during his last meeting with Mitya, in the evening by the tree, on the road towards the monastery, Mitya, smiting himself on the chest, 'on the upper part of his chest', had told him several times that he had a means of restoring his honour, that the means was here, 'here, upon his breast' . . . 'At the time I thought that as he smote his chest it was his heart that he was speaking of,' Alyosha continued, 'meaning that within his heart he could find the strength to extricate himself from the terrible disgrace that was in store for him and which he did not even dare to confess to me. I confess that I did in fact think at the time that he was speaking of father and that he was shuddering, as from disgrace, at the thought of going to father and perpetrating some violent act upon him, yet all the while it was as though it were something on his own chest he kept pointing at, and I remember it fleetingly occurring to me that the heart is not at all in that part of the chest, but further down, and he was striking himself much higher, here, right below the neck, and kept pointing to that place. That thought of mine seemed stupid to me at the time, yet it now occurs to me that perhaps what he was pointing to was the incense-bag in which the fifteen hundred was sewn up!'

'Precisely!' Mitya exclaimed suddenly from his place. 'That is so, Alyosha, that is so, at the time, I was striking it with my fist!'

Fetyukovich rushed towards him in a flurry, imploring him to calm himself, and at that same moment he fairly battened upon Alyosha. Alyosha, still in the grip of his reminiscence, vehemently expressed his supposition that the said disgrace most probably consisted in the fact that, having upon his person the said fifteen hundred, which he could have returned to Katerina Ivanovna as being half of the debt he owed her, he had none the less determined not to return that half to her and to use it instead for a different purpose, namely his elopement with Grushenka, if she would agree . . .

'That is so, that is precisely so,' Alyosha exclaimed in sudden excitement, 'my brother did indeed keep crying to me that evening that he could remove from himself at once a half, a half of the disgrace (he said it several times: "a half!"), but that he was so unfortunate in the weakness of his character that he would not do it . . . He knew in advance that he could not do it and had not the strength to do it!'

'And you firmly, clearly recall that it was on that part of his chest he smote himself?' Fetyukovich avidly inquired.

'Quite, quite sure, because I recall that I wondered at the time why he did it so high up, when the heart is lower down, but my thought seemed absurd to me then ... it only occurred to me fleetingly. And that is no doubt why I have recalled it again now. How, indeed, could I have forgotten it until now? It was that incense-bag he was drawing attention to, implying that he had the means with which to return that fifteen hundred, but was not going to do so! And at the time of his arrest in Mokroye he shouted − I know this, for I was informed of it − that he considered it the most disgraceful action of his whole life that, possessing the means with which to return a half (precisely a half!) of his debt to Katerina Ivanovna and thus not be a thief in her regard, he none the less could not bring himself to return the money, preferring to remain a thief in her eyes than to part with it! And how he tormented himself, how he tormented himself with that debt!' Alyosha concluded, loudly.

At this point the public procurator, too, stepped in. He requested Alyosha to describe once more the manner in which it had all taken place, several times asking with particular insistence whether the defendant, in beating himself upon the breast, had looked as though he were pointing to something. Perhaps he had simply been beating his breast with his fist?

'It was not really his fist that he used!' Alyosha exclaimed. 'He actually pointed with his fingers, and pointed here, very high up ... But how could I have so completely forgotten it until this moment?'

The chairman turned to Mitya and asked him for his comment on the testimony that had been given. Mitya confirmed that it had all taken place in precisely that manner, that he had been pointing to the fifteen hundred that had hung on his chest, just below his neck, and that, of course, it was a disgrace, 'a disgrace I do not disavow, the most disgraceful act of my entire life!' Mitya shouted. 'I could have returned the money but did not do so. I preferred to remain a thief in her eyes, and I did not return it, and my greatest disgrace was that I knew in advance that I would not return it! Alyosha is right! Thank you, Alyosha!'

With this the questioning of Alyosha was concluded. Important, and also characteristic, was the circumstance that at least one fact had been uncovered, one smallest piece of proof, if ever so small, so that it was not much more than a mere hint at a proof, but one which provided at least a drop of evidence that the incense-bag really had existed, that it had contained fifteen hundred and that the defendant had not lied at the preliminary investigation when in Mokroye he had declared that the fifteen hundred roubles were 'his'. Alyosha was pleased; flushed all over, he returned to his appointed place. Long afterwards he kept saying to himself: 'How did I forget? How could I have forgotten it? And how did it suddenly come back to me only now?'

The questioning of Katerina Ivanovna began. As soon as she made her appearance there was an unusual stir in the chamber. The ladies seized their lorgnettes and opera-glasses, the men began to show some signs of life, and several stood up in order to see better. Everyone subsequently asserted that Mitya had gone 'as white as a sheet' as soon as she came in. Dressed entirely in black, modestly and almost timidly she drew near to her appointed place. By her face one could not have guessed that she was excited, but determination glittered in her dark, moody gaze. It should be noted that very many people later asserted that she looked astonishingly beautiful at that moment. She spoke quietly, but clearly, to the whole chamber. She expressed herself with extreme calm or, at any rate, with an attempt at it. The chairman began his questions cautiously, with exceptional deference, as though he were afraid of touching 'certain strings' and out of respect for great misfortune. But Katerina Ivanovna herself, from her very first words, firmly declared in response to one of the questions put to her that she had been the affianced betrothed of the defendant 'until the time that he left me . . .' she added quietly. When she was asked about the three thousand she had entrusted to Mitya for dispatch by mail to her relatives, she said firmly: 'I did not intend him to post the money directly; I sensed at the time that he was in great need of money . . . at that moment . . . I gave him that three thousand on condition that he posted it off, if he cared to, at some time in the course of the month. He really tormented himself in vain over that debt later on . . .'

I do not mean to reproduce all the questions and the precise wording of her answers; I give merely the essential purport of her testimony.

'I was firmly convinced that he would always manage to send on that three thousand, as soon as he received it from his father,' she continued, replying to the questions. 'I was always convinced of his lack of self-interest and of his honesty . . . his great honesty . . . in pecuniary matters. He was firmly convinced that he would receive the three thousand roubles from his father and spoke of that to me several times. I was aware that he was in discord with his father, and I have always been convinced, and am so even to this day, that he was treated badly by him. I never remember him, for his part, having threatened his father on any occasion. At any rate, he never said anything when I was present, made no such threats. Had he come to me at the time, I should at once have calmed his anxiety concerning that wretched three thousand he owed me, but he did not come to see me any more . . . and I myself . . . I was placed in such a position . . . that I could not invite him to visit me . . . And indeed, I had no right to be exacting of him in regard of that debt,' she added suddenly, and something determined began to ring in her voice. 'I myself once received a pecuniary favour from him even greater than that three thousand, and accepted it, in spite of the fact that I could not at the time envisage that I should ever be in a position to repay my debt to him . . .'

In the tone of her voice one could almost feel a kind of challenge. At precisely that moment the questioning passed to Fetyukovich.

'This occurred not here, but at the outset of your acquaintance?' Fetyukovich caught up, with an instant premonition of something auspicious here. (I shall note in parenthesis that even though he had been summoned from St Petersburg in part by Katerina Ivanovna herself, he was as yet quite unaware of the episode concerning the five thousand that Mitya had given her in that other town, and the 'earthly prostration'. She had not told him of it, and had concealed it from him! This, too, was astonishing. One may with certainty suppose that she herself, until the very last moment, did not know whether she was going to relate that episode at the trial or not, and had been waiting for some kind of inspiration.)

No, never can I forget those moments! She began to relate, she related *everything*, the whole of that episode that Mitya had confided to Alyosha, leaving out nothing, neither the 'earthly prostration', nor its reasons, nor her father, nor her appearance at Mitya's lodgings, and not by a word or a single hint did she allude to the fact that Mitya, through her sister, had himself proposed that Katerina Ivanovna be, 'sent to him for the money'. This she magnanimously kept secret and was not ashamed to make it sound as though it were she, she herself who had gone running to the young officer that day with the aim of soliciting money from him. This was something shattering. As I listened, my blood ran cold and I shivered; the chamber froze, trying to catch every word. Here was something without precedent, as even from such a self-willed and contemptuously proud girl as she no one could possibly have expected such highly unguarded testimony, such sacrifice, such self-immolation. And for what, for whom? In order to save the man who had betrayed and insulted her, in order to do at least something, however little, to effect his salvation, creating a good impression in his favour! And indeed it was so: the picture of an officer giving away the last five thousand roubles he

possessed — all that remained to him in life — and respectfully bowing to
an innocent girl, emerged in a most sympathetic and attractive manner,
but . . . my heart was painfully wrung! I had a feeling that later the result
of it might be (and it was, it was!) slander! With a malicious titter it was
later said all over town that her account of the story was perhaps not
entirely exact, with particular reference to that part of it where the officer
dismissed the girl from his presence 'apparently with no more than a
respectful bow.' Allusion was made to the likelihood that something had
been 'omitted' there. 'And suppose it was not, suppose it was all true,'
said even the most respected of our ladies, 'what we still do not know is:
was it a particularly noble way for a girl to behave, even though in order
to try to save her father?' And was it really possible that Katerina
Ivanovna, with her intelligence, her morbid acumen, had not sensed in
advance that people would say such things? Of course she had, and now
she had determined to speak her mind! It goes without saying that all
these rather sordid doubts in the story's veracity began only later; at that
initial moment the effect of it was shock on all and sundry. As for the
members of the tribunal, they attended to everything that Katerina
Ivanovna had to say in reverential, not to say even bashful silence. The
public procurator did not permit himself one single further question on
that theme. Fetyukovich made her a deep bow. Oh, he had almost triumphed! Much ground had been won: a man giving away, on a noble
impulse, his last five thousand, and then the same man, murdering his
father by night with the aim of robbing him of three thousand — there
was something there that in part did not connect. At any rate, Fetyukovich
could at least now get the robbery out of the way. 'The case' was
suddenly bathed in a rather new light. A sympathetic factor had sprung
up in Mitya's favour. As for him . . . it was related of him that once or
twice while Katerina Ivanovna was giving her evidence he leapt up from
his place, but then sank back down on the bench again and covered his
face with both palms. When she had concluded, however, he suddenly
exclaimed in a sobbing voice, extending his arms to her:

'Katya, why have you ruined me?'

And he began to sob loudly, to the whole chamber. Though, as a
matter of fact, he regained instant control of himself and again shouted:

'Now I am doomed!'

And after that he seemed to grow rigid where he sat, his teeth clenched
and his arms pressed tightly against him in a cross. Katerina Ivanovna did
not leave the chamber, and sat down on a chair that was appointed to her.
She was pale and sat with her eyes lowered. It was related by those who

were near her that for a long time she shivered all over, as though in a fever. Now Grushenka made her appearance for questioning.

I am now closely approaching the catastrophe which, in its sudden onslaught, really did perhaps bring about Mitya's ruin. For I am convinced, as is everyone else, all the legal experts said so afterwards, that had it not been for this episode, the criminal would at least have received a lesser sentence. But of that in a moment. Just two words first about Grushenka.

She also made an appearance in the chamber dressed entirely in black, with her magnificent black shawl around her shoulders. Lightly, with her inaudible step, and a slight sway of the kind with which plump women sometimes walk, she approached the balustrade, gazing fixedly at the chairman and never once glancing either to right or to left. It is my view that she looked very beautiful at that moment and not at all pale, as the ladies asserted later on. They also asserted that her face bore a look that was somehow concentrated and malicious. I merely suppose that she was short of temper and feeling heavily upon her the contemptuously inquisitive eyes of our public, eager as it was for scandal. This was a proud character that would not tolerate contempt, one of that kind which at the merest suspicion of contempt from anyone immediately becomes inflamed with anger and the craving to administer a rebuff. Combined with this there was, of course, also timidity and an inner shame at this timidity, so it was not surprising that her discourse was uneven – now tinged with wrath, now contemptuous and intensely rude, now suddenly filled with a sincere and heartfelt note of self-condemnation and self-accusation. Sometimes, on the other hand, she spoke as though she were falling over some kind of precipice, as if to say: 'It makes no difference, whatever happens I am going to say it all the same . . .' With regard to her acquaintance with Fyodor Pavlovich, she commented sharply: 'It was nothing at all; am I to blame that he came pestering me?' And then a moment later added: 'I am to blame for it all, I laughed at the one and at the other – both at the old man and at that man there – and drove them both to it. It was because of me that it all took place.' Somehow the questioning touched on Samsonov: 'What business is that of anyone?' she at once bit off with a kind of brazen challenge. 'He was my benefactor, he took me barefoot when my kinsfolk had chucked me out of the *izba*.' The chairman, though ever so politely, reminded her that she must answer the questions directly, without embarking upon superfluous detail. Grushenka flushed, and her eyes glittered.

The envelope containing the money she had not seen, but had only heard from 'the evil-doer' that Fyodor Pavlovich had some kind of envelope in which there was three thousand. 'But it was all silly nonsense, I laughed, and would not have gone there for anything . . .'

'Whom did you refer to just now as "the evil-doer"?' the public procurator inquired.

'Oh, the lackey, Smerdyakov, who murdered his *barin* and hanged himself yesterday.'

She was, of course, asked in a trice what reasons she had for making such a positive accusation, but she, too, proved to have none.

'That's what Dmitry Fyodorovich himself told me, and you may believe him. It was the thief of friendship* who brought him to his ruin, so it was, she's the one who is the cause of it all, so she is,' Grushenka added, seeming to shudder all over with hatred, and a note of malice began to ring in her voice.

Again it was inquired whom she was alluding to.

'Why, the *baryshnya*, this Katerina Ivanovna who's here. She invited me to her house once, treated me to chocolate, tried to seduce me. She doesn't have enough true shame, no she doesn't . . .'

At this point the chairman, sternly now, made her pause, requesting her to moderate her language. But the heart of the jealous woman was already ablaze, she was ready to fly even down into the abyss . . .

'On the day that the arrest was made in the village of Mokroye,' the public procurator asked, reminiscing, 'everyone saw and heard you as you ran out of the other room, shouting: "I am the guilty one, let us go into penal servitude together!" I assume, then, that at that moment you were already convinced that he was the parricide?'

'I do not remember my feelings that day,' Grushenka replied. 'Everyone had started to shout that he had killed his father, and I felt that I was the guilty one and that he had killed because of me. And when he said he wasn't guilty I believed him immediately, and I still believe him now and I will always believe him: he is not the kind of man to tell a lie.'

The questioning passed to Fetyukovich. Among other things I remember that he asked about Rakitin and about the twenty-five roubles 'for bringing Aleksey Fyodorovich Karamazov to you'.

'What is so surprising about him having taken the money?' Grushenka said with a smile of contemptuous malice. 'He kept coming to scrounge money from me all the time, he used to take as much as thirty roubles a month, and it all mostly went on foolery: he had enough to be able to eat and drink without need of me.'

'And on what grounds were you so generous to Mr Rakitin?' Fetyukovich caught up, in spite of the fact that the chairman was very restless.

'Well, you see, he's my cousin. My mother and his mother are kindred sisters. Only he kept begging me not to tell anyone in the town about it, for he was very ashamed of me.'

This new piece of evidence turned out to be completely unexpected to all, no one in the whole of the town, not even in the monastery, not even Mitya, had known of it. It was said afterwards that Rakitin had turned crimson with shame in his chair. Even before entering the chamber, Grushenka had somehow discovered that he had given testimony against Mitya, and was therefore angry. The whole of the speech Mr Rakitin had earlier delivered, with all its nobility, all its outbursts against serfdom, on Russia's lack of civil order – all this was at last crossed out and cancelled in the general opinion. Fetyukovich was content: once again God had sent a windfall. On the whole, however, Grushenka was not questioned for very long, and she was, of course, unable to tell anything that was particularly new. She left a most unpleasant impression on the public. Hundreds of contemptuous stares were turned on her when, having concluded her testimony, she took her seat in the chamber rather a long way from Katerina Ivanovna. All during the time she was being questioned Mitya had kept silent, as if he had been turned to stone, his gaze lowered to the earth.

Ivan Fyodorovich made his appearance as a witness.

5

A Sudden Catastrophe

I should observe that an attempt had already been made to summon him, before Alyosha. But at that time the bailiff had informed the chairman that, because of a sudden indisposition or some kind of fit, the witness could not appear at once, but that as soon as he was restored would be willing to give his evidence at any time that was convenient. Though in fact, for some reason or other no one heard this, and it was only discovered subsequently. The initial moment of his appearance went almost unobserved: the principal witnesses, particularly the two lady rivals, had already been questioned; curiosity had, for the present, been satisfied. In the public one could even sense a certain weariness. There lay ahead the prospect of hearing several witnesses who most likely would have nothing in particular to relate in view of all that had already been related. Time was already on the march. Ivan Fyodorovich made his approach with a slowness that was somehow astonishing, without looking at anyone and even with his head lowered, as though he were frowningly reflecting on something. His dress was immaculate, but his face, on me at any rate, produced a painful impression: there was in it something that was almost touched with earth, something that resembled the face of one who is dying. His eyes were dull; he raised them and slowly surveyed the chamber with them. Alyosha suddenly sprang up from his chair and moaned out: 'Ah!' I remember that. But even that was caught by a few of those present.

The chairman began by telling him that as a witness he was not under oath, that he could give testimony or remain silent, but that, of course, all the testimony he offered must be in accordance with the dictates of his conscience, etcetera, etcetera. Ivan Fyodorovich listened and gave him a dull look; but suddenly his face began slowly to move apart in a smile, and no sooner had the chairman, who had been looking at him with surprise, stopped speaking, he suddenly burst out laughing.

'Well, and what else, then?' he asked loudly.

All became quiet in the chamber, it was as if something had been sensed. The chairman began to grow uneasy.

'You . . . are still possibly not very well?' he started to say, casting his eyes round for the bailiff.

'Do not be uneasy, your honour, I am sufficiently well and can tell you some interesting things,' Ivan Fyodorovich suddenly replied, quite calmly and deferentially.

'You have something in particular of which you wish to inform the court?' the chairman continued, still with suspicion.

Ivan Fyodorovich lowered his gaze, tarried for a few seconds and then, raising his head once more, replied with a kind of stammer:

'No . . . I do not. I have nothing in particular.'

Questions began to be put to him. He answered somehow altogether reluctantly, with a kind of intense brevity, a kind of revulsion, even, which grew greater and greater, though, as a matter of fact, his answers were intelligible enough. To much he pleaded ignorance. Concerning his father's private reckonings with Dmitry Fyodorovich he knew nothing. 'And I did not make it my business,' he pronounced. Of the threats made to kill his father he had heard from the defendant, of the money in the envelope he had heard from Smerdyakov . . .

'It is all one and the same thing again and again,' he broke off suddenly with a look of fatigue, 'I cannot tell the court anything in particular.'

'I perceive that you are unwell, and I understand your feelings . . .' the chairman began.

He had begun to turn to the sides, to the public procurator and the defence counsel, inviting them, if they found it necessary, to ask questions, when suddenly Ivan Fyodorovich in a voice of exhaustion asked:

'Let me go, your honour, I feel most unwell.'

And with these words, not waiting for permission, he himself suddenly turned away and began to walk out of the chamber. But, when he had taken some four steps, he stopped as though something had suddenly occurred to him, smiled a quiet, ironic smile and returned to his previous place.

'I, your honour, am like that peasant wench ... you know how it goes: "If I want, I'll jump, if I don't, I won't." They follow her around with a *sarafan* or a *paneva** or whatever, that she may jump up and they may bind her and cart her off to be wed, and she says: "If I want, I'll jump, if I don't, I won't ..." It is in some part of our national folk tradition ...'

'What do you mean to imply by this?' the chairman asked sternly.

'Look,' said Ivan Fyodorovich, suddenly producing a wad of money, 'here is the money ... the same money that was in that envelope' – he nodded towards the table on which lay the material evidence – 'and for the sake of which my father was murdered. Where may I put it? Master bailiff, please hand it to him ...'

The bailiff took the entire wad and handed it to the chairman.

'How is it possible that this money should be upon your person ... if it is the same money?' the chairman said in astonishment.

'I received it from Smerdyakov, the murderer, last night. I went to his lodgings and was with him before he hanged himself. It was he, not my brother, who murdered my father. He murdered him, and I put him up to it ... Who does not desire the death of his father? ...'

'Are you in your right mind?' broke from the chairman, in spite of himself.

'Oh, I am in my right mind, all right ... and it is a villainous mind, the same as yours, the same as theirs, the lot of them, those ... p-pug-mugs!' he said, turning suddenly to the public. 'A father has been murdered, and they pretend they are frightened,' he ground out with malicious contempt. 'They give themselves airs before one another. Liars! They all desire the death of their fathers. One vile reptile consumes the other ... Were it not for the parricide they would all lose their tempers and disperse in a rage ... Circuses! "Bread and circuses!"* As a matter of fact, I make a good one! Have you some water, give me a drink, in the name of Christ!' he said, suddenly clutching at his head.

The bailiff immediately came over to him. Alyosha suddenly sprang up and shouted: 'He is ill, do not listen to him, he has *delirium tremens*!' Katerina Ivanovna quickly stood up and, motionless with horror, stared at Ivan Fyodorovich. Mitya got up and with a kind of wild, distorted smile avidly examined his brother and listened to him.

'Calm yourselves, I am not mad, I am just a murderer!' Ivan began again. 'After all, one cannot ask eloquence of a murderer . . .' he added suddenly for some reason, with a distorted laugh.

The public procurator, in evident disarray, bent down to the chairman. The members of the tribunal exchanged bustling whispers with one another. Fetyukovich well and truly pricked up his ears, straining to hear. The chamber froze in expectation. The chairman suddenly seemed to recover his wits.

'Witness, your words are incomprehensible and impossible here. Calm yourself, if you are able, and tell us . . . if you really do have something to say. With what can you confirm such a confession . . . That is, if you are not raving?'

'That is just it, for I have no witnesses. The dog Smerdyakov will not send you his evidence from the other world . . . in an envelope. You keep wanting envelopes, one will have to suffice. I have no witnesses . . . Except possibly one,' he said with a thin, reflective smile.

'Who is your witness?'

'One with a tail, your honour, it would not do at all! *Le diable n'existe pas!* Pay no attention, he is a rotten, petty devil,' he added, suddenly ceasing to laugh and almost, as it were, confidentially. 'He is no doubt here somewhere, over there, under that table of material evidence – for after all, where would he sit, if not there? Look, harken to me; I told him I did not wish to sit in silence, and he began to talk about a geological revolution . . . stupid nonsense! But I say, why do you not just set the monster free? . . . If he has struck up a hymn, then it is because he feels cheerful! It is just as if a drunken blackguard had begun to bawl about how "Vanka's gone to *Piter*", while I would give a quadrillion quadrillions just for two seconds of joy. You do not know me! Oh, how stupid all this business of yours is! Look, I say, take me instead of him! I did come here for some reason, after all . . . Why, why is it that everything that is should be so stupid . . .'

And once more he began slowly and as if in reflectiveness to survey the chamber. But already a commotion had begun. Alyosha began to rush towards him from his place, but the bailiff had already seized Ivan Fyodorovich by the arm.

'And what is this now?' the latter exclaimed, fixedly studying the bailiff's face, and suddenly, grabbing him by the shoulders, knocked him violently to the floor. But the guards arrived in time, he was seized, and then he began to howl with a loud voice.* And all the time he was being led away he howled and screamed out something incoherent.

There was turmoil. I do not recollect it all in sequence, I myself was perturbed and could not follow. All I am certain of is that later, when all had grown calm once more and everyone had realized what it had all been about, the bailiff received a proper dressing-down, even though he provided a thorough explanation to the authorities, saying that all along there had been nothing the matter with the witness's state of health, that he had been seen by the doctor when an hour previously he had begun to feel slightly faint, but that until his entry into the chamber he had spoken coherently, so that none of this could have been foreseen; that on the contrary, he himself had insisted on giving evidence and had been absolutely set upon doing so. But before the chamber had had the least opportunity to calm itself and recover its wits, hot on the heels of this scene there had burst another: Katerina Ivanovna had had hysterics. Shrieking loudly, she began to sob, but refused to leave, desperately implored to be allowed to stay, and suddenly screamed to the chairman:

'I must submit one more piece of evidence, without delay . . . without delay! . . . Here is a document, a letter . . . Take it, read it quickly, quickly! It is a letter from that monster of cruelty, there, that one, that one!' she cried, pointing at Mitya. 'It was he who murdered his father, you will see it now, he tells me in this letter how he is going to murder his father! And the other one is ill, ill, the other one has *delirium tremens*! I have seen for three days that his brain is in fever!'

Thus did she shriek, beside herself. The bailiff took the document which she was holding out to the chairman, while she, sinking down on to her chair and covering her face, began convulsively and soundlessly to sob, shaking all over and suppressing the least murmur in fear of being sent from the chamber. The document submitted by her was that very same letter which Mitya had written from the Capital City inn, and which Ivan Fyodorovich had called a document of 'mathematical' importance. Alas! It was precisely this mathematical property of it that was recognized, and were it not for that letter, Mitya might possibly not have been undone, or been undone so dreadfully! I repeat, it was hard to follow the details. Even now it all appears before my mind as so much turmoil. Undoubtedly what happened was that the chairman at once communicated the contents of the new document to the tribunal of judges, the public procurator, the defence counsel and the jury. All I recollect is that the examination of the witness began. To the question: had she calmed down now, put to her gently by the chairman, Katerina impetuously exclaimed:

'I am ready, ready! I am quite able to give my answers now,' she added, evidently still dreadfully afraid that there would be some reason for her not being able to say all that she had to say. She was requested to explain in more detail: what was this letter, and in what circumstances had she received it?

'I received it the day before the crime itself, but he wrote it yet one day earlier, from the inn, in other words two days before his crime – look, it is written on some bill!' she exclaimed, gasping. 'He hated me then, because he himself had committed a vile action and had gone after that brute creature . . . and because he owed me that three thousand . . . Oh, he felt sore about that three thousand because of his own baseness, you see! That three thousand came about like this – I ask you, I implore you to hear me through: one morning, three weeks before he killed his father, he came to see me. I knew that he needed money, and I knew what for – yes, yes, for that very same reason, in order to seduce that brute creature and carry her off with him. I knew at the time that he had been unfaithful to me and intended to leave me, and I, I myself handed him that money that day, myself offered it to him ostensibly in order to send it to my sister in Moscow – and as I was giving it to him, I looked him in the face and told him he could send it whenever he liked, "even if only in a month's time". Well, how, how can it have been that he did not realize I was telling him straight to his face: "You need money in order to deceive me with your brute creature – well, here is that money, I give it to you myself, take it, if you are so without honour that you will take it! . . ." I meant to show him up in a bad light, and what happened? He took, he took it and carried it off and spent it down there with that brute creature, in a single night . . . But he realized, he realized that I knew everything, I do assure you that he even realized that, in giving him the money, I was merely putting him to the test: would he have so little honour as to take it from me, or not? Into his eyes I looked, and he looked into mine and he understood everything, understood everything, and took, took and carried off my money!'

'True, Katya!' Mitya suddenly cried. 'I looked into your eyes and understood that you were bringing disgrace upon me, and yet all the same I took your money! Despise the scoundrel, despise me, all of you, I have deserved it!'

'Prisoner,' the chairman exclaimed, 'one more word and I shall have you removed.'

'That money tormented him,' Katya resumed in convulsive haste, 'he intended to return it to me, he intended to, that is true, but he also needed the money for that brute creature. And then he went and murdered his father, but still he did not return the money to me, but took her to that village where he was arrested. There he also squandered the money he had stolen from his murdered father. And the day before he murdered his father he wrote me that letter, wrote it while he was drunk, I could see that immediately, wrote it out of spite, in the certain knowledge that I would never show anyone that letter, not even if he committed murder. Otherwise he would never have written it. He knew that I did not want to take vengeance and destroy him! But read it, read it attentively, please, you will see that he describes it all there, all of it in advance: how he will kill his father and where his father's money is. Please look now, do not miss it, there is one sentence there that says: "I will kill him if only Ivan has gone away." That means he had already planned in advance how he would carry out the murder,' with viperish *schadenfreude* Katerina Ivanovna suggested to the court. Oh, it was plain that she had carefully read this fateful letter in the most subtle nicety and had studied every minute detail of it. 'Had he not been drunk he would never have written to me, but look, it is all described in advance, all of it word for word in the way he later carried out the murder, the entire programme!'

Thus did she continue to vociferate, beside herself and, it goes without saying, with scorn for all the consequences it would have for her, though there was of course the possibility that she had foreseen them as far back as a month ago, for even then, shuddering with spite, she had possibly thought in her dreams: 'Should I not simply read it out to the court?' And now she had, as it were, gone flying over the precipice. I seem to remember that precisely at this juncture the letter was read out by the referring clerk, producing a shattering effect. To Mitya the question: 'Do you admit having written this letter?' was put.

'It is mine, it is mine!' Mitya exclaimed. 'Had I not been drunk I would never have written it! ... There were many things for which we hated each other, Katya, but I swear, I swear that even as I hated you I loved you, while you loved me – not!'

He sank back into his place, wringing his hands in despair. The public procurator and the defence counsel began to cross-question her, principally in the vein: 'What prompted you to conceal the existence of such a document earlier and to give your previous testimony in quite a different spirit and tone?'

'Yes, yes, earlier I lied, told nothing but lies, contrary to my honour and my conscience, but earlier I wanted to save him, because he hated me so much and despised me so much,' Katya exclaimed like a madwoman. 'Oh, he despised me dreadfully, despised me all the time, and you know, you know – he despised me from the very moment I prostrated myself at his feet for that money. I saw that . . . I sensed it at once, right there and then, but for a long time I did not trust myself. How many times did I read in his eyes: "All the same, it was you who came to me that day." Oh, he did not understand, he understood nothing of why I came running to him, he is capable only of suspecting baseness! He measured me by himself, he thought that all are as he is,' Katya ragingly ground out, in a perfect frenzy now. 'And the only reason he wanted to marry me was that I had received an inheritance, that was the only reason, the only reason! I have always suspected that was the reason! Oh, he is a savage beast! All his life he has been certain that all my life I would tremble before him in shame for having come to him that day, and that he would be able to despise me eternally for it, and thus take the upper hand with me – that is why he wanted to marry me! It is true, it is all true! I attempted to conquer him with my love, love without end, I was even willing to endure his unfaithfulness, but he understood none of it, none of it! And how could he understand any of it? He is a monster! This letter I received only on the evening of the following day, it was brought to me from the inn, and even that morning, even on the morning of that day, I had still been willing to forgive him all, all, even his unfaithfulness!'

Of course, the chairman and the public procurator did their best to calm her. I am certain that they were all possibly even ashamed to be exploiting her frenzy in such a way and to be listening to confessions of such a kind. I recall that I heard them say to her: 'We realize how hard it is for you, please be assured that we are capable of feeling too,' etcetera, etcetera, yet all the same they hauled the evidence out of the woman who had lost her mind in hysterics. She described, at last, with exceptional clarity, something which so frequently, if only for a second, flashes out even at moments of a strained condition such as this, how Ivan Fyodorovich had almost gone out of his mind during the past two months in his efforts to save 'that monster and murderer', his brother.

'He has tormented himself,' she resumed with vehemence, 'he has constantly tried to diminish his brother's guilt, confessing to me that he himself did not love his father, even possibly also desired his death. Oh, his is a deep, deep conscience! He has tormented himself with his conscience! He has revealed everything to me, everything, he has come to me and talked with me every day as with his only friend. I have the honour to be his only friend!' she exclaimed suddenly, almost with a kind of challenge, and her eyes began to flash. 'He went to see Smerdyakov on two occasions. One day he came to me and said: "If it was not my brother who committed the murder, but Smerdyakov" — because everyone in town was passing round that fable that Smerdyakov had done it — "then perhaps I, too, am guilty, because Smerdyakov was aware that I did not like my father and possibly thought that I desired my father's death." Then I produced that letter and showed it to him, and then he was completely persuaded that his brother had done it, and that struck him down completely. He could not endure it, that his own brother was a parricide! Even a week ago I saw that he was ill because of it. In the last few days, as he has sat with me, he has been in a delirium. I could see that his mind was disturbed. He has been going about raving, people have seen him like that out in the streets. The doctor from Moscow examined him at my request two days ago and told me that he is near to brain fever — all through him, all through the monster! And yesterday he found out that Smerdyakov had died — it shocked him so much that he has gone out of his mind . . . and all because of the monster, all of it from his efforts to save the monster!'

Oh, it goes without saying that thus may one speak and thus confess not more than once in one's life — at the moment before one's death, for example, as one ascends to the scaffold. But the fact was that Katya was quite in her character and in her moment. This was the same impetuous Katya who had rushed that day to the young libertine in order to save her father; that same Katya who a little earlier, before the whole of this public, proud and chaste, had made sacrifice of herself and her maiden's modesty by relating 'Mitya's noble deed', merely in order to attenuate at least in some small way the lot that awaited him. And now in exactly the same manner she again made sacrifice of herself, but already for another, and it was possible that only now, only at this moment did she for the first time fully sense and realize how dear to her was this other man! She had sacrificed herself in fear for him, suddenly imagining that he had brought ruin on himself by his statement that it was he who was the murderer, not his brother, sacrificed herself in order to save him, his good renown, his reputation! At the same time, however, a terrible thought fleeted by: had she not slandered Mitya in describing her former relations with him? That was the question. No, no, she had not slandered him intentionally when she had shouted that Mitya despised her for her earthly prostration! She herself believed this, she had been deeply convinced from the very time of that prostration that the open-hearted Mitya, who even then had worshipped her, was laughing at her and despised her. And only out of pride had she attached herself to him with a love that was cracked and hysterical, out of stung pride, and that love had resembled not love but vengeance. Oh, it was possible that that cracked love might have developed into one that was genuine, it was possible that Katya desired no other thing than this, but Mitya had wounded her by his unfaithfulness to the depths of her soul, and her soul did not forgive. As for the moment of vengeance, it descended unexpectedly, and all that had so long and painfully been amassing in the breast of the outraged woman at once, and again unexpectedly, broke loose to the surface. She betrayed Mitya, but also betrayed herself! And, it goes without saying, no sooner had she succeeded in speaking her mind than the tension snapped and she was crushed by shame. Again her hysterics began, and she fell down, sobbing and screaming. She was carried out. At the moment she was carried out, with a howl Grushenka rushed towards Mitya from her place before anyone could manage to restrain her.

'Mitya!' she began to howl, 'your snake has brought ruin upon you! There, she has showed you her true self!' she cried, shaking with malice, to the court. At a nod from the chairman she was seized and they began to lead her out of the chamber. She would not yield, but struggled and tore her way back towards Mitya. Mitya uttered a yell and also jerked his way towards her. He was taken hold of.

Yes, I dare say that our lady-spectators were content: the spectacle had been a rich one. After that, I remember that the doctor from Moscow made his appearance. It would seem that the chairman had before this sent the bailiff to arrange for help to be provided for Ivan Fyodorovich. The doctor reported to the tribunal that the patient was in a most dangerous fit of brain fever and that he must immediately be taken away. To questions from the public procurator and the defence counsel he confirmed that the patient had come to him of his own accord two days earlier and that he had then prognosed an imminent brain fever, but that the patient had been unwilling to accept treatment. 'And he was positively not in a healthy condition of mind, he himself confessed to me that he was having waking visions, meeting in the street various persons who were already dead, and that Satan came visiting him each evening,' the doctor concluded. Having given his evidence, the celebrated physician withdrew. The letter which Katerina Ivanovna had presented was added to the material evidence. Following consultation, the court decreed that the judicial investigation be continued, and that the two unexpected depositions (those of Katerina Ivanovna and Ivan Fyodorovich) be entered in the protocol.

I shall not, however, describe the further course of the judicial investigation. And in any case, the statements of the remaining witnesses were simply a reduplication and a confirmation of the preceding, though all had their characteristic peculiarities. But I say again: it will all be rounded upon a single point in the public procurator's speech, to which I shall in a moment proceed. All were excited, all were electrified by the latest catastrophe and with burning impatience awaited merely a swift denouement, the speeches of the two sides and the verdict. Fetyukovich had been evidently shaken by the testimony of Katerina Ivanovna. The public procurator, on the other hand, was exultant. When the judicial investigation was ended, a recess in the sitting was announced, which endured for almost an hour. At last the chairman opened the judicial pleadings. It was, I think, exactly eight o'clock in the evening when our public procurator, Ippolit Kirillovich, began his speech for the prosecution.

6

The Public Procurator's Speech. Characterization

IPPOLIT Kirillovich began his speech for the prosecution trembling all over with a nervous shiver, a cold, morbid sweat upon his brow and temples, feeling chill and fever by turns in all his body. He himself later described it thus. He considered this speech his *chef d'œuvre*, the *chef d'œuvre* of his entire life, his swansong. To be sure, nine months later he died of an acute consumption, and had he had an early premonition of his end, he really would with justification have been able to compare himself to a swan singing its final song. Into this speech he put all his heart and all the cleverness that he possessed, unexpectedly demonstrating that within him lay concealed both civic feeling and the 'accursed' questions,* at any rate so far as our poor Ippolit Kirillovich was able to accommodate them within himself. The principal reason that his address succeeded was because it was sincere: he sincerely believed in the guilt of the defendant; not to order, not out of duty alone did he accuse him and, in demanding 'revenge', he really did tremble with a desire to 'save society'. Even our lady public, which was when all is said and done hostile to Ippolit Kirillovich, did, however, acknowledge the exceeding nature of the impression that was received. He began in a cracked, breaking voice, but soon his voice grew stronger and began to resound over the entire chamber, continuing thus to the end of his speech. No sooner had he ended it, however, than he very nearly collapsed in a dead faint.

'Gentlemen of the jury,' the prosecutor began, 'the case before you has sent its thunder over all of Russia. But what, one may wonder, is the reason for such astonishment, such particular horror? Particularly to us, to us in Russia? After all, we are people who are so habituated to all this! No, our horror is that such sombre cases have almost ceased to inspire us with horror! That is what ought to horrify us, our habituation, and not the isolated evil-doing of this or that individual. Then where are the reasons for our indifference, our barely tepid attitude to such cases, to such portents of the time, prophesying to us an unenviable future? Are they to be found in our cynicism, in the premature exhaustion of the mind and imagination of our society as yet so young, but grown so untimely decrepit? In our moral principles that have been shaken loose to their foundations, or ultimately in the fact that we may perhaps not even have any of those moral principles at all? I do not intend to try to answer those questions, but none the less they are tormenting, and it is not only the duty, but also the obligation of every citizen to suffer on account of them. Our nascent, as yet timid, press has, even so, already performed certain services to society, for never without it should we have learned, in any completeness, of those horrors of unbridled liberty and moral degradation that it incessantly communicates upon its pages to all, and not only to those who visit a chamber of the new Public Court,* granted to us by the present reign. And what do we read, by the day, almost? Oh, of such things, by the minute, before which even the case now in consideration is rendered pale and presents itself as something almost commonplace. The most important thing of all, however, is that a large number of our Russian, our national criminal cases do indeed bear testimony to something universal, a kind of general misfortune that has struck roots among us and which, like all universal evil, it is difficult to combat. There, if you please, is a shining young officer of high society* who, hardly having begun his life and career basely, in silence, without any pang of conscience, knifes to death a petty civil servant, who was in part his benefactor, and his serving maid, in order to purloin his own letter of debt, and together with it the rest of the civil servant's money, more or less saying: "It will be useful for my society amusements and my future career." Having slaughtered them both with his knife, he withdraws, putting a pillow under the head of each corpse. There is a young hero, bedecked with medals for bravery, who in brigandish fashion slaughters on the highway the mother of his captain and benefactor and, as he incites his companions, assures them that "She loves me like her own son, and so will follow all my counsels and take no precautionary measures." Monster he may be, but now, in our time, I no longer dare to say that he is only an isolated monster. Another may not resort to the knife, but thinks and feels in just the same fashion as he, in his soul just as devoid of honour as he. In silence, along with his conscience, perhaps he wonders: "What, in any case, is honour, and is not murder a prejudice?" Perhaps some will raise their voices against me and say that I am a morbid, hysterical man, that I utter a monstrous slander, rave, exaggerate. Let them, let them – and my goodness, I should be the first to be glad! Oh, do not believe me, view me as one who is sick, but remember my words all the same: after all, if only one tenth, one twentieth part of my words is true, why, even then it is dreadful! Look, gentlemen, look how our young men shoot themselves: oh, without the slightest of Hamlet's questions about "what lies *beyond*", without so much as an indication of those questions, as though this point concerning the spirit and all that waits for us beyond the grave had long ago been cancelled out within their natures, buried and strewn with sand. Look, at last, at our depravity, our voluptuaries. Fyodor Pavlovich, the unhappy victim in the current process, is almost an innocent babe compared to some of them. Yet after all, we all knew him, "he lived among us"* . . . Yes, it may perhaps be that one day the psychology of Russian crime will be studied by the foremost intellects, both our own and those of Europe, for the subject merits it. But this study will take place at some later date, at leisure, when the entire tragic farrago of our present moment in time shall have receded to a more remote perspective, where it may be examined both more cleverly and more impartially than men such as I, for example, are able to do. For at present we either experience horror or pretend to, while on the contrary savouring the spectacle like amateurs of powerful and eccentric sensations that shake us from our cynically slothful idleness, or else, like little children, we ward off with our hands the fearsome ghosts and hide our heads in the pillow until the fearsome vision has passed, in order later to forget it instantly in mirth and games. One day, however, we too shall have to set out upon our lives in a sober and reflective manner, we too shall have to cast a glance upon ourselves and on society, we too shall have to comprehend something of our social task, or at any rate begin our comprehension. A great writer* of the era that preceded our own, in the finale of the greatest of his works personifying Russia in the aspect of a boldly dashing Russian *troika* galloping towards an unknown destination, exclaims: "Ah, *troika*, bird *troika*, who dreamed you up?" – and in proud rapture adds that before the headlong galloping *troika* all the nations deferentially stand aside. Yes, gentlemen, let them do so, let them stand aside, deferentially or no, but in my fallible view the inspired artist ended his work thus either in a fit of childishly innocent *belle pensée*, or simply from fear of the censor of those days. For, were his *troika* to be harnessed to his own heroes, the Sobakeviches, Nozdryovs and Chichikovs, then no matter whom one were to appoint *yamshchik*, with such horses one would never reach anything sensible! And those were only the old horses, at a far remove from those we have nowadays, which are rather more special . . .'

Here Ippolit Kirillovich's speech was interrupted by applause. The liberalism of his depiction of the Russian *troika* had gone down well. To be sure, only two or three claps of applause broke loose, and the chairman did not even deem it necessary to address the public with a threat to 'clear the chamber', merely casting a stern look in the direction of the *claqueurs*. But Ippolit Kirillovich took courage: never before until this day had he received applause! For all these years no one had wanted to listen to the man, and now here suddenly was a chance for him to speak his mind to the whole of Russia!

'Indeed,' he resumed, 'what is this Karamazov family that has suddenly earned such a sad notoriety in positively the whole of Russia? Perhaps I exaggerate too much, but it seems to me that in the general picture of this little family it is possible to glimpse here and there some of the principal common elements of our contemporary educated society – oh, not all its elements, and the glimpse is only of microscopic aspect, "as sun's orb in the waters' little drop",* but still something is reflected, something is revealed. Look at this unhappy, unbridled and debauched old man, this *père de famille* who has concluded his existence in so sad a manner. A hereditary nobleman who has begun his career as a poor sponge, by means of a chance and unexpected marriage gets his hands on a dowry, a small sum of capital, to begin with a petty cheat and a smooth-tongued buffoon with an embryo of mental faculties, rather strong ones, as a matter of fact, and before all else a usurer. With the passage of the years, or the accumulation of his capital, rather, he takes courage. His servility and ingratiating flattery disappear and there remains only a mocking and malicious cynic and a voluptuary. The spiritual side of him is entirely cancelled out, but his thirst for life is extreme. What it has come to is that he can see nothing in life beyond voluptuous pleasures, and thus he instructs his children, too. Fatherly, spiritual obligations of any kind there are none. He laughs at them, he rears his small children in the yard at the back and is relieved when they are taken away from him. He even forgets about them entirely. All the old man's moral principles boil down to – *après moi le déluge*. All that is the reverse of the concept of citizen, a most complete, even hostile isolation from society: "Let the whole world go up in flames, as long as I alone am comfortable." And he is comfortable, he is wholly content, he is eager to live thus for another twenty, thirty years. He short-changes his own son, and with that same money, the inheritance of the mother, which he is unwilling to hand over to him, he takes the mistress, the mistress of his own son, away from him. No, I do not intend to leave the defence of the accused to the highly talented defence counsel who has arrived from St Petersburg. I myself shall speak the truth, for I myself understand that sum of indignation he amassed within the heart of his son. But enough, enough of this unhappy old man, he has received his recompense. Let us, however, remember that he is a father, and a contemporary father. Do I offend society if I say that he is even one of many contemporary fathers? Alas, it is simply that so many contemporary fathers do not air their opinions as cynically as this one, for they are better reared, better educated, though in essence they share practically the same philosophy as his. I grant, however, that I am a pessimist, I grant it. We have already agreed that you will forgive me. Let us make the following arrangement in advance: you shall place no credence in what I say, no credence – I shall speak, but you shall place no credence in it. Still, however, let me speak my mind, for some of what I say, after all, you will not forget. But now here are the children of this old man, this *père de famille*: one sits before us now upon the bench of the accused, of him I have much yet to say; of the others, I shall speak merely in passing. Of these others, the elder is one of the contemporary young men with a brilliant education, with a mind that is rather powerful, but who now believes in nothing at all, having already rejected and cancelled out much, too much of life, in precisely the same fashion as his sire. We have all heard him, he has in friendly manner been received in our society. His opinions he has made no secret of, even the contrary, quite the contrary, a fact which now lends me the boldness to speak of him somewhat frankly, not as a private person, of course, but simply as a member of the Karamazov family. Here yesterday, in the environs of our town, there died by suicide a certain sickly idiot, who was strongly implicated in the case before you, the former manservant and, it may be, the natural son of Fyodor Pavlovich, Smerdyakov. He, with hysterical tears, described to me at the preliminary investigation how this young Karamazov, Ivan Fyodorovich, had horrified him with his spiritual immoderacy. "All things that were in the world, in his honour's view, were lawful, and henceforth nothing ought to be forbidden – that was what his honour was a-teaching me all the time." It appears that under the influence of this thesis, which he had been taught, the idiot finally lost his mind, though, of course, an influence was also exerted by his falling sickness and by all this fearsome catastrophe that had burst upon their household. But this idiot happened to let slip a certain most, most interesting remark, one that would have done honour to an observer cleverer than he, and indeed that is even the reason for my bringing it up just now: "If there is," he said to me, "one of the sons who is most like Fyodor Pavlovich in character, then it is he, Ivan Fyodorovich!" With mention of this remark I break off the characterization that has been begun, considering it indelicate to continue further. Oh, I do not wish to draw further conclusions and, like a raven, croak over a young fate naught but ruin. We have already seen today, in this chamber, that the spontaneous force of truth still lives within his young heart, that the emotions of familial attachment have not been extinguished in him by an unbelief and moral cynicism acquired more by inheritance than by genuine suffering of thought. Then the second son – oh, he is still a youth, devout and humble, in opposition to his brother's sombre and corrupting world outlook, seeking to adhere, as it were, to "popular fundamentals" or to what is designated among us by that ingenious little phrase in certain theoretical coteries of our thinking intelligentsia. He, you see, adhered to the monastery; he very nearly took monastic vows himself. In him, I believe, there found expression almost unconsciously and at such an early age that timid despair with which so many now in our poor society, in fear of its cynicism and depravity and erroneously ascribing all the evil to the influence of European education, rush, as they express it, to "the native soil", so to speak, the maternal embrace of their native land, like children frightened by ghosts, and at the withered breast of an enfeebled mother yearn only to fall peacefully asleep and even pass the rest of their lives asleep, if only they may not see the horrors that so frighten them. I, for my part, wish the good and talented youth all the best, I desire that his youthful *belle âme* and striving for popular fundamentals shall not subsequently be transmuted, as so often is the case, to a sombre mysticism from the moral point of view, and from the civic one to a narrow-minded chauvinism – two qualities that possibly threaten the nation with a greater evil than even the premature corruption, caused by European education falsely understood and pointlessly acquired, such as that from which his elder brother is suffering.'

For chauvinism and mysticism there were again two or three claps of applause. And of course, Ippolit Kirillovich had become carried away, and all of this had little bearing on the case before the jury, to say nothing of the fact that it had all come out rather obscurely, but the consumptive and embittered man had been unable to resist the opportunity of speaking his mind at least once in his life. It was said in our town later on that in his characterization of Ivan Fyodorovich he had let himself be led by an emotion that was even indelicate, because the latter had once or twice publicly got the better of him in argument, and Ippolit Kirillovich, recalling this, had now conceived a wish to get his own back. But I am not sure that it was right to conclude thus. In any case, all this was merely an introduction, and after it the speech proceeded more directly and more closely to the matter in hand.

'But here now is the third son of the father of a contemporary family,' Ippolit Kirillovich resumed. 'He sits upon the bench of the accused, he sits before us. Before us also are his exploits, his life and deeds: the time is at hand, and all has been unfolded, all made manifest. In opposition to the "Europeanism" and the "popular fundamentals" of his brothers he, as it were, represents natural Russia – oh, not all, not all of her, and God preserve us that it be all! And yet, here she is, our dear, sweet Russia, there is a smell of her, a scent of her, the mother. Oh, we are spontaneous, we are good and evil in an astonishing blend, we are lovers of enlightenment and Schiller and at the same time we go rampaging around the inns and tearing out the beards of the drunken sots, our boon companions. Oh, we too are good and beautiful, but only when we ourselves feel good and beautiful. Indeed, we are positively tempested – yes, tempested – by the most noble ideals, but only upon condition that they be attained of themselves, fall down upon our tables from the sky, and above all that they be gratis, gratis, so that nothing must be paid for them. Paying is something we dislike horribly, while on the other hand we love to receive, and this in everything. Oh, give us, give us every possible blessing of life (it must be every possible one, for more cheaply we will not be reconciled) and in particular do not hinder our disposition in any way, and then we too shall demonstrate that we are able to be good and beautiful. We are not greedy, no, but give us money, as much, as much, as much as possible, and you will see how magnanimously, with what contempt for the base metal, we can dissipate it within a single night in an immoderate spree. And if money is not given us, then we shall demonstrate how we are able to get our hands on it when we really want to. But of that later, let us proceed in proper order. First of all before us stands a poor, neglected boy, "in the backyard with no boots", as our venerable and respected fellow-citizen – alas, of foreign origin! – expressed it just now. Once again I repeat – to no one else will I leave the defence of the accused! I am both prosecutor and counsel for the defence. Yes, sir, we, too, are men, we too are human beings, and we are able to assess the manner in which the first impressions of childhood and the cosy little family nest may influence the character. But now the boy is become a youth, a young man, an officer; for unruly conduct and for challenging someone to a duel he is exiled to one of the small and distant frontier towns of our abundant Russia. There he serves, there, too, he goes upon the spree, and of course – great ships require deep waters. We need money, sirs, money first and foremost, and lo, after long arguments, it is settled between his father and him that he shall receive his last six thousand roubles, and they are sent to him. Observe that he has issued a document, and that a letter of his exists in which he almost forgoes his right to the rest of the money and with this six thousand concludes his altercation with his father. At this point occurs his meeting with a young girl of lofty character and education. Oh, I do not dare recount the details, you have only just heard them: here is honour, here is selflessness, and I say no more. The image of a young man, light-minded and depraved, but bowing before true nobility, before a higher idea, has fleeted before us with exceeding sympathy. But suddenly thereupon, within this very chamber, quite unexpectedly has followed the reverse side of the medallion. Once more I do not dare embark upon conjecture, and shall restrain myself from analysing why it has so followed. But all the same there were, after all, reasons why it has so followed. This same young person, in tears of an indignation long concealed, declares to us that he, he was the first to despise her for her incautious, possibly immoderate, but all the same exalted, all the same magnanimous impulse. In him, after all, in this girl's betrothed, before all others, first fleetingly appeared that mocking smile which only from him alone she could not bear. Aware that he has already betrayed her (betrayed her in the conviction that she now had a duty to endure anything from him, even his betrayal), aware of this, she purposely offers him three thousand roubles, and plainly, all too plainly, gives him to understand as she does so that she is offering him the money so that he may betray her: "Well, will you accept it, will you be so cynical?" she says to him silently with her judging and testing gaze. He stares at her, understands her thoughts completely (after all, he himself has admitted here in your presence that he understood everything) and without a scruple appropriates that three thousand and squanders it in two days with his new beloved! What then are we to believe? The first legend — the loftily noble impulse, a nobility giving away the last of its means of livelihood and prostrating itself before virtue, or the reverse side of the medallion, so detestable? Ordinarily in life it is the case that between two opposites the truth is to be sought somewhere in the middle; in the present instance that is literally not so. The most probable thing is that in the first instance he was sincerely noble, while in the second instance he was just as sincerely base. Why? For the very reason that we are a broad, Karamazovian nature — that is what I am leading up to, you see — capable of accommodating all kinds of opposites and of contemplating both abysses, the abyss above us, the abyss of the loftiest ideals, and the abyss below us, the abyss of the very lowest, stinking degradation. Remember the brilliant thought expressed earlier by the young observer who has deeply and closely contemplated the whole of the Karamazov family, Mr Rakitin: "A sense of the lowness of their fall is as necessary to these unbridled, immoderate natures as a sense of the loftiest nobility" — and it is true: it is precisely to them that this unnatural mixture is constantly and unceasingly necessary. Two abysses, two abysses, gentlemen, at one and the same moment — without that we are unhappy and unsatisfied, our existences are incomplete. We are broad, broad, as all our dear mother Russia, we shall accommodate all things and accommodate ourselves with all things! Talking of which, gentlemen of the jury, we have now touched upon that three thousand roubles, and I shall permit myself to run somewhat ahead. Imagine, if you will, that he, this man whom we are characterizing, having received this money that day, and in such a fashion, through such shame, through such disgrace, through degradation of the last degree — imagine that he could that very day apparently be capable of keeping back a half of it, sewing it into an incense-bag and for a whole month thereafter having the steadfastness to bear it around with him upon his neck, in spite of all temptations and extreme necessities! Neither in his drunken carousing about the inns, nor when he had to rush out of town in order to obtain, heaven knows from whom, the money he needed in order to take his beloved away from the wiles of a rival, his father — did he dare to touch that incense-bag. Why, even were it only in order not to abandon his beloved to the wiles of the old man of whom he was so jealous, he might have been expected to unseal his incense-bag and remain at home, the relentless guardian of his beloved, awaiting that moment when she would say to him at last: "I am thine," whereupon he would rush off with her somewhere as far away as possible from his present fateful surroundings. But no, he does not touch his talisman, and on what pretext? The original pretext, we have said, was namely so that when he was told "I am thine, take me where thou wilt", he should have the means to do so. This first pretext, however, paled, in the words of the defendant himself, into insignificance before the second. For as long as I bear this money upon my person, he said, "I am a scoundrel, but not a thief," for I may always go to my betrothed whom I have insulted and, placing before her this half of the sum deceitfully appropriated from her, may always say to her: "You see, I squandered half of your money and thereby proved that I am a weak and immoral man and, if you like, a scoundrel" (I use the language of the defendant himself), "but though I am a scoundrel, I am not a thief, for were I a thief, I should not have brought you this half of the money in question, but should have appropriated it as I did the first half." A remarkable explanation of the evidence! This most rabid, but weak man, unable to withstand the temptation of accepting three thousand roubles together with such disgrace – this same man suddenly feels within himself such stoic steadfastness that he can bear thousands around his neck, not daring to touch them! Does that even in any way conform with the character under investigation by us? No, and I will permit myself to tell you how the real Dmitry Karamazov would have behaved in such an instance, even had he actually brought himself to sew up his money in an incense-bag. Why, at the first temptation – oh, if only to once more divert that same new beloved with whom he had already blown the first half of that same money, he would have split open his incense-bag and removed from it – oh, let us suppose in the first instance no more than a hundred roubles, for why, he would say to himself, should he absolutely have to give back half, fifteen hundred, that is, fourteen hundred would be sufficient – in the end, you see, the result would still be the same: "a scoundrel," he would say, "but not a thief, because say what you like, I shall have brought back fourteen hundred roubles, while a thief would have taken the lot and brought back nothing." Then, after some time had passed, he would again have split open the incense-bag and again taken out a second hundred, then a third, then a fourth, and by the end of the month, no later, would at last have taken out the last hundred but one, saying that he would bring back one hundred, and the result would be the same: "a scoundrel, but not a thief. Nine-and-twenty hundred I squandered, but all the same I did return one, while a thief would not even have returned that." And finally, having squandered that last hundred but one, he would have looked at the last one and said to himself: "You know, it really is not worth returning one hundred – come, let us squander it, too!" That is how the real Dmitry Karamazov would have behaved, the one whom we know! As for the legend of the incense-bag – that is such a contradiction of reality that it can no longer be conceived. One may conceive anything, but not that. But to this we shall return again.'

Having listed in order all that was known to the judicial investigation concerning the disputes over property and the familial relations between father and son, and drawing again and again the conclusion that from the available information there was not the slightest chance of determining in this question of the division of the inheritance who had shortchanged whom or been shortchanged by him, Ippolit Kirillovich, apropos of those three thousand roubles which had lodged themselves in Mitya's brain as a fixed idea, mentioned the opinion of the medical experts.

7

A Historical Survey

'THE opinion of the medical experts sought to prove to us that the defendant is not in his right mind and a maniac. I assert that he is in fact perfectly in his right mind, but that this is the worst thing of all: had he not been in his right mind, then he might perhaps have turned out to have far more brains. As regards the opinion that he is a maniac, then with this I would concur, but only on one point – the same one to which the examination drew our attention, namely the defendant's view of that three thousand which had supposedly been withheld from him by his father. It may, none the less, be possible to discover a point of view incomparably closer to hand, in order to explain this customary frenzy of the accused in connection with that money, than his leaning towards insanity. For my part, I fully agree with the opinion of the young physician who found that the defendant enjoys and has enjoyed complete and normal mental faculties, but has merely been angry and embittered. In this lies the heart of the matter: not in the three thousand, not in a sum of money did the object of the defendant's constant and frenzied embitterment lie, but in the fact that there was here a particular reason that aroused his anger. That reason was – jealousy!'

At this point Ippolit Kirillovich extensively unrolled the entire picture of the defendant's fateful passion for Grushenka. He began right from the moment when the defendant had set off to see the 'young person' in order to 'beat her unmercifully', to use the defendant's own words,

Ippolit Kirillovich explained, 'but instead of beating her unmercifully he remained at her feet — there is the beginning of this love. At the same time the old man, the defendant's father, also casts an eye upon the same young person — a remarkable and fatal coincidence, for the two hearts were kindled suddenly, at the same time, though previously both one and the other had known and maintained acquaintance with this person — and these two hearts were kindled with the most unrestrained, the most Karamazovian passion. Here we have her own confession: "I," she says, "laughed at the one as at the other." Yes, she had suddenly conceived a wish to laugh at the one and at the other; previously she had not so wished, but now suddenly this intention had slipped into her mind — and the upshot of it was that both fell vanquished before her. The old man, who worshipped money as though it were God, immediately got ready three thousand roubles to give to her merely in exchange for visiting his abode, but was soon reduced to a point where he would have considered it happiness to place at her feet his name and all his fortune, if only she would agree to become his lawful spouse. Of this we have firm testimony. And as for the defendant, well, his tragedy is plain to see, it is before us. But such was the "game" played by the young person. To the unhappy young man the seductress did not even hold out any hope, for hope, genuine hope, was granted him only at the very last moment, when he, down before his tormentress on his knees, stretched out to her his hands already steeped in the blood of his father and rival: in that position, namely, too, was he arrested. "Send me, send me together with him into penal servitude, it was I who pushed him to it, I am more guilty than any!" this woman herself cried out, by now in sincere remorse, at the moment of his arrest. The talented young man who has taken it upon himself to write a description of the case before you — that same Mr Rakitin to whom I have already referred — defines in one or two compressed and characteristic phrases the character of this heroine: "An early disillusionment, an early deception and fall, a betrayal by the seducer who was her betrothed and who abandoned her, then poverty, the curse of a decent family and, at last, the patronage of a certain wealthy old man whom she, as a matter of fact, even now considers her benefactor. Within her young heart, which may perhaps have contained much good within it, anger was harboured from all too early an age. A calculating character was formed, one that stored up capital. A derisiveness and vengefulness towards society were formed." After this characterization it may be grasped that she was capable of laughing at the one and at the other solely for the sake of a game, a malicious game. And now in this month of hopeless love, of moral downfalls, of betrayal of the one to whom he was betrothed, of pocketing another's money that had been entrusted to his honour – the defendant, in addition to that, attains a state almost of frenzy, of rabid fury, because of constant jealousy, and of whom? His father! And to crown it all, the crazy old man is enticing and trying to seduce the object of his passion – with that same three thousand that his son considers his own, native inheritance from his mother, and which he holds against his father. Yes, I concur: that was hard to endure! In such a situation even mania might appear. Not in money lay the heart of the matter, but in the fact that with that same money his happiness was with such loathsome cynicism being smashed to smithereens!'

After this, Ippolit Kirillovich passed to the subject of how the thought of parricide had gradually arisen within the defendant, and retraced it by the evidence.

'At first we merely go shouting about the inns – we do it all that month. Oh, we like to pass the time among people and to waste no time in telling those people everything, even our most infernal and dangerous ideas, we like to confide in people and, we know not why, at once, immediately demand that those people at once respond to us with the most complete sympathy, enter into all our cares and anxieties, say "yes" to us and raise no hindrance to our disposition. Otherwise we shall grow angry and wreck the whole inn.' (There followed the anecdote concerning Second-Grade Captain Snegiryov.) 'Those who saw and heard the defendant during that month felt, at last, that now not only cries and threats against the father might be involved, but that in such a frenzy those threats might well pass into action.' (At this point the public procurator described the family meeting at the monastery, the defendant's conversations with Alyosha and the shocking scene of violence in the father's house when the defendant had burst in upon him after dinner.) 'It is not my intention to insist,' Ippolit Kirillovich went on, 'that before this scene the defendant had already, of malice prepense, decided to bring about his father's end by murdering him. None the less, this idea had already come up within his mind several times, and he had given it careful deliberation – for that we have evidence, witnesses and his own confession. I confess, gentlemen of the jury,' Ippolit Kirillovich adjoined to this remark, 'that even until today I have hesitated to impute to the defendant the complete and conscious premeditation of the crime that was suggesting itself to him. I have been firmly convinced that his soul had already more than once contemplated the fateful moment in advance, but only contemplated it, envisaged it only as lying within the realms of possibility, but had yet determined neither the term nor the circumstances of its execution. But my hesitation lasted only until today, until the appearance of this fateful document, presented to the court today by Miss Verkhovtseva. You yourselves, gentlemen, heard what she exclaimed: "It is the plan, it is the programme of the murder!" – thus did she describe the unhappy defendant's unhappy "drunken" letter. And indeed, behind this letter there lies all the import of a programme and premeditation. It was written two whole days before the crime – and, in this way, it is now definitely known to us that two whole days before the execution of his terrible design, the defendant declared with an oath that if he did not obtain the money upon the morrow he would kill his father with a view to taking the money from under his pillow "in the envelope with the red ribbon, if only Ivan has gone away". You hear? "If only Ivan has gone away" – here, in other words, it was all considered, the circumstances were weighed up – and what do we see: the whole thing was subsequently executed as if out of a book! Its premeditated and deliberate nature are beyond all doubt, the crime was to be committed for the purpose of robbery, that has been unequivocally declared, that has been written and signed. The defendant does not disclaim the presence of his signature. It will be said: these things were written by a man who was drunk. But that provides no extenuation, and is all the more important: while in a drunken state he wrote what he had conceived while in a sober one. Had it not been conceived in a sober one, it would not have been written in a drunken one. It will, perhaps, be said: why did he go about the inns shouting of his intentions? Anyone who determined on such a deed *with premeditation* would say nothing and keep it to himself. True, but he went and did his shouting when as yet he had no plans or forethoughts, but when there was in him but a certain desire, the mere maturing of an urge. Later he did less shouting about it. On the evening that this letter was written, having got drunk in the Capital City inn, he was, contrary to habit, taciturn, did not play billiards, sat to one side, spoke to no one and merely drove the assistant of one of our local merchants from his seat, but this almost unconsciously, out of a custom of quarrelling, without which now upon entering an inn he could no longer dispense. To be sure, together with his final resolution there must also have occurred to the defendant the apprehension that he had as a preliminary done too much shouting around the town and that this might greatly serve towards his conviction and prosecution when he carried out his design. But what was to be done, the fact of the publicity was now achieved, it could not be unmade, and if a lucky chance had rescued us before, so might it also now. We pinned our hopes upon our star, gentlemen! I am obliged, moreover, to admit that he did much to avoid the fateful moment, that he used a most considerable degree of effort in attempting to evade the bloody outcome. "Tomorrow I will obtain it from all men," as he writes in his curious language, "and if men will not give it me, then blood shall be spilt." Written, likewise, in a drunken state and likewise executed in a sober state, as if out of a book!'

Here Ippolit Kirillovich proceeded to a detailed description of all Mitya's endeavours to obtain money for himself, so as to avoid the crime. He described Mitya's adventures at the house of Samsonov, his journey to see Lyagavy – all of it from the documentary evidence. 'Exhausted, mocked, hungry, having sold his watch for that journey (while none the less carrying fifteen hundred roubles upon his person – and apparently, oh, apparently!), tormented with jealousy on account of the object of his love, whom he had abandoned in the town, suspecting that in his absence she would go to see Fyodor Pavlovich, he returns at last to the town. Thanks be to God! She has not been to see Fyodor Pavlovich. He himself escorts her to her protector Samsonov. (It is a strange fact that we are not jealous of Samsonov, and this is a highly characteristic psychological feature of this case!) After that, he rushes back to his observation post "at the rears" and there – there he learns that Smerdyakov is in a fit of the falling sickness, the other manservant ill – the way is clear, and the "signals" are in his hands – what temptation! None the less, in spite of it all he puts up some resistance; he goes to see that temporary resident of our town, so highly respected by us all, Mrs Khokhlakova. Having long regarded his fate with compassion, this lady offers him the most reasonable of counsels: to give up all this excess, this scandalous love, these idlings about the inns, this fruitless waste of his young strength, and to set off for Siberia, to the gold-mines: "There is the issue for your raging energy, your *roman*-esque character that craves adventure."' Having described the upshot of that conversation and the moment when the defendant suddenly received the news that Grushenka had not spent any time at Samsonov's at all, having described the momentary frenzy of the unhappy, jealous man whose nerves had been exhausted, at the thought that she had indeed deceived him now, there at the house of Fyodor Pavlovich, Ippolit Kirillovich concluded, directing attention to the fateful role played by chance: 'had the serving-maid had time to tell him that his beloved was in Mokroye, with her "former" and "beyond dispute" – nothing would ever have happened. But she was taken aback with fear, began to vow and to swear to God, and if the defendant did not murder her there and then, it was because he had gone dashing off headlong after the woman who had betrayed him. Observe, however: no matter how beside himself he may have been, he did, none the less, take the brass pestle with him. Why a pestle, in particular, why not some other instrument of murder? Well, if for an entire month we have been contemplating this scene and preparing for it, as soon as anything resembling a weapon flits before our gaze, we seize it as our weapon. And that some object of this kind might serve as an instrument of murder – that we have already envisaged for an entire month. That was why we so instantly and incontrovertibly recognized it as such! And so the fact remains that it was by no means unconsciously, by no means involuntarily, that he seized this fateful pestle. And so here he is in his father's orchard – the way is clear, there are no witnesses, but dead of night, murk, jealousy. The suspicion that she is here, with him, her rival, in his embrace and, possibly, laughing at him at that moment – takes his breath away. And indeed it is not only a suspicion – what suspicions can there be now, for the deception is manifest, plain to see: she is there, right there in that room from which the light is coming, she is in there with him behind the screen – and now the unhappy man steals over to the window, peeps deferentially in, docilely resigns himself and prudently withdraws, so as to get away as quickly as possible from trouble, in case something dangerous and immoral happens – and this is what they would have us believe, we who know the character of the defendant, who understand the condition of mind he was in, a condition that is known to us from the evidence, and above all in possession of the signals, by means of which he could at once unlock the house and enter!' Here, in connection with the signals, Ippolit Kirillovich let his prosecution rest for a while, deeming it necessary to enlarge on the question of Smerdyakov, with the purpose of exhausting completely this entire introductory episode concerning the suspicion that Smerdyakov was guilty of the murder, and to put paid to that idea once and for all. This he did most thoroughly, and everyone realized that, in spite of all the contempt he had expressed towards this supposition, he none the less viewed it as highly important.

8

A Treatise on Smerdyakov

'IN the first place, whence did the possibility of such a suspicion arise?' Ippolit Kirillovich began, taking this question as his starting-point. 'The first person to cry out that Smerdyakov had committed the murder was the defendant at the moment of his arrest, yet from that very first cry of his right to this very moment of the trial he has not brought forward one piece of factual evidence to support his accusation – not only that, but he has not brought forward so much as even a hint of such evidence that would in any way conform with human sense. His accusation has subsequently been confirmed by only three persons: the two brothers of the defendant, and Miss Svetlova. But the defendant's elder brother declared his suspicion only today, in a state of illness, in a fit of self-evident delirium and nervous fever, while earlier, throughout the whole two months, a fact of which we are positively informed, he totally shared the conviction concerning his brother's guilt, and did not even seek to oppose this idea. We shall, however, treat of this separately later. After this the younger brother of the defendant declared to us just now that he has no factual evidence whatever to support his notion concerning the guilt of Smerdyakov, not even the slightest, but finds grounds for his conclusion merely in the words of the defendant and "the expression on his face" – yes, this colossal demonstration of fact was twice pronounced just now by his brother. As for Miss Svetlova, she expressed herself in perhaps even more colossal manner: "Whatever the defendant tells you, please believe it, he is not the kind of man to tell a lie." There is all the factual proof concerning the guilt of Smerdyakov we have obtained from these three persons, who have all too great an interest in the fate of the defendant. And yet in spite of this the accusation that Smerdyakov is guilty has persisted and has been maintained, is maintained even now – can that be believed, can that be imagined?'

At this point Ippolit Kirillovich deemed it necessary to trace in brief outline the character of the deceased Smerdyakov, 'who cut short his own life in a fit of morbid delirium and insanity'. He presented him as a man weak-minded, with an embryo of some dim progressive education, unbalanced by philosophical ideas that were beyond the strength of his intelligence and frightened by certain contemporary theories concerning duty and responsibility in which he had been generously instructed from a practical point of view – by the reckless existence of his deceased *barin*, and possibly also father, Fyodor Pavlovich, and from a theoretical one – by various strange philosophical conversations with his *barin*'s elder son, Ivan Fyodorovich, who had willingly permitted himself this diversion – doubtless from tedium or a need for mockery that had found no better application. 'He himself described to me his mental condition during the last days of his sojourn in the house of his *barin*,' Ippolit Kirillovich elucidated, 'but others, too, have testified to the same thing: the defendant himself, his brother and even the manservant Grigory, that is to say, all those who might be expected to have known him most intimately. In addition to his being dispirited by the falling sickness, Smerdyakov was "cowardly as a hen". "He fell at my feet and kissed them," the defendant informed us at a moment when he had not yet apprised a certain disadvantage to himself in those words, "he is a hen with the falling sickness", was the way he expressed it in his own characteristic language. And yet he it is whom the defendant (as he himself has testified) selects as his trusted agent, bullying him so badly that the latter agrees, at last, to serve as his spy and message-carrier. In this capacity of domestic snoop he betrays his *barin*, informs the defendant both of the existence of the envelope containing the money and of the signals, by means of which it is possible to gain access to the *barin*'s chambers – and how could he not so inform? "His honour was going to kill me, sir, I could see plain as daylight he was going to kill me, sir," he said at the preliminary investigation, positively shaking and trembling before us, in spite of the fact that the tormentor who had bullied him was already under arrest at the time and could no longer come and punish him. "His honour suspected me every moment, sir, and I in fear and trembling, just in order to assuage his wrath, made haste to communicate to him all the different secrets, sir, in order thereby that he could see my innocence before him and let me go alive in peace, sir." Here are his own words, I noted them down and committed them to memory: "Whenever he used to shout at me, I just fell on my knees before his honour." Being by his nature a highly honest young man and entering thereby into the confidence of his *barin*, who had discerned in him this honesty when the latter had returned to him the money he had lost, the unhappy Smerdyakov was, one must suppose, horribly racked by remorse at having betrayed his *barin*, whom he loved as his benefactor. Those who suffer badly from the falling sickness invariably have, according to the testimony of the deepest psychiatrists, a tendency towards constant and, of course, morbid self-accusation. They torment themselves with their own "guilt" for something and in someone's regard, torment themselves with gnawings of conscience, frequently, even without any foundation, exaggerate and even dream up various culpabilities and crimes which they impute to themselves. And now here we have a case where a subject of this type really does become guilty and criminally involved, from fear and bullying. Moreover he had a premonition that because of circumstances that are forming themselves before his eyes, something unpleasant may ensue. When Fyodor Pavlovich's elder

son, Ivan Fyodorovich, travelled away to Moscow just before the catastrophe, Smerdyakov implored him to remain, not daring, however, in
keeping with his cowardly habit, to air all his misgivings to him in a clear
and categorical form. He merely made do with hints, but the hints were
not taken. It should be observed that in Ivan Fyodorovich he saw as it
were a protection, a guarantee that while the latter remained at home, no
trouble would take place. Remember the expression contained in Dmitry
Karamazov's "drunken" letter: "I will kill the old man, if only Ivan has
gone away"; in other words, Ivan Fyodorovich's presence in the house
appeared to all as a kind of guarantee of quiet and order in the house.
And lo, now he actually does go away, and Smerdyakov at once, no
more than an hour after the departure of the young *barin*, falls down in a
fit of the falling sickness. But that is perfectly natural. Here it needs to be
mentioned that during the final days, dispirited by fears and by a kind of
despair, Smerdyakov had a particular sense of the possible approach of
his fits of the falling sickness, which had invariably afflicted him before at
moments of moral tension and shock. The day and the hour of these fits
is, of course, impossible to predict, but all epileptics are able to sense
beforehand within themselves a disposition towards them. Medicine tells
us so. And lo, no sooner does Ivan Fyodorovich leave the threshold than
Smerdyakov, influenced by the effects of his, so to speak, orphaned and
defenceless state, goes down to the cellar on a matter of household
business, descends the staircase and thinks: "Am I or am I not about to
have a fit, and what if it comes right now?" And lo, precisely because of
this mood, this state of suspicion, these questions, he is seized by the
laryngeal spasm by which the falling sickness is invariably preceded, and
down he flies headlong, bereft of consciousness, to the floor of the cellar.
And here, in this most natural fortuity, some contrive to detect a suspicion, a sign, a hint that his illness was *purposely* feigned! But if that were
so, then there at once appears the question: why? On what calculation,
with what goal? Never mind medicine, now it is science, they say, that is
wrong, science that is in error, the doctors have been unable to distinguish
truth from feigning — let that be so, let it be so, but then answer me one
question: for what reason should he feign? Possibly so as, having schemed
the murder, to draw to himself by means of the fit he had suffered the
attention of those in the house in advance and as quickly as possible? You
see, gentlemen of the jury, there were or had been in the house of
Fyodor Pavlovich upon the night of the crime five people: in the first
place, Fyodor Pavlovich himself, but he did not kill himself, that is clear;
in the second, his manservant Grigory, but then he himself was very

nearly killed; in the third, Grigory's wife, the serving-maid Marfa Ignat-yevna, but to imagine her as the murderess of her *barin* is simply shameful. There remain, therefore, two people in view: the defendant and Smerdyakov. But as the defendant assures us that he is not the murderer, then consequently it must have been Smerdyakov, there is no other alternative, for no one else can be found, no other murderer may be selected. Here, here, therefore, is the origin of this "cunning" and colossal accusation against the unhappy idiot who yesterday did away with himself! It lies in one simple fact, namely that there is no other candidate! Given the existence of a mere shadow, a mere suspicion of another, of some sixth person, I am convinced that even the defendant himself would be ashamed to point to Smerdyakov, but would point to that sixth person, for to accuse Smerdyakov of this murder is a total absurdity.

'Gentlemen, let us abandon psychology, let us abandon medicine, let us abandon even logic itself, let us turn merely to the evidence, to the evidence alone and let us see what the evidence tells us. Smerdyakov committed the murder, but how? Alone or in association with the defendant? Let us initially examine the first possibility, that is to say, that Smerdyakov planned and committed the murder alone. Of course, if he did it, then surely he must have done it for some purpose, for some gain. Possessing, however, not a shadow of the motives for the murder such as those possessed by the defendant − that is to say, hatred, jealousy, etcetera, etcetera − it is beyond doubt that Smerdyakov could have committed it only for the sake of money, in order to appropriate that same three thousand he himself had seen his *barin* put away in the envelope. And so, having schemed the murder, he communicates in advance to another person − and, moreover, a person in the highest degree interested, namely the defendant − all the details concerning the money and the signals: the location of the envelope, the precise nature of the inscription upon it, the material with which it was tied, and above all, above all, communicates to him those "signals" by means of which one may pass into the *barin*'s chambers. Well, does he do this simply in order to give himself away? Or in order to provide a rival for himself, one who himself may wish to gain entrance and acquire the envelope? Ah yes, I will be told, but after all he imparted the information out of fear. But how can that be? The man who did not blink at devising such a fearless, brutal scheme and then executing it − communicates information which he alone in all the world is privy to, and which had he but kept silent about it, would never have been guessed by anyone in all the world? No, however cowardly the man may have been, had he devised a scheme like that then on no account would he have told anyone, at least about the envelope and the signals, for that would have meant to give himself away in advance. Had he been absolutely forced to impart information he would have devised something on purpose, concocted some fib or other, but about that he would have remained silent! On the contrary, I say again, had he kept silent only about the money, but then committed the murder and appropriated that money, no one in all the world would have accused him, at any rate, of murder for the sake of robbery, for after all no one but he had seen that money, no one but he knew of its existence in the house. Even were he to be accused, people would be bound to think that he had committed the murder from some other motive. But as no one had ever observed any such motives in him prior to the deed, and as everyone had, on the contrary, perceived that he was liked by his *barin*, honoured with his *barin*'s confidence, then of course he would be the last to receive suspicion, and suspicion would fall first and foremost upon such a one as had possessed those motives, one who had himself shouted that he possessed those motives, who had not concealed them, had revealed them to everyone, in a word, suspicion would fall upon the murdered man's son, Dmitry Fyodorovich. Smerdyakov would murder and rob, and the son would be accused of it — after all, that would of course be to Smerdyakov's advantage as a murderer, would it not? Well, and so now it is to this son Dmitry that Smerdyakov, having laid his scheme of murder, communicates in advance the information concerning the money, the envelope and the signals — how logical it is, how plain!

'There arrives the day of the murder planned by Smerdyakov, and lo, now he flies clean off his feet, *having feigned the whole thing*, in a fit of the falling sickness, and why? Well, of course, so that, in the first place, the manservant Grigory, planning to treat his injuries, and perceiving that there was no one at all to guard the house, might perhaps put off his treatment and settle down on watch himself. In the second place, of course, so that the *barin* himself, perceiving that no one was on watch, and in fearful apprehension, which he did not conceal, that his son might arrive, would redouble his mistrust and caution. Finally, and principally, of course, so that he, Smerdyakov, being incapacitated by the fit, would at once be carried from the kitchen, where he invariably passed the night separate from all the rest and where he had his own special entry and exit, at the other end of the outbuilding, to Grigory's little room, which both Grigory and his wife occupied behind the partition, three paces from their own bed, as had always happened, from time immemorial, as soon as he was incapacitated by the falling sickness, at the disposition of the *barin* and the compassionate Marfa Ignatyevna. There, as he lay behind the partition, in order to appear more truly ill, he would most probably, of course, begin to groan, that is, keep waking them up all night (as was indeed the case, according to the testimony of Grigory and his wife) — and all this, all this in order to be able to arise the more conveniently and then slay the *barin*!

'But, it will be said to me, perhaps he feigned his fit for the very purpose of evading suspicion as one who was ill, and communicated the information concerning the money and the signals to the defendant for the very purpose of luring him so that he would come and commit the murder, and when the latter, do you see, having committed the murder left and carried off the money, possibly making a noise and a commotion while doing so, arousing witnesses from slumber, then, you see, Smerdyakov too would arise and go — and what would he go in order to do? He would go for the very purpose of murdering the *barin* a second time, and a second time carrying off the money that had already been carried off. Gentlemen, you laugh? I myself am embarrassed to make such suppositions, yet, if you will credit it, it is this very thing that the defendant asserts is so: what he says is that after he had already left the house, having brought Grigory down and alarmed the entire neighbourhood, he rose, went, murdered and robbed. I say nothing of how Smerdyakov could have worked all this out in advance and predicted it all as though on his fingertips, that is to say that the angry and enraged son would arrive solely in order to cast a deferential glance in through the window and, though in possession of the signals, beat a retreat, leaving him, Smerdyakov, all the spoils. Gentlemen, I earnestly ask you this question: at what moment did Smerdyakov commit his crime? Please point out that moment, for without it there can be no indictment.

'But, you may say, perhaps the falling sickness was genuine. The sick man suddenly regained consciousness, heard a shout and went outside — well, and what of it? Did he take a look and say to himself: why do I not go and kill the *barin*? But how could he have discovered what was taking place, for, after all, he had until that moment been lying unconscious? And in any case, gentlemen, there is a limit even to fantasies.

'"Yes, sir," men of astuteness will say, "but what if the two were in complicity, and what if they both committed the murder together and divided the cash, what then?"

'Yes, indeed, that is a suspicion of major importance, and for a start there is colossal evidence to support it: one of the accomplices commits the murder and takes all the toil and trouble upon himself, while the other does nothing at all, feigning the falling sickness — for the very purpose of arousing suspicion in everyone beforehand, uneasiness in the *barin*, uneasiness in Grigory. One wonders what motives the two accomplices could have had for dreaming up such a crazy plan as this? But it may be that there was no active complicity at all on the part of Smerdyakov, but rather, so to speak, one that was passive and born of long suffering: perhaps the cowed Smerdyakov merely agreed not to oppose the murder and, sensing that he would in the end be accused of having let his *barin* be murdered, of having failed to shout or to oppose the deed, secured in advance from Dmitry Karamazov permission to spend that interval of time as though he were in the falling sickness, "and you can go and murder as you please, but my *izba* has walls". But if that were the case, then again, as this falling sickness must surely cause a flurry of alarm within the house, foreseeing this, Dmitry Karamazov would on no account agree to such an understanding. But I concede, let it be the case that he did agree: after all, even then the result would be that Dmitry Karamazov was the murderer, the outright murderer and instigator, and Smerdyakov only a passive accomplice, and not even an accomplice, but only someone who connived out of fear and against his will, something which, after all, the process of the law would be bound to perceive, and yet, lo, what do we see? As soon as the defendant is arrested he instantly unloads all the guilt on to Smerdyakov and accuses him *alone*. Not of complicity with him does he accuse him, but rather him alone: he did it on his own, he says, he committed the murder and the robbery, it is the work of his hands! But what kind of accomplices are they who at once begin to lay the blame upon each other — and in any case that never occurs. And observe what a risk Karamazov is taking: he is the principal murderer, while the other is not, the other has merely connived and lain behind the partition, and now he unloads all the guilt on to the recumbent man. But after all, the other, the recumbent one, might grow angry and out of a mere sense of self-preservation waste no time in declaring the genuine truth: that both had worked in complicity, but that he had not committed the murder, merely allowed it and connived at it because he was afraid. After all, he, Smerdyakov, might realize that the law would at once perceive the degree of his culpability, and consequently he might also calculate that if he were to receive punishment, then it would be of an incomparably lesser nature than that meted out to the other, the principal murderer, who wished to unload all the guilt on to him. But then he would perforce have made a confession. This, however, we did not see. Smerdyakov never even mentioned any complicity, though the murderer unequivocally accused him and all the time kept pointing to him as the sole murderer. Not only that: Smerdyakov even disclosed to the investigation that it had been *he himself* who had communicated to the defendant the information concerning the envelope of money and the signals, and that had it not been for him the other would never have discovered anything. Had he really been acting in complicity and been guilty, would he have given this information so lightly to the investigation, that is to say that all of this he had himself imparted to the defendant? On the contrary, he would have begun to deny it, and would be bound to distort the evidence and reduce its import. But he did neither. Only one who was innocent, who was not afraid that he would be accused of complicity, could have done as he did. And then, in a fit of morbid melancholy caused by his falling sickness and by the whole of this catastrophe that had burst upon him, yesterday he hanged himself. Doing so, he left a note, written in his curious style: "I exterminate myself by my own will and inclination, in order to blame no one." Well, why did he not simply add to the note: "the murderer is I, and not Karamazov". But this he did not do: did he have the conscience for the one but not the other? And what happens? Earlier today money was brought to the court, three thousand roubles — "the very same money", it was said, "that was contained in that very same envelope that now lies on the table of material evidence, and which I received yesterday from Smerdyakov". But you yourselves, gentlemen of the jury, remember that melancholy scene of earlier today. I shall not recapitulate the details, but shall nevertheless permit myself to make just two or three observations, selecting them from among the least significant — for the very reason that they are insignificant and so will not occur to everyone, and be forgotten. In the first place, and once more: because of the gnawing of his conscience, Smerdyakov yesterday returned the money and then hanged himself. (For had it not been for the gnawings of conscience he would not have returned the money.) And, of course, only yesterday evening did he for the first time confess his crime to Ivan Karamazov, as Ivan Karamazov has himself stated, for otherwise why should he have remained silent about it until now? So, then, he confessed, but why, I shall again repeat, in his suicide note did he not inform us of the whole truth, as he knew that for the guiltless defendant the last judgement was at hand upon the morrow? After all, the money alone does not constitute a proof. There did, for example, a week ago become known to myself and two other persons in this chamber a certain fact, namely that Ivan Fyodorovich Karamazov had sent to the principal town of our province for encashment two five per cent bonds, each with a value of five thousand, making up ten thousand roubles in all. I mention this fact merely in order to point out that money may come into anyone's hands on a given date and that, in bringing three thousand to the court, it is impossible to prove beyond doubt that this money came from this or that drawer or envelope. And lastly, Ivan Karamazov, having yesterday received such an important communication from the true murderer, does absolutely nothing. But why did he not declare it at once? Why did he postpone it all until the morning? I believe I am entitled to speculate why: his health undermined the past week, having himself confessed to the doctor and those close to him that he has been seeing visions, encountering people who are dead; on the eve of the *delirium tremens* which has struck him this very day, he, having suddenly learned of Smerdyakov's decease, suddenly constructs for himself the following argument: "The man is dead, the guilt may be placed upon him, and I shall save my brother. After all, I have money: I shall take a wad and say that Smerdyakov gave it to me before his death." You will say that this is dishonourable; that even though the man be dead, it is none the less dishonourable to slander him with lies, even in order to save one's brother? Yes, but what if he lied without being conscious of it, what if he himself, his reason affected by this news concerning the lackey's sudden death, imagined that such was in fact the case? After all, you saw the scene of earlier today, you saw what state this man was in. He stood on his feet and spoke, but where was his mind? That earlier testimony of a man in acute delirium was followed by a document, a letter from the defendant to Miss Verkhovtseva, written by him two days before the enactment of the crime, with a detailed programme of it drafted in advance. Well, and why do we seek this programme and those who devised it? Word for word according to this programme was the deed performed, and it was performed by none other than its deviser. Yes, gentlemen of the jury, "it was performed as though out of a book"! And in no wise, in no wise did we run deferentially and fearfully from the paternal window, in the firm conviction, moreover, that our beloved was with him now. No, that is preposterous and improbable. He entered and – put an end to the matter. It is probable that he killed in anger, afire with vicious hostility no sooner did he set eyes upon the one who hated him, his rival, but, having killed him, which he did, perhaps, with one blow, one stroke of his hand, armed with the brass pestle, and, having satisfied himself after a detailed search that she was not there, none the less did not forget to put his hand under the pillow and obtain the money in the envelope, the torn shreds of which now lie here upon the table of material evidence. I say this in order that you shall observe a certain circumstance, in my view an exceedingly characteristic one. Were this an experienced murderer, and in particular a murderer whose aim was robbery alone – well, would he have left the empty envelope upon the floor, in the aspect in which it was found beside the corpse? What I mean is that suppose it had been, for example, Smerdyakov, committing murder for the sake of robbery – why, he would simply have carried off the whole envelope with him, in no wise taking the trouble to unseal it over his victim's corpse; for he knew of a certainty that the money was in the envelope – after all, it had been put there and sealed in his presence – and had he carried off the envelope altogether, would not the existence of a robbery have remained unknown? I ask you, gentlemen of the jury, would Smerdyakov have acted thus, would he have left the envelope upon the floor? No, the one who acted thus would be a frenzied murderer, one whose reasoning was by this time poor, a murderer who was not a thief and until then had never stolen anything, one who even now pulled the money out from under the bedding not as a thief who was stealing, but as someone retrieving something that belonged to him from a thief who had stolen it – for precisely such were the ideas of Dmitry Karamazov concerning that three thousand, ideas which had attained within him the pitch of mania. And lo, having seized the envelope, which he has never seen before, he tears its cover in order to ascertain that the money is there, and then flees with the money in his pocket, even forgetting to think that he is leaving on the floor a most colossal accusation against himself in the form of the torn envelope. All because it is Karamazov, not Smerdyakov, he has not thought, has not considered, and indeed how could he? He tries to run away, he hears the cry of Grigory, the manservant who is catching up with him, the manservant seizes him, stops him and then sinks to the ground, felled by the brass pestle. The defendant leaps down to him out of pity. Imagine, he suddenly wants us to believe that he leapt down to him that night out of pity, out of compassion, in order to look and see if he could not assist him in some way. Well, was that a moment at which to display compassion of such a kind? No, he leapt down for the specific purpose of ascertaining whether the sole witness of his evil deed was alive. Any other emotion, any other motive would have been unnatural! Observe that he takes pains over Grigory, wipes down his head with his handkerchief and, ascertaining that he is dead, runs off again like a lost soul, covered in blood, back there, to the house of his beloved – how is it he has not considered that he is covered in blood and will at once be unmasked? But the defendant himself assures us that he did not even pay heed to the fact that he was covered in blood; that may be allowed, that is very possible, that invariably happens to criminals at such moments. On the one hand – fiendish calculation, and on the other an insufficient level of awareness. At that moment, however, he was thinking only of the whereabouts of *her*. He needed to learn in haste where she was, and now he runs to her lodgings and discovers a piece of news that is of unexpected and most colossal importance to himself: she has travelled away to Mokroye with her "former", her "beyond dispute"!'

9

Psychology at Full Steam.
The Galloping Troika. *The Finale of the Public Procurator's Speech*

REACHING this point in his speech, Ippolit Kirillovich, who had plainly opted for a strictly historical method of exposition, something to which all nervous orators are very fond of resorting in their deliberate search for strictly set limits within which to restrain their own impatient enthusiasm – Ippolit Kirillovich expatiated in particular on the subject of the 'former' and 'beyond dispute', expressing on this theme a number of thoughts in their own way engaging. 'Karamazov, who is jealous of all other men to the point of rabid frenzy, suddenly and in a trice seems to fall and dissolve before the "former" and "beyond dispute". All the more strange is it, as previously he had almost completely failed to pay any heed to this new danger to himself, looming into sight in the person of a rival he did not expect. But he had always thought of this as being so long ago, and Karamazov always lives only in the present moment. It is probable that he even viewed the man as a fiction. But, having in an instant grasped with his sick heart that, perhaps, for some reason this woman had been concealing this new rival and had for some reason earlier deceived him, that this newly-come-hurrying rival was all too little a fantasy and a fiction to her, but rather constituted for her all her hope in life – having in an instant grasped this, he submitted. Why, gentlemen of the jury, I cannot pass over in silence this sudden proclivity within the soul of the defendant, who might have been thought to be on no account capable of displaying it, for there was suddenly expressed an inexorable need for the truth, a respect for woman, a recognition of the rights of her heart, and when, pray? – at the moment when because of her he had steeped his hands in the blood of his own father! It is also true that the blood which had been shed was already at that moment crying for revenge, for he, who had brought ruin to his soul and all his earthly fate, found himself involuntarily obliged to feel and wonder at that instant what he meant or could mean to her *now*, this being more beloved by him than his own soul, when compared to this "former" and "beyond dispute", who had seen the error of his ways and had come back to this woman whom he had once ruined, with a love that was new, offers that were honourable, the promise of a life reborn and happy. And he, unhappy man, what could he give her *now*, what offer her? Karamazov grasped all this, grasped that his crime had closed all roads to him and that he was merely a criminal under sentence of doom, and not a man whose life still lay ahead! This thought overwhelmed and annihilated him. And lo, in a trice he settles on a certain frenzied plan which, given Karamazov's character, cannot but appear to him as the sole and fatal way out of his terrible position. That way out is suicide. He runs to retrieve his pistols which he has pawned with the civil servant Perkhotin and at the same time, on his way, as he runs, pulls from his pocket all his money, for the sake of which he has just splashed his hands with the blood of his father. Oh, money is now the thing most necessary to him: Karamazov is going to his death, Karamazov is going to shoot himself, and this shall be remembered! For not in vain are we a poet, not in vain have we burned up our life like a candle at both ends. "To her, to her – and there, oh, there I shall give a sumptuous feast, the like of which there has never been, so that it shall be remembered and long described. Amidst wild shouts, the reckless songs and dances of the gypsies we shall raise the toasting cup and toast the adored woman in her new happiness, and then – right there, at her feet, blow open our skull and bring retribution to our life! One day, she will remember Mitya Karamazov, will realize how Mitya loved her, will take pity on Mitya!" Much picturesqueness, *roman*-esque frenzy, wild Karamazovian unrestraint and emotionality – yes, and also something more, gentlemen of the jury, something that clamours in the soul, hammers untiringly in the mind, poisoning his heart to death; that *something* is conscience, gentlemen of the jury, its judgement, its terrible gnawings! But the pistol will reconcile all, the pistol is the only way out, and there is no other, for there – I do not know whether Karamazov thought at that moment about "*what will be there*", and is Karamazov capable of thinking, in Hamletian style, about what will be there? No, gentlemen of the jury, other lands have Hamlets, but so far ours has only Karamazovs!'

At this point Ippolit Kirillovich unrolled a most detailed tableau of Mitya's preparations, the scene at the home of Perkhotin, in the delicatessen, with the *yamshchiks*. He adduced a massive quantity of remarks, utterances, gestures, all of them confirmed by witnesses – and this tableau played a fearfully strong part in persuading his listeners. Most persuasive of all was the strength of the facts. The guilt of this frenziedly confused man who no longer cared about his own welfare emerged inexorably. 'He no longer had any reason to care about his own welfare,' said Ippolit Kirillovich. 'On two or three occasions he very nearly made a complete confession, almost alluded to it, simply hung back from saying everything' (at this point there followed the evidence of the witnesses). 'He even shouted to the *yamshchik* on the way: "Do you know that you are carrying a murderer?" But even so he was unable to say everything: first he had to get to the village of Mokroye, and only there would he complete his poem. But what lies in wait for the unhappy man? The fact of the matter is that when he has been in Mokroye only a few initial moments, practically, he realizes and, at last, understands completely that his rival "beyond dispute" is, perhaps, not at all so beyond dispute, and that felicitations upon a new happiness, and a toasting cup, are not desired of him nor would they be accepted. But you are already familiar with the facts, gentlemen of the jury, from the judicial investigation. Karamazov's triumph over his rival proved to be unquestionable, and here – oh, here there began an entirely new phase within his soul, a phase that was even perhaps the most terrible of all that this soul has ever experienced or will ever do so! It may be positively acknowledged, gentlemen of the jury,' Ippolit Kirillovich exclaimed, 'that desecrated nature and a criminal heart are avengers more complete than any earthly justice! And that is not all: justice and earthly retribution even lighten the retribution of nature, are even necessary to the criminal's soul at these moments as a salvation from despair, for I am unable even to imagine the horror and moral suffering experienced by Karamazov when he found out that she loved him, that for his sake she was rejecting her "former" and "beyond dispute", that it was he, he, "Mitya", whom she was calling with her to a regenerated life, promising him happiness, and this at what juncture? When already all was over for him and when nothing more was possible! In this connection I shall make in passing a certain observation most important to our understanding of the true essence of the defendant's position at that time: this woman, this love of his remained for him until this very last moment, until the very moment of his arrest, even, a being inaccessible, passionately desired, but unattainable. But why, why did he not shoot himself at that very moment, why did he abandon the intention he had conceived and even forget the whereabouts of his pistol? Why, it was this very same passionate thirst for love and the hope of assuaging it there and then that restrained him. In the intoxication of the feast he riveted himself to his beloved, who was also feasting with him, more charming and seductive to him than ever – he stayed beside her constantly, admired her, dissolved before her. This passionate thirst was actually able to quell not only his fear of arrest but even the very gnawings of his conscience! For an instant, oh, only an instant! I envisage to myself the condition of the criminal's soul at this time, in unquestioning and slavish submission to the three elements that had crushed it entirely: in the first place, a condition of drunkenness, the intoxication and noise, the stamping of the dance, the shriek of the singing and she, she, flushed from the wine, singing and dancing, drunken and laughing with him! In the second, the encouraging, distant hope that the fateful denouement was still far away, or at least not imminent – only the following day, only in the morning would they come and seize him. He had, therefore, several hours, that was a large amount of time, a dreadfully large amount! One may devise a great deal in several hours. I envisage to myself that what he experienced was something resembling what the criminal experiences as he is being driven to his execution, to the gallows: he must still ride down an inordinately long street, and at a slow trot, too, past a crowd of thousands, then there will be a turning into another street and only at the end of that other street the terrible square! Indeed, I think that at the beginning of the procession the condemned man, sitting upon his chariot of ignominy, cannot but feel that before him there still lies an infinity of life. But then, however, the houses go past, the chariot keeps moving forward – oh, it does not matter, to the turning into the second street there is still such a long way to go, and lo, he continues to gaze cheerfully to right and to left and at these thousands of indifferently curious people who are riveting their eyes upon him, and he still dreams that he is just such a man as they. But now here is the turning into the second street, but oh, that does not matter, does not matter, there is still a whole street. And however many houses go past, still he will think: "There are still many houses left." And so on right to the end, right to the square itself. Thus, I envisage to myself, did matters stand with Karamazov, too, that day. "They have not yet had time," he thinks, "it is still possible to hit on something, oh, there will still be time to make a plan of defence, to think up a rebuff, but now, now – now she is so charming!" His soul is troubled and afraid, but he succeeds, all the same, in putting aside half of his money and concealing it somewhere – otherwise I cannot think whither could have vanished an entire half of that three thousand that had just been removed by him from beneath his father's pillow. He had already been in Mokroye several times, he had already spent two whole days and nights on the spree there. That large, old wooden house was known to him, with all its sheds and galleries. I do indeed suppose that part of the money was hidden there and then, and in that very house, not long before his arrest, in some chink, some cleft, beneath some floorboard, in some corner, under the roof – to what purpose? What do you mean, to what purpose? The catastrophe may take place at any moment, and of course we have not yet considered how to meet it, and in any case we have no time, and there is a hammering within our head, and we are longing for *her*, yes, but money – money is necessary in every situation! A man with money is everywhere a man. Does such financial prudency perhaps appear to you unnatural at such a moment? But after all, he himself assures us that already a month before, at a certain moment that was also disquieting and fateful for him, he divided off a half of that three thousand and sewed it into an incense-bag, and if, of course, that is untrue, something which we shall in a moment prove, then none the less this idea is one familiar to Karamazov, he had contemplated it. Not only that: when he subsequently assured the investigator that he had divided off the fifteen hundred and put it in an incense-bag (something that never happened), it may be that he thought up that incense-bag, right there that instant, for the very reason that two hours before he had divided off a half of the money and hidden it somewhere down there in Mokroye, just in case, until the morning, simply in order not to have to keep it about his person, following an inspiration that had suddenly presented itself to him. Two abysses, gentlemen of the jury, recall that Karamazov can contemplate two abysses, and both of them at once! In that house we sought, but did not find. It may be that that money is there even now, or it may be that the following day it vanished and is now at the home of the defendant. Whatever the case, he was arrested beside her, on his knees before her, she lay upon a bed, he had his arms stretched out towards her and had so forgotten everything at that moment that he did not hear the approach of his arresters. He had not yet had time to make within his mind the preparations for an answer. Both he and his mind were taken by surprise.

'And lo, here he is before his judges, before the deciders of his fate. Gentlemen of the jury, there are moments when, in the course of our duties, we ourselves become almost afraid in the face of man, afraid also for man! These are the moments of contemplation of that animal terror when the criminal already sees that all is lost, but still struggles, still intends to struggle with you. These are the moments when all his instincts for self-preservation arise in him together and he, in his efforts to save himself, fixes you with a penetrating gaze, one full of questioning and suffering, devours and studies you, your face, your thoughts, waits to see from which side you are going to strike, and in a trice creates within his quaking mind thousands of plans, but none the less fears to speak, fears to give something away! These degrading moments of the human soul, this passage of it through the torments, this animal thirst for self-salvation are dreadful and sometimes provoke a shudder of compassion for the criminal even in the investigator! And lo, that day we were witnesses to all that. At first he was stupefied, and in his horror there broke loose some words that greatly compromised him: "Blood! I have deserved it!" But he swiftly held himself in check. What he should say, or what reply — none of that is ready in him yet, all that is ready is a single, unsubstantiated denial: "Of my father's death I am not guilty!" There for the moment is our fence, and there, behind the fence we shall perhaps arrange something else, some barricade. As for his initial compromising exclamations, he hurries, pre-empting our questions, to explain them by saying that he considers himself guilty only of the death of the manservant Grigory. "Of that blood I am guilty, but who killed my father, gentlemen, who killed him? Who could have killed him, *if not I*?" Do you apprehend it: it is us he is asking this, us who have come to him with this very same question! Do you apprehend that little remark that runs ahead of the game: "if not I", this animal cunning, this naïveté and this Karamazovian impatience? I am not the one who murdered him, and do not think that it was I: "I wanted to murder him, gentlemen, I wanted to," he confesses quickly (he is in a hurry, oh, a dreadful hurry!) "but all the same I am not guilty, I am not the one!" He concedes to us that he wanted to murder him: "You see for yourselves," he says, "how sincere I am, all the more reason, then, to believe that I am not the one who did it." Oh, in these cases the criminal sometimes becomes unbelievably light-minded and gullible. And lo and behold, at this point, as if quite by chance, the investigation suddenly put to him the most ingenuous question: "Well, was not Smerdyakov the murderer, then?" The very thing we had expected happened: he grew lividly angry at having been pre-empted and taken by surprise when he had not yet had time to prepare, select and seize the moment when to wheel out Smerdyakov would seem most plausible. In accordance with his nature he at once rushed to extremes and began to assure us with all his might that Smerdyakov could not have been the murderer, was not capable of being the murderer. But do not listen to him, that is merely his cunning: not at all, not at all does he relinquish Smerdyakov, on the contrary, he will advance him again, for whom can he advance if not him, but he will do it at another moment, as for the present this cause is spoiled. He will advance him only tomorrow, perhaps, or even only after several days, having found the moment at which he will cry to us: "You see, I discounted Smerdyakov more than you did, you recall that yourselves, but now I also am persuaded: he was the murderer, for how could he not have been?" But for the moment, in our presence, he sinks into a black and irritable denial, while impatience and anger lead him to offer the most clumsy and improbable explanation that he looked in through his father's window and then deferentially withdrew from it. Above all, he is not yet familiar with the details or the extent of the testimony submitted by Grigory, who has now regained consciousness. We proceed to an inspection of his person and a search of his lodgings. The inspection provokes his wrath, but also revives his spirits: not all the three thousand has been discovered, but only fifteen hundred. And, of course, only at this moment of wrathful silence and denial is it that, for the first time in his life, the idea of the incense-bag pops into his head. Without a doubt, he himself senses the utter implausibility of this fabrication and takes trouble, takes fearful trouble in order to make it more plausible, to compose it in such a manner that there results from it an entire and believable *roman*. In these cases the very first deed, the very first task of the investigation is not to allow any state of readiness to be attained, to catch unawares, so that the criminal may come out with his cherished ideas in all their give-away ingenuousness, improbability and contradictoriness. And the criminal may be compelled to speak only by suddenly and apparently by chance communicating to him some new fact, some detail of the case which is colossal in its significance but which until now he has not surmised and could on no account have perceived. This fact was held by us in readiness, oh, long had we held it ready: it was the testimony of the manservant Grigory, who had now regained consciousness, concerning the open door, out of which the defendant ran. About that door he had quite forgotten, and he had not surmised that Grigory could have seen it. The resulting effect was colossal. He leapt up and shouted to us suddenly: "Smerdyakov was the murderer, Smerdyakov!" – and lo, he had given away his cherished, his fundamental idea, in its most improbable form, for Smerdyakov could only have committed the murder after he, Karamazov, had cast Grigory down and run away. And when we notified him that before his fall Grigory had seen that the door was open and, as he came out of his bedroom, had heard Smerdyakov groaning behind the partition — Karamazov was, of a truth, overwhelmed. My colleague, our witty and esteemed Nikolay Parfenovich, subsequently related to me that at that moment he felt sorry for him to the point of tears. And lo, it is at this moment that, in order to repair the damage, he hurries to inform us of that notorious incense-bag, as if to say: "So let it be, now hear this tale!" Gentlemen of the jury, I have already explained to you the reasons why I consider all this fabrication concerning the money sewn up in an incense-bag a month before not only preposterous, but also the most improbable contrivance that could possibly be thought of in the given case. Even were one to hold a wager as to what more improbable thing might be said or imagined, even then it would be impossible to fabricate anything worse than this. Here, above all, one may by means of details check and reduce to dust the triumphant *romancier*, those same details in which reality is invariably so rich and which are invariably, as if they were completely insignificant and superfluous trivia, neglected by these unhappy and involuntary authors, and never even enter their heads. Oh, they do not care about such things at that moment, their minds are creating only the grandiose whole — and then people dare to suggest to them a trivial thing like that! But that is the very point on which they are caught out! To the defendant the question is put: "Well, and where were you so fortunate as to obtain the material for your incense-bag, who made it for you?" "I made it myself." "And where did you obtain the linen?" By now the defendant is beginning to take umbrage, he considers this almost an offensive insult to himself and, would you believe, sincerely, sincerely! But such are they all. "I tore it from my shirt." "Consequently, tomorrow we shall track down among your clothes this shirt from which a scrap has been torn." And consider, gentlemen of the jury, after all, if we really had found this shirt (and how could we have failed to find it in his trunk or chest of drawers if such a shirt did indeed exist?) — then it would be a fact, a tangible fact to support the veracity of his testimony! This, however, he is unable to fathom. "I do not recall, perhaps it was not from my shirt, I sewed it into one of my landlady's bonnets." "What sort of bonnet?" "One I took from her, it was lying around, a wretched old calico thing." "And you remember that definitely?" "No, not definitely . . ." And he is angry, angry, yet all the while, consider: how could he fail to remember it? At the most terrible moments of a man's life, when he is being driven to the scaffold, say, these are the very sort of trivia that are retained within his memory. He will forget about everything else, but some green roof or other that has fleetingly caught his attention on the way, or a jackdaw on the cross of a church – these things he will remember. After all, when he made his incense-bag he hid himself away from the other people in the house, he must remember how degradingly he suffered, as he held the needle, from the fear that someone might come in and catch him red-handed; how at the first knock he leapt up and ran behind the partition (there is a partition in his room) ... But, gentlemen of the jury, to what purpose do I inform you of all these things, all these details, trivia!' Ippolit Kirillovich suddenly exclaimed. 'Namely for the reason that the defendant has held stubbornly to all this preposterous nonsense right until this very minute! Throughout all the past two months, ever since that night so fateful for him, he has explained nothing, has not added one single explanatory or practical detail to his previous fantastic testimony, saying more or less: "Those are all mere trivia, and you will have to believe me on my honour!" Oh, we are glad to believe, we thirst to believe, even though it be only on your honour! After all, what are we – jackals, a-thirst for human blood? Give us, indicate to us one piece of evidence in the defendant's favour, and we shall rejoice – but it must be a tangible, practical one, and not a conclusion made by the defendant's own brother and founded upon an expression of the defendant's face or an indication of certainty that in beating his breast he must have been pointing to the incense-bag, and in the darkness, too. We shall rejoice in this new piece of evidence, we shall be the first to withdraw our accusation, we shall hasten to withdraw it. At present, however, justice cries out, and we insist, we can make no such withdrawal.' At this point Ippolit Kirillovich passed to his finale. He was like a man in a fever, he cried out in the name of the blood that had been shed, the blood of a father slain by his son 'with the base purpose of robbery'. He firmly pointed to the tragic and crying strength of the facts. 'And whatever you may hear from the defendant's counsel, so celebrated on account of his talent,' Ippolit Kirillovich was unable to keep back, 'whatever the eloquent and affecting words that may resound here, trained upon your sentimental feelings, remember all the same that at this moment you are in the holy sanctuary of our justice. Remember that you are the defenders of our truth, the defenders of our holy Russia, of her foundations, of her family, of all that in her is sacred! Yes, here you represent Russia at this given moment, and not only within this chamber will your verdict resound, but all over Russia, and all Russia will harken to you, as its defenders and judges, and will be reassured or dispirited by your verdict. But do not cause suffering to Russia and her expectations, our fateful *troika* is rushing headlong, and possibly to its doom. And long now in the whole of Russia have hands been outstretched and calls been made to stop the furied, impudent gallop. And if for the present the other nations still stand back from the headlong-galloping *troika*, then it is perhaps not at all out of deference to it, as the poet would like, but simply out of horror – please observe that. Out of horror, and possibly also out of loathing at it, and it is indeed good that they stand back, but perhaps they may decide to stop standing back and line up in a solid wall before the hurtling vision and bring to a halt the insane gallop of our unbridledness, in the interests of saving themselves, enlightenment and civilization! These anxious voices from Europe have already reached our ears. They are already beginning to resound. Then do not tempt them, do not accumulate their ever growing hatred by a verdict that justifies the murder of a father by his own son! . . .'

In a word, even though Ippolit Kirillovich had been greatly carried away, he none the less ended with pathos – and indeed, the impression he produced was an extraordinary one. He himself, having concluded his speech, hurriedly walked out of the chamber and, I repeat, in the adjacent room almost collapsed in a dead faint. The chamber did not applaud, but serious men were content. The only people who were not so content were the ladies, but none the less they too had enjoyed the eloquence, all the more so since they were not at all fearful of the sequel and expected everything of Fetyukovich: 'At last he will speak and, of course, conquer everyone!' All kept looking at Mitya; throughout the public procurator's entire speech he sat in silence, his teeth clenched, his gaze lowered. Only now and again did he raise his head, listening. Particularly when mention was made of Grushenka. When the public procurator informed the court of Rakitin's opinion of her, his face displayed a contemptuous and malicious smile, and he rather audibly articulated: 'Those Bernards!' And while Ippolit Kirillovich was describing how he had questioned and harassed him in Mokroye, Mitya raised his head and listened with terrible curiosity. There was one passage in the speech where he even seemed to be about to leap up and shout something, but mastered himself and merely shrugged his shoulders in contempt. Concerning this finale of the speech, alluding as it did to the public procurator's heroic achievements in Mokroye during the interrogation of the criminal, there was subsequent talk in the social circles of our town, and Ippolit Kirillovich was made fun of: 'The man couldn't keep himself from boasting of his abilities,' it was said. The session of the court was adjourned, but only for a very short period of time, a quarter of an hour, or twenty minutes at the outside. Among the public, arguments and exclamations rang. I have remembered some of them:

'A serious speech!' a gentleman in one group frowningly observed.

'He spun too much psychology into it,' another voice rang out.

'But I mean, it was all of it true, the irrefutable truth!'

'Yes, he's a master at that.'

'He summed it up.'

'And what about us, he summed us up too,' a third voice added, 'at the beginning of his speech, do you remember, when he said that we were all the same as Fyodor Pavlovich?'

'And at the end, too. But he was talking through his hat.'

'There were also some obscure parts.'

'He got a bit carried away.'

'Not true, not true, sir.'

'Well, no, I suppose it was clever enough. Long did he wait, then out he did speak, heh-heh!'

'Wonder what the defence counsel is going to say?'

In another group:

'Silly of him to rub the St Petersburg man up the wrong way: that bit about "trained upon your sentimental feelings", remember?'

'No, that was not very clever.'

'He was in a hurry.'

'A nervous fellow, sir.'

'All right for us to laugh, but what must the defendant be feeling like?'

'Yes, sir, what must Mitya-my-lad be feeling like?'

'But now I wonder what the defence counsel is going to say?'

In a third group:

'What lady is that, the one with the lorgnette, the fat one, sitting at the end?'

'That is a certain general's wife, a divorcée, I know her.'

'Aha, and with a lorgnette, too.'

'Riff-raff.'

'Oh no, rather *piquante*.'

'Two places along from her there is a little blonde, she's better.'

'Clever of them to catch him red-handed at Mokroye like that, eh?'

'Oh, clever, very clever. He told the story again. I mean, heaven only knows how many times he's told it in people's houses here.'

'And now he couldn't keep from telling it again. Vanity.'

'A man touched to the quick, heh-heh!'

'And touchy, too. Oh, too much rhetoric, too many long and windy phrases.'

'And he was intimidating, did you notice how he keeps intimidating? The *troika*, remember? "Other lands have Hamlets, but so far ours has only Karamazovs!" That was clever of him.'

'This was him courting liberal opinion. He's scared!'

'And he's scared of the advocate, too.'

'Yes, I wonder what Mr Fetyukovich is going to say?'

'Well, whatever it is, he won't get anywhere with our muzhiks.'

'You suppose?'

In a fourth group:

'But you know, that bit about the *troika* was all right, when he talked about the nations.'

'And it's true, after all, what he said, you remember – that the nations will not wait.'

'How do you mean?'

'Well, only last week in the English Parliament* one member got up on the subject of the nihilists and asked the Ministry whether it was not time to meddle with a barbaric nation in order to educate us. Ippolit said that about him, I know he did. He was talking of it last week.'

'It's a long way for the snipe to fly.'*

'What snipe? Why a long way?'

'Oh, we'll close Kronstadt* and not give them any grain. Where will they get it?'

'What about America? They get it in America now.'

'Nonsense.'

But the bell had begun to ring, all rushed back to their seats. Fetyukovich ascended the rostrum.

10

The Defence Counsel's Speech.
A Stick with Two Ends

EVERYTHING grew quiet as the first words of the celebrated orator rang out. The entire chamber glued its eyes upon him. He began exceedingly directly, in a simple and convinced manner, but without the slightest arrogance. There was not the slightest attempt at eloquence, at notes of pathos, at words that rang with emotion. This was a man who had begun to speak within an intimate circle of people who were sympathetic to him. His voice was magnificent, loud and likeable, and even in this voice alone one seemed to hear something sincere and open-hearted. All, however, came to grasp at once that the orator could suddenly rise to genuine pathos – and 'smite each and every heart with unknown power'.* He spoke, perhaps, less correctly than Ippolit Kirillovich, but without long, windy phrases and if anything even more precisely. One thing did not initially please the ladies: he kept somehow bending his back, especially at the beginning of his speech, not so much bowing as rather, as it were, surging and flying towards his listeners, something that involved a stooping of, as it were, indeed, a half of his long back, as though in the middle of this long and slender back of his there was affixed a hinge, so that it was able to bend at very nearly a right angle. At the beginning of his speech he spoke somehow distractedly, as though without method, seizing facts at random, but the ultimate result was an integral whole. His speech might have been divided into two halves: the first half – that was a critique, a refutation of the prosecution's case that was at times malicious and sarcastic. But in the second half of his speech he suddenly, as it were, altered both his tone and even his mode of treatment, and at once went towering up to the realms of pathos, while the chamber seemed to have been expecting this and began to tremble all over with ecstasy. He went straight to his task, and began by saying that though the field of his career was in St Petersburg, it was not the first time that he had visited a town of Russia to defend a prisoner, though he would only do so either when he was convinced of the man's innocence, or when he had a premonition of it in advance. 'The same thing happened to me in the present instance,' he explained. 'Even from the first newspaper reports alone I had already caught a fleeting glimpse of something that struck me exceedingly in the defendant's favour. In a word, my interest was first and foremost engaged by a certain juridical fact, though frequently recurring in legal practice, yet never, I believe, in such fullness or with such characteristic features as in the case before you. I ought really to formulate this fact only in the finale of my speech, when I conclude my address, but none the less I shall utter my reflection right at the outset, too, for I have a weakness for proceeding directly to the point at issue, without reserving effects or saving up impressions for later. This possibly demonstrates a lack of foresight on my part, but is on the other hand sincere. This reflection, this formula of mine is the following: the overwhelming weight of the facts is against the defendant and yet at the same time not one of those facts will withstand criticism if it is examined in isolation, on its own! As I followed the case further by means of rumours and the newspapers, I grew more and more confirmed in my reflection, and suddenly from the kinsfolk of the accused I received a request to defend him. I at once hurried here and here became finally convinced. You see, it is in order to smash this terrible weight of the facts and to demonstrate the unproven and fantastic nature of each incriminatory fact taken separately that I have taken it upon myself to defend this case.'

Thus did the defence counsel begin, and suddenly did proclaim:

'Gentlemen of the jury, I am fresh here. All my impressions have come to me without prejudice. The defendant, violent of character and unbridled, did not offend me beforehand, as he has, perhaps, a hundred persons in this town, which is why many have been warned against him in advance. Of course, I, too, admit that the moral feeling of this town's society has been justly aroused: the defendant is violent and ungovernable. He has, however, been received in the society of this town, even in the household of the highly talented prosecutor has he been shown much kindness.' (*Nota bene*. In the public at these words two or three titters were heard, swiftly suppressed, but noticed by all. Everyone in our town knew that the public procurator had admitted Mitya to his home against his will, for the sole reason that on some account he was found interesting by the public procurator's wife – a lady in the highest degree virtuous and respectable, but fantastical and capricious and fond in certain instances, primarily over trivia, of opposing her spouse. Mitya had, as a matter of fact, visited their house rather seldom.) 'None the less I shall make bold to consider it possible,' the defence counsel continued, 'that even in a mind as independent, a character as equitable as that of my opponent there might have formed against my unhappy client a certain erroneous prejudice. Oh, that is so natural: the unhappy fellow has all too richly deserved that others should treat him even with prejudice. As for outraged moral and, even more so, aesthetic feeling, it is sometimes implacable. Of course, in the highly talented speech for the prosecution we have all heard a strict analysis of the defendant's character and actions, a strict and critical attitude towards the case, and above all there have been advanced such psychological depths for the explanation to us of the essence of the case that the penetration of those depths could on no account have taken place in the presence of even the slightest intentionally and maliciously premeditated attitude towards the person of the defendant. But after all there are things which are even worse, even more fatal in cases of this kind than the most malicious and premeditated attitude towards the case. That is to say, if we are, for example, seized by a certain, so to speak, artistic game, by a need for artistic creation, so to speak, the making of a *roman*, particularly in the presence of a wealth of psychological gifts with which the Lord has endowed our faculties. While I was still in St Petersburg, as yet only making my preparations to come here, I was forewarned – and indeed I myself was aware without any forewarning – that I should encounter here as my opponent a deep and most subtle psychologist, who has by this quality long acquired by merit an especial reputation in our still young juridical world. But psychology, gentlemen, though it is a deep thing, none the less resembles a stick with two ends' (a titter in the public). 'Oh, you will, of course, forgive me my trivial comparison; of eloquent speaking I am anything but a master. But here, none the less, is an example – I take the first one I come across in the speech for the prosecution. The defendant, running away at night, in the garden, climbs the fence and casts down by a blow from a brass pestle the lackey who has seized him by the leg. Thereupon he immediately leaps back into the garden and spends an entire five minutes troubling himself over the man whom he has cast down, in an attempt to find out whether he has killed him or not. And now you see, the prosecutor is on no account willing to believe in the truth of the defendant's statement that he leapt down to the old man Grigory out of pity. "No," he says, "it is not possible that he could have felt such sentiment at such a moment; it would have been unnatural, and he leapt down for the specific purpose of ascertaining whether the only witness of his evil deed was alive or slain, thereby providing certain testimony that he had committed the evil deed, as he could not have leapt down into the garden on any other ground, inclination, or emotion." There is psychology at work; but if we take the same psychology and apply it to the case, only from the other end, what results will not at all be any the less probable. The murderer leaps down out of caution, in order to ascertain whether the witness is alive or not, yet he has only just left in the study of his own father, whom he has murdered, a – according to the testimony of the prosecutor himself – colossal piece of evidence against himself in the form of the torn envelope which bore upon it an inscription saying that there were three thousand roubles in it. "After all, had he carried off that envelope with him, no one in all the world would ever have discovered the existence of the envelope or of the money in it, and therefore also the fact that the money had been stolen by the defendant." That is an utterance of the prosecutor himself. Well, so on the one hand, you see, there was insufficient caution, the man lost his nerve, took fright and ran away, leaving the evidence on the floor, and yet when some two minutes later he struck and killed another man, there at once appears at our service a most heartless and calculating sense of caution. But let us allow, let us allow that it was so: for therein lies psychology's subtlety that in such circumstances I may be as blood-thirsty and vigilant as the Caucasian eagle at one moment, while at the next I may be blind and timid as the insignificant mole. But if I am so bloodthirsty and cruelly calculating that, having committed murder, my only thought in leaping down is to see whether the witness of my deed is alive or not, then why should I, so it would appear, trouble myself over this fresh victim of mine for an entire five minutes, and in addition possibly acquire new witnesses? Why should I wet my handkerchief, wiping the blood from the head of the one I had cast down, so that this handkerchief may later serve as evidence against me? No, if we are so calculating and cruel-hearted, then would it not be better, having leapt down, simply to discombobulate the cast-down manservant with that same pestle again and again about the head, in order to well and truly kill him and, having eliminated the witness, to remove all care from our heart? And, finally, I leap down in order to verify whether the witness to my deed is alive or not, and right there upon the path leave another witness, namely, that very same pestle that I snatched from two women, both of whom may at any time acknowledge that pestle as their own and begin to testify that it was I who snatched it from their kitchen. And it was not simply left on the path, dropped in absent-mindedness, perplexity: no, we made a special point of throwing our weapon away, because it was found some fifteen paces from that spot where Grigory was cast down. The question arises: why did we act thus? Oh, we acted thus for the specific reason that we were sick at heart at having killed a man, an old manservant, and so in vexation, with a curse, we threw away the pestle as being an instrument of murder, no other possibility presents itself, for why did we throw it with such an exertion of our might? As for the fact that we were able to feel pain and pity at having killed a man, that was really of course because we had not killed our father: had we killed our father, we should not have leapt down to the other whom we had felled, out of pity, then we should have felt another emotion, in that case it would not have been pity that we concerned ourselves with but self-salvation, and that is, of course, so. On the contrary, I repeat, we would have finally smashed his skull, and would not have spent five minutes troubling ourselves over him. A place for pity and kindly emotion appeared for the precise reason that until then our conscience had been clear. Here, therefore, is a different psychology. You see, gentlemen of the jury, I have now myself had recourse to psychology in order to show by means of graphic demonstration that from it one may infer whatever one may wish. All centres upon what hands it rests in. Psychology beckons even the most serious of men to the concoction of *romans*, and quite without their willing it. I speak of excessive psychology, gentlemen of the jury, and a certain abuse of it.'

Here once again approving titters were audible in the public, all of them addressed in the direction of the public procurator. I shall not adduce the entire speech of the defence counsel in detail, but shall merely select certain passages from it, certain of the most important points.

I I

There was No Money. There was No Robbery

THERE was one point that even astonished everyone in the defence counsel's speech, and that was the complete denial of the existence of that fateful three thousand roubles, and therefore also of the possibility that it had been stolen.

'Gentlemen of the jury,' the defence counsel began, 'any fresh and unprejudiced person coming to the case before you will be struck by a certain characteristic peculiarity, namely: the accusation of robbery and at the same time the complete practical impossibility of indicating just what exactly was stolen. We are told that money was stolen, and precisely the sum of three thousand – but whether it actually existed, no one knows. Think about it: in the first place, how did we first come to learn of this three thousand, and who saw it? The only person who saw it and indicated that it was put away in an envelope with an inscription was the lackey Smerdyakov. And he communicated this information to the defendant and his brother Ivan Fyodorovich before the catastrophe took place. Miss Svetlova was also made aware of it. None of these three persons, however, actually saw the money, and again the only person who did was Smerdyakov, but here the question asks itself: if it is true that it existed and that Smerdyakov saw it, then when was the last time he saw it? And what if his *barin* had taken the money from under his bed and put it back in the box without telling him? Please observe that according to the testimony of Smerdyakov the money was under the bedding, under the mattress: the defendant would have had to pull it out from under the mattress, and yet, none the less, the bedding was not rumpled in any way, and this has been painstakingly recorded in the protocol. How could the defendant have quite failed to rumple the bedding in any way and, in addition, with his hands that were still covered in blood to smear the most fresh and fine bedlinen with which the bed had been on this occasion specially made up? But, we shall be told: what of the envelope upon the floor? It is indeed this envelope that merits a few words. I was today somewhat astonished: the highly talented prosecutor, in approaching the subject of this envelope, suddenly himself – do you hear, gentlemen, himself – in his speech declared concerning it, precisely in that passage where he indicates the preposterous nature of the assumption that Smerdyakov was the murderer: "Had that envelope not been there, had it not remained upon the floor as evidence, and had the robber carried it off with him, then no one in all the world would ever have discovered that there was an envelope, and money in it, and that, therefore, the money had been stolen by the defendant." And so, even by the admission of the prosecutor himself, it is solely and exclusively this torn scrap of paper with the inscription on it that has served to accuse the defendant of robbery, "for otherwise," we are told, "no one would have discovered that there had been a robbery or even, perhaps, that there had been any money". But is the mere fact that this scrap was lying on the floor really a proof that it had contained the money and that the money had been stolen? "Well," we are answered, "after all, it was seen in the envelope by Smerdyakov," but when, when was the last time he saw it, that is the question I ask? I talked to Smerdyakov, and he told me he had seen it two days before the catastrophe! Why is it, then, that I cannot envisage, for example, the circumstance that the old man Fyodor Pavlovich, having locked himself up at home in the impatient and hysterical expectation of his beloved, might suddenly have taken it into his head, out of idleness, to take out the envelope and unseal it: "What," he might think, "if she does not believe a mere envelope? If I show her thirty rainbow bills in a single wad, that will have a more powerful effect, her mouth will water," and he tears open the envelope, takes out the money, and throws the wrapping on the floor with the masterful hand of a seigneur, of course without fear of leaving any evidence. I ask you, gentlemen of the jury, could anything be more within the bounds of possibility than such an assumption and such a factum? Why should it be impossible? But you see, if even something of the kind may have taken place, then the accusation of robbery is of itself destroyed: there was no money, and therefore there was no robbery either. If the envelope lay upon the floor as evidence that it had contained the money, then why may I not assert the reverse to be true, namely that the envelope lay upon the floor for the very reason that there was no longer in it the money that had been taken from it beforehand by the seigneur himself? "Yes, but what in that case became of the money, if it was taken from the envelope by Fyodor Pavlovich himself, it was not found in his house during the search?" For one thing, a part of the money was found in a box in the house, and for another, he might, might he not, have taken out the money that morning, or even the day before, in order to dispose of it in some other way, by paying it out, sending it away, in a word, to alter his idea, his plan of action at its very root, and in doing so not at all consider it necessary to inform Smerdyakov of it beforehand? And you see, if there exists even the mere possibility of making such an assumption, then how can one so emphatically and so firmly raise against the defendant the accusation of having committed the murder for the purpose of robbery and that a robbery did indeed take place? Why, in such manner do we enter the domain of the *roman*. After all, if we assert that such-and-such an object has been stolen, then we need to be able to identify that object or at least prove beyond dispute that it existed. But no one even set eyes on it. In St Petersburg recently a certain young man,* a boy practically, eighteen years old, a small-time hawker from a tray, entered a money-changer's shop in broad daylight with an axe and with extraordinary, typical boldness murdered the shop-owner and carried off with him 1,500 roubles in cash. Some five hours later he was arrested; upon his person, apart from fifteen roubles which he had already managed to spend, the whole fifteen hundred was found. Not only that, but the shop-owner's assistant, who had returned to the shop after the murder, informed the police not only of the sum that had been stolen, but of what precise denominations it had consisted, that is to say how many rainbow credit bills there had been, how many blue, how many red;* how many gold coins, and of what type; and then on the arrested murderer precisely the same banknotes and coins were found. In addition to all this there followed a complete and open confession by the murderer that he had committed the murder and had carried off that same money. Now that, gentlemen of the jury, is what I call evidence! For now I know, I see, I touch the money and cannot say that it does not or did not exist. Is it thus in the present instance? And yet after all, it is a matter of life and death, of a man's fate. "Yes," I shall be told, "but after all that same night he had been on a spree, squandering money, fifteen hundred roubles was found upon his person — whence did he obtain it?" But you see, it is precisely because only fifteen hundred roubles were discovered, while the other half could on no account be tracked down or discovered, it is precisely this that proves that that money must have come from a different source altogether, and had never been in any envelope. By a computation of time (and a most strict one) it was established and proven by the preliminary investigation that the defendant, having run out of the kitchen where the serving-maids were and having gone to the home of the civil servant Perkhotin, did not call in at his lodgings and indeed made no other calls, but was subsequently in the constant company of others, and so could not have divided off a half of the three thousand and hidden it somewhere in the town. It was precisely this consideration that formed the grounds for the prosecutor's assumption that the money was hidden in some cleft or crevice in the village of Mokroye. Why, might it not indeed be in the dungeons of the castle of Udolpho,* gentlemen? Oh, is it not a fantastic, a *roman*-esque assumption? And observe, if you will, that if this one assumption is proven groundless, that is to say, that the money is hidden in Mokroye — then the entire accusation of robbery is blown into the air, for where, then, whither has that fifteen hundred gone? By what miracle could it have vanished, if it is proven that the defendant made no call to any house? And with such *romans* are we prepared to bring ruin upon a human life! I shall be told: "But even so, he was unable to explain where he obtained the fifteen hundred that was found upon his person, and besides, everyone knew that until that night he had had no money." But who knew this? No, the defendant has given clear and firm testimony as to where he obtained the money from, and if you will, gentlemen, if you will — never could there be nor can there be a testimony more plausible than this, nor, in addition, one more compatible with the character and soul of the defendant. The prosecution took a liking to its own *roman*: a man of feeble will, having decided to accept the three thousand so disgracingly offered to him by his betrothed, could not, it is said, have divided off a half and sewn it into an incense-bag — on the contrary, had he done so, every two days he would have unpicked it and peeled off a hundred, and in such manner expended the whole within a single month. You will recall that all this was given exposition in a tone that would suffer no retort. Well, but what if the affair proceeded not at all this way, and what if you have created a *roman*, and in it a different personage? There is the rub: you have created a different person! It will perhaps be retorted: "There are witnesses who say that in the village of Mokroye he squandered the entire three thousand he had taken from Miss Verkhovtseva, a month before the catastrophe, all at once, like a single copeck, and therefore he could not have divided off a half." But who are these witnesses? The degree to which these witnesses may be trusted has already been made manifest at this trial. Moreover, the slice of pie always looks bigger in another's hand. And finally, none of these witnesses who say they saw the money counted it themselves, but merely judged it by eye. Why, the witness Maksimov testified that the defendant had twenty thousand in his hands. You see, gentlemen of the jury, as psychology is a thing with two ends, then permit me to supply the other end, and let us see if the result be otherwise.

'A month before the catastrophe the defendant was entrusted by Miss Verkhovtseva with three thousand roubles for dispatch by post, but there is a question: is it the case that it was entrusted to him with such disgrace and degradation as was proclaimed earlier? In her first statement on this same subject, Miss Verkhovtseva put it another way, another way altogether; while in her second statement we heard only cries of animosity, revenge, cries of a hatred long concealed. But even the mere fact that in her first statement the witness gave evidence that was incorrect gives us the right to conclude that her second statement too may have been incorrect. The prosecutor "does not wish, does not dare" (the words are his) to touch that *roman*. Well, so let it be, I shall not touch it either, but shall merely permit myself the observation that if a pure and highly moral person, such as the highly respected Miss Verkhovtseva indisputably is, if such a person, I say, permits herself, all at once, during the trial, to alter her first statement with the unequivocal aim of bringing ruin upon the defendant, then it is also clear that that statement of hers was not made without bias, in cool composure. Is it really proposed to deny us the right to conclude that a woman, in taking her revenge, may exaggerate many things? Exaggerate, indeed, that very shame and disgrace with which the money was offered by her hand. For, on the contrary, it was offered in just such a way as to make it possible for it to be accepted, particularly by a man as thoughtless as our defendant. Before anything else, he had that day in view the speedy receipt from his father of that three thousand that was owing to him in settlement. That was thoughtless, but by very reason of his thoughtlessness was he also firmly convinced that the latter would pay him the money, that he would receive it and, therefore, be able at any time to dispatch by post the money that had been entrusted to him by Miss Verkhovtseva and square the debt? On no account, however, will the prosecutor allow that he might that same day, the day of the accusation, have divided off a half of the money he had received and sewn it into an incense-bag: "Not thus," he says, "is this man's character, he was not capable of such emotions." But after all, you yourself have cried that Karamazov is broad, you yourself have cried of the two extreme abysses that Karamazov may contemplate. Karamazov is just such a nature with two sides, two abysses, that even in the grip of the most unrestrained need for a spree he is able to stop, if something makes an impression on him from the other side. And you see, that other side, it is love – that very same new love that ignited within him that day like gunpowder, and for that love he needs money, and more needfully, oh, far more needfully than even a spree with that same beloved. If she were to say to him: "I am yours, I do not want Fyodor Pavlovich," and he were to seize her and take her away – then he would need to have the wherewithal to do so. That, after all, would be more important than any spree. Did Karamazov not grasp that? Why, that was the very thing that had made him ill, that concern, so what is so improbable about his having divided off that money and hidden it away for any eventuality? Now, however, time is slipping away, and Fyodor Pavlovich has not paid the three thousand to the defendant, on the contrary, there is a rumour that he has allotted it to the specific purpose of enticing away his beloved. "If Fyodor Pavlovich does not let me have the money," he thinks, "I shall end up a thief before Katerina Ivanovna." And now there is born within him the thought that this same fifteen hundred, which he continues to carry around with him in the incense-bag, he will take, place before Miss Verkhovtseva and say to her: "I am a scoundrel, but not a thief." And so now, therefore, he has a double reason for guarding that fifteen hundred like the apple of his eye, and will on no account unpick the bag and peel off a hundred roubles at a time. Why will you deny the defendant a sense of honour? Nay, a sense of honour does indeed exist within him, even though it be an irregular one, even though it be very frequently a mistaken one, but it does exist, exists to the point of passion, and he has proved this. But now, however, the affair grows more complex, the torments of jealousy attain their highest degree, and still the same, the same two earlier questions appear ever more tormentingly, tormentingly within the inflamed brain of the defendant: "Shall I return the money to Katerina Ivanovna? With what means then will I take Grushenka away?" If he had been behaving like a madman so, getting drunk and raging about the inns all that month, then it was perhaps for the very reason that he himself was sick at heart, and it was more than he could endure. These two questions became in the end so aggravating that they finally drove him to despair. He made the effort of sending his younger brother to his father in order to ask him for the three thousand one last time but, not waiting for an answer, he himself burst in and ended by brutally beating the old man in front of witnesses. After that, consequently, there is no one from whom he may obtain money, his brutally beaten father will not give it. On the evening of that same day

he beats himself upon the breast, upon that very upper part of his breast
where the incense-bag is, and swears to his brother that he has the means
not to be a scoundrel, but that he will none the less remain a scoundrel,
for he can foresee that he will not take advantage of the means, has
insufficient inward strength, insufficient character. Why, why does the
prosecution not believe the testimony of Aleksey Karamazov, given so
purely, so sincerely, so without preparation, so plausibly? Why, on the
contrary, does it try to compel me to believe in the existence of money in
some cleft or crevice, in the dungeons of Udolpho's castle? On that same
evening, after his conversation with his brother, the defendant writes this
fateful letter, and it is this letter that is the most cardinal, the most
colossal fact that convicts the defendant of robbery! "I will ask for it
from all men, and if they will not give it me, I will kill my father and
take the money that is in the envelope with the pink ribbon from under
his mattress, if only Ivan has gone away" – a complete programme of the
murder, it is said, and who could it be, if not him? "It was performed the
way it was written!" the prosecution keeps exclaiming. But, in the first
place, it is a drunken letter, written in terrible anger; in the second, again
concerning the envelope he writes from what he has been told by
Smerdyakov, for he himself has not seen the envelope, and in the third,
the letter was written, and that there is no denying, but was what was
written performed, how may that be proven? Did the defendant obtain
the envelope under the pillow, did he find the money, did it exist, even?
For after all, it was not for money that the defendant had come running,
remember, remember! He had come running headlong not in order to
commit a robbery but merely to learn where she was, this woman who
had destroyed him with misery – not according to a programme, therefore, not according to what he had written did he come running, not, that
is, in order to commit a premeditated robbery, but came running suddenly,
suddenly, in a rabid frenzy of jealous rage! "Yes," it will be said, "but
even so, having run in and committed the murder, he took the money,
too." But there at last we have it: did he or did he not commit murder?
The accusation of robbery I reject with indignation: a man cannot be
accused of robbery if it is impossible to identify with precision what was
stolen, and that is an axiom! But did he even commit the murder, commit
it without any robbery? Is even that proven? Is not that, too, a *roman*?'

12

Nor was There Even Any Murder

'I must ask you to reflect, gentlemen of the jury, that a human life is involved here, and that it is necessary to be more careful. We have heard the prosecution itself testify that right up to the very last day, until today, the day of the trial, it hesitated to accuse the defendant of complete and outright premeditation of the murder, and that its hesitation lasted right until the presentation of this fateful "drunken" letter to the court today. "It was performed as out of a book!" But again I repeat: it was to her that he came running, for her, solely in order to learn where she was. Now that is an absolute fact. Had she happened to be at home, he would not have gone running anywhere, he would have remained with her and would not have fulfilled what he had promised in the letter. He came running haphazardly and suddenly, and as for his "drunken" letter, he may not have been thinking about it at the time at all. "He snatched the pestle," we are told – and you will recall how from this pestle alone an entire psychology was inferred for us: why he was bound to see that pestle as a weapon, snatch hold of it as a weapon, etcetera, etcetera. At this juncture there occurs to me a certain most commonplace thought: well, what if that pestle had not been lying in full view, and instead of being on a shelf from which the defendant was able to snatch it, had been put away in a cupboard – why, then it would not have flashed before the defendant's gaze, and he would have run off without a weapon, empty-handed, and then might perhaps never have murdered anyone. By what manner of means may I then make conclusions regarding the pestle as a proof of armament and premeditation? Yes, but he had gone shouting around the inns that he was going to kill his father, and two days before, on the evening he wrote his drunken letter, was quiet and quarrelled only with a merchant's assistant, "because", we are told, "Karamazov could not but quarrel". But, I will reply to that, if he had schemed such a murder, according to a plan, according to some written word, he would certainly not have quarrelled with the assistant and might perhaps not have visited the inn at all, because a soul that is scheming such a deed seeks silence and unnoticeability, seeks to disappear, so that it may neither be seen nor heard: as if to say, "Forget about me if you can", and this not from calculation alone, but from instinct. Gentlemen of the jury, psychology is a thing with two ends, and we are also able to understand psychology. And as regards all that shouting in the inns all that month, then surely it is not uncommon for children, or drunken layabouts emerging from the drinking-houses, quarrelling with one another, to shout: "I'm going to kill you!" – but they do not actually do it. And this very same fateful letter – well, is it not also drunken anger, the shout of a man emerging from a drinking-house: "I'm going to kill you, I'm going to kill the lot of you!" Why may it not be so, why could it not have been so? This letter, why is it so fateful, why, on the contrary, is it not ridiculous? For the very reason that the corpse of the murdered father was found, that a witness saw the defendant in the garden, armed and running away, and was himself cast down by him, and consequently it was all performed the way it was written and so the letter is not ridiculous, but fateful. Thanks be to God, we have arrived at the point of our endeavour: "If he was in the garden, that means he was the murderer." The whole thing, the entire case for the prosecution, may be reduced to those two expressions: *if he was*, followed inevitably by *that means*. But what if there is no *that means*, even though he was? Oh, I recognize that the weight of the facts, the concurrence of the facts are indeed rather eloquent. I should like you, however, to examine each of these facts separately, without being hypnotized by their combined weight: why, for example, is the prosecution on no account willing to admit the veracity of the defendant's statement that he ran away from his father's window? Recall the positive sarcasms upon which the prosecution embarks here with regard to the deference and the "pious" emotions that suddenly seized the murderer. But what if something of the kind actually did occur within him, that is to say, if not a deference of emotion, then a piety of one? "My mother must have been praying for me at that moment," the defendant testified at the investigation, and you see, he ran away as soon as he had ascertained that Svetlova was not in his father's house. "But he could not have done so through the window," the prosecution retorts to us. But why not? After all, the window was opened in response to the signals that were given by the defendant. At that point Fyodor Pavlovich might have uttered some word or other, let escape some cry – and the defendant would suddenly have received confirmation that Svetlova was not there. Why must we necessarily presume it to be as we imagine, or have presumed to imagine? In reality there may glimmer a thousand things that elude the observation of the most subtle *romancier*. "Yes, but Grigory saw the door open, and therefore the defendant must certainly have been in the house, and therefore he committed the murder." Concerning this door, gentlemen of the jury . . . You see, concerning this open door there is only one person who is able to give testimony, a person who was, however, at that time in such a condition that ... But let us assume, let us assume that the door was open, that the defendant denied it, told a lie about it out of a sense of self-preservation, so understandable in his position, let us assume, let us assume that he penetrated into the house, was in the house – well, what of it, why if he was there must he so certainly have committed murder? He could have burst in, run from room to room, pushed his father aside, even struck him, but, having ascertained that Svetlova was not within his house, run away, rejoicing that she was not there and that he had fled and had not killed his father. For that very reason also may he have leapt down a minute later from the fence to the side of Grigory, whom he had cast down in his extreme excitement, that he was in a condition to experience an emotion that was pure, an emotion of compassion and pity, for the reason that he had fled from the temptation to kill his father, had experienced within himself the emotions of a pure heart and the joy that he had not killed his father. Eloquently to the point of horror does the prosecutor describe to us the dreadful condition of the defendant in the village of Mokroye, when love had once more revealed itself to him, summoning him to a new life, and when it was already impossible for him to love, because behind him lay the bloodied corpse of his father, and beyond that corpse – retribution. Yet even so, the prosecutor still wishes to assume that there was love, which he explains in terms of his psychology: "The defendant's drunken condition," he tells us, "criminals have to be taken to the place of their doom, there is still a long time to wait, etcetera, etcetera." But Mr Prosecutor, again I ask you: have you not created another character? Is he so, so insensitive and callous, the defendant, that at that moment he was still capable of thinking at that moment of love and of prevarication before the court, if the blood of his father really lay upon his hands? No, no and no! No sooner was it revealed that she loved him, was summoning him to go with her, promising him new happiness – oh, I swear, he would have been bound to feel a double, a triple need to kill himself, and would indeed have done so without fail, had his father's corpse been lying there behind him! Oh no, he would not have forgotten where his pistols were! I know the defendant: the wild, wooden heartlessness that is laid by the prosecution at his door is not in keeping with his character. He would have killed himself, that is certain; he did not kill himself for the specific reason that "his mother prayed for him", and his heart was innocent of the blood of his father. He suffered torments, he grieved that night in Mokroye only for the old man Grigory whom he had cast down and prayed inwardly to God that the old man would arise and regain consciousness, that his blow had not been fatal and that retribution for it would not come to him. Why not accept such an interpretation of events? What firm proof do we have that the defendant is lying to us? Well, there is the father's corpse, it will be indicated to us once again: he ran outside, he committed no murder – well, who was it, then, murdered the old man?

'I repeat, here is all the logic of the prosecution: who could have committed the murder, if not he? "There is no one," it says, "whom we may put in his place." Gentlemen of the jury, is that really so? Is there really and truly no one at all whom we may put in his place? We heard the prosecution count on its fingers all who were in that house or who visited it that night. There were five people. Three of them, I agree, are completely excluded for obvious reasons: they are the murdered man himself, the old man Grigory, and his wife. There remain, consequently, the defendant and Smerdyakov, and now the prosecutor exclaims with enthusiasm that the defendant has identified Smerdyakov as the murderer because there is no one else whom he may so identify, that were there some sixth person, or even the ghost of some sixth person, the defendant would immediately, in shame, stop accusing Smerdyakov, and point to that sixth person instead. But, gentlemen of the jury, why may I not conclude that entirely the opposite is true? Two men stand before us: the defendant and Smerdyakov – then why may I not say that you accuse my client solely because you have no one else whom you may accuse? And that this is so only because you have in a completely prejudiced manner excluded Smerdyakov from all suspicion in advance. Yes, to be sure, the only people who point to Smerdyakov are the defendant, his two brothers and Svetlova, and they would appear to be the only ones. But in fact, there are also others: there is a certain, though obscure ferment in the social circles of this town with regard to a question, a suspicion, there is in circulation a kind of obscure rumour, there is a feeling that something may be expected to come to light. There is, finally, the testimony of a certain juxtaposition of facts, one thoroughly characteristic, though, I admit, also ill-defined: in the first place, this fit of the falling sickness on the very day of the catastrophe, a fit which the prosecutor was for some reason so painstakingly compelled to defend and vindicate. Then this sudden suicide of Smerdyakov on the eve of the trial. Then the no-less-sudden statement at the trial today by the defendant's elder brother, who until now had believed in his brother's guilt, and who suddenly came in with the money, and also again proclaimed the name of Smerdyakov as the murderer! Oh, I am completely convinced, together with the court and the public procurator's office, that Ivan Karamazov is ill and in acute fever, that his statement may indeed have been a desperate attempt, devised, what is more, in delirium, to rescue his brother by unloading the guilt on to the dead man. All the same, however, the name of Smerdyakov has been uttered, and again it is as though there were a whiff of mystery. It is as though something here had not been spoken to the end, gentlemen of the jury, and not concluded. And perhaps it will be spoken to the end. But let us leave that for the present, that still lies ahead. The court decided earlier to resume its sitting, but in the meanwhile, as we wait, I should like to make some observations, for example, concerning the characterization of the deceased Smerdyakov, so subtly and with such talent outlined by the prosecutor. Much as I wonder at his talent, I am, however, unable to concur entirely with the essence of his characterization. I went to see Smerdyakov, I saw him and spoke to him, he produced upon me an impression of quite a different sort. His health was weak, that is true, but in character, in heart – ah no, he was in no wise such a weak man as the prosecution has concluded in his regard. In particular, I found in him no timidity, that timidity that was described for us so characteristically by the prosecutor. As for ingenuousness, there was none of that in him at all, on the contrary, I found a terrible suspiciousness that lurked beneath an outward show of *naïveté*, and a mind that was capable of contemplating rather a great deal. Oh, too ingenuously did the prosecution consider him to be feeble-minded. Upon me he produced a very definite impression: I went away with the conviction that this was a being of decided malice, possessed of an inordinate ambition, a vengeful-ness and torrid envy. I have collected certain information: he had a hatred of his origins, was ashamed of them and would with grinding of his teeth recollect that he had "proceeded from the Stinker". For his former benefactors, the manservant Grigory and his wife, he had a lack of deference. Russia he cursed, and poured derision on her. He dreamed of going away to France, in order to transform himself into a Frenchman. Much and often had he talked of it before, saying that he had insufficient means thereto. I believe that he loved no one but himself, and had a strangely high regard for himself. Education he saw in good clothes, clean dickies and polished boots. Viewing himself as he did (there is factual evidence in support of his view) as Fyodor Pavlovich's illegitimate son, he might well have hated his situation when compared with that of his master's legitimate children: they, he might have reflected, would get everything, while he got nothing, they would get all the rights, the inheritance, while he was only a cook. He revealed to me that he himself had, together with Fyodor Pavlovich, put the money away in the envelope. The destination of this sum — a sum that might have made his career — was, of course, something hateful to him. To make it worse, he had seen the three thousand roubles in nice, bright rainbow credit bills (I made a special point of asking him about that). Oh, never show a vain and envious man a large amount of money at once; and this was the first time he had seen such a sum in a single hand. The effect of seeing the rainbow wad may have morbidly influenced his imagination, at first and for the time being without any consequences. The highly talented prosecutor has outlined for us with uncommon subtlety all the *pros* and *contras* of the supposition that it may be possible to accuse Smerdyakov of having committed the murder, and asked in particular: why should the latter have feigned the falling sickness? Yes, but after all he might not have been feigning at all, the fit might have come upon him quite naturally, but passed quite naturally, too, and the sick man regained consciousness. Not that he was entirely better, but that he none the less at some point came to himself and regained consciousness, as is often the case in the falling sickness. The prosecution asks: at what moment did Smerdyakov commit the murder? But to identify that moment is extremely easy. He might have regained consciousness, risen from a deep slumber (for he was only asleep: after fits of the falling sickness a deep slumber invariably ensues), at that very moment that the old man Grigory, having seized the defendant by the leg where, seated upon the fence, he was trying to run away, howled "Father-murderer!" so it could be heard all over the entire neighbourhood. This cry, unusual as it was in the quiet and the murk, might also have woken Smerdyakov, whose slumber by that time might not have been very sound: he might naturally have begun to wake up an hour before this. Having risen from his bed, he sets off almost unconsciously and without any plan in the direction of the cry, in order to see what has happened. In his head there is a morbid stupor, his reason is still a-slumber, but now here he is in the garden: he approaches the illumined windows and hears the dread tidings from his *barin*, who, of course, has rejoiced at his presence. From his frightened *barin* he learns all the details. And lo, by degrees, within his sick and disordered brain there forms a thought — one dreadful, but tempting and irrefutably logical: to murder him, take the three thousand in banknotes and afterwards unload all the guilt on to the young *barin*: to whom else will anyone think to impute the deed, if not the young *barin*, whom else will they accuse, if not the young *barin*? There is all this evidence, he was here! A terrible craving for money, for plunder might have seized his mind, together with the realization of impunity. Oh, these sudden and irresistible impulses so often arise on occasion and, above all, arise within the kind of murderer who even a moment earlier did not know that he intended to kill! And thus, Smerdyakov might have gone into the *barin*'s chamber and executed his plan; what with, by means of what weapon? With the first stone he picked up in the garden. But why, with what purpose? Well, three thousand, after all, that is a career. Oh, I do not contradict myself: the money might even have existed. And it is even possible that Smerdyakov alone knew where to find it, the very spot in his *barin*'s house where it lay. "Well, and the wrapping around the bills, the torn envelope on the floor?" Today, when the prosecutor, in speaking of that envelope, expounded his most subtle view that to have left it on the floor would be the action precisely of an unhabituated thief, precisely a thief such as Karamazov, and not at all that of Smerdyakov, who on no account would have left such evidence against himself lying around – today, gentlemen of the jury, as I listened, I suddenly felt that I was hearing something exceedingly familiar. And imagine, that same view, that surmise concerning the manner in which Karamazov might have acted with the envelope, I had already heard exactly two days earlier from Smerdyakov, and not only that, but he had even surprised me with it: indeed, I had the impression that he was affecting a false *naiveté*, running to forestall me, trying to thrust this idea upon me, so that I myself should come to this same view, and was as if suggesting it to me by implication. Did he not suggest the same idea to the investigation? Did he not thrust it upon the highly talented prosecutor? It will be said: but what about the old woman, Grigory's wife? After all, she had heard the sick man groaning beside her all night. Indeed, she had, but I must say that this argument is an exceedingly shaky one. I once knew a certain lady who bitterly complained that a mongrel in the yard outside kept waking her up all night and that she could get no sleep for it. And yet the poor little dog, as it transpired, had only yelped some two or three times throughout the entire night. And this is natural; a man is asleep and suddenly hears a groan, he wakes up in annoyance at having been woken, but falls asleep again an instant later. Some two hours thereafter comes another groan, he again wakes up and again falls back to sleep, then there is another, again two hours later, only three times in all throughout the whole of the night. In the morning the sleeper rises and complains that someone has been groaning all night, incessantly waking him up. But it is bound to seem to him this way; the intervals of sleep, each two hours in duration, he has passed in unconsciousness and does not remember, he remembers only the moments at which he was woken, and so it seems to him that he has been kept awake all night. But why, why, exclaims the prosecution, did not Smerdyakov confess in his suicide note? "For the one he had sufficient conscience, but for the other he did not," we are told. But permit me: conscience, that is already remorse, but the suicide may have felt no remorse, but only despair. Despair may be aggressively hostile and unappeasable, and the suicide, in placing hands upon his life, may at that moment have felt redoubled hatred for those whom all his life he had envied. Gentlemen of the jury, beware of making a judicial error! What, what is implausible in all that I have just presented and depicted to you? Find the error in my exposition, find that which is impossible, absurd. But if there is even a ghost of possibility, even a ghost of plausibility in my suppositions, then reserve your verdict. And is there here a ghost, merely? I swear by all that is sacred, I have complete faith in my own interpretation of the murder, which I have just presented to you. But above all, above all I am troubled, driven out of myself by the thought that of all the mass of facts that the prosecution has heaped on the defendant, there is not a single one that is in any way precise or irrefutable, and that the unhappy man is going to perish solely on account of the combined weight of those facts. Yes, that weight is a terrible one; that blood, that blood trickling from his fingers, those bloodstained clothes, that dark night, filled with the howl of "Father-murderer!" and a man shouting, falling with a broken skull, and then this mass of utterances, statements, gestures, cries — oh, that may exert such influence, may so suborn one's conviction, but is it able, gentlemen of the jury, is it able to suborn yours? Remember, you have been given an unbounded power, the power to bind and loose.* But the mightier the power, the more terrible its exercise! Not by one iota do I retreat from what I have just said, but let us suppose that it were so, suppose for a moment that I were to agree with the prosecution that my unhappy client steeped his hands in the blood of his father. This is only a hypothesis, I repeat that not for a second do I doubt his innocence, but say it were so, and I suppose my defendant to be guilty of parricide, but listen carefully to my words, even though I may admit such a hypothesis. There lies within my heart the duty to express to you yet something more, for I anticipate a great struggle within your hearts and minds . . . Forgive me this remark, gentlemen of the jury, concerning your hearts and minds. But I want to be truthful and sincere to the end. And let us all be sincere! . . .'

At this point the defence counsel was interrupted by a rather powerful burst of applause. Indeed, he had uttered his last words with a note of such sincere resonance that everyone felt that perhaps he really did have something to say and that what he was going to say now would be the most important part. But the chairman, upon hearing the applause, loudly threatened to 'clear' the chamber of the court if 'a similar instance' were to be repeated. All grew quiet, and Fetyukovich began in a kind of new, emotionally charged voice, not at all the same as the one he had used hitherto.

13

An Adulterer of Thought

'Not only by the combined weight of the facts is my client undone, gentlemen of the jury,' he proclaimed, 'no, my client is really undone by one mere single fact, and that is: the corpse of his aged father! Had this been a simple murder, then, faced with the insignificance, the unprovenness, the fantasticism of the facts, if each of them be examined in isolation, not combination, you too would reject the accusation, or would at least hesitate to undo a man's fate on account of mere prejudice against him, which, alas, he has so deserved! Here, however, we have not a simple murder, but a parricide! That impresses, and to such a degree that even the very insignificance and unprovenness of the accusing facts become less insignificant and less unproven, and this even to the most unprejudiced mind. But how can such a defendant be acquitted? Suppose he has committed murder and escapes unpunished – that is what each of us feels in his heart almost involuntarily, by instinct. Yes, it is a terrible thing to spill the blood of a father – the blood of the one who begot me, the blood of the one who has loved me, the blood of the one who has not spared himself for me, the one who has ached with my illnesses ever since I was a child, the one who has suffered all his life for my happiness and has lived only for my joys, my successes! Oh, to kill such a father – why, that is impossible even to think! Gentlemen of the jury, what is a father, a real father, what great word is this, what terrifyingly great idea lies in this designation? We have just indicated in part what a true father is and should be. But in the case before us now, the one with which we are so occupied, with which our souls ache – in the case before us the father, the deceased Fyodor Pavlovich Karamazov, in no way fitted that conception of a father which impressed our hearts just now. That is a misfortune. Yes, indeed, certain fathers resemble a misfortune. But let us examine this misfortune more closely – after all, we must fear nothing, gentlemen of the jury, in view of the importance of the decision we are about to make. We must especially fear nothing now and, as it were, wave certain ideas away, like children or like women easily frightened, to employ the highly talented prosecutor's happy expression. But in his impassioned speech my respected adversary (an adversary even before I had uttered my first word), my adversary several times exclaimed: "No, I will not let anyone else defend the accused, I will not leave his defence to the highly talented counsel who has arrived from St Petersburg – I am both prosecutor and counsel for the defence!" Thus did he several times exclaim, forgetting, however, to mention that if the fearsome defendant had for an entire twenty-three years been so grateful for a mere pound of nuts received from the only person who had shown him some affection as a child within the home of his progenitor, then, vice versa, such a man would not, would he, be able to forget, all those twenty-three years, that he had run about barefoot at his father's house "in the backyard without any boots on and with his little trousers held up by a single button . . ." in the expression of the philanthropic Herzenstube. Oh, gentlemen of the jury, why must we examine this "misfortune" more closely, repeat that which all already know? What greeted my client when he arrived there at his father's house? And why, why depict my client as unfeeling, an egoist, a monster? He is unrestrained, he is wild and violent, that is why we are trying him now, but who is to blame for his fate, who is to blame that with good inclinations, with a noble, feeling heart he received such a preposterous upbringing? Did anyone instruct him in sweet reason, was he educated in science and study, did anyone love him even just a little when he was a child? My client grew up under God's protection, like a wild beast, that is. Perhaps he had yearned to see his father after long years of being apart from him, perhaps a thousand times before, remembering his childhood as in slumber, he had driven away the repulsive spectres that had haunted his dreams as a child, and yearned with all his soul to excuse his father and to throw his arms about him! And what happens? He is greeted by nothing but cynical sneers, suspicion and chicanery concerning the disputed money; he hears nothing but talk and worldly maxims that make his heart turn over, every day "over some cognac", and at last, beholds his own father trying to take away from him, his son, by means of his son's money, his mistress – oh, gentlemen of the jury, that is repulsive and cruel! And this same old man complains to everyone about his son's cruelty and lack of deference, blackens his name in society, defames him, slanders him, buys up his letters of debt in order to have him put in prison! Gentlemen of the jury, these souls, these men who, like my client, seem outwardly cruel-hearted, violent and unrestrained, may very often be of an exceeding tenderness of heart, only they do not display it. Do not laugh, do not laugh at my idea! The talented prosecutor laughed today at my client without pity, exposing his love of Schiller, his love of "the beautiful and the lofty". Were I in his place, the place of a prosecutor, I would not laugh at those things! Yes, these hearts – oh, let me defend these hearts that are so seldom and so incorrectly understood – these hearts very frequently yearn for the tender, the beautiful and the just, and precisely as it were in contrast to themselves, their violence, their cruelty – they yearn unconsciously, but yearn they do. Passionate and cruel on the exterior, they are capable of loving to the point of torment, for example, a woman, and invariably with a spiritual, elevated love. Once again, do not laugh at me: that is the very thing that most often occurs in these natures! The only thing is that they are unable to conceal the passion of their temperament, which is at times very coarse – and it is this that strikes, this that is noticed, while the inside of the man is not seen. On the contrary, all their passions are quickly sated, but near the noble, beautiful being this apparently coarse and cruel man seeks renewal, seeks the possibility of correcting his ways, of becoming better, making himself lofty and honourable – "lofty and beautiful", however mocked those words may be! Earlier I said I would not permit myself to touch the *roman* of my client with Miss Verkhovtseva. For all that, however, half a word may be said: we heard today not a statement, but merely the cry of a frenzied and avenging woman, and not for her, oh, not for her is it to rebuke him for betrayal, for she herself has betrayed! Had she but had a little time to think it over, she would not have given such testimony! Oh, do not listen to her, no, my client is no "monster of cruelty", as she called him. The crucified lover of mankind, on the way to his cross, said: "I am the good shepherd, the good shepherd putteth his soul upon his sheep, and not one of them shall perish . . ."* Let us, also, not bring ruin to a human soul! I asked just now the question: what is a father, and exclaimed that this is a great word, a precious designation. But with the word, gentlemen of the jury, one must treat honourably, and I shall permit myself to name an object by its proper word, its proper designation: a father such as the murdered old man Karamazov cannot and is not worthy to be called a father. Love for a father that is not justified by the father is a preposterous, an impossible thing. It is impossible to create love from nothing, from nothing only God creates. "Fathers, provoke not your children to anger,"* writes the apostle out of his heart that is aflame with love. Not for the sake of my client do I cite these holy words now, I recall them for all fathers. Who has given me this authority, to instruct fathers? No one. But as a man and as a citizen do I appeal: *vivos voco!** We are not long upon the earth, we do many an evil deed and say many an evil word. Let us therefore pluck the opportune moment of our conjoined association in order to say, also, to one another a word that is good. Thus do I also: while I am upon this spot, I shall employ my moment to its advantage. Not in vain has this tribune been granted to us by a higher will — from it all Russia hears us. Not for the fathers of this town alone do I speak, but to all fathers do I exclaim: "Fathers, provoke not your children to anger!" Yes, let us first ourselves fulfil Christ's testament and then only shall we permit ourselves to ask it of our children. Otherwise we are not fathers but foes unto our children, and they are not our children, but our foes, and we ourselves have made them thus! "For with the same measure that ye mete withal shall it be measured out to you again" — not I do speak, but thus prescribes the Holy Gospel: measure in such measure as is measured out to you. And how can we blame our children if they measure to us as is measured out to them? Not long ago in Finland a certain unmarried girl, a serving-maid, was suspected of having secretly given birth to a child. A watch was kept upon her, and in the attic of the house, in a corner behind bricks, her trunk, which no one had known about, was found, opened and from it taken the corpse of a new-born infant, which she had slain. In the same trunk were found the skeletons of two infants she had brought into the world and slain earlier also at the moment of their birth, which fact she confessed. Gentlemen of the jury, is this a mother of her children? Yes, she bore them, but is she a mother to them? Will any of us be so bold as to pronounce over her the sacred name of mother? Let us be bold, gentlemen of the jury, let us be audacious, even, we are even obliged to be thus at the present moment and not go in fear of certain words and ideas, in the manner of those Moscow merchants' wives who go in fear of "metal" and of "brimstone".* Nay, let us prove, on the contrary, that the progress of recent years has also touched our moral development, and let us say outright: a begetter is not yet a father, while a father is a begetter and a deserver. Oh, of course, there is another meaning, another interpretation of the word "father", one which demands that my father, even though he be a monster of cruelty, a doer of evil unto his children, none the less remains my father, for the simple reason that he begot me. But this meaning is already, as it were, a mystical one, one that I may not comprehend with my mind but may only accept by faith, or, more correctly, *upon faith*, like much else which I do not comprehend, but which religion commands me, none the less, to believe. But in that instance let it then remain without the province of real life. Within the province of real life, which possesses not only its own rights, but itself imposes great obligations – within that province we, we wish to be humane, to be Christians, at last, must and are obliged to adhere only to convictions that have been justified in the light of intellect and experience, that have been passed through the crucible of analysis, in a word – to act in accordance with reason and not in a manner bereft of it, as in dream and delirium, that we may not bring harm to others, that we may not exhaust them with torment and bring ruin upon them. Then, only then will it be a genuine Christian act, not a mystical one only, but one that accords with reason and is now truly philanthropic . . .'

At this passage loud clapping broke forth from many areas of the chamber, but Fetyukovich even began to wave his hands, as though he were imploring that he not be interrupted and be allowed to finish. All of an instant grew hushed. The orator resumed:

'Do you suppose, gentlemen of the jury, that questions of this kind can possibly fail to affect our children, if, that is to say, they are already grown to youth, already beginning to think for themselves? No, they cannot, and let us not ask of them impossible forbearance! The sight of an unworthy father, especially when compared to other fathers, worthy ones, of other children, his coevals, involuntarily prompts a youth with tormenting questions. The official answer to these questions is: "He hath begotten thee, and thou art his blood, and therefore must thou also love him." Involuntarily the youth begins to reflect: "Did he love me when he begot me?" he asks, in greater and greater astonishment. "Was it for me that he begot me: he knew neither me nor even my gender at that moment, the moment of passion, inflamed perhaps by vodka, and passed on to me only a propensity for hard drinking – there are all his good deeds . . . Why then must I love him, merely because he begot me, and thereafter all his life did not love me?" Oh, to you, perhaps, these questions appear coarse, cruel, but then do not demand of a young mind impossible forbearance: "Drive nature out of the door, and she will fly in at the window"* – and above all, above all, let us not go in fear of "metal" and "brimstone", and let us decide the question as reason and philanthropy, not mystical concepts, prescribe. How then may it be decided? Like this: let the son stand before his father and ask him in good sense: "Father, tell me: why must I love you? Father, prove to me that I must love you!" – and if it is within that father's power and capability to reply and prove it to him, then this is a true and normal family, grounded not upon mere mystical prejudice, but upon foundations that are reasonable, self-accounting and stringently humane. In the contrary instance, if the father is unable to offer proof – then at once an end to this family: he is no father to him, and the son receives his freedom and the right henceforth to consider his father as one alien to him and even as his foe. Our tribune, gentlemen of the jury, must be a school of truth and plain concepts!'

Here the orator was interrupted by clapping that was uncontainable and almost frenzied. Of course, not all the chamber applauded, but all the same a half of the chamber applauded. The fathers and mothers applauded. From above, where the ladies sat, came shrieks and cries. Handkerchiefs were waved. The chairman began with all his might to ring the bell. He was evidently irritated by the conduct of the chamber, but to 'clear' it, as he had not long ago threatened, he decidedly did not dare; even the persons in high office, old men with stars upon their frock-coats, who sat in special chairs behind, applauded and waved handkerchiefs in the orator's direction, with the result that when the hubbub had abated, the chairman merely contented himself with his earlier most stern promise to 'clear' the chamber, and the triumphant and excited Fetyukovich again began to resume his speech.

'Gentlemen of the jury, you recall that dreadful night, of which so much has already been said today, when a son, by climbing a fence, penetrated into the house of his father and stood, at last, face to face with with the one who begot him, his foe and wronger. With all my might I insist – not for money did he come running at that moment: the accusation of robbery is preposterous, as I have already explained. And not to murder him, oh no, did he force his way into his house; had he with premeditation had that design, he would at least have seen to the matter of the murder weapon in advance, but he snatched the brass pestle instinctively, himself not knowing why. Even assuming that he had deceived his father by the signals, even assuming that he penetrated into his chambers – I have already said that not for one minute do I believe that legend, but assume that it were so, so let it be, and let us suppose it for a single moment! Gentlemen of the jury, I swear to you all, by all that is holy, had this not been his father, but another wronger to whom he was not related, he would, having run from room to room and ascertained that the woman was not within that house, have run away headlong, doing no harm to his rival, might have struck him, pushed him, possibly, but that is all, for that was not what was on his mind, he had not time for that, he needed to learn where she was. But the father, the father — oh, all was done by the mere sight of the father, his hater since childhood, his foe, his wronger, and now — his monstrous rival! A sense of hatred seized hold of him involuntarily, uncontainably, and reasoning was impossible: it all rose up in a single moment! It was an affect of mindlessness and madness, but also an affect of nature, avenging her eternal laws impetuously and unconsciously, like everything else in nature. But even now the murderer did not murder — I affirm this, I cry it — no, he merely brandished the pestle in sickened indignation, not desiring to kill, not knowing that he would kill. Had that fateful pestle not been in his hand, he might only have beaten his father, mercilessly, perhaps, but not killed him. Having started to run away, he did not know whether the old man whom he had cast down was dead or not. A murder of that kind is not a murder. Neither is a murder of that kind a parricide. No, the murder of a father such as that cannot be called a parricide. A murder of that kind may be classed as a parricide only out of prejudice! But did it happen, did this murder actually happen, I appeal to you again and again from the depths of my soul! Gentlemen of the jury, lo, we shall condemn him, and he will say to himself: "These men did nothing for my fortunes, for my upbringing, my education, in order to make me better, to make me a man. These men did not feed me and did not give me to drink, nor did they visit me as I lay naked in prison, and now they have sent me into penal servitude.* I am quits with them, I owe them nothing now and shall owe no one anything until the end of the ages. They are wicked, and I shall be wicked. They are cruel, and I shall be cruel." That is what he will say, gentlemen of the jury! And I swear: with your accusation you will only relieve him, relieve his conscience, he will continue to curse the blood he has spilt, and will have no remorse for it. At the same time, you will bring to ruin the man still possible within him, for he will remain wicked and blind all the rest of his days. But do you wish to punish him terribly, ferociously, with the most dreadful punishment that one may imagine, but with the purpose of saving and regenerating his soul for ever? If so, then crush him with your mercy! You will see, you will hear his soul shudder, show horror. "Am I to endure this mercy, am I to receive all this love, am I worthy of it?" — that is what he will exclaim! Oh, I know, I know this heart, this wild but noble heart, gentlemen of the jury. It will bow down before your pious deed, it will thirst for a great act of love, it will burn aloft and be resurrected for ever. There are souls that in their limitation accuse the entire world. But crush this soul with mercy, show it love, and it will curse its handiwork, for within it there are so many good beginnings. The soul will grow enlarged and will behold how merciful God is, how fair and just are men. He will be horrified and crushed by the repentance and the numberless debt that stands before him from this day. And then what he will say is not: "I am quits with them," but "I am guilty before all men and am the most unworthy of all men." In tears of contrition and burning, suffering tenderness he will exclaim: "Men are better than I, for they wished not to destroy me but to save me!" Oh, it will be so easy for you to perform it, this act of mercy, for in the absence of any evidence even slightly resembling the truth you will find it too painful to pronounce: "Yes, he is guilty." It is better to let ten guilty men go free than to punish one innocent one* – do you hear, do you hear that majestic voice from the previous century of our glorious history? Am I, who am insignificant, to remind you that Russian justice is not the retribution merely, but also the salvation of the ruined man? Let other nations have the letter and the retribution, we have the spirit and the sense, the salvation and regeneration of the ruined. And if it is so, if truly thus are Russia and her justice, then – forward, Russia, and intimidate, intimidate us not with your furied *troikas*, from which all nations stand aside in sickened loathing! Not a furied *troika*, but a majestic Russian chariot will solemnly and tranquilly attain its goal. In your hands lies my client's fate, in your hands lies, too, the fate of our Russian justice. You shall save it, you shall uphold it, you shall prove that there are those who care for its observance, that it is in good hands!'

14

The Muzhiks Stand Up for Themselves

THUS did Fetyukovich end, and on this occasion the ecstasy that burst forth from his listeners was uncontainable, like a storm. To check it now was not to be conceived: the women were weeping, many of the men were weeping also, and even two of the persons in high office were shedding tears. The chairman resigned himself and even tarried before ringing the bell: 'To have encroached upon such enthusiasm would have meant to encroach upon a sacred thing,' as the ladies of our town cried subsequently. The orator himself was sincerely moved. And lo, at such a moment did our Ippolit Kirillovich rise once more to 'exchange

objections'. Eyes fell on him with hatred: 'What? How can this be? That
fellow still dares to object?' the ladies began to babble. But even if the
ladies of all the world had begun to babble, and at their head the public
procurator's wife, why at that moment even then it would have been
impossible to restrain him. He was pale, he trembled with excitement; the
first words, the first phrases uttered by him were even incomprehensible;
he choked, articulated badly, lost his thread. As a matter of fact, though,
he swiftly recovered. But from this second speech of his I shall cite
merely one or two phrases.

'. . . We are reproached with having created *romans*. But what has the
defence counsel given us, if not *roman* upon *roman*? All that was lacking
was some poetry. In expectation of his mistress, Fyodor Pavlovich tears
up an envelope and throws it upon the floor. We are even quoted the
words he spoke on this remarkable occasion. Why, is this not a *poema*?
And where is the proof that he removed the money, who heard those
words he spoke? The feeble-witted idiot Smerdyakov, transformed into
some kind of Byronic hero, taking his revenge upon society for the
illegitimacy of his birth − is this not a narrative *poema* in the Byronic
taste? And the son, forcing his way into his father's chambers, murdering
him, but at the same time not murdering him, that is not even a *roman*,
not a *poema*, it is a Sphinx asking riddles, which it itself, of course, will
never solve. If kill he did, then he did kill, and how then can it be that he
did kill, yet kill did not − who will comprehend it? Thereupon it is
proclaimed to us that our tribune is the tribune of truth and plain
concepts, and lo, from this tribune of "plain concepts" resounds, with an
oath, the axiom that to call the murder of a father parricide is but mere
prejudice! But if parricide is a prejudice and if each child will interrogate
his father: "Father, why must I love you?" − then what will become of us,
what will become of the fundaments of society, whither will the family
turn? Parricide − why, do you not see, it is merely the "brimstone" of a
Moscow merchant's wife. The most precious, the most sacred precepts in
the destination and future of Russian justice are presented in distorted
and frivolous fashion, merely in order to attain a purpose, to attain the
justification of that which cannot be justified. Oh, crush him with mercy,
exclaims the defence counsel, while that is all that the criminal desires,
and tomorrow all will see how crushed he is! And is not the defence
counsel too modest in demanding only the acquittal of the defendant?
Why should he not demand the founding of a stipend in the name of
the father-murderer, for the perpetuation of his holy deed among posterity
and the younger generation? The Gospel and religion stand corrected: all

that is mysticism, he says, and only among us is there true Christianity, one verified by the analysis of reason and plain concepts. And lo, before us is erected a false likeness of Christ! *"For with the same measure that ye mete withal shall it be measured to you again,"* the defence counsel exclaims, and at that same instant infers from this that Christ commanded us to measure in the same measure in which it is measured to us — and this from the tribune of truth and plain concepts! We consult the Gospel only on the eve of our speeches in order to shine in our familiarity with what is after all a rather original composition, which may come in handy and serve to create a certain effect, in the measure to which it is required, always in the degree to which it is required! But that is the very thing that Christ commands us not to do, to beware of doing, because the wicked world does it, while we must forgive and turn the other cheek, and not measure in the same measure in which our wrongers measure to us. That is what our Lord hath taught us, and not that to forbid our children to murder their fathers is a prejudice. And we must not, from the pulpit of truth and plain concepts, correct the Gospel of our Lord, on whom the defence counsel is willing only to confer the name of "crucified lover of mankind", in contrast to all Orthodox Russia, which appeals to him: "For Thou art Our God . . ."'*

At this point the chairman stepped in and asked the *entraîné* to stop, requesting him not to exaggerate, to remain within due limits, etcetera, etcetera, as court chairmen usually do in such cases. And indeed, the chamber was unquiet, too. The public was stirring, even exclaiming in indignation. Fetyukovich did not even register any objection, but merely went up, his hand placed on his heart, to deliver himself in an injured voice of a few words full of dignity. Only slightly and mockingly did he again touch upon 'romans' and 'psychology', inserting at one point in a suitable place: 'Jupiter, thou art angry, therefore art thou wrong,'* provoking an approving and widespread titter in the public, for Ippolit Kirillovich did not now in any way resemble Jupiter. Thereupon, to the accusation that he had apparently given the younger generation permission to murder their fathers, Fetyukovich observed with profound dignity that he would not even make retort. As for the 'false likeness of Christ' and the circumstance that he had not conferred the name of God upon Christ, but had called him merely 'the crucified lover of mankind', this being, it was said 'against Orthodoxy and not to be uttered from the tribune of truth and plain concepts' — Fetyukovich alluded to 'slanderous insinuations' and to the fact that, in pursuing his intent to come here, he had at least supposed the tribune here to be secure from accusations 'that might jeopardize my standing as a citizen and loyal subject . . .' But at these words the chairman asked him, too, to stop, and Fetyukovich, bowing, concluded his reply, accompanied by a universal and approving ripple of voices from the chamber. As for Ippolit Kirillovich he had, in the opinion of our ladies, been 'squashed for ever'.

After this, the defendant himself was given the floor. Mitya stood up, but did not say much. He was terribly fatigued both physically and spiritually. The aspect of independence and strength with which he had appeared that morning in the chamber had almost vanished. It was as if he had experienced something that day to last him all his life, something that had taught him and made him understand something very important, which he had not earlier comprehended. His voice had grown feeble, and now he did not shout as earlier that day. In his words one could hear something new, reconciled, conquered and bowed down.

'What am I to say, gentlemen of the jury! My judgement has arrived, I feel the right hand of God upon me. An end to the licentious man! But, as though I were confessing my sins to God, I say to you: "Of the blood of my father – no, of that I am not guilty!" For the last time I say again: "It was not I who killed him!" I was licentious, but I loved the good. Every instant I strove to mend my ways, but lived like a savage beast. I thank the public procurator, much has he told me of myself that I did not know, but it is not true that I killed my father, the public procurator is mistaken! I thank the defence counsel also, as I listened to him, I wept, but it is not true that I killed my father, and it was not right to assume it! And do not listen to the doctors, I am fully in my right mind, only my soul is heavy. If you will spare me, if you will release me – I will pray for you. I will become better, I give my word, before God I give it. But if you will condemn – then I myself shall break the sword over my head,* and, having broken it, shall kiss the fragments! But spare me, do not deprive me of my God, I know myself: I shall make murmur! My soul is wretched, gentlemen . . . spare me!'

He almost collapsed into his place, his voice was strangled and cut short, he only just managed to articulate his final phrase. Thereupon the court proceeded to the formulation of questions and began to ask for concluding statements from defence and prosecution. I shall not, however, describe the details. At length the jury rose in order to retire for their deliberations. The chairman was much fatigued, and so he gave them a very feeble last instruction, saying: 'Be impartial, do not let yourselves be swayed by the eloquent words of the defence, but weigh up everything, and remember that on you lies a great responsibility,' etcetera, etcetera. The jurymen withdrew, and there was an adjournment in the proceedings.

It was possible to get up, walk out, exchange one's accumulated impressions, partake of a morsel at the buffet. It was very late by now, around one o'clock in the morning, but no one had departed. All were so strained and keyed up that they did not think of rest. All were waiting, all were heart in mouth, though, as a matter of fact, not all were heart in mouth. The ladies were merely in a state of hysterical impatience, while their hearts were calm: 'An acquittal,' they said, 'is inevitable.' All of them were getting ready for the spectacular moment of general enthusiasm. I will confess that even in the male half of the chamber there were exceedingly many convinced that an acquittal was inevitable. Some rejoiced, while others knit their brows, and yet others were simply crestfallen: they did not want there to be an acquittal! Fetyukovich himself was firmly convinced of success. He was surrounded, received felicitations, while people ingratiated themselves before him.

'There are,' he said in a certain group, as was subsequently related, 'there are these invisible threads that bind the defence counsel to the jury. They are formed and may be sensed even during the speech. I have felt them, they exist. The case is ours, have no concern.'

'What do you think those muzhiks of ours are going to say now?' said a frowning, fat and pock-marked gentleman, a landowner from near our town, going up to one group of conversing gentlemen.

'Not just the muzhiks, there are four civil servants there.'

'Yes, what about the civil servants?' a member of the *zemstvo* council said, walking up.

'But do you know Nazaryev, Prokhor Ivanovich, that merchant with the medal, who is on the jury?'

'Well?'

'He is as wise as Solomon.'

'But he never says anything.'

'That is as that may be, but actually it makes him even better. The St Petersburg fellow couldn't teach him anything, he himself will teach all St Petersburg. Twelve children, imagine!'

'Oh for pity's sake, do you really suppose they will not acquit him?' one of our young civil servants was shouting in another group.

'Of course they will,' a resolute voice was heard to say.

'It would be shameful, disgraceful, not to acquit him!' the civil servant continued to vociferate. 'Very well, say he did kill him, but after all, there are fathers and fathers! And anyway, he was in such a frenzy . . . He really might have only brandished the pestle, and the father went to the floor. The only bad thing was their bringing the lackey into it. That was just a laughable episode. If I'd been in the defence counsel's shoes I'd have just said straight out: he committed the murder, but he isn't guilty, and the devil with you!'

'Well, and so he did, except that he didn't say the devil with you!'

'Oh come on, Mikhail Semyonich, he as good as did,' a third small voice piped up.

'For pity's sake, gentlemen, I mean, they acquitted an actress* at Lent, didn't they, that one who cut the throat of her lover's lawful wedded wife?'

'Yes, but she didn't finish the job.'

'It doesn't matter, it doesn't matter, she started to do it!'

'And what did you think of the bit about children? Splendid!'

'Yes, it was.'

'Yes, but what about the part about mysticism, the mysticism bit, eh?'

'Oh, will you stop going on about that,' someone else exclaimed. 'You ought to be thinking of Ippolit, and his fortunes from today! I mean, the public procurator's wife will scratch his eyes out tomorrow because of Mitenka.'

'Is she here?'

'What do you mean, here? If she were here she'd have scratched them out long ago. No, she's at home with a toothache. Heh-heh-heh!'

'Heh-heh-heh!'

In a third group:

'You know, I think Mitenka may be acquitted.'

'I wouldn't mind betting that tomorrow he'll wreck the entire Capital City, he'll drink for ten days.'

'Hah, the devil!'

'Yes, well, the devil's the devil, you won't get by without the devil, where else should he be if not here?'

'Gentlemen, let's just say that's all eloquence. But I mean, one can't allow people to go breaking their father's heads with the scales of justice. Or else where would we end?'

'And what about the chariot, the chariot, do you remember?'

'Yes, he made a chariot out of a wagon.'

'And tomorrow it will be a wagon out of a chariot, "in the measure to which it is required, all in the measure to which it is required".'

'It's a clever lot we have nowadays. Do you think we have any truth or justice in the land of Rus', gentlemen, or does it not exist at all?'

But the bell had begun to ring. The jury had been out for exactly an hour, neither more nor less. As soon as the public had settled down again, deep silence reigned. I remember the jurymen entering the chamber. At last! I will not site the questions point by point, and in any case I have forgotten them. I remember only the reply to the first and principal question of the chairman, as to whether the defendant had committed the murder in premeditated fashion, with the purpose of robbery (the precise wording I do not recall). Everything froze. The foreman of the jury, who was of course the youngest of the lot, loudly and clearly, in the deathly silence of the chamber, proclaimed:

'Yes, guilty!'

And thereafter it was the same on every point: guilty, yes, guilty, and all this without the slightest recommendation for clemency! This, to be sure, no one had expected, almost everyone had been convinced that at least clemency would be recommended. The dead silence of the chamber was not broken, literally as though all had been turned to stone – both those who were thirsting for a conviction and those who were thirsting for an acquittal. But this was only in the initial moments. After that a fearful chaos arose. Among the male portion of the public there were many who turned out to be very well satisfied. Some even rubbed their hands, not bothering to conceal their delight. Those who were not well satisfied were as if crushed, kept shrugging their shoulders, whispering, but seemed not yet to have taken it all in. But, good Lord, what happened to our ladies? I thought they were going to cause a riot. At first it was as if they could not believe their ears. And suddenly, to the whole chamber, exclamations were heard: 'But what is this? What on earth is this?' They kept hopping up from their seats. They doubtless believed that it could all be altered and done all over again right there and then. At that moment Mitya suddenly got up and in a kind of tearing howl cried aloud, stretching his arms before him:

'I swear by God and by his Last Judgement, of my father's blood I am not guilty! Katya, I forgive you! Brothers, friends, spare the other one!'

He did not finish and began to sob to the whole chamber, in a voice, terrible to say, that was somehow not his own, but a new, astonishing one, that had sprung up in him God only knew from where. Up aloft, in the gallery, in the very furthest corner there resounded a piercing woman's wail: it was Grushenka. She had earlier gone to someone with entreaties, and had been readmitted to the chamber before the onset of the judicial pleadings. Mitya was led away. The pronouncement of sentence was postponed until the morrow. The entire chamber rose up in pandemonium, but I did not wait and did not listen. I recall only one or two exclamations, on the front steps, on my way out.

'He'll sniff twenty years down the mines.'

'Not less.'

'Yes, sir, our muzhiks stood up for themselves.'

'And put an end to our Mitenka!'

END OF THE FOURTH AND FINAL PART

EPILOGUE

I

Schemes for Rescuing Mitya

ON the fifth day after Mitya's trial, very early in the morning, before it was yet nine o'clock, Alyosha arrived at Katerina Ivanovna's house in order to come to a final arrangement concerning a certain matter that was important for them both, and, in addition, with an errand to discuss with her. She sat and talked with him in that same room where once she had received Grushenka; near by, in the next room, Ivan Fyodorovich lay in acute fever and unconscious. Immediately after the scene at the trial that day, Katerina Ivanovna had given instructions for the sick and unconscious Ivan Fyodorovich to be carried to her house, in disregard of all the future and inevitable talk of society and its censure. One of the two female relatives who lived with her had gone away to Moscow immediately after the scene at the trial, while the other remained. But even if both had gone away, Katerina Ivanovna would not have altered her decision and would have remained to tend to the sick man and sit with him night and day. He was being treated by Varvinsky and Herzenstube; as for the Moscow doctor, he had returned to Moscow, refusing to utter any prognosis with regard to the possible outcome of the illness. The doctors who remained, though they gave encouragement to Katerina Ivanovna and Alyosha, were plainly yet unable to offer any hope. Alyosha had been calling to visit his sick brother two times a day. This time, however, he had a particular, most troublesome matter to discuss, and he sensed in advance how hard it was going to be for him to talk about it, yet all the while he was in a great hurry: that same morning, in another place, another urgent matter waited, and he must be quick. They had already been conversing for some fifteen minutes. Katerina Ivanovna was pale, intensely fatigued and at the same time in an extreme state of morbid excitement: she had already sensed, by the way, the reason why Alyosha had come to see her now.

'With regard to his decision you must not worry,' she said to Alyosha with firm emphasis. 'This way or that, in the end he will come to this way out: he must escape! This unhappy man, this hero of honour and conscience – no, not him, not Dmitry Fyodorovich, but the other who is

lying behind this door and who has sacrificed himself for his brother,'
Katya added with flashing eyes, 'he long ago informed me of the whole
of this plan of escape. You know, he has already had dealings . . . I have
already informed you of some of it . . . Look, it will take place, in all
probability, at the third halt from here, when the party of convicts is
taken to Siberia. Oh, it is still a long way until then. Ivan Fyodorovich
has already made a trip to see the commander in charge of the third halt.
The only thing we do not know is who the commander of the party will
be, and it is impossible to find that out in advance. Tomorrow I shall
perhaps show you in detail the entire plan which Ivan Fyodorovich left
me on the eve of the trial, for some eventuality . . . It was that same time
when, you remember, you found us engaged in a quarrel: he was on his
way downstairs and I, catching sight of you, compelled him to return –
do you remember? Do you know what we were quarrelling about that
day?'

'No, I do not,' Alyosha said.

'Of course, he hid it from you at the time: it was nothing other than
this plan of escape. Three days before that he had revealed to me all the
principal parts of it – it was then that we began to quarrel, and we spent
the next three days quarrelling. We quarrelled because when he announced
to me that if Dmitry Fyodorovich were to be convicted he would run
away abroad with that brute creature, I suddenly grew angry – I will not
tell you why, I myself do not know why it was! . . . Oh, of course, it was
on account of the creature, that brute creature, and for the very reason
that she was also going to run away abroad together with Dmitry!'
Katerina Ivanovna exclaimed suddenly with lips that had begun to quiver
with wrath. 'No sooner had Ivan Fyodorovich realized that I was so
angry on account of that creature, in an instant he thought that I was
jealous because of Dmitry and that therefore I still continued to love
Dmitry. That was when our first quarrel arose. I was unwilling to give
explanations, to ask forgiveness I was unable; it was painful to me that
such a man could suspect me of a former love for that . . . And this when
I myself, long before, had told him straight that I did not love Dmitry,
but only him alone! It was only out of rage against that brute creature
that I grew enraged with him! Three days later, on that very evening
when you came in, he brought to me a sealed envelope which I was to
unseal at once if anything should happen to him. Oh, he had foreseen his
illness! He told me that in the envelope were the details of the escape and
that if he should die or fall dangerously ill, I was to rescue Mitya alone.
At the same time he left me money, nearly ten thousand roubles – the

same money that the public procurator, who found out from someone that he had sent it to be changed into notes, mentioned in his speech. I was suddenly horribly struck by the fact that Ivan Fyodorovich, who was all the while jealous because of me and all the while convinced that I loved Mitya, had not however given up his thought of rescuing his brother and was trusting me, me with that deed of rescue! Oh, that was a sacrifice! No, you cannot comprehend such self-sacrifice in all its plenitude, Aleksey Fyodorovich! I wanted to throw myself at his feet in veneration, but when I suddenly thought that he would merely construe it as an expression of my joy that Mitya would be rescued (and I know for certain that he would have thought that!), so irritated was I by the mere possibility of such an unfair notion on his part, that I again grew irritated and, instead of kissing his feet, again made a scene in front of him! Oh, unhappy that I am! Such is my character — a dreadful, unhappy character! Oh, but you will see: I will do it, I will drive him to the point where he gives me up for another, one with whom he will get along better, like Dmitry, but then ... No, then I would not be able to endure it, I would kill myself! And when you came in that day, and I called you, and made him return, then when he came in with you I was seized with such wrath at the hateful, contemptuous look he suddenly gave me that — you remember — I suddenly shouted to you that it was *he*, *he alone* who had made me believe that his brother Dmitry was a murderer! I went and told slanderous lies about him on purpose, in order to wound him again, while he, on the other hand, had never, never tried to make me believe that his brother was a murderer, on the contrary, it was I, I who had tried to make him believe it! Oh, it was all of it, all of it caused by my fury! It was I, I who prepared that accursed scene for him at the trial! He wanted to prove to me that he was noble and that though I loved his brother, he would none the less not ruin him out of vengeance and jealousy. So he appeared at the trial ... I am the cause of it all, I alone am to blame!'

Never before had Katya made confessions of this kind to Alyosha, and he had a sense that she was now at that very pitch of unendurable suffering when the proudest heart will with pain destroy its own pride and fall vanquished by grief. Oh, Alyosha was aware of yet one more dreadful cause of her present agony, however much she might have tried to keep it hidden from him during all these days since Mitya's conviction; but it would somehow have been too painful if she had determined to fall so low as to speak with him now about that cause. She was suffering on account of her 'perfidy' at the trial, and Alyosha had a premonition that conscience would draw her to confess before no one else but him, Alyosha, with tears, with shrieks, with hysterics, with beating upon the floor. He was, however, afraid of this moment, and desired to spare the suffering woman. All the harder did this make the errand on which he had arrived. He again began to speak of Mitya.

'It's all right, it's all right, don't be afraid for him!' Katya began again, obstinately and sharply. 'All this will last with him only a moment, I know him, I know that heart of his all too well. You may be certain that he will agree to escape. And the main thing is, it's not going to happen right now; there will still be time for him to make his resolve. By then Ivan Fyodorovich will have recovered and will himself take charge of it all, so I won't have to do anything. Don't worry, he will agree to escape. Why, he already agrees: do you think he is capable of leaving his brute creature behind? And they won't let her join him in penal servitude, so what can he do but escape? Above all, he is afraid of you, afraid that you will not approve of his escape from a moral point of view, but you must magnanimously *permit* him to do it, in view of the fact that your sanction is so indispensable here,' Katya added with venom. She fell silent for a moment and smiled an ironic smile.

'He goes on and on over there,' she set to again, 'about some hymns or other, about the cross he must bear, about some duty or other, I remember, Ivan Fyodorovich told me a great deal about it at the time, and if you knew how he said it!' Katya exclaimed suddenly with uncontainable emotion, 'if you knew how he loved that unhappy man at that moment, as he was telling me about him, and how he hated him, perhaps, at that same moment! And I, oh, I listened to his story and his tears with a haughty, disbelieving smile! Oh, brute creature! It is I who am the brute creature, I! It is I who have brought into being the fever in him! And the other, that convicted man – is he ready for suffering?' Katya ended, irritably. 'And can a man like that suffer? Men like him never suffer!'

A sense of what now felt like hatred and disgusted contempt sounded in these words. Yet all the while she had betrayed him. 'Well, perhaps it is because she feels guilty before him and at moments hates him,' Alyosha thought to himself. He wanted it to be only 'at moments'. In Katya's last words he had detected a challenge, but he did not take it up.

'That is why I summoned you here today, so that you yourself would promise to talk him round. Or, in your opinion, will to escape also be not honourable, not valorous, or whatever . . . not Christian, is that it?' Katya added with a challenge that was even stronger.

'No, it's all right. I shall tell him everything . . .' Alyosha muttered. 'He wants you to come and see him today,' he barked suddenly, looking her firmly in the eye. She shuddered all over and recoiled from him the merest way upon the sofa.

'Me . . . is that possible?' she mouthed, pale now.

'It is possible and it must be done!' Alyosha began insistently, in total animation. 'You are very necessary to him, particularly now. I would not begin to speak of this and cause you torment prematurely, if it were not essential. He is ill, he is like a madman, he keeps asking for you all the time. He asks for you not in order to make reconciliation, but wants you simply to come and show yourself on the threshold. Much has been accomplished within him since that day. He understands how incalculably guilty he is before you. It is not your forgiveness that he wants: "I cannot be forgiven," he says it himself, but wants you only to show yourself on the threshold . . .'

'You suddenly come and want me to . . .' Katya mouthed, 'all these days I have sensed that you would come with this . . . I knew that he would call me to him! . . . It is impossible!'

'Perhaps it is, but please do it. Remember that for the first time he has been shocked by how he has insulted you, for the first time in his life, never before has he perceived it in such fullness! He says: "If she refuses to come, then all my life now I will be unhappy." Do you hear: a convict who is going to serve twenty years still has plans to be happy – is that not pathetic? Just think: you will visit one who has been ruined without guilt,' burst from Alyosha with a challenge, 'his hands are clean, there is no blood on them! For the sake of his future suffering that is numberless, please visit him now! Come, say goodbye to him as he goes into the dark . . . stand on the threshold, and that is all . . . Why, you must, you *must* do it!' Alyosha concluded, underlining the word 'must' with incredible force.

'I must, but . . . I cannot,' Katya almost groaned. 'He will look at me . . . I cannot.'

'Your eyes must meet. How will you live for the rest of your life if you do not now make your resolve?'

'I had rather suffer for the rest of my life.'

'You must come, you *must* come,' Alyosha again underlined implacably.

'But why today, why right now? . . . I cannot abandon the one who is sick . . .'

'For a moment you can, after all, it is only a moment. If you do not come, by the time it is night he will fall ill with acute fever. I will not tell a lie, now have compassion!'

'Have compassion for me,' Katya said in bitter rebuke, and began to weep.

'So you will come, then!' Alyosha pronounced firmly, at the sight of her tears. 'I shall go and tell him that you are coming right now.'

'No, don't tell him that, not on any account!' Katya screamed in fear. 'I will come, but you must not tell him in advance, because I shall come, but I may not go in . . . I do not know yet . . .'

Her voice was cut short. She breathed with difficulty. Alyosha got up to go away.

'And if I meet someone?' she said suddenly, again turning pale all over.

'That is the reason why it must be right now, so that you do not meet anyone. There will be no one, I tell you truly. We shall be waiting,' he concluded insistently and walked out of the room.

2

For a Moment the Lie Becomes Truth

HE hurried to the hospital where Mitya now lay. On the second day after the sentence of the court, he had fallen ill with a mild nervous fever and was dispatched to the prisoners' section of our town hospital. The physician Varvinsky had, however, at the request of Alyosha and many others (Mrs Khokhlakova, Liza, etcetera), had Mitya put not with the prisoners, but separately, in that same little closet of a room where Smerdyakov had earlier lain. To be sure, at the end of the corridor stood a sentry, and the window was covered by an iron grille, and Varvinsky was able to rest easy with regard to his indulgence, one not entirely within the law, but he was a kind and compassionate young man. He realized how difficult it was for one such as Mitya to suddenly step straight across into the company of murderers and fraudsters, and that he would need to get accustomed to it first. But the visits of family and friends were allowed both by the doctor and by the chief warder, and even by the chief of police, all surreptitiously. In the past few days Mitya had, however, received visits only from Alyosha and Grushenka. Rakitin had twice endeavoured to get in to see him; but Mitya had emphatically requested Varvinsky not to admit him.

Alyosha found him sitting on his bunk, in a hospital dressing-gown, with a slight fever, his head bound with a towel that had been wetted with water and vinegar. With a look that was ill-defined he watched Alyosha come in, but in his gaze there also fleeted something that seemed akin to fear.

He had, on the whole, since the trial become dreadfully pensive. Sometimes he would say nothing for half an hour at a time, seemingly considering something slowly and tormentingly, oblivious to anyone and anything that were present. If, on the other hand, he emerged from his pensiveness and began to speak, he always did it in a way that was somehow unexpected and never on any account about what he really should have spoken about. Sometimes, with suffering, he would look at his brother. He seemed to find it easier to be with Grushenka than with Alyosha. To be sure, he hardly ever spoke to her, but no sooner did she come in than his whole face would be illuminated with joy. Alyosha sat down beside him on the bunk, and did not say anything. On this occasion he had awaited Alyosha with anxiety, but did not dare to ask any questions. He believed it to be out of the question that Katya would consent to come and at the same time felt that if she did not come then that would be something altogether impermissible. Alyosha understood his emotions.

'That Trifon,' Mitya began in agitation, 'you know, the Borisych fellow, they say he has wrecked the whole of that coach-house of his: he's been pulling up floorboards, tearing out planks, they say he has smashed the whole of his "gallery" to bits – he spends all the time hunting for treasure, for that same money, the fifteen hundred the public procurator said I hid there. As soon as he arrived back there, they say, he started getting up to his tricks. Serves the twister right! One of the warders here told me about it yesterday; he's from over that way.'

'Listen,' Alyosha said, 'she will arrive, but I do not know when, perhaps today, perhaps tomorrow, that I do not know, but she will arrive, she will, that much is certain.'

Mitya started, was on the point of saying something, but remained in silence. The news had had a fearful effect on him. It was plain that he had a tormenting desire to learn the details of what had been said, but that he was again afraid to ask about them immediately: anything cruel and contemptuous from Katya would have been to him like a blow from a knife at that moment.

'Here's what she said, among other things: that I should be sure to put your conscience at rest on account of the escape. Even if Ivan is not well again by that time, she herself will take charge of it.'

'You have already told me about that,' Mitya commented, thought-fully.

'And you have already repeated it to Grusha,' Alyosha observed.

'Yes,' Mitya confessed. 'She is not going to come this morning,' he said, looking timidly at his brother. 'She will only come in the evening. As soon as I told her yesterday that Katya was handling the matter, she held her tongue; but her lips twisted. All she did was whisper: "Let her!" She realized it was an important thing. I did not dare to probe further. After all, she really does seem to understand now that the other one loves not me, but Ivan.'

'Really?' burst from Alyosha.

'Though perhaps she doesn't. But she is not going to come this morning,' Mitya hurried to make clear again. 'I have given her a certain errand ... Listen, brother Ivan will surpass everyone. He is the one who must live, not us. He will get better again.'

'Imagine, even though Katya is afraid for him, she has almost no doubt that he will get better,' Alyosha said.

'That means she is convinced that he is going to die. It is her fear that makes her certain that he will get better.'

'That brother of ours has a strong constitution. I also hope very much that he will get better,' Alyosha observed, worriedly.

'Yes, he will get better. But she is certain that he will die. She has much grief ...'

A silence ensued. Something very important was causing Mitya torment.

'Alyosha, I love Grusha dreadfully,' he said all of a sudden in a trembling voice that was filled with tears.

'She won't be allowed to join you *there*,' Alyosha caught up at once.

'And there was another thing I wanted to tell you,' Mitya continued in a voice that was suddenly somehow charged with resonance. 'If they begin to beat me on the journey, or *there*, I shall not submit, but shall kill, and I will be shot. And I mean, it's twenty years! They are already beginning to address me as "thou". The warders say "thou" to me. All last night I lay passing judgement on myself: I am not ready! It is not within my strength to accept it! I wanted to start singing the "hymn", yet I cannot cope with the wardens' "thou's". For Grusha I would endure anything, anything ... except, come to think of it, beating ... But they will not allow her *there*.'

Alyosha quietly smiled.

'Listen, brother, once and for all,' he said. 'Here are my thoughts on

that score. And I mean, you know that I would not lie to you. Then
listen: you are not ready and not for you is such a cross. Not only that: it
is not necessary to you, who are not ready, such a grand martyr's cross.
Had you murdered father, I would have wished that you had not rejected
your cross. But you are innocent, and such a cross is too much for you.
You wanted to regenerate another man within yourself by means of
suffering; in my opinion, if only you will remember that other man all
your life and wherever you may flee to − that will be enough for you.
The fact that you have not accepted that great torment of the Cross will
merely help you to be aware within yourself of an even greater duty and
debt, and by this awareness henceforth, all your life, you will perhaps
assist your own regeneration more than if you had gone *there*. Because
there you will not endure and will make murmur and, perhaps, indeed,
will say to yourself at last: "I am quits." In this case the advocate spoke
the truth. Not for all are heavy burdens, for some they are impossible . . .
There are my thoughts, if you require them so badly. If others − officers,
soldiers, were to be held responsible for your escape, then I would "not
permit" you to flee,' Alyosha smiled. 'But they say and assure me (that
halt commander told Ivan himself) that if one knows how to go about it
the right way there will not be much of a punishment, and that it's
possible to get off with a mere trifle. Of course, it is dishonest to practise
bribery even in a case like this, but here I shall not on any account
presume to judge, because, as a matter of fact, if, for example, Ivan and
Katya were to encharge me with handling this matter for you, I know I
would go and give bribes; that is the whole truth, and I must tell you it.
And so it is not for me to be your judge and tell you how to act. Know,
however, that I shall never condemn you. And indeed it would be
strange, for how could I be your judge in this matter? Well, now I
believe I have considered everything.'

  'But I, in return, condemn myself!' Mitya exclaimed. 'I shall flee, that
has already been decided in your absence: can Mitka Karamazov do
otherwise than run away? But in return I condemn myself and there I will
pray forgiveness for my sin for ever! I mean, that is how the Jesuits talk,
is it not? The way you and I are doing now, eh?'

  'Indeed,' Alyosha quietly smiled.

  'I love you because you always tell the whole, unbroken truth and
never conceal anything!' Mitya exclaimed, joyfully laughing. 'In other
words, I have caught my Alyoshka as a Jesuit! I ought to smother you all
over in kisses for that, yes I ought! Well, then listen now to the rest of it,
I shall unfold to you the other half of my soul. Here is what I have

devised and determined: if I flee, even with money and a passport and even to America, then I will be encouraged by the thought that not to joy will I flee, not to happiness, but verily to another penal servitude, no worse, perhaps, than this one! No worse, Aleksey, verily I say, no worse! I now already hate that America of theirs, the devil take its hide. Very well, so Grusha will be with me, but look at her: I ask you, is she any sort of an American? She is a Russian, Russian, all of her, to the bone, she will start to pine for her native mother earth, and every moment I will see that she is doing it for me, has taken such a cross for me, and what guilt has she? And do you think I will be able to endure those stinking shits over there, even though they may all, every one of them, be better than I? I hate that America of theirs even now! And even though they are all, every single one of them, immense locomotive-drivers or whatever – the devil with them, they are not my kind of people, they don't have my kind of soul! It's Russia I love, Aleksey, the Russian God I love, even though I myself am a scoundrel! And I will choke and die there!' he exclaimed suddenly, his eyes flashing. His voice had begun to tremble with tears.

'Well, so this is what I have decided, Alyosha, listen!' he began again, having suppressed his excitement. 'Grusha and I will go there – and at once we shall till the land, work, with the wild bears, in solitude, somewhere as far away as possible. After all, there too there will be a place that is far away! They say there are also redskins there, somewhere over there in that land of theirs on the edge of the horizon, well, that is where we shall go, to the last of the Mohicans. Yes, and we shall at once get down to grammar, Grusha and I. Work and grammar, and so on for some three years. In those three years we shall learn the English language as well as any Englishmen there ever were. And as soon as we have learned it – an end to America! We shall escape back here to Russia, as American citizens. Have no fear, we shan't show our noses in this wretched little town. We shall hide somewhere as far away as possible, in the north or the south. By that time I will have changed my appearance, and so will she, back there, in America, a doctor will fake a wart on me, after all, they're not mechanics for nothing. And if not, then I'll put out one of my eyes, grow a beard an arshin long, a grey one (I'll have gone grey pining for Russia) – and perhaps no one will recognize me. And if they do, then let them send me into exile, it won't matter, it will just mean that fate did not allow! Here too we shall till the land in the wilds somewhere, and I will pretend to be an American all the rest of my days. In recompense, we shall die in our native land. There is my plan, and it is immutable. Do you approve?'

'Yes, I do,' Alyosha said, not desiring to contradict him.

For a moment Mitya fell silent, and then suddenly said:

'And what about the way they landed me in the soup at the trial? For they did, they landed me in the soup!'

'Even if they hadn't, they would still have convicted you,' Alyosha said, with a sigh.

'Yes, the public here have had enough of me! They can go to hang, but all the same it's hard!' Mitya groaned with suffering.

Again they were silent for a moment.

'Alyosha, tell me the truth now!' he exclaimed suddenly. 'Is she going to come now or isn't she, speak! What did she say? How did she say it?'

'She said she would come, but I don't know if it will be today. After all, it's difficult for her!' Alyosha said, giving his brother a timid look.

'Well, I do not wonder, I do not wonder that it's difficult for her! Alyosha, this is driving me out of my mind. Grusha keeps looking at me all the time. She understands. O God, O Lord, humble and restrain me: what do I ask? I ask Katya! Do I understand what I ask? The Karamazovian unrestraint, impious! No, I am not capable of suffering! A scoundrel, and all's said and done!'

'Here she is!' Alyosha exclaimed.

At this moment Katya suddenly appeared on the threshold. For a split second she paused, surveying Mitya with a kind of lost gaze. Mitya leapt headlong to his feet, his face displayed fear, he turned pale, but at once a timid, begging smile fleeted across his lips, and he suddenly, uncontainably, stretched out both arms to Katya. At the sight of this, she threw herself headlong towards him. She seized him by the hands, made him sit on the bed almost by force, herself sat down alongside and, still not releasing his hands, kept pressing them hard, convulsively. Several times both struggled to say something, but kept pausing and again silently, fixedly, almost as though riveted together, stared with strange smiles at each other; in this fashion some two minutes went by.

'Have you forgiven me or not?' Mitya mouthed at last, and that same instant, turning to Alyosha with a face that was distorted with joy, shouted to him:

'Do you hear what I ask, do you hear?'

'I loved you because you are generous of heart!' burst suddenly from Katya. 'And you do not need my forgiveness, nor I yours; it is all the same whether you forgive or not, all the rest of my life you will remain like a wound in my soul, and I in yours – and that is proper . . .' She paused to take breath.

'Why have I come?' she began again, frenziedly and hurriedly. 'To embrace your feet, to press your hands, like this, to the point of pain, you remember, the way I used to press them in Moscow, to say again to you that you are my God, my joy, to say to you that I love you madly,' she almost groaned in torment and suddenly avidly nestled her lips against his hand. Tears gushed from her eyes.

Alyosha stood speechless and embarrassed; he had absolutely not expected what he saw.

'Love is past, Mitya!' Katya began again. 'But dear unto pain to me is what is past. Know that for ever. But now, for one little moment, let there be what might have been,' she mouthed with a twisted smile, again looking joyfully into his eyes. 'Both you and I now love another, yet all the same I shall love you eternally, and you me, did you know that? Do you hear, love me, all the rest of your life love me!' she exclaimed with a kind of almost menacing vibration in her voice.

'I shall love and . . . you know, Katya,' Mitya began to say, taking breath at each word, 'you know, five days ago, that evening, I loved you . . . When you fell in a faint, and were carried out . . . All the rest of my life! So it shall be, so it shall eternally be . . .'

Thus did they babble to each other words that were almost without sense and uttered in frenzy, perhaps not even truthful, but at that moment all was truth, and they themselves believed themselves unstintingly.

'Katya,' Mitya suddenly exclaimed, 'do you believe that I killed? I know that now you do not believe it, but that day . . . when you gave evidence . . . Did you really, really believe it?'

'Even then I did not believe it! I have never believed it! I hated you and suddenly made myself believe, then, for that moment . . . When I gave evidence . . . I made myself believe it and believed . . . but when I had finished, I at once ceased to believe. Know that, all of it. I have forgotten that I came here in order to punish myself!' she said with a kind of wholly new expression, wholly unlike her recent amorous mouthings of a moment earlier.

'It is painful for you, woman!' suddenly burst from Mitya, wholly without restraint.

'Let me go,' she whispered, 'I will come again, but it is painful now . . . !'

She began to get up from her seat, but suddenly gave a loud scream and reeled back. Into the room suddenly, though very quietly, Grushenka had come. No one had expected her. Katya took an impetuous step towards the door, but, on drawing even with Grushenka suddenly stopped, turned white as chalk all over and quietly, almost in a whisper, moaned to her:

'Forgive me!'

The other stared at her and then, after a moment's wait, in a venomous, malice-poisoned voice replied:

'It's wicked we are, mother, you and I! Wicked, both of us! How can it be for us to forgive, you and I? Now if you'll rescue him, all the rest of my life I will pray for you.'

'But you do not want to forgive!' Mitya shouted at Grushenka in mad rebuke.

'Put your mind at rest, I will rescue him for you!' Katya whispered quickly and ran out of the room.

'And could you not forgive her, after she herself had said "Forgive" to you?' Mitya bitterly exclaimed again.

'Mitya, do not dare to rebuke her, you have no right!' Alyosha shouted warmly at his brother.

'Her proud lips spoke, but not her heart,' Grushenka pronounced with a kind of loathing. 'If she will deliver you – all will I forgive . . .'

She fell silent, as if she had crushed something in her soul. She had not yet managed to regain her wits. It later turned out that she had come in quite by chance, not suspecting anything at all and never supposing to encounter what she had encountered.

'Alyosha, run and follow her!' Mitya said, turning to his brother in a rush. 'Tell her . . . I don't know what . . . do not let her leave like that!'

'I will come back to you before evening!' Alyosha cried and he ran off in pursuit of Katya. He caught her up when she was already beyond the hospital wall. She walked swiftly, hurrying, but as soon as Alyosha caught her up, she said to him quickly:

'No, before that one I cannot punish myself! I said to her "forgive me", for I wanted to punish myself to the end. She did not forgive . . . For that I love her!' Katya added in a voice that was distorted, and her eyes flashed with a wild malice.

'My brother was not expecting her at all,' Alyosha began to mutter. 'He was certain that she would not come . . .'

'No doubt. Let us leave that,' she snapped. 'Listen: I am unable to go there for the funeral with you now. I have sent them flowers for the little coffin. I believe they still have money. If necessary, tell them that in the future I will never abandon them . . . Well, now leave me, leave me, please. You are already going to be late there, the bells for late liturgy are ringing . . . Leave me please!'

3

Ilyushechka's Funeral. The Speech by the Stone

HE was indeed late. They had been waiting for him, and even decided to bear the pretty little coffin, decorated with flowers, into the church without him. This was the coffin of the poor boy Ilyushechka. He had died two days after sentence was passed on Mitya. When he was still only at the front gate of the house, Alyosha was greeted by the cries of the boys, Ilyusha's companions. They were all waiting for him impatiently and rejoiced that at last he had arrived. In all there were about twelve of them, and they all had their satchels and shoulder-slung bags with them. 'Papa will cry, you must be with papa,' Ilyusha had made them promise before he died, and the boys had remembered this. At their head was Kolya Krasotkin.

'How glad I am that you have arrived, Karamazov!' he exclaimed, extending his hand to Alyosha. 'Things are dreadful here. Truly, it is painful to see. Snegiryov is not drunk, we know for a fact that he has had nothing to drink today, but he seems to be drunk all the same . . . I am forever resolute, but this is dreadful. Karamazov, if I do not detain you, may I, in addition, put to you one question, before you go inside?'

'What is it, Kolya?' Alyosha said, pausing.

'Is your brother innocent or guilty? Was it he who killed your father or was it the lackey? Whatever you say, so let it be. For four nights I have not slept for this idea.'

'It was the lackey who did it, and my brother is innocent,' Alyosha answered.

'And so say I!' the boy Smurov suddenly shouted.

'So he is going to his ruin as an innocent victim for truth and justice!' Kolya exclaimed. 'Though he is ruined, he is happy! I am ready to envy him!'

'What is this you are saying, how is it possible, and why?' Alyosha exclaimed, astonished.

'Oh, if only I, too, could some day sacrifice myself for truth and justice,' Kolya said with enthusiasm.

'But surely not in such a cause, not with such disgrace, such horror!' Alyosha said.

'Of course . . . I should desire to die for all mankind, and as for disgrace, then it is all the same: for our names will perish. Your brother I respect!'

'And so do I!' suddenly and now quite unexpectedly shouted from the crowd that same boy who had once declared that he knew who had founded Troy, and, having shouted, precisely as he had done that other day, blushed to his ears, like a peony.

Alyosha entered the room. In a blue coffin decorated with white ruche, his little hands folded together and his little eyes closed, lay Ilyusha. The features of his wasted face had hardly altered at all, and, strange to say, there was almost no smell from the corpse. The expression of his face was serious, and he looked as though he were reflecting about something. Especially beautiful were his hands, which were folded crosswise, as though they had been sculpted out of marble. Flowers had been put in his hands, and indeed the whole coffin had already been decorated both on the inside and on the outside with flowers that had been sent at break of day by Liza Khokhlakova. But flowers had also arrived from Katerina Ivanovna, and when Alyosha opened the door, the second-grade captain with a bunch of flowers in his quivering hands was in the process of scattering them, too, over his dear boy. He hardly glanced at the entering Alyosha, and was unwilling to look at anyone else either, not even his weeping, crazy wife, his 'little mother', who kept endeavouring to raise herself on her disabled legs and take a closer look at her dead boy. Ninochka had, on the other hand, been raised from her chair by the children, and they had moved her right up to the coffin. She sat pressing her head against it and was also, no doubt, quietly weeping. Snegiryov's face had a look that was animated but somehow confused, and at the same time desperate. In his gestures, in the words that escaped from him, there was something half-insane. 'My fellow, my dear fellow!' he kept exclaiming every moment, looking at Ilyusha. When Ilyusha had been alive he had had a habit of saying to him affectionately: 'My fellow, my dear fellow!'

'Little father, give me some flowers too, take one from his little hand, look there, that white one, and give it me!' the crazy 'little mother' begged, sobbing. Either it was that she had taken a fancy to the small white rose that was in Ilyusha's hands, or that she wanted to take a flower from his hands in memory, but she began to fairly throw herself about, stretching her arms out for the flower.

'To no one will I give them, to no one will I give them!' Snegiryov exclaimed hard-heartedly. 'The flowers are his, not yours! All of it is his, and none of it is yours!'

'Papa, give mamma a flower!' Ninochka said, suddenly raising her face that was moist with tears.

'Certainly not, and to her least of all! She did not love him. She took the little cannon away from him that day, and he gave — it — to — her,' the second-grade captain suddenly sobbed loudly, at the recollection of how Ilyusha had yielded his little cannon to his mamma. The poor, crazy woman fairly dissolved in quiet weeping, covering her face with her hands. The boys, seeing at last that the father would not release the coffin from his charge, even though it was now time that it be borne, suddenly surrounded the coffin in a tight mass and began to raise it up.

'I do not want to bury him in the cemetery,' Snegiryov suddenly cried out. 'By the stone I will bury him, by our old stone! Those were Ilyusha's instructions! I will not allow you to take him away!'

Even earlier, for this whole three days, he had been saying that he was going to bury him by the stone; but Alyosha, Krasotkin, the landlady, her sister and all the boys had taken a different view.

'Would you ever believe the idea he's dreamed up, to bury his son by some heathen stone as though he'd hanged himself,' the old landlady said severely. 'There's land there in the cemetery, with a cross. They will pray for him there. He'll be able to hear the singing from the church, and the deacon reads so clear and literate that it will all reach his ears every time, just as though it were being read over his little grave . . .'

At last the second-grade captain waved his hands, as if he were saying: 'Take him wherever you like!' The children raised the coffin, but, as they bore it past the mother, they paused before her for a moment and lowered it so that she might say farewell to Ilyusha. But, when she caught sight of that dear little face, close at hand, which all the three days she had beheld only from a certain distance, she suddenly started to shake all over and began to jerk her grey-haired head hysterically this way and that way over the coffin.

'Mamma, give him the sign of the Cross, give him blessing, kiss him,' Ninochka cried to her. But, like an automaton, she kept jerking her head and speechlessly, with a face that was distorted by burning grief, suddenly began to beat her breast with her fist. The coffin was borne further. When it was borne past her, Ninochka for the last time pressed her lips to the mouth of her deceased brother. Alyosha, on his way out of the house, was about to address the landlady with a request that she attend to those who would remain behind, but the landlady did not even let him finish:

'Stands to reason, I'll stay with them, we're Christians too.' As she said this, the old woman wept.

They had not far to bear him to the church, some three hundred paces, no more. The day was clear and still; there was a frost, but not much of one. The sound of the church bells was still booming out. Snegiryov, bustling and confused, ran along behind the coffin in his wretched old, short coat that was almost of summer lightness, his head uncovered and the old, broad-brimmed, soft hat in his hands. He was in a kind of irresolvable anxiety, and would now suddenly stretch out a hand in order to support the head of the coffin, thereby merely getting in the way of the bearers, now run to the side and see if he could not fit himself in there. One of the flowers fell on the snow, and he fairly hurled himself to retrieve it, as though God only knew what depended on that flower.

'And about the crust, we've forgotten the crust,' he suddenly exclaimed in terrible alarm. But the boys at once reminded him that he had taken a crust of bread earlier that day and that it was in his pocket. In an instant he jerked it out of his pocket and, having ascertained that it was there, regained his composure.

'It's Ilyushechka's instructions, Ilyushechka's,' he at once explained to Alyosha. 'He was lying in bed one night, and I was sitting beside him, and he suddenly told me: "Papa, when my grave is filled in, crumble a crust of bread on it so that the little sparrows will come and I will hear them and will feel happy that I'm not lying there alone."'

'That is very good,' said Alyosha, 'you must take bread there often.'

'Every day, every day!' the second-grade captain babbled, as if he had thoroughly brightened up.

They arrived, at last, in the church and put the coffin down in its midst. All the boys stood around it in a circle and continued to stand thus decorously throughout the entire service. The church was an ancient one and rather poor, many of the icons had no mountings at all, but in such churches one somehow prays better. As the liturgy was sung, Snegiryov appeared to grow a little hushed, though from time to time there broke forth in him the same unconscious and seemingly confused anxiety: now he would approach the coffin in order to adjust the pall, the fillet* or, once, when a candle fell out of the candle-holder, he suddenly threw himself to replace it, fussing over it for a dreadfully long time. After that he regained his composure and stood meekly by the head of the coffin with a dully anxious and seemingly bewildered face. After the reading from the Epistle he suddenly whispered to Alyosha, who was standing beside him, that the Epistle had been read *incorrectly*, but did not elucidate his meaning further. During the Cherubic Hymn he began to sing the words, but did not finish and, lowering himself to his knees, let his forehead cling to the stone church floor and remained thus prostrate for rather a long time. At last the funeral service proper began, and candles were handed out. The panic-stricken father began to fuss about again, but the moving, stupendous funeral singing woke and shook his soul. He somehow shrank all over suddenly, and began a rapid, staccato sobbing, at first under his voice, but towards the end loudly. And when the valediction began and the coffin was covered, he embraced it with his arms, as though he would not let them cover up Ilyushechka, and began rapidly and avidly, without cease, to kiss the lips of his dead boy. At last they managed to prevail on him and had already begun to lead him away from the step, when he suddenly stretched out an arm impetuously and took a few flowers from the little coffin. He looked at them, and it was as if he had a dawning of some new idea, with the result that he seemed to forget about the principal matter for a moment. Little by little he seemed to fall into a reverie and no longer offered any resistance when the coffin was raised up and borne outside to the little grave. It was not far away, in the cemetery, right beside the church, expensive; it was Katerina Ivanovna who had paid for it. After the customary ritual the gravediggers lowered the coffin. Snegiryov bent down so low, his flowers in his hands, over the open grave that the boys clutched hold of his coat in alarm and began to haul him back. But it was as though he no longer really understood what was being accomplished. When they began to fill in the grave, he suddenly began to point worriedly at the falling earth and even began to say something, but no one could decipher it, and he suddenly fell quiet of his own accord. At that point they reminded him that he must crumble the crust of bread, and he grew terribly agitated, whipped out the crust and began to break it in his fingers, throwing the morsels about the little grave: 'Now come flying, little birds, now come flying, little sparrows!' he muttered, worriedly. One of the boys started to observe to him that it was awkward for him to break the crust with the flowers in his hands, and that he ought to let someone hold them for him for a while. But he would not allow it, and even grew suddenly fearful for his flowers, as though they were trying to take them away from him altogether, and, having taken a glance at the grave and seemingly satisfied that all had been done, the pieces crumbled, he suddenly unexpectedly and even quite calmly turned and strolled off home. But soon his pace grew quicker and more hurried, he was in a rush, almost running. Alyosha and the boys kept up with him.

'Flowers for little mother, flowers for little mother! Little mother's been offended!' he began to exclaim suddenly. Someone cried out to him, telling him to put his hat on, that it was cold now, but, upon hearing this, he flung the hat on the snow as if in malice and began to say over and over again: 'I don't want my hat, I don't want my hat!' The boy Smurov retrieved it and carried it after him. Every last one of the boys was crying, Kolya and the boy who had discovered Troy most of all, and although Smurov, the captain's hat in his hands, was also weeping dreadfully, he managed none the less, almost at a run, to pick up a fragment of brick that lay red on the snow of the path, in order to throw it at a swiftly passing flock of sparrows. Of course, he missed his mark and continued to run, weeping. When they had gone half-way, Snegiryov suddenly came to a halt, stood for half a moment as though some sudden shock had overtaken him, and suddenly, turning back towards the church, set off at a run towards the little grave they had abandoned. The boys in an instant caught him up and clutched hold of him from every side. At that point, as if in helplessness, like a man overwhelmed, he fell on to the snow and, lashing about, howling and sobbing, began to cry out: 'My fellow, Ilyushechka, my dear fellow!' Alyosha and Kolya began to raise him up, entreating him and prevailing upon him.

'Captain, that will do, a man of courage has a duty to endure,' Kolya muttered.

'And what about the flowers, you'll spoil them,' Alyosha said, joining in, 'and "little mother" is expecting them, she is sitting crying because you did not give her any of Ilyushechka's flowers today. Ilyusha's little bed is still there . . .'

'Yes, yes, we must go to little mother, to little mother!' Snegiryov remembered again, suddenly. 'They'll remove the bed, they'll remove the bed!' he added, as though in fear that the bed might indeed be removed, leapt up and again ran off home. But it was quite near now, and they all came running together. Snegiryov impetuously opened the door and cried out to his wife, with whom he had earlier so cruelly quarrelled.

'Little mother, dear one, Ilyushechka has sent you flowers, for your bad legs!' he shouted, stretching out to her the little bunch of flowers, all frozen and broken from when he had lashed about on the snow a moment earlier. But at that same moment, before Ilyusha's little bed, in the corner, he caught sight of Ilyusha's boots that stood side by side, having only just been tidied up by the landlady — old, faded, stiffened boots, with patches. At the sight of them he raised his hands and threw himself towards them, fell to his knees, seized one boot and, pressing his lips to it, began to kiss it avidly, crying aloud: 'My fellow, Ilyushechka, my dear fellow, where are your little feet?'

'What have you done with him? What have you done with him?' the crazy woman began to wail in a heart-breaking voice. At that point Ninochka too began to sob. Kolya ran out of the room, and the boys, began to follow him. At last Alyosha, too, went out after them. 'Let them cry it out,' he said to Kolya. 'It is impossible to do anything that will console them now. Let us wait for a moment and then return.'

'Yes, it's impossible and that is dreadful,' Kolya confirmed. 'You know, Karamazov,' he said, suddenly lowering his voice so that none should hear, 'I am very sad, and if only it were possible to resurrect him, I would give everything in the whole world!'

'Ah, and I too,' said Alyosha.

'What do you suppose, Karamazov, should we come back again this evening? I mean, he will get drunk.'

'Perhaps he will. Only the two of us, you and I, will come, that will be enough, in order to sit with them for an hour or so, with the mother and Ninochka, for if we all come at once we'll just bring it all back to them again,' Alyosha counselled.

'The landlady is laying the table in there for them now – there's going to be a funeral meal, or whatever, a priest is coming; will we go back in for that now, Karamazov, or not?'

'Without question,' said Alyosha.

'Strange it is, all this, Karamazov, such grief, and suddenly some kind of *blinis*, how unnatural everything is in our religion!'

'They are going to have salmon in there, too,' the boy who had discovered Troy suddenly and loudly observed.

'I would earnestly request you, Kartashov, not to meddle any further with your stupid remarks, particularly when you are not being spoken to and when no one even cares whether you exist or not,' Kolya retorted irritably in his direction. The boy fairly turned scarlet, but did not dare to make any reply. In the meantime they were all quietly strolling along the path, and suddenly Smurov exclaimed:

'Here is Ilyusha's stone, the one under which they were going to bury him!'

They all came to a silent standstill beside the large stone. Alyosha looked, and the entire tableau of what Snegiryov had related once about Ilyushechka, how the latter, weeping and embracing his father, had exclaimed: 'Papa, dear papa, how low he made you fall!' at once presented itself to his memory. Something seemed to quake within his soul. With a serious and important air he took in with his eyes all these dear, bright schoolboy faces, the faces of Ilyusha's companions, and suddenly said to them:

'Gentleman, I should like to say a few words to you here, at this very spot.'

The boys surrounded him and at once turned on him their fixed, expectant eyes.

'Gentlemen, we shall soon be parted. I am going to be for a while yet with my two brothers, of whom one is about to go into exile, and the other is lying at the point of death. But soon I am going to leave this town, possibly for a very long time. And then, gentlemen, we shall be parted. So let us here, by Ilyusha's stone, agree that we shall never forget – in the first place, Ilyushechka, and in the second, one another. And whatever may befall us subsequently in life, even though we do not meet for twenty years hereafter – all the same let us remember how we buried the poor boy, the one at whom you formerly threw stones, do you remember, down there by the bridge? – but whom everyone came to love so later. He was a wonderful boy, a kind and brave boy, he had a sense of the honour and of the bitter insult that his father bore, and for which he rose up. So, in the first place, let us remember, gentlemen, all our lives. And even though we may be occupied with the most important matters, attain honours or fall into some great misfortune – all the same let us never forget how good we found it here, all of us in association, united by such good and happy feeling, which for this time of our love for the poor boy has possibly made us better than we are in actual fact. My little doves – allow me to call you little doves, for you resemble them very much, those pretty, warm grey birds, now, at this moment, as I gaze upon your kind, dear faces – my dear young children, it may be that you will not understand what I am about to say to you, because I often speak very incomprehensibly, but you will none the less remember it and later one day will agree with my words. Know then that there is nothing more lofty, nor more powerful, nor more healthy nor more useful later on in life than some good memory, and particularly one that has been borne from childhood, from one's parents' home. Much is said to you about your education, but a beautiful, sacred memory like that, one preserved from childhood, is possibly the very best education of all. If he gathers many such memories in his life, a man is saved for all of it. And even if only one good memory remains within our hearts, then even it may serve some day for our salvation. It may be that we shall later even grow wicked, have not the strength to keep ourselves from a bad action, laugh at human tears and at those men who say, as Kolya exclaimed today: "I want to suffer for all men" – and of those men we shall perhaps make wicked mockery. Yet none the less, however wicked we may be, though may God keep us from it, whenever we remember how we buried Ilyusha, how we loved him in his last days and how we spoke just now in such a friendly way and so together by this stone, then the cruellest and most mocking one of us, if thus we shall become, will none the less not dare to laugh within himself at the fact that he was kind and good at this present moment! Not only that, but perhaps this very memory alone will keep him from great evil, and he will have second thoughts, and say: "Yes, I was good that day, bold and honest." Let him smile to himself ironically, that does not matter, a man often laughs at what is kind and good; it comes of mere frivolity; but I want to assure you, gentlemen, that when he smiles that way, he will at once say within his heart: "No, I act badly in smiling ironically, for at those things one must never laugh!"'

'It will definitely be like that, Karamazov, I understand you, Karamazov!' Kolya exclaimed, his eyes a-flash. The boys had begun to grow excited, and also wanted to exclaim something, but they restrained themselves, gazing at the orator fixedly and with tender emotion.

'I say this for the risk that we may become bad,' Alyosha resumed. 'But why should we become bad, come to think of it, gentlemen? Let us, in the first place and above all, be kind, then honest, and then – let us never forget one another. This I repeat again. I give you my word, gentlemen, that I shall never forget a single one of you; each face that gazes on me now, this moment, I shall remember, even though it be for thirty years. Today Kolya tried to make Kartashov think that we did not want to know "whether he exists or not". As if I could forget that Kartashov exists and that he does not blush any more now, as he did that day when he discovered Troy, but looks at me with those wonderful, kind, merry eyes of his. Gentlemen, my dear gentlemen, let us all be as magnanimous and bold as Ilyushechka, as clever, bold and magnanimous as Kolya (who will be far cleverer when he gets a bit older), and let us be as modest, but as clever and dear, as Kartashov. But why do I speak of those two? All of you, gentlemen, are dear to me from this day, all of you I shall enclose within my heart, as I ask you to enclose me within yours! Well, and who is it who has united us in this kind and good emotion, one which we shall always, all our lives remember and are resolved to remember, if not Ilyushechka, that kind boy, that dear boy, a boy who shall be precious to us until the end of the ages! Let us never forget him, and let there be for him an eternal and good memory within our hearts, from this day forth and to the ends of the ages!'

'That's right, that's right, eternal, eternal,' all the boys shouted in their resonant voices, their faces filled with tender emotion.

'Let us also remember his face, and his clothes, and his poor little boots, and his coffin, and his unhappy, sinful father, and how he boldly rose up alone for him against the entire class!'

'We shall, we shall remember!' the boys shouted again, 'he was brave, he was kind!'

'Oh, how I loved him!' Kolya exclaimed.

'Oh, young children, oh, dear friends, do not be afraid of life! How good is life, when one does some good and upright thing!'

'Yes, yes,' the boys repeated in ecstasy.

'Karamazov, we love you!' one voice, apparently that of Kartashov, uncontainably exclaimed.

'We love you, we love you,' they all caught up. Teardrops flashed in the eyes of many.

'Hurrah for Karamazov!' Kolya proclaimed ecstatically.

'And eternal memory to the dead boy!' Alyosha added once more with emotion.

'Eternal memory!'

'Karamazov!' Kolya cried, 'is it really true what religion says, that we shall all rise up from the dead and come to life and see one another again, and everyone, even Ilyushechka?'

'Without question we shall rise, without question we shall see one another and joyfully tell one another everything that has happened,' half-laughing, half in ecstasy, Alyosha replied.

'Oh, how good that will be!' burst from Kolya.

'Well, and now let us finish our talk and go to his funeral meal. Don't let it trouble you that we shall eat *blinis*. After all, they are a thing that is ancient and eternal, and good for all that, too,' Alyosha laughed. 'Well, come on! Look, we shall go now hand in hand.'

'And eternally, like this, all our lives hand in hand! Hurrah for Karamazov!' Kolya shouted once more in ecstasy, and once more all the boys caught up his exclamation.

NOTES

p. xxxi   *Dedicated to Anna Grigoryevna Dostoyevskaya:* Anna Grigoryevna Dostoyevskaya, née Snitkina (1846–1918), Dostoyevsky's second wife, whom he married in 1867.

p. 4   *the 'fretting of a captive mind':* a quotation from a poem by Lermontov (1839):

> Trust, trust, young dreamer, not thyself,
> Fear inspiration like the plague . . .
> It is thy sick soul's fevered ague
> Or fretting of a captive mind.

p. 6   *Lord, now lettest thou!:* The beginning of an Orthodox prayer ('Lord, now lettest thou thy servant depart in peace, according to thy word', derived from Luke 2:29 – the *'Nunc dimittis'*).

p. 7   *izba:* here, a peasant's log hut.

p. 7   *Proudhon and Bakunin:* Pierre Joseph Proudhon (1809–65), French sociologist and economist, an anarcho-utopian socialist thinker. Mikhail Aleksandrovich Bakunin (1814–76), Russian populist and anarchist.

p. 7   *the old ratio:* the pre-1861 serf tally in 'souls' or heads, by which the value of an estate was calculated.

p. 11   *wailers:* in Russian, *'klikushi'* – Lev Tolstoy noted in his diary for 1889, while working on *The Kreutzer Sonata*, that 'the *klikushi* are always married women, never unmarried girls'.

p. 14   *the question . . . of the Ecclesiastical Court:* the Russian judicial reforms of 1864, which were based on the principle of equality before the law, also led to a discussion of the Ecclesiastical Court (*tserkovnyy sud*), which was felt to be out of harmony with the demands of the new age.

p. 16   *an early lover of mankind:* 'lover of mankind' is an Orthodox epithet for Christ, but during the nineteenth century, because of over-use by 'progressive' Russian thinkers and journalists, it acquired the character of a cliché.

p. 17 *the oblique rays of the setting sun:* one of Dostoyevsky's favourite and constantly recurring images.

p. 23 *what about those hooks?:* in Russian icons depicting the Last Judgement the sinners are often shown being dragged down into hell on hooks. The hooks also appear with a similar function in certain Russian religious verses.

p. 24 *J'ai vu ... l'ombre d'une carrosse:* 'I saw the shadow of a coachman who with the shadow of a brush was cleaning the shadow of a coach.' Some lines, well-known to Dostoyevsky's Russian readers, quoted in a parody of the sixth book of the *Aeneid*, by Perrault and Beaurain. The lines themselves come from an obscure work attributed to Scarron, entitled *Virgil Travestied* (*Virgile travesti*, 1648–52).

p. 25 *Except I shall see ... I will not believe:* cf. John 20:25.

p. 26 *if thou wilt be perfect ... follow me:* see, for example, Mark 10:21.

p. 27 *one of the great* podvizhniki*:* in the Russian Orthodox tradition *podvizhniki* are hermits or ascetics engaged over many years in the performance of a *podvig*, or great holy deed, involving the renunciation of the flesh. Paisy Velichkovsky (Pyotr Ivanovich Velichkovsky, 1722–94) was a Russian Orthodox luminary who travelled a great deal about the monasteries of Russia and lived for a time on Mount Athos. He is renowned for his translations into Church Slavonic and Moldavian of works by the Church Fathers.

p. 27 *the Kozelsk Optina:* Optina Vvedenskaya Makariyeva pustyn', a famous hermitage in the Kozelsk district of the province of Kaluga, founded in the fourteenth century. Dostoyevsky visited it together with the philosopher Vladimir Solovyov in June 1878, and Lev Tolstoy later had a considerable involvement with it.

p. 27 *It is related:* the story is from the Russian Orthodox Calendar of Saints (*Prolog*) for 15 October.

p. 28 *Ye learners, go forth!:* a quotation from the Orthodox liturgy. A 'learner', or 'catechumen', is one who has not yet been baptized into the Church. The 'learners' must 'go forth', or leave, before the Eucharist is performed.

p. 28 *one of our present-day monks:* according to Dostoyevsky's wife, Anna Grigoryevna, this was a monk named Parfeny, whose secular name was Pyotr Ageyev (1807–78), the author of a work entitled *Stories of a Pilgrimage and Journey through Russia, Moldavia, Turkey and the Holy Land*.

p. 29 *serving as an ober-officer:* in the Russian army the term 'ober-officer' was used to designate junior officers up to and including the rank of captain.

p. 33   *Who made me a judge or a divider over you?:* cf. Luke 12:14.

p. 38   *He looks like von Sohn:* the 'von Sohn murder' was a much-discussed case of homicide that was tried in the St Petersburg Circuit Court in 1870.

p. 40   *hieromonachs:* monks who are also priests (from Greek: *hiero-monachos*).

p. 41   *the Schism:* the schism in the Russian Orthodox Church brought about by the reforms of Patriarch Nikon (1605–81).

p. 42   *punctuality is the courtesy of kings: l'exactitude est la politesse des rois,* a remark attributed to Louis XIII.

p. 43   *Now then, Mr* ispravnik ... *our Napravnik!:* the pun is on the Russian word *ispravnik* ('police captain') and the name of the Russian composer E. F. Napravnik (1839–1916), who in 1869 became the first conductor of the Mariinsky Theatre in St Petersburg.

p. 43   *Have you been tickling her?:* A pun noted down by Dostoyevsky in his notebook for 1876–7: 'Women are dreadfully ticklish. Have you ever tried tickling one?'

p. 44   *the* philosophe *Diderot:* the French philosopher Denis Diderot (1713–84) made a visit to Russia in 1773, at the invitation of Catherine the Great.

p. 44   *the Metropolitan Platon:* the Metropolitan Platon of Moscow (Pyotr Yegorovich Levshin, 1737–1812) was a famous preacher, Church writer and leader.

p. 44   *The fool ... no God:* cf. Psalms 14:1.

p. 44   *Princess Dashkova ... Potyomkin:* Yekaterina Romanovna Dashkova (1743–1810) was an aide of Catherine the Great who helped her during the Palace Revolt of 1762, and who during her reign became President of the Russian Academy. She lived in Paris for several years and befriended many intellectuals, including Voltaire and Diderot. Grigory Aleksandrovich Potyomkin (1739–91) was a Russian statesman and military leader, a favourite of Catherine.

p. 46   *Blessed is the womb ... sucked:* cf. Luke 11:27.

p. 46   *What shall I do ... life:* cf. for example, Luke 10:25.

p. 47   *the Chet'i-Minei:* the *Chet'i-Minei* contain the lives of the saints and their teachings, arranged according to the calendar. There are several versions of them – Dostoyevsky owned an abridged one of a type commonly available. Fyodor Pavlovich is thinking of St Dionysus (Dénis) of Paris, of whom a story similar to the one he relates is told by Voltaire, among others.

p. 50   epitrachilion: the Greek word for an item of sacerdotal apparel.

p. 51   *others recited some lament:* the Russian verb is *prichitat'*, used to refer to a trance-like form of recitation employed in laments, dirges and incantations.

p. 52   *only three months more . . . three:* Dostoyevsky had lost his own son, Aleksey, who died at this same age in 1878.

p. 52   *Once upon a time:* a story drawn from the *Prolog* ('The Tale of the Reverend Father Daniil Concerning Andronicus and His Wife').

p. 53   *Rachel weeping for her children . . . not:* cf. Matthew 2:18.

p. 53   *Alexis the Man of God:* a reference to the Russian St Alexis (actually a Greek anchorite, who died *c.* 412) whose *vita* possessed a symbolic significance for Dostoyevsky, and was indeed one of the principal sources of inspiration for the plot of *The Brothers Karamazov.* 'Alexis the Man of God' leaves his family in order to devote himself to heroic asceticism (*podvizhnichestvo*) and salvation, and then returns to his family again. Returning to the secular world, he must remain faithful to God.

p. 55   *For it was said . . . just men:* cf. Luke 15:7.

p. 60   *'burdock growing on a grave':* Bazarov's words in Chapter 22 of Turgenev's *Fathers and Sons.*

p. 65   *the question of the Ecclesiastical–Civil Court . . . jurisdiction:* the 'person of spiritual authority' referred to is Professor M. I. Gorchakov of St Petersburg University, the author of an article entitled 'A Scientific Formulation of Ecclesiastic Law', which he published in a book that appeared in 1875 and of which Dostoyevsky possessed a copy. The article attempted to reconcile the 'Statists' (*gosudarstvenniki*) with the 'Churchists' (*tserkovniki*).

p. 66   *Ultramontanism:* a reference to the 'ultramontane' movement within the Catholic Church which in the fifteenth century strove to subordinate the Church entirely to the Pope, defending his right to intervene in the secular affairs of any state, and which in Dostoyevsky's day was still a powerful force. The Latin expression *ultra montis* from which the word 'ultramontane' derives here means 'on the other side of the Alps'.

p. 66   *a kingdom not of this world:* the words are taken from John 18:36, where they have a rather different meaning.

p. 68   *exclusively a Church and nothing other:* an idea that was later developed by the philosopher Vladimir Solovyov. Dostoyevsky considered that socialism and communism were alien to the Russian people, which believed that it would 'in the last analysis be saved only by an all-radiant unification in the name of Christ. There is our Russian socialism!' (*Diary of a Writer*, January 1881).

p. 71   *seven men of honest report:* cf. Acts 6:3.

p. 71   *the times or the seasons:* cf. Acts 1:7.

p. 72   *Not even Gregory VII dreamed of it:* a reference to Pope Gregory VII (1073–85), who strove to establish papal supremacy.

p. 72   *the third temptation of Satan:* cf. Matthew 4:1–11.

p. 72   *this star will shine:* an Orthodox formulation, apparently derived from Matthew 2:2 ('for we have seen his star in the east').

p. 72   *the December revolt:* the coup of 2 December 1851, in which Louis Napoleon Bonaparte of France came to power.

p. 76   *human beings ... in their own immortality:* an echo of one of Pascal's *Pensées*, which states that 'from the question of whether the soul be immortal or not there floweth a complete difference of morality'.

p. 77   *Schiller's* The Robbers *... Regierender Graf von Moor:* as many critics have pointed out, the plot of *The Brothers Karamazov* in some ways derives from that of Schiller's drama *Die Räuber* in that both concern the relation of brothers to a father. Fyodor Pavlovich is Dostoyevsky's 'Count von Moor'.

p. 78   *St Anne's Ribbon ... swords:* a lesser military decoration.

p. 80   *Across a handkerchief:* a reference to Schiller's drama *Kabale und Liebe* (1784), in which Ferdinand challenges the Hofmarschall von Kalb to a duel – each holding one end of a handkerchief in one hand, and a pistol in the other.

p. 81   *prey to her surroundings:* 'a prey to one's surroundings' was a stock phrase current in the radical and liberal journalism of Dostoyevsky's time. Dostoyevsky did not agree that human beings were the product of their social environment.

p. 81   *the woman who loved much:* cf. Luke 7:47.

p. 82   *gudgeons:* a species of small fish, lacking in nutritious content.

p. 83   *the holy calendar:* Fyodor Pavlovich did, after all, marry Miusov's cousin, and can prove it by referring to the records of the local church.

p. 86   *What means this dream:* a catch-phrase of the radical and liberal journalism of the 1860s and 1870s, often found in the works of Dostoyevsky's enemy Saltykov-Shchedrin. It derives from Pushkin's narrative poem 'The Bridegroom' (1825).

p. 86   *holy nonsense:* in Russian, *blagogluposti*, a word first coined by Saltykov-Shchedrin in an article of 1863 that attacked Dostoyevsky and the journal *Vremya*.

p. 87   *between two stools:* 'falling between two stools' was a favourite phrase used by Saltykov-Shchedrin to attack Dostoyevsky's position.

p. 88 *The bard of women's feet:* Pushkin was despised by the radicals of the 1860s and 1870s for his supposed lack of social engagement and for his frivolous leanings, which they characterized by reference to his poems about women's feet.

p. 91 *He was so good as to express ... fools:* all this is a résumé of the career of Dostoyevsky's enemy G. Z. Yeliseyev (1821–91), a radical journalist and critic who began as a 'seminarian', or divinity student, and ended as the editor of a powerful revolutionary journal.

pp. 91–2 *The end of my career ... in the capital:* several St Petersburg *littérateurs* including G. Ye. Blagosvetlov (1824–80) and A. A. Krayevsky (1810–89) did in fact build 'tenements' – the Russian expression employed by Dostoyevsky to refer to such a building is *kapital'nyy dom* (literally, 'capital house') – which they put to use in the manner described.

p. 94 *kisel':* a kind of starchy jelly.

p. 103 *In the Lackeys' Hall:* there is possibly a conscious reference here to the title of Gogol's short play *The Lackeys' Hall* (*Lakeyskaya*).

p. 104 *like an evil insect: kak zloye nasekomoye,* the first intimation of the Schillerean '*Wurm*'-theme: see below, note to p. 121.

p. 106 '*In the Meadows*': a Russian folk song.

p. 107 *a dragon:* 'dragon' and 'devil' are closely associated in Russian folklore. There is also possibly an association with the Schillerean *Wurm* (see below, note to p. 121).

p. 107 *the Godbearing Father St Isaac of Nineveh:* a sixth- or seventh-century stylite and ascetic known in the Russian Orthodox Church as 'Isaac the Syrian'.

p. 108 *the flagellants:* the 'Khlysty', a religious sect.

p. 109 *two arshins:* 1 arshin = 28 inches.

p. 110 *a boublik or kalatch:* a boublik is a thick, ring-shaped roll, and a kalatch is a kind of fancy bread.

p. 116 *a desyatina:* 1 *desyatina* = approximately 2.7 acres.

p. 116 *a few poods:* 1 pood = 16.38 kg (36 lb avoirdupois).

p. 117 *Trust not ... doubts that you have had:* a quotation from Nekrasov's poem 'Kogda iz mraka zabluzhden'ya' ('When From Out Delusion's Murk'), 1846.

p. 118 *like the golden fish ... in the fairy-tale:* a reference to Pushkin's Grimm-inspired 'Skazka o rybake i rybke' ('The Tale of the Fisherman and the Fish'), 1833.

p. 119 *Be thou noble, O man!:* a quotation from a Russian translation by A. Strugovshchikov of Goethe's poem 'Das Göttliche' ('The Divine'), 1783:

Edel sei der Mensch,
Hilfreich und gut!, etc.

p. 119   *And Silenus ... a stumbling ass:* the last two lines of Maikov's
poem 'Barel'ef' ('Bas-relief'), 1842.

p. 119   *I'm not Silenus ... strength in me:* in Russian, *'Ne Silen, a silyon'*,
an untranslatable pun on Silenus and the Russian word for strong.

p. 120   *Timid, naked, wild ... beholds:* the second, third and fourth
stanzas from Schiller's poem 'Das Eleusische Fest' ('The Feast of
Eleusis'), 1798, in Zhukovsky's translation. The original reads:

> Scheu in des Gebirges Klüften
> Barg der Troglodyte sich,
> Der Nomade liess die Triften
> Wüste liegen, wo er strich,
> Mit dem Wurfspiess, mit dem Bogen
> Schritt der Jäger durch das Land,
> Weh dem Fremdling, den die Wogen
> Warfen an dem Unglücksstrand!
>
> Und auf ihrem Pfad begrüsste,
> Irrend nach des Kindes Spur,
> Ceres die verlassne Küste,
> Ach, da grünte keine Flur!
> Dass sie hier vertraulich weile,
> Ist kein Obdach ihr gewährt,
> Keines Tempels heitre Säule
> Zeuget, dass man Götter ehrt.
>
> Keine Frucht der süssen Ähren
> Ladt zum reinen Mahl sie ein,
> Nur auf grässlichen Altären
> Dorret menschliches Gebein.
> Ja, so weit sie wandernd kreiste,
> Fand sie Elend überall,
> Und in ihrem grossen Geiste
> Jammert sie des Menschen Fall.

p. 120   *That from baseness' ... Mother Earth:* the first half of the
seventh stanza of the same poem (in Zhukovsky's version).

p. 121   *churn up her breast:* possibly a reference to a poem by Fet,
'Prishla vesna – temneyet les ...' ('The spring has come, the woods
are dark ...'), 1866.

p. 121   *but I too shall kiss . . . God enwraps Himself:* an image borrowed from Fet's translation of Goethe's poem 'Grenzen der Menschheit' ('Limits of Mankind'), 1778–81.

p. 121   *To the soul . . . faces God:* the fourth and third stanzas of Schiller's ode 'An die Freude' (1785). In Fyodor Tyutchev's translation, which Dostoyevsky used, and which Dmitry knows, the German word *Wurm* ('worm, dragon, reptile, maggot') is for some reason translated as *nasekomoye*, 'insect'. The reptilian, phallic associations of *Wurm* seem more apposite in the context of Dostoyevsky's novel, which includes both insect and non-insect imagery (centipedes, for example) – but since Dmitry does not know any German, it seems best to translate *nasekomoye* simply as 'insect'. Schiller's original stanzas read:

> Freude heisst die starke Feder
>   In der ewigen Natur.
> Freude, Freude treibt die Räder
>   In der grossen Weltenuhr.
> Blumen lockt sie aus den Keimen,
>   Sonnen aus dem Firmament,
> Sphären rollt sie in den Räumen,
>   Die des Sehers Rohr nicht kennt.
>
> Freude trinken alle Wesen
>   Aus den Brüsten der Natur,
> Alle Guten, alle Bösen
>   Folgen ihrer Rosenspur.
> Küsse gab sie uns und Reben,
>   Einen Freund, geprüft im Tod.
> Wollust ward dem Wurm gegeben,
>   Und der Cherub steht vor Gott.

For a detailed discussion of this theme, see Victor Terras, *A Karama-zov Companion*, 1981.

p. 123   à la *Paul de Kock:* Paul de Kock (1793–1871) was a French writer of romantic novels.

p. 124   *a line battalion:* a frontier battalion.

p. 130   *anonymous bond:* a bond on which the bearer's name had not been filled in.

p. 134   *There was dear . . . words:* the origin of these lines has not been established, but it may be that Dostoyevsky wrote them himself.

p. 134   *I bow to her:* Dmitry uses the Russian verb *klanyat'sya*, which is often used in the sense of 'to greet', 'to give one's greetings'. Here, however, the literal meaning, 'to bow', is all-important.

p. 135 *but at least I was a falcon:* a 'falcon' in Russian folklore is a synonym for 'hero'.

p. 137 *'draw up my soul out of hell':* cf. Jonah 2:6. The Authorized Version has 'and bring up my life from corruption'.

p. 138 *Chermashnya:* the name of the village in Tula which in 1832 was bought by Dostoyevsky's parents, together with another village which they acquired a year earlier. In 1877 Dostoyevsky made a visit to these villages.

p. 140 *kulebiakis:* pies with meat, fish or cabbage filling.

p. 141 *Balaam's ass . . . talk:* cf. Numbers 22:21–33.

p. 141 *you came out of the steam on the bathhouse wall:* one of the sayings noted down by Dostoyevsky in the *Siberian Notebook* he kept while living among the convicts.

p. 142 *Evenings on a Farmstead near Dikanka:* Gogol's first collection of short stories, published in 1831–2, of markedly rural and sentimental-folkish style and content.

p. 143 *Smaragdov's General History:* a textbook by S. N. Smaragdov, entitled *A Concise Outline of Universal History for the Primary School*, first published in 1845, but proceeding through several editions.

p. 143 *Skopets:* the Skoptsy were a religious sect practising castration.

p. 144 *'rainbow' hundred-rouble notes:* one-hundred-rouble banknotes had a rainbow colouring.

p. 144 *The Contemplator:* the painting was first exhibited in public in 1878. Ivan Nikolayevich Kramskoy (1837–87) was a member of the school known as the *peredvizhniki*. Dostoyevsky met him at Suvorin's in 1880. The artist painted a death-portrait of Dostoyevsky before his funeral in 1881.

p. 145 *a certain Russian soldier:* in real life, an NCO of the 2nd Turkestan Battalion of the Russian Imperial Army, Foma Danilov, who was taken prisoner by the Cossacks and tortured to death in Margelan on 21 November 1875. Dostoyevsky writes about the incident in his *Diary of a Writer* for January 1877, portraying Danilov as 'an emblem of Russia, all Russia . . .'

p. 152 *For with what . . . you again:* cf. Luke 6:38.

p. 152 *The thing we like best . . . sentenced them:* one of the reforms introduced after 1861 was the establishment of peasant courts, run by the peasants themselves as an adjunct to the State ones.

p. 154 *il y a du Piron là-dedans:* Alexis Piron (1689–1773), the French poet and dramatist who acquired the reputation early on in his career of being a pornographic writer, was refused membership of the Académie Française, and later in life became converted to Catholicism.

p. 155   *Arbenin, or whatever he's called:* Fyodor Pavlovich means Pechorin, the hero of *A Hero of Our Time* (1840). Arbenin is the principal character in Lermontov's play *Masquerade* (1835).

p. 156   *bare-legged dancers:* in Russian *bosonozhki*, a word that can also be used to describe girls who are poor ('barefoot').

p. 156   barin: a word that has no direct counterpart in English, sometimes translated as 'master', but after the Emancipation of 1861 really more akin to 'sir' or 'sire'.

p. 161   *he dursed me:* in Russian, *on menya derznul*, 'he "impudented" me', a phrase from Dostoyevsky's *Siberian Notebook*.

p. 176   La bourse ou la vie: 'Your purse or your life!', a quotation from Schiller's *Die Räuber* (Act I, Scene I).

p. 178   *the four cardinal points, or the five:* Dmitry is confusing the points of the compass with the continents, which in the nineteenth century were counted as five: Europe, Asia, Africa, America and Australia.

p. 185   *Crack-ups:* in Russian, *nadryvy* can be translated approximately as 'cracks', 'ruptures', 'harrowings', but also as 'hysterias'. *Nadryv*, like its French parent *déchirement*, connotes a breaking, tearing and straining beneath an intolerable weight of mental, emotional and spiritual suffering. It is a constantly recurring theme throughout the novel. 'Crack-up' is offered as a near equivalent.

p. 188   *Shall we yet behold:* a formulaic religious expression with the meaning 'Have we seen anything yet?'

p. 190   *He spoke . . . letter 'o':* a characteristic of Belorussian speakers from the north.

p. 190   armyak: a peasant's cloth coat.

p. 191   lapsha: noodles.

p. 191   *the Council of Laodicea:* the Council of Laodicea, held in AD 360 or 370, at which many tenets of the Christian ecclesiastical canon were established.

p. 193   *the spirit . . . of Elias:* cf. Luke 1:17.

p. 195   *the gates of hell:* cf. Matthew 16:18.

p. 204   *Monk, monk in silken pants:* this scene of jeering places Alyosha firmly within the tradition of the Russian *yurodivy*, or 'holy fool'.

p. 220   Den Dank . . . ich nicht: 'Your thanks, my lady, are not what I desire' (German) — a quotation from Schiller's narrative poem 'Der Handschuh' ('The Gauntlet'), 1797.

p. 223   *Crack-up in the* Izba: izba is either a peasant's hut or cottage, or a living room in such a cottage; here the two meanings, 'living room' and 'hut', tend to elide. The effect is hardly translatable, but is evocative of a rural kind of poverty. The *izba* is no more the type of place where one would expect to encounter the 'crack-up' or *nadryv* than is the drawing room.

p. 226   *a half-*shtof: a *shtof* was equivalent to approximately 1.2 litres. The vessel concerned was a quadrangular-shaped glass bottle-jug with a short neck.

p. 227   *lower depths:* in Russian *nedra,* a cliché of 'civic' parlance, favoured by left-leaning intellectuals.

p. 228   *I really ought . . . Slovoyersov:* in nineteenth-century Russian the *slovoyers* was a particle of speech ('-*s*' or 'sir') added to the end of words by persons of lower class or rank when addressing those in superior social positions. Snegiryov uses the word as a derogatory substitute for his own name.

p. 230   *And nothing . . . to bless:* a quotation from Pushkin's poem 'Demon' (1823).

p. 230   *Mr Chernomazov:* 'Chernomazov' is a Russian 'translation' of the Turko-Tatar-influenced 'Karamazov' — both are derived from words that mean 'swarthy' (literally 'black smear'). In Siberia Dostoyevsky had had the nickname 'Karasakal' ('Blackbeard') among the Tatar and Kirghizi prisoners. Here the 'translation' is probably unconscious and unintentional.

p. 233   *a coursiste:* in nineteenth-century Russia women were not allowed to enroll as students at the universities (many entered special female educational 'institutes' instead), but were admitted to certain courses there in a 'listening' capacity.

p. 241   kibitka: here, a hooded cart.

p. 244   *asthenia:* in Russian simply *slabost',* 'weakness', but used by Dostoyevsky here as a medical term.

p. 244   *brain fever:* Dostoyevsky uses the word *goryachka,* Latin *febris acuta,* in mid-nineteenth-century Russia still believed to be an inflammation of the blood, or of the brain and other organs.

p. 254   *Now I am like Famusov in the final scene . . .:* a reference to the final act of A. S. Griboyedov's comedy *Woe From Wit* (1824).

p. 257   *you opened her matrix:* cf. Exodus 13:2.

p. 258   *The Emperor of the French, Napoleon I, the father:* Napoleon I was in fact the uncle of Napoleon III.

p. 259   *the Petrovka:* a street in central Moscow.

p. 264   *the sticky leaf-buds:* a quotation from Pushkin's poem 'Yeshcho duyut kholodnye vetry . . .' ('Cold winds still blow . . .'), 1828.

p. 264   *Dear corpses lie there:* possibly a quotation from a poem by A. A. Fet, 'Ne pervyy god u etikh mest . . .' ('Not the first year about these parts . . .'), 1864.

p. 265   *In having . . . have died:* see Introduction, p. xxii.

p. 265   *a shade of decency:* a reference to Pushkin's epigram 'Skazali raz tsaryu, chto nakonets . . .' ('The tsar was once told that at last . . .'), 1825:

> Flatterers, flatterers, try to keep
> A shade of decency even in your baseness.

p. 268   *Believest thou, or dost thou not believe:* a question from the Russian Orthodox ritual attending the ordination of a bishop, in response to which the ordinand recites the 'Symbol of Faith', the Creed.

p. 269   *a certain old sinner:* Voltaire.

p. 271   *Ioann the Almsgiver:* John the Almsgiver, Patriarch of Alexandria from 611 until 619. The story related by Ivan occurs in Flaubert's *La légende de Saint Julien l'Hospitalier* (1876), Turgenev's translation of which had appeared in the *Messenger of Europe* (1877, No. 4).

p. 272   *epithimia:* the Greek word is used in Orthodox theology to denote an ecclesiastical penance.

p. 274   *down there in Bulgaria:* a reference to the events of 1875–6, when the conflict between the Bulgarians and the occupying Turks was at its height.

p. 274   *as Polonius says in* Hamlet*:* in Act I, Scene III of *Hamlet*, Polonius refers to 'the poor phrase', and 'implorators of unholy suits' – Ivan is presumbably quoting here from a Russian translation of the play.

p. 275   *the religious movement:* during the 1870s the philosopher and theologist Vladimir S. Solovyov gave a number of public lectures which attracted large audiences and around which a 'movement' came into being.

p. 276   *Nekrasov has some lines:* Nekrasov's poem 'Do sumerek' ('Before Twilight'), from his cycle *O Pogode* (*About the Weather*), 1859.

p. 277   *ablakat:* a Russian folk-word meaning *advokat*, or advocate, lawyer.

p. 278   *the* Archive *or the* Antiquity*:* names of Russian journals.

p. 279   *the Liberator of the people:* Tsar Alexander II (1855–81) was responsible for the emancipation of the serfs in 1861.

p. 279   *the general was put in ward:* a legal expression which means that the general had the administration of his estate and serfs taken out of his hands.

p. 279   *schemonach:* Ivan uses the Russian word *skhimnik*, a borrowing from the Greek *schemamonachos* – a monk who is a wearer of the *schema* (or habit), one who has taken upon himself the strictest religious vows. A 'hieroschemonach' is a priest or Elder of the same order.

p. 280   *that 'none does offend':* a quotation from *King Lear*, Act IV, Scene 6.

p. 282   *I hasten to return my entry ticket:* a near-quotation from Zhukovsky's translation of Schiller's poem 'Resignation', 1784.

p. 283   *the only sinless one:* Christ (a formulation from an Orthodox hymn).

p. 283   *a poema:* in Russian, the word *poema* can signify a prose narrative as well as a narrative poem.

p. 283   Nôtre Dame de Paris: the novel *The Hunchback of Nôtre Dame*.

p. 283   *to celebrate the birthday of the French Dauphin:* in fact, Hugo does not mention the birthday of the French Dauphin in this context – the national holiday celebrates the arrival of the Flemish envoys who wished to arrange a marriage between the Dauphin and Margaret of Flanders.

p. 283   *pre-Petrine antiquity:* i.e. pre-dating the reign of Peter the Great (1682–1721).

p. 284   The Journey of the Mother of God Through the Torments: one of the most popular of the apocryphal legends of Byzantium, which circulated early in Russia. There had been several publications of it in the Russian journals during the years before the writing of *The Brothers Karamazov*.

p. 284   *Behold, I come quickly:* cf. Revelation 3:11.

p. 284   *But of that day . . . Father in heaven:* a modified quotation from Mark 13:32.

p. 284   *Thou must have faith . . . pledges lend:* a quotation from Zhukovsky's translation of Schiller's poem 'Sehnsucht' ('Longing'), 1801.

p. 285   *a terrible new heresy:* the Reformation, with Luther and Protestantism as its driving-force.

p. 285   *An enormous star . . . bitter:* cf. Revelation 8:10–11.

p. 285   *O God the Lord, show us light:* cf. Psalm 118:27. Ivan's 'quotation' is somewhat distorted.

p. 285   *Weighed down . . . end to end:* a quotation of the third stanza of
Tyutchev's poem 'Eti bednye selen'ya' ('These poor villages'), 1855.

p. 285   *In resplendent . . . heretics:* a slightly modified quotation of lines
from A. I. Polezhayev's poem 'Koriolan' ('Coriolanus'), 1857.

p. 286   *hot streets and squares:* another quotation from Polezhayev's poem.

p. 286   ad majorem gloriam Dei: 'to the greater glory of God', the
motto of the Jesuits.

p. 286   Talitha cumi: cf. Mark 5:40–42. The words are Aramaic for
'Damsel, arise'.

p. 287   *of lemon and of laurel reeks:* a quotation from Scene 2 of Pushkin's
'Little Tragedy', *Kamennyy gost'* (*The Stone Guest*), 1826–30.

p. 288   *I want to make you free:* cf. John 8:32, *et seq.*

p. 289   *to bind and loose:* cf. Matthew 16:19.

p. 290   *Who is like . . . fire from heaven:* cf. Revelation 13:13.

p. 293   *If you would know . . . your Father:* cf. Matthew 4:6, *et seq.*; the
passage is a paraphrase of the biblical text.

p. 294   *your great deed:* the peculiarly Russian word used by Dostoyevsky is again *podvig*, with its echoes of *podvizhniki* and *podvizhnichestvo*,
and their attendant asceticism (see note to p. 27)

p. 294   *Come down from the Cross . . . it is You:* cf. Matthew 27:42,
though the passage is not quoted correctly.

p. 295   *your great prophet:* St John.

p. 296   *eight centuries:* a reference to Pope Stephen II's assumption of
secular power in AD 755.

p. 296   *the beast will come crawling to our feet:* a reference both to the
beast of the Apocalypse and to three lines from Scene 2 of Pushkin's
short play *The Covetous Knight.*

p. 298   *It is said and prophesied:* cf. Revelation 17:5–6.

p. 299   *fulfil the number:* cf. Revelation 6:11. Russian versions of the
Bible have 'fulfil the number' instead of 'be fulfilled'.

p. 302   *the town's dark streets and squares:* an inexact quotation from
Pushkin's poem 'Vospominanie' ('Reminiscence'), 1828.

p. 302   *all things are lawful:* cf. I Corinthians 6:12.

p. 303   Pater Seraphicus: a reference to the final scene of Goethe's *Faust*
(*Zweiter Teil*).

p. 309   *Licharda:* the Russian version of Richard – the name of the
servant of King Guidon in *Bova Korolevich* (*Prince Bova*), a chivalric
legend translated from medieval French.

p. 318   *dear kindred father mine:* a Russian idiom, *otets ty moy rodnoy* –
'father' in this mode of speech often signifies 'helper'.

p. 319   *poddyovka:* a man's long-waisted coat or jacket.

p. 320   *Lyagavy:* while the name Gorstkin suggests 'handful', the name Lyagavy means 'setter' (the breed of dog).

p. 326   *Kostroman monastery:* Kostroma is a district of northern Russia.

p. 330   *sixty paper roubles:* these were *assignatsii*, paper money introduced into Russia in 1769, but replaced in 1843 by credit bills ('banknotes'). Paper roubles were inferior in value to silver ones.

p. 334   One Hundred . . . Old and New Testaments: Anna Grigoryevna relates that this was the book Dostoyevsky used as a child when learning to read.

p. 334   *There was a man in the land of Uz:* cf. Job 1:1.

p. 334   *Hast thou considered my servant Job:* in Russian translations of the Bible this becomes 'Hast thou seen my slave Job?' (*A videl li raba moyego Iova?*), and in the original text of the novel the Elder Zosima stresses the word 'slave' in the passage that follows. The distinction was an important one to Dostoyevsky – see below, note to p. 365.

p. 335   *Let my prayer arise:* in Russian 'Da ispravitsya molitva moya, yako kadilo pred Toboyu' ('Let my prayer arise like incense before Thee'), a verse sung during the first part ('Vespers') of the Orthodox All-Night Vigil.

p. 337   *How dreadful is this place:* Genesis 28:17.

p. 337   *the very great pronouncement:* cf. Genesis 49:10 ('The sceptre shall not depart from Judah, nor a lawgiver from between his feet, until Shiloh come; and unto him shall the gathering of the people be').

p. 338   *Saul's conversion of the Jews:* cf. Acts 13:16–41.

p. 338   *Mary of Egypt:* an Orthodox saint who according to legend was a prostitute, but travelled to Jerusalem and became converted to Christianity, having spent forty-seven days in the wilderness.

p. 338   *help him voluntarily upon his field:* rural priests often augmented their income by means of small farming.

p. 339   *a bear came to a great saint:* St Sergius of Radonezh (1314–92) – the episode is taken from his *Life*.

p. 340   *for an hour, and . . . a year:* cf. Revelation 9:15.

p. 341   *the year 1826:* The Decembrist uprising had taken place in December 1825.

p. 349   *the sign . . . in heaven:* cf. Matthew 24:30.

p. 351   *on a campaign:* the year is 1812.

p. 352   *payment of the recruit-debt:* before the emancipation of the serfs, each Russian landowner was responsible for supplying the Imperial Army with recruits from among the souls in his possession.

p. 355   *the* Children's Reader: a Russian children's magazine.

p. 357   *As an outcast I cast myself out:* the play on words in Russian is more acute: *kak izverga sebya izvergayu*, where *izverg* means not only 'an outcast', but also 'a monster of cruelty'.

p. 360   *the long-suffering servant of God:* again, the Russian has 'the long-suffering slave of God', in keeping with Russian versions of the Book of Job (and in keeping with the general Russian tendency in Scripture to employ the word *rab* – 'slave' – where the English has 'servant').

p. 363   *'cursed be . . . cruel':* cf. Genesis 49:7.

p. 365   *Life without servants . . . than if he were not a servant:* Dostoyevsky elaborates this notion in his *Diary of a Writer* for 1880: 'Servants are not slaves. The disciple Timothy served Paul when they walked together, but read the epistle of Paul to Timothy: is he writing to a slave, or even to a servant, pray? For this is indeed "the offspring Timothy", his beloved son [The King James version has 'my own son in the faith', tr.]. Such, such will be the relation of masters to their servants, if both the one and the other become complete Christians! There will be servants and masters, but the masters will no longer be masters, and the servants no longer be slaves.'

p. 365   *described in the Gospels:* cf. Matthew 20:25–7, Mark 9:35, 10:43–4.

p. 366   *the stone . . . of the corner:* cf. Matthew 21:42.

p. 366   *they that take the sword . . . too:* cf. Matthew 26:52.

p. 366   *even unto the last two men upon the earth:* possibly an echo of Byron's poem 'Darkness' (1816), which Dostoyevsky knew in Turgenev's translation.

p. 366   *those days shall be shortened:* cf. Matthew 24.22.

p. 368   *inward form is well-apportioned:* in the ethically derived aesthetics that Dostoyevsky developed in his later years the concept of inward beauty, or 'inward well-apportionment' (*blagolepie*), is set in opposition to 'inward deformity' (*bezobrazie*).

p. 370   *fall to the earth and kiss her:* in Russian folklore, and in Dostoyevsky's novel, the earth is a mother.

p. 370   *be sorrowful, even unto death:* cf. Matthew 26:38.

p. 371   *the parable of Dives and Lazarus:* cf. Luke 16:19–31.

p. 372   *there shall be time no longer:* cf. Revelation 10:6.

p. 373   *like a hungry man . . . blood from his own body:* the source of this passage is the *Slova podvizhnicheskie* of St Isaac of Nineveh ('Isaac the Syrian'): 'The cur that licketh his own nostrils drinketh his own blood and, by reason of the sweetness of his blood, feels no harm. Likewise the monk who yields to the intoxication of vanity drinketh his own life.'

p. 375   *A Putrid Smell:* probably a quotation from Tyutchev's poem '*I grob opushchen uzh v mogilu*' ('And the coffin is now lowered into the grave'), 1836:

> And the coffin is now lowered into the grave,
> And everyone has crowded around . . .
> They push one another, breathe with difficulty
> A putrid smell constricts the breast . . .

p. 375   *sleeping:* more precisely, 'fallen-asleep' – in the Orthodox faith one who has died is considered to have 'fallen asleep' in the Lord.

p. 375   *the established rite:* in this passage Dostoyevsky made use of notes concerning 'the details of monastic burial' supplied to him by Konstantin Pobedonostsev, the head of the Holy Synod.

p. 375   *cuculus:* a cowl or hood.

p. 375   *aer:* the cloth with which the altar chalice and paten are covered.

p. 375   panikhida: requiem, service for the dead.

p. 376   *the instant power of healing:* such miracles are often recounted in the lives of the Orthodox saints.

p. 376   *an unquestionable temptation:* in Russian, the word for 'temptation', *soblazn*, also has an older meaning, that of 'scandal'.

p. 384   *Exorcising shall I exorcise:* literally, 'casting out I shall cast out' – *izvergaya izvergnu*. The scene is given an added comic flavour by the fact that in Russian *izverg* means 'a monster'.

p. 384   *the cruel chains:* chains or fetters worn as a penance.

p. 385   *Dost thou believe:* another reference to the ritual attending the ordination of a bishop.

p. 386   stikhira: a Russian form of Greek *stikhera*, a canticle on biblical themes.

p. 393   *Antidoron:* a part of the communion bread that is distributed to the faithful at the end of the liturgy.

p. 396   gesheft: a Yiddish word, meaning 'business'.

p. 398   nakolka: a kind of headdress.

p. 402   *estafette:* a special messenger, courier.

p. 413   *Cana of Galilee:* cf. John 2:1–11.

p. 420   *epistle from Siberia:* an ironic reference to Pushkin's verse epistle 'In the Depths of the Siberian Mines' ('*Vo glubine sibirskikh rud*'), 1827.

p. 439 *Othello is not jealous, he is trusting:* a quotation from Pushkin's 'Table-talk' (the title is in English, the genre borrowed from Hazlitt) of the 1830s.

p. 445 *'Enough!' as Turgenev said:* a reference to Turgenev's novella *Enough. A Fragment from the Notes of a Deceased Artist* (1865). Dostoyevsky had already parodied this tale in his novel *The Devils*.

p. 447 *the writer Shchedrin:* in this passage Dostoyevsky continues to spar with his adversary Saltykov-Shchedrin, though Mrs Khokhlakova's letter is modelled on one received by Dostoyevsky from an anonymous female correspondent.

p. 447 *The Contemporary:* the literary–political journal founded in 1836 by the poet Pushkin. Between the 1840s and 1860s the journal functioned as the organ of Russian revolutionary democracy and was subject to frequent incursions by the censor, being finally closed down in 1866.

p. 451 *and only silence whispereth:* a near-quotation from Pushkin's poem 'Ruslan and Ludmila' (1820).

p. 460 *Plotnikovs':* this grocery store or delicatessen is modelled on the one in Staraya Russa, where Dostoyevsky spent his childhood. His father was a regular customer at the shop.

p. 460 *sig:* a freshwater fish of the salmon species.

p. 460 *tyagushki:* candy 'icicles' – a kind of toffee.

p. 463 *Mastryuk . . . not a stitch:* a quotation from a historical folk ballad, 'Mastryuk Temryukovich' – Mastryuk's clothes are stolen as he lies asleep.

p. 463 *Easy led . . . deceiving:* a quotation from Tyutchev's poem 'The Funeral Banquet', 1851 (a free translation of Schiller's 'Das Siegesfest', 1803). The words are spoken by 'Odysseus inspired'.

p. 466 *yamshchik:* a coachman or driver.

p. 470 *One final tale:* a near-quotation from Pimen's monologue in Pushkin's tragedy *Boris Godunov* (1824–5):

> Yet one more, one final tale –
> And my chronicle is ended.

p. 476 *the Son of God:* the passage may be based on a Russian folk legend, *The Dream of the Most Holy Mother of God*, in which Christ, having come down from the Cross, visits hell.

p. 478 *Cherni:* possibly a reference to Cherni on the northern shore of the Caspian Sea, a noted fishing and angling region.

p. 481   Polish: *pan* = sir, Mr; *pani* = lady, Mrs; *panowie* = gentlemen. *Panie* is the vocative singular form of *pan*. The Polish sentences and phrases that follow are given by Dostoyevsky in Cyrillic, not roman characters. The 'Polish' is actually a mix of Polish and Russian; when the Polish would be completely unclear to a Russian-speaker, Dostoyevsky translated in the text. The Polish has mostly been translated in this edition.

p. 487   Dead Souls: see the end of Chapter 4 (Part One) of *Dead Souls*. The same chapter should be referred to in connection with the allusions that follow.

p. 488   *Piron:* See note to p. 134.

p. 489   *Is't thou, Boileau . . . travesty:* from Krylov's 'Epigram on a translation of the poem *L'art poétique*' (1814).

p. 489   *Thou'rt Sappho . . . dost not know:* a near-quotation of Konstantin Batyushkov's epigram. 'A Madrigal to the New Sappho' (1809).

p. 490   *dear little Russia, the dear old granny:* a sardonic reference to the concluding lines of Goncharov's novel *The Precipice* (1869), where Russia is evoked in the rather more imposing guise of a great and gigantic grandmother.

p. 490   *To Russia . . . 1772:* in the first partition of Poland between Russia, Prussia and Austria in 1772, Russia obtained the eastern part of Belorussia and the Catholic part of present-day Latvia, while the Polish lands proper went to Austria and Prussia.

p. 493   *Corner:* a card-playing term, meaning a quarter stake with the bending of one corner of the card.

p. 498   *hie thee . . . stove:* the words are from a *chastushka*, or Russian dance song.

p. 504   *Let this terrible cup pass from me:* cf. Matthew 26:39.

p. 509   *Oh, you passage, my passage:* a Russian folk song.

p. 511   *Jurisprudence:* the St Petersburg Imperial Law School.

p. 521   *yeralash:* a card-game.

p. 521   *our* zemstvo *doctor:* the *zemstvo* was an organ of local self-government, introduced after the electoral reforms of 1864.

p. 541   *a line of poetry:* the question is from Fyodor Tyutchev's poem 'Silentium' (1830?).

p. 578   *civil servant of the twelfth grade:* the twelfth grade was one of the lowest in the civil service.

p. 584   *zipun:* a homespun coat.

p. 586   *but the thunder has spoken:* the phrase evokes the Russian proverb 'Until the thunder speaks the muzhik will not cross himself.'

p. 588   *Forgive us, too:* the verbs for 'forgive' and 'say farewell' are closely related in Russian.

p. 591   *'dry and whetted':* a quotation from Nekrasov's poem 'Before the Rain' (1846).

p. 591   *progymnasium:* the lower part of a gymnasium (grammar school).

p. 595   *the section dealing . . . History:* in fact, Smaragdov's *History* (1843) does not give any information about the founders of Troy, though another textbook by him does.

p. 596   *Perezvon:* the name means 'Chimes', and has a very Slavonic 'ring' to it.

p. 601   *Oh children . . . years:* the beginning of Dmitriyev's fable in verse 'The Cock, the Tom-Cat and the Little Mouse' (1802).

p. 603   *Medelyansky hound:* the name derives from 'Mediolanum', the Latin name for the city of Milan. A mastiff.

p. 605   *boubliks:* thick, ring-shaped rolls.

p. 605   *to pick and choose:* possibly a reference to Saltykov-Shchedrin's *For Each to Pick and Choose. Stories, Scenes, Reflections and Aphorisms* (1863).

p. 611   *Zhuchka:* equivalent to the English 'Scamp', a common name for a house or 'yard' dog, male or female. In fact *zhuchka*, with a small letter, means a yard dog in Russian, though it also means 'little beetle'.

p. 627   *A Kinsman of Mahomet, or Salutary Folly:* a translation from the French, published in Moscow in 1785.

p. 631   *the mirovoy:* the *mirovoy sud'ya*, or Justice of the Peace.

p. 632   *Kolbasnikov:* the name is derived from *kolbasnik*, 'sausage-maker'.

p. 632   *a mug-whirler:* in Russian, *rylovorot*, slang for an ugly woman.

p. 634   *the naturals:* the natural sciences.

p. 638   *Belinsky . . . :* Vissarion Belinsky (1811–48), the radical and liberal critic who exercised a profound influence on the literary developments in Russia during the first half of the nineteenth century, and who in many ways made possible the beginning of Dostoyevsky's literary career. In his ninth article about Pushkin, Belinsky wrote concerning Pushkin's verse novel, *Eugene Onegin*, and in particular Tatyana's reply to its hero: 'There is the true pride of female virtue! But I am given to another — given, but have not given myself! Eternal faithfulness — to whom and in what? Faithfulness to such relations which constitute a profanation of the feeling and purity of feminine nature, because certain relations, which are not sanctified by love, are in the highest degree immoral.'

p. 638   *the Third Department:* the Tsarist secret police, which had its headquarters in a building near the Chain Bridge (now Pestel Bridge) across the Neva in St Petersburg.

p. 638   *the Chain Bridge:* Kolya quotes the first part of a 'radical' poem which had appeared in the journal *Polyarnaya zvezda (Pole Star)* in 1861, and was familiar to most of Dostoyevsky's readers.

p. 638   The Bell: the revolutionary newspaper published by Herzen and Ogarev in London between 1857 and 1867.

p. 646   *If I forget . . . cleave:* cf. Psalm 137.

p. 649   durachki: a card-game.

p. 661   *Skotoprigonyevsk:* the name means literally 'Cattle-Drive-Home-Place.'

p. 663   *a monument:* the question of the erection of a monument to Pushkin had been discussed in the Russian press since 1862, but the plan was not realized until 1880, when Dostoyevsky read his 'Pushkin Speech' at the unveiling.

p. 664   *A judicial affect:* 'affect' is borrowed from the German *Affekt*, a 'strong emotion, passion, impulse'. A crime committed under the influence of 'judicial affect' was akin to a *crime passionnel*.

p. 675   *like the Swede:* an instance of the Russian saying 'like the Swede at Poltava', which derives not from any criticism of the Swedish moral character, but rather from the defeat of Charles XII at the battle of Poltava by the Russians in 1709.

p. 675   *the Apocryphal Gospels:* Gospels not included in the New Testament (that of James is an example).

p. 677   *Claude Bernard:* a French natural scientist, physiologist and pathologist who lived from 1813 to 1878. Bernard's 'experimental' theories were of great importance to the writer Émile Zola, who utilized them in his literary theory and novels, and there is reason to believe that Dostoyevsky was much influenced by them also. Bernard is mentioned by Sigmund Freud in *The Interpretation of Dreams* as having advised the experimenters in a physiological laboratory: *'travailler comme une bête'* – Freud adds: 'he must work, that is, with as much persistence as an animal and with as much disregard of the result. If this advice is followed, the task will no longer be a hard one.' (*The Interpretation of Dreams*, 1900, translated by James Strachey, Pelican Books, 1983, p. 669.)

p. 678   De *thought*ibus non est disputandum: a rather 'unwitty' distortion of the Latin saying *De gustibus non est disputandum* (there is no point in arguing about taste).

p. 680 *Oh, this little foot ... head may:* the verses are a response by Dostoyevsky to a parody of Pushkin's poem 'Sumptuous city, city poor' (*Gorod pyshnyy, gorod bednyy*), 1828, by the 'poet-accuser' D. D. Minayev (1835–89). The civic 'accusers' (with Rakitin among them) here become the object of satire.

p. 684 *to the uttermost farthing:* cf. Matthew 5:26.

p. 706 *white room:* the guest room, or 'best room'.

p. 716 *Oh, now Vanka's ... wait: Piter* is slang for 'St Petersburg'.

p. 719 *Licharda:* see above, note to p. 309.

p. 732 *I am not a doctor ... illness:* in Dostoyevsky's Russian text, Ivan's illness is defined as *belaya goryachka*, or *delirium tremens* (DTs). There seems little doubt that Dostoyevsky wishes to stress Ivan's family nature – Ivan is a Karamazov, too, with the Karamazov vices. Although we see little or nothing of Ivan's drinking, hints of it are scattered throughout the novel (see, in particular, for example, Book V, Chapter 3, and Ivan's constant references to 'dashing the cup to the floor'). Dostoyevsky never managed to write the 'explanation' of Ivan's illness that was to form the subject of an article in *A Writer's Diary*, but from his letters it is clear that he consulted several doctors on the subject of *delirium tremens*, the symptoms of which Ivan unquestionably displays.

p. 733 *gospodin:* the Russian word for 'gentleman' – *dʒhentl'men*, used in the phrase 'a kind of Russian "gentleman"', has a decidedly pejorative ring.

p. 734 *Thomas believed:* cf. John 20:25–9.

p. 737 *pood:* see above, note (2) to p. 116.

p. 737 *Satan* sum et nihil ... *puto:* the Devil's variation on a celebrated line from Terence's comedy *Heautontimoroumenos* (*The Self-Torturer*): *Homo sum, humani nihil a me alienum puto:* 'I am a man, and nothing human is alien to me.'

p. 739 *which were above the firmament:* cf. Genesis 1:7.

p. 739 *Gattsuk:* A. A. Gattsuk (1832–91), publisher in the 1870s and 1880s of the Moscow periodical *A. Gattsuk's Gazette* and of the *Religious Calendar.*

p. 739 *something great and possibly even beautiful:* the 'great' and the 'beautiful' mentioned here derive, as earlier in the novel, from Schiller's *The Robbers.*

p. 740 *I can only cure your right nostril:* a variation on a theme from Voltaire's philosophical novella *Zadig ou la destinée* (1748), where it is the right eye that the doctor can cure.

p. 740   *you see . . . vaudevilles:* Khlestakov's words in Gogol's comedy *The Inspector General* (1836), Act III, scene 6.

p. 742   *a certain department:* the Third Department, or secret police.

p. 742   *rejected . . . faith":* the words are Repetilov's in the comedy *Woe from Wit* by Griboyedov (Act IV, Scene 4).

p. 743   *softening of your ways:* a progressive journalistic cliché derived from Voltaire and the French Enlightenment.

p. 743   *the prophet Jonah:* cf. Jonah, 2:1.

p. 745   *father . . . immaculate:* a quotation from a poem by Pushkin which begins with the same line, and is a poetic paraphrase of a prayer of St Ephraim the Syrian.

p. 745   *the actor Gorbunov:* I. F. Gorbunov (1831–96), an actor, writer and gifted narrator–improviser who was a personal friend of Dostoyevsky's.

p. 746   *Ça lui . . . de peine!:* the words apparently derive from an epigram on the famous French actress J.-C. Gaussin (1711–67):

> Tendre Gaussin, quoi! si jeune et si belle,
> Et votre cœur cède au premier aveu!
> – Que voulez-vous, cela leur fait, dit-elle,
> Tant de plaisir et me coûte si peu.

p. 747   *all that is great . . . beautiful:* see note to p. 739 (2).

p. 747   *a-thunder and a-glitter:* a paraphrase from an Apocryphal legend.

p. 747   *the Lion and Sun:* a Persian decoration, sometimes awarded to Russian civil servants in the Caucasus.

p. 747   *the Pole Star:* there is a play on words here – the 'Pole Star' was not only the name of a Swedish decoration, but also the title of a radical literary almanac that published the writings of the Decembrists, and also of a later journal published by Ogarev and Herzen.

p. 747   *the Sirius:* a decoration, but also a reference to the hero of Voltaire's novella *Micromégas* (1752), who lives on Sirius. The Devil's politics are very much of the conservative kind, and he is poking fun at Ivan for being a radical.

p. 747   *When Mephistopheles appeared to Faust:* the reference is to Scene 3 of Goethe's *Faust*.

p. 748   *The Geological Revolution:* the notion of a 'geological revolution' derives from Renan's *Vie de Jésus*.

p. 750   *Monsieur . . . chien dehors:* a joke noted down by Dostoyevsky in his notebook for 1876–7. The complete text is:

'Baptiste, tout de suite ce mot à son adresse.'

'Tout de suite? Madame ignore peut-être le temps qu'il fait, c'est à ne pas mettre un chien dehors.'

'Mais, Baptiste, vous n'êtes pas un chien.'

p. 751 *fortochka:* a small opening pane set in the main window, for purposes of ventilation.

p. 752 *pure cherub:* a quotation from Lermontov's narrative poem, 'The Demon' ('Demon'), I, I, 1839.

p. 768 *doors opened on heaven:* cf. Revelation 4:1 ('a door was opened in heaven').

p. 774 *Herrnhuter or 'Moravian Brother':* the Herrnhuters were a religious and social movement that emerged during the eighteenth century in the town of Herrnhut in Saxony and thereafter found its way to Russia, where it spread quite widely. It preached and practised the moral re-education of human beings, and many of its doctrines derived from the Czech 'Moravian Brethren', a religious sect that dates from the mid fifteenth century.

p. 788 *the thief of friendship:* in Russian *razluchnitsa*, a 'folk' word denoting a woman who destroys the happiness of others.

p. 791 *sarafan . . . paneva:* a *sarafan* is a kind of peasant dress without sleeves; a paneva the skirt worn by a peasant bride at her wedding.

p. 791 *Bread and circuses:* the common saying, derived from Juvenal's tenth Satire.

p. 793 *he began to howl with a loud voice:* in the Russian, the phrase has a New Testament ring to it, suggesting possession by devils.

p. 799 *the 'accursed' questions:* questions of life and death to which there is no answer.

p. 800 *the new Public Court:* as part of the judicial reforms of 1864, jury courts were introduced into Russia, and these were both open and public. The newspaper of the 1860s and 1870s contained transcriptions of speeches delivered by prosecution and defence at the open trials.

p. 800 *a shining young officer of high society:* a reference to the case, tried in 1879 and reported in the Russian press, of Karl Khristoforov von Landsberg, a retired ensign who was accused and found guilty of the murder of state councillor Vlasov and his maid Semenidova.

p. 801 *he lived among us:* the first line of a poem by Pushkin, dedicated to Mickiewicz (1834).

p. 801 *a great writer:* Gogol — the reference is to the finale of his *poema Dead Souls* (1842).

p. 802 *as sun's . . . little drop:* a quotation from Derzhavin's ode 'God' (1784).

p. 836   *in the English Parliament:* for a further discussion of this event, see Dostoyevsky's *Diary of a Writer* for 1876 (September, chap. 1).

p. 836   *it's a long way for the snipe to fly:* a Russian saying, somewhat akin to 'there's many a slip 'twixt cup and lip' – the other speaker does not hear properly.

p. 836   *we'll close Kronstadt:* the island of Kronstadt outside St Petersburg was one of Russia's main ports.

p. 837   *smite . . . with unknown power:* a quotation from Pushkin's 'Reply to Anonymous' (*'Otvet anonimu'*), 1830:

> And the suffered verse, with melancholy keen,
> doth smite . . . each heart with unknown power.

p. 843   *a certain young man:* this is based on an actual case (that of the peasant Zaytsev) which was tried in St Petersburg in 1878.

p. 843   *blue . . . red:* 'blue' notes were worth five roubles, 'red' notes ten.

p. 844   *castle of Udolpho: The Mysteries of Udolpho*, (1794) by Ann Radcliffe (1764–1823) was a Gothic novel popular in early nineteenth-century Russia.

p. 855   *the power to bind and loose:* cf. Matthew 18:18; also 16:19.

p. 858   *I am the good shepherd . . . perish:* cf. John 10:11, 14–15.

p. 859   *Fathers . . . to anger:* cf. Colossians 3:21. The defence counsel purposely omits the preceding verse: 'Children, obey your parents in all things: for this is well pleasing unto the Lord.'

p. 859   *vivos voco:* 'I call the living' (Latin). The motto, taken from the epigraph to Schiller's 'Song of the Bell' (*'Vivos voco. Mortuos plango. Fulgura frango'*), of Herzen's radical journal *The Bell*.

p. 859   *"metal" and of "brimstone":* a reference to Act II, Scene 2 of A. N. Ostrovsky's play *Hard Days* (1863). Two merchants' wives discuss their fear of these words, which come from the Bible. The passage is also a parody on a critical essay by Dostoyevsky's critic Ye. L. Markov, who accused the novelist of an excessively gloomy view of life.

p. 860   *Drive nature . . . window:* a quotation from Lafontaine's fable *La Chatte metamorphosée en femme*, in a free Russian translation by N. M. Karamzin.

p. 862   *and now they have sent me into penal servitude:* the passage derives from Matthew 25:35–43.

p. 863   *It is better . . . one innocent one:* a quotation in somewhat modified form of a sentence from Peter the Great's *Military Code* (1716).

p. 865   *For Thou art our God:* words addressed to Christ in many Orthodox prayers.

p. 865   *'Jupiter ... wrong':* a Russian saying. It appears in Turgenev's *Rudin* (1856), and its insertion here by Dostoyevsky may be satirical.

p. 866   *break the sword over my head:* a reference to the ritual breaking of the sword over the head of the man who has been condemned to death, something Dostoyevsky himself had experienced in 1849.

p. 868   *an actress:* the actress A. V. Kairova – the case was a real one. See the May 1876 issue of *Diary of a Writer*.

p. 887   *the fillet:* a band bearing the text of a prayer of absolution, put on the the dead person's head.

READ MORE IN PENGUIN

In every corner of the world, on every subject under the sun, Penguin represents quality and variety – the very best in publishing today.

For complete information about books available from Penguin – including Puffins, Penguin Classics and Arkana – and how to order them, write to us at the appropriate address below. Please note that for copyright reasons the selection of books varies from country to country.

In the United Kingdom: Please write to *Dept. EP, Penguin Books Ltd, Bath Road, Harmondsworth, West Drayton, Middlesex UB7 ODA*

In the United States: Please write to *Consumer Sales, Penguin Putnam Inc., P.O. Box 12289 Dept. B, Newark, New Jersey 07101-5289.* VISA and MasterCard holders call 1-800-788-6262 to order Penguin titles

In Canada: Please write to *Penguin Books Canada Ltd, 10 Alcorn Avenue, Suite 300, Toronto, Ontario M4V 3B2*

In Australia: Please write to *Penguin Books Australia Ltd, P.O. Box 257, Ringwood, Victoria 3134*

In New Zealand: Please write to *Penguin Books (NZ) Ltd, Private Bag 102902, North Shore Mail Centre, Auckland 10*

In India: Please write to *Penguin Books India Pvt Ltd, 11 Community Centre, Panchsheel Park, New Delhi 110017*

In the Netherlands: Please write to *Penguin Books Netherlands bv, Postbus 3507, NL-1001 AH Amsterdam*

In Germany: Please write to *Penguin Books Deutschland GmbH, Metzlerstrasse 26, 60594 Frankfurt am Main*

In Spain: Please write to *Penguin Books S. A., Bravo Murillo 19, 1° B, 28015 Madrid*

In Italy: Please write to *Penguin Italia s.r.l., Via Benedetto Croce 2, 20094 Corsico, Milano*

In France: Please write to *Penguin France, Le Carré Wilson, 62 rue Benjamin Baillaud, 31500 Toulouse*

In Japan: Please write to *Penguin Books Japan Ltd, Kaneko Building, 2-3-25 Koraku, Bunkyo-Ku, Tokyo 112*

In South Africa: Please write to *Penguin Books South Africa (Pty) Ltd, Private Bag X14, Parkview, 2122 Johannesburg*

READ MORE IN PENGUIN

A CHOICE OF CLASSICS

Leopoldo Alas	**La Regenta**
Leon B. Alberti	**On Painting**
Ludovico Ariosto	**Orlando Furioso** (in two volumes)
Giovanni Boccaccio	**The Decameron**
Baldassar Castiglione	**The Book of the Courtier**
Benvenuto Cellini	**Autobiography**
Miguel de Cervantes	**Don Quixote**
	Exemplary Stories
Dante	**The Divine Comedy** (in three volumes)
	La Vita Nuova
Machado de Assis	**Dom Casmurro**
Bernal Díaz	**The Conquest of New Spain**
Niccolò Machiavelli	**The Discourses**
	The Prince
Alessandro Manzoni	**The Betrothed**
Emilia Pardo Bazán	**The House of Ulloa**
Benito Pérez Galdós	**Fortunata and Jacinta**
Eça de Quierós	**The Maias**
Sor Juana Inés de la Cruz	**Poems, Protest and a Dream**
Giorgio Vasari	**Lives of the Artists** (in two volumes)

and

Five Italian Renaissance Comedies
(Machiavelli/**The Mandragola**; Ariosto/**Lena**; Aretino/**The
Stablemaster**; Gl'Intronati/**The Deceived**; Guarini/**The Faithful
Shepherd**)
The Poem of the Cid
Two Spanish Picaresque Novels
(Anon/**Lazarillo de Tormes**; de Quevedo/**The Swindler**)

READ MORE IN PENGUIN

A CHOICE OF CLASSICS

Jacob Burckhardt	**The Civilization of the Renaissance in Italy**
Carl von Clausewitz	**On War**
Meister Eckhart	**Selected Writings**
Friedrich Engels	**The Origin of the Family**
	The Condition of the Working Class in England
Goethe	**Elective Affinities**
	Faust Parts One and Two (in two volumes)
	Italian Journey
	Maxims and Reflections
	Selected Verse
	The Sorrows of Young Werther
Jacob and Wilhelm Grimm	**Selected Tales**
E. T. A. Hoffmann	**Tales of Hoffmann**
Friedrich Hölderlin	**Selected Poems and Fragments**
Henrik Ibsen	**Brand**
	A Doll's House and Other Plays
	Ghosts and Other Plays
	Hedda Gabler and Other Plays
	The Master Builder and Other Plays
	Peer Gynt
Søren Kierkegaard	**Fear and Trembling**
	Papers and Journals
	The Sickness Unto Death
Georg Christoph Lichtenberg	**Aphorisms**
Karl Marx	**Capital** (in three volumes)
Karl Marx/Friedrich Engels	**The Communist Manifesto**
Friedrich Nietzsche	**The Birth of Tragedy**
	Beyond Good and Evil
	Ecce Homo
	Human, All Too Human
	Thus Spoke Zarathustra
Friedrich Schiller	**Mary Stuart**
	The Robbers/Wallenstein

READ MORE IN PENGUIN

A CHOICE OF CLASSICS

Anton Chekhov	**The Duel and Other Stories**
	The Kiss and Other Stories
	The Fiancée and Other Stories
	Lady with Lapdog and Other Stories
	The Party and Other Stories
	Plays (The Cherry Orchard/Ivanov/The Seagull/Uncle Vania/The Bear/The Proposal/A Jubilee/Three Sisters)
Fyodor Dostoyevsky	**The Brothers Karamazov**
	Crime and Punishment
	The Devils
	The Gambler/Bobok/A Nasty Story
	The House of the Dead
	The Idiot
	Netochka Nezvanova
	The Village of Stepanchikovo
	Notes from Underground/The Double
Nikolai Gogol	**Dead Souls**
	Diary of a Madman and Other Stories
Alexander Pushkin	**Eugene Onegin**
	The Queen of Spades and Other Stories
	Tales of Belkin
Leo Tolstoy	**Anna Karenin**
	Childhood, Boyhood, Youth
	A Confession
	How Much Land Does a Man Need?
	Master and Man and Other Stories
	Resurrection
	The Sebastopol Sketches
	What is Art?
	War and Peace
Ivan Turgenev	**Fathers and Sons**
	First Love
	A Month in the Country
	On the Eve
	Rudin
	Sketches from a Hunter's Album